Random House

monster

CROSSWORD PUZZLE

OMNIBUS

VOLUME
ONE

Random House

monster
CROSSWORD PUZZLE
OMNIBUS

VOLUME
ONE

Edited by Stanley Newman

Random House
Puzzles & Games

1999

Jerry Cherry TANGY TAFFY® candy character
used with permission of Nestlé USA

ISBN 0-8129-3213-7

Random House Puzzles & Games website address:
www.puzzlesatrandom.com

Page design and typography by Mark Frnka
Manufactured in the United States of America
6   8   9   7
First Edition

1 FIRST THINGS FIRST by S.N.

ACROSS

1 Yodeler's place
5 "Get lost!"
10 Fill roles
14 Windless
15 Numerical goal
16 __ close to schedule
17 1/20/89, e.g.
20 Home room
21 Betz's TV wife
22 Rock bottom
23 Egg on
24 Choir member
25 In jeopardy
28 Uninteresting
29 Tiny colonist
32 Coin call
33 Elvis __ Presley
34 It may be pitched
35 Fine, so far
39 The Rams' league: Abbr.
40 Not at all nice
41 Spring up
42 Give the once-over

43 Polaroid pioneer
44 President __ of the Senate
45 Berth place
46 Job opening
47 Madame Curie
49 Ruin
50 Movie turkey
53 Cole Porter tune
56 Raised, as cats
57 Circus star
58 Chap, to Dundee
59 Give up
60 Nasal sensations
61 Fall heavily

DOWN

1 Corrosive chemical
2 Bowling area
3 Architect's work
4 Dallas sch.
5 Need oiling
6 As good as new
7 Turnpike

8 ABA member
9 California's locale, to Hawaiians
10 Apt. of a sort
11 The King __
12 Fly high
13 Take a stab at
18 Concerto __ (Baroque work)
19 Solemn promise
23 Gold-colored
24 Crazy as __
25 Make up (for)
26 Chewy candy
27 Long arm?
28 Not limited
29 Hang around for
30 Mythology branch
31 Indian carving
33 Author's rep
36 Almond-flavored drink
37 South Seas skirt
38 Easy run
43 Beef cut

44 Wire bender
45 Joy's partner
46 Self-controlled
47 Insignificant
48 Got older
49 Floor model
50 Ring up

51 "Render __ Caesar . . ."
52 Fraught with meaning
53 English channel?
54 Hoodwinked
55 Diamond judge

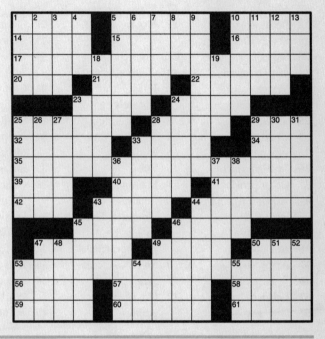

2 HANDIWORK by Shirley Soloway

ACROSS

1 Falcon feature
5 Singer Redding
9 Ferber et al.
14 Ohio city
15 Tennis star Sampras
16 Metal framework
17 Zest for life
18 Alternatively
19 Artful deception
20 New York resort area
23 On the __ (fleeing)
24 Majors and Trevino
25 Mouselike mammals
27 Firmly fixed
30 Mail again
32 Saudi Arabia's king
33 Speak highly of
35 Young fellow
36 R-V link
37 Controversial shortening

39 Sound a toreador adores
42 Gibson of Lethal Weapon
44 Slips into
45 Perfect match
46 Donkey, often
48 Concert instruments
50 Wool coat
52 Take wing
53 Fam. member
54 Foolish sort
60 Sheepish?
62 Dressed
63 Born Free lioness
64 French assembly
65 Past due
66 Stream forth
67 Golf hazards
68 Prayer end
69 Come in last

DOWN

1 Music marking
2 Caron role
3 __ Called Horse ('70 film)
4 Got by scheming

5 Victor Herbert work
6 Spills the beans
7 "__ deal!"
8 Look for
9 Yellowish white
10 Joanne of films
11 Settled once and for all
12 Attorney-__
13 Appears to be
21 Nighttime, in poems
22 Slalom curve
26 Cell substance: Abbr.
27 Preconditions
28 "Unforgettable" name
29 Hans Christian Andersen character
30 Gossipy tidbit
31 007's alma mater
34 Ye __ Tea Shoppe
37 Skirt slits
38 "Silence __"
40 Jar top
41 Pulver's rank: Abbr.

43 Palindromic preposition
45 North Carolinian
47 Kyoto cash
49 Norma __
50 "Mending Wall" poet
51 Pryer's need?

52 Rink footwear
55 CA sch.
56 Happy as a __
57 Seaman's saint
58 Without a warranty
59 Tropical fruit
61 Short snooze

PUT-ONS by Randolph Ross

ACROSS

1 Cut wires
5 BBs and bullets
9 Grassy field
12 Wall layer
15 __ and outs
16 Urban sharpie
17 Milk amts.
18 Road warning
19 D.C. VIP
20 Sign of imperfection
22 Marsh plant
24 Does farm work
25 Sticky stuff
28 Grazing areas
32 Wasp
36 Treeless tract
37 Color pros
41 North Carolina locale
43 Celebrants
46 Act angry
47 Actor Mischa
48 __ Entertainment!
52 Locks of hair
56 Drs.' grp.

57 Zsà Zsa's sister
60 Coll. club
61 Pioneer
64 Unclose, to the Bard
65 Leftover covering
66 Actor Beatty
67 Slips up
68 Notary's need

DOWN

1 Cultivated earth
2 Its HQ is in Brussels
3 Major ending?
4 Sheriff's band
5 Mimicking
6 Bub
7 Hammer of fiction
8 Unique individual
9 Rye, but not pumpernickel
10 Means of access
11 Size up
12 Dosage units: Abbr.

13 Hightailed it
14 Singing syllable
21 Closes down
22 Film editors, often
23 Clean-air org.
25 Defraud
26 "__ the fields we go . . ."
27 Slangy suffix
29 Official records
30 Your Show of Shows routine
31 Camping equipment
33 Kind of exam
34 Help with the dishes
35 Show displeasure
38 Chapter of history
39 Wasn't colorfast
40 JFK jet
42 He followed FDR
43 Acts the squealer
44 Part of the Old World
45 Turned sharply

49 Puts an end to
50 Word form for "both"
51 Powder materials
53 Gas-line additive
54 Agatha's colleague

55 German mining region
57 Poet Pound
58 Scaloppine ingredient
59 Dadaist painter
62 Neighbor of Syr.
63 Feeling of wonder

SIZES by Cynthia Lyon

ACROSS

1 Sentry's order
5 Phil Donahue's wife
10 Acclaim
14 Typee sequel
15 Like campus walls
16 The __ American
17 Harry Kemelman's detective
20 She "cain't say no"
21 Thinly populated
22 Author Sheehy
23 '69 landing site
24 Ruggedly built
27 Flimsy
30 Motorists' org.
31 __-kiri
33 Early Alaska capital
35 Séance operator
39 Iron, in Austria
40 Platter
41 One-fifth of DCCLV
42 Let back in

44 Haunted-house noises
47 South Pacific role
48 Mildred Pierce author
49 Bad-mouth
52 1910s or 1940s event
56 Jailbreak headline
58 Fails to be, informally
59 Author Remarque
60 Praise to the skies
61 Tacks on
62 Shabby and unkempt
63 NaOH solutions

DOWN

1 Romanian dance
2 Diary of __ Housewife
3 Timber wolf
4 Trinidad's neighbor
5 Cinderella's curfew
6 Use

7 Paris' __ gauche
8 Maui memento
9 Favored, as a bet
10 E.T., for one
11 Ice-cream ingredient
12 What Pandora unleashed
13 Actor Waggoner
18 __ instant (quickly)
19 Ring bearer?
23 What American Plan includes
24 Return-mail expediter: Abbr.
25 Rhino's relative
26 Poker ploy
27 Characteristic
28 New York city
29 Move furtively
32 Accountant's activity
34 Author Kingsley
36 Pragmatic ones
37 Spectrum component

38 A Bergen dummy
43 Fashion
45 Small brook
46 Ultimate purpose
48 Work together
49 Film-rating org.
50 Dry as a desert

51 The Swedish Nightingale
52 Court paper
53 King Kong actress
54 Fit of fever
55 National League team
57 Memorable period

5 WORKING OVERTIME by Donna J. Stone

ACROSS

1 Yonder folks
5 Shapeless masses
10 Darned thing?
14 Like some buildup
15 Evangelist McPherson
16 Jai __
17 "Excuse me!"
18 Sonia of *Moon Over Parador*
19 Social misfit
20 START OF A QUOTE
23 *Mal de __* (seasickness)
24 __ contendere
25 Trunks, for instance
30 Absentee
34 "Wild West" showman
35 Small band
37 It runs through Paris
38 Vein contents
39 MIDDLE OF QUOTE

41 Victory sign
42 TV host Robin
44 Clever remark
45 Bobolink's bill
46 Track events
48 Classical Greek teachers
50 Italian wine region
52 Joplin opus
53 END OF QUOTE
59 Horse's gait
60 "__ Kick Out of You"
61 O'Hara homestead
63 Indian-summer phenomenon
64 Funnel-shaped
65 Writer Hunter
66 Toe the line
67 Squirrel away
68 Resist boldly

DOWN

1 United rival
2 "That's a scream!"
3 Small businessman?
4 Al Jolson tune

5 The Yanks' #3
6 Italian bread?
7 General Bradley
8 Get cracking
9 Perk up the pot roast
10 Town in a Warwick tune
11 Butter substitute
12 Auto part, for short
13 Clown around
21 Scale notes
22 At __ for words
25 Chew out
26 *She __ Yellow Ribbon*
27 Brainstorms
28 OPEC member
29 Mr. Andronicus
31 Where the bees are
32 __ a time (singly)
33 Pay periods, often
36 Toledo's home
39 More than this?
40 Golf shot
43 Sea dog's ditty

45 Not at all fair-minded
47 Zeno's associates
49 Linden of *Barney Miller*
51 Gold bar
53 Take greedily

54 Percolate
55 Narrow shoe size
56 Elevator inventor
57 Place for pews
58 Big name in tennis
59 Even if, informally
62 Multiple-choice word

6 DOUBLE TALK by Trip Payne

ACROSS

1 Falls behind
5 Coffee man Valdez
9 Myra Hess, for one
13 "__ Ben Adhem"
14 Molten material
15 All tied up
16 Eddie Cantor tune of '26
19 Breath-freshener brand
20 Using staff facilities
21 Genesis character
23 Flue powder
24 Go separate ways
27 Frequent title beginning
29 Skirt features
32 Nabokov novel
33 Long look
35 "What's in __?"
37 Senior golf star
40 Where the Owl and the Pussycat went
41 Barely defeated
42 Links standard
43 Quick-witted

45 Enjoy a smorgasbord
46 Juno, to the Greeks
47 Arty New Mexico town
49 Confirmation or baptism
51 Cause
54 Theater district
58 Fifties Kenyan uprising
60 Alternatively
61 Harris storyteller
62 Jogger's gait
63 Makes a sheepshank
64 Walked on
65 Saint feature

DOWN

1 Chem-class locales
2 "Rock-__ baby . . ."
3 *Wheel of Fortune* daytime host
4 Math grouping
5 Holyfield punch

6 Tropical fruit
7 "__ home is his castle"
8 Tex-Mex treats
9 Making a premiere
10 Hertz rival
11 Unimportant
12 Come to a stop
14 *Amahl and the Night Visitors* composer
17 Hankering
18 Kids' drink
22 Stock unit
24 Bloc agreement
25 Kind of committee
26 Mrs. Gorbachev
28 Eat away at
30 Brownish gray
31 False charge
33 Fifties-music revival group
34 Candice's dad
36 Poet Pound
38 Franc portions
39 Calls it a day

44 Cultured food
46 Physical condition
48 More angry
50 "Open 9 __ 6"
51 Indonesian island
52 Put-on
53 Verne protagonist

55 Pisa dough
56 Hammer or hacksaw
57 "__ bigger and better things!"
58 Happened upon
59 Blossom-to-be

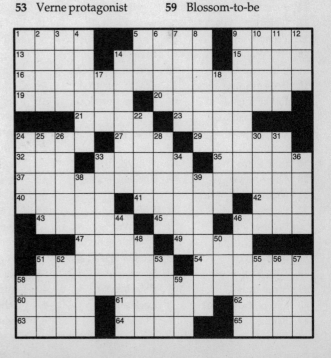

7 WHAT TIME IS IT? by Mel Rosen

ACROSS
1 Melville madman
5 Everglades bird
9 Director __ Lee
14 Doll's word
15 Chunk-light fish
16 Spud
17 Fifties TV mayor
20 Casual footwear
21 Yes, to Yvette
22 Go one better
23 Hog haven
24 Swimsuit part
26 Throws out a line
29 Bring on board
31 Machine part
34 Abdul-Jabbar's alma mater
35 Fifties TV clown
38 Getz or Musial
39 Texas NFLer
40 Rock's partner
41 Fifties TV marionette
43 Pesky insect
44 Many mos.
45 Transgressions
46 Byron and Browning
47 What RNs dispense
48 Heavenly body
49 Chairman of the '50s
51 "This __ fine how-do-you-do!"
54 Residences
58 Fifties TV host
61 The Addams Family star
62 Herbert sci-fi classic
63 Analogy phrase
64 In an irritable mood
65 Part of U.S.A.
66 Enjoy gum

DOWN
1 Fuse units
2 Sound of amusement
3 Evil Idi
4 Orchestra's place
5 NATO member
6 Kramden's workplace
7 Sondheim's __ the Woods
8 Elephant Boy star
9 R-V center?
10 Ristorante course
11 "Tell __ the judge!"
12 Hang on to
13 Go astray
18 Diner sign
19 Bibliophile's pride
25 Confederate soldier
26 Easy and comfortable
27 Audition attendee
28 Side dishes
29 Heavenly headgear
30 Vexed
31 Genetic copy
32 __ once (suddenly)
33 Turns to slush
35 Will addition
36 Pride member
37 Well-suited for the workplace
42 Fashion monogram
46 Alehouses
47 "Strain the facts __ the rules": Tolstoy
48 Fencer's choice
49 Think over
50 P.M. periods
52 Malt-shop order
53 Hallelujah, I'm __
55 Reception aid
56 Feminine suffix
57 Revue, e.g.
58 Baseball club
59 Whichever
60 Unspecified person

8 APT MUSIC by Karen Hodge

ACROSS
1 Toward the left, at sea
6 Tree branch
10 Not a lot
13 Tougher to find
14 Admired one
15 Getting __ years
17 French flapjack
18 "__ Want for Christmas . . ."
19 Beef-grading agcy.
20 Police music?
23 Hardwood tree
24 Big name in theaters
25 Like a pro
28 Olympics org.
31 Memorable period
32 George's big brother
33 Casals' instrument
35 Ghostbusters goo
39 Strait music?
42 Cross one's heart
43 Romantic episode
44 __ Lanka
45 Hosp. professionals
47 Pa Cartwright
48 Put up with
49 Baby birds
53 "__ the fields we go . . ."
55 Charitable music?
61 Meal: Lat.
62 Nutritive mineral
63 Tower material
64 It grows on you
65 Straw vote
66 Atlas was one
67 Fort __, NJ
68 Whirlpool
69 Reckless speed

DOWN
1 Foot part
2 __-mutuel betting
3 Pitcher Hershiser
4 Sportscast showing
5 Lock of hair
6 Deceitful one
7 Doing nothing
8 Double agents
9 Coward's __ Spirit
10 Ump's call
11 Come next
12 Having more breadth
16 Early political cartoonist
21 "Beggarman" follower
22 College official
25 Puts on TV
26 Furrowed feature
27 Fine fabric
29 Gymnast Korbut
30 Tackle Everest
33 The eyes have it
34 Bassoon's cousin
36 "__ Miracle" (Manilow tune)
37 Goodson of game shows
38 Toledo's lake
40 Lenin's inspiration
41 __-the-mill (ordinary)
46 Skunk feature
48 Miscellaneous facts
49 Scratch the surface
50 In the lead
51 Guardian spirits
52 Hyannis entrée
54 Mrs. Bunker
56 Wait on the phone
57 Nothing more than
58 Bons __ (witty remarks)
59 Part of QED
60 "Auld Lang __"

9   M&Ms by Eric Albert

ACROSS
1 Apollo's twin sister
8 Come through
15 Deadline
16 Venezuelan river
17 *Time* piece
18 Seascape painter __ Homer
19 Memorable mime
21 Venetian-blind component
22 Greenish blue
23 *ER* network
26 Electrically versatile
29 Bibliography abbr.
30 Atty.'s title
33 Grille material
36 Detective Wolfe
37 "The Morning After" singer
40 Lendl of tennis
41 Big cheese, maybe
42 Deli bread
43 Prepare salad
44 Assistant
45 __ Lanka
46 Kukla's colleague
49 Folksinger Phil
53 *Some Like It Hot* star
58 Fairly, in a way
60 Broadcast slot
61 Belly
62 Soft-shell clam
63 Elsa was one
64 Santa's elves, e.g.

DOWN
1 First one-term president
2 Part of RFD
3 Tropical fish
4 King's order
5 Ceremonial club
6 "__ never work!"
7 Appear
8 Bridal goods
9 Author Jong
10 Bed sheets or bath towels
11 "Last one __ rotten egg!"
12 Step forward
13 Prefix for system
14 Ticket word
20 Go with
24 Senator Goldwater
25 High-tech replica
26 Poker "bullet"
27 Huntley or Atkins
28 First 007 film
29 Addr. loc.
30 Gives off
31 Really enjoy
32 Hugo character
34 Last year of Queen Victoria's reign
35 "Zounds!"
38 White-hat wearers: Abbr.
39 Indivisible
46 Compose, as a constitution
47 Ceremonial procedures
48 Alda and Arkin
49 Waiting in the wings
50 Nonpaying activity
51 Bart Simpson's dad
52 Crystal gazers
54 Elvis __ Presley
55 "One-l lama" poet
56 Tiny bit
57 Hurler Hershiser
58 Good buddy
59 Box-score stat

10   SHORTENED STATES by Wayne R. Williams

ACROSS
1 One person's opinion
6 Packs away
11 Sylvester, to Tweety Bird
14 Moral principle
15 Pitch
16 Sluggers' stats: Abbr.
17 Sprang up
18 Board at parties
19 Before, poetically
20 Sherwood Anderson opus
22 Boater or bowler
23 Asian celebrations
24 Golf-bag contents
26 Strength of character
30 Nebraska river
31 Olympic skier Phil
32 Neil Simon play
35 Three, to Steffi
36 Middle measurement
37 Misfortunes
40 McMurtry novel
42 Actress Braga
43 Rack partner
45 Fitted together
46 Small wheel
47 Zeus' mother
49 Lupino or Tarbell
50 Mark Twain book
57 Zilch
58 Singer Adams et al.
59 Brimless hat
60 Cable channel
61 Baker's need
62 Unethical one
63 "Oh yeah, __ who?"
64 Fills completely
65 Corrects copy

DOWN
1 *Rich Man, Poor Man* author
2 Actress Singer
3 Unknown author: Abbr.
4 Rocket top
5 Train bridge
6 Nero Wolfe's creator
7 Calendar col. heading
8 Innovative: Abbr.
9 *Barney Miller* character
10 Kenyan language
11 John Irving novel
12 Out-and-out
13 Dangerous fly
21 Quilting party
25 Sines, cosines, etc.
26 C times XXV
27 Musical discernment
28 Alan Cheuse book
29 Mrs. Ed Norton
30 Word after "stay" or "shot"
32 Baseballer Ripken
33 Feel poorly
34 Compass dir.
36 Come out on top
38 __ low (stay hidden)
39 Blue
41 Tennis shots
42 The Seahawks' home
43 Some collectible art
44 Antiseptic substance
45 Guys
47 Della or Pee Wee
48 Party givers
51 Flash of inspiration
52 Italian auto
53 Parka part
54 Prefix for distant
55 Something vital
56 Gets the point

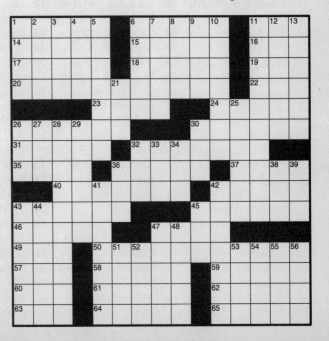

11 TWAIN TIME by Mel Rosen

ACROSS

1 ASCAP rival
4 Thompson of *Family*
8 Major-__ (steward)
12 Get wind (of)
13 *Joie de vivre*
14 Wear away
16 Cuts prices on
18 Boys, in Barcelona
19 Mork's planet
20 Hungry feeling
21 Does fingerpainting
22 Cake finish
24 Biggers' detective
25 Soccer-shoe features
27 Hoarding cause, perhaps
31 Runs easily
32 Armor flaw
33 Peas purchase
34 Like __ of bricks
35 Rich cake
36 Mideast missile
37 Part of TGIF
38 Wanders about
39 Battle strategy
40 Was nurturing
42 Spread (out)
43 Sharif of films
44 Salad-dressing bottle
45 *Charlie's Angels* name
48 Sand and such
49 Came upon
52 Keep __ to the ground
53 Brand-name's protection
55 Pile up
56 Called up
57 Allegro con __
58 Midmonth day
59 Conversation filler
60 Pedigree org.

DOWN

1 Put up with
2 *Night Court* actress
3 Rub the wrong way
4 Family cars
5 Beside
6 Deputy __ (cartoon canine)
7 Hoofer Miller
8 Hamlet's land
9 Get situated
10 "__ Lisa"
11 Fragrance
12 Medical-insurance co.
15 Ending for host or heir
17 Barbecue adjuncts
21 Was outstanding
23 Columnist Herb
24 Promissory notes
25 Assertion
26 Numbers game
27 Minimal evidence
28 Musical notation
29 Measuring device
30 All over
32 Deal with
35 Synagogue scroll
36 Trig ratio
38 Casual comments
39 Fry lightly
41 Roman odist
42 Latter-day icebox
44 Construction-site sight
45 Musical notes
46 Thumbs-down voter
47 Scanned through
48 Mardi __
50 Author Ambler
51 WBC result
53 Numerical prefix
54 Finance deg.

12 GLOBAL GEOMETRY by Randy Sowell

ACROSS

1 Borders on
6 Sail support
10 Hard journey
14 Seasonal song
15 Lebanon's locale
16 Slow flow
17 London landmark
20 Pep up
21 Everlasting
22 Presidential prerogative
23 Actor Beatty
24 Nagging pain
27 __ Vegas
29 Big bankrolls
33 Bikini top
34 Author Cornelia __ Skinner
36 Small piano
38 Mysterious Atlantic region
41 Furry fish-eaters
42 Monopoly payment
43 Connecticut collegian
44 High schooler
45 Smidgen
46 Allison of '50s TV
47 Snake with a squeeze
49 Christie's *Postern of __*
52 In the wrong role
56 Charge in court
60 Cook crossed it in the 1770's
62 Defeat soundly
63 Topnotch
64 Sour expression
65 They may be split
66 __ *to Morocco*
67 Watered the lawn, perhaps

DOWN

1 Part of a French play
2 *Green Acres* structure
3 Russian river
4 Nine-__ shift
5 Dred Scott, e.g.
6 Louisiana's state flower
7 Stubborn-mule link
8 Warning devices
9 Aesthetic discernment
10 Travel agent's offering
11 Chestnut horse
12 Old Testament book
13 Boat part
18 Allow
19 Proof-ending initials
24 Monastery head
25 Minotaur's home
26 Author Bret
28 *Ad __ per aspera*
29 Finish first
30 *Look Back in __*
31 Perry's aide
32 Toklas' colleague
34 __ *Man Flint*
35 Football scores: Abbr.
36 Moral wrong
37 Butter portion
39 Chess pieces
40 Visibly embarrassed
45 Arm art
46 "I will __ evil . . ."
47 Watering hole
48 Pianist Levant
50 Fly-ball's path
51 Actress Van Devere
52 Stable parent
53 Privy to
54 Poker variety
55 Abyssinians and Burmese
57 Tops a cake
58 Cheerfulness
59 Nonsocial sort
61 ". . . partridge __ pear tree"

13 ON YOUR METAL by Karen Hodge

ACROSS

1 Prods, in a way
6 Road feature
10 Bible prophet
14 Limber
15 Neck of the woods
16 Composer __ Carlo Menotti
17 Pittsburgh Steelers' rival?
20 Omit in pronunciation
21 Missile housing
22 Debate side
23 Alluring
25 New England capital
27 Take down a __
30 Runs wild
32 Colonial descendants' org.
33 Perched on
35 Mangy mutt
36 Defeats
39 Singer Guthrie
40 Nasal input
42 Make fun of
43 Phone feature
45 Filmdom's Nora Charles
46 Locale
47 Winter bug
48 Can be read effortlessly
50 Moe's hairstyle
51 Düsseldorf dessert
54 Statistical info
56 Great grade
57 "__ restless as a willow . . ."
59 Semidiameters
62 Pewter-maker's directives?
66 Kind of sax
67 Up to the job
68 Wears a hole in the carpet
69 Take five
70 __ good example
71 Criticizes

DOWN

1 Lobbying org.
2 Make eyes at
3 German port
4 "All Shook Up" singer
5 Farm machine
6 Sheep sound
7 Coffeemakers
8 China Beach extras
9 Cellist Casals
10 Psyche section
11 Metalworker's motto?
12 Prop for Figaro
13 Put __ to (stop)
18 Word-related
19 Sonata movement
24 "__ Cheatin' Heart"
26 Hauls (off)
27 Carson's predecessor
28 Raison d'__
29 Weather veins?
31 Grimm villain
34 French soldier
36 Disobedient
37 Name in Yugoslavian history
38 Short distance
41 Mind-set
44 Telecast component
48 Like Cherries Jubilee
49 They take a licking
51 Shankar's instrument
52 Transparent linen
53 Bovary and Samms
55 Let's Make __
58 Shaker contents
60 Peruvian ancestor
61 Gossipy tidbit
63 Barracks bed
64 Tchrs.' grp.
65 Draft org.

14 PLACES OF INTEREST by Eric Albert

ACROSS

1 Copacetic
5 Man and Capri
10 Friday and Columbo
14 Tel __
15 Protester's litany
16 Trim a photo
17 Famous false front
20 Woolly mama
21 Sty cry
22 Keep out of sight
23 Peter Pan pirate
24 Beau Bridges' brother
25 Dulcimer, e.g.
28 Mini-meal
29 E, to Morse
32 Nile city
33 Shoe strip
34 Actor from India
35 Carouse
38 Cub Scout group
39 What the snooty put on
40 Midnight Cowboy character
41 Bandage brand
42 Nimble
43 Coded message
44 Parting words
45 Makes lace
46 Tack on
49 "That hurts!"
50 Service charge
53 Police film of '81
56 Toward the dawn
57 Daphnis' love
58 Not quite closed
59 Opening day?
60 Penney rival
61 Carpet surface

DOWN

1 Taunt
2 Declare openly
3 Windborne toy
4 Actress Arden
5 More distasteful
6 Do very well
7 Long and lean
8 Part of SASE
9 Heel style
10 Musical symbol
11 Kind of hygiene
12 Walt Kelly creation
13 Gush forth
18 Short time
19 Vivacity
23 Beef cut
24 Falters at the altar?
25 Mothers of Invention leader
26 Singer who won the Nobel Prize
27 ". . . checking it __"
28 The Champ Oscar winner
29 __ Vader
30 Of great weight
31 Henry VIII's house
33 Spins noisily
34 Button alternatives
36 Auto audio accessory
37 Twist out of shape
42 In __ (harmonized)
43 Official seal
44 Predilections
45 One-on-one instructor
46 Mountaintop
47 Brit's baby carriage
48 Tower town
49 Man __ Mancha
50 Pacific island group
51 List-shortening abbr.
52 Brontë heroine
54 Bit of resistance?
55 Budget limit

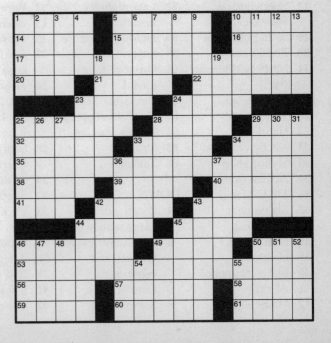

15 — SPIRITUALISM by A.J. Santora

ACROSS
1 Biblical kingdom
5 Overhead-__ engine
8 It may be rattled
13 Shade source
16 Carol start
17 The spirit of the time
18 Sand bar
19 Actress Merkel
20 Eva and Zsa Zsa
22 Volcano name
23 Pat and Vanna's boss
25 Thread holder
27 High-tech scanner
28 Indo-Europeans
31 Appease
33 Tasty tidbit
36 Patronized a casino
37 Team spirit
40 Shorten sleeves, maybe
41 Public opinion, for short
42 Tony Curtis film role
44 Like a bump __
48 Extremity
49 Iwo Jima terrain
52 Actress Singer
53 Years and years
55 Nova __
58 Actor Alastair
59 *Divine Comedy* writer
61 Philosophical spirit
63 River mammal
64 Florida product
65 Holiday
66 "For shame!"
67 Biol. dept. course

DOWN
1 Simoleons
2 First act
3 Where the bees are
4 Deli order
5 Corn holders
6 Man of morals
7 Dallas-Fort Worth area, e.g.
8 Maritime message
9 Smart
10 Where marines train
11 Arises (from)
12 In the same category
14 Meringue ingredient
15 Scones' partner
21 Scale note
24 Improvised, in jazz
26 South Seas spot
29 *Missing in Action* star
30 __ Lanka
32 Wrist-related
34 West Indies isle
35 Tokyo's former name
37 Stretch out
38 Tuition payers
39 Nav. officer
40 Leading
43 *Emerald Point __* ('80s prime-time series)
45 __ thought (daydreaming)
46 Writer Fallaci
47 Gin drink
50 Parcels (out)
51 TV's Eliot Ness
54 Proofreader's notation
56 S&L payment
57 Ms. Gardner
60 Pitcher's stat
62 Author Levin

16 — CALLING COSTNER by Richard Silvestri

ACROSS
1 The West had one
5 Otherwise
9 Astor's wares
14 The third man
15 Sea swallow
16 *Cats* inspiration
17 Sherwood Forester
19 Soda-bottle size
20 Pupil's chore
21 *North by Northwest* star
23 Pick-me-up
26 Tongue-lash
28 Handcuff
31 Kitchen utensils
33 Styling shop
34 Actress Burstyn
36 Mr. DiMaggio
37 Big name in basketball
38 Pine product
39 Isolated
40 In the manner of
41 Alacrity
42 Maine senator
43 Painter Thomas Hart __
45 How ships may run
47 *Our Gang* girl
48 Film holder
49 Actress Burke
51 Late-night TV host Bob
56 Hold accountable
58 Sherwood Forester
61 Grounds for a medal
62 Devastate
63 Opposition prefix
64 Textile workers
65 Drop
66 Take ten

DOWN
1 Poet Sandburg
2 Large woodwind
3 Cotillion attendees
4 Wallach and Whitney
5 Kind of pride
6 Summer sign
7 Hit-show letters
8 Winds down
9 One with a large food bill
10 Donahue of *Father Knows Best*
11 Sherwood Forester
12 Boot part
13 Orch. section
18 Pitcher Ryan
22 Colorado high spot
24 Heads for the hills
25 Satellite of '62
27 Spoke monotonously
28 Sent away
29 Sherwood Forester
30 "I should say __!"
32 Spotted
33 Stick it in your ear
35 Feudal lord
38 Attacked
39 Bud's buddy
41 Cries out
42 Use crayons
44 Seismic disturbance
46 Eat one's words
50 Bushy hairdo
52 Magi's guide
53 Maintain the piano
54 New Testament book
55 Vaudeville routine
56 Hanes competitor
57 Set (down)
59 Daiquiri need
60 VI halved

17 BASEBALL SUCCESSES by Mel Rosen

ACROSS
1 Watered-down
5 Canyon of the comics
10 Carpet style
14 Presley's middle name
15 Out-and-out
16 Evening hour
17 Succeed without swinging?
19 Blues singer James
20 Transparencies
21 *Rhoda* star
23 Director Brooks
24 Must, informally
25 Get a move on
29 Toto's creator
30 Nay neutralizer
33 Choir members
34 Abby, to Ann
35 Economist Smith
36 Carrying a grudge
37 Impress indelibly
38 Beer-label word
39 "You must remember __"
40 Zillions of years
41 Splits up

42 __ Ridge, TN
43 Parting word
44 Potato-chip alternatives
45 Civil rights leader Medgar
47 Joanne of films
48 Asian temple
50 Gives VIP treatment to
55 Like crazy
56 End up succeeding?
58 White as a sheet
59 Hope or Jessica
60 Step __ (hurry)
61 "No ifs, __, or buts!"
62 Not broadside
63 Vet patients

DOWN
1 Radner character
2 Rock star Clapton
3 Top-rated
4 Make a sweater
5 __ Island (Big Apple borough)
6 Beach need

7 Greek vowels
8 Kilmer of *The Doors*
9 Gray dog
10 Hägar's pooch
11 Score a lode of runs?
12 Penny, perhaps
13 Transmission choice
18 Appoints
22 24-hour cash source: Abbr.
24 Picks up
25 Is forced
26 Oahu greeting
27 Get a whiff of success?
28 Stocking stuffers
29 Safari boss
31 __ *Win* (diet book)
32 Making __ of things
34 Harness races
35 Jai __
37 Better than awful
41 Cut back
43 Media mogul Turner

44 Immovable
46 Casts a ballot
47 Don __ de la Vega (Zorro)
48 Hemingway's nickname
49 Actor Ladd

50 __ a hand (assist)
51 Flapjack chain, initially
52 Torrid, for one
53 Send forth
54 Salon jobs
57 Hightailed it

18 SAY CHEESE by Emily Cox & Henry Rathvon

ACROSS
1 Redcoat general
5 Passover feast
10 Fairy-tale baddie
14 Something pumped
15 ". . . is as good as __"
16 Campus guys' group
17 Extol
18 Cheesy destiny?
20 Give up the throne
22 Deep chasm
23 State with conviction
24 Buffalo hockey pro
27 African nation
30 Bond of a sort
34 Intrinsically
35 Positive sign
37 Yonder folks
38 Parisian pal
39 Bratlike
42 Three-faced woman?

43 Teaching both genders
45 Film critic James
46 Of longer standing
48 Back up with muscle
50 Not too hotly
52 Man with a Principle
54 Robin Cook book
55 Unexplainable
58 For the few
62 Cheesy fight?
65 "Waterloo" band
66 Pieces' partner
67 Radium researcher
68 Blockhead
69 Shooer's word
70 Office fill-ins
71 Spouses no more

DOWN
1 Arizona river
2 The A of UAR
3 Cheesy exclamation?
4 Salad greens

5 African expedition
6 Send forth
7 Processes veggies
8 BPOE member
9 Fam. member
10 Unconventional
11 Western novelist
12 "Phooey!"
13 Greek letters
19 Have coming
21 Largest asteroid
25 Good-luck charm
26 Army outpost
27 Speedily
28 Clunky car
29 Orbital point
31 Cheesy talker?
32 Carpenter's tool
33 Polishing agent
36 Pinocchio's bane
40 International agreement
41 Bus station
44 Least prudent
47 Summer drink
49 Hazard to navigation

51 French schools
53 Get new guns
55 Suffers recession
56 Leif's dad
57 She was Gilda in '46
59 Lose one's footing
60 Gull's tail?
61 Long-running musical
63 Fall mo.
64 McClanahan of *The Golden Girls*

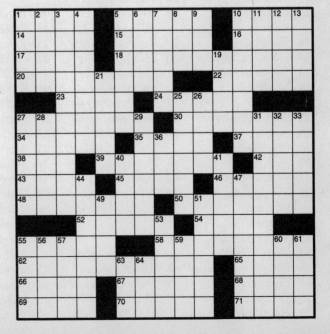

19   BALANCING ACT by Cynthia Lyon

ACROSS

1 NFL team
6 Allowing a draft
10 Dossier
14 Summarizing paragraph
15 Gossipy info
16 Skunk's weapon
17 What Hillary did
20 Personnel data
21 Con
22 Tried for office
23 __ move on (rush)
24 Devoid of dirt
27 Dry oneself
31 Music category
32 Boring item
33 Dessert choice
34 Making minimum wage
38 Hula instrument
39 Law-school course
40 Shade sources
41 Mrs. and Mrs.
43 Overall total
45 "I cannot tell __"
46 Actress Caldwell
47 __ the dumps (feeling blue)
50 Snails, squids, etc.
55 How things may be rated
57 Singer/composer Laura
58 Collaborating group
59 Lily variety
60 The yoke's on them
61 Sargasso Sea swimmers
62 "All __ Up" (Elvis tune)

DOWN

1 Not so much
2 Pizarro victim
3 Roundish
4 Vincent Lopez's theme
5 __ Nevada mountains
6 Jingle writers
7 Writes (down) quickly
8 Imitate
9 Critic
10 Black-tie affair
11 Germ of inspiration
12 Totally confused
13 Art Deco artist
18 Sigourney role in '88
19 Signs up for
23 "We Got the Beat" group
24 *Masterpiece Theatre* host
25 Tackle-box contents
26 Large deer
27 Massachusetts university
28 Fiery stones
29 Topics for 9 Down
30 Attorney's earnings
31 Emulated Ederle
32 Come to terms
35 A stressful type?
36 Propose, in a way
37 Corp. bigwig
42 *Cheers* star
43 Greg Norman's game
44 Souvenirs of the past
46 Increases sharply
47 __ harm (be innocuous)
48 Figurine mineral
49 Piece of merchandise
50 Grain product
51 Zion National Park site
52 Fly alone
53 Metric weight
54 Lie in the tub
56 *To Kill a Mockingbird* author

20   RUSH, RUSH, RUSH by Eric Albert

ACROSS

1 Kind of point
8 And the like: Abbr.
11 H. Rider Haggard novel
14 It started about 1000 B.C.
15 Company, it's said
16 Singer Ritter
17 Lana Turner film
18 Badge material
19 Modern music
20 Chap
21 Surf, in a way
23 Stupefy
26 Chinese belief
28 Famous Washington
29 Eye-fooling pictures
31 Boorish
33 Take on tenants
34 Eden character
35 It may be extended
37 Corp. bigwigs
38 Ex-TV E.T.
39 Harmonize
43 Keyless
45 Cornhusker city
46 Butter ringer
49 Ignoble
50 Be suitable
51 J.R. Ewing's foe
53 Check
55 Woods locale?
56 Top-blower of '80
58 Baseball's Brock
60 Zsa Zsa's sister
61 Prepare pancakes
62 Doctorow novel
66 Hitchcock's title
67 "__ Gotta Be Me"
68 Plane part
69 Down
70 Take-home
71 Prepared fowl

DOWN

1 Lower the lights
2 Hurler's stat
3 Seafood order
4 OLD GERMAN SAYING, PART 1
5 __ Cass Elliot
6 Bond, for one
7 Luthor or Barker
8 Sundance's girlfriend
9 King's smaller version
10 African river
11 Lane success
12 Paradise
13 Old pro
21 MIDDLE OF SAYING
22 END OF SAYING
23 Venetian official
24 High point
25 Western name
27 Secret stuff
30 Try out
32 Do a vet's job
36 "Time __ the essence"
40 Hoop star Archibald
41 Smart
42 Aaron's nickname
44 Watch
46 Haunt one's thoughts
47 Baltic republic
48 Est founder Werner
52 Small and spritely
54 *The Exorcist* star
57 Novgorod negative
59 Impolite look
62 "Awesome, dude"
63 1040 folks: Abbr.
64 Curly's brother
65 Complete

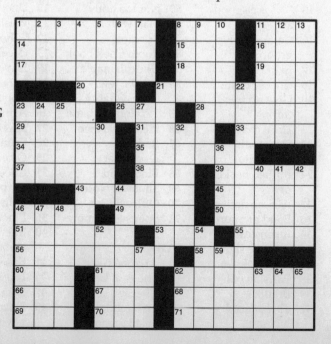

21 CAR POOL by Randy Sowell

ACROSS
1 Eban of Israel
5 Snake sound
9 Fills film roles
14 Ring event
15 Nabisco nosh
16 National Leaguer
17 "This one's __!"
18 Apple-pie partner
20 Cong. member
21 Rummy variety
22 Bobby of hockey
23 "Harper Valley __"
24 Like the prairie
27 King, in Cannes
29 Bring up
30 John Major's predecessor
35 Liner levels
37 Sci-fi film of '82
38 It has its ups and downs
39 Incoming plane: Abbr.
40 "__ Folly" (Alaska)
43 Richard Skelton
44 Apollo objective
46 Fictional Lane
47 Works at a bar
49 Grass-roots politician
51 Achy or angry
52 __ Tac Dough
53 Date time
57 Author Fleming
60 Third word of "America"
62 One way to stand
63 Delta competitor
64 New York City neighborhood
67 Complain
68 House of Lords member
69 "I cannot tell __"
70 Kennel comment
71 Fine wood
72 __ the lily (overdo it)
73 Tags on

DOWN
1 Scrub a mission
2 Big mistake
3 Farmer's delight
4 Chowed down
5 More comfy, in a way
6 Golf-bag contents
7 Fixed
8 London district
9 Lunch for Bugs
10 Blonde shade
11 Cool it
12 Easy run
13 Kid's pop
19 Trip for Mom, maybe
21 Corning's concern
25 "A mouse!"
26 They may be dire
28 Unfriendly
31 __ d'oeuvres
32 Western lizard
33 Looked at
34 Steiger and Stewart
35 Clammy
36 Slangy suffix
37 Ark arrivals
41 Bring out
42 Ale relative
45 Filbert, e.g.
48 Go wrong
50 Prolonged account
51 Refused to go
54 Shower time
55 Oscar, e.g.
56 Americans, to Brits
57 "Let __" (Beatles tune)
58 Ishmael's skipper
59 Pianist Peter
61 Woodland creature
65 __ vivant
66 Yale student
67 Finance deg.

22 FEBRUARY BIRTHDAYS by Mel Rosen

ACROSS
1 Watch the grandchildren
4 Etchers' needs
9 Walked through water
14 Excessively
15 Riveter of song
16 More frosty
17 Charged atom
18 Comedian born 2/2
20 True-blue
22 Round: Abbr.
23 Sub weapon
26 Unstressed vowel sounds
30 Not to be believed
32 Card game
34 Funnyman Murray
36 Did cobbler's work
38 Twine fiber
39 Actor Ray
41 Up to now
43 Sleuth Wolfe
44 Castle defenses
46 Student's jottings
48 Just published
49 Ran away
51 Sign of spring
53 Overly ornate
55 "__ to Watch Over Me"
58 Declare to be true
60 Taj __
61 Actor born 2/18
67 Wheel of Fortune purchase
68 Nostalgic tune
69 Less encumbered
70 Digital-watch type: Abbr.
71 Revenge of the __
72 Tex-Mex treats
73 Soapmaker's need

DOWN
1 Circus prop
2 Ten grand
3 Actor born 2/26
4 Naive
5 Bill's partner
6 Doctrine
7 Computer storage device
8 Highway rigs
9 Macbeth trio
10 Essen exclamation
11 Gaming cube
12 Election suffix
13 AMA members
19 Theater section: Abbr.
21 LAPD alert
24 Twosomes
25 Synthetic fabric
27 Farm wagon
28 Talk-show host born 2/12
29 Long look
31 Clear the windshield
33 Leisurely
34 Doorway part
35 Indifferent
37 Takes out
40 Director Preminger
42 San __, Italy
45 Mexican wraps
47 Cooks on low heat
50 Opera star
52 Teachers' org.
54 Dutch earthenware
56 Mrs. Reagan
57 Omit in pronunciation
59 __ avis (something unusual)
61 Actor Voight
62 British beverage
63 Nav. rank
64 Barnyard baby
65 IBM competitor
66 Bus. bigwig

ACROSS
1 Small snake
4 Belief
9 Ore chore
14 Desktop devices: Abbr.
15 Sank, as a putt
16 Church top
17 Willie Mays' nickname
19 Airport lineup
20 Banquet officiator
21 Yucatan's capital
23 Basketball, essentially
25 Paul Whiteman tune of '27
26 Cir. statistic
27 Nav. rank
28 Singer Sumac
31 *No, No, Nanette* tune
35 Very impressed
36 Rights grp.
37 Quite devout
39 Cause of ruin
40 Dice toss
41 Make a hasty escape
43 Industrious insect
44 RR stop
45 Pasture plaint
46 *The __ Experiment* (Rimmer novel)
49 Dramatist Rostand
53 Worthy of a medal
54 Artoo __
55 Revere's co-rider
56 *Billboard* success
60 Vacuous
61 Where the blissful walk
62 Language ending
63 Pyramid builders
64 Singer James et al.
65 Checkers side

DOWN
1 Church areas
2 Untrustworthy one
3 __ out (intimidate)
4 "Ta-ta!"
5 Western Bean
6 Lodge brother
7 "*Agnus __*"
8 Fifth wheel
9 The Jetsons' dog
10 Seville's setting
11 Event in the news, 6/67
12 Oratorio piece
13 "You bet!"
18 Attentive
22 Printer's measures
24 O.K. Corral visitor
25 Reversed film
29 Waiter's offering
30 Mideast gulf
31 *Scarlett* locale
32 A soc. sci.
33 Sinatra tune
34 *Hollywood Squares* inspiration
35 Belly
38 Just the __ (even so)
42 Silent assenters
44 __ Lanka
47 Sports venue
48 American Beauties, e.g.
50 *The __ Side of Midnight*
51 Sort of pollution
52 Overdid the affection
53 Tennis pro Mandlikova
55 Poorly lit
57 Que. neighbor
58 Butter portion
59 Aunt, in Acapulco

ACROSS
1 Fringe benefit
5 Toddler's transport
10 Gripe (about)
14 Mystery writer Rendell
15 Travels by train
16 Forearm bone
17 Actor Sharif
18 START OF A QUIP
20 Enigmatic types
22 "__ dream . . .": King
23 Eshkol's successor
24 Fed
25 PART 2 OF QUIP
28 Order-form word
32 Be superior
33 Oligarchic group
34 GM car
35 Boardwalk structure
36 "Do That to __ More Time" ('79 tune)
37 *Carte*
38 Suffix for form
39 *__ Carats* (Ullmann film)
40 Helicopter part
41 Discipline
43 PART 3 OF QUIP
44 Duck soup
45 Take into account
46 __ alone (solos)
49 Raga musician
53 END OF QUIP
55 How some sit by
56 Knock off
57 Push gently
58 Light filler
59 Heavy weights
60 Nasty look
61 Comic Kaplan

DOWN
1 Old hands
2 Sugar portion
3 Area code 801
4 Fishing vessel
5 Mrs. Ed Norton
6 Kitchen gadget
7 Lupino and Tarbell
8 Barbie's beau
9 Size up
10 Ninja Turtle, e.g.
11 Norse royal name
12 Green Gables girl
13 Nothing, in Navarre
19 Author Alexander
21 Singer Carter
24 Sack cloth
25 Animate
26 Send packing
27 Where the buoys are
28 Bartlett bit
29 "__ Kick Out of You"
30 Operatic hero, often
31 "__ telling me!"
33 Novelist Kosinski
36 Humidifies
37 '60s fad
39 Grain implement
40 Perlman of *Cheers*
42 __ *Fables*
43 Not as dry
45 Cabinet part
46 Nitty-gritty
47 In the know about
48 Peter Wimsey's school
49 Marquis de __
50 Brainstorm
51 Mess specialist
52 Actress Daly
54 Flow along

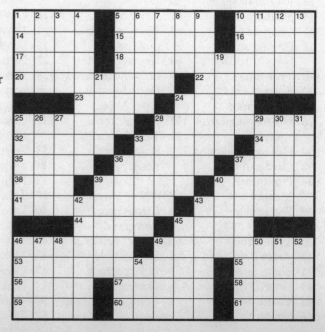

25 SLIPS by Eric Albert

ACROSS

1 Player
6 Lansbury Broadway role
10 Bushy hairdo
14 Hot stuff
15 Party to
16 Self-admiring
17 SLIP
19 Friend in a fight
20 Orestes' sister
21 Gun-lobby grp.
23 __, lies, and videotape
24 Ball, for one
25 Distinguishing mark
27 Cartoonist Peter
28 As a group
31 Dogpatch creator
34 With polished planes
35 Smelting substance
36 Middle area
39 Brain-wave rdg.
40 Bounty crewman
42 Agile
43 Like some protesters
44 "... oh where can __?"
47 Not moving
48 Russian inland body of water
52 Mythical beast
54 Patriot descendants' org.
55 Adjective for Sears Tower
56 Free space
58 SLIP
60 Toning target
61 Fishing fly
62 Monteverdi opera
63 Goat cheese
64 Store-sign abbr.
65 Beasts of burden

DOWN

1 Actress Sharon
2 Santiago's land
3 Forklike
4 Good fellow
5 Mob-scene member
6 Nanki-Poo's father
7 Raggedy one
8 Night light
9 Charm
10 Gardner of Mogambo
11 SLIP
12 Raise the dander of
13 Cameo stone
18 Kukla's costar
22 Pitchers?
26 Hood's heater
29 Omen observer
30 Tense
31 Robin Cook book
32 Make __ for it
33 SLIP
34 Debate side
36 Started a pot
37 Within one's tolerance
38 Right-handed, originally
41 "... kerchief, and __ my cap"
42 Clouseau portrayer
44 Having headgear
45 Important periods
46 Panama money
49 Vassal's crew
50 Cosmetician Lauder
51 A Musketeer
52 Carmina Burana composer
53 Customary function
57 Wharton deg.
59 Museum material

26 PAUL'S PICTURES by Mel Rosen

ACROSS

1 Kind of excuse
5 Fix socks
9 Govt. agent
13 Comic Idle
14 Lumberjacks' competition
15 Sitarist Shankar
16 Former soccer org.
17 Late-blooming plant
18 Actor Baldwin
19 Newman/Field film of '81
22 Coral island
23 Presidential nickname
24 Out of practice
27 Droop
30 Mideast nation
34 Italian wine region
35 SAG members
37 UN workers' agcy.
38 Newman/Cruise film of '86
41 Poetic nighttime
42 Bank (on)
43 Sotto __
44 Dickens character
46 Shoe width
47 "Phooey!"
48 Salesperson, for short
50 Galley implement
51 Newman/Woodward film of '76
60 Travel widely
61 Plumed military hat
62 Ms. Moffo
63 Part of AFL
64 Cut off
65 Champagne bucket
66 Hankerings
67 Gives the twice-over
68 Anchorman's spot

DOWN

1 Olin of Havana
2 Jordanian, e.g.
3 Long for
4 Choosy, in a way
5 Vitamin amount
6 Sax range
7 Sand bar
8 __ Rae
9 County Kerry capital
10 Niger neighbor
11 With: Fr.
12 Delightful
14 Slightly improper
20 Thumbs-down vote
21 Bottomless pit
24 Had some standing
25 Show to a seat
26 Office skill, for short
27 Sub device
28 "A poem lovely as __"
29 __ better (top)
31 Not important
32 Single out
33 British poet Alfred
35 Hearty brew
36 Postal-service abbr.
39 Comparatively peculiar
40 Was owed a credit
45 Military papers
47 Old horse
49 Western band
50 __ about
51 Serving prop
52 Native land
53 Uniform
54 Curds' partner
55 Church area
56 Turner and Pappas
57 Some time ago
58 Till contents
59 Carefree escapade

STOOGE SETTING by Fred Piscop

ACROSS
1 Simon and McCartney
6 Corn eater's throwaway
9 Language of the Yucatán
14 Postulate
15 Ms. Gardner
16 Occupied
17 Laugh scornfully
18 Kilmer of *The Doors*
19 Low-calorie
20 Poetic stooge?
23 Barnyard parent
24 It's split for soup
25 African snakes
28 "__ Entertain You"
32 "Later, dude!"
36 *The Hustler* prop
37 Arouse, as interest
38 Remote computer user's ritual
39 Magazine stooge?
42 Think-tank output
43 River in Pakistan
44 Indivisible

45 Jury member
46 Hiccup, e.g.
47 Lemon-lime concoctions
48 Mrs. Nixon
50 Cambridge sch.
52 Actor stooge?
59 Turning point
60 Bossy comment
61 Battery part
63 Acid type
64 Peanut product
65 From the __ (from square one)
66 Expand, in a way
67 Foxlike
68 Slalom curves

DOWN
1 Second ltr. addendum
2 Outstanding
3 Pre-owned
4 Feudal lords
5 Adobe ingredient
6 Vena __
7 Roundish
8 *Cinderella* scene

9 Pooh's creator
10 Disney staffer
11 Imported auto
12 Arthur of tennis
13 Badminton need
21 Historical souvenir
22 Go __ (rant)
25 __ off the old block
26 Leather variety
27 Martinique volcano
29 Rig out
30 __ profit (make money)
31 Blends
33 ". . . __ cigar is a smoke"
34 *Chinatown* screenwriter Robert
35 Queen __ lace
37 IOU relatives
38 Freight amts.
40 Radio plug-in
41 Scrumptious
46 Cardinal's insignia

47 Makes amends
49 Playwright Chekhov
51 Public persona
52 Guitarist Hendrix
53 Roman poet
54 Big name in cookies

55 Make muddy
56 Poly preceder
57 Spoils
58 __ out (barely beat)
59 Ben, to Hoss
62 Aurora's counterpart

24 DOWN by S.N.

ACROSS
1 Kind of radio
5 Reagan Attorney General
10 Gent
14 __ *Richard's Almanack*
15 Also called
16 Playwright David
17 Musical work
18 Gives autographs
19 Scat-singing name
20 According to
21 Wishy-__
22 *60 Minutes* reporter
23 Stand in good __
25 Began to like
27 Bandleader Les or Larry
29 Donald Sutherland's kid
32 Parson __ (Washington biographer)
34 Brought out in the open
36 Egg-yong link
37 Florence's river

38 Shatner's costar
39 Rhine city
40 Taylor or Torn
41 O'Neill's "Emperor"
42 "Semper Fidelis" composer
43 31-game winner in '68
45 Combat zone
47 Optimistic
49 Tears apart
51 Hurry-scurry
53 Meek followers
55 Fall mo.
57 Kick in
58 Bar-mitzvah dances
59 Industrial bigwig
60 Eisenhower's namesakes
61 Not moving
62 Soccer great
63 Make a scene
64 Formative years
65 Hardy boy?

DOWN
1 Each, so to speak

2 Acts apathetic
3 24
4 *The Ghost and __ Muir*
5 Siege site of 73 A.D.
6 Wallach and Whitney
7 24
8 Sony competitor
9 Capital of Somalia?
10 Dream up
11 24
12 Masterly
13 Nectar source
21 Witty ones
22 Lose traction
24 Admiral Zumwalt
26 __-doke
28 London forecast
30 Zillions of years
31 Author Jaffe
32 Open-hearted
33 Leif's pop
35 Climbed
38 "__ but the brave . . ."

39 Blessing
41 Be in harmony
42 Short distance
44 Most relevant
46 Wave heights
48 In unison
50 Parboil

51 "Aquarius" musical
52 Paul the singer
54 Have coming
56 Three-spot
58 Miss' partner
59 Payroll pro: Abbr.

CHEF'S SPECIAL by Eric Albert

ACROSS

1 Super Bowl camera locale
6 Part of a Stein quote
11 Jazz specialty
14 Aviator Markham
15 Shaving accidents
16 Have chits out
17 Administrative charge
19 Cartoonist's staple
20 Missouri mountains
21 Liz role of '63
22 He was caricatured in *The Clouds*
25 Hang together
27 Trudge
28 Bank patron
29 "Me, me!"
30 The ilium
34 Flavor enhancer: Abbr.
37 Cartoon cry
38 Literally, "equator"
39 Discoverer's cry
40 __ Lanka
41 Seasonal worker
42 London area
43 Examines electronically
45 Smell awful
46 Rectangular
48 Candle-wax source
52 Picture of health?
53 Newspaper name
54 Grain holder
55 Banquet VIP
60 Weird
61 City captured by van Gogh
62 Furry Aussie
63 Unseld of basketball
64 Ms. Boop
65 Fortune 500 firm

DOWN

1 Certain ammo
2 Stand for
3 Anger
4 "Goodness gracious!"
5 Shopping center
6 Maestro Previn
7 Takes a chance
8 Folksinger Phil
9 Enjoy Vail
10 Uncommon sense?
11 Whiskey + beer chaser
12 Title holder
13 Indian tea
18 Be a fink
21 Fidel's friend
22 Gets a glimpse of
23 Born first
24 New Zealand territory
25 Nikon rival
26 Out in the open
28 Malt-shop pop
30 Virility personified
31 Cake cover
32 Small dogs
33 Keep out
35 Diaphanous
36 Like newborn colts
44 Affecting innocence
45 1918 World Series winners
46 U-shaped river bend
47 Woman in white
48 Hemmed in
49 Pretentious, in a way
50 Fall veggie
51 Director Edwards
53 Parade command
55 Bill
56 Mine find
57 Put a strain on
58 "Xanadu" rock group, initially
59 Was the manager of

LETTER CARRIERS by Wayne R. Williams

ACROSS

1 First name in homespun humor
5 Expensive
9 Hoopster Olajuwon
14 Artery of a sort
15 Exile isle
16 Hal of baseball
17 *Laugh-In* regular
19 Emulate Hamill
20 Elevation standard
21 Working hard
22 Cursor starter?
23 Seditious acts
27 "Mashed Potato Time" singer
31 Model Macpherson
32 __ *kleine Nachtmusik*
33 Goldfinger's creator
38 Rawls or Reed
39 Diarist Nin
40 Sticky stuff
41 *Same Time Next Year* star
44 Old-fashioned humor
45 __ carotene
46 Steve Lawrence's partner
49 Dashing young man
53 Actor Wallach
54 Racetrack boundary
55 Franchise holder
60 Vicinities
62 Silents leading lady
63 Lively dance
64 Get moving
65 Gemini org.
66 Put a stop to
67 Is in the red
68 Author Shirley Ann

DOWN

1 Botches up
2 Memorization method
3 Goya's *The Naked __*
4 Menjou of the movies
5 He was Gilligan
6 Otherwise
7 Like __ from the blue
8 Campaigned (for)
9 Morning hrs.
10 Syndicated deejay
11 Poetic muse
12 Kind of kitchen
13 Bumps into
18 Mrs. Zeus
24 Add polish to
25 Building wings
26 *Cakes and __*
27 Farmer's locale
28 "Runaround Sue" singer
29 Cold-shoulder
30 Five of a kind
34 Roll-call response
35 Inventor Sikorsky
36 *Cheers* character
37 Vamoosed
39 Dashiell's dog
42 "I'm Just Wild About Harry" composer
43 Fam. member
44 Making money
47 Windshield adornments
48 Highland valley
49 Jam flavor
50 Biblical brother
51 Investor's concern
52 Poke, in a way
56 Frivolous
57 Burn slightly
58 Actress Lanchester
59 Biblical brother
61 Heavy-hearted
62 Good buddy

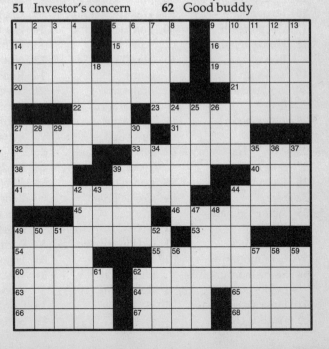

31 CAPITAL IDEA by Richard Silvestri

ACROSS

1 Former filly
5 Likable Lee
9 Freeway entrance
13 Part of BTU
14 Actress Papas
16 "... baked in __"
17 Midwestern capital
20 __ Haw
21 Auxiliary verb
22 Nattily dressed
23 Trap material
24 Macabre
25 Copyright kin
28 "Slippery" trees
29 Barbara __ Geddes
32 Due
33 "You're __ Need to Get By"
34 Scope starter
35 Midwestern capital
38 Cover the inside of
39 Mesabi products
40 Make joyful
41 Oink spot?
42 Walkie-talkie word
43 Former 007
44 End of a CSA signature
45 Installs a lawn
46 Hitching post?
49 Turn on a pivot
50 Trifle (with)
53 Midwestern capital
56 Glee-clubber
57 Disney's "Little Mermaid"
58 Mildred Pierce author
59 More than half
60 Bar mem.
61 Difficult voyage

DOWN

1 Go, to the dogs?
2 Pot payment
3 Ready for picking
4 Greek letter
5 Mum
6 Packing a rod
7 Equine restraint
8 Miller who dances
9 Hoarse-voiced
10 Each, slangily
11 Little bit
12 Christmas tree?
15 Localized
18 African river
19 Head set of a sort
23 Feel the presence of
24 Immigrants' island
25 Straw votes
26 Stay for
27 Cheap-sounding
28 Bugs' nemesis
29 Sired
30 Poets' muse
31 Irish product
33 Come to terms
34 Vitamin forms
36 Short fictional work
37 Face-first fall
42 Bogus butter
43 Extra
44 Magic Kingdom neighbor
45 Winter fall
46 Steamed seafood
47 Aloha State city
48 Aardvark's entrée
49 Bad mood
50 Romanov ruler
51 Steinbeck character
52 Tug hard
54 New Deal agcy.
55 Take steps

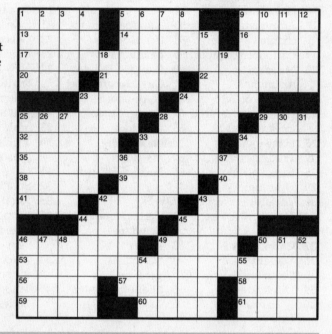

32 TALKING SENSE by Shirley Soloway

ACROSS

1 Hemingway's nickname
5 No gentlemen
9 Boca __, FL
14 "Too bad!"
15 __ end (over)
16 Be penitent
17 Deep breath
18 Home-repair pro Bob
19 Talks up
20 Understand at last
23 Army bed
24 Implore
25 "To __ His Own"
27 Snack on
28 Least resonant
32 Sire
35 Actor Keenan
36 Smith of economics
37 Commotion
38 Some inadmissible evidence
41 Hula instrument
42 Author Uris
44 Story line
45 Rockies resort
47 Comes out for
49 Farm female
50 Small band
51 Gets even for
55 Ms. Gardner
57 Was suspicious
60 Tomato product
62 Small bottle
63 The O'Hara home
64 Make an appearance
65 TV award
66 Unlidded
67 Mr. __ Goes to Town
68 Lunch time
69 Comic Foxx

DOWN

1 No longer chic
2 Totally unfamiliar
3 Debra of films
4 Hardwood source
5 Word of warning
6 Slanting
7 Spanish surrealist
8 Fly in the ointment
9 Chair material
10 From __ Z
11 Improved a bit
12 Not fooled by
13 Roosting place
21 Seventies prime minister
22 Redhead's secret, maybe
26 FBI counterpart
28 Fledglings
29 Meet Me __ Louis
30 Benefit
31 Some govt. agents
32 Farm package
33 Heaven on earth
34 Aesthetic discernment
35 Corduroy texture
39 Sort of salts
40 Went off course
43 Eur. nation
46 Glenn's title
48 Stair parts
49 Actress Keyes
51 Hertz rival
52 Juice choice
53 Golden-__ corn
54 Get up
55 Imitated
56 Housetop sight
58 On a par
59 Wheels of fortune?
61 Newsman Koppel

SINGING THE BLUES by Eric Albert

ACROSS

1 Flying stingers
6 "Hey, you!"
10 Three tsps.
14 Newsboy's cry
15 Hockey great Gordie
16 Jai __
17 Fats Domino tune of '57
19 Nancy of *The Beverly Hillbillies*
20 Garden spots
21 Complain
22 "Pet" complaint
23 Bridge feat
25 Come through
27 Pirate, e.g.
30 Author de Beauvoir
31 Nome home
32 Dyed-in-the-wool
33 Potassium hydroxide solution
36 Steady change
37 Gunning for
39 Mr. Knievel
40 Lawyer's charge
41 Play prize
42 Dickens' __ *House*
43 Accepts, as a credit card
45 Babies do it
46 "Care to dance?"
48 Loud sound
49 Opry greeting
50 Become boring
52 Touch up against
56 Porter's "Well, Did You __!"
57 Dinah Shore tune of '53
59 *Star Wars* role
60 Burgers' surroundings
61 Temporary currency
62 Skim along
63 Some NCOs
64 Intrinsically

DOWN

1 Friday's portrayer
2 Wheel shaft
3 Poker variety
4 Sportscaster's place
5 Snead of golf
6 __ Penh
7 Scotch partner
8 Lovely leap
9 Mystery writer Josephine
10 Hoodwink
11 Bobby Vinton tune of '63
12 Soothing substance
13 One who must be paid
18 Barbra's *Funny Girl* costar
22 Walk heavily
24 Count Tolstoy
26 Kuwait's ruler
27 Jazz phrase
28 Sly look
29 Bing Crosby tune of '37
30 Gratifies completely
34 Slangy assent
35 Actress Sommer
37 Take __ (acknowledge applause)
38 Hydrant
39 High style
41 __ *the Lonely* ('91 film)
42 Pa Cartwright
44 Passé
45 Baby-powder ingredient
46 Book holder
47 Humble home
48 Smile upon
51 Charley had one
53 Roseanne, née __
54 *Exodus* author
55 Use a keyboard
57 Airgun ammo
58 Nile slitherer

THROUGH THE YEAR by Trip Payne

ACROSS

1 Roman moralist
5 *Kon-Tiki* material
10 Breakfast-in-bed prop
14 *Hawaii Five-0* star
15 Out of this world
16 Where "you are"
17 Oklahoma town
18 Air sprays
19 Stuffs one's gut
20 MARCH
23 Kimono sash
24 Zilch
25 Pueblo material
28 High __ kite
31 Doll's word
34 Family member
35 Sudden raid
38 Squash potatoes
40 MAY
43 Lamb's pseudonym
44 Sullivan's student
45 Taunter's cry
46 Splinter group
48 Billy __ Williams
49 Televised
51 Bested in the ring
53 Actress Jillian
54 AUGUST
62 Bee, to Opie
63 Had a show of hands
64 Forearm bone
65 Calf-length
66 Dancing Castle
67 Service-club member
68 Pour __ (exert oneself)
69 Fernando of films
70 Diminished by

DOWN

1 Mr. Kadiddle-hopper
2 Top-rated
3 Where sines are assigned
4 *Goldfinger* heavy
5 Thumper's playmate
6 Tell __ (falsify)
7 Letter to Santa
8 Clockmaker Thomas
9 Williams of *Happy Days*
10 "Cradle of Texas Liberty"
11 Twenty quires
12 Avant-garde
13 Sportscaster's exclamation
21 Overly large
22 Canyon edge
25 Arthur of tennis
26 Microwave features
27 Actor Davis
28 Ready to fight
29 Subway entrance
30 Pew separator
32 Medieval estate
33 __ crow flies
36 Mork's home
37 Compass dir.
39 Oregon peak
41 Give up
42 Rafsanjani, e.g.
47 Nursery-schooler
50 Completely
52 Prepare eggs, in a way
53 Vicunas' home
54 Call it a day
55 Counteract
56 Copperfield's wife
57 Agenda part
58 Actress Rowlands
59 Netman Nastase
60 Genesis character
61 Rather and Rowan
62 "__ my brother's keeper?"

35 WRITE ON! by Cynthia Lyon

ACROSS

1 On vacation
4 Back talk
8 Emulate Brian Boitano
13 *South Pacific* role
15 Twice *cuatro*
16 Courteous
17 START OF A QUIP
19 Writer Cleveland
20 Have no reason to
21 Old hag
22 City on Pearl Harbor's shore
24 Blueprint
25 PART 2 OF QUIP
30 One from Mars
31 What we share
32 Pack away
34 Predetermine the outcome
35 "Enough!", to Enrique
36 Lead to a seat, jocularly
37 Memorized
39 The same
40 Explorer Polo
42 PART 3 OF QUIP
45 Past due
46 Bit of business
47 Cheddarlike cheese
49 Ms. Bloomer
53 Structural
54 END OF QUIP
57 Sun-dried brick
58 Sea shade
59 Auctioneer's cry
60 Hart and Collins
61 Transmit
62 Aye canceler

DOWN

1 Lena of *Havana*
2 Drum partner
3 Actress Alice
4 Tone down
5 Expert
6 Yon maiden
7 Scale member
8 Egyptian amulet
9 What obis accessorize
10 The Bard's river
11 Ersatz swing
12 Ron of TV's *Tarzan*
14 "The will to do, the soul __": Scott
18 Norma Rae's concern
21 Elegance
23 "An oldie, but __"
24 Cheops' edifice
25 David's weapon
26 Princeton mascot
27 Film director Sidney
28 Automotive one-eighty
29 Puccini opera
30 Genesis craft
33 Personal question?
35 Swell
38 Midsize kangaroo
40 Orange Bowl home
41 Shoelace tips
43 Aesop's repertoire
44 In chairs
47 Musical postscript
48 Bloodhound's trail
50 Admired celebrity
51 Kansas city
52 Mayberry sheriff
53 Periodical, for short
54 Home of *Sesame Street*
55 Robin Hood's quaff
56 Baseball score

36 CARPENTRY by Karen Hodge

ACROSS

1 Shish __
6 Datum, for short
10 G.P. grp.
13 Ms. Trump, once
14 Protagonist
15 Rude ones
17 Rock bottom
18 PC owner
19 Columnist Bombeck
20 How some fight
23 Cereal topping
26 Conductor Toscanini
27 "Are you a man __ mouse?"
28 Catchall abbr.
30 Five-star monogram
31 Home room
32 Sondheim musical
36 Canadian flier
37 Noise pollution
38 Assistant
42 American industrialist
47 Classified contents
50 Crew-team prop
51 Pro golfer Woosnam
52 Arabian Baba
53 Duplicates, in a way
55 Block deliverer of old
57 Realizer's cry
61 *Andy Griffith Show* kid
62 End-of-semester event
63 Butler in-law
67 Dried out
68 Do followers
69 Fall tools
70 Hallucinogen letters
71 Read quickly
72 Midmorning munch

DOWN

1 The family
2 __ Marie Saint
3 Acting up
4 *West Side Story* role
5 Minor peer
6 Seal up
7 *Entertainment Tonight* cohost
8 Vicinity
9 Oz transport
10 Without __ (broke)
11 Act the pirate
12 Look up to
16 Ritzy shop
21 Inauguration highlight
22 The __ Scott Decision
23 Start to bubble
24 Cartoonist Peter
25 Alliance acronym
29 Closet lining, often
30 Adoptee of the comics
33 *Strangers __ Train*
34 Carry the day
35 Dave's singing partner
39 Muslim leader
40 Oscar __ Renta
41 Green land?
43 Cheer (for)
44 Kitchen tools
45 Reagan cabinet member
46 Popeye's tattoos
47 Parting word
48 Drive away
49 Elevator alternative
54 Suit material
56 Frome of fiction
58 Co. bigwig
59 Shangri-la resident
60 "__ the Mood for Love"
64 Alias: Abbr.
65 __ room
66 Seek to know

37 SONGS OF '72 by Mel Rosen

ACROSS
1 Surrealist painter
5 Oil-bearing rock
10 Cheese choice
14 Stratford's river
15 Eroded
16 Pastrami parlor
17 God: Lat.
18 Gilbert O'Sullivan '72 tune
20 __ spumante
21 Used a fax
22 Dig (into)
23 Pvt.'s superior
25 Organic compound
26 Sammy Davis, Jr. '72 tune
33 One who wanders
34 __ to Utopia
35 African nation
39 Water pitcher
40 Powerful sharks
41 Actor's quest
42 Something __ (unusual)
43 AT&T employee
44 Mint-family herb

45 Don McLean '72 tune
47 High country
51 Genetic material
52 Have life
53 Ray of films
56 Strait-laced
60 Nilsson '72 tune
62 Rate of speed
63 Gin flavoring
64 Buenos __
65 Mortgage, e.g.
66 Longings
67 "__ not amused"
68 Some footballers

DOWN
1 Nursery word
2 Urban rtes.
3 Impolite type
4 Like crocodile tears
5 Spring, e.g.
6 Patriot Nathan
7 Like __ of bricks
8 Fast time
9 Compass dir.
10 Sidles (toward)
11 Passed out

12 Still in the game
13 Clementine's dad was one
19 Mideast port
24 Train unit
26 Genealogy diagram
27 Wolf's cry
28 Two December days
29 Window treatment
30 Oxen handler
31 New Zealand native
32 Marketing-budget items
35 Juice blend
36 Med. facility
37 Et __ (and others)
38 Proofreader's directive
40 Mr. __ (Teri Garr film)
44 Outlaw
45 Vocal range
46 Lindsay's writing partner

47 Worth gossiping about
48 Cast out
49 Climber's spike
50 Cookout residue
53 End in __ (require overtime)

54 Vega's constellation
55 Active person
57 Come down in buckets
58 Topped a cupcake
59 Clothing department
61 Reuther's org.

38 TRADE NAMES by Wayne R. Williams

ACROSS
1 Wild guesses
6 Run for health
9 Hebrew scroll
14 Classic Gene Tierney film
15 Oklahoma city
16 Wear down
17 Messed up
18 Veteran baseball broadcaster
20 Overacts
22 "My __ Sal"
23 Scalp line
24 Pâté base
27 Doorway side
31 Strikebreaker
32 Contemporary soul singer
34 Prefix for violet
36 __ acids
37 Tenon's complement
40 Waits on
42 Olympics star Zatopek et al.
43 Zurich folk
44 "Night and Day" composer

47 Greek-salad ingredient
51 Farmer, frequently
52 VCR button
53 MacGraw and Baba
54 Shriner's headgear
55 Mother Goose couple
57 Dudley Moore's ex-partner
63 More than enough
64 Martini garnish
65 Norma __
66 Some responses
67 Game-show host
68 Hog's home
69 Lock of hair

DOWN
1 Nods off
2 Landing strip
3 Arctic lights
4 Dodgers' #1 hitter in '91
5 Marquis de __

6 Jam holder
7 Poetic piece
8 Handy tool
9 Blue shade
10 Bobby of hockey
11 Stick up
12 Citrus drink
13 __ Alibi (Selleck film)
19 Silents vamp
21 Chair parts
25 Regarding
26 By way of
27 Founder of CORE
28 Related (to)
29 Patch up
30 Partnership abbr.
33 Dugout stack
35 Speak like Daffy Duck
37 Engineering branch: Abbr.
38 Melville novel
39 Make angry
40 Overwhelms
41 Road rollers
43 Three before V
45 Cartel in the news

46 Barbershop needs
48 Slip by
49 Auto documents
50 Weigh, in a way
54 At large
56 Mtge. installment

57 "Ulalume" writer
58 "Nightmare" street
59 __ Tac Dough
60 Actress Arden
61 Cereal grain
62 Anthem author

ONE-UPMANSHIP by Eric Albert

ACROSS

1 Chili con __
6 Do fingerpainting
10 Make a complaint
14 Liner's "highway"
15 __ facto
16 Singer Fitzgerald
17 Disposes of?
19 *Green Card* director
20 Seeing that
21 What's black and white and Red all over?
23 Falls behind
24 Velvet Underground singer
25 Main road
28 Soup holder
29 Nevada resort
30 Existentialist author
31 In favor of
34 Chance to play
35 Wears a long face
36 Lose energy
37 Pub drink
38 Apartment sign
39 Groundbreaking
40 Paper boss
42 Just
43 Stop-sign shape
45 "The Rape of the Lock" writer
46 Kindergarten book
47 California city
51 Secretary for a day
52 Ecstatic?
54 Fencing need
55 *Dies __*
56 Medium-sized band
57 Laura of *Rambling Rose*
58 Some shortening
59 Deteriorate

DOWN

1 Musical conclusion
2 Old pros
3 Movie division
4 Layered pastry
5 Trap
6 Aria artists
7 *Planet of the __*
8 Halsey's org.
9 Turkish strait
10 Yard-sign start
11 CB radio response?
12 Slur over a syllable
13 Electrical unit
18 Like meringue
22 Bewails
24 Director Sidney
25 "__ girl!"
26 Julia of *The Addams Family*
27 Unfaithful sort?
28 Come to a point
30 List introducer
32 Moundsman Hershiser
33 Bank (on)
35 Service-station supply
36 *Carmen* character
38 Buster Brown's dog
39 Fourth largest planet
41 Make moist
42 Stereo ancestor
43 Made a selection
44 Parisian pancake
45 Went white
47 Lasting impression
48 __ cost (gratis)
49 Pine for
50 Part of A.M.
53 Gun grp.

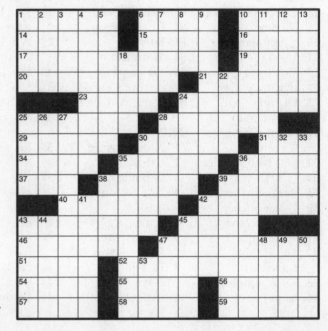

LEFT OUT by Matt Gaffney

ACROSS

1 Golf Hall-of-Famer
6 Fortuneteller
12 *Cats* or *King Kong*
13 Bound by affection
15 Spike Lee film of '89
17 "That's amazing!"
18 Top or train
19 B-F link
20 __-Sheikh (former pro footballer)
24 Smart portrayer
26 Life milestones
30 Admits freely, with "up"
31 Hispanic American
32 Wipe clean
34 Arm
37 __ the test (tries out)
43 Air pair
45 Macbeth was one
46 Lacking power
47 Famous Alley
48 Coffee brewer
50 Wash. neighbor
51 Beatles #1 tune of '66
58 Midwestern college town
59 Dine at home
60 December birthstone
61 Make into law

DOWN

1 Police informer
2 Ding-a-lings
3 Ordinal ending
4 Malt beverage
5 Article written by Kant
6 Baseball great Mel
7 Hamelin menace
8 Otto's "Oh!"
9 Jim Belushi's hometown
10 __ *a Tenor*
11 Beats barely
13 In the past
14 Your ancestor?
15 Tower over
16 "You can do __ you try"
21 Bucks, for instance
22 Enzyme ending
23 Biblical prophet
24 "Just __ suspected!"
25 Actor Dailey
27 Backup strategy
28 __ in "apple"
29 Crush, in a way
33 Go to pieces
34 Candy covering
35 *"Ich bin __ Berliner"*
36 Historical period
38 Tony-winner Hagen
39 Useful article
40 Language group
41 Dentyne rival
42 Mr. Hammerstein
43 Amnesiac's question
44 Out-and-out
45 Leon Uris novel
48 Detroit-based org.
49 Victor's partner
52 Computer-keyboard key
53 Carnival locale
54 __ vivant
55 Minuscule
56 Made a getaway
57 "Make __ double!"

41 THE BOLD ONES by Trip Payne

ACROSS
1 Distaff soldier
5 Hosiery shade
10 Box a bit
14 Verdi opera
15 German industrial city
16 Give a hoot
17 FBI agent
18 Gather wool
19 Not care __
20 Brecht title character
23 Not so many
25 90-degree letter
26 Johnson of *Miami Vice*
27 Pub pour
28 "*La donna è mobile*" is one
32 16th-century council city
34 Platter
36 Becomes beloved
39 Southern sluggers
43 Footrest
44 Vitamin unit
46 Make fit
49 Highfalutin' one
51 Moo __ gai pan
52 The P of "wpm"
53 She's "sweet as apple cider"
56 Extremely pale
58 Classic comic
63 Simpson sibling
64 Not even once
65 Dynamic prefix
68 Preceding periods
69 No longer cutting-edge
70 Iambs and anapests
71 Faxed, perhaps
72 Sportscaster's numbers
73 Take apart

DOWN
1 Shake a finger
2 Marksman's must
3 He played Batman
4 Crusoe carved one
5 *Entertainment Tonight* cohost
6 Arthur of tennis
7 Computer worker
8 Dove's goal
9 Sign up
10 Lasting aftereffect
11 5/30 event
12 Catherine's home
13 Feel contrition
21 Singing syllable
22 "Infra" opposite
23 Craze
24 Lamb's alias
29 Lessee's payment
30 Fascinated by
31 Monroe's successor
33 Invitation abbreviation
35 Hoofbeat sound
37 Statesman Abba
38 Florence's river
40 Rarely visited room
41 Just old enough to vote
42 __ gin fizz
45 Many-faced Chaney
46 Granny Smiths
47 Trace the origin of
48 Gotten out of bed
50 What ewes say
54 Fender flaws
55 Head off
57 Major mess
59 Early cartoonist
60 Nike rival
61 Riga resident
62 Infuriates
66 Beaujolais color
67 __ 60 (acceleration standard)

42 SMOOTH SOLVING by Alex Vaughn

ACROSS
1 Enliven
6 Get past the goalie
11 Affectedly shy
14 Senate's colleagues
15 Today's craze
16 Actress Merkel
17 Draw a conclusion
18 Walters spot
20 Smooth
22 "Who __ kidding?"
24 Satisfied sounds
25 Former Belgrade bigwig
27 Redeems, in a way
30 Belly muscles
33 A Bobbsey twin
34 Stick back together
35 Sha Na Na personae
37 Environmental headaches
39 Garage work
42 Tabernacle tables
46 *Wheel of Fortune* buy
47 __ glance (quickly)
48 Bottomless pits
49 Take to the cleaners
51 Topmost *numero*
52 Ms. Gardner
53 Pennsylvania university town
59 Sylvester Stallone role
60 Corn-chip name
63 Yoko __
64 Mischa of music
65 __ *Attraction* ('87 film)
66 Intuition, plus
67 Wood tool
68 Borg or Ekberg

DOWN
1 __ Beta Kappa
2 L-o-n-g time
3 Breathing hard
4 Software buyer
5 Scope starter
6 Craftspersons
7 Caesar's dog
8 Not fooled by
9 Nothing: Fr.
10 Jazzman Hines
11 Cooking style
12 Brigadier's insignia
13 Go off-course
19 American Legion member
21 Loewe score
22 Part of ETA
23 Dogpatch's Daisy __
26 Light-switch positions
28 Plum variety
29 Board at parties
30 Onassis' nickname
31 Harp on
32 Charlie Brown's sister
35 Some MDs
36 Heathrow craft
38 Little-firm agcy.
39 Chem room
40 Unharmonized passages
41 Hotel staffer
43 High __
44 Race the motor
45 Retiree-payment org.
48 Whoever
50 Family group
51 Sort of sprawl
54 Get ready, for short
55 Grow tiresome
56 Actress Samms
57 Bake-__ (cooking contests)
58 Stick in one's __ (rankle)
59 Doakes or DiMaggio
61 Tiny bit
62 Flamenco dancer's shout

43 PSHAW! by Mel Rosen

ACROSS
1 Send by truck
5 *Oklahoma!* aunt
10 "Cry __ River"
13 Behan's land
14 "Tough!"
15 Spade's namesakes
16 From a distance
17 Physics branch
19 The little things
21 Nobel's homeland
22 Merchandise
25 Church areas
26 Flock of fish
30 *Mermaids* star
32 Praises highly
33 Literary alias
38 Peace Prize city
39 Irrigate
40 Street performer
41 Northern grouse
43 Mohammed's birthplace
44 Word of regret
45 Kind of descendant
46 Comes out for
50 Hose material
52 Northern hemispheres?
54 Eccentric character
59 Former *Candid Camera* cohost
62 Mixed bag
63 Inventive: Abbr.
64 Brunch choice
65 *Close Encounters* craft
66 Former Mideast nation: Abbr.
67 Lent a hand
68 Catches some rays

DOWN
1 Clothes line?
2 Old sound system
3 Turkey neighbor
4 Lima's land
5 Observation
6 Astronomical adjective
7 Actor Marvin
8 Ostrich look-alike
9 Dream phenomena: Abbr.
10 Damsels
11 Game-show host
12 NBA and NCAA
15 Short distance
18 Trophy, at times
20 "Terrible" age
23 Rapturous delight
24 Martin of movies
26 Feed the pigs
27 Playbill listing
28 Luau act
29 Bakery enticement
31 Common Mkt. locale
33 Irreligious
34 Seer's signal
35 Good-natured
36 Fitness club
37 Ground grain
39 Wheaton of *Star Trek: The Next Generation*
42 Lodge member
43 Take exception to
45 Kept safe
46 Old-time theater name
47 Athens civic center
48 "__ de Lune"
49 King follower
51 Jeweler's need
53 Humane org.
55 Main event, for one
56 __ Romeo
57 Columbia athlete
58 At a __ for words
60 Work wk. end
61 Showed the way

44 FILM HAND by Wayne R. Williams

ACROSS
1 Sharp punch
4 Play the guitar
9 Biblical king
14 *The Name of the Rose* author
15 Lasso
16 Castle or Cara
17 With *The*, Heston classic
20 __ Aviv
21 Small bottle
22 Go one better
23 Cruelty, and then some
26 Actress Irving
27 Verse starter?
28 Reynolds film of '83
31 War god
32 Mystery writer Josephine
33 Water pitcher
34 Leather type
35 Laughlin film of '71
38 Store group
41 Ambience
42 Just released
45 Actor Julia
46 Elvis film of '58
49 UFO pilots
50 D.C. official
51 Something whispered
52 Do something
53 Fiery offense
56 Outer edge
57 Bogart/Hepburn classic
62 Spooky
63 Tour of duty
64 Endangered antelope
65 Winding devices
66 Charlie Chan portrayer
67 ABA member

DOWN
1 Black shade
2 Clear plastic
3 Arid
4 Box office abbr.
5 Cratchit kid
6 Freeway access
7 Area code 801
8 Overzealous one
9 Indistinctly
10 "All the Things You __"
11 Business deal
12 Chanted
13 Can't stand
18 Muse of history
19 Myra Hess' title
23 Air France flier
24 Goose group
25 Cry like a baby
29 Fam. member
30 Indo-European
31 Razor-billed bird
34 Sudden alarm
35 Puppeteer Baird
36 Moonshine holder
37 Circle sections
38 Brings into being
39 Little axe
40 Forbidding
42 Former leader of Panama
43 Mercury, but not Venus
44 Drenched
46 *From Here to Eternity* actress
47 Be unyielding
48 Brown shade
50 Bank boxes
54 Numerical prefix
55 Tooth partner
58 Prepare to fire
59 Vane dir.
60 Acctg. period
61 Brazil, e.g.

ACROSS

1 Doorframe part
5 Blind as __
9 Guitarist from Spain
14 "Dies __" (Latin hymn)
15 Between-meal bite
16 Aficionado
17 Bête noire
18 Defense grp.
19 Dress style
20 START OF A QUOTE
23 Asleep at the switch
24 Mule's father
25 Lama land
28 Attention-getter
30 Mass expression
34 Airline to Tokyo
35 H.S. jrs.' exam
37 Nome native
39 END OF QUOTE
42 Mechanic's concern
43 Interoffice note
44 Bristol brew
45 Observed
46 Take five
48 __ up (got smart)
50 Wine word
51 Bear lair
52 SPEAKER OF QUOTE
59 Johnson of Brief Encounter
60 Well-ventilated
61 "Puttin' on the __"
63 Peel it and weep
64 Sacred cow
65 Buffalo's water
66 Miniskirt Mary
67 "The __ of the Ancient Mariner"
68 Laura of Rambling Rose

DOWN

1 Mainsail's neighbor
2 King Fahd, e.g.
3 Countless
4 Private Bailey
5 Edifice add-on
6 Gravy holder
7 __ spumante
8 Doubting disciple
9 Crow's toes
10 Trevino's target
11 Tel __
12 Actor Auberjonois
13 Vein contents
21 Old-fashioned sticker
22 Put on a pedestal
25 Subdues Simba
26 Cockamamie
27 Scout's honor
28 Lassie's offering
29 Sunflower supports
30 Rap-sheet abbr.
31 He had a gilt complex
32 Monsieur Zola
33 Big-name
36 Audiophile's equipment
38 April occurrence
40 Wagner's one
41 Dachshund doc
47 Napoleon's cousin
49 Instinctive
50 Barely enough
51 Holmes' creator
52 Course listing
53 Inter __ (among other things: Lat.)
54 Pride papa
55 Skirt length
56 One __ the Heart (Coppola film)
57 Green land
58 Swizzle
59 Vin partner
62 Buddhist sect

ACROSS

1 Cold period
5 Fast planes, briefly
9 Rural structures
14 Roll-call response
15 Luau spread
16 Single-masted boat
17 Storied sword
19 Entertain
20 Beale and Bourbon: Abbr.
21 Vote in
22 Over again
23 Last name in plows
24 Deck worker
26 Inquisitive types
29 Type of birthday card
32 Maui mementos
33 U.S. artifacts
35 Storage container
36 Lerner and Loewe musical
38 "It's cold!"
39 Like a cad
41 Mailbox feature
42 Sadistic sorts
43 Thin cereals
45 Goes like lightning
46 "Get lost!"
48 Bons __ (witty remarks)
50 Free of errata
51 NFL gains
54 Cookout residue
56 Quest object
58 Mystery data
59 Gilligan's home
60 "__ Want for Christmas . . ."
61 Large group
62 Hammer hurler of myth
63 Fuse metal

DOWN

1 "__ a Lady" (Tom Jones tune)
2 Deli-counter call
3 Circle segments
4 Soup ingredient
5 Rural crossings
6 Cavalry weapon
7 Cease-fire
8 Put in order
9 Eagles' org.
10 Fact book
11 Business conference
12 Small margin of victory
13 Throw out
18 Sly expression
23 __ Moines, IA
24 Gutsy chap
25 Touched down
26 Photo holder
27 Paris' river
28 Malory character
29 Clobber
30 Place on a list
31 Pub game
33 Amo, __, amat
34 Guys
36 Cut out
37 Malt beverages
40 Liqueur flavoring
41 Bottom line
43 Comparatively cloudy
44 Called up
46 Move through water
47 Casals' instrument
48 __ 1 (speed of sound)
49 Cold capital
50 IOU
51 Bush's alma mater
52 Pickle choice
53 Lost traction
55 Vane dir.
57 Not refined

47 BRR! by Shirley Soloway

ACROSS
1 Mardi __
5 Spheroid hairdo
9 Disaster film?
13 Latvia's capital
14 Prepares presents
16 Out-of-the-ordinary
17 Opening remark
19 In the past
20 San __, CA
21 Minimal money
22 Burn the surface of
23 Rat follower
25 Toward the dawn
27 Under-the-table cash source
31 Upright, for one
35 Barnyard sitter
36 Bombay wear
37 "If You Knew Susie" singer
38 Craving
40 Actress Berger
42 Was generous
43 Least ruddy
45 Dame __ Chaplin
47 Author Buscaglia
48 Barbecue order
49 Grows rapidly
51 Circle meas.
53 Stage pullers
54 Author Ambler
57 Pause in the action
59 Hangs ten
63 Lorre's detective
64 Excludes from participation
66 Admired one
67 Blazing
68 *Born Free* character
69 Be disposed (to)
70 Ltr. writer's courtesy
71 Forest dweller

DOWN
1 Hold tight
2 Chinese-restaurant freebie
3 Matured
4 Native-born Israelis
5 Impress a lot
6 Break
7 Garden tool
8 Broke into
9 Cake feature
10 Country path
11 Whale of a '77 film
12 Mr. Gynt
15 Sp. miss
18 Author Philip et al.
24 Pull __ one (try to cheat)
26 Health club
27 Armada members
28 Permit access to
29 Defeated one's cry
30 Curtain fabric
32 In any way
33 Innovative
34 Black-and-white snacks
37 "__ talk?": Rivers
39 Sneezing cause, maybe
41 Whistle blowers
44 Emulate Killy
46 Take down a peg
49 Blue cartoon characters
50 Gratified
52 __ Romeo (auto)
54 Send forth
55 Took the bus
56 Take __ the chin
58 *Star Wars* princess
60 Portrayal
61 Circuit device
62 Hollywood Boulevard embedment
65 Last letter

48 REPEATERS by Wayne R. Williams

ACROSS
1 Track circuit
4 Kind of energy
9 Sounded sheepish
14 __ Miss (southern school)
15 Came up
16 Dropped the ball
17 Thoroughgoing
19 Brings under control
20 Show the pearly whites
21 Giraffe's cousin
23 Joins up
25 Suffix for form
26 Santa __, CA
28 Conks out
29 Kind of combat
33 Lofty poem
34 Mezzo Marilyn
35 Mil. address
38 Cheer of a sort
41 Tillis or Tormé
42 Asian capital
44 Genetic letters
45 Gradually
48 Boorish one
52 Short distance
53 __-jongg
54 Provoke passion
56 Fireballer Ryan
58 Spoke and spoke
59 Yonder folks
61 Ruthless competition
65 Bowling alleys
66 April-like
67 Recipe phrase
68 Kasparov's game
69 Van Gogh locale
70 Choice: Abbr.

DOWN
1 Set free
2 Homecoming guests
3 Women's clothing size
4 More rational
5 California fort
6 Old card game
7 Tempe sch.
8 Passed gossip
9 VHS alternative
10 Plains tribe
11 Like strolling lovers
12 Shoebox letters
13 Shingle letters
18 Pub preferences
22 *Krazy* __
24 Chase away
25 Bring to light
27 __ of Cleves
30 Nav. rank
31 Taunter's cry
32 Penna. neighbor
35 Contented comments
36 Woodland way
37 Basketball variety
38 Strait place: Abbr.
39 SSW opposite
40 Open-mouthed stare
43 Runs against
46 Singer Sumac
47 Dee or O'Connor
48 Ella's style
49 Evans and Blair
50 *My Favorite Year* star
51 Asia's Bay of __
55 They see right through you
57 Not so much
59 RN's specialty
60 Doubter's exclamation
62 Rowing-team member
63 Gerard or Hodges
64 Chemical ending

49 ALL AT SEA by Karen Hodge

ACROSS

1 Do a slow burn
5 Throat-clearing sound
9 Wool-coat owners
13 Hamilton Burger's nemesis
15 Church area
16 Fe, to a chemist
17 Modern prefix
18 Country singer Campbell
19 Utah resort
20 Scottish sailboat?
23 Contemptible sort
24 Quick to learn
25 Chanel's nickname
28 Get ready for dinner
31 Board's partner
34 Garden shrub
36 *Atlantis* org.
38 LaSalle or DeSoto
40 Why ritzy ships are made?
43 Compass dir.
44 "I cannot tell __"
45 __ as the driven snow
46 National League division
48 Something boring
50 Miner's treasures
51 Spherical veggie
53 Hawk
55 Female barge crews?
62 Pavarotti piece
63 Crowd noise
64 Looks leeringly at
66 Breathe hard
67 Bible book
68 Nero's instrument
69 Ultimate objectives
70 Refuse to acknowledge
71 Rag-doll name

DOWN

1 Dallas sch.
2 Powder ingredient
3 Are, to Pilar
4 Timber defect
5 Ms. Lansbury
6 *Let's Make a Deal* host
7 Mr. Knievel
8 The brainy bunch
9 Theater district
10 Guthrie the younger
11 Marquand's sleuth
12 Cereal sound
14 Back of the neck
21 Lament
22 Uses an aerosol
25 Beer purchase
26 Layer in the news
27 __ cropper (failed)
29 Curl the lip
30 "Bali __"
32 Take place
33 Skier Phil
35 Lifts one's spirits
37 Impresario, e.g.
39 Hwys.
41 Clown around
42 Literary justification
47 Sounds of impact
49 Off the track
52 Landed, as gentry
54 Stunt-plane maneuver
55 Appear stunned
56 OPEC member
57 Orange cover
58 Seep slowly
59 Raise a red flag
60 Look ahead
61 Mail out
65 Sauce source

50 COST OF LEAVING by Eric Albert

ACROSS

1 Temporary currency
6 Lose control
11 Sharp turn
14 Came to power
15 The Jetsons' dog
16 Whitney patriarch
17 START OF A QUIP
19 Ms. Ullmann
20 Fragrant legume
21 Big family
23 Marvin of movies
24 Popular cordial
26 Business patterns
30 Indiana's state flower
31 "Very funny!"
32 Pioneer impressionist
33 Frontiersman Carson
36 MIDDLE OF QUIP
40 Get-up-and-go
41 Ben on *Bonanza*
42 Laundry loss, maybe
43 Fairway flaw
44 Hate heartily
46 Traveling group
49 About 907 kilograms
50 Where you live
51 Supported
56 Wild spree
57 END OF QUIP
60 Take advantage of
61 Girder of a sort
62 Flight part
63 Badminton need
64 *Tootsie* star
65 Expedition

DOWN

1 Fresh talk
2 Cornfield preyer
3 Tiber town
4 "It's clear now!"
5 Grinder
6 Check getter
7 Nonspeaking part in *The Thin Man*
8 Advanced degree?
9 Annuity alternative
10 Gain affection for
11 Allen film of '83
12 Suspect's out
13 Basic assumption
18 Tarzan's neighbors
22 *The Bridge of San Luis __*
24 Touch, for one
25 Leopold's colleague
26 Bloke
27 Ivy League school
28 Block part
29 Run for it
30 Main idea
32 Comic Cohen
33 Running bowline, e.g.
34 Restless desire
35 Toddler
37 Pesto ingredient
38 Science show
39 NATO member
43 Dear old one?
44 Weaver's machine
45 Headlong dash
46 Cooking style
47 Humiliate
48 Best-known synonymist
49 Musical motif
51 Kind of carpet
52 Kett of the comics
53 *"Buenos __"*
54 Troop group
55 Combustible heap
58 Mavericks' org.
59 Hamilton's bill

SPORTS HIGHLIGHTS by Wayne R. Williams

ACROSS

1 Made logs
6 Ambience
10 Taj Mahal site
14 Luncheonette's lure
15 Like horses' hooves
16 Bread unit
17 Blood part
18 Football event
20 Huntz or Arsenio
21 Roman playwright
22 Plains Indian
24 Thurber dreamer
28 Pro golf event
30 Sci-fi author James
32 Revoke, in law
33 Comic DeLuise
34 One __ million
35 Čapek play
36 Hockey event
40 Extra ltr. addendum
41 MDX divided by X
42 Road hazard
43 Used used candles

45 Make a list
48 Tennis events
50 Part of PGA
51 Full of aphorisms
52 Fanatical ones
55 Boast
58 NCAA semis teams
61 Mrs. Helmsley
62 Nasal sensation
63 Change the decor
64 Single
65 Simpson kid
66 Bk. after Amos
67 Burn, in a way

DOWN

1 Beauty-pageant accessory
2 Vicinity
3 Baseball event
4 Take after
5 Beaver project
6 Selling points
7 *Enterprise* crew member
8 Cowboy's accessory
9 Mideast port

10 Even if
11 Infant's syllable
12 Sushi-like
13 CIO's partner
19 Sergeant Preston's grp.
21 Rocky crag
23 Bush cabinet member
25 Horse-racing event
26 Bowler's target
27 Leavening agents
28 Actress Strassman
29 Eighteen-year-olds
30 As well
31 UN currency agcy.
33 Commercial coloring
37 Designer Claiborne
38 Sure shot
39 Gift-tag word
44 Unisex
46 Salieri's tormentor

47 N. Atlantic nation
48 Not walked upon
49 Sea plea
51 Soft cheese
53 Hendrix's hairdo
54 Leopold's colleague

56 Till contents
57 Walk in water
58 Watch pocket
59 Ms. Lupino
60 Negative conjunction
61 Director Jean-__ Godard

MEN OF LETTERS by Trip Payne

ACROSS

1 Legume holders
5 Après-ski spot
10 Turn-of-the-century ruler
14 Devilish doings
15 Sports stadium
16 Tropical spot
17 "since feeling is first" poet
19 Author Hunter
20 Gussies up
21 Agent 86's series
23 Authoritative statement
24 Undergrad degs.
25 Prime-time hour
26 Hymn book
29 Trivial Pursuit need
32 __ Paulo, Brazil
35 XIII qvadrvpled?
36 Bearer's task
38 "The Four Quartets" poet
40 *Beasts and Super Beasts* author
41 Parthenon dedicatee

42 Curly poker?
43 Spelling meet
44 Soldier-show sponsor
45 Sissyish
48 Battleship letters
50 Deluge refuge
51 __ living (work)
56 Don't fret
59 More grainy, perhaps
60 Soprano Gluck
61 *Women in Love* author
63 Ladder-back chair part
64 Electron tube
65 "__ silly question . . ."
66 Glass square
67 Sneetches' creator
68 Fine kettle of fish

DOWN

1 Looks through the door
2 Has __ barrel
3 Unpredictable

4 Pivots
5 Rotating pieces
6 *Exodus* hero
7 Language of India
8 Absorb food
9 Magazine magnate Condé
10 "__ Kangaroo Down, Sport"
11 Philo Vance's creator
12 Controversial tree spray
13 Office expense
18 Pre-Q queue
22 Senator Thurmond
24 Worms, often
27 Novelist Wilson
28 Merman or Mertz
30 Memo heading
31 I, to Claudius
32 Jet-set jets
33 "A Shropshire Lad" poet
34 Grand __ Opry
37 Bathday place
38 Greek letter
39 Occupied
40 Use the horn

42 Ms. Retton
46 Golfer's iron
47 Datebook duration
49 Put forth
52 Mr. T's ex-group
53 Shampoo-bottle instruction

54 Bottle parts
55 Geometrician's finds
56 Grate upon
57 Actress Joyce of *Roc*
58 Interjects
59 Is beholden to
62 TV spots

53   SUCCESSES by Randolph Ross

ACROSS
1 With suspicion
8 Placing in combat
15 Precarious perch
16 Tuscany, long ago
17 Was successful, in the ring
19 Begley, Jr. and Sr.
20 Chemistry Nobelist Harold
21 Service charge
22 Russia's __ Sea
25 Here: Fr.
26 To-do
27 Was successful, like a pelican?
32 Cable TV's Emmy
33 Civil War shade
34 __ way (sort of)
35 Public platforms
37 Shop machine
41 NBA arbiter
42 Civil unrest
44 Beauty preceder
45 Was successful, at the deli?
48 Circular word
50 Memorable time
51 Kimono accessories
52 United rival
53 Pérez de Cuéllar's home
55 High-tech banking serv.
57 Was successful, in the air
63 Treeless region
64 Black eyes
65 Sonnet parts
66 Offers up

DOWN
1 "Eureka!"
2 Charles, to Philip
3 Ship's mph
4 Too
5 Yearn for
6 Train components
7 Hot time in Le Havre
8 *Dick Van Dyke Show* family name
9 Spillane's __ *Jury*
10 Low card
11 Oleo holder
12 Easily angered
13 McKinley's hometown
14 Stiff winds
18 Luxembourg, e.g.
22 Worshipper's place?
23 Puerto __
24 Tavern brews
25 "Give __ rest!"
26 Flying standard
28 Leggy bird
29 Working manuscript
30 Once-popular theater name
31 Monogram parts: Abbr.
36 Loyal
38 Swedish auto
39 Culture starter
40 Joins together
42 Second showing
43 "__ Yankee Doodle dandy"
45 Ms. Barton et al.
46 Day savers
47 Comes __ (is recalled)
48 Assembly instructions
49 In the know
53 Louis XVI, to Louis XVII
54 Polish prose
55 Arthur of tennis
56 Bed size
58 Coll. hoops contest
59 Superlative suffix
60 Society-page word
61 Cur's comment
62 Draft org.

54   BIRTHDAY BOY by Mel Rosen

ACROSS
1 Word often mispunctuated
4 Cars for hire
8 Carrot-family spice
13 Big party
15 State openly
16 Sound off
17 Earth sci.
18 Sandwich shop
19 Basic measurements
20 Cult series starring 40 Across
23 "I should say __!"
24 *2001* computer
25 It may be common
27 Likely to be bought
31 Musical combo
35 Greek letter
36 Cotton bundles
39 Do roadwork
40 Actor born March 19th
44 *Aida* piece
45 Reaches new heights
46 Top ranking
47 Doorframe topper
50 Most intimidating
52 Hogan rival
55 Supplement, with "out"
56 Woody's frequent costar
59 Spy series starring 40 Across
64 Computer-data format
66 It gets high twice a day
67 Cheese choice
68 David's weapon
69 At any time
70 Résumé, for short
71 Family auto
72 Home rooms
73 Heavy weight

DOWN
1 "__ a Kick Out of You"
2 Dash dial
3 Gin flavoring
4 Michigan city
5 Rosary prayers
6 Heavy knives
7 Boars and sows
8 Salad, for one
9 Coffeemaker
10 Most important
11 "Tell __ the judge!"
12 Cozy home
14 __ Centauri
21 Temple leader
22 Printing measures
26 Montreal pro
27 Calyx part
28 Nintendo forerunner
29 Cicero's language
30 Lodge members
32 Resort lake
33 Linda or Dale
34 Article of faith
37 Comic Philips
38 Con game
41 Hamelin pests
42 Receptionists, e.g.
43 Japanese metropolis
48 Annapolis graduate
49 Singer Brenda
51 Israeli desert
53 Played a scene
54 Transmission gear
56 It abuts Vt.
57 Land in the ocean?
58 Low-pH stuff
60 Genesis setting
61 Splice film
62 U.S. alliance
63 Fed. agent
65 Once __ blue moon

55 NO CHANGE by Cynthia Lyon

ACROSS

1 Comic Conway
4 In need of caulking
9 Kennel cries
13 Indivisible
14 *L.A. Law* role
15 Peter, in Panama
16 Bookkeeper: Abbr.
17 Poison
18 Delight in
19 START OF A FRAN LEBOWITZ QUOTE
22 Job tyro
23 Conditional conjunction
27 Mid.
28 La __ Tar Pits
30 Navigational aid
31 Malt-shop order
34 PART 2 OF QUOTE
37 Lummoxes
39 Rock singer Rose
40 Terry or Burstyn
41 PART 3 OF QUOTE
44 Western wear
45 Pinocchio's undoing
46 Within arm's reach
47 Pierre's pal
49 Chicken
51 Tart in tone
55 END OF QUOTE
58 Trembling
61 Ring championship
62 Dixie st.
63 Stephanie Zimbalist's dad
64 Ibsen's __'s *House*
65 Weightlifting units: Abbr.
66 They're often connected
67 Mead need
68 Loos' Lorelei

DOWN

1 Hoist glasses
2 Bring upon oneself
3 Tourist magnet
4 Hidden
5 Pencil-box contents
6 Ouzo flavoring
7 Well-meaning
8 Himalayan hulk
9 Barbra role
10 N. modifier
11 Paid player
12 Oil source
15 Alias of a sort
20 Noisy bug
21 Where you may see a second helping
24 *South Pacific* character
25 Is frugal
26 Exhausted
28 Popular pooch
29 Rub the wrong way
31 Fishlike
32 Kukla's colleague
33 Wooden peg
35 Sunblock substance
36 __ *Madigan* ('67 film)
38 Like word
42 Does darning
43 Balloon basket
48 Just
50 Personal preferences
51 River of rhyme
52 Cagers' game, for short
53 "__ darned!"
54 Put an end to
56 Logan's locale
57 Rover's playmate
58 Proof letters
59 E.T.'s craft
60 Museum material

56 HARD-HITTING by Eric Albert

ACROSS

1 It cools your head
7 Parisian pal
10 Big shot
13 City on Lake Erie
14 Blueprint
15 Dublin's loc.
16 Like a mosaic
17 *Soufflé* ingredient
18 Use the microwave
19 Round a rink
20 Snoop's motivation
22 LBJ son-in-law
24 Central sections
25 Poodle name
28 Unpaired
29 Pittsburgh player, for short
30 "Get a load of that!"
31 European airline
32 Request
36 On the summit
37 British playwright Joe
39 Consequently
40 In sad shape
42 Tampa clock setting: Abbr.
43 Course length
44 Have vittles
45 Recording label
46 Shed tears
47 Slyly malicious
50 Hue and cry
52 Bow material
54 Katmandu's country
58 George's brother
59 Sea swallow
60 Conventional city?
61 Handy Latin abbr.
62 Sharp taste
63 Milk holder
64 Baseball commissioner Vincent
65 Before, in palindromes
66 Walk of life

DOWN

1 Like __ (candidly)
2 Bop on the bean
3 Singer Fitzgerald
4 Ferlinghetti and Ginsberg, e.g.
5 Parting word
6 Saturn or Neptune
7 Police bulletin
8 Hawaiian isle
9 Ready to use, as a camera
10 Arabian Nights bigwig
11 Really steamed
12 British diarist
14 British cash
20 Closet lining
21 Mechanic's tool
23 Become mellow
25 Unwanted fat
26 Tiny speck
27 Alimentary input
29 Small chicken
33 At large
34 Mean man
35 Easy victory
38 *Sesame Street* grouch
41 County in 11 states
47 Foremost
48 It comes from the heart
49 Beatty role
50 Chile partner
51 Slightly ahead
53 Pay attention to
55 Lap dog
56 Declare
57 Behind time
60 *Pygmalion* monogram

57 VERTICES by Mel Rosen

ACROSS

1 Fill fully
5 Show amazement
9 *Person to Person* network
12 Brick worker
13 Earthly extremes
14 Move quickly
15 Short of cash
17 Chicken-king link
18 *Much __ About Nothing*
19 Bring up
20 First name in glue
22 Open-hearted
24 Drawer attachment
25 Talks too much
30 Singer Lane et al.
33 Simple Simon's yens
34 Seafood delicacy
35 Litigious one
36 Old hat
38 Brassy Horne
39 Under the weather
40 Nibble on
41 Was helpful
42 Every available means
46 "As __ going to St. Ives . . ."
47 Seltzer-making gadget
51 Fudge nut
53 Small role
55 Major rte.
56 Swear words?
57 Foundation element
60 USO visitors
61 Large antelope
62 Sahara stopovers
63 Sault __ Marie, MI
64 Makes a dress
65 Told a whopper

DOWN

1 Riyadh resident
2 __ Martin (007's auto)
3 One __ customer
4 Menu choices
5 Lots and lots
6 Skin-cream additive
7 Church bench
8 Ancient ascetics
9 Having rooms
10 Peevishness
11 Burn the outside of
12 Extinct birds
13 Worked at a trade
16 Be worthy of
21 Spanish article
23 "Good buddy"
24 Baby bouncer
26 Give rise to
27 Wildcat strike
28 First-rate
29 Audition (for)
30 Korea, China, Iran, etc.
31 Wall Street optimist
32 Eager to fight
36 *__ Gotta Have It* ('86 film)
37 Afternoon ritual
38 "Mona __"
40 Raffle tickets
41 Spray can
43 LAX client
44 Patronized a casino
45 A certain smile
48 "__ Were the Days"
49 Had the deed to
50 Bologna breads
51 Swine
52 Work in the cutting room
53 Stick in one's __ (rankle)
54 Sothern and Miller
58 Señor's "Hurrah!"
59 Skater Babilonia

58 GOING METRIC by Fred Piscop

ACROSS

1 As such
6 Dog-paddled
10 Farm cribs
14 "Hi" or "bye"
15 Rock group Motley __
16 Mary Kay rival
17 Raw __ (crayon color)
18 Auto part
19 *Rikki-Tikki-__*
20 Getting beat
22 Eighth, e.g.
24 A few Z's
25 Metric dessert?
28 Discipline
31 Soprano __ Gluck
32 Boathouse gear
33 Rickenbacker was one
35 "There is many __ twixt . . ."
39 Metric working hours?
44 Alley "oops"
45 Did lunch
46 __ de cologne
47 Moby Dick's foe
50 Dry wine
53 Metric haberdashery?
57 "Am I a man __ mouse?"
58 Native Canadian
59 Droopy-eared dog
63 Engine enclosures
65 Molecule component
67 Type of heating
68 Yemen seaport
69 "Would __ to you?"
70 "Time in a Bottle" singer
71 Nothing
72 Singer Carter
73 "Casey __ Bat"

DOWN

1 Peter __ Rubens
2 *Blondie* kid
3 Holds up
4 Arab rulers
5 Make money the old-fashioned way
6 Univ. or acad.
7 Off by a mile
8 Arctic sight
9 Intellectual
10 Cave dweller
11 Ms. Trump, once
12 Evans' partner
13 Take potshots
21 Look in your eye
23 Samms and Lazarus
26 Some time ago
27 Bread or cabbage
28 Gear teeth
29 Lamp part
30 Sea of Russia
34 Hellenic H
36 Claim against property
37 "__ first you . . ."
38 Tobacco-chewer's sound
40 Tiny container
41 Set of values
42 Use acid, maybe
43 Recovery regimen, for short
48 *Strangers on __*
49 Common bug
51 Mississippi River source
52 Classify
53 Mercury model
54 Wear away
55 *Unsafe at Any Speed* author
56 Apply more lubricant
60 Job opening
61 Price-list word
62 Locust or lime
64 __-Cone (cool treat)
66 Gibson of *Lethal Weapon*

59 NATIVE SPORTSMEN by Randolph Ross

ACROSS
1 Love __ the Ruins
6 Gandhi's bane
14 Richards of tennis
15 Pirate-ship post
16 American Leaguer
18 Alts.
19 Transparent gemstone
20 Choice word
21 Arizona State city
22 Army outposts
23 Game judge
26 Inventor Sikorsky
28 Russian river
29 Gymnast Comaneci
31 Supplement, with "out"
34 Georgia Dome, in '92
38 Sturgeon-to-be
39 Anatomical pouch
40 "Read 'em and __!"
41 Thin and strong
42 Swell, to Eliza
45 Spongelike cakes
48 __ Peak
49 Piece of steelwork
50 Orthopedist's adjective
52 Dallas sch.
55 NFLer
58 Ups the ante
59 Aaron Copland work
60 Bestowed lavishly
61 *Golden Boy* writer

DOWN
1 Paris landmark
2 Lose solidity
3 Some change
4 Cal. neighbor
5 Old coot
6 Ball's sidekick
7 __-European
8 Getting __ years
9 Mr. Chaney
10 Make beloved
11 Simon and Diamond
12 Break off
13 Fish-eating birds
15 Bob Vila's field
17 Ade flavoring
21 Type starter
22 Big pig
23 German valley
24 Switch suffix
25 Series set at a high school
26 High-minded folks
27 Strait loc.
30 Contented sounds
31 At all times
32 Howard of *Dallas*
33 Catch sight of
35 Sapporo sashes
36 Beethoven's "__ Elise"
37 Leaves openmouthed
41 European capital
43 Give the go-ahead
44 Zipper's descendant
45 Health-spa gear
46 Embarrass
47 Where *el dinero* is
48 Was nosy
50 Old-time autocrat
51 Entr'__
52 Join (with)
53 Have a session
54 Sky sightings
56 Stout alternative
57 Coal carrier

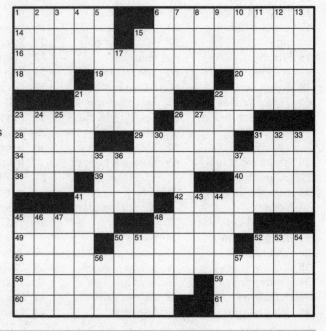

60 HIDDEN ISLANDS by Wayne R. Williams

ACROSS
1 Nutmeglike spice
5 Rodeo rope
10 Highlander
14 Book after Joel
15 Cast member
16 Race driver Yarborough
17 Fast season
18 Aquanaut hides Caribbean island
20 Ancient Peruvians
22 Stalk topper
23 AAA suggestion
24 Invitees
26 Musical group hides Mediterranean island
29 Ten to one, e.g.
33 Auction unit
34 __ Blair (Orwell)
35 Shamir's nation
37 Supped
38 Musician hides New York island
40 *Little Women* monogram
41 Golf-ball material
43 Novelist Ferber
44 "The Boy King"
45 Roy Rogers' real name
46 Eastern seaport hides Indonesian island
48 Made over
51 Turned tail
52 Cried out excitedly
55 Greek letter
58 Medicine growers hide Indonesian island
62 Put to sea
63 Dextrous starter
64 Comb, in a way
65 Regarding
66 Catchall cat.
67 Quaking tree
68 Self-images

DOWN
1 Landlocked African nation
2 Prayer conclusion
3 Actually hides Mediterranean island
4 Ritzy home
5 __ Palmas
6 IRA, e.g.
7 R-V hookup?
8 Expressed sorrow
9 Talking tests
10 Use cutters
11 Cleveland team, to fans
12 Spread in a tub
13 Period of office
19 Morse symbol
21 Make a choice
24 Writer Sheehy
25 Sullied
26 Granite blocks
27 Across-the-board
28 La __ Tar Pits
30 Western outlaws hide Pacific islands
31 Hold back
32 Board of education?
35 Doesn't exist
36 Way up
39 Do nothing
42 Type of dancing
46 Letter parts
47 Ann Sothern film role
49 Ecology org.
50 Actress Burke
52 "POW!"
53 Fractional prefix
54 Spheres
56 Spanish painter
57 Pub servings
59 Maple product
60 Mao __-tung
61 Sun Yat-__

61 WEATHER REPORT by Wayne R. Williams

ACROSS

1 Take for granted
7 Foolishly fond
11 Actress Ullmann
14 Slo-mo showing
15 *Topaz* author
16 Hole-in-one
17 *The Invisible Man* star
19 __ Tin Tin
20 Jannings or Zatopek
21 Computer command
22 Part of Cohan's signature
23 Delany and Carvey
25 *My Little Margie* star
29 Tug's offering
31 Drink for two?
32 *Scarlett* predecessor
41 Continental abbr.
42 Gallagher's vaudeville partner
43 Actor Beatty
44 Florida collegians
49 Penultimate Greek letter
50 One on the beat
51 Stroke of luck
57 Visual aid
61 Historic time
62 Midday
64 Digestive-system word form
65 Break in the action
66 Sudden noise
69 Had a snack
70 Peter the pianist
71 Filmdom's T.E. Lawrence
72 Directed
73 Prepares to drive
74 Cleared, as salary

DOWN

1 Moved in a curved path
2 Alabama town
3 Columbus' sponsor
4 Lament loudly
5 Hatterlike
6 Spud features
7 Tropical fruit
8 Prospero's servant
9 Rummy game
10 Horse's cousin
11 Slow tempo
12 More aloof
13 Malice, so to speak
18 Dustcloth
24 Scatter seeds
26 Kind of pride
27 "Understand?"
28 Fancy marble
30 "__ and Hopin' "
32 Precious stone
33 Arles assent
34 New Deal grp.
35 Calendar abbr.
36 One of the ladies
37 Sea dog
38 Rustic hotel
39 Society-page word
40 Graduate deg.
45 Velocity abbr.
46 Adherent's suffix
47 Machine tooth
48 Brandy flavor
51 Statutory
52 Seeing red
53 Opened wide
54 Habituate
55 Child's taboos
56 Vulcan, e.g.
58 Parcel out
59 Norman Vincent __
60 Had aspirations
63 Light gas
66 Explosive letters
67 __ *Haw*
68 Hwy.

62 BIKE RACK by Randolph Ross

ACROSS

1 Play parts
5 Kipling character
8 Pet-shop purchase
12 Café au __
13 __ *kleine Nachtmusik*
14 Figurine mineral
15 Logic
16 Throw for a loop
17 Totally attentive
18 PR representative
21 Big-time operators
24 Actress Garr
25 Pseudonym
27 "Now I gotcha!"
30 __ of passage
32 Burning
33 Up-to-date
34 Make __ of the tongue
36 At this time
37 Most important
40 Draft status
42 *The Joy Luck Club* author
43 Murrow's __ *Now*
44 Stock speculators, for short
46 Economist's concerns
53 Slacks style
54 Ring out
57 Thine: Fr.
58 CAUTION: __ WORK
59 Coffee
60 Property claim
61 Writer Kingsley
62 Chop __
63 Nav. rank
64 Kent's coworker

DOWN

1 Hebrew letter
2 Kayak kin
3 "A __, a tasket . . ."
4 NFLer
5 Flew, in a way
6 Accustom (to)
7 High-IQ group
8 Ivy League school
9 Santa __, CA
10 Take to the cleaners
11 Phone no. abbr.
13 Lively qualities
15 Vane dir.
19 Episodic show
20 Norwegian royal name
22 Cheerful
23 Dr. Mead's hangout
26 Basted, perhaps
27 Fuse units
28 Biblical peak
29 French farewell
31 "Xanadu" rock group
32 Brief glimpse
35 Reeling
38 Do wrong
39 End in __ (require overtime)
41 Just awful
45 Conceptual framework
47 Chip __ (Disney cartoon pair)
48 Avoid restaurants
49 Plumlike fruits
50 Bolshevik bigwig
51 Wipe out
52 Orly bird?
54 Evening wear
55 __ de toilette
56 St. crosser

63 THE WORD FOR TODAY by Mel Rosen

ACROSS
1 Mornings: Abbr.
4 Mr. Marner
9 Copes with
14 Once around
15 "Once upon __ . . ."
16 Psi follower
17 Improve, as wine
18 Lead astray
20 Flash's foe
22 Soup ingredient
23 Mao __-tung
24 Creatures of the deep
26 "__ I say . . ."
27 Diamond home
29 Stock-market participant
34 Funny Charlotte
37 Battery terminal
39 Bring together
40 Western gullies
42 Bridge boo-boo
44 Hägar's pooch
45 Wesson's partner
47 Stallone's nickname
48 Lofty area
50 "__ the bag!"
52 Actor Holliman
54 20 Questions category
58 Cagney costar Clarke
61 Sidekick
63 Lounge around
64 April 1st
67 Pie ingredient
68 *Arroz* partner
69 *Les __-Unis*
70 S.A. country
71 Great buy
72 Country bumpkin
73 Get a load of

DOWN
1 You must remember this
2 Penn and Teller's specialty
3 Went through
4 *Cheers* role
5 *Napoli* native
6 Such as
7 Modified
8 "From __ shining . . ."
9 Rick Nelson tune of '63
10 Latin I verb
11 Boston hoopster
12 Hollywood giants?
13 Out of harm's way
19 Imported auto
21 Political initials
25 Act zany
28 Play horseshoes
30 Beatles' "__ I Love Her"
31 Cutting tools
32 List-shortening abbr.
33 Be certain of
34 Hasty
35 "Rule Britannia" composer
36 ". . . __ saw Elba"
38 Send forth
41 Special-interest grp.
43 "See you then!"
46 "And __ go before I sleep"
49 Poi source
51 Zilch
53 *The Life of __*
55 Half a '60s singing group
56 Sky blue
57 Narrow shelf
58 Prospectors' drawings
59 "Little Things Mean __"
60 *Glamour* rival
62 Bismarck's loc.
65 Ga. neighbor
66 Fashion monogram

64 SERIES BUSINESS by Trip Payne

ACROSS
1 Arkbound son
5 Scrub the launch
10 32-card game
14 Cocoon contents
15 No social butterfly
16 "*Clair de __*"
17 Wallach and Whitney
18 Gladiators' spot
19 It may be pumped
20 Series start
23 Massage needs
24 Thin streak
25 Challenge the polygraph
26 Game-show worker
28 Gift-tag word
29 Banana oil, e.g.
31 Part of TGIF
32 "It's __ for Me to Say"
33 Actor O'Brien
34 Series start
41 Rock singer __ Rose
42 Apt. units
43 &
44 Is without
47 Lots of energy
48 Made pay
50 Author Levin
51 Court order?
53 Outer limit
54 Series start
59 Slightly
60 Computer-screen symbols
61 End in __ (be drawn)
62 Give as an example
63 *On the Beach* author
64 Kind of sign
65 Starr and Kyser
66 "Great blue" bird
67 They're often liberal

DOWN
1 Gush forth
2 Waikiki wiggle
3 Loosely connected
4 Five iron
5 Shepard and Arkin
6 Bjorn of tennis
7 Series start
8 French impressionist
9 Prefix for port
10 Dove into second
11 CBS traveler
12 Lawlessness
13 Less relaxed
21 Unkindly
22 Anchor position
26 Graduate deg.
27 Scepter top, often
28 Visibility problem
30 Cardinals' loc.
32 Cardinals' org.
33 Some nightwear
35 Mr. McGrew
36 Special edition
37 Mischief-maker
38 Certain shark
39 Polar to SSW
40 Mighty strange
44 Commandeer
45 Asian peninsula
46 Reason
47 Analyst's concern
48 WPA mastermind
49 *Night of the __*
52 Coffee variety
53 *Barnaby Jones* star
55 Western Indians
56 Word form meaning "within"
57 Free-for-all
58 Cravings

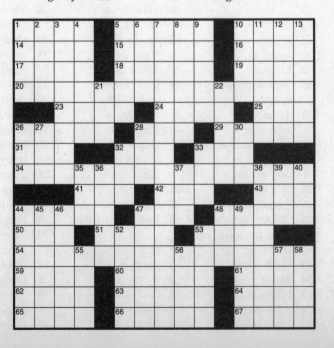

65   HARD LESSONS by Eric Albert

ACROSS

1 One of the Titans
6 Pugilist's punch
9 Mongol monk
13 Filch
14 Lose one's cool
15 Frankenstein's gofer
16 Casino's video game
17 "__ partridge in a pear tree"
18 Self-centered
19 START OF A QUIP
22 Lwyrs.' grp.
24 Mag execs.
25 Cotton cloth
26 Toreador's fear
28 Pasty-faced
30 PART 2 OF QUIP
32 Dandy
35 Ancient Peruvian
36 "__ note to follow sew . . ."
37 Zhivago's love
38 Cry of fear
39 PART 3 OF QUIP
43 Tapered boat
44 Ran wild
45 Business bigwigs
48 __ Lingus
49 Is multiplied?
50 END OF QUIP
54 Table extender
55 River in Asia
56 Surpass
59 Cat's-paw
60 Khartoum river
61 Trojan tale
62 Flow forth
63 "Spring forward" period: Abbr.
64 Mother-of-pearl

DOWN

1 Egyptian snake
2 Early afternoon
3 Bob Seger tune of '86
4 Pinnacle
5 Eve's deceiver
6 Songwriter Mitchell
7 Man Friday
8 *A Streetcar . . .* character
9 Kind of maid
10 Another time
11 A bit damp
12 Actress Lucie
14 Bullion units
20 Perimeter
21 *Moonstruck* star
22 Texas A&M student
23 Paladin portrayer
27 Director Lupino
28 Has __ (may win in court)
29 Persian ruler
31 Sax range
32 Out of this world
33 Law's partner
34 __ deux
37 Actor Gorcey
39 Healing substance
40 Flawed, in a way
41 ". . . __ saw Elba"
42 Steak cut
43 Closing time
45 Blends together
46 Slightly ahead
47 Run amok
48 Competent
51 *The Haj* author
52 Seagoing sort
53 "Be-Bop-A-__" ('56 tune)
57 Patriot descendants' org.
58 Poem of praise

66   WORLD HUES by Mel Rosen

ACROSS

1 Onetime inkwell sites
6 Was in front
9 At the apex
13 Immigrants' island
14 Safety feature
16 NHL team
18 Real doozy
19 Beau Bridges, to Lloyd
20 So long, in Salerno
21 Burden
23 ASAP relative
25 __ Brownell Anthony
29 *Dances with Wolves* home
31 Shake up
34 Happy state
37 "That hurts!"
38 Exotic houseplant
42 CIO's colleague
43 One at large
44 Glacier feature
47 Interstate exits
51 Terry product
52 Wine word
55 Drained of color
56 Vessel of 1492
59 Bar bill
61 Novelist Kesey
62 Some chickens
67 Plant classification
68 Blue __ Mountains
69 Samoa studier Margaret
70 Wind up
71 Commented, cattle-style

DOWN

1 Tyrannical one
2 Actress Stritch
3 Make a mistake
4 They're related
5 Heathrow sights
6 Brooklyn, NY school
7 Clapton of rock
8 Lucy's son
9 Total
10 Upsilon preceder
11 It's in the veins
12 Aft. periods
14 __ of (sweet on)
15 Take down a peg
17 Cut (off)
22 Nostradamus, for one
24 Marmalade fruits
26 Eye problem
27 "Little Things Mean __"
28 Improved's partner
30 New Haven student
32 PBS series
33 Use scissors
35 Virtuosos
36 USSR news agcy.
38 Big hairdo
39 Soloed in the sky
40 "__ the fields we go . . ."
41 Spring up
42 Behave
45 Offered at retail
46 Quite unfamiliar
48 Get along somehow
49 Frat hopeful
50 Had an inkling of
53 List abbr.
54 Corn holder
57 Clementine's shoe size
58 P __ "pneumonia"
60 Apt. unit
62 Spinning-rate abbr.
63 __ *Haw*
64 "Are you a man __ mouse?"
65 Little boy
66 South American port

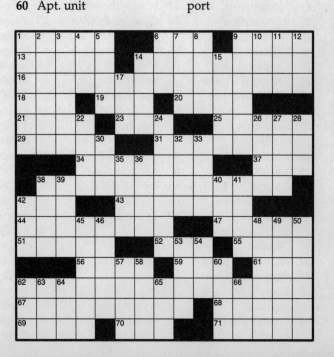

67 SHIPMATES by Randy Sowell

ACROSS

1 Le Sage's *Gil* __
5 Iraqi port
10 Citrus drinks
14 Ready to pick
15 Fields of expertise
16 Noel trio
17 Violin virtuoso
19 Stratford-on-__
20 Actress Mason
21 Tree-to-be
23 Latched onto
25 Police operation
26 Important
29 Slalom curve
32 Repair software
35 Product patron
36 Each
38 Stop __ dime
39 Leave one's seat
40 Of interest to Peary
41 Loretta of *M*A*S*H*
42 Radio spots
43 __ *Rides Again*
44 Yugoslav statesman
45 Somewhat suspicious
47 Look at
48 Ms. Garson
49 This: Lat.
51 Be bold
53 Amusing story
57 Theater district
61 Columbo portrayer
62 *Dallas* star
64 "Don't throw bouquets __"
65 Ice rink, e.g.
66 To be, in Paree
67 What's left
68 Socially inept
69 "__ Me" (Roger Miller tune)

DOWN

1 Hat edge
2 Actress Hartman
3 On __ with (comparable to)
4 Resort locale
5 Kind of metabolism
6 Sculptures and such
7 Gets the point
8 Seldom encountered
9 *JFK* actor
10 Charlotte __, VI
11 British rock star
12 Designer von Furstenberg
13 Vocalize
18 Chastity Bono's mom
22 Miami's county
24 Topple from office
26 Diego Rivera work
27 Short digression
28 Southern senator
30 Sedimentlike
31 Burned, in a way
33 Bring together
34 Florida collegian
36 Big lummox
37 Hue's partner
41 Went quickly
43 Recolored
46 Annoying noise
48 Football field
50 *George M.* subject
52 Orderly grouping
53 Worship from __
54 Hoops star Thurmond
55 Ripped
56 Water pitcher
58 "I __ Song Go . . ."
59 Gull relative
60 Designer Cassini
63 Common conjunction

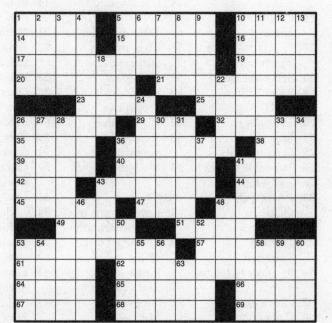

68 PECULIARITIES by Trip Payne

ACROSS

1 Women's magazine
5 Ship staff
9 *Star Trek* engineer
14 Needle case
15 Pasta entrée
16 West Point senior, at times
17 Cropland unit
18 The Bard's river
19 Hardwood tree
20 Camus novel
23 Cardinals and ordinals: Abbr.
24 Manx cat's lack
25 Tijuana Brass leader
27 *Damn Yankees* tune
29 Tagalong's cry
31 "Monkey suit"
32 Fanatic's feeling
34 Barton or Bow
38 Rock-video parodist
42 Word form for "bone"
43 Anderson of *WKRP*
44 Shelley selection
45 Actress Samantha
47 Persian's weapons
50 Clock sound
53 Forget about
54 Clark's *Mogambo* costar
55 Paraphernalia
61 Maintained a spinet
63 Teensy bit
64 Additional
65 C.S. Lewis' first name
66 Lean-looking
67 All over again
68 No fan
69 Vanilla holder
70 Dozes (off)

DOWN

1 Musical-chairs quest
2 Impress deeply
3 Angler's buy
4 Panama party
5 Alexandra, for one
6 Disraeli, to Gladstone
7 Scholar collar
8 White House section
9 Role for Basil
10 Airport transit
11 Atmospheric layer
12 Voice range
13 Sub-rosa meeting
21 Coal product
22 Have a bite
26 Prince Charles' sport
27 Gradations of color
28 Leave the stage
29 Tom Bradley's title
30 Lively spirit
31 __ *for the Seesaw*
33 Ms. Fitzgerald
35 Declare openly
36 Frees (of)
37 Blackjack card
39 Smell bad
40 Naive reformer
41 Tom, Dick, or Harry
46 Ares or Eros
48 Jar top
49 Tarzan, for instance
50 Concealed drawback
51 Palate neighbor
52 "Be quiet!"
53 Sheet material
56 Cassette alternative
57 Aria, usually
58 Kid's taboo
59 The __ Scott Decision
60 Does needlework
62 Second name?

69 BUZZERS by Wayne R. Williams

ACROSS
1 Berate
6 Castaway's construction
10 City vehicle
13 Thin candle
14 Lamb's alias
15 Ending for insist
16 Claudius' portrayer
18 Put on TV
19 Bartlett's abbr.
20 Hamlet was one
21 NBA's Archibald
22 *Poltergeist* director
25 Work gang
26 __ good deed
27 Lovers' quarrel
29 Garden sphere
32 Alps river
36 1986 Indy 500 winner
39 Coffee brewer
40 *Do the Right Thing* actress
42 Western Indian
43 *Deliverance* "dueler"
45 Winter wear
46 Critic Reed
47 Farm structure
49 *Viva __ Vegas*
51 Disney dog
53 Centenarian composer
60 Tarbell and Lupino
61 Slaughter of baseball
62 Prayer end
63 *Bonanza* setting: Abbr.
64 *Zoo Story* writer
67 Mr. Whitney
68 Deviate
69 Oceanic ring
70 __ Moines, IA
71 States further
72 Powell/Keeler film of '34

DOWN
1 Office skill
2 Chocolate substitute
3 Bid first
4 Albanian money
5 Erving's nickname
6 Hit the high points
7 *Home __*
8 Cloth makeup
9 Skater Babilonia
10 *Maude* star
11 Make one
12 Scatter about
16 CD's rival
17 Botheration
21 Coll. sports org.
23 Film genre
24 Hawaiian isle
28 Home type
29 Alehouse
30 __ of Good Feeling
31 *The Brady Bunch* actress
33 Dict. notation
34 Bklyn.'s locale
35 Writer LeShan
37 Munched on
38 Tarzan portrayer Barker
41 __ Stanley Gardner
44 Blue birds
48 Had to have
50 Skiing race
51 Paper choice
52 Designer Simpson
54 Single
55 Pig papas
56 Leb. neighbor
57 Take a stroll
58 Hull parts
59 Vane dir.
64 Zsa Zsa's sister
65 Dear old one?
66 Straining __ gnat

70 NEIGHBORLY ADVICE by Eric Albert

ACROSS
1 Indian chief?
6 Disconcert
10 __ vu
14 In reserve
15 Midterm, for one
16 Change, often
17 START OF A QUENTIN CRISP QUIP
20 Wonderment
21 Pokes fun at
22 Point of view
23 Vitamin unit
24 Star follower
26 PART 2 OF QUIP
30 German sausage
31 Tamarind and tangerine
32 Keats creation
33 Wild and crazy time
35 Sprat's no-no
38 Small crown
40 Singer Moore
42 PART 3 OF QUIP
46 Sounded like a chick
47 Actress Skye
48 Give a speech
49 Piece of work
50 Not quite oneself
53 END OF QUIP
57 One seeing red?
58 Southeast Asian
59 Make merry?
60 X-ray dosage units
61 Chance to participate
62 Sound of impact

DOWN
1 Columnist Barrett
2 Once more
3 Baloney, so to speak
4 Hotshot pilot
5 Vet-turned-author
6 Frail
7 Lumbering needs
8 Heat in a microwave
9 Big bird
10 Depressing experiences
11 Perplexing person
12 Globe-trotter's risk
13 White-faced
18 Potter's oven
19 __ deux
23 Slumberwear
24 *The Way We __*
25 "Of course!"
26 Company, it's said
27 Western film of '63
28 Preceding, in poems
29 Backbreaker, perhaps
33 "Smooth Operator" singer
34 Stir into action
35 Billie's hubby
36 __ Dhabi
37 Feathers precursor
38 Rides a seesaw
39 Drive forward
40 Micky Dolenz's group
41 Pinkerton logo
42 __ tantrum (got mad)
43 Raised with effort
44 A B vitamin
45 Brit's "Nonsense!"
46 Vivid quality
49 Old autocrat
50 Milky stone
51 Cow : cheddar :: goat : __
52 Guitar ridge
54 Communications corp.
55 Calendar abbr.
56 Eisenhut, e.g.

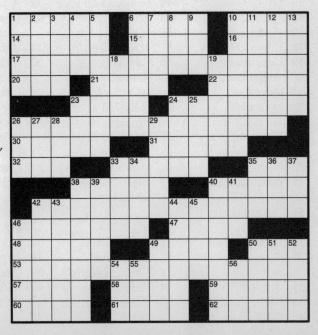

BAR FARE by Bob Sefick

ACROSS

1 Deep cut
5 *Love Story* author
10 Boone portrayer Parker
14 Run in neutral
15 Hispaniola part
16 Bound
17 Bouncy standard
20 Made beloved
21 Second-place finisher
22 Wine category
23 "__ she blows!"
25 Sampled some soup
29 Any day now
30 Provide firepower to
33 Reactor part
34 Mall unit
35 Lamb comment
36 Sailor's saying
40 __ Grande
41 Has the impression
42 Mental picture
43 Way down yonder
44 Master stroke

45 Promising ones
47 Medicinal medium
48 Mauna __
49 Donkey's uncles
52 End of the instructions
57 With *The*, Salinger novel
60 Puccini piece
61 *Boléro* composer
62 Glance from Groucho
63 *Green Acres* structure
64 Oboelike
65 "__ we forget"

DOWN

1 Taunt
2 Mideast port
3 Snow vehicle
4 Wherever I am
5 Divvied up
6 Golden-__ corn
7 Hem in
8 Absorbed, as costs
9 __ *Abner*

10 Wax target
11 Sushi selection
12 Japanese drink
13 Practice boxing
18 Unadorned
19 Wood smoothers
23 Roger Rabbit and colleagues
24 Israeli dance
25 Winter warmer
26 Old Aegean region
27 *Stir Crazy* star
28 Vivacity
29 Clown's prop
30 Lodging place
31 Blue moon, vis-à-vis full moon
32 "Last of the Red Hot __" (Sophie Tucker)
34 Super buy
37 Aloof
38 Film holder
39 Baseball star Raines
45 Not at all cheap
46 Solemn word

47 Pie ingredient
48 Like highways
49 Hailing __ (urban action)
50 Lee of cakedom
51 Agitate
52 Electrically charged
53 Part with, perhaps
54 Genealogy chart
55 Seeing things
56 Boldly forward
58 "To __ is human"
59 Comedienne Charlotte

CAR-ICATURES by Fred Piscop

ACROSS

1 Mardi __
5 Performs like L.L. Cool J
9 Heats and dashes
14 Carson's successor
15 Jai __
16 "__ a River"
17 __-deucy
18 Lily-pad locale
19 Courtyards
20 Sentimental journalist?
23 Pool-table covering
24 Mayo and marmalade
25 Naval officer
27 Belly muscles
28 City in *Italia*
31 Pro golfer __ Stewart
34 Errand person
37 Former Mideast org.
38 Burden
39 Actor's words
40 Gin flavoring

41 Siamese twin
42 Traffic cone
43 Bridle and primrose
44 Whistle blower
46 Frat symbol
47 Mild acid
49 Book section
53 Baby elephant
55 Walk-on parts?
57 Lettucelike
59 Run like heck
60 Journalist/ reformer Jacob __
61 Followed a circular path
62 Hydrox rival
63 Borge, for one
64 __ around (pries)
65 High schooler
66 Jet-set jets

DOWN

1 Sand product
2 Summarize
3 Lend __ (listen)
4 Versatile veggies
5 White-water locale

6 At __ for words
7 Breathe heavily
8 LP surface
9 TV name
10 Like Dickens' Dodger
11 Rostand hero?
12 Actor Jannings
13 Government center
21 Kemo __
22 McIntosh relatives
26 Letter starter
29 Lye, chemically
30 Bauxite and galena
31 Ode writer
32 Part of A.D.
33 Former Supreme Court justice?
34 Hodges of baseball
35 Yoko __
36 Boggy area
39 Ode-like
40 Redd Foxx's TV family
42 __ capita

43 Docking place
45 Candy type
46 Hydrogen atoms have one
48 Henry __ Lodge
49 Martinique volcano
50 Assumed name

51 Dirty Harry portrayer
52 Mississippi quartet?
53 Thunder sound
54 Prefix for space
56 *Utopia* author
58 NFL distances

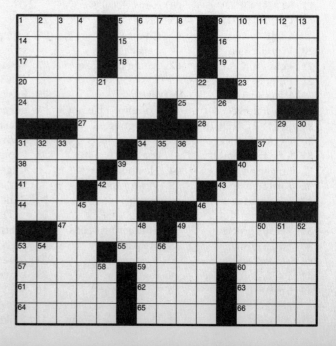

73 SIBILANCE by Eric Albert

ACROSS
1 Joint problem
5 Use fingerpaints
10 The third man
14 It's not clear
15 Intoxicating
16 Rex's detective
17 Place for stock talk
20 Practice playing
21 He's light-headed
22 Be a busybody
23 *Strangers on a Train* star
24 Catcher's catch
28 Rapierlike
29 See eye to eye
30 Louise of *Gilligan's Island*
31 Distort, as facts
35 Fight
38 Held on to
39 All-knowing
40 Singer Page
41 Soak in the sun
42 Settle a spat
43 Bright with light
47 Disseminate
48 Young hunk
49 Film-set staffer
54 "My gosh!"
56 The Kingston __
57 Nary a soul
58 Author Kingsley
59 Splinter group
60 Eva or Magda
61 Carry on

DOWN
1 E.g., e.g.
2 Whodunit game
3 Call for quiet
4 Superior companion
5 Four Seasons #1 song
6 Like Oscar Madison
7 Palliate
8 Words from the sponsor
9 Caraway carrier
10 Bruckner or Rubinstein
11 *The Unbearable Lightness of* __
12 Eat into
13 Solo practitioner
18 South Florida city
19 Highlands group
23 Literary category
24 Load luggage
25 Mean sort
26 Onstage phone, for instance
27 Ending for song or slug
28 Brit's phone booth
30 Dickens hero
31 Envelope acronym
32 High-flying toy
33 *Brute* preceder
34 Defeat decisively
36 Last act
37 Produces in profusion
41 Scott of *Charles in Charge*
42 Feline specialist
43 Flat boats
44 Worship
45 Kind of column
46 Gold brick
47 Pool person
49 Hoity-toity one
50 Kaiser's kin
51 *I Remember* __
52 Similar
53 Hatchling's home
55 Quaid thriller of '88

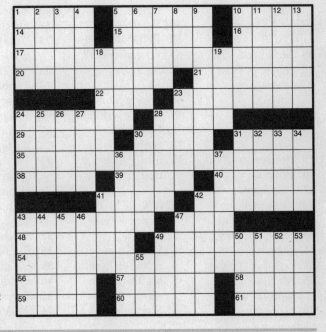

74 BIRTHDAY BOY by Mel Rosen

ACROSS
1 Cousin of PDQ
5 Bumps into
10 Kind of tense
14 Theater box
15 God of Islam
16 Pitch-black
17 1963 hit for 32 Across
19 Cut coupons
20 Good-for-nothings
21 Manageable
23 Morning moisture
24 Removes rind
25 To no __ (useless)
29 Cookout remains
32 Singer born April 16th
35 Do some damage
38 Kadiddlehopper
39 Deeply felt
40 Comic Kaplan
41 Norm: Abbr.
42 1962 hit for 32 Across
44 Garden flower
45 Set a spell
46 Area code 208
49 Sis' sibling
51 Meal
53 High-steppers
58 Swiss peaks
59 1963 hit for 32 Across
61 Tall story
62 Wimbledon opener
63 Hard to hold
64 Stared at
65 Propelled a gondola
66 Cameo stone

DOWN
1 Church vestments
2 Ford's role in *Star Wars*
3 Water, to Juan
4 Hammer part
5 Minister's house
6 Pasta shape
7 Building wings
8 Sigma follower
9 Small building
10 Zodiac sign
11 Warbucks' charge
12 Know-how
13 Does word processing
18 In a weird way
22 Ready for business
25 Foundation
26 Electrical unit
27 In the sack
28 Business' "Big Blue"
29 Add on
30 Canonized *Mlles.*
31 Tel Aviv dance
33 Stringed instrument
34 Not __ many words
35 Engels' colleague
36 Busy as __
37 Comedian Foxx
40 "That's incredible!"
42 Greek letters
43 River through Lake Geneva
44 __ out (discontinued)
46 Ticked off
47 Put off
48 Granny Smith, for one
49 Diacritical mark
50 Made a scene
52 Cookbook qty.
53 Knitting instruction
54 Role for Liz Taylor
55 Roulette bet
56 __ on (trust)
57 Infernal river
60 Composer Delibes

75 STRESS TEST by Donna J. Stone

ACROSS

1 Chalet shape
7 *The People's Choice* dog
11 Mensa data
14 Compulsive
15 Univ. marchers
16 The word, at times
17 START OF A QUIP
19 Stole style
20 Stable parents
21 Prepare eggs, in a way
23 Arp's art
26 Greases the wheels
29 Border on
30 Put out
32 Old science
34 Photo tint
35 Bountiful setting
36 MIDDLE OF QUIP
41 Breach
42 Gymnast Cathy
45 Maxilla or mandible
49 Bit of wit

51 Soprano's showcase
52 "Wings of __" (Husky hit)
54 Spouse of 67 Across
55 Philosophy
57 Coat-of-arms figure
59 Relatives
60 END OF QUIP
66 First offender?
67 Spouse of 54 Across
68 Funny faux pas
69 Article written by Kant
70 Sidle
71 Old __ (Disney dog)

DOWN

1 Paper pitches
2 To and __
3 Wheel part
4 Schubert hymn
5 Southwestern sight
6 Menu listing

7 Mustard greens
8 Sodom escapee
9 King of Siam's favorite word
10 Folksinger Phil
11 Tipple
12 Minimum of a sort
13 Wisenheimer
18 Hit the books
22 "That's what you think!"
23 __ Plaines, IL
24 Timber tool
25 Johnny of *Edward Scissorhands*
27 "I could __ horse!"
28 Eastern European
31 *The Addams Family* dance
33 Deneuve's darling
35 "Weird Al" Yankovic film
37 Sandwich salad
38 Runners carry it
39 No early bird
40 Evildoer
43 Keep out
44 Singer Sumac

45 Raised, as prices
46 Make the grade
47 Frank
48 Evil-minded
49 At any time
50 '50s "Awesome!"
53 Too large
56 Gooey stuff
58 Pump, for one
61 Actor Danson
62 Greet warmly
63 Out of sorts
64 Artichoke heart?
65 Make a blunder

76 NICKNAMES by Max Hopkins

ACROSS

1 Kemo Sabe's trademark
5 High-interest activity
10 Open a bit
14 ". . . __ saw Elba"
15 Word not used in *The Godfather*
16 Big party
17 Riotous brawl
19 Makes a decision
20 Copier chemical
21 Short distance
23 Sennett staffer
24 One being used
26 Barber's need
28 Compass pt.
29 Chatter
31 Pirate's chant
34 __ *from a Mall* (Woody Allen film)
37 Up and around
38 Cremona craftsman
41 Do lunch
42 Sail holders

43 Breakfast fruit
44 Stylish
46 *Batman* butler
48 Fall guy
49 Norton's namesakes
52 Make a new chart
54 Small sum
57 Lamb's mama
59 Atmosphere
61 Get in
62 Durante's claim to fame
64 Girl of the '40s
66 Savage and Severinsen
67 Banquet host
68 Swampy ground
69 Job opening
70 Gave medicine to
71 Billion-selling cookie

DOWN

1 Army healers
2 Odors
3 Where Dole deliberated

4 David and Solomon
5 What the miffed take
6 Mediterranean isl.
7 Strange sightings
8 Barrels of laughs
9 Yak preceder
10 __ Khan
11 Big prizes
12 Vocal range
13 Scrape
18 Slangy assent
22 Some golf tourneys
25 Petered out
27 Anthem starter
30 NFL team
32 Stage success
33 Hosp. locales
34 Put away
35 Film world
36 Place
38 *I __ Camera*
39 Gibson of *Lethal Weapon*
40 Out-of-doors
45 Used an atomizer

47 Painted poorly
49 Cure-all
50 Actress Trish Van __
51 Sound system
53 PR gimmick
55 Treas. Dept. agcy.
56 Headache remedy, familiarly
57 Winds up
58 Yarn material
60 Fundamentals
63 Adjective ending
65 Little stinger

77 EXPLORERS CLUB by Mel Rosen

ACROSS

1 Walk through water
5 Mouth off
9 Like the polo set
14 Actress Barbara
15 Dull pain
16 Oahu greeting
17 __ Called Horse
18 NYSE alternative
19 Stair post
20 Alaska explorer
23 Compass pt.
24 Moral standard
25 Lulu
27 Greenland explorer
33 Dowser's tool
36 Newspaper notice
37 Admit frankly
38 *Arabian Nights* character
40 War-prone
43 Office note
44 Mountain lion
45 Vast amount
46 Florida explorer
50 Operatic solo
51 Like some pitchers
56 Guys
59 Africa explorer
62 Kitchen come-on
64 __ instant (quickly)
65 Bookie quote
66 Exodus mount
67 Corsica neighbor
68 Mild-mannered
69 Villain's look
70 Method: Abbr.
71 Puts in a lawn

DOWN

1 Work at the loom
2 Let in
3 __ of a Salesman
4 Boredom
5 Swedish auto
6 Top of the mountain
7 Dessert choice
8 More alluring
9 Mental block
10 Grand __ Opry
11 Ticket details
12 "__ a Lady"
13 Bush's alma mater
21 Boston entrée
22 Abolitionist Turner
26 Ship wood
28 Oriental sash
29 Coal container
30 Hertz competitor
31 Got up
32 Ladies' club of a sort
33 Freeway exit
34 Bread spread
35 __ *Yankees*
39 Medicos
40 Cry's partner
41 I love: Lat.
42 Eases off
44 Without adornment
47 Rich dessert
48 "*Agnus __*" (hymn)
49 Would like to be
52 Cyclotron fodder
53 Copland work
54 Finished
55 School furniture
56 Church service
57 "__ go bragh!"
58 Not a soul
60 Captures
61 Small fly
63 Ginnie __ bonds

78 ENTOMOLOGY by Shirley Soloway

ACROSS

1 Toddler perches
5 *Father of the __*
10 Periodic-table stat.
14 Conditioner ingredient
15 Extend a lease
16 Bass instrument
17 Against the rules
19 Start of the show
20 *The Third Man* star
21 Gridiron spheroid
23 Bad marks
24 Objective
26 Marquee word
27 Cheap quarters
30 Cotillion attendee
33 "Battle Hymn of the Republic" writer
36 Small brook
37 "__-Loo-Ra-Loo-Ral"
39 Some exams
41 *Red October*, for one
42 Bulgaria's capital
43 Jai-alai basket
44 "Oh"
46 One-stripe GIs
47 Keystone character
48 Oversize dos
51 Home appliance
53 "Open 10 __ 6"
54 Wyo. neighbor
57 Barcelona bucks
60 Copies, in a way
62 Feel sore
63 Tony Randall Broadway role
66 Convinced
67 Beast of Borden
68 Outlaw Younger
69 Stallone et al.
70 Like some jackets
71 Smell __ (be suspicious)

DOWN

1 Knight weapon
2 Unconcerned
3 Annie of *Designing Women*
4 Religious group
5 More like seawater
6 __ room
7 Variety
8 Far-reaching
9 Singer Ruth
10 Sailor's shout
11 Quite miffed
12 Reply to the Little Red Hen
13 Lena of *Havana*
18 Honest-to-goodness
22 Main points
25 Sothern role
27 Fedora fabric
28 Makeup variety
29 Even if
31 Actor Stoltz
32 Farm sounds
33 Debt
34 Treat with milk
35 In a petulant manner
38 Clumsy one's comment
40 Wooden shoe
45 Put out
49 Glossy finish
50 Fashion mag
52 Orchestra section
54 __ it (trouble-bound)
55 Perry's aide
56 To date
57 Go by
58 Earth sci.
59 Bank ins. initials
61 Killer whale
64 Nimitz's grp.
65 Music marking

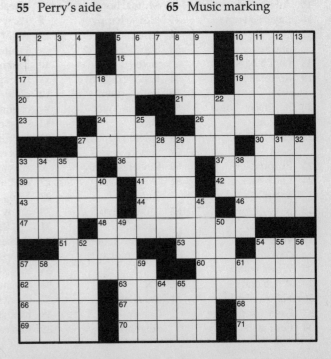

79 ALO-HA by Donna J. Stone

ACROSS
1 Jockey's prop
5 It may suit you
10 *Hook* pooch
14 Top-notch
15 Horned in
16 Abba of Israel
17 Diamond Head dessert?
19 Cardinal's home
20 Sedan season
21 "It's a Sin to Tell __"
22 Cut canines
24 MacLachlan of *Twin Peaks*
25 __ Fein (Irish political group)
26 Photo tints
29 Robert Taylor film of '51
33 Sourpuss
34 Wreak havoc on
35 Fictional captain
36 Cut __ (dance)
37 Stops trying
38 And more of the same: Abbr.
39 Breakfast bread
40 Exploits
41 Play area?
42 James Galway, e.g.
44 Went by SST
45 Cooper's tool
46 Just adorable
47 Downhill run
50 Sandy stuff
51 Audiophile's purchase
54 Piltdown man was one
55 Swaying aircraft?
58 Tel __
59 Bleaching agent
60 Kenyatta of Kenya
61 Food store
62 Blade type
63 Chilly powder

DOWN
1 Dracula's wrap
2 Defeat decisively
3 *Lean __* ('89 film)
4 Zing
5 Toddler's mishaps
6 Sergeant Bilko
7 Ready to pick
8 Prizm or Storm
9 They may be limited
10 Maui musical?
11 Foster a felon
12 *Bed Riddance* author
13 Kick in
18 Palindromic craft
23 Part of SASE
24 Hawaiian ruler?
25 Fills the bill
26 Boa, but not cobra
27 Robin of '38
28 Pop singer Abdul
29 Peace's partner
30 Coup __
31 Public persona
32 Did cobbling
34 Charlotte __ (dessert)
37 *Jeopardy!*, for example
41 Scrap
43 NFL stats
44 Kitchen appliance
46 Stick one's neck out
47 Large herring
48 Harbor locale
49 Hard rain?
50 Gooey mess
51 Like __ of bricks
52 Short note
53 Freighter front
56 *Raid on Entebbe* weapon
57 Dr. Dentons

80 THREE IN A ROW by Eric Albert

ACROSS
1 Short swims
5 "That's awful!"
10 Lab runners
14 *To Live and Die __*
15 All possible
16 Layered stone
17 Give the once-over
18 Lent a hand
19 Roughen, in a way
20 It rains on some parades
22 *New York Enquirer* boss
23 Purpose
24 Look back in anger
25 Jerry of the Chicago 7
26 Whiskey cocktail
28 White water
29 Witch craft
30 Yellow shade
33 Green's opposite
34 Poor taste
37 Bed clothes
40 Catches cold?
41 Cuts close
45 No longer edible
47 Mini-mistake
48 Mutual home
49 Not so happy
52 Oomph
53 Stare slack-jawed
54 Behave oneself
56 Fully grown
57 Mad as a wet hen
58 Solemn appeal
59 Service scores
60 Reviews highly
61 Dog in *Beetle Bailey*
62 "A grand old name"
63 Put into action
64 Persian plaint

DOWN
1 Break in on
2 Canine neighbor
3 Control substance
4 Went underwater
5 Per annum
6 Señora Peron
7 Chest material
8 Party paper
9 Actor Wilfrid __-White
10 Test model
11 Occupy
12 Gold-extraction chemical
13 Cost item
21 I strain?
25 Test result, before curving
27 Go bad
28 *Norma __*
30 Enjoy Sun Valley
31 "__ Reveille" (Kyser tune)
32 Hosp. pros
35 Rascal
36 Theater abbr.
37 Create software
38 Kingston's locale
39 Red catch
42 Make unnecessary
43 Indicate
44 By hook or by crook
46 Fifth-rate
47 Command
49 Detergent ingredient
50 Hit the road
51 Unqualified
54 Grow weary
55 Be vaguely menacing

81   COUNTS by Mel Rosen

ACROSS
1 "__ Lisa"
5 Abraham's wife
10 Cry loudly
14 Roberts of Tulsa
15 Wear gradually
16 Lebanon's locale
17 Anger, pride, etc.
20 Trifle (with)
21 Old oath
22 Balances evenly
23 Historical periods
24 Imported autos
25 Argentina steppes
28 Business transaction
29 "Telly" network
32 Cancel a mission
33 Layer of paint
34 Court statement
35 Athos and company
38 Heavy weights
39 Mars' counterpart
40 Ledger entry
41 Mos. and mos.
42 Singer Kristofferson
43 __ Berry Farm
44 Put on an act
45 Eye coverings
46 Tests metal
49 Hollywood Boulevard crosses it
50 Binet's concerns
53 Grist for DeMille
56 Essential point
57 Art stand
58 Revue piece
59 Work units
60 Indigent
61 Recipe amts.

DOWN
1 The lion's share
2 Sandwich snack
3 Dark blue
4 Potent potable
5 Marsh plants
6 Fields of expertise
7 Byway
8 Tack on
9 Companion/ assistant
10 Supporting factor
11 Sale caveat
12 Bordeaux or Beaujolais
13 Glasgow gal
18 Bring to naught
19 Cry of pain
23 __-ski outfit
24 Nestlings' noses
25 Hamburger unit
26 Can't stand
27 Pre-noon times
28 Vitamin amounts
29 Declared holy
30 Toulouse topper
31 Playbill listings
33 Radium discoverer
34 Cancún cash
36 Skilled shots
37 Kind of bicycle
42 Boxing result
43 Good-hearted
44 Hard data
45 Like some paper
46 "Ma, He's Making Eyes __"
47 Omen observer
48 Hidden obstacle
49 Posy holder
50 Printer's purchases
51 Stick it in your ear
52 Atl. speedsters
54 Dogpatch's Daisy __
55 Superlative suffix

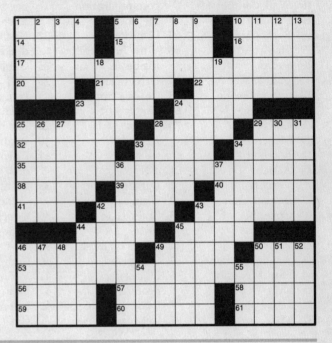

82   HARDWARE by Richard Silvestri

ACROSS
1 Curved letters
6 Ego
10 Ring rocks
14 Monetary gain
15 Word form meaning "thought"
16 Came to earth
17 Soft hat
18 In the vicinity
19 __ 18 (Uris novel)
20 Wolfed down
21 Storm phenomenon
24 Burton's birthplace
26 "Uncle" of early TV
27 Highwayman
29 Macbeth's title
31 Whitish stone
32 Adventuresome
34 Acknowledge applause
37 Edmonton athlete
39 Moving vehicle
40 Beetle Bailey's boss
42 Actress Harris
43 Throws out
46 Hill's partner
47 Head off
48 Knocked for a loop
50 Pygmalion product
53 Turbaned seer
54 Laundress
57 Baton Rouge campus
60 "... __ forgive those ..."
61 First name in whodunits
62 Turner and Louise
64 Ollie's pal
65 Latvia's capital
66 Stinker
67 Some brooders
68 Get top billing
69 Register for

DOWN
1 Mediterranean isle
2 Tallow source
3 Eccentric
4 Palindromic preposition
5 Come to terms
6 Hole in your head
7 Paradise
8 Heavy metal
9 Boxer George
10 Take a chance
11 Mr. Ness
12 Metric prefix
13 Union member?
22 Bovine bunch
23 Circus trio
25 Up to the task
27 Leeway
28 *Andy Griffith Show* kid
29 Brief treatise
30 Subtle indication
33 Assert
34 Three-sided snack
35 Make eyes at
36 Garden bane
38 Show with sketches
41 *Bonanza* brother
44 They give a hoot
45 "I never __ purple cow"
47 European capital
49 Yankee great
50 Buckle starter
51 Try a tidbit
52 Nile dam
53 Mudslinger's specialty
55 Court order
56 Ms. Korbut
58 Letter encl.
59 Computer owner
63 Electrovalent atom

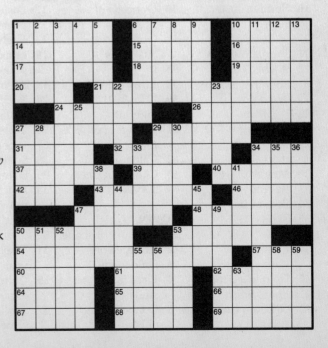

83 SATIRIZATION by Peter Gordon

ACROSS

1 Half a sawbuck
4 Grad
8 Floor connectors
14 Lennon's lady
15 Ms. Barrett
16 Walk daintily
17 Pi follower
18 Part of MIT
19 Star in Aquila
20 Satire publication
23 She, in Seville
24 __ Alamos, NM
25 Catch flies
29 Most profound
32 Boo-boo
35 Actress Verdon
37 Emend again
38 Cover boy of 20 Across
42 Worshiped
43 A whole bunch
44 Florida county
46 Ships or pots
51 Leave out
52 Mao __-tung
54 Smell __ (be suspicious)
55 Catchphrase of 38 Across
59 Exodus locale
63 Competent
64 Gallaudet U. communication method
65 Contrite one
66 With "up," spill the beans
67 Driving area
68 Crack a cipher
69 Guitar part
70 Calvin __ Hobbes

DOWN

1 Put together
2 Gasp or sniff
3 Brain, so to speak
4 Opera highlight
5 Outspread
6 Like some peanuts
7 Passover staple
8 Getz of jazz
9 Word-game piece
10 Prone (to)
11 "Give __ rest!"
12 King, en France
13 Sun. oration
21 Former gas-station freebie
22 Distinctive doctrine
25 Goblet part
26 "If I __ Hammer"
27 Related
28 Lay hold of
30 Wading bird
31 Bjorn Borg is one
33 Actress Cara
34 Grinch creator
36 Court divider
38 Eliot's __ Bede
39 Burt's wife, once
40 Campus club
41 Voting time
42 Latin I word
45 Incoming-plane stat.
47 __ Paulo, Brazil
48 Typo list
49 "The Sea Wolf"
50 Fixed up, as hair
53 Employees
55 Dandelion, e.g.
56 Fabled race loser
57 Otherwise
58 TV's Batman
59 Swell, in slang
60 Hot time in Tours
61 Bashful's brother
62 __-Cone

84 EGOMANIA by Eric Albert

ACROSS

1 Wasteland
6 Chew the fat
10 Humorist Bombeck
14 Gallic goodbye
15 Praise crazily
16 Sudden ouster
17 I
20 House drawing
21 Rural hotel
22 Awkwardly situated
23 Went down
25 "__ Ideas"
26 Bette role of '90
29 Munch mousily
30 Money player
33 Be ready for
34 Boxer Max
35 Skip
36 I
39 Pound unrelentingly
40 Help in a crime
41 Photo finish
42 Gridiron gains: Abbr.
43 Jacques __ Cousteau
44 Kind of roll
45 Tops and trains
46 Sticking point?
47 Grammatical category
50 Opposite of 51 Across
51 Opposite of 50 Across
55 I
58 Bring home
59 "Has 1001 __"
60 Fighting
61 Change another's mind
62 Catch sight of
63 Choreographer Twyla

DOWN

1 Bend out of shape
2 Admired one
3 Ohio town
4 Place for a good student
5 Donne's "busy old fool"
6 Thick piece
7 Song of praise
8 Gibbon or orangutan
9 Short Time star
10 Great acclaim
11 Mouth part
12 Pasteur portrayer
13 High point
18 Hirschfeld's daughter
19 All over
24 Vocal range
25 Maladroit
26 Too sentimental
27 Wool fabric
28 Some peers
29 Strong winds
30 Hatches a scheme
31 Way to go
32 "For sale by __"
34 Toyland visitors
35 Cultural organization
37 Service shade?
38 General Bradley
43 Andrew's dukedom
44 Jackson or Smith
45 Really small
46 First name in flags
47 A long time
48 Pull out a pistol
49 Miles of film
50 __ down (resign)
52 Sioux City's state
53 Stage-door symbol
54 Tombstone lawman
56 Superman's insignia
57 Scoundrel

85 BODY FOOD by Randolph Ross

ACROSS
1 __ a doornail
7 Buck or stag
11 Cheese partner, often
15 Salad ingredient
16 Dirty air
17 Author Calvino
18 *Concentration* conjunction
20 Pastoral god
21 Pub quaff
22 Car-radiator part
25 Give the once-over
26 Sheena's role on *Miami Vice*
27 __ *Like It Hot*
29 Driver's place
31 Brubeck of jazz
32 Partner in crime
33 Addition column
34 Circuit breakers
36 Chan's remark
37 Great deal
38 Vane dir.
39 Trainee
40 *"Mein Gott!"*
41 It's bagged at the market
44 Brian of rock
45 *Kama* __
48 Tub toy
49 Spaghetti's thinner kin
53 Salad ingredient
54 Minor quarrel
55 Army: private :: navy : __

DOWN
1 Stuffed delicacy
2 Mr. John
3 "... carry __ stick"
4 Medico
5 Some time
6 Struck down
7 Diana Ross film of '75
8 *You __ There*
9 Mauna __
10 Matriculants
12 Initials on a post-office poster
13 Animation frame
14 *Napoli* native
15 Nile snake
19 Lets out
21 Scotsman's "sure"
23 Slow down, in mus.
24 __ *Great Pumpkin, Charlie Brown*
25 Come out
26 Arguments against
27 Grassland region
28 Shades of meaning
29 Football great Tarkenton
30 Staff colleague
31 TV role for Dwayne
32 Soda-machine feature
35 Actress __ Park-Lincoln
36 Hardwood tree
38 Two-person card game
40 The Ram
41 Puccini opus
42 Gobbled up
43 __ loss for words
46 Channels 14 and up
47 Russian chessmaster
48 Lyman Frank __
50 Cumberland, for one
51 Columnist LeShan
52 Harper Valley org.

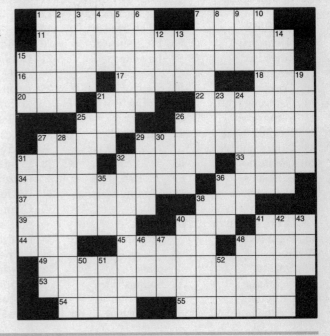

86 SHORT STORY by Trip Payne

ACROSS
1 River in Spain
5 *M*A*S*H* star
9 Bring in crops
13 Villainous expression
14 Black and Baltic
15 Author Seton
16 Arachnid of song
19 Forest females
20 Cowardly types
21 Paramedic: Abbr.
22 Summertime cooler
23 Sidelong look
27 Soak up
29 Tommy of Broadway
31 Galley paddle
32 Prepared to drive
34 "My Way" composer
35 Horn blower of rhyme
39 Martin's nickname
40 Game-show groups
41 Not quite right
42 Plate officials
44 Attractive person
48 Name of two presidents
50 Motherly attention, briefly
51 Yoko __
52 Fast tempo
55 Guzzlers
56 Runner of rhyme
60 Roundish shape
61 Olympian Korbut
62 Prides' pads
63 Moistens
64 Be patient
65 Foil alternative

DOWN
1 Cover with earth
2 Harasses
3 Actor Alejandro et al.
4 Scepter topper
5 TV's Gomez Addams
6 Diminished by
7 Journal pages
8 Give homework
9 Mikhail's wife
10 Finish off
11 Mate's reply
12 Duffer's goal
13 Front of an LP
17 Sanford of *The Jeffersons*
18 Soccer great
22 Guitar ridge
24 Not well-to-do
25 Soap unit
26 Historic time
28 Herr von Bismarck
29 Deep winds?
30 Bone __ (study)
33 Actor Johnny
34 Not to mention
35 "__ is but a dream"
36 Hard facts
37 Like sapsuckers' bellies
38 Political group
39 Shepherd or schnauzer
42 Tangelo variety
43 Laid-back
45 Edd Byrnes role
46 All-inclusive
47 Pasadena-parade posies
49 Singer Lou
50 Pay for dinner
53 First name in scat
54 Leslie Caron musical
55 Something easy
56 "That's amazing!"
57 Second name?
58 Scarf down
59 __ de France

ELEMENTARY by Shirley Soloway

ACROSS
1 Fur piece
5 Flexible armor
9 The Babe's sultanate
13 __ close to schedule
14 Country singer Travis
15 Othello's adversary
16 Top-rated
17 Starlike flower
18 Corner sign
19 Get things out in the open
22 Swelled head
23 How some try
24 Do the pots
26 Bank jobs
29 Newsman Vanocur
32 Drum's partner
35 Paint layer
37 Bucks
38 Onassis' nickname
39 Pet rodents
41 See the point of
42 Greene of *Bonanza*
44 Right-hand person
45 On a cruise
46 Prepares for prayer
48 Mideast desert
50 Cooks, in a way
52 Of an eye part
56 Pullman, e.g.
58 Levelheaded
61 "Woe is me!"
63 Song of joy
64 Unlikely to bite
65 Carry on
66 Falls loudly
67 Actor Sharif
68 *60 Minutes* name
69 Sudden urges
70 Mouthy Martha

DOWN
1 Prepare eggs
2 __ *Gay* (WWII plane)
3 Solitary one
4 Foot control
5 Moonshine-to-be
6 Part of A.M.
7 Mental flashes
8 Hammerstein's forte
9 Family member
10 Retrievers, for instance
11 Excited
12 "__ the morning!"
14 The daily grind
20 Antique auto
21 Goes here and there
25 Important "numero"
27 Writer Ephron
28 Vaccine discoverer
30 "Waiting for the Robert __"
31 Pro follower
32 Columbo portrayer
33 Nutritive mineral
34 Hothead
36 Oxydol competitor
39 Ice-cold
40 Great numbers
43 New beginning?
45 Rickenbacker or Wright
47 Not carefully done
49 Prior to, in poems
51 Lowland
53 Molière's milieu
54 "Be that as __ . . ."
55 Dear, in Deauville
56 Irene of *Fame*
57 King of comedy
59 Light gas
60 A little night music
62 Hog's home

LOSERS by Fred Piscop

ACROSS
1 This: Sp.
5 Adding devices
10 Burger side dish
14 Dough
15 Turn yellow, perhaps
16 Poi source
17 Loser of '64
20 Palmer, for short
21 UN license plate abbr.
22 Mr. T's former group
23 Word form for "height"
25 Proficient
27 *Mal de* __
30 True to fact
32 Roadster, e.g.
35 Chester __ Arthur
37 %
38 Where it's at
40 Loser of '68
43 Slow tempo
44 *Wheel of Fortune* purchase
45 First-rate
46 Tennis call
47 Hero's lover
50 Word preceding *amis*
51 Quintessential pirate
52 Rock singer Clapton
54 *Our Miss Brooks* star
57 Stirrup's site
59 __ del Sol
63 Loser of '72
66 Mimicry specialist
67 Ale kin
68 Stage direction
69 Actor Calhoun
70 Green sauce
71 Prepare memos

DOWN
1 Napoleon slept there
2 Fly high
3 Actor Rip
4 Some courtyards
5 Sweater part
6 "Clinton's __" (Erie Canal)
7 Each
8 Last place
9 Sen. Lugar's home
10 Frame of mind
11 Overdue
12 Linoleum measurement
13 Despicable one
18 Belt out
19 Clobber
24 Went gingerly
26 Milder, weatherwise
27 Taj __
28 Get away from
29 African capital
31 __ *Frome*
32 Billiards shot
33 Coeur d'__, ID
34 Point __ National Seashore
36 Electron's charge: Abbr.
39 Half a dance?
41 Making angry
42 Beat another's price
48 "__ *Fideles*"
49 Edward G. role
51 Irish county
53 Want for oneself
54 Ice-cream ingredient
55 __ *Man* (Estevez film)
56 Person of action
58 Bible book
60 Alluring
61 Fall down, maybe
62 Prefix for date
64 Telepath's power
65 Onetime Pontiac model

ACROSS

1 Undeniable data
6 George Burns' cigar, e.g.
10 Tag or War
14 Contract negotiator
15 Run easily
16 Track shape
17 Social class
18 '56 hit for 24 Across
20 Zsa Zsa's sister
21 Test a jacket
23 A bit creepy
24 "Music! Music! Music!" singer
27 Actress Anderson
28 Fire up, enginewise
29 Guide to treasure
32 Without paying attention
36 Scoff at
38 Diving bird
39 __ Abner
41 Payout ratio
42 Picket-sign word
45 Grass-roots candidate
48 Came upon
49 Toys __ (pre-Xmas mecca)
51 "With malice toward __ ..."
52 '54 hit for 24 Across
57 "Cross of Gold" orator
60 Extreme
61 Compass pt.
62 '57 hit for 24 Across
64 French menu
66 Be the boss
67 Antiquing medium
68 All over
69 Antlered animal
70 Salon order
71 Supermarket section

DOWN

1 Gem surface
2 Yucca kin
3 Composer Franck
4 Boulder breaker
5 Western hat
6 Usher's handout
7 Helicopter part
8 Kitchen tool
9 Soup ingredient
10 Errand runner
11 Declare true
12 African nation
13 *Vogue* rival
19 *Superman* star
22 Make a scene
25 Actress Verdugo
26 Joined together
29 Skirt length
30 Tots up
31 Pain in the neck
32 Grad
33 __ up (cram)
34 Easily swayed
35 Pup's plaint
37 Logger's contest
40 Capital-gains category
43 Dunne of films
44 Daily grind
46 Below average
47 Loosened
50 Dirty spot
52 High-tech beam
53 Mr. Gantry
54 *Rigoletto* composer
55 Computer key
56 Like an oboe's sound
57 Polar explorer
58 Cad
59 Christmastime
63 Kindergarten break
65 Santa __, CA

ACROSS

1 Puzzle fanatic
7 Monster in the closet
14 The fun of it
15 Freezing
16 Greek dessert?
18 Takeoff
19 Dry red wine
20 Numbers game
21 Trigger puller?
22 Patriots' org.
25 Showpieces
26 Party member?
27 Yard event
31 Accomplished
32 *Phaedo* subject
33 Greek challenge?
36 Contractual out
37 Horned hooter
38 Points of view
39 Larry King's locale
40 Charlie Parker's specialty
43 Submissions to eds.
44 Fidel's colleague
45 Deckhand
46 Call it a career
50 Santiago "sir"
51 Greek greeting?
54 Stamps
55 Gets to the bottom line
56 What one wears
57 Gershwin's only hit song

DOWN

1 "Seward's Folly"
2 Smartly dressed
3 Delaware dynast
4 Snow place like home
5 White-hat wearer
6 One-third tbsp.
7 Onion-topped roll
8 Kareem's college
9 Tackle and such
10 Pinnacle
11 Italy's shape
12 Previously used
13 __ *to Billy Joe*
17 Sect's symbol
21 Up-to-the-minute
22 Org. founded in '49
23 Make a run for it
24 Guitarist Paul
26 Soprano's note
27 In addition
28 Opera opener
29 No longer a kid
30 Humorist Mort
31 Patsy
32 Haggard romance
33 Give a fling
34 "Uh-oh!"
35 *Kidnapped* monogram
36 Make a run for it
39 Use the molars
40 Tropical tree
41 Filmdom's Lawrence
42 Read carefully
44 Mean and nasty
45 Conductor Zubin
46 Rough file
47 Soul singer James
48 Boris Godunov, e.g.
49 *Bus Stop* writer
50 Put away
51 FDR program
52 Short flight
53 "__ Now or Never"

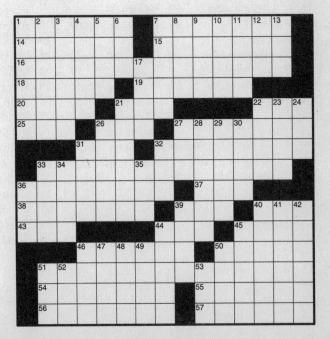

91 TAKE OFF by Wayne R. Williams

ACROSS
1 Poker stake
5 Got up
10 African nation
14 Old codger
15 Pygmy antelope
16 Latvia's capital
17 Take off
19 Menu listing
20 Correction spots
21 Likes and dislikes
23 Actor Beatty
24 Tissue fluid
25 Wheel-alignment measure
29 Neuwirth of *Cheers*
30 McBain and McMahon
33 Symbol of achievement
34 Take off
36 Oven setting
37 Indicate indifference
38 Characterization
39 Take off

41 Serenity
42 So far
43 Lady Chaplin
44 More incensed
45 Disprove a point
47 __ Paulo, Brazil
48 Concentrating viewer
50 Heel style
55 Ms. Chanel
56 Take off
58 Places of refuge
59 Bring joy to
60 Otherwise
61 Army outpost
62 Became the father of
63 Highland loch

DOWN
1 Dull pain
2 Roulette bet
3 Frat-party attire
4 Ordinal endings
5 One flying high
6 Sampled
7 Art medium

8 Kimono sash
9 Sailor's tote
10 Crunchy
11 Take off
12 Film critic James
13 Boulder and Aswan High
18 Adjusted plugs and points
22 Hemsley sitcom
24 Diminishment
25 Hack driver
26 In the know
27 Take off
28 La __ Tar Pits (L.A. locale)
29 Mandalay's locale
31 Sweet, in Seville
32 Smile derisively
34 Protester's litany
35 __ Scott decision
37 Causes of calamity
40 Japanese metropolis

41 Director Pier __ Pasolini
44 Injured severely
46 Irregularly worn
47 Put into words
48 Strikebreaker
49 Synagogue scroll

50 Arcturus or Aldebaran
51 All tied up
52 Scope starter
53 Prepare salad
54 Washington bills
57 Yale student

---

92 BASEBALL FILMS by Mel Rosen

ACROSS
1 Recedes
5 Room's companion
10 WWII date
14 Actress Russo
15 Bowler's milieu
16 __ Lackawanna Railroad
17 Reverse, e.g.
18 Family member
19 Chance to play
20 '89 Costner film
23 Integers: Abbr.
24 Biol. or astron.
25 '76er or Celtic
28 For each
31 Open up, in a way
35 Computer "reading" method: Abbr.
36 Caught in the act
39 Syllogism word
40 '76 Matthau film
43 Natural eyewash
44 Be a sign of
45 Use the peepers
46 Put __ to (halt)

48 Marino of football
49 Comes in second
51 Humorist Shriner
53 Kind of camera, initially
54 '27 Beery film
61 Biblical stargazers
62 Loverboy
63 Tennessee's state flower
65 Ready for business
66 Having no point
67 Salad base
68 Hazard to navigation
69 Change components
70 All-in-one dish

DOWN
1 Bit of work
2 Complaint
3 __ B'rith
4 Cool and collected
5 Parade participants

6 Mixed bag
7 Hebrew letter
8 Bill-of-lading abbr.
9 Textile workers
10 Hostage, euphemistically
11 Instrument for Ringo
12 Affectations
13 Kyoto cash
21 Doone of fiction
22 Old French coin
25 Terra __
26 Yearns (for)
27 *All Creatures __ and Small*
28 Yearned for
29 Actress Verdugo
30 Took back in battle
32 Heavy metal
33 Reach accord
34 "Everything's Coming up __"
37 Say more
38 April setting: Abbr.
41 Window-shopping

42 Snoopy's sister
47 Slapstick missile
50 Planetary paths
52 Sammy Cahn creation
53 Mules and pumps
54 Batman's accessory
55 Maturing agent

56 First-class
57 Fed. agent
58 Bivouac shelter
59 In __ (stuck)
60 Fork point
61 Unruly bunch
64 Wood processor?

ACROSS

1 Once owned
4 Butter bit
7 Hairstyling goo
10 Garfield's hand
13 GI show sponsor
14 Hard to catch
16 "It must be him, __ shall die"
17 Jack Lord cop series
19 *The A-Team* muscleman
20 Turner's pride
21 10th grader
22 Short drive
23 Takes to the cleaners
26 Ace place?
28 Swab's target
29 Some NHLers
30 Printer's widths
31 __ firma
34 Ehrich __ (Houdini)
35 Journalist/muckraker
37 Arm of the sea
40 Shades of color
41 *L.A. Law* characters
44 Biblical language
46 Intertwine
48 Taking it easy
49 "Me and Mamie __"
50 Mr. Nastase
51 Former UN member
54 Hoop group: Abbr.
55 Greek letter
56 Resort sport
60 Gentlemen
61 "My pleasure!"
62 *Foucault's Pendulum* author
63 Newsman Donaldson
64 Jazz instrument
65 Convent dweller
66 Swell place?

DOWN

1 "What was that?"
2 Happy __
3 Depressing situations
4 Architect I.M.
5 Hall-of-Fame boxer
6 Boston-area school
7 Say "Uncle!"
8 Nevertheless
9 Sign of summer
10 Vesuvius victim
11 Gets in
12 Oath taker
15 "Sprechen __ Deutsch?"
18 Freshly
22 Capriati foe
23 Service charge
24 Romance language
25 Corporate VIP
27 "Ignorance of the __ excuse"
29 Senator Jake
32 Coll. mil. grp.
33 Slugger's stat
35 Farr of *M*A*S*H*
36 Anatomical passage
37 Arabian Nights rulers
38 World's fourth largest lake
39 Allies' anathema
41 Felt hats
42 With suspicion
43 Yon sloop
45 Large lizard
47 Pasteur portrayer
49 Senator Hatch
52 Mythical river
53 Adjust the clock
56 Has been
57 Dallas inst.
58 Barbie's beau
59 __ long way (last)

ACROSS

1 Phyllis Diller's hubby
5 Soccer great
9 Slow tempo
14 ". . . maids all in __"
15 Wellington's alma mater
16 Burger topping
17 *What's My Line?* host
18 Grade-school gamut
19 Rocket brake
20 *The Flintstones'* address
23 "Uh-uh"
24 __ *culpa*
25 Selling point
28 Stead
30 '75 Wimbledon winner
34 Books pro: Abbr.
35 Appear to be
37 Khyber Pass, e.g.
39 *The Munsters'* address
42 Mom's mission, maybe
43 Pre-owned
44 Short story?
45 Galley directive
46 Perlman of *Cheers*
48 *Peer Gynt* playwright
50 "__ Sera Sera"
51 Old pro
52 *The Kramdens'* address
60 Message board?
61 Bristol brews
62 Prepare to fly
63 French city
64 Yothers of *Family Ties*
65 Provoked
66 A deadly sin
67 A piece of cake
68 Alternatively

DOWN

1 Rages
2 Smell __ (be suspicious)
3 __ contender
4 *Car 54, Where Are You?* star
5 Lipstick shade
6 Sundance's sweetie
7 Canadian flier
8 Food processor
9 Liza's half sister
10 From the top
11 Ms. Moreno
12 Like some R-rated movies
13 Yoko __
21 Sends out for food
22 Hors d'__
25 High points
26 Show off
27 Stravinsky's *Le __ du printemps*
28 Pantyhose part
29 Permeate
30 Cheer rival
31 Thick slices
32 Skater Sonja
33 Keep one's __ (watch)
36 Gridiron ploy
38 Devoted fan
40 *Krazy __*
41 "The Lady __ Tramp"
47 Greek goddess
49 Wodehouse's Wooster
50 Put the kibosh on
51 Size up
52 Permanent effect?
53 Hawaii's #2 city
54 "Leaving on __ Plane"
55 Literary alias
56 Itches
57 Viscount's better
58 Spouses no more
59 Ebb and flow
60 Hemispheric alliance: Abbr.

95 HORSING AROUND by Eric Albert

ACROSS
1 Goldbrick
6 English assignment
11 Jazz session
14 Disturbingly weird
15 In the know
16 Reverent dread
17 START OF A QUIP
19 How some stand
20 Best-selling game
21 Anti-Dracula device
23 "Olé" or "bravo"
24 Stephen King thriller
26 Field hand?
30 Fuse blower
31 Houyhnhnm subject
32 Quid pro quo
33 Mary's boss at WJM
36 MIDDLE OF QUIP
40 Compass pt.
41 No-good sorts
42 $10 gold piece
43 Really excited
45 Soft stroke
46 Mom, so to speak
49 *Rocky III* foe
50 *A Place in the Sun* star
51 Light in the dark
56 Commencement wear
57 END OF QUIP
60 Plate cleaner, often
61 Usher's beat
62 Shoe material
63 Mr. Milland
64 Remote target?
65 Chuck, for one

DOWN
1 Line of clothing?
2 Protagonist
3 Islamic republic
4 Puerto __
5 Don't fret
6 Primeval
7 Move in the breeze
8 Defense-system initials
9 Indiana Jones quest
10 Order response
11 Perry opened it
12 Rise
13 Basement reading
18 Thatcher, e.g.
22 It does a bang-up job
24 Spring events
25 Arizona Indian
26 Computer-storage unit
27 Displays delight
28 What you used to be?
29 Conk on the noggin
30 Nobel was one
32 Spine-tingling
33 Mezzanine section
34 Barn dwellers
35 "Has 1001 __"
37 Tart-tasting
38 Felix's concern
39 Org. founded in 1890
43 Campaign name of '36
44 Moneybags
45 Duster's target
46 Come to mind
47 Wool-coat owner
48 A bit foolish
49 Haystack painter
51 __ bonding
52 Bad spell
53 Fencing need
54 *Betsy's Wedding* director
55 Hardly overbearing
58 Actress Ullmann
59 Road curve

96 NO SOUR NOTES by Mel Rosen

ACROSS
1 Sore spot
5 Hot tub
8 Boston NBAer
12 Cozy spot
13 Paid out
15 He raised Cain
16 3/4 of a dozen
17 Tall bird
18 Cathedral area
19 Grand __ Opry
20 Sammy Davis, Jr. tune
22 Judaism's Allah
24 Twosome
25 Ornamental flower
27 Turndown
31 Elementary particles
32 Cartoon creature
34 GI's hangout
35 Large amounts
36 __ with faint praise
37 Not "fer"
38 Compass dir.
39 Ports and such
40 Foil, for example
41 Fox's name
43 Not as well-done
44 Directional ending
45 Added attractions
47 Eurythmics tune
51 Former Mideast org.
54 Some shortening
55 Ease
56 Mean monster
57 Similar (to)
58 Early cataloguer
59 Miss the boat
60 Bump into
61 Ga. neighbor
62 Set-to

DOWN
1 __ Domini
2 Wrap around
3 Abba tune
4 Supplement, with "out"
5 Wild escapade
6 Yellowish pink
7 Magnani of film
8 __ *Top This?* (old game show)
9 Wax-coated cheese
10 It's enlarging Hawaii
11 Fed. agents
13 Vowel sound
14 Makes an offer
20 "__ Magic Moment"
21 Actor Howard
23 Charity
25 Library stamp
26 Seeing eye to eye
27 Hose mishaps
28 Archies tune
29 Out of the way
30 Antisocial type
32 True grit?
33 Sra., in France
36 Tyrolean skirts
37 Skin-cream additive
39 Toad feature
40 Factory manager
42 Have no obligation to
43 Some shoes
45 "She loves me" scorekeeper
46 Singer Branigan
47 Bridge coup
48 Greet the day
49 Toledo's lake
50 Sailing hazard
52 Domingo melody
53 Bank (on)
56 Switch position

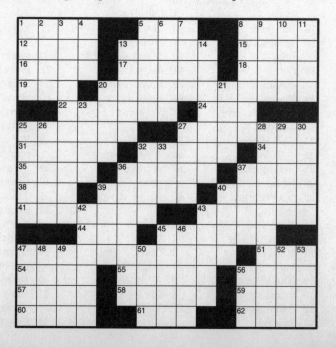

ACROSS

1 Itty-bitty branch
5 Say "guilty," say
10 Green __ and Ham
14 Whale of a movie
15 Rent
16 Leave flat
17 Ritzy New York store
20 Be a mole
21 Hamelin menaces
22 Pull up stakes
23 Small liqueur glass
24 Guitarist Atkins
25 Utterly hopeless
28 Max of *The Beverly Hillbillies*
29 Book after Esther
32 Haunted-house sound
33 Gymnast Korbut
34 Asian desert
35 '80s police series
38 They're slippery when wet
39 Conform to
40 Rope ring
41 High's partner
42 Cut quickly
43 Lend an ear
44 Comply with
45 Makes a wager
46 Ancient
49 Sweater eater
50 Phi-psi link
53 Centrist
56 Theater award
57 Hawaiian "Hi!"
58 Bewilder with a blow
59 Look to be
60 Not at all tame
61 Lumber choppers

DOWN

1 Sleep unsoundly
2 Stole, for example
3 Revolting
4 Argon or neon
5 Easily bent
6 *Waiting for __*
7 Gulps down
8 Volcano output
9 Racetrack tie
10 Kick out
11 Ms. Lollobrigida
12 Down in the mouth
13 "That's one small __ . . ."
18 Monks' wear
19 Change course
23 Rings out
24 Sly as a fox
25 Felt pity
26 Bramble, e.g.
27 Bread spread
28 Delete an expletive
29 Go lance to lance
30 Overly large
31 American buffalo
33 Go around
34 It'll hold water
36 Poor at crooning
37 Gay and cheerful
42 Bear's advice
43 __ *Weapon* (Gibson film)
44 Computer-telephone device
45 South Africa's former PM
46 Football's __ Alonzo Stagg
47 Taunt
48 Adams or McClurg
49 *Dial __ Murder*
50 Try to influence
51 Visibility problem
52 March 15th, for one
54 ". . . Round the __ Oak Tree"
55 Nutrition stat.

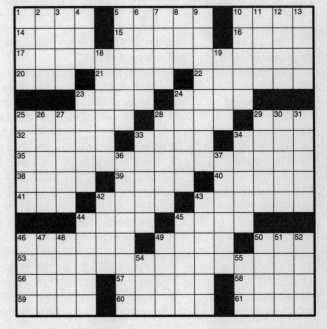

ACROSS

1 Banned chem. sprays
5 PAT
8 Back of the neck
12 PAT of *The Karate Kid*
14 Ostrich kin
15 Alaska's first governor
16 Missing link, maybe
17 DDE's rank
18 Receive an IOU for
19 Home of the NFL's "PATS"
21 Subtraction word
22 Start of spring?
23 Pool gear
24 Give, as odds
26 Soft palates
27 *PAT and Mike* actress
31 __ carotene
34 Boy or girl preceder
36 Home on the range
37 Tennis surface
38 German wine region
40 Ford models
41 Sheeplike
43 Environmental sci.
44 Game-show winnings
45 Pop singer PAT
47 Half of VP
49 Director Craven
50 Dole (out)
51 RR stop
54 College major
57 PAT of *One Day at a Time*
60 ". . . __ saw Elba"
61 Eur. country
62 "Cut that out!"
63 Deli-counter call
64 King of France
65 Periodic-table components
66 Go out with
67 Cribbage prop
68 Deteriorates

DOWN

1 Chuckleheads
2 Pearson and Barrymore
3 Fourth dimension
4 Political position
5 *The Ballet Class* artist
6 Prayer end
7 Washer load
8 PAT's jeep on *The Roy Rogers Show*
9 *The African Queen* screenwriter
10 0-star reviews
11 Extremities
12 Thick head of hair
13 Bony
20 Chair material
25 Quick to learn
26 PAT Sajak's colleague
27 George I's house
28 Capable of
29 Hire a decorator
30 Chick's home
31 Shapeless mass
32 Roof overhang
33 Dead ringer
35 __ *Tac Dough*
39 Prideful feeling
42 Somme summer
46 B neighbor
48 Hoops position
50 Head honcho
51 March honoree
52 Works hard
53 Tiny workers
54 Patch up
55 Field of expertise
56 Schoolbook
58 Lotion additive
59 __ it (start work)

99 ORDINAL ARRAY by Wayne R. Williams

ACROSS

1 Old Testament heroine
8 Thespians' union: Abbr.
11 Part of TGIF
14 Raise
15 Treeless tract
17 First followers
19 __ Khayyám
20 Likewise not
21 Rosie O'Neill portrayer
22 Exclude
25 Board member, often
26 Second followers
33 The "al." in "et al."
34 __ Na Na
35 Maiden name indicator
36 Barn bellow
37 Soup sample
39 Get one's goat
41 Zilch
42 Miller or Jillian
43 __ es Salaam
45 Entertainer MacKenzie
47 Third followers
51 Morning hrs.
52 City on the Po
53 Ease up
56 Sportscaster Scully
57 Right-hand person: Abbr.
61 Fourth followers
65 Desperate
66 Seeing red
67 Draft org.
68 Compass dir.
69 Rental customers

DOWN

1 Display model
2 Jack of old movies
3 VHS alternative
4 Past the deadline
5 Bleacher cheer
6 One-time connection
7 Red dyes
8 Practice punching
9 *Exodus* character
10 Doohickey
11 "*Dies __*"
12 Conway and Cratchit
13 Matches a bet
16 How cars go up hills
18 A Day at the movies
23 Commits a blunder
24 Moreover
25 Hero's mount
26 Rambling sort
27 Make amends
28 Sandal piece
29 4 on the telephone
30 Like some sanctums
31 Actor Sam
32 Edited out
38 Preceder of excellence
40 Fruit with green pulp
44 10 to 1, e.g.
46 Beethoven pieces
48 Film critic, e.g.
49 Makes corrections to
50 Bridge alternative
53 States further
54 Pix about people
55 Cookie tycoon Wally
56 Room's asset
58 Wise one
59 Trick or game ending
60 Turner and Koppel
62 Boom-bah preceder
63 Chemical suffix
64 Mrs., in Madrid

100 QUITE A CASE! by Cynthia Lyon

ACROSS

1 Booty
5 Olympian's award
10 Typewriter settings
14 Columbus' home
15 Handy
16 "__ want for Christmas . . ."
17 START OF A QUIP
20 Sphere of influence
21 Party roamers
22 Liked, slangily
24 Prior to
25 PART 2 OF QUIP
33 Eucalyptivore
34 Holds the deed to
35 A question of manners?
36 Senator Hatch
37 Big bankroll
38 Simpson of fashion
40 Peach product
41 Treat meat
42 Slaves away
43 PART 3 OF QUIP
47 Bud's buddy
48 Caviar, essentially
49 Property recipient
54 Loosen, in a way
58 END OF QUIP
61 Start of Caesar's claim
62 Upstanding
63 "__, a thousand times . . ."
64 H.S. exams
65 Sample recordings
66 Hammerhead feature

DOWN

1 Suburban turf
2 Copter's noise
3 Adjutant, e.g.
4 *The Naked Maja* painter
5 Hawaiian housedress
6 Ordinal suffix
7 Per follower
8 Jai __
9 Kin of Loewe's collaborator
10 Pad
11 Popular houseplant
12 Indistinct sight
13 Occupies an ottoman
18 Hemingway's Santiago
19 Taj Mahal city
23 Mature
25 *Flying Down __*
26 Ran quickly
27 Harvarder's rival
28 Create bonsai
29 Make beloved
30 __ *Finest Hour* (Churchill book)
31 Hall decker
32 Rams' ma'ams
33 Sennett squad
38 Show up for
39 "Cock-a-doodle-__!"
41 Made a difference
44 Legal outs
45 Kelly critter
46 Judicial arenas
49 They'll travel anywhere: Abbr.
50 National League park
51 Dismissed
52 Raison d'__
53 Grades K-6
55 Galvanization need
56 Pedestal percher
57 __ colada
59 A soc. sci.
60 AAA job

101 GOING PLACES by Shirley Soloway

ACROSS

1 Sch. at Tempe
4 Dieter of rhyme
9 Ms. Verdon
13 Connery role
15 Author Jong
16 Hard to find
17 Yearbook inscriptions
19 Spanish I verb
20 Tip over
21 Golf gadgets
22 *Moonstruck* Oscar-winner
23 Some makeup
25 Majestic story
27 Lawyers' grp.
28 Eased
31 Church official: Abbr.
34 Repair a tear
37 Mom's brother
38 __ *American Cousin*
39 Dining-room staffers
41 Research room
42 Make a speech
44 Half a Samoan city
45 Flexed
46 Noisy celebration
48 Central mail loc.
50 Nathan Hale's alma mater
51 Office tyros
56 Pats lightly
58 Prefix for dynamics
60 Move laterally
61 Orchestral instrument
62 Geometric intersection
64 Fish-story teller
65 Omit in pronunciation
66 Market rise
67 "Shall we?" answer
68 Boca __, FL
69 Antique car

DOWN

1 Demean
2 Silly Sales
3 Loosen a knot
4 Sun. talk
5 Empty talk
6 More mature
7 Dull pain
8 Mortarboard attachment
9 "Ode on a __ Urn"
10 Launderer's concern
11 Art Deco artist
12 In the neighborhood
14 Canadian cash
18 Smooth-talking
24 Whale of film
26 In addition to
28 Sick as __
29 Lively spirit
30 Obligation
31 Othello was one
32 Free of doubt
33 Dinner-service piece
35 Catch sight of
36 Hoop group: Abbr.
39 Ameche role
40 Meditative discipline
43 Little puzzles
45 __ up on (studying)
47 Cyrus McCormick invention
49 Tower town
51 Characteristic
52 Concerto movement
53 Seer Cayce
54 *Dallas* mama
55 "__ evil . . ."
56 Well-behaved kid
57 Rose's beau
59 Singer Fitzgerald
63 Poetic night

102 ENOUGH! by Mel Rosen

ACROSS

1 Shopping prop
5 Get off, on the gridiron
11 Banned pesticide
14 Theater award
15 Spice things up
16 Seafood delicacy
17 Put a stop to, with "on"
19 Pussycat's companion
20 Took the wheel
21 Force forward
23 Jaguar or Cougar
24 Appeals-court rulings
26 Goes bad
29 Knock down
30 Get together
31 Clark's colleague
32 No gentleman
35 Sprightly tune
36 Turn (to)
37 Hailing call
38 Wright wing
39 Quail quantity
40 Norwegian coin
41 Molecular variation
43 Flew like an eagle
44 Afternoon performance
46 Draw on
47 Video-game name
48 Provides comfort
52 Near the center
53 Cease
57 Resembling
58 Heavens-related
59 Nobel Peace Prize city
60 Squalid quarters
61 Prying needs
62 *Pygmalion* playwright

DOWN

1 Friday and Drummond
2 Border upon
3 Get one's goat
4 Put on the air
5 They lead you on
6 Must have
7 Unsubstantial food
8 Catalina, for one: Abbr.
9 Singer Rawls
10 Fire trucks
11 Prepare to rest
12 Wooden rod
13 Spills the beans
18 Hors d'oeuvres holders
22 Actress Farrow
24 __ decimal system
25 Kuwaiti prince
26 Hill's partner
27 Runner Zatopek
28 Close up shop
29 Take a back seat (to)
31 River structure
33 High-grade
34 __-in-the-wool
36 "The Eternal City"
37 Wyoming Indians
39 Funnel-shaped
40 Arboreal Aussie
42 *To __ with Love*
43 Bar seating
44 __ *Family* ('80s sitcom)
45 At an angle
48 Top draw
49 Pocket money
50 Scat queen
51 Pack away
54 Sugary suffix
55 VH-1 rival
56 Sooner than

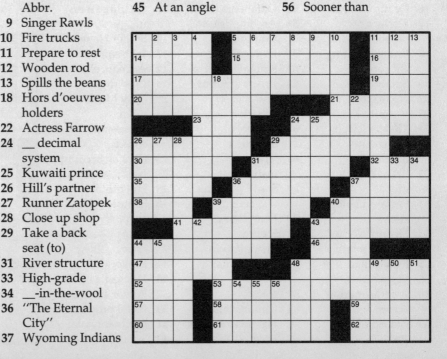

GREEK CLIQUE by Wayne R. Williams

ACROSS
1 Dispensed
6 Keg feature
9 Campfire remains
14 Stradivari's teacher
15 __ glance (quickly)
16 Fulton's power
17 *Antigone* playwright
19 __ Haute, IN
20 Shoshonean Indian
21 Sha Na Na member, e.g.
23 Suffix for scram
24 It had a part in Exodus
26 Greek comedy writer
28 Pot starter
30 Spread for bread
31 French river
34 Brewery vessels
37 Broadway souvenir
40 Moves emotionally
41 Wedding vow
42 German plane
43 Matching
44 Ink mess
45 Sportscaster Merlin
46 *Typee* sequel
48 In the past
50 *Anabasis* author
54 Bonehead plays
58 Brit. record label
59 One of TV's Snoop Sisters
61 __ Tin Tin
62 Delaware senator
64 Plato's student
66 French student
67 "__ been had!"
68 Summon up
69 Union man Chavez
70 Rule: Abbr.
71 More rational

DOWN
1 Conductor Kurt
2 Chew the scenery
3 Used a camcorder
4 Ordinal ending
5 Greek philosopher
6 __ of woe
7 Mr. T's former outfit
8 Old hat
9 From the stars
10 Canonized *femme*: Abbr.
11 Father of History
12 Baseball great Combs
13 Sling mud
18 Political ending
22 Seth's son
25 Riviera resort
27 Snuggling one
29 Satanic
31 Equine beast
32 Call __ day
33 Greek poet
35 Fuss
36 Dorothy's dog
38 Arthur Godfrey's instrument
39 Make illegal
42 Plato's mentor
44 Physicist Niels
47 First game
49 NBA team
50 Three-masted ship
51 Monsieur Zola
52 Radio-studio sign
53 Effrontery
55 Playwright Joe
56 German poet
57 Curl one's lip
60 Victory, in Vienna
63 Spacewalk, initially
65 Caesar's eggs

PROCRASTINATORS by Fred Piscop

ACROSS
1 June honoree
4 Paper packages
9 Not quite right
14 Metal in the rough
15 Glorify
16 Group doctrine
17 Hodges of baseball
18 Procrastinating TV cop?
20 Smooth singer
22 Up (to)
23 Visigoth king
24 Theater letters
26 Lioness in *Born Free*
29 "What's __ for me?"
31 Parapsychology subj.
33 Hereford hotel
34 Reggae relative
36 Iceboat necessity
38 Pluto's path
40 Procrastinating actress?
43 Get rid of the suds
44 "Ciao, baby!"
45 Mediocre grade
46 Dancer Miller
47 Have to pay
49 Cubic Rubik
51 Gardener's bane
53 Oklahoma town
55 Accomplish, so to speak
59 Evil look
61 Snuggling sorts
63 Procrastinating preacher?
66 Wharton deg.
67 Symbol of leakiness
68 "Taps" instrument
69 Stand __ (don't waver)
70 Lent a hand
71 Sloppy precipitation
72 __ and outs

DOWN
1 Church belief
2 Historian Durant
3 Perry's assistant
4 Come back to
5 Expel, in a way
6 "Up and __!"
7 Heston role
8 Hearst's kidnappers: Abbr.
9 "...three men in __"
10 Singer Haggard
11 Like some ink
12 Aegean, e.g.
13 Pigs' digs
19 New Mexico town
21 Three-tone chords
25 Give an account of
27 Nasty, as remarks
28 Hill builder
30 Sampled the steak
32 Campy sound effect
34 Porkers
35 Housed a hound
37 Writer Tarbell
39 Pistol property
41 Prefix for natal
42 Suburban event
43 Bitterly cold
48 Getting close
50 Later, maybe
52 Do research
54 Set aside
56 Metronome settings
57 Sort of sprawl
58 H.S. exams
60 *One-__ Jacks* (Brando film)
62 Beat by a whisker
63 Cubs' org.
64 Second-sequel letters
65 Dictionary abbr.

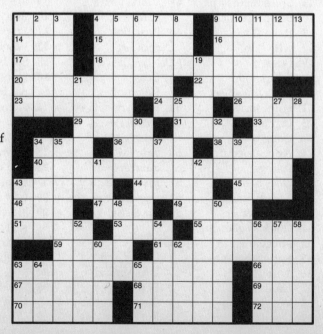

105 CAESAR AT THE MALL by Eric Albert

ACROSS

1 Spill the beans
5 Western capital
10 Electrically versatile
14 Get up
15 *South Pacific* role
16 Allegro con __
17 Similar (to)
18 Really miffed
19 Not at all shy
20 START OF A QUIP
23 International aid org.
24 Author Umberto
25 Imported auto
27 Actress Taylor
28 Golfer Woosnam
30 Moth's lure
32 Inspire wonder
33 Vaudeville bit
34 Gem-studded headgear
35 MIDDLE OF QUIP
38 Sweet-talk
41 Swiss spot
42 High ball?

45 Count Basie's instrument
46 Rub the wrong way
47 Recurring idea
49 Coffee brewer
50 "Smoking or __?"
52 Dance to rock
53 END OF QUIP
57 Green stone
58 Airport control center
59 *Peter and the Wolf* "duck"
60 Eden's earldom
61 Video-game maker
62 Chimney channel
63 Pesky plant
64 __ around (snoops)
65 Parker who played Boone

DOWN

1 Showy display
2 Car-ad phrase
3 Ludicrous

4 "... but it's more important to __"
5 Line on a letter
6 In the thick of
7 "__ Marlene"
8 Late morning
9 Corpsman
10 Golda's colleague
11 What a pryer uses
12 Two-horned thing
13 Not prepaid
21 Neckline shape
22 European capital
26 Unseld of basketball
28 Sparklers
29 In conflict
31 F. Lee's field
33 "Botch-__" (Clooney tune)
34 Recipe amt.
35 Debate side
36 Without equal
37 Lodge member
38 PC's "brain"
39 Radio-signal medium

40 Mystery woman
42 Easy to read
43 Threatening
44 *Saturday Night Fever* group
46 Altogether
47 Add icing to

48 Dismount quickly
51 Available in kegs
52 Netman Becker
54 Direct (one's way)
55 Love letters?
56 Roll response
57 Vise part

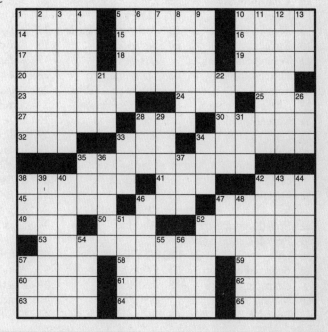

106 SMALL TALK by Shirley Soloway

ACROSS

1 Real money
5 Become blurry
9 Dirty air
13 Racqueteer Arthur
14 By __ (barely)
16 Point out
17 Of limited duration
19 Poker payment
20 Part of TLC
21 __ Na Na
22 Rivers, to Roberto
23 Derisive look
24 Take away (from)
26 Ready to pick
28 Actress North
31 Chem rooms
34 Lee of cakedom
37 Wipe out
38 Nest-egg letters
39 '60s pop singer
41 An NCO
42 Dietary need
44 Put on the market
45 "The __ the limit!"
46 *Butterfield 8* star

48 __ mater
50 Dresses up
53 Roundish shapes
57 Powder ingredient
59 Memorable time
60 When *Dallas* was on
61 Touch against
62 Clam variety
64 Jury member
65 It divides Paris
66 Happiness
67 Actress Lanchester
68 Ship out
69 Makes a statement

DOWN

1 Throws out a line
2 Pale-colored
3 Was all aglow
4 Sheepdogs, for instance
5 Jamie or Felicia
6 "Eureka!"
7 __ Macabre

8 Dinnertime of film
9 Less common
10 Satellite-locating system
11 Director Preminger
12 The Bee __ (rock singers)
15 Brings up
18 Ms. Garr
24 College officials
25 "Excuse me!"
27 Greek letter
29 Catch sight of
30 Long swimmers
31 Pick-me-up
32 Oratorio piece
33 Some eyes, so to speak
35 Deli bread
36 Earth bound?
39 Walked over
40 Under the weather
43 Agamemnon's daughter
45 Nest eggs
47 Country dances

49 Last word of "I Got Rhythm"
51 Shouts out
52 *The Sons of __ Elder* (Wayne film)
54 Writer Rogers St. Johns
55 Cagney's TV partner
56 Actress Brenda
57 Finish-line prop
58 Genesis son
60 Took off
63 Country-music cable sta.

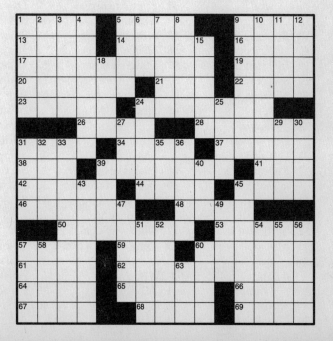

107 BEARDS by Cynthia Lyon

ACROSS
1 Plumb crazy
5 Stroller, in Sussex
9 S.V. Benét's Farmer Stone
14 The Bard's river
15 Big fuss
16 Unanimously
17 Eatery listing
18 Bearded leader
20 Rural sts.
21 Wasn't colorfast
22 Police-blotter abbr.
23 Citric quencher
24 Cereal grain
25 Darth Vader's side
28 Trees akin to cashews
31 Has the potential to
32 Freud's concern
33 Bearded monarch
36 Up
38 Bearded cartoon character
40 Macho type
43 Bearded sibs
47 Thurman of *Henry & June*
48 Squid squirt
50 *This __ Life*
51 Percussion gourd
53 Mineo of movies
55 High range: Abbr.
56 Zilch
57 Paris hotel
59 Airborne Dracula
60 Bearded gift-bearer
63 "Dueling," to "indulge": Abbr.
65 Mr. T's former group
66 Actress Sedgwick
67 Gross
68 Madison vice president
69 "Wait __!" ("Hold on!")
70 Abound

DOWN
1 Felon's flight
2 Past the deadline
3 Judge unfit
4 Responsibility
5 Harper Valley org.
6 Actor Benson
7 Astaire's sister
8 Double agent
9 Funnyman Murray
10 Songwriters' org.
11 Bet middlers?
12 Blow up
13 Buddhist sect
19 Thought
23 Fire wood?
24 Write that you're coming
26 Yule aromas
27 Zillions of years
29 Instrument for an *angelo*
30 Bluish
31 *La Bohème* character
34 "And all __ is a tall ship . . ."
35 Doctrine
37 "One __ land . . ."
39 Electric co., e.g.
40 Render a tune
41 Flow forth
42 American Leaguer
44 Harlequin genre
45 Movie-set blooper
46 Grads-to-be: Abbr.
49 Antidrug officer
52 Wedding setting
53 Collar inserts
54 Sky's color
58 Chase of Hollywood
59 Worms, often
60 Lose firmness
61 *Little Women* girl
62 Air Force org.
64 Prom locale

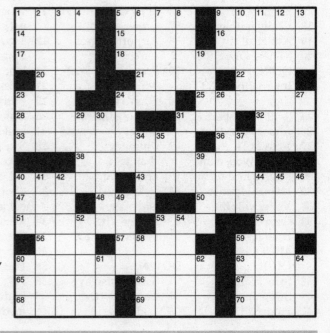

108 TWO THEMES IN ONE by Alex Vaughn

ACROSS
1 Mrs. David Copperfield
5 Seed source
10 Air pollution
14 Words of worry
15 "With this ring, __ wed"
16 Casino city
17 Riviera resort
18 Wakes up
19 Irritated mood
20 Sweet wine
22 Newspaper notices
24 __-disant (self-styled)
25 Desire deified
27 Republicans' symbol
29 House pet, informally
32 Sufficient space
33 Mss. polishers
34 __ the elbows (shabby)
36 "__ fightin' words!"
39 Canal chamber
41 Riverbank earthworks
43 Fail to include
44 Made a living at
46 Suit component
48 Bikini part
49 Makes a boo-boo
51 Popular stuffed animal
53 Novelty dance
56 Nectar source
57 Make choices
58 Kind of energy
60 Syrian leader
63 Singer Redding
65 "__ Peak or Bust"
67 Elisabeth of *Soapdish*
68 Diet successfully
69 Pizzeria fixtures
70 Irish Republic
71 Part of A.M.
72 Dunaway et al.
73 Tune up for a bout

DOWN
1 Advice, often
2 Glenn's state
3 Smarty
4 What the Tin Man wanted
5 Greek letters
6 Dog in *Beetle Bailey*
7 Smarty's trinket
8 Jeopardy
9 Day starter
10 S.A.T. takers
11 Smarty's attainment
12 Omelet extra
13 "I understand!"
21 It drops from palms
23 Catch sight of
26 Mideast missile
28 Happy sounds
29 Sort of seaweed
30 Loved one
31 "Take __ from me"
35 "A __ 'clock scholar"
37 "Look at that, Luis!"
38 Have the lead
40 *Show Boat* composer
42 Cut it out
45 Prohibition backers
47 Flushing, NY field
50 *Little __ Horrors*
52 String section
53 "Rah!" relative
54 Author Sinclair
55 Tony of baseball
59 Actor Auberjonois
61 Ambience
62 Whitetail, e.g.
64 Go on dates with
66 Draft org.

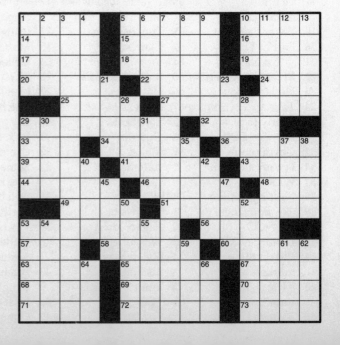

109 SOLVE WITH "EASE" by Randolph Ross

ACROSS

1 Designer Schiaparelli
5 In the past
8 Army outpost
12 Witches' brew need
13 Quick flash
15 Theater sign
16 Smell __ (be suspicious)
17 *Oklahoma!* aunt
18 Marine life
19 Indicated
21 Not around
23 Overtime cause
24 Calendar col. heading
25 Nutritionist's concern
26 *Joie de vivre*
28 Flown the coop
29 Beatnik's home
32 __ *Under the Elms*
34 Rank too highly
36 Take __ the chin
37 Carousal
39 Western author Wister
40 Romeo's surname
42 Mr. Dangerfield
44 Chang's brother
45 State on the Long Isl. Sound
46 Yorkshire river
47 Datum, for short
48 Sapporo sash
49 Vane dir.
52 Hale and hearty
55 Makes do
57 Lendl of tennis
58 Make happy
60 Bar order
61 Acquire
62 Champing at the bit
63 Answering-machine sound
64 Comrade-in-arms
65 Card game
66 Letters near 0

DOWN

1 Pass legislation
2 Poet Jones
3 Jolson's specialty?
4 Envelope abbr.
5 Green Mountain Boys leader
6 __ the lily
7 What *unum* means
8 Cruel sort
9 Wheel shaft
10 Give an autograph
11 Coup d'__
13 Buy a fake beard?
14 Apprentice outlaw?
20 General Bradley
22 Pabst product
25 Swooped down
27 Washer residue
28 Bridge name
29 Tribal emporium?
30 Suit to __
31 Declare untrue
32 Canadian coin
33 Venerable prep school
35 Angling gear
38 Fourth-down play
41 New Testament book
43 Arles assents
47 Phoenix forecast
48 Peripheral
50 Precious gem
51 Organic compound
52 Latvia's capital
53 Face shape
54 It may be posted
55 Long story
56 "It __ laugh"
59 Grad-school major

110 WORDS WORTH by Donna J. Stone

ACROSS

1 Present day?
5 Vegan's no-no
9 Swab brand
14 Auld lang syne
15 Perry's creator
16 Not turn __ (remain calm)
17 Global band
18 Forgo the fries
19 Conductor's concern
20 START OF AN IRVIN COBB QUIP
23 Drivers' org.
24 Canal zone?
25 Give rise to
28 *Sesame Street* character
30 Goya's *Duchess of* __
34 Cocks and bulls
35 Mob member
37 *The __ the Rose*
39 MIDDLE OF QUIP
42 Joan of Arc, e.g.
43 Haydn epithet
44 *Murder in the Cathedral* monogram
45 Christie concoction
46 Singer James
48 More mirthful
50 Sault __ Marie, MI
51 Fire preceder
52 END OF QUIP
59 Old hat
60 Marina's place
61 Installed, as tile
63 More than enough
64 Roman and Christian
65 Nevada city
66 Gould of *The Prince of Tides*
67 Expected back
68 Single buyer

DOWN

1 Affair of 1798
2 Sky light
3 *New Yorker* cartoonist
4 It takes two
5 Euripides tragedy
6 Buffalo's county
7 Actor Baldwin
8 Restrict Rover
9 Gulf nation
10 In that case
11 Foot of a sort
12 Mammy Yokum prop
13 Sign of stage success
21 Larder
22 Sylvester's snooze
25 Curly's brother
26 Kind of code
27 Houston ballplayer
28 News brief, briefly
29 Tut's turf
30 "What Kind of Fool __?"
31 Koufax, for one
32 Gem State capital
33 In search of
36 *From __ Eternity*
38 Leisurely, to Liszt
40 Conglomerate letters
41 Bond rating
47 Toyota model
49 It's charming
50 TV bishop
51 "__ of robins . . ."
52 *My Friend* __
53 Samples the Chablis
54 Normandy town
55 Made tracks
56 Novelist Hunter
57 Stiff wind
58 Summer-camp activity
59 __ Mahal
62 Pardo or Johnson

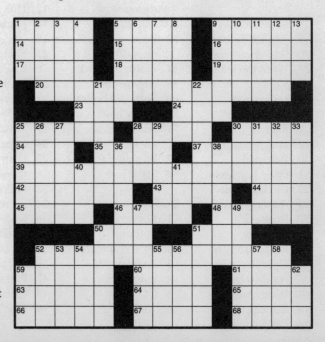

111 ALLITERATION by Mel Rosen

ACROSS

1 Ump's call
5 Llama land
9 *Misery* star
13 Singer Guthrie
14 Church area
15 Bring to naught
16 Mr. Connery
17 Low-priority place
19 Owns
20 Love-neighbor link
21 London section
22 Some sandwiches
24 Teachers' org.
25 Roof support
27 Pre-meal drink
32 Meadows' hubby
33 *The Plains of Passage* author
34 Milan money
35 As well
36 Summer spell
39 Abolitionist Turner
40 Genesis character
42 Bridal wear
43 Fake jewelry
45 They make conclusions
47 Like baby food, often
48 Neither fish __ fowl
49 Strike a pose
50 Tenderly, in music
54 "Absolutely!"
55 Lacrosse-team complement
58 Small stitch
60 Ace in the __
61 Diner sign
62 Machu Picchu people
63 Night fliers
64 Wild plum
65 Some votes
66 Tiny fly

DOWN

1 Waistband
2 General vicinity
3 Heavy-rain result
4 Very long time
5 Stage shows
6 List-ending abbr.
7 Croupier's gadget
8 In a suave manner
9 Shorten
10 Last Stuart monarch
11 Yemen seaport
12 *L'Etoile du __* (Minnesota's motto)
14 Can't stand
18 __-friendly computer
20 The way things are going
23 French season
25 Appraised
26 Without equal
27 German cars
28 Ring out
29 Hollywood's nickname
30 Hopping mad
31 Destined
33 Worry, it's said
37 Tennis effect
38 Taters
41 Crowing time
44 "Chances __" (Mathis tune)
46 Old geezer
47 Yeats and Keats
49 Caged talkers
50 Joe Young's family
51 It may be square
52 Football great Graham
53 Mrs. Chaplin
56 Jazz-singing name
57 Bird house
59 Not at all friendly
60 Monopolize

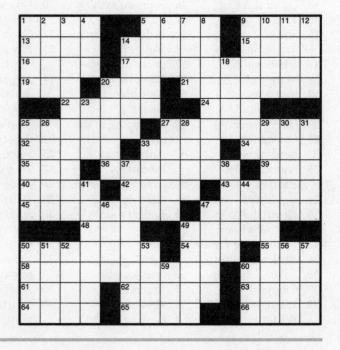

112 INSTRUMENTAL by Shirley Soloway

ACROSS

1 South __, IN
5 Platter
9 At a distance
13 One more time
15 Roman orator
16 Where the grapes are
17 Interfered with
19 Author Ferber
20 Scenery suffix
21 Went too far with
23 Kept up the criticism of
26 Bandleader Brown
27 Pregrown grass
30 Reclined
31 Oxen harness
33 Circular dance
35 Absorbed with
37 Roebuck's partner
40 Responsibility
41 Operetta composer
43 Water holder
44 Circus star
46 Fully convinced
47 Breathe heavily
48 *Serpico* author
50 D.C. 100
52 Roll-call vote
53 Beer kin
55 "Quiet!"
58 Fashion designer
60 *Salvador* star
63 Pour __ (exert oneself)
64 Biology branch
68 Amaze
69 Software buyer
70 Sticky stuff
71 Sound-stage areas
72 Be abundant
73 Stack role

DOWN

1 Ebenezer's outburst
2 Swelled heads
3 Antidrug cop
4 Singing Shore
5 CCC plus CCCI
6 Author Fleming
7 Got to one's feet
8 Escort fleet
9 Declare
10 Waste, as time
11 Musical of "Tomorrow"
12 Hits the books
14 High land
18 Get off the track
22 Slaughter of baseball
24 Some evergreens
25 Show excitement
27 Took a photo of
28 Charlie's wife
29 Dismissed from the service
32 Hold on to
34 En route, in a way
36 Used paddles
38 M. Descartes
39 Sp. miss
42 Fame or acclaim
45 Criticizes
49 Don't participate in
51 Descend rapidly
53 Not quite right
54 Singer Lenya
56 By itself
57 "The Man Without a Country"
59 Traveler's stops
61 Medicine amount
62 Some NCOs
65 Wide-eyed remark
66 Furnish weapons to
67 "__! We Have No Bananas"

113   J & X by Eric Albert

ACROSS

1 Not naked
5 Ringlike things
10 Well-protected
14 Actress Turner
15 Wide-awake
16 Decorative molding
17 Rabbi's religion
20 Boyer/Bergman thriller
21 City on the Missouri
22 Large amount
23 Complain constantly
25 Cause to be
29 Raise to the third power
30 Dog doc
33 Allies' foes
34 Muslim palace area
35 Eddie's *Green Acres* costar
36 Close together
40 Shakespeare title word
41 Loudly, in music
42 Goose call
43 Mrs. Turkey
44 Romantic gift
45 Easily broken
47 Drum accompanier
48 Nanki-__ (*The Mikado* role)
49 Elemental
52 Thanksgiving choice
57 Outside the court
60 "Oh, woe!"
61 Old enough
62 Save, as coupons
63 Lane's coworker
64 Played cat-and-mouse (with)
65 *Kiss Me __*

DOWN

1 Stop up
2 *Dr. Zhivago* role
3 Farm workers
4 Writer Roald
5 Wisconsin native
6 Love, to Leilani
7 Teller call
8 Erving's nickname
9 RV center?
10 Make an impression
11 What a diva delivers
12 Perch or piranha
13 Austen novel
18 French river
19 Scale starters
23 Radium researcher
24 Help in a heist
25 Punjab prince
26 Give off
27 *Six Crises* author
28 Franklin invention: Abbr.
29 Hindu stratum
30 Puff-adder's poison
31 *Dynasty* star
32 Loquacious
34 Gymnastics device
37 Lesotho's locale
38 Magical sound effect
39 "__ believe in yesterday"
45 Compulsory
46 Thor's foe
47 Leading the line
48 Singer Janis
49 Nestling's nose
50 Wheel joiner
51 Ollie's partner
52 6/6/44
53 Big name in trucks
54 '40s leading lady Raines
55 Came to earth
56 Hunt and peck
58 Write hurriedly
59 Tabloid topic

114   CAJUN KOOKERY by David A. Rosen

ACROSS

1 Extra
6 Long rides?
11 Preservative: Abbr.
14 One way to get information
15 Arden of poetry
16 Sleep phenom.
17 Vegetarian TV host?
19 Idle talk
20 Sondheim's __ *the Woods*
21 Makeup buy
23 Old witches
26 Table listings
27 Bart's dad
28 Debate side
29 Persist suffix
30 Worrier's word
31 Ad __ committee
32 Sketcher's eraser
35 Comparative ending
36 Fraternity parties
38 New Mexican Amerind
39 Excessively ornate
41 Short dog, for short
42 Obscene stuff
43 Hardwood tree
44 German article
45 Buffalo iceman
46 Party stalwart
49 Hardened criminals
50 "__ that remark!"
51 Computer selection screen
52 Short time?
53 Nutty film critic?
58 __ vivant
59 Kind of jury
60 Wispy clouds
61 George's bill
62 Stunk
63 *You __ for It*

DOWN

1 Fuss
2 Cartoonist Browne
3 Colonial descendant's grp.
4 May and Stritch
5 It bums you out
6 Jocular Jay
7 Gershwin's *Concerto __*
8 Young follower
9 Indian, e.g.
10 Dewey, Cheatham & Howe, Esqs.?
11 TV host in the soup?
12 What "you've gotta have"
13 Oscar-awarding org.
18 "__ Impossible" (Como tune)
22 Copper
23 Preside over
24 The old birl game
25 Spicy poet?
26 Concorde compartment
28 Talk fondly
31 Medical insurance grp.
32 Prepare for action
33 Road reversal
34 Parcels (out)
36 Lugs around
37 Uncountable years
40 She-bears: Sp.
42 Asian hunting dogs
44 Big property
45 Roman philosopher
46 Competitive dance
47 Heavenly hunter
48 Against property, in legalese
49 Low land
51 Hand, slangily
54 *Diamond __*
55 Boat of refuge
56 Prior to
57 Box top

115 FLAG DAY by Randolph Ross

ACROSS
1 Big parties
6 Quite humid
10 Lose traction
14 Greek : alpha :: Hebrew : __
15 Lotion ingredient
16 French father
17 Gene Krupa portrayer
18 Canadian flag emblem
20 U.S. flag, familiarly
22 Shaker __, OH
23 Enjoy the buffet
24 __ in the Dark
27 Wanders about
29 Signed off on
32 Estranged
34 Two of a kind
35 Soviet flag, familiarly
38 Famous name?
39 Finding offensive
40 Rock star Jon __ Jovi
41 The bottom line
43 Clever ploys
44 Old French coin
45 Lizzie material
46 French flag's colors
55 British flag
56 Got out of bed
57 Composer Rota
58 North-forty unit
59 Terry product
60 Idyllic spot
61 Amaze
62 Water jugs

DOWN
1 Legs, so to speak
2 Touched down
3 Actress Olin
4 Impressionist?
5 Wyoming Indian
6 __ with faint praise
7 "When I was __ . . ."
8 Washing needs
9 Hailed on
10 Get lost
11 Don't give up
12 "Dies __" (hymn)
13 Dict. entries
19 Important periods
21 Rose-petal oil
24 San Antonio landmark
25 Lost in Yonkers writer
26 Clothes lines
27 Citizen __
28 Interjects
29 Chaplin costar in The Great Dictator
30 Ceramic ovens
31 Small remnant
32 Ishmael's captain
33 Sea dogs
34 Police stns.
36 Canary's cousin
37 Overrun
41 McCarthy aide
42 Message boards of a sort
44 React to Frankie
45 Subtracted
46 Mystical poem
47 Oklahoma city
48 Sup in style
49 Savoir-faire
50 Stocking shade
51 It may be knitted
52 St. Elmo's Fire star
53 Spreadsheet worker
54 Snakelike fish

116 MID-JUNE BIRTHDAYS by Mel Rosen

ACROSS
1 The word, at times
4 Scale a peak
9 Pa Clampett
12 "I beg your pardon!"
14 Traffic-report source
15 Opera star
16 Film critic born June 18th
18 Give off
19 Transparent act
20 Okay as food
22 Cairo waterway
24 Zilch
25 Complain in court
29 Beef cut
31 Detective Archer
34 Truth, old-style
35 Animation frames
36 As __ (therefore)
37 What the suspicious smell
38 Silently understood
39 Cuba, por ejemplo
40 Auction word
41 "Do __ others . . ."
42 Taj __
43 Letter carrier: Abbr.
44 Harris' __ Rabbit
45 Mideasterner
46 Mideasterner
48 Sore spot
50 Deer meat
53 Skilled worker
58 Vaccine type
59 Comedian born June 17th
61 Shredded
62 Barkin of The Big Easy
63 "What __ is new?"
64 Native Alaskan: Abbr.
65 Claude's cup
66 __ Monte

DOWN
1 Mr. Antony
2 "Oops!"
3 Bytes or bucks lead-in
4 Bank offering
5 Recording company
6 Chemical suffix
7 Swampland
8 Plant pro
9 Actor born June 15th
10 Demonic
11 See socially
13 Mal de __
15 Senior member
17 Western spread
21 32,000 ounces
23 Orestes' sister
25 Missouri river
26 Element #5
27 Actress born June 16th
28 Leather ending
30 Mixed bag
32 Showy display
33 Migratory mammal
35 Walking stick
36 Anna's adopted home
38 Airplane engine
42 Bumps into
44 Coll. degrees
45 Holy place
47 Get one's goat
49 Superheroes' wear
50 Have one's say, in a way
51 Greek Cupid
52 Novelty piano piece
54 Rink surface
55 Real-estate sign
56 Cathedral area
57 Coward of the theater
60 High trains

117 ISLANDERS by Randy Sowell

ACROSS
1 Piano practice
6 Army leaders
11 Mature
14 War hero Murphy
15 News summary
16 *Pillow Talk* star
17 Indonesian singer?
19 Pub potable
20 __ kleine Nachtmusik
21 *For the Boys* actor
22 "A Boy __ Sue"
24 Pooh's pal
25 Rhyme for fizz
26 "You bet!"
27 Mediterranean actor?
33 Prayer beads
36 Cruise in films
37 Feedbag fill
38 Stay clear of
39 Morning moisture
40 Kind of rate or rib
41 Architect Saarinen
42 Coach Parseghian
43 Left port
44 Indonesian crooner?
47 Short sleep
48 Collection agcy.
49 Brobdingnagian
52 Fictional flying monster
55 *Born Free* roarer
57 It often turns
58 Charlottesville sch.
59 Mediterranean actress?
62 __ Aviv
63 Make amends
64 Hole __
65 Whichever
66 Seasons, maybe
67 Word on a nickel

DOWN
1 *60 Minutes* reporter
2 Unusual art
3 *A Bell for* __
4 Bank sight
5 Comics cry
6 Poultry part
7 Singer McEntire
8 Open up __ of worms
9 Actor Mineo
10 Small piano
11 First-family member
12 High wind
13 Looked at
18 In an unfriendly way
23 Oregon city
25 __ Krishna
26 Sweet tuber
27 Rock megastar
28 Work as __ (collaborate)
29 Cut the lawn
30 Pellets of a sort
31 "Don't look __!"
32 No longer new
33 Coral creation
34 Ham's word
35 FDR's mom
39 Actress Joanne
40 Botches the birdie?
42 Nile reptile
43 Leave the path
45 Dole's home
46 Bridal paths
49 American buffalo
50 "__ Want to Walk Without You"
51 Chromosome parts
52 Actress Lee
53 Hot spot
54 See 57 Down
55 Earth sci.
56 Washer fuzz
57 With 54 Down, *Cagney & Lacey* star
60 Call-day link
61 __ *Tac Dough*

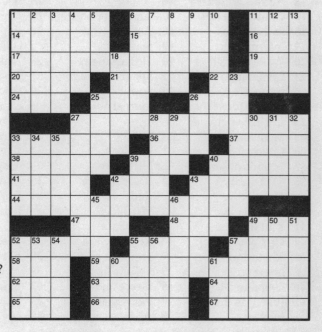

118 LATIN 101 by Bob Lubbers

ACROSS
1 Sitting on
5 Rather and Blocker
9 Knitting-book word
13 Bring up
14 Mideast ruler
16 Ersatz butter
17 Powerful shark
18 Famous physicist
19 Ford models
20 Marines' motto
23 __ *Gay* (WWII plane)
24 Antitoxin
25 Indian carving
28 *The Blood on __ Claw* ('71 horror film)
31 Shoreline sight
34 "Zounds!"
36 __ stone (immovable)
37 In the past
38 *Andrea* __
40 Form prefix
41 Michener bestseller
44 Rigel, for one
45 "... __ a man with seven wives"
46 Photo tones
48 Old Mexican civilization
50 Planet's path
52 How others see us
55 Coin phrase
58 Down in the dumps
59 Actress Verdugo
60 Runs in
62 Portrait medium
63 Washday challenge
64 Done with
65 Warts and all
66 JFK landers
67 Where Scarlett lived

DOWN
1 Tattoo place
2 Ruffle, as hair
3 "The Old __ Bucket"
4 Engage in hype
5 Clobbered
6 Part of AFT
7 Soft-ball brand
8 Some tourney games
9 Sully
10 Threatening words
11 Half the checkers
12 __ Alamos, NM
15 Carnival attractions
21 UN observer grp.
22 Historic times
26 Analyst's concerns
27 *I Remember Mama* mama
29 Midevening
30 Miffed mood
31 Finicky eaters
32 Curved molding
33 Public opinion
35 Gustavo __ Ordaz (former Mexican president)
39 Glassblowers, e.g.
42 Stuffy
43 *Elephant Boy* star
45 "__ tell a lie"
47 Becomes a daddy
49 Big bird
51 Pinball mishaps
53 Tropical fruit
54 Live coal
55 Ivy Leaguers
56 Arthur and Lillie
57 Curriculum section
58 Feathery stole
61 Mrs., in Málaga

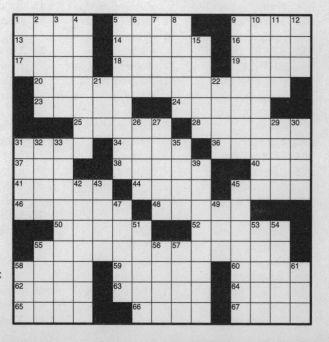

119 GENDER BENDER by Eric Albert

ACROSS

1 Come to pass
6 Benchley book
10 Fit together nicely
14 WWI battle site
15 Laos' locale
16 Actress Sommer
17 Olfactory input
18 Sash stopper
19 Infernal river
20 Wake-up call?
23 Commands respect from
24 Discomfort
25 *L.A. Law* network
28 Baby fox
30 College choice
32 Sounds of surprise
35 "The Last Frontier"
40 Burned up
41 Klutz?
44 God of passion
45 Rhetorical question
46 Compass pt.
47 Just __ in the bucket

49 __ *Dalmatians*
51 Nancy Drew's boyfriend
52 Singer Lennon
57 Find fault
61 Avoiding blame?
64 Bantu language
66 Annul
67 Alpha's opposite
68 A ways away
69 Stage strap
70 Origami need
71 Spanish painter
72 Supplicate
73 Journal note

DOWN

1 Astaire's birthplace
2 Baseball great Rod
3 Witchlike woman
4 Reveal to the world
5 "__ my lips!"
6 Fleece finder
7 Notwithstanding
8 Author Cather

9 Pie-throwing comic
10 "You've Made __ Very Happy"
11 "Rocket Man" singer
12 Aurora locale
13 Bad spell
21 James, for one
22 Rep.'s colleague
26 Light element
27 Posh pancake
29 Oddjob's creator
31 Beast of burden
32 Canoe anagram
33 Moving pack
34 Fairbanks' fighting
36 "__ du lieber!"
37 Reserved
38 Blood relatives
39 Apply oil to
42 Equi- kin
43 From __ Z
48 Nightwear

50 O'Neill's comer
53 Take by force
54 LP holder
55 Kipling's homeland
56 *The __ and the Ecstasy*
58 Well-trained one
59 "Message received"
60 Pole star?
62 Atmosphere
63 U.S.O. stalwart
64 Go off course
65 Strange sighting

120 WADING GAME by Trip Payne

ACROSS

1 Donutlike roll
6 Dickens character
9 Battling
14 *Without __* (Caine movie)
15 Vitamin-bottle abbr.
16 More than a nudge
17 START OF A RIDDLE
20 Carson's successor
21 Alamogordo event
22 Car scar
23 Loft bundle
25 "From __ 60 in 8.2 seconds"
27 MIDDLE OF RIDDLE
35 Sports palace
36 Entrée "bed"
37 Bro or sis
38 Tourney ranking
39 "The Thief of Bad Gags"
41 Water carrier

42 Guinness Book suffix
43 Hydrox rival
44 Gets ready (for)
45 END OF RIDDLE
49 __ Ridge, TN
50 Extinct New Zealand birds
51 Greek vowels
54 Wonderland-cake sign
57 Rock-band gear
61 ANSWER TO RIDDLE
64 Miscalculated
65 Roseanne's TV husband
66 Singer Della
67 Wanton looks
68 Citrus drink
69 Append

DOWN

1 Have a cry
2 Post-workout feeling
3 Hidden valley
4 Foreign debt of a sort

5 Appomattox attendee
6 President __
7 __ *fixe*
8 Bridge call
9 Blond shade
10 It may be put on
11 Eroded
12 Name that may ring a bell
13 First-of-month payment
18 Actor Robertson
19 Pronto
24 GP's org.
26 Mao __-tung
27 Sahara stopovers
28 Not canned
29 Take care of
30 Mr. Flynn
31 Feel poorly
32 Willow tree
33 Melanie's mama
34 Too large
39 One with lots to sell
40 Sonnet ending
41 Told the future
43 Three __ kind

44 Masters grp.
46 Dorm decor
47 Not susceptible
48 Some votes
51 Daredeviltry name
52 Get bored
53 Cropland measure
55 Leontyne Price role
56 Frog kin
58 Loquacious equine
59 Monterrey money
60 British gun
62 "__ bodkins!"
63 Generation

121 KID STUFF by Trip Payne

ACROSS
1 It's often filed
5 Hold at fault
10 Some
14 Farming word form
15 Company takebacks
16 Sgt. Friday's employer
17 Burn the surface of
18 "This is only __"
19 Greek consonants
20 Kids' activity
23 Weaver sci-fi film
24 Sea shocker
25 Anderson's *High* __
27 Hwys.
28 Dutch cheese
32 G&S title character
34 Lawrence's locale
36 Actor Baldwin
37 Kids' activity
41 Ashbrook of *Twin Peaks*
42 Bulls, at times
43 Come out
46 Droops down
47 Promgoers: Abbr.
50 Outdated discs
51 College major
53 Actor Milo
55 Kids' activity
60 Right-hand person
61 Furnace fodder
62 One chip, often
63 Ship's staff
64 *Fiddler on the Roof* star
65 Hwys.
66 Turner and Danson
67 Huge number
68 Legal wrong

DOWN
1 Auto-racing org.
2 From time immemorial
3 Rafsanjani's followers
4 Greene of *Bonanza*
5 Bric-a-__
6 Riga resident
7 In __ (peeved)
8 General Dayan
9 High regard
10 Kal Kan competitor
11 Con man's specialty
12 Serial parts
13 Dict. entries
21 January, to Juan
22 Flavius' 551
26 Mythical bird
29 __ es Salaam
30 ". . . __ fat hen"
31 Cretan king
33 *Get Smart* baddies
34 Controversial tree spray
35 Taj Mahal city
37 Wiener-roast spot
38 Unbalanced
39 Canine command
40 Mr. Welles
41 Wilm.'s state
44 One-liner
45 Puts up a building
47 Japanese religion
48 Leaseholder
49 Most worldly-wise
52 Scout group
54 Maze word
56 11:00 feature
57 Hemingway's nickname
58 Plenty
59 Capri, for one
60 Make a decision

122 CAR-NATION by Wayne R. Williams

ACROSS
1 Nightwear
8 Left undone
15 Admire a lot
16 Cane cutter
17 Silverdome home
19 *Gorillas in the Mist* director
20 Visitor from space
21 Rating unit
22 Free-for-all
24 Mini-army
28 Self-satisfied
30 Vacation spot
32 __ Baba
35 Rachins of *L.A. Law*
37 Eagle's nest
38 W.J. Bryan's home
42 Furnishings
43 Architect of St. Paul's
44 Slippery catch
45 Common mushroom
47 Like some Fr. nouns
49 Meeting: Abbr.
50 Mad. Ave. guy
53 Virginia dance
57 Moffo and Magnani
59 Desert Storm target
60 Marshal Dillon's home
65 Adds territory
66 Most creepy
67 Not at all polite
68 Power et al.

DOWN
1 __ *Delicate Condition* ('63 film)
2 Take up
3 Ruling group
4 Lets out, maybe
5 __ Marian
6 One-time connection
7 Wine word
8 Funt's request
9 More like a fine fabric
10 Rue one's run
11 Arm of the Pacific
12 Beer barrel
13 Schedule abbr.
14 Retreat
18 __ *de mer*
22 Comic Martin
23 First governor of Alaska
25 Mythology branch
26 Toddler's transportation
27 Big bargain
29 Native New Zealander
31 Has coming
32 Robert and Alan
33 Hamlet, to Horatio
34 Ancient Peruvians
36 Dir. opp. SSE
39 Formal flowers
40 Columnist Bombeck
41 High-fiber food
46 Stamp a stamp
48 Head-y word form
51 Henry James' __ *Miller*
52 CO clock setting
54 Ruhr Valley city
55 Wipe clean
56 Holds up
58 Waiting-room call
59 Roseanne, née __
60 Bit of butter
61 Top ranking
62 Genetics letters
63 To date
64 Cipher code

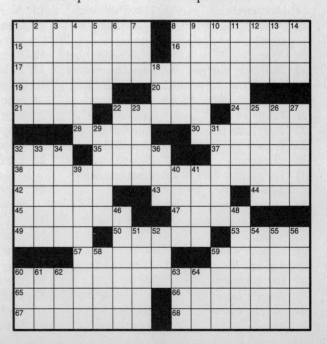

123 ANIMAL FAMILIES by Mel Rosen

ACROSS

1 Spanish mark
6 Kennel order
9 Football great Tarkenton
13 *Play It __, Sam*
14 Sapporo sport
15 Captain Kirk's home
16 "Nothing __!"
17 Be a bellyacher
18 Show appreciation
19 Primate family
22 Director Howard
23 Shaving-cream type
24 Barnyard family
32 Misrepresent
33 At hand
34 Say more
36 Seth's son
37 Get duded up
39 As well
40 As well
41 Disorderly conduct
42 Platte or Pecos
43 Desert family
47 Furniture wood
48 Young boy
49 Primate family
58 Insensitive one
59 Book-jacket part
60 Field boss
61 Slots city
62 Christmas trees
63 __ *Get Your Gun*
64 Churchill successor
65 Porker's pen
66 Sales prospects

DOWN

1 Vocal fanfare
2 "__ a Name" (Croce tune)
3 Hibernation station
4 Flintstones' pet
5 Eat too much
6 Waves at the beach
7 Moslem cleric
8 Long sled
9 Hardly loyal
10 Cast slot
11 Not home
12 Breaks of a sort
14 Tea biscuit
20 Office seeker, for short
21 __-do-well
24 Help in a crime
25 Columbus' hometown
26 Above it all
27 *M*A*S*H* extras
28 __ a customer
29 Legal charge
30 Soothing ointment
31 Collectible car
35 '50s actress Diana
37 Pitcher's coups
38 Korean soldier
39 Draw a bead on
41 *Tobacco __*
42 Profoundly different
44 BBC's headquarters
45 Broadway failures
46 Caboose, e.g.
49 Zoning unit
50 Ran in the wash
51 First-rate
52 Move like a butterfly
53 City SE of Chicago
54 Solitary
55 Turner of Hollywood
56 Battery fluid
57 __ *Having a Baby* ('88 film)

124 GREEK ALPHABET by Fred Piscop

ACROSS

1 Razor brand
5 "Halt!" to a salt
10 Talk like Daffy Duck
14 Icy coating
15 The __ Kid (Romero role)
16 Arabian Nights count
17 Alien?
19 Men-only party
20 Sofa fabric
21 Company abbr.
22 Plants a bug
23 Telephone triad
25 Pulsate
27 Fact facer
31 They go for the gold
34 __ ease (antsy)
35 __ pants (women's wear)
38 "The Boy King"
39 Server's rewards
40 Lamb's mom
41 Angelic headgear
42 Mt. St. Helens output
43 *La Belle __* (Jolson show)
45 Kitchen gadget
46 Spiritualist's session
48 Height
50 Tropical fish
52 Profit follower
53 Mackintosh, for one
55 Spider-web type
57 Fertilizer variety
62 Be adjacent to
63 Food preservative?
65 Ade flavoring
66 Occupied
67 Boxer's wear
68 Long-standing argument
69 Port holders
70 Musical work

DOWN

1 Throat-clearing sound
2 "__ the mornin'!"
3 Poorly thought-out
4 *Tosca* tune
5 Squirrel's stash
6 Coq au __
7 Italian wine center
8 Barely sufficient
9 Doors tune of '69
10 Ali KO'd him
11 Computer company?
12 Bathday cake
13 Kiddie-lit trio
18 Sale-ad word
24 Significant __
26 Tire attachment
27 Hayworth and Coolidge
28 Beethoven's "*Für __*"
29 Bank convenience?
30 __ Cruces, NM
32 Foot-long device
33 *Who's Minding the __?*
36 Reverence
37 Dodger Hall-of-Famer
41 Smash show
43 %
44 Type of dancing
45 Seer's deck
47 Took home
49 Mobile homes
51 Wrestling locale
53 Knee neighbor
54 Theater award
56 Air-cond. units
58 Root for Hawaiians
59 On
60 *Song of India* actor
61 Rainbow segments
64 "Go __ your mother"

125 SHORT WEEKEND by Eric Albert

ACROSS

1 Big blowout
5 Figurine mineral
9 Poet's feet
14 "Omigosh!"
15 Love, in the flesh
16 Go bad
17 Hood's confessor
19 Jessica or Hope
20 *Anne __ Gables*
21 Say again
23 Pigeon perches
24 X-rated stuff
25 Attack viciously
26 One with examples
27 007's alma mater
28 High point
29 Some Chicago trains
30 Soffit location
32 Old Testament heroine
34 Tiros or Echo
36 Mideast capital
39 Singer Cantrell
40 Batter's need
43 Pedestal occupant
44 Give the nod to
46 Language of India
48 Little: Fr.
49 Barbra's *Funny Girl* costar
50 Timex competitor
51 Crew-team crew
53 Adds oxygen to
54 No longer crisp
55 Breaking apart
57 Mortise filler
58 Winemaking center
59 Lorre film role
60 Outer limits
61 Look to be
62 White Christmas need

DOWN

1 Using the army, maybe
2 Plane part
3 Taps
4 The Munsters' family car
5 *Swan Lake* leaps
6 Make __ for it (flee)
7 Grumpy colleague
8 Kayak builder
9 Land in the sea?
10 On __ with (equal to)
11 Lepidopterist's catch
12 Major-league
13 Woody Allen film of '73
18 Overhauled tire
22 Set the dial to
24 Outstanding
27 *The Three Faces of __*
28 Packed away
31 Comfortable
33 Prestige level
34 Actor Mineo
35 Nonclerical
36 Sharp answer
37 Thought about
38 Butler's question
40 Pride or joy
41 In the habit of
42 Scotland's largest city
45 Jayhawker State
47 Waker-uppers
49 Signs of things to come
50 Turn down the lights
52 Fizz flavoring
53 Start stud
56 Put to work

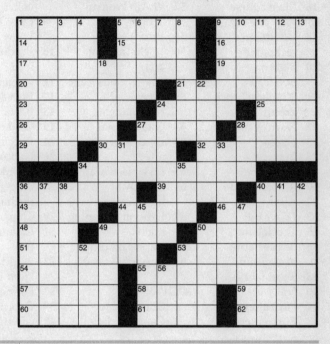

126 FIRST LADIES? by Mel Rosen

ACROSS

1 VHS alternative
5 Hens or mares
9 Not quite closed
13 Cheer words
14 Packs down
16 Path or phone opener
17 Satan's doings
18 __ asst. (office aide)
19 "You're So __" (Simon song)
20 Comic actress
23 Ping-Pong need
24 Common Mkt. money
25 Big-beaked birds
27 Conducts (oneself)
32 Ski lift
33 Lawyers' org.
34 Reaches quick conclusions
36 __ nous
39 Civil case
41 Hogan rival
43 Revue, e.g.
44 *One Touch of __*
46 Wish granter
48 Put to work
49 Finished a cake
51 States
53 Makes minor adjustments
56 Decimal base
57 "What __ doing?"
58 *Charlie's Angels* actress
64 Skirt length
66 *Glengarry Glen Ross* playwright
67 Soil additive
68 Psyche sections
69 Nimble-legged
70 New Haven students
71 Make a bad impression
72 Building wings
73 Two-year-olds

DOWN

1 *Song of the South* title
2 Chalet overhang
3 Rarefied
4 Out like a light
5 Heights
6 "If I __ Hammer"
7 Small-screen award
8 Like some milk
9 Off-road transport, in short
10 *Shane* star
11 Martian, e.g.
12 Leases out
15 Snobbish type
21 EPA concern
22 Cartoonist Goldberg
26 Preserves, in a way
27 HBO's system
28 Bassoon's relative
29 Audrey Hepburn's singing stand-in
30 Sharp taste
31 Ten-__ bicycle
35 Sensible
37 Mrs. Kennedy
38 Woolly beasts
40 Nip's partner
42 Gives orders
45 Go after
47 TVA product
50 Stage production
52 Bobby-sock relative
53 Brought under control
54 Mental picture
55 Rocket section
59 Actor Jannings
60 Congeal
61 Grain building
62 Skip over
63 Capone's nemesis
65 -arian relative

AMAZING PHRASING by Wayne R. Williams

ACROSS

1 Dawber or Shriver
4 *Exodus* author
8 Removed soap
14 Southern st.
15 Window glass
16 Main course
17 Flap one's gums
18 Goodman's nickname
20 Before, poetically
21 "Xanadu" rock group
22 Narrow opening
23 Overact
25 In force
27 Make one
30 Ali technique
32 Altar words
33 Flows out
35 Greek letter
36 Beatle in the background
38 Sheet fabric
40 Soil
42 Earn after taxes
43 Eur. nation
44 Chocolate products
45 Pay stub?
46 Charity race
50 Tongue-clicking sound
51 Classic sagas
52 "I Am Woman" singer
55 Prof.'s rank
56 __ chi (martial art)
58 Anonymous John
59 Meet requirements
63 Quaint hotel
64 Excessively affected
65 Like Nash's lama
66 "Ready or __, here I come!"
67 Lyndon's running mate
68 Important times
69 Important time

DOWN

1 Check name
2 Cause anxiety
3 Be critical
4 Maintenance cost
5 Support bar
6 Do something new
7 Portion: Abbr.
8 Toss another coin
9 Ones in the know
10 Product package info.
11 __ Lanka
12 Poet's dusk
13 BA or MBA
19 Cold capital
24 Puccini opera
26 Nabokov novel
27 Entertain lavishly
28 Bergen or Buchanan
29 Cabinet features
31 Cave-dwelling fish
33 Florida attraction
34 Hour indicators
37 Permeate
39 Cop, at times
40 Giving a leg up to
41 Go wrong
43 Super Bowl team's div.
47 Outcome
48 Marquee word
49 Superfluous items
53 Philanthropist
54 Overinquisitive one
55 Old one: Ger.
57 Nautical direction
59 Six ft., at sea
60 Debt letters
61 Seles shot
62 Long scarf

ALTERED STATES by Matt Gaffney

ACROSS

1 __-mo replay
4 Adorns
11 Erving's sobriquet
14 Photo or film
15 Wife-related
16 Wallaby, for short
17 Ted Koppel's network
18 Cotton?
20 Ultimate rewards
22 Acetaminophen alternative
23 Quickness
24 Went quickly
26 Some breads
27 Pennsylvania city
28 Come into one's __
29 Went quickly
31 Oaxaca uncle
32 Proficiency
34 Midmorning
38 "How about a trip to Opryland?"
41 Candidate's concern
42 "The Rain in Spain" is one
43 Ted Turner's pride
44 QB's scores
46 Compete
47 Pound, for one
48 H.S. class
51 Prayer word
53 __ Clara, CA
54 Part of IRS
56 Rhymer's foot
57 Northwestern philanthropist?
60 Actor Wallach
61 Took the gold
62 Pre-tourney activity
63 Salon order
64 Driller's deg.
65 Jailbreaker
66 Give it a whirl

DOWN

1 Long lunch?
2 One of Carnegie's causes
3 They may be special
4 Army horn
5 Onetime spouses
6 "Inka Dinka __"
7 Make a mistake
8 Havana export
9 Wilhelm was one
10 Rebuke, so to speak
11 *Advise and Consent* author
12 *The Trials of __ O'Neill*
13 Painter Jasper
19 Meredith Baxter __
21 Suffix for Brooklyn
24 Checker's claim to fame
25 Off base, perhaps
28 Gives the thumbs-up to
30 __ time (never)
32 Future flower
33 First Red head
35 Plea possibility
36 *The Accidental Tourist* author
37 Frame of mind
39 Cake spice
40 Ripen
45 Spa features
47 Cong. contributor
48 Large number
49 *Salome* character
50 Makes level
52 Corpsman
53 NCO, for short
55 Slangy turndown
56 All finished
58 Man-mouse link
59 Short snort

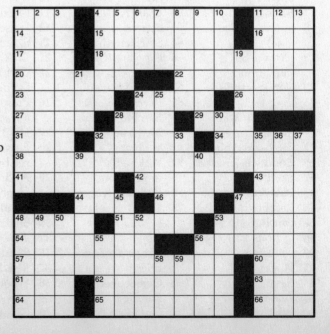

HOMOPHONES by Mark Diehl

ACROSS

1 Capital of Equatorial Guinea
7 Oolong, e.g.
10 Soak (up)
13 One of the kingdoms
14 Equine entrée
15 Big galoot
16 Actress __ Sue Martin
17 Cop, often
19 PARE
21 Goes a round (with)
22 Yen
23 Inventor Rubik
24 Auto pioneer
25 Dull pain
26 12-year-old, for instance
27 Golf prop
28 London neighborhood
29 Partygoers
30 PAIR
32 Austrian composer Oscar

35 __ mater (brain covering)
36 They may be small
39 Attack time
40 Drop suddenly
41 Overcharged
42 Elvis __ Presley
43 Display model
44 Bed material
45 PEAR
48 Tub accessories
49 Bitter feeling
51 Eroded
52 *The Name of the Rose* author
53 *Truth __* (Madonna film)
54 __-Bol (bathroom cleaner)
55 Mail-motto word
56 Drew closer to

DOWN

1 Traveler's aid
2 "__ a day . . ."
3 Citrus drink

4 Mideast rulers
5 Formal dances
6 Norwegian royal name
7 Three times
8 *The Good __*
9 Positive replies
10 Lampoons
11 Ice-hockey situation
12 Folks
17 *PÈRE*
18 Obliquely positioned
20 Nouveau __
21 Guzzler
25 Astronaut's answers
26 Salad base
28 Tart-tasting
29 Robin Williams role of '82
30 Potbelly
31 Bombeck's genre
32 Hebrews' Saturday

33 Like Tallulah's voice
34 Perched
36 Train component
37 Put back
38 Football dist.
40 One with a mortgage

41 Starr character?
43 Northern constellation
44 Raucous sound
46 Seer's discovery
47 Disney film of '82
50 Herring hue

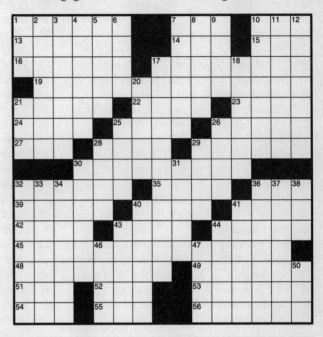

EXACT QUOTE by Eric Albert

ACROSS

1 Reduce drastically
6 Retractor's meal?
10 Samoa studier
14 Author Bret
15 Zero, to Zina Garrison
16 Mrs. Lindbergh
17 Mouth-to-mouth recitation
18 Seth's brother
19 __ St. Vincent Millay
20 START OF A SAMUEL BUTLER QUOTE
22 Pea place
23 Insignificant
24 Bank breaker
25 Devout
27 Act the snoop
28 Road-sign warning
29 Kael the reviewer
31 Make faces
32 Well-defined

33 MIDDLE OF QUOTE
36 Grab greedily
37 CARE package, e.g.
38 Fully attentive
39 "The racer's edge"
40 Flower-to-be
43 Former Met Jones
44 MIT-trained architect
45 Actress Rowlands
46 Tool set
47 END OF QUOTE
50 It's a long story
52 Put in piles
53 Copycat's comment
54 Stir
55 Spread in a tub
56 __ the back (compliment)
57 Emulate Etna
58 He played Klinger
59 Panache

DOWN

1 Creole dish
2 Makeup maker
3 War store
4 Fourteen pounds
5 Man of the hour
6 Button one's lip
7 Spring singer
8 Bread chamber
9 Join metal
10 Fannie __
11 Terminus
12 Tell the world
13 Stubbornly determined
21 Roy's ride
25 Give the lowdown to
26 Homeric tale
28 *Macbeth* character
29 Peach center
30 Kind of elephant
31 Actor Sal
32 Press for payment
33 Good ship of song
34 Santa's season

35 Derek and Diddley
36 Small bundles
39 Military zone
40 *Bugsy* star
41 Not at all rad
42 Beginning

44 Kitchen tool
45 High-minded
47 "Time __ the essence"
48 Vincent Lopez's theme
49 Strike callers
51 Black Angus, e.g.

131 CONTRASTS by Shirley Soloway

ACROSS
1 First vice president
6 Use a camcorder
10 *Born Free* roarer
14 Make a new wager
15 Astronaut Shepard
16 Follow behind
17 Quite clearly
20 __ distance (far away)
21 Comedienne Charlotte et al.
22 Where llamas roam
23 Musical breather
24 "__ but known!"
26 Is inconsistent
33 Bring down the house
34 Starchy side dish
35 Sticky stuff
36 Santa __, CA
37 Had hopes
40 Mr. Chaney
41 Headline of '14
42 Caviar versions
43 Laura of *Blue Velvet*
44 Total difference
49 Takes home
50 Oklahoma Indians
51 Reference book
54 Cartoonist Peter
55 *The Golden Girls* name
58 Completely
62 Make angry
63 Screenwriter James
64 Kind of kitchen
65 Milky gemstone
66 Forest growth
67 Room to maneuver

DOWN
1 Diva's solo
2 Fender bender result
3 Eban of Israel
4 Blanc or Brooks
5 Takes a long look
6 Learn to like
7 "Too bad!"
8 Review poorly
9 Put a stop to
10 Kind of pride
11 __-back (relaxed)
12 Locale
13 Pub servings
18 Legal tender
19 In a clump
23 "Concord Hymn" monogram
24 Hide's partner
25 Suffix for attend
26 Rowdy to-do
27 Polynesian porch
28 Arkansas range
29 Actress Van Devere
30 Eyed rudely
31 "Too-Ra-__-Loo-Ral"
32 Marie Osmond's brother
37 *Gunsmoke* star
38 "And __ goes"
39 Board inserts
43 Shingle letters
45 Nail polish
46 Rich cakes
47 __ time (never)
48 Rope loops
51 Oversized hairdo
52 Game-show prize
53 Entertainer Falana
54 Iowa city
55 Greek letter
56 Author Ambler
57 Diarist Frank
59 Scottish topper
60 Swelled head
61 Beer barrel poker?

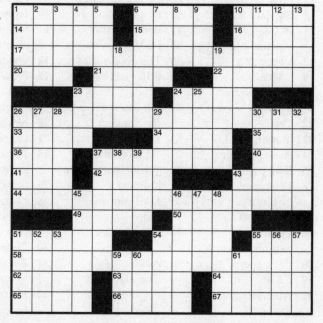

132 NEW WORDS by Mel Rosen

ACROSS
1 Not fully shut
5 Track circuits
9 Evert of tennis
14 Mexican nosh
15 Give off
16 Port-au-Prince's land
17 Musical work
18 Meatless patty
20 Back of the neck
21 USNA grad
22 Put away
23 Infuriated
25 Plaster paintings
29 LAX stats
30 Little bits
31 Away from the office
32 Soda buys
34 Sidekick
35 Colorado Indian
36 Hirt and Pacino
37 Like Cajun food
40 Computer screen: Abbr.
41 Winter bug
42 Big cheeses
43 Barbecue leftovers?
45 Musical discernment
46 Reminiscent of port
47 Get ready, for short
48 The whole shootin' match
50 Signify
53 Business abbr.
54 "My __ Sal"
55 Surmounting
56 Jet-setters
60 Roll on the tarmac
61 Nick of *48 HRS.*
62 "__ a man with seven wives"
63 Ear-related
64 Lost color
65 Cut back
66 Mythical birds

DOWN
1 Make up (for)
2 Honshu's land
3 Massage method
4 Optimistic
5 Protective embankments
6 Make a change to
7 Pen pals?
8 Relig. title
9 Mail channels
10 Rabbit's cousins
11 Predetermine the outcome of
12 Mineral suffix
13 Military address
19 Figaro's job
24 Huff and puff
25 Loses color
26 TV addict
27 Bizarre
28 Leaves in the manuscript
30 A little weird
32 Sidewalk eateries
33 God of Islam
34 Impressionist's work
38 Show plainly
39 Tall tale
44 Hill figure
46 On a poster, perhaps
47 Nice to deal with
49 Please, in Potsdam
50 Provide food (to)
51 Poisonous
52 Grand tales
54 Explorer Vasco da __
56 Econ. datum
57 Mauna __
58 Unsatisfactorily
59 Actor Torn

BOX OFFICE by Wayne R. Williams

ACROSS

1 Skin feature
5 Flash of light
10 Aussie birds
14 "Excuse me!"
15 Heart connection
16 __ avis
17 Boxing film of '80
19 Cheese coat
20 Poetry Muse
21 "Old Blood and Guts"
23 Blocker or Rather
24 Narrow cuts
27 On the lookout
30 Boxing film of '49
32 Contend (for)
33 Donut shapes
36 Partnership word
37 School break
39 Rust causer
41 Knight's superior
42 Second showing
43 Chip off the old block

44 Some ships: Abbr.
45 Page-setting job: Abbr.
46 Boxing film of '82
49 Take care of
51 Actor Quinn
52 President pro __
55 Mr. Duck
57 Desire badly
59 Melville novel
61 Boxing film of '37
64 Falling out
65 Freeze, as roads
66 Musical ending
67 Bumbling sorts
68 From Oslo
69 __ over (capsize)

DOWN

1 Cut corners
2 *Pal Joey* writer
3 *King Lear* character
4 Give off
5 One-liner
6 Tennis shot

7 Broke out
8 Finally
9 Beer ingredient
10 Flynn of films
11 Boxing film of '79, with *The*
12 Vase with a base
13 Blue
18 Between-meal food
22 Get narrow
25 Simple shelter
26 "__ It Romantic?"
28 Narrow platform
29 Trial runs
30 Ocean motion
31 Astronomy Muse
33 Law-school course
34 Type of daisy
35 Boxing film of '71
38 __ *fan tutte* (Mozart opera)
40 The Braves' #44
41 *Ben-Hur* costar
43 Racing car, at times

47 Patterned cloth
48 Contents abbr.
50 Horn honks
52 Western resort lake
53 Skirt
54 Olympics prize

56 Related (to)
58 Billiards prop
59 Gold, in Guatemala
60 Actress Farrow
62 Astronaut Grissom
63 Simian

CELEBIRDIES by Trip Payne

ACROSS

1 General Alexander et al.
6 NBC drama
11 Magnavox rival
14 African capital
15 Tony of baseball
16 Special-interest grp.
17 *Cheers* star
19 Actor Gazzara
20 Enlistees' food
21 Not appropriate
22 Lab assistant
23 Lost calf
25 TV commercial cry
27 "Do it again!"
30 Not very strong
31 "Go, team!"
32 Giraffe's cousin
35 Yorkshire town
38 "Do __ say . . ."
39 Late-night star
41 Onassis' nickname
42 Spinal parts
44 Something awful

45 "Silent" president
46 Sort of, slangily
48 "You bet!"
50 As a precaution
52 Spelunking fan
54 Plane or pliers
55 Cowboy star Lash
57 *Battle Cry* author
61 Make a misjudgment
62 *The Cosby Show* star
64 Dogpatch's Daisy __
65 Bungling
66 With speed
67 Retirees' agcy.
68 Drills a hole
69 Feathered talkers

DOWN

1 Maltreat
2 Sore spot
3 Cools down
4 Former Connecticut governor

5 Maple goo
6 __ *Doone*
7 Ease one's fears
8 Lacking firmness
9 Hindu incarnation
10 Pale-faced
11 *Lifestyles . . .* host
12 Guiding principle
13 '70s veep
18 "I've got it!"
22 End in __ (be drawn)
24 Pac-10 team
26 Heat unit
27 Historical periods
28 *Atlantis* group
29 Jazz pianist
30 Old-time interjections
33 Auel heroine
34 Arafat's org.
36 "Phooey!"
37 Farm building
40 The jitters
43 Irani money

47 Part of FDR
49 Doc's roommate
50 List parts
51 Dunn and Ephron
52 Decorative paper
53 Anagram of "tunas"

56 Say with certainty
58 Reddish-brown horse
59 Old Peruvian
60 Meets with
62 Poke fun at
63 Sweet potato

135 LOOKING BACK by Eric Albert

ACROSS
1 Catch some rays
5 Pasta shape
10 Gymnast Korbut
14 Jazz singer James
15 Woody's *Play It Again, Sam* costar
16 Noble gas
17 He had a hammer
18 Itty-bitty bay
19 Not at all amiable
20 START OF A QUIP
22 Starr of the strips
24 Bryant or Baker
25 Gloria Vanderbilt's logo
27 Ode object
28 Sun __-sen
29 Wild spree
32 Keogh cousin: Abbr.
33 Tire track
34 Knight spot
36 In the know
37 MIDDLE OF QUIP
41 Aware of
42 He made some good points
43 "Gotcha!"
44 Malt drink
46 Can material
47 "__ Love You"
50 Dream acronym
51 Roman foe
53 Viscounts' superiors
55 Peke, for one
57 END OF QUIP
60 "Back to you"
61 Springs
63 Far's partner
64 Give up rights to
65 Sandy's owner
66 On a cruise
67 Grasped
68 Calliope et al.
69 Propeller-head

DOWN
1 Double-cross
2 Wisdom personified
3 Restraining order?
4 Gold measure
5 Blue-pencil
6 Occupation
7 Makes a bundle
8 __ *from the Heart*
9 Rec-room fixture
10 A while back
11 *Exodus* author
12 Event of 1849
13 Tempo marking
21 Punjab potentate
23 Cell material: Abbr.
26 Prevail
30 MGM name of the '40s
31 Go predecessor
34 Noah's number
35 Pocket filler?
36 Funny fellow
37 Ecstatic
38 Calgary happening
39 Site of the Tell legend
40 Sank
41 Rowboat device
44 In the past
45 Impasse
47 Kind words
48 Kind of pitch
49 ". . the witch __"
52 Sunday songs
54 Dam site
56 Kiddie-lit detective
58 Andy's son
59 Brings to bear
62 Burmese statesman

136 MUSIC LESSON by Mel Rosen

ACROSS
1 Woolly beasts
5 __ Penh, Cambodia
10 Prefix for light
13 Newspaper section, for short
14 Residence
15 Span. ladies
16 Musical embellishments
18 Break the news
19 Kind of kick
20 Worth salvaging
22 Bradley and Sullivan
23 Light into
24 Good relations
27 "His Master's Voice" co.
28 Say "howdy" to
31 Say it isn't so
32 Paper Mate rival
33 Brawn
34 Dict. abbr.
35 Musical conclusion
37 Perjure oneself
38 Whom Simple Simon met
40 Actor Beatty
41 Ponce de __
42 Seer's deck
43 Off-rd. transportation
44 Portsider's nickname
45 Glove leathers
47 Battery size
48 Swizzle stick
50 Eccentric senior
54 Roger Rabbit, for one
55 Ultra-loud, musically
58 Jillian and Sothern
59 Receded
60 Kimono closers
61 Roll-call response
62 Bridle straps
63 After-tax amounts

DOWN
1 Therefore
2 Put on
3 Greek letters
4 It may be high
5 Window glass
6 Cable channel
7 *Wayne's World* catchword
8 Black Sea port
9 Western hills
10 Musical symbol
11 Berlin had one
12 Seagirt land
15 Cellar access
17 Nelson of old films
21 Not specific
23 Musical stresses
24 Keep up with the times
25 __ event (photo op)
26 Chord transpositions
27 Free (of)
29 *Silas Marner* author
30 Smaller than small
32 Throw out
33 1400, in old Rome
35 Supply food for
36 Calif. neighbor
39 Bewails
41 Entices teasingly
43 Kind of bacterium
44 Southeast Asian land
46 Put aside
47 Etching liquids
48 Stand pat
49 Musical sound
51 Taunt
52 Give off
53 "It's My Turn" singer
56 Slugger's stat
57 Perfect score, often

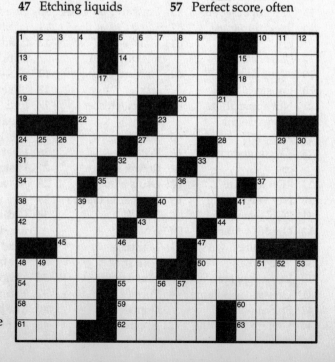

SIMPLE FARE by Wayne R. Williams

ACROSS
1 Health haven
4 Barn baby
9 Call up
14 Floral loop
15 String-quartet member
16 Ancient Greek region
17 Simple, foodwise?
19 Put into effect
20 __ Stanley Gardner
21 Asian celebration
22 Movie parts
23 Satisfy
25 To be, in Toulouse
27 Polite word
28 Catcallers' compatriots
33 CIA forerunner
36 Pope's crown
39 Che's colleague
40 With 64 Across, simple, foodwise?
43 Noted violinmaker
44 Mural starter
45 Citrine quaff
46 Stocking style
48 Pedigree org.
50 Small fly
52 Of the nerves
56 *War of the __*
60 Out of the ordinary
62 Singer McEntire
63 Parting word
64 See 40 Across
66 Municipal
67 Hollywood's golden boy?
68 Poor grade
69 Move furtively
70 Good-guy group
71 Isr. neighbor

DOWN
1 Nod off
2 Irritation creation
3 Congregation separation
4 Eggs: Lat.
5 Climbing shrub
6 Easy gait
7 Privileged few
8 Inventor's initials
9 Something simple, foodwise?
10 Sharpen
11 __ even keel
12 Riviera resort
13 Breaks a fast
18 Some votes
22 Sellout sign
24 Something simple, foodwise?
26 Waldheim's predecessor
29 Aunt, in Alicante
30 Novelist Ferber
31 Funny Foxx
32 Roy Rogers' real name
33 Norwegian king
34 __ Valley, CA
35 Jamaican tunes
37 Japanese dog
38 __ Tin Tin
41 Ordinal ending
42 Some doters
47 USN rank
49 Street edge
51 Sort of sculpture
53 Studies
54 Historic Dublin theater
55 Hen, for one
56 Fem. soldiers
57 Valhalla VIP
58 Bank of France?
59 *Star Wars* princess
61 Medicos
64 Vain man
65 "You __ what you eat"

ROACHES! by Trip Payne

ACROSS
1 Tropical spot
6 Family members
10 Big chunk
14 Hawaiian veranda
15 Organic compound
16 CIA agent, maybe
17 He wrote about a cockroach
19 Official proceedings
20 Squealed
21 Sci-fi vehicle
22 Alpo rival
24 "Till death __ part"
26 Phone patrons
27 His best friend is Cockroach
31 Buffalo NHLer
32 Right-angle shape
33 Court order?
37 Pitch __-hitter
38 Max Roach, for one
42 Theology subj.
43 Pressed the doorbell
45 Mentalist's claim
46 "When the moon hits your eye ..."
48 Hal Roach sci-fi movie
52 Nelson in the news
55 *Coal Miner's Daughter* subject
56 Mutate, maybe
57 Raft propeller
58 Actress Swenson
62 Use grindstones
63 He wrote about a cockroach
66 Personal quirks
67 Original thought
68 Bizarre
69 Roadside quaffs
70 Costner role
71 Famed physicist

DOWN
1 Landon et al.
2 *Scarlett* estate
3 __ upswing (rising)
4 Sluggishness
5 Columnist Smith
6 Large shark
7 Hard facts
8 __ choy (salad veggie)
9 Like thirst
10 More minuscule
11 Actress Sondra
12 Preacher's spot
13 Knocks on the noggin
18 African antelope
23 Every last bit
25 Place for wood
26 Unexcited
27 Ruler in 1900
28 Mandlikova of tennis
29 Deep black
30 Largo and lento
34 Mill input
35 Eastern European
36 Half of GE
39 Did an angler's job
40 West Point sch.
41 Come down
44 Heathen descriptor
47 Actress Van Vooren
49 Ariz. neighbor
50 Camel cousins
51 Vega's constellation
52 Bombay-born conductor
53 Steer clear of
54 Present time
57 *The Defiant __*
59 Bar food
60 Little lady
61 On the ocean
64 Horace work
65 Deteriorate

139 ROMAN-TIC MOVIES by Eric Albert

ACROSS
1 Drum partner
5 Scale a peak
10 Exercise target
14 Laze about
15 Spanish poet
16 *The Jungle Book* star
17 Roman-tic movie of '35?
20 Get larger
21 Workshop hardware
22 Hard to solve
23 Christian Science founder
24 Fizz preceder?
25 Baghdad natives
28 Withdraw (from)
29 Pug's punch
32 In progress
33 Letter opener
34 Unadorned
35 Roman-tic movie of '72?
38 Diner sign
39 Paris airport
40 Lab copy
41 Actress Carrie
42 Surrounded by

43 Lacking a key
44 Cut closely
45 Play the horn
46 Achieve through effort
49 Emulate Niobe
50 Swear solemnly
53 Roman-tic movie of '80?
56 Pull apart
57 New Zealand native
58 Brisbane buddy
59 Give the nod to
60 Shirt inserts
61 Novel need

DOWN
1 Diamond imperfection
2 Tiny bit
3 Fiber source
4 Architectural add-on
5 Makes indistinct
6 On a high plane
7 Pupil's surroundings

8 AT&T competitor
9 Violent reaction
10 Lens setting
11 Café au __
12 Assist in illegality
13 In use
18 Finale
19 Privy to
23 Peter Shaffer play
24 Erle's lawyer
25 *Peer Gynt* playwright
26 Hand off
27 Playing marble
28 Use as a weapon
29 Medea's husband
30 Sports site
31 Cut at an angle
33 *Peanuts*, for one
34 Claus von __
36 Freeze and frieze
37 Inky animals
42 Sills solo

43 *Dynasty* role
44 Tea container
45 *The Champ* Oscar winner
46 '60s hairstyle
47 Hard journey
48 Singer Turner

49 Stallion stopper
50 Small vessel
51 Mr. Preminger
52 Stimulate
54 Tit for __
55 Diminutive demon

140 SERVICE CHARGE by Donna J. Stone

ACROSS
1 Job opening
5 Haarlem export
10 Bogus Bach
13 Coffee-break time
15 Slezak of *One Life to Live*
16 Singer Rawls
17 START OF A QUIP
19 Porter's kin
20 Italian squares
21 In reserve
23 "Later!"
25 English cathedral city
26 Nod or wink
29 Talk-show host Friedman
31 Jai __
32 Parliament members
33 Ski wood
36 PART 2 OF QUIP
39 PART 3 OF QUIP
41 Lines of thought?
42 It comes from the heart
44 Pack provisions

45 Jewelry material
46 Fly the coop
48 Pyramus' lover
51 "Big Three" site
53 Acid type
54 __ rat (is suspicious)
58 __ spree
59 END OF QUIP
63 Gladiator's item
64 Monteverdi opera
65 Handbag part
66 Spud bud
67 Debra of *Love Me Tender*
68 Head set

DOWN
1 Put one's foot down
2 One of Jacob's sons
3 Recruit-to-be
4 Kilimanjaro's setting
5 Rib
6 Spoon-bender Geller

7 Glowing
8 He was liked in '56
9 Conniption fit
10 Hair braid
11 Sweet, to Solti
12 Pretty peculiar
14 Toyota rival
18 Keen
22 PBS benefactor
24 Troop troupe
25 Word form for "within"
26 Free from danger
27 Bjorn opponent
28 Social clique
30 Whale of a tale
32 Apollo's instrument
33 Dashiell's dog
34 Put an end to
35 Redcoat general
37 Shari Lewis puppet
38 Stud site
40 Magnify
43 Go for it
45 "__ was saying, . . ."

46 Film Tarzan Lincoln
47 Bouillabaisse and burgoo
48 Porterhouse alternative
49 Mead need
50 Fuming

52 __ *in the Dark*
55 Cremona currency
56 Feature
57 Snake charmer's crew
60 Keogh kin
61 One of 3M's M's
62 Mini, to McTavish

141 POWER PLAY by Mel Rosen

ACROSS

1 Raced Mark Spitz
5 "__ Ha'i"
9 F-sharp's alias
14 __'-shanter
15 Puts to work
16 Green hue
17 Abbr. in Bartlett's
18 Clock face
19 Judge's prop
20 Powerful, in the weight room
23 Musical transition
24 Comic Philips
25 Work with acid
29 Not for
31 Do cobbling
33 West of *Batman*
36 DeLuise film of '80
39 Underwater shocker
40 Powerful, in business
44 Eur. nation
45 Stratum
46 Aware of
47 Business-page listings
49 Stable baby
52 Twelve Oaks neighbor
53 Get __ for effort
56 Hallow
59 Powerful, in a crisis
63 1492 vessel
66 Cabbagelike plant
67 Jai __
68 Quite mature
69 __ on (goads)
70 Kindergarten breaks
71 Is overfond
72 Vast amounts
73 Three, in Toledo

DOWN

1 RR terminals
2 Wish-list items
3 Love, Italian-style
4 Marital fidelity
5 Spending plan
6 Laos' locale
7 Tenant's pact
8 Mideast belief
9 Full of energy
10 Linen plants
11 Actress Ullmann
12 Rosary prayer
13 __ Aviv
21 Convent dweller
22 Scandinavian
26 Wheel-alignment term
27 Soccer-shoe feature
28 Conversation starter
30 Not certain
32 Very long time
33 Sailor's shout
34 River region
35 __ Day (tree-planting time)
37 Tankard filler
38 Surf partner
41 Sort
42 Nose-related
43 Open-minded
48 Big house
50 Preoccupy
51 Chicken __ king
54 Alternative to Reeboks
55 Old truism
57 Kind of power
58 Land or sea ending
60 Bran source
61 Aquatic organism
62 Show of affection
63 Paper tablet
64 Oath words
65 Fanatic follower

142 STATELY SOLVING by Trip Payne

ACROSS

1 *Hill Street Blues* actress
6 Health hangout
9 4/1 victims
14 Out of the way
15 Some votes
16 Parks and Bonheur
17 What "they call the wind"
18 Capp and Capone
19 North's nickname
20 Washington's state gem
23 Maryland's state sport
24 Plant part
28 Stay in hiding
32 Cockpit person
33 Started the hand
36 Hardwood tree
37 Abba of Israel
38 Modine movie of '84
39 *To Live and Die __*
40 Free (of)
41 Actor Willie
42 Slow mover
43 Giuliani and Riordan
45 Pom or pug
46 Wisconsin's state domestic animal
50 Alaska's state fossil
55 Two-faced god
56 Tread the boards
57 24-book poem
59 "Not on __!" ("Never!")
60 Highlands refusal
61 Slow tempo
62 High-IQ group
63 Snake's sound
64 Misplaces

DOWN

1 Amateur-radio operator
2 Memo abbr.
3 Swampland
4 Revise copy
5 Corporate plane
6 Messed-up situation
7 Greek city-state
8 Good quality
9 Show disapproval of
10 Bird's-egg study
11 Chilly capital
12 Installed carpeting
13 Vane dir.
21 Charged atom
22 Lalapalooza
24 With 31 Down, Connecticut's state animal
25 Leg bone
26 "Luck Be __"
27 Calendar abbr.
29 Pearl City porch
30 Country singer K.T. __
31 See 24 Down
33 Not well-lit
34 Palindromic preposition
35 Paid notices
38 Pesto ingredient
39 Lodging place
41 Asian inland body of water
42 Lumber center
44 Aromas, in Exeter
45 Part of FCC
47 __ *Hope* (old soap)
48 Workout places
49 Actress Phoebe
50 Step through water
51 __ even keel
52 Muffin spread
53 Some containers
54 Can't stand
55 Freeway snarl
58 __ and don'ts

143 HOLLYWOOD & OVINE by Richard Silvestri

ACROSS

1 Hammett hound
5 Placed on display
10 Open a crack
14 Honest-to-goodness
15 Lake craft
16 Encrypt
17 Sheepish actress?
19 And __ There Were None
20 Years and years
21 Got ready for a bout
23 Butler of fiction
26 Put aside
27 Famous family of Virginia
28 Self-image
30 Prepared prunes
33 Pierce portrayer
34 Out-of-the-way
36 Language suffix
37 Easy basket
39 Profit chaser?
40 Dreadlocks wearer
42 Part of NATO
43 Puzzle word
46 Oliver's colleague
47 Abundant supply
49 "__ on a bet!"
50 Young 'uns
51 Metamorphose
53 TV exec Arledge
55 Awe-inspiring
57 Feel poorly
58 Kind of exam
59 Sheepish actor?
65 Folklore villain
66 First name in cosmetics
67 Light and graceful
68 Geek
69 Orchestra members
70 Make public

DOWN

1 Hand holder
2 Get an eyeful
3 Put down a road
4 Ms. MacGraw
5 Kid's transport
6 Jessica or Otto
7 Three __ match
8 Mary of comics
9 Proximate
10 On the go
11 Sheepish director?
12 "Zip-__-Doo-Dah"
13 Tear apart
18 Bottom-line gain
22 Make changes in
23 Spin a yarn
24 Sheepish actress?
25 Biblical twin
26 "__ to Watch Over Me"
27 Dey-time drama?
29 Grandpa Walton portrayer
31 House and grounds
32 Campus bigwigs
35 Approximately
38 Singer Page
41 In the matter of
44 Lawmaking body
45 Takes steps
48 Soothed
52 Say "Nyah-nyah!"
54 José's hurrah
55 Before you know it
56 Cheer on
57 In the sack
60 Noshed on
61 Make an arrest
62 By means of
63 Make a mistake
64 Ham holder

144 LITERALLY SPEAKING by Eric Albert

ACROSS

1 Sing the praises of
5 The Art of Loving author
10 Coal carrier
14 Moreover
15 Ms. McPherson
16 Palindrome place
17 DE(LOST)ED
20 __ in the Park
21 Spot remover?
22 It flies in fights
23 Hit the mall
24 Narrow waterway
28 Exude odors
29 Pro-wrestling org.
32 Mail device
33 Mrs. Dithers
34 Tosca tune
35 SEN(FLAW)SE
38 Tide type
39 Language expert Chomsky
40 Give a response
41 Sea slitherer
42 Farm dwellers
43 Elephant's counterpart
44 Movie based on a board game
45 It's furry and purry
46 Shoe support
49 SW California city
54 ORDI(NIL)NARY
56 Kandinsky colleague
57 He thought up Friday
58 Essay on Man writer
59 Betray boredom
60 Furry swimmer
61 Depict unfairly

DOWN

1 Mary's pet
2 Et __ (and others: Lat.)
3 Former UN member
4 Doctor's order
5 Make a spreading search
6 Strictness
7 Leave out
8 What boys will be
9 Mike, to Archie
10 Make possible
11 Rapid pace
12 Double reed
13 Taper off
18 Not as certain
19 Make dinner
23 Blood component
24 Movie part
25 __ Men and a Baby
26 Part of RFD
27 On the apex
28 Mel of baseball
29 Inflict
30 Show fear
31 Arbuckle's nickname
33 Big bill
34 Solemn assent
36 Veiled venom
37 Subterranean passage
42 "__ want for Christmas . . ."
43 Comet's colleague
44 Comic Myron
45 Kayak, e.g.
46 Pitch-black
47 Les Paul hit of '50
48 Mixed bag
49 Search (through)
50 Current units
51 Out of control
52 "Uh-uh"
53 Once again
55 Procure

145 BODY WEAR by A.J. Santora

ACROSS
1 Abbott or Costello
9 __ Antilles
15 Losing money
16 Natural-gas compound
17 Hoopster's wear
18 Swell, '60s-style
19 Shoe-box letters
20 __ Dhabi
21 Little squirt
22 Part of USNA
24 Poet Teasdale
26 Finish-line prop
29 Whole bunch
30 More vigorous
31 Court party
32 XIII quadrupled
34 Beret kin
36 Author Buscaglia
37 Umps' wear
42 __ Gatos, CA
43 Pittsburgh river
44 Copacabana locale
45 One against
47 Forearm bones
49 All ears
53 Lemon skin
54 Transmission choice
55 Up __ (stuck)
56 Gray work
58 Point (at)
60 Columnist LeShan
61 Literary comparison
63 MPs' wear
65 Kitchen tool
66 Carpenter's creation
67 "Good Night __" (old song)
68 Swore (to)

DOWN
1 Equates
2 Treat glass
3 Load cargo
4 Shoot-breeze link
5 High land
6 King Hussein, e.g.
7 Hairdresser's nightmare?
8 Ames and Jaymes
9 Dancer's wear
10 French infinitive
11 Blows a circuit
12 South America's largest city
13 It may be SWAK
14 Bandleader Alvino
21 Special pleasure
23 Cobbler's piercers
25 Pennsylvania city
27 Social equal
28 An asteroid
30 '60s casual wear
33 "How was __ know?"
35 Fi preceder
37 Thunder sound
38 Sharpen
39 Highly regarded
40 William Bendix TV role
41 Wrongful act
46 Big Ten team
48 Biblical landfall
50 "We __ amused"
51 Hawk
52 Ruffled the hair
55 Walk slowly
57 Gen. Robt. __
59 Fake, for short
61 Scale note
62 Phoneticist's symbols: Abbr.
63 Get __ for effort
64 Satisfied sounds

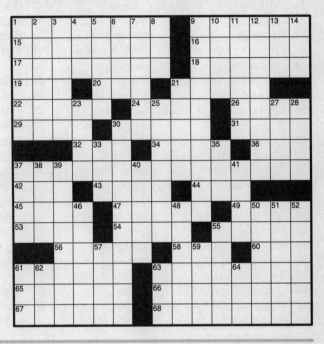

146 CULT CARTOON by Mel Rosen

ACROSS
1 Fast-food drink
5 Proficient
9 Mr. Kadiddlehopper
13 Wading bird
14 Grande and Bravo
15 Give up
16 Flying cartoon hero
19 Wide shoe width
20 Something funny
21 React to a pun
22 Place
23 Come up short
24 Destructive one
27 Eat well
28 Undergrad degs.
31 Make a complaint
32 Varieties
33 Bonn exclamation
34 Spy foes of 16 Across
38 Compass pt.
39 Dairy-case buys
40 Tall grass
41 Alert color
42 Feels bad about
43 Adjective for Merman
45 Rifles and revolvers
46 Appear to be
47 Maestro's stick
49 Psychic's sight
50 Work to do
53 Best friend of 16 Across
56 Territories
57 Jazz phrase
58 Castaway's home
59 Circle segments
60 Med-school subj.
61 Author Uris

DOWN
1 Become a father to
2 Bassoon's kin
3 Monopoly items
4 Seek knowledge
5 More Bohemian
6 Old theater name
7 At sea
8 Atty.'s title
9 Yuletide music
10 Milan money
11 Equally balanced
12 Singer Tormé
15 Most lean and strong
17 Buffalo's lake
18 Kampala's country
22 Mrs. Burt Reynolds, once
23 Helsinki natives
24 Earth tone
25 Rope loop
26 Took a chance
27 Foolish capers
28 Diamond sacks
29 Dull pains
30 Not really legit
32 Pants parts
35 Misfortunes
36 Reunion invitees
37 Composer Khachaturian
43 Deprived (of)
44 Paper measure
45 Man of the world?
46 Bacteria fighter
47 Jefferson's VP
48 Actor Baldwin
49 Related
50 San __, CA
51 European capital
52 "I've __ had!"
53 Cote comment
54 New Deal agcy.
55 Tin Man's need

147 FRUCTIFEROUS by Bob Lubbers

ACROSS
1 Rat-__
5 Break off
9 Uses a VCR
14 Solemn ceremony
15 La __ aux Folles
16 Without __ (broke)
17 Kemo __ (Tonto's pal)
18 Waikiki wiggle
19 Rent document
20 Tea variety
23 Tea holder
24 Singer Cole
25 Creeps along
27 Chew the fat
28 The __ the earth (kindly one)
30 Made a stack
33 Mrs. Roy Rogers
34 Big brass
37 Actress Meyers
38 Half a ten-spot
39 Buddhist sect
40 __ Cass Elliot
42 Peggy and Pinky
43 Nodded off
45 Marsh birds
47 Cratchit's kid
48 Heavenly lights
50 D.C. landmark
54 Bordeaux buddy
55 Clam variety
58 __ Carta
60 Hud Oscar winner
61 Three of a kind
62 Vermonter Allen
63 "__ each life . . ."
64 British prep school
65 Supple
66 Active one
67 Family rooms

DOWN
1 Fiery ambition?
2 Royal crown
3 Facing the pitcher
4 __ Mutant Ninja Turtles
5 Earl of car-painting fame
6 Brown shade
7 Give the eye
8 Highest level
9 Scout's quest
10 Old pro
11 Adolescent's "beard"
12 Come next
13 Flights have them
21 Pleased
22 NFLer or NHLer
26 Army bed
28 Puts away
29 Pub supply
30 Robin's Mork & Mindy costar
31 Author Levin
32 Chaplin film of '52
33 Calorie counter's concern
35 Nectar collector
36 "__ then I wrote . . ."
38 What pols press
41 Opposite of hence
43 Sour-cream concoctions
44 Skipped over
46 Repair a chair
47 "You've Got a Friend" singer
48 Veronica of Hill Street Blues
49 Fine fiddle
50 Rickety auto
51 Rich cake
52 Burger topping
53 Spinks and Uris
56 Oklahoma city
57 Betting setting
59 Slangy refusal

148 JOURNALISM 101 by Alex Vaughn

ACROSS
1 Beet variety
6 Some seaweed
11 Ruefully ironic
14 Western show
15 Brings up
16 Farm chopper
17 Classic comedy routine
19 __ Khan
20 Unspecified folks
21 Chicken choice
23 Rented an alley
26 Their work is filling
27 Felt sore
28 Actor with the shortest name
29 Salamander
30 Canonized femmes: Abbr.
31 __-Locka, FL
32 Wet Williams
35 Tokyo honorific
36 Besieged one's remark
38 "Xanadu" rock group
39 Dad, so to speak
42 NASA affirmative
43 Southwest predator
44 North Slope quest
45 Back in time
46 Brian of skating
47 Map boundary
50 Makes a face
51 Cube clutcher
52 Pizzeria products
53 Menlo Park monogram
54 Bestselling kids' book series
59 Fashioned like
60 Specialized angler
61 "Encore!"
62 Rebellious Turner
63 Lose stiffness
64 Safecrackers, slangily

DOWN
1 Intimidate
2 "That's what you think!"
3 From __ Z
4 Fixes wingtips
5 Spoke monotonously
6 Canine comments
7 Aloha token
8 Small attic
9 Fiery felony
10 Probate concerns
11 Quitter's remark
12 Famous synonymist
13 Long time
18 Actor Beatty
22 Make flour finer
23 __ profundo
24 Based on eight
25 Children's remark
26 Carting cost
28 Speedometer reading: Abbr.
31 Hold the deed to
32 Reaction to a rodent
33 Bugs' pursuer
34 Laughs heartily
37 Pasture plaint
40 After-dinner snack
41 Permissible
43 Give portents of
45 San __, TX
46 Words on an arrow
47 Mighty one of myth
48 Florida city
49 "I didn't know she had it __"
50 Boom-bah preceder
52 Wrongdoer, to cops
55 Antique auto
56 Hang back
57 Appreciate jazz
58 Light-switch positions

ANGLERS by Randolph Ross

ACROSS
1 Mixologist's milieu
4 Didn't like
9 Bread spread
13 Hwy.
14 Los __, NM
16 Actor Arkin
17 Chapter in history
18 He reached his peak
20 Mrs. Flintstone
22 Mauna __
23 Texas city
27 Shiite belief
32 *The Way We Were* director
34 Dopey's brother
35 Climbing vines
36 Hall-of-Fame pitcher
41 *Do __ Waltz?*
42 Common Market abbr.
43 *Wild Kingdom* host
48 MP's quarries
49 Nineveh native

51 USSR successor
53 "__ Theme" (*Doctor Zhivago* tune)
55 Lincoln's Chief Justice
62 Byron work
63 Part of WATS
64 Ho Chi Minh City, once
65 French diarist
66 Tailless cat
67 Rent out
68 Hood's "heater"

DOWN
1 Cook up
2 Large courtyards
3 Kingdoms
4 Take a chance
5 It may be pale
6 Typewriter setting
7 Down Under bird
8 Small blob
9 Glove-box contents
10 __ Baba

11 Asian ox
12 "__ for the money . . ."
15 Jack of *Barney Miller*
19 Trap, in a way
21 Director Elaine
24 Cree or Crow
25 Most with August birthdays
26 Chinese nuts
28 Chair part
29 Short street
30 Rent-__
31 Ger. currency
33 __ *Man!* ('73 film)
36 Tobacco chunk
37 Dynamic start
38 Sky-high
39 __ Kid (Cagney role)
40 Towel word
41 "__ Believer"
44 French philosopher
45 A Mandrell sister

46 Singer Peeples
47 Lamour outfit
50 Gymnast Comaneci
52 Officeholders
54 Mailed away
55 *Cheers* role

56 Southern constellation
57 Author Deighton
58 Factor of makeup
59 Go quickly
60 Khan opener?
61 Morse message

ON LITERACY by Eric Albert

ACROSS
1 Spa feature
10 Savalas role
15 Frozen dessert
16 Lloyd Webber hit
17 START OF A DISRAELI QUOTE
18 Delicious
19 List item
20 European airline
21 Get moving
24 *The __ Hawk* (Flynn film)
25 Phone bug
28 "__ heeere!"
29 Meat cut
31 Drink a bit
32 Argentine region
33 MIDDLE OF QUOTE
37 London square
39 Schedule abbr.
42 Darkroom device
43 Abandon
46 Beast of burden
47 Make public
48 Salary standard

49 Sask. neighbor
50 Mr. Goldfinger
51 Comedian Smirnoff
54 END OF QUOTE
58 Legal defense
59 Court addict
60 British diarist
61 Booth and Guiteau

DOWN
1 Put in stitches
2 Bat material
3 Hula strings
4 Four-and-a-half score
5 C-major's analog
6 Pasta shape
7 In pieces
8 Diminutive
9 __ up (in a lather)
10 Bogart thriller
11 Egg cell
12 Kirk, to McCoy
13 Cash device: Abbr.

14 Bandleader Kyser
20 Skewered meat
21 Alts.
22 "__ believe in yesterday"
23 Pregame speech
24 Shankar's instrument
25 Casual shirt
26 "__ was saying, . . ."
27 School grp.
29 DC-10 device
30 Hockey-shutout box score
32 Message unit
34 "The Tears __ Clown"
35 Uncommon sort
36 Hoopster Baylor
37 *Miss Pym Disposes* author
38 Cell molecule
40 Furry scarf
41 Whichever

43 Boat basin
44 Unchanged
45 School break
48 Gets real angry
49 __ *Dick*
50 Puts fear into
51 Jabber

52 Fermented drink
53 Runner Keino
54 "Let's call __ day"
55 __-Wan Kenobi
56 Sister of a sort
57 Printer's units

151   PRECISELY! by Mel Rosen

ACROSS
1 Was an agent
6 Daytime TV fare
11 Three, in Turin
14 Like a washing-machine filter
15 Part of a ream
16 Free (of)
17 Precise, as to facts
19 Half of bi-
20 Day laborer
21 __ in "apple"
22 Most up-to-date
24 "What's __ for me?"
26 Take turns
27 Jazz fan
30 Paid escort
31 Cobbler's tool
32 Rose portion
34 Multiperson race
37 Teachers' grp.
38 Evans and Robertson
40 "__ Got Sixpence"
41 Practice routine
44 Ziti or rigatoni
46 Five-spot
47 __ Off (Burnett film)
49 Implants
51 Soda-shop order
52 Johnson of Laugh-In
53 Mecca pilgrim
54 Mao __-tung
55 Close loudly
59 Like Methuselah
60 Precise, as to appointments
63 __ glance (quickly)
64 Nintendo forerunner
65 Easy victories
66 Poodle size
67 Madagascar mammal
68 Flooded with water

DOWN
1 Feed the pigs
2 Maine's state tree
3 Enthusiastic about
4 Kind of pride or food
5 Use henna
6 Short and wide
7 Inning's sextet
8 River islet
9 Play intro
10 State representative
11 Precise, in painting
12 Car-wash step
13 Use a blue pencil
18 Set a trap
23 It may be tall
25 Short snooze
26 Gets one's goat
27 Poker holding
28 Vase-shaped pitcher
29 Precise, in speaking
30 Festive events
33 Patched, perhaps
35 Rarin' to go
36 Hankerings
39 Hi-fi system
42 Lounge about
43 Not exaggerated
45 Tsp. or tbsp.
48 Middle Easterner
50 Give a gift
51 Very, in music
52 Up and about
53 Castle adjunct
54 Finished, for short
56 Peru's capital
57 Audio boosters
58 Fit together
61 School of whales
62 Gun org.

152   OUT OF THIS WORLD by Trip Payne

ACROSS
1 Fergie's first name
6 Sudden sound
10 Lie in the sun
14 Uneven
15 MP's quest
16 Not fooled by
17 Sprang up
18 Give an assessment to
19 Singer Redding
20 Aliens, supposedly
23 Second person
24 Crossed out
25 Grammarian's concern
27 Baggage handlers
30 Play a part
32 Golf prop
33 Hearty brew
34 What some play by
35 Sharp pull
36 Alien vehicles
40 Get Smart group
41 Drain, as energy
42 Actress Caldwell
43 Quite cold
44 Author Du Bois
45 Goulash spice
49 Gettysburg general
51 Assistance
52 The bottom line
53 Meeting with an alien
58 Household helper
59 Sharp pull
60 TV exec Arledge
61 Words of approximation
62 Cleveland's lake
63 Loudness units
64 Banned pesticides
65 Husky's burden
66 Concerning

DOWN
1 Paint basecoat
2 Get in
3 Showed team spirit
4 Helper: Abbr.
5 Ladder base
6 Trash boats
7 Bestow
8 Mini-missive
9 High-spiritedness
10 Ship poles
11 Picnicker's pet?
12 Brandy cocktails
13 Boxing stats
21 Outlay
22 Eccentric type
26 Squealing shout
28 Low islands
29 __ Baba
30 They go tow-to-tow: Abbr.
31 Old Portuguese coin
34 Mentalist's claim
35 Scoff at
36 King, but not prince
37 Spanish Civil War fighter
38 Chatter
39 Beverly Hills __
40 Kipling novel
44 Director Craven
45 Settled on
46 Chant
47 Actor __ Ivory Wayans
48 Not moving
50 Extinct birds
51 Potts of Designing Women
54 "I Only Have __ for You"
55 Viscount's superior
56 Bear, to astronomers
57 Darkness at __
58 Stylish, for short

153 MOVIE DIRECTION by Wayne R. Williams

ACROSS
1 In addition
4 Elevator inventor
8 Poirot, e.g.
14 Coffee server
15 Roof device
16 Country singer Nelson
17 Crouse movie of '77
20 *My Name Is __ Lev*
21 Tip or hip ending
22 Backtalk
23 Diminutive suffix
25 Pants man Strauss
27 *My Three Sons* grandpa
29 Can't stand
31 Wrap up
36 Chemical ending
37 Wear away
39 Haitian rum
40 Kind of triangle
42 Parody writer
44 Spanish hero
45 Train station
47 "The Boy King"
48 Pennsylvania school
50 Legendary tale
51 Shaker __, OH
52 O.K. Corral lawman
54 Golfer Ballesteros
56 West et al.
60 Poi base
62 Shady spot
65 Finney movie of '84
68 Hereditary
69 *Enterprise* crewman
70 Kitchen topper
71 Hole enlarger
72 *Hook* role
73 The Mormons: Abbr.

DOWN
1 *Tubby the __*
2 Raw minerals
3 Peck movie of '59
4 Dillon movie of '79
5 Inventor's initials
6 Quaint hotels
7 Reached an agreement
8 Veer
9 __ *Abner*
10 Wallach and Whitney
11 Arm bone
12 Some football results
13 Dame Myra __
18 Drenched
19 __ *Haw*
24 Work for
26 Wilding movie of '50
27 Swiss city
28 Ted, to JFK, Jr.
30 __ the line (obeyed)
32 Toy-store magnate Schwarz
33 Sorvino movie of '83
34 West Pt. grad
35 Pub fliers
38 Catch sight of
41 XIII quadrupled
43 Prize monies
46 Josephine was one
49 Tea-party host
53 Bowl cheer
55 Trade-training abbr.
56 *The Ghost and Mrs. __*
57 Charles' sister
58 Author Ferber
59 Cloth line
61 Egg cell
63 Novelist Bagnold
64 Curtain hardware
66 Hwy.
67 Grand __ Opry

154 U-U-U by Eric Albert

ACROSS
1 Clear tables
4 Wife of Jacob
8 Handy
14 Give __ whirl (try)
15 Egg
16 South American
17 YEW
20 Letter from Paul
21 *Boyz __ Hood*
22 Heart of the matter
23 __ *supra* (see above)
25 A bit immodest
29 For example
30 Mine find
33 Quaid film of '88
34 Sedate
35 The one left standing
37 EWE
41 Safari land
42 "__ River"
43 Goon's gun
44 Crack a code
47 Radio regulators: Abbr.
50 Shapeless mass
52 Speak roughly
53 "Ooh __!"
54 Person with a PC
56 Obsolete eatery
59 YOU
63 Thriller of '60
64 One revolution
65 Yanks' home
66 "__ they run . . ."
67 Perry's creator
68 Cal. page

DOWN
1 Weightlifter's pride
2 Perfect place
3 One's marbles
4 Yuppie abode
5 Mr. Knievel
6 "Till we meet again"
7 Med. ins. co.
8 Irish province
9 Merit-badge holder
10 Old anesthetic
11 Cone producer
12 Burmese statesman
13 Tennis stroke
18 Comedian Kabibble
19 Reverse the effects of
24 Not alfresco
26 Rib relinquisher
27 Rooster's topper
28 Chatter
30 "__ to Be You"
31 Comedienne Charlotte
32 Dazzling display
34 Foul spot
36 Harrison's *Star Wars* role
37 Ground grain
38 Latch __ (get)
39 Bug-zapper ancestor
40 Fuse word
41 Soviet spies
45 Before
46 Actress Irene
47 Known to all
48 Contract part
49 Forty winks
51 Big name in beer
53 Chaney of film
55 London section
57 Caspian Sea feeder
58 Ripped up
59 Second ltr. addendum
60 Vane dir.
61 Ham holder
62 Soap ingredient

155 BRASS TACTICS by Donna J. Stone

ACROSS

1 Machine parts
5 Sudden spurt
10 King's mad dog
14 Foster a felon
15 F. Scott's spouse
16 Birdsong of basketball
17 Munich mister
18 History homework
19 Computer command
20 START OF A QUOTE BY RICHARD STRAUSS
23 Sushi-bar selection
24 Society-column word
25 Lysol target
28 Wine word
31 __ mater
34 Corn portion
35 Cover stories?
38 Exeter elevator
40 MIDDLE OF QUOTE
43 Nest or burrow
44 Slogan of a sort
45 Symbol of sturdiness
46 Prepare to fly
48 "How was __ know?"
49 Ersatz emerald
51 Under the weather
53 Foreman's forte
54 END OF QUOTE
62 Field of study
63 Excite
64 Euro Disney attraction
65 Spice-rack item
66 Everyday
67 Worshiper's place?
68 Salami shop
69 Sordid
70 Lifesaver flavor

DOWN

1 "All the Way" lyricist
2 Busy as __
3 Mr. Griffin
4 *Julia* actress
5 Conductor George
6 Uruguayan coin
7 To boot
8 Sitting Bull's st.
9 Guatemalan language
10 Singer Elvis
11 Hatch's home
12 Teasing talk
13 Sugar suffix
21 Recovery regimen, for short
22 Scones partner
25 Genesis character
26 Mystical deck
27 Luncheonette lure
28 Exodus locale
29 Siskel's partner
30 The __ Kid (Western hero)
32 Cretan king
33 Black key
36 Dachshundlike
37 Word of salutation
39 Little guy
41 Baja city
42 Errata
47 UN branch
50 In the heavens
52 *Mission: Impossible* actor
53 Singer Smith
54 Perry's victory site
55 Singer Carter
56 Get up
57 Blue hue
58 Magellan discovery
59 Stereo's ancestor
60 Gouda alternative
61 Unimportant
62 Slap on

---

156 AMENDMENTS by Shirley Soloway

ACROSS

1 Reach across
5 Mardi __
9 Free rides
14 Angel topper
15 Make a scene
16 Soaps actress Slezak
17 Scandinavian city
18 Sicilian spewer
19 Anglo-__
20 Transfer ownership
23 Compass pt.
24 Jay's follower
25 Top pilots
26 Funny Foxx
28 Done with
29 *Raging Bull* star
31 Anti-Dracula weapon
34 Winslow Homer painting
36 Ceramic square
37 Waker-upper
39 From Florence: Abbr.
40 Scared off
42 Bell sound
43 Alludes (to)
44 Sharp pain
46 Make over
47 Fizzy drink
48 Deli meat
51 British brew
53 Lighting accessory
56 Sired, old-style
58 Day's receipts
59 Olympian warmonger
60 __ *Gay* (WWII plane)
61 At any time
62 Nifty
63 Last-place finisher
64 Parcel (out)
65 Jane Austen novel

DOWN

1 Surprise, and then some
2 Turkish title
3 Calm down
4 Lunch time
5 Corfu's country
6 CBS anchorman
7 Christie and Karenina
8 Getz of jazz
9 Abates
10 Author Levin
11 Kind of mortgage
12 Ring decisions
13 Fully competent
21 Made a donation
22 Dorothy's Oz visit, e.g.
27 Processing veggies
28 '40s actor Dennis
29 __ *Rosenkavalier*
30 Whitish gem
31 Part of MST
32 Wedding-cake level
33 Inseparable friends
34 Having the blues
35 Plumber's connection
37 Traffic-sign shape
38 Guitarist Paul
41 Soviet symbol
42 Prefix for sack
44 Shirt feature
45 Stick (to)
47 Barrel part
48 Sultan's pride
49 First-string players
50 *Call Me Madam* inspiration
51 Second son
52 Emcee Jay
54 Gossipy tidbit
55 Country road
57 Chilean cheer

157 DO SOMETHING! by Trip Payne

ACROSS
1 Blessed events
7 Wax-coated cheese
11 Reb general Stuart
14 Third of an inning
15 Levee kin
16 Bunyan's tool
17 Olmos movie of '87
20 Paris *aeroport*
21 True-blue
22 Brewery hot spot
23 May honoree
24 Video room
25 He went east of Eden
27 Least dangerous
29 __ Monica, CA
33 Nepal native
36 Personal quirks
38 Campy exclamation
39 Become brave enough
42 Refrain bit
43 Martin Mull's *Roseanne* role
44 Donkey's comment
45 Work a puzzle
47 Depressed sorts
49 Not on the job
51 Fleur-de-__
52 Actor Kilmer
55 Not to mention
58 Mr. Doubleday
60 Tractor-trailer
61 Take up arms
64 Mamie's man
65 Blackjack cards
66 Eerie get-together
67 Marked out
68 Congressman Gingrich
69 Attacks

DOWN
1 __ buddies (close pals)
2 Preface, for short
3 Kingdom
4 Cereal tiger
5 Paul Newman role
6 Chess result
7 Sea swirl
8 Preachy, as literature
9 Scouting leader
10 Director Brooks
11 Coffee, so to speak
12 Former spouses
13 Ernie's roommate
18 Not a soul
19 New York college
24 Spotted, as a horse
26 Distributors
27 Capote's nickname
28 Person in a pool
30 Biblical sailor
31 Forum wear
32 Several
33 "Master" NCOs
34 Man of the hour
35 Bibliography abbr.
37 Estate sharer
40 Do-it-yourself beer
41 Scale notes
46 Shop clamp
48 First-year cadet
50 Joust weapon
52 Leaf channels
53 Chevron rival
54 Irish export
55 Grand __ racing
56 Delight in
57 Pre-owned
59 Hummingbird's home
60 Chair part
62 Ziering of *Beverly Hills 90210*
63 Golfer Trevino

158 CAPITALISM by Bob Lubbers

ACROSS
1 Mineo and Maglie
5 Pale-faced
10 Rotisserie need
14 __ happens (incidentally)
15 Banal
16 Mitchell mansion
17 South Korean singers?
19 Algerian port
20 *The Messiah* composer
21 Coming to terms
23 Capri, for one
25 Gets the point
26 Toyland visitors
29 "What's __ Pussycat?"
32 Composers' org.
35 Cookie tycoon Wally
36 Mini-river
38 *Ben-__* (Heston film)
39 __ Jose, CA
40 Plays for time
41 Western Indian
42 Rural lodging
43 Arab rulers
44 Cut short
45 Part of USNA
47 Teacher's deg.
48 Karpov's game
49 Move slowly
51 Diamond Head's home
53 Sinatra specialty
57 Country, to Caesar
61 Imported cheese
62 Italian lovers?
64 Author Morrison
65 Villain's expression
66 Greek letters
67 Sp. miss
68 Group doctrine
69 Budget component

DOWN
1 Miss America wear
2 Taking a cruise
3 NFLer
4 Bones up on
5 Bikini, for one
6 __ Lanka
7 Derisive sound
8 Suffix for leather
9 Duck dwellings
10 Fur wraps
11 French skydiver's gear?
12 OPEC member
13 Sharp taste
18 Not so much
22 Workhorse groups
24 Main course
26 Washbowl
27 Hotpoint competitor
28 German jet-setter?
30 Slipped up
31 Kook
33 Saturn and Mercury
34 Gets ready, for short
36 Newsman Donaldson
37 DDE opponent in '56
40 Soft minerals
44 Camera part
46 Tiredness cause
48 Number-one son's surname
50 Actor Buchholz
52 In two
53 "Shall we?" response
54 Nasal appraisal
55 Zilch
56 FBI agents
58 Solemn ceremony
59 Optimist's words
60 Exec. aide
63 Shoe width

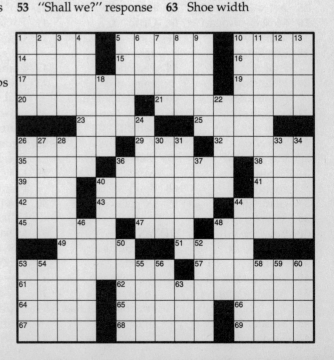

AQUARIANS by Eric Albert

ACROSS
1 Needed a massage
6 Cutting comment
10 Bush Cabinet member
14 Triangle, e.g.
15 Healing plant
16 Superman's mother
17 Apple implement
18 Frat event
20 *Stand by Me* star
22 Cola cooler
23 Weight
24 Refuser's phrase
28 Won out over
31 Epic '59 film
32 Ms. Lauder
33 Peruvian place
36 Fool's wear
37 Twain portrayer
41 Old hand
43 "My Way" composer
44 Signals for a cab
47 Eagerly accept
50 Small stinger
51 Render illegible
52 Actor O'Shea

55 Glasgow "go"
56 *Sullivan's Travels* actress
60 *Cosmos* author
63 Kidney-related
64 Producer De Laurentiis
65 South African native
66 Commercial manicurist
67 Serb or Croat
68 Building add-ons
69 More self-conscious

DOWN
1 Chalk up (to)
2 Options
3 Tryon novel
4 Fencing need
5 Author Earl __ Biggers
6 Wash down
7 Standoffish
8 He's synonymous with synonyms
9 Noodle, so to speak

10 Harsh horn
11 Stirrup site
12 *The A-Team* heavyweight
13 Fork over
19 Needle dropper
21 Advanced deg.
25 "Hello, Young Lovers" show
26 Beer holder
27 Physics unit
29 "__ for Two"
30 Snakelike swimmer
31 Bullion shape
33 Mr. Chaney
34 Sort
35 Wall St. employee
38 Boater or skimmer
39 Shout of surprise
40 Boat propeller
41 Nightwear
42 Jamaican export
45 Trickle-out amount
46 NFL player

48 His name may ring a bell
49 Zeus' son
50 Ad follower
52 Industrialist
53 As a total
54 *Peanuts* character

57 Tear down
58 Munitions
59 Rachel's sister
60 LP successors
61 Be under the weather
62 Geneticist's letters

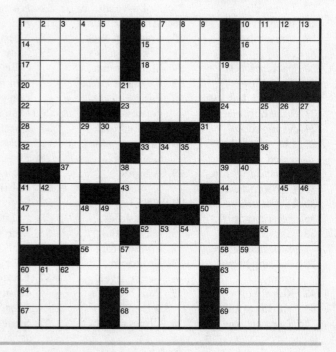

ANAGRAMMING by Wayne R. Williams

ACROSS
1 Hindu title
4 Scare away
9 Mississippi quartet?
14 Checkers
15 Actor Andrew
16 Mother-of-pearl
17 Military asst.
18 Oscillation anagram
20 Helmsley's namesakes
22 Spherical bodies
23 Garr of *Tootsie*
24 Stevedores' grp.
27 Los __ , NM
31 Permutation anagram
34 Giant great
35 Kimono sash
36 Pet-shop buy
37 Ballet wear
38 Pruned
40 Not up to snuff
41 Ariadne's father
42 "__! poor Yorick"
43 Yucatán Indian
44 Feedbag tidbit

45 Allow
46 Desecration anagram
50 Wild cat
52 __ kwon do (martial art)
53 Puts on TV
54 Grub
56 Close a purse again
58 Percolation anagram
63 Biblical judge
64 Sports figures
65 Benefit
66 Wide width
67 Marriage-vow word
68 Spills the beans
69 Bolshevik

DOWN
1 Mosaic pieces
2 Cash in
3 Procreation anagram
4 Friends of faunae: Abbr.
5 German toast

6 Black gold
7 "Sail __ Ship of State!"
8 Casino game
9 Make possible
10 Spanish beat
11 Part of M.S.
12 Pause fillers
13 Complete collection
19 Fuming
21 Mythical crier et al.
25 Greek satirist
26 Number-cruncher
28 Enumeration anagram
29 Director Preminger
30 Erwin and Gilliam
32 Make free (of)
33 One of the Graces
37 Crownlets
38 __ Alto, CA
39 Baldwin or Guinness
41 Shemp's brother

43 Words to live by
46 Not refined
47 Jump the tracks
48 Irish city
49 Sighted
51 Baltic residents
55 Minor fight

57 Building wings
58 Austral. state
59 DDE's arena
60 Propel, in a way
61 "__ been had!"
62 White House nickname

161 GETTING PHYSICAL by Mel Rosen

ACROSS

1 One or the __
6 Historical period
9 Auction actions
13 Panda land
14 Wernher __ Braun
15 TV and radio
16 Carryalls
17 Catchall abbr.
18 Salad veggie
19 On the town
20 Start work, perhaps
23 Split __ (be too fussy)
25 Orchestra member
26 Onetime deliverers
28 Hee-haw
29 Airline to Tokyo
32 Bill on a cap
33 Venetian-blind part
34 Author Victor
35 Norwegian king
36 Brown shade
37 Parisian pals
38 Pasta alternative
39 Church area
40 Twofold
41 Asian ox
42 Picnic pests
43 Landlord's client
44 In the old days
45 20 percent
46 Child's song
50 Lodge member
53 Sandy's owner
54 Shout disapproval
55 Cosmic Carl
57 Adjust a lens
58 Easily deflated item
59 Piano piece
60 Student's hurdle
61 Free (of)
62 Closely packed

DOWN

1 Prefix meaning "eight"
2 Holier-than-__
3 Go to bed
4 Helmsman's dir.
5 More throaty
6 Makes level
7 Coll. army program
8 Alaska city
9 Uncle Miltie
10 Word form for "thought"
11 Platter
12 Can. province
15 Hatfield foe
21 Coffee maker
22 Ease up
24 Get __ on (rush)
26 Scrimshaw stuff
27 Eyelashes
28 Elated state
29 Make a false start
30 Quick on one's feet
31 Also-ran
33 Start to fall?
34 Visit often
36 Baccarat announcement
40 Did a bomb-squad job
42 Chips in
43 Carioca's home
44 Yves Saint Laurent fragrance
45 Inundate
46 Sound's partner
47 Fort __, KY
48 Ancient Peruvian
49 Person in the lotus position
51 Small boys
52 Patella's site
56 Had a bite

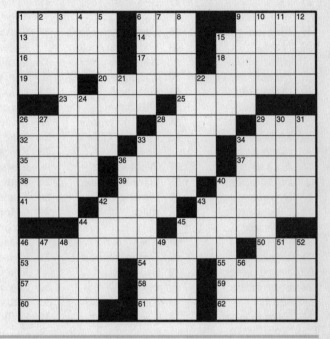

162 COUNTRY FOLKS by Alex Vaughn

ACROSS

1 Finance degs.
5 Texas A&M rival
8 Leaves out
13 Utah resort
14 The census, e.g.
15 __ noir (red wine)
16 Betray boredom
17 Part of BTU
18 Lauder of lipsticks
19 Literature Nobelist in '21
22 Gets lost
23 FDR's dog
24 Vitamin quota: Abbr.
27 Old horse
29 Toddler swaddler
31 Witch
34 WBC middleweight champion, 1988
37 Plains natives
39 Easiness epitomized
40 Irene of Fame
41 Life Wish author
46 Ginza gelt
47 Seasoned veteran
48 Ms. Farrow
49 Aves. cross them
50 To be: Lat.
53 NL team
58 Basketball star
61 Miss something?
63 Insanity, at times
64 Painter Joan
65 Rocket brake
66 Cribbage need
67 Latch __ (get)
68 Quite pale
69 Mos. and mos.
70 Yawl pole

DOWN

1 Early Americans
2 He spoke for Daffy
3 Doing battle
4 December flier
5 Actor Franchot
6 Cheers character
7 Extremist
8 Out-of-doors
9 File category: Abbr.
10 Give-and-take
11 Sock part
12 Sault __ Marie, MI
14 Celestial object
20 Atlanta arena
21 M*A*S*H star
25 Plowman John
26 Indo-European
28 Stare open-mouthed
30 Pedigree org.
31 Orange-roof eatery, familiarly
32 Like Pisa's tower
33 Locket artisan
35 Zilch
36 Smile radiantly
38 VCR speed setting
42 Countrified affirmative
43 __ Hashanah
44 Kiddie turtle tetrad
45 Belafonte's holler
51 Oversentimental
52 Fishing specialist
54 Keaton/Garr film of '83
55 Minneapolis suburb
56 Knave's booty
57 Stuck-up one
59 Legalese phrase
60 Chippendale quartet
61 Swimsuit part
62 Congressman Aspin

163 THAT'S A WRAP by Eric Albert

ACROSS
1 Thick rug
5 African tree
11 G&S princess
14 Rail rider
15 Senescence
16 Sort of sauce
17 French revolutionary
19 Fine and dandy
20 Noble principles
21 Marshy area
22 "It's cold!"
23 Like a non-rolling stone?
24 Mah-jongg piece
26 Carson replacement
27 Bouquet
28 Like some hair
29 Slow up
30 __ Hari
31 Winker
32 Space center
36 Song of the south
37 Take to heart
38 Striking object
39 Court jester
40 Chicago NBAer
44 Party cheese
45 Numerical suffix
46 Melville book
47 Be a stool pigeon
48 Lend a hand to
49 Footballer/actor Alex
50 __ Dhabi
51 Hot stuff
54 Oil source
55 Put into words
56 Dorothy Gale's dog
57 Wool source
58 Harbor builder
59 Playing-fields place

DOWN
1 Barbie seafood
2 Bad-luck bringer
3 Convent head
4 Use restraint
5 Conks on the noggin
6 Mideast name
7 Coleridge composition
8 Sot
9 Come to terms
10 "I've __ Lonely Too Long"
11 Columbus' queen
12 Simile hardware
13 *Driving Miss Daisy* actor
18 Underhanded
24 "See ya!"
25 Rowena's husband
26 Rude look
28 Texas city
29 Colored cloth
30 Become engaged
31 Risk-taker Knievel
32 She had "It"
33 Native ability
34 Walk the floor
35 One billion years
36 Hold tight
39 Felt hat
40 From memory
41 Eradicate
42 Bring about
43 Instruction unit
45 Church offering
46 License plate
48 Egyptian snakes
49 Athlete's trouble spot
52 Scientist's place
53 WNW opposite

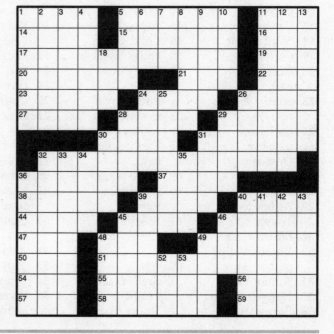

164 DAILY PLANETS by Matt Gaffney

ACROSS
1 French states
6 Kept a low profile
9 Reference-book name
14 Biblical verb
15 White House nickname
16 Glue variety
17 MARS
19 Quite disgusted
20 Computer command
21 Keats work
22 Asset adjective
25 Kind of beef
29 Road reversal
30 Ogle
32 Where most folks live
33 End-of-day rituals
35 Chapel Hill sch.
36 Passed out
38 Musical taste
40 Gunfight site
42 Ratio phrase
43 Space Needle's city
44 Golf's "Slammer"
45 Baltimore team
47 Some Tuscans
48 "For Me and My __"
49 Impromptu outing
51 Army, to Navy
54 PLUTO
58 Winter month, in Mexico
59 __ Marie Saint
60 Mrs. Kramden
61 Assad's land
62 "Uh-huh"
63 Religious belief

DOWN
1 Flow out
2 __ Aviv
3 Jack Benny's 39, e.g.
4 Japanese food style
5 Add, perhaps
6 Ms. Jessica
7 "Yeah, sure!"
8 __ Moines, IA
9 Grid judge
10 Unseal, old-style
11 NEPTUNE
12 Send out
13 Hunted and pecked
18 Silly Caesar
22 Polynesian party
23 "__ skin off my nose!"
24 MERCURY
25 Ranch beasts
26 "Be good __ gone"
27 Look over
28 Rebel Turner
30 Men's shop buys
31 Melodic
34 Exemplar of evil
36 Stable infant
37 Comic Johnson
39 Serling and Stewart
41 Corp. boss
42 How jet-setters travel
44 Singer O'Connor
45 Folklore beasts
46 Pluvial
47 Groan evoker, maybe
49 Baloney, so to speak
50 PDQ
52 *Exodus* character
53 Mauna __
54 *L.A. Law* actress
55 CCLI doubled
56 Lt.-to-be's place
57 The __ State (Idaho)

165 WILDE ADVICE by Wayne R. Williams

ACROSS

1 Columnist Bombeck
5 Sounded shocked
11 Police dept. alert
14 Hood's knife
15 *Taxi* role
16 *Horton Hears a __!* (Seuss book)
17 START OF AN OSCAR WILDE QUOTE
20 Hindu group
21 Simon and Tsongas
22 Jason's objective
25 Position troops
26 Rodeo rope
27 Climb up
30 UFO pilots
31 Of a leg bone
33 Kind of hygiene
37 MIDDLE OF QUOTE
40 Stock order
41 Ukrainian port
42 Fire preceder
43 Hold back
45 National Leaguer
47 Comrades in arms
50 Deep singers
51 Gorby's missus
52 Coral island
54 END OF QUOTE
60 Vane dir.
61 Phoneticist's marking
62 Light gas
63 Sun. homily
64 Brown ermines
65 Watch over

DOWN

1 Cornerstone abbr.
2 Greek P
3 $1,000,000, for short
4 Shorebird
5 Formation fliers
6 Like crazy
7 Rational
8 Bakery buy
9 USN rank
10 Dig out
11 Fifth-rate
12 Sleuth Vance
13 Overbearing
18 Leave empty
19 Peke or pom
22 Guitar ridges
23 Limber
24 Studio support
25 Cold-cut emporia
27 Put up with
28 Trig functions
29 *Hamlet* contraction
32 Sikorsky and Stravinsky
34 WPA projects
35 Burning
36 Metallic fabrics
38 M. Pascal
39 Incendiary substance
44 Bailiwicks
46 On an angle
47 Van Gogh locale
48 "Jezebel" singer
49 Birdman of Alcatraz, e.g.
50 Good things
52 Taj Mahal site
53 Quick pace
55 Meal ingredient
56 Cpl. or Sgt.
57 Born, in Bordeaux
58 Swindle
59 Last word

166 S-CAPADE by Fred Piscop

ACROSS

1 Quasimodo creator
5 Pipemaker's material
8 Hiccup, e.g.
13 Right away: Abbr.
14 Raw metal
15 __ *of the Jackal*
16 THE STAR
18 Expose to the atmosphere
19 Commandment
20 Sitting room
21 Neighbor of Isr.
22 "We aim to __"
25 Cravings
26 __ Blow (average guy)
27 Hat material
29 __ Spumante
32 Glum drop
34 Cronies
38 Jail, so to speak
40 Skilled worker
42 Hindu's destiny
43 __-de-camp
45 Tijuana nosh
46 Baker's need
48 "*C'est la __!*"
50 Prefix for space
53 Bird, often
55 Trophy shape
58 __ *17* ('53 film)
60 Alphabet inventor
62 "Could __ Magic" ('57 tune)
63 STAR'S LADY FRIEND
64 Close again
65 Tavern
66 Tehran's land
67 Charlie Chan portrayer
68 Wooden pin
69 __ out (supplements)

DOWN

1 Some fasteners
2 Loan-sharking
3 Sort of starer
4 Oil cartel
5 All-in-one
6 Speak on a soapbox
7 Mr. Jonson
8 Mets' stadium
9 STAR'S BOSS, AT TIMES
10 Allan-__
11 Squashed, maybe
12 Bristol's partner
15 Come to a point
17 Take-back, for short
23 Simile center
24 Valuable violin
26 STAR'S MALE FRIEND
28 Give a show
29 Pop a question
30 Hearst's kidnappers: Abbr.
31 Pavement material
33 Wipe out
35 UN member
36 Bub
37 __-cone (cool treat)
39 Ginnie __
41 Respecting deeply
44 "For what __ worth . . ."
47 Play backer
49 Some nest eggs: Abbr.
50 National Leaguer
51 Mrs. Mertz
52 Mrs. Gorbachev
54 Steak order
55 Lewis' partner
56 Forearm bones
57 Hammer parts
59 "I'm __ boy!" (Costello)
61 Nastase of tennis
63 Back talk

167   SPORTSMANSHIP by Shirley Soloway

ACROSS

1 Cotton fabric
5 Yard tool
9 "So be it!"
13 Gusto
14 Preceding nights
15 St. Kitts-__ (Caribbean nation)
17 Takes chances on the rink?
20 Beret relative
21 Bordeaux *et* Champagne
22 Lucky charm
23 Drapery support
24 Singing sound
25 Start a swan dive?
32 Cool spot
34 Day saver
35 Piano piece
36 Helen's abductor
37 Prior to, in poetry
38 Furry fish-eater
39 Cupid's equivalent
40 Inflated psyches
41 Loud shouts
42 About to score on serve?
45 Pigpen
46 Days of yore
47 Mortar mate
51 __ cost (free)
53 Copacabana city
56 Getting close, in a race?
59 Vacancy sign
60 Beloved
61 Prince of opera
62 __ *and Lovers*
63 "__ forgive those . . ."
64 Actress Rowlands

DOWN

1 Pain in the neck
2 Chase of films
3 Polite address
4 Aardvark tidbit
5 Live
6 Stratford's river
7 Teen dolls
8 Cleve.'s zone
9 Barbarian
10 Bistro list
11 Morally wrong
12 Riviera resort
16 Stuck in place
18 Calls forth
19 Silent screen star?
23 Salad veggie
24 Singer Brewer
25 Clairvoyant's card
26 *Zorro, __ Blade*
27 Crane's cousin
28 Never walked on
29 "__ I can help it!"
30 Cheerfulness
31 What walls may have
32 Shoot forth
33 Mata __
38 It's spotted in the zoo
40 Make an appearance
43 Cartographer's dots
44 London hub?
47 Dutch oven, e.g.
48 Genesis man
49 Normandy town
50 Afterwards
51 A long time
52 Spring event
53 Intense anger
54 Sect's symbol
55 Gumbo ingredient
57 Wyo. neighbor
58 Nautical gear

168   ALL THE NEWS by Trip Payne

ACROSS

1 Author Seton
5 Surfeit
9 Toss out
14 Felt bad about
15 *Goodbye, Columbus* author
16 Library no-no
17 Leading man?
18 At a distance
19 Moving about
20 Supporting a London paper?
23 Charlotte et al.
24 Mr. Guthrie
25 Mail again
28 Snacked on
29 Con game
33 Opening words
34 Make __ (achieve some progress)
36 One-time link
37 Baltimore paper's condiments?
40 Botch up
41 Danny and Stubby
42 __ nous
43 Goes to seed
45 Dallas sch.
46 Commencement
47 Cavs or Bucs
49 Gin flavoring
50 Surround a Boston paper?
56 Plotting group
57 Bleachers level
58 Fall birthstone
59 R&B singer Adams
60 "__ Petite" (Jackie Wilson song)
61 Bill-signing needs
62 Reach
63 Talks and talks and talks
64 *The Razor's __*

DOWN

1 A man from Amman
2 Hosiery shade
3 "No problem!"
4 Stage-door Johnnies, e.g.
5 Gave marks
6 Some apartments
7 A Four Corners state
8 Appears menacing
9 Sluggish sort
10 Sagan book
11 Confirmation, for one
12 Yard-sale sign
13 __ annum
21 Northerner of film
22 Italian city
25 Stair part
26 Start of a Spanish year
27 React with surprise
28 It's often bid
30 Brahmans, e.g.
31 Take __ for the worse
32 *Olympia* artist
34 Unevenness
35 Put on __ (act snooty)
38 Kind of congestion
39 Award-show prop
44 Nested layers
46 States of warning
48 Bright display
49 Mindless followers
50 Auto racer Yarborough
51 Phrase of doubt
52 "__ Yellow Ribbon . . ."
53 Newspaper page
54 Sudden noise
55 Ultimatum word
56 Vital part

169 POSTSCRIPTS by Randolph Ross

ACROSS
1 Brit's raincoat
4 Complain
8 Nicolas of *Moonstruck*
12 Verdi opera
13 Mild cigar
15 Quite excited
16 Early Beatles song
18 Math course
19 "__ you so!"
20 Boards Amtrak
22 "Sausage" anagram
25 Hard work
26 Biblical song
31 Bottle tops
34 Dessert wedge
35 __ Gay
36 Have a bug
37 You may mind them
40 Come out first
41 First-quality
43 College in NYC
44 On the briny
45 Artful liar
49 Casino implement
50 WWII camps
54 In the cellar
58 Bowling-alley button
59 Auto rod
60 Freud's line
63 Couturier Christian
64 Ancient Aegean region
65 In a snit
66 Sorbonne summers
67 Beatty and Buntline
68 Hear a case

DOWN
1 Spritzes
2 Bolivian bye-bye
3 Draft orders
4 20% of MXXV
5 Draft order
6 Mirthful Martha
7 Immediately if not sooner
8 Majorcan lanugage
9 Culture commencer
10 Enter
11 Meringue ingredients
12 Samoan capital
14 __ sorts (peevish)
17 Harem quarters
21 Six Flags attractions
23 Open spaces
24 Director Kazan
27 __ Park, NJ
28 They may be exchanged
29 Nastase of tennis
30 Carvey or Delany
31 Yokum's creator
32 Snobs' put-on
33 Ballet move
37 Step on it
38 Archaeological expeditions
39 Bow out
42 Columbo's cases
44 Minimally
46 Giraffe's cousin
47 Tutoring session
48 Asian apparel
51 Early American tycoon
52 Madison VP
53 Eye problem
54 Miami's county
55 Way out
56 Spiny houseplant
57 Actress Daly
61 El __ (Spanish hero)
62 Gives birth to

170 OPINION OPINION by Eric Albert

ACROSS
1 Get the hang of
7 Like some victories
15 C to C, e.g.
16 Defeat
17 START OF A QUIP
19 Wield an axe
20 No longer new
21 Hoop star Thurmond
22 Razor's asset
24 Addams uncle
26 PART 2 OF QUIP
31 Slalom curve
32 Thwart a thrust
33 Pours down
35 Day-care denizen
36 Bird call
38 '60s hairstyle
42 Western resort
44 League rule
45 Crowded, initially
48 PART 3 OF QUIP
51 Orion's trade
53 Ex-Yugoslav leader
54 Wine region
55 Fly rapidly
57 "__ the ramparts . . ."
60 END OF QUIP
65 Honored one
66 Turns of phrase
67 New one in town
68 Astaire/Rogers classic

DOWN
1 Sweater muncher
2 Sign of strain
3 Worried state
4 Little bit
5 Night before
6 Safe place
7 Unpartnered
8 Roman poet
9 Gerbil, maybe
10 __ Lanka
11 Holy symbols
12 Chip in
13 Feigns feelings
14 Puts off
18 "Aha!"
22 Swamp dweller
23 Finish with the dishes
24 Wacky Wilson
25 Poet's nighttime
26 Inclined (to)
27 One opposed
28 Biblical boat
29 Sky sign
30 Watering hole
34 Authority
36 *Mermaids* star
37 Opp. of vert.
39 Follies name
40 Controlled
41 Be in the red
43 Friend of Tarzan
44 Drill insert
45 Shoulder garments
46 Head headlong for
47 In a road show
49 Big name in elevators
50 Silly-willy
52 Jeweled headdress
55 Fancy party
56 Lustful look
57 "Oops!"
58 Madame Bovary
59 Take five
61 Col. superior
62 Joplin opus
63 Altar vow
64 Tout's offering

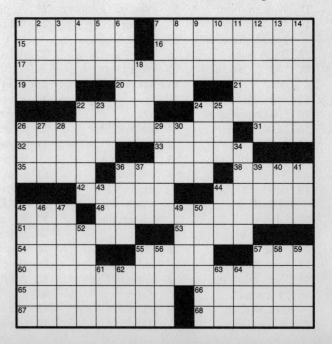

171 FRUIT SALAD by Mel Rosen

ACROSS
1 Iceberg part
4 "Sink" or "swim"
8 Ranks high
13 Pisa dough
14 Roundish
15 Wear away
16 "What's the big __?"
17 *Doctor Zhivago* heroine
18 Mongol invader
19 Not fem.
20 Loud firecracker
22 Gibson of tennis
24 Gather in
25 Big jerk
27 Masters, for one
32 Office areas
37 Sketched out
38 Skin-cream additive
39 Sprinter's must
41 Made an unreturned serve
42 Sweeps upward
44 Harvesting machines
46 Complained
48 Fairway warning
49 Camp beds
52 Behind-the-scenes
56 "Nonsense!"
61 "Would __ to you?"
62 Told the world
63 Present time?
64 Church area
65 Crème de la crème
66 Treat meat
67 Greek letters
68 Houston's home
69 Makes a choice
70 Choose: Abbr.

DOWN
1 Kind of wave
2 "__ my case"
3 "Dandy!"
4 Pinatubo and Krakatoa
5 "Well, Did You __!" (Porter tune)
6 Less common
7 Loud sound
8 Did a letter over
9 Bedouin
10 Oz visitor
11 Dutch cheese
12 Belgrade native
13 Succotash bean
21 Teen's exclamation
23 Dumbo's wing
26 Keystone __
28 Info sources
29 Dash or relay
30 Water pitcher
31 Some footballers
32 On the toasty side
33 Mixed bag
34 Sub __ (secretly)
35 Came upon
36 Feudal worker
40 Bishops' districts
43 Withdraws (from)
45 Big leaguer
47 Big parties
50 Mexican resort
51 Provide a recap
53 Tickle pink
54 Be a match for
55 Some shirts
56 Aid in crime
57 Lose color
58 __-fixe menu
59 "__ Smile Be Your Umbrella"
60 Tea table

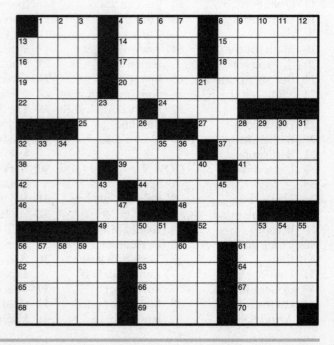

172 CHILD'S PLAY by Eric Albert

ACROSS
1 Mensa qualifier
7 Boy Scout's reference
15 Swain
16 Open to discussion
17 Western hero
19 "__ Smile Be Your Umbrella"
20 Boffo show
21 "No __, ands, or buts!"
24 Brit's greeting
26 Lose brightness
30 Dust-jacket text
33 Frolicsome
34 Grandchild of Adam
35 Governmental system
37 Gizmo
39 Square-dance song
41 Sort of sword
43 Turn into steam
46 "Famous" cookiemaker
47 Actor Cariou
48 Artist's A-frame
49 Ancient story
50 *Andrea* __
52 Clothes line
53 Cranberries' place
54 PDQ relative
57 Whoopi Goldberg film of '86
65 Silk headgear
66 Wears away
67 Wearying
68 Squirrel, for one

DOWN
1 Mr. Kabibble
2 Status __
3 Inside info
4 List-ending abbr.
5 Where the rubber meets the road
6 Faithfulness
7 Old witch
8 In a mischievous manner
9 Mystery writer Marsh
10 Wipe the woodwork
11 __-relief
12 Japanese sash
13 Of long standing
14 Important
18 Nothing at all
21 Apple rival
22 Andy Capp's wife
23 Astronomer's sighting
25 Pilot's break
26 It's often felt
27 Great suffering
28 Deer's daughter
29 Superlative suffix
31 Debonair
32 French cheese
36 EMT specialty
37 Rip off
38 Spiny succulent
40 Zealous sort
41 Wool source
42 A Little Woman
44 Last letter
45 Shade source
47 Big blockage
50 "Tiny Bubbles" singer
51 One with a query
53 Slant
55 Oversized hairdo
56 Walk wearily
57 Make a note
58 Wire-service abbr.
59 *Mal de* __
60 Prefix for fix
61 Corroded
62 Citrus drink
63 State rep.
64 FDR's successor

ROCK CONCERT by Bob Lubbers

ACROSS
1 Western actor Jack
5 Makeshift store
10 Straw vote
14 Name for a poodle
15 Japanese-American
16 Part of B&O
17 How geologists take things?
19 Tach readings
20 Noisy napper
21 Park art
23 Ignore the script
26 GI entrée
27 Highway hangings
30 John __ Passos
32 Upper crust
35 Refuses to
36 Genderless
38 Mannerless man
39 Vane dir.
40 Protective coats
41 __ out a living
42 Half of CIV
43 Pencil's place
44 Govt. agents

45 Sci-fi weapon
47 Choose: Abbr.
48 Civil-rights leader Medgar
49 Fumble one's speech
51 Lively dances
53 Wealthy woman
56 Don't act up
60 ''Nova'' anagram
61 Geologist's assay gear?
64 Frying medium
65 What you see
66 Twist out of shape
67 Some brothers
68 Wyoming range
69 Collar insert

DOWN
1 Gees' preceders
2 Elsa's dad
3 Continental prefix
4 Itinerant worker
5 Traffic tie-up
6 Foil material
7 ''__ live and breathe!''

8 NBA team
9 Eating plans
10 Mine entrance
11 Geologist's favorite song?
12 Pie ingredient
13 Investor's bane
18 Bright shades
22 Sound-alikes of a sort
24 High standards
25 More daring, like a geologist?
27 ''Peachy keen!''
28 Old Aegean region
29 Geologist's encouraging words?
31 Brosnan role
33 Bet acceptor
34 Perfect places
36 Classical prefix
37 Make a mistake
40 Shoulder movement
44 *Maude* and *Rhoda*

46 Four-legged Kenyans
48 TVA power
50 Send simoleons
52 *The Beverly Hillbillies* star
53 Broad valley

54 Roundish shape
55 Coleridge work
57 Get __ on the back
58 Ms. Miles
59 Catch sight of
62 *The __ in the Hat*
63 In olden days

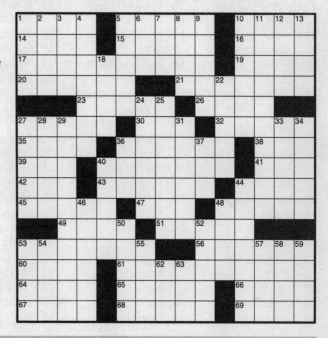

SPORTS CENTER by S.N.

ACROSS
1 Oil initials
5 __ Hari
9 Drink deeply
14 Canadian prov.
15 *Jeopardy!* name
16 Excessive
17 Klinger portrayer
18 Undaffy
19 Aircraft walkway
20 Comes home, sort of
22 Scout Carson
23 Wedding-column word
24 ''If __ a Hammer''
26 Road ''beetles''
29 __ *bene*
31 Absolute ruler
32 Schnozz
33 Pirate Hall-of-Famer
36 1980 Wimbledon winner
37 Midwestern hockey team
38 __ *Wonderful Life*
39 Manor master
40 Troubleless

41 Badminton boundary
42 A little change
43 Graceful tree
44 Shake up
45 Antebellum Confederacy
50 Kiddie-lit elephant
53 Hawaiian holiday spot
54 '60s spy airplane
55 Flabbergast
56 RBI, e.g.
57 Charlotte et al.
58 Posh
59 Slangy turndown
60 ''__ a Lady'' (Jones tune)

DOWN
1 Clumsy folk
2 Urban map
3 Raison d'__
4 CBer's need
5 En __ (as a group)
6 Jai __
7 French Revolution event

8 Tree cutter
9 Dennis of *Innerspace*
10 Single thing
11 Paid notices
12 Spoon or joy ending
13 Professional payment
21 Absorbed, as a school subject
22 Writer Čapek and director Reisz
25 Saltlike
26 Not arterial
27 British alemaker
28 Keel-rudderpost connectors
29 Replace an old obligation
30 Orchestral member
31 Have nothing __ (get stuck, detective-wise)
32 Makes alluring
33 Varnish ingredient
34 Penn's partner

35 Mercer and Normand
42 Singer Mariah
43 Mrs. Bunker
44 Dizzy's genre
46 Waikiki feast
47 Western state

48 Bird call
49 Cartwright boy
50 Ingot
51 ''What a good boy __''
52 Mr. Masterson
53 College at E. Lansing

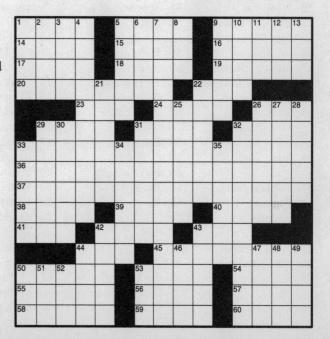

AUTO SUGGESTION by Donna J. Stone

ACROSS

1 Greek-salad ingredient
5 *Soapdish* star
10 __ of the Roses
14 Court-martial candidate
15 *Unsafe at Any Speed* author
16 Seer's sign
17 Floor model
18 Boston Symphony leader
19 Printing process
20 START OF A QUIP
23 Frome of fiction
25 Morse message
26 Show follower
27 Bud's buddy
28 Sound of shock
32 Old saw
34 Poet's foot
36 "OK with me!"
39 MIDDLE OF QUIP
42 Sea World attraction
43 Spitz sounds
46 Gandhi, e.g.
49 Spirited steed
51 Letters of credit?
52 *Wheel of Fortune* buy
53 Erich __ Stroheim
56 Capp character
58 END OF QUIP
63 Dilatorily
64 Philip Nolan's fate
65 Just around the corner
68 *Dukes of Hazzard* deputy
69 Term-paper need
70 The Fatman's friend
71 Bears' lairs
72 First sign
73 *Kismet* setting

DOWN

1 In thing
2 Flock female
3 Barnum attraction
4 Ho "Hi!"
5 Chest gripper
6 Be idle
7 Lupino and Tarbell
8 Small salamanders
9 Thalia's sister
10 Despicable one
11 It multiplies by dividing
12 Tommy of *Lassie*
13 Cop some z's
21 MIT grad
22 Hayes or Stern
23 Gin name
24 __ T (perfectly)
29 "I've Got __ in Kalamazoo"
30 Pea product
31 Turkish title
33 Action time
35 Melville character
37 Successor
38 Author Ferber
40 "__ Got a Friend"
41 Slickers and such
44 "The Gold Bug" author
45 Big __, CA
46 Rained hard?
47 Crackers
48 Vegas singer
50 Do away with
54 __ a customer
55 *Six Crises* author
57 Dog star
59 Musical Myra
60 Counter change
61 Bjorn opponent
62 Splinter group
66 Alias letters
67 Purchase paperwork: Abbr.

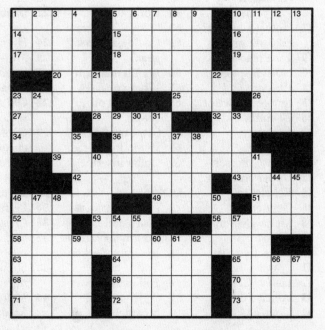

COMPARISONS by Mel Rosen

ACROSS

1 Practice boxing
5 Break up
9 Work out on ice
14 Wash up
15 Bassoon relative
16 Heaps up
17 Voice of America org.
18 Wildcat
19 Showy display
20 Quick-witted
23 Plane holders
24 Datsun, nowadays
28 AP rival
29 New York stadium
31 Cable choice
32 Sagacious
36 Sounds of delight
37 Oath words
38 Sun. speech
39 Seafood delicacy
40 Bro or sis
41 Unfettered
46 "Annabel Lee" author
47 Hitchcock's __ *Window*
48 Cutesy suffix
49 Wimpole or Wall
51 Sponsors of a sort
55 Really irate
58 Have a nosh
61 Solitary
62 Tibetan monk
63 Blender setting
64 Rom. Cath. official
65 Estrada of *CHiPs*
66 Fed the kitty
67 Bean plants
68 Be worthy of

DOWN

1 Semi-melted snow
2 Turkish title
3 Bird-related
4 Debate again
5 The North Star
6 Chasm
7 Writer Jaffe
8 Schoolbook
9 Short-term sale
10 Soccer shots
11 The whole nine yards
12 1773 jetsam
13 Part of i.e.
21 "__ Doc" Duvalier
22 Over again
25 Puppeteer Lewis
26 Dislike a lot
27 __ around (snooped)
29 Scornful look
30 Israeli dance
32 Filmy strands
33 Dostoyevsky's *The __*
34 Levelheaded
35 On a cruise
41 __ out (went berserk)
42 On a pension: Abbr.
43 Volcanoes, e.g.
44 Top-notch
45 Soda maker
50 Variety-show host
51 Mean and low
52 Tara family name
53 Send money
54 Idaho river
56 Charity
57 Just fair
58 Hot tub
59 Convent resident
60 Mr. Buchwald

177   NAME-ING NAMES by Eric Albert

ACROSS
1 Quite stylish
5 Wood-trimming tool
9 Monastery head
14 Late-night TV name
15 Make money
16 Zero people
17 Harsh, as weather
19 These times
20 BING
22 Choir offerings
23 Jimmy Carter's daughter
24 Sample soda
27 The night before
28 On edge
31 Jupiter's wife
32 Bring together
34 Civil-suit subjects
35 MING
40 Flatten
41 Up, on a map
42 State with confidence
43 Sir Newton
45 Shoot the breeze

48 Basinger of *Batman*
49 African snake
50 Delicate purple
52 RING
57 Man with a horn
59 Tropical fish
60 Basic belief
61 Stare stupidly
62 Dennis, to Mr. Wilson
63 Has in mind
64 *Born Free* character
65 Genealogy diagram

DOWN
1 Overused phrase
2 Shakespearean subject
3 What you earn
4 List-introducing punctuation
5 Peak
6 Person of action
7 Galvanization need
8 Catch, in a way

9 Champing at the bit
10 Hapless one
11 Ride the waves
12 "__ Clear Day"
13 Mystery writer Josephine
18 USN rank
21 "Peg __ Heart"
25 Excited by
26 Sit for shots
28 Lively dance
29 ET vehicle
30 Leading lady Loy
31 Kid around
32 Software runner
33 Gretzky's org.
34 Explosive initials
35 Hostile reaction
36 Jeans name
37 Common prayer
38 Film-noir classic
39 Mythical beast
43 Funnyman Kabibble
44 Sea creature

45 Author Grass
46 Not willing
47 Scold severely
49 Building blocks of matter
50 Gold-chained actor
51 Highly skilled

53 Familiar with
54 Honest-to-goodness
55 Nadirs
56 "My Way" singer
57 Rye partner
58 What a feller needs?

178   CARRY ALL by Alex Vaughn

ACROSS
1 Way to address a lady
5 *M*A*S*H* character
10 Exxon's ex-name
14 __ *La Douce*
15 Run off and wed
16 Zhivago's love
17 Mortgage, e.g.
18 Something extra
19 Radiate
20 Joey carrier
23 Bullfight "bravo"
24 Had what __ (measured up)
27 Syrup source
30 Because you were challenged
34 French "one"
35 They kiss
37 Direction, in Durango
38 Neighborhoods
39 Introduction to metrics?
40 Sup at home

41 At __ (wholesale)
42 Visigoths' doing
44 Bard's "before"
45 He really kneads you
46 Actor Beatty
47 *Cheers* star
49 Wine word
51 Matter-of-taste remark
58 Himalayas' home
60 Still in contention
61 Rubik's device
62 Visual signal
63 Sham artist
64 Recline idly
65 Keyed up
66 Makes level
67 Peers at

DOWN
1 Cereal partner
2 Moffo solo
3 Solemn assent
4 Tropical fruit

5 Kind of collision
6 Actor Ray
7 Unprogressive one
8 Each
9 Louvre display
10 Vote in
11 Revered Texan
12 __ Lanka
13 Bran source
21 Spiny houseplants
22 Western Indian
25 Airline-board phrase
26 Wailed
27 Skipped a line
28 __ borealis
29 Ringmaster's word
31 Assumed name
32 They're round and flat
33 Buy a pig in __
36 Rode the bench
37 Lobe's locale
40 Mr. Zimbalist
42 Southwestern capital

43 Dismissals
45 Bird Maoris once hunted
48 Not very secure
50 Repetitive pattern
52 Croat, for one
53 Reebok rival

54 Pizza place?
55 Harbor bobber
56 Well-qualified
57 Solidifies
58 Wide-eyed wonder
59 Imogene's cohort

MAP OF THE STARS by Randolph Ross

ACROSS
1 Congressman Aspin
4 __ facto
8 Mr. Waller
12 Clinton's home
14 Touch against
15 *Arsenic and Old Lace* actress
17 "You're __ and don't know it"
18 CIA predecessor
19 *Exodus* hero
21 *Monitor* foe
25 Learner's need
27 Media revenue source
28 Simile center
29 Sushi-bar selections
30 *Cheers* actress
35 *Perry Mason* role
36 *The Big Chill* actress
38 Aid in crime
39 __ for "apple"
40 Reb inits.
43 *All __* (Miller play)
46 Gets rid of
49 Slalom curve
50 Shoe specification
52 Employee's last words
53 Wimbledon winner in '70
58 Golden-__ (senior citizen)
59 Astronomical event
60 One of Jacob's sons
61 Bartlett's abbr.
62 Night spot

DOWN
1 Drank like a cat
2 Scoreboard column
3 Killy, for one
4 Business-letterhead letters
5 Greek letter
6 "My Gal __"
7 Cold capital
8 Like some bottoms
9 Lawyers' org.
10 Sandwich order
11 Germfree
13 Italian wine region
16 Small snake
17 *I __ Fugitive from a Chain Gang*
20 Bitsy preceder
22 Comic actress Gibbs
23 Ore analysis
24 Unwitting dupe
26 Civil War signature
30 __ the city (mayor's bestowal)
31 Sort
32 Let __ (don't touch)
33 Make a clean slate
34 NRC predecessor
35 Equine event
36 Jerry Herman musical
37 Just awful
40 Golf links
41 Was right for
42 Member of 9 Down
44 Silents siren
45 Diver's place
47 "New Look" designer
48 Short news item
51 Author Bombeck
54 Gun the engine
55 Lunch ending
56 As well
57 Where to see Larry King

HEAVEN FOR BID! by Donna J. Stone

ACROSS
1 Analyzed sentences
7 Clammy
11 Race downhill
14 Pianist de Larrocha
15 Bridge support
16 Groan producer
17 START OF A QUIP
19 Part of SBLI
20 Robert __ Marley
21 Cleanse
23 *Three Men __ Baby*
26 Admitted, with "up"
29 *Scarface* star
30 Last word in fashion
32 Mythical twin
34 Cartoon cat
35 Boss' note
36 MIDDLE OF QUIP
41 Cut out cake
42 Giggle sound
45 Most promptly
49 Tile game
51 Behold, to Brutus
52 Jeweler's measure
54 As a result
55 Mideast nation
57 Tall story?
59 Dos Passos trilogy
60 END OF QUIP
66 Velvet finish
67 Get-up-and-go
68 Crewel tool
69 Drain-cleaner ingredient
70 D'Artagnan prop
71 Whirled

DOWN
1 Pastoral god
2 Inn quaff
3 *6 Rms, __ Vu*
4 Game plan
5 Irish republic
6 *Family Feud* host
7 Armless sofa
8 Justice Fortas
9 Framing need
10 Play thing?
11 Inflationary pattern
12 Martial art
13 Atlas features
18 Periodic-table info: Abbr.
22 Montevideo's loc.
23 Campaign name of '36
24 Dundee denial
25 Punctually
27 "... __ saw Elba"
28 St. Paul's feature
31 Ooze
33 March, but not mazurka
35 *The A-Team* star
37 Go for broke
38 Salad cheese
39 Feeling low
40 Restaurateur Toots
43 MIT grad
44 Inflated feeling
45 *Batman Returns*, e.g.
46 *Purple Dust* playwright
47 Gas rating
48 PBS benefactor
49 __ Hari
50 Bring into harmony
53 Alto or bass
56 Tear down
58 Completed the cake
61 Helpful hint
62 *Wheel of Fortune* buy
63 A mean Amin
64 Message to a matador
65 Nancy Drew's boyfriend

181 SACK TIME by Bob Lubbers

ACROSS
1 Short letter
5 No longer trendy
10 Did the butterfly
14 General Idi
15 Dangerous whales
16 Mexican money
17 Doris Day film of '59
19 Mr. Preminger
20 What you wear
21 Kenyan capital
23 Parking aide
25 Steel factory
26 Pasta shapes
28 Dwarf trees
31 Like __ of bricks
32 Rat-race result
34 FDR agency
35 Seamstress Ross
37 Corn unit
38 Accurate, pitchwise
40 Outs' partners
41 __ of Jeannie
44 Poetic nighttimes
45 Hats, so to speak
47 So far
49 Part to play
50 Pavarotti, for one
51 Elizabeth II's house
53 Beethoven opus
57 Author Morrison
58 Ductwork material
60 Suggest strongly
61 Floor, in France
62 Shaker contents
63 Porgy's love
64 Copter part
65 Normandy town

DOWN
1 Western wine region
2 Leave out
3 Pinball problem
4 Perks up
5 General Colin's family
6 Whistler works
7 Barely enough
8 Room, to Roberto
9 Kayak builders
10 Thread holders
11 Party pooper
12 Italy's answer to 1 Down
13 Pasture plaint
18 Evangelist Roberts
22 Duz rival
24 Organic compounds
26 Dictation taker
27 Arkansas resort
28 Chew out
29 Actress Dunne
30 Simon follower
31 Just slightly
33 Norma __
36 Investor's concern
39 Proximity
42 Bedroom piece
43 Godzilla or Rodan
46 Shetlands, e.g.
48 Unavoidable fate
50 Pick up the tab
51 Got tiresome
52 "__ be in England . . ."
54 Rat-__
55 Hard to believe
56 Palo __, CA
57 Rickety ship
59 Self-image

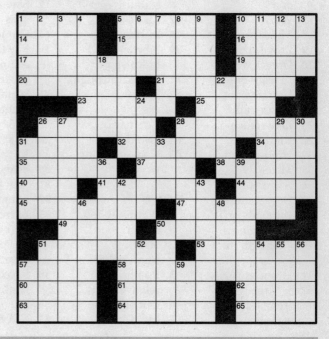

182 IT'S SHOW TIME! by Eric Albert

ACROSS
1 Johann Sebastian __
5 Dick and Jane's dog
9 Son of Seth
13 .405 hectare
14 Knee-bone neighbor
16 Norway native
17 Jane Fonda film of '86
20 Chop down
21 Anti-flood structure
22 Senselessness
23 Beauteous group
24 Mr. Laurel
25 Sale sweetener
28 Smile broadly
29 Fast way to England
32 Eye-bending designs
33 All in
34 Concerned with
35 Pacino film of '75
38 Cools down, in a way
39 "Working or not"
40 Marry in haste
41 Bobby Orr's org.
42 Englishman, for short
43 Belmont Stakes winner in '75
44 Brought into being
45 Chicken fixin's
46 Girl, to Dundee
49 "Excuse me!"
50 Sundial's 7
53 Randy Quaid film of '78
56 Exodus author
57 Country singer Steve
58 Kind of vaccine
59 Nerd
60 African nation
61 Little shaver

DOWN
1 Shower alternative
2 Liniment target
3 Stagehands
4 Fabric border
5 Work hard
6 Little finger
7 Off-Broadway award
8 Soft metal
9 Like leprechauns
10 Post-WWII alliance
11 Powerful cartel
12 Energetic
15 Stir up
18 Folk-blues singer
19 Economist Smith
23 Epic poets
24 Does ushering
25 The Thinker sculptor
26 Noteworthy period
27 Roll with a hole
28 Are suited for
29 Snobby one
30 "His face could __ clock"
31 Copier need
33 Count of jazz
34 Bride's acquisition
36 Gridiron gain
37 Make over
42 It's east of Java
43 Karamazov brother
44 Capital of Belarus
45 Nut case
46 Too confident
47 Take on
48 Singer Adams
49 Razor brand
50 Oft-used adverb
51 Meryl, in Out of Africa
52 Capri, for one
54 Swiss partner
55 Balderdash

183 YES, YES, YES! by Trip Payne

ACROSS

1 *Casablanca* role
4 Lobster eater's wear
7 Lustrous fabric
13 Pretended to be
16 Geronimo, for one
17 Warn
18 Mine workers
19 Prove false
20 Dry, as wine
22 "This is only __"
23 Haughty one
24 Tissue cell
26 Like some pots
28 Kind of file
32 Hindu chant
35 Males
36 Aware of
37 Does as told -
38 Winner's prize
39 Coming next
40 "Whip It" rock group
41 __ and aah
42 __ Creed (religious statement)
43 Rebekah's son
44 Cactus type
46 Not up
48 Mail agcy.
52 Fuel nuggets
55 4/15 org.
56 Floorboard sound
57 Like some inspections
59 Tibetan hideaway
61 Riffled (through)
62 *The Moon and __*
63 Gets narrower
64 Gaming cube
65 Understanding words

DOWN

1 Warms up for a bout
2 Standish stand-in
3 Rumba relative
4 Out of shape
5 Mr. Amin
6 Droopy dog
7 Fish, in a way
8 Bee-related
9 Logically expected event
10 Top level
11 "__ a Lady"
12 Superman's alias
14 Groucho show
15 Ray Charles' commercial backup
21 Social pariah
24 Hunters' org.
25 Offs' opposite
27 __ *gratia artis*
29 Kitty starter
30 British gun
31 Skin feature
32 Manner
33 Burrows and Vigoda
34 St. Petersburg's river
38 Raccoon relative
39 Put on TV
41 CIA forerunner
42 Shrewish type
45 Tacit
47 Nitrate, e.g.
49 "__ evil . . ."
50 Shrivel with heat
51 Some terriers
52 Stable youth
53 Draftable person
54 PDQ kin
56 Horn, for one
58 Bradley and McBain
60 1011, to Tacitus

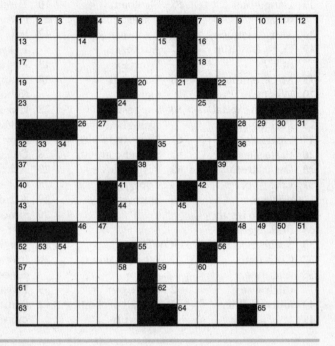

184 SIX FIFTEENS by Mel Rosen

ACROSS

1 __ Romeo
5 Complete victory
10 Not processed
13 Mother of William and Harry
15 Jeweled headpiece
16 Miss. neighbor
17 Newspaper staffer
20 Speedometer's meas.
21 Make (one's way)
22 Knock for a loop
23 "__ Old Cowhand"
25 Tough test
29 Check total
31 Trumpet effect
32 Sixth sense
35 Sperry's partner
36 Changes shades
37 Sault __ Marie, MI
38 Iowan, for one
43 Half and half?
44 Clapton of rock
45 A big jerk
46 Home, in the phone book
47 Chihuahua child
48 Plumed military hats
50 Dry-cleaning worker
52 Lancastrian symbol
53 Inner drive
55 Prefix for focus
57 *Die Fledermaus*
60 Carpentry contraption
65 Early gardener
66 Pleasure boat
67 Couldn't stand
68 Round Table address
69 Miller rival
70 Evergreen shrubs

DOWN

1 Hockey star Oates
2 Emulate Daffy
3 Dior, for one
4 *Wheel of Fortune* buy
5 Mr. Musial
6 Department-store staffer
7 Do lunch
8 Poetic preposition
9 Mini-notebook
10 Hiker's risk
11 Manager Felipe
12 Put on notice
14 Dam in Egypt
18 Bivouac quarters
19 "This __ fine how-do-you-do!"
24 Newsman Roger
26 Beams of light
27 Eat more sensibly
28 Additional
29 Jouster's protection
30 Memorable vessel
33 Office skill, for short
34 Job benefits
39 Carson successor
40 Moran of *Happy Days*
41 Cellar stock
42 Thick-piled rugs
48 Mex. miss
49 Cheap booze
51 Alert color
53 Puts to work
54 Sitarist Shankar
56 Judges of a sort
58 Once more
59 Koppel and Turner
61 Coll. deg.
62 "Xanadu" group
63 Old card game
64 Loft material

185 WATER MUSIC by Donna J. Stone

ACROSS
1. British buggy
5. Window sticker
10. Bridge charge
14. Old bird
15. Display conspicuously
16. "__ Around" (Beach Boys tune)
17. College courtyard
18. Wagner's father-in-law
19. Loquacious equine
20. Italian water music?
23. Pine product
24. R-V hookup?
25. Texas state tree
28. "So that's your game!"
31. Tire Town, USA
35. Epoch
36. Cantaloupe's cousin
39. Narrow shoe size
40. French water music?
43. Czech river
44. Singer Brewer
45. Sleeve contents?
46. Ball-bearing attractions?
48. Neighbor of Jord.
49. *Gaslight* star
51. Inept sort
53. Wine and dine
54. Chinese water music?
61. Jupiter's alias
62. Michelangelo subject
63. Hardly hyper
65. Sacred cow
66. Cockamamie
67. Raison d'__
68. Scads
69. Vacuum-tube gas
70. Pants part

DOWN
1. Pronto, initially
2. No gentleman
3. *Queen for __*
4. Pavarotti's birthplace
5. Dutch pottery
6. Way out
7. Old Testament kingdom
8. Cooper's tool
9. Baltic natives
10. Faraway place
11. Mythical monster
12. Lascivious look
13. Inc., in Ireland
21. Light weight
22. "Make __ double!"
25. Señorita's shekels
26. Carve a canyon
27. __ cropper (failed)
28. Grate stuff
29. Like Esau
30. Capp character
32. Settle accounts
33. In reserve
34. *Unsafe at Any Speed* author
37. ABA member
38. Horse cousin
41. Bobby Vinton #1 tune
42. Off-limits
47. Lose energy
50. Lots and lots
52. Recruit's NJ home
53. Valhalla VIP
54. Skywalker's teacher
55. Revlon rival
56. Big name in westerns
57. Writer Hunter
58. Producer De Laurentiis
59. Hung up
60. Pound of poetry
61. Dandy's first name?
64. Even so

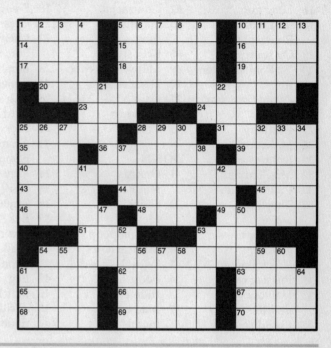

186 GOOD SKATES by Randolph Ross

ACROSS
1. Actress Gardner
4. Shipboard officers
9. TV host Donahue
13. Like a wet rag
15. Some exams
16. Not well-done
17. __ above (minimally)
18. '88 Olympics skater
20. Of a lord's estate
22. Beginning
23. '68 Olympics skater
26. Actor Alejandro
27. *Exodus* role
28. Mauna __
31. Grimm villain
34. Utmost, so to speak
36. '92 Olympics skater
40. Shares secrets with
41. Converse
42. It's inspiring
43. Get __ of (eliminate)
44. Suns do it
46. '84 Olympics skater
52. Crazy as __
55. Paint solvents
56. '32 Olympics skater
59. Ms. Barrett
60. "Cheerio!"
61. *Look Back in __*
62. Tree knot
63. Haywire
64. Impolite looks
65. Els' followers

DOWN
1. ". . . __ unto my feet"
2. Curriculum __ (résumé)
3. In the company of
4. Make changes to
5. "And we'll have __ good time"
6. Postpone
7. Actor Wallach
8. Sleek plane
9. Fork tine
10. Deli meats
11. "*Dies __*" (hymn)
12. "__ we forget"
14. Go forward
19. Sharpening
21. Whiskey type
24. Address after "yes"
25. Film role for Shirley
28. Polish political name
29. Workplace agcy.
30. Working hard
31. Ark. neighbor
32. Got taller
33. Communion, e.g.
34. Marino or McGrew
35. Air carriers
37. Albania's capital
38. Monogram part: Abbr.
39. *The Empire Strikes Back* teacher
44. Shows contempt
45. Stop for a bite
46. Savalas role
47. Kitchen appliance
48. More frosty
49. Make a hole __
50. Midmorning
51. Peter and Nicholas
52. Nick Charles' pooch
53. Sandy soil
54. Familiar with
57. *2001* computer
58. Compass pt.

SO WHAT? by Trip Payne

ACROSS

1 Barely open
5 Con game
9 Paper layers
14 U.S. national flower
15 Balsa or balsam
16 Long gun
17 '77 Linda Ronstadt tune
19 Oil source
20 '82 Pointer Sisters tune
22 *Falcon Crest* star
26 Binge
27 Draft org.
28 Makes up (for)
30 Dolores __ Rio
32 Mrs. Truman
33 Cajun veggie
37 They hold water
40 '83 Lauper album
43 Kiss follow-up?
44 Piece of cake
45 Halves of quartets
47 Could possibly
49 Heavy-hitting hammer
51 Pedigree grp.
54 Snake poison
58 "__ my case"
59 '73 Carly Simon tune
62 Gourmand
63 '63 Chiffons tune
68 Skirt style
69 Midwestern tribe
70 Hertz rival
71 Gave a PG-13 to
72 Go down
73 College book

DOWN

1 Onassis, familiarly
2 Scribble (down)
3 Nincompoop
4 Musical notes
5 Wineglass part
6 Boorish and rude
7 Man with morals
8 Mr. Lansky
9 Goes forward
10 Caron movie
11 __ *Tuesday, This Must Be Belgium*
12 Arctic assistants
13 Burpee products
18 French river
21 Crossed out
22 Chemist's second home
23 Bomb tryout
24 General Dayan
25 11th-century saint
29 "Send help!"
31 Cosmetics name
34 Wins the bout
35 10-K, for one
36 Santa __ , CA
38 Bea Arthur sitcom
39 Walks heavily
41 Drooled
42 Pkg. co.
46 Matched group
48 "Without a doubt!"
50 Floor covering, for short
51 Once __ (annually)
52 Eucalyptus muncher
53 Make the grade
55 "Never!"
56 __ Culp Hobby
57 Bricklayer
60 Russo of *Lethal Weapon 3*
61 "Uh-huh . . ."
64 What *gras* means
65 "__ been had!"
66 Put the kibosh on
67 Guinness Book suffix

HIGH HOPES by Shirley Soloway

ACROSS

1 Get away from
7 Colorful shell
14 Footstool
15 New Jersey river
16 Wishful pursuit
18 Gary and Mary
19 *Dallas* matriarch
20 Ottawa's prov.
21 Sword handle
24 Make a choice
28 Clairvoyant ability
30 Slow mover
32 Caviar
33 Bea of vaudeville
35 *One Day at* __
37 Wishful pursuit
41 O'er opposite
42 Expenditure
43 One-third of MCCIII
44 Blossom holder
45 Art, to Antony
48 Mr. Melville
52 Wedding vows
54 Comic Philips
56 "You __ be congratulated!"
58 Mint jelly
60 Wistful pursuit
65 Large wardrobe
66 Is indicative of
67 Hold back
68 Hams it up

DOWN

1 Fuel gas
2 Gets underway
3 The bottom line
4 Pennsylvania sect
5 Hook's nemesis
6 Liberia's lang.
7 Asian inland sea
8 __ out (uses a chute)
9 *L.A. Law* guy
10 Suit grounds
11 Western Indian
12 Slangy refusal
13 Printer's widths
14 Acapulco octet
17 Payback
22 Punching tools
23 Paper sheets
25 Buffalo's lake
26 Robin Cook book
27 Be abundant
29 Evil scheme
31 Turned gooey
34 Self suffix
35 Tooth pros' grp.
36 "__ Little Tenderness"
37 About 2.5 centimeters
38 Old-time Persian
39 Matched set
40 Brat in *Blondie*
46 Fame
47 Strikes down
49 Feudal estate
50 Bandleader Shaw
51 Gets close to
53 Antidrug advice
55 Folk singer Phil
57 Laces up
59 Flue dust
60 A long way off
61 Raw metal
62 Man behind the catcher
63 Commemorative verse
64 Neither masc. nor neut.

189 · SO THEY SAY by Eric Albert

ACROSS
1 Deep black
4 Leading lady Lamarr
8 Borgnine role
14 *Messiah* is one
16 Tooth covering
17 Pedestrian path
18 Unremarkable
19 HOME
21 Fish eggs
22 When Paris sizzles
23 Glimpse
26 Declare openly
28 British baby buggy
32 Farrow of films
33 Scandinavian city
35 *My Favorite Year* star
37 FAMILIARITY
40 Writer Welty
41 Ms. Sommer
42 Unit of energy
43 Checkup
44 Music symbol
46 Lavish attention (on)
47 Ave. crossers
48 Ram's mate
50 MISS
58 Get back
59 One with a marker
60 Chinese philosopher
61 Hungry for company
62 Oscar-winner as Mrs. Kramer
63 Picnic predators
64 Before marriage

DOWN
1 Kid around
2 Pennsylvania port
3 "Voila!"
4 Bookstore section
5 Clean the boards
6 Pickle flavoring
7 __ Ono
8 Cautionary sign
9 100-buck bill
10 Mata __
11 Clips and shells
12 Incline
13 Building extension
15 Towel material
20 Corp. boss
23 Patter provider
24 Crazy Horse, for one
25 Bamboo bruncher
26 Swiss peak
27 Marks a ballot
28 "El Dorado" writer
29 Cowpuncher competition
30 Make aware of
31 Join forces
33 "__ the ramparts..."
34 Get wise
36 Pipe type
38 Piper's son
39 PBJ alternative
45 Leg. title
46 Salami shops
47 Take by force
48 Major happening
49 Walks through water
50 Essential point
51 Composer Stravinsky
52 Recent
53 Pac-10 member
54 Common supplement
55 Kind of collar
56 Dome home zone
57 Kite nemesis
58 *Kidnapped* monogram

190 · SECURITY RISK by Donna J. Stone

ACROSS
1 Dict. abbr.
4 Epsilon follower
8 Coeur d'__, ID
13 Perrins' partner
14 Cheese choice
15 Partonesque
16 START OF A QUIP
19 Calculator ancestor
20 Ale place
21 Sapphire side
22 Make up (for)
24 Citrus cooler
26 Busy as __
27 Napoleon's fate
28 Aftereffect
29 "Cool!" in school
30 Numerical suffix
31 Folklore being
32 MIDDLE OF QUIP
35 Menotti title character
38 Tropical tuber
39 Sine __ non
42 Scads
43 Former African country name
45 Hair balls?
46 Parker product
47 They may be greased
48 Shearer of *The Red Shoes*
49 '60s dance
51 Short snooze
52 END OF QUIP
55 Take __ at (attempt)
56 Make a buck
57 Vane reading
58 Bedtime reading
59 Eye problem
60 Cherry shade

DOWN
1 Morgiana's master
2 Wrote graffiti
3 Local booster
4 *The Odyssey* character
5 Actor Byrnes
6 Asian philosophic ideal
7 Explosive
8 Superior to
9 Mechanic's job
10 Chef's concentrate
11 Kind of sun
12 Funnyman Philips
17 No longer in style
18 Maureen O'Sullivan role
19 Out of range
22 Skating maneuver
23 Dickens character
25 Go wrong
27 *Sea Hunt* shocker
28 Actor Mineo
30 __ Aviv
31 Exit-ramp word
32 Kid's query
33 Crew-team members
34 Ending for press
35 Audiophile's purchase
36 Cary Grant's '33 costar
37 Food coloring
39 Malaria medicine
40 Like some movies
41 Urgent letters
43 Ms. Pitts
44 __ *Restaurant*
45 Pain in the neck
47 Reserve
48 Foot wiper
50 Kaiser's counterpart
51 French film
52 Great time, so to speak
53 *Krazy* __
54 Ironic

191   ORAL EXAM by Bob Lubbers

ACROSS
1 Emerald Isle
5 "This is only __"
10 Open slightly
14 Author Vidal
15 Use pointlessly
16 Prohibition
17 Litter bit
19 Is in debt
20 Two-__ (small plane)
21 Show fear
23 Verdi work
26 Kuwaiti ruler
27 Cow quarters
30 Poem of praise
32 Pop singer Billy
35 Yale athletes
36 Mixed drink
38 In the past
39 Actress Ullmann
40 Leaf-covered
41 Josh around
42 Peggy or Pinky
43 European airline
44 Soccer great
45 Sign up
47 Dapper __
48 Peels off
49 Trumpet accessory
51 Not bogus
53 Stifle
56 Unfinished rooms
60 Serve tea
61 Just misses a putt
64 Caesarean phrase
65 Select group
66 Ms. McEntire
67 Attorney Roy
68 French painter
69 Sp. ladies

DOWN
1 Ham partners
2 Libertine
3 *My Friend* __
4 Isaac and Wayne
5 Cognizant (of)
6 Beer device
7 Mind reader's talent
8 Editor's notation
9 __ Haute, IN
10 Kind of energy
11 Very hard candy
12 Genesis son
13 Ploy
18 Agts., e.g.
22 Overdo a role
24 Stirred up
25 Nimitz's title
27 Ball girl?
28 Little green man
29 Delta's locale
31 Director May
33 Fast on one's feet
34 Junction points
36 Sailor, slangily
37 Greek letter
40 Dirty stuff
44 Talks quickly
46 Beat in a heat
48 Essential part
50 Fished, in a way
52 Fence openings
53 Chance-taking, for short
54 Lorre role
55 Make angry
57 Cake topper
58 *Havana* locale
59 Fitness centers
62 Pen dweller
63 RR stop

---

192   KID STUFF by Eric Albert

ACROSS
1 Ralph __ Emerson
6 Lifeline locale
10 Wine barrel
14 Belted constellation
15 __ vera (shampoo ingredient)
16 Put money in
17 Kid-lit gold spinner
20 Leg joint
21 English prep school
22 Symbol of love
23 Vanquish a dragon
25 Potter's material
27 Squeezing snake
30 Make bubbles
31 Actress Dawber
34 Exclaimed in delight
35 Put something over on
36 Lucid
37 Kid-lit builders
40 Eccentric guy
41 St. Louis landmark
42 Fork parts
43 A question of method
44 Logan of Broadway
45 Sweet-smelling place
46 Dinner giver
47 Walesa, for one
48 __ von Bulow
51 Untrustworthy sort
53 Cluckers
57 Kid-lit siblings
60 Sty cry
61 Aroma
62 Copycat's phrase
63 The hunted
64 Actress Daly
65 Hurled

DOWN
1 Put in effort
2 Make __ for it
3 Jell-O flavor
4 Racetrack info
5 I, to Claudius
6 __-faced (pale)
7 Sax range
8 Tarzan's garment
9 Director Brooks
10 Deejay Kasem
11 "Diana" singer
12 Mix a martini
13 Superman's alter ego
18 Low in fat
19 Defrost
24 Mine find
26 Lounge lazily
27 Cover a hole
28 Exuberant cry
29 Lose on purpose
30 Make a mess of
31 *Common Sense* writer
32 Make mad
33 Needing cleaning
35 Mamie or Rosalynn
36 Shoe projection
38 Myanmar neighbor
39 Latin abbr.
44 "No way, __!"
45 Net star Bjorn
46 Sled dog
47 Army spiritual leader
48 Piece of pork
49 Den
50 Diarist Frank
52 Privy to
54 "__, Brute!"
55 Noble gas
56 Walk through mud
58 Unimproved land
59 Real-estate ad wd.

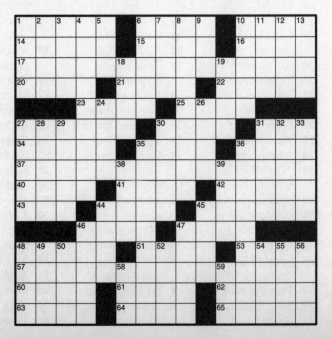

193 ALPHABETS by Lois Sidway

ACROSS

1 Way off
4 Orchestral areas
8 Alabama city
13 "Isn't It a __?" ('32 tune)
14 Conversation filler
15 Burger topping
16 Folklore baddie
17 Blind part
18 Shakespearean forest
19 Key letters
22 Actor's quest
23 __ de corps
27 A: Ger.
28 O.R. personnel
30 Matador's foe
31 Young hog
34 Message from Morris
36 Top bond rating
37 Behave
40 Vane reading
41 A Kentucky Derby prize
42 Postulate
43 "I've Got __ in Kalamazoo"
45 A Bobbsey twin
46 Evildoing
47 Tell
49 Ruse victims
53 Victory sign, to Morse
56 Where you live
59 Matured
60 __ Camera (basis for Cabaret)
61 Western capital
62 Extra
63 Prepare to swallow
64 San Diego baseballer
65 James Bond's alma mater
66 Holyfield stats

DOWN

1 Night's work for Holyfield
2 Awesome hotel lobbies
3 Deli need
4 Car part
5 Eastern religion
6 Thailand export
7 __ precedent
8 Midday TV fare
9 Filled with delight
10 It may be flipped
11 A Stooge
12 Actress Jillian
13 Ice-cream buys
20 Perry White's occupation
21 They'll buy burritos
24 Interstates
25 OPEC delegate
26 Breakfast order
28 Elevated
29 Gets some z's
31 Sloppy brushstroke
32 Be contingent
33 Peyton Place star
34 Western plateau
35 American elk
38 Musical group
39 Like Teflon
44 Painter's need
46 Depress
48 "__ Kangaroo Down, Sport"
49 Word form for "wing"
50 Spud country
51 Furniture designer
52 Henry Higgins' creator
54 British title
55 "__ the sun in the morning . . ."
56 Cleo's cobra
57 Ewe said it
58 Like Mother Hubbard

194 BODY SOUNDS by Fred Piscop

ACROSS

1 __ it up (overacts)
5 Wilma's hubby
9 Birch relative
14 Blind as __
15 Like some hair
16 Superman star
17 Ms. Barrett
18 Krugerrand, for one
19 Like some fences
20 TOE
23 Phonograph needles
24 Form of wrestling
25 Gun grp.
28 Ave. crossings
30 Melee starter
33 "Do __ say . . ."
36 Aid partner
39 Pelvic bone
40 EYE
44 Toyota model
45 Fuss
46 Composer Rorem
47 Plain as day
49 Deviate from the course
52 Temp. unit
53 Bridges or Brummell
56 Well-dressed
60 NOSE
64 Barber's offering
66 __ pas (mistake)
67 Hard to believe
68 Navel type
69 Wings: Lat.
70 Thpeak like thith
71 Spiral-shelled creature
72 Legendary apple splitter
73 Greek H's

DOWN

1 Ethereal instruments
2 More or less
3 Macho
4 Stable units
5 Central points
6 Civil disturbances
7 Root or Yale
8 Blew up
9 Jason's craft
10 __ day (2/29)
11 School kid's punishment
12 Cain's mother
13 Richard Skelton
21 Clever chap
22 Author L. __ Hubbard
26 Meet the old grads
27 Gave guns to
29 __ Jose, CA
31 Org. once led by Bush
32 Under the weather
33 Traveled a curved path
34 Italian wine
35 Join the melting pot
37 Milk component
38 Comedian Philips
41 Suffix with drunk or dull
42 Humorist Bill
43 Mr. Rogers
48 Warriors' org.
50 Part of Q&A
51 Turkey-throat feature
54 Allan-__
55 Business as __
57 Genetic feature
58 Oral Roberts U. site
59 Canine's cries
61 Emulating Lucifer
62 Oddball
63 Rink jump
64 Mama pig
65 "What did you say?"

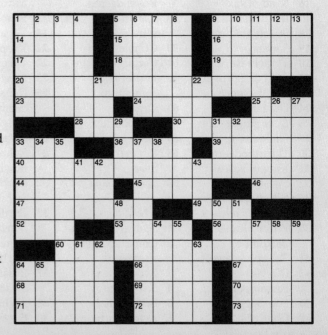

195 NOTTINGHAM REVISITED by Randolph Ross

ACROSS

1 Skyline sight
6 Some tires
13 __ *Knowledge* ('71 film)
14 Loathed one
16 Nottingham lithographs?
18 Upswing
19 In the matter of
20 Silvery fish
21 Meet with
23 Repressed, with "up"
25 Gin name
26 Nottingham bride?
31 Had a bite
32 Midmonth day
33 Garry and Melba
37 Make a bad pact
39 Hindu salvation
40 Middle of *Macbeth*
41 "__ Be Cruel"
42 Enthusiasm
43 Nottingham gangsters?
46 TV initials
49 Reliever's stat
50 Big __, CA
51 Separates socks
54 Grande and Bravo
56 Mount Snow machine
59 Nottingham merchant?
62 Popular sitcom
63 Palate projections
64 Introvert's trait
65 Like Mr. Universe

DOWN

1 Calcutta clothing
2 Most prim
3 Destitute
4 Hamelin pest
5 Ms. Lanchester
6 Roof holders
7 *Julius Caesar* character
8 Bit of Morse code
9 Like __ (candidly)
10 "Psst!" relative
11 Flood preventer
12 Common sense
13 EMT training
15 Italian wine region
17 Fish hawk
22 Charlie Sheen's brother
24 Comedian's need
26 One of the Bears
27 Suffix for problem
28 Quick-thinking retorts
29 Oliver and Sheree
30 Pataki's title: Abbr.
34 Auk feature
35 Oklahoma city
36 Undermines
38 Broadcast medium
39 Preceder of "the above"
41 Goes through mitosis
44 Captains of industry
45 Beat on the track
46 V.I. Lenin's land
47 Cheerful sounds
48 Just-picked
52 Deuce beater
53 Exemplar of grace
55 Urban-renewal target
57 Have __ in (influence)
58 Numbered hwy.
60 *A Chorus Line* number
61 Eggs

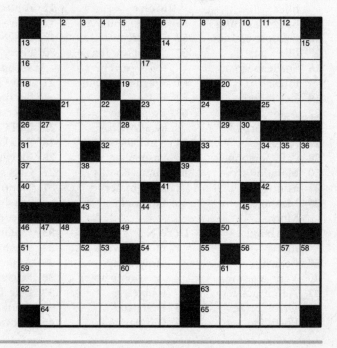

196 FIND AWAY by Trip Payne

ACROSS

1 Mr. Selleck
4 Filibuster
9 Glove-box items
13 Gray's field: Abbr.
15 Poet Elinor
16 Kind of sax
17 Bethlehem trio
18 Sports stadium
19 Satiate
20 TV accessory
23 Start of a proverb about silence
24 Digger's tool
26 Rock singer John
27 Nicklaus' grp.
30 The other team
31 King of Norway
32 Swiss home
34 White alternative
35 Hippie's remark
38 White House nickname
41 Shopping sprees
42 Director Preminger
46 Fourbagger
48 Chariot suffix
49 Smug expression
50 Barbarian
52 Porcupine features
53 Midler top-10 tune of '90
57 Royal decree
58 *The Prince of Tides* star
59 Gobbles up
61 Comic Johnson
62 Perrier competitor
63 Organic compound
64 Have to have
65 "__ evil, hear . . ."
66 Secret stealer

DOWN

1 Scottish headgear
2 Continuously successful
3 Red shade
4 Sharp blows
5 Brit's radial
6 Actor Baldwin
7 Carpet alternative, for short
8 Relies (on)
9 Long-vowel indicator
10 Everywhere
11 Ancient astronomer
12 Sauce variety
14 Vacation period
21 Keep for oneself
22 Greek letter
23 New beginning?
25 Caustic chemical
27 Ring up
28 Measure
29 Raise the hem, maybe
32 Dernier __ (latest fashion)
33 Printer's measures
36 James __ Garfield
37 Possible award-winner
38 "What ho!"
39 Big blaze
40 Kuwait, for one
43 Soup holders
44 Lullaby locale
45 Signs off on
47 Hammed it up
49 Health resort
51 Bowling places
52 Office worker
54 Hawk's opposite
55 "Would __ to you?"
56 Ollie's pal
57 Ardent watcher
60 Foxlike

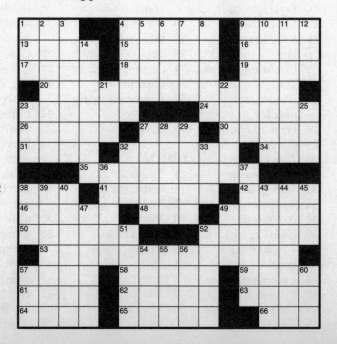

197 FICTIONAL PHYSICIANS by Randolph Ross

ACROSS

1 Opera star Merrill
7 Prince Charles' sport
11 Wild blue yonder
14 Have __ many
15 Literary VIP
16 Hasten
17 MD once on ABC
19 Switch settings
20 Fruity dessert
21 Biblical twin
22 Illiterate endorser
24 Mlle. of Madrid
26 Combustible heaps
29 Recipe direction
32 *Star Trek* doctor
35 Send to cloud nine
36 Usually
37 Babysitter's banes
39 Memos
40 Scatterbrained sort
43 Gives testimony
45 MD once on NBC
47 Controversial tree spray
48 Thai or Mongol
49 Cub Scout units
53 Speedwagon maker
55 Starting
57 Mauna __
58 Oliver Stone film
60 Conan Doyle doctor
64 Pub order
65 Greek theaters
66 Chore
67 Future flower
68 Bastes or hems
69 Ear pollution

DOWN

1 Easy victories
2 TV studio sign
3 Artist's topper
4 List ender
5 No gentleman
6 Drunkard
7 Lung lining
8 Tulsa product
9 Slow pitch
10 Figurine mineral
11 Timesavers
12 Relatives
13 "You bet!"
18 *True Grit* Oscar-winner
23 Placed in a third-party account
25 *Compos mentis*
27 Chapter in history
28 '60s radical org.
30 Hercules' captive
31 Bakery buys
33 Lets up
34 Lord's land
35 Singled out
37 Mexican peninsula, for short
38 Irani money
41 Blotter initials
42 Insult, in current slang
43 "Add __ of salt . . ."
44 Dey's *L.A. Law* role
46 Forest vines
50 Lanchester et al.
51 All's opposite
52 Time, metaphorically
54 Eyes: Sp.
56 Old card game
58 Holyfield hit
59 Winter bug
61 Tribute in verse
62 Chop down
63 Pod prefix

198 OCTOBER ACTIVITIES by S.N.

ACROSS

1 Wants to know
5 Switch positions
9 Purina rival
13 Dalmatian's name
14 Bowling term
15 *Mommie Dearest* name
16 Walk nervously
17 Reddy to sing?
18 Kick in a chip
19 October activity
22 Once around the track
23 Wilm. is there
24 *Wheel of Fortune* purchase
27 Stinky cigar
30 Thrill
35 Entertainer Falana
37 Acapulco gold
38 Made night noises
39 October activity
42 Oblivious to ethics
43 One __ customer
44 Ltr. enclosure
45 Critic, often
46 Divine food
48 Sun. speech
49 __ de cologne
51 Head stroke
53 October activity
61 Notorious Ugandan
62 __ *for the Misbegotten*
63 PDQ, O.R.-style
65 Retail
66 Set-to
67 Ingrain deeply
68 Quite dark
69 Van __, CA
70 Give's partner

DOWN

1 Nile reptile
2 Minor disagreement
3 *Mayor* author
4 Mill output
5 Phone letters
6 It may be free
7 Elm Street name
8 Good judgment
9 Open a crack
10 Actress Anderson
11 Crown of the head
12 Some bills
14 Lathe, e.g.
20 Had been
21 Hurricane of '85
24 Wedding platform
25 __ *Rae*
26 *The Waste Land* poet
28 Hockey Hall-of-Famer
29 "Ya __ have heart . . ."
31 A whole bunch
32 Opera highlights
33 Suffering stress
34 Gardener's device
36 Suburban square?
38 *Colors* star
40 Black or Valentine
41 Director Howard
46 Waikiki wear
47 Travel grp.
50 Larry Storch's *F Troop* role
52 Rec-room piece
53 Sitarist Shankar
54 Prayer ending
55 Eccentricity
56 May event, familiarly
57 Ride for a kid
58 Colleague of Clark and Jimmy
59 Feminine-name ending
60 Pillage
64 "__ end"

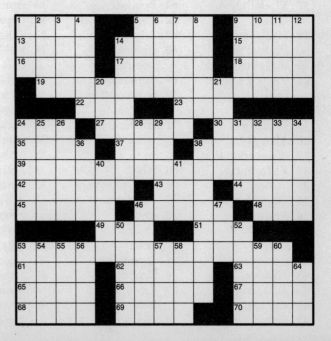

199 REVERSALS by Wayne R. Williams

ACROSS
1 Onetime Wimbledon winner
5 Ecology org.
8 Least risky
14 Faster way
16 Said grace
17 Interrupt
18 Stair elements
19 Furry swimmer
20 Deepest
22 Calendar letters
23 Make a choice
25 Australian area
29 Hot tub
30 Turndown vote
31 Jeff Bridges film of '84
32 $2 exacta, e.g.
33 DDE defeated him
34 Life of Riley
35 Gets tiresome
38 Ornery equine
39 *Inferno* writer
40 Model Macpherson
41 Friday was one
42 __ Ridge, TN
43 Teddy's niece
45 Coral islet
46 Sphere
49 Withdraw
50 Killer whale
51 Act dovish
52 Cattle food
54 Fur tycoon
56 Musical chords
59 Catch up to
61 Tight spot
62 Corporate buyout
63 Overacts
64 Olsen of vaudeville
65 Makes one

DOWN
1 Classy neckwear
2 Pipe down
3 Devon drink
4 Irish Gaelic
5 Author Umberto
6 Virtuousness
7 Env. abbr.
8 Alfalfa form
9 Manilow's record label
10 Basketball maneuver
11 Look over
12 Sun. homily
13 NFL scores
15 Power seats
21 Charlton role
24 Bit of butter
26 To __ (unanimously)
27 The players
28 Leg flexer
32 Morning meal
33 Egyptian cobra
35 Coach Ewbank
36 Ms. Fitzgerald
37 Sir Guinness
38 Major artery
39 Tot service
41 Soup and salad
42 Long paddle
44 Brain, so to speak
45 Contemporary
46 From C to C
47 Flimflammed
48 Drills, e.g.
53 Arrive at
55 Put away
56 Kin of *les* and *der*
57 Hit head-on
58 Prefix for metric
60 __ out a living

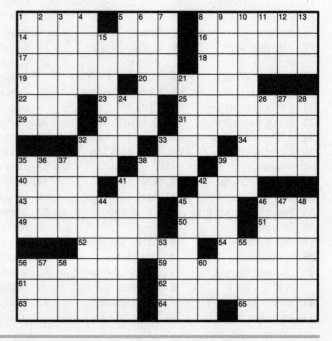

200 MUSIC APPRECIATION by Eric Albert

ACROSS
1 Sop ink
5 FDR topic
9 Film sensitivity
14 Tasty tubers
15 __ California
16 Genghis' gang
17 START OF A QUIP
19 Sigourney Weaver film
20 Flagpole topper
21 PART 2 OF QUIP
23 Expects
25 March ender
26 Messy Madison
29 Nasal-sounding
33 Kid around
36 "Oops!"
38 Napoleon, twice
39 Mideast name
40 PART 3 OF QUIP
42 __-de-sac
43 National Zoo attraction
46 Cry like a baby
47 Computer noise
48 Swallow up
50 Peruvian beast
52 Close with force
54 "__, you fool!"
58 PART 4 OF QUIP
63 Price twice
64 Bouquet
65 END OF QUIP
67 Like a lot
68 Immense volume
69 Enthusiastic
70 Some cookies
71 Turn aside
72 All those in favor

DOWN
1 Two, to Revere
2 Legal drama
3 End-all
4 Prufrock's poet
5 Agents' org.
6 Simplicity
7 Trojan War hero
8 House style
9 Invitation to dance
10 Amendment XXIV subject
11 Canal of song
12 Land west of Nod
13 Auto mark
18 Pups and parrots
22 Take a loss in
24 Flat-bottomed boat
27 *Pequod* skipper
28 Fit for a queen
30 Jet-set resort
31 Stick together
32 Short shout
33 Make fun of
34 Zesty spirit
35 Birds do it
37 Allen Ginsberg opus
41 Strong rebuke
44 Tidying tool
45 Eager to hear
47 Pre-overtime amount
49 Low-tech cooler
51 Spanish surrealist
53 Diamond gloves
55 "Wild and crazy" Martin
56 *West Side Story* song
57 "Dear me!"
58 Falls behind
59 Common diet supplement
60 Convertible, maybe
61 Cranny's colleague
62 Jacks, but not Jills
66 Recently arrived

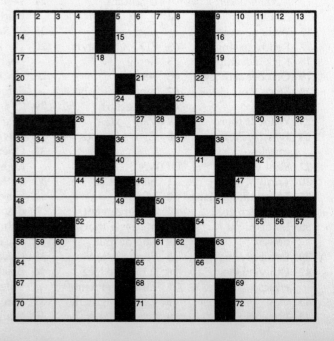

201 STRIKE IT RICH by Shirley Soloway

ACROSS

1 Beach surface
5 Western writer on a $5 stamp
10 Acting job
14 Small band
15 Factory group
16 Water pitcher
17 Part of CPA
18 Sober-minded
19 *Bus Stop* writer
20 Get rich quick
23 Button directive
24 After six
28 Grass purchase
29 Liza's Oscar film
33 Coral or Caribbean
34 Baseball exec Al
35 School grps.
36 Get rich quick
41 Cathedral area
42 Charlie Chan portrayer
43 British brew
44 Brain part
47 Señora Perón
50 Not at all friendly
52 Female fox
54 Get rich quick
58 A real clown
61 __ Boothe Luce
62 Environmental sci.
63 Genesis site
64 Floor installer
65 "Don't look __!"
66 Heredity unit
67 Derisive look
68 Church service

DOWN

1 Philatelist's fodder
2 Jockey Eddie
3 Cut a little
4 Is overfond of
5 Corn covering
6 Opposing one
7 Mideast money
8 Hard worker
9 Salad vegetable
10 Have sovereign power
11 __ up to (admit)
12 Turkey part
13 Prior to, in poems
21 Wide tie
22 Court barrier
25 Ratio phrase
26 Well-ordered
27 Regular, e.g.
30 Hardwood
31 Flying buzzer
32 Pear variety
34 Line on a map: Abbr.
35 Not COD
36 Saintly ring
37 Currier's partner
38 100 percent
39 White House nickname
40 Scoundrel
41 Slangy refusal
44 Russian space station
45 Votes in
46 Sell
47 Track bet
48 Some poisons
49 Bracelet holders
51 Steak order
53 Construction girder
55 Moolah
56 Nut source
57 Kohl's title
58 Canine command
59 Kind of poem
60 Buddhist sect

202 TODAY'S PUZZLE by Randolph Ross

ACROSS

1 Apply (to)
8 Keep at it
15 Hillary's height
16 Replenish inventory
17 Former *Today* cohost
19 Child pleaser
20 Oklahoma Indian
21 Els' followers
22 Mel of baseball
24 Gibbon, e.g.
25 Pitcher's stats
26 Former *Today* cohost
31 Smith of Rhodesia
32 Green land
33 Fit for farming
37 Led to the barn, Dogpatch style
39 Frying pan
40 Lady of Spain
41 Oil acronym
42 "__ Clear Day..."
43 *Today* regular
46 African nation
49 Popular suffix
50 Some magazine pages
51 Ms. MacGraw
52 Levee kin
54 Leb. neighbor
56 *Today* cohost
62 Command stratum
63 Veal dish
64 Causing bias
65 Still standing

DOWN

1 Urban walker: Abbr.
2 Night before
3 Soldier in gray
4 TV reporter Liz
5 Prefix for space
6 Brit's exclamation
7 Ultimate degree
8 President __
9 Architect Saarinen
10 Gad about
11 __ Lanka
12 Lazybones
13 Alabama city
14 Lock of hair
18 "__ intended"
22 "__ Ben Jonson"
23 Critic Kenneth
24 Not "fer"
25 Mideast airline
26 Chest protectors
27 Silents star
28 Error's partner
29 Like Alaska?
30 Ambler and Idle
34 *Captain __* (Flynn film)
35 Fasting times
36 Coup d'__
38 "__ lay me down..."
39 Energetic
41 Like some cereals
44 Partiality
45 Opera immortal
46 Puts together
47 Word of regret
48 Easily bent
52 Sandwich shop
53 Barbell material
54 "If __ make it there..."
55 Gather, in chemistry
57 Use an axe
58 Big bird
59 Not refined
60 Spot for a *cartographe*
61 Good-for-nothing

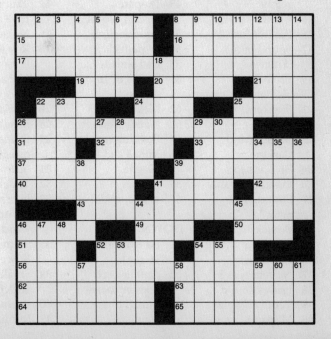

203 FULL OF BEANS by Eric Albert

ACROSS
1 Mr. Sharif
5 Persian potentate
9 Kind of orange
14 Raging blaze
16 Tony of baseball
17 '70s auto
18 It "keeps on ticking"
19 Tattletales
20 Ewe's partner
21 To some extent
24 Employment aid
28 Baby Snooks portrayer
29 Papergirl's path
31 Mai __ (cocktail)
32 Paper puzzle
33 Circus shooter
34 Likely (to)
35 *On the Town* lyricist
38 Golfer's goal
40 Jacket parts
41 Guns the engine
44 Corn holder
45 "If __ a Rich Man"
46 Bit of salt
47 Unspecified person
49 Exhaust one's creativity
50 Was in front
51 Entity
53 Highly motivated
56 Knee tendon
60 Monk's cloister
61 Avant-garde composer
62 Minnie of Nashville
63 Dampens
64 Bush's alma mater

DOWN
1 Out of synch
2 "O Sole __"
3 Part of ETA
4 Blushing
5 Be frugal
6 Bumper-sticker word
7 Tatum and Carney
8 Med. ins. plan
9 Prose alert
10 Out on __ (vulnerable)
11 Vitality
12 Actress Arden
13 Overeasy
15 Church top
20 Brake parts
21 Computer co.
22 New Deal org.
23 Inca conqueror
24 Tarzan's home
25 Concluded
26 Grab forty winks
27 Radio to assemble
29 Ice-T, e.g.
30 __ Majesty's Secret Service
33 Like old bathtubs
36 *Thimble Theater* name
37 *Silver Spoons* star
38 *Treasure Island* character
39 Display delight
42 Taper?
43 Avoiding fame
46 Kicks, in a way
48 Berry tree
49 Takes a flier
51 Unornamented
52 Give out
53 Casual topper
54 Justice Fortas
55 Hoop group: Abbr.
56 Take an axe to
57 Call __ day
58 Nada
59 "That's awesome!"

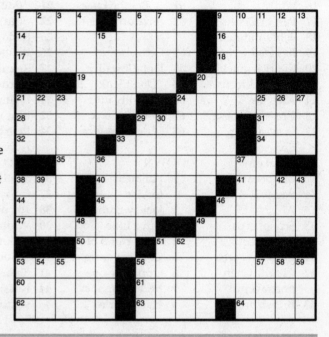

204 GYM NEIGHBORS by Wayne R. Williams

ACROSS
1 Puppeteer Lewis
6 Harm, in a way
10 Be up and about
14 More than ready
15 *M*A*S*H* star
16 Painter Joan
17 Sound of a critic?
19 Erelong
20 Sicilian landmark
21 *Superman* villain Luthor
22 Burstyn and Barkin
24 Broker's lots
26 Handle capably
27 Sound of an actor?
30 Be sick
33 Lucy's landlady
36 Entreaties
37 Novelist Levin
38 Heavy sound
39 Toothy displays
40 Map out
41 Make leather
42 Got up
43 Emitted beams
44 Army insect
45 Sound of a ballplayer?
47 Out-and-out
49 Prepare
53 Disarm a bull
55 Squeak curer
57 __ podrida
58 Old lament
59 Sound of an actress?
62 Melancholy
63 Nautical adverb
64 Ike's missus
65 Mineo and Maglie
66 Desires
67 Winter gliders

DOWN
1 Ed Norton's workplace
2 Author Bret
3 Booster rocket
4 Brought back
5 Nettle
6 Stable female
7 *Jeopardy!* name
8 Actress Lupino
9 Portuguese wines
10 T-shirt size
11 Sound of an actress?
12 Tailor's need
13 Howard and Nessen
18 Roy Rogers' real last name
23 Not as many
25 Up to, briefly
26 Hot dog
28 Brouhaha
29 Prime social category
31 "Dies __"
32 Touch down
33 Jazz singer James
34 Comparative word
35 Sound of a Bowery Boy?
39 Smallest city with an NFL team
40 Beethoven's Sixth
42 Mimic
43 Sage of Concord's monogram
46 Eye amorously
48 Fuel-line components
50 *Ghostbusters* goo
51 Spanish hero
52 Walks off with
53 Pats lightly
54 Joyce of *Roc*
55 Author Wister
56 March time
60 Bullring cheer
61 Apt. ad abbr.

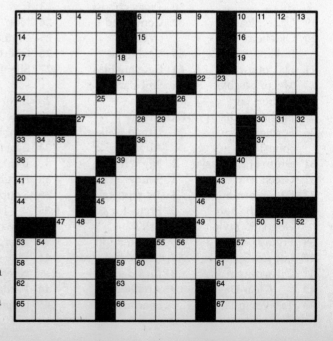

205 GREEN LIGHT by Matt Gaffney

ACROSS
1 Act testily
7 Yerevan native
15 Bob, but not Joe
16 "Misty" start
17 Open an envelope
18 Captain Stubing's command
19 Guys' dates
20 "Our __ your gain"
22 Met Life's bus.
23 Computer key
25 Storage unit
26 Yon bloke's
28 In __ (disheveled)
30 Inn offerings
35 Summer drink
36 Well-executed
37 Just plain awful
38 Green-light phrase
41 Barbecue areas
42 Gator's home, maybe
43 Free (of)
44 Merlin of TV
45 In unison
46 Sea plea
47 Farrow et al.
48 Know-nothing remark
50 Obstinate equine
53 Beer holder
55 Vaccine name
58 Perry victory site
60 Visigoth leader
62 Book's edition
63 Saskatchewan's capital
64 "Diagnose" anagram
65 Donald Sutherland's kid

DOWN
1 The Color Purple character
2 Barrie barker
3 Theater spots
4 Egg on
5 Oklahoma city
6 Ring a bell
7 Green-light phrase
8 They're often ruled
9 Z or M
10 Supplements, with "out"
11 Catch a crook
12 Even odds
13 __ for All Seasons
14 Is left with
21 West Indies belief
24 Aviator of the comics
26 Duck Soup soloist
27 Optimal
29 Kitten's cries
30 Rose up
31 Buckeyes' sch.
32 Filmdom's Zhivago
33 Ex-governor Cuomo
34 Snow gliders
37 Actress Cannon
39 Stamping tool
40 Rope feature
45 Musty house's need
47 Madame Curie
49 The way we word
50 Swiss range
51 Lee of cakedom
52 Spud covering
53 "You __ do!"
54 Carefree frolic
56 Reinforce, in a way
57 Former Chrysler category
59 Last part
61 Aiea adornment

206 BODY LANGUAGE by Bob Lubbers

ACROSS
1 Acting job
5 Greek column style
10 Aid in crime
14 On top of
15 Stew style
16 Cabbie's take
17 Sports stadium
19 USC rival
20 Capture a fish
21 Mean one
23 Church area
26 Billboard entry
27 Alda and King
30 Bible line: Abbr.
32 Father Knows Best actress
35 Stable parent
36 Western capital
38 __ Zedong
39 Nimitz's rank: Abbr.
40 Chafes
41 Sprint rival
42 Iced drink
43 La Cosa __
44 Planting ground
45 Gold bar
47 Shoe width
48 Batters' ploys
49 Oklahoma city
51 Faint
53 Back-of-book sections
56 Brook's big brother
60 Pedestal part
61 Small rodent
64 Venerable prep school
65 Divided nation
66 Thailand, once
67 My Three __ (sitcom)
68 Take the wheel
69 Relaxed state

DOWN
1 German valley
2 Ronny Howard role
3 Run easily
4 Board a Boeing
5 "They __ Believe Me"
6 Bobby of hockey
7 __ de Janeiro
8 Doctrines
9 Atkins and Huntley
10 __ Thing Happened on the Way . . .
11 Board game
12 Writer Gardner
13 Run like crazy
18 Stops from squeaking
22 Midwest Indians
24 Reluctant (to)
25 Tells a story
27 Violin maker
28 Burdened
29 Ultimate battle
31 Made a new sketch
33 Not spoken
34 Works hard
36 Cable channel
37 Teachers' grp.
40 Playful trick
44 __ at Campobello
46 Burger topping
48 The two of them
50 Ship strata
52 Mr. de la Renta
53 Midmonth day
54 Alliance acronym
55 Took a photo of
57 Director Kazan
58 Regretful word
59 Fictional aunt
62 Anger
63 Society-page word

207 AGES by Wayne R. Williams

ACROSS
1 Part of speech
5 Map collection
10 Smack hard
14 *Beetle Bailey* dog
15 Requirements
16 Lamb's pen name
17 Yuppie '80s TV series
20 Common Market abbr.
21 Deep voices
22 Lets up
23 Northern constellation
25 Statuesque
27 Poker stakes
31 In advance
35 Milne book
39 Steno book
40 Egyptian bird
41 First course
42 British Isles republic
43 Gold container
44 Janis Ian tune of '75
46 Turkish export
48 Car choice
49 *Scarlett* setting
51 Noted virologist
55 English racecourse
58 Sugary
62 Yoko __
63 Beatles tune of '67
66 Solitary
67 Eagle's nest
68 Old Testament book
69 Drunkards
70 Editorial commands
71 Sleep symbols

DOWN
1 Widely recognized
2 Additional
3 New York city
4 Scand. land
5 Writer Seton
6 Hardy heroine
7 Most August-born folks
8 Own up to
9 Compass dir.
10 Sake
11 Wallach and Whitney
12 "Come here often?" is one
13 Merchandise labels
18 Steak cut
19 Fax ancestor
24 Crow cries
26 Tolerated
28 Winery worker
29 Time periods
30 Graf rival
32 Mayberry kid
33 Few and far between
34 First place
35 Puppy bites
36 Bassoon kin
37 Clever people
38 Computer command
42 Sicilian volcano
44 Cremona craftsman
45 Villainous
47 Makes amends
50 Selling feature
52 Rotgut
53 Become accustomed
54 Dunn and Ephron
55 Hole-making tools
56 "Skedaddle!"
57 Minimum change
59 Cable element
60 Cinema sign
61 Summers on the Somme
64 Bell and Barker
65 Shriner's topper

208 "GEEZ!" by Fred Piscop

ACROSS
1 Some sandwiches
6 Blue-ribbon event
10 Tijuana cheers
14 __-garde
15 Discourteous
16 Mr. Hackman
17 Rho follower
18 Flash of brilliance
19 Research info
20 Mom's rock-pile admonition?
22 Daredeviltry name
23 Smoke-detector output
24 Mean and nasty
26 Condescended
30 Comb impediment
31 Reddish apes
32 Application phrase
36 Succotash bean
37 Novelist Rand
38 Sills solo
39 Service holder of a sort
42 *Tobacco Road* family name
44 In this way
45 Simple life
46 It's spotted in the zoo
49 Turin "Ta-ta!"
50 Get an __ effort
51 Antelope city?
57 West German capital
58 Forsaken
59 Stan's cohort
60 __-dry (arid)
61 ". . . __ saw Elba"
62 Frosted, in recipes
63 Controversial tree spray
64 "Dagnabbit!"
65 Some votes

DOWN
1 Door fastener
2 Sinful
3 Shankar genre
4 "__ honor, I will do my . . ."
5 Producing plays
6 "__ or foe?"
7 Imported automobiles
8 March 15th, for instance
9 Justifications
10 Angry poet?
11 Go out
12 Go in
13 Mattress name
21 Opposers of 65 Across
25 Beans spiller
26 Knucklehead
27 Buffalo's county
28 __ *Camera* ('55 film)
29 Pesky rebellion leader?
30 __ Clemente, CA
32 Caustic stuff
33 Comic Johnson
34 Appearance
35 Shucker's needs
37 Capp and Capone
40 "*Now* I see!"
41 Stole from
42 Pinocchio, often
43 Save-the-earth science
45 *The __ Winter*
46 __ the Hutt (Lucas character)
47 "__ and his money . . ."
48 "You're __ Hear from Me"
49 Healer
52 Author Ephron
53 *Cosmopolitan* competitor
54 Word of woe
55 Jet-set city
56 Bishops' realms

209 PARALLEL BARS by Eric Albert

ACROSS

1 Turn away
6 *Pygmalion* playwright
10 Camel feature
14 Resort isle
15 Short note
16 Laos' locale
17 BAR
20 *Joy of Cooking* abbr.
21 Guitar kin, for short
22 Clear a channel
23 Southpaw's sobriquet
26 Joyride
27 Red wood
29 Floor covering
30 Block a broadcast
33 High home
34 Actress Delany
35 Brouhaha
36 BAR
39 Director Kazan
40 Wines and dines
41 *Where's __?* ('70 film)
42 Howard of *Happy Days*
43 Big jerk
44 Dressing table
45 Pretentiously picturesque
46 Puts on the payroll
47 Mr. Kosygin
50 Golfer Woosnam
51 *Murphy Brown* network
54 BAR
58 G&S character
59 Walk out
60 *Lost Horizon* director
61 Pipe part
62 Painter Magritte
63 Makes meals

DOWN

1 Large quantity
2 Love god
3 Prince tune of '84
4 Decline
5 Chou En-__
6 Great __ Mountains National Park
7 "I'm present!"
8 Rock-band gear
9 Punny business
10 Safe place
11 Practiced
12 Flash's foe
13 Top of the head
18 Import tax
19 Border lake
24 *All My Children* character
25 Ad word
26 Hole in your head
27 Silly prank
28 Surprised exclamation
29 Something banned
30 *SNL* alumnus
31 Well-practiced
32 Coral-reef denizen
34 Humdinger
35 Kind of steak
37 Unfaithful one
38 On __ with (equal to)
43 Brought up
44 *Trattoria* offering
45 Universal truth
46 Rapidity
47 Proposes as a price
48 Spoils of war
49 Sommer of *The Prize*
50 "When the moon __ the seventh house . . .''
52 Tree feature
53 Mineral springs
55 Tin Woodman's tool
56 Radio regulator: Abbr.
57 __ Paulo

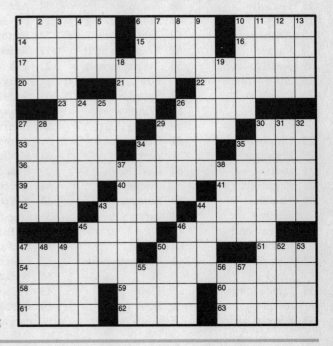

210 WHAT A DOG! by Trip Payne

ACROSS

1 Syrup source
6 Elbow room
11 Walk like pigeons
14 Vermont town
15 Condor's claw
16 Vane abbr.
17 With 62 Across, a 1991 award winner
19 New-style "Swell!"
20 *Hamlet* phrase
21 *Faust* writer
23 British maid
26 Award won by 17 Across
29 Garfield's middle name
31 "For shame!"
32 Bits of butter
33 Hexer's belief
35 React to yeast
38 With 53 Across, 26 Across' awarder
42 Wild guess
43 New Orleans school
46 Woodpile spot
50 Zodiac animal
52 Words of consolation
53 See 38 Across
57 Stash away
58 Mysterious knowledge
59 Poi source
61 Viscount's drink
62 See 17 Across
68 UFO pilots
69 "Oh, hush!"
70 Plumber's prop
71 Anonymous Richard
72 Door joint
73 Barely defeated

DOWN

1 Kittenish sound
2 Gray shade
3 "__ Love You" (Beatles tune)
4 Doyle's inspector
5 Montreal player
6 Mason's assistant
7 Handle roughly
8 Arabian Nights name
9 Brazzaville's land
10 The __ the line
11 Cannon's name
12 *Cat __ Tin Roof*
13 Sprinkles, in a way
18 Head away
22 Seer's sense
23 Cleveland NBAer
24 Showtime rival
25 "Pretty maids all in __"
27 Of interest to Bartleby
28 Dimelike
30 Rolling stone's lack
34 Mel of baseball
36 Fast flier
37 Needle case
39 Playwright Connelly
40 Norwegian dog
41 Sari wearer
44 Doze (off)
45 Female antelope
46 Hamill or Witt
47 Bit of legalese
48 Box up
49 Genetic letters
51 Change genetically
54 Methuselah's father
55 Hawaiian island
56 Totally outlaw
60 U.S. national flower
63 __ Arbor, MI
64 Smoke, for short
65 Droop
66 __ out a living
67 Was in first

211 ON HAND by Randolph Ross

ACROSS
1 Jocular sounds
5 Stopwatch, for instance
10 Counterfeit
13 __ *Three Lives*
14 Pull out
15 Lea lady
16 California city
18 Anchorman Rather
19 Nearly alike
20 Auto center
22 Dwelt
24 Small salamanders
25 Chipped in
28 Physique, for short
29 Rag-doll name
30 "Boola" relative
31 Jarreau and Jolson
32 Like short plays
35 Punch in the mouth
39 African native
40 UN agcy.
41 Bit of deceit
42 __ around (wander)
43 *Playboy* founder's nickname
44 Washbowl
46 Asian sea
48 *Pinta* was one
50 Tries to persuade
52 Young or Swit
56 "What a good boy __!"
57 Sponge cakes
59 Wine variety
60 "On __ Day..."
61 Curriculum part
62 Rudolph's mother
63 Sharpens
64 Comics possum

DOWN
1 Pants supports
2 Jai __
3 Pilot's place
4 Look up to
5 Like Ivan
6 __ on parle français
7 Repaired
8 Moved sideways
9 Take it easy
10 Fakir's mattress
11 Anticipate
12 Fender benders
14 Fitness centers
17 Snow glider
21 Extend a subscription
23 Secret file
25 Places of refuge
26 Prefix for second
27 Hitchhike
29 In addition
31 Mr. Baba
32 Yoko __
33 One-fifth of MX
34 At that time
36 Seal a tub
37 Dutch airline
38 Forage plants
43 Teacup part
44 European capital
45 Give __ (assist)
46 Honor
47 Shakespearean teen
48 Football job
49 __ dire (jury-selection process)
51 Cabbage product
53 __ 'clock (midmorning)
54 Math subject
55 Legalese phrase
58 So far

212 THE DOCTOR IS IN by Eric Albert

ACROSS
1 Small songbird
5 Societal no-no
10 Quite luxurious
14 Give a job to
15 Squirrel snack
16 Singer Guthrie
17 Dr. Seuss book
20 Wind instrument
21 Make mad
22 Newsman Koppel
23 Hoosegow
24 Trite writings
28 Like some hair
29 Mouth piece
32 Series of steps
33 *Of __ I Sing*
34 Mediocre
35 Dr. Seuss book
38 Actress Bancroft
39 Tehran's country
40 Leered at
41 NBA coach Unseld
42 Half hitch or bowline
43 Expressionless
44 Meditate (on)
45 Sock part
46 Formal wear
49 Latin prayer
54 Dr. Seuss book
56 Words of understanding
57 Fencing swords
58 Moore of *Ghost*
59 People
60 Mean and malicious
61 Kemo __

DOWN
1 Propeller's sound
2 Teeming (with)
3 Author Ambler
4 Roman emperor
5 Two-person bike
6 Played a part
7 Physicist Niels
8 Lode load
9 Cursory cleaning
10 Ward off
11 '77 whale movie
12 Hit hard
13 Stockings
18 Conductor Toscanini
19 Deep black
23 Song of praise
24 "Fiddlesticks!"
25 Make up (for)
26 Where livestock live
27 Beer adjective
28 Golden grain
29 Bloodhound features
30 Embers, eventually
31 *Bananas* name
33 Lose on purpose
34 It's a long story
36 XIX
37 Serious and somber
42 Aga __
43 Take it slow
44 Kiss target
45 Station receiver
46 End-of-week remark
47 Roughly
48 Orange cover
49 Ripens, as cheese
50 Tags on
51 Perlman of *Cheers*
52 Poetic foot
53 French friend
55 Valedictorian's pride: Abbr.

213 THREE OF A KIND by Matt Gaffney

ACROSS
1 Slows down
8 Slugger's tool . . .
11 . . . and what it's made of
14 Tony Knowles, for one
15 Cornered
17 Versatile one
19 "Who am __ argue?"
20 H.S. class
21 Franklin et al.
22 Hunters' wear
25 Grazing land
26 Forearm bones
27 Sounds of relief
29 M. Descartes
31 Word before driver or school
34 Campaign staffer
35 Blazed trails
38 Bogie's Oscar film
41 Fore's opposite
42 Show anger
43 Colorado city
44 *Edward Scissorhands* star
45 Lose rigidity
46 Fast car
49 Circle section
52 Norman and Edward
56 Jai __
57 Grammy-winner Irene
59 Nothing at all
60 Lion
65 Scott hero
66 Like some basements
67 Singer Tillis
68 Stylish, '60s-style
69 Goes over

DOWN
1 Indira's son
2 Fill with delight
3 Baja noshes
4 Pose an issue
5 *King Kong* studio
6 Off one's rocker
7 Traffic tie-up
8 Warsaw Pact member
9 Fitting
10 Punish severely
11 Eve or Elizabeth
12 "You look like you've just __ ghost!"
13 *Steppenwolf* writer
16 Casino furniture
18 Be duplicitous
23 Mock fanfare
24 *Amadeus* playwright
26 Not uniform
28 IHOP freebie
30 Ferber and Best
31 El stop: Abbr.
32 Channels 14 and up
33 After taxes
34 Hole in one
35 Author Buscaglia
36 Always, in verse
37 Spiral molecule
39 Had an effect on
40 Sudden impulse
44 Lower oneself
46 Eric B. & __ (rap group)
47 Still in it
48 Ear feature
50 Bowl yell
51 Fancy flapjack
53 Conniver's quest
54 Stirred up
55 Gravity-powered vehicles
58 Trojan War fighter
61 Bit of resistance
62 Egg __ yong
63 Chapel Hill sch.
64 Wedding-announcement word

214 WHERE YOU LIVE by Cathy Millhauser

ACROSS
1 Bullring cheers
5 Winter weather
9 Something easy
14 Old Testament book
15 Bread spread
16 Sky blue
17 Prefix for social
18 Dressed
19 Broadway awards
20 Cape Canaveral structure
23 High-fashion mag
24 Slippery one
25 Family member
28 Think alike
30 Rank beginner
32 "Snow" veggie
33 Failing totally
37 "Rule Britannia" composer
39 Wee bit
40 Toad feature
41 Does mining work
46 Mr. Lombardo
47 Bring back the line
48 Fictional Jane et al.
50 Tee's preceder
51 Singer Peeples
53 Double curve
54 Beef selections
59 Richard's *Pretty Woman* costar
62 Family member
63 Word form for "thought"
64 Trimming
65 *An American Tail* characters
66 Zilch, to Zapata
67 Bagpipers' wear
68 Fits to __
69 Frenzied

DOWN
1 Evangelist Roberts
2 Moon goddess
3 Caesar said it
4 Black eye
5 Inner-ear part
6 North's nickname
7 Low in fat
8 Sly trick
9 Library fixture
10 Polo rival
11 Convent dweller
12 Hue's partner
13 Gentlemen
21 Music mark
22 Colony founder
25 Farm storage
26 Mythical flier
27 Rosalynn followed her
28 Hawks' homes
29 Sacred river
31 Ex-GI org.
32 National Leaguer
34 USPS delivery
35 Fall behind
36 Wedding words
38 Immigrant's course: Abbr.
42 Furniture ornaments
43 Getting __ years
44 Bequest receiver
45 Fabric worker
49 Eye feature
52 *Battlestar Galactica* commander
53 Prevention unit
54 Dagger handle
55 Cut it out
56 Gouda alternative
57 Make over
58 Drench
59 NYC airport
60 Mentalist Geller
61 __ *Abner*

215 SMART QUOTE by Wayne R. Williams

ACROSS

1 Painter Edgar
6 Jell-O spokesperson
11 Geom. shape
14 Antilles isle
15 Jacques, for one
16 She-bear: Sp.
17 START OF A QUOTE
19 Go bad
20 Minimal
21 Treats seawater
23 Odds' colleagues
24 Folklore beasts
27 Mexican city
28 Shingle letters
29 Defense org.
30 Ski spot
31 Fictional exile
32 Calls
33 MIDDLE OF QUOTE
36 Source of quote
37 Inner disposition
38 Societal standards
39 Steamed
40 Writer Sinclair
41 CO clock setting
44 Lunar plain
45 Well-behaved kid
46 Washed-out
47 Profession of 36 Across
49 Cartoonist's need
51 __ Aviv
52 END OF QUOTE
55 Dir. opp. WSW
56 Boredom
57 Biko of South Africa
58 Draft letters
59 Musical notation
60 All in

DOWN

1 Touched lightly
2 Short trip of a sort
3 Some hoopsters
4 __ Irish Rose
5 __ serif
6 Wall St. analyst's designation
7 Bobby of hockey
8 Like some rolls
9 Highland hillsides
10 Cravings
11 Brando Oscar role
12 U-235 and U-239
13 Tangled mess
18 Squealer
22 Stands for
25 Rival of Navratilova
26 Became unraveled
29 __ Dame
30 The Rookie star
31 "It" is this
32 Released, in a way
33 Brings to life
34 Crusaders' adversaries
35 Makes jump
36 Wee speck
38 Auto stat.
40 Never praised
41 Kitchen tool
42 Record holder
43 Designated
45 Unanimously
46 Singer LaBelle
48 Spud's buds
50 Be idle
53 Destructive one
54 CX

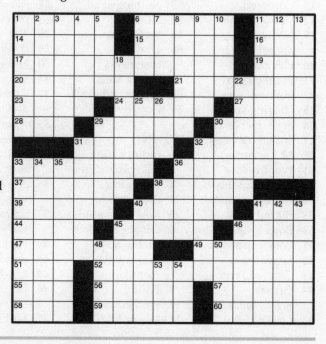

216 PLACES TO PLAY by Wayne R. Williams

ACROSS

1 Jazzman Waller
5 Nonfilling dessert
10 Confused states
14 Vicinity
15 More frosty
16 Honolulu shindig
17 Fruit coat
18 Palmer's place
20 Country's count
22 Recording medium
23 Inventor Howe
24 Second ltr. addition
26 Open, in a way
30 Al Capp beast
32 Fur wrap
33 Gretzky's place
37 Clever person
38 Yoko __
39 Go bad
40 Miami Beach hwy.
42 Pasture
43 Hosp. area
44 Holyfield's place
47 More certain
50 Evasive maneuver
51 Tropical fish
52 Author LeShan
53 Barely beat
56 Filled with breezes
58 Small tree
59 Winter Olympics place
64 Past due
65 Cleveland's lake
66 Explosive, for short
67 Genesis name
68 Fetches
69 Prepare to drive
70 Family rooms

DOWN

1 Broad comedy
2 Statesman Sharon
3 Seles' place
4 Inept soldier
5 Lively dances
6 Coll. major
7 Diamond lady
8 Some jabs
9 Dangerous whale
10 Well-versed
11 __ Miss Brooks
12 Flivver fuel
13 Take to court
19 Musical work
21 Stadium seater
24 __ Alegre, Brazil
25 Taro product
27 Striker's place
28 Little green man
29 Price twice
31 Advice-column initials
33 Lifting device
34 When actors enter
35 Mrs. Yeltsin
36 Good-natured
41 Think alike
45 Marked a ballot
46 Became flushed
48 Wipes off
49 Metal rod
52 Singer Gorme
54 Iacocca's successor
55 Clothe oneself
57 Monthly check
58 Queue before Q
59 Canine command
60 Unrefined metal
61 Wee amount
62 Hwy.
63 S.A. nation

217 TWENTY QUESTIONS by S.N.

ACROSS

1 Spill the beans
5 MacLeod of *The Love Boat*
10 Word on a fuse
14 Actress Anderson
15 Singer Cara
16 Kingly address
17 Rolaids target
18 Light beer
19 Get __ the ground floor
20 What the Mets play at Shea
22 Least usual
24 Fuss
25 Addams Family cousin
27 Comparative suffix
28 Twelfth letter
30 Has at
33 Writer Burrows
36 Filmed a new version of
38 Ankle adornment
40 Ending for opt
41 Charles' princedom
43 First name
44 Scout's asset
46 "Be __ your school"
48 Thesaurus find: Abbr.
49 Punctilious
51 Omega's preceder
52 Mr. Wallach
54 Slinger's handful
55 Word form for "equal"
57 Sense
60 Court players
64 It's east of the Urals
65 Governor Stevenson
67 Robert De __
68 Catch some rays
69 Runner Steve
70 __ end (over)
71 Grade-school homework
72 Where things are
73 Cosby's first series

DOWN

1 Not very interesting
2 Plumb crazy
3 Charisma
4 Waited awhile
5 Arizona river
6 One of the Musketeers
7 Meatless main course
8 -esque relative
9 Pianist Peter
10 Out of the way
11 Ore veins
12 Big leaguers
13 Transmitted
21 Egg on
23 Half of DJ
26 Akron product
28 Onetime Indians
29 General Curtis __
31 Underground passage
32 Holds up
34 Overcomes
35 "Me too," in Montreal
37 100%
39 __ de Cologne
42 Morning, à la Winchell
45 Grand-scale
47 Jockey's controller
50 Have thoughts
53 Pipe problems
56 Mideast region
57 Little bits
58 Jacob's twin
59 New Mexico town
61 What criticizers pick
62 Corner
63 Panasonic rival
66 A third of MDXVIII

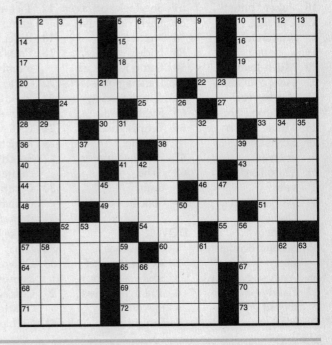

218 THUMB-THING ELSE by Trip Payne

ACROSS

1 *West Side Story* heroine
6 Skater Thomas
10 "__ she blows!"
14 Man from Muscat
15 Author Hunter
16 Make angry
17 Thumb user
19 __ impasse
20 Supplement, with "out"
21 Frozen rain
22 Draw forth
24 Washington paper
25 Sea foam
26 Wheedle
29 Japanese vehicle
32 Clear the board
33 Asian capital
34 "What's __ name?"
35 Two cubes
36 Reservation symbol
37 Peel an apple
38 Be the interviewer
39 Lauren of *The Love Boat*
40 Birds in formation
41 Fixed leftovers
43 Viewed with alarm
44 Skunks' weapons
45 Smidgens
46 Actress Berenson
48 Arp's genre
49 By way of
52 "__ It Romantic?"
53 Thumb users
56 *Cosby Show* son
57 Flow slowly
58 Actor Lew
59 Geog. region
60 Poor grades
61 Baker's ingredient

DOWN

1 *Utopia* author
2 One way to run
3 Uncontrolled anger
4 Chemical ending
5 Pet-carrier need
6 Accounting entry
7 Mr. Knievel
8 Keep out
9 Room-to-room device
10 Characteristics
11 Thumb user
12 Jai __
13 Dollars for quarters
18 Lessen the load
23 Mischievous god
24 Prepare to be shot
25 Court assessments
26 Fragrant wood
27 Come to mind
28 Thumb user
29 Put a value on
30 Licorice flavor
31 Didn't wax
33 Gordie and Elias
36 Frog or cat, e.g.
37 Black and Baltic
39 New Mexico art colony
40 Vacation motive
42 Journal boss
43 Clichéd dog moniker
45 Toyland visitors
46 Catcher's gear
47 Laver contemporary
48 Catch some Z's
49 Actress Miles
50 Makes furious
51 Helper: Abbr.
54 Caviar
55 Caustic solution

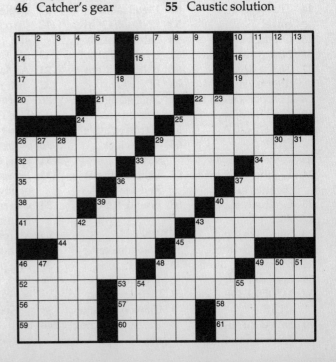

219 DANCE BAND by Randolph Ross

ACROSS
1. __ Aires
7. "Hey you!"
11. Pa Clampett
14. Tie score
15. Mustang, but not stallion
16. Poker "bullet"
17. Dancing animator?
19. __ de mer
20. Much-loved
21. Final course
23. Purina rival
26. Diet-food phrase
28. Movie pooch
29. Davis of *Thelma & Louise*
31. Thumbs-down vote
32. Wallace and Douglas
33. Witness
35. Second Beatles film
36. AAA suggestion
37. Candy-bar ingredient
39. Man-mouse link
42. Farmer's friend
44. Flower parts
46. Thumper's friend
48. Put a top on
49. Adidas alternatives
50. Nobelist Wiesel
51. Sherlock portrayer
53. Early cartoonist
54. Night light
56. Hideaway
58. Baton Rouge sch.
59. Dancing pollster?
64. __ out a living
65. Rubberneck
66. Tennis great Pancho
67. Watched Junior
68. "The __ the limit!"
69. Folksinger Pete

DOWN
1. Gift feature
2. Actress Merkel
3. Sushi selection
4. Still in progress
5. Eleven: Fr.
6. Family car
7. __ de deux
8. When *60 Minutes* is on
9. Cutlery metal
10. Stocking stuffers
11. Dancing president?
12. Two-handed card game
13. River features
18. Press corps member?
22. Go to sea
23. Ice-cream ingredient
24. Riga resident
25. Dancing colonist?
27. South American capital
30. Computer-data format
32. Breakfast fruit
34. Make leather
35. *Leave __ to Heaven*
38. Down in the dumps
40. Comedienne Charlotte et al.
41. Coll. prof. rank
43. Help do wrong
45. Connection
46. __-lettres
47. "Seward's Folly"
48. Storefront feature
51. Referee's order
52. Windblown soil
55. Coop group
57. Curved molding
60. Scale notes
61. Big galoot
62. Vein contents
63. Something to shoot for

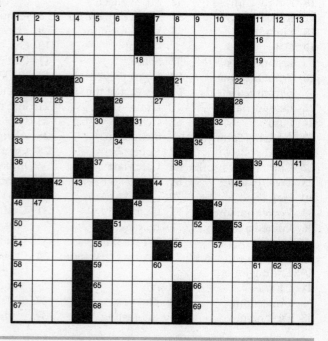

220 INJECTING HUMOR by Donna J. Stone

ACROSS
1. Lays down the lawn
5. Godunov or Badenov
10. Bassoon kin
14. Throw in the towel
15. On the ball
16. Nice or Newark
17. The __ Reader (literary mag)
18. Trooper's tool
19. Auel heroine
20. START OF A QUIP
23. Fathered a foal
24. "__ the Walrus" (Beatles tune)
25. Graduation gear
27. Alts.
28. Swig like a pig
32. *Shogun* costume
34. Missionary, often
36. Boot out
37. MIDDLE OF QUIP
40. Sailed through
42. Author Smollett
43. Copier supplies
46. Prepare to fly
47. Cover-girl Carol
50. Speedometer abbr.
51. __ jiffy
53. Metal fabrics
55. END OF QUIP
60. Saltwater fish
61. Ryan or Tatum
62. Baltic resident
63. El __, TX
64. Michelangelo masterpiece
65. Heron relative
66. "__ o'clock scholar"
67. Land on the Red Sea
68. Bound bundle

DOWN
1. Wet-sneaker sound
2. Wearing apparel
3. Bistro patrons
4. Canyon of fame
5. Roseanne Arnold, née __
6. Oil of __
7. Overhaul
8. OPEC representative
9. Make tracks
10. Whitish gem
11. Eagle, for one
12. Joan of Arc site
13. SFO stat
21. Adds fringe to
22. Brit. record label
26. Florist's need
29. Dos Passos trilogy
30. Actress Lorna
31. Spec episode
33. Brahman bellows
34. Oriental-art material
35. Marching-band member
37. Egg plant?
38. Pack complement
39. __ Selassie
40. S&L convenience
41. Mimic
44. Free (of)
45. A bit too curious
47. It multiplies by dividing
48. Soup ingredient
49. Fearsome fly
52. *Oklahoma!*'s Ado __
54. Off-the-cuff
56. Knowledgeable
57. Be abundant
58. Hoopster Archibald
59. Pizzazz
60. Exercise place

221   CLEANUPS by Trip Payne

ACROSS
1 Behold, to Brutus
5 James and Kett
10 Prejudice
14 "__ I say, not . . ."
15 Precious kids
16 Mrs. Lindbergh
17 Book protector
19 Thurmond of basketball
20 Country music?
21 Makes captive
23 Act as pilot
24 Chicago's zone: Abbr.
25 Santa __, CA
26 Bring up
28 Geronimo, for one
31 Cornfield cries
34 Some cars
37 Former Mideast nation: Abbr.
38 High __ kite
39 Ratfink
40 Coffee brewer
41 __ Misérables
42 Quitter's word
43 Iowa city
44 Composer Gustav
46 Jamie of M*A*S*H
48 Franklin's nickname
49 Dietary component
51 Actress Slezak
55 Outer limit
58 Dotes on
59 Pasturelands
60 Important time for networks
62 Memo phrase
63 Gives for a time
64 Feminine ending
65 Pea holders
66 Use the delete key
67 Owner's proof

DOWN
1 Icelandic classics
2 Make a difference
3 Social position
4 Williams and Rolle
5 Gouda alternative
6 Gumshoe
7 Can hold
8 Don't exist
9 Concordes, e.g.
10 Split need
11 Where sound can't travel
12 Chip in
13 Understands
18 Burns of *Dear John*
22 Slip-up
24 *Antigone* king
27 "Swinging on __"
28 Ms. Bryant
29 Krishna preceder
30 Ocean fliers
31 Not upset
32 Taking a cruise
33 Kind of stomach
35 Put on
36 High above
39 Bloodhound's track
43 Like a one-way sign
45 Camera parts
47 Cincinnati team
49 Not so many
50 Sports palace
52 Actress Dunne
53 New Hampshire city
54 Was inquisitive
55 Gymnast's maneuver
56 Betting setting
57 Capri is one
58 Church area
61 Bradley and Begley

---

222   WALL COVERING NEEDS by Bob Lubbers

ACROSS
1 *Casablanca* role
5 Pay out
10 Practice punching
14 Arthur of tennis
15 Rarin' to go
16 Top of the head
17 Loco
19 Enjoying the Love Boat
20 Like some steel
21 Bent a fender
23 __ October (fictional sub)
24 Painter/inventor
25 Sitter hirer
29 Board-game pair
30 Troop grp.
33 Likeness
34 Rope twist
35 Hockey target
36 Judy's daughter
37 Mails away
38 Rajah's spouse
39 School founded in 1440
40 Poker card
41 __ blanche
42 Leb. neighbor
43 Phobos orbits it
44 Make angry
45 Not much, so to speak
47 Josh around
48 Was generous
50 Work together
55 Elite alternative
56 Harmless loudmouth
58 Varieties
59 Way to the altar
60 Scarlett's home
61 Airplane tip
62 Equine gaits
63 Pretentious

DOWN
1 All ears
2 Cartographer's speck
3 Good buddy
4 Bush Cabinet member
5 Covert
6 Peeled off
7 Old oath
8 Pince-__ glasses
9 Ship-repair spots
10 Reaches across
11 Paper product
12 Suited to __
13 Perused
18 Swiss city
22 Poetic preposition
24 Mork's friend
25 Lots (of)
26 Friendliness
27 Arkansas athletes
28 Actor Richard
29 Eats in style
31 "À votre __!"
32 Green-card holder
34 Deborah and Graham
35 Alumnus
37 Take no more cards
41 West Pointer
43 Miss West
44 British bishops' hats
46 Rub out
47 Prepared to be knighted
48 Joyride
49 Hawaiian city
50 __ facto
51 Comedian Rudner
52 Seaweed product
53 Part of CD
54 Serving piece
57 Make public

223 HUMAN ANIMALS by Shirley Soloway

ACROSS

1 Western wear
6 Line of poetry
11 Increases
14 Troy lady
15 Artist Matisse
16 Society-page word
17 Overachiever
19 Newsman Rather
20 Small songbird
21 Billboard displays
22 Walk out on
24 Fountain in Rome
26 More prudent
27 Edith, to Archie
30 *I Dream of Jeannie* star
33 Gee's preceder
36 Burmese or Bornean
37 Make a hole __
38 Part of RFD
40 U.S. summer setting
41 Canceled projects
42 Up for __ (available)
43 Standing tall
45 Orly lander
46 Mixed bag
47 Highway menace
49 *Max __ Returns* ('83 film)
51 Blue ribbon, e.g.
54 Whirlpool rival
56 Supply troops to
58 Extra
60 Circle segment
61 WWII aviator
64 Recipe phrase
65 Hard to see
66 Lend __ (listen)
67 Drunkard
68 Bandleader Skinnay
69 Hair jobs

DOWN

1 __ out (discipline)
2 *Damn Yankees* tune
3 Inspirational author
4 Hammered, in a way
5 SAT taker
6 Backyard building
7 Afternoon socials
8 Bill to pay: Abbr.
9 Attribution
10 Brings on board
11 Nonfavored ones
12 Nectar source
13 Conveyed
18 Barbara and Conrad
23 "__ evil, hear . . ."
25 Perfume bottles
26 Poster word
28 Biblical judge
29 Port of Iraq
31 Hazzard deputy
32 Robin's roost
33 As a result
34 Roll up
35 Timid soul
37 Being dragged
39 More or less
44 Tennis pro Michael
47 Sleeve style
48 Mischievous girl
50 Faux pas
52 Reviewer Ebert
53 Wild fancy
54 *Serpico* author
55 Mr. Guthrie
56 Skirt length
57 Farm animals
59 Goes awry
62 Chinese principle
63 Dance genre

224 REVERSE ENDINGS by Wayne R. Williams

ACROSS

1 Tip over
5 Circle fully
11 Actress Gardner
14 Software buyer
15 Carolina river
16 Super __ (Lee Trevino)
17 Crooked heath?
19 "Black gold"
20 Rocking-chair locales
21 Patch a wall
23 Quite perceptive
24 Compass pt.
25 Life preserver?
33 Sour-cream product
36 Author Anita
37 Wed in haste
38 Time to remember
39 Wearing a cloak
41 Use the microwave
42 Light wood
44 Oblique line: Abbr.
45 Chicago trains
46 Where grouches worship?
50 Word after want
51 Battle of the __
55 Small generator
59 Barrymore and Richie
61 Tuscaloosa's loc.
62 Slots jackpot?
64 Forceful stream
65 Barrymore and Merman
66 Concerning
67 Woodsman's need
68 Usher again
69 Some votes

DOWN

1 *Mea __*
2 Part of PGA
3 Indian statesman
4 Land areas
5 Dueling sword
6 Beatty et al.
7 Precious stone
8 Wedding vows
9 Start up again
10 Moonstruck
11 Run __ (lose control)
12 Bridal wear
13 Wheel shaft
18 Close-call comment
22 Amoeba, for one
26 Stevedores' grp.
27 __ *Cane* ('63 film)
28 Dominant idea
29 Shiite's belief
30 Percolate
31 Milky mineral
32 __ up (livens)
33 Something owed
34 "*Dies __*"
35 Tropical tree
39 Landlubber's woe
40 Psyche part
43 C-__ (cable channel)
47 House and grounds
48 Orchestra member
49 Shorebird
52 Mrs. Helmsley
53 "Battle Hymn" word
54 Senator Kefauver
55 Goya subject
56 *Family Ties* role
57 Entryway
58 Protest-singer Phil
59 Actress Kedrova
60 *Meet Me __ Louis*

225 COMPOSITION by Eric Albert

ACROSS
1 Neon, e.g.
8 Avoided the issue
15 Bring up
16 Part at the start
17 START OF A ROSSINI QUOTE
18 Free
19 Handle badly
20 Sounded the horn
21 Falsification
22 I is one
27 Feminine ending
28 PART 2 OF QUOTE
33 Regarded with reverence
34 New York county
35 New York county
38 Gas rating
40 High-school outcast
41 Hardly touch
44 PART 3 OF QUOTE
47 Doctor's charge
50 Got too big for
51 Rule, in India
52 Donnybrook
56 Too big
58 Rice dish
60 END OF QUOTE
62 Nickname of a sort
63 Police ploy
64 Last course
65 Detection devices

DOWN
1 Provide a feast for
2 Outs
3 Casino shows
4 Nights before
5 Careful strategy
6 Munched on
7 Vast expanse
8 FDR program
9 Dudley Moore film
10 Major crime
11 Kind of custard
12 Wait in the shadows
13 Competitive advantage
14 Action
23 Off-color
24 __ Town
25 Vane reading
26 Off-the-wall
29 Riga resident
30 Keogh alternative
31 Beelzebub's business
32 Ball holder
33 Literary alias
35 __ Khan
36 Author Deighton
37 Garden spot
38 "__ from Muskogee"
39 Pfeiffer role
41 S.F. setting
42 Line of thought?: Abbr.
43 Mid.
45 Can't stand
46 Hair quality
47 Raisin center
48 Less trouble
49 Tosses out
52 Ginger's partner
53 Perfect for picking
54 Warts and all
55 Folding beds
57 Elmer's nemesis
59 Mel of Cooperstown
60 6-pt. scores
61 Mine rocks

226 PULLING RANK by Gus Black

ACROSS
1 Social blunder
6 "This can't be!"
10 Mistake-maker's cry
14 Expect
15 Way out
16 Give a hand
17 Doctor's career
20 Brontë heroine
21 List entry
22 Extend a subscription
23 Tuna holders
25 Touch against
27 State strongly
30 Trojan War hero
31 Violinist's need
34 Classic Western film
35 Computer owner
36 Clown character
37 Bob Keeshan role
40 European range
41 Weave a web
42 In unison
43 Single layer
44 Day laborer
45 Gas-range part
46 Cry
47 Eight furlongs
48 In the know
51 In the know about
53 Not at all stiff
57 Long-running soap opera
60 Hardwood trees
61 Couple
62 Knot again
63 Irritating insect
64 First name in mysteries
65 Days __ (yore)

DOWN
1 Stare open-mouthed
2 Out of whack
3 County event
4 Words on a nickel
5 Greek letter
6 Waiting for Lefty playwright
7 Clinton's hometown
8 Marilyn's real name
9 "... man __ mouse?"
10 Eightsome
11 Lena of Havana
12 Leaders set it
13 Gush forth
18 Delicate color
19 Key point
24 General vicinity
26 Horse's home
27 Composers' org.
28 "__ We Dance?"
29 Foolish
30 Invite to stay
31 Element #5
32 Layer in the news
33 Swain
35 Not much liked
36 Sculpture variety
38 Understanding words
39 Caesar's conquest
44 Jury member
45 Storage boxes
46 Take by force
47 007 portrayer
48 Excited
49 Withdraw (from)
50 "Lonely Boy" singer
52 Mr. Donahue
54 "Tell __ the judge!"
55 Body armor
56 Said "guilty," perhaps
58 Tailless simian
59 In favor of

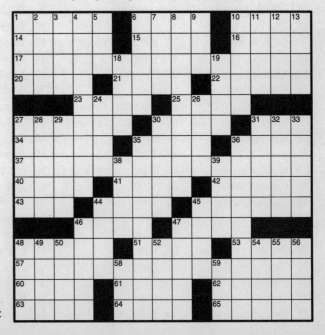

227 FLAG-WAVING by David A. Davidson

ACROSS

1 Lip service of a sort
5 'Tis, in the past
9 Wearied
14 Add to the pot
15 Indian chief
16 Green shade
17 Ballet bend
18 Russian river
19 O-shaped roll
20 Flag-hoisting contests?
23 Storm
24 Adorn an i
25 Cry of contempt
28 Kon-Tiki Museum locale
31 Cash alternative
33 Arctic or antarctic
37 Director Preminger
39 Boxer Max
40 "Flag Factory Robbed"?
43 Pain in the neck
44 Change course
45 Gets an apartment
46 St. Francis' home
48 Ready to pick
50 Author Buscaglia
51 Summer in Quebec
53 Pacific island
58 Flag day?
61 Set firmly
64 Adverse fate
65 Eban of Israel
66 Having knowledge
67 Science mag
68 Bridge support
69 Less outdated
70 Shoe inserts
71 Injury

DOWN

1 Key letter
2 Shore recess
3 Be frugal
4 "You look as if you've __ ghost!"
5 Swimwear
6 Toad feature
7 Open a bit
8 Bar food
9 Williams of *Poltergeist*
10 Word of regret
11 Use a backhoe
12 Garden dweller
13 Pa. neighbor
21 Squash variety
22 Tropical bean
25 Einstein
26 Artist's rep
27 Toast beginning
29 Traditional knowledge
30 Supplementary
32 Well-qualified
33 From John Paul
34 Corpulent
35 Cow catcher
36 One of the opposition
38 Actress Garr
41 Señora Perón
42 Be apprehensive about
47 Bird dog
49 Authorize
52 The __ the line
54 Bacterium type
55 Leg bone
56 Barbecue leftover
57 Get guns again
58 Kingly address
59 Circular roof
60 First-rate
61 Omelet cooker
62 Be a mortgagor
63 Got a peek at

228 GROUNDKEEPERS by Wayne R. Williams

ACROSS

1 Health resort
4 Hotshot
7 Kind of camera: Abbr.
10 Singer Stafford et al.
13 Steam engine
15 DMV procedure
17 Set up
18 Thankless one
19 Chopin's *chérie*
21 Blood quantity
22 Stitched
23 Teachers' org.
24 Latin 101 verb
25 Hindu mystics
29 Genetic letters
30 Shade source
33 Came to earth
34 Sell out
37 Bossy's comment
38 *Aida* guy
40 That girl
41 Throbs
43 Irrigation need
44 Calls one's own
45 Bandleader Brown
46 Short snooze
48 Forks over
50 Tammy Faye's former grp.
51 Take off
55 Novelist Seton
56 *Steel Magnolias* star
60 Speak hesitatingly
62 Too old
63 Saved, as a mag article
64 Old pro
65 Partnership word
66 Paid notices
67 Compass dir.
68 Mos. and mos.

DOWN

1 Some deer
2 Blender setting
3 Hood's missile
4 Building add-on
5 *Picnic* playwright
6 Ultimate letters
7 Fishing nets
8 Actress Carter
9 Rule: Abbr.
10 *Upstairs, Downstairs* star
11 Caesar's port
12 Doesn't dele
14 Hayloft locales
16 Hooky player
20 Testifier of '91
26 Merchandise
27 "Woe is me!"
28 Ctr.
29 Bowler's button
30 Nero, for one: Abbr.
31 Bud's partner
32 Famous feminist
34 Mrs. Truman
35 Light-dawning cry
36 "Absolutely!"
39 Shemp's brother
42 Turkish staple
46 Is taken aback
47 Burning
48 Rigatoni, e.g.
49 Singer Susan
50 Alias: Abbr.
52 Psychedelic doctor
53 *Pomp and Circumstance* composer
54 Idyllic places
57 Tennis term
58 Actor Montand
59 Honor with a party
61 Extinct bird

BODY BEATERS by Randolph Ross

ACROSS
1 Dieter's entrée
6 Ran into
9 Fitting
12 Handsome guy
14 Home to billions
16 Bowl sound
17 Rousing hoedown tune
19 LP filler
20 Sixth sense
21 Tough puzzle
23 Laissez-__
24 "Life Is Just __ of Cherries"
25 Terrestrial
28 Middle Easterner
29 Comet and friends
32 Salinger girl
35 Current unit
36 Took a rip (at)
38 *Shop __ You Drop*
39 Disoriented
41 Side dishes
44 Chagall and Antony

47 Code of silence
48 Craze
49 One of the Chipmunks
51 Unfaithful friend
53 Vane dir.
56 Lodge member
57 Funny joke
59 Pub choice
60 Royal address
61 Second banana
62 *Mal de __*
63 Poker pile
64 John of rock

DOWN
1 Out of danger
2 Fusses
3 Airplane maneuver
4 Hill builder
5 Break up
6 Ike's missus
7 Fox Sports Net rival
8 Clasp of a sort
9 Threatening one

10 Expert group
11 Hammer wielder
13 Long steps
15 Isle off Venezuela
18 Boathouse hanging
22 Unit of sound
23 Summer appliance
25 Like Sabin's vaccine
26 Verne character
27 Tasty morsel
28 "Small world, __ it?"
30 Mas that baa
31 Winning streak
33 Oven accessory
34 Designer Schiaparelli
37 Kowtows
40 Scuba gear
42 Bahrain, for one
43 *Tin __* ('87 film)

45 Takes a chance
46 Siamese attraction
48 *Atlantic City* director
49 Red as __
50 Butcher's wts.

51 Smile broadly
52 Space starter
53 Dalmatian's name
54 Utah state flower
55 British architect
58 Campaign pro

MONSTROUS by Trip Payne

ACROSS
1 Vinegar acid
7 On the __ (fleeing)
10 Eye part
14 Texas city
15 College climber
16 Hockey player's protection
17 European airline
18 Make known
19 Tavern buys
20 Monster you can't fool?
23 Become one
26 Part of TNT
27 Squeaker or squealer
28 High transport
29 Dodger Hershiser
31 Ethereal
33 Church areas
35 Smart aleck
37 Tiny, to Burns
38 Monster's game equipment?
42 __ in "nudnik"
43 Raymond Burr role

45 Dull hues
48 __ uproar
49 Work hard
50 Tiriac of tennis
51 "__ your old man!"
53 Crumpet complement
55 Napoleonic marshal
56 Monstrous novel?
60 Melville opus
61 __ *Kapital*
62 Wild equine
66 Become winded
67 Sign a contract
68 Soda units
69 Red and Black
70 Both Begleys
71 Go AWOL

DOWN
1 Ms. MacGraw
2 Bandleader Calloway
3 Prior to, in poetry
4 Period of office
5 Dostoevsky character

6 Where to park your parkas
7 Taleteller
8 Oversized birdcage
9 *The Thin Man* name
10 __ the crack of dawn
11 Holds dear
12 Channel swimmer
13 Determine worth
21 "Sacred" word form
22 Cossack leader
23 "That's super!"
24 Actor Estrada
25 Lucie's dad
30 Comedian Bruce
32 Kidney enzyme
34 Coors rival
36 '92 Wimbledon winner
37 Absolutely
39 *Persona non __*
40 Zodiac beast
41 McClurg of movies

44 Bridge expert Culbertson
45 Legs of lamb
46 Dormmate
47 Mother on *Bewitched*
48 Bali, but not Mali
52 Goody, maybe

54 Palmer, to pals
57 Caldwell et al.
58 Suggests a price
59 Scarfs down
63 "__ whillikers!"
64 Make a miscue
65 Q-U connectors

231   ZOO FILMS by Eric Albert

ACROSS

1 __ *Having a Baby*
5 Suitor
10 Iced dessert
14 Roof edge
15 "Stormy Weather" singer
16 Ballerina Pavlova
17 Hepburn film of '68
20 Music character
21 Unbind
22 "__ the season . . ."
23 Emmy-winner Daly
24 Mature woman
28 Cuts the grass
29 *Touched by an Angel* network
32 Circle the earth
33 Toll road
34 Dr. Jonas __
35 Hogan film of '86
38 Bumper-sticker word
39 Religious image
40 *M*A*S*H* extra
41 Inspire wonder
42 Sounds of censure
43 Optimally
44 Slow and dull
45 Act human?
46 Professional penman
49 Help hatch
54 Heston film of '68
56 Become a landlord
57 Locker-room garment
58 Milan money
59 __ Ono
60 Nail-board stuff
61 Entrée list

DOWN

1 Abel's brother
2 Laughing sounds
3 Mr. Knievel
4 Prefix for propelled
5 Sure winner
6 Usual practices
7 Auto-racer Luyendyk
8 Tavern or hotel
9 Yesterday's groom
10 Lake craft
11 Picnic pests
12 Anatomical hinge
13 Deserve for deeds
18 Wholly
19 Charged particles
23 Small souvenir
24 Fudge flavor
25 Quiver contents
26 Steak cut
27 *Casablanca* character
28 Director Forman
29 Core group
30 Glorify
31 Trapshooter's target
33 Overly exacting
34 Social slight
36 Data holder
37 Not so
42 Fit-tied link
43 In a mischievous manner
44 Kind of bean
45 Go into
46 Vigorously active
47 Singer Laine
48 Foul-smelling
49 "__ Only Have Love"
50 Soothing cream
51 ". . . baked in __"
52 Sea swallow
53 Birthright seller
55 Pah-pah preceder

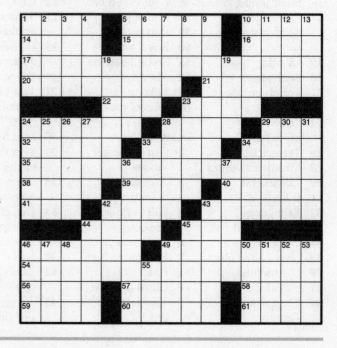

232   STAGE NAMES by Fred Piscop

ACROSS

1 Señor's squiggle
6 __ *Richard's Almanack*
10 Sp. woman
13 Indian, for one
14 __ snuff (acceptable)
15 Recipe component
16 BERNARD SCHWARTZ
18 Order for dinner
19 Cool treat
20 More harsh
22 Taurus preceder
24 As Darth Vader would
25 Gunboat feature
28 Discoverer's cry
30 Patella locale
31 At any time
33 Extends one's enlistment
36 Peculiar
37 "Inner" word form
38 U.S. draftees
40 Cheerleading word
41 __ as a judge
43 Small songbird
45 Prefix for nautical
46 Turmoil
48 Man with a megaphone
50 George C. Scott role
52 Mideast rulers
54 Decks out
56 South American airline
60 Gator kin
61 RICHARD STARKEY
63 Fork prong
64 Secluded valley
65 Lama land
66 __ in "solve"
67 Exercise system
68 Caravan stops

DOWN

1 Little shavers
2 Sect's symbol
3 Letterman's rival
4 Preschoolers' supervision
5 Bonus piece
6 Thick soup
7 Pick
8 Elevator man
9 Player list
10 ARTHUR JEFFERSON
11 Party hearty
12 Mimic's skill
15 Gray bird
17 Puts together
21 New York's Medgar __ College
23 Visualize
25 Ring results
26 Take apart
27 AARON CHWATT
29 Egg on
32 Solemn promises
34 Trim off
35 Brake device
37 Shortstop's slip
39 Not outside the body
42 Tempt
44 Numbered hwy.
45 Old French region
47 Get-up-and-go
49 Brit noble
50 Nation's agreements
51 High-ceiling courts
53 __ Carta
55 Missile housing
57 Captures
58 Native Canadian
59 They may be liberal
62 Electron's chg.

233 SOMETHING'S BREWING by Trip Payne

ACROSS
1 A Leno predecessor
5 Picket-line crosser
9 Beef-rating org.
13 Cartoonist Peter
14 There's nothing in it
15 Stuck-up person
16 Reviewer Rex
17 Essayist's alias
18 Practice piece
19 Voice of the teapot in *Beauty and the Beast*
22 Rabbit-sized rodent
23 Publicize loudly
24 Carroll's teapot dweller
29 Buffalo NHLers
33 Overwhelming emotion
34 Gene carriers
35 Van Gogh locale
36 Author Rand
37 Assail
38 WWII contingent
39 I love, to Livy
40 Travel-guide name
41 Teapot Dome figure
44 Freight hauler
45 Utter bomb
49 Tempest in a teapot
53 Two-time Nobelist
54 Assemble a film
55 Caron film
56 Fort Knox bar
57 Dinner bed, often
58 Made a misstatement
59 Yemen seaport
60 Spree
61 Foal's father

DOWN
1 Graph lead-in
2 Field of battle
3 "Wall Street Lays __"
4 Copland opus
5 Knife cases
6 Lassie, e.g.
7 *Inter* __ (among other things)
8 Boston's nickname
9 Not schooled
10 Like lime pie
11 Comedienne Goodman
12 Feasted on
15 Organic lubricant
20 Guitars' ancestors
21 Miffed
25 *The __ the Jackal*
26 Golden Rule word
27 European valley
28 Guesses: Abbr.
29 "I never __ purple cow"
30 Asian sea
31 Tell all
32 Economic downturn
36 Sometimes-shy person
37 Kind of eclipse
39 Word form for "air"
40 Move to and fro quickly
42 Bowl-O-Rama button
43 Somalia's home
46 Operadom's "Bubbles"
47 IV x XXVII
48 Tanker
49 It may be mutual
50 Exhort
51 Singer Adams
52 __-de-camp
53 Espionage grp.

234 TIMELY ADVICE by Donna J. Stone

ACROSS
1 Coral and Red
5 Discombobulate
10 Church area
14 David's instrument
15 Producer Ponti
16 Thailand neighbor
17 As a result
18 Right: Fr.
19 "__ forgive those . . ."
20 START OF A QUIP
23 Soothes
24 Junior, for one
25 '20s auto
28 Fish-and-chips partner
29 "If I __ Hammer"
33 Telescope view
35 Hairdresser's nightmare
37 Pianist Gilels
38 MIDDLE OF QUIP
42 Jupiter's alias
43 Watering hole
44 Jittery
47 Be important
48 Supermarket-scanner data: Abbr.
51 Teut.
52 Baseball great Mel
54 Dogpatch dweller
56 END OF QUIP
61 It's nothing
63 Coleco competitor
64 Blue hue
65 Eternally
66 __ so many words
67 Wear a long face
68 Florida county
69 Pass a law
70 Sound-stage areas

DOWN
1 Aussie woman
2 Sharp scolding
3 Sock style
4 Spinning-reel part
5 Electrically versatile
6 Theda of the silents
7 Elvis __ Presley
8 Opens an envelope
9 Frank
10 Jai __
11 Deli delicacy
12 Piglet's mom
13 Vane dir.
21 Leading man?
22 *Strangers __ Train*
26 Leave the stage
27 *Thimble Theatre* name
30 Citrus cooler
31 Air conduit
32 __ *Is Born*
34 Boxer Spinks
35 TV talker
36 Peace Nobelist Myrdal
38 Lane marker
39 Like some nobility
40 Even so
41 Sheer fear
42 Run for the health of it
45 Came by
46 Natural gas component
48 Inimitable
49 Next-to-last syllable
50 Haunted-house sounds
53 Rocky Mountain range
55 Bill of fashion
57 Knight time
58 Bank deposit?
59 Author Ambler
60 "__ She Sweet?"
61 Last letter in the OED
62 Zsa Zsa's sister

235 STRANGE QUARTERS by Randolph Ross

ACROSS

1 Havana honcho
7 Tennis pro, often
14 Wind instrument
16 Take a rest
17 Defensive wall
18 Stockpiles
19 Rock stars, to teens
20 *Bolero* composer
22 *Pinta* partner
23 Tiny touches
24 "__ 'em!" (coach's exhortation)
29 Bit of comedy
30 Make repairs to
31 Lead astray
32 Efficiency apartment?
34 High-rise fortuneteller?
35 Deluxe aerie?
37 Sandinista leader
38 Some sisters
39 Blushing
42 Rear parts, in anatomy
43 Reagan Secretary of State
44 "__ Ha'i"
45 Shed, in Sheffield
47 Stalagmite fan
48 Winery acivity
52 Hard to catch
54 Rashly
55 Troop group
56 Loud speaker
57 Fairly good

DOWN

1 Managing somehow
2 Maine national park
3 Lamour costume
4 Song refrain
5 They'll be darned
6 "Let Me Be the __"
7 Eastern Europeans
8 Precious resource
9 Val Kilmer film of '85
10 "__ bodkins!"
11 Ring stats
12 Lea lady
13 TLC dispensers
15 Willy-nilly
21 In the gut
23 Neural branches
25 Hatred
26 Judy Garland, née __
27 Old French coin
28 President pro __
30 No philanderer
31 It may be on the house
32 Secret messages
33 Soup or salad
34 It holds a qt. of milk
35 *The Bride Came __*
36 Coronado's quest
39 Deep ditch
40 News time
41 Worst-case descriptor
43 More immense
44 Fundamental
46 Aware of
47 Medical discovery
48 "__ the season . . ."
49 Hill builder
50 That girl
51 Summer shade
53 Youngster

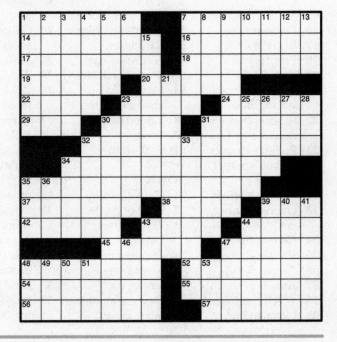

236 ALL WET by Gus Black

ACROSS

1 Historical period
4 Cup of coffee
8 Betrayed boredom
14 Actor Herbert
15 *Exodus* author
16 *The List of __ Messenger*
17 Rock Hudson film of '68
20 Oedipus' mother
21 Maui strings
22 Needing a massage
23 __ *en scène* (stage setting)
25 Diplomacy
29 Farm tool
30 Tornado, so to speak
33 Pigeon sound
34 18th president
35 Wife's mom, e.g.
37 Chinese-food ingredient
41 Family car
42 Indian corn
43 Night before
44 *La Mer* composer
47 "Tea for __"
50 Horn sound
52 Sleeveless garment
53 Impatient one's query
54 Clark's coworker
56 Color close to cranberry
59 Old-time engine
63 French mathematician
64 Owl outburst
65 Singer Damone
66 Main road
67 Poet Millay
68 Doe beau

DOWN

1 Biblical prophet
2 Art genre
3 *Cocoon* Oscar-winner
4 Sticks out
5 Smell __ (be suspicious)
6 Pauling's specialty
7 "__ was saying . . ."
8 American Leaguer
9 Ax cousin
10 Twist violently
11 Pen point
12 Corn unit
13 Heredity letters
18 Pronounce
19 Kick out
24 Panama, for one
26 Rights org.
27 Paint layer
28 Aspen machine
30 Tendency
31 Kid's card game
32 Real swank
34 Onetime sports car
36 Compass pt.
37 Sand-castle destroyer
38 Film critic James
39 Dirty Harry portrayer
40 Sibling, for short
41 Spider product
45 As Satan would
46 Kiss: Sp.
47 Be prosperous
48 Cotton killer
49 At bat next
51 Finish second
53 Drenched
55 Actor Sharif
57 "__ Fire" (Springsteen song)
58 __ *bene*
59 Health center
60 Paving material
61 Superlative suffix
62 Señor Guevara

237 ALL THINGS BRIGHT by Richard Silvestri

ACROSS

1 Carnival attraction
5 Sound of fright
9 Robin Cook book
13 In a while
14 No-no
15 More than
16 Bowling, New England-style
18 Zola novel
19 Charm
20 Chow down
21 Black card
22 Echo
24 Standard charge
26 Heads the cast
28 Parking place
32 Lorenz or Moss
35 Facial feature
37 "Born in the __"
38 Procedure
39 Pub potation
40 Attacking with satire
45 Cleveland or Washington: Abbr.
46 Come into view
47 Hefty
49 Real bummer
51 As __ pin
55 '60s TV talker
58 __-Magnon man
60 Gets around
61 Univ. unit
62 Barge crew
64 Up to it
65 New York island
66 Where to see FDR
67 __-do-well
68 Gravity-powered vehicle
69 Ending for joke or game

DOWN

1 Indy entrant
2 Senseless
3 Ladies of Spain
4 Last
5 Big difference
6 Rose lover of fiction
7 Sub device
8 Mail-order extra
9 Anxiety
10 Sort of circular
11 Café handout
12 Riyadh resident
14 Threefold
17 Boorish fellow
23 Tied
25 Roof goo
27 Slowpoke
29 Not quite shut
30 Strong wind
31 Flock females
32 Luau lesson
33 PDQ kin
34 Gangplank
36 Critic Kenneth
41 Pushcart proprietor
42 Regatta need
43 Wise guys
44 Welcomes
45 Kinds of firecrackers
48 Was resilient
50 Cross-examine
52 Own up to
53 "Come up and __"
54 Actor Ed
55 Thom of shoedom
56 After-bath wear
57 Fashion mag
59 Make eyes at
63 Took cover

238 CITRUS MUSIC by Cathy Millhauser

ACROSS

1 Make an exchange
5 Mardi __
9 Bette, in *All About Eve*
14 Prepare (the way)
15 Roof runoff
16 Nautical adverb
17 Son of Zeus
18 Dismantle
19 Potter's finish
20 Citric Dylan tune?
23 Mighty peculiar
24 Three, in Capri
25 Goat quote
28 Court cry
31 In
36 Creator of Boy
38 Keep at it
40 Alamo rival
41 Citric Welk group?
44 Reagan and Howard
45 Like Nash's lama
46 Half of deca-
47 Armed swimmers
49 Wonderland bird
51 Averse to mingling
52 African slitherer
54 Rap-sheet letters
56 Citric Glen Campbell tune?
64 All over
65 Be a kvetch
66 Revolution line
68 Word expert Peter Mark __
69 Musical tempo
70 Greek philosopher
71 Make an LP
72 Preeminent
73 Churchill's successor

DOWN

1 Springs are here
2 Nice and friendly
3 State confidently
4 Green sauce
5 Solomon of rhyme
6 Called up
7 Go-fer
8 Quick drink
9 Fridge device
10 *M*A*S*H* nurse
11 Stationery stack
12 Mideast region
13 Soothsayer's sign
21 Find smashing
22 Qum resident
25 Part of MGM
26 Literally, "for this"
27 Catalyst, e.g.
29 Mr. von Furstenberg
30 Marked off, in a way
32 Find awful
33 Bakery hardware
34 Jolly feeling
35 Opinion piece
37 To boot
39 Peace Prize city
42 Humid
43 Piped up
48 Palette set
50 Flue feature
53 Warsaw et al.
55 Make gape
56 Distort
57 Inventor Sikorsky
58 Hockey structure
59 Goes quickly
60 French milk
61 __ *la Douce*
62 Cut down
63 Midevening
67 Chip off the old block

MONETARY POLICY by Eric Albert

ACROSS

1 Jezebel's husband
5 Disconcert
10 *Ghost* name
14 Lose appeal
15 He-manly
16 Beasts of burden
17 Birthright barterer
18 Dampen with drops
19 __ Hari
20 START OF A QUIP
23 Key with one flat
25 Wedding walkway
26 Of a sense
27 Summon silently
31 Black as night
32 *The Third Man* actor
33 Class-rank stat.
36 Baseball great Speaker
37 MIDDLE OF QUIP
38 Biceps exercise
39 Darling
40 Catch in a lie
41 Frozen raindrops
42 Made a quick note
43 Ms. Gaynor
44 Yellowish-brown
47 Bad temper
48 END OF QUIP
53 Spread in a tub
54 Oil source
55 Be stunning
58 Founding father?
59 Ward off
60 First name in fashion
61 Sandbox patron
62 Put to use
63 Criminal crowd

DOWN

1 *The Naked __*
2 Is owner of
3 *Freebie and the Bean* star
4 Toronto team
5 Fossil resin
6 Boxer Max
7 Aussie rock group
8 New York ballpark
9 Bay
10 Field of activity
11 Checkups, for example
12 Oxide component
13 Foolish
21 Encyclopedia bk.
22 Myanmar neighbor
23 Orchestra leader Percy
24 Saki's real name
27 Suit
28 Marry in haste
29 Make murky
30 Iodine source
32 Toad feature
33 OAS member
34 Hold dear
35 Dead tired
38 Sidewalk vendor's offering
40 Corrida cry
42 Robbins of Broadway
43 Speed-limit letters
44 WWII craft
45 Antiquated
46 Piece of luck
47 Refine ore
49 Was dressed in
50 Bend an elbow
51 Pickable
52 Recovered from
56 Buddhist belief
57 Silly Putty holder

IN THE MOOD by Randolph Ross

ACROSS

1 Rummy variety
8 Seed coverings
13 Fellow employee
14 They have brains
15 Cooperating in crime
16 "__ Mountain High Enough"
17 Kennedy matriarch
18 Dali feature
20 Binge
21 Half the world
22 __ *Championship Season*
25 Pitcher feature
28 Seventh-century date
30 Cosmic countenance
35 Judge's shout
36 Spiteful ones
37 Expected
38 Match a raise
39 Informal refusals
40 Govt. purchasing org.
42 Reference-book name
46 Congealment
49 Normandy town
53 "Amen!"
54 Rational thinker
56 "¡__ días!"
57 May birthstones
58 Rose oil
59 Saw again

DOWN

1 Michigan arena
2 Inspires grandly
3 Bit of marginalia
4 Mr. Carney
5 Economize
6 Sax range
7 State one's case
8 Met highlight
9 Southfork, e.g.
10 Wealthy
11 Ball-game summaries
12 __ Paulo, Brazil
13 Sleeper, for one
14 Garfield, but not Roosevelt
19 Stew
20 *A __ Born*
22 Completely
23 Limits risk
24 Home of Iowa State
26 "Excuse me!"
27 Eat one's words
29 Kind of verb: Abbr.
30 Mike or Mary
31 Half the course
32 Trainee
33 Unspecified degree
34 "__ Lisa"
41 Field of battle
43 Texas tackler
44 Folklore being
45 __ on (urged)
47 Big name in fashion
48 UFO crew
49 "Get lost!"
50 Bathroom square
51 *Shane* star
52 Switch settings
53 Entrepreneur's govt. agcy.
55 S&L offering

241 WEATHER-WISE by Shirley Soloway

ACROSS
1 Five-time Wimbledon champ
5 Hurt badly
9 Small pieces
13 Lhasa's locale
14 Ms. Abzug
15 "Put a lid __!"
16 Doesn't exist
17 TV studio sign
18 Theda of silents
19 Quite appropriate
22 Dr. Casey
23 Leave behind
24 Singer Barbara
26 Beef cut
28 __ Field (old Brooklyn ballpark)
31 Breakfast order
34 Vicinity
37 Tatum or Ryan
38 "That's awesome!"
39 Act of deception
41 San Diego attraction
42 Conductor Dorati
44 Withdraw (from)
45 Constant irritant
46 Wetter, in a way
48 Hire a decorator
50 Thrust (upon)
53 Draws out
57 Play on words
59 Make a great impression
61 *M*A*S*H* star
63 Yes ending
64 Sea flier
65 Privy to
66 Took a crack at
67 Vex
68 Flat craft
69 Dance move
70 Editor's instruction

DOWN
1 Puppeteer Bil
2 Actor Davis
3 Christmas-song quintet
4 Gets together
5 Haberdashery department
6 Warning sound
7 Sacro follower
8 Leatherneck
9 Short haircut
10 Very easily
11 Grow weary
12 Ollie's buddy
14 Rudder operator
20 Capote's nickname
21 Big shot
25 King __ Saud
27 Ship's forepart
29 New Mexico town
30 Pigeonhole
31 Old oath
32 Heredity unit
33 Hear about
35 Ram's mate
36 Slightly open
39 Sacked out
40 Kind of jack
43 Purpose
45 Sulky ones
47 Cooks chestnuts
49 Tooth pro's deg.
51 Mini, for one
52 Very strange
54 French painter
55 Comic Kovacs
56 Refine metal
57 Matched set
58 Forearm bone
60 Horn sound
62 Ubiquitous bug

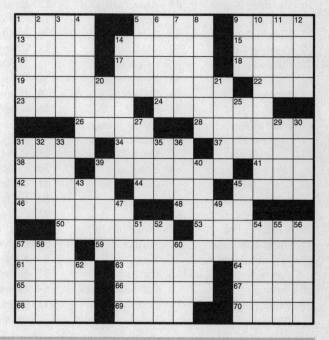

242 POLITICS AS USUAL by Richard Silvestri

ACROSS
1 Pompous people
6 Where the Vikings landed
10 Riga resident
14 Written exercise
15 Smart guy?
16 Hodgepodge
17 Gobbled up
18 *Educating* __ ('83 film)
19 Secluded valley
20 Political PR person
22 Hard to find
23 It may be legal
24 Slots spot
26 Change chemically
29 Make happy
33 Spheres
37 Hodges of baseball
38 Something to sneeze at?
39 Collect the crops
40 Alpha's antithesis
42 Major Hoople's cry
43 Prohibit by law
45 Bern's river
46 NFL team
47 Connecting flight
48 Opposition group
50 Principal role
52 MCI rival
57 Not as much
60 Political operative
63 Grad
64 Author James
65 More than
66 Crib cry
67 "Them" or "Us"
68 Mystic writings
69 In a while
70 One of the gang
71 Oscar-night sight

DOWN
1 Bikini event
2 Physical condition
3 Become established
4 Correct a text
5 "Return to __"
6 Painter Chagall
7 Came to earth
8 Snappy comeback
9 Make quake
10 Political crony
11 Ms. Fitzgerald
12 Section of seats
13 Color variation
21 The Beaver State
25 Modernizing prefix
27 Fire preceder
28 Unsullied
30 Pond life
31 Stagecoach puller
32 Tackle's colleagues
33 Metallic rocks
34 Find a tenant
35 __ California
36 Political opportunist
38 Louisiana county
41 Gunsel's weapon
44 Fury
48 Musically slow
49 Asparagus units
51 Flooded
53 Answer a charge
54 Actress Massey
55 "When pigs fly!"
56 Lock of hair
57 Prayer-wheel user
58 Zing
59 Big-time wrestling?
61 Take it from the top
62 Homeowner's holding

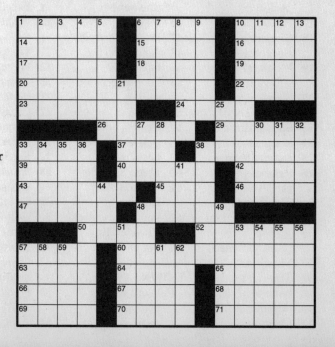

243 PLAY BALL! by Eric Albert

ACROSS

1 Indonesian island
5 Decision-making power
10 Finn's floater
14 __ vincit omnia
15 Body of soldiers
16 Gardner of mystery
17 Kids' game
20 Compass pt.
21 Sills solo
22 Pick up on
23 Motley __ (rock group)
24 Fischer's opponent
25 Pack up and leave
28 On __ with (equal to)
29 Blue as the sky
30 Close-fitting
31 Mess-hall meal
35 Woody Allen, in *Bananas*
38 Fuss
39 River Napoleon navigated
40 Par minus two
41 Stare slack-jawed
42 *Mr. Ed* is one
43 Take a wrong turn
47 Renders speechless
48 Assert without proof
49 "Oh!"
50 "Mamma" follower
53 Deteriorating
56 State strongly
57 Full
58 Singer Fitzgerald
59 Sleuth Wolfe
60 Dark hardwood
61 Become lachrymose

DOWN

1 Make fun of
2 Author __ Kingsley
3 Cast a ballot
4 Circle segment
5 Foment
6 *L.A. Law* lawyer
7 Exercise system
8 Soak (up)
9 Where columns are found
10 Landlord's loot
11 First sign
12 Small bit
13 Easily irritated
18 Did damage to
19 Not far off
23 Composer Gian __ Menotti
24 White of a wave
25 Plumb loco
26 Singer Pinza
27 Signaled an anchor
28 Point of view
30 Cuts quickly
31 Course meeting
32 Lofty
33 Scandinavian city
34 Sigh of relief
36 Kind of
37 River embankments
41 Chevalier musical
42 Like a suit fabric
43 Cartoonist Wilson
44 Martini garnish
45 Make a change
46 Part of MGM
47 Very pale
49 "Take __ the Limit"
50 Track distance
51 Wait at a light
52 Without delay: Abbr.
54 Chew the fat
55 Royal Botanic Gardens site

244 SHELL SHOCK by Fred Piscop

ACROSS

1 Boxer Max
5 __ to stern
9 Teases
14 Choir member
15 "__ a heart!"
16 Exemplar of perfection
17 Police, slangily
18 Cheater's sleeveful
19 Montreal's subway
20 Newscaster on the half shell?
23 Spot to drive from
24 Long. crosser
25 Lubricate anew
28 Animal-product eschewer
31 *The __ and I*
34 Petroleum giant
35 __-pop (family-owned)
36 Mr. Onassis
37 Trapper on the half shell?
40 Summer drink
41 Overjoys
42 Banana throwaway
43 "And I Love __" (Beatles tune)
44 Tom Jones' birthplace
45 Finches and pheasants
46 Make a dress
47 Wag's wordplay
48 Actress on the half shell?
55 Food-processor setting
56 Sullen
57 Oolong and pekoe
59 Less cordial
60 Lively subjects
61 Admiral Zumwalt
62 Pains in the neck
63 Chess ending
64 Bread and booze

DOWN

1 Word from Scrooge
2 Actor Baldwin
3 Latin list ender
4 Earth's action
5 *Evening __* (sitcom)
6 Sonora snack
7 Neck and neck
8 Arizona city
9 Excellent
10 What "i.e." stands for
11 Turn down
12 Have coming
13 __-mo replay
21 Blanc or Tillis
22 Grassy plains
25 Indian chief
26 Wear away
27 Earthy color
28 Soundtrack component
29 Overact
30 Comic Kaplan's namesakes
31 Buffet patron
32 Conquistador's quality
33 Half the third-graders
35 African nation
38 Ring bearers
39 She never married
45 Kramden's vehicle
46 Sloppy precipitation
47 Prize money
48 *Time* founder
49 Crocus kin
50 __ *Bede* (Eliot novel)
51 Vaudevillian Bayes
52 Jeff's partner
53 Slippery
54 Like some excuses
55 Dickens character
58 Sea plea

245 HOLD THAT TIGER by Trip Payne

ACROSS
1 Trick takers, often
5 Moves diagonally
9 Where to detrain
14 With the exception of
15 *Mirabella* rival
16 Kind of football
17 No contest, e.g.
18 Circus musician
19 Stuck in the mud
20 Cereal with a tiger mascot
23 Vaudevillian Eddie
24 __ up (be honest)
25 Play for time
28 Go nuts, with "out"
30 Circumference segment
33 Indulging in revelry
34 Roger of *Cheers*
35 *Jacta* __ *est*
36 Comic strip with a tiger
39 Swiss artist
40 Screenwriter James
41 Computer accessory
42 In the dumps
43 Crop pest
44 Stocked with weapons
45 Cook book
46 Corn or form starter
47 Description of Blake's tiger
53 Perry destination
54 Rocky spot
55 New York college
57 Without company
58 __ *kleine Nachtmusik*
59 Any thing at all
60 *The Maids* playwright
61 Zipped along
62 Singer James

DOWN
1 Little viper
2 Barn baby
3 For all time
4 Pacino film
5 Like some sauces
6 Nautical adverb
7 Pleased as punch
8 Livestock device
9 Linen fabric
10 Satie and Estrada
11 *Fils'* parent
12 *The Defiant* __
13 Lincoln son
21 Conductor Georg
22 Pet-shop purchase
25 Loots
26 Refrain sounds
27 Was under the weather
28 Room fresheners
29 Richards of tennis
30 Obsolete platter
31 Singer Della
32 Scoped out
35 Goolagong is one
37 Wynonna's mother
38 Muscat fellow
43 Easter finery
45 Poet Hart
46 Egged on
47 Loft cube
48 Fairy-tale word
49 Film worker
50 Poison
51 A lot of fun
52 Cross-shaped fastener
53 Wild tear
56 Airline to Tokyo

246 GETTING GOOFY by Fred Piscop

ACROSS
1 Puccini opera
6 Biblical king
11 __ Paulo, Brazil
14 Detest
15 Full of energy
16 "__ a boy!"
17 "That's All, Folks!" series
19 Meadow
20 Ponce de __
21 Conger
22 Mark again
24 Mr. Sharif
26 "__ Back to Old Virginny"
27 Max of makeup
30 Convertible, slangily
31 *The Lady* __
32 Rayburn and Kelly
33 Unexplained sighting
36 Greek H's
37 Hand-cream additives
38 Short distance
39 Shriner's topper
40 Ships' staffs
41 Absolute
42 Naval aide
44 Drearily
45 Bone-dry
47 "Purple __" (Prince tune)
48 Come (to)
49 Dinghy need
50 Info
54 __ es Salaam
55 Sunday-news insert
58 Foolish fellow
59 Poetic muse
60 Shriver of TV
61 Mao __-tung
62 __ *Seed* ('77 movie)
63 Jazz dance

DOWN
1 Hard to believe
2 Orchestra member
3 "Get lost!"
4 Implies
5 "__ you serious?"
6 Bigot, for one
7 Hebrew month
8 __ Tin Tin
9 Excess supplies
10 Just __ (punishment)
11 Pliable toy
12 *The* __ (Mr. T series)
13 American Indian
18 Planetary lap
23 To opposite
25 Stylish, so to speak
26 Bamboolike grasses
27 Feudal estate
28 Feed the kitty
29 Custer opponent
30 Take title to anew
32 Gather slowly
34 Sense
35 Grand Ole __
37 Generator part
38 Maintain one's position
40 Like some beef
41 Mentalist Geller
43 __ Claire, WI
44 Robin Williams role
45 Camp David Accords signer
46 Collect
47 Semi-synthetic fabric
49 Aware of
51 Dynamic start
52 Barbershop order
53 PDQ
56 Asian nation, for short
57 Mornings: Abbr.

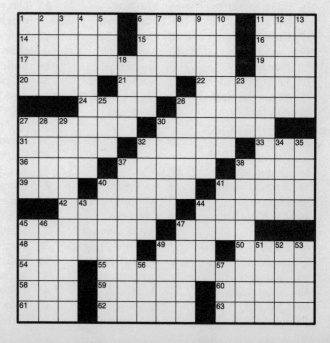

247 WATER PIX by Alice Long

ACROSS
1 Go for a rathskeller record
5 __ as a hatter
10 Hacienda home
14 Looking up
15 __ la Paix (Paris street)
16 Polly or Mame
17 "Excuse me!"
18 More fitting
19 The Lettermen, e.g.
20 Book of pride and Joy?
22 Sham
24 Controversial tree spray
25 Feed the hogs
26 Action film of '80
33 Ham it up
34 Steno's boss
35 Hamper fill
36 "Uh-uh!"
37 Loft lava
38 Actress Zetterling
39 Airport stats.
41 Rocky peaks
42 Gather bit by bit
44 War film of '60
47 Woolly moms
48 Bridge section
49 Drawing room
52 Hold one's hand?
56 End-of-scene direction
57 Gourmand
59 *Star Trek VI* captain
60 Chorus singer
61 States
62 Iowa State address
63 Low in fat
64 Breach of judgment
65 Staple to a board

DOWN
1 Hermit by the sea
2 Jocular sounds
3 Computer owner
4 Olympics entrant
5 Ark docking site
6 Comics crew
7 Distribute
8 Wine-cooler base
9 Ghost ship
10 Unwitting tool
11 Ambiance
12 Ornery mood
13 The gamut
21 Hightail it
23 Balderdash
25 *Cinderella* characters
26 Clair and Auberjonois
27 Stradivari's teacher
28 Grant Wood was one
29 Commuter's home
30 Finger-pointer
31 Esau's father
32 Armor flaw
37 Otherworldly
40 Hope contemporary
42 FBI employee
43 Map-making Earth orbiter
45 Early afternoon
46 Thinly distributed
49 Ring out
50 Linchpin locale
51 Beatles' meter maid
52 Plan part
53 Wild cat
54 Actor Guinness
55 Walrus feature
58 Rock-video award

248 HORSING AROUND by Karen Hodge

ACROSS
1 Bit of barbecue
4 Author Ferber
8 Carpenter's tool
13 Just standing around
15 Former sr.
16 Take __ (throw the bout)
17 Colt's stable?
19 Carnation containers
20 Beast of Borden
21 Nag's sickness?
23 Attack
25 Bowling surface
26 Ski-resort machine
28 Distinct styles
33 Sound sheepish
36 Hairdo
39 *My Three Sons* role
40 Newlywed horses' dream?
44 Take care of
45 Asian fruits
46 Q-U link
47 Fords of the '50s
49 Sewer line?
52 Seep slowly
55 Con jobs
58 Equine charm?
63 Captures on paper
65 Neighborhoods
66 Mustang menagerie?
68 Oscar de la __
69 Assigned function
70 Admired one
71 Alpine strain
72 Jean Auel character
73 Be a landlord

DOWN
1 Swarming (with)
2 Admired ones
3 Great time
4 Freud's concern
5 Tap one's fingers
6 Kind of congestion
7 Author Rogers St. Johns
8 Pale purple
9 Wax-covered cheese
10 Passport stamp
11 At any time
12 __ majesty (high crime)
14 Mr. Ness
18 Dagwood's neighbor
22 Police-blotter abbr.
24 Nutmeg spice
27 It's over your head
29 Like some vbs.
30 __ about
31 Farrow et al.
32 Shipped off
33 Army post
34 Imitated
35 Potent potables
37 "__ Were a Rich Man"
38 Confused states
41 Polished off
42 Movie-hype word
43 Takes off the shelf
48 Soak (up)
50 Current letters
51 Wetlands
53 African equine
54 Jetson kid
56 "__ tov!"
57 Made a vow
58 Grant from Hollywood
59 Hydrox rival
60 Libraries do it
61 *Little Man __* (Foster film)
62 Take it easy
64 Flue grime
67 Teachers' org.

249 ACTING CLASS by A.J. Santora

ACROSS

1 Women's mag
5 Overcharge
9 General Dayan
14 Witt maneuver
15 *Star Trek* propulsion
17 Betting setting
18 *Death Becomes Her* star
19 Coach Parseghian
20 Electrical units
21 Fencing sword
22 __ a dime
24 Last year's plebe
26 Real-estate abbr.
27 Smarmy to the max
29 Most unhappy
31 Works hard
32 Cashmere kin
35 Moffo of opera
36 Batter of verse
37 "__ a man with . . ."
41 Makes fun of

43 Kroft of *60 Minutes*
44 Chapter XI column
47 Gives in
49 Area code 302: Abbr.
50 Start off
53 Rogers' rope
54 Ed or Nancy of TV
56 Having troubles
58 Dernier __ (latest fashion)
59 *Thelma & Louise* star
61 Green stone
62 Poll subject of '92
63 Mars' alias
64 Percolates
65 Yale students
66 Polite bloke

DOWN

1 Ringling Brothers' home
2 Elbow grease
3 *Havana* star

4 Eb's wife
5 *Cosmos'* Carl et al.
6 __ close to schedule
7 U.S. booster rocket
8 Buddy
9 Author Rita __ Brown
10 Will-__-wisp
11 Food basic
12 Ax handlers
13 Mariel's grandpa
16 Bungle
20 The enemy
23 *The Greatest Story Ever Told* role
25 __ polloi
28 Govt. agent
30 Mailer's profession
33 East, in Essen
34 "__ real nowhere man"
36 Some teeth
38 Health program
39 *Our Miss Brooks* star

40 Most peevish
42 From __ Z
43 Swindle
44 Old sayings
45 Dionysus' mother
46 Floppy-disk holder
48 Envelope attachments

51 Maternally related
52 Part of USNA
55 Cut quickly
57 Rock legend Hendrix
60 Foolish sort
61 Binge

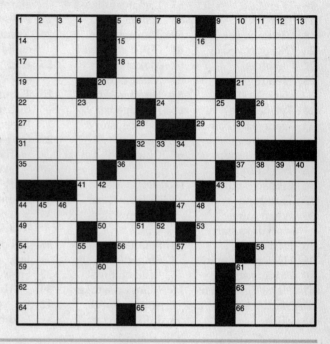

250 ANOTHER FINE MESS by Randolph Ross

ACROSS

1 *Uno* follower
4 Scads
8 Engine cos.
11 Additional phones: Abbr.
13 Nintendo forerunner
14 Long journey
15 With *The*, Lee Marvin film of '67
17 Replete (with)
18 Australian city
19 Musical transition
20 Murphy had one
21 Buttons or Barber
22 Certain psychologist
24 ME-to-FL hwy.
25 Hero of the '54 World Series
27 Posted
29 Work on a persistent squeak
30 Hash house

35 Some carolers
36 Letter opener
39 Blues great
45 Animation frame
46 Agitated states
47 Cut (off)
48 Bear: Sp.
49 Bjorn Borg, e.g.
50 Fertilizer chemicals
52 Moa relative
53 Loaded
55 "The doctor __"
56 Author James et al.
57 Pre- kin
58 Hallow ending
59 Actress Diana
60 Slalom curve

DOWN

1 Joyce hero
2 Enzyme class
3 Spreading around
4 Disagreeing

5 Use a hammock
6 Vein contents
7 Badge material
8 Quite cold
9 Disarm
10 Shooting events
12 "Gateway to the West": Abbr.
13 Parting word
14 Operatic effects
16 Feminist Molly
19 Amoco rival
22 They may have it
23 De __ (too much)
26 Secret meeting
28 Redeemed
31 *Family Ties* mom
32 Periodic-table no.
33 In order (to)
34 $C_{10}H_{14}N_2$
37 Takes out, in a way
38 Muddles through puddles

39 Carter secretary of state
40 Not so smart
41 Attracted
42 Exclusive groups
43 David Lee and Philip

44 Like a gymnast
50 Padre or Pirate, for short
51 Southern constellation
53 Mania
54 "__ to Extremes" (Billy Joel tune)

251 BOXER SHORTS by S.N.

ACROSS
1 Hemingway's nickname
5 Petty
10 Paper package
14 "Son of __!"
15 Check receiver
16 Therefore
17 Tear apart
18 Circus emcee
20 Disapproved of
22 Cat breed
23 Wedding-song start
24 Tylenol rival
25 Trademark coined by Eastman
27 Sow's quarters
28 Track offerings
32 Like some dicts.
33 Threshold
35 When some workdays start
36 First course
38 Hosiery material
40 Hosiery shade
41 Playwright Ibsen
43 Martial art
45 Zilch
46 *Jeopardy!* contestant
47 One's wheels
48 Interstate stopover
50 *Coffee, __ Me?*
52 Parcel (out)
53 Lacking fullness
56 Femme fatale
59 Tourney type
61 Gallic girlfriend
62 Makes mad
63 Merman of song
64 Desideratum
65 Put together
66 Labor-history name
67 Chip in the pot

DOWN
1 Cowboy's pal
2 Screenwriter James
3 Slaphappy
4 Singer McArdle
5 Wild outburst
6 Mansion worker
7 Author Rand
8 Info gatherer
9 Wallace's running mate
10 Stifle
11 Art Deco artist
12 A long time
13 Twist's request
19 Cause for alarm
21 Pesters
24 Vacuum container
25 Buckwheat side dish
26 Tubular instruments
27 Paper layer
29 Coffee-shop worker
30 "__ Was a Lady"
31 Common sense
34 Squid's weapon
35 Abbott-Costello link
37 Sham
39 __ *Miss Brooks*
42 "__ you" (radioer's reply)
44 Sign of the future
47 Road Runner's foe
49 Canadian capital
51 To the point
52 Macho
53 Barbershop job
54 Bar-mitzvah dance
55 Felt remorseful
56 Appearance
57 "__ We Got Fun"
58 Rose or Rozelle
60 Food-preservative initials

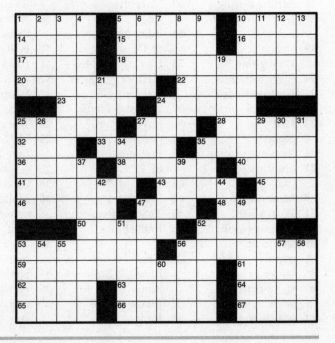

252 APT ANAGRAMS by Eric Albert

ACROSS
1 Repeated idea
6 Unflinching
11 Refuse to commit
14 On the whole
15 Rallying cry
16 Dorm covering
17 AN ORAL EDICT anagram
19 Storage receptacle
20 Type of triangle
21 Actress Scacchi
23 Unruffled
24 Ardently enthusiastic
25 Do some damage to
29 Writer Runyon
30 Pitcher's place
31 Donut covering
33 Sponsored messages
36 Small horse
37 Mondale's nickname
38 Telegram term
39 __ Lanka
40 The sauce
41 Yerba __, CA
42 Pool-hall predator
44 Schoolwork holder
45 Church split
47 Uncovered wagon
49 Arizona city
50 Thatcher's group
55 Lyric poem
56 NAME FOR SHIP anagram
58 Was in charge of
59 Bridge phrase
60 Be a squealer
61 *D.C. Cab* actor
62 Midafternoon
63 Deuce beaters

DOWN
1 Skirt style
2 Small bills
3 Mexican munchie
4 Evils
5 Soft and limp
6 Rabbi detective
7 Eskimo carving
8 Elevator inventor
9 "Who am __ complain?"
10 Sting, e.g.
11 BEAR HIT DEN anagram
12 Juan's wife
13 Caged talker
18 Bring up
22 Pi follower
24 Heckle
25 Mischievous kids
26 Othello, for one
27 NINE THUMPS anagram
28 __ *Which Way You Can*
29 See regularly
31 Understand, in sci-fi slang
32 Claiborne of fashion
34 Sufficiently cooked
35 Sail supporter
37 Make up
38 Grab some rays
40 Average improver
41 Walk-on
43 With it
44 __ Mawr
45 Rant and rave
46 Chest material
47 Small-tree thicket
48 Get out of bed
50 Former Russian ruler
51 At a distance
52 Learning method
53 Aeneas' home
54 Strong longings
57 Dashboard letters

253 TRUE GRID by Fred Piscop

ACROSS
1 Air conduit
5 Crockett defended it
10 Are: Sp.
14 Job-safety org.
15 Sand bit
16 Time-machine destination
17 Footballer's detention center?
19 "__ first you don't . . ."
20 *The War of the Worlds* visitor
21 Make out
23 Church area
24 Grove
25 Printer's proof
28 Temple quorum
31 Where it's at
34 Melon cover
36 Answer back
37 NOW cause
38 Debate side
39 Mr. Carney
41 Native: Suffix
42 Ice-cream flavor
44 High-flying toy
46 Agitated state
47 Stamp-pad devices
49 TV option
51 Taoism founder
53 Photographer Adams
57 Harsh-tempered
59 Ninepins pin
61 Blubbers
62 Footballer's magazine photo?
64 Turkey __ (dance)
65 Prepare to be knighted
66 Cassini of fashion
67 Aussie rockers
68 Walk heavily
69 French statesman Coty

DOWN
1 Tenet
2 Run-of-the-mill
3 Visual aid
4 Steak order
5 Turkish official
6 Author Hubbard
7 Track-meet org.
8 Botch up
9 Egotistic belief
10 Unisex
11 Footballer's fastener?
12 Ivan, for one
13 Envelope abbr.
18 Grievous
22 Avoid, as an issue
24 __ voyage
26 __ bono (free)
27 Orr's milieu
29 Word form for "height"
30 Nikolai's negative
31 Trucker's wheels
32 Mashie or niblick
33 Footballer's fishing gear?
35 *Star Trek* character
38 Chocolate substitute
40 Confederate
43 Publishing family
45 Freezer product
46 Bought by mail
48 Stays on
50 Hibernation station
52 Skunk's trademark
54 Made off with
55 Novelist Glasgow
56 Narrow shelf
57 Wine region
58 Country humor
59 Watch part
60 Some seaweed
63 Classical beginning

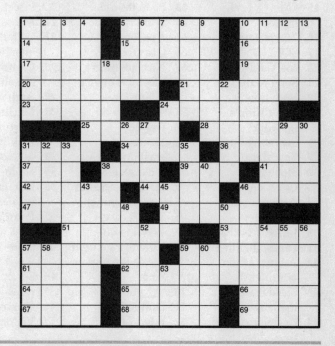

254 FROM THE HORSE'S MOUTH by Trip Payne

ACROSS
1 Eyeglasses, for short
6 Red-tag event
10 Blue shade
14 Marsh bird
15 Mr. Love?
16 Phoenix team
17 "What's that bird overhead, Tonto?"
19 South American monkey
20 Lots of quires
21 Romania, once
22 Retro singing group
25 Pay attention
26 *Mommie* __
27 Actor Gerard
28 '60s protest grp.
29 Forgets about
30 Brief beachwear
32 Puts on TV
33 Blackmore character
35 Joyce of *Roc*
38 Secretary's task
40 Spelunking fan
41 Part of MPH
43 Slaloming shape
44 Sign of the future
46 Baal's challenger
48 Some promgoers
49 Magi
50 Temple's trademark
51 Smokes, for short
52 "How was that joke, Gumby?"
57 Tighten __ belt
58 Supplements, with "out"
59 Pica alternative
60 Subjunctive word
61 TV's Batman
62 Stay a subscriber

DOWN
1 Get the point
2 Faldo's grp.
3 Unit of work
4 Animation art
5 Author Laurence et al.
6 Trig term
7 Bouquet
8 Gehrig and Gossett
9 Atlanta's zone: Abbr.
10 __ *Is Born*
11 "How fast should I go, Lone Ranger?"
12 Let loose
13 Mongols, e.g.
18 Half-__ over (tipsy)
21 Melting-watch painter
22 Prefix for sweet
23 "What's my mane made of, Roy?"
24 Bohemian
25 Price rise
26 Quaid film of '88
27 Juniper product
30 Cranberry spot
31 "How keen!"
33 Couch potato's dream device
34 Switch positions
36 Microscope part
37 Thou follower
39 Soup ingredient
40 Fridge section
41 Donna of *Angie*
42 Stritch or May
44 Most pristine
45 Sale-ad word
47 Senator Helms
48 Record machines
50 Royal Crown rival
52 Chop down
53 Word a matador adores
54 Relatives
55 Somme time
56 Bow wood

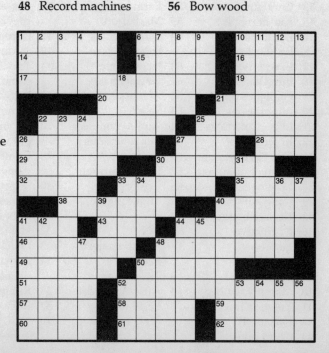

255 NOW HEAR THIS by Matt Gaffney

ACROSS
1 Explorer Amundsen
6 Applies grease to
11 Some ammo
14 Telecast component
15 "Me, __ I call myself"
16 "Certainement!"
17 SOUND SLEEPER
20 Ms. Caldwell
21 Song refrain
22 Seep slowly
23 Larry King's network
24 Sarge's shout
27 Taxi star
30 Slobber
33 Glass square
34 America's Cup contender
38 LEAKY TIRE
41 Fan, sometimes
42 August Moon offerings
43 Basketball maneuver
44 Casino naturals
47 Russian refusals
50 Grill's partner
51 Tough spot
54 Thumbprint feature
56 Douglas, e.g.
59 GHOST
63 Be in the red
64 War cry
65 Apartments
66 Old crony
67 Barn adjuncts
68 Electrical device

DOWN
1 Deride
2 Moussaka washdown
3 Pickaxe relative
4 Columnist Smith
5 A whole bunch
6 Take it easy
7 WWII town
8 Gillette invention
9 Cease-fire region: Abbr.
10 "__ you!"
11 Dunderhead
12 Edwin Aldrin
13 Shoe clerk's query
18 Canadian export
19 Religion founder
23 Louder, to Liszt
25 Banned insecticides
26 Messes up
27 Cellar-door attachments
28 Cartographic closeup
29 Archaic verb
31 Merlin of TV
32 Hartman and Kirk
33 Ltr. addenda
35 For the Boys grp.
36 Ukr. and Lith., formerly
37 Pompous sort
39 Stick around
40 Store-window word
45 Spain's longest river
46 Grounds for the Victoria Cross
48 __ a kind (poker hand)
49 "Go ahead!"
51 Cartoon coquette
52 Tom Harkin's state
53 "The First __"
55 "Uh-oh" cousin
56 Thwart a plot
57 Tiny amount
58 Promising
60 Athena's symbol
61 "What have we here?"
62 A Chorus Line finale

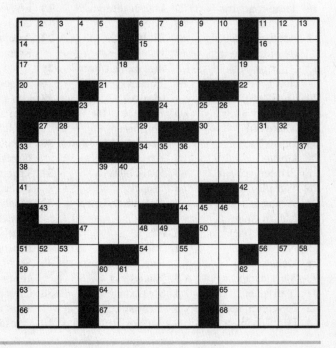

256 PLACE SETTING by Ronnie K. Allen

ACROSS
1 Yodeler's perch
4 "__ to you!" (buck-passer's words)
9 Genghis, e.g.
13 Coral formation
15 Kid-lit rabbit
16 Local theater, for short
17 Exxon rival
18 Introduction
19 Gilligan's home
20 Impolite one
21 Like __ of bricks
22 In pursuit of
23 Ebert's colleague
25 Form of pollution
27 Employees
29 Rang out
33 Kind of boom
36 Distinctive quality
38 Cairo's waters
39 "__ in Rome . . ."
40 Man-made fiber
41 Yuletide buy
42 Part of MIT
43 Court jester
44 Bird call
45 __ City (Batman's base)
47 Highway alert
49 Civil-rights leader Medgar
51 Farm horse
55 Ms. Barton
58 Quasimodo's creator
60 Jason's ship
61 Hawaiian city
62 Active strength
63 Select
64 Author Bombeck
65 Just ridiculous
66 Tie feature
67 Leafed through
68 Customs
69 "Little piggie"

DOWN
1 Sheiks' subjects
2 Poet Jones
3 Texas river
4 African speedster
5 Legal wrong
6 Mary Poppins tune, with "A"
7 "__ hooks" (crate phrase)
8 Miss __ Disposes (Tey novel)
9 Metaphorical treachery
10 Possess, previously
11 Competent
12 __-do-well
14 Traveler's choices
22 Bat wood
24 Handy abbr.
26 Optimistic phrase
28 Gambling game
30 Soggy bog
31 General Robert __
32 Heartfelt
33 Quick gulp
34 Remark of dismay
35 Robin's home
37 Rock partner
40 "All __" (Sinatra tune)
44 __-Magnon man
46 Actress Gardner
48 Idolizes
50 Horned herbivore
52 Main impact
53 Northern hemisphere?
54 The Prince of Tides star
55 One-name singer
56 Pisa dough
57 __ mater
59 Auctioneer's last word
62 See 62 Across

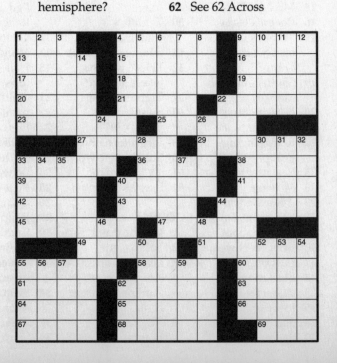

257 CARD TRICKS by Karen Hodge

ACROSS

1 Beaver's project
4 *M*A*S*H* star
8 Tend to the turkey
13 Composer Bartók
14 Nuthatch's nose
15 Sandwich snacks
16 Rack's partner
17 One opposed
18 Ferber novel
19 Baseball star?
22 Literary class
23 Undergrad deg.
24 RR stop
27 Golfer's iron?
32 D.C. lobby
35 Mah-jongg piece
36 Teasdale et al.
37 "I've Got __ in Kalamazoo"
39 High spirits
42 Used to be
43 Less easy to find
45 Neckline shapes
47 Atl. flier
48 World-class lover?
52 Santa __, CA
53 Busy buzzer
54 Select few
58 Hammett trilogy?
63 ". . . I say, not __"
65 Burglar's take
66 NBAer, for short
67 Kind of prize
68 Poet Pound
69 Cabbage kin
70 Bops on the bean
71 Hind or hart
72 Foxy

DOWN

1 Two in a deck
2 Out of this world
3 Feudal estates
4 "I'm __ boy!"
5 Director Riefenstahl
6 Computer input
7 With hands on hips
8 After-dinner drinks
9 Dry as dust
10 Comforts
11 Wernher __ Braun
12 Superlative suffix
13 Toot one's own horn
20 Verse syllables
21 Taking a vacation
25 Ski lifts
26 Something desirable
28 Get-up-and-go
29 Actor Wallach
30 Daredevil's need
31 Long-armed entity
32 Juneau jacket
33 Once more
34 Lapel flower
38 Trip component
40 Crumpets' colleague
41 Yonder yacht
44 Scotch cocktails
46 Start walking
49 Service charge
50 Well-__ (loaded)
51 Pants
55 Ultimate standard
56 Brit's boob tube
57 Italian princely family
59 Manual: Abbr.
60 Exude
61 Fairway warning
62 Top-billed one
63 Letter openers?
64 Jack of *Barney Miller*

258 SHIP SHAPE by Shirley Soloway

ACROSS

1 Head over heels
5 Devonshire drinks
9 Flowers-to-be
13 Actor Richard
14 "__ we all?"
15 On a cruise
16 Incline
17 Makes wait, in a way
19 Feeling poorly
20 California county
21 High-school student
23 Modify copy
27 Ginza gelt
28 Dogpatch's Daisy __
30 "__ out? Decide!"
31 Cassette player
34 Army priests
36 *Hawaii Five-O* star
37 More cunning
39 Byron works
40 Seals' singing partner
42 Least lax
44 Guided trip
45 Retirees' org.
46 One's partner
47 On fire
49 Fashion expressions
52 Halogen salts
55 Crude cabin
56 Acknowledging applause
60 Garage job
61 Grand in scale
62 Road reversal
63 Author Wiesel
64 Love too much
65 Gives permission to
66 Iditarod vehicle

DOWN

1 See the light
2 Well-coordinated
3 Typesetter's sheet
4 Strong bug
5 Make __ for it (flee)
6 Baltic resident
7 Give guarantees
8 Put away
9 "Nonsense!"
10 Soldier-show grp.
11 DuPont's HQ
12 Down in the dumps
14 Little or Frye
18 Gymnast Comaneci
20 Some machines do it
22 Necessary
24 "My One __"
25 FDR confidant
26 Boulevard liners
28 CCXXX quintupled
29 *Prelude to __* ('92 film)
31 Close attention, for short
32 Heart line
33 Pothook shape
34 Ante- kin
35 Jet-set plane
38 Frat letter
41 Get into condition
43 "Darn it!"
45 Unruffled
48 Business bigwig
49 Created clothing
50 James Blake's nickname
51 Fine mount
53 Be adjacent to
54 Craggy hills
56 Danson of *Cheers*
57 Overseas addr.
58 Baby beaver
59 Rocks at the bar
60 Bandleader Brown

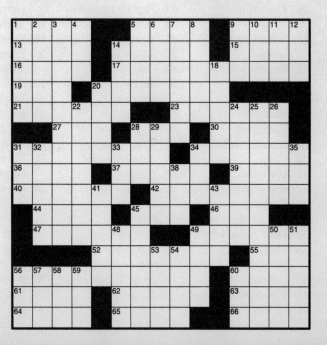

TOP BANANAS by A.J. Santora

ACROSS

1 *Bells __ Ringing*
4 Actress Dalton
8 __ deux
13 Pol. party
14 Silents star
15 Market for goods
16 Rocks with rye
17 Top banana in baseball
19 Top banana in movies
21 Scale notes
22 Overwhelm
23 Dublin distances
25 Fits to __
26 Clumsy one
29 Mrs. Kovacs
31 Acts to excess
34 First woman M.P.
35 Top bananas at concerts
39 *Tugboat __*
40 Went fishing
41 Phaser setting
42 Bishop's domain
43 *Twelve O'Clock High* grp.
47 Stand __ stead
51 Bantu language
53 Religious deg.
54 What top bananas get
57 Top banana in vaudeville
59 Name in UN history
60 Shaw et al.
61 Slightly open
62 Brittany season
63 "__ is human"
64 Singing syllables
65 Bolshevik

DOWN

1 __ dozen (abundant)
2 Say it isn't so
3 Come out
4 Song star Paula
5 Sockless
6 Highland hill
7 Sleepy sign
8 Sound of the West
9 Control-tower staff: Abbr.
10 Scheduling phrase
11 Mockery
12 Airport stats.
15 "You can count __"
18 Seneca's *sum*
20 Chess promotion
24 Leftover
27 "__ way to go!"
28 Flowerless plants
30 Hesitator's syllables
32 Ginnie __
33 Cooking herb
34 Noshed on
35 Barker and Bell
36 Clark Kent or Ratso Rizzo
37 Overwhelm
38 Kind of error
44 "The Duke of Brooklyn"
45 Grown together
46 Tired out
48 Noted Canadian physician
49 Singer Redding
50 Comic actor Aykroyd
52 *Ne plus __*
53 One of those things
55 Genuine
56 __ California
58 Film-set VIP

SPECIALIZATIONS by Randolph Ross

ACROSS

1 Small towns
6 Nonclerical
10 Radar image
14 Biblical patriarch
15 Siam visitor
16 Four-star review
17 Soda-jerk's specialty?
19 Brainstorm
20 Take aback
21 Sought office
22 Marty portrayer
24 Literary initials
26 Cozy
27 Writer's specialty?
33 Path's beginning
34 German article
35 Hang in the balance
37 AP rival
38 Court procedure
41 Golfer's position
42 Full of calories
44 Theater attendee
45 Words to the audience
47 Egyptian's specialty?
50 Lauder rival
51 Female pheasant
52 Fireworks name
55 Be shy
57 Sandy stuff
61 Doozy
62 Tour-guide's specialty?
65 "Pronto!"
66 Sped away
67 Allow to ride
68 Family rooms
69 Chop __
70 Idolize

DOWN

1 Loman's son
2 Voice of America org.
3 Make fun of
4 Newspaper name
5 __-fi
6 Tra trailer
7 Sometime soon
8 "Minuet __"
9 Hot peppers
10 Raise
11 Fill a hold
12 Currier's partner
13 Marsh material
18 Treat with milk
23 Place to be stuck
25 Restaurateur Toots
26 Mexican state
27 Dinner jelly
28 New York city
29 Transcribe again
30 More desperate
31 Archaeological find
32 Bagnold et al.
33 __ *Town*
36 Actress Wallace
39 Vanity cases
40 Fill
43 Vocal reflexes
46 Got to first base
48 Fabulous flier
49 Guitarist Atkins
52 Bag brand
53 Scheme
54 __ Bator
55 Grimm character
56 Cheese product
58 Mag printing process
59 Fictional aide
60 Tony-winner Daly
63 Chit
64 Slangy suffix

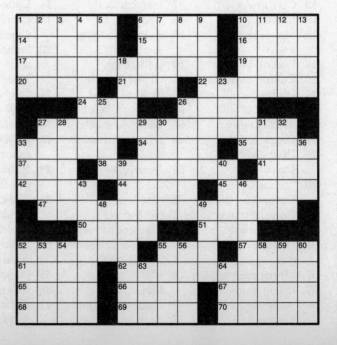

261 SPORTS FIGURES by Trip Payne

ACROSS
1 Funny one
5 Slack-jawed
10 Does in
14 Melville novel
15 Cato, for one
16 Sing lightly
17 Tippling baseballer?
20 Ottawa's prov.
21 "__ only as directed"
22 Billy __ Williams
23 Earth-conscious org.
24 Fred Astaire's sister
26 Unadorned
27 Mah-jongg tile
28 Actress Thompson
29 Fourth estate
31 Cat's-paw
32 They may be aquiline
34 *I Know Why the __ Bird Sings*
35 Former Soviet footballer?
39 Sheets of glass
40 Calendar page
41 Hts.
42 Put up with
44 Goofs up
48 Tell a whopper
49 Read quickly
50 High-minded
51 __ Arbor, MI
52 Plant pouch
53 Alley follower
55 RR destination
56 Serious basketballer?
60 Biblical brother
61 Love, Italian-style
62 __ *fixe*
63 Noticed
64 Toyland visitors
65 Social misfit

DOWN
1 Hot drinks
2 Donohoe of *L.A. Law*
3 Went bad
4 Happy's brother
5 Greek warmonger
6 Quayle's successor
7 "__ Blue?"
8 National Zoo beasts
9 Puts in one's diary
10 Bullring cheer
11 Pyromaniacs
12 Swatter alternative
13 Really mad
18 Cry's partner
19 __ *Haw*
25 Jousting needs
26 Wedding figure
29 Greek letter
30 Stimpy's cartoon pal
31 Prancer's sleighmate
33 Approves of
34 Director's yell
35 Indonesian islander
36 Ant's receptors
37 Sweetie pie
38 Put a stop to
39 Royal residences
42 Ancient amulet
43 City on Puget Sound
45 Occupy a spot
46 Cat, often
47 Didn't move
49 Compass pt.
50 Coll. student's pride
53 Mean one
54 Mines' lines
57 Cask of wine
58 Vest pocket
59 Word on Burgundy bottles

262 MEN OF LETTERS by David Owens

ACROSS
1 Phony
5 In the center of
9 Gourmet James
14 Sprint need
15 Tough to find
16 Beer variety
17 *Joie de vivre*
18 Yoked team
19 Big family
20 Lower-case poet
23 Chihuahua cheers
24 Pastrami surroundings
25 Life of Riley
26 Togs' tags
28 Job to do
29 Actress Anderson
30 Jingle writers
33 Unsuitability
38 Bubble up
39 It may be purple
40 Break sharply
41 Tubular tobacco
43 Actor McDowall
44 Clever folks
45 Cowboy's strap
47 Cash alternative
50 "I'm __ boy!": Costello
51 H.S. subj.
54 Weak, as excuses
55 *Monkey Business* screenwriter
58 "__ ear and out . . ."
60 Arkin or Alda
61 Broadcasts
62 Present time
63 Moore of *Ghost*
64 Gin flavoring
65 Aggressive sort
66 Toward Tangier
67 Circus structure

DOWN
1 Direct
2 *Roots* author
3 Quite quickly
4 Diner's directory
5 Olfactory inputs
6 Ankle coverers
7 "Goodnight __"
8 Former Chinese leader
9 Sandwich order
10 "Miniver Cheevy" poet
11 Fleet-footed
12 Mutineer, e.g.
13 Cassini creation
21 Intend
22 Ski spot
27 Army or carpenter
28 Peter O'Toole portrayal
29 High-tech tools
30 Disney's network
31 "Why __ Love You?"
32 Russian plane
34 "__ on your life!"
35 Grid player
36 Regrettable
37 Catch sight of
39 __ *Dragon* (Disney film)
42 Oil apparatus
43 Sally in space
46 Make money the old-fashioned way
47 Dirty Harry
48 Asian capital
49 Surrounded by
50 Cop __
51 Your umbrella?
52 *Gigi* star
53 Mini-map
56 Green gem
57 Ultimate
59 Mountain ending

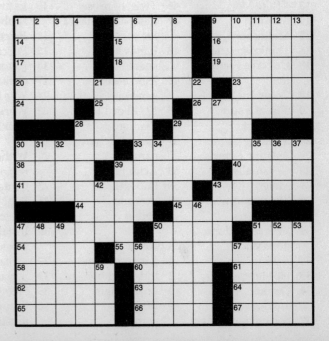

263 TOO WISE FOR YOU by Shirley Soloway

ACROSS

1 Caesar's sidekick
5 Football play
9 Kind of shark
13 "Famous" cookiemaker
14 Picker-upper
15 Moistureless
16 Sour-tasting
17 Wiser, maybe
18 Funny Foxx
19 Dairy-case buy
22 "I've __ up to here!"
23 Bubbled again
27 Anchor's place
30 Slyly disparaging
31 Earring holder
34 Dogpatch patriarch
38 Actor Vigoda
39 Open courtyards
40 Prefix for system
41 Annually
44 Citrus drinks
45 Cosmetics name
46 One with airs
48 Firmly determined
52 Dow Jones component
56 Sunny shade
59 Soft mineral
62 Homeric epic
63 Gymnast Korbut
64 Baseball manager Felipe
65 Clock sounds
66 *Hud* Oscar-winner
67 Become fuzzy
68 Fresh talk
69 Flying piscivore

DOWN

1 Angler's haul
2 Astaire's hometown
3 Prepared apples
4 Not sidesaddle
5 Fabric, for short
6 Choice words
7 Prolonged attack
8 Use steel wool
9 Singer Al
10 *People __ Funny*
11 Little goat
12 Out-of-the-ordinary
14 Trifle (with)
20 Hwy.
21 Full of promise
24 Found pleasing
25 Draw out
26 Test recordings
28 Do a vet's job
29 Actress Jurado
31 Paint coat
32 Too heavy
33 Finishes ahead of
35 Judge's intro
36 Zadora et al.
37 Tall story
42 Happen again
43 Eerie Lugosi
44 Colorful shell
47 Miner's find
49 Inventory count
50 Shire of *Rocky*
51 Ambler and Blore
53 Not as hale
54 Utah city
55 Low-lying land
57 Talks too much
58 PGA distances
59 File-folder feature
60 Winner's take, often
61 Gossett or Gehrig

264 PHYSICAL FORECAST by Randolph Ross

ACROSS

1 Take notice, maybe
6 Variety-show fare
10 Toy-magnate Schwarz
13 "Take Me __"
14 Braid
15 Matterhorn, e.g.
16 Thinking lucidly
18 Dot on a French map
19 Cools one's heels
20 Slip of a sort
22 Pinpoints
25 Melding game
27 Atlantic islands
28 Get smaller
29 Meted (out)
30 "Entertainment" preceder
31 "When __ door not a door?"
34 Extremities
35 Hot-tempered
36 Oxlike antelopes
37 Society newcomer
38 Rolling, in a way
39 Makes a scene
40 Pop star Richie
42 Et __
43 Wound in a reel
45 Mideast capital
46 Twist of prose
47 Baseball manager Joe
48 It may be spared
49 Kind and generous
55 12/24 or 12/31
56 Clamorous
57 Farm-machine name
58 Actor Beatty
59 Pull (in)
60 Best and Ferber

DOWN

1 Air Force org.
2 Ind. neighbor
3 Lower digit
4 Without warning
5 Like some movies for preteens
6 "Too bad!"
7 No gentleman
8 Overtime reason
9 Patron of Fr.
10 Easily sunburned
11 Parcel out
12 Puccini work
14 Favorites
17 Gets moving
21 Was in charge of
22 Worked on the docks
23 O₃
24 Without remorse
25 Quite careful
26 Bohemian
28 Beach find
30 Installed mosaics
32 *Kama __*
33 Syrian leader
35 Stooge Larry
36 Brought together
38 Crusade, e.g.
39 Mark again
41 Charged atom
42 Relief org.
43 Squad-car feature
44 Make one's case
45 Danish physicist
47 Fed. agent
50 *Bells __ Ringing*
51 *Louis Quatorze* was one
52 First-down yardage
53 Fab competitor
54 __ Moines, IA

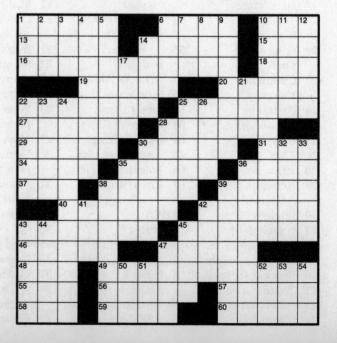

KINSHIP by Cynthia Lyon

ACROSS

1 Art style
5 Put off
10 "What __?"
14 *Lucky Jim* author
15 Toothpicked delicacy
16 Cry of acclaim
17 START OF A QUIP
20 Consoles
21 Coat of arms
22 Joad family member
23 Went left
26 PART 2 OF QUIP
32 Analyze sentences
33 Skip
34 Spill the beans
36 __-disant
37 Magnani and Moffo
38 Harvarder's rival
39 Austen's Miss Woodhouse
41 Paraphernalia
42 Like __ (50-50)
44 PART 3 OF QUIP
47 Fry's *The __ Not for Burning*
48 Monastery address
49 Arnaz autobio
52 The Syr Darya feeds it
56 END OF QUIP
60 See 8 Down
61 Stable worker
62 Hollywood clashers
63 Baseballer Sandberg
64 Medieval guild
65 Everything else

DOWN

1 Roast table
2 Shot
3 TV knob
4 __ a pig
5 Scale starter
6 Flora in an O'Neill title
7 Little lie
8 One of two raft riders?
9 Pron. type
10 Work on a soundtrack
11 Quitting time for some
12 "A Little Bitty Tear" singer
13 Cutting
18 "__ to bury Caesar . . ."
19 Nation in the Atl.
23 Mass-market books?
24 It's for the birds
25 Long-dist. line
26 *Dixit* lead-in
27 Fashion model Campbell
28 "Donkey Serenade" composer
29 Unfrequented
30 Kate Nelligan film of '85
31 Chic shop
35 Small snack
37 Improved, cheesewise
40 Sinatra tune
42 Kind of comprehension
43 Less
45 Munro's alias
46 "Time will doubt __": Byron
49 Place of worship?
50 Substance
51 Yves St. Laurent's birthplace
52 Bustles
53 Wise one
54 Piccadilly statue
55 A.D.C.
57 I may follow them
58 Refrain fragment
59 Way out there

SCUBA SIGHTINGS by Bob Lubbers

ACROSS

1 Barrymore or Pearson
5 Singer Vikki
9 They often overrun
14 Be concerned
15 *M*A*S*H* star
16 Bracelet locale
17 Lawn intruder
19 Come in second
20 Algiers district
21 Bandleader's "Go!"
23 Fly high
26 More sensible
28 Paint with dots
31 "*Ach du __!*"
33 Stays away from
34 Actress Barkin
36 Flamenco shout
37 Drops a fly, e.g.
38 Pick up the tab
39 Hazel, for one
40 *Wayne's World* word
41 Sp. misses
42 Took a chance
43 New Orleans school
45 Duelists' aides
47 Evil spirit
48 Love god
49 Geeks
51 Monster's nickname
56 Process ore
58 He takes a lot of interest in his work
61 Desi's daughter
62 Willing partner
63 Popular houseplant
64 Actor Werner
65 Pleasingly warm
66 Repair

DOWN

1 800, to Antony
2 "Ta-__-Boom-De-Ay"
3 Historic times
4 Friday portrayer
5 Drive-in server
6 Pie-mode link
7 Hwys.
8 Too swift to act wisely
9 Bligh's title
10 Working, as a computer
11 *Back to the Future* prop
12 RN's specialty
13 Get the point
18 Sounds of shock
22 Geographic speck
24 Wide awake
25 Set free
27 Banks (on)
28 Cover in mystery
29 Sweater style
30 __ and outs
32 Funny Foxx
33 Mailed away
35 Medical beam
38 General course
39 __ *of La Mancha*
41 Bull, often
42 Vitamin amounts
44 Aviator Earhart
46 Fleeced
50 Bridge coup
52 Something phony
53 12/26 event
54 Tailor's tool
55 Supplemented, with "out"
56 __-mo replay
57 Greek letters
59 Sapporo sash
60 Completely

267 FARM CAMP by Wayne R. Williams

ACROSS
1 Hankering
5 Tonsorial tool
10 Flat-bottomed boat
14 Cairo's river
15 Attu resident
16 Star stage
17 Race edges
19 Hebrew measure
20 Boom times
21 Pavarotti, e.g.
22 Unwritten promise
23 Cleaned the deck
25 Persian Gulf fed.
28 Funny Charlotte
29 State of readiness
30 One way to win
33 Junction point
34 Salon job
35 Speakers' platforms
36 Department of Agriculture unit
39 Court business
42 Smeltery stack
43 Put up a fuss
47 Sincere
49 Kukla's colleague
50 Mess up
51 Possesses
52 Bring into being
53 Confess
55 Impassive one
58 Kingsley or Jonson
59 Landscape dip
60 Political issue
62 Pindar's output
63 Battery terminal
64 Latin 101 verb
65 Poetry syllables
66 Thumbs-up answers
67 Beer ingredient

DOWN
1 Monstrous
2 Fresco painter
3 Held tight
4 Contraction with two meanings
5 Scored
6 King of comedy
7 Love, to Laver
8 Win a chase
9 Civ. liberties
10 Bamboozle
11 Nation off Mozambique
12 Frighten into defeat
13 Game officials
18 Proofreading term
24 Like better
26 Confuse
27 Jacob's twin
30 __ Alibi (Selleck film)
31 Dramatist Fugard
32 Gardener's tool
34 Antibiotic precursor
37 Solemn vow
38 TV screen
39 Before
40 Spread throughout
41 Former convict, perhaps
44 "Heart of Dixie"
45 Word-for-word
46 Most sharp
48 Ancient Palestinian
49 Theater sec.
52 Summons to court
54 Author Nathanael
56 Southwest art colony
57 Ye __ Tea Shoppe
60 Foal feed
61 Machine part

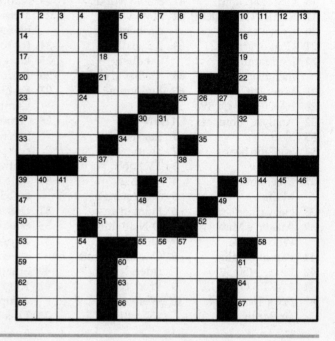

268 PUN JABS by Randolph Ross

ACROSS
1 Call for help
4 NFLer, e.g.
7 Angle measure
13 Daley's city, for short
14 Finish third
15 Third of an inning
16 Squealer
17 Indian children's game?
19 Lunchroom lure
21 Tide type
22 Indian stocking stuffer?
26 Long ago
30 Peter, Paul and Mary's "Day __"
31 Bar furnishing
32 Brutus' breakfast?
35 Important time
36 Fraught with pitfalls
37 Indian lunches?
41 Blackmail, perhaps
42 GM auto
43 Compass pt.
44 Bulls and Bears
45 Ocean floor
48 Garfield dog
49 Indian pirate flag?
53 Jeff Bridges' brother
55 Habituate
56 Indian farming?
62 Archaeological expedition
63 Toxic substance
64 Gstaad gear
65 "Wow!"
66 Squirrel, for one
67 Beer barrel
68 Pipe shape

DOWN
1 Beanpole
2 Butler's wife
3 Squash, maybe
4 Greek letter
5 Stewart or Serling
6 Use credit
7 Actress Blakley
8 Forever __ day
9 Tyrannical
10 __ Dalmatians
11 Razor-billed bird
12 Ultimate degree
14 Persian potentates
18 Green Gables girl
20 16th-century start
23 I.e., for long
24 Mrs. Dithers
25 I Married __ ('42 film)
27 Nogales night
28 Polar bears pitch them
29 Family Ties mom
31 Indian honorific
32 "__ Billie Joe"
33 Overwrought
34 Mongolian range
36 __-four (standard plank)
38 Headquarters
39 Taxing org.
40 "Let's shake on it!"
45 Aretha's realm
46 Eastern Indians
47 Cupid or Quayle
49 Pleasure trip
50 Beauty-pageant VIP
51 The Little Mermaid
52 German philosopher
54 Wharton subj.
56 Fool's mo.
57 Sticky stuff
58 Be free (of)
59 "For shame!"
60 Mini-guitar
61 Apparatus

269 DON'T WALK by Fred Piscop

ACROSS
1 Fuel-gauge reading
6 Got blubbery
10 No Honest Abe
14 Comic Anderson
15 Football's __ Alonzo Stagg
16 "Der __" (Adenauer)
17 RUN
20 Not fem.
21 Days of Heaven star
22 Like week-old bread
23 Moe's cohort
25 Darning __ (dragonfly)
26 War fleets
29 Sow's mate
30 Play reveille
31 Animation frame
32 __ tai cocktail
35 RUN
40 Radical campus org. of the '60s
41 Atty.'s title
42 Consequently
43 Meets with
45 Ceramic servers
47 Decathlon components
50 Craze
51 Joshua of Broadway
52 Sportscaster Albert
53 Ratio phrase
57 RUN
60 "Waiting for the Robert __"
61 Rep. Mary __ of CA
62 Quotable catcher
63 X-ray units
64 Goose kin
65 Shady place

DOWN
1 Jr. high preceder
2 "__ Lisa"
3 Propels a shot
4 Haberdashery buy
5 The Beatles' "__ Blues"
6 '40s baseball brothers
7 Rough stuff
8 Lech Walesa, for one
9 Lao-__
10 Second of two
11 Its hero is Achilles
12 Bikini, e.g.
13 Richards of tennis
18 Taj Mahal site
19 Government workers' org.
24 "Zip-__-Doo-Dah"
25 Vincent Lopez's theme
26 Eyebrow shapes
27 Crucifix
28 "__ the word!"
29 Actor Vereen
31 __ au vin
32 __' War (racehorse)
33 C.P.A.
34 Turner and Pappas
36 Golfer's pocketful
37 Feminine suffix
38 Bangkok resident
39 Mr. Fixit
43 Bags
44 Sicilian spewer
45 Game fish
46 #10's, e.g.
47 Bugs' pursuer
48 "Success!"
49 Urged, with "on"
50 Polynesian peak
52 Persian's plaint
54 Belgradian, for one
55 Poi, essentially
56 General Bradley
58 Cable-network letters
59 Unfilled time-slot abbr.

270 FRANKLY SPEAKING by Cathy Millhauser

ACROSS
1 Hold up
5 PC owner
9 Flavorful
14 Sonic clone
15 __ contendere
16 Madrid museum
17 START OF A QUIP
20 Doc
21 Quo Vadis? role
22 Reuben's bread
23 Mag. execs
24 Wartime offense
26 Actress Freeman
27 It gets letters
32 Finished, in a way
35 Hit the bell
38 The Neverending Story author
39 PART 2 OF QUIP
42 Yours, in Tours
43 British servant
44 Continents' divider
45 Big shot
47 Nix, in a way
49 PART 3 OF QUIP
52 PART 4 OF QUIP
55 Fidel's friend
58 Sgts., e.g.
59 Lower (oneself)
61 END OF QUIP
64 '50s record
65 Insignificant
66 Old one: Ger.
67 Did modeling
68 Some votes
69 Hideout

DOWN
1 "__ Be the One"
2 Felt sore
3 Loses one's coat
4 Writer Morrison
5 Awaiting delivery
6 Acapulco warmer
7 Ms. Verdugo
8 Popular posies
9 Folksy instruments
10 Canine comment
11 Up to __ ('50s game show)
12 For no reason
13 Senate VIP, once
18 Army creatures?
19 Animal feeder
25 Planet of the Apes, really
26 College major
28 Film studio, for short
29 "Shave __ haircut, two bits"
30 Admired one
31 Chippendale quartet
32 Esau's wife
33 Baum barker
34 One of the Ghostbusters
36 "That's it!"
37 Chutzpah
40 Water partner
41 Square one
46 Gave clues
48 The Courtship of __ Father
50 Big-headed, sort of
51 Helena's competitor
52 Inventor Nikola
53 West Indies nation
54 ATM key
55 Pork order
56 Nativity-play prop
57 Remnants
60 Ground grain
62 Stamping machine component
63 Top at the pool

271 ON TIME by Shirley Soloway

ACROSS
1 Wilander of tennis
5 Guns the engine
9 "Oh!"
13 Working hard
14 Shake off
15 Iowa city
16 Fast-food drink
17 Mrs. Perón
18 Shopping center
19 No time at all
22 Golf ball's position
23 Yule song
24 Casino employee
26 Latter-day
29 College major
31 Get away from
32 Copycat
33 Guided trip
36 Nothing at all
37 Go backwards
40 Suffix for press
41 __ podrida
43 Salad to sundae
44 Shirt size
46 Swallow
48 Removed the suds
49 Fast talk
51 __ good example
52 *Strangers __ Train*
53 Beef cut
59 Mayonnaise covers
61 Weather satellite
62 Aware of
63 Rat-__
64 Functional
65 Circus cat
66 Beams of light
67 Ltr. encl.
68 Author Ferber

DOWN
1 Brit's raincoats
2 On the summit
3 Cash drawer
4 Dyed furniture
5 Have a blast
6 Monumental
7 Turn down
8 Does a hatchet job on
9 Time after midnight
10 Time after midnight
11 Unearthly
12 Organic compound
14 Adjust your clock
20 Skin cosmetic
21 Actress Ruby
25 Burlesque bit
26 Casino city
27 Villainous
28 Go home
29 Dieter of rhyme
30 Fruit cover
32 Long time
34 Do lobbying
35 Oboe insert
38 Honorary title
39 Narrow openings
42 Opp.-meaning word
45 Author France
47 Precious stone
48 Singer Della
49 Of interest to Peary
50 Ms. Bryant
51 Fur piece
54 Silents actress Naldi
55 *Exodus* author
56 Oklahoma city
57 Like __ of bricks
58 Hawaiian resort coast
60 Canonized ones: Abbr.

272 THEY'RE NUMBER ONE by Trip Payne

ACROSS
1 Loft cube
5 Emergency call
8 Young haddock
13 Squashed circle
14 Lunch container?
16 Butler's concern
17 National Leaguers
18 Reunion attender
19 A clue like this has four of them
20 Wage earners
23 Language ending
24 Vane dir.
25 Batman and Penguin, e.g.
29 Star in Cygnus
31 Riveter of song
33 "I don' wanna!"
34 Zombie ingredient
36 Smoke, for short
37 Raison d'__
38 Movie-musical dancer
42 Sushi-bar selections
43 Rocky peak
44 Tire contents
45 Company quota?
46 Straightens out
48 "Horse behind bars"
52 It goes to your head
54 From A __
56 Squeal (on)
57 *The Robe* star
60 Pop-jazz singer
63 Olympic weapon
64 Hurries along
65 Kick out
66 Real bummer
67 Igor, for one: Abbr.
68 Shows the way
69 Sumac of song
70 Volstead opponents

DOWN
1 Failed badly
2 Disinclined
3 Triangular-sailed ship
4 Klensch of CNN
5 Bring forth
6 More overtly suave
7 Totally surprise
8 Dinner party
9 Deep gorge
10 Zodiac animal
11 Eye, to a poet
12 Legal offs.
15 Soap-opera gimmick
21 Fix a program
22 Puzzlement
26 Excited by
27 Make worthy of
28 Yonder yacht
30 Fouls up
32 Earthy color
35 Kilo's system
37 Homonym of 44 Across
38 Back street
39 Not quite straight
40 Made a difference
41 Pie before dessert
42 H's ancestor
46 *The Practice* scenes
47 Steady succession
49 Black-and-blue mark
50 Least common
51 Explosive experiments
53 Like Yale walls
55 The end
58 Grand Ole __
59 Spring event
60 Author Kaufman
61 Tin Woodman's tool
62 Evian or Bath

273 GROWING THINGS by Wayne R. Williams

ACROSS

1 Magazine layout
7 Tight spots
11 Have more to say
14 *Ruby* star
15 Brainstorm
16 Martial-arts legend
17 At home
18 Gilding material
20 Shop equipment
21 In a careless way
22 Coffee servers
24 Meat dish
26 Sherlock's hat
30 Unite
33 Woody's son
34 Frog kin
35 __ one's time
36 Division word
37 Does paper work
38 Israeli guns
39 Free-for-all
40 Ripped up
41 Poker pack
42 Craving
43 Electricity sources
46 William or Sean
47 Singer Wooley
48 Mountain lions
51 Greyhound pacer
55 Skier's maneuver
59 Guarantee
60 Feeling blue
61 Son of Isaac
62 Small sofa
63 Word that filers ignore
64 Landlord's due
65 Word form for "intestine"

DOWN

1 Go to sea
2 __ colada
3 Remainder
4 Peace Nobelist of 1912
5 Birch-family trees
6 *Alice __ Live Here Anymore*
7 Lively dance
8 Fuss and feathers
9 Gibson or Tillis
10 "The Ballad of the Green Berets" singer
11 Emcee Trebek
12 Business arrangement
13 Challenge
19 Belli's field
23 Took a chair
24 Fleming and Hamill
25 Kennedy and Koppel
26 Holstein's home
27 Bert's buddy
28 John of rock
29 French river
30 Dry up
31 Proclamation
32 Class furniture
35 *Buck Privates* costar
37 English prep school
43 Annoy
44 *Wheel of Fortune* category
45 Use yeast
46 Actress Dawber
48 Attention-getting sound
49 Home of the Jazz
50 Ancient Persian
52 Scottish island
53 Champagne bucket
54 *Vincent & __* ('90 film)
56 Put to work
57 Hightailed it
58 Obsessive fan

274 TASTE TEST by Scott Marley

ACROSS

1 Kind of chop
5 Trucker, often
9 Guff
13 Western show
14 Bank (on)
15 Aware of
16 Cousteau's domain
17 Make eyes at
18 A Four Corners state
19 Saves
21 Reply to *gràzie*
22 Pub order
23 "__ She Sweet?"
24 Keep score, in cribbage
25 Gielgud's title
26 Watering hole
30 Hobo's dinner
33 Night sight
36 Hunter's need
37 Comic Johnson
38 Kilmer classic
39 Feel no __ (be tipsy)
40 Franklin's flier
41 Quick summary
42 Art Deco name
43 Space-race starter
45 Signs off on
47 Shirt or blouse
48 Be audacious
50 *Playbill* paragraph
53 Like some keys
56 To the __ (all the way)
58 Butter alternative
59 Football score
60 *Arroz* partner
61 Move like a hummingbird
62 __ Eleanor Roosevelt
63 Out-and-out
64 Certain Hindu
65 Honey bunch
66 Annoying one

DOWN

1 Union group
2 Designer Simpson
3 Walnut's innards
4 Dwarf tree
5 Promote, in checkers
6 Bible word
7 Jed Clampett's daughter
8 Ham's mate
9 Poor loser's attitude
10 Put into the pot
11 For men only
12 London district
13 Singer Julius La __
20 Landing place
21 According to
24 Globetrotter's need
25 Fondness for desserts
26 La __ Tar Pits
27 Mr. Sharif
28 Drop off
29 Semiautomatic rifle
30 Fifth Avenue store
31 Fall clumsily
32 Caesarean phrase
34 Difficult journey
35 '60s nuclear agcy.
44 Likewise not
46 Maintain
48 Newsperson Sawyer
49 World book
50 Sings like Merman
51 Small bay
52 Telltale sign
53 Mary Quant and colleagues
54 Jai __
55 Schmo
56 Shade of white
57 Instructional method
59 Yak away

PENNY-WISE by Donna J. Stone

ACROSS
1 Door part
5 Parish priest
10 Roads scholar?
14 Israeli airline
15 __ Gay
16 At any time
17 Moore of *G.I. Jane*
18 Get __ (eliminate)
19 Nelson's river
20 START OF A QUIP
23 Soft metal
24 Spruce up
25 Brainy brats?
30 Offer an opinion
34 '75 Wimbledon winner
35 Tipped off
37 *Peanuts* character
38 Menlo Park monogram
39 MIDDLE OF QUIP
41 Tom, for one
42 Striped stone
44 Heavy metal instrument
45 Heart's desire
46 Go over again
48 Acts like Attila
50 Cremona cash
52 Actor McShane
53 END OF QUIP
61 Intaglio material
62 Cantaloupe or casaba
63 Easy stride
64 Grimm creature
65 Coeur d'__, ID
66 Brainchild
67 Call the shots
68 Filled to the gills
69 __-do-well

DOWN
1 Champions of the Force
2 Pianist Templeton
3 Early sitcom
4 Crepe cousin
5 Betty's rival
6 "What's __ for me?"
7 Musical postscript
8 Overhead
9 Basket fiber
10 Shakespearean subject
11 *Metamorphoses* author
12 Endless band
13 Hydrox rival
21 Relative of -ist
22 In a weird way
25 Saudi Arabia neighbor
26 Grammarian's concern
27 "Do __ a Waltz?"
28 Take the Pledge?
29 Frame
31 Disguised, for short
32 Smooth-spoken
33 Senator Kefauver
36 Skater Thomas
39 "__ to please"
40 Dumped on
43 Wired, in a way
45 Hand-lotion ingredient
47 Some TV shows
49 On the __ (fleeing)
51 Cub Scout leader
53 Gimlet, but not daiquiri
54 *Picnic* playwright
55 Pianist Hess
56 "__ a Song Go . . ."
57 Not a soul
58 Centering point
59 Piece of fencing?
60 Century segment

PRECIOUS by Eric Albert

ACROSS
1 Quick kiss
5 Columnist Herb
9 "Nattering nabobs" veep
14 Singer Guthrie
15 Actor Alan
16 Play genre
17 Muffin ingredient
18 *Pal* __
19 Kind of kitchen
20 Stevenson character
23 Mork's planet
24 Styled like
25 Comrade
26 Parting word
27 Gomer of TV
28 Famous first baseman
31 Jokingly
34 *The Bridge of San Luis* __
35 Induce
36 Exec's protection
40 Roman poet
41 Writer Rand
42 Pulitzer poet Conrad
43 Music style
44 Merlot stopper
45 Current unit
46 Show anger
47 Justice Fortas
48 Chat
51 Marilyn Monroe, for one
55 *Ulysses* writer
56 Noted canal
57 Author Victoria
58 Ms. Moorehead
59 Morning meal
60 Leave out
61 TV Hall of fame
62 Storied septet
63 Goddess of youth

DOWN
1 Picasso or Casals
2 Inaccuracy
3 Chain sound
4 Movie monster
5 Wheedle
6 Hawaiian greeting
7 Perfect place
8 One opposed
9 Fitness expert Davis
10 Unexpected extra
11 Hoopster Archibald
12 Kuwaiti ruler
13 Pallid
21 Mansfield of movies
22 *The Man from U.N.C.L.E.* character
26 Melville hero
27 4/1 action
28 *The Winds of War* author
29 Can't stand
30 Plow pullers
31 Composer Stravinsky
32 TV science show
33 Go crazy
35 Pot item
37 Mama Judd
38 European range
39 "Ship of the desert"
44 Affectedly attractive
45 Convent head
46 Diamond plane
47 Garcia's girlfriend
48 Folklore being
49 Extemporize
50 Margo, in *All About Eve*
51 Cartoon possum
52 Vanessa's sister
53 Advocate strongly
54 "Yikes!"
55 Bread spread

277 SISTER CITIES by Rebecca Alexander

ACROSS

1 Luce's creation
5 Unornamented
10 Actor Mineo
13 Maturing agent
14 Sonata movements
16 Sen. Sessions' state
17 City on the Mohawk
19 Tasseled topper
20 The way things work
21 Gray work
23 Tit for __
24 Ballet bend
26 City on the Ohio
32 Band section
33 Vladimir's vetoes
34 Dine
36 "__ to differ!"
37 Words to the audience
38 Seles' org.
39 West ender
40 Fetch
41 Like krypton
42 Bulldogs' hometown
45 Clan man
46 Mixologist's milieu
47 Capital way down south
50 Capital management
54 Coffee brewer
55 Northwestern lumber town
59 In the past
60 Beethoven's Third
61 Not irregular
62 Osaka scratch
63 Interrupt dancers
64 Flower droplets

DOWN

1 Infield cover
2 Composer Stravinsky
3 Office note
4 Putting up
5 Magic word
6 Weather fronts
7 Unspecific amount
8 Oath response
9 Postal-creed word
10 In the clear
11 Hasn't __ to stand on
12 Slothful
15 Hanks of yarn
18 Closes in on
22 Summer sign
24 Fraternity hopeful
25 Lo-cal
26 Charmer's snake
27 Don't exist
28 Refuse to budge
29 Using a chaise
30 Japanese-American
31 *Kama* __
32 Move quickly
35 Butter bit
37 Cartoonist Peter
38 Still to be marked
40 Suit well

41 Qum resident
43 FDR VP
44 Luke's mentor
47 Berth place
48 Push along
49 A party to
50 Central points
51 Church area
52 Prepare to swallow
53 Many a millennium
56 Mythical monster
57 Old French coin
58 Summer-camp apprentice: Abbr.

278 SPICE RACK by Richard Silvestri

ACROSS

1 Young fellow
4 *WarGames* group
9 Scored well on an exam
13 On the rocks
15 Puff up
16 Quite positive
17 Procession VIP
19 Place for corn
20 Examined thoroughly
21 Airline-board info: Abbr.
22 Metal sources
23 16 and 21, e.g.
25 Delight in
27 From the heart
31 Iron man?
34 Cove relative
35 Gentleman's gentleman
37 "What Kind of Fool __?"
38 Comment conclusion
39 British diarist
40 Sinful
41 Ariz. neighbor
42 Dropped pop, e.g.
43 Made away with
44 Threatener's words
46 Rankled
48 Anne, to Margaret
50 German coal region
51 Huck's transport
53 Prefix for skeleton
55 Colored slightly
59 Like crazy
60 Dawdle
62 One of the strings
63 Born first
64 Ear part
65 -kin kin
66 Gary Cooper role
67 A fistful of dollars

DOWN

1 Wilted
2 Rent-__
3 Art follower
4 One in want
5 Ending for scram
6 Hard to get
7 Tête-__
8 Makes mad
9 Comparable to a cucumber?
10 Seek through flattery
11 The __-Lackawanna Railroad
12 American Socialist Eugene
14 Candidate, at times
18 Sired
24 Bank client
26 Trifling amount
27 Manilow's instrument
28 Go in
29 Devil feature
30 In the __ luxury
32 M. Zola
33 Got one's goat
36 Guitars' ancestors
39 Came before
40 Timeless

42 Compass pt.
43 Sober-minded
45 Chicken or Rich
47 Bacchus' attendants
49 Nolan's fate
51 Enthusiastic review
52 Got down
54 Antiquated "antiquated"
56 Incandescence
57 Island near Corsica
58 Applied henna
61 Held first

279 THE ELEMENTS by Wayne R. Williams

ACROSS

1 Canseco or Ferrer
5 Lends a hand
10 NYC cultural attraction
14 Grub
15 Nicholas Gage book
16 From the beginning
17 EARTH
20 Started up: Abbr.
21 Jean Renoir film
22 Tearful woman
26 Emcee's job
30 AIR
34 Board material
35 Classic car
36 Singer Kitt
38 Not fer
39 CIO's partner
40 CCXXV + CCCXXVI
41 Out of sorts
43 Hood's heater
44 Witty remark
46 Dundee of boxing
48 Santa __, CA
49 Up to
51 FIRE
53 Paradisiacal
55 Wish granter
56 French 101 verb
58 "Eye" word form
62 WATER
68 Pitts of comedy
69 Church honoree
70 Highway division
71 Object
72 Turner and Louise
73 Hazzard deputy

DOWN

1 Ballet movement
2 Thole inserts
3 RBI or ERA
4 Juan Carlos' realm
5 Playboy nickname
6 "Xanadu" group
7 Superman foe Luthor
8 Nabokov novel
9 Mideast region
10 Hindu sage
11 "Sail __ Ship of State!"
12 Actress Harris
13 Dumbfound
18 Stood for
19 Bancroft or Boleyn
23 Florida city
24 Showing off
25 Erhard's discipline
27 Jamaican music
28 Writer Fallaci
29 Language structure
30 Violin and Palette painter
31 Money back
32 Limestone variety
33 Be a bandit
37 William __ White
42 Tanner's need
45 Conifer arbor
47 Band engagement
50 Vilnius' loc.
52 Pester the comic
54 High point
57 Morales of Bad Boys
59 __ Bator
60 Late-night name
61 Assayer's material
62 Israeli gun
63 Tended tots
64 Weather-vane dir.
65 Brooch, e.g.
66 Genetic letters
67 Part of TGIF

280 MATH ANXIETY by Randolph Ross

ACROSS

1 Headquarters
6 Most wise
12 Piece of needlework
14 Competed on the Charles
15 Basement entrance
16 Predestines
17 START OF AN OLD JOKE
19 Big Apple initials
20 Dreamer's phenom.
21 Ms. Lupino
24 Arm of the Riviera?
27 Impressionist
29 Signs up
31 __ Palmas
32 Kind of blade
33 Hall-of-Fame pitcher Fingers
34 PART 2 OF JOKE
36 PART 3 OF JOKE
37 Makes up (for)
38 Shortfall
39 Agnew's nickname
40 Contract details
41 Haul away
42 Mamie's predecessor
43 AAA suggestion
44 Taunter's cry
45 Shooter ammo
47 THE PUNCH LINE
53 Pugilist
56 Eye opener?
57 Hospital resident
58 Soirée time
59 Hollow stones
60 Clear the tape

DOWN

1 Italian port
2 NYSE rival
3 Gives rise to
4 Quarterback John
5 Ocean views
6 Get lost
7 Imported auto
8 Iris' cousin
9 Actor Wallach
10 Sun Yat-__
11 6-pt. plays
12 European airline
13 Scandinavian rug
14 Comparatively steamed
18 Unencumbered
22 Water down
23 Liqueur flavorings
24 Swell up
25 Roof beam
26 Classify
28 Bill-signing souvenir
29 Dallas daddy
30 Tournament placements
32 Arden et al.
33 Open to suggestion
35 Caught in a net
36 Baseball club
38 Bird on a Canadian $1 coin
41 Word of comfort
42 Cereal topper
44 Bakery equipment
46 Fishing specialist
48 Raison d'__
49 Lemony quencher
50 "Oh, what a relief __!"
51 And Then There Were __
52 Bit of work
53 Fruit tree
54 Feminine-name ending
55 Onetime sports car

281 EASY AS PIE by Richard Silvestri

ACROSS

1 Spruce cousin
4 All by oneself
8 Reads carefully (over)
13 *Coffee, Tea __?*
14 Enjoy gum
15 Accustom
16 Pizza topping
18 Zoo attraction
19 Addison colleague
20 Author Seton
22 Works too hard
24 Attic
28 Hair jobs
30 1850s war site
32 Pile up
35 Pizza topping
37 Actor Ayres
38 Sports-shoe attachment
39 Explosive letters
40 Pizza topping
43 Rodeo rope
45 Flow
46 Ade ingredient
48 Shut carefully
50 Corrupt
53 Belt holder
55 Be a snitch
57 Bakery emanation
61 Pizza topping
63 First-discovered asteroid
64 Alpine comeback
65 Pillage
66 Big happening
67 Homeowner's holding
68 McMahon and Sullivan

DOWN

1 Worries
2 Drive forward
3 Summer TV fare
4 Slide-show need
5 Cry of contempt
6 Singing Horne
7 Due (to)
8 Peru conqueror
9 __ in a million
10 Massage
11 Make a blunder
12 Dead or Red
13 Co-__ (urban apartments)
17 Bill Clinton's idol
21 Big boat
23 Play for time
25 *6 Rms __ Vu*
26 Sends forth
27 Freezing temperatures
29 Fishhook fastener
31 Regarding
32 Charitable donation
33 Bumps into
34 In the know
36 Looked over the joint
38 Engraved gem
41 Darjeeling export
42 Sub stabilizer
43 Of a lung division
44 Mr. France
47 Stanislavsky teaching
49 Like planetaria
51 Arose
52 *St. __ Fire*
54 Purple shade
56 Superlative suffix
57 Top-notch
58 Gun the motor
59 Bedrock deposit
60 Old boys?
62 "__ loves me . . ."

282 LETTERS FROM ATHENS by Bill Swain

ACROSS

1 Tends the soup
6 Climbing gear
11 Ritzy rock
14 Celestial transient
15 Rock ridge
16 Pub pour
17 Relaxation waves
19 Ms. Farrow
20 Tells about
21 Hoffman Oscar film
23 Composer Jule et al.
24 Garden bloom
25 Actress Scacchi
27 Worthy of reverence
30 Short hairdo
33 Peruses
35 Get away
36 State with conviction
38 Musical combos
40 Pitcher Nolan
41 Germanic invaders
43 Conical quarters
45 Mach 2 traveler
46 Explosive mixture
48 Outcropping
50 Hooky player
52 Mariners
56 '92 World Series winner
58 Southwest sight
59 Fuss
60 Like some sleek jets
62 Author Kesey
63 John of rock
64 Pizza topping
65 Hesitater's sounds
66 Fabric workers
67 Assays, e.g.

DOWN

1 Lasting impressions
2 Apartment sign
3 Use subtlety
4 Put back pictures
5 Ancient Greek coins
6 Cheerleading yells
7 Adjective suffix
8 Lab's __ dish
9 Allen and Frome
10 Highly original
11 Atomic photons
12 Director Kazan
13 Have in mind
18 Excise
22 More simpatico
24 Most wacky
26 Sour-tasting
28 Spacewalks: Abbr.
29 Push in
30 __ California
31 Egg cell
32 Particle accelerators
34 Second-year student
37 Nostalgic clothes style
39 Vacillate
42 Rang, as a bell
44 Gray was one
47 Since last week
49 Animals
51 *Affliction* star
53 Caspar was one
54 Standing tall
55 Focal points
56 Carry off
57 German river
58 __ *souci* (carefree)
61 Rocky crag

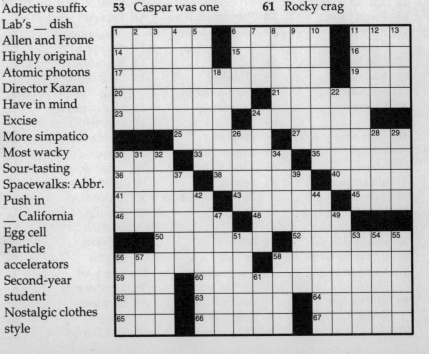

283 HARD TO SWALLOW by Randolph Ross

ACROSS
1 Knocks for a loop
6 Caesar's 300
9 *King Kong* costar
13 "It's the end of __!"
14 Parlor, for one
16 Roll-call response
17 Less, in La Paz
18 "__ se habla español"
19 Geometric lines
20 Practiced restraint
23 Lost
27 Shoe holder
30 PC screen
31 Fashionable Drive
32 Tear apart
33 Men and boys
34 Warning signals
35 "Gotcha!"
36 Quilters' convention
37 Middling grade
38 Scale notes
39 Talkative type
41 Talent for music
42 Nastase of tennis
43 Capri and Wight
44 Pod preceder
45 Beatty and Buntline
46 Talked idly
50 Retracted a remark
54 Pasta choice
57 Have __ (know somebody)
58 Actor Patrick
59 Wickedness
60 Stand up to
61 __-car
62 Turns colors
63 Mind-altering drug
64 Wild fancy

DOWN
1 Door frame
2 "Dedicated to the __ Love"
3 Fast time
4 Ran slowly
5 Prokofiev's bird
6 Apple bearer
7 Acts the flirt
8 *The Little Engine That* __
9 A question of motive
10 Reviewer Reed
11 *Diamonds __ Forever*
12 "Without a doubt!"
15 Not at all spicy
21 Artist/illusionist
22 Bizarre
24 Swimmer Gertrude
25 Virgilian epic
26 Plays horseshoes
27 Like *Hamlet*
28 Go over old ground
29 Make possible
34 Letter flourishes
36 Attack on all sides
37 Heeled over
40 Moans and groans about
41 Immigrants, e.g.
42 Vocalizer
47 Unwilling to listen
48 On key
49 In __ (briefly)
51 Russo of *Lethal Weapon 4*
52 Bank deposit?
53 Verbal attack
54 Londoner's last letter
55 Wall climber
56 Music marking

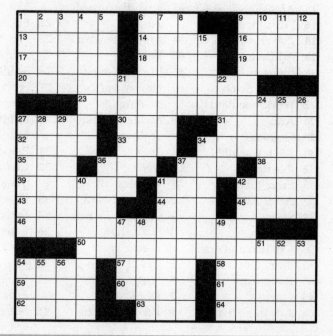

284 PUNCTUATIVE by Wayne R. Williams

ACROSS
1 From a distance
5 They're serious
11 Package letters, often
14 Painful
15 Bathroom bottle
16 Word form meaning "sharp"
17 Exodus directive
19 Majors or Marvin
20 Lawrence portrayer
21 Department-store section
23 Major annoyance
24 Aftward
25 Nasal expression
27 Sports venues
30 Forceful trends
33 Prefix for while
35 Jenny in *Love Story*
36 Muckraker Tarbell
37 Sleep inducers
40 Research thoroughly
41 Raised trains
42 Starter chips
43 Gear features
45 Disarm a bull
48 Wheat variety
50 Prepares cutlets
52 Mideast liquor
56 In proportion
58 Just about
59 "Eureka!"
60 Gum-related
63 According to
64 Old Testament prophet
65 Urgent
66 Launch counter?
67 French Revolution leader
68 Gets it

DOWN
1 British racecourse
2 Civil War expert Shelby
3 Knight clothes
4 Deep regret
5 Bucks
6 Measuring stick
7 Nav. rank
8 Bearings
9 Write in the margin
10 Gordon or Irish
11 Portico's companion
12 Cart team
13 Recolors
18 *The Tempest* king
22 High dudgeon
24 Fills with fizz
26 Hold your horses
28 Came down
29 Sound bored
30 In deadlock
31 Running in neutral
32 Driver's display
34 Pipe part
38 Slender cigar
39 Speaker system
44 Quick trips
46 Bobby of hockey
47 Gathered in
49 Robert of *Soap*
51 "Mack the Knife" singer
53 Bandleader Shaw
54 __ Boothe Luce
55 Rote and Rote, Jr.
56 *Hair* producer
57 Big bird
61 Shakespearean contraction
62 "Now I see!"

285 SILVER LINING by Donna J. Stone

ACROSS
1 Pugilistic pokes
5 Grating
10 *Casablanca* setting
14 Square measure
15 Bring bliss to
16 Blind as __
17 Analyze poetry
18 Light beer
19 Run the show
20 START OF A QUIP
23 Adams and McClurg
24 Put in stitches
25 __ *Rosenkavalier*
27 Fam. member
28 Hollywood clashers
32 Hardly hyper
34 Proofer's findings
36 In the know about
37 MIDDLE OF QUIP
41 Asian desert
42 Legendary quarterback
43 Verdi opera
46 Moon Mullins' brother
47 Antipollution grp.
50 Bear's lair
51 Peter out
53 Diverse
55 END OF QUIP
60 Gooey stuff
61 Join up
62 Part of Batman's garb
63 Coward of drama
64 *Cheers* chair
65 Nautical adverb
66 Creole veggie
67 Celica model
68 Runners carry it

DOWN
1 Artist Johns
2 Give consent
3 __ '66 (Sergio Mendes group)
4 Have a hunch
5 Dean Martin role
6 Jai __
7 Old clothes
8 Sunflower supports
9 Caduceus carrier
10 "__ Mia" ('65 tune)
11 A dime a dozen
12 Tiny Tim's trademark
13 When Strasbourg sizzles
21 Grenoble's river
22 Flock female
26 Auto acronym
29 Terrier threat
30 Iolani Palace locale
31 Reeked
33 Kennel critters
34 Depraved
35 Reebok rival
37 Seven-pound computer
38 Jacob's partner
39 Ending for prior
40 David's great-grandmother
41 Neptune, but not Earth
44 Kapaa keepsake
45 Preoccupy
47 Sing the praises of
48 Mr. Reese
49 Rattled one's cage
52 Malawi native
54 Pizarro victims
56 Oscar __ Renta
57 Play thing
58 Third-rate
59 __ podrida
60 *Starpeace* artist

286 BREAKFAST ORDERS by Randolph Ross

ACROSS
1 Reiner or Lowe
4 Last word in prayer
8 Delicious or Granny Smith
13 Major work
15 Singer Falana
16 Polynesian parties
17 Breakfast order
20 "Get lost!"
21 San Diego attraction
22 *Casablanca* character
23 European capital
26 Queue after Q
28 Breakfast order
36 Luxurious
37 Arkin or Alda
38 Win by __
39 Sculptures and such
40 Most clichéd
42 Hwy.
43 Mythology branch
45 Maryland collegian
46 __ off (angry)
47 Breakfast order
50 Cambodia's Lon __
51 Genesis locale
52 Datum
55 Cable network
58 Becker of tennis
62 Breakfast order
66 Cook's wear
67 Brainstorm
68 Filet fish
69 Othello's countrymen
70 Told tall tales
71 Danson of *Cheers*

DOWN
1 Fabled birds
2 Cartel initials
3 Perry Mason portrayer
4 100%
5 Lower the lawn
6 Brit. monarch
7 Post-WWII alliance
8 Governor Landon
9 Overly moral one
10 Name of six popes
11 Director Buñuel
12 "¿Cómo __ usted?"
14 Hunt
18 Run __ (go crazy)
19 Hirt's instrument
24 Castle protection
25 Some black keys
27 Sing like Ella
28 Point of view
29 *Burden of Proof* author
30 National Leaguer
31 Archaeologist's word form
32 Hit __ (affect)
33 '88 Olympics host
34 Adlai's '56 running mate
35 Run-down
40 Utah's state flower
41 Exceeded the limit
44 Summoned
46 Parts of wood joints
48 Sticky stuff
49 Country singer McEntire
52 Con game
53 "__ the mornin'!"
54 Spheroid hairdo
56 Leave port
57 *The King* __
59 Melee
60 Capri, for one
61 Tool building
63 Nav. rank.
64 Poor grade
65 June honoree

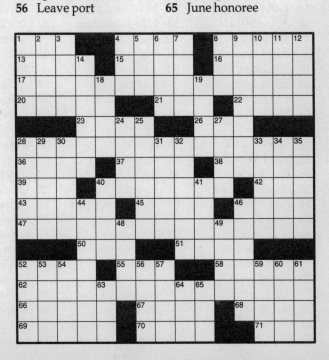

287 CLUB SONGS by Scott Marley

ACROSS
1 Sheepish remarks
5 Art Deco artist
9 Thanksgiving celebration
14 __ cost (free)
15 Forecast word
16 Flirt
17 Song for an intergalactic golf course?
20 Was a model
21 San __, TX
22 How some order lunch
23 Mideasterner
25 Start the pot
27 Fix, as a copier
31 Purposeful trip
35 Soprano Moffo
38 Declare openly
40 Cool quarters
41 Song for an overused golf course?
44 Some kin
45 __-do-well
46 Wheel connector
47 Cow, often
49 Pipe problems
51 Half a fortnight
53 Desirable possession
57 __ Major
60 Beetle or bee
64 Inventor Whitney
65 Song for a fancy golf course?
68 Dieter's no-no
69 Telegram
70 "He's the Wiz and he lives __"
71 "Casey __ Bat"
72 Stern's opposite
73 Nix

DOWN
1 Baritone's colleagues
2 Fighting
3 Ms. Bryant
4 Henry VIII's desire
5 Leprechaun land
6 Called up
7 Buster Brown's dog
8 __ Gay
9 Prescription agcy.
10 Spring-basket material
11 Sax range
12 Smeltery leftovers
13 First-timer
18 Acquire
19 "__ but the brave . . ."
24 It doesn't wind up
26 Math subject
28 Golfer Stephenson
29 The Bard's river
30 Roadside inn
32 Haley of *Roots*
33 Yuletide
34 Cooked enough
35 Expressing pleasure, as a dog's tail
36 Word form for "nerve"
37 Grandma
39 "What fun!"
42 Understanding words
43 NOW cause
48 Steed's strap
50 Actress Capshaw
52 Has down cold
54 Paris divider
55 Singer John
56 Frenzied state
57 "__-daisy!"
58 Least of the litter
59 Baseball record
61 Foul mood
62 Raison d'__
63 Sci. class
66 Five-star nickname
67 Free (of)

288 HOLLYWOOD REPORTER by Wayne R. Williams

ACROSS
1 Sentence break
5 Change for a five
9 Manhandled
14 Rights grp.
15 Storm of *My Little Margie*
16 Actor Milo
17 First Henry Aldrich movie
19 Dueling tools
20 Some anchors and stringers
21 Nonviolent protest
23 Babylonia, today
25 Read a poem
28 Rommel et al.
32 Shoshone tribe
34 Profit figure
35 Boorish one
36 Sore spots
37 Bleacher yell
38 Neck and neck
39 Glynnis O'Connor TV film
40 Stood up
41 Geom. shape
42 Blue shades
43 Sahara mount
44 Function
45 Roll-call call
46 Isn't colorfast
47 Duke of Edinburgh
49 Ms. Teasdale
51 Like a standoff
53 Priest's hat
58 Stone worker
60 Abbott and Costello film
62 Nonsensical
63 Ireland's alias
64 European capital
65 Rose essence
66 Paramount structures
67 Blossom support

DOWN
1 Tony Orlando's backup
2 Charley horse
3 Shredded side dish
4 Crude dwellings
5 Lustful lookers
6 Mrs. Yeltsin
7 Pixie
8 Gets a load of
9 49 Across, e.g.
10 Spicy jelly
11 Van Johnson movie
12 Wide-shoe letters
13 Pub. defenders' foes
18 __ acids
22 Peaceful Greek
24 Gores' predecessors
26 Back-combed
27 Merman and Barrymore
28 Ocular device
29 Fill with joy
30 David Janssen movie
31 Charged atom
33 Kazurinsky and Conway
36 __ Lap ('83 film)
39 Bawls
40 Actress Charlotte
42 Stephen King novel
43 Mild cigar
46 Half the honeymooners
48 Hotelier Helmsley
50 Scrub a mission
52 She sheep
54 Genesis name
55 Evaluation
56 Roof piece
57 Energy source
58 *Mamma __!*
59 Grasshopper's colleague
61 Hurry up

289 HOW CUTE! by Trip Payne

ACROSS
1 Color Me __ (pop group)
5 Courtly dance
10 Michigan, e.g.
14 BSA part
15 A Trump ex
16 Yoked team
17 Lopez's theme
18 Asocial one
19 Parker products
20 SPEAKER OF QUOTE
23 Sumatran ape
24 Edmonton player
28 Dover dish
31 Half-grown herring
33 Baby food
36 START OF A QUOTE
38 "I smell __!"
40 *Gaslight* star
41 Florida county
42 MIDDLE OF QUOTE
45 British Airways craft
46 Equestrian's cry
47 Fix typos
49 Prized violin
50 Gets warm
54 END OF QUOTE
60 It brings people closer
63 Compel
64 U.S. alliance
65 See 43 Down
66 Electrolysis particle
67 Statuesque model
68 Marquis or viscount
69 Shows team spirit
70 Ltr. enclosure

DOWN
1 *Deliverance* dueler
2 "My Cherie __"
3 Reese of *Touched by an Angel*
4 Tuckers out
5 Arizona river
6 What Stratford's on
7 Homestead Act offering
8 Unique item
9 Trim, as expenses
10 Hardly close
11 Firefighter's need
12 Barbie's beau
13 Nav. rank
21 They may be colossal
22 Spineless one
25 Bonet and Simpson
26 Bagnold et al.
27 Convened again
29 Earring spots
30 Ham it up
31 Eydie's singing partner
32 Ran on TV
33 Shells or spirals
34 __ *With a View*
35 Turkish title
37 Pinkerton logo
39 Philanderer
43 With 65 Across, Monty Python member
44 Columbus ship
48 Pete Sampras' field
51 *Battlestar Galactica* name
52 Moreno and Coolidge
53 *Basic Instinct* star
55 Worshiping place?
56 Words for Nanette
57 Small band
58 Kilt wearer
59 Sawbucks
60 State follower
61 Wordsworth work
62 Flamenco cry

290 WHERE'S MR. LINCOLN? by Eric Albert

ACROSS
1 Swerve or twist
5 Attorney-__
10 Pillow cover
14 Curb cry
15 Tibetan capital
16 *Our Gang* dog
17 *Butterfield 8* star
20 Drenched
21 Hardly exciting
22 "Olde" store
23 Highway marker
24 Prepare
25 Virginia, once
28 Babe's bed
29 Holyfield's pride
32 Island greeting
33 Animated character
34 Delany of *China Beach*
35 Filed wrong, maybe
38 Squared away
39 Stand up
40 Director Walsh
41 Above, in verse
42 Cream buy
43 The sky, so to speak
44 Pawn
45 Jupiter's alias
46 Again and yet again
49 FDR's place
50 Shake up
53 Gung-ho expression
56 Finely appointed
57 Packing a rod
58 Barn dance
59 Crude cartel
60 Styne show
61 Brisk

DOWN
1 Lamb dish
2 Green veggie
3 Way to go
4 Expert
5 Hudson River city
6 English homework
7 Past due
8 Timber tree
9 Phone service
10 Secretly observe
11 Samaritan's offering
12 At the zenith
13 Nothing more than
18 Lacking a key
19 Ishmael's boss
23 "Over There" writer
24 Investigate thoroughly
25 Walk-on
26 Green shade
27 Dangerfield persona
28 Run by gravity
29 Informal instrument
30 Better
31 With low spirits
33 Use your noodle
34 Ladd or Lane
36 Bob Barker prop
37 Become broader?
42 Somewhat: Mus.
43 Improv offering
44 Soprano's attainment
45 Is in accord
46 Galley glitch
47 Earring variety
48 Trick
49 Mildly moist
50 Off-road vehicle
51 Declare formally
52 Bank (on)
54 Stab
55 Returns org.

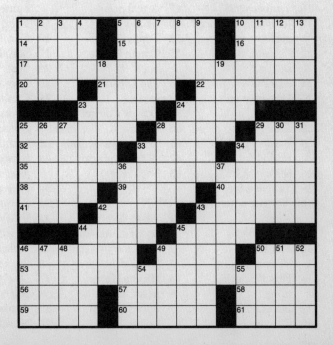

LAST COURSE by Randolph Ross

ACROSS

1 High country
6 Enthusiastic
11 Fireman's tool
14 Really go for
15 Castle or Cara
16 Samovar
17 Something simple
19 Little bit
20 "__ boy!"
21 Sleeveless tops
22 Santa's stockpile
23 French king
25 __ something (scheming)
27 Favor-currying credits
33 Be situated
34 City light
35 Western range
37 __ Raton, FL
39 Juan's "one"
41 Popular cookie
42 Less fresh
45 Golden Rule word
48 OAS member
49 Neat situation
52 Medieval menial
53 Social-page word
54 Binges
57 Intermission follower
60 Scientist Sagan
64 Need to pay
65 Clever one
67 Moving vehicle
68 Taylor of *The Nanny*
69 Barcelona bye-bye
70 CBS logo
71 Beasts of burden
72 Clark's foster parents

DOWN

1 Wine valley
2 Correct copy
3 Frost, for one
4 Jockey Eddie
5 Grant's foe
6 Filled (with)
7 Rainbow shapes
8 Pummel
9 Blotter mark
10 Poor grade
11 Geo or Reo
12 Diagnostic device
13 Pass catchers
18 Sheeplike
22 Kemo Sabe's pal
24 Have title to
26 Even up
27 Regional fauna and flora
28 Short summary
29 Chit
30 Listless feeling
31 Musical Mel
32 Nasty look
33 Many oz.
36 Boston Red __
38 *Suisse* sights
40 Top ranking
43 Overhead trains
44 Titles differently
46 Elixir
47 Mine find
50 Ice-cream topping
51 Puzzle out
54 Roman god
55 Not home
56 Barry or Rayburn
58 Shade source
59 Inhabitants' suffix
61 Related
62 Funny joke
63 Not as much
65 Sp. lady
66 Symbol of might

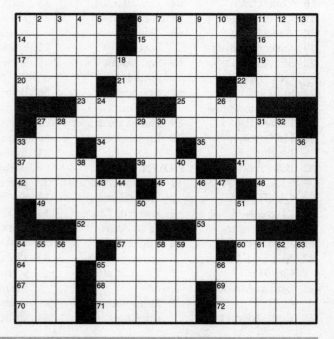

SEEING RED by Eric Albert

ACROSS

1 Chasm
6 They have their points
10 Pronto
14 Small stream
15 Calendar row
16 Timber wolf
17 Justice, prudence, etc.
20 "__ pin, pick it up, . . ."
21 Annoy
22 Like heaven's gates
23 Carry on
25 Radio "good buddy"
26 Make stick
29 Take it easy
30 Ad-free network: Abbr.
33 Soup stock
34 Places
35 Metric weight
36 Fats Waller tune
39 Done with
40 Cafeteria carrier
41 Liking, and then some
42 Scale notes
43 Go bankrupt
44 Caustic comment
45 Look after
46 Out of control
47 A real nut
50 Relatives
51 Top with tar
55 Conan Doyle book
58 *The King and I* locale
59 Duster's target
60 Deceive
61 Thing with strings
62 Actress Jurado
63 Shell rival

DOWN

1 Basic elements
2 Scottish hillside
3 Time long past
4 Drink diluter
5 Hit the slopes
6 In the know
7 Bubbly band leader
8 *My Name Is Asher __*
9 Lam before trial
10 Sacred spot
11 Off-pitch
12 Genesis name
13 Bouquet
18 Coming soon
19 Ship hazard
24 Sore
25 Too confident
26 Can't stand
27 Booty collection
28 Sound qualities
29 Express alternative
30 Fork part
31 Count of jazz
32 Vilify
34 Of interest to tabloids
35 Big race
37 *Double Indemnity* star
38 Actor Jannings
43 Nosebag fill
44 __ oxide ointment
45 Beat badly
46 Fine and filmy
47 Redeem
48 Kubla Khan's continent
49 Rigel is one
50 Speed unit
52 Emcee Trebek
53 Kill a bill
54 School founded in 1440
56 Keogh cousin
57 British brew

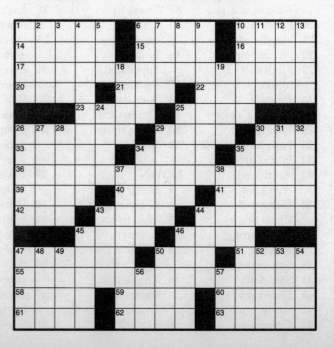

293 INTRODUCTIONS by Scott Marley

ACROSS
1 Political movement
6 Bar in a car
10 "__ Ha'i"
14 A, as in Athens
15 Like a bishop's move: Abbr.
16 "The doctor __"
17 Classic movie line, supposedly
20 Prefix meaning "outside"
21 Fireplace tool
22 Singer Trini
23 "Get lost!"
24 Qty. of heat
25 Do or sol
27 Have the lead
29 Sound beater?
32 '83 play
36 Soccer target
37 Nightfalls
38 __ upswing (rising)
39 Hit tune of '65
42 *Padre*'s sister
43 Contentment
44 Barbershop sound
45 It runs when broken
46 Encouraging remarks
48 Make __ out of (disprove)
51 Earth tremor
53 Armstrong affirmative
56 Cohan-tune end
59 To __ (unanimously)
60 *The Wizard* __
61 Gobbled up
62 Outdoor meals, for short
63 Moist, in a way
64 City on the Rhône

DOWN
1 Checked in
2 Actor Karras
3 Till
4 __ Na Na
5 Made of clay
6 *A Bell for* __
7 PED __ (corner sign)
8 Troubadour's repertoire
9 Rational mind
10 Theater name
11 "The earlier, the better!"
12 Occupation
13 Don Juan's mother
18 Gnu home
19 Extreme
23 Copy editor's concern
24 Deep voices
25 Mama Judd
26 Midwest city
27 Set starter
28 Hawaiian idol
29 Mideast region
30 Rascal
31 Lacrosse-team complement
33 "What __!" (bored one's remark)
34 Willie of baseball
35 Beef cuts
36 "Vamoose!"
40 Pola of the silents
41 *Pequod* survivor
45 Brings home
46 Posh
47 Holmes clue
48 41 Down's captain
49 Helpless one
50 Baghdad's country
51 Not out
52 Sufficient, in poems
53 Regarding
54 Sign of tomorrow
55 Some dolls
57 George Burns role
58 Scottish river

294 POSSESSIONS by Wayne R. Williams

ACROSS
1 Fiery crime
6 Actor Erwin
9 French priests
14 Martin's toy
16 Ruth's mother-in-law
17 Edith's dessert
18 Diamond boot
19 Ms. Ono
20 Singing voices
22 Fast food
23 Change color
24 Elements
26 Small band
30 Astrologer Sydney
32 Likes a lot
34 Pearl's family
38 Post-WWII strongman
39 *Jagged Edge* star
41 Bigotry
42 C.P.'s gardening tool
44 Drunk as a skunk
46 High times
47 Mimics
48 Magic word
51 *Nova* network
53 Miami team
54 Moe victim
57 To be, to Marie
61 Org.
63 Margaret's joint
65 Office skill
66 Edwin H.'s wrap
67 Ruhr Valley city
68 Half of *deux*
69 Fly-eating bird

DOWN
1 Drained of color
2 Word form for "current"
3 Water well
4 *Novus* __ *seclorum*
5 P.M. periods
6 Hackneyed
7 Wrongful act
8 As far as
9 *Wheel of Fortune* buy
10 Red's dance
11 __ acid
12 Chew the scenery
13 Becomes a dad
15 Collar insert
21 Open spots
23 Female rabbit
25 Peeve
26 "Memory" musical
27 Valhalla VIP
28 Lorre role
29 Jerry's pitch
30 Orchestra group
31 Greek M's
33 Training center
35 Welles character
36 Way: Lat.
37 Beatty et al.
40 Either Chaney
43 Tippler
45 Prof.'s aides
48 Look of the moon
49 Takes breaks
50 Does gently
51 Trim a tree
52 West Virginia senator
55 Rights grp.
56 Chestnut horse
57 Ending for opal
58 Spring event
59 Opportune
60 Dueling sword
62 Issue side
64 Recipe meas.

295 ROADSIDE VERSE by Cathy Millhauser

ACROSS

1 Exile isle
5 Hashhouse spheroid
10 Complaining sort
14 Bartlett or bosc
15 Up __ (stuck)
16 Attract
17 Top of the head
18 Tome home
19 Singer Redding
20 START OF A VERSE
23 5 Across feature
24 Brewer's oven
25 A Bobbsey
26 Retain
27 Dennis' neighbors
31 Make beam
34 Line that isn't there
36 Floral garland
37 PART 2 OF VERSE
41 Director Howard
42 Pot covers
43 Groups of two
44 Necessitates
47 Old oath
48 Genetic material
49 Orion has one
51 Word before sister or story
54 END OF VERSE
59 "__ the mornin'!"
60 Where the blissful walk
61 Livy's love
62 Inventor Sikorsky
63 Handy
64 Slave away
65 A lot
66 Broadway bestowals
67 "Smooth Operator" singer

DOWN

1 __ Lederer (Ann Landers)
2 Spinach descriptor
3 Enjoy the ocean
4 2-D extent
5 South Seas explorer
6 Aramis' colleague
7 Italian city
8 Hard to hold
9 Stain again
10 Troupe group
11 Old Testament name
12 Scotto solo
13 Top-rated
21 Kayak user
22 __ ammoniac (ammonium chloride)
26 Nonprescription: Abbr.
27 Mental faculties
28 Ms. Korbut
29 Requirement
30 Remains idle
31 Rochester's love
32 Doctorow's __ Lake
33 Polly, e.g.
34 Rental name
35 Marked a ballot
38 __ Eve
39 Deles, maybe
40 Comic Louis
45 Shaded spots
46 One-million link
47 Distress signals
49 Conk
50 Post of etiquette
51 Pago Pago's land
52 Egg-shaped
53 *Texaco Star Theater* star
54 Working hard
55 Order phrase
56 Familiar with
57 Golden Rule word
58 Bartholomew Cubbins' 500

296 METALLURGY by Shirley Soloway

ACROSS

1 Gymnast's maneuver
6 "It's __-win situation!"
9 The basics
13 Dress style
14 Sprightly tune
16 W. C. Fields' "Phooey!"
17 Fortune hunter
19 Jutland resident
20 Singer Adams
21 Elephant keeper
23 Sault __ Marie, MI
24 Puppy bite
26 Tailor's tool
28 Ingenue, e.g.
32 Rope feature
33 __-mo replay
34 New York city
36 Composer Carmichael
39 Of Swiss peaks
41 Coach Parseghian
42 How actors enter
43 Family members
44 High-tech beam
46 Gold meas.
47 Ireland's alias
49 Bring under control
51 Make a __ difference
54 Explorer Johnson
55 Stadium shout
56 Wiped off
59 Knocks sharply
63 Agenda element
65 Tarpon, for one
67 Sign of sorrow
68 Author Wiesel
69 Murphy of WWII
70 Leftovers
71 Blooming time: Abbr.
72 *Cagney & Lacey* star

DOWN

1 Cook's herb
2 Tramp along
3 Leslie Caron role
4 Start a paragraph
5 Turner of CNN
6 Seaweed
7 Close-by, in poems
8 Butter substitutes
9 Total up
10 The nitty-gritty
11 Poem part
12 Man the helm
15 18-wheeler
18 Drive forward
22 Petty gamblers
25 Raymond Burr role
27 Any time now
28 __ breve (music marking)
29 American snake
30 Ball balancer
31 Mrs. Brady
33 Maple product
35 *Atlantis* org.
37 Courage
38 "May I help you?"
40 British nobleman
45 Wear away
48 Ancient Scandinavian
50 "Cheerful Little __"
51 Put on paper
52 Made of grain
53 Lays an egg
57 Vocal gaffe
58 At any time
60 Assistant
61 Greek letters
62 Ewes and mares
64 First Lady's title
66 Duster's need

297 BON VOYAGE by Alfio Micci

ACROSS
1 Musical finale
5 Inclined paths
10 Carnegie or Evans
14 Eager
15 *Silas Marner* author
16 Lupino and Tarbell
17 Ultimatum phrase
20 __ Miss
21 Trigonometric function
22 Make clear
23 Prefix for graph
24 Algerian port
25 Punjab capital
28 Small pianos
31 How others see us
32 Word on a penny
33 Point at the target
35 War god
36 In the center of
38 Comic Rudner
39 Dug in
40 Israeli statesman
41 Kind of eclipse
42 Thoroughly soak
44 Kitchen closet
45 Smell __ (be suspicious)
46 Math course
47 Wheel inventor
50 One of these days
51 Supplement, with "out"
54 Classic sitcom
57 Comic Johnson
58 Sheer fabric
59 Warble
60 Yule song
61 Went astray
62 Choir voice

DOWN
1 Roman VIP
2 Track shape
3 Netherlands sight
4 Summer quaff
5 Fix the roof
6 By oneself
7 Bog
8 Campaigning one
9 At the helm
10 Just heavenly
11 Mideast gulf
12 Not of the clergy
13 Spanish direction
18 French river
19 __-garde
23 Apparel
24 Dentist's request
25 Green bean
26 Violin maker
27 Ladies' room
28 Tea partner
29 Spoil
30 Shankar's instrument
34 "A grand old name"
36 Harsh-talking
37 Sloop pole
38 Ladder part
40 Macabre
41 "Mule Train" singer
43 Comics Captain
44 Looked into
46 Peter O'__
47 Iberian dessert
48 Architect Saarinen
49 Size up
50 Recipe verb
51 Hardly angelic
52 Town near Cleveland
53 Thus
55 Rocky peak
56 Cool __ cucumber

298 A CROSSWORD by Wayne R. Williams

ACROSS
1 Joke around
5 Fleming and Carney
9 English racecourse
14 Assert positively
15 Stare open-mouthed
16 Take off
17 July 1, in Moose Jaw
19 Tiberius' tongue
20 Not quite right
21 Pencil-box items
23 Take a total
24 Sully
26 Fermi's concern
28 S.A. nation
29 Japanese novelist
33 Trajectories
36 Talked like
38 "Encore presentation"
39 Resting spot
40 *Bolero* composer
42 Scotland __
43 __ *Bulba* (Gogol novel)
45 City on the Arno
46 Deep black
47 Hank Aaron, for one
49 Cliburn or Morrison
51 Arrived
52 Skycap's tote
56 Actress Arthur
58 Brief bio
61 Coll. basketball tourney
62 Flynn of films
64 Indian chief
66 Board of education?
67 Nordic name
68 Singer Sonny
69 Lab work
70 Gumbo ingredient
71 Album tracks

DOWN
1 Reformer Riis
2 Get around
3 Dispatches
4 La-la lead-in
5 Culture medium
6 Detection device
7 "__ brillig . . ."
8 Actresss Ione
9 Top player
10 __ of Marmara
11 Racing boat
12 *Metamorphoses* author
13 Look after
18 Moose cousin
22 Uncooked
25 Islamic bench
27 Following directions
29 Kline or Costner
30 Fruity quaffs
31 Ottoman
32 *60 Minutes* name
33 Cinema canine
34 Honest-to-goodness
35 Falconlike birds
37 Haydn's nickname
41 South Seas skirt
44 Bakery freebies
48 Debussy's *La* __
50 Teen ending
52 State of India
53 Type of pear
54 James Dean film
55 Cultural spirit
56 Highest-quality
57 Perry's penner
59 Melville novel
60 *Columbo* star
63 Mel of baseball
65 Telephonic 2

SING SING by Trip Payne

ACROSS
1 DeMille production
5 Well-qualified
9 Hoop star Thomas
14 It's undeniable
15 Clothes line?
16 John __ Garner
17 Regrets
18 Barbara Mason tune of '65
20 Actor Wallach
21 "__ Lang Syne"
22 Using chairs
23 Like Poe's stories
25 Small cobras
26 Mr. Wiesel
27 Aid in crime
28 Hitter's stat
31 New World explorer
33 Shutterbug's buy
35 Pearl Buck character
36 Sevareid et al.
37 "Dedicated to the __ Love"

38 Beef cut
40 Parachute parts
41 Jimmy's daughter
42 Cool treats
43 Ballet garb
44 Bolger costar
45 Hose material
48 Taxing subject
51 Sisters or mothers
52 Recipe phrase
53 UB40 tune of '88
55 MP's quarry
56 Former Dodge
57 Actress Swenson
58 Back of the neck
59 Library no-no
60 Hideaway
61 Goes blonde

DOWN
1 Zimbalist of *The F.B.I.*
2 Singer Abdul
3 Vanilla Ice tune of '90
4 Dol. parts
5 Guarantee

6 Blues street
7 Alan or Cheryl
8 Dash lengths
9 Kind of interview
10 Long stories
11 "You're soaking __!"
12 Land measure
13 Hung onto
19 Make judgments
21 Slightly
24 Without company
25 How some are taken
27 Wanted-poster word
28 Slade tune of '84
29 Extorted
30 Wading bird
31 Caesar's partner
32 Reunion attendee
33 Less restrained
34 Salvation Army founder
36 Was artistic with acid
39 Popular cat
40 Ornery sort

43 Unmusical quality
44 Bodies of knowledge
45 Molds and mushrooms
46 Take the honey and run

47 *Twice-Told __*
48 OPEC member
49 Rex's sleuth
50 Half of DCCCIV
51 Ricci or Foch
54 Comic Shriner
55 &

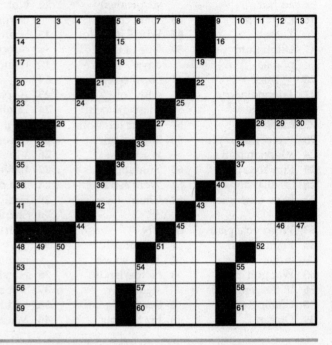

STOCK ANSWERS by Harvey Estes

ACROSS
1 Collins of rock
5 Manner of walking
9 "Excuse me!"
13 Mystical poem
14 Brit's 14 pounds
15 What love may mean
16 Stock company?
18 Miscellany
19 Racy beach?
20 Hollywood hopeful
22 Adored ones
24 Spread in a tub
25 *Café* cup
28 Soup sample
30 Grump's exclamation
33 *Ordinary People* actor
35 Captures
37 Zsa Zsa's sister
38 Desire deified
39 Apollo 11 module
41 Become boring
42 Damage
43 *M*A*S*H* nurse

44 Sell wholesale
46 Vote in
48 Part of TNT
50 Eat away
51 Porcine meal
53 Entanglement
55 Columbus' landfall
58 Hare __
62 U.S.
63 Stock option?
65 Cleo's queendom
66 Musical sounds
67 Pablo's love
68 Well-handled
69 Medium
70 Flintstones' pet

DOWN
1 Stir to action
2 Kona dance
3 Jones' nickname
4 Radicals
5 Makes off with
6 Carload
7 Ultimate aims
8 Spaghetti sauce

9 Portuguese possession
10 Stock exchange?
11 Northeast port
12 Not worth arguing about
14 Word form for "Chinese"
17 Copland ballet score
21 *The Sound of Music* scenery
23 Lounge entertainers
25 Main focus
26 Ear-oriented
27 Stock holder?
29 Chum
31 Flee from
32 Batman's alias
34 S. Dak. neighbor
36 Hyacinth's home
40 SST concern
41 Southern California town
43 Bit of matter
45 Spooky

47 Bordeaux beverage
49 More black
52 Solemn agreements
54 Parentheses' shapes
55 Shortwave, e.g.

56 Gallic girlfriend
57 Smithy's item
59 Sphere starter
60 Inert gas
61 __-American Symphony (Still opus)
64 Wee hour

CRAZY by Bob Lubbers

ACROSS
1 Truck maker: Abbr.
4 Toy-truck maker
9 Bit of gossip
14 __ de cologne
15 Diamond miscue
16 __ nous (confidentially)
17 Wall St.'s home
18 Train pullers
20 Director's shoots
22 Scope starter
23 Long-__ (anteater-like)
26 Washes well
30 Public speaker
32 Put in fizz
34 English channel?
36 Hair cutter
38 Hair shop
39 Feels poorly
41 Kids' blocks
43 K-P filler
44 Impassive
46 "Forget it!"
48 *Oui* or *da*
49 Battle zone
51 Sound effect, for short
53 Biased
55 News stories
58 Vigoda and Burrows
60 Red as __
61 Almond accessories
67 Ecology org.
68 Pigtail, e.g.
69 Wild cat
70 Move sideways
71 Christie and Karenina
72 First vice president
73 Mag. bosses

DOWN
1 Fellows
2 Yucatán culture
3 German export
4 '60s satellite
5 Spanish gold
6 AEC successor
7 Former Surgeon General
8 Weapons: Fr.
9 Hits the hay
10 Mono- kin
11 VH-1 rival
12 Crude copper
13 Musical notes
19 Killer whale
21 Lisbon's loc.
24 Latin abbr.
25 Jury complement
27 Range dividing Europe and Asia
28 Some summer air
29 Hard stuff
31 Radioer's response
33 Genesis name
34 Sport fish
35 Small snacks
37 Fido's friend
40 Construction area
42 Golfer Ballesteros
45 No heroes
47 Meals
50 Singer McEntire
52 Director Reiner
54 Crosby record label
56 Lukewarm
57 Half the deer
59 Lose traction
61 Dr. J's league
62 Tea brewer
63 Brown shade
64 Spy grp.
65 Miss Gabor
66 Sleep phenom.

SOMETHING FOR ALL by Eric Albert

ACROSS
1 Dennis the Menace's dog
5 Glance through
9 Sibilant sound
14 Kind of vaccine
15 Broad-based
16 *Cheers* role
17 TOM
20 Start the pot
21 Wet dirt
22 His, to Henri
23 Family member
24 Wild guess
26 Bishop of Rome
27 Restore to health
28 Water pipe
29 Actor Farr
30 Printing measures
31 Small eatery
32 Remnant
33 DICK
35 Singer Vic
38 Buddhist monk
39 Israeli airport
42 Dizzying designs
43 Help with the dishes
44 Kind of admiral
45 Hard and unyielding
46 Joke
47 Full of filth
48 Remain quiet
49 Anchor Rather
50 Contribute to a cause
51 HARRY
55 Sports site
56 Kampuchea's continent
57 Let loose
58 No longer bothered by
59 *What's My Line* host
60 Donkey dinner

DOWN
1 Cartland offering
2 Heavy metal
3 Breaks stride
4 Clip
5 Give tit for tat
6 Modeling buy
7 Common vow
8 Broadway star Ethel
9 Mideast victim
10 Go Fish alternative
11 Annoying
12 Get up late
13 Hick
18 Subtle suggestion
19 Soaking spot
24 Not out
25 Father's Day gift
26 Errand doer
28 Buddy, in Britain
29 Indonesian island
31 Bit of change
32 *Newsweek* rival
33 Quad building
34 Use a VCR
35 Sirius
36 Independent of experience
37 Headwaiter
39 Smiley's creator
40 Hardwood source
41 Unmoved
43 "FOR SALE: Refrigerator, like new, $140 or best offer. Call 555-7826 evenings"
44 Head for the hills
46 Funnyman Murray
47 Cut the lawn
49 Unwilling to listen
50 6/6/44
52 LP center?
53 Stiff __ board
54 Zilch

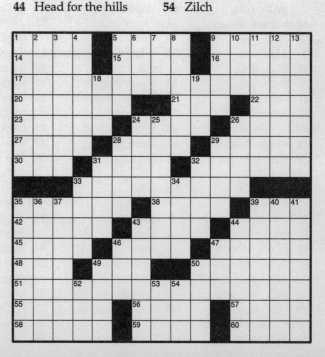

303 ON FOOT by Shirley Soloway

ACROSS
1 Skim and 1%
6 Balance center
9 Put together
13 TV studio sign
14 Make eyes at
15 Expended
16 Asian evergreen
18 Barnum's singer
19 Author Bagnold
20 Come after
21 A piece of cake
22 Eastern Indians
24 VT clock setting
26 Gun the engine
27 Infused with zeal
32 Photo
35 Utility device
37 Like lettuce
38 Pueblo material
40 Rap-sheet letters
41 Flynn of films
42 Clunky car
43 Streisand costar in '91
45 Mao __-tung
46 Hitchcock film of '36
48 Election winners
50 Recipe amt.
51 Lack
55 Pear choice
58 Painter Rembrandt
61 Inflight offering
62 Utah resort
63 British collegians
65 Close loudly
66 Kingly address
67 High-ceiling halls
68 Orchestra member
69 WWII region
70 Finishes ahead of

DOWN
1 Heston role
2 Senseless
3 Bandleader Lester
4 Joking sort
5 Sp. lady
6 Swelled heads
7 Felipe of baseball
8 Cash in
9 Driver of a sort
10 Where most people live
11 Family rooms
12 Sea swirl
14 Keeps
17 GI's time off
23 Bonds together
25 They may be vented
27 Tea type
28 River to the Caspian Sea
29 Move quickly
30 Strange sightings
31 Nabors role
32 Good buddies
33 Inspiration
34 Search thoroughly
36 Sharp flavor
39 Marine base
44 Rome's river
47 Place side by side
49 Mideast resident
51 Spiny houseplant
52 Closes in on
53 "Shut up!"
54 Lanchester and Maxwell
55 Big party
56 __ podrida
57 Lead player
59 Leave the stage
60 Continental prefix
64 Bit of hair cream

304 DIAMOND CRIMES by Randolph Ross

ACROSS
1 June dance
5 Inferior
9 Allan-__
14 Verdi heroine
15 Skating maneuver
16 Mideast desert
17 What the runner did
20 Picketers, perhaps
21 Wipes out
22 Actor Frobe
23 Applications
24 Vegas hotel
26 Guinness Book suffix
27 Agatha's colleague
31 5th-century pope
32 National spirit
34 Poetic adverb
35 What the third-base coach did
38 Pitch __-hitter
39 Copier chemical
40 Exigencies
41 Laugh heartily
43 Headline of '14
44 Nursery sounds
45 Lends a hand
47 Reagan confidant
48 Harmonize
51 Zeppelin's forte
55 What the slugger did
57 Nosey Parker
58 Fancy wheels
59 S-shaped curve
60 Bullish sound
61 Dance routine
62 Highway

DOWN
1 Written permission
2 Director Martin
3 Skunk's weapon
4 Libeled
5 Sci-fi weapons
6 Put out
7 Short times
8 Thruway warning
9 Conductor Previn
10 Insult
11 Turkish leaders
12 __ majesty (high crime)
13 Nights before
18 Squeezed by
19 Greek sage
23 Wedding-party member
24 Office worker
25 Say OK to
26 The upper atmosphere
28 Richards of tennis
29 It's on the Aire
30 Messes up
31 Persian potentate
32 Lab burners
33 Daily event
36 Snow form
37 One next door
42 Cosmetics queen
44 Drive-in server
46 Unmoving
47 Casino order
48 Bits of current
49 Chance to play
50 The Andrews Sisters, e.g.
51 Mine entrance
52 Shakespearean villain
53 No contest, perhaps
54 Albertville vehicle
56 Chi-town trains

305 FIRST PERSONS by Wayne R. Williams

ACROSS

1 Union bane
5 Calendar abbr.
9 Tavern orders
14 Unpunctual
15 State with authority
16 Actor Delon
17 Individuals
18 Big car exec
20 Wedding tradition
22 Harsh-looking
23 In the know
24 Tailor, often
26 Nosed out
28 Roll-call count
30 Speaks grandiloquently
34 Red-headed riot
39 Star's stage
40 Colorado Rockies owner
41 Fellow
42 Chips, at times
43 Seth's son
44 *Kate & Allie* costar
46 Evita's title
49 *Discovery* agcy.
50 Student's souvenirs
53 At the ready
57 Ipanema's locale
60 *North Dallas Forty* star
62 Author Benchley
63 Reagan aide
66 Folk tales
67 Nicholas Gage book
68 Govt. training program
69 Margot role
70 Thickheaded
71 Waste allowance
72 Poetic works

DOWN

1 Indolence
2 Tippy transport
3 Mr. T and crew
4 Miss America of '45
5 Actor Mineo
6 Arden et al.
7 Pro golfer Calvin
8 Group of three
9 One with the funds
10 "Xanadu" rockers
11 For one
12 Edgar __ Burroughs
13 Crackle's colleague
19 Mythical ship
21 Rains cats and dogs
25 Actress Charlotte
27 *The Purple Rose of Cairo* actor
29 Epic tale
31 Lug around
32 At any time
33 Fresh language
34 Hotshot pilots
35 Nary a one
36 Palindromic time
37 Čapek play
38 Hebrew letter
42 Famed fabler
45 Atlas page
47 What Nancy calls her hubby
48 Ion source
51 Choose
52 Handle the helm
54 Got up
55 Spooky
56 Prepare for work
57 Musical mouthpiece
58 Not busy
59 Author Wister
61 Spanish direction
64 Officeholders
65 Dig in

306 FIGHTING WORDS by Shirley Soloway

ACROSS

1 Soup holders
5 Rams and roosters
10 Saudi native
14 Support in crime
15 Have __ (participate)
16 Angler's device
17 Negri of silents
18 Gold bar
19 Diminutive suffix
20 Hold back
23 Have a bite
24 Ecology agcy.
25 Santa __, CA
28 Comet part
31 Screenplay
36 Ballad subject
38 "What's __ for me?"
40 Wild West show
41 Well-positioned
44 Respectful refusal
45 Fashion mag
46 Relaxation
47 High regard
49 Make an engraving
51 Showed the way
52 "Unforgettable" name
54 Put-it-together buy
56 Act unethically
65 Neighborhood
66 Ritzy headpiece
67 Spiny houseplant
68 Broadway bestowal
69 Actress Burstyn
70 Get up
71 Last vestiges
72 Removed from copy
73 Caught in the act

DOWN

1 Abner's creator
2 Mideast name
3 Singer Carter
4 No longer fresh
5 Keep up
6 British composer
7 Captains' diaries
8 Wed in haste
9 Installations
10 Sir Guinness
11 Old Testament book
12 Comic Johnson
13 Honey bunch
21 Sort of cereal
22 Mother-of-pearl
25 Skirt style
26 Forbidden things
27 Sea shout
29 *Bus Stop* playwright
30 Sock material
32 Garden growth
33 Made in heaven
34 "__ porridge hot . . ."
35 Dragged around
37 Pennsylvania city
39 Pinball woe
42 Dunne or Castle
43 Crew member
48 Soda-shop order
50 Make tracks
53 Cotton fabric
55 Ski lifts
56 Despise
57 Heavy metal
58 Take care of
59 Hudson and Baffin
60 Financial street
61 Fruit producer
62 Author Wiesel
63 Come in second
64 SAT taker

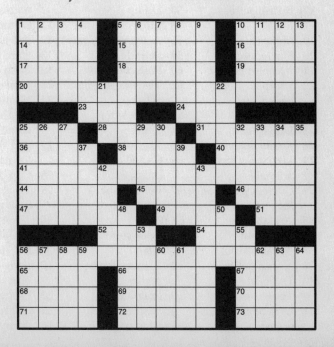

307 SPREAD IT AROUND by Carol Fenter

ACROSS

1 A summer place
5 Start for breadth
10 Week-ending cheer
14 Actor Sharif
15 Marsh bird
16 "Rule Britannia" writer
17 Spread it around
19 Trim back
20 Wild donkey
21 Removed varnish
23 Rogers and Clark
25 Loosen
26 Frome of fiction
29 Luxury, so to speak
31 Pear type
34 Gift-card word
35 Work on a soundtrack
36 Writer Horatio et al.
37 Daily grind
38 Auto options
40 Bigger than med.
41 Fine fur
43 Praiseful poem
44 Big family
45 Pitcher's place
46 School org.
47 Nancy Reagan's advice
48 Mall tenant
50 Young lady
52 Garden chore
55 Explains
59 Lendl of tennis
60 Spread it around
62 President in '76
63 Sully
64 Unlikely story
65 Some 49ers
66 Robert and Alan
67 Writer Gardner

DOWN

1 "It's Impossible" singer
2 To __ (unanimously)
3 Ancient Mexican
4 Theater freebie
5 Tudor name
6 __ Khan
7 Spring bulb
8 Take it easy
9 Violinist Isaac
10 Using a keyboard
11 Spread it around
12 Memo phrase
13 Cater to
18 Light gas
22 Type like *this*: Abbr.
24 Speak indistinctly
26 Mr. Zimbalist
27 Cape Cod town
28 Spread it around
30 Monastery head
32 Stadium instrument
33 __ hooks
35 Trivial Pursuit need
36 Historical time
38 Choice words
39 Hoss' brother
42 Has in mind
44 Girl Scout rank
46 Foreign correspondent?
47 Farm structure
49 Gaucho's rope
51 S&L items
52 Kate, to Petruchio
53 Name that may ring a bell
54 Electric-power network
56 Open slightly
57 Slow down, in mus.
58 Hook's henchman
61 Once __ blue moon

---

308 FARM TEAM by Wayne R. Williams

ACROSS

1 Take up
6 Antonym: Abbr.
9 Jack the dieter
14 Jason's wife
15 Aussie leaper
16 Dress style
17 British actress Joan
19 Makes a scene
20 Sun. speech
21 Inventor Nikola
22 Pampas backdrop
23 Train unit
24 Diplomacy
26 Really enjoy
29 Like some farm animals
34 Currency-exchange fee
35 Arafat's grp.
36 Switch on
37 Abrasive tool
38 Not as polite
40 To be, in Toulouse
41 One-celled animal
43 Tax agcy.
44 Poverty
45 Very scary
47 Tries out
48 Sothern and Sheridan
49 Track action
50 Let up
53 Little green man
56 Actress MacGraw
59 Sound
60 Hull collection
62 *The Maltese Falcon* actress
63 Greek letter
64 *Cannery Row* star
65 Rock-strewn
66 Cariou of musicals
67 Poke fun at

DOWN

1 Rock-concert gear
2 Remove from text
3 Fragrance
4 Basilica bench
5 Kind of sauce
6 Assns.
7 Sci-fi writer Frederik
8 It may be hot
9 Crusader's opponent
10 British royal house
11 Outer covering
12 Pot starter
13 Hardy heroine
18 Cash ending
23 Joint effort
25 Mimics
26 Fergie's first name
27 Old World lizard
28 Cap part
29 TV actor Gulager
30 *The Age of Bronze* sculptor
31 Merits
32 Long-plumed bird
33 Property records
35 Shrimp kin
39 Unit of work
42 Parched
46 Señora Perón
47 One renting
49 Pa Cartwright
50 Gardner et al.
51 Rope fiber
52 Singing voice
54 Past due
55 Pro boxer Barkley
56 __ breve
57 "Why not?"
58 Comment of clarity
61 Iowa college

309 ENGLISH MAJORS by Randolph Ross

ACROSS

1 They're often exchanged
5 __ Raton, FL
9 Asian priest
13 Gulf state
14 Gem weight
15 Riviera seasons
16 Stead
17 Clear as __
18 They fly by night
19 Raven rhymster?
22 Big belly
23 Concert closers
24 Letter getter
29 Negotiations
30 Rhyming wisecracker?
32 Ring result
33 Menlo Park monogram
34 Ms. MacGraw
37 Actress doing screenplays?
43 Minneapolis suburb
45 New hires
46 Salon work
48 Peak
49 Autobiographer president?
54 Disassemble
55 Leans (toward)
56 Given the boot
58 Slay
59 George of *Star Trek*
60 Ship out
61 Nine-digit IDs
62 H H H
63 Extremities

DOWN

1 Actor Kilmer
2 Garfield's canine pal
3 Unwelcome growth
4 Cozy up
5 Rum cake
6 Pitcher Hershiser
7 Spanish street
8 Home of the Hawks
9 Maestro Stokowski
10 Busy
11 Free-for-alls
12 ADCs
14 Egg holder
20 Subtle glow
21 Sen. Helms' state
24 A-Team member
25 NASA assent
26 Bar's beginning
27 In the know about
28 Had in mind
31 Yogi, for one
34 Went to Wendy's
35 *To Kill a Mockingbird* author
36 Auditing org.
37 Dennis' neighbors
38 Monogram part: Abbr.
39 Ms. Fabray
40 '60s dance
41 Something hysterical
42 Synchronous
43 Cultural group
44 __-the-wool
46 Desert Storm targets
47 Tony the Tiger's favorite word
50 "Times of your Life" singer
51 Citrus drinks
52 Draft team
53 Tear apart
57 Tooth pro's deg.

310 ON CUE by Matt Gaffney

ACROSS

1 Shriver of tennis
4 "Delicious!"
7 Obi-Wan, for one
11 De Niro role
13 Smooth
15 50-year-old
17 Hypnotized
18 Smoke, for short
19 JFK's predecessor
20 Shake, in prescriptions
21 Strength
24 __ majesty (sovereign crime)
25 Wine word
26 Debater of '92
27 Yearned (for)
28 Run-of-the-mill
29 Pizarro victim
30 Southwest city
33 Nutrition stats.
34 Santa __
35 Heartless one
36 Glide on ice
37 B&O stop
40 High point
41 Moriarty's creator
42 K-6
43 Promulgate
44 *Flying Down to* __
45 In unison
46 Colorado Avalanche, once
51 Touch-and-go
52 Leads
53 Sundance's love
54 LAX client
55 Questioning comments

DOWN

1 Dive in
2 Low-pH
3 *Olympia* painter
4 Pronoun with two homonyms
5 Actress Merkel
6 Ryan or Foster
7 Discombobulate
8 Prints, perhaps
9 World's lowest lake
10 Destitute
11 Blue shades
12 O followers
13 Nasty mood
14 Witchlike woman
16 Real, in Regensburg
21 Course listing
22 Basra's land
23 Happy-__
24 *Peanuts* character
26 Budweiser rival
27 Arouse ire
28 Nonchalant
30 TV's Batman
31 Mideast carrier
32 Unit charge
33 Loser's demand
35 Pyrenees resident
36 Any minute now
37 Pushover
38 Group principles
39 In __ (disheveled)
41 Chop up
42 -ish relative
44 Grid official
45 Lend a hand
47 Lea plea
48 UN Day mo.
49 Ducat word
50 Genetic material

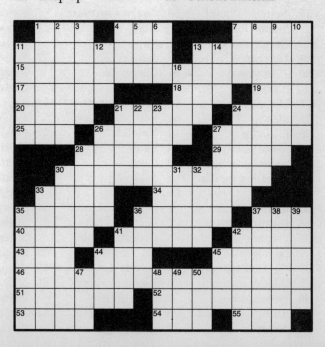

311 AT THE RODEO by Shirley Soloway

ACROSS
1 Practice boxing
5 Country singer Davis
8 Not refined
13 Ashen
14 British noble
15 Mighty strange
16 "__ Mommy Kissing . . ."
17 Aleutian island
18 Frankie or Cleo
19 Tell lies
22 Tire town
23 Fully grown
27 Be conversant
31 Religious believer
34 Chess castle
35 National Leaguers
36 Right-angle shape
37 Serial starter
38 Comic Louis
39 Soften up
41 Rat-__
42 Standish stand-in
44 Acting haughty
47 *Mad* genre
48 "Thereby hangs __"
51 Gamble recklessly
56 Heavy metal
59 Tibia, for one
60 Before an audience
61 Room group
62 Withstand
63 __ out a living
64 Griffith and Rooney
65 ID of a sort
66 Soviet news agency

DOWN
1 Barbecue need
2 Turkish title
3 Happy as __
4 Does over
5 SAT section
6 Johnson of *Laugh-In*
7 Wood or iron, e.g.
8 Storage area
9 House agent
10 Onassis' nickname
11 Transgression
12 Get the point
14 "His wife could __ lean"
20 Refuses to
21 Actress Miyoshi
24 Turn over
25 Change color
26 German city
28 Intense anger
29 Synagogue scroll
30 Too __ handle
31 Floor models
32 Actress Verdugo
33 __ ease (stressed)
37 Called for
40 Parched
42 Fictional terrier
43 Info sheet
45 Spring flowers
46 Less common
49 '50s space dog
50 Arctic aides
52 Flows back
53 Antagonists
54 __ even keel
55 Not as much
56 "Be Prepared" org.
57 Dash off
58 Lend a hand

312 ON THE MOVE by Trip Payne

ACROSS
1 Letter requirement
6 Women's mag
10 Beer ingredient
14 Singer Osmond
15 "Pants on fire" preceder
16 Nobelist Wiesel
17 Indian, for one
18 Oratorio solo
19 Tide cause
20 __ long way (last)
21 Move quickly
24 Idée __
25 Encircles
26 Move slowly
31 Actor Fernando
32 "Waiting for the Robert __"
33 Barracks bed
36 Riyadh resident
37 Prepares a package
39 "__ Don't Preach" (Madonna tune)
40 Hoosegow
41 Really exhausted
42 Taken in
43 Move quickly
46 Safe place
48 Diamond stats
49 Move slowly
52 List-ending abbr.
55 Ore source
56 Zimbabwe, once: Abbr.
57 Midwest metropolis
59 Cheers for toreros
60 Nary a thing
61 Wandering one
62 Hair line?
63 Exceeded 55
64 Nectarous

DOWN
1 Urban problem
2 Crunchy snack
3 General vicinity
4 Ms. Farrow
5 Solvers' tools
6 Works too hard
7 Emerald Isle
8 Cougar's home
9 HBO puppets
10 *Cats* song
11 Orally
12 NFL team
13 Take care of
22 Gas' word form
23 Make mad
24 Exerciser's concern
26 Show offense, perhaps
27 Word in many Bugs Bunny titles
28 "__ Old Cowhand"
29 Wasteland
30 Heidi's hangout?
33 Roman statesman
34 Available to the public
35 Sharp flavor
37 *Shane* and *Silverado*
38 Bleachers cry
39 Bosom buddies
41 *Night Court* character
42 Masthead names
43 Least civil
44 Ate away
45 __ Dhabi
46 String-quartet member
47 Poisonous reptile
49 Unpopular play
50 "Just __, skip, and a jump away"
51 Doggie munchie
52 Roof feature
53 Quaker pronoun
54 Golfer's vehicle
58 Cut lawns

313 · FAMILY TV by Mark Ryder

ACROSS
1 Extensive
5 Saharan transport
10 PBS science show
14 Come up against
15 "What __ is this": Pepys
16 Actor Bates
17 Classic '50s sitcom
20 Go for it
21 Revealing pictures
22 Score part
23 GI address
24 Yale student
25 '60s Arden sitcom
34 Distorts
35 Sale condition
36 Storm or Gordon
37 The Big Band __
38 Snitch
41 Parts of qts.
42 Exxon's former name
44 __ gin fizz
45 Perturb
47 '70s Natwick detective drama
50 Shipping unit
51 Govt. purchasing org.
52 Closet hangings
54 Singer Cleo
57 P.O. poster people
60 TV psychologist
63 Polynesian carving
64 Kid-lit elephant
65 Mr. Roberts
66 Realtor's sign
67 Chevy __, MD
68 In the past

DOWN
1 Travel, as an aroma
2 Construction piece
3 It may call
4 Ordinal ending
5 Metaphorical temptation
6 "Diana" singer
7 More than a few
8 Personalities' parts
9 Actor Ayres
10 Arrester's activity
11 Tub in the fridge
12 Flower holder
13 Industrious insect
18 __ facto (retroactively)
19 One-person performances
23 Fuse unit
24 To be: Lat.
25 Sing like the birdies sing
26 Irritating
27 Clear a tape
28 *Little Iodine* cartoonist Jimmy
29 Bar legally
30 Irks
31 Boo-boo
32 Take in, e.g.
33 Adam and Rebecca
39 ". . . unto us __ is given"
40 Autumn apple
43 Bonelike
46 School org.
48 A bit too interested
49 Pay no mind to
52 Work for three
53 H-M link
54 Jacob's first wife
55 Eban of Israel
56 Tax-deferred accts.
57 Flowerless plant
58 Bric-a-__
59 Global speck
60 Wino's bane
61 Ont. network
62 "Yoo-__!"

314 · PLACE NAMES by Wayne R. Williams

ACROSS
1 Hostess Perle
6 Homecoming attendees
11 Tie-up
14 Blood of the gods
15 Thurmond and Archibald
16 Shoshonean
17 Actress from Peking?
19 Mauna __
20 Sound a horn
21 Troop's camp
22 Window ledge
23 Tiny amounts
25 Sand bars
27 Kind of assault
30 After-shower powder
31 Hasty flight
32 Word form for "skull"
35 Western lake
38 Composer Khachaturian
40 Iberian river
42 Ship of 1492
43 Columbus' home
45 Uses a fork
47 French article
48 Be up and about
50 Proximate
52 On land
54 Warren Beatty role
55 Lead player
56 Rocky debris
58 False god
62 Comparative ending
63 Film director from Warsaw?
65 "Agnus __"
66 Zoo beast
67 Missouri mountains
68 Sprightly character
69 Stair post
70 *Corrida* beasts

DOWN
1 GM's home
2 Reverberation
3 Kicker's target
4 Asia's Gulf of __
5 Coach Parseghian
6 Playwright from Vientiane?
7 Vesuvian flows
8 Texas sch.
9 Slightest
10 123-45-6789 org.
11 Cook from Santiago?
12 Coral ring
13 What American Plan includes
18 Slow down
22 Large seabird
24 Where some stks. trade
26 Bowler or boater
27 Get tired
28 Few and far between
29 Actor from Muscat?
33 Weirdo
34 Tennis pro from Teheran?
36 Till contents
37 Bridge position
39 It's under the hood
41 Toed the line
44 Make public
46 Blue
49 Do cobbling
51 Nixon pal
52 Stage whisper
53 Girder material
54 Construction machine
57 Hammer part
59 From a distance
60 Bushy do
61 Albanian currency
63 Pig's digs
64 Tiny amount

BRIGHT SAYING by Eric Albert

ACROSS
1 *Blondie* boy
5 100 centavos
9 Just for this
14 Slay
15 Declare true
16 *Thelma & Louise* name
17 Lollygag
19 Put up with
20 START OF A QUIP
22 Gathers up grain
23 Be obliged
24 Part of TGIF
27 Carrie Nation, e.g.
28 Overly sentimental
31 Had in mind?
32 Seed or germ
34 Sulu, on *Star Trek*
35 MIDDLE OF QUIP
40 Column order
41 Kind of daisy
42 S&L concern
43 Actress Moorehead
45 Popinjay
48 __-jongg
49 Seaport, for short
50 Troop group
52 END OF QUIP
57 Riyadh resident
59 Judo award
60 *Glengarry Glen Ross* star
61 "Rama __ Ding Dong"
62 Sacred cow
63 Religious devotion
64 Recedes
65 London gallery

DOWN
1 Composer Elgar
2 Do-nothing
3 Lose for a bit
4 Available
5 Forest way
6 Not at all noble
7 18-wheeler
8 Nevada neighbor
9 Playing marble
10 Salami seller
11 Cold capital
12 Sean Lennon's mom
13 Crow cry
18 Start's start
21 Rte.
25 Marky Mark fan
26 Big gulp
28 Speak lovingly
29 Bobby of hockey
30 Party's purpose, perhaps
31 Comedian Stubby
32 Huff
33 Cpl.'s inferior
34 Make an attempt
35 __ *Bede*
36 Caesar's partner
37 Ferdinand was one
38 Cancel suddenly
39 Dos' followers
43 Succor
44 Talk turkey?
45 *Peanuts* character
46 Wild cat
47 Club-shaped tool
49 Pluvial
50 Boggy ground
51 Moon's track
53 Mark copy
54 Fine steed
55 Pyramid, essentially
56 Christmas-poem beginning
57 Somebody's fool
58 Onassis, informally

LAUGHING MATTER by Richard Silvestri

ACROSS
1 Beyond repair
5 Big chunk
9 Number-picking game
14 Mountain lion
15 Tra trailer
16 G-man Ness
17 River to the Caspian
18 Cookie king Wally
19 Well-versed
20 Comedy classic of '31
23 Isolate
24 I, to Claudius
25 Columnist Bombeck
28 Like *Macbeth*
33 Dam site in Egypt
37 Love, in Latin
39 Actress Rowlands
40 Stars of 20 Across and 57 Across
43 Bog
44 Gets a move on
45 Comic actor Jack
46 Taking that into account
48 Colorful horse
50 Junk mail
52 Starter's gun
57 Comedy classic of '30
62 It takes a licking
63 Came to earth
64 __ *Christie*
65 Man-made waterway
66 College department
67 Harbor sound
68 Without rhyme or reason
69 Fluctuate
70 Tolkien creatures

DOWN
1 Sea foam
2 Superior neighbor
3 Muscat resident
4 Schmoozes
5 David, to Goliath
6 Moussaka ingredient
7 Baseball family name
8 Low man at the opera
9 Horseshoes score
10 Merrie __ England
11 Connections
12 A-one
13 Giant Hall-of-Famer
21 Actress Verdugo
22 Musical lead-in
26 Ankle-length
27 Color of caution
29 Turkish title
30 Nerd
31 Letters at Calvary
32 Detective work
33 "Don't throw bouquets __"
34 Thug's knife
35 *The Way We __*
36 Word of approval
38 Approximately
41 Valerie Harper role
42 Popular mixer
47 Those polled
49 Lack of concern
51 Shuts with a bang
53 Glide on the ice
54 Mortise mate
55 Ripley ending
56 Atty.-to-be's exams
57 __ impasse
58 Grandma
59 African-born supermodel
60 Hammer type
61 Ms. Moreno
62 Bot. or bio.

317   KERN TUNES by Scott Marley

ACROSS
1 Coup __
6 Dressing-room door symbol
10 Summertime sweets
14 Sky blue
15 Gondolier gear
16 __ E. Coyote
17 Soda size
18 "How sweet __!"
19 Chief Norse god
20 1928 Kern tune
22 Clears
23 Add'l phone
24 Shade source
26 Berth place
30 Band aid?
32 Inc., in England
33 Pressure
34 Denver's height, more or less
36 Passover piece
40 Garage-sale words
41 Discount drastically
43 "High" time
44 *Divine Comedy* poet
46 High-flying toy
47 Old fool
48 Broad-antlered deer
50 Candlelit
51 Fire man?
52 *Gypsy* wardrobe
56 Like Lucia di Lammermoor
58 Newspaper page
59 1928 Kern tune
65 Casserole ingredient
66 Serve food
67 Out of the way
68 It may take a deuce
69 Unfounded
70 Canine canines
71 Pants inhabitants
72 Koppel and Kennedy
73 Bird sound

DOWN
1 *Cagney and Lacey* star
2 Singer Pinza
3 '84 Peace Nobelist
4 Geometry problem
5 __ Haute, IN
6 What can't be undone, metaphorically
7 Kansas canine
8 Kicking partner
9 Act as a distributor
10 1934 Kern tune
11 Fruit product
12 Cream of the crop
13 Sight or smell
21 Course completers
25 TV production company
26 Campus region
27 __ Major (constellation)
28 Not "fer"
29 1933 Kern tune
31 Tartan pattern
35 Pre-repair data
37 Decorate, as leather
38 Move rapidly
39 Aware of
42 Model of virility
45 Actor Wallach
49 __-all (smart aleck)
52 "I __ Right to Sing the Blues"
53 Reject disdainfully
54 Doctrine
55 Forest clearing
57 Unwelcome wind
60 Not sharp
61 *Vidi*
62 It intersects Hollywood
63 __ out (defeat narrowly)
64 Take a break

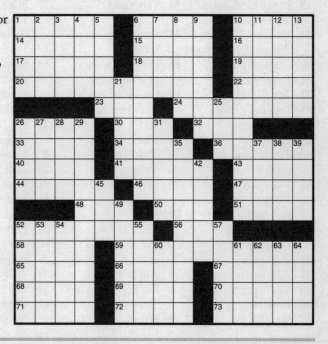

318   VIRTUOUS PEOPLE by Randolph Ross

ACROSS
1 Sea "king"
5 Goya subject
9 Invites to the penthouse
14 Apollo's mother
15 Get an __ effort
16 Glorify
17 Obsessed by
18 "__ first you don't . . ."
19 Imported auto
20 Virtuous newswoman?
23 Iraqi coin
24 "__ live and breathe!"
25 __-cat (winter vehicle)
26 Stanford-Binet scores
29 Point of view
31 Campus mil. grp.
33 Tropical isle
34 Ordinal ending
36 Cardboard creations
38 Virtuous film buddies?
41 Witty exchange
42 Big bird
43 Russian city
44 Sea dogs
46 Carrying a carbine
50 Buddhist sect
51 Military address
52 Have the title
54 Santa __, CA
55 Virtuous Neil Simon character?
58 *Amerika* writer
61 La Scala solo
62 Touched down
63 Back way
64 Apply wax to
65 Countdown end
66 Comic-book cries
67 Cast opening?
68 Idyllic place

DOWN
1 Dover attraction
2 Fix a carpenter's mistake
3 Legendary conqueror
4 Italy's shape
5 Milkers of song
6 *An __ to Remember*
7 Shaw title character
8 Creative
9 Opening word
10 Wood choppers
11 Jazz instrument
12 Eskimo knife
13 Gal. parts
21 Mad milliner
22 Concert bonus
26 Piece of poetry
27 Wharf
28 Bro's sib
30 High country
32 More peculiar
33 Conductor Kurt
35 *Panama __* (Merman musical)
37 __ clef (fiction genre)
38 Roll response
39 Ready for retailing
40 Asian region
41 Russell's nickname
45 Church party
47 Posted
48 All-inclusive
49 Wright brothers' hometown
51 Changes another's mind
53 Marine mammal
55 Turn aside
56 Shoe holder
57 Knock down
58 Arthurian knight
59 Hearty brew
60 Mr. Ziegfeld

BEAUTIFICATION by Alex Vaughn

ACROSS
1 Sweet side dishes
5 West Point mascot
9 Marsh wader
14 "There oughta be __!"
15 Large land mass
16 Make ecstatic
17 Holding forth on the good old days
20 Hamlet's title
21 Be lacking
22 Try to learn
23 Driving game
25 Blithe romp
27 Faux __
30 Trudge through mud
32 Most achy
36 Hockey great's nickname
38 Taj Mahal site
40 Pound portion
41 Paragons
44 Alaskan art form
45 Pup's protest
46 Breathe quickly
47 Russian plain
49 Scissorhands portrayer
51 Noun suffix
52 Star in Cetus
54 Vaccine pioneer
56 Peak A/C time
59 Dried up
61 Televised ribbings
65 Shea Stadium's locale
68 First name in photography
69 Designer von Furstenberg
70 Jai __
71 Disheveled
72 Didn't hang onto
73 Did hang onto

DOWN
1 Uncouth cry
2 Controversial orchard spray
3 Ankle-length
4 Big Band music
5 Strait man
6 Nimitz's org.
7 Largest shareholder?
8 Three-legged stand
9 Clearance height
10 Building wing
11 Shankar specialty
12 Birdsong of basketball
13 Bottle part
18 Sgts. and cpls.
19 Afternoon events
24 Socked in
26 Big Bertha's maker
27 Those who bug
28 Like __ (fast)
29 Nastiness
31 Midas' quality
33 China's Chou __
34 Part of the Lauder line
35 Short-tempered
37 Early aft.
39 Car bars
42 With a saucy twinkle
43 Plain to see
48 "... __ saw Elba"
50 Clear of snow
53 Synthetic fiber
55 Ketchikan craft
56 A remote distance
57 Arm bone
58 Puff of wind
60 Frozen-waffle name
62 Cod alternative
63 Loaded question
64 Playlet
66 In readiness
67 Discouraging words

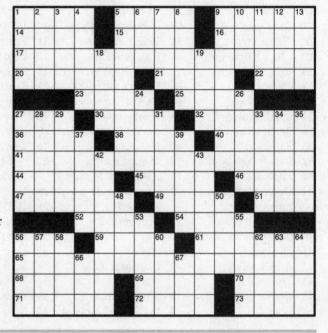

FULL SCALE by Wayne R. Williams

ACROSS
1 More, to Morales
4 Resort activity
8 SMU's home
14 Worshiper of a sort
16 Set properly
17 Sorrowful, in music
18 Gas figure
19 Canine comments
20 Medieval singer
22 Snick-and-__ (old knife)
23 Suffix for pun
25 In __ (actually: Lat.)
26 Meal prayer
28 Lasting impression
31 Soggy ground
33 National League park
35 Howard of GWTW
39 Wallach or Whitney
40 Tonal qualities
42 Indy Jones' quest
43 Worships
45 Tax-free bond, briefly
46 Norma __
47 Ms. Bombeck
49 Lean one
51 Spoiled kid
54 Ore. neighbor
56 Advanced degs.
59 Recurring verses
62 Vault
63 Eurasian language group
64 Tiny Tim's range
68 Tailor's tool
69 Ran
70 Play up
71 Change the decor
72 Wordsworth work

DOWN
1 Exemplar of greed
2 Embellish
3 Vocal exercise
4 Needle-nosed fish
5 Word form for "ear"
6 Guitarist Paul
7 Wharton hero
8 Scot's preposition
9 Eyebrow shapes
10 Pup groups
11 Women's mag
12 Frank and Tyler
13 Inscribed stone
15 The hare, for one
21 4/15 payee
23 Disunion
24 Pour profusely
27 Fall flower
29 Grip tightly
30 Norse pantheon
31 Actress Arthur
32 "__ Hickory" (Jackson)
34 Defensive weapon: Abbr.
36 Slow tempo
37 Novelist Levin
38 __ out a living
41 Actor Tamblyn
44 Make a second swap
48 Grain beard
50 Cop __
51 Grain coverings
52 Find a new tenant
53 Following
55 With regard to
57 Passé
58 China name
60 Feels poorly
61 Sews up
65 Tailless mammal
66 Ran first
67 Sellout sign

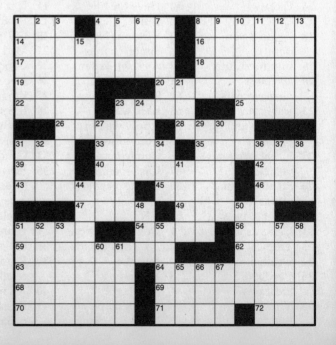

321 NATURE WALK by Bob Lubbers

ACROSS

1 Volcano output
5 Stay away from
9 Go bad
14 Take on
15 __ Nostra
16 Therefore
17 Verbal sigh
18 Supremes leader
19 Bandleader Shaw
20 Get going
23 That girl
24 Fortas and Lincoln
25 Fudd et al.
27 Supermarket saver
30 Big to-do
32 Purina rival
33 Raison d'__
35 Scout group
38 On Soc. Sec.
39 Pencil ends
41 Naval rank: Abbr.
42 Pale
44 Narrow street
45 Related (to)
46 Make possible
48 Brought a smile to
50 City near Seattle
52 "Shoo!"
53 Basic education?
54 Past one's prime
60 On __ (spreeing)
62 Lettuce piece
63 Oil of __
64 Feudal lord
65 Venus de __
66 Dough does it
67 Popped the question
68 Unique person
69 Tennis segments

DOWN

1 Persian ruler
2 "Hi __, Hi Lo"
3 Smell __ (be leery)
4 WWII secret police
5 Projectionist, e.g.
6 Derisive cries
7 Former UN member
8 *Discovery* org.
9 Onions' kin
10 __ capita
11 In ruins
12 More frosty
13 Lustful looks
21 Cable network
22 Cash ending
26 Damage
27 Irene of *Fame*
28 Cheers for the matador
29 In big trouble
30 Bears, to Brutus
31 Hammer end
34 Like some tales
36 Mayberry boy
37 Duck's home
39 Infatuated
40 Try to grab
43 Rock producer Brian
45 Mailer and Michener
47 German region: Abbr.
49 Ginnie __
50 Singing syllables
51 *Ars Gratia* __
52 No longer fresh
55 Kid in *Blondie*
56 Mount's strap
57 Mr. Nastase
58 Remain active
59 Cleaning solutions
61 Mature

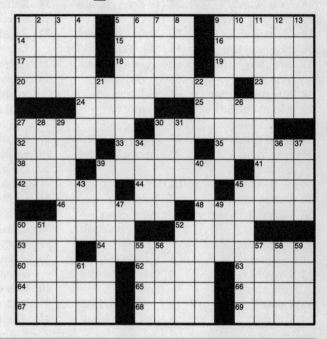

322 MALE CALL by Eric Albert

ACROSS

1 Cement a deal
6 Athlete's bane
10 Eject
14 Available for rental
15 Corn country
16 Early zookeeper
17 Western film of '70
20 Out of shape
21 Singer Tillis
22 Grocery store
23 The least bit
25 Red wine
26 Adds decorations
29 Best buddy
30 Remain quiet
33 Mata Hari portrayer
34 Kaput
35 Batman's creator
36 Whodunit film of '36
39 Got hold of
40 City on the Brazos
41 Turns unfriendly
42 Poetic contraction
43 *Dallas* patriarch
44 Setting
45 Provide support for
46 Nursery color
47 On the move
50 Dazzling expert
51 Product showing
55 Adventure film of '32
58 Ronny Howard role
59 Blow your horn
60 Three-line verse
61 Pain in the neck
62 Undulate
63 Kills time

DOWN

1 Wild guess
2 Habitat
3 Defender Dershowitz
4 Veteran infielder
5 List shortener
6 Beef cut
7 Lounge about
8 Fear + wonder
9 Disparage
10 Quick swig
11 Political patronage
12 Life of Riley
13 Make keener
18 Cookie tycoon
19 Do damage to
24 __ about
25 Glossy, e.g.
26 Playing marble
27 *Mississippi Burning* star
28 Dramatist Joe
29 "Your king is threatened"
30 Mead subject
31 Combined
32 Feeling the strain
34 Crude cabin
35 Impress mightily
37 Conversation contribution?
38 Religious image
43 Indonesian island
44 Judy's daughter
45 *L'Arlésienne* composer
46 Dutiful respect
47 Surmounting
48 Horn, for one
49 Baseball great Speaker
50 Steed stopper
52 Actor Jannings
53 Put together
54 Difficult duty
56 Drag behind
57 Frat letter

323 SEASONING by Matt Gaffney

ACROSS
1 LP speed
4 Botch the job
10 Angkor __
13 *A Passage to India* director
15 Diner, e.g.
16 Vow words
17 Rock's "Boss"
19 Certain sister
20 National Leaguer
21 In a nifty way
23 Will ritual
28 Suggestion start
29 Moral obligation
32 Salami shop
33 Card game
34 I, as in Innsbruck
35 __ the finish
36 Puttin'-Ritz link
39 Flamenco shout
40 Return
42 A question of method
43 Decathlete Johnson
45 Dealing with a full deck
46 Application
47 Ramsgate refreshment
48 Author Ludwig
49 Mars' alias
50 Woes
52 Passed a law
54 *Le Roi* __ (Louis XIV)
56 Most important
59 Silly Putty holder
60 Queen of disco
66 __ de toilette
67 Sedative
68 Except for
69 One or more
70 Horseshoes shot
71 To catch a thief

DOWN
1 *Kidnapped* monogram
2 Cartoon skunk Le Pew
3 Engels' colleague
4 Command to Spot
5 __ Cruces, NM
6 Mel of baseball
7 Minuscule
8 Peace goddess
9 Actress Daly
10 Swiss city
11 Grown-up
12 Neil Simon collection
14 Rather cold
18 Swed. neighbor
22 Rachins of *L.A. Law*
24 Garfield's pal
25 Clinton Cabinet member
26 First state, alphabetically
27 Immense
29 Fashion name
30 *Daily Bruin* publisher
31 Lee Majors series
33 Chinese cooker
37 Footwear
38 Wool-coat owners
40 Coll. srs.' test
41 Boston NBAer
44 Alternatively
49 Revolutionary Sam
50 Prediction start
51 Boston's airport
52 Run off, in a way
53 Grounded Aussie
55 Admired one
57 "__ Old Cowhand"
58 Leningrad's river
61 Singer Peeples
62 A Bobbsey
63 Wolfed down
64 Rev.'s address
65 Civil War soldier

324 TREE TOWNS by Randolph Ross

ACROSS
1 Winds do it
5 Lose buoyancy
9 Fixes the outcome
13 Skywalker's mentor
14 Motley __ (rock group)
15 Author Ferber
16 Physical, for one
17 Actress Veronica
19 Business arrangement
20 City near Little Rock
23 Imported auto
25 Hawks' org.
26 Where Sonny Bono was mayor
31 Iron in the rough
32 Trig ratios
33 Author Bombeck
36 Craggy ridges
38 Sault __ Marie, MI
39 "Phooey!"
40 Perturbed mood
41 Dandelions, e.g.
43 CPR expert
44 2nd largest Hawkeye city
48 Poetic night
49 Postman's path
50 Atomic research center
56 Square measure
57 Actress Braga
58 Stephen King beast
62 Engird
63 Difficult situation
64 Easily bruised items
65 Fill fully
66 Midmonth day
67 Mother and daughter

DOWN
1 Parting word
2 Smoked salmon
3 Harem quarters
4 Bead money
5 Slivovitz or aquavit
6 "*Dies* __"
7 Desensitize
8 Capsize, with "over"
9 Obviously embarrassed
10 Light bulb, symbolically
11 Snarl
12 Breakthrough bacteriologist
18 Inhalers of a sort
21 Treas. Dept. agcy.
22 Football positions: Abbr.
23 Carradine, in *The Ten Commandments*
24 Man of the cloth
26 Garden-store supply
27 Stage platform
28 Prefix for cede
29 "I __ drink!"
30 Run in
34 Ike's missus
35 "__ boy!"
37 Ship accommodations
41 Magic sticks
42 Big ranches
45 "*Agnus* __"
46 Charged atom
47 Coneheads?
50 Shell propellers
51 Scotto solo
52 Reeve role
53 Asian desert
54 Author Bagnold
55 Pitchfork part
59 "That's yucky!"
60 Coffee, so to speak
61 CIA precursor

325 SAY WHAT? by Shirley Soloway

ACROSS
1 Part of ABM
5 Hoss' big brother
9 Union bane
13 Sea of Tranquillity site
14 Dressed to the __
16 El __, TX
17 Good goose?
19 Chimp snack
20 Greet, in a way
21 Adaptable
23 Inform performers?
26 Type widths
27 Drill sergeant's syllable
30 Vaudevillian Tanguay
31 First shepherd
33 Actor Roberts
35 Falls from grace
37 . . . __ Man, Charlie Brown
40 Wide neckwear
42 Baton Rouge sch.
43 Start of 37 Across
44 Harness horse
45 Feinstein and Glenn: Abbr.
47 Reach across
48 Hebrew month
50 Piece of the action
51 TV's Tarzan
52 Part of PST
54 Veggie buy?
58 Cookery genre
60 Free
64 Bank (on)
65 Doctor duo?
68 Running in neutral
69 Carved stone
70 Considerably
71 Spring times
72 Tributes in verse
73 Sawbucks

DOWN
1 Rock-concert gear
2 Author Ephron
3 Plane, but not train
4 Contribution of ideas
5 Half of L.A.
6 Prefix for meter
7 Governor Richards
8 Jason's wife
9 Hot tubs
10 Are forbidden to run off?
11 Gomez Addams portrayer
12 Some pears
15 Nacho topping
18 Eroded
22 No longer a threat
24 Lesser of two __
25 Jose of baseball
27 Bucket of bolts
28 Bear: Lat.
29 Get lucky in one's choice?
32 Self-images
34 Like some dorms
36 First light
38 Kind of exam
39 Say it's false
41 Make an outline
46 Marks of infamy
49 Rubs roughly
52 Curtain fabric
53 Bara of silents
55 "Super!"
56 Two-way preposition
57 Peace Prize sharer
59 Louis and Carrie
61 Floor covering
62 Sacred image
63 Sleek fliers
66 Radical
67 Tabard Inn serving

326 ELECTION DAY by Trip Payne

ACROSS
1 Tiny coin
5 Bird call
10 Russian range
14 Egyptian goddess
15 Pay tribute to
16 Zilch
17 Election-day sights
20 Take a look at
21 "__ helpless . . ."
22 Sound-effects specialty
23 English architect
24 Pavlov's signal
25 Makes furious
28 __ and void
29 Wanted-poster abbr.
32 Parisian aunt
33 Wooded valley
34 Give __ (care)
35 Election-day mail-ins
38 The __ Seasons
39 Early automaker
40 Kate's roommate
41 Lex Luthor, to Superman
42 Supercomputer company
43 Women's scarves
44 Pretentious
45 Made a landing
46 Crybaby's sound
49 Don __ (legendary lover)
50 Get the point
53 Election-day focus
56 Hold as an opinion
57 __ Hawkins Day
58 Theater sign
59 Smart-mouth's talk
60 Gives off
61 Unit of force

DOWN
1 Casino cubes
2 Englishman's "Golly!"
3 Street performer
4 Psychic ability
5 Doorbell sounds
6 Golfer Ben
7 Bed-and-breakfast spots
8 Pilfer
9 Fawlty Towers actress Scales
10 Wait __ Dark
11 Down Under leapers
12 Novelist Tyler
13 Not as much
18 Lindbergh and Yeager
19 Road charge
23 Restaurant freebie
24 Onion plants
25 Walking stick
26 It's a no-no
27 Come afterward
28 Indigent
29 On __ (hot)
30 Couric of Today
31 Church areas
33 Gap in time
34 Ration out
36 Famous race-winner
37 Hispanic
42 Gator's kin
43 Works like a horse
44 Throat-clearing sounds
45 Taxpayer's fear
46 Flowers-to-be
47 Draft status
48 Keats' creations
49 Return of the __
50 Alluring
51 Actress Moran
52 Italian clan
54 Hoover or Grand Coulee
55 Senator Kennedy

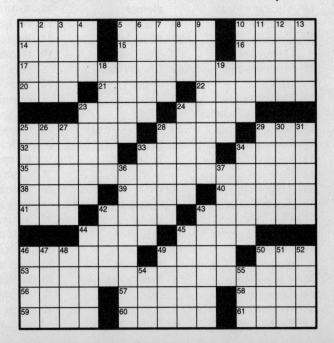

327   IN PLACE by Shirley Soloway

ACROSS

1 Singer Patti
5 Realty sign
9 *Bonanza* brother
13 *The Good Earth* wife
14 Inventor Howe
16 Fruit center
17 Nonclerical
18 Cup, in Caen
19 The __ McCoys
20 Happy as a lark
23 Newsman Rather
24 Prosecutors: Abbr.
25 Indy participant
28 Ave. crossers
31 Envelope requirement
35 Notable period
36 Overly decorative
39 Brainstorm
40 Nebraska natives
43 Software buyer
44 Submerged
45 Engineers' univ.
46 Sting operation
48 __ Vegas
49 Graff of *Mr. Belvedere*
51 Little one
53 Ghostly sound
54 Where to seal a deal
63 Additional
64 Shakespearean sprite
65 "__ a Little Prayer" ('67 tune)
66 At all times
67 Sign a new lease
68 Trunk item
69 Anti votes
70 Smaller amount
71 Makes an inquiry

DOWN

1 Royal sport
2 Actor Ladd
3 Trot or gallop
4 Send a secret message
5 Author Anya
6 Norwegian monarch
7 Shopping aid
8 Take off
9 Puzzle type
10 Hard worker
11 Asian sea
12 Canasta objective
15 Plant start
21 Word of mouth
22 Used to be
25 Fictional uncle
26 Get up
27 West Point student
28 Slowpoke
29 Florida city
30 Escalator alternative
32 "There Is Nothin' Like __"
33 __ blue (police)
34 Glue
37 Silly Skelton
38 Prior to, in poetry
41 One's own way
42 Turn of phrase
47 "The Raven" author
50 Nabokov novel
52 Ski lift
53 Fastens securely
54 Seer's sign
55 PBS science show
56 Low card
57 Hurler Hershiser
58 Floor covering
59 Casual shirts
60 Wife of Osiris
61 Vice agent
62 Spud buds

328   FULL DECK by Matt Gaffney

ACROSS

1 Basic skills
5 Sea World attraction
10 Lounge around
14 Boxing match
15 Fireballer Ryan
16 Muscat's locale
17 Stadium feature
20 Crooner Garfunkel
21 Stretches the truth
22 Flower holders
23 Like Nash's lama
25 Mass response
27 *White Palace* star
31 Legal matter
34 St. __ Fire
35 "The King"
36 Actor Wallach
37 Pie __ mode
38 Senator Specter
39 Medication instrn.
40 Actor Beatty
41 Glue guy
42 Astronomer Tycho
44 CBS symbol
45 "Yeah, tell me about it!"
47 Borscht ingredient
48 Jai __
49 Committee type
52 Bluish-white element
54 "Eureka!"
57 #1 hit by 35 Across
61 Choir voice
62 Spree
63 Tide type
64 "Très __!"
65 Animal's track
66 Christiania, today

DOWN

1 "Dancing Queen" group
2 Wild hog
3 Specially-designed
4 Sault __ Marie, MI
5 *Escargots*
6 Duffer's target
7 Start of a Shakespeare title
8 Satire magazine
9 Cycle starter
10 *Death of a Salesman* character
11 Andy's pal
12 Author Grey
13 Wraps up
18 React to a sneeze
19 Declares positively
24 Recent, in combinations
25 Comment upon
26 Chow __
27 Stateswoman Kirkpatrick
28 Kirstie of *Cheers*
29 Give the go-ahead
30 *Manhattan* director
31 Gets back
32 Nobelist Root
33 Half a cassette
38 Soothing plant
41 Escape button
42 Spew smoke, as a volcano
43 GE acquisition
46 Long for
47 Element #5
49 *Moby-Dick* captain
50 Sandwich shop
51 Can't stand
52 Founder of Stoicism
53 *Othello* villain
55 Get better
56 Purina rival
58 Gun pellets
59 Move like lightning
60 Lennon's lady

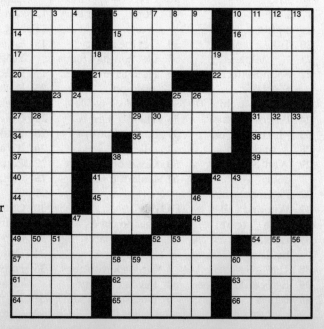

329   NET ANATOMY by Wayne R. Williams

ACROSS
1 Drops dramatically
6 Eyed lasciviously
11 Lumberjack's tool
14 Stand by
15 Wharton character
16 Coach Parseghian
17 Where the strings are
19 Study
20 *Our Man in Havana* author
21 Capriati's weapon
23 Track figures
24 CO clock setting
26 Garbo and Scacchi
27 Appropriate
28 Game units
29 Lobber's target
34 Follow closely
38 Kukla's friend
39 Evergreen tree
40 Break in the audience
41 St. Paul, once
42 Service error
44 Fail to hit
47 Do-it-yourself purchase
48 Least
51 Cave-dwelling fish
52 View quickly
56 Smashing shot
58 Theatrical group
60 Court divider
61 Hacker's malady
63 Sked abbr.
64 Church feature
65 Ward off
66 Farm enclosure
67 Actress Della
68 Nuisances

DOWN
1 Singer Donna
2 Oscar, e.g.
3 Spiked the punch
4 Is partial to
5 Anna of *Nana*
6 Slightly askew
7 Political payoff
8 Wacky
9 Come forth
10 Namib or Negev
11 Former Egyptian leader
12 Sports venue
13 Magic sticks
18 Musical pace
22 Greek hearth goddess
25 Packs to capacity
27 Perfect service
28 Seles swing
29 Jackson and Derek
30 So. state
31 Actor Gulager
32 "Trees" poet
33 *Blame It on __*
35 Sun Devils sch.
36 Out of sorts
37 Voided serve
40 Sternward
43 Pinball miscues
45 Beatty/Hoffman movie
46 Founder of *The Tatler*
48 Lisa and others?
49 Navratilova rival
50 Make a second attempt
51 Ferber and Best
52 Figure out
53 Sugar shapes
54 Nautical direction
55 Small salamanders
57 Poker stake
59 Swing a sickle
62 Wrath

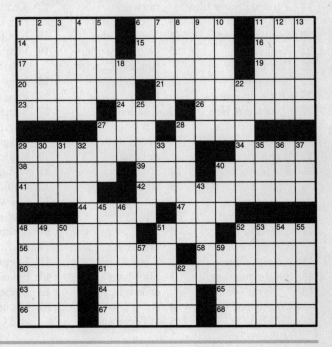

330   BORED GAME by Donna J. Stone

ACROSS
1 Prudhomme's cuisine
6 Took off
10 Pianist Templeton
14 Bryant or Ekberg
15 Valhalla villain
16 Lower California
17 Valhalla VIP
18 Perfect place
19 Does Little work
20 START OF A QUIP
23 Dug in
25 "For shame!"
26 Like a lummox
27 Rake over the coals
29 English diarist
31 Mosey along
32 Manuscript book
33 Service member?
36 Act like Etna
37 MIDDLE OF QUIP
38 Physicist Niels
39 Take everything
40 __ apso
41 Stimulate
42 New Hampshire campus
43 Job security
44 Right-fielder Tony
46 Halloween decoration
47 Actor Carmichael
48 END OF QUIP
52 Toto's creator
53 Gray or Moran
54 "The Man Without a Country"
57 Grimm creature
58 Bring down the house
59 Grenoble's river
60 Sidereal, e.g.
61 Petty clash?
62 Selling point

DOWN
1 Cornfield cry
2 Pitch __-hitter
3 '40s dance
4 Hatch's home
5 Actress Fabray
6 Sweeney Todd's street
7 City near Stockton
8 Gets by, with "out"
9 Manitoba's capital
10 Puts down
11 Accept eagerly
12 Tape-deck button
13 "The Man in Black"
21 Wish undone
22 Jet-black
23 Discombobulate
24 Conductor's concern
28 Fish-and-chips quaff
29 Self-confidence
30 Author Ferber
32 *The Black Camel* sleuth
33 __ St. Jacques
34 *Star Trek* character
35 Gussy up
37 Play grounds?
38 Coal container
40 Stubbs or Strauss
41 Porky's pal
42 Val of *Thunderheart*
43 Smidgen
44 Inedible orange
45 Singer Branigan
46 "John Brown's Body" poet
48 "__ Named Sue"
49 Rope in
50 Ms. Minnelli
51 It's often total
55 *Hearts __ Wild*
56 Gladiator's item

331 SPACE VEHICLES by Bob Lubbers

ACROSS
1 Apropos of
5 Dunderhead
9 Florida city
14 Machine parts
15 Garfield's pal
16 Sandwich cookies
17 Tyrone Power film of '57
20 Pacific current
21 Rocky hills
22 Part of DA
23 Raison d'__
25 Stuck-up one
27 __ as a wet hen
30 Popular pasta sauce
32 Haifa's locale
36 Bordeaux bye-bye
38 Pesky insect
40 __ de Pascua (Easter Island)
41 Charlton Heston film of '68
44 Actress Olin
45 Single quantity
46 "__ You Glad You're You"
47 Puts up
49 Scottish caps
51 Technical advisory org.
52 Clock sound
54 Charlotte and Norma
56 Peter Jennings' network
59 Stick around
61 Noisy to-do
65 George Sanders film of '42, with *The*
68 Of interest to Peary
69 Challenge
70 Carter of Broadway
71 Word with grand or band
72 Sp. ladies
73 Greenish blue

DOWN
1 Entr'__ (musical interlude)
2 Witty Mort
3 Eliot Ness' colleagues
4 Actor Davis
5 Mexican state
6 Actress Lupino
7 Cartoonist Caniff
8 Acapulco pocket money
9 Sculpted trunks
10 Onassis' nickname
11 Flattop of a sort
12 Keats or Byron
13 Off. helper
18 Not for real
19 Word form for "bird"
24 Urge into trouble
26 Pipe wood
27 Sappy tree
28 Harmonica virtuoso Larry
29 Keaton of *Interiors*
31 Not qualified
33 Colorado ski resort
34 Ms. Verdugo
35 Endures
37 Make into law
39 Perfume ingredient
42 Florentine fellow
43 Relax
48 In the area of
50 Groucho, Harpo, and Chico
53 Notorious pirate et al.
55 Bloodhound motivator
56 Fuse word
57 Overshoe
58 Soft-drink flavor
60 Russian despot
62 __-jerk reaction
63 West Coast campus: Abbr.
64 Put on the market
66 A Bobbsey twin
67 Author Levin

332 JUST DESSERTS by Eric Albert

ACROSS
1 Padlock places
6 Bowling-alley button
11 Fast flier
14 Lane's colleague
15 Famed architect
16 Dogpatch's Daisy __
17 Cinch
19 Ulna location
20 German astronomer Johann
21 Shawl or stole
22 Clever conversation
25 Coward's __ *Spirit*
27 Stage direction
28 Voice of Bugs Bunny
29 Go head to head
30 Fishing wear
34 Furniture wood
37 Gin inventor Whitney
38 2.54 centimeters
39 Wordsworth work
40 Writer Deighton
41 Dick of *Mary Poppins*
42 Kyser or Starr
43 General tendency
45 Greenish yellow
46 Stick fast
48 Like most stockings
52 Bird food
53 It's north of Java
54 Dan Rather's network
55 Sammy Davis #1 hit
60 Biblical boat
61 Enjoys a bath
62 The Gem State
63 Remuneration
64 By itself
65 Egyptian city

DOWN
1 High-school dance
2 Ex-ring leader?
3 Compass pt.
4 Eat sparingly
5 Nasty smile
6 Ransack and rob
7 Act introducer
8 Box a bit
9 Cartoon cry
10 Dead heat
11 Shrewd one
12 Miles of movies
13 Phoenix suburb
18 Make a choice
21 Finish first
22 Make merry
23 Napoleon's fate
24 Unrealistic plan
25 City unit
26 Woodworking machine
28 Emaciated
30 Emulate a dragonfly
31 Lamebrained
32 Await judgment
33 Two hearts, e.g.
35 Photographer Ansel
36 *Flowers for Algernon* author
44 Lipstick shade
45 Bridges and Bentsen
46 Songwriter's org.
47 Winger of *Leap of Faith*
48 Darned things?
49 Clear the slate
50 Advisor Landers
51 Radio and TV
53 Put up with
55 Recipe abbr.
56 Weeding tool
57 Cavernous opening
58 Exclamation of triumph
59 Rouen rejection

333 VOWEL CLUB by Shirley Soloway

ACROSS
1 Wilander of tennis
5 Horse's gait
9 Bank grants
14 Touched down
15 Director Clair
16 Nepal's neighbor
17 Individual performance
18 Heron kin
19 Blows a horn
20 PAT
23 Driver's purchase
24 Easy desserts?
25 *Tonight Show* host
27 Marching musicians
30 Soaks up
33 Cell part
34 Word form for "Chinese"
36 Feathered missile
37 Bovine bellow
38 PUT
41 Actor's signal
42 Remnants
44 Uris or Trotsky
45 Take the podium
47 Guinness statistics
49 Calorie counter
50 Tony relative
51 Letter enc.
52 In the past
54 PIT
60 Theodore of *The Defiant Ones*
62 Night light?
63 "I Want __ Happy"
64 Coeur d'__, ID
65 Sleuth Wolfe
66 Actor Richard
67 Uncovered
68 "So be it!"
69 South African currency

DOWN
1 Opposite of fem.
2 Expos manager Felipe
3 Lean to one side
4 Bent over
5 Family groups
6 Picture puzzle
7 Step __ (hurry)
8 Try out
9 Petrol measures
10 Mrs. Lennon
11 PET
12 Naldi of the silents
13 Answer back
21 Lets go
22 Funny bone's locale
26 Doze off
27 Hall of __ (sports star)
28 Hole __ (ace)
29 POT
30 Ever's partner
31 He's no gentleman
32 Take the reins
34 Canonized *Mlles.*
35 Wedding words
39 Church official
40 Rock music, to some
43 Show sorrow
46 Come back in
48 Plundered
49 Man-made fabric
51 Gaze steadily
52 Rhyme scheme
53 Southwestern lizard
55 Annapolis inst.
56 Single unit
57 Caesar's garb
58 Abba of Israel
59 Tear apart
61 Chemical ending

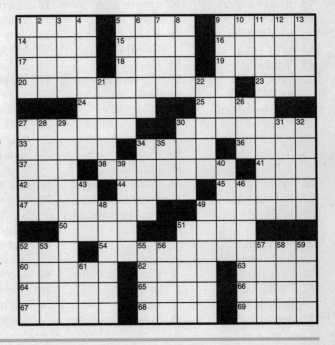

334 BODY LANGUAGE by Donna J. Stone

ACROSS
1 North Eur. airline
4 Military materials
9 Bosc alternative
14 "Evil Woman" rockers
15 Hazardous gas
16 Circus jugglers
17 *Diamond* __
18 Puppetry?
20 Novelist Binchy
22 Tallow source
23 Descend upon
26 Import tax
30 Oust from office
32 Tire type
34 Drink like a dachshund
36 Calcutta clothes
38 Busybody
39 Montreal player
41 Michelangelo masterpiece
43 Ice-cream ingredient
44 As a companion
46 Tremble
48 Caribou kin
49 Batman and Rin Tin Tin
51 Undercoat
53 Meryl of *Death Becomes Her*
55 Football equipment
58 Spineless
60 Get to
61 Lips?
67 Skater Midori
68 Muscat native
69 Peachy-keen
70 *Wayne's World* word
71 Frawley role
72 Actress Burstyn
73 Sect starter

DOWN
1 Alabama city
2 *America's Most Wanted* info
3 Shoe?
4 Cubbins' creator
5 College bowl roar
6 Big scene
7 Giftwrap items
8 Newfoundland's nose
9 Auto accessory
10 PBS benefactor
11 Actress Smithers
12 Time-honored
13 Nav. designation
19 Cold feet
21 Allied vehicle
24 Hippety-hop
25 Aziz of Iraq
27 Brainchild
28 Nail polish?
29 __ *Attraction*
31 Traffic jam
33 High old time
34 Rachel's sister
35 Wheel shafts
37 Very simple
40 __ about
42 Related
45 "Holy cow!"
47 "The Sage of Concord"
50 Trickle
52 Shoe width
54 Pamphleteer Thomas
56 Part owner?
57 Gandhi garb
59 Boat bottom
61 She's tops with Pops
62 Doolittle's digs
63 Former Mideast alliance: Abbr.
64 Big bang letters
65 Presidential nickname
66 Sedan season

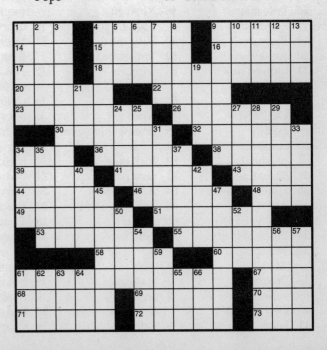

JUMP FOR JOY by Cynthia Lyon

ACROSS

1 Drunk, in W.S.'s day
4 Noggin
8 Necklace part
13 New Zealander
14 Casino city
15 Joust weapon
16 START OF A COMMENT
18 Chips in
19 Big step
20 PART 2 OF COMMENT
22 Passover feast
23 "Lest we lose our __": Browning
25 "__ Blu Dipinto di Blu"
26 Wages, old-style
27 Popeye's foe
28 Wallenda's walkway
29 Wind up
30 Little look
31 "Hi, sailor!"
32 PART 3 OF COMMENT
35 Somewhat
37 Pipe problem
38 1955 merger initials
41 Sustenance
42 "__ to the wise . . ."
44 Jazz flutist Herbie
45 The __ Khan
46 Don or John
47 Booty barterer
48 PART 4 OF COMMENT
50 Decreased?
51 "__ an arrow . . ."
52 END OF COMMENT
55 Anti-vampire weapon
56 Bide-__
57 Otherwise
58 Rusty of *Make Room for Daddy*
59 Explosive sound
60 Deli buy

DOWN

1 First-point value, in tennis
2 Gave
3 Was sympathetic
4 Party nosh
5 Alway
6 Ques. opposite
7 Sometime in the near future
8 Pole star?
9 Crow's-nest cry
10 The merchant of Venice
11 Vistas
12 Mortar mate
13 __ *Kate*
17 10¢ profile
21 Yoko
23 Half of GE
24 York or Edinburgh
27 Bird's bill, in Brest
28 Hammerstein-Kern song
30 Call's colleague
31 Warbucks henchman, with "The"
32 Part of RSVP
33 Screws up
34 Accomplished
35 Cold capital
36 Stephanie of *The Colbys*
38 With shrewdness
39 Joss stick
40 Wound up
41 Starve
42 Big fuss
43 Concerto setting
44 "Hey, Look __"
46 Thin side of a weight-loss ad
47 Calendar abbr.
49 Baloney
50 The same
53 Utility bill abbr.
54 Verily

AUTO PARTS by Mary Brindamour

ACROSS

1 Table accessory
5 Barcelona residences
10 Dull sound
14 Region
15 Alpha's opposite
16 Like magic
17 Bug barrier
19 Blow one's top
20 Jockey seat
21 Slowed down
23 Dryer fuzz
25 Adds up
26 Desirable quality
29 Some are personal
31 52, to Caesar
32 House members: Abbr.
33 Master hand
34 Tropical fruits
37 Tax specialist: Abbr.
38 Prolonged sufferings
40 Deli buy
41 Hard-and-fast
43 Chip off the old block
44 Major ending
45 Word form for "outside"
46 Cozy room
47 Out-of-date
48 *Remington __* ('80s TV show)
50 Sling mud
52 Immature
54 Director Hitchcock
58 Steakhouse word
59 Engine energizers
61 Tarzan's pals
62 Rich cake
63 First person
64 Army meal
65 Be at the wheel
66 Hosiery purchase

DOWN

1 Statutes
2 Soprano's showcase
3 Patch up
4 Canoe power?
5 Comic Myron
6 "What a good boy __!"
7 Fortuneteller
8 Shoelace parts
9 __ say (regrettably)
10 Tract of land
11 Interstate illuminators
12 Persuades earnestly
13 Colored Easter eggs
18 Narrow opening
22 Cartographer's book
24 Pedro's snack
26 Curved lines
27 Labor Day mo.
28 Trunk contents
30 Closely packed
33 PR man
34 Game pieces
35 Feedbag filler
36 *Hook* pirate
38 Did something
39 Charged atoms
42 Defrosted
44 Cap feature
46 Absolute ruler
47 Papermaking material
48 Square or circle
49 Shopping agendas
51 Los Angeles cager
52 Pull an all-nighter
53 Jackrabbit, for one
55 Boorish
56 Mild oath
57 Mil. awards
60 Highway: Abbr.

337 FAMILY BUSINESS by Shirley Soloway

ACROSS

1 Outer edges
5 Formal agreement
9 Prohibit by law
14 Ear-related
15 __ breve
16 *I Was __ War Bride*
17 Small food markets
20 Elementary-school book
21 Affirmative answer
22 Brewery kiln
23 Shelley specialty
25 Large tub
27 Cowgirl Evans
30 Women's group
36 General Bradley
37 Cool spot
38 Take off
39 Washer cycle
41 That girl
42 Stable unit
44 "The Lady __ Tramp"
45 Watch faces
47 Pitcher Hershiser
48 Easy job
51 Barber and Buttons
52 Motorists' org.
53 Fill the hold
55 Slight fight
58 Psyche sections
61 Church leader
65 In a scolding way
68 Cake topping
69 Detective's discovery
70 Jeff Bridges film of '82
71 *"La Plume de Ma __"*
72 Legal wrongdoing
73 The unelected?

DOWN

1 Frisky frolic
2 *Ripley's Believe __ Not*
3 Chevalier song
4 Runs quickly
5 San Diego team
6 Heidi's home
7 Surfeit
8 Use the VCR
9 Have a snack
10 Like marble
11 Fictional plantation
12 Corrida cries
13 Pain in the neck
18 Word form for "recent"
19 Set aside
24 Little accident
26 Olympian warmonger
27 Kind of column
28 Pennsylvania sect
29 Pearl City patio
31 Shore find
32 Of the anklebone
33 Chicago airport
34 Lubricated
35 Small valleys
40 Norse verse collection
43 Attacked viciously
46 "I Am . . . __" (Neil Diamond tune)
49 Potential
50 Kotto of *Alien*
54 Actress Joanne
55 Skirt feature
56 Type of type
57 Similar
59 Air vent
60 Normandy battle site
62 Light tan
63 Coin depository
64 Hamilton's bills
66 Get mellow
67 Mongrel

338 ODDBALLS by Matt Gaffney

ACROSS

1 Hummingbird's home
5 Deli delicacy
8 Kind of point
13 World's fair
14 Be different
15 Video-game name
16 General Custer's nemesis
19 Sylvester, to Tweety Pie
20 Sportscaster Cross
21 What the nose knows
22 On the lookout
24 Rights org.
27 Caustic chemicals
30 Change the decor
31 Actress Garr
32 Swiss miss
33 Broadcast
35 Gymnast Korbut
37 Turn down
38 Golf star
42 Jazz style
43 Catcalls
44 __ of Aquarius
45 Usher's beat
47 Peach feature
49 Cottage or castle
53 Feed the kitty
54 Daddy
55 La Scala locale
56 Highly excited
58 Chum
60 Lyricist Gershwin
61 Pop parodist
66 Botched up
67 Snead stroke
68 Car scar
69 Infield corners
70 Health club
71 Desire deified

DOWN

1 Ambrosia partner
2 Complete a sigh
3 Acted meanly
4 Stocking stuffer?
5 Caterpillars and tadpoles
6 ". . . man __ mouse?"
7 Affair of 1798
8 Saudi King
9 *King Ralph* star
10 Hod job?
11 __ *longa, . . .*
12 Stretch the truth
14 TV taper
17 In shape
18 __ *Asked for It*
23 Sound like Simba
25 Confuse
26 Cheerful song
28 Actress McClurg
29 Early evening
31 Peter, Paul & Mary, e.g.
32 Den __ (Holland's capital)
34 "Let __ Me"
36 Schwarzenegger's birthplace
38 It's hard-pressed for money
39 On the second floor
40 Couch potato's place
41 Radar's drink
42 Ram's remark
46 Stowe villain
48 *Viva __!* (Quinn flick)
50 Twist or North
51 Dolphin Dan
52 Lays down the law?
54 Green org.
55 "I have a dream" initials
57 Track data
59 Carpenter, e.g.
61 Charlotte's pride
62 Pitcher's stat
63 CD ancestors
64 "Uh-huh"
65 Keats creation

339 RLS REVISITED by Fred Piscop

ACROSS
1 Forty winks
4 Dauntless
8 *Pomp and Circumstance* composer
13 Wading bird
15 Where most Indians live
16 Stiller's partner
17 Bottle part
18 "That was close!"
19 Jolson's "My __"
20 R.L. Stevenson duo
23 *Victory* __ (TV oldie)
24 __ Alamos, NM
25 Numbers man?
28 Wore
32 On one's __ (alert)
33 SAT takers
36 Ms. St. Vincent Millay
37 Makes little cubes
38 Cartoon magpies
42 Hand-cream additives
43 "__ me in!"
44 Draft agcy.
45 Commiserate with
46 Purchase plan
49 Catchall abbr.
50 Electrified swimmer
51 Fits neatly together
55 Children's game
60 Turning ripe
62 Teed off
63 Kitchen ending
64 Driving area
65 Welles role
66 In the bag
67 April 1 exploder
68 Out of control
69 Singer Benatar

DOWN
1 Turtle type?
2 As red as __
3 Guitar accessories
4 Blubber
5 Industrial-safety grp.
6 Mortgage, e.g.
7 Waste time
8 TV awards
9 Call the shots
10 Fighting roosters
11 Pitcher's asset
12 Actor Bolger
14 Some terriers
21 Boutonniere locales
22 Mason's device
26 Banana throwaways
27 Biblical beasts
29 Pindaric poem
30 Genetic info
31 *Driving Miss Daisy* star
32 Sudden spasm
33 Pentagon, for one
34 Fired up anew
35 Squelching
37 Presidential middle name
39 A or E, but not I
40 Narc's org.
41 Bone of contention?
46 "Light-Horse Harry"
47 "Seward's Folly"
48 *Oui* and *ja*
50 Lawn-trimming gadget
52 Inept opponent
53 Aquarium fish
54 Trapshooting
56 Actress Swenson
57 Social critic Chomsky
58 Bond flick
59 Carnival creep
60 Compass drawing
61 Moo goo __ pan

340 FOLLOW THE NUMBERS by Bob Lubbers

ACROSS
1 Neck and neck
5 Save a bundle
10 Revlon rival
14 Spanish surrealist
15 Jousting weapon
16 Floor model
17 ONE
19 Next in line
20 Nelson Eddy hit
21 Singer Flack
23 __ Plaines, IL
24 Large quantities
25 Disney art
28 TWO
33 Ham's platform?
34 Tizzy
35 Cured a kielbasa
36 Roll with the punches
38 Jacket feature
40 Season
41 Moses' sister
43 Out of the rat race: Abbr.
45 Actor Chaney
46 THREE
48 Bulldogs
49 Color characteristics
50 Hasty escape
52 Moderately, to Mehta
55 Dexterity
59 Mata __
60 FOUR
62 Robert Craig Knievel
63 Green lights
64 *State Fair* state
65 Acts kittenish
66 Accomplished
67 As recently as

DOWN
1 Bahrain bigshot
2 *Ristorante* refresher
3 Swing and Big Band
4 Desert drifters
5 Tillstrom colleague
6 Buck or bull
7 Sajak sale
8 Ironing accident
9 Mexicali misters
10 Stickiness
11 Turn sharply
12 Fail to mention
13 Asta's mistress
18 Tahiti, *par exemple*
22 Grinned from ear to ear
24 Dolls up
25 Charley horse
26 Mrs. Steve Lawrence
27 Get the idea
29 Loon lips?
30 Jolly Roger visage
31 Poet Jones
32 Barbara and Anthony
34 Beat the bronc?
37 Freshwater ducks
39 "__ the ramparts . . ."
42 Guitarist Carlos
44 Most exaggerated
47 Shaped with a hammer
48 Designer Gucci
51 Pershing's grp.
52 "May I get a word in?"
53 Place for pews
54 Actress Barrymore
55 Bandleader Fields
56 Hired hood
57 Beagle bellow
58 Waiter's item
61 Mao __-tung

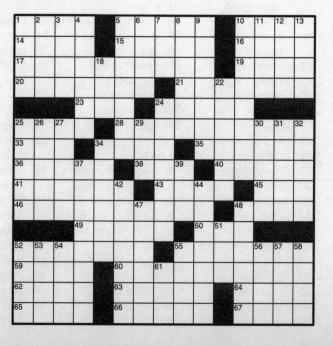

341 NUMISMATICS by Shirley Soloway

ACROSS
1 Pulls a fast one
5 Sharp blow
9 Fountain fizzes
14 Attention-getter
15 Scarlett's estate
16 West Indian nation
17 New Testament sages
18 Former African dictator
19 Knight wear
20 Lots of money, with "a"
23 Nav. rank
24 Hard-hearted
25 Use for support
27 Actor Byrnes
29 Summer fruits
32 Brimless hat
36 Nurse's __ (hospital worker)
39 Tony-winner Judith
40 Be adjacent to
41 Prepared a press
42 Ernest's pal
43 Word with trench or house
44 Country dance
45 Fuses metal
46 Singer Brewer
48 Lawyers' org.
50 Groups of three
53 They get squirreled away
58 Farm tool
60 Cable channel
62 Cook's coverup
64 Frees (of)
65 Theater award
66 *The Picture of Dorian Gray* author
67 Forearm bone
68 Trick
69 __ up (nervous)
70 Close forcefully
71 Spin suffix

DOWN
1 Vacation sites
2 Illinois airport
3 Mideast desert
4 Strike down
5 Remained
6 Light source
7 Sharon of Israel
8 Velvety fabric
9 Sleuth Michael
10 Kayak propeller
11 Paperback book
12 Like __ of bricks
13 Gentlemen
21 Shady character?
22 Christened
26 Martini additive
28 Hamlet, for one
30 Picked-on student
31 Thesaurus entries: Abbr.
32 Diplomacy
33 Woodwind instrument
34 Certain periodical
35 Make a remark
37 34th president, to pals
38 Oscar __ Renta
41 Teheran native
45 Texas town
47 Fell from grace
49 Evergreen
51 Shades of beige
52 Abundant ability
54 Aromas
55 Prove false
56 Disturbing sound
57 Look down one's nose
58 Bird of prey
59 Mayberry boy
61 __ May Oliver
63 "__ to Joy"

342 BABY TALK by Bob Lubbers

ACROSS
1 Rope fiber
5 Sawyer of *Prime Time Live*
10 Prayer finale
14 Insist on
15 Andean Indian
16 *I Remember __*
17 Report from the field
19 Analogous
20 Helps develop
21 Chemical compounds
23 "__ the fields we go . . ."
24 Fundamental
25 Back a motion
29 Fills road cracks
30 Old crone
33 Scottish families
34 Construct
35 Shopper's paradise
36 One of the Aleutians
37 Handled clumsily
38 Aware of
39 Novelist Macdonald
40 Country hotels
41 Theater sections
42 SASE, e.g.
43 Quite a few
44 Kenny of country
45 Sorrel steeds
47 Cambridge univ.
48 Leisurely, to Liszt
50 They're crackers
55 Pie à la __
56 Capital of Arkansas
58 Small burrower
59 Like some triangles
60 Tennis great Arthur
61 Mine finds
62 Trig functions
63 Broadway offering

DOWN
1 David's instrument
2 "If __ I Would Leave You"
3 Post-it message
4 High-school formal
5 Passed the butter?
6 Draw a conclusion
7 The Four __ ('50s group)
8 Dundee denial
9 Won over
10 Fancy fiddle
11 Break a buck
12 Kuwaiti ruler
13 Merriman and Grey
18 The Simpsons, for instance
22 Cobra's comment
24 Makes muffins
25 Fill with fright
26 Singer __ John
27 Children's game
28 Burden
29 Yellowish-brown
31 Shorten the sleeves
32 Lipstick type
34 Nobelist Thomas et al.
35 Electronic synthesizer
37 Automatic uprights
41 Singer Lenya
43 Actress Zetterling
44 Moon valleys
46 Curved moldings
47 Dull finish
48 Bullets, for short
49 Entryway
50 Shake up
51 Keogh alternatives
52 Snack
53 Sound effect
54 Swerve sharply
57 Here, in Havre

343 HARMONIZATION by Harvey Estes

ACROSS

1 Starring role
5 Madame Bovary
9 Former Atlanta arena
13 Differential part
14 Give the slip
15 Wreak havoc on
16 Nero's seat
18 "That __ excuse"
19 Ring championship
20 From Valdosta
22 Gentleman of leisure?
24 Smart
25 At __ for words
28 Sports noncombatant
30 Square one
33 Upright: Abbr.
34 Took it easy
36 Gridiron gadget
37 Part of ERA
38 Pull one's leg
39 "Born in the __"
40 Ovid's __ Poetica
41 Swell place?
42 Sibling's daughters
44 Huff
45 Nervous about verbs?
47 Rowan or Rather
48 Ore deposits
49 Look intently
51 Strait-laced
53 Frying pans
56 Emulate Arachne
59 Surveyor's item
60 Strumming accessory
63 Actor Guinness
64 Drive up the wall
65 The __ and Future King
66 __ egg (savings stash)
67 Dresden denial
68 Hammer head

DOWN

1 Once around the track
2 Way out
3 Jai __
4 Filling pro
5 The night before Christmas
6 Westminster reject
7 Pixie and Dixie
8 Type of committee
9 The __ of Species
10 Orchestra easel
11 1492 vessel
12 Privy to
14 Cain's victim
17 Auto pioneer
21 Valerie Harper sitcom
23 Wore down
25 "Cut it out, Popeye!"
26 River embankment
27 Sacred-music makers
29 Skillful in a language
31 Spooky
32 Exams and quizzes
34 Half of CIV
35 Feminine suffix
38 Prepare to propose
43 Couturier Oleg
44 Bubbly beverage
46 Choose
48 Sleeper or bench-presser
50 King Lear character
52 Out of town
53 Ollie's buddy
54 Leafy green veggie
55 Adjust an Amati
57 Climbing plant
58 __ homo
61 Heavy weight
62 Barbie's boyfriend

344 TRIPLE PLAY by Eric Albert

ACROSS

1 Former Iranian ruler
5 Bring up
9 Waste material
14 "Whatever __ Wants"
15 The Neverending Story author
16 Sermon subject
17 Round shape
18 Unheeding
19 Give an extension
20 PLAY
23 A Nightmare on __ Street
24 No vote
25 Be a barbarian
26 Garden site
27 Teller's cry
28 Big flap
31 "Later!"
34 Singing mayor
35 Homeric hero
36 PLAY
39 Ann Landers, for one
40 Fawn's father
41 Actress Sophia
42 Link letters?
43 Gala gathering
44 Continually carp
45 Poppycock
46 Hanks or Cruise
47 Cribwear
50 PLAY
54 Guitarist Eddy
55 Piece of one's mind?
56 Bluish green
57 Highway maneuver
58 Orange outside
59 Missile-crisis name
60 Bearded rock group
61 Sews up
62 Hustler Rose

DOWN

1 Be inclined
2 Poor house
3 Eyeopener?
4 One, to two
5 Sketch again
6 Us, according to Pogo
7 Economist Smith
8 Russian who couldn't leave
9 Severe
10 Endorsed item
11 Truckee River city
12 The last word?
13 Praying place
21 Seize an advantage over
22 Ancient German
26 Quick-witted
27 V-shaped cut
28 Open a bit
29 British title
30 Yokemates
31 "__ boy!"
32 Crowing time
33 "__ you not!"
34 Sudden flare-up
35 Fascinated
37 Bring down
38 Memorable building?
43 One prone to sheepless nights?
44 Moving men?
45 What a beatnik beats
46 General direction
47 Irritation
48 Horsed combat
49 Moccasin, e.g.
50 Egyptian port
51 Horse and __
52 Wednesday's warrior
53 Ballfield protector
54 Vietnam War initials

345 POULTRY IN MOTION by Cathy Millhauser

ACROSS

1 Delhi wrap
5 Montezuma, for one
10 Small bottle
14 Candid
15 Hoosier State flower
16 *The Neverending Story* writer
17 Drink for the newly-hatched?
20 __-Whirl (carnival ride)
21 Initials, perhaps
22 Praying figure
23 Dada founder's family
25 Some temps
26 Hart part
29 Severed trunks
31 Like raunchy roosters?
33 New Haven tree
36 Hertz competitor
37 Bill and coo
38 Bank of Scotland?
39 Made tracks
40 Hens' hot rods?
42 Spectacle
43 Bottom decks
44 Garage description
47 City in Oklahoma
48 Kind of candle
49 Lay down the lawn
51 Links master Sam
55 What the shapely chick did?
58 Key
59 Mrs. Claus von Bulow
60 Mason's wedge
61 Links gizmos
62 Cropped up
63 '60s sitcom trio

DOWN

1 Out of condition
2 2nd Q. start
3 Rod's partner
4 Places, as fixtures
5 PD alert
6 Goose eggs
7 Pilfered
8 Baseballer Slaughter
9 Charisse of *Silk Stockings*
10 Swerved swiftly
11 Pre-Pizarro Peruvian
12 Hersey town
13 Tough turns in traffic
18 Pants style
19 Lavished attention (on)
24 Make it big
25 Inga of *Benson*
26 At a distance
27 Celestial flash
28 Bed type
29 Salt away
30 *Cat on __ Tin Roof*
32 Well-informed
33 Suffix with switch
34 Finnish northerner
35 Unger upsetter?
38 Chutzpah
40 Barely there
41 Like autumn weather
42 Libra's symbol
44 Planetary path
45 "It's __!" (quitter's comment)
46 Monsieur Zola
47 Heavenly spots
49 Urge on
50 Cry of despair
52 Canyon comeback
53 Comparable
54 Brit. war awards
56 NATO member
57 Reuben ingredient

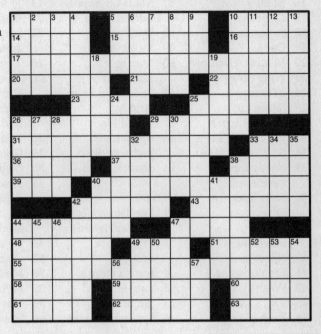

346 TABLE TALK by Shirley Soloway

ACROSS

1 Treats leather
5 Irritated
10 Arkin or West
14 Busy as __
15 Minneapolis suburb
16 100 centesimi
17 Astonished
19 "Now it's clear!"
20 Jesse James, for one
21 Buckwheat dish
23 "From __ 60 in 8.2 seconds"
24 Becomes unusable
27 Kitchen addition?
28 Nosy types
30 Newsman Rather
33 __ Romeo (auto)
36 Mrs. David Copperfield
37 Deep black
39 Mrs. Helmsley
41 Small piece
42 In for __ awakening
43 Challenged
44 Part of MIT
46 Rat-__
47 Noah's craft
48 Most humid
51 Café au __
53 Break suddenly
54 Coal container
57 Spotted steed
58 Containing NaCl
60 Skillful
61 Printer's apparatus
65 Italian wine region
66 More sickly
67 Nonpayment takeback, for short
68 Office kingpin
69 __ *Irish Rose*
70 Garfunkel and Fleming

DOWN

1 Forbidden
2 Approximately
3 Recently involved with
4 Hawk
5 California giant
6 Altar words
7 Actress Ullmann
8 Chemical ending
9 More shaded
10 "He's making __ . . ."
11 Dispensed freely
12 Region
13 West of Hollywood
18 Make a buck
22 Confused
25 Poorly fitting, in a way
26 Leaps up
28 Logical
29 Has dinner at home
31 *A Man __ Woman*
32 Raisa's refusal
33 Alan of *Betsy's Wedding*
34 TV producer Norman
35 Warehouse vehicles
38 Spoiled kid
40 Own up to
45 Advertising lures
49 Perfect place
50 Sandwich meat
52 Pros' foes
54 Tour-de-France participant
55 Clumsy
56 Franco and Peter
57 Tijuana currency
59 *Doctor Zhivago* character
60 Apply lightly
62 Legal deg.
63 "The Greatest"
64 Shirt style

347 BASEBALL ROOKIES by Peter Gordon

ACROSS

1 Kind of heating
6 Man-mouse link
9 Divulged, as facts
14 Eat away at
15 Lowe of *Wayne's World*
16 In the know
17 Legitimate
18 Sailor, in slang
19 Dens
20 Miami newcomers
23 Long time period
24 In demand
25 Show up
29 Rotisserie part
31 Jim Bakker's org.
34 Sociologist Hite
35 Ready for business
36 New York City area
37 Denver newcomers
40 Norse god
41 Prepare a meal
42 Wash cycle
43 *Tic __ Dough*
44 Earn a living
45 Focus
46 Above, to Keats
47 Constricting snake
48 20 Across and 37 Across, e.g.
56 Land measures
57 Madison Avenue output
58 Dark
59 Be generous
60 Manager Durocher
61 Sports producer Arledge
62 True-blue
63 Clinton's instrument
64 Senator Kefauver

DOWN

1 Egotist's concern
2 Pitcher Hershiser
3 Trademark design
4 Jewish month
5 Late-inning pitcher
6 Choir instrument
7 *Make __ for Daddy*
8 Swedish rock group
9 Candidate list
10 Expect
11 Picnic bane
12 Botches up
13 __ Moines, IA
21 Unknown John
22 Large horned animal
25 Tie type
26 Valerie Harper sitcom
27 Archaeologist's find
28 Heavy metal
29 Ghost or goblin
30 Bonus
31 Heart of the matter
32 "__ Boots Are Made for Walkin' "
33 Ne'er-do-well
35 Disagreeable smell
36 Membrane
38 Future oak
39 Man or monkey
44 Sneaky sort
45 Pro's antithesis
46 Verdi production
47 Fenway Park club, for short
48 Reverberation
49 Medical photo
50 Bando and Maglie
51 Mental image
52 Genesis name
53 Scads
54 Ore store
55 Canonized Mlles.
56 Marlee Matlin medium: Abbr.

348 STYLISH by Bob Lubbers

ACROSS

1 __ up (got in shape)
6 Baby food
9 Winter warmer
14 Battery terminal
15 Songwriter Gershwin
16 In need of a plumber
17 Jocular Jerry
18 Sushi fish
19 Bandleader Shaw
20 Reduces expenses
23 Loser to DDE
24 Tiger tracks
25 __ of Capricorn
27 Where Cleo barged in?
29 Furrier family
32 Mornings: Abbr.
35 *The Wizard of Oz* actor
38 Winged walker
39 Simpletons
41 Snickers shape
42 Set jewels, e.g.
43 Body beginner
44 Extreme cruelty
46 '60s college org.
47 *The __ House* (Pfeiffer film)
49 Entre __ (confidentially)
51 Over, in Orvieto
54 Points the finger
58 GI hangout
60 Goofs on stage
62 Wild partying
64 A/C measure
65 Arles aunt
66 Poetic beat
67 Cot or crib
68 Islamic prince
69 Pines (for)
70 Puget, for one: Abbr.
71 Fashionable frocks

DOWN

1 Soft minerals
2 Seize an advantage over
3 CNN transition phrase
4 "The Wizard of Menlo Park"
5 Picture verbally
6 Wharf
7 "__ we all?"
8 Less colorful
9 Joins hands
10 "__ the fields we go . . ."
11 Underground passageways
12 *The Grapes of Wrath* figure
13 Yes votes
21 Norwegian capital
22 Crowd noise
26 Bit of gossip
28 Exile island
30 Actress Donna
31 Beer, slangily
32 Ice-cream ingredient
33 Restaurant roster
34 Begins a journey
36 Move about
37 "__ go bragh!"
40 Most definitely, in Durango
42 Attempted to equal
44 Be a boatman
45 Reacts to soaps?
48 Draws a conclusion
50 Deli meat
52 Heavyweight Tony
53 Frequently
55 Sal of *Exodus*
56 Computer key
57 Crystal gazers
58 West Pt.
59 Build on __ (chance a profit)
61 Animated Elmer
63 Shoe width

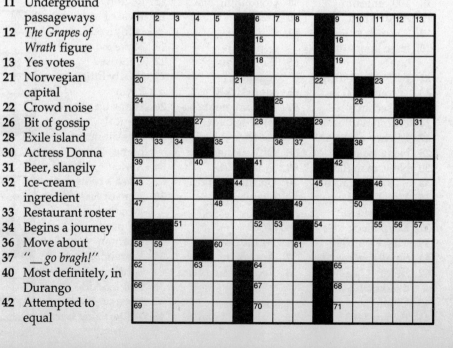

349 PRESS YOUR LUCK by Richard Silvestri

ACROSS

1 Beer ingredient
5 Training inst.
9 Home or visitors
13 Operatic solo
14 Polio vaccine pioneer
16 Put on the payroll
17 Press your luck
20 Harshness
21 Run in
22 *You __ There*
23 Pulitzer Prize author James
24 Lodge
28 Kind of hammer
29 Three-time ring champ
32 Hold forth
33 Raft-traveler Heyerdahl
34 Angry state
35 Press your luck
38 Actress Barbara
39 Eight furlongs
40 Something to stake
41 Roulette bet
42 Laze about
43 Major triads, e.g.
44 Takes a chair
45 *Little Red Book* author
46 St. Francis' home
49 Binge
54 Press your luck
56 Suspend
57 Out of the ordinary
58 Fabric fuzz
59 Kitchen end
60 Trophy rooms, perhaps
61 Word of woe

DOWN

1 Spy name
2 God who sounds like a Zodiac sign
3 Like a wet noodle
4 Finish line
5 Have great hopes
6 Metz menu
7 "__ Named Sue"
8 Roman 504
9 Soothing word
10 __ *kleine Nachtmusik*
11 Parabolic paths
12 Bump into
15 Falls for lovers
18 Interteam deals
19 Sketched
23 Companionless
24 His name is Mudd
25 Wear down
26 Gorged
27 Pour __ (try extra hard)
28 Prepare champagne
29 Lend __ (listen)
30 Hopping mad
31 List components
33 Coin-flip call
34 Farm structure
36 Rush of feeling
37 No place for Mary's lamb
42 Call a spade a "thpade"
43 Yule tunes
44 Prolonged attack
45 Expert
46 Arthur of tennis
47 Jalousie feature
48 Dispatched
49 Headquarters for Batman and Robin
50 Home of the Bruins
51 Leave port
52 Eleanor Roosevelt's first name
53 A great deal
55 Affirmative action?

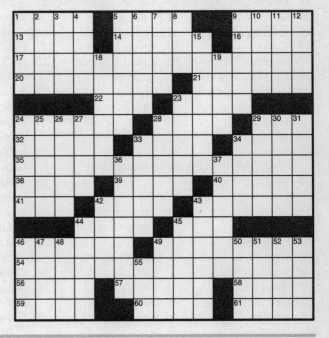

350 MAKING SENSE by Randolph Ross

ACROSS

1 They're often cast
7 "__ the Beautiful"
14 Giants' home
15 Venezuelan hero
16 Unwelcome comment
18 Start of MGM's motto
19 Like dishwater
20 Happening
21 Currier's partner
23 Red-ink entries
25 Make a comeback
28 Bit of negativity
29 Say please
32 Popeye, e.g.
34 It's often tacky
35 Trial
40 Words of comprehension
41 Head for bed
42 Fathers and grandfathers
43 Princess tester
45 Feral
49 Caliph's kin
51 Eye drop
52 Capital of Tibet
54 Meryl's *Out of Africa* role
57 From __ Z
58 Dial-less devices
61 Increasingly upset
62 Pencil box items
63 Taps out the same message
64 Montana's team, for short

DOWN

1 Deprive
2 Free admissions
3 Summer setting in NY
4 Committed perjury
5 Humdinger
6 Detected a traitor
7 Pecs' partners
8 Additionally
9 NFL side
10 Covers with frost
11 Terrible name
12 Shopper's aid
13 Scroll holder
14 Flight segment
17 Road sign
22 "If You Knew __"
24 Without inspection
26 __ room (family place)
27 Moo goo __ pan
29 He flattened Foreman
30 Eastern riser
31 Beer barrel
33 Acclamation for Escamillo
34 Tony the Tiger's adjective
35 Dandy dude?
36 Exploit
37 Bear's lair
38 Aachen article
39 Pottery or poetry
43 Apply a thumbtack
44 Walking on air
46 More like a junkyard dog
47 Restaurant patrons
48 Refuse
49 "__ bleu!"
50 Feel poorly
52 Solitary
53 Warm greetings
55 Foolish date: Abbr.
56 Tatar top man
58 Pine product
59 Hesitator's syllables
60 Sugar suffix

351   WHAT-KNOT by Bob Lubbers

ACROSS

1 Karate kin
5 Agt.'s take
8 Tijuana treats
13 PDQ, politely
14 Hand-cream additive
15 Helmsman's term
16 Opinion taker
18 *Odyssey* siren
19 Tusked sea mammals
21 Cocktail cheese
22 Sodium solutions
25 Public-__ television
27 Thinks
28 Fairy-tale youngster
30 Jessica of *Cape Fear*
31 Movie director Alexander
32 Little fellow
35 High cards
36 Scrumptious
37 Chan's assent
38 Gettysburg soldier
39 Crowd maker?
40 Singer Springsteen
41 Far and wide
43 Formal living room
44 Holy
46 Volcanic rocks
47 *Kon-__*
48 Pain reliever
51 Sports palace
53 First-__ (game starters)
57 Brink
58 Tiny amounts
59 Actor Estrada
60 Road curves
61 Draft agcy.
62 Say it isn't so

DOWN

1 Jelly container
2 Troop troupe: Abbr.
3 Drink like a sparrow
4 First nights
5 Blizzard fleet
6 Fizzy favorite
7 Spill the beans
8 Tic-__-toe
9 For each
10 UN founding father
11 Aquarium denizens
12 Sunflower supports
14 __-ski party
17 Calcutta queen
20 Hall of Famer Koufax
22 Kind of calculator
23 Quickly
24 Defensive players
26 Jefferson Davis' dom.
28 Watered the lawn, e.g.
29 Jocular Johnson
31 Malden or Marx
33 Fashionable neckwear
34 Active ones
36 Bara of the silents
37 Put in order
39 Father's Day gift
40 "__ Street Blues"
42 Surrey trim
43 Bastille locale
44 Barrel part
45 Buenos __
46 Condor and canary
49 Fast fliers
50 School grps.
52 DDE opponent
54 Before, in verse
55 __ Tin Tin
56 The wild blue yonder

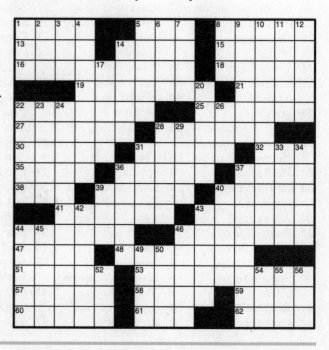

352   SHOCKING SUBJECTS by Eric Albert

ACROSS

1 Block bit
5 Stress-free
9 Easy __
14 In the pink
15 Mayberry boy
16 Mike of *Wayne's World*
17 Where most people live
18 Actress Perlman
19 Puts up
20 WWII partisans
23 Tie the knot
24 Lawyer's letters
25 Ice-T's music
28 Chess maneuver
32 Root beer alternative
33 Flowery necklace
34 Bounding main
35 Asian tongue
36 Ping-__
37 Diplomatic official
41 Feels ill
42 Mouth piece?
43 Fat-eschewer of rhyme
44 No longer working: Abbr.
45 Ball callers
46 Fourth-rate
47 Numeric prefix
48 Parisian possessive
49 *Peggy __ Got Married*
50 Pitch woo
57 Hindu ascetic
59 "If __ a Hammer"
60 Kind of history
61 Like Nero Wolfe
62 Form loops
63 38 Regular, e.g.
64 Pizzeria patron
65 MacLachlan of *Twin Peaks*
66 Mist

DOWN

1 Light talk
2 Mess-hall meal
3 Tennis player Nastase
4 Still-life subject
5 It's a cinch
6 Plant pest
7 Bears false witness
8 Diner fare
9 Blake of *Gunsmoke*
10 In __ (meshing well)
11 *M* man
12 Make mad
13 Start start?
21 *Dallas* family name
22 "__ Me" (Sinatra tune)
26 Vergil's hero
27 Foul spot
28 Kid's racer
29 Needing massage more
30 Means of support
31 Forbids
32 Gives a hand
36 Organ piece
38 Glue guy
39 Oil-level indicator
40 Grate stuff
45 Shylock, e.g.
46 Hug affectionately
49 Slow mover
51 Belgian river
52 Crow's-nest cry
53 Elegant
54 Pavarotti piece
55 Make fun of
56 Swiss artist Paul
57 Hostile force
58 Perry Mason's org.

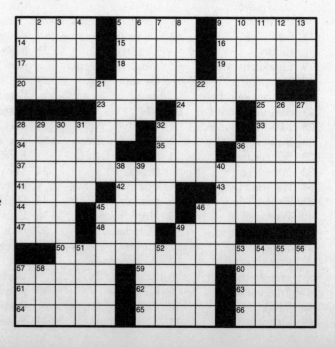

353 MOVING RIGHT ALONG by Trip Payne

ACROSS

1 Pull into traffic
6 Play with bubble wrap
9 "__ an idea!"
14 *Paper Moon* Oscar winner
15 Aussie critter
16 Not so hot
17 Clamming up
20 Botanist Gray et al.
21 Vain act
22 Literary monogram
23 Former Dodger third-baseman
24 Tailor's measure
28 Quartet
30 Mao __-tung
32 Invisible helix
33 "Lady Soul"
35 Beans on the bean
37 Disney refrain
40 Settles down
41 Don of *Trading Places*
42 What did ewe say?

43 Drink with bangers
44 Loafer adornment
48 Detergent ingredient
51 Director Howard
52 Vane dir.
53 Brace oneself
56 Game Boy rival
57 Bill Griffith comic strip
61 Worried
62 Huzzah of sorts
63 Imitate a signature
64 Chaplain
65 Take a gander at
66 Also-ran

DOWN

1 *Amadeus* role
2 Send to Elba
3 Big spread
4 Generational problems
5 Yale student
6 Actress Ashcroft
7 Herman Melville novel

8 Fourth-down option
9 "__ the bag!"
10 Gives a hand
11 Word form for "bee"
12 Bigwig, for short
13 The two Begleys
18 Required
19 1813 battle site
23 Singer Irene and family
25 Author Ferber
26 Egyptian symbol
27 Bell and Barker
29 Fascinated
30 School paper
31 The Marquis de __
34 Dabbling duck
35 Cagney role
36 Dedicated poems
37 Strong fervor
38 Author Dinesen
39 Squids' kin
40 Hoop grp.
43 "And that __ hay!"

45 Mocking looks
46 Attract
47 King of the hill
49 Bond-value phrase
50 Philippine island
51 Shankar simoleon

54 Sabot or clog
55 Pretty slippery
56 "Get out!"
57 Laser-beam sound
58 "Make __ double!"
59 __ XING (street sign)
60 Patriots' assn.

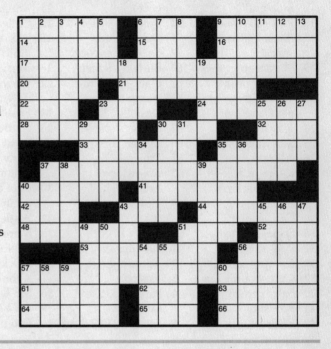

354 FRACTURED FILMS by Shirley Soloway

ACROSS

1 Hits hard
5 Attired
9 Palm readers
14 Mideast gulf
15 Buddhist bigwig
16 *Dallas* matriarch
17 Singer Julius La __
18 From the top
19 Full of pep
20 James Stewart film
23 Flat hat
24 Journal ending
25 Paint-shop purchases
27 Tilting, to a tar
30 XC
32 "Unforgettable" name
33 Seal group
34 Provide oxygen to
38 Liz Taylor film
42 Winter weasel
43 Gladiator's item
44 __ polloi
45 Tried out
47 Pull away

49 Canadian province
52 Skater Babilonia
53 Mauna __
54 Paul Newman film
60 French menu word
62 Reveal all
63 Dorothy's dog
64 Heart parts
65 Caspian's neighbor
66 Cabell of baseball
67 Pie part
68 Pie apple
69 Actor Auberjonois

DOWN

1 Fishhook feature
2 Bouquet
3 Chihuahua coin
4 Asp and anaconda
5 One beside himself?
6 Volcanic flow

7 Part of U.S.A.
8 McGavin of *Kolchak*
9 Brine
10 Building wing
11 Upper crust
12 Adversary
13 Appears to be
21 Superlative suffix
22 Kind of play
26 __ *Breckinridge*
27 Date starter
28 Cowardly Lion portrayer
29 Particular
30 Neither's neighbor
31 "What have __?"
33 Magic word
35 Flu symptom
36 Spinks stats
37 Prepare for the press
39 Wee being
40 Listless
41 Cherry or cranberry

46 Sole sauce
47 Ares' area
48 John of *Hearts Afire*
49 Ocean organisms
50 Unwilling (to)
51 Wilkes-__, PA
52 Tutu fabric

55 Caligula's nephew
56 Chowder ingredient
57 Couldn't be better
58 *Blame __ Rio*
59 The scenter of your face
61 Zip

BLACK AND WHITE by Harvey Estes

ACROSS

1 The good old days
5 Indian chief
9 Small cut
13 Regretful one
14 "Never __ moment"
16 Roll-call response
17 Black-and-white snack
19 She sheep
20 Type of pear
21 Trattoria beverage
23 Play by ear
25 Maryland athlete
26 Allstate rival
29 John __ Passos
31 Grammarian's concern
34 Org. leader
35 Social butterflies
37 Pod occupant
38 Computer in *2001*
39 Cutesy suffix
40 Salty spread
41 Sch. subj.
42 British suffix
43 Crept slowly
45 Cheeseboard choice
46 Harass
48 Over there
49 Brainteaser
50 __ instant (at once)
52 Bull Run victor
54 Deli delicacy
57 Carve a canyon
60 Buffalo's water
61 Black-and-white stumper
64 Unskilled laborer
65 Milker's seat
66 Dweeb
67 True grit?
68 Grandson of Adam
69 Blows away

DOWN

1 Paid player
2 Atmosphere
3 Taken in
4 Paris and Priam, for two
5 *Eating __* ('82 film)
6 Hubbub
7 Single file?
8 Ms. MacGraw et al.
9 Goes off course
10 Black-and-white dailies
11 Brings to a boil?
12 Chilean money
15 Word form for "thin"
18 Musical finale
22 Wear hand-me-downs
24 Foolishness
26 Gardener's bane
27 Blank a tape
28 Early black-and-white medium
30 Cool as a cucumber
32 Bottle dweller
33 More than willing
35 Workweek start: Abbr.
36 Mr. Serling
39 Diva Lorengar
44 End of the world?
45 Joseph of *My Favorite Year*
47 Mean
49 Parisian papa
51 Takes forty winks
53 With __ on (eagerly)
54 Animates, with "up"
55 Geometry calculation
56 Trombone accessory
58 Actress Barrymore
59 Joyce's homeland
62 Beastly place?
63 Driller's deg.

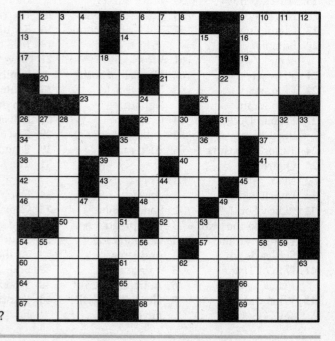

HURRY UP! by Shirley Soloway

ACROSS

1 __ *La Douce*
5 Paid performers
9 Actress __ Jessica Parker
14 Genuine
15 Steakhouse word
16 Spread joy
17 British composer Thomas
18 At any time
19 Government takebacks
20 Mercury
23 __ and outs
24 Twangy
25 Large antelope
27 *Empty* __
30 Work forces
33 Famous feline
37 Century segment
39 Novelist Zola
40 Pulls apart
41 Jazz instruments
43 Gray or Moran
44 Upright
46 Monthly expenditure
47 Adjusts a clock
48 Takes the wheel
50 Dried out
52 Window covering
54 Wed in haste
58 __ and don'ts
60 Con artists
64 *Some Like* __
66 Got hold of
67 Thicke or Alda
68 Shoulder scarf
69 Border
70 __ *Can* (Davis, Jr. book)
71 Managed somehow
72 Down the __ (in the future)
73 Trickle slowly

DOWN

1 Desert Storm locale
2 Summer TV show
3 Excessive enthusiasm
4 Actor Baldwin et al.
5 Elvis and Priscilla
6 Sitarist Shankar
7 Pitcher Hershiser
8 Dish out dinner
9 Notched like a saw
10 Bar order
11 Occurring swiftly
12 Like __ of bricks
13 Musician Myra
21 Topeka's st.
22 Aboveground trains
26 Prospective parents' concerns
28 Scorch
29 Levies a tariff
31 Dart about
32 Capitol VIPs
33 Aphrodite's son
34 __ filter (dryer feature)
35 Hot-rodder's store
36 *Lou Grant* star
38 Monsieur Clair
42 Moved like lightning
45 Sketched an outline
49 Dieter's resort
51 Pipe type
53 Chemical compound
55 Rubber-stamps
56 Martinique volcano
57 Use the pencil end
58 Kind of brake
59 Producer Preminger
61 Big fuss
62 Roman garment
63 Small bit
65 Bilbao bravo

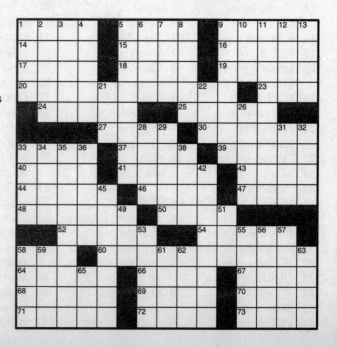

357 LILAC TIME by Eric Albert

ACROSS

1 Mandlikova of tennis
5 Polychrome parrot
10 Piece of truth
14 Trojan War hero
15 Make self-conscious
16 Felipe, Jesus, or Matty
17 Crooks in a '51 film
20 Boil in oil?
21 "Zip-__-Doo-Dah"
22 Roughhouse
23 Piece for two
24 *Pretty Woman* man
25 Quit office
28 Vane silhouette
29 Tom or tabby
32 'Umble Heep
33 Living-room piece
34 Cotton quantity
35 Having royal blood
38 Piece of one's mind?
39 Approach
40 Peer-group member?
41 Director Russell
42 Tribal division
43 Molar hole
44 Virtuous
45 Italian river
46 Conductor Toscanini
49 Tangle up
50 *Murphy Brown* network
53 Shy one
56 Ring out
57 Sociologist Durkheim
58 On guard
59 Alike in amount
60 Gave a score to
61 Bobcat

DOWN

1 One, to two
2 Open a bit
3 Dark blue
4 Tin Man's tool
5 Drive crazy
6 Red as __
7 International help org.
8 Hard wood
9 Breaking wave
10 F, on some tests
11 Donations to the poor
12 Under control
13 Subway, in Suffolk
18 Zilch
19 Move furtively
23 Paul Anka hit
24 Errand runner
25 Cube man
26 Cause to decay
27 Wailing warning
28 *Yankee Doodle Dandy* subject
29 __ pants (casual slacks)
30 Mete out
31 Smaller than small
33 Place
34 Crowd cry
36 Witness
37 Congo tributary
42 Husky vegetable?
43 Hungered after
44 Artful deception
45 Sharp corner
46 Venomous vipers
47 Mrs. Danny DeVito
48 London streetcar
49 Fit of anger
50 Terra cotta
51 Switzerland's capital
52 Charon's river
54 "Baby __ Want You" ('71 tune)
55 He gives a hoot

358 GOING UNDER by Shelley Wolfe

ACROSS

1 Receipt stamp
5 Niches for riches
10 Small pie
14 Aware of the plot
15 Rigg of *The Avengers*
16 Jai __
17 Winter forecast
18 __ *Me* (Tomlin film)
19 King of gorillas
20 Barbera's partner
22 Actress Raines
23 *Picnic* playwright
24 Asian metropolis
26 Horseshoe toss
28 Cancel
31 In competition
33 Came down to earth
34 Have __ in one's bonnet
36 Map collection
40 Long-running sitcom
41 Bayes and Ephron
43 Corned-beef concoction
44 Nasty smile
46 Santa __, CA
47 Spanish direction
48 Greek physician
50 Actress Loren
52 Cavalry advance
55 Lucy's landlady
57 Angelic topper
58 Portable container
60 Grapevine item
64 Not worth __ (valueless)
65 General course
67 Place for pews
68 Send into shock
69 Removed a squeak
70 Pleased
71 Parents' org.
72 River transports
73 Architectural add-ons

DOWN

1 Ritzy
2 *The King and I* character
3 "Blame __ the Bossa Nova"
4 Completely
5 '60s coll. grp.
6 Choreographer Alvin
7 Be overeager
8 Organic compound
9 Pay hike?
10 Getting married, maybe?
11 By the side of
12 Grazing ground
13 Circus cat
21 NASA affirmative
25 Shakespearean actor Edmund
27 __ manner of speaking
28 Merino males
29 High spirits
30 Carpentry grip
32 Affirmative votes
35 Wet blanket
37 Mascara site
38 __ Spumante
39 Mets' playground
42 Waist definer
45 Joplin piece
49 Church reader
51 "__ the ramparts . . ."
52 Yawning gulf
53 "¡__ mañana!"
54 Audibly
56 Article of faith
59 Soprano's showcase
61 Shopper's paradise
62 Gem shape
63 Beatty/Keaton film
66 Periodontist's deg.

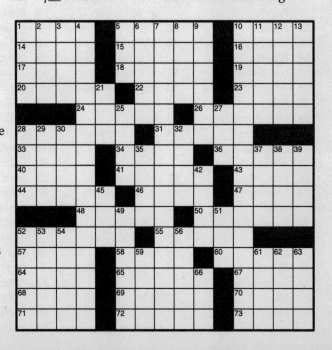

359 FAMOUS FICTION by S.N.

ACROSS

1 Prerecorded
6 Greetings for the villain
10 Young lady
14 Bart or Ringo
15 General's assistant
16 "__ girl!"
17 Card-game pot
18 Game-show winnings
19 Actress Celeste
20 Alice Walker novel
23 McMahon and Sullivan
24 Metal-laden rock
25 Repress
29 Exact duplicate
31 Superman's insignia
34 Erie or Suez
35 Broad smile
36 __ Hari
37 Lorraine Hansberry play
40 Unintelligent one
41 Takes into custody
42 For days __ (interminably)
43 Missouri city: Abbr.
44 Suburban plot size
45 Kind of photo
46 It's between "fa" and "la"
47 Gloomy
48 Willard Motley novel
56 Printing process, for short
57 Actress Miles
58 Propelled a canoe
60 Concerned with
61 Composer Satie
62 Squawk
63 Chimney dirt
64 Took the bus
65 Off-the-wall

DOWN

1 Sound of reproach
2 Working hard
3 Route
4 Art Deco artist
5 Battery types
6 Fancy dances
7 1 A.M., Army-wise
8 Stench
9 Crucial tennis situation
10 Olympic skier Phil
11 Surmounting
12 "__ never work!"
13 Knight's counterpart
21 Poem of praise
22 Coffee brewer
25 Lots
26 Fortune-telling card
27 Considering everything
28 __ accompli
29 Native American group
30 Sports statistic
31 Simplifies
32 Bowls over
33 Annie's dog
35 Snarl
36 Send __ Flowers
38 Well-to-do
39 Minimize
44 Swell, in space
45 Cheerful
46 Rush off
47 Pipe cleaner?
48 Singer Kristofferson
49 Taboo
50 Maestro Klemperer
51 Pianist Peter
52 Dry as a desert
53 Honolulu's island
54 "It either rains __ pours!"
55 Pay for the use of
59 Actress Susan

360 GOOD "O" FOLKS by Randolph Ross

ACROSS

1 Classroom no-no
4 Nonclerical
8 Game participants
13 The Plastic __ Band
14 Easter
15 Hardware item
16 Hugh's constellation?
19 Scroll site
20 Itch
21 Jolie daughter
22 Computer command
23 Anita's dawn?
26 Prayer
29 It's sometimes bitter
30 Take a look at
31 Code-cracking org.
32 Pie nut
34 Impressionist John
35 Peter's hammer holder?
37 "__ home is his castle"
40 Hebrew month
41 Salutation word
44 Meet event
45 They're rated in BTUs
46 Zero
48 Madalyn Murray's coifs?
51 Writer Hart
52 Former Mideast confed.
53 Goof
54 Olive stuffing
57 Elusive, like Ryan?
60 Helping hand
61 Boxer Griffith
62 Sault __ Marie, MI
63 Rawhide prop
64 Great dog
65 John Jr.'s uncle

DOWN

1 Todman's partner
2 Removes a checkrein
3 Czech territory
4 Stroller's spot
5 Take __ (try)
6 I, in Essen
7 Montana Indians
8 Reeked
9 __ Saud
10 Made much of
11 Heighten
12 Dropout from the flock
14 __ de deux
17 Bad day for Caesar
18 Leader
24 Practical person
25 Jet black
27 Goes (for)
28 Classical beginning
33 Agreed
34 Pro __ (without fees)
35 "Dedicated to the __ Love"
36 Secret rival
37 Excitement
38 Gospel singer Jackson
39 Mites and ticks
41 Most promptly
42 Establish
43 Did cobbler's work
45 Square measure
47 Ness' crew
49 Copy, for short
50 1992 Olympics site
55 Capri or Man
56 Shemp's sib
58 Footlike part
59 Singer Sumac

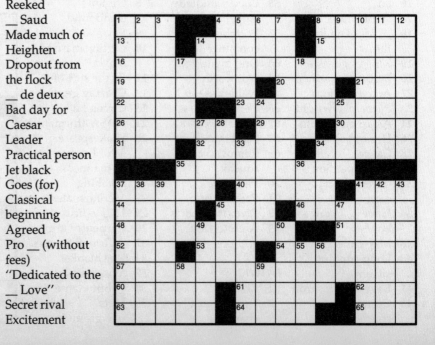

ACROSS AND DOWN by Trip Payne

ACROSS
1 Yuppie car
4 Are able to, to Shakespeare
9 Go a few rounds with
12 Actress Bernhardt
14 Make merry
15 Zombie's punch?
16 Like some cases
18 Frozen dessert
19 Noun suffix
20 Matador's foe
21 Funk pianist
23 Amahl's creator
25 Jeff Bridges' brother
26 Good and bad times
31 Casey Kasem countdown
34 Little carpenter
35 Family card game
36 Popular theater name
37 FedEx rival
38 Poem division
40 "Sprechen __ Deutsch?"

41 Columbus sch.
42 __ cream pie
43 Spread out
47 "Last one __ rotten egg!"
48 Rubs the wrong way?
52 Anytown, U.S.A. locale
55 Poi party
56 Strike sharply
57 Mensa measurements
58 Tolstoy novel
61 Total cost
62 Tut's turf
63 "Grody __ max!"
64 Profs.' aides
65 Marsh flora
66 Leaky-tire sound

DOWN
1 Danny of *Not Necessarily the News*
2 Chesspiece
3 "And after that?"

4 Actor Hardwicke
5 Not to mention
6 Slangy negative
7 Notetaker, often
8 Group of four
9 Vivacity
10 "Hey, that smarts!"
11 Comic-book hero group
12 "__ told"
13 Church area
17 "__ a million years!"
22 Stick out
24 __ von Bismarck
25 Prohibits
27 Not working
28 Search for
29 Fascinated by
30 High time
31 Brit's baloney
32 Garfield's canine pal
33 Jury member
37 Milk grader, for short
38 Leads astray
39 All confused

41 Acting, perhaps
42 Misbehave
44 One, to Wagner
45 Response
46 Regular hangouts
49 Mild oaths
50 Every one

51 *Graf* __
52 Driving hazard
53 Blue hue
54 Beliefs
55 Sgt. Friday's outfit
59 Bread or booze
60 Dawn goddess

SOMETHING FISHY by Shirley Soloway

ACROSS
1 Doll's word
5 *Butterfield 8* author
10 Cookie keeper
13 Brutus' birds
14 Showed again
15 Window glass
16 Misleading clue
18 Makes believe
19 Musical chord
20 Boat trip
21 Comic sketch
22 Flower segment
24 Sofas and stools
26 __ Gay
29 Skiing areas
32 West Coast cops, for short
35 Fixes the outcome
37 Quiver item
38 Mr. Baba
39 Ore processor
41 Santa __, CA
42 Stage star Theodore
44 Vincent Lopez theme

45 __-bitsy
46 Shorthand specialists
48 Have __ (argue)
50 Meat and veggie combos
52 Soap opera, for one
56 __ in (victimize)
58 Andy Taylor's son
61 Zoo attraction
62 Finished
63 Patti Page hit
65 *Serpico* author Peter
66 Metrical foot
67 Cooking fat
68 Caribou kin
69 Get up
70 Leicester lodgings

DOWN
1 Shopping centers
2 Ward off
3 Radio and TV
4 Humiliated

5 Bobby of hockey
6 Towel inscription
7 Sills solo
8 Sari sporters
9 Ulterior motives
10 Lean-cuisine eater
11 Opposed to
12 Take five
15 Religious leader
17 *East of* __
23 Comedian Crosby
25 Controversial tree spray
27 Mortgage, e.g.
28 Shining brightly
30 Ages
31 Move in the breeze
32 Research rooms
33 Touched down
34 Western mountain
36 Normandy town
39 __ gin fizz
40 Be all __ (listen)
43 Becomes a participant
45 Haifa native

47 Descends swiftly
49 Johnny of *Edward Scissorhands*
51 Tomato-throwing sound
53 Peruvian Indian
54 Decorate

55 Alan and Cheryl
56 "The Eternal City"
57 Like Humpty Dumpty
59 Notion
60 Coll. major
64 Compound-sentence connector

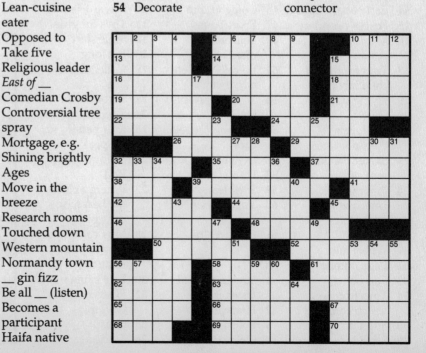

363 PLAYING IT SAFE by Bob Lubbers

ACROSS

1 Fond du __, Wisconsin
4 En __ (all together)
9 Mexican munchies
14 Comic Kabibble
15 Indo-European
16 Pullman choice
17 Like zeppelins: Abbr.
18 Night scenes
20 *Tosca* tunes
22 Head set?
23 Solidify
26 Global specks
30 Hide oneself
32 Restrict Rover
34 Language suffix
36 Weather outburst
38 Fry lightly
39 Rock star David Lee __
41 *Cheers* chair
43 Give the cold shoulder to
44 Chorale members
46 Poke around
48 Infielder's stats
49 Noon nap
51 Perforated screen
53 REM events
55 Curled one's lip
58 Bring up
60 Mosey along
61 Orphan Annie's trademark
67 Slanting: Abbr.
68 Augusta's state
69 Leno or Letterman
70 Whole bunch
71 Fowl family
72 Joyrides
73 USAir rival

DOWN

1 Fragrant bush
2 Houston player
3 Mail scheme
4 Ilona and Raymond
5 Onassis' nickname
6 Thesaurus offering: Abbr.
7 Wise guy
8 Chou __
9 Scuffles
10 PD alert
11 Tax pro, for short
12 Above, to Arnold
13 Last year's jrs.
19 Prefix for while
21 Turkish title
24 Hts.
25 Acts piratical
27 Sched. guesses
28 Zeus' zapper
29 Arrangement
31 Off target
33 Confederates
34 Historical periods
35 Three-dimensional
37 Secures the ship
40 Argyles and anklets
42 Meat cut
45 Headed the bill
47 Fills the bill
50 Congregation response
52 Moon vehicle
54 Willy Loman's concern
56 Pasta shape
57 Actress Burke
59 Cavort
61 UN post
62 Egypt and Syr., once
63 Book-jacket feature
64 Numero __
65 201, to Tiberius
66 He's a real doll

364 CHILD'S PLAY by Alice Long

ACROSS

1 Shades worn at the beach?
5 Fleet
10 "__ pinch of salt"
14 Early boatwright
15 Post of propriety
16 *Mission Earth* author Hubbard
17 Toys for foes of child labor?
19 Flying start?
20 Show
21 California volcano
23 Skater Babilonia et al.
24 Piper units
25 Unacquainted with ethics
28 Filer's aid
31 Wheel hub
32 Page number
33 Succor
34 Toys from a watch company?
38 Slip up
39 Seaside swoopers
40 Palo __, CA
41 Steps onto the platform
43 Robert Guillaume sitcom
45 Injures
46 Cologne coin
47 Breastbones
49 Unusual distrust
53 Lo-cal's modern adjective
54 Toys for juvenile hall?
56 "Famous" cookie cook
57 Delight
58 He and she
59 Shed tears
60 Yugoslavian coin
61 *In __* (really)

DOWN

1 Square-topped fastener
2 First-quality
3 Polish place
4 Oxford form
5 Give a second sentence to
6 Pile up
7 Illus.
8 Sort
9 Reading disorder
10 Seward setting
11 Toys for girls?
12 Scale start
13 Ere long
18 College sports org.
22 Part owner?
24 Lifeline locales
25 Chipped in, so to speak
26 Slalom champ Phil
27 Where a child may exercise control?
28 Musical chimes
29 Stay in place, nautically
30 Pelé's first name
32 Hosts of the '52 Olympics
35 Grasp
36 Made a face
37 Dough, of sorts
42 Least usual
43 Sweeney Todd's occupation
44 Of an historic time
46 Valletta's locale
47 Cabbage dish
48 *Newsweek* competitor
49 Blueprint
50 Protest singer Phil
51 Store on *The Waltons*
52 "__ sow, so . . ."
55 Yale player

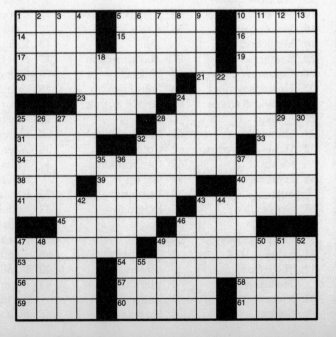

365 SOUND OF MUSIC by Harvey Estes

ACROSS
1 Drinks like a doberman
5 *The Prince of Tides* star
10 __ weevil
14 Singer Guthrie
15 Nebraska city
16 Ma Joad, for one
17 String-section curtsies?
19 Genealogy diagram
20 Montezuma was one
21 Cal. col.
22 Piece of work
23 Phone starter
26 Overhaul
28 Watch stem?
34 Adjectival suffix
35 __ *Abner*
36 *Roots* Emmy winner
37 Casserole cover
38 Criminal
41 Travel org.
42 *Par* __
44 He raved about a raven
45 Hue's partner
46 Heavy-metal instrumentalists?
51 Studies
52 Down the drain
53 *Laura* actor Clifton
56 *Hearts __ Wild*
58 Ancient Greek region
62 Blue shade
63 Fishing line?
66 Interlude
67 "__ Be Me"
68 In addition
69 *To __ a Mockingbird*
70 Tickle pink
71 Installs

DOWN
1 Pelée output
2 Cal. neighbor
3 Map out
4 Sober
5 *Persona __ grata*
6 Govt. finance org.
7 Vientiane's country
8 Frustrate
9 Egg-roll time
10 Timothy of *The Last Picture Show*
11 Gumbo ingredient
12 Is inexact?
13 Scallion's big brother
18 Decorated the cake
24 Porgy part
25 Indigo plant
27 Twofold
28 Relinquish
29 World's largest democracy
30 Caught some Z's
31 Legislate
32 Moves toward
33 Cafeteria item
34 Middle East airline
38 *Bus Stop* playwright
39 Aim
40 Dynamic start
43 Character
47 Incapable of
48 Where shekels are spent
49 "__ something I said?"
50 Stashes away
53 Pathway
54 Word form for "identical"
55 Male elephant
57 "¿Cómo __ usted?"
59 Shade of green
60 Part of MIT
61 Matures, like wine
64 Plop down
65 Sault __ Marie, Ont.

366 DOG DAY by Shirley Soloway

ACROSS
1 *Diary of __ Housewife*
5 Theater turkey
9 Curved
14 Photogravure process, for short
15 "The __ of the Ancient Mariner"
16 Actress Dern
17 Canine pedigrees?
19 Italian bread?
20 __-Barbera cartoons
21 Place in one's care
23 Mrs. Perón
24 *My Three __*
26 Form a concept
29 Gets a new tenant
31 U.S. native
32 Outfits
35 Inc., in England
36 Canine documentaries?
40 Tempe coll.
42 Sound system
43 Golden raisin
47 Shop machine
51 Jai-alai ball
52 Superstar
54 __ carte
55 Aerosol gas
57 He keeps lions in line
59 Catch container
61 Canine devotion?
63 Cancel
64 Ratio words
65 Change for a five
66 Grating sounds
67 Adventure story
68 Left the premises

DOWN
1 Private eye Lew
2 California desert
3 Musically untraditional
4 Quilt filling
5 Part of TGIF
6 Napkin fabric
7 Seer's signs
8 Nuisance
9 Refer (to)
10 Hair-__ (scary story)
11 Canine appendages?
12 Century 21 rival
13 Prosecutors: Abbr.
18 Stretchable thread
22 Edge
25 Word form for "bone"
27 Explosive initials
28 Actor Byrnes
30 Big head
31 Tennis great Arthur
33 __ Major
34 Oregon hrs.
36 Terrier enclosures?
37 Approximately
38 Lots
39 Heavy weight
40 Cleo's attacker
41 Lyon of *Lolita*
44 Ripped to shreds
45 Coral islands
46 Short snooze
48 Singer Vic
49 Dice throw
50 Most unusual
52 Occupied
53 Store divs.
56 Buy __ in a poke
58 In the hold
59 Sedan or coupe
60 Heredity letters
62 Saucepan

367 LANGUAGE CLASS by Bob Lubbers

ACROSS
1 Psyched up
5 Come to light
10 Type of map
14 Actress Velez
15 Mortise's mate
16 "__ Lama Ding Dong"
17 Shirt feature
19 "Put __ writing"
20 Cherry-topped treat
21 Siege activity
23 Liqueur flavoring
25 Bank offering
26 Convalescent's need
29 Canadian currency
32 Reunion attendee
33 Least
36 Lode load
37 Less caloric, in ads
38 Part of USNA
39 Cosmetics company
40 Bomber grp.
41 Snow __ (shovel alternative)
44 Sleeveless garment
45 On land
47 Worships
49 Govt. agt.
50 Step
51 Like mom and dad
54 Cellist Pablo
58 Rod attachment
59 Tablecloth material
61 "Dies __"
62 Desi's daughter
63 "The __ Love" ('87 tune)
64 Feminist Lucretia
65 Bergen dummy
66 Tree house?

DOWN
1 Politician Landon et al.
2 Spiritual guide
3 Unlocked
4 Cannes cop
5 Godlessness
6 __ room (family hangout)
7 Temporarily unavailable
8 Like a plush toy
9 Hugs, in a way
10 Basic
11 Valentino, for one
12 Ugandan dictator
13 Sharp taste
18 Walking stick
22 Tooth part
24 Office worker
26 Hobbyist's wood
27 Inventor Howe
28 Split bill
30 Gertrude Stein phrase
31 Landlord's take
34 Damp and cold
35 Three-time Wimbledon winner
39 Loathing
41 Fiber source
42 Soup legumes
43 Arrived at
46 Brunch basic
48 Perfume bottle
50 Pizza piece
51 Stiffly formal
52 Space starter
53 __ for one's money
55 Ms. Bancroft
56 Wine dregs
57 Grumpy mood
60 To __ With Love

368 PEOPLE OF HONOR by Cynthia Lyon

ACROSS
1 Soup server
6 James __ Garfield
11 Cubs' home, for short
14 Serve
15 Rooster Cogburn's portrayer
16 Try (for)
17 Oldies deejay
19 Army grp.
20 Garden bloomer
21 Yule refrain?
23 Checker color
24 Reagan or Colman
25 Has it out
29 Nursery noise
30 Fess Parker role
31 "Use __ My Girl" ('78 song)
32 Go out of control
35 Lummox
36 Winter archer
37 Jackson 5 member
38 Actress Goodman
39 Plow pullers
40 __ Goes to College
41 Mortised
43 Plane place
44 Judgmental criteria
45 Fez's land: Abbr.
46 Tarzan's home
47 San Francisco Bay city
52 Alias abbr.
53 Fictional tec
55 Dopey colleague
56 Frank composition?
57 Quitter's cry
58 "We __ the World"
59 Randi of CHiPs
60 Anesthetic

DOWN
1 Code content
2 Declare
3 Mrs. Rogers
4 Long sentence?
5 New Haven symbol
6 Having bristles
7 Mexican region
8 Scandinavian rug
9 Emulated Brokaw
10 Vietnam delta
11 "It's Too Late" singer
12 Note of note
13 "__ be Queen o' the May"
18 Kong's kin
22 Pillbox-hat designer
24 Jerry of the Chicago 7
25 Front four?
26 Chewy candy brand
27 Renowned radio comedy writer
28 Eternal
29 Opened wide
31 Penguins' garb?
33 Chichén __, Mexico
34 Way in
36 __ Otis Skinner
40 Like Bach's works
42 Ohio city . . .
43 . . . and its description?
44 Director George
45 The Bells of St. __
46 Silly song of 1918
47 Dijon dad
48 Charley's alter ego?
49 Solidarity's Walesa
50 Boob tube, for short
51 Dilly
54 "Mighty __ a Rose"

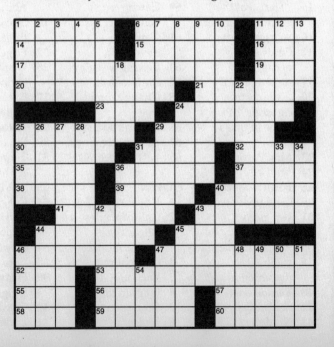

369   DON'T HOLD YOUR BREATH by Scott Marley

ACROSS

1 Swindle
5 Tobacco wad
9 Homes for *hombres*
14 First-rate
15 Big wheels?
16 Computer company
17 Unlikely occurrence
20 Deli equipment
21 Get the point
22 Rival of 16 Across
23 Like the Sahara
25 The Emperor's clothes
28 __ au vin
31 Close
33 Actor Mineo et al.
34 Credit slips?
36 The E in QED
38 Yellow stone
41 Unlikely occurrence
44 Emerson opus
45 Muscle quality
46 SALT talks subject
47 __ *Well That Ends Well*

49 Fruit holder
51 Little one
52 Humbleness
55 Steinbeck character
57 What's missng?
58 Feel unwell
60 Largest U.S. tribe
64 Unlikely occurrence
68 Eng. Dept. course
69 Mistruths
70 German port
71 A lot
72 Pops
73 Catch sight of

DOWN

1 Band and table
2 Kind of mine
3 Con
4 Hajji's aim
5 Humorous poem of a sort
6 Wasn't it
7 Electrical units
8 Suitor
9 __ in "cat"

10 Police notice, briefly
11 Wet blanket
12 Cover story?
13 Historic march setting
18 Word often embroidered
19 Driver's needs
24 Was audacious, once
26 Proceeds
27 Hilo hello
28 Refer to
29 They accompany aahs
30 Tortilla melt
32 Yucatán yummies
35 Butcher-shop fixture
37 Lone Ranger's companion
39 Magazine's contents
40 Relish
42 Olive's kin
43 Lamblike quality
48 She takes the lead

50 Farrow and Sara
52 Taj __
53 __ *Time* ('80s Broadway show)
54 Give in
56 Suggest, artistically
59 *Star Wars* character

61 Hertz competitor
62 Army vehicle
63 Paris airport
65 Topper
66 Dix and Worth, for short
67 Last letter in London

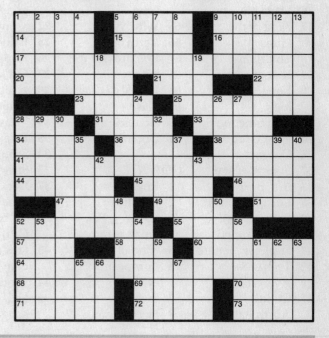

370   APT SNACKS by Cathy Millhauser

ACROSS

1 Self-confidence
6 Word on a keyboard
11 Pen pal?
14 Wrench type
15 Former Mets manager Joe
16 Mine material
17 Sage's snack?
19 Relatives
20 Enjoy the Jacuzzi
21 "Two-by-two" structure
22 Worrell or Hemingway
24 Radiates
26 Use a ewer
27 "Two-__ action!" (movie-ad promise)
30 Pipe type
33 Holy crosses
34 __ about (nearly)
36 Pump, e.g.
37 Ugandan heavyweight
38 Witch's snack?
41 Final finale
42 She liked Ike

44 Truman or Bush, once
45 Kind of crust
47 Surfer's term
49 Impudent
50 It's spun by mouth
51 Cop-show wailer
53 Plaid fabric
55 __ Alicia of *Falcon Crest*
56 Find fault
60 "Yes," to Yvette
61 Clone's snack?
64 Cheerleader's quality
65 Blake of jazz
66 Triptych images
67 Loop loopers
68 Cut corners
69 Terminal

DOWN

1 Kitten's mitts
2 Mixed bag
3 *Casablanca* role
4 "Love __ not itself to please...": Blake
5 Herein, in brief

6 Get down to business
7 Pawns
8 Rub the wrong way
9 Bahamas town
10 Sheer fear
11 Snoop's snack?
12 Author Murdoch
13 Nice chap
18 Sudden attack
23 __ *on the Run* ('90 film)
25 Become engaged
27 Confidence
28 Julie Christie's birthplace
29 Twiggy's snack?
30 __ *de grâce*
31 Moves like molasses
32 Tipsy, maybe
34 The yoke's on them
35 Compass pt.
39 Makes smooth
40 Foolproof
43 Bacteriologist's base

46 Edible floppy disk?
48 Carpentry and printing
49 Strathclyde hillside
51 Salk colleague
52 Narrows
53 Wear a long face
54 *The Mammoth Hunters* writer
57 Perched on
58 Paradise for a pair of dice?
59 "Ahem!"
62 Where: Lat.
63 Executed

371 SOLID STATE by Shirley Soloway

ACROSS

1 Fitness farms
5 Pitchfork part
10 Daily drama
14 Come to the rescue
15 Solitary soul
16 Little pie
17 King of the Huns
18 Entertain
19 Kett of comics
20 Long, cold look
23 Trig functions
24 Played for time
28 Coronet
32 *Superman* star
33 Inc., British-style
36 European sable
39 Exist
40 Easily duped
41 Explosive letters
42 Teen scene
46 Ave. crossers
47 Cuddly Australian
48 Singer Presley
50 Indulge oneself
53 Household job
57 Like Andy Devine
61 Quiet sort
64 *West Side Story* song
65 Wine valley
66 Verdi opera
67 Prepares for the press
68 Jack of *Rio Lobo*
69 Nasty
70 Actress Taylor
71 Declares

DOWN

1 Rug types
2 Lab dish
3 Edgar __ Poe
4 Small piano
5 Kind of map
6 European capital
7 Burden
8 Heron homes
9 Terrific
10 Pittsburgh player
11 Cereal grain
12 Museum display
13 School org.
21 Egyptian goddess
22 __ avis
25 Baltic natives
26 Happening
27 Car scars
29 __ time (never)
30 Equine shade
31 "Have __ day!"
33 Escapades
34 Scout unit
35 Stick-on
37 Daredevil Knievel
38 TV tycoon Griffin
43 Jack of *The Odd Couple*
44 Singer Vikki
45 Half a Latin song
49 Radiates
51 More courageous
52 Stay away from
54 Florida city
55 Clear a loan
56 Dutch exports
58 "__ go bragh!"
59 Lo-cal, in ads
60 Bouquet holder
61 Machine part
62 Tell a fib
63 Nabokov novel

372 HEAD GAMES by Dean Niles

ACROSS

1 United group
5 Sow chow
9 Oral
14 Bowling alley
15 Feel concern
16 Make merry
17 Enlightening experience
19 Loose-limbed
20 Actor Wallach
21 Bring to ruin
22 Fiddle around
23 Hang down
25 Just out
26 Attacked
29 Dusting cloth
32 Think the world of
35 Rope in
36 Run-of-the-mill
37 Dryer deposit
38 Puts on
39 Throw out a line
40 Butterfly kin
41 Sheep shed
42 Terra __ (clay)
43 Blonde shade
44 Speak boastfully, in a way
46 Pass over
48 Cracked dish?
52 Mortise mates
54 Ray of light
56 Chopping tool
57 Wed in haste
58 Kept in reserve
60 Selling point
61 Soft cheese
62 Social misfit
63 Thin-voiced
64 Gave rise to
65 Pretentiously highbrow

DOWN

1 Run in the wash
2 Derek and the Dominos hit
3 __ a million (rare)
4 Corporate VIP
5 Play parts
6 Real estate
7 Layered cookie
8 According to
9 Made much of
10 Fails to mention
11 Ruthless
12 Tennis great Arthur
13 Wolfish expression
18 Life sign
22 Makes ready
24 Singer Brooks
25 Burned brightly
27 In
28 More than mad
30 Helper: Abbr.
31 "I __ Name" (Croce tune)
32 __ mater
33 God, in Guadalajara
34 To a tee
36 Range of view
38 Jillions
42 Punctuation mark
44 XC
45 Wandered
47 Cantered easily
49 L.A. hoopster
50 Put into use
51 Kennedy or Roosevelt
52 Pull apart
53 Otherwise
54 Roseanne, née __
55 A Great Lake
58 Tides do it
59 Genetic info

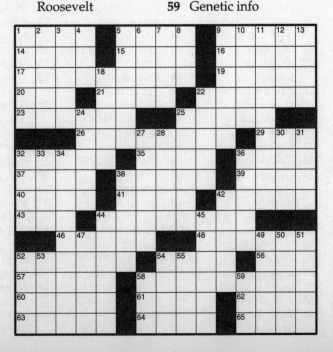

373 INKA DINKA DO by Trip Payne

ACROSS
1 Cabbage concoction
5 Beer ingredient
9 TV exec Arledge
14 Peter of reggae
15 Toe the line
16 Lot measures
17 Billy Ray Cyrus song
20 __ Tse-tung
21 Tennis champ Gibson
22 Forever __ day
23 Gives satisfaction
25 Suspend
27 Actor Alejandro
28 New Mexico resort
30 Have brunch
33 Business attire
36 Mead locale
37 Literary omnibus
38 Children's song
42 Bosom buddy
43 Textbook headings
44 Frog relative
45 __ Na Na
46 Very dry
47 Laura __ Giacomo
49 Bonkers
51 A jack beats it
55 At __ (differing)
57 Yummy
60 Comic Charlotte
61 Notes in 17 and 38 Across?
64 Rogers' partner
65 Glinda's creator
66 "__ Ideas"
67 Ballads
68 French resort spots
69 "Wild West" showman

DOWN
1 Official seal
2 Townsman
3 ". . . who lived in __"
4 Kid's query
5 Safer of *60 Minutes*
6 Helps a hood
7 Rachel's sister
8 Little one
9 Supportive scream
10 Indian, for one
11 Sweet drink
12 Geeky type
13 Wife in *Bugsy*
18 Really vile
19 Philistines
24 Overly theatrical
26 Quickly, in memos
28 Try a bit
29 Carter and Irving
31 Once again
32 Sour
33 Tries a bit
34 Bountiful setting
35 Hawaiian or Cuban
36 Move a muscle
39 Spree
40 Actually existing: Lat.
41 Rural stopovers
47 Watery fluids
48 Novelist Seton
50 Employing
51 Brimless hat
52 Ragu rival
53 Propelled a shell
54 Short-tempered
55 Lyric poems
56 Robotic rockers
58 Prefix meaning "both"
59 Beaker's kin
62 Draft agcy.
63 Actor Tayback

374 BATTLE ORDERS by Bob Lubbers

ACROSS
1 Sphere starter
5 Pen pals?
9 Plant part
13 S. Europeans
15 Court-martial candidate
16 Flying-related
17 Go gaga
19 Hibiscus garlands
20 Argument riposte
21 Diatribes
23 Frost intro
25 Valuable stone
26 Guerrilla Guevara
28 Seasonal gales
33 Trolley sound
35 Lt. Kojak
36 Word of wonder
37 Pawn of a sort
40 Hostile
42 Legendary Giant
43 Get bigger
45 Roof edges
46 One way to pay
50 Lay down the lawn
51 Pie __ mode
52 Raccoon relative
54 Spigots
58 Actress Jackson et al.
62 Defeat
63 Hook and ladder
65 At rest
66 Single quantity
67 Stereo component
68 __ moss
69 Beatty and Buntline
70 Rocker Townshend

DOWN
1 Stereo's ancestor
2 Coup d'__
3 African nation
4 Wasted
5 Designer Picasso
6 __ Jima
7 Part of GI
8 Traveled on snow, in a way
9 Submarine part
10 Prepared to drive
11 Buffalo's county
12 Speedster Stirling
14 Construction area
18 Comic Crosby
22 Darned
24 __ nouveau
26 Bolt material
27 "¡__ mañana!"
29 Half a dance
30 Jazzman Red
31 Gave an Rx
32 Cows and sows
33 Flavor abbr.
34 Group of geese
38 Whale of a time
39 Natl. rights grp.
41 Abating
44 Fem. soldier
47 Gerulaitis gear
48 __ *Thesaurus*
49 Chip's chum
53 Camper's shelter
54 Wacky Wilson
55 __-de-camp
56 Bruins' sch.
57 __ qua non
59 Eat elegantly
60 Without __ (riskily)
61 Withered
64 Free (of)

375 — KNOTS by Fred Piscop

ACROSS
1 Animated Elmer
5 18-wheeler
9 Rare violin
14 On a cruise
15 Formal dance
16 __ Selassie
17 KNOT
20 Classroom projectile, perhaps
21 From
22 Word form for "outer"
23 Orly lander
24 Cheer
26 One of the Lincolns
28 __ Breckinridge
29 Off-the-wall
33 Correo __
36 Restrain
38 Ferrigno and Rawls
39 KNOT
42 Quick snack
43 Daminozide brand
44 Ill-tempered
45 Loud sleepers
47 Clinches
49 Olivier title
50 Wimbledon champ of '75
51 WWII craft
54 Saddler's tool
57 Beam bender
59 "Tell __ It Is"
61 KNOT
64 Kate's partner
65 Numbskull
66 Verne captain
67 Self-evident
68 Four Seasons tune of 1964
69 Part of NAACP

DOWN
1 Preferences, briefly
2 PC enthusiasts
3 Rid, à la the Pied Piper
4 Happy __
5 Not as plump
6 Goof up
7 Form-related
8 Little devils
9 Biblical instrument
10 Actor Hunter
11 Irritate
12 Ex-footballer Karras
13 Floor model
18 "Psst!"
19 Bad to the core
25 Record companies
27 Polk's veep
28 Dashboard display
29 A __ Born
30 Entre __
31 Worsley of hockey fame
32 Catch sight of
33 PD broadcasts
34 Actress Moran
35 Printing process, for short
37 Coach Parseghian
40 Group of monkeys?
41 Sylvester's costar
46 Actress Brennan
48 Start of a Dick Van Dyke film
50 Tie type
51 Actor's delivery
52 Reads quickly
53 Grand __ National Park
54 PDQ
55 In good health
56 Tra-__
58 Dozes off
60 __ moth
62 Sundial numeral
63 Dock workers' org.

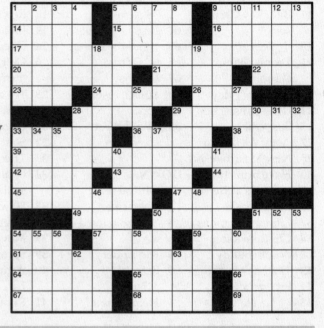

376 — FIGURE IT OUT by Eric Albert

ACROSS
1 Baseball gloves
6 Small bay
11 Traveler's need
14 Pinhead
15 Grown-up, legally
16 Altar vow
17 The best
19 Platoon setting
20 The Big Chill director
21 "And I Love __"
22 Foul person?
23 Sneaky
24 Taped sports event?
27 Mix a salad
29 Violinist Perlman
31 Central point
34 Everyman Doe
37 Epsilon follower
38 Five clubs, e.g.
39 Cry of pity
40 Pleasure cruiser
42 Bread spread
43 Computer problem
45 Quiz choice
46 Cozy retreat
47 Conductor Kostelanetz
48 Author/critic Susan
50 Take care of
52 Beaver's dad
53 Flow back
56 Tai __ (martial art)
58 Snaky swimmer
60 Open acknowledgment
62 Dress border
63 Famed watershed
66 It's all the rage
67 Residence
68 Burn a bit
69 Northern Exposure network
70 Onetime Hollywood Square
71 Moved sideways

DOWN
1 Small weasels
2 Without a flaw
3 Slightly sloshed
4 Recounted
5 Actor Whitman
6 Red letters?
7 Patriots' org.
8 Strip of wood
9 Plumed bird
10 Run away
11 Super-small
12 First person
13 Regal magnificence
18 Stylish
25 Con men
26 Admit an error
28 "Toodle-oo!"
29 Guarantee
30 Hawaiian honcho
32 Puts to work
33 Ammo
34 It's south of Borneo
35 Ken of thirtysomething
36 Dickens novel
41 Group of four
44 Dakar's nation
49 Counsel
51 Bat Masterson's hat
53 Dallas surname
54 Lawman's symbol
55 Feel sympathy
56 Elegant
57 Parsley or peppermint
59 Boxer Spinks
61 Roman poet
64 Append
65 Casual shirt

HEAVE-HO by Fred Piscop

ACROSS
1 Thunder sound
5 Pleasure craft
10 Explode
14 Mata __
15 Be off
16 Ms. Lenska
17 Emulate Perry White
18 Aquatic mammal
19 Mo. expense
20 Undergo chemical change
22 Small carpets
24 Fit
26 Porker's pad
27 Brigitte's brother
29 Six-line stanza
34 Ajax alternative
37 Comics villain Luthor
38 Break one's back
39 Petri-dish filler
40 Decree
43 Turner et al.
44 Lifts a barbell
46 "Rub-a-dub-dub" craft
47 Loch __

48 "__ Fideles"
50 Comedian Arnold
52 Feeling poorly
54 Glacial effect
58 Lightning bugs
63 Push
64 Shaquille of the courts
65 Armor type
67 Change for a five
68 Wipe out a diskette
69 First name in daredeviltry
70 Pale color
71 Fathers
72 Eastern European
73 Back talk

DOWN
1 Dijon darling
2 Full
3 *Norma* numbers
4 Farm tools
5 __-mo
6 Used a stencil
7 "Dang!" e.g.

8 Excess production
9 Ross and Margot
10 __ Rabbit (Harris character)
11 Humdinger
12 Designer Cassini
13 Female mil. personnel
21 Paving material
23 YYY
25 Soccer great
28 Walks out
30 Schoolboys' shooters
31 Appropriate
32 Holiday preceders
33 __ of the D'Urbervilles
34 Lower California
35 Matured
36 Bring to light
41 Cloyingly prettier
42 Ski lift

45 Puts an end to
49 Building wing
51 Denials
53 Drink garnishes
55 Ancient Greek colony
56 Pizzeria equipment

57 Tree houses?
58 Adversaries
59 Calvary inscription
60 Parent
61 Peace of mind
62 Icicle locale
66 Law deg.

SYMPHONIC VARIATIONS by Ronnie Allen

ACROSS
1 Carried away
5 Enthusiasm
10 Mr. Addams
14 Baseballer Cabell
15 Go on stage
16 Sacred
17 Penitential period
18 Bogged down
19 Actress Gray
20 Nerd
22 Kitchen ticker
24 Sgt. Bilko, e.g.
25 Stir sir
27 Awakened
29 Got steamy
31 Word form for "stomach"
33 Sternward
34 __ Attraction
36 Less risky
39 Gospel writer
41 "Big Three" site
43 Composer Schifrin

44 Montezuma, for one
46 Eucalyptus eater
48 Bear's lair
49 Set
51 Final syllable
53 "My __ Amour" ('69 tune)
55 Frolic
57 Cut down
58 Messed up
60 Expert
63 Spring bloom
65 1860s Blues
67 French friend
68 Tot's taboo
69 "Me, too!"
70 Secret Service agts.
71 Actor Griffith
72 A real knockout
73 __ of Eden

DOWN
1 Moolah
2 From the top
3 Opus for oboe?
4 Stellar

5 Prized person
6 Join forces
7 Follow the fiddler?
8 Abound
9 They may be marching
10 *Evita* character
11 Trumpeter's trouble spot?
12 Woody Allen film
13 Church council
21 Stk. description
23 Goes bad
26 6/6/44
28 Orenburg's river
29 American peninsula, for short
30 *The Wizard __*
32 Utah resort
35 Adopt
37 School before jr. high
38 Gossipy Barrett

40 Close-by
42 Grad
45 Baby bed
47 Goya's patron
50 Mislead
52 So far
53 Cabinet members?

54 Blue bird
56 Make __ of it
59 "Step __!"
61 Slapstick stock
62 Mobile home
64 Sauce source
66 Hide-hair connector

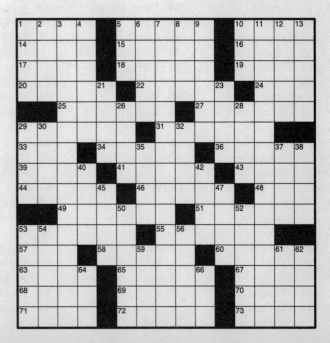

DOOR OPENERS by Harvey Estes

ACROSS
1 Equally
5 Czechs and Poles
10 Word form for "Chinese"
14 Cadabra preceder
15 Blender setting
16 Handle
17 Car-door opener
19 "Clinton's Big Ditch"
20 With-it
21 As a result
22 Detective Queen
24 Objective, for one
25 Pants part
26 Struck down
28 Countdown conclusion
32 Passing fancy
33 Fibbed
34 Egg-shaped
35 Saudi, e.g.
36 Head-turner
37 Reebok rival
38 Actress Moore
39 Sign of the future

40 Was certain of
41 Takes to the cleaners
43 Exceed 55 mph
45 Down the line
46 Full of pep
47 Mini-chicken
50 Card game
51 In thing
54 Jai __
55 Door opener of last resort
58 Flintstones' pet
59 Ancient Aegean region
60 Sand bar
61 Short jacket
62 Lent a hand
63 Defeat

DOWN
1 Big name in baroque
2 Bassoon relative
3 *The Parent* __
4 Fez or fedora
5 Few and far between

6 Thrust
7 Fleece-seeking ship
8 Victory sign
9 Alfresco aria
10 Versatile door opener
11 Concerning
12 Film __
13 Carry out orders
18 Race division
23 Bandleader Brown
24 Locker-door opener
25 Couturier Calvin
26 Virago
27 Gloria Estefan's home
28 Takes the bait
29 Just like ewe
30 Put on an act
31 Took off
32 Crumpled papers
33 Light unit
36 Coffee country

42 Trait transmitter
43 Margarine or marmalade
44 Univ. teacher
46 *Parade* composer
47 Commanded
48 Came down to earth

49 Second starter
50 Provide bread
51 Let go
52 Master hands
53 Dexterous
56 "Le __ Soleil"
57 Sphere

'92 IN REVIEW by Matt Gaffney

ACROSS
1 Capital of Iceland
10 "The Lady __ Tramp"
13 Naturalized *señoras*
15 Revolutionary
16 Leno's inheritance
18 Sellout letters
19 Cpl.'s superior
20 Feminine suffix
21 "Open 9 __ 6"
22 Collar a crook
25 Satyric trait
27 Import tax
29 Texas city
31 "I hate to break up __"
32 Senate Minority leader, once
33 One of 3 in '92
38 Do-nothing
40 Lyricist Gershwin
41 Game of chance
42 Witness' task
45 He makes it all up to you

46 Impart
47 Fools with photos
49 Tolerated
51 Muscovite, e.g.
52 Society-column word
53 Party animal?
54 Actor Morales
56 Coat part
58 Cambridge coll.
59 Midyear getaways
64 Past
65 Raul Julia's birthplace
66 Cozy room
67 One of 3 in '92

DOWN
1 Inform
2 Comedian Philips
3 Japanese cabbage?
4 Mr. Kristofferson
5 Rock lightly
6 "Attention!" in Augsburg

7 Dye container
8 Atlas feature
9 Madeline of *Clue*
10 Familiar fixture
11 Printing stroke
12 __ in sheep's clothing
14 *The Benefactor* author
17 Sneaky sort
22 Rock bottom
23 Dwelling
24 One of 3 in '92
26 "As I __ . . ."
28 Lock up again
30 Looked like Lothario?
34 ". . . __ shall die"
35 Amazing name
36 Gawk
37 Traveler or Trigger
39 Richards and Taylor
43 Makes sense
44 Wheels for kids

48 Drive-in employee
49 Sportscaster Rashad
50 Almond kin
51 Graph opener
55 East Asian river

57 *Mondo Cane* tune
60 Hosp. areas
61 Peace, in Petrozavodsk
62 Author Umberto
63 Drunkard

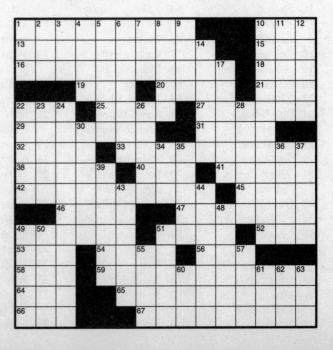

PACK TALK by Shirley Soloway

ACROSS
1 Slightly moist
5 Prepares to fire
9 Extreme
14 McClurg or Adams
15 Sudden thought
16 City on the Seine
17 Mattress platform
19 Confused
20 Caesar's foe
21 Predetermine
23 Slangy affirmative
24 Health resort
26 Fuel container
27 Roasted treat
30 Badminton stroke
33 Just fair
36 Reverberation
37 Upper crust
39 Hebrew month
40 Back areas
42 "What's __ for me?"
43 Sways
45 Greenish blue
46 "Untouchable" Eliot
47 Genesis vessel
48 Social worker's duties
51 Family group
53 Naval off.
54 Bandleader Calloway
57 Made arrangements
60 Graceland, e.g.
62 Audibly
63 Table game
65 Tropical fish
66 Writer Stoker
67 Strip of wood
68 Taj __
69 Big rig
70 Respond rudely to

DOWN
1 Pat Boone's daughter
2 Love madly
3 Snafu
4 Pain in the neck
5 Pilot's concern
6 Dictator Amin
7 Repair a rip
8 Spice-rack item
9 To the north
10 Livy's language
11 Telephone channel
12 Chinese staple
13 Make an inquiry
18 Shove
22 Letters after R
25 Fancy neckwear
27 Bottle stop
28 *My __ Sons*
29 Cash-register key
31 Singer Redding
32 Wagers
33 Poet Teasdale
34 Cologne characteristic
35 Coarse fabric
38 "The Swedish Nightingale"
41 "All __" (Brenda Lee hit)
44 Public disgrace
49 Tapper Miller
50 Exec. aide
52 Designer Ashley
54 __ lily
55 Book of maps
56 Borscht ingredients
57 Court action
58 Dwindles
59 Throw down the gauntlet
61 Dick Tracy's lady
62 Fast money source: Abbr.
64 Actress Rita

AD DICTION by Trip Payne

ACROSS
1 __ Vanilli
6 Lingerie item
9 Cafeteria selections
14 Zodiac sign
15 __ room (den)
16 Foreword or overture
17 One way to advertise
20 Dash lengths
21 Less speedy
22 Concerning
23 Kansas city
24 __ *That Jazz*
26 One way to advertise
32 Milk measures
33 Bauxite and galena
34 Treasure-hunt need
36 Ruin
37 Challenging one
39 Holyfield's defeater
40 Famed architect
41 Moore of *A Few Good Men*
42 Joan of Arc site
43 One way to advertise
47 "__ was saying . . ."
48 Polly or Esther
49 First name
52 Call __ (remember)
55 __ double take
58 One way to advertise
61 Says for sure
62 + or &
63 Actress Anouk
64 It gives you a rise
65 Auto acronym
66 Computer fans

DOWN
1 Full-grown filly
2 Where Shiraz is
3 Mason-jar toppers
4 Ring around the collar?
5 Marine crustaceans
6 NBC newsman
7 Two after do
8 Highest point
9 Douglas tree
10 Ready for summoning
11 Inventor Elisha
12 "Phooey!"
13 One-man show
18 Aspen's st.
19 Delete key's ancestor
23 Fascinated by
25 CD predecessors
26 Reds and whites
27 Calcutta's country
28 Column style
29 Fury
30 Love affair
31 Deviated
32 Baby basset
35 Cross product
37 Statesman Clinton
38 "__ Blue?"
39 Gravy vessel
41 Shingle letters
42 Short poem
44 Title assigners
45 Bob or beehive
46 A lot of rot
49 *Queen for __*
50 Seedy joint
51 General vicinity
53 General Bradley
54 Pride of lions?
55 Tiny coin
56 Unique person
57 Long periods
59 Chicago's zone: Abbr.
60 "Deck the Halls" word

383 PRESLEY PLATTERS by Randolph Ross

ACROSS

1 Head of France
5 West Indian
10 Unruly group
13 "Over The Rainbow" composer
14 Cara or Castle
15 Zsa Zsa's sister
16 Presley platter of '56
19 Pragmatic
20 Tony or Edgar
21 Cal. segments
22 Nitrous oxide, e.g.
23 Slim and trim
24 Classic cars
27 Hot time on the Riviera
28 __ Alamos, NM
29 Incapacitate
33 Public disturbance
34 Presley platter of '57
37 Sugar shape
38 Fired up
39 Genetic protein
40 Godfrey's instrument
41 Cat call
44 Take a space
46 H.S. grp.
49 Fish lightly
51 Baffle
52 Collar makers?
55 Presley platter of '69
57 Before, to Byron
58 Lincoln's in-laws
59 Like some gemstones
60 __ Moines, IA
61 Brewer's ingredient
62 MTV viewer

DOWN

1 Aftershock
2 Go by
3 Garr of *Young Frankenstein*
4 __'acte
5 About
6 They're coded
7 Nonfictional
8 Squid's defense
9 Act appropriately
10 Like gold and silver
11 Caught up to
12 Most worn, as a tire
13 Interrupter's word
17 Hanks film
18 Be behind, in a way
23 Take the reins
25 Garfield's friend
26 Part of RSVP
27 "So what __ is new?"
30 Unsteady
31 Top-notch
32 Hidden microphone
33 Teased
34 Turning point
35 You can count on them
36 Sleep stage
37 Betrayed
40 Full of oneself
42 Danish seaport
43 Leavenworth leader
45 Diamond authority
46 Urges
47 *Who Do You __?*
48 DDE opponent
50 "Hey, you!"
52 Radames' love
53 X-rated material
54 Fork part
56 Speedy Sebastian

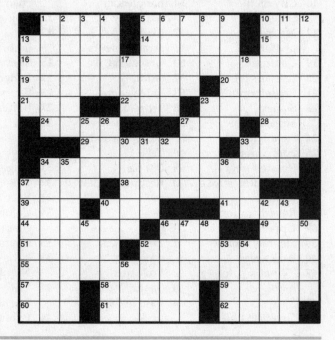

384 CAREER MOVES by Robert H. Wolfe

ACROSS

1 Guesses: Abbr.
5 Mexican fare
10 Theater man Hart
14 Singer Campbell
15 Conform
16 *Falstaff* feature
17 What gymnasts try to do
20 Warhorses
21 Eastern canal
22 Mayday, to Morse
23 Leander's love
24 Visit abroad
26 *Norma* __
28 Makes calm
32 Nurtured
37 Sp. miss
38 What a mimic tries to leave
42 Disney sci-fi film
43 12:50
44 Handpicks
48 Lemony drink
49 Put in order
51 Meander
55 Sixth sense
58 Cookware coating
59 Cookware coating
61 What basketball players do on an airplane
64 Unburden
65 "Go fly __!"
66 Arden and Plumb
67 Call it quits
68 Feel
69 Take a break

DOWN

1 Basket filler
2 A deadly sin
3 Snicker sound
4 Scoff
5 Little ones
6 Hoo-ha
7 Underground explorer
8 Classical musicals
9 Try hard
10 *The* West
11 Mine finds
12 Grain building
13 Get smart
18 Venerated
19 Take notice of
24 Swarm
25 Rodeo rope
27 *Exodus* hero
29 The Magi, e.g.
30 007's school
31 Rational
32 Gym equipment
33 Fairy-tale monster
34 Hammer or hoe
35 Sharpens
36 Govt. div.
39 Scan
40 Final point
41 Sound system
45 Soft drink
46 Musical syllables
47 Caress
50 Meese or Booth
52 Propose
53 Survival film of '93
54 Certain spies
55 Supplements, with "out"
56 "Ush"
57 Uruguayan coin
59 Corner
60 *Empty* __
62 Get-up-and-go
63 Half qts.

385 MISSING THE BUSS by Donna J. Stone

ACROSS
1 Graduation gear
4 Conductor Karl
8 *Ragged Dick* author
13 Half and half?
14 Field of study
15 African capital
16 START OF A COMMENT BY BOB HOPE
19 Filled the bill
20 Strauss stuff
21 Mid-size band
22 Cuttlefish kin
24 Little lie
26 Action figure
27 Prepare home fries
28 Get an __ effort
29 Slap on
30 Sulk
31 Actress Verdugo
32 MIDDLE OF COMMENT
35 Appendix neighbor
38 Singer Simone
39 *La Fanciulla __ West*
42 Not (one), with "a"
43 Mess around
45 Goldberg rival
46 Merger inits. of 1955
47 Cassandra, for one
48 Dog star
49 Religious beads
51 Zone
52 END OF COMMENT
55 He picks pix
56 Author Angelou
57 Center of Shintoism?
58 He had a gilt complex
59 British gun
60 Remnant

DOWN
1 *Mayflower* landing site
2 Flagged
3 Lapwing, for one
4 Smooth-pated
5 Lodestuff
6 Fell
7 Elephant man?
8 Put on
9 Bolger/Haley costar
10 African skyscraper?
11 Agronomist's concern
12 Fracas
17 Hound or hamster
18 Mayberry mite
19 Cream or cola
22 Easy marks
23 Dignified
25 Bikini half
27 Sea plea
28 Wayfarer's whistle wetter
30 Betty Crocker product
31 Century 21 competitor
32 Essential
33 Doorway part
34 Whichever
35 Stateside Ltd.
36 *Out of Africa* setting
37 Sank down
39 Regular customer
40 Had a ball
41 Meat cut
43 Dreadful
44 Gaping gorges
45 Consul's assistant
47 Deices, in a way
48 Writer Kaufman
50 Antitoxins
51 Tatum's dad
52 Minify a midi, maybe?
53 Plopped down
54 Pipe cleaner?

386 FILM FORECAST by Eric Albert

ACROSS
1 Twist in wood
5 Do the decks
9 Spanish seaport
14 Composer Stravinsky
15 Tiny amount
16 Pure, fresh air
17 Speak without words
18 Nursery furniture
19 Cleanse
20 Eastwood movie of '71
23 Strong craving
24 Pub potable
25 __ Grit
26 Some jump for it
27 Overshoe
28 Turkish topper
31 Love, in Lyons
34 Pairs
35 Be an omen of
36 Kelly movie of '52
39 Misfortunes
40 Foot feature
41 Have as a goal
42 The blue yonder
43 The one and the other
44 Madness?
45 Chevalier song
46 Farm worker
47 Tabloid subject
50 Poitier movie of '61, with *A*
54 Knight fight
55 Advantage
56 Kind of kick
57 Dweller in Dogpatch
58 Noticed
59 *Othello* villain
60 Subway
61 Common condiment
62 Cut out coupons

DOWN
1 Popeye's pal
2 Sprightly
3 Type type
4 Hunted animal
5 Palermo is its capital
6 Inferior
7 Go __ (fight)
8 Fairy's purchase?
9 Duck responsibility
10 Light blue
11 Quad building
12 *Bus Stop* playwright
13 Our omega
21 New Zealand native
22 First-class person?
26 Earthenware vessels
27 *The Brady __*
28 Bubbles
29 Rework words
30 Founder of Stoicism
31 "Functioning or not"
32 Cookies' accompaniment
33 As recently as
34 Filth
35 Cheeseboard choice
37 Country singer Judd
38 Your home
43 Small restaurant
44 Firmly fixed
45 Dough nut?
46 Heavenly being
47 Customary
48 Mold and mildew
49 Doing best
50 After-bath wear
51 Cousin's mother
52 Light-bulb lighter?
53 Homeric specialty
54 Bread spread

387 ECHOIC ADDRESSES by Bob Lubbers

ACROSS
1 Tacks on
5 Statesman Eban et al.
10 CLIV + XLVII
13 IHOP rival
14 Knots
15 Supply with weapons
16 Zoo performer
17 Deft
18 Pom's perch
19 Last Frontier city
21 Location
22 World-weary
24 Wrote graffiti
26 Suffix with profit
27 Opens to view
31 "That's __" (Dean Martin hit)
32 Anti-colonist?
34 Arafat's grp.
35 L.A. suburb
39 Vietnamese holiday
40 Blow up
42 Sellers or Fonda
45 *King Lear* daughter
46 AAA offering
47 Supervise
49 Sitcom afterlife
51 Lion lairs
52 Eastern capital
56 Officeholders
57 *Remington* __
58 Agree (with)
61 Western Indian
62 Scotto or Tebaldi
63 Element
64 Edit. submissions
65 Song opener
66 Omelet ingredients

DOWN
1 Joyful sounds
2 Buck's mate
3 Indonesian capital
4 Arias, e.g.
5 *Three Men* __ *Baby*
6 Conifer covering
7 Studio lamps
8 Similar
9 Heathrow arr.
10 Gingham alternative
11 Volcano feature
12 Block
14 Moo goo __ pan
20 Lincoln and Douglas, e.g.
21 Polynesian islander
22 Actress Arthur
23 Camera part
25 Medieval sport
28 Rat-__
29 Sleep phenom.
30 Wear away
33 Comes in
34 Pocket bread
36 Photog's orig.
37 __-on (wild behavior)
38 Westernmost Aleutian
41 Sundown, to Shelley
42 Speaker's platform
43 Occurrences
44 Tightens up
45 Give way
48 Gobbled up
50 Happen next
53 Yogi or Smokey
54 Choir member
55 Teachers' org.
57 __ Lanka
59 Excavate
60 UFO crew

388 NEAR-MISSES by Karen Hodge

ACROSS
1 Crystallize
5 "What __ mind reader?"
9 Strip in Asia
13 Jai __
14 Protracted
15 Colonial newsman
16 Not quite a thoroughbred?
18 Dance under a bar
19 Sixth sense
20 ". . . ground, to scratch it with __": Warner
21 Actuaries, e.g.
22 Less-than-perfect aide?
24 Committee
28 Mork's planet
29 Suspect's need
30 Cook book
32 Barely open
36 Below-par postal service?
39 Eager
40 Jury member
41 Edge along
42 South American tuber
43 "Farewell, Fernando!"
44 Game-show also-ran?
51 Elate
52 Not as much
53 Confused feeling
56 Really mad
57 Poorly attended party?
59 Disheartening one?
60 Thai tutor
61 Team mates?
62 Baseballer Slaughter
63 Suds from a bar
64 Brontë's governess

DOWN
1 Shade of green
2 Yalies
3 Light source
4 Recline
5 Hi, in HI
6 Nitwit
7 Atlas closeup
8 Get better in the bottle
9 Southern staple
10 Intended
11 Referee, slangily
12 "Ring around __ . . ."
15 Singer Petula
17 Lincoln's first VP
21 Part of RFD
23 Mr. Simpson
24 Cram
25 Healing plant
26 Shade of green
27 Browning's black
30 Lucid
31 Poem of praise
32 Ardent
33 *Star Wars* knights
34 Folk singer Guthrie
35 Bread and booze
37 Florida attraction
38 "Because __!" (authoritarian response)
42 Hold out
44 Electricity
45 Cook wear
46 Mild cigar
47 March toys
48 Coeur d'__, ID
49 Patriot Silas
50 __ as the eye can see
53 Sly
54 Unusual sort
55 Critic Shalit
57 Bill
58 Unhatched fish

389 COOK'S TOUR by Cathy Millhauser

ACROSS

1 Stole stuff
5 Gloomy
9 Guitar accessories
14 Gouda alternative
15 Toy brick brand
16 Hokkaido city
17 Zip, to Zapata
18 West-Coast sch.
19 Bandleader Prado
20 Bake belongings?
23 TV Tarzan
24 Cardiac exits
25 Take five
27 With 47 Across, massage one's pal?
31 Mine car
34 It may be acute
38 Married Mlles.
39 Painter Magritte
40 Made to yawn
41 Prohibition
42 Banks hold them
43 Fava or lima
44 Mare fare
45 Lightens
46 Palo __, CA
47 See 27 Across
49 Student's ordeal
51 Paul Hogan, for one
56 Old witch
58 Char lollipops?
62 Arm
64 Reagan Cabinet member
65 Teamwork obstacles
66 Charge
67 Keystone site
68 Fade away
69 Brick worker
70 Unsurpassed
71 Stallone et al.

DOWN

1 Group of brains
2 Spud state
3 The pits
4 Sears competitor
5 It makes bread tough
6 Mr. Walesa
7 Tangelo type
8 Sound of distress
9 Thicket
10 Had, in a way
11 Skin oaks?
12 Turgenev's birthplace
13 Skier Chaffee
21 Played croupier
22 Mardi __
26 Narrow ridge
28 Imprison
29 String king?
30 Packed
32 "Snowbird" singer Murray
33 Army meal
34 Israel's Eban
35 Greeting-card word
36 Shred pieces?
37 Tanglewood town
42 __ Tho (Vietnamese statesman)
44 *All* __ (Tomlin film)
48 Zero
50 Cottonwood kin
52 Swerves
53 *Love Story* teller
54 Wit with a twist
55 Strauss trio?
56 Skipper's place
57 Blue hue
59 *Pequod* captain
60 Uncommon
61 Unleashes, perhaps
63 "__ to Pieces" ('65 tune)

390 GEOMETRICAL by A.J. Santora

ACROSS

1 Stylish
5 *Fame* name
9 Down with, in Dijon
13 Half steps
15 Suppressed
17 Rehab practitioner
18 Sneezing sound
19 Ed Sullivan's network
20 Pop container
22 Vegas game
23 __-Prayer (phone service)
26 Butcher's special
28 Rocket feature
30 Flat-backed fiddles
31 Plying away
32 Surgeon's request
34 Chimney bottom
36 Euphrates people
39 "Che" Guevara
41 Golden Rule word
43 Pulled one's crate?
45 Colin Powell's bailiwick
47 Increased gradually
49 Envelops
50 "He's __ Picker" (Berlin song)
51 Brad tool
52 Antagonist
53 Helicopter part
55 Simultaneously
60 "Comin' __ Wing and a Prayer" ('43 tune)
61 Use logic
62 Prefix for "while"
63 Glaze basis
64 *Cope Book* aunt

DOWN

1 AR zone
2 Scornful sound
3 __ *Mine* (Harrison bio)
4 Prepare to resist
5 Fox documentary show
6 Sajak sale
7 Damsel's hero
8 Take __ at (try)
9 King of Judah
10 Starting-over direction
11 Close behind
12 Part of ASAP
14 *Cigare* filler
16 Alcove
21 __ *Sunday* ('60 film)
23 Genes designer?
24 Speck
25 Sale condition
26 Hundred-dollar bill
27 "To __ little glass of wine . . ."
29 "Song __" (Rimsky-Korsakov)
33 Made footnotes
35 Ins. abbr.
37 Ms. Swenson
38 Check
40 Bee participant
42 Come-__ (lures)
43 Guthrie of theatre
44 Protagoras or Pericles
46 "It takes __ tango"
47 __ *passu* (fairly)
48 Tower over
52 Stop food
54 Scoundrel
56 *Love Story* composer
57 Scand. country
58 __ laude
59 Homeric character

391   IN THE MAIL by Shirley Soloway

ACROSS
1 Tater
5 Irene of *Fame*
9 Starts fishing
14 Rocker Turner
15 Cassini of fashion
16 "__ of Old Smokey"
17 Hertz competitor
18 Director Wertmuller
19 *A Bell for __*
20 Precisely
23 Ran into
24 *Remington __*
25 Assembles
27 Deep breath
29 Becomes rigid
32 The Cumberland __
35 Actress Durbin
38 Kansas senator
39 Wed impulsively
41 __ de Janeiro
42 Mickey or Mighty

43 Passable
44 Blake of *Gunsmoke*
46 Highlander's hat
47 Aquarium denizens
49 Long periods
51 "__ go again!"
54 Write in the margins
58 Actress Lupino
60 Union member, e.g.
62 Jai alai basket
64 __ were (so to speak)
65 Poet Khayyám
66 Join up
67 Sampras of tennis
68 Mexican money
69 Office worker
70 Winter vehicle
71 Crystal gazer

DOWN
1 Sports data
2 Turn on an axis
3 Bring together

4 Short races
5 Prof's place
6 "I cannot tell __"
7 Landlords' income
8 Striped stone
9 Rough
10 *Sanford __ Son*
11 Eradicates
12 Musical quality
13 Catch sight of
21 Leave out
22 James or Place
26 Take apart
28 Injure
30 *Born Free* lioness
31 Appear to be
32 Adventure story
33 Healing plant
34 ASAP
36 Dancer Peeples
37 *And Then There Were __*
40 Skin opening
42 Feudal estate
44 On a cruise

45 Made a contribution
48 Jockey Eddie
50 Razor sharpeners
52 Envelops
53 Defunct car
55 Actress Anouk
56 Poke fun at
57 Bad move
58 Frozen desserts
59 Car scar
61 Refer to
63 Perfect rating

392   WRITERS CRAMPED by Dean Niles

ACROSS
1 Theater success
5 Repairs
10 Labor Day mo.
14 Frosted
15 Principle
16 Llama land
17 *Sons and Lovers* author
19 Religious image
20 Tippler
21 Employ
22 Bean or pea
24 Dollar division
25 Actress Claire
26 Swear in
29 Leading advocate
32 Sneak along
33 Cautions
34 "__ Got Rhythm"
35 Ancient history
36 *Peer Gynt* composer
37 Tackle a bone
38 A pig __ poke
39 Chan portrayer
40 Bear and Berra
41 Unmarried
43 Picayune

44 Setter type
45 Musical group
46 "__ Army" (Palmer's fans)
48 Mr. Disney
49 Hoopsters' org.
52 Old clothes
53 *The Hobbit* author
56 Canadian Amerind
57 Shot and __ (bar order)
58 Network
59 Towel word
60 Like Chicago
61 Very slender

DOWN
1 Commands
2 __ Rios, Jamaica
3 Fedora fabric
4 Pharm. watchdog
5 Gomer Pyle, for one
6 Put into use
7 Workday start, for many

8 "What's up, __?"
9 __ salts (stimulant)
10 Faucet
11 *Tulips and Chimneys* author
12 High-school formal
13 Melody
18 "__ or When"
23 Forever and ever
24 Religious sect
25 Stifling a yawn
26 Meat jelly
27 Arbus or Sawyer
28 *The Catcher in the Rye* author
29 Pamphleteer Thomas
30 Be of use
31 Full of the latest
33 Rage
36 Boxer's bane
37 Egg on
39 Theater award
40 Streisand film

42 Spring bloomers
43 *Le Morte d'Arthur* writer
45 With __ breath (in suspense)
46 Curved structure
47 Seldom seen
48 Small songbird
49 Robert De __
50 '60s lovefest
51 Rooney or Griffith
54 Slugger's stat
55 USSR CIA

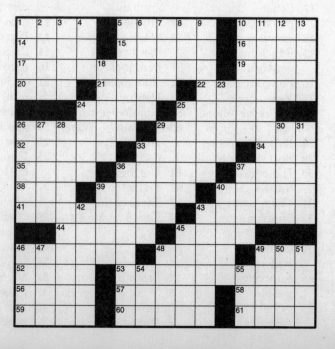

393 NAME THAT TOON by Matt Gaffney

ACROSS
1 Italian bread?
5 Downhill equipment
9 Fuzzy
12 Like Nash's lama
13 Actress Louise
14 Do a double take, perhaps
16 Wascally wabbit . . .
18 . . . and his cwazy enemy
19 Botched effort
20 Umpire's call
22 Santa __, CA
23 Wallace of *Cujo*
24 Bat wood
27 Danish cheese
29 Candy __ (hospital volunteer)
32 Heat again
33 *Año* opener
34 Farm measure
35 Batty bird
41 World's Fair

42 Reeves of *River's Edge*
43 Indirect route
46 Hoards
49 Appalachian range
51 __ *Rosenkavalier*
52 Tear apart
54 Lean-__ (sheds)
55 Follow closely
57 "__ for yourself!"
59 Author Jong
61 Demented drake
64 Helicopter part
65 Nobelist Wiesel
66 Margarine
67 Hot off the press
68 Level-headed
69 Hard to find

DOWN
1 Like ears
2 Habituates
3 Kick oneself
4 To boot

5 R-V link
6 Relatives
7 Rural hotels
8 Doctor's directive
9 Md. neighbor
10 Simon & Garfunkel hit
11 Reba of country music
14 Superman portrayer
15 Mobile home
17 Intellectual
21 Out of the way
25 Gush forth
26 Man of the hour
28 Problem solver?
30 Hardwood tree
31 Swindles
35 Emmanuel Lewis sitcom
36 Jumbo shrimp, e.g.
37 Antonym
38 With 45 Down, scroll site
39 Do the driveway

40 Get-up-and-go
44 Shankar's specialty
45 See 38 Down
47 Actress Andress
48 Two-__ (swimsuit)
50 Teams

53 Tea type
56 Tra-__
58 Foul stench
60 Bull's beloved
62 Shark giveaway
63 Lawyer's charge

394 ALL THAT JAZZ by Charles E. Gersch

ACROSS
1 Go __ for (defend)
6 Summer cooler
9 Ignoble
13 "Softly, __ dream"
14 New Orleans jazz style
17 New Orleans' nickname
19 Liqueur flavoring
20 Gets to
21 Pro-gun grp.
22 Capillary kin
24 British gun
25 Short drive
27 New Orleans cuisine
30 Adjectival suffix
31 G.B., for one
33 Visionary
37 New Orleans university
39 Bonzo nosh
40 Euripides heroine

42 "For shame!"
43 Fix a fight
44 Raspy
46 Slaps on
47 The A train?
50 Nehru's successor
53 Herr's hearer
54 __ strict line (conform rigidly)
56 Town
58 "__ New Orleans" ('20s tune)
62 Where New Orleans is
63 Eared seal
64 Harbors: Abbr.
65 Stand for
66 Sits down

DOWN
1 Make lace
2 Job-safety org.
3 New Orleans' founder
4 __ régime (pre-1789 French rulers)
5 Ankles

6 Classified info
7 More risky
8 Put out
9 Casino action
10 Chem. compound
11 New Orleans footballer
12 __ nous
15 Squid's weapon
16 Actress Cannon
18 Shelley's sundown
23 Exp. opposite
24 Penn or Young
25 Where it's at
26 Actor Newman
28 Baby blues
29 Security problem
31 Up on
32 Antitoxins
34 New Orleans party time
35 Oklahoma town
36 Joplin pieces
38 Rubdown target
41 Magazine
42 Japanese export
45 Gumshoe Mike

46 Stopped, in the French Quarter
47 Go for strikes
48 Total disorder
49 "Quit babbling!"
51 Book's ID no.
52 Royal house

54 Prepare salad
55 WWII news agcy.
57 New Orleans trumpeter
59 E, to Morse
60 Quaker grain
61 Gov. Cuomo's concern

395 QUIET INSIDE! by Randolph Ross

ACROSS
1 Slightly open
5 Trotter's tootsy
9 Kitchen gadget
14 Mustached modern artist
15 Jai __
16 __ Gay
17 Broadway successes
19 Coach/commentator Hank
20 Lake Michigan city
22 Pro foe
23 A Touch __ ('73 film)
26 Big-boy sizes
28 Smoked or salted
29 Mini-mounts
30 Scare up
31 Marks a map
32 Bowler, for one
35 Not as much
36 Makes mulligatawny
37 Thanksgiving abbr.
38 Ski material
39 First-place medals
40 Kid stuff?
41 Tweed type
43 Miss Hannigan's charge
44 "Peace Train" singer
46 Arden and Sherwood
48 Ferrer musical
49 Easton and others
51 Gluck et al.
53 Greasy spoon
57 Canines, e.g.
58 Piedmont province
59 Component
60 Helena's competitor
61 Tsp. or in.
62 __ up (get in shape)

DOWN
1 Pitches
2 Toast topper
3 Pie __ mode
4 Safe
5 Otto and Jessica
6 Grab bags
7 Flicka food
8 Cod catchers
9 __ Plaines, IL
10 Absorption
11 Poultry variety
12 Bring bliss
13 Ghostbusters actor Harold
18 Cabbage and lettuce
21 Family members
23 Central Florida city
24 Pollution
25 Indy gear
27 Jackie, to Roseanne
29 Trudges along
31 Easter dinner, perhaps
33 Look at the books
34 Stand fillers
36 Toe travails
37 Ignores
39 SAT's big brother
40 Purcell of Real People
42 Emulate Earhart
44 Roofing material
45 Mah-jongg pieces
46 Roman holiday?
47 "__ Blindness" (Milton work)
50 Life of Riley
52 Yonder yacht
54 Juan's one
55 Transgression
56 When Strasbourg sizzles

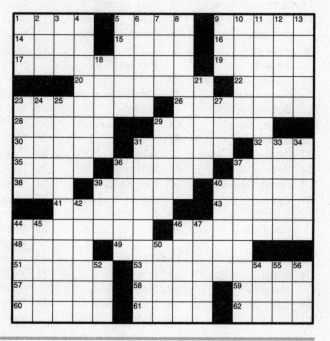

396 ZILCH by Eric Albert

ACROSS
1 Require a rubdown
5 Grate stuff
10 Shopper's paradise
14 Donkey's cry
15 Canary's cry
16 Bassoon relative
17 '60s phrase
20 Lamb's kin
21 In the bag
22 Surrounded by
23 James of Brian's Song
24 Soft cheese
25 Descend upon
28 Asks for alms
29 Janitor's item
32 Valerie Harper sitcom
33 Bill of fare
34 Of sound mind
35 Fin de siècle epithet
38 Archer or Jackson
39 Birdhouse visitor
40 Elevator tunes
41 Oxford omega
42 Funnyman Sahl
43 Actress Tyson
44 Racer's gauge
45 Stocking material
46 Glacial period
49 Singer of Hollywood
50 "The Greatest"
53 Hanks/Gleason drama
56 Chanel of fashion
57 Indian language
58 Crazed
59 Tennis ace Arthur
60 "The final frontier"
61 Slow

DOWN
1 Fit for the job
2 Emulate a rooster
3 __ Gun Will Travel
4 Spud bud
5 Bona fide
6 Fleeced
7 Roll-call response
8 Sushi selection
9 Thunderball prop
10 The reel thing
11 Undercover?
12 The Daily Planet's Lane
13 Latvian
18 Biblical prophet
19 Brest buddies
23 Bum
24 Dahomey, today
25 Ball's costar
26 1953 western
27 Talkies' attraction
28 Stephen Vincent __
29 Indian ears
30 Ryan or Tatum
31 Kid-brotherish
33 42 Down gift
34 Puzzled
36 Conversation contribution?
37 Actor Estevez
42 Star followers
43 Hem in
44 Resort lake
45 Type of boom
46 Pizarro victim
47 Speaks softly
48 Engrave
49 Kind of bean
50 Bullets and bombs
51 Take a peek
52 Totally black
54 Breach
55 Put on the __ (make famous)

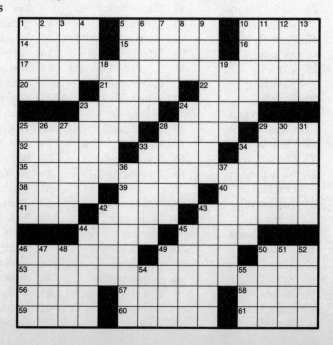

397 MORE ZILCH by Fred Piscop

ACROSS
1 ABC rival
4 "__ Breaky Heart"
8 Group of lions
13 Secular
14 Tried-and-__
15 *Bolero* composer
16 Egyptian cross
17 Mrs. Chaplin
18 Basketballer Shaquille
19 They may be whispered in your ear
22 *Amateur Hour* host
23 Society-column word
24 *People __ Funny*
25 North Pole worker
27 Mess specialist
31 __ Domingo
34 Zorba or Jimmy
36 Drivers' org.
37 Claims to public land
40 "The Boy King"
41 Mules and moccasins
42 Telegraphy code
43 Window frame
45 Olden times, in olden times
46 Workweek start: Abbr.
47 Superlative suffix
49 Beach footwear
53 *Song of the South* tune
56 Israeli seaport
58 Hoss' brother
59 Actress Anderson
60 Doubleday or Yokum
61 __ 18 (Uris novel)
62 St. Louis sight
63 Bolivian city
64 Hammer part
65 "I told you so!"

DOWN
1 "__ talk?": Joan Rivers
2 Did the Tour de France
3 Plans
4 Right away
5 Shepherd's staff
6 Peck partner
7 "She Loves You" word
8 Lying flat
9 Kitchen appliances
10 Currier's partner
11 Narc's org.
12 Building addition
13 Wear well
20 Seer's cards
21 Have a hunch
25 Slipped up
26 Minus
28 Cowardly Lion portrayer
29 Feedbag filler
30 Foundation
31 JFK landers
32 Blue hue
33 Bonkers
34 An earth sci.
35 Japanese robe
38 Eta follower
39 Venetian traffic
44 Young cow
46 Lunatic
48 Trunk item
49 '60s activist Bobby
50 Idolize
51 Jousting weapon
52 __ Tzu (Tibetan dog)
53 Brass component
54 Clammy
55 Singer Adams
56 Owns
57 __ Dhabi

398 THIS BUD'S FOR YOU by Matt Gaffney

ACROSS
1 Stomach flattener
6 Genetic letters
9 Become engaged
13 Largest artery
14 Sgts. and cpls.
15 Montreal player
16 Lover
18 Don't dele
19 Bronco's lunch
20 "__ Woman" (Reddy hit)
21 Mosque feature
23 Lust after
25 Filmed again
26 Run-of-the-mill
29 Exist
30 __ *Solemnis*
31 Strong as __
32 *Wayne's World* word
33 Southwestern sight
34 "It Had to Be __"
35 Munich's locale
37 Youngster
40 Nutritional amts.
42 Actor Beatty
43 *Beetle Bailey* bulldog
44 Zeus' shield
46 Coupe grp.?
47 Yes votes
48 Sipped slowly
50 Cunning
52 First Triumvirate member
54 "__ Were a Carpenter"
55 Shot
58 Clinton's hometown
59 Idaho-Montana range
62 Store-window sign
63 Sore
64 Confection
65 Musical symbol
66 Turner or Pappas
67 Wing

DOWN
1 Waist band
2 *State Fair* state
3 Deck member
4 Colorado Indian
5 Barbecue area
6 Zenith rival
7 Comic Crosby
8 Bustling
9 Avignon address
10 Pretzel variety
11 Does 85
12 Scones' accompaniment
14 Pulitzer poet Howard
17 Fine cigars
22 Herculean labor site
23 Peepers portrayer
24 Lockjaw
26 For instance
27 Lennon's lady
28 Fox's rationalization
33 Birthing specialist
35 Triangle parts
36 It's the truth
38 Wolfed down
39 John __ Passos
41 Conflict
43 Mighty tree
44 Brokaw or Rather
45 Common Market locale
49 One of the Emirates
51 Around, datewise
53 Under the weather
55 Beethoven's birthplace
56 Portend
57 Charon's river
60 Common article
61 Kurosawa epic

FIRST FAMILY by Trip Payne

ACROSS
1 Indian state
6 Physique, for short
9 Ina of *The Black Orchid*
14 *The Great __ Pepper*
15 Silly Charlotte
16 Singer Turner's autobiography
17 Three-time Masters winner
18 "__ no wonder!"
19 Porous
20 Tenzing Norgay's companion
23 Wild plums
24 All-purpose exclamations
25 Sound sleepers?
28 Maximally
31 Numbers for one
32 Josip Broz
33 Shooter ammo
35 AFC champs in '91
40 Toper
41 Drug buster
42 Ewes' guys?
43 Slogan
45 Try to hit
48 Actress Taina
49 Disdain
50 Thomas Carlyle's sobriquet
55 Miles of jazz
56 Card game
57 Seeps out
59 Ring or rink
60 Plastic __ Band
61 Engine sounds
62 Grant's real first name
63 Toothpaste type
64 Collar needs

DOWN
1 "Isn't that cute!" sounds
2 All there
3 Iditarod vehicle
4 Hepburn/Tracy movie
5 The "M" of LEM
6 They're given away
7 "Egad!" and "Zounds!"
8 Lucie's father
9 Thornton of *Hearts Afire*
10 Colonel's command
11 He's fabulous
12 Pitch-black
13 Senate vote
21 Postal Creed word
22 Bingo relative
25 VIP transports
26 Not at all
27 Singer Adams
28 Be out of sorts
29 Water-balloon sound
30 Actress Hopkins
32 *Tic __ Dough*
34 Little helper?
36 Poster pointer
37 Red River city
38 Use a spider
39 Resolves a problem
44 Taylor of *I'll Fly Away*
45 Porpoise pack
46 Weed beater
47 Low decks
49 Teatime treat
50 Gujarat garb
51 Maintain
52 Beat hard
53 Old Testament book
54 Eaglet's home
55 Morse click
58 Draft agcy.

BIRTHRIGHT by Donna J. Stone

ACROSS
1 Ms. Minnelli
5 Clanton foe
9 Kitchen kingpin
13 Mr. Hershiser
14 Take in, perhaps
15 Vegetate
16 START OF A QUIP
19 Writer Hentoff
20 "... __ shall die"
21 Left no stone unturned
22 Places for patches
24 Antiquity, in antiquity
25 Select
28 Fabric ornament
33 Slowly, to Solti
34 *M*A*S*H* star
35 Em or Bee
36 Chemical suffix
37 SPEAKER OF THE QUIP
40 Columbus campus, briefly
41 Hose mishap
43 Thailand neighbor
44 "¿Cómo está __?"
46 California city
48 Belong
49 Ending for Capri
50 Warbucks, for one
52 *Marcus Welby, M.D.* actress
56 Patriotic org.
57 Symbol of wisdom
60 END OF QUIP
63 Shoot down
64 Rocket starter
65 *Show Boat* composer
66 Dumb __ ox
67 "Hey, you!"
68 Intaglio material

DOWN
1 Kind of roast
2 Role for Shirley
3 Citrus peel
4 *Freedom Road* star
5 J.R.'s mama
6 Had some hash
7 Confederates
8 Moral laws
9 Mrs. Lyndon Johnson
10 Appointment-book division
11 In addition
12 Hightailed it
14 Come to terms
17 Sarge, e.g.
18 Dict. type
22 Baby beaver
23 Snore
25 Anklet feature
26 Eastern dye
27 *Superfly* star Ron
29 Mrs. Smith's specialty
30 Bartlett bit
31 Big name at Indy
32 Clementi piece
34 Pants part
38 *Moby-Dick*, for instance
39 Permafrost area
42 Todman's partner
45 Deficient
47 "... three men in __"
48 Spud state
51 Texas athlete
52 __ *Villa!*
53 Meadow mamas
54 Pro follower
55 Hydrox competitor
57 Writer Wister
58 Guarded
59 Mercury model
61 Ultimate
62 Bowe stat

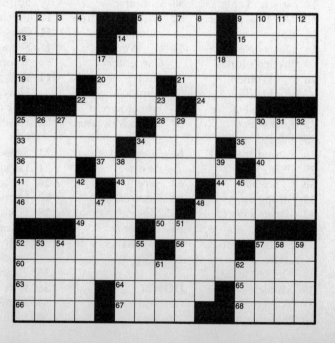

401 ELEMENTARY by Dean Niles

ACROSS
1 Jr.-year exam
5 Wove a web
9 Dawn goddess
12 French girlfriend
13 Domingo, for one
15 __ *Ado About Nothing*
17 Lady's man?
18 Lift up
19 Meany
20 __ foo yung
21 Fertility symbol
23 Combine
25 Kind of punch
26 Three in one
28 Macadamized
30 Big name in applesauce
31 Fresco, for one
32 Pugilists' org.
35 Greek vowels
36 Quebec city
37 Columnist Herb
38 Hide-hair link
39 Tropical fish
40 Filled to the gills
41 Greets, in a way
42 Defensive back
43 Sock style
46 Passover meal
47 Fourth of July item
50 Actress Farrow
53 "__ a Name" (Croce tune)
54 Hailing from Honshu
55 Practical jokes
56 Overdo the sentiment
57 "Whole __ Love" ('70 song)
58 Fox follower?
59 Letter additions: Abbr.
60 Service charges
61 Creole veggie

DOWN
1 Colorless
2 Urban blight
3 Invisible instrument
4 Senator Kennedy
5 Attack from above
6 Pole star?
7 Moon __ Zappa
8 Snack
9 Chewed the scenery
10 Must
11 Tighten with a tool
14 Elimination
16 Submarine sandwich
21 One, in Wiesbaden
22 Scott Turow book
24 Sundae topping
26 Govt. agents
27 Printing process
28 Catty remarks?
29 Region
31 Speck of dust
32 Stationery feature
33 Borscht ingredient
34 Actor Garcia
36 More than a couple
37 __ au lait
39 Lauder powder
40 Iran's Bani-__
41 Artistic family
42 Regarded to be
43 Not give __ (be indifferent)
44 Construct haphazardly
45 Before deductions
46 Emulate Kristi
48 From
49 Make a footnote
51 Composer Stravinsky
52 Movie terrier
55 Former Pontiac model

402 FOUR GO by Shirley Soloway

ACROSS
1 October birthstone
5 Strike ignorer
9 Lord or Lady
14 Capital of Peru
15 Hercules' love
16 *The Woman __* ('84 film)
17 Superman's sweetie
18 Wordy Webster
19 Changes the text
20 DINGO
23 Filming session
24 Bud's buddy
25 Step on the __ (hurry)
28 LINGO
32 Rock band's need
35 Slightly moist
36 Jocular Johnson
37 Campus digs
39 Watery fluid
42 Critic Rex
43 Pavarotti piece
44 ". . . baked in __"
46 Shingle letters
47 BINGO
52 Catch sight of
53 *Norma __*
54 "To __ human . . ."
57 RINGO
62 Silvery fish
64 *Doctor Zhivago* character
65 Concerned with
66 Singer Della
67 Egg-shaped
68 High time?
69 Strongboxes
70 Puts in stitches
71 Sicilian spewer

DOWN
1 __ podrida
2 Reverent
3 Pennsylvania sect
4 *The __ the Mohicans*
5 Frank and Nancy
6 Self-possessed
7 Jai __
8 On __ of (representing)
9 Unavailable
10 __-European
11 Set off
12 Give permission
13 Asner and Wynn
21 Crucifix
22 Calculator figs.
26 Made believe
27 Lean-tos
29 Married Mlle.
30 Talk-show host Winfrey
31 Corn portion
32 Proverb
33 Tropical eel
34 Top-quality meat
38 West of Hollywood
40 "__ Lazy River"
41 Iron and calcium
45 Light tan
48 Speaks one's piece
49 Dieter's no-no
50 Stringed instruments
51 Winter weasel
55 *__ Rappaport*
56 Novelist Anya
58 "What __ can I say?"
59 Icicle site
60 Sketch
61 Gossipy Barrett
62 SAT takers
63 "Cry __ River"

403 WHERE'S LADY BIRD? by Matt Gaffney

ACROSS

1 Amazing act
5 Muffin topping?
9 Schwarzenegger's hometown
13 Tear down
14 Dizzying designs
16 Seize the day
17 Part of QED
18 The winter's tail?
19 Unlocked
20 Top fashion model
23 "__ is me!"
24 Word on a dime
25 Hot topic
27 Humiliate
29 Fond du __, WI
31 Oolong, e.g.
32 __ Can (Sammy Davis book)
33 Corinth's country
36 GA's zone
37 *The Golden Girls* actress
40 Clear (of)
43 Emulate Fred Noonan
44 Pieces' partners
48 Be in debt
49 Mousse alternative
50 Delaware senator
51 Clavell's __ *House*
53 Grass à la mowed?
55 Triumphant exclamation
56 West Virginia senator
61 One of the Jacksons
62 Celebrity bash
63 Joyce's land
64 Sherman Hemsley sitcom
65 Shampoo-bottle word
66 Nicholas or Ivan
67 Ezio Pinza, for one
68 Shifty glance
69 Chicks' moms

DOWN

1 Express road
2 Stud site
3 Showy shrubs
4 Head of France?
5 __ *Holiday*
6 Quickly
7 Irving hero
8 Keystone's place
9 Sheen
10 Clever comeback
11 Boulevards
12 Buddhist movement
15 Useful article
21 Curly poker?
22 Houston coll.
26 Feast on fries
28 Bro or sis
29 Riga resident
30 Flu symptom
33 Donated
34 Staircase part
35 History division
38 Gung-ho
39 Baseball stat
40 Director Howard
41 WWII locale
42 Lincoln-Douglas encounters
45 Put on a pedestal
46 Mideast capital
47 Noisy nappers
50 "See ya!"
52 City on the Rhone
53 *Steppenwolf* author
54 In search of
57 Hockey legend Bobby
58 Wind
59 *Citizen* __
60 Mr. Walesa
61 Filing aid

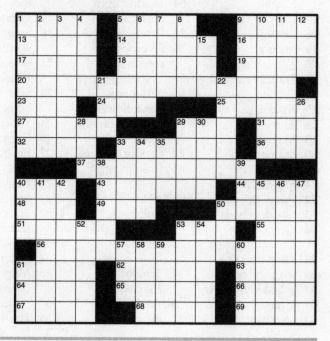

404 GEOLOGIZING by A.J. Santora

ACROSS

1 Coal container
4 Ailing, perhaps
8 Exercise target
12 "It's __-win situation!"
13 Tower town
15 Melodious McEntire
16 Geometry suffix
17 California course
19 New Hampshire's nickname
21 Monastery heads
22 "I never saw __ cow . . ."
26 __ *Happy* (Elvis film)
27 Driller's deg.?
29 Decrease?
30 Dulles abbr.
31 Mouthy Martha
33 Impassioned
35 Like some jeans
38 Inner self
40 Show
41 "This __ test"
44 Pumice source
45 Hearty bread
46 Luke's book
47 "Diddle Diddle Dumpling" footwear
50 From the heart?
52 Carole King song
55 Bakery favorites
58 Deli choice
59 *Rigoletto* rendition
60 Lineal start
61 Kapaa keepsake
62 Peteman
63 Boggy stuff
64 Computer key: Abbr.

DOWN

1 Impediments
2 Like *Galileo*
3 Emollient
4 Fosters a felon
5 Woods dweller?
6 Abates
7 Mouth features?
8 Something for nothing
9 Actress Thompson
10 Easy as __
11 Crank's comment
14 *Quantum* __
17 Cherry center
18 A/C measure
20 See 24 Down
23 Easily forecast
24 With 20 Down, Cambodian leader
25 Otolaryngologist's field: Abbr.
27 Tint
28 Truman opponent
31 *Palais* personage
32 Tiny toiler
33 Nile reptile
34 Letter from Athens
36 Refuse repository
37 Medieval weapon
38 Exit letters
39 Critic's god?
42 Puts down
43 Epicure's antithesis
45 Porter
46 Eyebrow shape
48 Holbrook or Roach
49 Utah city
50 Make the grade
51 Certifies
53 Rank high
54 Gumbo thickener
55 New Jersey cape
56 Live
57 Equipment

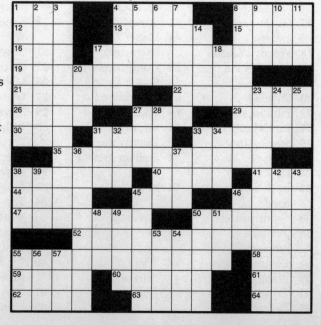

405 SOUNDS OF THE CITIES by Bob Carroll

ACROSS
1 Reply to the Little Red Hen
5 Iraqi port
10 Study hard
14 Gemayel of Lebanon
15 Functioned
16 __-my-thumb
17 Inventor visibly aged?
19 Brainstorm
20 Not as far
21 Make out
23 Snare
24 Diogenes, for one
25 Had a meeting
28 "There __ crooked man . . ."
30 Looks daggers
34 Very French?
36 Yrs. and yrs.
38 October 31 option
39 Em, to Dorothy
40 *Songs in the __ Life* (Stevie Wonder album)
42 Bananas
43 Speaker's request

45 Barbie or Ken
46 Nev. neighbor
47 They buy hot stuff
49 Roulette bet
51 *The Ghost and __ Muir*
52 Handles
54 Bite a bit
56 "__ Fire" (Doors hit)
59 Gas asset
62 Singer Pinza
63 Thorn in the Enlightened One's side?
66 Standard
67 NYC neighborhood
68 __ *Called Horse*
69 Unemployed
70 Fix the brakes
71 Yahoo

DOWN
1 Arrest
2 Straw in the wind
3 Word-game piece

4 Altar acquisition
5 Sans saddle
6 Rent-__
7 Grunter's grounds
8 Sounding like an oboe
9 Calculating
10 Truckload of Diors?
11 Took a trolley
12 Impressionist
13 Horror-film sound effect
18 Shot up
22 Delta stuff
24 Grand and Bryce
25 Crook
26 As __ (usually)
27 Mortise's mate
29 Origin
31 Get guns again
32 Rarin' to go
33 Forest males
35 Cattle ranch?
37 Unaccompanied
41 Pulled back

44 Flat rate?
48 Grave
50 Ms. Moreno
53 __ of (through)
55 Kind of cross
56 Director Riefenstahl
57 Sportswear maker

58 Beatles tune of '65
59 "How __ coincidence!"
60 *Nautilus* skipper
61 Jacob's twin
64 Pickpocket
65 It's a real blast

406 TIMELY PHRASES by Eric Albert

ACROSS
1 Dismal dwelling
6 '60s dance
10 Exercise aftermath
14 Mrs. Kramden
15 Greek liqueur
16 Egg on
17 Dotage
20 Currently popular
21 __ *Man Flint*
22 Too sentimental
23 Desert refuge
26 Slog along
27 Soul singer Gaye
29 Horn honk
30 *60 Minutes* network
33 White as a sheet
34 *Scarlett* setting
35 Not give __ (be indifferent)
36 Coveted shape
39 Wild revelry
40 Drama award
41 Grayish tan

42 New beginning?
43 Banned insulators: Abbr.
44 Made a muscle
45 Puttering
46 Singer Lenya
47 Houston team
50 Binge
51 __ Lanka
54 Thriller of '73, with *The*
58 Short swims
59 Viscount's superior
60 Pull a fast one
61 __ gin fizz
62 Freshwater fish
63 Bashful colleague

DOWN
1 Leftover dish
2 Butter substitute
3 Quasimodo's creator
4 Author Umberto
5 Spy-novelist Deighton

6 Adjust a camera
7 German valley
8 Israeli weapon
9 Gilding metal
10 Plant pest
11 Cut short
12 Earring shape
13 Circular current
18 Rub out
19 Quit, as a course
24 Comic Schreiber
25 Vocalize
26 In itself
27 Ed Mc__
28 Stick out like __ thumb
29 Foundation
30 *Pacific Princess*, for one
31 Freight boat
32 Risk a ticket
34 Striped cat
35 Bond or Smart
37 March style
38 "Yeah, sure"
43 Vanishing sound

44 West African country
45 Everyday language
46 Big dipper
47 Appends
48 Leave port

49 Secretary's error
50 Pull sharply
52 Pilaf ingredient
53 Dark as night
55 "Bali __"
56 Inc., in England
57 Favoring

407 BOX SCORE by Dean Niles

ACROSS

1 Author Kingsley
5 How-to part
9 Find fault
13 "__ you be my neighbor?"
14 Actress O'Neal
16 Exploits
17 *Against All __*
18 Basketball venue
19 Without
20 Hawaiian garland
21 Satisfies
23 Lee of *The Fall Guy*
25 Gobbled up
26 Pecs' partners
27 Drop out
32 Bandleader Artie
35 *__ Shelter* (Rolling Stones film)
36 "The loneliest number"
37 Outdoes
41 Baba beginning
42 Adult insect
43 Some necklines
44 Digestive gland
46 Doctor's charge
48 Augsburg article
49 Painted or drew
52 Non-mechanical failures
57 Quick punch
59 Colorful fish
60 Swarms
61 He may be up to Paar
62 Sun. magazine section
63 Camp David visitor
64 Septi- successor
65 Hill dwellers
66 Coloratura Lily
67 Hold back

DOWN

1 Army offender
2 Computer accessory
3 *A Passage to __*
4 Ave. crossers
5 One way up
6 Little pies
7 Soissons seasons
8 Soccer kick
9 Said "Dang!"
10 Relative of PDQ
11 Casino city
12 "Hey, you!"
15 Gandhi honorific
21 Prefix for "goblin"
22 Early anesthetic
24 Gripping movie?
27 Eccentric
28 "__ Excited" (Pointer Sisters hit)
29 Libertine
30 Novelist Rice
31 Takes the plunge
32 Sp. ladies
33 A shake in the grass?
34 Indigo plant
35 Snarl
38 Split apart
39 Turkish inns
40 Hot spot
45 Baking potatoes
46 Guinness specialties
47 Some dashes
49 Miller's Willy
50 Kick out
51 Beatrice's beau
52 Israeli dance
53 "Once __ a time..."
54 Actor Dillon
55 Harvest the crop
56 Try again
58 Explosive sound
61 __ Alamos, NM

408 NO END IN SIGHT by Alice Long

ACROSS

1 Terrible time?
5 B-vitamin acid
10 Smoker and diner
14 Act the drifter
15 __ ten (rating scale)
16 Touched down
17 Stretch
18 Indian, e.g.
19 Refute
20 Cause for a draw at the board
23 S-shaped molding
24 Bolt down
25 Inches along
28 Medic
33 "__ quack, there..."
34 *Planet of the Apes* setting
35 Tin Woodsman prop
36 Staple of melodramas
39 Confessional confession
40 Film-set shots
41 Divided, in a way
42 Commit arson
44 Plague
45 Grid position
46 Membrane opening
47 Long, long time
54 Retreat
55 *Home __*
56 Trig term
57 Doing nothing
58 Dialer's concerns
59 Microwave, for one
60 Gusto
61 Prepared to be knighted
62 Brokaw's beat

DOWN

1 Drainpipe part
2 Sported
3 "Moon __ Miami"
4 Strong nation, nautically
5 Author Shelby and family
6 Perfectly timed
7 Mr. Iacocca
8 Type type, for short
9 Orchestral offerings
10 Plebes, e.g.
11 Evelyn's brother
12 Ice Capades workplace
13 Boar-ed room?
21 Sweetbrier
22 Helter-skelter
25 Topic of 20 Across
26 Fix a cravat
27 "__ we all?"
28 Phoebe of *Gremlins*
29 Hockey's Bobby et al.
30 __ Carta
31 Wheel shafts
32 Essentials
34 Actress Sommer
37 Early animal, alphabetically
38 "Just 'cause I felt like it!"
43 Black weasel
44 "No, really!"
46 Game-show group
47 Wash out
48 Canvas cover?
49 Oomph
50 Learning method
51 Seedy joint
52 From the top
53 Itches
54 Designer Claiborne

409 OPTICAL ALLUSIONS by Cathy Millhauser

ACROSS
1 Bow or Barton
6 Rigatoni kin
10 Toody and Muldoon
14 Actor Warren
15 __ impulse (spontaneously)
16 Field of study
17 Putting tattersall on a tote?
20 Sandwich cookie
21 Compete
22 Chula __, CA
23 Pakistan neighbor
25 Hot chamber
27 Making lines on a perch?
33 Honored with a party
34 Trace
35 "Am I right?"
36 Sailed through
37 Genesis disaster
39 Analyze poetry
40 Pine product
41 Rosenberg of *Civil Wars*
42 In pieces
43 Adding polka dots to slips?
47 Can't stand
48 Evasive phrase
49 Mystery award
52 Rhoda's mom
53 George or Victoria
57 Depicting drapery?
61 Scrutinize
62 Bar order
63 Dome home
64 "Good grief!"
65 Cryptographer's concern
66 Nuisances

DOWN
1 Ms. Chanel
2 He had a mane role
3 To __ (precisely)
4 Drew back
5 Say please
6 City-planner's concern
7 *Bus Stop* playwright
8 Way, out East?
9 Bedding setting
10 Betting setting
11 Shakespeare's spheres
12 __ moss
13 It's a long story
18 Director Reitman
19 Turn inside out
24 Free (of)
25 Columbus' milieu
26 Peddle
27 News in a nutshell
28 In __ (unborn)
29 Flip-flop
30 Prize of a guy
31 Burns a bit
32 It may be pitched
33 Antoine Domino
37 Dart about
38 Cugat ex
39 Summer food problem
41 Coleco competitor
42 Graphic stuff?
44 Became friendlier
45 Wear well
46 Sound like Simba
49 On __ (tense)
50 Wet blanket
51 Mideast strip
52 Topped a cake
54 Troubles
55 Long-hair hassle
56 Those, in Toledo
58 *SNL* network
59 Prizm or Storm
60 Prepare to pour

410 ROMANESQUE by Trip Payne

ACROSS
1 Viking name
5 Reduced
10 Early TV comedy
14 Hawaiian seaport
15 Steal the spotlight, maybe
16 "Look __ this way . . ."
17 After-school treat
18 *Roots* role
19 Tahoe town
20 54
23 News detector?
24 Davis of *Evening Shade*
25 Common expression
28 Muffin ingredient
31 Chariot terminus
32 30
36 Captain Hook's sidekick
37 Sprang up
38 Amneris' opera
42 1101
45 __ Altos, CA
48 Snake charmer's crew
49 Election or anniversary
50 Tilting, to a tar
52 "Dies __"
54 1009
60 One of a pair
61 Follow, as advice
62 The mad scientist's assistant
64 Suit to __
65 __ Ste. Marie, Ontario
66 Agatha's colleague
67 Popularity-contest loser
68 Ship crew
69 The mind's I?

DOWN
1 Melodramatic cry
2 Papal money?
3 Actor Baldwin
4 Paper feature
5 Lap dogs
6 Tickle one's fancy
7 Guidry and Santo
8 Caesar said it
9 Wheel partner
10 Schoolhouse employees
11 Relaxed, in the army
12 She's a Pearl
13 Repentant one
21 "Arrivederci, __"
22 Burt's ex
25 Taggers
26 Turn down
27 Pushcart purchase
28 Big helps
29 Hinge
30 Blows away
33 Saturn and Mercury
34 Lose one's footing
35 Green qualities
39 "__ got it!"
40 Actor Castellaneta
41 Supermodel Carol
43 Popular hors d'oeuvre
44 Parent
45 Sheriff or deputy
46 Ester type
47 *My __ Eileen*
51 Silver or Scout
52 "__ you so!"
53 Carries on
55 Hasty
56 Mar. madness sponsor
57 Phaser setting
58 Grimm creature
59 Gunsel's gal
63 Foul caller

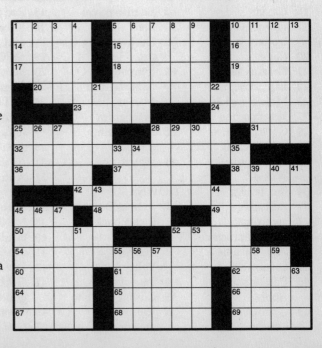

411 AT THE OFFICE by Mary E. Brindamour

ACROSS

1 Rosemary or thyme
5 Fancy cravat
10 Chits
14 Screenwriter James
15 Trouser material
16 Slow-witted
17 Secretary's machine
19 Sicilian volcano
20 Antipollution grp.
21 Up-front
22 Blind as __
23 Fashions
25 Bruins' sch.
27 Fiery felony
30 Grapple, down South
33 Archbishop of Canterbury's headdress
36 Like a lion
38 Actress Novak
39 Got by, with "out"
40 Uses a stopwatch
41 Trucker's rig
42 Toothpaste type
43 *For __ Sake* ('74 film)
44 Cook for a crowd?
45 Letter sign-off
47 Begin
49 Jack of *The Tonight Show*
50 Playground fixture
54 Diamond Head's island
56 Sergeant's order
60 Lawyers' org.
61 Army offender
62 Accountant's tool
64 Camper's shelter
65 Hot coal
66 Earsplitting
67 Observes
68 Shovel's kin
69 Industrious insects

DOWN

1 Despises
2 Tut's territory
3 Settle a debt
4 Opie's aunt
5 Puzzle heading
6 Leg part
7 Summon to court
8 Dollar bills
9 Plagues
10 Standards of excellence
11 Messenger's pickup point
12 Forearm bone
13 Strip of wood
18 __ *the Boys Are*
24 Cooking fat
26 Scoundrel
28 Leave out
29 Tom, Dick, and Harry
31 Lifesaver flavor
32 Kuwaiti ruler
33 Byte beginning
34 Turner and Pappas
35 Receptionist's device
37 Heron's home
40 Patios' kin
41 Satisfy completely
43 Tiny green veggie
44 Angler's basket
46 Strongboxes
48 State confidently
51 Suppressed
52 More or less
53 City divisions
54 Feedbag filler
55 Bide-__ Home
57 Pat down
58 Exile isle
59 Made a hole in one
63 Pie __ mode

412 FEATHERED FRIENDS by Fred Piscop

ACROSS

1 Daddies
6 Musical finales
11 __ *My Children*
14 Raise a fuss
15 Saint Theresa's home
16 Caviar
17 Former Globetrotters star
20 Rage
21 Grazing land
22 El __, TX
23 Make a racket
27 Number one
29 Galley feature
30 Illinois city
33 "We __ the World"
34 Ref. books
37 Research awards
39 *Roots* character
43 "I __ tell a lie"
44 Unsuspecting
46 Caesar's tongue: Abbr.
49 Gymnast Mary Lou
51 Actress Arthur
52 Disinclined
54 Seer's sign
57 Stuff to the gills
58 Nicklaus' org.
61 Sonny and Cher, once
62 English naval hero
68 Dockworkers' grp.
69 John or John Q.
70 Lamb output
71 Man of Steel monogram
72 Ethyl acetate, for one
73 Way to go

DOWN

1 Actress Dawber
2 Rickenbacker, e.g.
3 "Harper Valley __"
4 Taxpayer's fear
5 Curling, for one
6 "Silent" president
7 Track shape
8 __ Straits (rock group)
9 Caustic
10 Mr. Mineo
11 Warship fleet
12 Less restrictive
13 Poe poem
18 "Read 'em and __"
19 MPG testers
23 Fish dish
24 Secular
25 St. Louis sight
26 University honcho
28 Actress Shirley
31 *Believe It __*
32 Auto style
35 Personal quirk
36 Traumatizes
38 Mexicali Mrs.
40 Gridder's gear
41 Scoff at
42 Level
45 Gobble up goodies
46 Timmy's pooch
47 Is of use
48 Aquarium denizens
50 Dozes off
53 Third man in the ring
55 More boorish
56 Trunk
59 Pesky insect
60 Pinnacle
63 Silly Charlotte
64 Neighbor of Syr.
65 Tempe sch.
66 *Krazy __*
67 Potato bud

413 SOUNDALIKES by Matt Gaffney

ACROSS
1 West Indian
6 Spout forth
10 Cheer competitor
14 Home __
15 ME-FL highway
16 Opponent
17 Enjoys Emerson
18 Make bread?
19 Slugger Musial
20 Make peace
23 Mil. sch.
24 Singer Davis
25 That woman
26 Peter Pan author
32 Descendant
35 Secretaries set them
36 Employ
37 Be bent upon
38 Rivers and Baez
40 German Buick
41 Gore and Yankovic
42 Do Europe
43 Poker stakes
44 Bakery favorite
48 Thompson of Back to the Future
49 Musical ability
50 Cpl.'s superior
53 Lyndon Johnson opponent
58 Rigatoni relative
59 Countess' husband
60 Basketball venue
61 Scott Turow book
62 Away from the wind
63 Long for
64 Canoeist's pitfall
65 Clasped
66 Silly Soupy

DOWN
1 Hydrate starter
2 Alaska native
3 Emulates Leo
4 The __ 500
5 Ring holder
6 Never on Sunday setting
7 Hatch's home
8 Antitoxins
9 Drop clues
10 Major appliance
11 Barge in
12 Pronto, to Ben Casey
13 Relatives
21 He acts badly
22 Mr. Addams
26 Tiny bit
27 He put the beat in the Beatles
28 Isle of __
29 Gun pellets
30 "Understood!"
31 Slippery swimmers
32 Ear cleaner
33 Ring up
34 Added fireproofing
38 Average guy
39 __ Miss Brooks
40 Individual
42 Ski lift
43 Frequency band
45 In a macabre manner
46 Hollered
47 Paw part
50 Incredible bargain
51 Category
52 Prefix for port
53 Tie up
54 "She Loves You" refrain
55 Strong wind
56 Hurler Hershiser
57 __ code
58 Akins or Caldwell

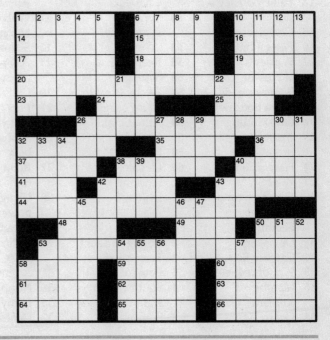

414 GIANT STEPS by Dean Niles

ACROSS
1 Respectful address
5 Clump of dirt
9 Actor Sebastian
14 Host
15 Bear or Berra
16 Nixon in China, e.g.
17 The __ Hunter
18 Baby whale
19 Talk out of
20 Friday's creator
23 Tilling tool
24 Big scene
25 Ontario's neighbor
27 Shark attack
33 Tavern
34 Eye drop?
35 Angel on high
38 Rivals of LeSabres
40 Music measure
42 Skin moisturizer
43 The __ Balloon (David Niven book)
46 Some apples
49 Shoe part
50 Make a mistake
53 Celt
54 Half and half?
55 Southern constellation
58 Certain ads
64 Russian city
66 Golda of Israel
67 Actress Verdon
68 Dumbstruck
69 Pay one's share, with "up"
70 Sphere starter
71 Bacchic attendant
72 Lobe probe?
73 Stumble

DOWN
1 Parents' org.
2 General location
3 "You said it!"
4 Innumerable
5 Weather phenomenon
6 Burden
7 Give the eye
8 Stand apart
9 Cough suppressant
10 Act like Cheetah?
11 One of the March girls
12 Sandwich cookie
13 Grocer's measure
21 Rephrase, perhaps
22 Galena and bauxite
26 Poet Pound
27 Flick
28 Word form for "within"
29 Make an __ (stop)
30 Chew the fat
31 Chassis
32 "Big Three" site
36 Shooting match?
37 Achilles' weak spot
39 Close-fitting
41 Willard extra
44 Buck
45 First shepherd
47 Led the meeting
48 Egotist's darling
51 Peruvian pack animals
52 Affliction
55 You love, to Livy
56 Latvia's capital
57 Med. sch. subj.
59 Transmitted
60 In __ (originally positioned)
61 Water jug
62 Actress Moore
63 Small cut
65 Bond, for one

415   PUZZLED STATES by Randolph Ross

ACROSS
1 Put on
5 Music to Shankar's ears
9 Offended
13 *Bat Masterson* prop
14 Peter Wimsey's school
15 Carroll critters
16 Fixes a fight
17 Wolsey's successor
18 Some spreads
19 Tulsa housewife?
22 Outstanding
23 *Exodus* protagonist
24 Hera's home
27 W or S?
29 For some time
32 Classical beginning
33 Davis' org.
34 Catches flies
35 Wd. of request
36 Member of Kareem's team
38 Geom. figure
39 "Xanadu" group
40 Goes to pieces
41 Fayetteville ten?
45 Moral law
46 Leb. neighbor
47 William, to Charles
50 Syracuse symphony?
53 "Give it __!"
55 Reebok rival
56 Side
57 "Achy Breaky Heart" singer
58 Atlantic isl.
59 Chip in
60 Fastener
61 Elevator units
62 Stocking stuffers?

DOWN
1 Young haddock
2 Terse verse
3 Point of view
4 Southwestern sight
5 Sorrow
6 Very, very, very small
7 Skirt shaper
8 Wild flowers
9 Sober as a judge
10 Stuffs a suitcase
11 Wolverine automaker
12 Slalom shape
15 Asian metropolis
20 Calls a cab
21 Plus
25 Not yet firm
26 Alpha and beta
27 Removable top
28 Using little power
29 Broadway org.
30 Helicopter noise
31 Attentive ones
35 Nonphysical
36 Filthy __
37 Genesis craft
39 Catch a glimpse of
40 Packs of pecks
42 High two-pair
43 Small salamanders
44 Argue
47 Pool person
48 Get on a soapbox
49 Identifies
51 Costa __
52 Photo finish?
53 Essen expletive
54 Scandinavian rug

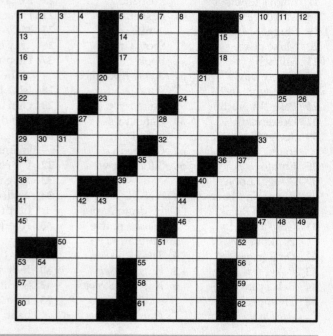

416   KEEP IT SIMPLE by Shirley Soloway

ACROSS
1 Shoestring
5 Perlman and Howard
9 Once again
13 Actor Richard
14 Make happy
16 Singer Falana
17 Indian tourist town
18 Tropical tubers
19 Whirl around
20 "Nothing to it!"
23 *The Hunt for __ October*
24 Sporting dog
25 Portable fuel
27 Art Deco designer
29 Bow material
32 Nourish
35 Dutch cheese
38 __ lily
39 Actress Gardner
40 Envelope info
42 Med. test
43 Frisbees, e.g.
45 Pull sharply
46 Famous fellow?
47 Most cunning
49 Conn of *Benson*
51 Ancient
54 Befitting a baron
58 Bandleader Brown
60 Nothing to it
62 Pearl Buck heroine
64 Fred Astaire's sister
65 Falls behind
66 French clergyman
67 Spartan slave
68 Tom Joad, for one
69 Piece of information
70 Transatlantic planes
71 Waters down

DOWN
1 Bounds
2 Playing marble
3 Insertion symbol
4 Legislated
5 Answered testily
6 Norwegian monarch
7 Drug busters
8 Summer ermine
9 Pacino and Smith
10 "Nothing to it!"
11 Nobelist Wiesel
12 Magician's prop
15 Sandy ridge
21 Always, to Byron
22 Idle and Clapton
26 Hoopsters' org.
28 Whirlpool
30 Dairy-case purchase
31 Henpecks
32 Temporary trends
33 Depraved
34 Nothing to it!
36 Coach Parseghian
37 Darn a rip
40 Strong point
41 Frying pans
44 Beer barrel
46 Vent output
48 Synagogue scroll
50 Fawn's mother
52 Gold deposits
53 Sword fights
55 Daddy duck
56 On the up-and-up
57 Affirmative responses
58 Lie around
59 Island off Italy
61 Soak up moisture
63 Fish catcher

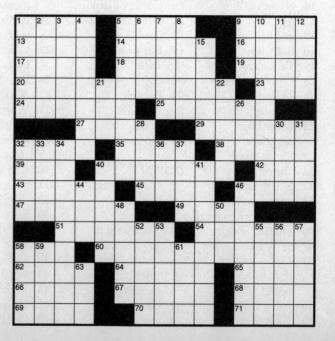

417 SEA IT NOW by Bob Lubbers

ACROSS
1 Aircraft abbr.
5 Dole (out)
9 Searches for treasure
14 "Whatever __ Wants"
15 *Scarlett* setting
16 "It's the end of __"
17 Figurine material
19 Mexican "monsters"
20 Make a patriotic display
22 '60s radical grp.
23 Slender
24 Out of order
26 Movie openers
29 Darned again
31 Singer Adams
32 Blue hue
34 Coral communes
37 Maiden-name indicator
38 Sound films
40 Islet, on a globe
41 No-no
43 Connery or Penn
44 LXVII x VI
45 Moon valleys
47 Ionospheric high spot
49 Gets a whiff of
51 Fly high
52 Split __ soup
53 Ice-cream flavor
59 L.A. dunker
61 Like some votes
62 *Die Fledermaus* maid
63 See red
64 Gossipy Barrett
65 Sharply to the point
66 Tracy's Trueheart
67 Govt. agents

DOWN
1 Deli side-dish
2 *Welcome __* ('77 film)
3 Patron saint of Norway
4 Singer Patti
5 CA volcano
6 Consumed
7 Not kosher
8 James __ Jones
9 Some bargainers
10 Cycle starter
11 *Naughty Marietta* star
12 Play the market
13 Fresh
18 Suit to __
21 Pecs' partners
25 Must pay
26 __ caterpillar
27 Concept
28 Tennis shoot-off
29 Leaf gatherers
30 Director Kazan
33 "What __ is new?"
35 Pâté de __ gras
36 Tend the sauce
38 Like an 800 number
39 Puts into effect
42 Vinegar's partner
44 Garage alternative
46 Shreveport coll.
48 Café au __
49 *Killer Tomatoes* sound
50 Gettysburg victor
51 Appears to be
54 Dexterous
55 Sticky stuff
56 High-school formal
57 Bowling alley
58 *Joie de vivre*
60 Overhead rails

418 NATIVE INTELLIGENCE by Randolph Ross

ACROSS
1 BLT spread
5 Emulated Arachne
9 Candied, as fruits
14 Decrease?
15 SSS classification
16 Worked up
17 *Entre __* ('83 film)
18 Horse course
19 Tolerate
20 Disney duck
22 In stitches?
24 Moving vehicle
25 Crest competitor
27 Woodworking tools
29 Rooftop toppers
32 *Rhoda* character
33 Grant or Gehrig
34 Fool
35 Zero in on
39 Lie in wait
41 Moxie
43 Waiter's item
44 Similarly
46 Space starter
48 Sixth sense
49 "__ Hear a Waltz?"
50 Cut short
52 __ of Alcatraz
56 Stylish neckwear
57 Benz chaser
58 Don Juan's mom
60 "Return to __" (Elvis tune)
63 Make true
65 Arabian channel
67 Actress Thompson
68 Richards of tennis
69 Literary pseudonym
70 Textbook heading
71 Condition
72 Director David
73 "Why don't we?"

DOWN
1 Babysit
2 Buck ender
3 Progressive thinker
4 Discounted
5 Unemotional type
6 Out __ limb
7 Doberman docs
8 Greases the wheels
9 Alhambra's locale
10 Women's __
11 Survival film of '93
12 Closet material
13 Anthony and Barbara
21 Beam bender
23 Kahlua cocktail
26 Russell role
28 Split hairs?
29 "__ Want for Christmas"
30 It's often modified
31 Nursery-rhyme dieter
36 Working dog
37 Orient
38 Italics or agate
40 Choreographer Michael
42 Actress Miles
45 Convention winner
47 Way back when
51 Embassy official
52 Wall Street pessimists
53 Small bay
54 Isabella or Ena
55 Stair post
59 Middleweight champ Tony
61 Correct copy
62 *Peanuts* expletive
64 Understand
66 Cir. bisector

419   I STRAINS by S.E. Booker

ACROSS

1 Urban fleet
5 Have in mind
9 Raise the price
14 Stage telephone, e.g.
15 __ mater
16 Sheepish?
17 "I __": Popeye
19 Tattooed lady of song
20 Sacked out
21 Ground grain
23 __ a Wonderful Life
24 Encouraging word
25 Aimless
27 Bound by contract
31 Lumberjack
34 FDR measure
35 Outdoorsy
37 Actor Waggoner
38 Surrendered
40 Author Levin
41 "__ brillig . . ."
42 Supplemented, with "out"

43 Tumbledown
46 Garfunkel or Fleming
47 Makeshift shelter
49 "Black" and "white"
51 Movie mogul Zanuck
53 Bemoan
54 Make public
56 *My Life as __*
57 Cornered
60 Work a mill, maybe
62 *I __*: Paar
65 Picture
66 Ohio lake
67 Go for
68 Less feral
69 Toboggan
70 Strong as __

DOWN

1 Spring summer?
2 Munitions
3 Orange or Sugar
4 Globe
5 Poet Arnold

6 Actor Wallach
7 "I __": Madonna
8 Appointed
9 Mess (up)
10 It goes up walls
11 "I __": Sinatra
12 Kind of pricing
13 Soup starters
18 Separated
22 Like __ of sunshine
26 Pool-table top
27 Well-behaved kid
28 *Golden Hind* skipper
29 "I __": King
30 Dog on *Topper*
32 Eye opener?
33 Retreats
36 Rhett's last word
39 Author Ferber
43 Assembly-line inventor
44 Rambled about

45 "I Want __ Want Me"
48 Stock market participant
50 Cosmic cloud
52 Harnesses
54 Keep __ (persevere)

55 *My Friend __*
58 Has __ with (knows well)
59 Mrs. Lennon
61 Generation
63 Fade out
64 Country singer Ritter

420   WHAT'S IN A NAME? by Eric Albert

ACROSS

1 Unruly bunch
4 Pinza, for one
8 "The Scourge of God"
14 Easy to love
16 It should be looked into
17 Kitchen covering
18 Tearjerkers?
19 What "Emily" means
21 Neon or nitrogen
22 Supply weapons to
23 Purple shade
26 Stone film
28 Characters in *Antigone*
33 Blonde shade
34 Female rabbit
35 Excess formality
36 What "Robert" means
40 Western capital
41 First mate?
42 *A Raisin in the Sun* star

43 *As You Like It* locale
44 *Oklahoma!* baddie
45 Egg container
46 Pussycat's companion
48 Watchdog org.
50 What "Amanda" means
58 Luau site
59 Luau interrupter?
60 Makes nervous
61 Visionary views
62 Mason's assistant
63 Quiz
64 Cyclone center

DOWN

1 French Sudan, today
2 Thor's boss
3 Become buddies
4 Model-airplane material
5 Helps on a heist
6 Play legato
7 Rig

8 __-propre
9 Pot maker
10 Crowd?
11 Geritol ingredient
12 Solitary
13 __ longa, vita brevis
15 Blusher kin
20 Acorn, in time
23 Turkish official
24 Leading man?
25 "The French Chef"
26 Revive
27 Not as many
29 Bumbler
30 Line of business
31 High points
32 Piece of paper
34 Heredity letters
35 Sault __ Marie, MI
37 Born
38 Very quickly
39 College climber
44 House guest?

45 Ship-related
47 Bridge ancestor
48 Chimney channels
49 He played Mr. Chips
50 Mickey's creator
51 Man __ (thoroughbred)

52 Partly pink
53 Fail to mention
54 Wash out
55 Mr. Nastase
56 Prying
57 Ready and willing
58 Owns

TRINITY QUARTET by William A. Hendricks

ACROSS

1 "Hell __ no fury . . ."
5 Dundee denizen
9 "Ma! (He's Making Eyes __)"
13 Tennist Arthur
14 Canine, e.g.
15 National League stadium
16 Wiry
17 Port-au-Prince's land
18 Hound and hamster
19 Cravat
20 Soft-ball brand
21 Din
23 They're spotted in the wild
25 Ike's opponent
26 Ocean sound
27 Stash
28 Frost bite?
31 Tony
33 Early explorer
34 Savanna antelope
35 Macho man
36 Optics item
38 An NCO
39 Dairy spheroid
40 Fringe benefit
41 Thrills
43 Sinbad's bird
44 Not as much
45 Chihuahua child
46 How to pack fish
48 Utah performing clan
51 Lifework
53 Castor, to Pollux
54 Piece of advice
55 Circular sections
56 University of Maine town
58 Jocular Johnson
59 Total defeat
60 Part of NOW
61 *Educating __* ('83 film)
62 Call the shots
63 __-do-well
64 Weirdo

DOWN

1 Must
2 Savory jelly
3 Indoor attraction
4 "Wait a minute!"
5 Flies like an eagle
6 Hair style
7 Giant with 511 homers
8 Depth
9 Adoption org.
10 "Tom Dooley" singers
11 Apportion, with "out"
12 __ *of Eden*
14 Horseracing coup
20 Wordy Webster
22 Obi-Wan portrayer
24 Latch
25 What snobs put on
27 Skater Carol
29 *Picnic* playwright
30 Places
31 *Mask* star
32 Science-fiction award
37 Pretense
38 __'War (racehorse)
40 Ballet bend
42 Delineate
47 Bird houses
48 Title holder
49 Likewise
50 Pipe up
51 Auto part, for short
52 Slangy suffix
53 Big book
57 Richard the unidentified
58 Joan Van __

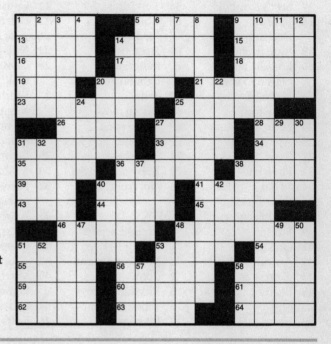

THAT TEARS IT by Trip Payne

ACROSS

1 Miller rival
6 __ *Trek*
10 Former Irani ruler
14 More competent
15 Spelunking spot
16 Chaplin prop
17 Heavenly woman
18 Slaughter of baseball
19 Author Haley
20 Droopy tree
23 Be decisive
24 Use a straw
25 Colorful ring
29 "Oh, phooey!"
31 Spending maximum
34 Sentimental journalist
36 Lowly worker
38 Reggae singer Peter
39 Goes out on one's own
41 Flamenco cries
42 Inspirations
44 Scolded loudly
46 Form of ID
47 The hunted
49 Danger warnings
50 Crumpet accompaniment
51 Indefinite pronoun
52 Hit '92 film
59 Piltdown Man, for one
60 Head set?
61 Acid in proteins
63 Opera highlight
64 Fizz flavoring
65 For the __ (currently)
66 Stylist's stock
67 Loose-fitting dress
68 In a difficult position

DOWN

1 "You sicken me!"
2 Take __ (acknowledge applause)
3 In the dumps
4 Saharan
5 Libya's largest city
6 __ *of a Woman*
7 Sharp taste
8 Solemnly proclaim
9 Hold off
10 Resell tickets
11 Sign of sanctity
12 From the top
13 Witch's curse
21 "Not me, thanks"
22 Speech problem
25 Some wines
26 Crucifixes
27 Actor Buddy
28 Work-safety grp.
29 Kind of race
30 In __ (lined up)
31 Plum or melon
32 Attu resident
33 Aphids and gnats
35 Director Hooper
37 Took the bus
40 Streetspeak
43 On __ (riskily)
45 Posh
48 Least typical
50 Big Bend's location
51 Square one
52 Zipped along
53 It comes down hard
54 Connecticut campus
55 Driving need
56 Love personified
57 Go for the gold
58 Depend end
59 Old crone
62 Multi-vol. ref. work

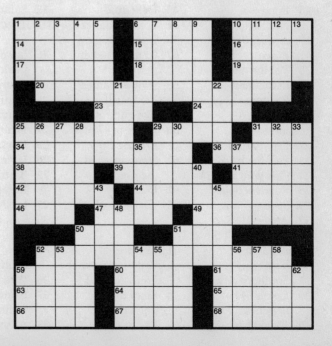

423 NAMESAKES by Fred Piscop

ACROSS
1 Attempt
5 Early man
9 Hold out
14 Soccer great
15 Lincoln or Ford
16 Physicist Enrico
17 Sect's symbol
18 __ Scott Decision
19 Jung friend
20 Freddie and __ ('60s rockers)
23 Heart of Houston?
24 Long, long time
25 Appropriate
27 Bend, in a way
31 Powerful
34 "That's __, folks!"
35 Distributed
38 Flight segment
39 Flutter
41 One Stooge
42 Author Ferber
43 Course ender
45 Beethoven wrote one
48 Some MIT grads
49 Adriatic peninsula
51 Takes off the rough edges
53 Brazilian dance
55 "Slippery when __"
56 Tiny circle
58 Child star Freddie
64 Hacienda material
66 Othello, for one
67 Trim
68 Dumb move
69 Paper page
70 Egyptian goddess
71 Stretches
72 Ruby and garnet
73 No. cruncher

DOWN
1 Rotisserie part
2 Part of RIT
3 Medicinal plant
4 Toot
5 Rhythmic flow
6 Vibes
7 Bit of gossip
8 Junction points
9 Compensates for
10 Not "agin"
11 Skelton's "Freddie the __"
12 Ostrich cousins
13 Disencumbers
21 __ to Rio
22 NFL positions
26 Commedia dell'__
27 Kiddie-music singer
28 Immigration island, once
29 Bedrock's Fred
30 __'shanter
32 Forty-__ (prospector)
33 Astroturf alternative
36 Chop off
37 __ off (sore)
40 Mitchell homestead
44 Loosens (up)
46 Edits, maybe
47 Explorer Tasman
50 With 56 Down, "Honeymoon" preceder
52 No man's land?
54 Knight wear
56 See 50 Down
57 Stench
59 Hit the bottle
60 Did garden work
61 Not fem.
62 Colorful Viking?
63 Greeley's direction
65 Ms. Arthur

424 HORSE SENSE by Eric Albert

ACROSS
1 Austen offering
5 It often has one line
9 Score symbol
14 Out of gas
15 Doing business
16 Popeye's girlfriend
17 April, 1961 fiasco
19 Put the check in the mail
20 Response evoker
21 Mangle a message
22 Dandy dude?
23 Feel the heat
24 One way to park
28 Roads scholar?
29 Spree
32 At rest
33 He knew all the Angles
34 Fuss
35 Southern city
39 Rescue 911 network
40 13 witches
41 Profound
42 Drill sergeant's shout
43 Actress Barbara
44 Phidias product
46 Misery star
47 Corporate VIP
48 Debt fluid
51 Spanish dance
56 Upscale region
57 Chili ingredient, perhaps
58 Hall-of-Famer Lombardi
59 Not quite closed
60 Elwes of The Princess Bride
61 Stand in good __ (be useful)
62 Like a fox
63 "Babe" rockers

DOWN
1 Declines
2 Potatoes' partner
3 Polite request
4 Bit of the universe
5 Rag man
6 Designer perfume
7 Barroom barrels
8 Navy rank: Abbr.
9 Very cheaply
10 Salesperson
11 An arm or a leg
12 Satan's bag
13 Throw a party for
18 Japan's peak peak
21 Hungarian leading lady
23 Confine
24 White wood
25 Brick base
26 Hold tight
27 Barbie's beau
28 Refuge
29 Jackson or Leigh
30 "Au revoir!"
31 Flip
33 The __ Percent Solution
36 Wreck location
37 Famous filmmaker
38 Author Tarbell
44 Watch
45 "What __?"
46 About that time
47 Ear feature
48 Acts racy?
49 Leave the stage
50 Sci-fi classic
51 Pacific island group
52 Basics
53 Pinlike?
54 Coleman or Cooper
55 Semiprecious stone
57 Dog's dog

425 HEAD START by Donna J. Stone

ACROSS
1 Pugilistic pokes
5 Huff and puff
9 "__ Excited" (Pointer Sisters hit)
13 Perched on
14 In all respects
15 "Cheerio!"
16 Fountain order
17 Brought to ruin
18 Kaiser's counterpart
19 START OF A DEFINITION
22 European capital
23 Winter malady
24 Advanced deg.
26 Metric start
27 Rat pack
31 Interference
33 Run the show
35 Valhalla villain
36 SUBJECT OF DEFINITION
40 Zilch, to Zina
41 Earl Grey's place
42 Astoria's locale
45 "Confound it!"
46 Scorpius' neighbor
49 Keatsian crock
50 Baby beaver
52 Saint-Saëns trio
54 END OF DEFINITION
59 Out of town
60 Run a risk
61 First victim
62 Common possessive
63 Cockamamie
64 Prego competitor
65 "Zip-__-Doo-Dah"
66 Mobile home
67 Prepare cherries

DOWN
1 Derek of I, Claudius
2 Makes up (for)
3 Fandango kin
4 Give rise to
5 Weaponry
6 Nurse's helper
7 Packing a wallop
8 Powers a trike
9 Poison ivy symptom
10 Katz's congrats
11 Astral
12 Propel a shell
14 Quid pro __
20 Bittern relative
21 "For shame!"
25 601, to Tiberius
28 "__ Gotta Be Me"
29 Coming up
30 Midas' sin
32 Got off
33 Diver Louganis
34 So. state
36 Used the library
37 Kitchen gear
38 "__ Lazy River"
39 Pole star?
40 Bud's buddy
43 Endorses
44 Dumb ox
46 Blind __
47 Weasel out
48 Sanctuary
51 Cawdor big shot
53 Boom and gaff
55 AMEX rival
56 Love Me Tender star
57 Canadian coin
58 Vein contents
59 "Gotcha!"

426 HARD PUZZLE by Norma Steinberg

ACROSS
1 Bough
5 Toyland visitors
10 Bowling-equipment maker
13 M
14 Hem and haw
15 Festive
17 Salisbury attraction
19 Diver Louganis
20 Oriental tower
21 American Uncle
22 "Oh, sure!"
23 Stowe girl
25 James Dean persona
27 Advisory body
31 Leave in the lurch
34 Jeremy of Damage
35 Overused
38 Mean mongrel
39 Part of RSVP
40 Billy Joel's instrument
41 White-faced
42 Aruba or Atlantis: Abbr.
43 Gem surface
44 Benefits
45 Fragrant trees
47 Josephine's title
49 Prepares for publishing
51 Sugarloaf Mountain city
52 God's Little __
54 Sounds of recognition
56 Western desert
61 Little fellows
62 Popular hymn
64 Level
65 Diarist Nin
66 Sort of school
67 Mrs., in Marseilles
68 __ hand (help)
69 Five __ Pieces

DOWN
1 Speak like Daffy Duck
2 Minimal amount
3 __ synthesizer
4 Sonny or Chastity
5 Act
6 "__ Maria"
7 Makes illegal
8 Mortimer's master
9 __ be (appeared)
10 Texas A&M students
11 Bakery treat
12 Attorney Bailey
16 FBI man
18 Paradises
24 Toys in the __
26 Hum bug?
27 Kind of pride
28 Went up
29 Colorado power source
30 Part of SBLI
32 Calls the shots
33 Lock of hair
36 Norma __
37 Word form for "between"
40 Idyllic
41 __ excellence
43 Calendar abbr.
44 Takeoff
46 "__ Fideles"
48 Tropical tree
50 Gleamed
52 Sitcom alien
53 Serenity
55 Read hastily
57 Mock
58 Taj Mahal town
59 Neckline shapes
60 Notice
63 Baby goat

427 MUSICAL SOUNDS by Fred Piscop

ACROSS

1 Von __ (*The Sound of Music* surname)
6 Flaccid
10 Limber with language
14 Courtyards
15 Sneaking suspicion
16 Descartes or Clair
17 DO
20 Cuts prices
21 Worries
22 President pro __
23 __ Spumante
24 Bans
27 Teen socialite
29 Compass points
33 Hunk of gunk
34 Alluring ad
36 Barroom spigot
37 RE
40 Gas-pump abbr.
41 Horse operas
42 Birdbath organism
43 Hagar's pooch
45 Attorney's deg.
46 Part owner?
47 "__ does it!"
49 Japanese sash
50 Sharp
53 It's often direct
57 MI
60 __-Lackawanna Railroad
61 Venetian-blind part
62 Ms. Rogers St. Johns
63 Undermines
64 Dagwood's neighbor
65 Mess around

DOWN

1 Highlands headgear
2 1 and 66: Abbr.
3 Asian inland sea
4 Philippine erupter
5 Free tickets
6 *One __ to Live*
7 Day to beware?
8 Tex-__ cuisine
9 Duelists' units
10 *Ars __ artis*
11 Microscope part
12 Actress Swenson
13 Sugar source
18 Resistance unit
19 Bigots
23 Totally ridiculous
24 Aspen apparatus
25 Standish's stand-in
26 Witty pianist
27 Skillfully
28 Steen stand
30 Wading bird
31 It requires two
32 Opera prop
34 *Prelude __ Kiss*
35 Printer's measures
38 Starchy staple
39 Mexican estate
44 Gets more mileage from
46 Overseas
48 It may be common
49 Hockey great Bobby
50 Does Little work?
51 *Buona __, Mrs. Campbell*
52 Junket
53 Silent sort
54 Capable of
55 Playwright Coward
56 Rock group Jethro __
58 __ *That Jazz*
59 Negative vote

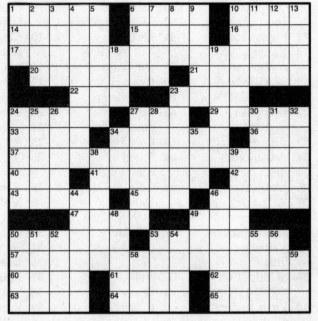

428 CUTTING EDGE by Randolph Ross

ACROSS

1 Sorcerer
6 Put up with
11 Deli meat
14 Nicholas Gage book
15 Lyons lid
16 Turkish VIP
17 Hugh Beaumont role
19 Pine product
20 Acted surreptitiously
21 Crossworder's need
23 John Ritter's dad
24 Playwright's ms.
26 Reaction to bad news
27 Light beer
30 Streaky
32 Roman author
33 Arm holder
34 United rival
37 Actress Ullmann
38 Helicopter
39 Sharp projection
40 Lemon cooler
41 Hatted Hedda
42 Top-notch
43 Evening galas
45 Bumpkins
46 Ballpark figs.
48 Mr. and McMahon
49 Help a waiter
50 Porpoise pack
52 Pawn
56 Lower digit
57 Sgt. Pepper bandleader
60 Century 21 competitor
61 "You're All __ to Get By"
62 "To __ human"
63 Reviewer Reed
64 Wired
65 Take care of

DOWN

1 Kitten cries
2 Actor Rachins
3 *Power* star
4 Like some memos
5 In worse health
6 Undercover?
7 Maude portrayer
8 Sportscaster Cross
9 Spiritual tune of '17
10 Raison d'__
11 Malicious attack
12 A second time
13 Mrs. Donahue
18 Archvillain Luthor
22 *Wayne's World* word
24 Russian grasslands
25 Fancy flapjacks
27 Notorious Montez
28 Psyched up
29 Fires
30 Obliquely positioned
31 __ Lingus
33 Coast
35 Peter out
36 Stone and Golden
38 The Windy City, for short
42 Spartan
44 Barcelona bear
45 Makes haste
46 Organic compound
47 20
49 Diddley and Derek
51 Newspaper notice
52 London park
53 Alps river
54 Pluck
55 Sinclair rival
58 Dawson or Deighton
59 Guitarist Paul

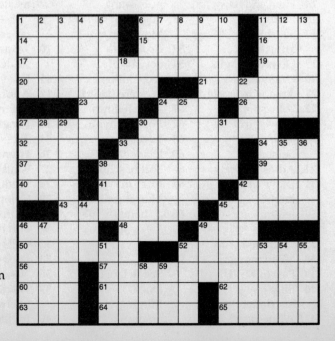

429 E.T. by Dean Niles

ACROSS
1 '70s hairdo
5 IBM products
8 Like some rocks
13 Barcelona bull
14 Aim
15 Woody Allen film of '90
16 Spirited steed
17 Poet Wilcox
18 Tijuana tykes
19 Early E.T. hit
22 Stimpy's pal
23 Seeded bread
24 Sheer fear
28 Knucklehead
31 Interstate, e.g.
35 Playwright Oscar
36 Formal agreement
38 Slugger's stat
39 E.T., in full
43 Took command
44 One of the Strausses
45 Nary a soul
46 Strong alkalis
48 Violin part
50 Dead duck
51 Catch some rays
53 Cousteau shocker
55 One of E.T.'s mates
63 *Taras Bulba* author
64 Cartoonist Peter
65 Skye of *Say Anything*
66 Full of energy
67 Lament
68 Urgent appeal
69 They're easy to see through
70 Pipe type
71 Astrology-hotline worker?

DOWN
1 Loony Laurel
2 Israeli dance
3 Smell __ (be suspicious)
4 Asian desert
5 Where to spend a zloty
6 "__ Me Irresponsible"
7 Eastern European
8 Virile
9 Stone or Reed
10 Trig term
11 James Herriot, for one
12 "Certainly!"
14 Actor Hackman
20 Trying experience
21 Standing tall
24 Reside
25 Bendix role
26 Slur over
27 Cooper's tool
29 Eye-related
30 Oom-__
32 Acrylic fabric
33 Have __ to pick
34 More urgent
37 Hair hassle
40 Classic comedian
41 First lady?
42 "__-hoo!"
47 Made an effort
49 Ear part
52 Van Gogh locale
54 Short jacket
55 Actress Albright
56 Opposed to, in Dogpatch
57 Improvise, in a way
58 Russian city
59 Puppy bites
60 Filet fish
61 On bended __ (begging)
62 Sidereal or solar
63 Opening

430 PRODUCTIONS by Matt Gaffney

ACROSS
1 Cooler company
9 "Over There" composer
14 Darwin site
15 "Oh, give me __..."
16 Grocery-store option
17 Societal values
18 Gardner et al.
19 Make up
21 Aardvark's prey
22 Monthly expense
23 Mus. medium
24 Heaps
26 Refrain starter
27 Impair
29 Caesar and Vicious
32 Swell place?
35 Hawaii has one
37 Patient person's motto
41 Song dedicatee, with "the"
42 3 times, to a pharmacist
43 Feminine suffix
44 Part of USAR
45 Gibson or Harris
48 Mr. Eban
50 Churchill's "so few"
53 Soft-drink choice
54 Squealer
56 "__ day's work"
58 Sophoclean tragedy
59 Von Bulow portrayer
61 Drive up the wall
63 Go along
64 Wheeling sight
65 Misplaces
66 Church points

DOWN
1 More debonair
2 *Nación*
3 Eniwetok event
4 Terrier threat
5 Beyond zealous
6 __-Dale
7 Bully's motto
8 Manuscript enc.
9 Bedouin's transport
10 "What have we here?"
11 Alger and Nelson
12 Mass word
13 Fit together
14 In pieces
20 Least common
25 Actor Homolka
28 It may follow you
30 Banned pesticide
31 "I told you so!"
32 Pitcher Dave
33 Elver's elder
34 Lacking principles
36 Blow away
37 Garden tool
38 Actress Jillian
39 Ford and Rockefeller
40 Madison or Fifth: Abbr.
45 California desert
46 Makes merry
47 Less severe
49 Supports
51 Dickinson of *Police Woman*
52 __ Islands (Danish possession)
53 Nitpick
54 Irani money
55 Craft of myth
57 Vientiane's land
60 Born: Fr.
62 Poet/painter Jean

431 FABRICATIONS by Shirley Soloway

ACROSS

1 "You __ mouthful!"
6 WWII females
10 Open a bit
14 Pilgrim John
15 Beige
16 Blood components
17 Daydream
19 Actor Kristofferson
20 Vendor
21 Duel tool
23 Easy mark
24 __ Baba
25 Clear the slate
27 Bracketed word
30 Composers' org.
33 Fit for a king
36 Hubbubs
38 "I could __ horse!"
39 Error
40 Religious ceremony
41 Loses one's footing
43 Tower town
44 Small amounts
46 "Since __ You Baby" ('56 tune)
47 Ginger cookie
48 Struck down
49 Corny goddess?
51 Ames and Asner
52 Jazz musician Red
54 Moon craft
56 Lab animal
58 Beer choice
60 Foliage
64 Old-time oath
66 Wild duck
68 Imported cheese
69 Over
70 Bad-tempered
71 Peddler's goal
72 Amphibious vehicles: Abbr.
73 Bread spreads

DOWN

1 Carpentry tools
2 Soothing plant
3 Superstar
4 Perry's secretary
5 Actress Lansbury
6 Rainy
7 Painful sensation
8 Party decoration
9 More certain
10 Inquire
11 Eastern conifer
12 *Tosca* tune
13 Grating sound
18 Gets up
22 British nobleman
26 Daily dramas
27 Delhi wraps
28 Set phrase
29 Little rabbit
31 Multicolored felines
32 *One Day at __*
34 Syrian leader
35 By __ and bounds (rapidly)
37 "From __ shining . . ."
42 __ *Dallas*
45 Belgrade native
50 Is responsible for
53 Oral
55 Silent star Normand
56 Confederate soldiers
57 Indian city
59 Sheepshank, for one
61 Bouquet holder
62 Word form for "outer"
63 "The __ the limit!"
65 Poor grade
67 D.C. second bananas

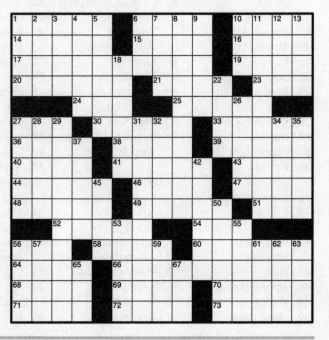

432 PULLING RANK by Matt Gaffney

ACROSS

1 Practice boxing
5 "__ 'em, Rover!"
8 Decorates cupcakes
12 Buenos __
14 Comic Philips
15 Break to smithereens
16 Landowner's sign
19 Peace, in Panama
20 Actress Zetterling
21 There's no charge for it
22 007's school
24 Apprentice
26 "__ Fine Day" ('63 tune)
27 Jeans material
29 Crystallize, as an idea
30 Yalies
31 Andrews and Carvey
33 Lend a hand
35 "Woe is me!"
36 Tory leader
39 Big bash
42 O.R.'s locale
43 Have a hunch
46 Lincoln and Vigoda
47 Massage
49 Holds as an opinion
51 Spare part?
52 Pitched a tent
55 Heartfelt
56 Mobile home?
58 Mauna __
60 Lanka lead-in
61 NBC owner
64 __ *Gay*
65 Pipe cleaner?
66 Mediterranean island
67 Dispatched
68 "Absolutely!"
69 "What __ for Love" (*A Chorus Line* tune)

DOWN

1 Weakened
2 Copied illegally
3 Painted Desert locale
4 Priest's title: Abbr.
5 "__ is believing"
6 Mischief-maker
7 __ Otis Skinner
8 "__ a man with . . ."
9 Actor O'Connor
10 Latvia neighbor
11 Introvert's quality
13 Our uncle
15 Gyrated
17 Skater Babilonia
18 "__ the fields . . ."
23 Sapporo spies
25 Joins forces
28 __ Zedong
30 Was the breadwinner
32 "Quiet!"
34 Record players
37 As a rule
38 Brit. ref. work
39 Auto shops
40 Texas city
41 Mideast land
44 Gets steamed
45 Certain retirees
48 Lovely ladies
50 Seasoned
52 *Fame* name
53 Cardiologists' org.
54 Buck's mate
57 Sash or cummerbund
59 Part of IRA
62 CBS symbol
63 Angle starter

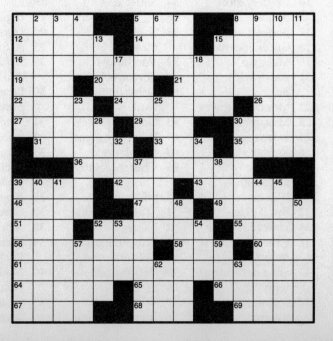

433 SHOOT THE WORKS by Fred Piscop

ACROSS
1 Part of CPA
5 Adam's little brother
9 Disconcert
14 Starch source
15 Hercules' love
16 Muscovite moolah
17 READY
20 Hold __ (corner)
21 Mac
22 Palmer's pocketful
23 TV scanning lines
26 Ruminate
28 Sky stalker
30 Import duty
34 *M*A*S*H* extras
37 Bullring cheers
39 Actor Murphy
40 AIM
44 Substitute
45 Minn. neighbor
46 Inc., in Ipswich
47 Tankard material
49 Take the reins
52 Collar type
54 Graceland and Tara
58 9 inches
61 Miss Piggy's pronoun
63 Field worker
64 FIRE
68 Furry fisher
69 __-Ball (arcade game)
70 Caligula's nephew
71 Garden intruders
72 *Jane* __
73 Turned right

DOWN
1 Financial phrase
2 Magna __
3 Baby beds
4 Missile from the audience, perhaps
5 Evaded the seeker
6 Punch line?
7 Neatnik's nemesis
8 __ cholesterol
9 Rainbow shape
10 Go for some Brownie points
11 Irish Rose lover
12 Wild plum
13 Party animals?
18 Viewer
19 Border on
24 Free-for-all
25 Athenian statesman
27 __ Basin (German region)
29 *Revenge of the* __
31 Rocker Billy
32 Ali weapon
33 Chicken chow
34 Reagan role
35 Concerning
36 Put away
38 Outpouring
41 Spread out
42 *Da* opposite
43 Luau instruments
48 Easy win
50 Handy bit of Lat.
51 Running amok
53 Ear pollution?
55 Wigwam kin
56 __ nous (confidentially)
57 Put up with
58 Tell's partner
59 Fancy appetizer
60 Prefix for diluvian
62 Black
65 Ovid's __ *Poetica*
66 Plunk preceder
67 "Now __ here!"

434 W by Randolph Ross

ACROSS
1 Piglet's creator
6 Mexican region
10 Singer Zadora
13 "She's __" (Lesley Gore tune)
14 Snug as __ . . .
15 Moses or Peter
16 Tubby's pal
18 Dentist's order
19 Coach Ewbank
20 Maestro Toscanini
22 Bother
25 Honshu seaport
28 Fuel-gauge reading
29 Man or stallion
31 Advent
33 Cannon shot
35 With 30 Down, Yorkshire breed
38 Tulsa coll.
39 Extreme
41 Clothe, with "up"
42 Went back to the drawing board
44 Living-room piece
46 Cordial flavoring
48 Chemise or tent
49 Intrinsically
51 Wet blanket
53 Prefix for "while"
54 __ form (unusually good)
56 Any day now
58 Catch in the act
59 Peace Nobelist
65 Oklahoma tribe
66 Cheeseboard choice
67 Imbibes excessively
68 Thrice: Pharm.
69 __ packing (dismiss)
70 Derogatory

DOWN
1 __ de mer
2 "__ Ruled the World"
3 Sodom escapee
4 Ailing
5 *Mirabella* rival
6 Stallone role
7 __ Dhabi
8 Cal. page
9 Juan's water
10 Luau appetizers
11 Like some gases
12 Pester
15 Blew one's top
17 Cartoon cry
21 Enjoyed a party
22 Support
23 Put on a pedestal
24 South African fighter
26 Pigtail stylist
27 Author Ambler
30 See 35 Across
32 Eaker and Levin
34 Blabs away
36 Windblown soil
37 Discharge
40 House paper
43 Discounted
45 Delaware River city
47 Destroyed, as hope
49 Champagne grape
50 Related to Mom
52 Sticky stuff
55 Dwindles
57 Goes (for)
60 High dudgeon
61 Moral wrong
62 AP competitor
63 Actor Danson
64 Apply

435 SHOWS WITHIN SHOWS by Trip Payne

ACROSS
1 Petty clash
5 A, in Arabic
9 He had a gilt complex
14 Cabbagelike veggie
15 Mediocre
16 Shelved for now
17 Loy costar
18 Big sport?
19 Extend, in a way
20 Play-within-a-play in *Hamlet*
23 Teacup part
24 Vociferate
25 Ring master?
29 "Boy, that's something!"
30 Scarfs down
31 Enzyme ending
32 Dallas County city
35 Naysayer, e.g.
36 Farm animals
37 Film-within-a-film in *The Bodyguard*
40 __ Bator
41 Shoshoneans
42 *A Lesson from* __
43 Loser to DDE
44 Old ending
45 Home terminals, for short
46 Visionary
48 "Wow, look at that!"
49 Tack on
52 TV-show-within-a-TV-show in *Newhart*
55 Holiday song
58 Stout relatives
59 Raggedy
60 To no __ (useless)
61 Austin or Copley
62 Perry victory site
63 Wedding performers
64 Socks
65 Family rooms

DOWN
1 Execute axels
2 Turkish title
3 Let out, maybe
4 Gilbert & Sullivan, e.g.
5 Confirm
6 Really bad
7 "Oh, woe __!"
8 Tootsy soaks
9 Marshy ground
10 Klutzy
11 Awful noise
12 __ bandage
13 Stitch up
21 Vast quantity
22 Fix a shoelace
26 Chutney ingredient
27 __ *World Turns*
28 Settles down
29 Federal agts.
30 Log
32 Platoon subdivision
33 Swiss mathematician
34 Pad's paper?
35 Upshot
36 Feels troubled
38 Exterior
39 "*Stille* __"
44 Odors
45 *Happy Days* character
47 Steer clear of
48 They're inimitable
49 Love to pieces
50 "Splish Splash" singer
51 Units of force
53 Pat on the buns?
54 Was behind, in a way
55 Hack
56 Video award
57 Took off

436 JUST DESSERTS by Norma Steinberg

ACROSS
1 Actress Irene
6 Impertinence
10 Cathedral seating
14 Mrs. Ralph Kramden
15 Teheran's country
16 Swear
17 Michelangelo masterpiece
18 Ms. Lollobrigida
19 Krupa or Kelly
20 See 13 Down
21 Dessert
24 Beef cuts
26 Pot top
27 Ariel of Israel
29 Expression of disgust
33 *Pretty* __
34 Swamp whooper
35 Actor Holbrook
37 MP's quarry
38 Static problem
39 Prefix for "hit" or "bucks"
40 Glove leather
41 Impertinence
42 Use skillfully
43 Liquidate
45 Went after
46 Yves' "yes"
47 "The City of Trees"
48 Dessert
53 Truck part
56 Awestruck
57 Feathered scarves
58 Exchange
60 "Second Hand __"
61 Science magazine
62 Compare
63 Gave rise to
64 Affirmative votes
65 Happening

DOWN
1 Theater producer Joseph
2 "It's a Sin to Tell __"
3 Dessert
4 Put-on
5 Zoo favorite
6 Leo, Libra, etc.
7 Cal. neighbor
8 Sensible
9 Going "Grrr!"
10 Thai tower
11 Even once
12 Refuses to
13 With 20 Across, Popeye's kid
22 Bed-and-breakfast establishment
23 Use a stopwatch
25 Spoken
27 Love letters?
28 "__ that possible?"
29 Anguish
30 __ and file
31 Dessert
32 Top Scout
34 *Roman à* __
36 Actress Cheryl
38 Robed singer
39 Sara and Farrow
41 Whodunit board game
42 Bobby's prop
44 Emulated Paul Bunyan
45 *Beverly Hills* __
47 Foundation
48 What you wear
49 Frankenstein's flunky
50 Snoop, with "about"
51 A few
52 Grandma
54 Mideast gulf
55 Crooked
59 *6 Rms, __ Vu*

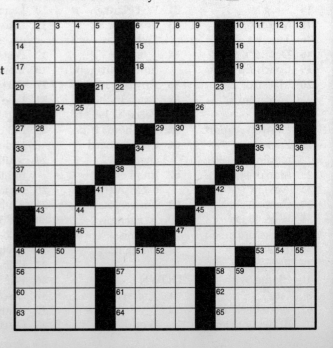

437 TRINITY by Dean Niles

ACROSS
1 Lauder powder
5 Dance, to Deneuve
8 Spill the beans
12 Staying power
13 Russian river
15 __ Music (British group)
16 Pay the penalty
17 Let go
18 "That's clear!"
19 Two-pair beater
22 Cousteau's workplace
23 Bear down
24 Defeats
28 __ were (so to speak)
29 Part of PST
31 Twice XXVI
32 VIP
35 Sky light?
36 Singer Eartha
37 Soap-opera staple
40 Off-the-wall
41 *Seven Days in __*
42 Teatime treats
43 Inventor Whitney
44 Actor Alastair
45 Marsh matter
46 Windblown soil
48 Propelled a raft
50 African snake
53 Club sandwich
56 New York stadium
59 Musical finale
60 Curie or Osmond
61 Rip
62 Egyptian goddess
63 Subtle sarcasm
64 Cheer (up)
65 Pipe fitter's union?
66 Walking stick

DOWN
1 Religious donation
2 Greek marketplace
3 Solitary
4 Enters furtively
5 Sideboard supper
6 Costa Rican Nobelist
7 Buttercup variety
8 __ *of Frankenstein*
9 __ Alamos, NM
10 Bunyan's tool
11 "Toodle-oo!"
12 Large tubs
14 Luau neckwear
20 Japanese art
21 Brokaw's employer
25 Adjust the car wheels
26 Ring championship
27 Locations
28 Off-center
30 Liqueur flavoring
32 Watch part
33 Author Calvino
34 Bottled spirit
35 Pigpen
36 Tie the __ (marry)
38 It may hold you up
39 Theoretical
44 Lith., formerly
45 Tickle pink
47 Very simple
49 Any Elvis recording
50 Ohio city
51 Notre Dame's river
52 Sitting duck
54 __ *on parle français*
55 Actress Williams
56 "The racer's edge"
57 __ *Haw*
58 Lend an __ (listen)

438 THERMOMETRY by Shirley Soloway

ACROSS
1 Imported cheese
5 Hoax
9 Graceful bird
13 Melodious McEntire
14 Watering holes
16 Bed of roses
17 Frosted
18 TV commercial, e.g.
19 Genealogist's output
20 No consolation
23 Damage
24 Holliman or Scruggs
25 Stitch over
27 Talk like Daffy Duck
29 Trick ending
31 Tilted, to a tar
34 Italian noblewoman
36 *The __ Kid* ('79 film)
37 "How adorable!"
38 Stage whisper
40 Luke and Leia's friend
41 Novelist Marcel
44 Peacefully
47 Prince of Darkness
48 Diet component
49 Medicine measure
50 More ironic
52 Discharge
54 Silly Lillie
56 Remains calm
61 Kind of sax
63 Gaiters
64 Hawaiian port
65 Toboggan
66 __-ski party
67 Verve
68 *From __ to Eternity*
69 Whirlpool
70 "Auld Lang __"

DOWN
1 Author Ambler
2 Art __
3 First herdsman
4 Least rational
5 Lethargy
6 Like a paper tiger
7 From
8 *Cats* tune
9 Solidify
10 Greeting-card contents
11 On a whale watch, perhaps
12 __-do-well
15 Achy
21 Drac's wrap
22 Russian autocrat
26 Ransom __ Olds
27 "Too-Ra-__ . . ."
28 Having difficulties
30 Mikhail's missus
32 It'll give you a weigh
33 Cereal-eating tiger
34 Cagney and Lacey
35 Grabbed a chair
36 __-de-lance (viper)
39 Loathed
42 Mideast inits.
43 Trim, in a way
45 Trim, in another way
46 Degrees
48 Ice-cream concoction
51 *Born Free* lioness
53 Gold of *Benson*
54 Gala event
55 *Vogue* competitor
57 Dry-goods measure
58 Fawning
59 *The Good Earth* heroine
60 Isolated
62 Pindaric poem

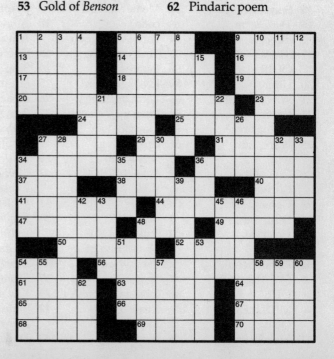

439 GRIDIRON ACTION by Harvey Estes

ACROSS
1 Shed tears
5 Church service
9 Socks
13 Part of OAS
14 *Wait __ Dark* ('67 film)
16 Grandpa McCoy
17 Sack
18 Fright site?
19 Piece of cake
20 Control closely
23 Payable
24 AAA offering
25 Tallahassee coll.
28 Mesmerize
31 Hogan dweller
36 Prince Charles' sister
38 Hatch's home
40 Wyoming range
41 Party hearty
44 Runs without moving
45 Dudley Do-Right's darling
46 Be important
47 __ Pieces (E.T.'s munchies)
49 Constructed a cobweb
51 Yellowstone hrs.
52 Plutarch character
54 Birthstone, e.g.
56 Seder
63 A shake in the grass?
64 Old hat
65 Shipshape
67 Gulf state
68 Eastern Europeans
69 Ghost or golf
70 Fade away
71 Apt. bldg. worker
72 Sign of the future

DOWN
1 Female flier
2 Mideast monarch
3 Condor country
4 In thing
5 Summon
6 Contra- kin
7 Dateless deer?
8 Use cross hairs
9 Corned-beef concoction
10 Atlanta arena
11 Bathday cake
12 Eerie insight
15 Reveal
21 Holidayless mo.
22 Lawn-mower path
25 Muslim mendicant
26 Mean
27 Ben or Sam
29 "Blame __ the Bossa Nova"
30 You can see through them
32 Swerve
33 Peppard series, with *The*
34 Shakes up
35 Kickoff
37 Gets by, with "out"
39 Beatles flick
42 PC enthusiasts
43 Bowe bout
48 Has a ball at the mall
50 Born
53 Racetracks, e.g.
55 Chutney fruit
56 Cougar
57 Thicke or Alda
58 All there
59 Jacob's twin
60 Invitation letters
61 Line of clothing?
62 Hardly feral
63 Interrogative adverb
66 Jack's predecessor

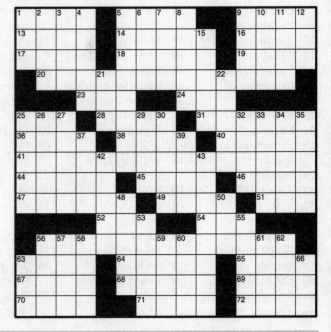

440 PAST MASTER by Donna J. Stone

ACROSS
1 Chan portrayer
6 Tach meas.
9 *All My Children* siren
14 Sleep disorder
15 Sundial numeral
16 *The Champ* director
17 START OF A QUIP
20 Utter
21 Way off base?
22 From __ Z
23 Billing area?
25 Wang Lung's wife
26 One of the Cleavers
29 Gone
31 Benz chaser
32 Dos Passos trilogy
34 Pusan people
38 SPEAKER OF QUIP
40 MIDDLE OF QUIP
41 Muscle type
43 Speedy solution?
44 Nephrologists' org.
45 Least eminent
47 Out of control
48 Author Grey
51 Medieval legal code
54 Fortas or Vigoda
55 Town meetings
56 Fuming
59 END OF QUIP
63 Lorre or Lupus
64 Luau instrument
65 Lummoxlike
66 Cropped up
67 Seer's gift
68 Raleigh's rival

DOWN
1 "Uh-uh!"
2 Talks just like
3 Monogram pt.
4 Tahini base
5 "¡__ la vista!"
6 Ipanema's locale
7 Rice dishes
8 Wednesday
9 First name in stunts
10 Fix a fight
11 Standard
12 Terra __
13 Punishable pyrotechnics
18 Above, to Arnold
19 Country dance
24 Sine __ non
25 Up-front
26 Be a wise guy
27 Bring to ruin
28 Tailed amphibian
30 *Battle Cry* author
32 "Render __ Caesar..."
33 Wales peak
35 *Divine Comedy* figure
36 Megalomaniacal captain
37 Sitting Bull's st.
39 Key signature?
42 State one's case anew
43 Had a bite
46 Has a bite
47 Comes around
48 Mothers of Invention founder
49 More competent
50 Peachy-keen
52 Be inexact
53 __ Triomphe
55 Hot stuff
57 Some bills
58 Irish tongue
60 "Be my guest!"
61 With-it
62 Gender

441   UP A TREE by Shirley Soloway

ACROSS

1 Musical disk
5 Brazilian state
10 Food wrap
14 Hebrew month
15 Inventor Howe
16 Atmosphere
17 Gossipy Barrett
18 Model Cheryl
19 Sunflower support
20 Expanded one's business
23 "Just __ of Those Things"
24 Bambi's mom
25 More malicious
27 Joins up
30 Richard of *The Real McCoys*
32 Actress Thompson
33 Foy or Fisher
35 Tennist Monica
38 H.H. Munro's pseudonym
40 Assistants
42 Lose freshness
43 Take for __ (deceive)
45 Surrendered
47 Farrow of *Radio Days*
48 More orderly
50 Car's safety feature
52 *The Marriage of __*
54 Jack of *Barney Miller*
55 MTV music
56 Peruse
63 Highly excited
65 Irish county
66 Swiss artist Paul
67 Bovine bellows
68 April in Paris
69 Balin and Claire
70 Singer James
71 Word of mouth
72 Head set?

DOWN

1 Apparel
2 What the nose knows
3 Grandmother
4 Rio __
5 D.C. suburb
6 "I cannot tell __"
7 Rushed off
8 *Othello* villain
9 Take for granted
10 Musical notes
11 In a difficult situation
12 "Goodnight __"
13 Less plausible
21 Fruit center
22 Some perfect scores
26 Once again
27 Actress Lanchester
28 In the vicinity
29 Becoming established
30 Apple drink
31 Woodwind instrument
34 Casino cubes
36 Director Kazan
37 Bambi's dad
39 Thought
41 Shore find
44 British nobleman
46 Couturier Christian
49 Shoe tip
51 Raw recruit
52 Chassis
53 Gold bar
57 Thomas __ Edison
58 Jamie of *M*A*S*H*
59 The Kingston __
60 Forearm bone
61 Equipment
62 Musician Myra
64 Young women's org.

442   GLOVE BOXES by Mary E. Brindamour

ACROSS

1 Boston or Bangkok
5 Ulan __
10 Scottish family
14 Dept. of Labor div.
15 Omit, in speech
16 Hit the ceiling
17 Grad
18 Gentlemanly gestures
20 Pro __ (for now)
21 Renown
22 Impossible to miss
23 Shout of approval
25 *Jane __*
27 Mountain-related
29 Rolls along
33 Action word
34 Abrasion
36 Rock-band's need
37 Start the day
39 __ Vegas
40 Spokes, e.g.
42 *Sanford and __*
43 Teacher, at times
46 Talbot or Waggoner
47 Small songbird
49 Tower builder
51 Goals
52 Maui neighbor
53 Makes a buck
56 Ailing
57 Pro-gun grp.
60 Jewelry item
63 Like kids at Christmas
64 Major ending
65 *Kate & __*
66 Animal skin
67 Bread and booze
68 Job openings
69 Trams transport them

DOWN

1 Paint layer
2 Gilligan's home
3 Unique impression
4 Sweet potato
5 Acts properly
6 Texas landmark
7 Fork prong
8 Unconventional
9 Legal matter
10 Longed for
11 Erie or Ontario
12 Stress, perhaps
13 Oriole's home
19 "Little Jack __"
21 Devotee
24 Umbrella parts
25 Clear the slate
26 Slangy assent
27 "Stop, sailor!"
28 "*Vive __!*"
29 Line of work
30 Small sponge cake
31 Novelist Zola
32 Sales pitch
35 *A Touch of __* ('73 film)
38 I specialist?
41 __ Romeo (auto)
44 Daiquiri ingredient
45 Gets to
48 Parsonages
50 Printer's purchase
52 Permissible
53 Ornate pitcher
54 Pretentious
55 Religious ceremony
56 WWII battle site
58 Actor's goal
59 FBI men
61 Used to be
62 The whole enchilada
63 Mil. address

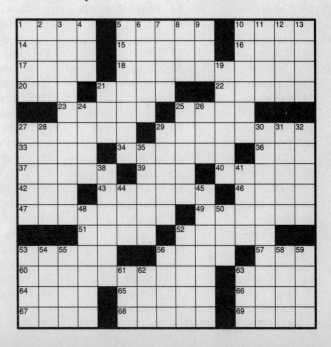

443 SEASON'S GREETINGS by Eric Albert

ACROSS

1 Fancy flapjack
6 Fill with fear
11 Unfriendly
14 Backpack wearer
15 *The Threepenny Opera* star
16 Blue Eagle agcy.
17 Albino rock star
19 Tuck's mate
20 After-school treat
21 City sound
22 Actress Turner
25 Sundae topper
27 On vacation
28 Enlists
29 Tibetan ox
30 Blank
34 School org.
37 Mine find
38 Cartridge holder
39 5.5 yards
40 Arrange type
41 Pasta description
42 Soreness?
43 Call opener
45 Lead-pipe cinch
46 Crooked
48 Bitter brawl
52 Float on the breeze
53 *Green Eggs and Ham* character
54 Frank's ex
55 "Bad Girls" singer
60 Brooks or Blanc
61 Guatemalan good-bye
62 Permission
63 Out of sorts
64 Broods
65 Tire part

DOWN

1 *Evita* role
2 Disencumber
3 Med. test
4 '50s "Awesome!"
5 Robin of 1938
6 Peas-in-a-poddish?
7 October Revolution name
8 Put a penny in the pot
9 Livestock feed
10 Render imperfect
11 Mattress type
12 Court official
13 Like a lap dog
18 Great grief
21 Hogan of golf
22 Sends to slumberland
23 In the know
24 Serve a prison sentence
25 Woo
26 "Another card!"
28 Soprano Sutherland
30 Rhubarb unit
31 Ornamental shrub
32 Loosen a fastener
33 Driving need
35 Pentateuch
36 Very skilled
44 Put away
45 Almost boil
46 Turbaned teacher
47 Orange variety
48 Light boat
49 Put together
50 "__ the season . . ."
51 Service error
53 Use scissors
55 Lassie's mother
56 *Deep Space Nine* character
57 Rita __ Brown
58 Zsa Zsa's sister
59 Blushing

444 FACTOR-IZATION by Matt Gaffney

ACROSS

1 Utah senator
6 Karate wear
10 Hwy.
13 Heart parts
14 Chef Child
15 Witch's curse
16 Gable role
18 Bonanza material
19 Baseballer Dykstra
20 Like some nuts
21 Bank org.
22 Pass catchers
24 Flour variety
25 South Korean city
26 *The __ of Casterbridge*
28 Eyes lasciviously
30 Border
32 Formal agreement
33 Rage
34 Bill Clinton was one
38 Even if, informally
39 In __ (positioned)
40 Lennon's lady
41 Pop poets
43 *Wheel* host
47 Jessye Norman's forte
48 Mineral spring
51 Bedtime, in ads
52 Sonja Henie's birthplace
53 Miser
56 Game pieces
57 "Annabel Lee" author
58 *Cheers* actress
60 Sullivan and O'Neill
61 Role for 58 Across
62 Gem State capital
63 Function prefix
64 Olympic hawk
65 Fortify

DOWN

1 Manhattan district
2 Parthenon dedicatee
3 In
4 Pasadena coll.
5 Beaver and bowler
6 Montana city
7 Model Macpherson
8 Rearranged the facts?
9 __ *Baby* (Morrison novel)
10 Zimbabwe, formerly
11 *Tootsie* star
12 Carry out
14 Caesar's month
17 Tight spot?
21 Remote
23 London area
25 Wyoming peaks
27 Big part of the Bible?
28 Fond du __, WI
29 Sonic rebound
31 Eshkol's successor
32 Paterno sch.
34 Musical genre
35 Lost
36 Ave. crossers
37 Bank's offering
38 Flocked together
42 Paid player
44 Comic Walker
45 Relaxed
46 Husky home
48 Circus barkers
49 Daddy
50 Go __ (flip out)
53 Burn a bit
54 Roll-call reply
55 Spheres
58 JVC competitor
59 Fate

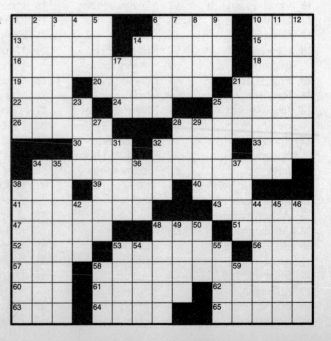

445 SOUND ARGUMENTS by Karen Hodge

ACROSS
1 Mass place
6 Until now
11 Boxing blow
14 Hex
15 Japanese board game
16 NATO member
17 Where to file armor suits?
19 Ctr.
20 Pure Sir
21 Go by
23 Categorize
24 PA 76, I-80, etc.
25 Fresh words
27 Will be: Sp.
29 Lock part
33 Sad, to Simone
35 Author Hunter
38 King of Broadway
39 Suit spec.
40 Litigation capital?
42 Personal opinion
43 Show to a seat
44 Exam for H.S. jrs.
45 Room to maneuver
47 Maximum
49 Sleeper, maybe
51 Business-letter word
52 Working
55 Put into effect
57 *Moby-Dick* ship
60 West and Keaton
62 Discharge
63 Result of religious conviction?
66 Architect I.M.
67 Head: Lat.
68 "I fear'd __ might anger thee": Shak.
69 Pressure unit: Abbr.
70 At __ for words
71 Old-time auto

DOWN
1 Exclamation of disgust
2 Breath holder
3 Case losers' sounds?
4 Smooth __
5 Detox center's objective
6 "On __ of one to ten . . ."
7 Booted?
8 One of the "Three Little Words"
9 Plume source
10 *Wheel of Fortune* category
11 Checkers move
12 Defects and all
13 Commanded
18 The Minotaur's downfall
22 Ski wood
24 Mr. Shankar
25 Play the uke
26 "You __ beautiful to me"
28 Right-hand page
30 Affirmative testifier?
31 Term of endearment
32 Stratagems
34 1/48 c.
36 Braves' home
37 TV comedian Louis
41 Sunrise spot
46 Houdini specialties
48 Greek cross
50 Scrumptious spreads
53 Puccini masterwork
54 Perfect
56 Abundant
57 Shakespeare producer
58 Sonny and Cher, e.g.
59 Big boat, initially
60 AC power units
61 Fill up
64 Nav. rank
65 CII – XLIII

446 TOO MUCH NOISE by Alex Vaughn

ACROSS
1 Corn holder
4 Certain Slav
8 He takes things easily
14 Get a move on
15 Vicinity
16 Supply of wine
17 Furry TV alien
18 Dines at eve
19 Emulate Earhart
20 Extreme urgency
23 Mound
24 __ the line (obeyed)
25 Estrada or Satie
28 Radiant
30 AMA members
33 Yoko __
34 Le Duc __ (Vietnamese statesman)
36 Landed
37 Gave the green light
38 It followed WWII
41 Bonfire residue
43 Lo-cal
44 Hose on a ball field
45 Wildebeest
46 For each
47 Honeybee's foothold, maybe
51 Stately shaders
53 Wife of Osiris
57 Om study course?
58 Cosmological explanation
62 Kitchen implement
64 Shielded, at sea
65 Golfer's aid
66 Big lizard
67 Highway marker
68 Woman treated as an object?
69 Opinionated list
70 Former Surgeon General
71 Gridiron units: Abbr.

DOWN
1 Mambo relative
2 Offshore platform
3 Happen to
4 Cummerbund
5 Let out the lava
6 Printer's proof
7 Musical Count
8 '80s Chrysler product
9 Stubbs or Strauss
10 Not just anyone
11 Ping-Pong place
12 "I tawt I taw a puddy __"
13 Lode load
21 Arboreal idler
22 Strange to say
26 Squid's squirt
27 Sent down for the count
29 Whipper-snapper
31 Soul-food order
32 Crouch
35 Theater award
36 Tad's dad
38 The go-ahead
39 Swanky lobbies
40 Daisy type
41 Get mellower
42 NBC comedy showcase
48 Like some smiles
49 "It's a deal!"
50 Thicknesses
52 __ the captain's table
54 Carrot stick or candy bar
55 Nanook's nook
56 Pool person
59 Actor Hackman
60 Fiber source
61 Nasty Uriah
62 Harness part
63 Past

447 — NATIONALISM by Randolph Ross

ACROSS

1 Prepare vegetables
6 Compass dir.
9 Calendar abbr.
12 Delphic VIP
14 Ark architect
15 Cato's eggs
16 Warsaw angler?
18 Casserole cover
19 Asian holiday
20 Scandinavian with his back up?
22 Language suffix
23 WY setting
24 *Peyton __*
25 Ridge
27 Conduct a meeting
31 Vital statistics
32 Graf's game
34 Acidity
36 Prague publication?
38 Slowness to anger
41 Refines metal
45 Bravo and Grande
46 Strikebreaker
48 Unrestrained
49 Slipped up
51 Service div.
53 Damage
54 Stockholmer's courage?
58 Author LeShan
59 Chinese principle
60 Bangkok kin?
63 Tulsa coll.
64 *The Art of Love* author
65 Sidesteps
66 Speedy flier
67 Understand
68 Sociologist Hite

DOWN

1 Most lenient
2 Italian seaport
3 Oriental
4 Essen expletive
5 Half of MMCII
6 Goes to court?
7 Ramon's room
8 Have a puppy
9 Fall scenery
10 Brings to light
11 Evil
13 Calls it a day
14 PBS affiliate
17 Ancient barbarian
21 Offensive football position
23 Corn color
26 Cut into
28 Actor Milo
29 Badminton stroke
30 Pairs
33 D.C. 100
35 Type style
37 New Deal agcy.
38 Magic words
39 Sky battles
40 Removed, as pages
42 Summer cooler
43 Sycophant
44 Spandau street
47 Singer Ives
50 Clarify, in a way
52 Eye problem
55 Possess
56 Send out
57 Lend a hand
61 Watching machines?
62 Multipurpose exclamation

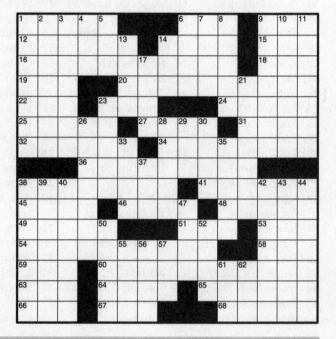

448 — FLIGHT FORMATION by Sally R. Stein

ACROSS

1 Chicago jetport
6 Air traveler's bane
10 '60s TV talker
14 Lint collector
15 Ending for attend
16 Flying prefix
17 "Anything goes!"
20 Tobacco oven
21 Chowed down
22 New York city
23 Fairy-tale meanie
25 Mr. Lugosi
27 Doubled up
30 American and rivals
34 Accountant, at times
35 Hold back
36 Suffix for verb
37 Executive's takeover insurance
41 Before
42 Some seafood
43 Like freeways
44 Early NASA rocket
47 Big Big Band name
48 No-no negative
49 Bugs Bunny's pursuer
50 In any way
53 Retainer
54 French silk
58 Sign of safety
62 Stravinsky's *The __ of Spring*
63 Hawaiian strings
64 "*Deutschland über __*"
65 Stinky
66 Pinball problem
67 Texas shrine

DOWN

1 Aware of
2 Some laughter
3 City rtes.
4 Made over
5 Fraternal member
6 Haste result
7 Pay to play
8 "*__ bin ein Berliner*"
9 Hole start
10 Potent potable
11 Do followers
12 Newsman Sevareid
13 Beard, once of ITT
18 It's behind the house
19 Calm down
24 Actor Richard
25 Catafalques
26 Columnist Bombeck
27 It beeps
28 Like a lot
29 Wasn't busy
30 "Thereby hangs __"
31 Any old things
32 Cosmetician Lauder
33 Less then luxurious
35 Exhausted
38 Light gas
39 Schlemiel
40 Persuasion to purchase
45 Shook out from the shaker
46 Word-game piece
47 Four-handed piano piece
49 Quite a meal
50 Natural hairdo
51 Follow
52 Italian wine region
53 Sense
55 __ podrida
56 Particular
57 "Tiger in your tank" company
59 Weirdo
60 Enjoy Aspen
61 Call of the mild?

449 FILMS OF THE MONTH by Trip Payne

ACROSS

1 Easy dessert?
4 Bundy and Hirt
7 Suit badly
14 Ali Kafi's land
16 Acura model
17 Eye-related
18 On the way out
19 French menu word
20 *A Passage to India* subject
22 Look at again
23 Clockmaker Thomas et al.
25 Stew server
28 Long-term goal
30 Indeed
31 Like cavern walls
35 Rodeo animal
38 Threshold
39 Soothing substance
40 Popular solecism
41 James Dean type
43 Luke's teacher
44 Zip along
45 Boathouse item
46 Moveable feast
48 Runners carry it
49 __ Lanka
50 ___-Star Pictures
51 Lineup
54 Photographer Adams
58 Fiesta Bowl city
61 Krueger's street
63 Put together
64 Supervised
67 Trattoria treat
69 Armed force
70 Calendar period
71 *Being There* star
72 Singer Ritter
73 Draft agcy.

DOWN

1 White-spotted rodents
2 "__ the Nightlife" ('78 song)
3 Snowy bird
4 Modern art?
5 Leg-puller
6 Dresden diet dish
7 Wire gauge
8 Chemical ending
9 Look too long
10 Burt Lancaster film of '64
11 Sponsorship
12 Ocean flier
13 Sorcerer
15 Joan Plowright film of '92
21 Bette Davis film of '48
24 Bracketed word
26 Come unglued
27 Shoelace hole
29 Down in the dumps
32 Oodles
33 Pie à la __
34 Compote component
35 Cell blocks?
36 Mideastern bread
37 Long ago
42 Bring home
47 Sportsman Parseghian
52 *Beau* __
53 Hand out
55 Wise guys
56 *Dame __ Hollywood*
57 Women's magazine
58 He-cats
59 *Howards End* role
60 Pell-__
62 Lion's pride
65 Strain
66 *How the West __ Won*
68 Dr. Ruth's field

---

450 NOT SO HOT by Eric Albert

ACROSS

1 Rocker Jett
5 It comes from the heart
10 Harass a pledge
14 Skilled
15 Navigation danger
16 Execute
17 Dispassionate?
20 Tumbler turner
21 Enterprising captain?
22 "Relax, soldier!"
23 Galileo's birthplace
24 Mast or boom
25 Upward slope
28 "Oops!"
29 Service member?
32 Shy
33 Bates or King
34 Bond foe
35 Just out?
38 Seasons firewood
39 Bladed poles
40 Teases unmercifully
41 Mint
42 Whale of a tale
43 Diet-ad caption
44 Summer-camp activity
45 Dexterous
46 Peace of mind
49 Long story
50 Hen or pen
53 Capote book?
56 Papal name
57 It's often delivered
58 Improve oneself, in a way
59 Singer Adams
60 Asparagus helping
61 Alluring

DOWN

1 Trunk tool
2 Bassoon cousin
3 Sheedy of *Only the Lonely*
4 Composer Rorem
5 Pitch in
6 Butler's bride
7 Symbol of steadfastness
8 Kind of cross
9 De Niro role
10 *The Gulf Stream* artist
11 Israel's Eban
12 Sleepers catch them
13 Rochester's love
18 Resembling
19 Bountiful setting
23 Salon offerings
24 Persian rulers
25 It's near Lake Nasser
26 Put on
27 Hall-of-Fame hitter Rod
28 *Ne plus* __
29 Philosophy
30 Racing surname
31 Oater extras
33 __ *in the Crowd*
34 Tenor
36 One way to play
37 Factory-assembled
42 French river
43 Alms requester
44 Neighsayer?
45 *Who's the Boss?* star
46 Ready to eat
47 Geraint's lady
48 "Rats!"
49 Economy, for one
50 Tender
51 Piltdown man, e.g.
52 Uptight
54 Vim and vigor
55 Barbell letters

451   IN THE CARDS by Shirley Soloway

ACROSS
1 Cotton bundle
5 Health clubs
9 Woodworking tool
14 Whiff
15 Soft-drink choice
16 Allen or Frome
17 __' War (racehorse)
18 Stir up
19 Silvery fish
20 Battle positions
23 Castilian cheer
24 Before, to Byron
25 More amusing
27 Emulate Hines
32 Author Bagnold
33 "Where Do __?" (*Hair* tune)
34 Atlantis or Long
36 Actor Sharif
39 Accepted
41 Gone by
42 Kind of drum
43 Pitcher Hershiser
44 *Tarzan, the* __
46 __ manner of speaking

47 Barbecue favorite
49 Taped
51 Gets the better of
54 *Exodus* hero
55 __ carte
56 Bar order
62 Ruffled trim
64 Busy as __
65 Barcelona bull
66 Perfect
67 Study all night
68 Pizazz
69 Tree houses?
70 Actress Jurado
71 Great dog

DOWN
1 Dismal failure
2 Hebrew month
3 Actress Anderson
4 Wore away
5 Room dividers
6 *Winnie-the-*__
7 Catch in __ (unmask)
8 Dieter's dish
9 Textbook division

10 Sun. banker?
11 Bette Davis film
12 Berry of *Boomerang*
13 Computer key
21 Midwest product
22 __ Scott Decision
26 Pride papa
27 Former Yugoslavian leader
28 Ice-cream ingredient
29 Inscrutable expressions
30 Applaud
31 Champing at the bit
35 Alaskan seaport
37 English composer Thomas
38 Enjoy a novel
40 Author Wiesel
42 Stallion sound
44 Italian wine region
45 *Police* __ ('84 film)

48 Deli rolls
50 Caused a commotion
51 "Mack the Knife" singer
52 Dodge
53 Light bite
57 "Cadabra" preceder
58 Orderly
59 Vincent Lopez theme
60 Pakistan neighbor
61 Ice-cream holder
63 Tam or turban

---

452   WINNING PAIRS by Carol Fenter

ACROSS
1 October implement
5 Stuffy
10 "Doorman, call me __"
14 "Peek-__!"
15 Puccini opera
16 Musical conclusion
17 Winning pair in '64
20 Leatherworker's item
21 Deck member
22 Streisand song
23 Campus female
24 Took a rest
25 Goes bad
28 Ruination
29 Parisian pie
30 Postcard message
31 Greek cheese
35 Winning pair in '56
38 Walked
39 *The Defiant* __
40 "Untouchable" Ness

41 Trudge
42 __ cry (slogan)
43 Inserts more film
47 Soap setting?
48 International agcy.
49 Elaborate party
50 Cry of discovery
53 Winning pair in '44
56 *Et* __ (list ender)
57 Top-drawer
58 Forced to go
59 Wash
60 More mature
61 Wraps up

DOWN
1 Punjabi prince
2 Take __ (acknowledge applause)
3 German chancellor Helmut
4 Forever and a day
5 Salts away
6 __ down (softened)

7 Pale
8 Hosp. area
9 Laundry worker
10 Nose noise
11 Esprit de __
12 An Astaire
13 Howled like a wolf
18 Hot
19 Le Moko or Le Pew
23 Quoted an authority
24 Evaluates a movie
25 Galley notation
26 Couple
27 Approximately
28 Like a cowpoke's legs
30 Taboos
31 Foul matter
32 Way out
33 *Home Improvement* prop
34 Kick in
36 Extend an engagement
37 Tidier

41 Trot or canter
42 Pancake starter
43 Urban's opposite
44 __ *Gay*
45 7th-century pope
46 Actor Davis

47 Actress Davis
49 Wacky Wilson
50 Sunday shout
51 Ranch worker
52 Hill dwellers
54 Yalie
55 Take advantage of

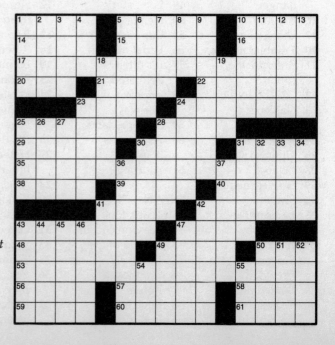

453   PARDON MY FRENCH by Trip Payne

ACROSS

1 Thornburgh's predecessor
6 Isfahan's locale
10 Criticize harshly
14 At full speed
15 Wine's aroma
16 Spelling of *90210*
17 1958 shocker
20 Catch sight of
21 Finish second
22 Clear a video
23 Little legume
25 Victor
26 Inauguration highlight
32 Toymaking tycoon?
33 *Common Sense* writer
34 Raven relative
37 Leaps
38 Walked in the woods
39 Loft cube
40 "So there!"
41 Dead duck
42 Buffalo coat?
43 Stubborn sorts
45 1990 Cy Young winner Doug
48 Inclined
49 *College Bowl* host Robert
50 Debtors' letters
53 Mosque official
57 Promise to never use again
60 Dress style
61 Cold capital
62 Hitching place?
63 *Harper's Bazaar* artist
64 Kiwis' kin
65 Plowmaker John

DOWN

1 Its punch is spiked
2 Green-egg layers
3 Tombstone figure
4 His rock kept rolling
5 Chemical suffix
6 Scoop, for short
7 Deteriorates
8 '68 U.S. Open champ
9 Society-page word
10 Shandy's creator
11 Theatrical salesman
12 Got up
13 He gets down to work
18 Viking name
19 Clear the frost
24 Dawn goddess
25 Reset a watch
26 Folksinger Phil
27 Lotion additive
28 Finish-line marker
29 Have thoughts
30 Charlatan
31 Passionate
34 They hold the mayo
35 Actress Sommer
36 Drinks from bags
38 Skein sound
39 Paris fortress
41 Actress Garson
42 Baby basenji
43 Like some spheroids
44 Event, in El Salvador
45 Tivoli's Villa __
46 Less polished
47 "You __ serious!"
50 Then
51 *Man __ Mancha*
52 Tabloid topics
54 Tiny thing
55 Out of range
56 Only
58 ___-pah-pah
59 "Cool!"

454   FASTENATION by Bob Lubbers

ACROSS

1 *Betsy's Wedding* director
5 Till
9 Jack and jenny
14 Debt security
15 Architect Saarinen
16 Buck or Bailey
17 Mainer, e.g.
19 Webber's partner
20 SNAP
22 Shadowy site
23 Encouraging word
24 Museum pieces
26 Rep. or dep.
29 Bulldogs
32 PDQ relative
33 Cuts across
36 Actor Stu
39 Puerto __
40 Dirties
42 __ up (judge)
43 Bracelet site
45 Elementary particles
47 Tra-__
49 Antitoxins
50 Oral examiner: Abbr.
51 Jacks, often
54 Part of Q&A
56 __-jongg
57 TAPE
63 Dumbstruck
65 Microwave, for one
66 Swamp stalker
67 State strongly
68 Wedding cake layer
69 __ Ababa
70 __ souci (carefree)
71 Dutch portrait painter

DOWN

1 Baldwin of *Prelude to a Kiss*
2 Truth twister
3 Lucie's dad
4 Fidgety
5 Sheet fabrics
6 Carson's successor
7 Hydrox competitor
8 Inner mechanism
9 Quiet
10 Coral or Red
11 TACK
12 Bert's pal
13 Husky loads
18 Duel tools
21 "Make __ double!"
25 Foot bones
26 Gillette product
27 Beam broadly
28 NAIL
30 Religious image
31 Pigs' digs
34 Pitcher Ryan
35 Swing around
37 Shirt brand
38 Nitti's nemesis
41 Certain airmen
44 Casino naturals
46 Carries on
48 Fly trajectory
51 Nebraska city
52 Called for
53 Girls of Guat.
55 Reaped row
58 Hindu deity
59 Portent
60 Reebok rival
61 Sprightly dance
62 Drops the ball
64 Ho dish

455 AROUND THE ZODIAC by Bob Carroll

ACROSS
1 Jai __
5 Kind of statistics
10 Fells
14 Smith and Fleming
15 Hole __
16 __ the crack of dawn
17 American League team?
20 Minutiae
21 Speed demon
22 Turf
23 Make money
25 Sports conference
29 O'Hara estate
30 Silvery-gray
33 From the top
34 Attack
35 __ and Sympathy
36 Exaggerates?
40 Word form for "same"
41 Green-card holder
42 Light rain
43 They're out of this world

44 Far from swarthy
45 Robbins hit
47 Author Shere
48 So. state
49 Tonto's horse
52 The bridge on the river Kwai
56 Yuppie nosh?
60 From a distance
61 Expect
62 Catches 40 winks
63 Count (on)
64 Reed and Harrison
65 "The __ the limit!"

DOWN
1 Crest competitor
2 Put down
3 Archer or Jackson
4 Ain't right?
5 Foresight
6 __ Chicago ('38 film)
7 They toddle

8 Santa __, CA
9 Journey part
10 Person
11 Grand-scale tale
12 Decline
13 Tend the sauce
18 Facility
19 Book boo-boos
23 Ingested
24 Smell __ (suspect)
25 Enjoy the beach
26 __ water (troublebound)
27 Lysol target
28 Brace
29 Mini-guffaw
30 Open courtyards
31 Dr. for children
32 Must
34 Steps in a field
37 Elk
38 Chair piece
39 Plate cleaner
45 Chooses
46 Cowboy actor LaRue

47 Get the lead out
48 Palmer, to pals
49 Indelible impression
50 Bagdad __
51 October birthstone

52 Recordings, MTV-style
53 Sawbucks
54 Security problem
55 Notice
57 Elevator unit
58 Attribute
59 Tee preceder

456 CULINARY COMBOS by Bob Lubbers

ACROSS
1 Lettuce variety
5 Vogue competitor
9 Less
14 Actor Jannings
15 Fashion name
16 By oneself
17 Competent
18 Asta's mistress
19 Canterbury headdress
20 Little girl's makeup
23 Saw serrations
24 Visualized
25 B&O and NY Central
28 Asp gasp?
29 She-bear, in Seville
32 Vendor
34 Put on a pedestal
37 Mrs. Chaplin
38 Everyday dinner
42 Jocular Johnson
43 Persian potentates

44 Short snooze
46 Kitchen meas.
47 Author Levin
50 Language suffix
51 Mad as a hatter
54 Less plausible
56 Common condiments
60 Copycat's cry
62 Taleteller
63 As a __ (usually)
64 Happening
65 Ore source
66 Eye part
67 Walks through water
68 Ginger cookie
69 Gave temporarily

DOWN
1 Burden bearers
2 Permeates
3 Ship sections
4 Act sheepishly?
5 Best of films
6 Jungle king
7 Some nobles

8 Remove graphite
9 Feast or __
10 DeMille specialty
11 Napoleonic defeat site
12 "To __ is human . . ."
13 Hwy.
21 Valerie Harper sitcom
22 Coins of Spain
26 Russo of Lethal Weapon 3
27 Mexican Mmes.
30 Solar occurrence
31 M*A*S*H man
33 Oodles
34 "__ o'clock scholar"
35 Fitting
36 Legal wrong
38 Medieval weapon
39 Historical periods

40 Swore (to)
41 Tell target
45 Portions out
47 Tainted
48 Retrieve a trout
49 Clap in cuffs
52 Rings up

53 Burger topper
55 Taxing time?
57 Top-notch
58 Doll's word
59 Make ready
60 Kitten's comment
61 __ Marie Saint

457 WATER LOG by Dean Niles

ACROSS
1 Holey roll
6 Choir member
10 Actor Auberjonois
14 Toughen up
15 NASA destination
16 *Tosca* tune
17 Book of maps
18 1961 invasion site
20 Grid judge
21 Cast off
23 Restive
24 Animal trail
26 Olympic runner Lewis
28 Pacino's profession
30 Wedding dance
34 Weight allowances
35 Takes off
36 Baseball stat
37 Wedding-cake layer
38 Paper measures
39 Lowdown
40 Lyricist Gershwin
41 Accordingly
42 Journalist Joseph
43 Clever retort
45 Playful
46 Traditional knowledge
47 Renaissance fiddle
48 Texas __ University
51 California city
52 *Norma* __
55 Linda Ronstadt hit
58 Tenth-graders
60 Wagers
61 Viet __
62 Colosseum contest
63 Take a breather
64 TV's Downs
65 Fall tools

DOWN
1 Put up with
2 Pay to play
3 Warm current
4 Distinct period
5 Textbook topics
6 Light color?
7 Fill up
8 Plaything
9 Yoko __
10 With total absorption
11 __ the Red
12 Imminent
13 No sweat
19 Pink-slips
22 Take everything
25 Docking place
26 Weather condition
27 Pub orders
28 Top level
29 Mubarak's city
30 "Woe is me!"
31 Mary Steenburgen film
32 "You can't judge __ ..."
33 Unsteady
35 Yard barrier
38 __ *Window*
39 Ballet bend
41 Nuclear weapon
42 Go-between
44 Firstborn
45 Invited to dinner
47 Unrefined
48 Short form, for short
49 Sheltered, at sea
50 "Phooey!"
51 Stretched out
53 Actress Baxter
54 Guesses: Abbr.
56 Essen expletive
57 "__ don't say!"
59 Gabor sister

458 DIGITAL READOUT by Shirley Soloway

ACROSS
1 Ann __, MI
6 Kett of the comics
10 Cpl.'s subordinates
14 Former NYC mayor
15 Nadirs
16 Daytime drama
17 Best and Ferber
18 Small cut
19 __ *La Douce*
20 Piano-key count
23 Actor Danson
24 Drivers' org.
25 Sock style
27 Billboard displays
30 Light preceder
32 Crazy as __
33 Greek island
35 Retirement age for some
39 Mountain refuge
40 Lon of Cambodia
41 Comparison: Abbr.
42 Blackjack
45 Complete a salad
46 Not in any way
47 Dallas coll.
49 *The Crying Game* star
50 __ of (eliminate)
52 The whole lot
54 TV Tarzan
55 Convenience chain
62 Throw lightly
64 Easter bloom
65 Dodge
66 Mayberry youngster
67 Author Hunter
68 Transmits
69 Coming up
70 Depend (on)
71 Low cards

DOWN
1 Have __ in one's bonnet
2 "Handy" product-name prefix
3 Explosive sound
4 Nebraska city
5 Say it again
6 Otherwise
7 Singer Tennille
8 Branch bit
9 Paving material
10 Chi follower
11 Prospector
12 Moroccan mount
13 Hammett detective
21 Deviate
22 Hector's home
26 Succeed
27 Part of CPA
28 Close the curtains
29 Year of the spirit
31 "The time __"
32 Wheel shafts
34 Domingo, for one
36 Charged atom
37 Bud holder
38 *Born Free* lioness
43 "__ Magic Moment"
44 Vocal mountaineer
45 Least stimulating
48 West of Hollywood
50 Make progress
51 Wed in haste
53 Move with a fulcrum
56 "__ la France!"
57 Mideast airline
58 The Big Apple, for short
59 Windmill part
60 Whirlpool
61 "Untouchable" Eliot
63 Make waves?

459 BEANS by Fred Piscop

ACROSS

1 Seeing red
6 "__ me up, Scotty"
10 Sported
14 Coeur d'__, ID
15 __-Seltzer
16 "Zip-__-Doo-Dah"
17 WAX
20 Certain ammo
21 Berry bushes
22 Stand for
23 Manage somehow
24 __ plexus
27 It's usually four
29 Get one's goat
33 Ever and __
34 River feature
36 G.P. grp.
37 KIDNEY
40 LAX abbr.
41 Nutritional need
42 Forget
43 Boom type
45 Cal. page
46 Celts
47 "Make my day," e.g.
49 Drunk follower
50 Clock again
53 Chewy confection
57 GREEN
60 Datum
61 Dairy-case item
62 Old toothpaste
63 __ d'oeuvres
64 Flair
65 To be: Sp.

DOWN

1 Big dog
2 "__ a Song Go Out . . ."
3 Swerve
4 Type of medicine
5 Plane spray
6 Actor Max
7 New Haven hardwoods
8 Rap-sheet abbr.
9 San __, CA
10 Prison honcho
11 Garfield's pal
12 Bring up
13 Snaky fish
18 Dachshund doc
19 Ciudad Juárez neighbor
23 Siskel or Ebert
24 Presses, as flowers
25 __ a customer
26 Navigational device
27 3/17 event
28 Rapidly
30 "__ with a spoon!"
31 High-tech memo
32 Goes ballistic
34 Box-score abbr.
35 Scout group
38 Pitch tents
39 Glove-box contents
44 Numskulls
46 "Say good night, __"
48 Cultivate again
49 Onassis' nickname
50 Get cracking
51 Word form for "within"
52 Ivan, e.g.
53 Govt. workers' org.
54 Like __ of bricks
55 French state
56 Actress Olin
58 Out of sorts
59 Colonial descendants' org.

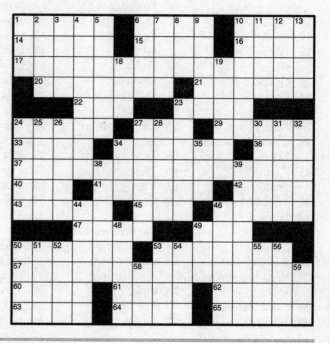

460 SMALL-TIME by Bob Carroll

ACROSS

1 Factory teeth
5 Jet set?
9 Orlando's backup
13 Beef cut
14 Throw in the towel
15 De Klerk's predecessor
16 Small-time poet?
18 A trip around the world
19 Catty?
20 Give off
22 Whopper concocter
24 Heroic romance
25 Heel
28 Prone to bumbling
31 Awaken
33 Hard work
34 Painting medium
38 "My Way" composer
39 Treacherous
40 Zion National Park state
41 Suds
42 "Up and __!"
43 Audience cheer
44 Come before
47 Patsy
48 A Musketeer
50 "Ooh __!"
52 Editor Fadiman
54 Easily solved
58 More qualified
59 Small-time race?
62 Donnybrook
63 Right-hand person
64 Caspian Sea, technically
65 Unwanted guest, e.g.
66 Canned
67 Spud buds

DOWN

1 Staff member?
2 Move like molasses
3 Young woman
4 Slow one
5 Rat
6 Star of the day
7 Start of a game?
8 Occupational suffix
9 Small-time actress?
10 Up
11 E.B. or Betty
12 Hoopster Archibald
15 Presages
17 In reserve
21 Light on one's feet
23 Take turns
25 Kvetch
26 Top-rated
27 British nobleman
29 Parceled (out)
30 Dreadful
32 Small-time actress?
35 "Take __ a compliment!"
36 Barbecue rocks
37 Have a ball at the mall
39 DeLuise film
43 Misrepresent
45 __ Dame
46 Experienced
48 *The Zoo Story* author
49 Dough drawers
51 Generous
52 A summer place
53 Sports org.
55 Beseech
56 Cotton to
57 They left the union
60 Veto
61 William Wordsworth work

461 SWAP MEET by Trip Payne

ACROSS
1 Inner personality
6 Loft cube
10 __ carotene
14 Secondary
15 Colorado tribe
16 Burly Burl
17 Pupil from abroad
20 Face lifts?
21 It can be common
22 UN branch
25 *Wheel of Fortune* buy
26 Clever repartee
27 __ on the chin
29 Prudish person
31 Former jrs.
32 Versatile batter
35 On the briny
36 Bunyan's whacker
37 Gymnast Korbut
41 Job-training places
46 Squeal
49 Russian river
50 First stage
51 Steamy
53 Meditative words
54 Scone partner
55 Decide about
56 Actress Tomei
59 Reason for travel
64 Scrabble piece
65 Poi base
66 Absurd
67 Cong. meeting
68 School on the Thames
69 Ephron and Dunn

DOWN
1 Soul, in Soissons
2 Prohibit
3 Stateside Ltd.
4 __ scale (hardness index)
5 Old Semitic language
6 Troop tooter
7 To __ (just so)
8 Not as much
9 Guinness Book ending
10 Delaware Democrat
11 Contests
12 More nervous
13 Autumn bloomers
18 Baseball climax, usually
19 Grammarian's concern
22 __ *Wonderful Life*
23 Statutes
24 Joad, for one
26 Small amount
28 "L'__, c'est moi"
29 TV-display speck
30 Hwys.
33 "If I __ hammer . . ."
34 Carrot or radish
38 Out of sight?
39 Untamed joy
40 *The Thin Man* terrier
42 Regretting
43 Lob path
44 Crystal or Carlin
45 Jordan's king
46 Does a double take
47 Jughead's pal
48 Thoroughly destroys
52 Vocal sounds
53 Bean or Welles
56 Castle ditch
57 Bushy do
58 Part of A.D.
60 Bastille Day season
61 Canal zone?
62 Genetic material
63 "You bet!"

462 GRID PLAY by Matt Gaffney

ACROSS
1 Shed, in Shrewsbury
6 French bread?
11 That woman
14 Potts or Oakley
15 Houston athlete
16 Sleeve contents?
17 Part of the NFL
20 In the style of
21 Architect I.M.
22 Switzerland's capital
23 Comic DeLuise
24 Thesaurus man
28 *My Life as __* ('85 film)
29 States emphatically
32 Couch
33 Alaskan seaport
34 Soldier's awards
36 Wonka's creator
38 Part of CBS
39 3 points in football
42 Slightly spoiled
45 Request
46 Head and Wharton
50 Train track
52 Painter Chagall
54 Jacobi of *I, Claudius*
55 __ way (not at all)
56 Legal catchall
58 Woodsman's tool
59 Missouri range
61 Physique, for short
63 Dershowitz specialty
64 Football placement
69 SASE, e.g.
70 Jazzman Chick
71 Bravery
72 "I told you so!"
73 Garden tools
74 Reads quickly

DOWN
1 Paving material
2 Carpenters tune
3 Not indicated
4 Ignited
5 Univ. of Maryland player
6 Page numbers
7 Free (of)
8 "The Greatest"
9 Calif. neighbor
10 Baby furniture
11 Beehive and bob
12 Election issue
13 Goes back on a promise
18 __ Lingus
19 Penn or Young
25 Actress Paulette
26 H.S. math course
27 Western lake
30 *Luftwaffe* opp.
31 Lose one's footing
35 Alabama city
37 Actress Cheryl
40 Fit and trim
41 Stretch the truth
42 Baltimore players
43 Aficionado's periodical
44 MBA major
47 Sung syllables
48 Geometric figure
49 Spits
51 Folk tail?
53 Snake charmer's crew
57 Louis, *par exemple*
60 Dinkins' predecessor
62 Auto offs.
65 Egg __ yong
66 Promgoers: Abbr.
67 Average grade
68 Ringo's raincoat

463 JEWELRY STORE by Harvey Estes

ACROSS

1 Confederate president
6 *Li'l Abner* cartoonist
10 Crane or Cummings
13 Author Jong
14 See eye to eye
16 Broad st.
17 Site for scouring
19 Affirmative vote
20 Not on the sched.
21 Actor Pickens
22 Oak nut
24 Wd. part
25 Pool tool
26 Hazardous gas
28 Evidence of angst
32 Porpoise pack
35 East, in Essen
36 Make a knot
37 Some roasts
38 Article written by Pascal
39 Shoe material
41 "__ hands on deck!"
42 *Wheel of Fortune* purchase
43 Hoopster Michael
44 Prison paraphernalia
48 European capital
49 Inclined
50 Audiophile's purchase
53 "Later!" in Lyons
55 Hindu avatar
57 "*O Sole __*"
58 *Diamond __*
59 Kegler's targets
63 Buddy
64 Expect
65 Egg containers
66 Like a fox
67 AMEX rival
68 Old hat

DOWN

1 Obligations
2 Sheik site
3 Essential
4 I, in Augsburg
5 Posed for pics
6 Wired
7 Cultural start
8 Yellow flower
9 Cross product
10 Stabbed in combat
11 Above
12 Hit the batter
15 "Good heavens!"
18 Nothing special
23 Grass eater
25 Corp. kingpins
27 Sternward
28 "__ voyage!"
29 Part of SST
30 Verdi opera
31 MTV viewer
32 Thick slice
33 Fountain order
34 Jed Clampett, e.g.
38 Now happening
39 "__ would seem"
40 Keatsian crock
42 Landers or Jillian
43 *Shogun* setting
45 Director Spike
46 Caribbean island
47 Berber, for one
50 Out of kilter
51 Coins
52 Oater group
53 Hannibal's route
54 Face
56 Baba and MacGraw
60 Hold the deed
61 Economist's abbr.
62 Chick chaser

464 TONY WINNERS by Rich Smreker

ACROSS

1 Jupiter's neighbor
5 Seaside sidler
9 Steep slope
14 "The wolf __ the door"
15 Word form for "blood"
16 Puzzle with pictures
17 Tony-winning play of '84
20 Be in a bee
21 Canadian tribe
22 For fear that
23 Spoils
25 Prego competitor
27 Lays down the lawn
30 Tony-winning play of '70
35 __-Magnon
36 Soprano Te Kanawa
37 In short supply
38 Arrested
40 '60s campus org.
42 Susan Lucci role
43 AA offshoot
45 Galley features
47 Tom or tabby
48 Tony-winning play of '88
50 Seas, in Sedan
51 '75 Wimbledon winner
52 Dynamic start
54 "Back in the __"
57 Kicked oneself
59 Minneapolis suburb
63 Tony-winning play of '60
66 Uncanny
67 Author Bagnold
68 Teddy trim
69 Opera prop
70 Ramon's room
71 Peepers

DOWN

1 Wire measures
2 PDQ relative
3 Burn up the road
4 Stable compartments
5 Señor Guevara
6 Nuclear devices
7 Manchurian river
8 They take seconds
9 Sign of success
10 Kind of phone
11 Skilled
12 French streets
13 Attention-getter
18 Day-__ pigment
19 Bold acts
24 Oriental sash
26 Stares open-mouthed
27 "Get lost!"
28 Toothbrush brand
29 Danube, in Dresden
31 Get __ (throw out)
32 Streisand played her . . .
33 . . . and then won this
34 Abbey Theatre director
36 Trunk features
39 Decorating technique
41 Dressing part
44 Outmoded jacket
46 "Comin' Thro' the __"
49 What an alumnus does
50 Spacecraft segment
53 Sleep stage
54 Western Indians
55 Limelites leader
56 Withered
58 __ May Oliver
60 Brit's phrase
61 Congenial
62 Tennis points
64 Poetic word
65 U.S. Govt. agency

KNIT WIT by Shirley Soloway

ACROSS

1 Hammer part
5 __ breve
9 Tall story?
13 Apple variety
14 Peach products
15 Burr or Copland
16 START OF A QUIP
18 Watching machine?
19 Al __ (firm)
20 Defer
22 Casserole cover
23 PART 2 OF QUIP
29 Spanish queen
30 Cockney endearment
31 Actor Borgnine
32 Emulates Ice-T
35 Reach
36 Nest-egg abbr.
39 PART 3 OF QUIP
41 Smash letters
42 Alabama city
44 Peau de __
45 Michael of *Broken Arrow*
47 151, to Tacitus
49 Loser's locale
52 PART 4 OF QUIP
55 Fictional collie
56 Bow or Barton
57 Fuming
59 Moll Flanders' creator
62 END OF QUIP
65 Fall birthstones
66 Key
67 Out of shape
68 Not so hot
69 Tetra type
70 Comic Johnson

DOWN

1 Hold tenderly
2 One from Column A
3 Plummer or Blake
4 Took off
5 Chest pounder
6 Golfer's concern
7 Resulted in
8 Syrian leader
9 Penny Marshall role
10 Hosp. areas
11 Antagonist
12 Cable channel
15 Loose
17 *The Subject Was Roses* actress
21 "See ya!"
24 Spiritual guide
25 Some tracks
26 New Jersey athletes
27 Kaiser's counterpart
28 Director Preminger
33 Arafat's grp.
34 1991 Wimbledon winner
36 "__ Her Again" ('66 hit)
37 Attorney General
38 To boot
39 Releases conditionally
40 Port preceder
43 __ X
46 Actress Gardner
48 Horus' mom
49 Cain, for one
50 Crystal-clear
51 "__ Fideles"
53 Comic Stu
54 Move up
58 Melodious McEntire
59 Chemical company
60 MPG monitor
61 Out of reach
63 Mr. Ziegfeld, familiarly
64 Browning's bedtime?

UP-TO-THE-MINUTE by Shirley Soloway

ACROSS

1 Bedtime story
5 "__ It Romantic?"
9 Let up
14 "In the twinkling __ eye"
15 Scorch
16 *Concentration* feature
17 "And __ goes"
18 "¿Cómo __ usted?"
19 Thrill
20 It's news
23 Firm, pasta-wise
24 Greek letter
25 Traveler's guide
28 Up-to-date fashion
31 La __ Opera House
35 AAA way
36 Monogram pt.
37 Hawaiian island
38 Oriental sauce
39 Moccasin or mamba
40 Shortly
41 Poke fun at
42 A real knockout
43 Contemporary furnishings
47 Get the message
48 Shoe width
49 Opening
54 Avant-garde movies
56 Yucatán yummies
59 "I'm __ girl now!"
60 Danson and Kennedy
61 Striped stone
62 Carson's successor
63 Concerning
64 Head tops
65 Shakespearean actor Edmund
66 Noted loch

DOWN

1 Puccini opera
2 In a tangle
3 Scottish landowner
4 __ nous
5 __ *Letter to My Love*
6 Sonnet part
7 Hoopster Thurmond
8 Poor imitation
9 Sports stadiums
10 Swig
11 Belli org.
12 "The Boy King"
13 Compass pt.
21 Chou __
22 Diminutive suffix
25 Sociable starling
26 Similar
27 Newsman Jennings
29 Wear away
30 Subtle shade
31 Closes noisily
32 Light boat
33 Battery part
34 Stroller's spot
38 Stroller's spot
39 Printer's stroke
41 Was acquainted with
44 __ Pieces (candy)
45 California town
46 Idaho neighbor
50 Be part of the crowd
51 Actress Graff
52 Naval offs.
53 Road curves
54 Postcard message
55 Busy as __
56 Keyboard stroke
57 __ Khan
58 Felix, e.g.

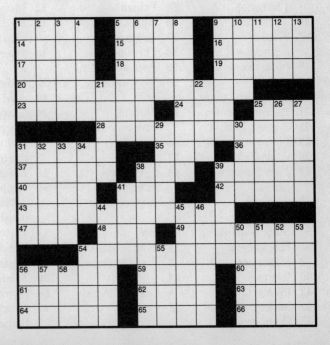

467 — BODY LANGUAGE by Harvey Estes

ACROSS
1 Old pro
4 Urban eyesore
8 UAW stronghold
12 Sweater muncher
14 Cash for Carlos
16 Worship
17 Arctic sight
18 Like some combat
20 Made threats
22 Unit of energy
23 Maiden-name indicator
24 __ Rosenkavalier
25 Short notice
27 Like some smiles
31 More prized
35 Baja bye-bye
36 Metallic fabric
38 Ice-cream holder
39 Waist band
40 __ metabolism
41 Leg joint
42 Duel tool
43 Brezhnev's dom.
44 Sunflower supports
45 Handbag parts
47 Like most agreements
49 Some secretaries
51 Catch a crook
52 Classified info
55 Chowed down
56 "__ two to tango"
60 Like some meetings
63 Bat habitat
64 Dash
65 Actress Laurie
66 Swiss artist Paul
67 Amusing sorts
68 Beatty flick
69 Final point

DOWN
1 Radio type
2 __ slaw
3 007's school
4 Area of influence
5 Starring role
6 Service div.
7 Reproduction
8 Speedometer abbr.
9 Persia, today
10 Walking stick
11 Jekyll's bad side
13 Like some competitions
15 Apple pastry
19 Fairy-tale monster
21 Corporate VIPs
25 Bright metal ornaments
26 Like some victories
27 Gently maneuvers
28 Learn the ropes
29 Step part
30 "Woe is me!"
32 Singer Blakley
33 Foe
34 Shortstop Pee Wee
37 New Testament figure
40 Inge drama
44 "Hurry!" in a hospital
46 Marsh matter
48 Records in a ledger
50 Fermented milk
52 __ Good Men (Cruise film)
53 Surrealist Salvador
54 "Beat it!"
56 Finished the cake
57 Leafy vegetable
58 Level
59 Plant-to-be
61 Pulver's rank: Abbr.
62 Mimic

468 — FOWL PLAY by Bob Lubbers

ACROSS
1 Radioer's word
6 Quickly, in memos
10 Some NCOs
14 "Farewell!"
15 "__ Don't Preach" ('86 tune)
16 Third-rate
17 Kind of withdrawal
19 New Rochelle college
20 Pacino and Gore
21 Account entries
23 Actress Ursula
27 Fireman's need
28 __ de Cologne
29 New Jersey's capital
32 Cop grp.
35 Side dishes
37 Roger Rabbit, e.g.
38 H.S. subject
39 __-Seltzer
40 Gem
41 Pianist Gilels
42 Make tracks
43 Coop group
44 Syrup source
45 East ender?
46 Napoleon's birthplace
48 Author Deighton
49 Lab lackey
51 Fellers?
53 Agreeable sort
57 Undivided
58 Play quoits
59 Back away
64 Wipe off the map
65 Biblical preposition
66 Museum piece
67 Fit to __
68 __ the line (obeyed)
69 Kitchen wrap

DOWN
1 Fem. soldier
2 Wedding words
3 __ Abner
4 Chest material
5 Current connectors
6 Cal. page
7 Benefit
8 Top
9 Place for street talk?
10 Turns around
11 Sign of a chill
12 Muscle quality
13 Niñas' moms, for short
18 Warsaw Pact ex
22 Years on end
23 Add fizz to
24 Carpenter, frequently
25 Avoid commitment
26 Hunting dog
30 High times?
31 Adenoid neighbor
33 Water heater
34 Steve and Ethan
36 Talent for music
38 Actress Arthur
40 Quick way home
44 Fridge-door doodads
46 Take in
47 Make a fricassee
50 Beau __
52 Salami type
53 Gillette product
54 Chimney lining
55 Cry of dread
56 Formality
60 Parcel letters
61 Hockey great Bobby
62 "Born in the __"
63 Heavy weight

469 SLIPPERS by Dean Niles

ACROSS
1 Actress Russell
5 Biological body
9 Might
14 Hurler Hershiser
15 Caspian feeder
16 Likeness
17 "Gracious!"
18 Transmit a signal
19 Nixon Defense Secretary
20 Sarandon film
23 Bandleader Brown
24 Get a load of
25 Sports org.
27 Yellow-flowered plant
33 Mil. address
34 Ms. Parks
35 Run off the tracks
38 Meter maid of song
40 Galahad or Gawain
42 *The Sun __ Rises*
43 Weakness
46 Feudal domain
49 Certain sib
50 Legendary hustler
53 Pillow cover
54 Strain
55 Draft agcy.
58 Work need
64 Blush
66 "Waiting for the Robert __"
67 Worthless
68 Convenient excuse
69 Bring up
70 Stuff
71 Mail money
72 Painful
73 They act badly

DOWN
1 "Uptown Girl" singer
2 Mythical vessel
3 Around the corner
4 Primogenitary
5 Arctic adjective
6 Sandwich cookie
7 *Serpico* author
8 Nut tree
9 Hamlet
10 "__ Believer" ('66 tune)
11 Author Godwin
12 Frightening fellow
13 Bolsheviks
21 __-do-well
22 Sealed the deal
26 Taj Mahal site
27 Actress Theda
28 __ *Smoke* ('78 film)
29 Aleut carving
30 Palm Sunday beast
31 Innocents
32 Hot stuff
36 "__ something I said?"
37 It's often total
39 Author Kingsley
41 Copacabana city
44 Come into
45 Simile kin: Abbr.
47 Bric-a-brac stand
48 County event
51 Smoldering remains
52 College major
55 Trauma aftermath
56 Food fish
57 Willowy
59 Toast topper
60 Put on
61 A certain something
62 Bridge bid
63 *Desire Under the __*
65 Kimono accessory

470 NOSING AROUND by S.E. Booker

ACROSS
1 Nag
5 Quarterback Starr
9 Cryptography work
14 Latin love
15 At a distance
16 Ms. Winfrey
17 __ stick
18 Allegro con __
19 Bushed
20 START OF A QUOTE
23 Goes astray
24 Actress Meyers
25 Casual shirt
26 Busybody
31 Artificial waterway
34 Cold-storage candidates
35 Chow
36 __ *Bravo*
37 SPEAKER OF QUOTE
40 Tina's ex
41 Cain raiser
43 Elizabethan epithet
44 Less refined
46 Big beast
48 Actor Chaney
49 Scandinavian rug
50 Tennis type
54 END OF QUOTE
58 Comb contents
59 Total
60 Tubby's tootsie
61 Bizarre
62 Take it easy
63 Qum's country
64 Out-and-out
65 Liquidate
66 Suffragette Carrie

DOWN
1 "The __ Crusader" (Batman)
2 Get __ on (begin)
3 Maris or Moore
4 Proportionately
5 Drivel
6 Bushy styles
7 Sudden attack
8 Paris' home
9 Chicken
10 Employment opportunity
11 "Fiddlesticks!"
12 Some pitchers have them
13 Withdrawn
21 Give in
22 It may be belted
26 Put the kibosh on
27 Coffeemakers
28 *Exodus* author
29 Use the microwave
30 Driver with a handle
31 Bellyache
32 Office assistant
33 Wordy Webster
34 Worry
38 Axis sub
39 Treasury certificate
42 Business-section fodder
45 Heavenly
47 "You can't pull the wool over __!"
48 Jazzman Hampton
50 To this day
51 Singer Branigan
52 Publicity
53 *Beat the Clock* action
54 Do Europe
55 Aware of
56 Author Murdoch
57 In the flesh?
58 Monopolize

471 · AIM OF THE GAME by Mary E. Brindamour

ACROSS

1 Charitable donation
5 Police raid
9 Emulate a bloodhound
14 Chimney dirt
15 Way off
16 Peter of *Casablanca*
17 Golfer's aim
19 In front
20 Come in
21 Filler/driller
23 Landlords' income
26 Even so
27 *Lou Grant* star
30 __ as a board
34 Cartwright or Matlock
35 Timeless, to Tennyson
37 Islamic prince
38 Malaise, with "the"
40 Place
41 Teheran native
42 Director Kazan
43 Felt sorry for
45 "Holy cow!"
46 Mean coward
48 Jimmy and Rosalynn
50 *TV Guide* abbr.
51 Late bloomer
52 Decked out
55 Supermarket path
59 Nectarine or kumquat
60 Olympian's aim
63 Clear the windshield
64 Sting like __
65 L.A. footballers
66 Echelons
67 Rep. rivals
68 __-Ball (arcade game)

DOWN

1 Tennis great Arthur
2 Diving bird
3 Shed feathers
4 Takes the reins
5 Forbid
6 Flying saucer
7 __ of Iwo Jima
8 Genealogy chart
9 Blackboards
10 Pitcher's aim
11 Gets one's back up
12 College club
13 Nourished
18 Papas and Dunne
22 NASDAQ rival
24 After taxes
25 Fearful
27 Flowed back
28 Perry's secretary
29 Diarist Nin
30 Playful pranks
31 Icon
32 Better quality
33 Burger partner
36 Tire track
39 Gretzky's aim
41 __ of Jeannie
43 Implore
44 Dig in
47 Winds down
49 Wine tasters, e.g.
51 Hacienda material
52 __ rug
53 Devastate
54 Mild oath
56 Pierre's st.
57 Metallic material
58 "So what __ is new?"
59 HST predecessor
61 Apollo craft
62 __ Moines, IA

472 · PLAYING 'ROUND by Harvey Estes

ACROSS

1 Oriental wrestling
5 Gouda alternative
9 African country
13 How-to part
14 Marry on the run
15 Comedian Foxx
16 Press down
17 Indifferent
18 Ransom Eli __
19 Play basketball
22 Noticed
23 Northern seabird
24 '60s singer
27 Mardi Gras follower
29 Star Wars abbr.
32 Borders on
33 Conservative skirt
34 Holstein's home
35 Where clowns play
38 Billions of years
39 __-deucy
40 Solemn music
41 AMA members
42 Congregational comeback
43 Not quite
44 PD alert
45 Pub drinks
46 Wordplay game show
53 Prejudice
54 *Dallas* matriarch
55 White stone
56 Natural hairdo
57 Brings up
58 Comic Crosby
59 Profound
60 Unit of loudness
61 Pass catchers

DOWN

1 JFK landers
2 Hatch's home
3 Office note
4 They attract
5 Vocalist John
6 Condemn
7 ". . . baked in __"
8 Skilled technician
9 Shepherd's staff
10 Beatles movie
11 Slaps on
12 Driller's deg.
14 German city
20 Needle
21 End of an inning
24 Destined
25 Strongly dislike
26 Allen's partner
27 Flax fabric
28 Uptight
29 Orthopedic prefix
30 Pharmacopoeia
31 Map in a map
33 Mickey's kin
34 Sermon ingredient?
36 Wanderers
37 Gentleman of leisure?
42 Orang, e.g.
43 Medicinal plants
44 Moral man?
45 Blazing
46 Chaucer's __ of Bath
47 "__ Krishna!"
48 Butter substitute
49 Spanish dessert
50 Familiar with
51 Biblical ointment
52 Shade trees
53 Spoiled

ACROSS
1 Act like Cheetah?
4 Use scissors
8 Good-natured humor
14 Shark giveaway
15 Charlie's fourth
16 Sarge's "Relax!"
17 *Interview with the Vampire* author
19 Eden, e.g.
20 Bram Stoker character
22 Geraint's lady
23 Un- relative
24 "Now I see!"
27 __ Paulo, Brazil
30 Score a four, perhaps
33 Atom part
38 Eye-opener?
39 Vampire-movie spoof
42 Cake topper
43 Annoyed
44 Heiden and Witt
47 Inlet
48 Sundown, to Shelley

49 "The Lady __ Tramp"
51 Now, to Cicero
55 Vampire's homeland
60 Actress Hemingway
63 Overhauled Lugosi's role?
64 Degree
65 Short jacket
66 Water cooler
67 Takes care of
68 Fake knockout
69 Profit preceder

DOWN
1 __ *in the Crowd*
2 Western tree
3 Extreme boredom
4 Categorize
5 Why the bar patron wasn't served
6 Enl.
7 Hymn of praise
8 __ Beach, CA
9 Handy bit of Latin

10 Actress Miles
11 Year in Augustus' reign
12 Mao __-tung
13 Ginza gelt
18 Wrap up
21 Capt.'s subordinate
24 Price-tag words
25 Author Bret
26 Dangerous partner
27 Plan part
28 Comic Carney
29 Campy exclamation
31 Actress Bates
32 German river
33 "Für __"
34 Actress Sondra
35 French spa
36 Canadian coin
37 Bird beak
40 Lowe or Reiner
41 Police hdqrs.
45 Theater district
46 Form 1040 entry: Abbr.

50 __ as a beet
51 *Platoon* setting
52 Remove a brooch
53 Heir, maybe
54 Junior officer
55 Connections

56 Some income
57 Tibetan beast
58 Ukrainian city
59 Wind monitor
60 "__ amis"
61 Viking weapon
62 AAA offering

ACROSS
1 Blow for a bounder
5 Of interest to Nelson
10 Prepare potatoes
14 Plumb crazy
15 Nitrous __
16 Marine leader?
17 Lea ladies
18 Lots of paper
19 Psychology pioneer
20 START OF A QUIP
23 African land
24 Shirt style
25 Recline
27 List-ending abbr.
28 Angler's danglers
32 Ethnic
34 Joked around
36 Just
37 MIDDLE OF QUIP
40 Confront

42 Neck of the woods
43 Fantastic
46 Spits, e.g.
47 Fashion model Carol
50 Sgt. or cpl.
51 Buck's beloved
53 Furniture designer Charles
55 END OF QUIP
60 Jubilee
61 Out of gas
62 Smell __ (be suspicious)
63 "I'm working __"
64 __ *Gay*
65 Intervals
66 Emulate Whistler
67 Actor Quaid
68 Gen. Robert __

DOWN
1 Tawdry type
2 Like some yogurt
3 Vinegary
4 Tough nut to crack

5 *A Doll's House* heroine
6 Skating jump
7 Pharmacy bottle
8 Come clean
9 __ Antilles
10 Goya subject
11 Hooked
12 Old timer?
13 Crone
21 Bridge term
22 Main
26 TV Tarzan
29 Recipe word
30 Sacred cow
31 Operatic hero, often
33 Transformer part
34 Patella's place
35 Art __
37 Puzzle variety
38 Beyond balmy
39 FTD pitchman
40 Lots of laughs
41 Antediluvian
44 Nabokov heroine
45 Hang around

47 Lacking standards
48 Delaware tribesman
49 Fearsome fly
52 Minneapolis suburb
54 Saw

56 Clockmaker Thomas
57 Jeff Bridges film of '82
58 Stayed put
59 *Queen for __*
60 Competitor

475 ZIP! by Trip Payne

ACROSS
1 Stimulate
5 Wander about
9 Large tangelos
14 Inauguration highlight
15 Get off the stage
16 Unskilled workers
17 Long-tailed flier
18 Force
19 Barbaric sort
20 Shakespearean comedy
23 Put an edge on
24 Directional suffix
25 Lava rock
28 Relating to dinner
33 Magician's phrase
35 Narcs' grp.
36 Turn on, in a way
37 Holm of *Chariots of Fire*
38 Gawain and Guinness

39 Bowler, for one
40 "Piece of cake!"
44 Losers
46 Hams it up
47 Kennel feature
48 "__ See Clearly Now"
49 Sartre treatise
55 Judean king
56 Director Joel
57 Hit the ground
59 "Dash __!"
60 Devour Dickens
61 Mideast strip
62 Helena's rival
63 Corner shapes
64 Looked at

DOWN
1 Chinese vessel
2 Actor Corey
3 Caesar's recrimination
4 Wallace Beery movie
5 Biting insects

6 Chemical compound
7 Asti product
8 Sundance's sweetie
9 Raised on high
10 Reading or writing
11 Lummox
12 Excited by
13 Vane dir.
21 Sacred
22 Mathers' role, for short
25 South African statesman
26 Hearing-related
27 Roasting rods
28 Still-life subjects
29 Director Clair
30 __ savant
31 Eagle's base
32 Shoemaking tools
34 Legal claim
38 Hard time?
40 Small roller
41 Dangle

42 Sale goods, often
43 Muscat's land
45 Brightly colored bird
48 Standard
49 Puts up
50 Roman auxiliary?

51 Farmland unit
52 Playwright Coward
53 Do in
54 Scope
55 Hurry along
58 Small amount

476 HAVE A FLING by Eric Albert

ACROSS
1 Polite request
5 Camera-lens setting
10 Forest male
14 *East of* __
15 San Antonio landmark
16 "Gosh!"
17 Help prepare dinner
19 Riding stick
20 Green club
21 Devout
22 Fancy fronts
25 Take a bad turn
26 Introduction
27 Promotion, plus
29 Selling point
30 Furniture wood
31 Pear-shaped fruit
34 Goes bad
35 Stupefied
36 __ qua non
37 Antipollution grp.

38 Defraud
39 Bobby of tennis
40 Bladed tool
42 Sizzling
43 Borgnine role
45 *No, No, __*
46 Kipling's Kim
47 Dress parts
49 Fizzy drink
50 Camp out
54 God of love
55 Just right
56 Great lake
57 Evergreen trees
58 Poor
59 Hemingway's nickname

DOWN
1 Ran into
2 Big scene
3 "Okay!"
4 Extremely
5 "__ your seat belts"
6 Venetian-blind parts

7 Narrative
8 Poet Khayyám
9 Engine enclosure
10 Get-together
11 Take a dive
12 Love, in Lyons
13 Natalie Wood musical
18 Check the books
21 Bishop of Rome
22 Breakdown beacon
23 Famous fabulist
24 Block the sun
25 It's often panned
27 Eye color
28 Serving customers
30 Labyrinth
32 Metal bar
33 *Beau* __
35 Cote creature

36 Dodge
38 Soft drink
39 Oscar de la __
41 Bug
42 Without caution
43 Amble
44 Tedious task

45 Battery type
47 Of great extent
48 Suit to __
50 Wrestling win
51 Period
52 Bit of a bite
53 Coffee alternative

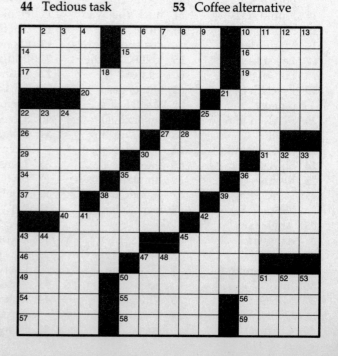

477   TERRAINIANS by Randolph Ross

ACROSS

1 Director Sergio
6 Keats or Pindar
11 Commotion
14 "A House __ a Home"
15 Tony of tennis
16 Dublin dance
17 Milton Caniff character
19 100%
20 Afternoon delight?
21 Fabulous birds
22 Channel-swimmer Gertrude
24 Highly original
26 Fill the hold
27 He knew how to win friends and influence people
32 Roll with a hole
35 Falsifies
36 Unspecified amount
37 Nest eggs
38 Exchange
40 Hot stuff
41 Tot's time-out
42 Dates regularly
43 Ached (for)
44 "Gentle on My Mind" singer
48 *Alice's Restaurant* character
49 Sweet girl of song
53 Sign of neglect
56 Citrus cover
57 Watched junior
58 *A Chorus Line* number
59 Margaret Hamilton role
62 Caustic substance
63 Aromatic seed
64 *Año* opener
65 Switchboard abbr.
66 Olympic skater Carol
67 Locations

DOWN

1 Shopping aids
2 First name in cosmetics
3 Wee hr.
4 Fall mo.
5 Perpetual
6 Delphic VIP
7 Adams and Ameche
8 Slick
9 Pump stuffer
10 Sinews
11 Slightly open
12 Pickling herb
13 Check out, in a way
18 Barbecue fuel
23 Flock female
25 Bad day for Caesar
26 Uttered
28 Envelope closer
29 Profit
30 Memo words
31 Observed
32 Cherry choice
33 Russian sea
34 Rubberneck
38 Aquatic shade
39 San __, Italy
40 Pump gas
42 Shrill sound
43 Oaths
45 Slangy negative
46 Scottish youngsters
47 __ St. Vincent Millay
50 Cay
51 Mother-of-pearl
52 Group morality
53 Nat or Natalie
54 Black stone
55 Borscht veggie
56 Journalist Jacob
60 Lexington sch.
61 Verse starter

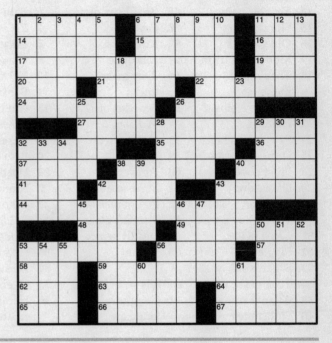

478   GROCERY JINGLES by S.N.

ACROSS

1 Time periods
5 Southern deseeders
9 Wielded
14 Barn adjunct
15 Flawlessly
16 M. Matisse
17 Chocoholic's nosh
20 Bewildered
21 Revlon rival
22 "Be my guest!"
23 __ facto
26 "Has __ uses"
28 Salad veggie
32 "Confound it!"
36 Boxing legend
37 Songstress James
38 TV tec Remington
40 Confess
42 Peter, Paul, and Mary: Abbr.
44 Producer Spelling
45 Way out
47 Go on the road
49 Linking word
50 Cloth worker
51 Fast-food fare
54 Fit
56 Deutschland denial
57 X
60 Auditioner's goal
62 Ms. Comaneci
66 Junk-food treat
70 Concede
71 Eye amorously
72 Skin-cream additive
73 Chick talk
74 Poverty
75 Strong cravings

DOWN

1 "¿Cómo __ usted?"
2 Laugh-a-minute
3 Shakespeare title start
4 Sun: Fr.
5 Sports car, for short
6 Debtor's letters
7 Launch org.
8 Wonder or Nicks
9 Record player
10 Composer Delibes
11 Deep black
12 Ontario's neighbor
13 Conks out
18 Takes place
19 Beer brand
24 Salon request
25 Goes for
27 Brainstorm
28 Worked the hay
29 Gray matter?
30 Petrol unit
31 Singer LaBelle
33 Showed again
34 "Take Me __"
35 Takes care of
39 Prefeathering preparation?
41 "__ perfumed sea": Poe
43 Any day now
46 One's performances?
48 Article in *Le Monde*?
52 Golfer Byron
53 "Rome wasn't built __"
55 Makes tea
57 Bloke
58 *A __ in the Head*
59 Man, e.g.
61 Advantage
63 Ford's running mate
64 Privy to
65 Census data
67 Outdo
68 __ de France
69 Actor Beatty

479 MAKERS by Harvey Estes

ACROSS
1 Fence piece
5 Dove for the base
9 Halloween mo.
12 Spirited steed
13 Make amends
14 Terrible name?
15 Storage bin
16 Old geezers
17 Moment of truth
18 They make money
21 Change clothes?
22 Damage
23 Sajak or Trebek
25 Jamie __ Curtis
26 Frost-covered
28 Davis' dom.
30 *One Day __ Time*
31 Costa del __
32 Piggie
33 Sagan's subj.
34 They make time
39 Atlanta arena
40 Scale notes
41 Zag's counterpart
42 Roman deck count?
43 Wapner's field
44 Tyrannosaurus chaser
45 Paw part
48 Broadway org.
50 Payable
52 Kukla's colleague
54 They make tracks
57 Benedict of *The A-Team*
58 Homeric epic
59 Not feral
60 Forever
61 Make a call
62 PC enthusiast
63 Printer's measures
64 Deadly septet
65 Shut up

DOWN
1 Computer language
2 Maryland state bird
3 Greet the general
4 Porterhouse alternative
5 "... a dark and __ night"
6 Bath accessory
7 PA system
8 Lucy's love
9 Cloudy
10 CD alternative
11 Big-bang letters
13 Old hand
14 News bit
19 Some combos
20 Bath brew
24 Head set?
27 Santa __, CA
29 Take captive
31 __ Lanka
32 Montana stats
33 Holidayless mo.
34 Hernando's "Hi!"
35 Oversight
36 Heraldic creatures
37 Capital of India
38 *Six Crises* author
43 Hosp. employee
44 Lear's daughter et al.
45 Tickle pink
46 Pilots
47 Leave flat
49 Arctic birds
51 Accord
53 Ease off
55 Short swims
56 Chemical suffix
57 Wallace of *E.T.*

480 SOUND BITES by Bob Lubbers

ACROSS
1 Big-eyed Betty
5 Butte kin
9 James Herriot, e.g.
13 Eugene O'Neill's daughter
14 Hokkaido city
16 Forehead-slapping words
17 Worker bees?
19 Blubber
20 Appeared to be
21 Knee slappers
23 Lake tribe
25 Swing a sickle
26 Peanut man
29 Clinton Cabinet member
32 Sentry's cry
33 Insurance workers
35 Kyser or Starr
36 Gardner et al.
37 Cul-de-__
38 London gallery
39 Sun. talk
40 Astoria's locale
43 Simone's state
44 January stoats
46 They're attractive
48 Algonquian language
49 Ledger entry
50 Little Dipper twinkler
53 Wild ass
57 __ for one's money
58 Toad's drink?
60 Shoestring
61 Cellular salutation
62 Installed tile
63 Lodge brothers
64 Eastern European
65 *Odyssey* characters?

DOWN
1 Ducks a jab
2 Seep slowly
3 Eleven, at the Elysée
4 Remittances
5 Less even-tempered
6 JFK info
7 Shoves off
8 Zone
9 "Who cares?"
10 Tight chick?
11 Unique individual
12 Shirts and sweaters
15 Loan shark, e.g.
18 Parks or Convy
22 Army VIPs
24 Gets the lead out
26 Moon state
27 Tennis great Rod
28 Rooster rouser?
29 Suit
30 Make anxious
31 Rostov refusals
34 Running game
38 Arm of the sea?
40 Washington bills
41 Outline more sharply
42 *Lolita* author
45 Castle and Cara
47 Ms. Lollobrigida
49 Full of whimsy
50 Uncolorful
51 Test type
52 Ornery Olympian
54 Nanny or billy
55 Literary pseudonym
56 Geom. measures
59 Pie __ mode

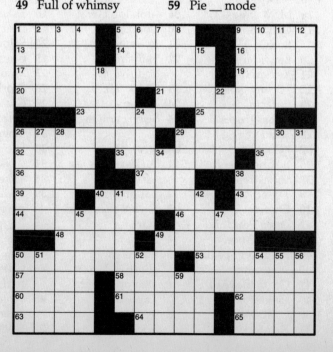

481 SPOTLESS by Shirley Soloway

ACROSS

1 __ lazuli
6 Unruly youngster
10 Gentle __ lamb
13 Smart __ (wise guy)
14 Architect Saarinen
15 "__ bien!"
16 Dump the unnecessary
19 Chemical ending
20 Revealed
21 Kunta __ (Roots role)
22 Singer Shannon
23 Gets closer to
25 Search thoroughly
30 Eyelets
31 Send out
32 Mineo and Maglie
36 Egg-shaped
37 Steer clear of
38 Suit to __
39 Wallet bills
40 Actor Wilder
41 Mideast coin
42 Disposed of quickly
44 Compensation
48 Birth __ Nation
49 Assumed name
50 Land measure
52 Actress Lupino
55 Walk away from
59 RSVP cards, e.g.
60 Choir member
61 Perry's secretary
62 Aves.
63 Drop heavily
64 Nasty smile

DOWN

1 Metallic fabric
2 Arkin or Alda
3 Chinese pooch
4 Winter hazard
5 Fleming and Witt
6 Classroom clanger
7 Woodwind
8 Coach Parseghian
9 "This weighs a __!"
10 Israeli statesman Moshe
11 Take care of
12 Colorado resort
15 Castor or Pollux
17 Carbonated cooler
18 Go out of control
22 Sword fights
23 Tour leaders
24 Poker stake
25 Took a picture
26 Small bay
27 Pearl Buck heroine
28 Makes merry
29 Muscat native
32 "You __ mouthful!"
33 __ time (never)
34 Book page
35 Medieval worker
37 Swelled heads
41 Stands up for
42 Mexican money
43 Israeli dance
44 Less experienced
45 African antelope
46 Computer accessories
47 Team screams
50 Concerning
51 Karate blow
52 Tropical spot
53 Kansas senator, once
54 At a distance
56 Short snooze
57 Building wing
58 TV room

482 UP TO SPEED by Randolph Ross

ACROSS

1 Bandleader Lombardo
4 Assail
9 Spartan slave
14 Downed dessert
15 Poetry Muse
16 "Have __ day!"
17 Flock word
18 Mercury
20 Turin relic
22 Lorenzo's __
23 Qom's country
24 Reformer Jacob
26 Abates
28 American armada
32 __ kwon do
33 Shoe width
34 Prepped a banana
38 Civil-rights leader Medgar
41 Rainbow shape
43 Brigham Young U. home
44 Madrid money
46 Čapek play
48 A Bobbsey twin
49 Harvard society
53 Royal officials
56 __ gin fizz
57 Vicinity
58 Pleased sounds
60 South Fork family
64 Good buddies
67 Cereal grain
68 Chemical compound
69 Temple teacher
70 __ Miss
71 Thin-sounding
72 Canape holders
73 "Unforgettable" name

DOWN

1 Chews the fat
2 Hatch's home
3 Century segment
4 Costume sparkler
5 Scholarly
6 Skater Babilonia
7 Airport worker: Abbr.
8 __ a Mockingbird
9 "Bali __"
10 Army recruiter
11 Sorbonne book
12 Expanse
13 Seabirds
19 Nod off
21 Mine find
25 Mets' stadium
27 Trickle
28 How-to part
29 Roof edge
30 Some necklines
31 Boat for cars
35 Actress Anderson
36 Author Hunter
37 Bell sound
39 Used a microwave
40 Getz or Musial
42 Service members?
45 __ Is Born
47 Subject to
50 Casual top
51 Uses a divining rod
52 "Agnus __"
53 '60 Olympian Johnson
54 Clear the slate
55 Beau __
59 Soothsayer
61 High time?
62 Festive
63 Editor's order
65 Cook bacon
66 Jordan's org.

483 SPREADING OUT by Dean Niles

ACROSS

1 Arm or leg
5 *Suspect* star
9 Open country
13 What a nose knows
14 Wash
15 Frozen over
16 Sociable starling
17 Region
18 Pull together
19 LaBelle tune
22 Sweet potatoes
23 Binds the hay
24 El __ (Heston role)
27 Graphics-software acronym
30 Doll up
32 Scale notes
33 Half an island
37 Restricted lands
41 Pizazz
42 Caviar
43 Roentgen's discovery
44 Common speech
47 Mil. boat
48 High-tech missives
51 Stomping ground
53 Gregory Hines musical
58 Beat around the bush
59 Goals
60 Fail to mention
62 More distant
63 Genuine
64 Cameo, for one
65 Lead player
66 Green Gables girl
67 Historic Scott

DOWN

1 Actor Herbert
2 Pastoral poem
3 __ *Lisa*
4 Reagan press secretary
5 Unpleasantly moist
6 Pick on
7 At all times
8 Enlarge a hole
9 On the take
10 Leave out
11 Some beers
12 SHAEF commander
15 *The __ Archipelago*
20 Signs of boredom
21 Bottomless pit
24 Espresso spot
25 Matinée figure
26 Mrs. David Copperfield
28 Like some sale mdse.
29 Tiny
31 Stimpy's pal
33 "I'm freezing!"
34 Like Humpty Dumpty
35 Fernando and Alvino
36 Office helper: Abbr.
38 In reality
39 Campaigner
40 Put out
44 More repulsive
45 Cossack chief
46 Go at each other
48 Kick out
49 Radio and TV
50 *Ragged Dick* author
52 Sea arm
54 Poet Teasdale
55 Legal claim
56 Love, to Livy
57 Relay length
58 That guy's
61 Newsman Koppel

484 SEZ WHO? by S.E. Booker

ACROSS

1 Tractor-trailer
5 Spruce up
10 Bang the door
14 Satan's specialty
15 "__ cockhorse . . ."
16 __ *18* (Uris novel)
17 "Politics is applesauce"
19 Nays' opposite
20 Colorado Indian
21 "__ deal!"
22 Songbird
24 Show off
26 Yemeni capital
27 "I got a million of 'em!"
33 Tableland
36 Western show
37 Wildcat strike?
38 Special edition
40 Greek letters
41 Squiffed
43 Make like
44 Patton portrayer
46 Pot filler?
47 "So long until tomorrow"
51 Downing St. address
52 Horrified
56 Scattered about
59 Singer Vannelli
61 Schmooze
62 Gardener, often
63 "I want to be alone"
66 Designer Cassini
67 City in Italy
68 Noticed
69 Sea swirl
70 Upright
71 At this point

DOWN

1 Conclude
2 Señora Perón
3 Roger Bannister, for one
4 Out of sorts
5 Short term for short-term
6 Fixes
7 Mental picture
8 Debussy's sea
9 Delinquent
10 Fig type
11 Stead
12 "Woe is me!"
13 Prepare potatoes
18 "__, *Pagliaccio* . . ."
23 Biblical king
25 Open a little
26 Supplements
28 Peter Lorre role
29 Kid
30 "Fish" or "fowl"
31 Cast
32 Actress Sommer
33 Ground grain
34 World's fair
35 Brood (over)
39 "On __ Boat to China"
42 Hasty
45 Hold tight
48 Get-up-and-go
49 ". . . pronounce you __ wife"
50 Psyched up
53 Come to terms
54 Cavalry weapon
55 Beef cut
56 It's left half the time
57 Snitched
58 Bamboo, essentially
59 *Breathless* star
60 Pack __ (finish)
64 Jog
65 Ski material

485 WHAT'S NEWS by Matt Gaffney

ACROSS

1 Sicilian rumbler
5 __-fi
8 Party wear, perhaps
13 Continue
14 Like old knives
15 Giraffe cousin
16 Schwarzenegger's birthplace
17 Fall birthstone
18 Liverpudlians, e.g.
19 Start of a headline cited by Jay Leno
22 Threaten
23 __ Rosenkavalier
26 Bat material
29 Monk houses
30 Epoch
31 Shocking affairs
33 Turning point
35 Witch work
36 __ résistance
38 Slip of the tongue
39 Traded barbs
40 Defendants: Lat.
41 Seat cover?
43 Lith., formerly
44 Montana stats
45 Lens shapes
47 End of headline
51 Paperboy's path
53 Actor Stoltz
54 Don __ (legendary lover)
56 Nimbi
57 Color lightly
58 Where most people live
59 Strength
60 Sink down
61 Iodine source

DOWN

1 Tomorrow's turtle
2 Legal wrong
3 Wordy Webster
4 WWII site
5 In a wonderful way
6 Conflicts
7 "Tell me about it!"
8 "Ain't Too Proud __" ('66 tune)
9 Gumbo thickener
10 U.S. track star
11 Likely (to)
12 Bro's sib
14 Frozen treat
20 Tax cheat
21 Heavy wts.
24 Wears away
25 Not for kids
26 Own
27 Made a point
28 Keystone capital
32 Cpl., e.g.
33 Marine bird
34 Cover the cupcakes
36 Decorator's task
37 Not quite right
39 Oktoberfest area
41 Follow closely
42 Small bays
45 Cardinal point?
46 White's colleague
48 Bountiful setting
49 Clever ploy
50 Letters
51 Pound a portcullis
52 Yves' assent
55 Forty winks

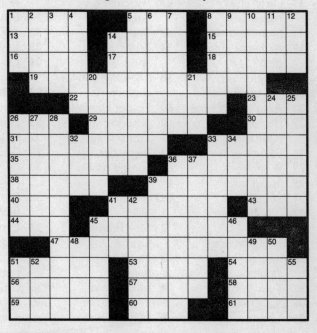

486 ON THE RISE by Shirley Soloway

ACROSS

1 La __ Opera House
6 Actor DeLuise
9 Game-show prize
13 Immigration island
14 Emmy-winner Imogene
15 Mrs. Charlie Chaplin
16 Have high aspirations
19 Silly talk
20 Shoe part
21 Explosive initials
22 __ of Eden
24 Lemon skin
26 Not yet decided
30 Killer whale
34 Griddle
35 Thesaurus wds.
36 Sleep stopper
37 Throb
39 Chef's meas.
41 Maui patio
42 Actress Verdugo
43 Jai __
45 Negative prefix
46 Computer info
47 Extremely happy
50 Graph starter
52 Singer Simone
53 Make a request
56 Insertion marks
58 Bad bottom line
62 "Money is no object!"
65 Sleuth Wolfe
66 Long time periods
67 Of service
68 Boat movers
69 Genetic letters
70 Be buddies

DOWN

1 Slav
2 Singer Laine
3 "Too bad!"
4 Rock coating
5 Bonfire remains
6 Actress Diana
7 Sea animals
8 Composer Gustav
9 Cruise of The Firm
10 Cheer (for)
11 Aware of
12 Breathe rapidly
14 At peace
17 Suspicious
18 Shoe-box letters
23 Off the track
25 "Whatever __ Wants"
26 Raised the stakes
27 Abdul or Prentiss
28 Narrow passage
29 Size up
31 The Amazing __ (magician)
32 Roger of baseball
33 Pennsylvania sect
36 Set straight
38 Break suddenly
40 Foundation blocks
44 Liqueur flavoring
47 Ragged
48 Cartoonist Gary
49 Rock salt
51 Antiaircraft-gun sound
53 __ time (never)
54 NY ballpark
55 Actress Deborah
57 Sicilian spewer
59 Leave out
60 Grain holder
61 British weapon
63 Sea plea
64 Drag along

487 BODY FOOD by Bob Lubbers

ACROSS
1 Moreno or Coolidge
5 *Brian's Song* star
9 Leading man?
14 Actor West
15 Girls' club: Abbr.
16 Stone marker
17 Barbecue side dish
19 Vulgar
20 "__ the Barrel"
22 Actress McClurg
23 Heavenly bodies
26 Brunch order
28 Wobble
29 Stand for
31 *Les* __-*Unis*
32 "Nevermore" bird
33 Useful article
36 Roman emperor
37 Trencherman
38 Male deer
39 Table scrap
40 Pronounce
41 Flier's floater
42 Plains Indians
44 Vestiges
45 Jungle jaunt
47 Least friendly
48 Real lulus
49 Albany or Augusta
52 Boise's locale
54 Bump on a spud
58 *The Color Purple* character
59 Hurler Hershiser
60 Stocking stuffers?
61 Toting a gun
62 Legis. period
63 Ginger cookie

DOWN
1 *Norma* __
2 Mrs. Eddie Cantor
3 Paving material
4 Little cupid
5 Pedal pusher
6 MP quarries
7 Word form for "height"
8 Ork talk
9 L.A. coll.
10 Wall or Wimpole
11 Salad foundation
12 Beast of Borden
13 Adjust a timer
18 Links alerts
21 Cosmetic purchase
23 Office worker
24 Flying Pan
25 Exotic veggie
27 Calendar abbr.
29 Goes with
30 "If __ I Would Leave You"
32 Pro __ (proportionately)
34 Can't stand
35 Discharge
37 Moral standard
38 Onion relatives
40 Former Mideast nation: Abbr.
41 Eastern European
43 #5 iron
44 Destroys the Dodge
45 Star in Virgo
46 Assistance, in court
47 Makes a footnote
50 Mil. addresses
51 Skin opening
53 Brit. lexicon
55 Years on end
56 Affirmative vote
57 Sixth sense

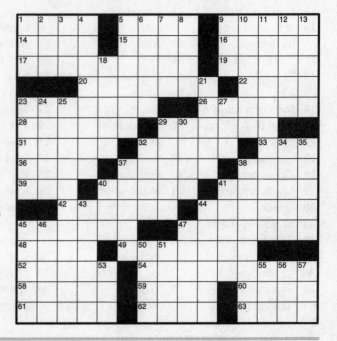

488 GOOD VS. EVIL by Trip Payne

ACROSS
1 Ethereal instrument
5 Almost never
9 Specialist
14 Bridge support
15 Lament
16 Garlic section
17 Disinterested proponents
20 "Maria __" ('41 tune)
21 Deceive
22 Dash lengths
23 No. cruncher
25 Discovered
27 Venezuelan attraction
31 Landon et al.
35 "Inka Dinka __"
36 District
37 Play for time
38 Actress Rita and family
40 Tallinn's land
42 __ of itself (per se)
43 On the safe side
44 Turner network
45 "... a __'clock scholar"
46 Popular hors d'oeuvre
49 Tea of *Flying Blind*
51 Mr. Ziegfeld
52 Dogpatch's Daisy __
55 Like a foal
57 Novelist Shaw
61 1993 Tony-winning play
64 Barrel part
65 Writer Ephron
66 Jet-black
67 Auto type
68 Extremities
69 Robin Williams film

DOWN
1 Sock away
2 First victim
3 Four-star review
4 "Purple Rain" man
5 Approves
6 Actress Patricia
7 French diacritical mark
8 Cover up
9 Singer Marilyn
10 Pie __ mode
11 Go to the polls
12 Tied
13 Nitti's nemesis
18 Reindeer country
19 Baseball's Ed and Mel
24 Bushy do
26 16-nation grp.
27 Let in or let on
28 Nary a soul
29 Tennis star Ivanisevic
30 DDE's rival
32 Joust weapon
33 Brief indulgence
34 Street talk
37 Kind of marble
39 Chemical compound
40 Actor Wallach
41 Ego
43 Papal city, once
46 They spawn fawns
47 Locomotive
48 Dickens' *Little* __
50 Actress Barkin
52 Church service
53 Pot starter
54 "My word!"
56 Linear measure
58 Port authority?
59 Very unpleasant
60 Opposing votes
62 __ Marie Saint
63 Bell and Kettle

489 CRAZY by S.E. Booker

ACROSS
1 Bivouac
5 Blew away
9 Tease
13 Colossal commotion
14 In the flesh
15 Together, to Toscanini
16 Cookie favorites
17 Cool it
18 Position
19 Director Reitman
20 Crazy
22 House party?
24 Leander's love
25 Cafeteria burden
27 Kind of comedy
32 Crazy
36 Hue and cry
37 Doozie
38 Course requirement?
40 Traffic sound
41 Taken __ (startled)
43 Crazy
46 Namby-pamby
49 Frame of mind
50 Terrible times?
52 Be that as it may
56 Crazy
61 "Give __ little earth for charity": Shak.
62 It grows on you
63 Ballerina Pavlova
64 Hopeless case
65 Creole veggie
66 Goes bad
67 Improve
68 Dickensian clerk
69 Hit a fly
70 Mrs. Truman

DOWN
1 Tricky pitch
2 Geometry calculations
3 Crazy
4 Seven, on a telephone
5 To boot
6 Oz heavy
7 Conjures up
8 Cut out
9 "Ta-__-Boom-De-Ré"
10 Eliot's Bede
11 Western Indian
12 Wizard of Oz role
13 Fencing weapon
20 Overpack
21 Haunted-house sound
23 Mork's home planet
26 Big mouth
28 Crazy
29 God, to de Gaulle
30 Exploits
31 Le Pew of cartoons
32 Close noisily
33 Tubby, for one
34 "There oughta be __!"
35 Smidgen
39 Zombie ingredient
42 __ and kin
44 Object
45 Sweetie
47 Promises
48 "__, brown cow?"
51 Nick name?
53 Grape expectations?
54 Prayer finales
55 Back grounds?
56 "Oops!"
57 Phony
58 Red menace
59 Rope in
60 Stand up
64 Chatter

490 TRAVELER'S CHECK by Donna J. Stone

ACROSS
1 Actor __ Cobb
5 Havana, for one
10 Bible book
14 M*A*S*H star
15 Out of the way
16 Crooner Jerry
17 Scheme
18 Like some jackets
19 Turgenev Museum site
20 START OF A QUIP BY HENNY YOUNGMAN
23 Machine part
24 Mitchell homestead
25 Conduit
30 Hook's mate
34 Beyond help
35 Zhivago's love
37 Linen fabric
38 __ Mahal
39 MIDDLE OF QUIP
41 Makes one's mark
42 1970 World's Fair site
44 Brace
45 Movie theater
46 Italian port
48 Tie
50 Present, in the future
52 Corporate VIP
53 END OF QUIP
60 Burn remedy
61 Opera cheer
62 The King and I setting
64 Director Peter
65 More competent
66 __ Taft Benson
67 Costner role of '87
68 Savanna sounds
69 He's abominable

DOWN
1 Drink like a dachshund
2 Actress Raines
3 Dutch treat
4 Czech composer
5 I, Claudius character
6 Horus' mom
7 Ms. Lollobrigida
8 Proficient
9 Phone button
10 Guacamole base
11 Full-grown filly
12 Toast topper
13 Egotist's darling
21 Seal school
22 Ovid's Muse
25 Maltese Falcon star
26 Resembling
27 Free, in a way
28 Li'l Abner creator
29 Riser's relative
31 D.D. Emmett tune
32 Ms. Verdugo
33 Adjust a watch
36 Auto-racer Luyendyk
39 One of the Philippines
40 Plow pullers
43 Smoked fish
45 Fastidious
47 Meteorology line
49 Dolores __ Rio
51 Jet starter
53 Housesitter star
54 Gen. Robert __
55 Superman's sweetie
56 Extravaganza
57 At any time
58 __ up (evaluate)
59 Trenchant
63 Actress Zetterling

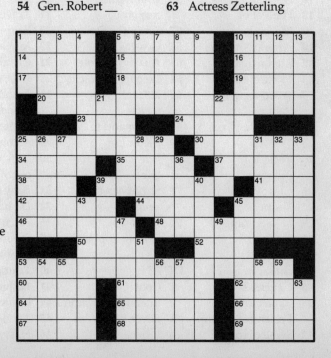

491 WORDS OF A FEATHER by Harvey Estes

ACROSS
1 Smart talk
5 Plant pest
10 Dove sounds
14 Horse's gait
15 Spot for sports
16 Head line?
17 Reverberation
18 One way to quit
20 Race like the wind
22 Farrow and Sara
23 One of two baseball teams
24 Tells fibs
26 Busy as __
28 Latin
32 Where the Ark parked?
36 Dizzy
37 Turner and Cole
39 Singer Lesley
40 Foundry refuse
41 Light boat
42 Alan of *Shane*
43 French bean?
44 Daffy has one
45 Fix the lawn
46 On the beach
48 Wall hanging
50 Shipshape
52 Bluish-white element
53 High card
56 Level
58 Keeps the home fires burning
62 Back down
65 Textbook heading
66 Ike's ex
67 Rocket slower
68 Garr of *Tootsie*
69 Made tracks
70 Car metal
71 Oracle

DOWN
1 Do a slow burn
2 Curved structure
3 London district
4 Squealer
5 German city
6 Paid player
7 Pilot's place
8 Calcutta's country
9 Computer's collection
10 EMT course
11 Mighty trees
12 Sandwich cookie
13 Underworld river
19 __-friendly
21 Thailand, formerly
25 Six-Day War site
27 Estimable young men
28 "¡__ la vista!"
29 Dots in the ocean
30 Path in the grass
31 Art able
33 Dean Martin specialty
34 Passion
35 Bear in a crib
38 Yellow gem
41 Ward and Wally
45 Monthly expense
47 Stink
49 Small gun
51 Article of faith
53 Pretends
54 Cookie nugget
55 __ *kleine Nachtmusik*
57 Postcard message
59 Leg joint
60 Green land
61 Use a teaspoon
63 Scoundrel
64 Noun suffix

492 CHINA SYNDROME by Trip Payne

ACROSS
1 __ *the Horrible*
6 Entreated
10 Toot one's own horn
14 Absurd
15 Hamlet or Macbeth
16 Artemis' mother
17 Ziti or rigatoni
18 Make eyes at
19 Word form for "within"
20 Vanity tags, e.g.
23 __ Baba
25 Porkpie or pillbox
26 Clear videotapes
27 Toupees
29 NASA ship
33 Inc. kin
34 Cultural character
36 Gaucho's rope
38 "The Great Pretender" group
42 Swell place?
43 Stallone role
46 Cul-de-__
49 Like zombies
52 It may be posted
53 Very loud
55 Uninformed response
57 Serling or Steiger
58 Gossips
63 Analogy words
64 Prepare a present
65 He took two tablets
68 Command to Fido
69 Bee or Em
70 *Peter Grimes*, for one
71 Soviet news agency
72 Implores
73 Gold or copper

DOWN
1 Cool
2 Literary collection
3 Boyer film of '44
4 Pro foe
5 Arrive at
6 On the double
7 Fireplace fuel
8 *Vogue* rival
9 Profound
10 Become teary
11 Traveler's car
12 Bear out
13 Moved to action
21 Canal zone?
22 I, for one
23 Emotion at Stonehenge
24 Ignited
28 Manhattan area
30 Stick one's neck out
31 Baby beaver
32 Do lunch
35 Anchored
37 Riyadh resident
39 Cross product
40 Young man
41 Fashionable group
44 Life story
45 Time-honored
46 Nasty sort
47 Record label
48 Sportscaster Bob
50 Skilled people
51 Big flop
54 Mariners' cries
56 Unauthorized TV greeting
59 Deck cleaner
60 Test choice
61 Install a door
62 Catch a calf
66 Prime time?
67 Actor Mineo

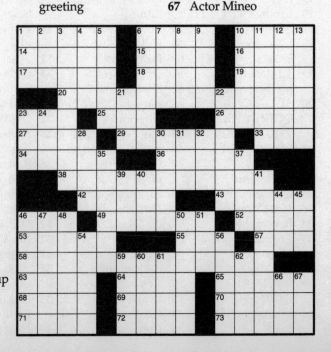

493 THE OTHER CLINTON by Dean Niles

ACROSS
1 Lip lash?
5 Common contraction
8 Actress Harris
11 1492 caravel
12 Pants part
14 Mah-jongg piece
15 Eskimo kin
16 Official records
17 "__ Rock" ('66 song)
18 Eastwood's *Rawhide* role
20 Feds
21 Pilaf ingredient
22 Informal wear
24 Slip away
28 Southern Butler
30 Actress Miles
31 Director Adrian
33 Golfer Palmer
37 Invite along
39 Seasoned stews
41 Shakes off
42 Nicholas or Alexander
44 Painter Mondrian
45 Equip again
47 "__ in St. Louis, Louis"
49 Walk like a giant
52 Shortly
54 Urge on
55 Eastwood Oscar-winner
61 Eat up
62 Dexterous
63 Literary device
64 Declare positively
65 Prophet
66 Without guile
67 "Sure!"
68 ETO commander
69 Whirlpool

DOWN
1 Storage tower
2 From the top
3 Earring type
4 Old goats?
5 Author Asimov
6 Reading desk
7 Tardy
8 Dade County city
9 Glue guy
10 Inclined
11 Golf guideline
13 Try a mouthful
14 Eastwood thriller
19 Traffic sign
23 Without a date
24 Depraved
25 Carson follower
26 Circle segments
27 Eastwood western
29 Mrs. Zeus
32 Tibetan Frosty?
34 Night: Fr.
35 Bit of news
36 Punta del __
38 Hand-me-down
40 Knight wear
43 Filled positions
46 Vendettas
48 Auto need
49 Spread out
50 Valuable collection
51 Emulates Sinbad
53 __ Dame
56 Require
57 Son of Enoch
58 Not valid
59 A deadly sin
60 Comic Louis

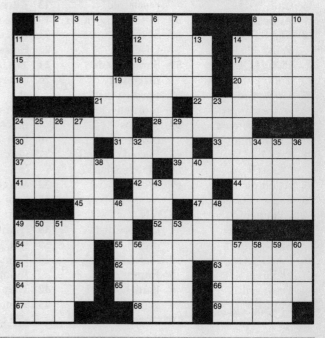

494 KNOCK THREE TIMES by Eric Albert

ACROSS
1 Omit
5 Wing it
10 Racquetball target
14 Novelist Rice
15 Refuse
16 Mitch Miller's instrument
17 KNOCK
20 Meadow muncher
21 Singer Redding
22 Michael Jackson hit
23 Forked out
24 Getz of jazz
25 Two on the aisle, e.g.
28 Tater
29 Ave. crossers
32 Diminish
33 Stigmatize socially
34 Oil cartel
35 KNOCK
38 Clownish
39 Pool accessory
40 Barkin or Burstyn
41 Put away
42 Opus
43 Slender and sleek
44 Headed for the bottom
45 Niger's neighbor
46 Classical hunk
49 Coasted
50 Male swan
53 KNOCK
56 Big boss
57 Actress Keaton
58 Catch forty winks
59 Unload
60 Fiery fragment
61 Swerve

DOWN
1 All there
2 Grasped
3 *Picnic* playwright
4 Schoolboy's shot
5 Already
6 Michelangelo subject
7 Caustic substances
8 Entrepreneur's mag
9 TV, slangily
10 __ of the Year
11 Help on a heist
12 Ms. Anderson
13 Riga resident
18 Precisely
19 Samoa studier
23 Bag holder?
24 Pluck
25 Tony of TV
26 Wolf-pack member
27 *What's It All About?* author
28 Peanuts or popcorn
29 Small fall
30 Principle
31 Play part
33 Carroll creature
34 Eyed amorously
36 Role for Burr
37 Silver State
42 Ragamuffin
43 Black eye
44 Act surly
45 Genetic duplicate
46 Bow lines?
47 Bewilderment
48 Black or white gem
49 Dagger thrust
50 Prepare pasta
51 Emulate the Blob
52 Make tea
54 Actor Alastair
55 Driller's deg.

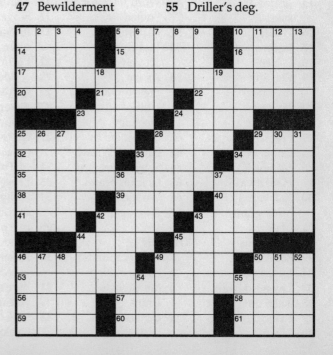

495 SHORT AND SWEET by Penny A. Roman

ACROSS
1 Fisherman
7 Cream measure
11 Babble on
14 Leatherneck
15 Man __ (racehorse)
16 Call __ day
17 Actress Blake
18 START OF A WINNIE-THE-POOH QUOTE
20 Yellow slippers?
22 *Carmen* setting
23 Actress West
25 "A" in Arabic
27 Churchman
28 PART 2 OF QUOTE
32 Attempts
33 Gray, in Grenoble
34 Channel designation
37 Skein sound
38 PART 3 OF QUOTE
40 Draft status
41 Vane dir.
42 Visionary

43 Sand bar
44 PART 4 OF QUOTE
47 Sign of balance?
50 Peeved
51 Salon stuff
52 How land is measured
55 Gettysburg victor
57 END OF QUOTE
59 Some arcade machines
62 Benz chaser
63 Journalist Jacob
64 Roman philosopher
65 Blazed the trail
66 Matchmakers?
67 Worn down

DOWN
1 Orthopedists' org.
2 *Platoon* setting
3 Rumor mill
4 Bank holdup?
5 Wins over
6 "Are you sure?"

7 Luau staple
8 "__ only kidding!"
9 Identify
10 Sees the world
11 Triangular sign
12 __ *of Two Cities*
13 Kitchen gadget
19 Ill temper
21 Part of RSVP
23 Closet pests
24 '60s hairstyles
26 Operatic barber et al.
29 Word to a mouse
30 Part of TNT
31 Canterbury can
34 Mixed up
35 Exhilarating
36 Two-faced
38 Night spot
39 Kin, for short
40 Palindromic shout
42 They trap
43 Something to slip on

44 Paris sight
45 __ de plume
46 1972-80 Broadway hit
47 Defame
48 Hole __ (ace)
49 With __ breath

53 Albany-to-Buffalo canal
54 Struck, once
56 "Book 'em, __!"
58 Slalom maneuver
60 Diamonds, slangily
61 Down

496 BEACH DAY by Shirley Soloway

ACROSS
1 Foundation
6 Eastern European
10 Trade
14 Let up
15 Junior dress size
16 Hindu queen
17 Jason's wife
18 __ 'acte
19 Elevator inventor
20 Halt an advance
23 Frat letter
24 Cook, in a way
25 Marine leader?
27 Haul away
30 *Kidnapped* monogram
31 Eyes flirtatiously
32 Meager
34 Lifted, as spirits
37 Lay a sidewalk
38 Keep out
39 Relocate
40 Make payment

43 Response
45 Depends (on)
46 In favor of
47 __ "King" Cole
48 "__ to the Church on Time"
49 Word form for "outer"
51 Pastoral god
52 Participate actively
58 Assns.
60 French river
61 Janis of *Silk Stockings*
62 Not fooled by
63 Nobelist Wiesel
64 Shining brightly
65 Cracker brand
66 Wooded valley
67 *Bambi* extras

DOWN
1 Impact sounds
2 Foster a felon
3 Marquis de __
4 Units
5 Ushers and hostesses

6 Mean looks
7 Dryer fuzz
8 Counter to
9 *Marcus Welby, M.D.* actress
10 Sign of success
11 Dilutes
12 Singer Bryant
13 Italian tower town
21 Patriot Nathan
22 __ May Clampett
26 Rains hard
27 Baker's amts.
28 Colorful fish
29 On the same __ (in accord)
31 __ *Town*
33 Lease again
34 Halloween decoration
35 Eye part
36 Saucy
38 Kramden's vehicle
41 Ewe's youngster
42 Like the Cyclops

43 St. Louis landmark
44 Memo book
46 Shorebird
48 French menu word
50 Inedible orange

51 *Winnie-the-__*
53 Capri, e.g.
54 Simon or Diamond
55 Sly trick
56 Composer Stravinsky
57 Kitten cries
59 Jack of *Barney Miller*

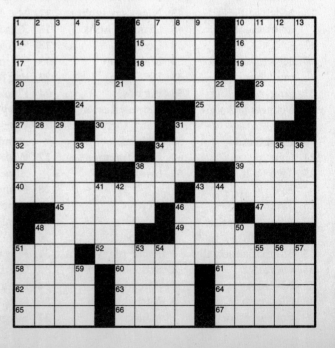

497 ON THE ALLEYS by Fred Piscop

ACROSS
1 Ruin a reputation
6 Pinafore opening?
9 Dunks for apples
13 *Cheers* waitress
14 Actress Nina
15 Frenzied
16 Valuable violin
17 Overhaul
18 Tear down
19 Kindled
20 Proverb start
23 Ancient Greek
25 Regretted
26 __ and outs
27 Calls the balls
28 Astern
31 Jets or Mets
34 __ Gigio
36 Hawkins or Thompson
38 Start conducting
41 Actress Ekberg
42 Head of France?
43 Iowa city
44 Groovy, these days
45 Crucifix
47 Atomic energy grp.
49 Iron fishhook
50 Keds product
54 Go Dutch
58 Bristol brew
59 Egyptian port
60 Jackrabbit, e.g.
61 Defense Secretary
63 Metric weight
64 MIT grad
65 Confidence
66 "... a __'clock scholar"
67 Begley and Marinaro
68 Senator Kefauver

DOWN
1 La __ (opera house)
2 Ike's lady
3 Clio's sister
4 Model Carol
5 Shriveled grape
6 Gardener, at times
7 Scottish actor Hugh
8 Grew quickly
9 Exposed
10 General Bradley
11 TV clown
12 Timetable, for short
14 Tarkenton of football
21 Ersatz emerald
22 *Steppenwolf* author
24 Stopping point
27 Increased
28 Actor West
29 Just great
30 Koppel and Kennedy
31 Russian ruler
32 Sicilian volcano
33 Saharan
35 Beyond control
37 Manila hemp
39 Jeweler's measure
40 Eastern dye
46 "... __ I sing"
48 Money back
49 Doodad
50 Pun add-on
51 Ruined
52 Beethoven's "*Für __*"
53 Picks up a videotape
54 Certain NCO
55 Immaculate
56 Director David
57 Energy units
62 SAT takers

498 SOB STORIES by Dean Niles

ACROSS
1 Cast off
5 Cuckoo
9 Hiding place
14 Actor Waggoner
15 At rest
16 Curly coifs
17 Church recess
18 German valley
19 Burdens
20 Riverbank tree
23 Mini, to MacTavish
24 Vent
27 Wander off
30 Arm: Fr.
32 Compass pt.
33 Greenish blue
34 Side
35 Adoption org.
36 Miracles tune, with "The"
39 October implement
40 Tabloid fliers
41 Texas town
42 Consumed
43 Self-satisfied
44 Slugger Rod
45 Country star Kathy
47 PC linkup
48 Stephen Rea film
55 Ran the show
57 Orient
58 Astronaut Shepard
59 French river
60 Model Macpherson
61 Frying need
62 Prepared to be shot
63 Mailer's *The __ Park*
64 Proposes

DOWN
1 Cabbage concoction
2 PR job
3 Otherwise
4 Full of meaning
5 Big name in entertainment
6 Saw
7 Diamond defect
8 Actress Garr
9 Roughened skin
10 In progress
11 Cellar substitute
12 Brick carrier
13 Curvy letter
21 "__ the Line" (Cash tune)
22 Full of rich soil
25 Real-estate account
26 Moore opener
27 Planes
28 Range toppers
29 Soapbox derby, e.g.
30 Obfuscate
31 Merino males
34 Soybean product
35 Scorch
36 Mine car
37 Poisonous plant
38 Pluck
43 Removed the pits
44 Easy pace
46 Comforting word
47 Cotton thread
49 Actor Oliver
50 New Haven campus
51 Wing-ding
52 "Oh, woe!"
53 A+ or C-
54 Some footballers
55 Tear
56 Troop troupe

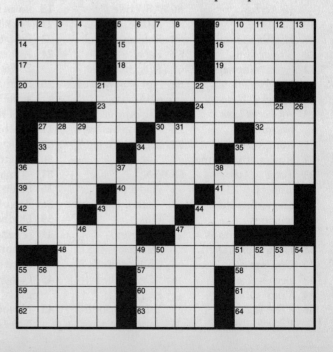

499 KITCHEN STARS by Bob Lubbers

ACROSS
1 Mil. decorations
5 Took care of
10 Army vehicle
14 Range Indian
15 Once more
16 Coax
17 Melodious McEntire
18 Fuming
19 Tetra type
20 Flip singer?
23 Self-assurance
24 TV Tarzan
25 Pasture sound
28 Stand for
29 Overshoe
32 Boxer's helper
34 County Kerry port
36 Biblical preposition
37 Cheesy star?
40 Sign of sainthood
42 Nile god
43 Avoids capture
46 "¿Cómo __ usted?"
47 PD alert
50 "__ Willie Winkie"
51 Sarnoff's org.
53 *Roma*'s land
55 Drippy actress?
58 Proficient
61 Dwight's opponent
62 Major-__ (headwaiter)
63 Jogger's gait
64 Corpsman
65 Terrible name?
66 Facility
67 Saw wood
68 Some bills

DOWN
1 Fin type
2 Russian plain
3 Blue hue
4 "From __ shining . . ."
5 Tub toy
6 Taj turf
7 WWII aux.
8 Deed
9 Ryan and Tatum
10 Refuse
11 Prior to, to Prior
12 Identity
13 Cob's mate
21 Eclipse shadow
22 Bread or booze
25 Singer Sonny
26 Hill dweller
27 Flap
30 Dairy-case purchase
31 Short
33 Den denizens
34 Walked
35 Sponsorship
37 It's often tacky
38 Cunning
39 *Bonanza* prop
40 Fell
41 Porter's kin
44 Century 21 competitor
45 Hightails it
47 Nook
48 Simple Simon's acquaintance
49 Twirlers' tools
52 *As You Like It* setting
54 Check the books
55 Jubilee
56 Actor Ray
57 Noodle topping?
58 Dug in
59 Bikini half
60 __ Alamos, NM

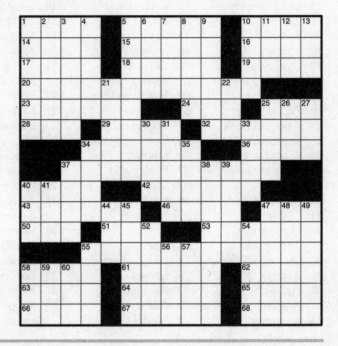

500 ANAGRAMS by Randolph Ross

ACROSS
1 Jai __
5 NYC div.
9 Date with a dr.
13 Darling, e.g.
16 Rajah lead-in
17 Apt anagram of 13 Across
18 Goofs
19 Highlands tongue
20 Singer Janis
22 __ in "elephant"
23 No gentlemen
26 Smears
28 *A Chorus Line* number
29 Ration
32 Rose's other name
33 Tone __ (rap singer)
34 She took a shine to shoes
37 Satisfied sounds
38 Francis and Dahl
40 Courses
43 Bern's river
44 Void
46 "The Racer's Edge"
47 Author Hubbard
49 Locality
50 Sundial numeral
51 Least taxing
54 "__ It Romantic?"
55 Erie hrs.
56 ABA title
57 Morse bits
60 Reformer Jacob
62 Penalty
67 Sgts. and cpls.
68 Apt anagram of 62 Across
69 Lab burner
70 Actress Moore
71 Scale starters

DOWN
1 Had a pizza
2 Author Deighton
3 Plus
4 Sorbonne concepts
5 Chilly sounds
6 "This round is __!"
7 Silly Charlotte
8 __ *vincit amor*
9 "Botch-__" ('52 song)
10 Prose symbol
11 Apt anagram of 10 Down
12 *Pravda* source
14 Musical knack
15 Latin abbr.
21 Tuck's mate
23 Fountain order
24 Apt anagram of 25 Down
25 Formal statement
26 Brooks or Blanc
27 Machine part
29 Noisy racket
30 Augury
31 __ majesty
35 Steep
36 Kin of pre-
39 Divine archer
41 Japanese export
42 Rotisserie rod
45 Gangster's gun
48 Never, in Nuremberg
52 Sports network
53 Cuttlefish kin
54 "My name __" ("I'm ruined")
55 Sea eagle
57 *Carpe* __
58 __ spumante
59 LBJ's VP
61 Pub. pension payer
63 Vane dir.
64 Comedian Philips
65 Radio's PBS
66 Poet's monogram

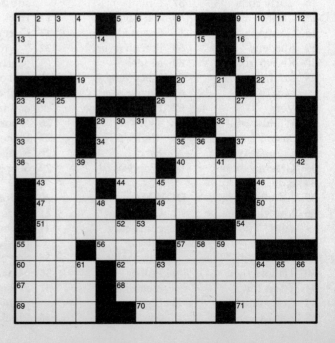

501 WHAT'S COOKIN'? by Harvey Estes

ACROSS
1 Obligation
5 Clock sound
9 Russian czar
13 At any time
14 German sub
16 Risqué
17 Dean Martin specialties
20 Trainee
21 Earth
22 Make a knot
23 "Vaya con __"
25 Soft drink
27 Ex-soldiers' org.
30 Nights before Christmas
32 Arrow part
35 Hipbones
37 Directional suffix
38 Sharon of Israel
40 Higher priorities
44 Patriot Allen
45 "The Gold Bug" author
46 Fiery fiddler?
47 Mixes

49 Rug style
51 __ Jose, CA
52 Alaskan seaport
54 Baltic tributary
56 Common article
59 Mythical mom of twins
61 Prepares pork chops
65 Become quite annoyed
68 Teheran's country
69 Reveal
70 "For Pete's __!"
71 Fedora fabric
72 Come down to earth
73 Looked at

DOWN
1 Liter leader
2 Neck and neck
3 Sash, e.g.
4 Cornered, in a way
5 Breakfast pastry
6 __-Wan Kenobi

7 Canvas beds
8 Ring wins
9 Lyricist Gershwin
10 Far-flung
11 Play start
12 AMEX rival
15 Some combos
18 Soft, white cheese
19 Dated
24 Medieval menial
26 Moses' brother
27 Bad __ (uneasy feeling)
28 Flies like a canary
29 England's Isle of __
31 Small cuts
33 Drums' companions
34 __ cotta
36 One more time
39 French city
41 Sign up
42 London area
43 Tennis accessory

48 Sniff the air
50 Microbe
53 Ford flop
55 Shortstop Pee Wee
56 End-of-week initials
57 Roll-call response

58 List ender
60 "__ boy!"
62 Queen for __
63 British nobleman
64 Rushed
66 Industrious insect
67 Years on end

502 DOUBLY QUIET by Shirley Soloway

ACROSS
1 Church officer
6 Pleased
10 Mil. female
13 Singer Branigan
14 Almost there
15 "__ Were a Rich Man"
16 Some knots
18 Turf
19 Actor Carney
20 "__-porridge hot . . ."
21 Resort lake
23 Highways and byways
24 Pastoral poem
25 Hebrew month
27 Up __ (yet)
29 Kind of communication
33 Venomous viper
36 Singing Mama
37 Sews a toe
38 Tennis star Arthur
39 Adjectival suffix
40 Couture event
42 America's Most Wanted host

44 "__ sow, so shall . . ."
45 Former New York senator Al D'__
47 Premiere performance
50 Assail
51 Price twice
52 Used to be
55 Crank's comment
56 Little or no attention
59 Mine find
60 Actress Anouk
61 __ firma
62 Paving material
63 Unassuming
64 String toys

DOWN
1 Martinelli or Lanchester
2 Comedian Bert
3 Performance for two
4 Before, poetically
5 Good relationship
6 Tumbler

7 Solitary
8 Make an inquiry
9 Preordain
10 On the fence
11 "__ Such as I" ('59 song)
12 Castro of Cuba
14 Niger's neighbor
17 Cousteau's workplace
22 Big fuss
23 Knocks sharply
25 Discovery shouts
26 Kitchen appliance
27 Singer Tennille
28 Approximately
29 Anat., e.g.
30 Harem rooms
31 Dress accessory
32 Prince Charles' title: Abbr.
34 Oxford or brogan
35 Church bench
38 Helper: Abbr.

40 Ocean wreckage
41 Mischievous
43 Had a bite
45 Monastery head
46 Stiller's partner
47 John or Bo
48 Novel ending

49 __-relief
51 European capital
52 Lean and sinewy
53 Curly coif
54 Depots: Abbr.
57 Rush off
58 Vintage car

503 BIG STAR by Dean Niles

ACROSS
1 Scale notes
4 Knife handle
8 *West Side Story* song
13 Mandela org.
14 Competes
15 Kate Nelligan film
16 See 43 Down
19 Strong-arm
20 Actor Morales
21 Navy rival
22 Maynard's good buddy
25 Sail site
29 Actress Remick
30 Of interest to Lord Nelson
31 Nile feature
32 Bathroom worker
33 __ *Mame*
34 BIG STAR FILM
37 Witches
38 Items in the fire
39 Holstein homes
40 New Hampshire campus
41 "Gotcha!"
44 "Auld Lang __"
45 Verbose
46 Controversial tree spray
47 Peasant fellow
49 Cotton fabric
51 BIG STAR FILM
55 Inch along
56 Distant start
57 Hair goo
58 Don one's duds
59 Mgr.'s helper
60 "Kookie" Byrnes

DOWN
1 Alfalfa or Buckwheat
2 "Play it again, Sam!"
3 Plot
4 Blueprint inits.
5 Some terriers
6 Hakim's hat
7 Poetic monogram
8 Thornburgh's predecessor
9 Pond organism
10 Disciplines
11 Chemical suffix
12 Televise
17 Bitingly funny
18 Mr. Simon
23 Finished
24 More daft, in Devonshire
26 Sax type
27 Prod to activity
28 __ kwon do
30 Evenings, on marquees
31 Guitarist Eddy
32 Crockett country
33 Unsigned
34 Shallow server
35 Beeper
36 Provoked thoroughly
37 Dan Rather's network
40 RC group
41 Assert
42 Pilose
43 WITH 16 ACROSS, BIG STAR
45 Envelops
46 Sturdy wood
48 Summers on the Seine
50 Platoon, e.g.
51 Math. term
52 Flight stat.
53 Afternoon drink
54 Mensa measures

504 NAME THAT TUNE by Trip Payne

ACROSS
1 Pit for a pump
5 Not quite straight
9 Beat it
14 Draftable
15 Comic Kaplan
16 Basketball venue
17 Da-da-da-DUM . . .
20 Ms. Lauder
21 Favorable opinion
22 Settle a deal
23 Grew tiresome
25 Storm warnings
29 Sluggish
31 TV Tarzan
32 Smeltery stuff
33 Cracker shape
36 Mock
37 DUM-da-DUM-DUM . . .
41 French designer
42 Navy rank
43 Actress Gardner
44 Period
46 Funds a college
50 Chanter's utterance
52 __ serif
54 By way of
55 Burger topping
57 Hot spots
59 DUM-DUM-da-DUM . . .
63 "__ mud in your eye!"
64 Sporting blade
65 Birth of a notion?
66 Put out
67 Gobi-like
68 Snooping about

DOWN
1 "Amen!"
2 Cultural agcy.
3 Convention-goer
4 Popular hors d'oeuvre
5 In the past
6 Two-time Grand Slam winner
7 Too heavy
8 __ up (confined)
9 Without harm
10 Felony, e.g.
11 Ring judge
12 Farm animal
13 __-jongg
18 Conforming (to)
19 Circus barker
24 Valhalla VIP
26 Wander about
27 Quiz option
28 Dr. Ruth's specialty
30 Carson's predecessor
31 *Lohengrin* heroine
34 Big flattop?
35 Noshed on
36 Ward (off)
37 Prima donna
38 Horse color
39 Ness and company
40 Horse-drawn cab
41 Holder like Boulder
44 Actor Borgnine
45 Sudden assault
47 Lay it on
48 Draws back
49 Glide easily
51 Lighthouse or minaret
52 Marsh bird
53 *Roots* Emmy-winner
56 Dedicatory verses
58 Prone to preening
59 Popular article
60 Spell
61 Before, to Byron
62 "Well, I'll be!"

505   OLD JOKE by Matt Gaffney

ACROSS
1 Cherbourg crony
4 Darling dog
8 Ohio town
13 Also-__ (losers)
15 WWII alliance
16 Boost in bucks
17 START OF A QUIP
20 Kids
21 Selfsame
22 The Lion in summer
23 Ipanema's locale
24 Base stuff?
25 Dos Passos trilogy
26 PART 2 OF QUIP
30 Cry of discovery
31 Cryptic org.
32 Sword part
35 Molly Brown's boat
38 *Vogue* concern
41 Competition
42 Austrian ice
43 Broadway sign
44 PART 3 OF QUIP
49 Good times
51 Be important
52 Stout relative
53 Architectural addition
54 Zenith
55 Record player
58 END OF QUIP
61 King Gillette invention
62 Alphabet sequence
63 __ *Can* (Davis book)
64 Repose
65 Co. compensation program
66 "HELP!"

DOWN
1 Host
2 It's sometimes held
3 Really tick off
4 Casual refusals
5 Medieval weapon
6 Ultimate state
7 Resources
8 Roentgen's discovery
9 Musical acumen
10 Physicist Bohr
11 "__ bad moon rising . . ."
12 Flying start?
14 Subbed
18 Odin's son
19 Zodiac animal
24 Platter
25 Bountiful setting
26 ". . . __ the whole thing!"
27 Switchblade
28 Verse lead-in
29 Hesitation sounds
33 Wharf sights
34 Sped
36 Picnic intruders
37 Ultimate degree
38 Colonial flute
39 "Just __ suspected!"
40 Data: Abbr.
42 Looks up to
45 Roguish
46 Hot stuff
47 Western defense grp.
48 Gray matter?
49 Arm bones
50 Square
53 Masterson colleague
54 Farm measure
55 Sow chow
56 Exxon's ex-name
57 Singer Redding
59 Bird of myth
60 Lennon's lady

506   FAMILY REUNION by Carol A. Fenter

ACROSS
1 Asian desert
5 Autumn fruits
10 Exec. degrees
14 "__ the Mood for Love"
15 Strong point
16 Give a yes-__ answer
17 Man with a scythe
19 New Rochelle college
20 __ water (stays afloat)
21 Menacing
23 Borscht veggie
25 Up in the world?
26 Oat or wheat
29 Find the sum
31 Wails
34 Utter defeat
35 Broad st.
36 Search, with "out"
37 Plant part
38 Looked for oil
40 Regret
41 Prepares to frame
43 Midmorning
44 Find fault
45 Troy's last king
46 Dracula's alter ego
47 Choir members
48 Brazier bit
50 Utah's state flower
52 Fruit cocktails
55 State for casinos
59 Russian range
60 Storyteller of the South
62 Renown
63 Turn of phrase
64 Pool triangle
65 Ran away
66 Fresh
67 Fr. holy women

DOWN
1 Present
2 First name in tents
3 Light snack
4 Occupy
5 Describe grammatically
6 NY hours
7 Sale sign
8 Jog one's memory
9 Office worker
10 Not as dry
11 Reagan film of '38
12 Novelist Tyler
13 Fly high
18 Paradise
22 Really annoyed
24 Rikki-Tikki-__
26 Hold on to
27 Oarsman
28 Rosalind Russell role
30 Actress Burke
32 Medical prefix
33 Dance moves
35 Dadaism founder
36 Bog
38 Disney pachyderm
39 "Why don't we?"
42 Toured a smorgasbord
44 St. Pat's plants
46 Singer Lee
47 Worry, for one
49 Needle cases
51 Foe
52 Sleeve end
53 Kind of exam
54 Biol. and chem.
56 *Amo, amas,* __
57 Mussolini moniker
58 Requests
61 __ Angeles, CA

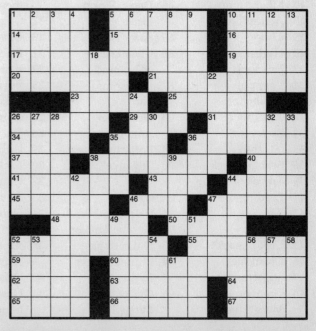

DOWN TO EARTH by Bob Lubbers

ACROSS

1 Vocalist Vikki
5 __ Flow (British naval base)
10 Tabloid topics
14 Slangy suffix
15 Race postings
16 Wren den
17 Score big
19 Pastrami palace
20 Aircraft housings
21 Paper chief
23 "__ the ramparts . . ."
24 Madrid museum
25 Nag politely?
29 Tragic fate
30 Scale tones
33 Entertain
34 Garr of *Tootsie*
35 *God's Little* __
36 Congenial
37 Words to live by
38 Shine
39 Actress Sommer
40 Ventilates
41 Clear the slate
42 Auction ending
43 Model Macpherson
44 Chewed out
45 Hydrocarbon radical
47 Lawyer's charge
48 Cost of care
50 Most cheerful
55 Adolescent
56 Beach building
58 Gillette product
59 Oklahoma native
60 Meat cut
61 Musical Myra
62 Wise guys
63 Winds up

DOWN

1 "All the Way" lyricist
2 Sills solo
3 Coll. troops
4 Heavy cord
5 Created a coif
6 Juice in a jug
7 Author Kingsley
8 __ diem
9 Minor planet
10 Brought to ruin
11 Hidden flaws
12 Scandinavian capital
13 Tend the sauce
18 Isolated
22 Beaver bulwark
24 Reads intently
25 Hindu queen
26 Author Zola
27 Investigators
28 "Understood!"
29 Plow name
31 Got up
32 Mended
34 Warbling sound
35 Taj Mahal town
37 Belafonte numbers
41 Actress Verdugo
43 __ out a living
44 August Wilson play
46 Horne and Olin
47 Sundae sauce
48 Hatch's home
49 Fountain or Seeger
50 Hose mishap
51 Capri, for one
52 Short jacket
53 Glided smoothly
54 Sawbucks
57 Fit __ fiddle

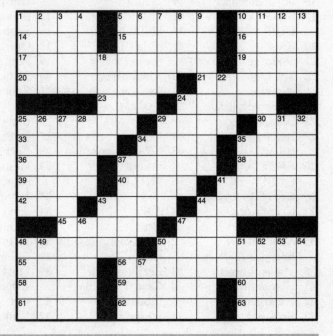

SNACK PACK by Randolph Ross

ACROSS

1 Mutt's pal
5 Petal oil
10 Fancy horseplay?
14 Russian river
15 Doorbell
16 Black stone
17 Milano moola
18 Actress Shire
19 Chop __
20 Hacker snack?
23 Jazz form
24 Very popular
25 Parabolic
28 Atlas abbr.
31 Sweeping
35 __ canto
36 Scholar snack?
39 Trebek or Karras
41 Leading
42 *The __ of the Rose*
43 Crook snack?
46 Crash site?
47 Supernumerary
48 Grant or Meriwether
49 Newspaper notices
51 Barcelona bear
53 Elevator unit
54 Carpenter snacks?
61 Bear or Berra
62 Bring up
63 Desert Storm locale
65 Actor Arkin
66 Chemical compound
67 Dachshund's dad
68 Heartstring sound
69 Porterhouse, e.g.
70 "By Jove!"

DOWN

1 Cal. page
2 Author Ambler
3 Old card game
4 Burned dinner?
5 Misbehave
6 One of those things
7 Mah-jongg piece
8 Mideast royalty
9 Get to
10 Atomic antiparticle
11 "Moving __" (*The Jeffersons* theme)
12 Caustic chemicals
13 Lumbering
21 Places for peas
22 Rail rider
25 Put down
26 Take five
27 Chin feature
28 Taj __
29 Unlucky *numero*
30 Back financially
32 Giraffe cousin
33 Set as a goal
34 Heroic feats
37 Disfigure
38 Alphabet sequence
40 Office activity
44 Hernando's house
45 Chestnut horse
50 Hurt
52 Mean ones
53 Help Her Honor
54 Day starter?
55 Actor Richard
56 Hops heater
57 Evening, on a marquee
58 Cruising
59 Math course
60 Poet Teasdale
61 Red Sox great, for short
64 Proof letters

509 MANE EVENT by Penny A. Roman

ACROSS

1 "__ Not There" ('64 tune)
5 Shacks
9 Start the slaw
14 Give a hoot
15 Organic compound
16 __ Selassie
17 B __ "boy"
18 Brunei's locale
19 "Live Free __" (NH's motto)
20 Possessed hairpiece?
23 Cartoonist Silverstein
24 Building wings
25 Nightclub bit
28 Curled one's lip
30 Bottle top
33 Flapjack chain
35 Curve in a ship's plank
36 Lady of Spain
38 Loverboy
40 Japanese export
42 Kwai, for one
43 Nerds
45 Baseball stat
47 Shut in
48 CIA's predecessor
49 En __ (chess maneuver)
52 Charles or Conniff
53 Misplaced
54 Knock off
56 *Hair* practice?
62 Caribbean nation
63 Similar
64 Fearful words
65 Wide neckwear
66 Marshes
67 Active sort
68 "This __ for the books!"
69 Lip
70 In stitches?

DOWN

1 "Get lost!"
2 Jumble
3 Buffalo's water
4 Mails
5 "My goodness!"
6 Yapping away
7 Hard work
8 Actor Christian
9 Take upon oneself
10 Angelic instruments
11 Harass
12 Nobelist Wiesel
13 Billy __ Williams
21 Interrogative exclamations
22 Bullring cheers
25 __-surface (missile route)
26 Chinese canines
27 Big books
29 Witnesses
30 Vegetation, often
31 Fight site
32 Bash
34 For each
37 Little bite
39 Stem, to stern
41 Embarrassing
44 Mouth off
46 Earnest
50 Attack from above
51 "__ Skylark" (Shelley ode)
53 Admit
55 Urges on
56 Source for *Pravda*
57 Puerto __
58 Managed, with "out"
59 Loafer, e.g.
60 Once again
61 Desolate
62 "Bali __"

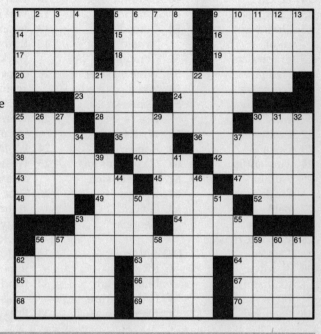

510 GETTING TO WORK by Matt Gaffney

ACROSS

1 Peters out
5 "Coffee, __ milk?"
10 Side
14 John Irving character
15 Ostracized animal
16 "Eat your carrots __ dessert!"
17 START OF A QUIP BY GEORGE WILL
20 In the bag
21 Arts' partner
22 Entryway
24 Gabor et al.
25 Wilde, for one
28 Cut of bacon
30 Puts up
34 Trams transport it
35 Philosopher's inventory?
37 Singer Sedaka
38 Hoot and holler
40 MIDDLE OF QUIP
41 See socially
42 Pack away
43 Pop in
45 Despondent
46 Opera singer Stratas
48 Place to play
50 Annapolis grad.
51 Literary pseudonym
53 Denials
55 Kilimanjaro's setting
59 California athletes
63 END OF QUIP
65 At a distance
66 Try to be safe?
67 Spread-out
68 Stoolies
69 Presidential nickname
70 Beef dish

DOWN

1 Basket fillers
2 Unadorned
3 Cauldron contents
4 Shell out
5 Libyan city
6 Dawn goddess
7 "Rock of __"
8 Prevention dose
9 Brings back
10 Actor/director Robert
11 Mr. Sevareid
12 Pay to play
13 __ scale (mineral measure)
18 Pairs
19 Time for a revolution
23 Spokes
25 Defeat decisively
26 Fuming
27 Operatic hero, often
29 Golfer King
31 Stop
32 Real big guy
33 Goes downhill
36 Laotian native
39 Splinter remover
43 Least humble
44 Streetcar
47 Eastern European
49 Do business
52 Supermarket pathway
54 Turns aside
55 Kaiser's counterpart
56 __ Romeo (auto)
57 Shipshape
58 Dry-as-dust
60 Revise a manuscript
61 Uncouth
62 Act like Etna
64 Unmatched

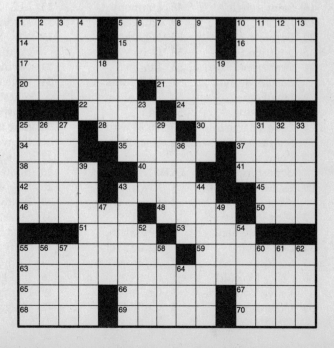

511 ANY WHICH WAY by Mary E. Brindamour

ACROSS

1 Closed
5 Canonized Mlles.
9 Interrogative pronoun
12 Uses a VCR
14 Lo-cal
15 Camp food
16 Drained of color
17 Emphasize
19 Hedge sculpture
21 "__ With a Kiss"
22 Ease
23 Got a D
24 Tiny critter
26 Author Sinclair
27 Belfry resident
28 Paul of *Crocodile Dundee*
30 __ wave (tsunami)
34 Bit of gossip
36 Factions
38 Caesar's costar
39 Column style
41 Tide types
43 Ironic
44 More cunning
46 Makes amends
48 South Americans
50 Comedian Arnold
51 Convincing
52 Wine mavens
54 Weed-covered
56 Nebraska city
58 Writes
59 Roman poet
60 Hazardous gas
61 Pitcher's stat.
62 Droops
63 Gingrich of Georgia

DOWN

1 RR stop
2 Biblical verb
3 Pad furniture
4 Plains abode
5 Drink noisily
6 Littler than little
7 Airport abbr.
8 Teeter-totter
9 During the time that
10 Sharpened
11 Was in debt
13 Informant
15 Revered work
18 Convene again
20 Sedans
23 Word form for "five"
24 Footnote abbr.
25 Western alliance
26 Shoe salesman, at times
29 Kelly and Hackman
31 Reduce in importance
32 Land measure
33 Puts down
35 Gentlemen
37 Run-ins
40 Hold on
42 Machine part
45 Prelims
47 Kind of band
48 Sweetheart
49 Booster rocket
50 Smooths
51 Deal (with)
52 Baby branch
53 Put on display
55 Cicero's eggs
57 Picnic pest

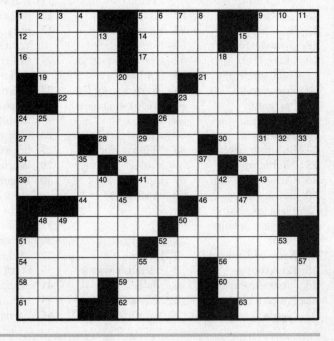

512 TRIPLE FEATURE by Eric Albert

ACROSS

1 Unclear
5 Hot lunch
10 Con game
14 Drama award
15 Great destruction
16 Saint's circle
17 Ignore
20 Barbie's boyfriend
21 *Gentlemen Prefer Blondes* author
22 Small part
23 Actor Arnaz
24 Give a name to
25 Smitten
28 Point of departure
29 Radio regulator: Abbr.
32 Memorable ship
33 Unadulterated
34 2-D extent
35 Scold
38 "If __ I Would Leave You"
39 Of enormous extent
40 Huey, Dewey, and __
41 Writer Deighton
42 Sword handle
43 Like a puppy
44 Ship's tiller
45 Singer Patti
46 Harmony
49 Hunger pain
50 Nightwear
53 Defy
56 Être
57 Obliterate
58 Poet Alexander
59 Out
60 Tools with teeth
61 Once more

DOWN

1 Pawn
2 Ready, willing, and __
3 Jerusalem, figuratively
4 Affirmative answer
5 Opt for
6 Capital of Vietnam
7 Composer Charles
8 __ Alamos, NM
9 Cold drink
10 Unfilled pie
11 Barrel
12 Voice range
13 LEM locale
18 Huddle count
19 New Haven campus
23 Giving person
24 Jeweler's measure
25 Constrain
26 Like a babe in the woods
27 Cotton items
28 Invitee
29 Impostor
30 Beany's buddy
31 Sweet and crumby
33 Sacred song
34 Home
36 Bad guy
37 Nancy's pal
42 Oregano, for one
43 French port
44 Cozy and comfortable
45 Like Nehru jackets
46 "__ girl!"
47 Medium-sized dog
48 Castro's country
49 High point
50 Laborer
51 Wisecrack
52 Fret and fume
54 Gun-lobby grp.
55 Whirlpool bath

513 CRAFTY by Bob Lubbers

ACROSS

1 Medal metal
5 Made a footnote
10 Top guns
14 Woodwind
15 Do dais duty
16 Taxi-ride tab
17 Wabash feeder
19 Scurry about
20 Game fish
21 Prepares a pump
23 Beer mug
24 Bring up
25 Kitchen worker
31 Bible book
34 Abound
35 Lamb product
36 Dem.'s opponent
37 Word form for "split"
39 Adjective suffix
40 Thoughts
43 "Cheerio!"
44 Be a brat
45 One-man rule
48 Ski lift
49 Set __ for (try to trick)
52 Chosen field
55 Agricultural land
57 Where buns bake
58 Like some tapes
61 Lemon skin
62 Lofty spaces
63 Hornet house
64 Citrus drinks
65 Takes off
66 Nor. neighbor

DOWN

1 I've __ a Secret
2 Newspaper pieces
3 '50s pitcher Eddie
4 Push in
5 Tropical treats
6 Mideast power
7 Soaks up rays
8 WWII arena
9 More profound
10 Declares
11 Cool-headed
12 Part of HOMES
13 Prepares the table
18 Homeric
22 Merry Martha
24 Sends cash
26 Church reader
27 Composer Franz
28 Land east of the Urals
29 Fleming and McShane
30 Turns blue
31 Parched
32 Word form for "center"
33 Crude cartel
38 Babe Didrikson __
41 Is present
42 Kemo __
44 Sports injuries
46 Podiatric adjective
47 Particular
50 Former VP
51 "__-porridge hot . . ."
52 Mrs. Dithers
53 Eager
54 Actress Russo
55 Start of a spell
56 Cut coupons
59 Western Indian
60 Inc., in Ipswich

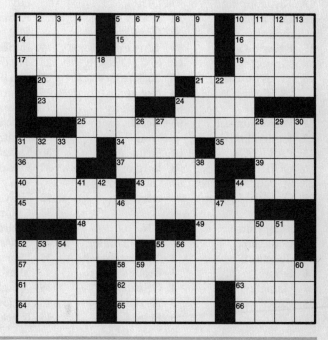

514 KITCHEN SET by Trip Payne

ACROSS

1 Rhone feeder
6 Prudish person
10 Imitated
14 Singing chipmunk
15 Atmosphere
16 Greek philosopher
17 Peter's Friends actor
19 The gamut
20 Layer of eggs
21 A, in Arabic
22 In a feeble way
24 __ and Old Lace
26 Chair man
27 GE company
28 "__ Bill the Sailor"
31 It'll give you a weigh
34 Shimon of Israel
35 Away from home
36 Cryptogram
37 Shred cheese
38 Dorothy's dog
39 Drillers' org.
40 Golf clubs
41 Memento
42 Singer Elliot
44 "That's it!"
45 __ de Chine
46 Leaving the stage
50 Thelma's friend
52 Thin
53 Director Spike
54 Teacup handles
55 "I Feel Good" singer
58 To be, in Tours
59 Revlon rival
60 Flood barrier
61 Wide Sargasso Sea author
62 Biblical trio
63 Renowned reviewer

DOWN

1 Peter and the Wolf bird
2 Change
3 Hot spots
4 Tuck's mate
5 Add value
6 Hysteria
7 Fancy collar
8 Kind of verb: Abbr.
9 City's nickname
10 Showy shrub
11 Beyond the Fringe star
12 Chemical compound
13 Half asleep
18 Director Kazan
23 Sothern and Jillian
25 Perry's creator
26 Hauls
28 Casserole components
29 Stringed instrument
30 Harrow's rival
31 Racket
32 Musical ending
33 Former MTV host
34 Novel medium
37 Toast spread
38 Perfectly
40 Covers cupcakes
41 Sewing item
43 Comes up
44 Imaginary line
46 Nicholas Gage book
47 "__ a Parade"
48 Less established
49 The Maids playwright
50 Suggestive look
51 Vow
52 Urban problem
56 Gardner of Mogambo
57 Dixie fighter

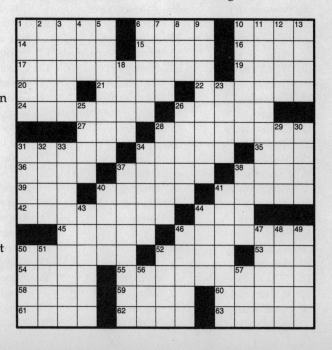

515 JAM SESSION by Emily Cox & Henry Rathvon

ACROSS
1 Snack spot
5 Before
10 Exemplar of redness
14 Cadabra preceder
15 Taco topping
16 Like a blue moon
17 Ballerina's support
18 START OF A QUIP
20 Depose
21 Poetic pugilist
22 Trellis climbers
23 PART 2 OF QUIP
27 St. Paul's architect
28 Chocolate Town, U.S.A.
32 Blueprints
34 Cookbook direction
36 Before
37 Hamelin pest
38 PART 3 OF QUIP

41 Chicken __ king
42 Grand __ Opry
43 Flying grp.
44 Following
46 Vast holdings
49 Angers
50 PART 4 OF QUIP
54 Rouen's river
57 Gone by
58 Tonsorial request
60 END OF QUIP
63 Back from work
64 Not apt to bite
65 Was slimy
66 Gets by, with "out"
67 Sirius, e.g.
68 Borg or Bergman
69 Garnet and ruby

DOWN
1 Roman orator
2 Approximately
3 Trout's milieu
4 Oriental
5 As right __
6 Plant stem

7 Borden bovine
8 Barbecue remains
9 Lah-di-__
10 NHL squad
11 Deserve
12 Canal, lake, or city
13 Roman Polanski film
19 Ended
24 Try out
25 Smell
26 Word form for "sun"
29 Summertime health hazard
30 Della's creator
31 Once around the sun
32 Univ. staffer
33 Composer Schifrin
34 Swiss city
35 "Son __ Preacher Man" ('68 tune)
39 __ tight ship
40 Patio server
45 It tickles

47 Metal worker
48 Hand-me-down
49 Tristan's love
51 Corn color
52 Looked like Lothario
53 Intended

54 Barrier breakers
55 French state
56 __ *Fugitive from a Chain Gang*
59 Military meal
61 Call for help
62 Drag

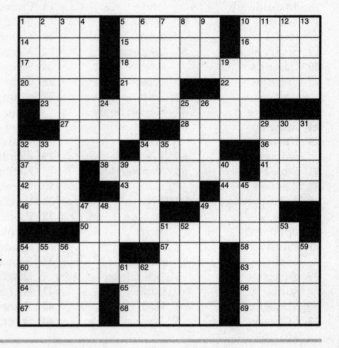

516 SHOOTING STARS by Janie Lyons

ACROSS
1 Freshwater fish
5 Shame
10 Burn slightly
14 Felipe of baseball
15 Italian bowling
16 Nevada city
17 *Butch Cassidy and the Sundance Kid* star
19 Word form for "within"
20 Car-radio feature
21 Captivated
23 Helper: Abbr.
25 Middle
26 Printer's directions
29 Irving or Carter
31 Tips a hat
34 Story
35 Arafat's org.
36 Previously
37 "The Greatest"
38 Helium holder
40 Society column word

41 Poet William
43 Atty.'s degree
44 Pierre's st.
45 Tree bumps
46 Deli bread
47 Hardwood trees
48 __ as a goose
50 Aroma
52 Aetna rival
55 Senator Muskie
59 Harvest
60 *High Noon* star
62 Noun suffix
63 Cop __ (bargain, maybe)
64 Mrs. Nick Charles
65 Danish physicist
66 Oozing
67 Winter forecast

DOWN
1 *Li'l Abner* cartoonist
2 Winglike
3 Don Juan
4 Throb

5 Helps a hood
6 Violinist's need
7 Highest point
8 Meager
9 Siva worshiper
10 __ the crop (finest)
11 *The Tin Star* star
12 Poker stake
13 Crucifix
18 Noted loch
22 German seaport
24 Lofty
26 Pile up
27 Claw
28 *The Magnificent Seven* star
30 Actress Ringwald
32 Anomaly
33 Searches for
35 Golf goal
36 Hope or Newhart
38 Intoxicate
39 Bread spread

42 Flourish
44 Sunday talks
46 Record again
47 Hubbub
49 Adventure stories
51 Corrode

52 Jordanian, for one
53 *Tonight Show* host
54 __ Stanley Gardner
56 Knowledgeable about
57 Pianist Peter
58 Sketch
61 Slangy assent

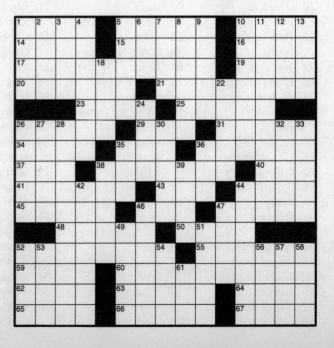

517   MATTERS OF TASTE by Dean Niles

ACROSS
1 Dull
5 Bogged down
10 "Waterloo" group
14 Leak slowly
15 Rub out
16 Wedding-cake level
17 Disdain for the unobtainable
19 List entry
20 EMT procedure
21 Gave temporarily
22 Insignificant
24 Serengeti sillies?
26 Please, in Potsdam
27 Serious cinema
30 Gun an engine
33 It makes waste
36 *Picnic* playwright
37 Brooks and Gibson
38 Part of QED
39 Burn
40 Yardstick org.
41 Comrade
42 Tom Joad, for one
43 Appendix neighbor
44 Little child
45 Deviating
47 Aviator Post
49 Calf
53 More economical
55 Headliner
57 1300 hours
58 Courtly instrument
59 Widespread craving
62 Sign of the future
63 Rockies range
64 Floundering
65 Peel an orange
66 Roman parent
67 Balkan

DOWN
1 Painter Hieronymus
2 Daft
3 Blue hue
4 __ *Alibi* ('89 movie)
5 Slightest
6 Isfahan's country
7 Engrossed
8 Journal ending
9 Very unpopular
10 Leaning
11 Furthest extremity
12 Bar order
13 Troops
18 Annoying light
23 Dined
25 Cooper hero Bumppo
26 Morning musician
28 *The Iceman Cometh* character
29 Studio sign
31 Otherwise
32 Engine option
33 Solar output
34 Singer Guthrie
35 Taffy type
37 Devilfish
39 Regains control
43 Motionless
45 Bristol brew
46 Personification
48 Actress Worth
50 On the prowl
51 Computer key
52 Fix up
53 Hog food
54 Mountain lion
55 Transmitted
56 Head: Fr.
60 Mil. stat.
61 U.S. alliance

518   CALIFORNIANS by Harvey Estes

ACROSS
1 Caprice
5 "My Heart Skipped __" ('89 tune)
10 Mighty trees
14 Scottish isle
15 Skedaddle
16 Sneaker or sandal
17 Soybean product
18 Like *The Twilight Zone*
19 Knowledge
20 Skelton character
23 Mideast desert
24 Eye problem
25 Oil-can letters
26 Arrange type
27 __ out (removed)
30 Ram's ma'am
31 Finale
32 Botches up
34 Bark sharply
36 CT summer hours
38 Bugs Bunny adversary
42 Revolutionary
43 Griddle
44 Statue stone
47 Smidgen
50 Pen point
52 Bad deal
54 Stolen
55 *You __ There*
56 Head the cast
58 Oxygen isotope
60 Computer-game name
64 Kandinsky colleague
65 "Peter, Peter, Pumpkin-__"
66 Sitarist Shankar
68 *Born Free* lioness
69 *Ghostbusters* goo
70 __ even keel
71 Actress Cannon
72 Put up with
73 Harmony

DOWN
1 Cleverness
2 Muncie resident
3 Troop group
4 __ Loa
5 Away from the wind
6 Keg contents
7 Makes a buck
8 Fly a fighter
9 Really small
10 Christiania, today
11 "My kingdom for __!"
12 Seoul man
13 Gardened
21 Get even with
22 Titles
23 Compass pt.
28 Viewer
29 Hoover or Grand Coulee
33 Bart, to Homer
35 Card dot
37 __ Mahal
39 Have a hunch
40 Playground game
41 Furniture wood
45 "Mellow Yellow" fellow
46 When the French fry
47 Raised, as prices
48 By word of mouth
49 Saint of Spain
51 Lava rock
53 Hawaiian dish
57 2 to 1, e.g.
59 WWII planes
61 Nasty
62 Verne captain
63 __ Scott Decision
67 Business abbr.

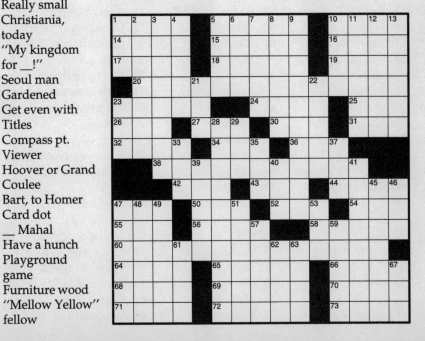

519 SMARTY PANTS by Randolph Ross

ACROSS
1 Nutritionist Davis
7 Rich soil
11 Turkish dignitary
14 Sell to consumers
15 Oklahoma city
16 Let go
17 Beach pants
19 Family members
20 Farm building
21 Actor Tamblyn
22 It's a cinch
23 __ for Sergeants
26 Art supporter
27 Outdoorsmen's pants
31 Sound of surprise
32 Rest rm.
33 Baltimore athlete
37 Alfresco
39 Meara's partner
40 __ of Innocence (Wharton novel)
41 Apply
42 Bear's lair
43 Girls' pants
47 Cuttlefish cousin
50 Taken care of
51 Cheese chunk
52 "__ she blows!"
53 Algeciras aunts
57 Joplin composition
58 Mod pants
61 Presidential nickname
62 Smell __ (be suspicious)
63 "We __ amused"
64 T-shirt size: Abbr.
65 Active
66 Potters, at times

DOWN
1 Circle sections
2 Knish noshery
3 Latin abbr.
4 Mr. Cranston
5 Eye cover
6 Yalie
7 Protein source
8 "Just __!" ("In a moment!")
9 Melodies
10 Hosp. personnel
11 Prepares potatoes
12 Napoleon's fate
13 Streisand role
18 Mourn
22 Pesto ingredient
24 In debt
25 Bartered
26 Most chilling
27 Funny fellow
28 "No dice!"
29 Distinction
30 Summer feature
34 Ye __ Booke Shoppe
35 Lascivious look
36 Marine flappers
38 Tasty
39 Exceptionally good
44 Building stone
45 Fidelity, to Macbeth
46 Not as bland
47 Theater drop
48 Tremble
49 Egged on
52 Univ. of Md. player
54 Actress Skye
55 __ patriae
56 JFK jets
58 __-relief
59 Fathead
60 Pod preceder

520 ARRESTED DEVELOPMENT by Donna J. Stone

ACROSS
1 Mighty mite
5 Search for prey
10 Not quite shut
14 Come unglued
15 Correspondence
16 Bone-dry
17 Bend
18 Foreword
19 No gentleman
20 START OF A HENNY YOUNGMAN QUIP
23 No gentleman
24 Steep
25 Level off
30 Hackney's home
34 Fictional sleuth
35 __ kleine Nachtmusik
37 Polk's predecessor
38 Baby bark
39 MIDDLE OF QUIP
41 Actor Tognazzi
42 Jazzman Louis
44 Bjorn opponent
45 Nail type
46 Lodger
48 Cute as a button
50 Lobe probe?
52 Bleak critique
53 END OF QUIP
60 D-Day site
61 Rosey of football
62 Borrow permanently?
64 Winglike
65 Touch up
66 Articulated
67 __ a soul (no one)
68 Pub game
69 The Mikado character

DOWN
1 Pound plaint
2 Lauder powder
3 Finished
4 Hailing from Hermosillo
5 Nun's kneeler
6 Durban dough
7 Conductor Klemperer
8 On edge
9 Sets free
10 Auto accessory
11 Army vehicle
12 Geometry calculation
13 Bank (on)
21 Bad beginning
22 Well-dressed
25 Tut's turf
26 Ream component
27 Remove a brooch
28 Rigatoni relative
29 __ Gay
31 Brief ad
32 On the up and up
33 Carve a canyon
36 Writer Bagnold
39 Namibia native
40 Dotted lions?
43 Stonework
45 Asian capital
47 Pulled (on)
49 Writer Santha Rama __
51 Word form for "skin"
53 "Not if __ help it!"
54 Presidential pooch
55 Calendar period
56 Story
57 Coin in Kenya
58 Superman's lunch?
59 Furniture wood
63 Mideast grp.

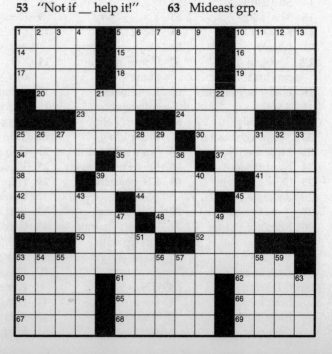

521   COUPLES by Shirley Soloway

ACROSS

1 Birthday figures
5 Talks wildly
10 "__ boy!"
14 Burrowing rodent
15 Similar
16 Clean the deck
17 Poker hand
19 Become winded
20 Step
21 Hummingbird's home
22 Picnic pests
23 Out of kilter
25 Spew forth
27 Serves the soup
30 __ David (religious symbol)
32 Greek love god
33 Border on
36 Whines
38 R-V center
39 Car coloration
41 Shoe width
42 Rome's river
44 Neck part
45 Soho streetcar
46 Screenwriter May
48 '92 Wimbledon winner
50 Therefore
51 Hunt or Hayes
53 Env. notation
55 Designer Cassini
57 Carpenter's items
61 French silk
62 Simon and Garfunkel, e.g.
64 Diminutive dogs
65 "Untouchable" Ness
66 *Desire Under the __*
67 Editor's word
68 Office worker
69 Taken-back auto

DOWN

1 Electrical units
2 Capricorn symbol
3 Director Kazan
4 Ongoing dramas
5 Brit. fliers
6 Thicke and Young
7 Bad habits
8 Gets by, with "out"
9 Six-line verse
10 Rogers' partner
11 Trade Center buildings
12 Fruit pastry
13 Vigoda and Burrows
18 *Coffee, Tea __?*
24 "__ Mommy Kissing Santa Claus"
26 Fictional aunt
27 For fear that
28 Bandleader Shaw
29 Holiday pay rate
30 Corner sign
31 Dog lovers?
34 Skeleton part
35 Actress Hagen
37 Big rig
39 Math subject
40 Actress Patricia
43 Purposeful
45 Scarlet bird
47 Rope loops
49 British actor Leo
51 Skater Sonja
52 Encourage vigorously
53 Vipers
54 Horn-blower's sound
56 Cheerful song
58 Run in neutral
59 Sugar serving
60 Mediocre
63 "How was __ know?"

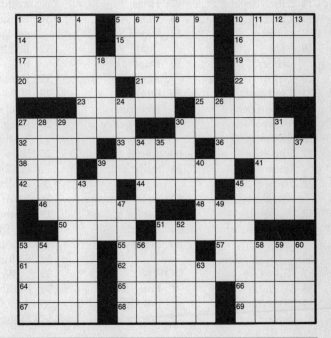

522   COURSE WORK by Nancy Salomon

ACROSS

1 Toe woe
5 Fundamental
10 Duel tool
14 Peek-__
15 Luncheonette lure
16 Pop
17 Pest-control devices
19 Tend the sauce
20 Shortstop Reese
21 Back-pedals
23 *Born Free* lioness
25 Tilted
26 Roman garments
29 Faux __
31 Disdain
34 Ache
35 Buck and bull
36 Coins
37 Chowed down
38 Terrestrial
40 "In what way?"
41 Lofty goals
43 Rogers or Clark
44 Cherry stones
45 Tunes
46 Hilarious Hope
47 Slightly stewed
48 Nimble
50 Just for the fun __
52 Add to
55 Summaries
59 Wear out
60 Battle of 1775
62 Dollar bills
63 Do-__ situation (crisis)
64 Buffalo waterfront
65 Famed loch
66 Musical pauses
67 Turned blue?

DOWN

1 Summer place
2 Woodwind
3 Libertine
4 "Piece of cake!"
5 Last name in motels?
6 Part of ETA
7 Fly high
8 Forces
9 Social class
10 Lifeblood
11 TV snack
12 Prepare for publication
13 Head set?
18 Slippery swimmers
22 Grating
24 Copycat
26 Bangkok natives
27 Exceed
28 Gabor sitcom
30 Houston ballplayer
32 Uproars
33 Full of the latest
35 Owns
36 Like a fox
38 Beast of Borden
39 Freight-car hopper
42 Start a fight
44 Threw a strike
46 "How Can I __?" ('67 tune)
47 Row
49 Sweat and slave
51 Releases
52 Pour __ (strive)
53 Workday start
54 Pass catchers
56 Well-ventilated
57 Ballet bend
58 Toboggan
61 Hobby-shop buy

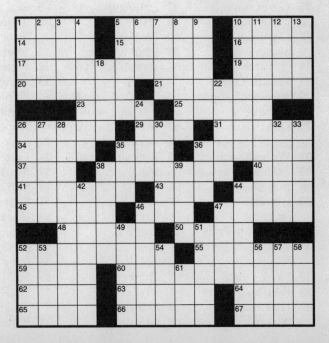

523 NUMBER, PLEASE by Dean Niles

ACROSS

1 Stands up
6 *Moby-Dick* captain
10 Run away
14 Numskull
15 Red herring
16 Hops dryer
17 Contiguous-state count
19 "Do __ others . . ."
20 Before, to Byron
21 Swit sitcom
22 Prison boss
24 Balky
26 Genie's gift
27 Shoebox letters
28 Brown-bag alternative
32 Piano size
35 Recreational racecar
36 __ contendere
37 Take five
38 Antique
39 Spot of liquor
40 "Zounds!" or "Egad!"
41 Rat, to a cat
42 *The __ Bunch*
43 More rad
45 Stain
46 Western coll.
47 Hags
51 Men: Abbr.
54 Word form for "half"
55 Dance, in France
56 Official records
57 Emergency number
60 Avoid
61 Sufficient, slangily
62 Actor Murphy
63 Taylor spouse
64 Dustcloths
65 Hearty meal

DOWN

1 Long-term inmate
2 Love a lot
3 Fathers
4 Little guy
5 Frustrated
6 Come up
7 Actor O'Brian
8 Fire aftermath
9 Caught in the middle
10 Exclusive social set
11 Bring the plane in
12 Punta del __
13 007's school
18 Roof edge
23 Lang. for Marlee Matlin
25 Bill with Salmon P. Chase
26 Prolix
28 Farm machine
29 Author Ephron
30 Outfitted
31 Comfy and cozy
32 Sailor's quaff
33 __ *Window*
34 In the matter of
35 Asian nation
41 Light beer
42 Credits in articles
44 Rec-room item
45 Floor model
47 Complaints
48 Where you live
49 Frenzy
50 Glossy
51 Rigging support
52 Talk back?
53 Earring type
54 Cozy
58 One __ million
59 SC summer setting

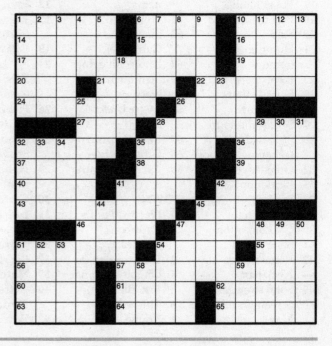

524 BIG SHOTS by Trip Payne

ACROSS

1 Assessment: Abbr.
5 Enjoy the buffet
10 General Bradley
14 First name in tennis
15 Cover story?
16 Congenial
17 Citation abbreviation
18 __ *macabre*
19 Paradise
20 He played Frank CANNON
23 One-person performances?
24 Writer Kaufman
25 Exhausted
28 *In medias __*
30 Guinness Book ending
32 Prior to, to Prior
33 *The CANNONball Run* actor
38 Hook's mate
39 Reed instrument
40 How fish are packed
41 Crew member
42 Rain buckets
43 CANNONball Express engineer
45 Alf and Mork, for short
46 Toothpaste type
47 __ Lingus
48 Fishes for
50 Prof.'s aides
53 Hold-up man?
57 Dyan CANNON movie
60 Classical figure?
62 Ask for a steak
63 North Indian city
64 Dry-as-dust
65 Rock singer __ Marie
66 Swerve
67 Truckle to
68 Car bomb?
69 Gaelic

DOWN

1 Thinks (over)
2 2:1, e.g.
3 Everything included
4 Hard assignment
5 Actress Thompson
6 Gentle as __
7 Baseballer Coleman
8 Become outdated
9 Zip, to Zola
10 *The Main Event* actor
11 Intermediary
12 Expert
13 Cartoon chihuahua
21 Psychiatrist's response
22 Squealer
26 Cara of *Fame*
27 Must-haves
29 Part of life?
31 "Later!"
33 Blockheads
34 Amin's predecessor
35 Jerry's place
36 Still the same
37 Film-sequel designations
38 Radio type
44 Playwright Anouilh
46 Govt. purchasing org.
49 Green shade
51 Llama's peaks
52 Part of an act
54 Pub order
55 Buenos __
56 Blank look
58 Decide
59 Russian sea
60 Linking words?
61 Do film-editing work

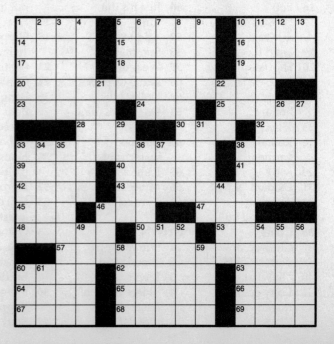

CHASED LADIES? by Emily Cox & Henry Rathvon

ACROSS
1 Cut a little
5 Saharan mount
10 Gear tooth
13 Cuckoo
14 Left the sack
15 Waste
16 Perched on
17 "Whole __ Love" ('70 tune)
18 Level
19 Lombardi or Edwards
21 START OF A QUOTE
23 Gold, to Cortés
25 Attack
26 PART 2 OF QUOTE
30 Human beings
34 Smooths
36 It has its ups and downs
37 Pine tree
38 PART 3 OF QUOTE
40 Bonanza material
41 Proven reliable
45 Contempt
49 Cap and dolman
51 PART 4 OF QUOTE
52 A lot
54 Links goal
55 END OF QUOTE
59 Pundit
63 Ill-boding
64 Chopper
66 Western team?
67 Jejune
68 "__ you" (radioman's reply)
69 Give temporarily
70 Tex-__ (southwestern cuisine)
71 Dweebs
72 Santa's route?

DOWN
1 Eastern European
2 Reply to the Little Red Hen
3 Byzantine art form
4 Theater fare
5 Presidential nickname
6 ". . . maids all in __"
7 Closet pests
8 Prize
9 Humble sheds
10 Happy as a __
11 Seep
12 Dancer Verdon
15 *Agnes Grey* author
20 Passion deified
22 Sported
24 Lennon's love
26 Presents
27 Projecting window
28 Further downhill
29 Bubble maker
31 "With __ in My Heart"
32 Pine tree
33 Treacly
35 Danson of *Cheers*
39 Electron's chg.
42 Gave a giggle
43 For all time
44 "__ Venice" (Mann story)
46 Dandy
47 Nest eggs
48 '80s Borgnine series
50 Globe
53 Ed Norton's workplace
55 Early apple eater
56 Passion
57 Cereal brand
58 Samoa studier
60 Yamaguchi maneuver
61 Lunchtime reading
62 "Massa's __ Cold, Cold Ground"
65 Sts.

WHAT'S COOKING? by Shirley Soloway

ACROSS
1 "Too bad!"
5 *Butterfield 8* author
10 Freshwater fish
14 Marquis de __
15 Boca __, FL
16 Mata __
17 Become calm
19 Gymnast Korbut
20 "For want of __ . . ."
21 Mornings: Abbr.
22 High-pitched flutes
23 Mouth pros
25 Restrain
26 Have a bite
27 Prohibited
30 Pinky or Peggy
33 "My lips are __"
36 Creole veggie
37 Shade trees
39 Make corrections
40 Century segment
41 Singer Lane
42 Waistline
44 Two-bagger: Abbr.
45 Marched up Main
47 Wynn and Asner
49 Had a mortgage
50 Kept harassing
55 Court session
57 A long way off
58 __ Gay
59 Shopping center
60 Lost one's temper
62 Daredevil Knievel
63 Tears down
64 Geom. shape
65 Sparks and Beatty
66 Prayer endings
67 Sciences' partner

DOWN
1 Syrian leader
2 Singer Frankie
3 Jingle guy
4 Hebrew, e.g.
5 Hockey great Bobby
6 Attacked
7 Particles
8 Moves a skiff
9 Actress Jillian
10 Church vocalist
11 Poorly planned
12 Give encouragement
13 Diagonal
18 Inventor Howe
22 Mink or beaver
24 Irritated
25 Fussed over
27 Ward (off)
28 Dreary
29 British nobleman
30 Spring
31 Exile isle
32 In a state of confusion
34 In the thick of
35 Went first
38 Beach barriers
43 Sidled
46 Dover's home: Abbr.
48 Hacienda housewife
50 Pool-table fabric
51 Songwriter Harold
52 Fido's friend
53 Put in office
54 Pub game
55 Nitti nabbers
56 Boffo review
57 Shaving cream
60 Swimsuit top
61 Road curve

AS EASY AS... by Harvey Estes

ACROSS
1 Basics
5 Word used in dating
10 Spoken
14 Republican name
15 Intense hatred
16 Red in the middle
17 Slot machines
20 Youth org.
21 Bunch together
22 Light brown
23 Range of hearing
25 Gum ingredient
28 "Absolutely!" in Baja
29 "O'er" opposite
32 Cranny companion
33 Fleur-de-__
35 Oz coward
37 Hot-shot pilot
38 Opinion
42 Wrath
43 With respect to
44 Matter for future generations?
45 Noun suffix
47 Noncom, for short
49 Row
53 Soup pot
55 Mickey's Florida home
57 Before, in verse
58 Put a match to
60 Ran for cover
61 Picnic contest
65 Scottish isle
66 Name on a plane
67 Choir member
68 Classroom furniture
69 Inserted a gusset
70 Army eatery

DOWN
1 Desert bricks
2 Teensy tree
3 Frees from blame
4 Neptune's domain
5 Practical smarts
6 Have a notion
7 Gets free (of)
8 Baby bears
9 G.P. grp.
10 Install a minister
11 April apparel
12 Carney or Linkletter
13 __ Misérables
18 Stadium shout
19 To the __ degree
24 Farm building
25 Dunce
26 __ Lomond
27 Just manage, with "out"
30 Change
31 "__ the season..."
34 Here, in Le Havre
36 Persona __ grata
38 Family framework
39 Zane Grey works
40 New Deal org.
41 Pro __ (proportionately)
42 Squid's squirt
46 Silver __ ('76 film)
48 Stare with bulging eyes
50 Take a breath
51 Royal decrees
52 Cowboy competitions
54 Martial arts master
56 Inc., in England
58 Late-night name
59 Frankenstein's assistant
61 Dosage schedule: Abbr.
62 Weeding tool
63 Chicken piece
64 Zodiac symbol

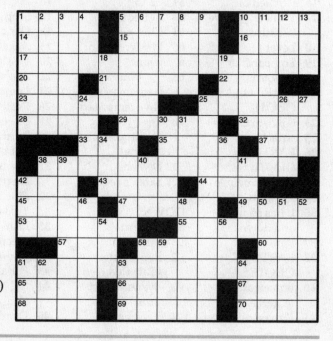

WAYS TO GO by Dean Niles

ACROSS
1 State positively
5 European streakers?
9 Worn-out
13 Magic charm
14 Rice dish
15 Royal sport
16 Drained
17 Take __ for the worse
18 German auto
19 Catchall abbr.
20 At a disadvantage
22 Tot's toys
24 Capp and Capone
25 "__ a Rebel" ('62 tune)
26 Had significance
31 __ homo
34 Hiding place
35 Hebrew priest
36 Path to power
40 Overly
41 No longer fresh
42 Pupil's place
43 Fondness
45 '88 Dennis Quaid film
47 Moon lander
48 Endocrine output
52 Suspect
57 Party to NAFTA
58 Ukraine capital
59 Colorado company
60 Judd Hirsch sitcom
61 Women's magazine
62 Lose one's tail?
63 Closed
64 Witnessed
65 Florida county
66 Quarterback option

DOWN
1 Cautionary color
2 West African river
3 Kick out
4 Stewart or Laver
5 Locations
6 Aspersion
7 Scarlett setting
8 Catch some rays
9 Thinly scattered
10 Psychiatrist's slot
11 Antique adjective
12 Drudgery
14 Finishes the road
20 Tijuana tribute
21 Let out, perhaps
23 Lieutenant Kojak
26 Dull finish
27 Dull pain
28 Philosopher Descartes
29 Fraternal group
30 Record
31 Singer James
32 Ax stroke
33 Jockey's item
34 Voucher
37 Complete
38 Made a face
39 __ Clayton Powell
44 Football team
45 Soak
46 California base
48 Gang of Goths
49 Cornhusker city
50 Heart of a matter
51 Theater signs
52 Hawaiian strings
53 Longest river
54 Strike out
55 Fountain order
56 Noisy
60 1/3 tbsp.

529 WHOMEVER by Matt Gaffney

ACROSS
1 Mensa stats
4 Multimedia corp.
7 __ -down (topsy-turvy)
13 Pecan or cashew
14 __ one's toes (stay alert)
15 Infernal
16 By means of
17 *Cuatro y cuatro*
18 Gawky guy?
19 "To whom __:"
22 Spanish stores
23 New Mexico neighbor
27 Sicilian rumbler
28 Sea dog
30 Olympic hawk
31 Bread or booze
34 Blemish
37 Freudian concepts
38 "With whom __?"
41 Tiffany treasure
43 Soccer great
44 "I told you so!"
45 Melville work
47 Wolfed down
49 Much of Mongolia
53 Thornton Wilder classic
56 Trumpet call
59 *For Whom __*
61 Bring to a boil?
64 Term of address
65 Got together
66 '50s music style
67 Evergreen tree
68 Exist
69 Some chords
70 Broadway sign
71 Alphabet sequence

DOWN
1 Be hospitable
2 "Stop that!"
3 Flower part
4 Hajj destination
5 Share a dais
6 Ever and __
7 Indy winner Al
8 Lab dish
9 Poem part
10 Her, in Hamburg
11 Wallace of *E.T.*
12 Go astray
14 William of *Hopalong Cassidy*
20 Cost __ and a leg
21 *Cheers* role
24 Not a dup.
25 Composer Rorem
26 Donkey
29 Red as __
32 Baby bark
33 Language suffix
35 Endorses
36 Men's accessory
38 Cupid
39 Backup
40 South American river
41 Sticky stuff
42 Australian bird
46 Ontario city
48 Rich pastry
50 Texas tycoon
51 Jacket type
52 Shoe part
54 George Burns film
55 Cries
57 Latin American plain
58 "Ma! (He's Making Eyes __)"
60 Realms: Abbr.
61 Erie hrs. in Aug.
62 Postal creed word
63 French king

530 PARENTAL RESORT by Donna J. Stone

ACROSS
1 Silences
5 Unit of loudness
9 "You can __ horse to . . ."
14 Gillette product
15 Campus court
16 Drive forward
17 Attempt
18 *The __ Reader* (literary publication)
19 Second to none
20 START OF A QUIP
23 Actor Maximilian
24 __ Alamos, NM
25 Purrfect pet?
27 Hen or pen
28 Lowliest cadets
31 __ *de vivre*
32 Mr. Koppel
33 Flying start?
34 Singing cowboy
35 MIDDLE OF QUIP
38 Fictional swordsman
41 Teddy trim
42 PD alert
45 Composer Satie
46 Setup
48 Cornhusker st.
49 Be too encouraging?
50 Smash letters
51 Ty Cobb's team
53 END OF QUIP
57 Capone's crony
58 Southern campus
59 Gobble (down)
61 Nip
62 Pulmonary organ
63 Place for a patch
64 De Mille of dance
65 Dates
66 Risqué

DOWN
1 Helium or hydrogen
2 Lawyer's case?
3 Drew an equation
4 Dark color
5 Cried like a baby
6 Inning components
7 Ork talk
8 Swimmer Gertrude
9 Filches
10 Kuwaiti ruler
11 It's often in a jam
12 Hit rock bottom
13 Cockpit fig.
21 Marty Robbins hit
22 Dawn goddess
23 Fast way to the U.K.
26 *The Daughter of Time* author
29 Be human?
30 Cooks in a cauldron
31 Hooch holder
34 Listless
35 Rub the wrong way
36 Napa Valley vessel
37 Bar tool
38 Asian sect
39 Holding forth
40 '60s affirmation
42 Sea animal
43 Confuse
44 Shot
46 __ Lanka
47 Tyrolean tunes
50 Short shows
52 Stares stupidly
54 To be, in Toulouse
55 Turn about
56 Actor Franchot
57 Cryptic bur.
60 Whimsical

531 FAMILIAR TRIO by Dean Niles

ACROSS
1 Mike problem
5 Stoneworker
10 Not quite closed
14 Failure
15 Low joint
16 Hold sway
17 Prerecord
18 Nasty
19 Some agents
20 C-__ (cable channel)
21 Drill-sergeant's shout
22 __ down (shut up)
23 Be
25 Showy shrub
28 Copied perfectly
30 Richard of *Pretty Woman*
31 Sugar qty.
34 Cowboy country
35 Hostess Perle
36 Tango quorum
37 Omelet ingredients
38 Emcee Hall
39 "__ a Lady" ('71 tune)
40 Wine word
41 __ Island (Brooklyn resort area)
42 Touches
43 Choral syllable
44 Gardener, at times
45 Forecaster
46 Sonoran snooze
48 One of the musical B's
49 Sun screen
51 __ Mahal
53 Reagan Cabinet member
56 Go over a manuscript
57 France's longest river
59 Professor 'iggins
60 Helen's mother
61 Impassive
62 Read quickly
63 __ of Our Lives
64 Mr. Chips portrayer
65 Camper's shelter

DOWN
1 Salamanders
2 Show approval
3 Early TV cowboy
4 Job slots
5 Prepared potatoes
6 Singer Murray
7 Some traits do this
8 __ Maid (card game)
9 Society-page word
10 Bandleader Shaw
11 Consent avidly
12 On the sheltered side
13 Pull apart
22 Urgent appeal
24 Kind of neckline
26 Full of pep
27 Pretentious
28 Wave top
29 Bar order
32 Bulge
33 Sheriff's band
35 French impressionist
38 Cattle calls
39 Naval footlocker
41 *Silkwood* star
42 __ Angelico
45 Beg to differ
47 Tiny bits
49 Prairie, in Pretoria
50 Notion
52 *Aida* selection
54 Teheran's country
55 *Peer* __
57 Psychedelic letters
58 Word form for "ear"

532 BEACH PARTIES by Trip Payne

ACROSS
1 Star in Orion
6 Squint (at)
10 *Sesame Street* subject
14 Love a lot
15 Gen. Robt. __
16 Heap
17 Chopin's favorite novelist
19 Ken of *thirtysomething*
20 Weaken
21 It's a small matter
22 Voting sheet
24 School grps.
25 With merriment
26 Labor leader Gompers
29 Stout spots
32 Dumbstruck
33 Metric weights
34 Dovecote sound
35 Pisa dough
36 __ the Barbarian
37 Blackbird
38 Caribou kin
39 Jeans alternative
40 Put a halt to
41 French ladies
43 Cautioned
44 Florida city
45 Chaplin prop
46 Eye part
48 *Casablanca* role
49 Brown shade
52 *Diary of __ Housewife*
53 Smooch-throwing TV hostess
56 Jennifer on *WKRP*
57 "Oh, fiddle-faddle!"
58 Bulova rival
59 Pie à la __
60 Baseballer Cabell
61 Alamogordo event

DOWN
1 Old clothes
2 Birth of a notion?
3 Sticky stuff
4 Foul up
5 Heir
6 Chihuahua cash
7 Western star Jack
8 Sundown, to Shelley
9 Snoopy's foe
10 Artemis' twin
11 "Caribbean Queen" singer
12 Advertising award
13 Faxed or telexed
18 List ender
23 Superciliousness
24 Insect stage
25 Big bashes
26 Hawthorne's hometown
27 Well-coordinated
28 Former U.S. poet laureate
29 Ties up
30 Code name?
31 Did some cobbling
33 Seoul site
36 Buddy
37 Only
39 Showed up
40 Rummy variety
42 __ Dinmont terrier
43 Do the laundry
45 Social stratum
46 Self-possessed
47 *Typee* sequel
48 Fascinated by
49 Big book
50 Bellicose deity
51 Waiting-room cry
54 Scottish John
55 Song that sells

533   M*A*S*H NOTES by Matt Gaffney

ACROSS

1 Iron fishhook
5 Emulate Mahre
8 "So what __ is new?"
12 Divvy up
14 Vandyke site
15 Journalist Jacob
16 Reserve
17 Hockey player Gordie
18 Little devils
19 M*A*S*H surgeon
22 Some bills
23 Dispensed the deck
25 Purcell and Miles
29 Usual: Abbr.
30 Cross letters
32 Keep __ (persist)
33 ". . . who lived in __"
35 "Golly!"
36 M*A*S*H nurse
40 __ nutshell
41 L.A. athlete
42 "Let __!" ("Who cares?")
43 Impact sound
44 Taxing org.
45 Smart ones, to Wilhelm
47 Dietetic, in ads
49 Naturalist Fossey
51 M*A*S*H clerk
57 Mideast canal
59 Marx or Malden
60 Mikhail's missus
61 Actress Bancroft
62 Devil's thing
63 Available
64 Golf club
65 Certain sib
66 Theater constructions

DOWN

1 Wound
2 Utah resort
3 Ebb's partner
4 Service member?
5 Has a ball at the mall
6 Fuzzy fruit
7 Beatles song from Help!
8 Author Jong
9 Spots for stars
10 Use a straw
11 Snaky letter
13 Canines and molars
14 Joan of Twin Peaks
20 Sí or oui
21 Drive away
24 __ of Innocence ('93 film)
25 Master, in Madras
26 Like Schönberg's music
27 West Side Story star
28 Part of A&P
29 Norse god
31 Man of La Mancha
33 Inquires
34 Cow or sow
37 Homeric epic
38 Shares, with "in"
39 Sundial numeral
45 Kids' card game
46 Año opener
48 Stunned
49 Actress Day
50 "__ be seeing you!"
52 Sitarist Shankar
53 Smith and Fleming
54 See 47 Across
55 GRE relative
56 Spitz sounds
57 Carpenter's tool
58 Juan's "one"

534   FARM STAND by Shirley Soloway

ACROSS

1 Doggie delights
6 Word of woe
10 IL hours
13 Deal maker
14 Petunia part
16 Rowing need
17 CORN
19 Actress Merkel
20 Montana's capital
21 Hypersensitivity
23 Frolic
25 __ Now (Murrow show)
26 Red and Coral
29 CABBAGE, with 47 Across
31 Mil. awards
34 SASE, e.g.
35 Combustible heap
36 Train station
37 __ Dame
39 Murals or mobiles
41 Cropped up
42 Sailing vessel
43 Heavenly bodies
45 AAA offering
46 Lady's man?
47 See 29 Across
49 Movie great
50 Pedro's pots
52 Kitchen addition?
54 Bravery
56 Youth lodging
60 Pacino and Smith
61 PEA
64 Carnival city
65 Uptight
66 At full speed
67 Cross product
68 Action time
69 Artist Matisse

DOWN

1 Tub ritual
2 Grimm creature
3 Diamond or Simon
4 Logs
5 Office skill
6 GI's address
7 Apollo vehicle
8 Colonel's command
9 "Ballad of the Green Berets" singer
10 SQUASH
11 Vocalized
12 Cafeteria carrier
15 Actor Waggoner
18 Amusingly passé
22 Duck down
24 Legal starter
26 Have a hunch
27 Col. Tibbets' mom
28 BEAN
30 Argentine dictator
32 __ Rica
33 Take the reins
35 Zest
36 __ Rheingold
38 Norse chieftain
40 Shady character?
44 "Down __ Riverside"
47 Fixed spuds
48 Donny or Marie
49 Tahini base
51 Shopping aid
53 Hebrew scroll
54 David's instrument
55 Nobelist Wiesel
57 Gov. employee
58 Kuwaiti leader
59 Anderson of Nurses
62 She-bear: Sp.
63 Mystery writer Josephine

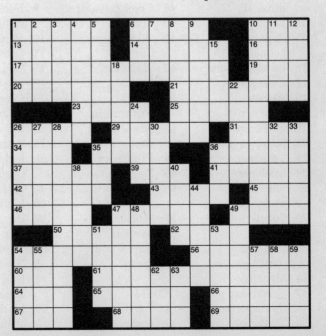

535 FUNNY CARS by Robin & Norman Landis

ACROSS

1 Write quickly
4 Melville monomaniac
8 Little ones
12 Coin word
14 Floor covering, in Falmouth
15 Caribbean country
17 Frank place
18 Song-and-dance vehicle?
20 Seer
22 The good earth
23 __ U.S. Pat. Off.
24 Prefix for "plunk"
25 Stick together
27 Plane engines
31 Electrical unit
32 "What __ mind reader?"
33 Water works?
37 Page number?
38 Rajput's wraps
39 Be bold
40 À la *Swann's Way*
42 Religious image
43 Expeditious
44 Poseidon's prop
47 Ad-lib comedy
49 Self-esteem
50 "No, __ thousand times no!"
51 Smack in the mouth?
54 Lamebrain
58 Red Corvette?
61 Mrs. Copperfield
62 __ Martin (007's auto)
63 Author Wiesel
64 Berra or Bear
65 To be, to Tiberius
66 Yodelers' perches
67 Spearheaded

DOWN

1 Martial art
2 Lollapalooza
3 Toltec city
4 Francis __ Sinatra
5 Go quickly
6 Landers and Sheridan
7 Galoot
8 "Praise __ and Pass the Ammunition"
9 Boathouse item
10 Wedding dessert
11 Navigate
13 Rockmobile?
16 *Bus Stop* playwright
19 British priests
21 David __ Roth
26 Buffalo Bob's vehicle?
27 Talk hoarsely
28 *Omnia vincit __*
29 Walk-ons
30 Solemn
31 Pass out
34 Special time
35 Disney sci-fi film
36 Posted
38 *All in the Family* surname
41 '74 World's Fair site
45 Colors over
46 "Where Do __?" (*Hair* tune)
47 Actress Swenson
48 Bullwinkle, for one
52 Mets' stadium
53 Peddle
55 Hoodwink
56 Egg on
57 Stated
59 Derek and Diddley
60 Hotshot

536 MOVIE MARATHON by Shirley Soloway

ACROSS

1 Adam of *Batman*
5 Prepares to shoot
9 Mr. Brinker
13 Psychedelic musical
14 Legal paper
15 Repetitive behavior
16 Land measure
17 Top-quality
18 Actress Verdugo
19 '86 Fonda film
22 Sugary suffix
23 Tach meas.
24 Intelligent
27 Fluffy neckpiece
29 Tobacco dryer
33 Charged particle
34 Menace
37 __ consequence (unimportant)
38 '75 Pacino film
41 Popular cookie
42 Idle
43 Mine find
44 Actress Carter
45 Cat or canary
46 Politician picker
48 Greek consonant
50 Mongrel
51 '50 Widmark film
60 Warbucks' waif
61 Diva's performance
62 Israeli dance
63 Daring act
64 Tailor's tools
65 Privy to
66 The biggest Cartwright
67 Fencing weapon
68 Unpleasantly damp

DOWN

1 Start of a query
2 Apiece
3 Kingly address
4 Aftershock
5 Having knowledge (of)
6 Heavy metal
7 Short skirt
8 British gun
9 Heavenly sight
10 Help a hood
11 Baseball team
12 Head the cast
15 Pile high
20 Caesar's port
21 School records
24 Lebanese city
25 Actress Demi
26 Jockey Cordero
27 Suit
28 In the know about
30 In progress
31 Nap noisily
32 Copier need
35 Nearsightedness
36 Fancy appetizer
39 Marineland attractions
40 Variety show
47 Tropical flower
49 Printer's notation
50 Go after
51 Poet Ogden
52 Division word
53 Wildebeests
54 Back of the neck
55 Faucet fault
56 Fork point
57 New Rochelle college
58 '82 Jeff Bridges film
59 Pull sharply

537 SKULL SESSION by Bob Lubbers

ACROSS

1 Ameche role
5 Socialist Eugene
9 Actor Buddy
14 Bread spread
15 Dynamic start
16 Bingo alternative
17 Foothold
19 Navigation system
20 One after another
21 Cover story?
23 Inlets
26 "I Let __ Go Out Of My Heart" ('38 tune)
28 Make Mickey move
31 __ Howser, M.D.
33 Sikorsky and Stravinsky
34 Devoured
36 Prohibit
37 Sunburn soother
38 Fills to the gills
39 Deflect, with "off"
40 Actor Beatty
41 Send payment
42 Mild oaths
43 Seasoned
45 Ideas
47 French river
48 Pesky insect
49 Drink noisily
51 Maximum
56 Sand bar
58 Texas arena
61 Dracula's title
62 __ En-lai
63 Bumbler
64 "High __" ('59 song)
65 Spud buds
66 Falls behind

DOWN

1 Boyish cuts
2 "Waiting for the Robert __"
3 Producer Norman
4 Places
5 Showy flower
6 Foot width
7 Lingerie item
8 Bar supply
9 Sci-fi writer Harlan
10 Small error
11 Skinny veggie
12 Airport abbr.
13 __ sequitur
18 Injures
22 Fills the hold
24 Hannibal Smith and company
25 Usher's activity
27 Jets' rivals
28 Shining brightly
29 Lunch favorite
30 Fury
32 Extremities
33 Fleming and McShane
35 Rockies range
38 Exodus commemoration
39 To and __
41 Final tallies
42 "Same here!"
44 New Orleans campus
46 Zodiac sign
50 Gallop or trot
52 1650, to Tiberius
53 Oop's girlfriend
54 Polluted air
55 Knight and Turner
56 Tchrs.' workplace
57 Yoo or boo follower
59 Bashful
60 Sock part

538 GLOBAL LETTUCE by Harvey Estes

ACROSS

1 Poet Teasdale
5 White House pooch
9 To __ (unanimously)
13 U.S. leader
14 Kind of heating
15 Govern
16 Dramatic beginning
17 Game site
18 Brink
19 Money for Maoists?
22 Velvet finish
23 Bandleader Brown
24 Seize power illegally
26 Clog clearer
28 Legal wrongs
32 Word on a pump
33 Center prefix
35 Corporate VIP
36 Act like an ass
37 Franc or centime?
40 The Kingston __
42 Scoundrel
43 Canadian prov.
44 Musical note
45 Meadow munchers
47 Windy City airport
51 Self-confidence
53 Pussycat companion
55 Ovine whine
56 Low pay in Madrid?
61 Have a go __ (try)
62 Stringed instrument
63 Punta del __
64 Director Clair
65 Commercial constructor
66 Hot spot?
67 Walked
68 __-do-well
69 March 15th, for one

DOWN

1 __-out (dazed)
2 Hood or Tell
3 Eye liner?
4 V __ "Victor"
5 Arden or Sherwood
6 Actor Guinness
7 Turner or Wood
8 Damascus dude
9 Fields of study
10 Fender
11 North African nation
12 Born
14 Manuscript enc.
20 Wed secretly
21 Clear tables
25 Be nosy
27 Evil emperor
29 Earth tone
30 CSA soldier
31 Barcelona bull
34 Move very slowly
36 Soap setting?
37 Man from Manila
38 Actor's signal
39 __ Gay (WWII plane)
40 Kitchen meas.
41 Farm alarm?
45 PAC-money recipient
46 Tulip tree
48 Mistreated
49 Baby's toy
50 Atelier items
52 Stuffed
54 Withdraw
57 Terrible tsar
58 Play favorites
59 Diamond place
60 Nostalgic soda name
61 College major

539 AIRPORT COUNTERS by Randolph Ross

ACROSS
1 Use a crowbar
4 Strong
10 Clock face
14 Chinese philosophy
15 Slit in the sod
16 "Understood"
17 Presidential number-crunchers
20 SSS classification
21 Flight of steps
22 Geog. abbr.
23 "On __ Day"
26 Pay proportionately
28 Something to remember
31 Malicious type
32 Isr. neighbor
33 Monogram pts.
35 Miss Trueheart
36 One million cycles per second
39 Not that great
42 Bristles
43 Ex of Frank
46 Happenings
49 Uncommon sort
51 Excessive bureaucracy
53 Burstyn and Barkin
54 Pitching stat
55 Moves about at a party
58 Fairy tale opener
59 Cardinal or Padre
63 Sedan seasons
64 Nudges
65 Med. specialty
66 Start over
67 Avers
68 Peter, Paul and Mary: Abbr.

DOWN
1 WWII craft
2 Vulgar
3 Alpine singer
4 Numbered hwy.
5 Crumb
6 River bottoms
7 Textbook heading
8 Throw away
9 Belonging to others
10 Bit of code
11 Quarantine
12 Fills with bubbles
13 Flatt and Pearson
18 Mother of the Titans
19 Cut short
24 "It's a Sin to Tell __"
25 Called up
27 "Puttin' on the __"
29 Farrow and Sara
30 Different
34 __ precedent
36 __ Blanc
37 Undercooked
38 Blue hue
39 More peaceful
40 Celebrated Thanksgiving?
41 Calmed
43 Boulevards
44 *Irises* signature
45 States
47 __-shanter
48 Backbones
50 Sleep like __
52 Put on a pedestal
56 Italian isle
57 Pay-phone feature
60 Bar opener
61 Lea lady
62 Long-eared equine

540 KEEP OUT by Matt Gaffney

ACROSS
1 Japanese emperors
8 "Honey" singer Carey
14 Southwesterner
16 Bet at the track
17 Rocky Mountain state
18 Turned away
19 Broadcast
20 Big landholder?
22 Never, in Nuremberg
23 Heavenly
25 __ Gigio
29 Minor difficulty
31 Printing measures
32 Mideast gulf
33 __ bell (is familiar)
35 Scandinavian toast
36 KEEP OUT!
40 Boston airport
41 *Watership Down* home
42 Second-hand
43 Metric wts.
44 African tree
48 __ bad example
49 Egyptian leader
51 Baseball stat
52 Mensa taboo
53 Foreign flier
54 __ on thick (exaggerates)
58 Pain in the neck
61 Consecrate
62 Quit trying
63 Like an oak
64 Moisture

DOWN
1 French wines
2 Like an O. Henry story
3 Proper order
4 Black Sea arm
5 Rimsky-Korsakov's *Le Coq* __
6 Out __ limb
7 Mideast peacemaker
8 Olympic awards
9 Some lines
10 Sought office
11 It's here in France
12 Supped
13 Possessed
15 KEEP OUT!
21 Actress Hedy
23 Like a bee
24 Mailed out
25 __ prisoners (behave aggressively)
26 Bouquet
27 Lawn fertilizer
28 Just
30 Denver suburb
34 Showy trinket
35 Simple weapon
36 Fringe benefit
37 Deep pink
38 "__ Around" ('64 tune)
39 Kill __ killed
43 Like some problems
45 Heathcliff's creator
46 Basic calculator
47 Weightlifter's pride
50 __ Valley, CA
52 "The Swedish Nightingale"
53 Conrad of *Diff'rent Strokes*
54 __ Cruces, NM
55 Aardvark tidbit
56 Second person
57 General's address
59 __ *Got a Secret*
60 Arrange type

541 ALL SMILES by Shirley Soloway

ACROSS
1 Notice
5 "I've Got __ in Kalamazoo"
9 Taj Mahal town
13 Siamese
14 Flag holders
16 Israeli airline
17 Birth, e.g.
19 Author Sheehy
20 Pencil end
21 In an impassive way
23 Aspin or Paul
24 __ standstill
26 Whiskey type
27 Gum-drop brand
29 __ rule (usually)
32 Rampur royalty
35 __ Tin Tin
36 Daisy Mae's man
38 "__ Rhythm"
39 Revises a text
42 Inactive
43 Assertion
45 Service charge

46 College degs.
47 Make a mistake
48 Choral group
52 Thoughts
54 Ocean vessel: Abbr.
55 Mythical bird
58 Auto-racer Mario
61 Performer Pia
63 Scott of *Charles in Charge*
64 Loud guffaw
66 Stopping places
67 One who watches
68 Mr. Laurel
69 One-liners
70 Transatlantic planes
71 Coop critters

DOWN
1 Lucy's landlady
2 Be generous
3 The Mamas and the __
4 Puppy sounds
5 Opening
6 State VIP

7 Bristol brews
8 Soup ingredient
9 Sponsorship
10 Seeks votes
11 Support on the stairs
12 Comrade-in-arms
15 Pack away
18 Slangy assent
22 Hartman or Bonet
25 Battery contents
27 Feline musical
28 Butter spreader
30 Ward of *Sisters*
31 Greek war god
32 Come up in the world
33 Thickening agent
34 Teenage pastime
37 Lettuce choice
40 Gumshoes
41 Carbonated drinks
44 Architectural detail
49 Wood strips

50 Bars legally
51 Russian range
53 Metal waste
55 Highway
56 Church instrument
57 Lyricist Sammy et al.

58 __ *Hand for the Little Lady*
59 *Peter Pan* pooch
60 Eye part
62 Short race
65 Congeal

542 COLORFUL FOOD STORIES by Dean Niles

ACROSS
1 Pizazz
6 Trombone accessory
10 For fear that
14 Light weight
15 In __ (stuck)
16 Curtain-raiser
17 Seuss tale
20 Put in stitches
21 Dehydrates
22 Solo
23 Photog.'s item
24 Behind schedule
26 Dervish
29 Plain to see
31 __ kwon do
34 Healing plant
35 In accord
36 Verbal noun
38 Anthony Burgess book, with *A*
41 Offer shelter to
42 Collection
43 Harness part
44 Timid
45 Cantaloupe or casaba

47 Ancient Persians
48 Soft drink
49 Melody
50 Oriental
53 *Jaws* menace
56 Soft touch
59 '68 Beatles movie
62 First name in daredeviltry
63 Sign on
64 *Divine Comedy* poet
65 Alluring
66 Holler
67 Furry fish-eater

DOWN
1 Beclouds
2 Entice
3 Once again
4 The __ Capades
5 Hand over
6 Biblical trio
7 Coax
8 Scuffle vigorously
9 Frat letter

10 Serve the minestrone
11 Reverberation
12 Ollie's other half
13 Use a stopwatch
18 Energy unit
19 Talk and talk
23 Family member
25 Tech talk
26 The truth
27 God of Islam
28 Eccentric
29 Lennon's lady
30 Left-hand page
31 Brought into pitch
32 Actress Dickinson
33 Happy places
35 Possessed
37 Less available
39 Kurosawa costume
40 Barbie's beau
46 Timmy's pet
47 G&S character
48 "Long Tall __" ('56 tune)

49 Supply with weapons
50 Some votes
51 Golfer Ballesteros
52 Holly shrub
54 Throw forcefully

55 Cain's victim
56 Add some color
57 Poker stake
58 Jury member
60 Youngster's query
61 Inform (on)

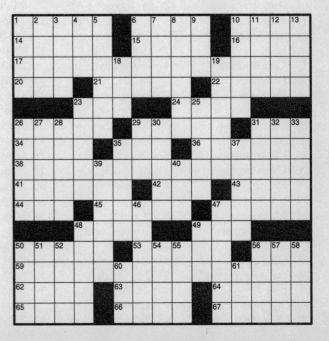

543 CLERK WORK by Randolph Ross

ACROSS
1 Carroll girl
6 Dad's lad
9 Zuider Zee sight
13 *Peter and the Wolf* bird
14 Cad
16 Step __ (hurry)
17 What legal secretaries keep?
20 Overwhelmed by
21 Bo and John
22 President pro __
23 Sell chances
26 Halfhearted welcome at a TV station?
32 Scents
35 Bits of time
36 "King of the Road"
37 American elk
39 Usher
41 Part of HOMES
42 Backtalk
46 Related to mom
47 The sound of many secretaries?
50 Without a key
51 Disfigure
54 Corrida creature
58 Newborn
61 Bad-mouth the boss' visitors?
64 Levin and Gershwin
65 Perry's creator
66 Musical of "Tomorrow"
67 Acerbic
68 Lettuce layer
69 Do a double-take

DOWN
1 __ as a fiddle
2 Cleo or Frankie
3 Muslim religion
4 Masticate
5 Smooth the way
6 Rams' horns
7 "__ the fields we go . . ."
8 Buntline or Beatty
9 Entryway
10 Memo words
11 Shot to the shins
12 Parisian's seasons
15 Without a cover
18 Carter's predecessor
19 Gore, informally
24 Cost
25 TV regulators
26 Prickly plant
27 Newfoundland clock setting: Abbr.
28 Sandal type
29 *State Fair* state
30 News notice
31 Zilch
32 Has obligations
33 Move like a mouse
34 Mayberry boy
38 U-238, e.g.
40 Egg maker
43 From __ Z
44 Thesaurus wd.
45 Stretched over
48 Legendary lawman
49 "__ a Song Go . . ."
51 Exodus food
52 Room at the top
53 Bowler's button
54 Touch up a text
55 Cremona cash
56 Russian despot
57 Kiln
59 Actor Sharif
60 Hawaiian goose
62 Celestial body
63 __ du Diable

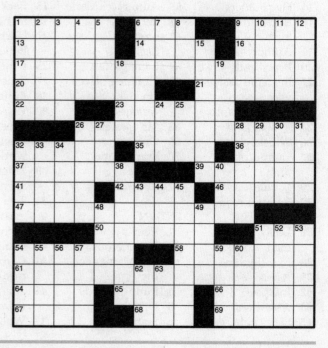

544 SILENT FEATURE by Richard Silvestri

ACROSS
1 Willing
5 Croc's cousin
10 Run the stereo
14 Over again
15 Creighton University site
16 Protuberance
17 Scenter of your face?
18 Conditions
19 Humorist Bombeck
20 Contorting
22 Gardener, at times
24 Wrapped up
26 Hints for the future
27 Lively dance
31 Layers
33 "__ for your thoughts?"
35 Sun. talk
36 Buster Brown's dog
40 Signifies
42 Clear-cut
44 Ground cover of a sort
45 Pioneered
47 Esoteric
48 Like some tiles
51 Germany's Pittsburgh
52 Type type
55 Mrs. Gorbachev
57 Give an account
59 Memory aid
64 Marsh bird
65 Sierra __
67 Enthusiastic review
68 Not quite round
69 Formed a fillet
70 Congregational comeback
71 Cincinnati sluggers
72 __ as dust
73 "__ we forget"

DOWN
1 The Jets, e.g.
2 In a bit
3 Butte kin
4 Washstand item
5 Entered
6 Puts right
7 Clay pigeons
8 Resistance unit
9 Kind of file
10 Branch of physics
11 Greene or Michaels
12 Commercial creators
13 *Two __ Before the Mast*
21 Inclined
23 Get moldy
25 The __ Scott Decision
27 Writing tablets
28 Amenable (to)
29 Funnyman Jay
30 Smart alecks
32 Region
34 Shout
37 Lupino and Tarbell
38 Splicer's material
39 Macmillan's predecessor
41 Burn
43 Defeat decisively
46 Ring rock
49 Bottom line
50 Banquet meal
52 Glitch
53 Be off
54 Greek epic
56 Run-down
58 Mediterranean isle
60 Articulated
61 June, April, or August
62 Currier's partner
63 Coin
66 Dawn goddess

545 FOOD FOR THOUGHT by Eric Albert

ACROSS
1 Fling
5 Bottom of the barrel
10 Stick in the mud
14 Prime the pot
15 Hit the high points
16 From the top
17 Tragic monarch
18 Stronghold on high
19 Abide
20 START OF A QUIP
23 Asimov genre
24 Salt element
27 List ender
28 *Reversal of Fortune* star
33 Rub clean
34 Bach composition
36 Couturier Cassini
37 MIDDLE OF QUIP

39 Borodin prince
41 "__ you do!"
42 Philanthropist
44 After-school treats
45 Spoil
48 Speak frankly
50 Archie's better half
52 END OF QUIP
57 Oil cartel
59 Serenity
60 Sour substance
61 Genuine
62 Bit-part performer
63 Melody
64 *Casablanca* setting
65 Quite dear
66 Pianist Myra

DOWN
1 *Honor Thy Father* author
2 A bit of drama?

3 Interference
4 Letter line
5 Pass slowly
6 Stagger
7 Neutral tone
8 Dieter's dread
9 Set of requirements
10 Clumsy
11 Approves, in a way
12 Gun
13 Woolly woman
21 Pigeonhole
22 Garden tool
25 Exploit
26 Ryan or Tilly
29 Author Anita
30 Monteverdi character
31 *60 Minutes* correspondent
32 Upper crust
34 Record
35 Be a parrot
37 Unmusical
38 Relaxed
39 Altar answer

40 Republicans, collectively
43 Jog along
45 Error
46 Guitarist Chet
47 Aegean isle
49 Organ pieces

51 __ *Valley Days*
53 On deck
54 Door to a garden
55 *God's Little* __
56 Spring
57 Hobbit foe
58 Princess perturber

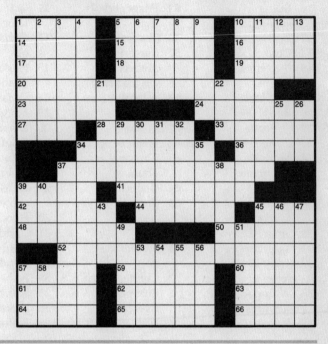

546 IN HIS POCKET by Mary Brindamour

ACROSS
1 Movie terrier
5 Guru
10 Not quite closed
14 Sudden idea
15 __ of Troy
16 Colorless
17 Elastic device
19 Computer symbol
20 Pub potable
21 Sneezer's need
22 Got by, with "out"
23 WWII general
25 Peanuts or popcorn
27 Signed an agreement
30 Prevailing tendencies
33 French impressionist
36 Light beer
38 Debtor's letters
39 Greek love god
40 Philanthropist
41 Canadian prov.
42 Building wing
43 Polite refusal

44 Borscht ingredient
45 Braves the bully
47 Electrical inventor
49 Orchestra section
51 Compassionate ones
55 Jai __
57 NHL player
60 Mauna __
61 Officeholders
62 Staples alternatives
64 Ready, willing, and __
65 Crème de la crème
66 March 15th, e.g.
67 Mrs. Dick Tracy
68 Derby and dash
69 Extremely

DOWN
1 "That's __!" ("All done!")
2 Former Miami coach Don

3 Lama land
4 Diplomatic off.
5 Grow smaller
6 Spider's snares
7 "Woe is me!"
8 Waiter's handouts
9 Typesetter, at times
10 For each
11 Whittling tool
12 Lotion additive
13 Tear apart
18 Short jackets
24 Acapulco aunts
26 O'Hare abbr.
28 Yale students
29 Ship's crane
31 Blockhead
32 Soapy water
33 Feat
34 __ Stanley Gardner
35 Tee toppers
37 Richard of *Pretty Woman*
40 Blabbermouth
41 At hand
43 Teachers' org.

44 Mont __ (French peak)
46 Eye parts
48 Intimidates
50 La __ Opera House
52 Skip over
53 Cowboy, at times

54 Impertinent
55 Get __ on the back
56 Earring locale
58 *The Aeneid*, for one
59 Apportion, with "out"
63 Actress Ullmann

547 ASTRONOMICAL by Fred Piscop

ACROSS
1 Stowe sight
6 Boxcar rider
10 Shed
14 Quinn of *Reckless*
15 Daredevil Knievel
16 Butter substitute
17 Ecumenical Council site
18 "__ 'em and weep!"
19 Gulf state
20 Birds' prey
22 __ Scotia
23 Coffeemaker
24 Mortarboard ornament
26 Bold
30 Sportscaster Musburger
32 Singer Lenya
33 Tater topper
37 Tony Musante series
38 Whipped-cream servings
39 Forearm bone
40 Put in the autoclave
42 Offspring
43 Foul liquid
44 Turnstile fodder
45 Drives back
48 Moray
49 Fitzgerald of jazz
50 Shades
57 Carson predecessor
58 On the briny
59 Adorable one
60 Ear-related
61 __ *Poets Society*
62 Major happening
63 Clockmaker Thomas
64 Goofs up
65 Coolidge's veep

DOWN
1 Stuff to the gills
2 Cremona cash
3 European river
4 Huff and puff
5 Bubble over
6 Wading bird
7 Above
8 "__ me up, Scotty!"
9 Seniors
10 '87 Cher film
11 Actor Edward James __
12 Corporal's time off
13 Having musical qualities
21 Twisted
25 Mandela's grp.
26 Diner orders
27 Plant part
28 "Ma! (He's Making Eyes __)"
29 Ed McMahon show
30 Hooch
31 Cartoonist Goldberg
33 Slender
34 Nobelist Wiesel
35 Shortly
36 Picks a crew
38 Ballet slide
41 "Well, __ be!"
42 Consoled
44 __ Aviv
45 Seized autos
46 Thrill
47 *S'il vous __*
48 "Zounds!"
51 __-friendly
52 Around the corner
53 Fiji's capital
54 Fret
55 __ *kleine Nachtmusik*
56 Collections

548 TAILOR-MADE by Randolph Ross

ACROSS
1 Have to have
5 O'Hara estate
9 Sonora snacks
14 Comic Johnson
15 Wedding vows
16 Absurd
17 Made amends
20 And others
21 Poetic contraction
22 Kiln
23 Country stopovers
25 Actor Mineo
27 Was apathetic
34 Zodiac sign
35 Prima __
36 Dawn goddess
38 Prejudice
39 "Get __!" (remark to a snoop)
40 Small cut
41 Form of ID
42 Stone monument
43 "Some of __ Days"
44 Hesitated
47 Travel org.
48 Prepared to drive
49 Beer
52 __ Paulo, Brazil
55 Villainous looks
59 Insisted
62 Come to terms
63 Entryway
64 Aural
65 High-strung
66 Posted
67 Stadium fillers

DOWN
1 Back of the neck
2 Part of QED
3 Kett of the comics
4 Says no
5 Evening the score
6 Contribute (to)
7 Learning method
8 Tennis great Arthur
9 __ Pan Alley
10 Namibia neighbor
11 Hernando's house
12 Responsibility
13 Opening mo. in H.S.
18 Allusions
19 Crackers
24 Moved stealthily
26 Nabokov heroine
27 Light touches
28 Like the Blarney Stone
29 Actress Keaton
30 "Look at this!"
31 __ *terrible*
32 Extend a subscription
33 Dissonance
37 Floored it
39 Relaxed
40 __ meaning (nuances)
42 Little, in Edinburgh
43 "And __ wrote..."
45 Hoi polloi
46 Wasteland
49 Petty clash
50 Press
51 Laura or Bruce
53 Totals up
54 Oklahoma tribe
56 "¿Cómo __ usted?"
57 Wreak havoc upon
58 Short times, for short
60 Look at
61 Sweetie

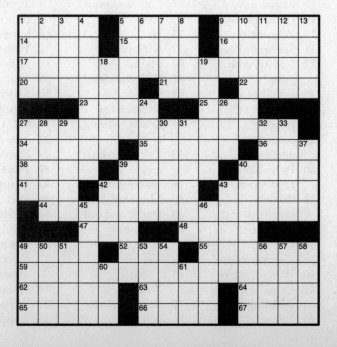

549   AFTER THE COLON by Trip Payne

ACROSS
1 Library sound
5 "With __ in My Heart"
10 Geometry calculation
14 Capable of
15 Flight part
16 Journey segments
17 *Daily Planet* name
18 Brief argument
19 Labels
20 Subtitle of Thoreau's *Walden*
23 Actress Barkin
24 Part of EST
25 "Eureka!"
27 Mao __-tung
28 Raised cattle
32 Busy place
34 Illinois city
36 __ *Well That Ends Well*
37 Subtitle of Kazantzakis' *The Odyssey*
41 Shepard or King
42 Show to the door
43 Chose one's phrasing
46 *Hawaii Five-O* role
47 Zombie base
50 Rent out
51 Quarterback's resource
53 Kid a bit
55 Subtitle of Richardson's *Pamela*
60 Stoic Greek philosopher
61 Newspaper type
62 *The Egg __*
63 Bellicose deity
64 Schoolroom spinner
65 __ precedent
66 Look deeply
67 __ Park, CO
68 Matchmaker from Olympus

DOWN
1 Young hen
2 Booty
3 Put a lid on
4 "We're Off __ the Wizard"
5 Part of NAACP
6 Galley word
7 Inauguration highlight
8 Informal evenings?
9 Development
10 Choir member
11 Clearly written
12 Off-white
13 Simpleton
21 Sleeping
22 *Deep Space Nine* character
26 Show stoppers?
29 Caviar source
30 Miscalculates
31 Feasted
33 Tightly drawn
34 Swimming hole
35 Cruising, perhaps
37 Skin softener
38 *L.A. Law* actor
39 Long, long time
40 Necessary amount
41 Leatherworking tool
44 Wolf down
45 Menial worker
47 Comic Gilda
48 Familiar with
49 *In __ res*
52 Times at the table
54 Rub out
56 Shade of red
57 Run amok
58 Czech river
59 Exes' followers
60 Turn sharply

550   PARADOX by Shirley Soloway

ACROSS
1 Part of EMT
5 Melville captain
9 Gray matter
14 Place for pews
15 Roy's missus
16 Mikhail's missus
17 Historic Scott
18 Dross
19 Phil's colleague
20 Singer K.T.
22 Author Angelou
24 START OF A QUERY
31 Roget wd.
32 TV monogram
33 Get up
34 Does road work
37 In accord
38 MIDDLE OF QUERY
43 Deli draw
44 Ballerina's supports
45 Offshoots
47 Took nourishment
49 VMI or UCLA
52 END OF QUERY
56 Ontario native
57 Animated
58 Hearty entrée
62 Praise highly
65 Privy to
66 In the know
67 "Now __ me down . . ."
68 Indian tourist city
69 Prepared an apple
70 Kitchen addition?
71 Fast fliers

DOWN
1 Bestows
2 Like the Everglades
3 Actress Keyes
4 Made over
5 Pitches
6 Holbrook or Linden
7 Texas landmark
8 Started
9 NYC thoroughfare
10 Talk to the music
11 Ventilate
12 "Rose __ rose . . ."
13 Slangy negative
21 __ de plume
23 Affirmative vote
25 James or Place
26 Hurt
27 Pro __ (proportionately)
28 Sacred image
29 Sell
30 Chem. suffix
35 '30s movie studio
36 Make a vow
38 Whale of a tale?
39 Black, to Chirac
40 Out of control
41 Lost control
42 Piedmont city
43 Bit part in Shakespeare?
46 H.S. student
48 Space walk: Abbr.
49 Playground favorites
50 Prance about
51 Laughing carnivores
53 High home
54 Gave out cards
55 Inventor Howe
58 Cul-de-__
59 Deuce
60 Musical sensitivity
61 Exist
63 Napa vessel
64 Spud bud

551 CARTOON COUPLES by Fred Piscop

ACROSS

1 Shortstop Pee Wee
6 Iowa city
10 Comic Sahl
14 Magna __
15 Church section
16 Region
17 Specialized lingo
18 Genealogy diagram
19 *Jurassic Park* beast, for short
20 Cartoon couple
23 Wave top
24 Slugger Ralph
25 Confront boldly
28 To __ (without exception)
30 Ice-cream flavor: Abbr.
31 Lively dance
33 Climbing plant
36 Cartoon couple
40 Ecology org.
41 Hostess Perle
42 Western sch.
43 Window frame
44 Actress Rolle
46 Valuable violin
49 More sensible
51 Cartoon couple
56 Fall
57 __ *Three Lives*
58 Taxi device
60 Fill with cargo
61 Give a hoot
62 Bring together
63 *For Your __ Only*
64 Famous pirate
65 Landing area

DOWN

1 Communications co.
2 Lawman Wyatt
3 As a result
4 Hand-operated valve
5 Diner patrons
6 Feeds the kitty
7 French Revolution name
8 Level
9 Bird food
10 Actress Marlee
11 Senator Hatch
12 Superman portrayer
13 Congress, e.g.
21 "Are we there __?"
22 Giraffe relative
25 Pinnacle
26 Cookie nugget
27 Caesar's partner
28 *M*A*S*H* star
29 Family member
31 Nasty cut
32 Aardvark morsel
33 Ruler marking
34 Disgusting
35 Fiscal span
37 High-tech memo
38 __-man (toady)
39 Vitamin or mineral
43 Ear bone
44 Conclusion
45 Irish poet Heaney
46 Confuse
47 Tropical eel
48 Battery terminal
49 Memorable Mortimer
50 Threw in
52 Clark or Cavett
53 Jai __
54 Recipe instruction
55 Himalayan legend
59 Agent, for short

552 ROUND AND ROUND by Shirley Soloway

ACROSS

1 Heated tubs
5 Knightly titles
9 Lassoed
14 Verb tense
15 Take a tumble
16 La Scala performance
17 Tennis great Arthur
18 Barrett or Jaffe
19 Significant others
20 Negotiate
23 Breadthless?
24 Big rig
25 Hit the slopes
28 Dos Passos trilogy
30 Harness up
32 Wide-awake
36 Middle weight?
39 Ward of *Sisters*
40 Pulls apart
41 Take __ (snooze)
42 Maytag function
44 Spiner of *Star Trek: The Next Generation*
45 Gets up
46 Cardiologists' org.
48 Vane dir.
49 Paint layer
52 African antelopes
57 Ideal perspective
59 Go to pot
62 Prego rival
63 Antitoxins
64 Foot bones
65 Desire deified
66 Touch up articles
67 Confused
68 "¿Cómo __ usted?"
69 Actress Daly

DOWN

1 Generate
2 Turkish title
3 *My Name Is __ Lev*
4 Take the reins
5 Soda sippers
6 Golf club
7 Lemon peels
8 Detective Sam
9 Lettuce variety
10 Iridescent birthstone
11 Favorite
12 Prior to, in poetry
13 Trial VIPs
21 Oaf
22 Mideast rulers
25 Book part
26 Designer Donna
27 Maladroit
29 "Just __!" ("Hold on!")
31 Play the lead
32 City on the Nile
33 Absorb
34 Borden bovine
35 Cheerleader shouts
37 Good buddy
38 Vicinity
40 Emmy-winner Cicely
43 Patron saint of music
44 Cotton bundle
47 Mythical menace
50 Go along (with)
51 Peter and Alexander
53 Valuable property
54 Wanting
55 "Mack the Knife" singer
56 Give an opinion
57 Upswing
58 "__ Rhythm"
59 RR depot
60 Bit of butter
61 Hosp. areas

OUT OF CONTROL by Manny Nosowsky

ACROSS

1 Speculation
5 Sounds of wonder
9 Curly coifs
14 Lay __ thick
15 Med. sch. subj.
16 Duplicity
17 Lose control
20 Bring bliss to
21 Rabbit kin
22 Senior member
23 Bring on board
25 Greek Cupid
27 Lose control
31 Spanish article
34 October stone
35 Winter bug
36 Downright
38 Lévesque or Clair
39 Damascus' state
42 Advantage
43 Take hold of
45 __ and outs
46 Deli side dish
47 Cheer for a team
48 Lose control
52 Garfield's pal
53 Lee or Teasdale

54 16th-c. queen
57 "Darn!"
59 Nebraska city
63 Lose control
66 Sheeplike
67 Basso Pinza
68 Supreme Court count
69 Tendon
70 Fax, perhaps
71 License plates

DOWN

1 Teeming
2 "__ never work!"
3 Kind of bean
4 Lumber flaws
5 Lout
6 Covertly
7 It's a laugh
8 Sound investment?
9 Palindromic potentate
10 Endows
11 Take public transportation
12 __ podrida

13 Noticed
18 Sinn __ (Irish political group)
19 Mister, in Munich
24 Ring judges
26 Approvals
27 Gershwin character
28 *Tosca*, for example
29 Philippine island
30 Radium researcher
31 Punch server
32 Bach's instrument
33 Distorts
37 One of two Bible portions
40 Washday challenge
41 Where most people live
44 The third degree?
49 General assistant?

50 Parts of poems
51 Stepped on
52 Ecology concern
54 Identities
55 First name in jeans
56 Put __ writing
58 Wood trimmer

60 *La Traviata* highlight
61 Suspended
62 Does impressions
64 Fresh from the store
65 Signal assent

NON-NOBELISTS by Matt Gaffney

ACROSS

1 Auction action
4 From A __
7 Kitchen wear
12 Skater Thomas
13 Golfer Ballesteros
14 Augusta's state
15 Poker pair
16 Augury
17 Lobbied for
18 Non-Nobelist for literature
21 Ransom __ Olds
22 Madison or Fifth: Abbr.
23 Disparages testimony
27 Skier Phil
29 Offspring
31 Low digit?
32 Admitting, with "up"
34 James Dean classic
36 Non-Nobelist for peace
39 AL team
40 Backbone-related
41 Zsa Zsa's sister
42 Yellow moths

43 Garbo or Nobel
46 Send home, in a way
49 Lamb's mom
50 __ nutshell
52 Non-Nobelist for physics
56 Desert flora
59 Ex-UN member
60 Closed
61 Sigourney Weaver film
62 Women
63 Race parts
64 Trumpet sound
65 Witch's curse
66 Bat wood

DOWN

1 Deprive of wind
2 Michener opus
3 Platter
4 Arizona State site
5 Ended
6 Founder of Stoicism
7 Bring a smile to
8 Second section
9 Fix the outcome

10 Undivided
11 Nancy Drew's boyfriend
12 Knight's counterpart
13 In the black
19 Canal blocker?
20 Poetic vase
24 Provo's state
25 Author Morrison
26 Arrange type
28 Santa sounds
29 Breaks under pressure
30 Today, in Turin
33 "__ Excited" (Pointer Sisters tune)
34 Tackled a bone
35 Comic Eric
36 Maneuver a bishop
37 PDQ relative
38 *Jeopardy!* questions
39 Place to plant
42 "Am __ understand . . ."
44 Restaurant offerings

45 "No more!"
47 Playful animal
48 North Sea feeder
49 English county
51 Unpopular picnickers
53 Husky command

54 '75 Wimbledon champ
55 __ de Pascua (Easter Island)
56 Hack
57 Every single one
58 Spy grp.

555 OUT OF OFFICE by Tony Stone

ACROSS
1 Navigator need
4 Rough it
8 Star flower
13 Fancy horseplay?
14 Puccini piece
15 Resort lake
16 *Exodus* author
17 Camera's eye
18 Forebodings
19 Trivia buffs?
22 Bones' partner
23 Roof extension
24 U.S. union
27 *Sí* or *oui*
28 Dadaism founder
31 Lisbon cash
33 Tiny animals
36 Dry-as-dust
37 Halloween need?
41 Aware of
42 Greek sea god
43 Spirited session?
45 Jillian or Sothern
46 No. cruncher
49 Sea dog
50 Popular snack
53 Guide down the aisle
55 Slovenly soothsayers?
59 Self-move firm
61 Walked all over
62 Architect Saarinen
63 Ms. Q?
64 Relaxation
65 "Unto us __ is given"
66 Make changes to
67 Does and ewes
68 Fam. member

DOWN
1 Troops' zeal
2 __ *Restaurant*
3 Stations sentries
4 Unruffled
5 Space
6 Pie filling
7 High-muck-a-muck
8 Expiates
9 Identical
10 Synonym sources
11 Long time
12 Scale notes
13 Swollen
20 Sea World whale
21 "Nobody Knows de Trouble __"
25 Bank agcy.
26 Big vein
29 Babes in motion
30 Jury member
32 NBA team
33 "This weighs __!"
34 Street salutation
35 Hammett hound
37 Outlay
38 Draft status
39 Look to heaven?
40 Accumulate
44 Lost ardor
46 Omelet filling
47 Rolls fuel
48 Bad lighting?
51 Senator Kefauver
52 Talk tycoon
54 Start gathering wool
56 Destroy
57 Deep pink
58 Poems of praise
59 UN member
60 Buzz

556 LEND A HAND by Trip Payne

ACROSS
1 Nile slitherers
5 Lease charge
9 Razor sharpener
14 Actor's goal
15 Singer Adams
16 Billy Joel's instrument
17 Astronaut Shepard
18 Impressionist Carvey
19 Drive forward
20 *Cheers* nickname
23 Finish the cupcakes
24 Victory symbol
25 Snuggle
29 Suit fabric
31 Identical
34 Wreak havoc on
35 Work unit
37 *Reine's* husband
38 Woodwind instrument
39 Schoolyard retort
43 *Elephant Boy* actor
44 Baden-Baden, for one
45 Mauna __
46 Related
47 Foots the bill
49 "I give up!"
53 Tease a bit
55 Silly Putty container
57 Swiss river
58 '65 Beach Boys tune
62 Comic Myron
65 Corporate symbol
66 Writing tablets
67 Expect
68 All over again
69 Fencer's choice
70 Italian sauce
71 Ripped
72 Unpopular kid

DOWN
1 A Musketeer
2 Comfort
3 Team member
4 Put in the mail
5 Change colors again
6 *Daniel Boone* actor
7 1492 vessel
8 Greenish blue
9 Backbone
10 This typeface
11 Knock sharply
12 *A Chorus Line* number
13 Campaigner, for short
21 Olympics official Brundage
22 *Anna Christie* playwright
26 "Oom-pah" instrument
27 Jungle king
28 Chemical suffix
30 Post-sneeze remark
32 Deck out
33 Cry from the pasture
36 Mahalia's music
39 Rice wine
40 Drama award
41 "__ Lazy River"
42 Moolah
43 __ Luis Obispo, CA
48 Folk singer Pete
50 Party snack
51 Roofer's need
52 Rubbed out
54 Slowly, to Solti
56 No longer a child
59 Land map
60 Uni- relative
61 Unlocked
62 Mortarboard
63 Must pay
64 Possesses

557   SLOW DOWN by Dean Niles

ACROSS

1. Sot's sound
7. Dog doc
10. Baltimore player
11. Main character
12. Comic Conway
15. Seeing someone
16. Part of A.D.
17. Record label
18. __ *Man Answers* ('62 film)
19. Corporate raider's payoff
21. Timber tool
23. Lions' pride
24. First name in daredeviltry
25. Hamelin hero
27. Go-getters
28. Dad's lad
29. Wordsworth works
30. Coyote cry
31. Pulver's rank: Abbr.
32. Green garnish
34. List abbr.
37. African snakes
39. Steak state
40. Greek letter
41. Whoop it up
43. Tough and shrewd
45. Mesopotamian deity
46. Chelsea's cat
47. Coll. sports org.
48. French Canadian
50. Hardwood
51. Network in *Network*
52. Mountain pool
53. Where to spend a drachma
56. Scarf down
57. Rugged rock
58. *Seinfeld*, for one
59. "Hold it!"
60. "A-Tisket A-__"

DOWN

1. Coal scuttle
2. One of the Gershwins
3. Legal recourse
4. Arranged a do
5. Arm bone
6. Wooden pin
7. Thin coating
8. Sea birds
9. Fudd, for one
11. Track activity
12. Vacation convenience
13. Less friendly
14. Shopping places
19. Staring one
20. Kitty's comment
21. Church recess
22. The Belmonts' leader
23. He had the touch
26. Seed source
27. Senior member
30. Cattle groups
33. Carefree excursions
35. __ *Team* (Mr. T series)
36. Musical conclusion
38. Wild guess
41. Irritate
42. Caribbean island
43. Cry of joy
44. Beginnings
46. Frighten
49. Engrave a design
50. Opera offering
53. Canadian levy: Abbr.
54. Runner Sebastian
55. CPR expert

558   HUE DOWNS ETC. by Shirley Soloway

ACROSS

1. PD alerts
5. Speak ill of
10. Farm measure
14. Token taker
15. Took a chance
16. Lean-to
17. Mandlikova of tennis
18. Demeanors
19. __ colada
20. GREEN __
23. Fluffy canine
24. Chad, e.g.
25. Sampras shots
27. Join forces
30. Supreme Court member
33. Tranquil
36. Egotist's love
38. Emporium
39. British beer
40. Lab worker
42. Spy org.
43. Earl Hines' nickname
45. Largest amount
46. Slate, for short
47. Chemical compounds
49. Radiate
51. Part of CEO
52. Very best
56. That woman
58. YELLOW __
62. Ye __ Gift Shoppe
64. Norman Vincent __
65. __ rug (dance)
66. Vivacity
67. James and Kett
68. Hebrew month
69. Sunbeams
70. Mine duct
71. D.C. figures

DOWN

1. Pale-faced
2. Beach: Sp.
3. Lisa of *The Cosby Show*
4. Arena
5. Warn
6. Barbara or Conrad
7. Greek war god
8. Transmitted
9. Ford follies
10. Poisonous reptile
11. BLUE __
12. Casino city
13. Dutch cheese
21. Calendar abbr.
22. Birds do it
26. However
28. Really rain
29. St. __ *Fire*
31. Pennsylvania port
32. Peruse the news
33. Eatery
34. "How awful!"
35. RED __
37. Throw out a line
40. Considerate one
41. Most rigid
44. Jinx
46. New York Indians
48. Extents
50. Coll. hoop contest
53. Give off
54. Evil one
55. Peter and Nicholas
56. Gardener, at times
57. Actress Raines
59. Adam's third son
60. "I could __ horse!"
61. Norwegian king
63. Naval off.

559 TRICK-STERS by Cathy Millhauser

ACROSS
1 Union bane
5 Irish county
10 Canadian Indian
14 English composer
15 Spiral
16 Unctuous
17 BOO-STER?
19 Snoot
20 Nile feature
21 HAM-STER?
23 Record protector
25 Clear a tape
26 Caligula's nephew
28 Spread out
32 Terre Haute coll.
35 Seated Beatle
38 Locust, e.g.
39 SHY-STER?
43 Rumple
44 Shroud site
45 Approvals
46 Race between poles
49 Word form for "within"
51 Humble
54 Burns a bit
58 LOB-STER?
62 Movies' Superman
63 Alligator label
64 OY-STER?
66 Joyce's homeland
67 Emulate Bryan
68 Yearn
69 Den din
70 *The Gondoliers* character
71 Overdue

DOWN
1 Bits of time, so to speak
2 Catch holder
3 Secret motive
4 Shellacked
5 Letter from Xenophon
6 Opposite of dextro-
7 Animated
8 Stand for a soprano
9 Supernumeraries
10 Musical composition
11 Run wild
12 Additional
13 Ogler
18 Watering hole
22 Egyptian snake
24 Estrada of *CHiPs*
27 "Step __!"
29 Woody's boy
30 Work period
31 "Why don't we?"
32 Tenets
33 Synagogue
34 Heavenly bear
36 Dik-dik's cousin
37 Baddie
40 NHL player
41 French wines
42 Jawaharlal's daughter
47 Kimono sash
48 Animal on the gridiron
50 *The Hairy Ape* playwright
52 Future fern
53 *Aunt __ Cope Book*
55 Columbus' birthplace
56 Olympic contest
57 Coat material
58 Bleacher feature
59 Pinza of *South Pacific*
60 Writer Ephron
61 Makes a choice
65 Meadow

560 FOWL-MOUTHED by Donna J. Stone

ACROSS
1 Stayed put
5 Heston role
10 Actress Chase
14 Pinza of the Met
15 Sierra __
16 Slave
17 *Alice's Restaurant* name
18 THE WORD DEFINED
20 Retreat
21 Elsa's mistress
22 Fermented tea
23 Actress Stapleton
25 Black plus white
26 Place for a blade
29 Linen in the beginnin'?
30 Dawber of *My Sister Sam*
33 Fate
34 Job opening
35 Mrs. Zeus
36 START OF A DEFINITION
39 Red ink
40 Skirt shaper
41 Pipe cleaner
42 Mislead
43 Dame Hess
44 Wine home
45 Clean a counter
46 Sheet of stamps
47 Unmitigated
50 D.C. bigwig
51 Call it a day
55 END OF DEFINITION
57 Provo's home
58 Safe place?
59 Well's partner
60 *Bus Stop* playwright
61 Man from Mayberry
62 Artist's subjects
63 Light gas

DOWN
1 Get better
2 Pound of poetry
3 Caron role
4 Entryway features
5 Biblical prophet
6 Bucket of bolts
7 Clone
8 Chemical suffix
9 Pretty up
10 Land of lasagna
11 Timber wolf
12 Potter's need
13 Shake __ (hurry)
19 Wheedle
24 Handy bit of Latin
25 Library fixture
26 Cranium
27 Asian capital
28 Rub out
29 Plant life
30 Pansy part
31 Fight site
32 Estate house
34 Salt away
35 Comic character
37 Tut or Mubarak
38 Temptation location
43 Ho Chi __
44 Jet-set site
45 Off-the-wall
46 Get one's goat
47 "Waterloo" group
48 Nolan of baseball
49 Durban dough
50 Lose control
52 *The __ Reader* (literary publication)
53 *Othello* heavy
54 Not now
56 Actor Gulager

561   NEATLY DONE by Randolph Ross

ACROSS

1 __ seed (deteriorate)
5 __ & Moe (Gleason film)
9 Give forth
13 Actor Mischa
14 __ Now (Murrow TV show)
16 Congenial
17 Stain remover
19 Aware of
20 Throw forcefully
21 Abates
23 Cause a riot
26 Values
27 Late, in La Paz
28 Part of SBLI
29 Licentious
31 Andy's friend
32 Mornings: Abbr.
33 Cash in
35 Sass
36 Has hopes
38 Inventor Whitney
39 Next to hit
41 Family member
42 Peak
43 Spiritual leader

44 Fast plane
45 Seven, in Seville
46 Junior's custodian
48 Repaired a road
49 Parlor furniture
51 Feels off
52 "__ the Rainbow"
53 Tanners
58 Swampland
59 Roman river
60 Sweet sandwich
61 Actress Lanchester
62 "So long!"
63 Like some buildup

DOWN

1 Wander (about)
2 __ Town (Wilder play)
3 Mystery writer Josephine
4 Prom flowers
5 Grenoble's river
6 Enthusiasm
7 Eastern discipline

8 Gives way
9 Shipwrecked, perhaps
10 Naval vessel
11 Religious symbol
12 Perfect scores, at times
15 Oak or elm
18 Early guitar
22 Silly Soupy
23 Author Calvino
24 Identifying
25 Rural aircraft
26 Knowledgeable one
28 Troublesome tyke
30 Strike out
32 Invite
33 Buttons or Barber
34 Made cocktails
36 Sharp
37 Snitch
40 African region
42 Aviation display
44 Georgetown educator

45 Common seasoning
47 Try out
48 Ornate headwear
49 "__ Enchanted Evening"

50 Satanic
51 Cooperate with criminals
54 O'Neal's org.
55 Southpaw stat
56 Reviewer Reed
57 Oriental sauce

562   CUTESY by Matt Gaffney

ACROSS

1 To be: Lat.
5 Nest egg, for short
8 Mensa stats
11 Pesky bug
13 Southwestern sight
15 Slashes the budget
17 Managed to include
19 Employ
20 Bilko and Kovacs
21 Wilander of tennis
23 Zuider __
24 Emulate Cicero
26 Little troublemakers
28 Jumping-peg game
31 Old Testament book
32 Eastern discipline
33 Burden
35 Plops down
37 Chores
40 Warm up the oven

42 Love the attention
44 __ up (evaluates)
45 Cable channel
47 Pianist Peter
48 Approximately
50 Medical suffix
52 Tell (on)
53 '87 Danny DeVito film
55 More adventurous
57 Eyebrow shape
58 Con
60 Saudi __
64 Short play
66 Evening out
68 Falls below the horizon
69 Family member
70 Compel
71 Hair coloring
72 Summer quencher
73 Dietitians' amts.

DOWN

1 Facility
2 Roman initials
3 Cold-shoulder
4 Rural refrain?

5 __ Mine (George Harrison book)
6 Beef or lamb
7 It's east of the Urals
8 I, in Innsbruck
9 Game-show host
10 Throat germ
12 Tractor name
14 On edge
16 Understands
18 Eva's sister
22 Ivanhoe man
25 Hackneyed
27 Another time
28 Beer ingredient
29 Calvary inscription
30 Former Philippine capital
34 Colonel Potter, to friends
36 They may be deviated
38 Turkish river
39 Primer pooch
41 Road curves
43 Beast

46 Doctor Freud
49 "Christmas comes but __ year . . ."
51 Letter stroke
53 Russian news agency
54 Annoyed

56 Stubble scraper
59 Blue hue
61 Finch, e.g.
62 Peruvian Indian
63 "Rock of __"
65 Poetic monogram
67 Devoured

563   BRACE YOURSELF by Dean Niles

ACROSS

1 Triumphant cries
5 Latin parent
10 Prepare potatoes
14 Hamlet
15 *M* man
16 The younger Guthrie
17 Good match
19 Journalist Jacob
20 Full-blown
21 "__ Up Before You Go-Go" ('84 tune)
23 Jury member
25 Insignificant quantities
26 Historic period
29 Southeast Asian
30 Sufficient, poetically
31 Kind of game
33 Leaves
37 Marsh plant
38 "__ Rock" ('66 song)
39 '92 Disney film
43 Computer peripheral
46 Movie theater
47 Sleep stage
48 Conclude
49 Ode division
52 Strikebreaker
54 "Born in __" ('84 song)
55 Selfishness
59 Masterson colleague
60 Stand-in
64 Freud subj.
65 Fuming
66 Ger.
67 Biblical graffito
68 Mans the bar
69 Fr. holy women

DOWN

1 "__ boy!"
2 Wolf wail
3 Way off base?
4 Be nosy
5 Tableland
6 NASA affirmative
7 Angle starter
8 Seabird
9 Claret, e.g.
10 Samuel Clemens
11 Sharon of Israel
12 *Ghostbusters* goo
13 Wets (down)
18 Gas and coal
22 On
24 Computer acronym
25 Koppel or Kennedy
26 Bible book
27 Stagger about
28 Neck of the woods
32 Simon smash, with *The*
34 Assess
35 Govt. agents
36 Gemstone
40 Short swims
41 Occupy
42 Formerly known as
43 Sock units: Abbr.
44 Falls back
45 Adult insect
49 Cook veggies
50 Macbeth's title
51 Showed again
53 Matches
56 Cynical rejoinder
57 Swing around
58 Shea men
61 Mine find
62 Mr. Quayle
63 Since 1/1, to a CPA

564   JUST ADD WATER by Eric Albert

ACROSS

1 Green stone
5 Journalist Joseph
10 Handle Bazookas?
14 Evangelist Roberts
15 Longest French river
16 Solemn assurance
17 JUST ADD WATER
20 Tee preceder
21 Tyler's successor
22 Kobe robe
23 Piece
24 Postwar alliance
25 Pooh's pal
28 Die
29 *Dallas* network
32 Culinary by-product
33 Green Hornet's assistant
34 Baldwin of *Malice*
35 JUST ADD WATER
38 Their jobs are on the line
39 Black as night
40 Composer Copland
41 Deli preference
42 Hill dwellers
43 Ninja Turtle, for one
44 Trek among the trees
45 Actor Richard
46 Obscures
49 Cabbage cousin
50 Actor Vigoda
53 JUST ADD WATER
56 Singer Guthrie
57 Like Yale's walls
58 Union Jack, for instance
59 __ *Gynt*
60 Easy mark
61 Big bash

DOWN

1 San __, CA
2 Large boats
3 Honoree's platform
4 North Pole worker
5 Total
6 Lazes about
7 Under the weather
8 Great Bruin
9 Baby game
10 Women's mag
11 Angel topper
12 Thames town
13 Owl howl
18 Show up
19 Locale
23 *Stand and Deliver* star
24 Missing marbles
25 Sulky horse
26 Dramatic device
27 Tevye's wife
28 Wine vats
29 Bow or Barton
30 "Don't __ it!"
31 Bouquet
33 Kunta of *Roots*
34 Hard stone
36 Firing notice
37 Hardy's other half
42 Hired helper
43 Tune
44 Indulge
45 Opens wide
46 Applaud
47 Group knowledge
48 Stare at
49 Craft a cardigan
50 Proficient
51 Cop's route
52 Border
54 Eggs
55 Deviating from

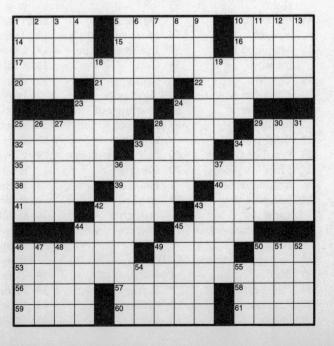

565   SAFARI SIGHTS by Bob Lubbers

ACROSS

1 Dreary
5 Get better
9 Music org.
14 Double agent
15 *Casablanca* character
16 Yale yell
17 Pith helmets?
19 Singer Skinnay
20 Truth
22 Curved molding
23 Jaguars, e.g.
26 Pink tones
28 Actor O'Shea
29 Boom-bah preceder
32 Rich soil
33 "What's in __?"
35 Hang around
37 Little devil
40 Damp
41 Lennon's lady
42 *L.A. Law* character
44 9-digit ID
45 Sword handles
47 "Jezebel" singer
48 Devour Dickens

50 Blonde shade
52 Regretful one
53 Prime-time choice
56 Los __, NM
58 Sgt. Friday's employer
59 Tropical malady
62 Meat jelly
64 Kenyan claret?
68 Martin or Lawrence
69 Hawaiian city
70 Religious image
71 ". . . after they've seen __"
72 One-pot dinner
73 Ago, to Burns

DOWN

1 Auto bur.
2 Caviar
3 One's partner
4 Realtor's concern
5 Drummer's cymbals

6 Mideast airline
7 __ spumante
8 Holds up
9 Fortas or Burrows
10 California city
11 Home with a river view?
12 Foreign
13 Matador maneuvers
18 Painter __ Borch
21 Southern address?
23 Muslim leaders
24 Underworld judge
25 Serengeti singer?
27 True-blue
30 Object of worship
31 Yearly visitor
34 Fictional Frome
36 Setback
38 *Exodus* actor
39 Looks intently
43 Unique character

46 The same as before
49 Salad ingredient
51 '30s film vamp
53 Anklet feature
54 "¡__ mañana!"
55 Wood strips

57 Fracture facts
60 Café au __
61 Skilled
63 Passing grade
65 Frosty
66 __ sequitur
67 Vane letters

566   VOCALIZING by Fred Piscop

ACROSS

1 USAir competitor
4 Catlike animal
9 *M*A*S*H* character
14 Mil. unit
15 Not so congenial
16 Make reparation
17 Get mellower
18 Newscast image
20 Get together
22 Revives
23 Kett of the comics
24 *Sophie's Choice* author
26 Bumpkin
29 Fix a flat
33 Clothing
36 Arafat's grp.
38 __ Claire, WI
39 Musical message
43 Hosp. area
44 "Inka Dinka __"
45 Saps
46 __ *Is Born*
49 Tugboat or gravy boat

51 Least suntanned
53 Anthem starter
57 Unwelcome guest
60 Chosen child
63 Dental deadener
65 Supply with weapons
66 Roast host
67 Some tournaments
68 Compete
69 Willing one
70 Bronco show
71 Evening, in poetry

DOWN

1 Identify a caller
2 "Ain't __ Fun?"
3 007, e.g.
4 Give as an example
5 "Not if __ help it!"
6 Most disgusting
7 "A mouse!"
8 Tot's transport

9 Ames Brothers tune of '50
10 Daughter of Zeus
11 "Easy __ it!"
12 Med. student's course
13 Make over
19 Neither's partner
21 Flier to Rio
25 Treads softly
27 Geller the spoonbender
28 Transmit
30 Actress Garr
31 James of *Brian's Song*
32 Sings with closed lips
33 India's continent
34 Spasms
35 Hardware item
37 Early automaker
40 State's head
41 ". . . __ I saw Elba"
42 Lively dance
47 Orbit point

48 Bacon serving
50 Put on a play
52 Hawaiian souvenir
54 Barrel part
55 Raptor's nest
56 Mideast land

57 "__ a Song Go . . ."
58 Cass, for one
59 Hockey need
61 "Great" dog
62 __ buco
64 Main mail place: Abbr.

567 DAIRY CASE by Shirley Soloway

ACROSS

1 Uncooked
4 *Little Women* character
8 Stands behind
13 Western actor Jack
15 Fencing weapon
16 Lofty spaces
17 Top-notch
18 Pharmacy bottle
19 Very small
20 Open-textured fabric
23 Classifieds
24 Drapery ornament
25 Rivulet
27 "__ go bragh!"
29 Takes on
32 Impact sound
35 Twist
38 Actor Russell
39 Boxing bigwig
40 Bookworm, maybe
43 Disgusted expression
44 Resort place
46 Actress Braga
47 In favor of
48 Subway coins
51 Young Guthrie
53 Free
56 Seasonal songs
60 Coolidge, for short
62 Seeking favor
64 Texas landmark
66 Israeli dance
67 Olympian Korbut
68 Skinflint
69 Scandinavian king
70 MTV viewer
71 Nuisances
72 Try out
73 Med. personnel

DOWN

1 Show one's feelings
2 Oahu greeting
3 Decreases
4 Cutting on a slant
5 Grand work
6 Marsh ducks
7 Spartan slave
8 Used the tub
9 Had a bite
10 Used-car descriptor
11 Good-natured
12 Articulates
14 Reagan appointee
21 Suit fabric
22 __-la-la
26 Response from space
28 Henpecks
30 Peter, Paul and Mary, e.g.
31 Occupational suffix
32 Angler's worms
33 In addition
34 Translucent tableware
36 Greek consonant
37 Actress Olin
41 Copters and fighters
42 __ Lama
45 Always, to Keats
49 Gomer Pyle portrayer
50 Letters after R
52 "Ready __, here I come!"
54 *Some Like* __
55 Swiped
57 Eyed excessively
58 German weapon
59 Extends across
60 Army outpost
61 "I cannot tell __"
63 Memorable times
65 Encountered

568 FOUR DOWN by Dean Niles

ACROSS

1 Atlas material
5 Third Greek letter
10 Con game
14 First shepherd
15 Sky hunter
16 Mountain lion
17 Bring up
18 Full of sediment
19 Mine extracts
20 Latin abbr.
21 DOWN
23 Chicago Bears coach George
25 Tackled the trail
26 Signal once more
28 Verdon et al.
30 Feverish feelings
31 Subatomic particle
32 Indicate approval
35 Steady stare
36 Eccentric
37 Body, in biology
38 Cabinetmaker's tool
39 Cease, to a sailor
40 __ on (fussed over)
41 Gray poem
42 Reno business
43 Engine
45 Wading bird
46 DOWN
49 Writing tablet
52 "Hi-__, Hi-Lo"
53 On the lookout
54 Dog-food name
55 Actor Baldwin
56 Have a feeling
57 Folk singer Joan
58 Combats
59 Passover meal
60 *Jane* __

DOWN

1 Full-grown filly
2 Help a hood
3 DOWN
4 Type of camera: Abbr.
5 Attend unaccompanied
6 Opera highlights
7 Pepper holder
8 Lorre role
9 No place in particular
10 Scares
11 Nobelist Marie
12 Make a change
13 Sail support
21 "Woe is me!"
22 In the __ (healthy)
24 Sheltered, at sea
26 Indian music
27 Old-fashioned oath
28 Having moxie
29 Imperfection
31 Marsh, for short
32 DOWN
33 Harbinger
34 Column part
36 Cloverleaf feature
37 Mediocre
39 Matty or Felipe
40 Pub projectile
41 Moral principles
42 Middle
43 __ letter (use the post office)
44 Famous Canadian physician
45 Pinto or palomino
46 Talon
47 Run away
48 Tear apart
50 Mimic
51 Snooze
54 Presidential nickname

569 INDEPENDENT LADIES by Matt Gaffney

ACROSS
1 Epic stories
6 Walled city
13 Senator Lott
14 Senate topic
15 Act before Madonna
17 Longfellow subject
18 Cross product
19 "It's a Sin __ a Lie"
21 City on the Rhone
22 Smack
24 Jagr's grp.
25 Pug or Peke
27 Star Wars abbr.
28 Asleep on the job
30 Used to be
33 Jonas Savimbi, e.g.
35 Singer Bonnie
37 Independent ladies of TV
40 Zinc __ (skin protector)
41 Pulled a scam
42 Affirmative answer
43 Furrier family
45 NFL div.
47 And so on: Abbr.
48 Actress Hagen
49 Bridge coup
51 Get better
54 Sweet snack
57 Undivided
58 Some numbers
60 Noted naturalist
62 Domino's delivery
63 Good, to Garcia
64 Cold spells
65 Broadcast

DOWN
1 Telegram interruptions
2 Van Cleef's partner
3 A League of Their Own actress
4 Landers or Sothern
5 Editor's order
6 Throw in the clink
7 Honors
8 Born yesterday
9 The Name of the Rose setting
10 Paris or Hoboken
11 Santa sounds
12 __ even keel
14 Independent ladies of film
16 "Da Doo __" ('63 tune)
20 Liberals
23 Longed (for)
26 Hamlet character
29 Some ads
30 Roadside blossom
31 Had for dessert
32 Pig pad
34 Like Gatsby
36 Bailiwicks
37 Actress Myrna
38 Timber tool
39 __, She Said ('91 film)
44 Rasp
46 Feline nemesis
47 Role for Audrey
50 "Nothing can stop __!"
51 Kachina craftsman
52 Comic Idle
53 Woodworking tool
55 MacGraw and Baba
56 Collars a crook
59 Coax and coax
61 Groove

570 BEDSIDE MANNER by Donna J. Stone

ACROSS
1 __ Krishna
5 Ran, as dyes
9 Bates' bailiwick
14 Churchill's successor
15 Key signature?
16 Duck
17 Singer Falana
18 Elvis' daughter
19 Statement entry
20 SUBJECT OF DEFINITION
23 Bell ringer
24 Mrs. Dick Tracy
25 Coffee break
28 "Old Blood and Guts"
32 Boxer Jake La__
36 Killer whale
38 Strong desire
39 START OF DEFINITION
42 Pasteur portrayer
43 Identify
44 "And Jill came tumbling __"
45 Sudden emotions
47 Lily locale
49 Stocking stuffers
51 __ pie
56 END OF DEFINITION
60 Perhaps
61 Show favoritism
62 Hideaway
63 Little women
64 Mystery man?
65 Comic Johnson
66 Winter weather
67 Forest fauna
68 Ginger cookie

DOWN
1 Pitches in
2 Really like
3 Let up
4 Legislate
5 Column credit
6 Secular
7 Actress Lanchester
8 Dispensed
9 A Gorgon
10 Cram
11 Can openers
12 Singer Adams
13 "__ bygones be bygones"
21 Bar mitzvah reading
22 High kingdom
26 Couch
27 Walk heavily
29 Run lightly
30 Grimm creature
31 Within earshot
32 Some PTA members
33 "Moving __" (Jeffersons theme)
34 Narrow shoe size
35 Like some watchbands
37 Role for Liz
40 Beginning
41 Peace Nobelist of '78
46 Annoy
48 Less messy
50 Tatter
52 Marner of fiction
53 Hunger
54 Singer Bryant
55 Throat bug
56 Howl
57 Thornfield governess
58 The old days
59 Rod
60 Booker T. and the __

571   LISTENING IN by Shirley Soloway

ACROSS
1 Out of control
5 Cooking odor
10 Russian ruler
14 On the ocean
15 Very cold
16 Lhasa __
17 Close-by
19 Art __
20 Not so hot
21 Daredevil Knievel
22 NASA affirmative
23 Wine valley
25 Sharp answers
28 Curved line
31 __ Pass (Uris novel)
33 Mr. Kabibble
34 On __ Pond ('81 film)
36 Wartime signal
40 Duel tool
41 Bit of bread
43 __ Camera ('55 film)
44 Come back
46 Father goose?

48 Down Under jumper
49 Physician of antiquity
51 Retirees' org.
52 Letting up
55 Objectives
57 __-relief
58 French river
60 Very fancy headgear
64 A Farewell to __
66 Oxymoronic display
68 Boxing event
69 First name in cosmetics
70 Unlikely to attack
71 Griffith or Rooney
72 Strict
73 Sp. ladies

DOWN
1 Desire
2 "Oh!"
3 Ballet move
4 Singer Bobby
5 Rep.

6 Use the microwave
7 Norwegian monarch
8 Ores, e.g.
9 Shake up
10 Smidgen
11 Leads the way
12 Wide neckwear
13 Corner chess pieces
18 "There Is Nothin' Like __"
24 __-nez
26 Start of a pencil game
27 K.T. of country music
28 Worry, perhaps
29 Use a lariat
30 Totally confusing
32 Gene Tierney thriller
35 Station
37 U.S. Grant's rank
38 Iowa college town
39 __ avis
42 Most tattered

45 Luau dish
47 "... __ all a good night"
50 Unwelcome admirer?
52 Addis __
53 Nobleman
54 Short messages

56 Prepares flour
59 Fill to the gills
61 Unlatched, maybe
62 Capital of Italia
63 Yes votes
65 Hog home
67 D.C. figure

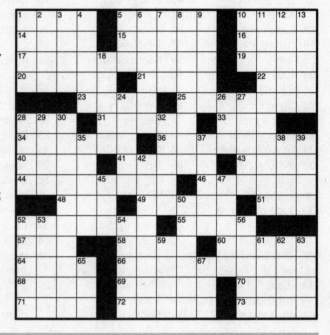

572   GO-GETTERS by David Owens

ACROSS
1 Nickname for Hemingway
5 Lhasa __
9 One at __ (singly)
14 Declare
15 Jungle home
16 Horse papas
17 How go-getters go
20 Our Miss Brooks star
21 Spirited session?
22 Popeye's girl
23 Cots on wheels
24 They may be split
28 Sting
30 Swamp
32 Seer's asset
33 __ facto
37 What go-getters do
40 Eye problem
41 Detective story pioneer
42 Ceremony
43 Stir up
45 Trunk

46 Shore specialty
50 Kimono cummerbund
52 Bays
53 Blackens
58 What go-getters have, with "a"
60 Lilting syllables
61 Egotist's obsession
62 Commedia dell'__
63 Parisian legislature
64 __-European
65 Misplace

DOWN
1 Wan
2 Tel __
3 Moplike pooch
4 Region
5 "Luck Be __" ('50 tune)
6 Den wood
7 Autograph
8 Poetic eye
9 State
10 Big fellow

11 Actress Dunne
12 Clemency
13 Snaky shapes
18 Concerto __ (musical form)
19 Coup leader
23 Deep cut
24 Rock-band equipment
25 Recommend
26 Concorde destination
27 Gander or cob
29 Rhythm
31 Postulate
33 "Tell __ the judge!"
34 Rain hard
35 Aerobics centers
36 Scandinavian city
38 Frog kin
39 Protests that went nowhere?
43 Phrasal conjunction
44 Germanic gnome
46 Winnows

47 Acclimate
48 Comic __ Sherman
49 The Most Happy __
51 Smashing, à la Variety
53 Paradise

54 Slanted type: Abbr.
55 Goose egg
56 Gobbles up
57 Hook's henchman
59 "Unaccustomed __ am . . ."

573 FOOD INDIGO by Dean Niles

ACROSS
1 Two tuba toots
7 Chore
10 Lose tension
13 Curly or Moe
14 Physically sound
15 Zero
16 Tea man
17 Broad sts.
18 He stung like a bee
19 Greek mountain
20 Music category
22 Nourished
23 Choreographer Tharp
25 Piano piece
27 Vietnamese capital
30 Major mess
33 Puts into office
35 Just begun
39 Bibl. book
40 Socrates' student
42 Revolve
43 Where one stands
45 Took the measure of
47 Locker-room hangings
49 Uprisings
50 Romantic expedition
53 Grammarian's concern
55 Keats' container
56 Classical hunk
59 Equal
63 Turkish title
64 Drug buster
65 High-class hound
67 Wine word
68 Move slowly
69 Got a look at
70 Adherent suffix
71 Rebel grp.
72 Settled down

DOWN
1 Cold capital
2 Elevator man
3 Swabs
4 Blue snack
5 Past
6 Funny Youngman
7 Al Hirt tune
8 Couturier Cassini
9 Ask on bended knee
10 Complete botch
11 Felt unwell
12 Sail along
14 Blue drink
21 Subordinate Claus?
24 Wilde was one
26 Blue candy
27 Dickensian clerk
28 Not to mention
29 Clears
31 Social worker?
32 Highlander
34 Quick trip
36 Vehicle
37 Waste allowance
38 Wraps up
41 Singer Rawls
44 Really huge
46 Work unit
48 Govt. assistance
50 Resembling
51 Prods along
52 Put into law
54 Ski spot
57 Rather and Quayle
58 Bo Derek film
60 Modify text
61 "Waiting for the Robert __"
62 Comic Foxx
66 Sweet suffix

574 MOVIE TITLES by Manny Nosowsky

ACROSS
1 Sarcastic salutation
7 Takes off
14 Congenital
15 Beg
16 MacLaine film
18 Crack up
19 __-pocus
20 "__ the fields we go . . ."
21 Knight time?
22 Napoleon's troops
23 Monogram ltr.
24 Undivided
25 Lingerie items
26 Solemn peal
27 Hwys.
28 Phnom __
29 Steed seat
30 Milan money
31 Peppy
32 Not in class
35 Put-on
36 Scepter's sidekick
39 Electronics device
40 Tara resident
41 PBS benefactor
42 "Rabbi Ben __" (Browning work)
43 Spare spot
44 Went like hotcakes
45 Move like molasses
46 Water pipe
47 Aries month
48 Tati film
51 Murmuring
52 Rise and shine
53 Unbeatable foes
54 Assembly instruction

DOWN
1 Grinding material
2 Toughs it out
3 Humiliate
4 Tiber town
5 Outrage
6 Vote into the Hall of Fame
7 Low cards
8 Come after
9 School grps.
10 Some collectibles
11 Did planning-commission work
12 Get sick
13 Surprise
16 Daley, e.g.
17 Pizazz
22 Tip off
23 Place to race
25 Back of the book
26 Destiny
29 Initiate ignition
30 Castor's mother
31 Enlist the unwilling
32 NBA coach Rick
33 Really weird
34 Cereal grass
35 Cold-shoulders
36 Not in stock
37 Plymouth model
38 Not well
40 Speechifies
43 Oar pin
44 Director Lee
46 Some sandwiches
47 Word of woe
49 Take advantage of
50 Have property

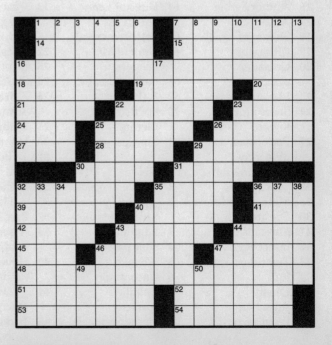

575 EGO TRIP by Bob Lubbers

ACROSS
1 *Cheers* order
5 Foxy
8 Make a choice
14 Stamped over
16 Asian ass
17 Self-defense testifier?
18 Oblique maneuvers
19 Barracks assignments
20 Make a match
21 Do a Little bit
22 One of the Great ones?
23 Greek vowels
25 Worker's ID
26 Classic cars
27 Remnant
28 Runs second
30 Subjective lady?
32 Himalayan people
34 A mean Amin
37 Conscience?
39 Atl. crosser
40 Under __ (tranquilized)
42 Photographer's abbr.
44 Long-eared leapers
45 Some ships: Abbr.
47 "__ a Song Go . . ."
51 John __ Passos
52 Durango dough
53 Prefix for "drama"
54 Mountain peak
55 __ Moines, IA
56 Actor Rod
59 "__ Through the Tulips"
61 Self-awareness?
62 Kind of play
63 Sporty Chevy
64 Read carefully
65 Craving
66 Dorothy, in *The Wiz*

DOWN
1 Corruptive one
2 Fix a lamp
3 Designer Gucci
4 Dull
5 Dele's opposite
6 __ Antilles
7 Football stats.
8 Medicine measures
9 Oklahoma town
10 Dishonorable sort
11 Mirrors?
12 Profundity
13 Gaelic
15 Compass dir.
20 Carried on
24 Room renters
25 Mercury's sun
27 Actor Arnaz
28 Suburbanite's obsession
29 Arrange type
31 Pelts
33 Poet's family
34 Sort of: Suff.
35 Due date
36 Self-promoter?
38 Waters down
41 Loser to DDE
43 Restrainer
46 __ Lee Browne
48 Smooth, to Solti
49 Votes in
50 Rich cakes
52 Golfer Calvin
54 At the summit
55 Physicians, for short
57 Actor Rip
58 Part of SASE
60 Frat letter
61 Frosty

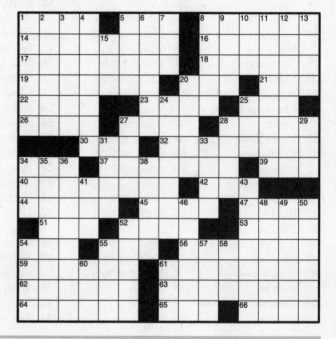

576 CATTY by Shirley Soloway

ACROSS
1 Actress Virna
5 Belief
10 Garage item
14 Ken of *thirtysomething*
15 Daily delivery
16 Author Ferber
17 Auto maker
18 Sharon of Israel
19 Citric sips
20 Crusader symbol
23 I-beam material
24 Show pique toward
27 Performed diligently
31 Exploding stars
33 Tiny speck
36 Mohair producers
39 Eye area
41 More mirthful
42 Insect eggs
43 Tightly-curled fur
46 Caustic substance
47 Went awry
48 '50s Ford
50 Opera performers
53 Thompson or Hawkins
57 Chang and Eng
61 Singer Adams
64 Director Lean
65 Solidifies
66 Letterman rival
67 Graff of *Mr. Belvedere*
68 Folklore heavy
69 Fall faller
70 Sportscaster Merlin
71 Lunchtime

DOWN
1 Weavers' needs
2 __ ease (uncomfortable)
3 Edge along
4 Shoe part
5 IRS men
6 Uncommon
7 DeMille specialty
8 Horned animals
9 Synthetic fabric
10 Kitchen measure
11 Unusual
12 *A Chorus Line* number
13 *Viva __ Vegas*
21 Fitzgerald of jazz
22 Vocalized
25 Be of use
26 Shabby
28 Actress Swenson
29 Actor Richard
30 Holmes' creator
32 To be: Lat.
33 Con
34 In the open
35 __ Haute, IN
37 Peruse
38 Arsenal supplies
40 Have __ (understand)
44 __ Do (Mary Martin musical)
45 Top-of-the-line
49 Sofa style
51 Dashboard feature
52 Little
54 San __, CA
55 Prelim
56 German city
58 Arden and namesakes
59 __ qua non
60 Genesis locale
61 Building wing
62 Poor grade
63 __ way (sort of)

577 COMMAND MEN by Dean Niles

ACROSS
1 Ran in the wash
5 Ran easily
10 Take it easy
14 Helper
15 Sound off
16 A Great Lake
17 Use the scissors
18 Dreadlocked cultist
19 Swedish soprano
20 Ray Charles song
23 Corrida cry
24 Boston ballplayers, familiarly
25 Weasel relative
28 MTV viewer
30 French friend
33 Woody Allen film
36 Register drawer
37 Give a squeeze
38 Creole vegetable
39 Star Trek order
44 Hardwood tree
45 Advocate
46 Black-and-white snacks
47 __-Cat (winter vehicle)
48 Canadian prov.
49 Disillusioned one's lament
57 Cotton holder
58 Unaffiliated company
59 Sunscreen chem.
60 Radar image
61 Punctuation mark
62 Component
63 "__ Sides Now"
64 In the matter of
65 Becomes firm

DOWN
1 Baroque composer
2 Leslie Caron film
3 Redact
4 Cabinet grp.
5 Rhine siren
6 "__ Ben Jonson"
7 El __, TX
8 Singer James
9 Scroll site
10 Chill out
11 Actor Roberts
12 Swim alternative
13 Newsman Koppel
21 Sacred
22 Folk singer Mitchell
25 Eavesdroppers
26 Islamic deity
27 Palliative
28 Stocking shade
29 Omelet ingredient
30 Seek permission
31 The Bells of St. __
32 "__ Believer" ('66 tune)
34 Gangster
35 Jot down
36 TV Guide abbr.
40 Paul of Scarface
41 Nin's works, e.g.
42 Subject matter
43 Table scraps
47 Slender one
48 Pungent plant
49 By oneself
50 Landed
51 Soon
52 Out of commission
53 Musical composition
54 Tarzan's partner
55 Newspaper notice
56 Grub
57 Consumer org.

578 SOLVE FOR X by Fred Piscop

ACROSS
1 Musical chord
6 Engine part, for short
10 Guitar device
14 Esther of Good Times
15 Controversial tree spray
16 Arabian sultanate
17 X
20 Develop slowly
21 Hon
22 Involved with
24 Making a racket
25 Richardson novel
29 Globetrotter Meadowlark
32 2001, for one
33 Lifting device
34 __ Lanka
37 X
41 __ Life to Live
42 Norse pantheon
43 Sty cry
44 Old-fashioned footwear
45 Fish hawk
47 Cornhusker city
50 "__ Enchanted Evening"
52 Former NFL commissioner
55 Jay and the Americans tune
60 X
62 __ of Eden
63 San Marino simoleon
64 Tibetan beast
65 Horse-drawn cart
66 Former Senator Simpson
67 Moral infrastructure

DOWN
1 Math subject
2 Macbeth or Mork
3 Woes
4 Came down
5 Report fully
6 Proofer's mark
7 Pie __ mode
8 Squealers
9 Make beer
10 Inducement
11 Valuable violin
12 Is __ Burning?
13 Musically correct
18 Sicilian peak
19 Latino lady
23 Southern school, familiarly
25 Word form for "fire"
26 A long, long time
27 Russell role
28 Pitcher's stat
30 "Be it __ so humble . . ."
31 Mal de __
33 Satyric trait
34 Recipe instruction
35 M. Descartes
36 Very dark
38 Incendiary substance
39 Teachers' org.
40 Chop off
44 Like some rock formations
45 General Bradley
46 Mexican shawl
47 Rounded
48 Tooth type
49 California town
51 Most of the world
53 "Whatever __ Wants"
54 Wicked
56 Rat-__ (drum sound)
57 Ho Chi __
58 __-European
59 Turkish rulers
61 Lyricist Gershwin

MR. SUSPENSE by Matt Gaffney

ACROSS

1 Film by 35 Across
7 Film by 35 Across
15 Approximately
16 "See ya!" in Sapporo
17 __ scales (influence)
18 Sets up
19 Summer quencher
20 Dinner course
22 Emulates Ross
23 Journalist Jacob
24 A little too suggestive?
25 Gouge the gullible
28 It falls in fall
30 Star Wars princess
31 Coll. cadets
32 G-men
35 Master of suspense
40 Deli order
41 Tear up the track
42 __-de-camp
43 Squeakers
44 Pint-size
47 Portuguese protectorate
50 Pay-stub abbr.
51 Footnote abbr.
52 More courageous
54 Where blokes get news
57 Film by 35 Across
59 Gather together
61 Man on M*A*S*H
62 Colonel's command
63 Picked
64 Film by 35 Across

DOWN

1 __ Hari
2 Like a desert
3 Film by 35 Across
4 Pecan or cashew
5 "Where are you?" reply
6 Ideal
7 Nicholas and Alexander
8 Rabbit relative
9 Brontë heroine
10 Sort of snake
11 __ Court (British legal societies)
12 Rants and raves
13 Ms. Barrymore et al.
14 Fresh
21 Suit accompaniment
24 P.D.Q. __
25 Destructive
26 Pickpocket
27 Musical ability
28 Place to park
29 51 Across rel.
30 Chem room
31 Edge
32 Nip in the bud
33 Alphabet sequence
34 '50s nickname
36 Bass Pinza
37 Bashful's colleague
38 Garden tool
39 Purrer
43 Dorothy of Peyton Place
44 Actress Ullmann
45 Martian feature
46 Seer's cards
47 Arizona sights
48 __ of Two Cities
49 Conspiracy
50 Capacitance unit
52 Slug
53 Discourteous
54 Bric-a-__
55 Big party
56 The People's Choice basset
58 Tic-__-toe
60 Spanish king

CAPITAL PUN-ISHMENT by Trip Payne

ACROSS

1 Long gone
5 Non-elite types?
10 Reverberate
14 Hankering
15 Stupefy
16 Wet forecast
17 Reverse, e.g.
18 Croc kin
19 Russian-born artist
20 Italian hotel feature?
23 Masticates
25 Comes back
28 French leeches?
31 M*A*S*H country
32 Part of NAACP
33 Young fella
34 Individual
35 Band instrument
36 Flowers' home
37 Plump
41 Because
42 Swedish rock group
46 Enthusiast
47 Chow from 31 Across?
49 In a singular way
51 "__ Romance" (Kern tune)
52 Irish backgammon equipment?
55 Bread spread
57 Slogan specialist
58 "__ la vie"
61 Actress Anderson
62 Annoy
63 Office hangings?
64 Computer input
65 Marine raptors
66 Rapid City's st.

DOWN

1 Porky or Petunia
2 Did lunch
3 Trick-or-treaters, perhaps
4 Add as an extra
5 Patti of music
6 "__ corny as Kansas . . ."
7 Provided the banquet
8 Possession of Portugal
9 Start a match
10 Builder
11 Vocations
12 Top-10 song
13 Wee hour
21 Bks.-to-be
22 Signed a contract
23 Acct.
24 Possesses
26 Old-time auto
27 __ Angelo, TX
29 "Now __ me . . ."
30 Put a strain on
34 Cuzco's country
35 Bush
36 Show disapproval
37 Winter bug
38 Nol of Cambodia
39 Clear
40 Big Californian
41 Nobelist Richard
42 Influences
43 W. capital
44 __ vivant
45 Fables in Slang author
47 Curving fastball
48 Dr. Frankenstein's workplace
50 Cheer
53 Beer buy
54 French article
55 Antique
56 Mauna __
59 Vast expanse
60 "Naughty, naughty!"

581   LARGE-SCALE by Shirley Soloway

ACROSS
1 Bible book
5 Avant-__
10 Last word in church
14 "__ Be Cruel" ('56 tune)
15 UFO pilot
16 Willing
17 Diva rendition
18 Sire
19 Theater sign
20 Visible to the naked eye
23 __ a Wonderful Life
24 Nasty smile
25 Summer TV shows
27 Visored hat
30 Reprimands
33 Likens
38 Archie's wife
39 Czech river
40 Big box
43 Art Deco designer
44 Cancellations
46 Came to a halt
48 Financial recipient
51 Dover's st.
52 Firefly, for one
54 Actress Emma
59 Texas coll.
61 Ethnically diverse
64 Mexican snack
66 Actor Reginald
67 __ avis
68 "Diana" singer
69 Rub out
70 "__ the Mood for Love"
71 Chivalrous deed
72 Methods: Abbr.
73 Forgo the fettuccine

DOWN
1 Photographer Ansel
2 Erin of Happy Days
3 In reserve
4 Gaze intently
5 Chews the fat
6 Actor Guinness
7 Austerity
8 More profound
9 Whole
10 Make cheddar better
11 Full-length garment
12 Send out
13 Fishing devices
21 Largest dolphin
22 Sugar shape
26 Artistic subjects
28 Rainbow shape
29 For each
31 Diminutive suffix
32 Lean-to
33 Viet __
34 Nasal appraisal
35 Big money
36 Disposed
37 In a blue mood
41 Slugger Williams
42 Compass letters
45 Sunflower support
47 Casablanca character
49 Classical pieces
50 Queen of mystery
53 Lab burners
55 Pungent
56 Orange Bowl's home
57 Donny's sister
58 Lean
59 Bambi's father
60 Horse hair
62 Meet Me __ Louis
63 Deli breads
65 Cereal grain

582   ENVELOPE, PLEASE by Randolph Ross

ACROSS
1 Bates or King
5 Johnny's successor
8 He ran against Bill and George
12 Shade of green
13 Lennon's wife
14 Jacob's wife et al.
15 Envelope info
18 Before, to Byron
19 A Bobbsey twin
20 Examines the books
21 Former U.S. territory
22 Silent okay
23 Patina
27 Invitees
31 Envelope info
33 Exodus protagonist
34 Dundee denial
35 Anger
36 Envelope info
43 Finish behind
44 Neatens (up)
45 Southern constellation
46 "What Kind of Fool __?"
47 Lay __ (disprove)
50 Motel freebie
51 Bread spread
54 Envelope handlers
57 Sends
58 Diamond __
59 Traffic-light color
60 Sentence part: Abbr.
61 Pinky or Peggy
62 Fabricated

DOWN
1 Orchard spray
2 Ade flavor
3 "__ Maria"
4 Newborn
5 Bennett or Blondell
6 Plus
7 Jedi instructor
8 Occupant
9 Kiln
10 Mother and daughter
11 Compass pt.
12 Washington bill
14 Ushered, perhaps
16 Muslim ascetic
17 Ladder steps
21 Small amount
23 Cabinet item
24 Forgets
25 Hook pooch
26 Flying pests
28 Grab
29 Garr and Copley
30 Dance movement
31 Salt, to a chemist
32 Serious
37 Two-__ (tot)
38 Emphasis
39 Breakfast bread
40 __ against time
41 M, C, or I
42 Half of MCCII
47 Autocratic ruler
48 Mayberry boy
49 Lofty
50 Dot in the sea
51 Be in harmony
52 Served well
53 Sea, to Seurat
54 Strike caller
55 First head of the UN
56 Old Dominion campus: Abbr.

583   FINAL THREESOME by Dean Niles

ACROSS

1 Newts
5 Pull a con
9 Indian chief
14 "It's a Sin to Tell __"
15 Sign of sanctity
16 Send packing
17 Stuff to the gills
18 __ instant (at once)
19 *Dancer at the Bar* artist
20 Reproductive material
23 Foot part
24 Take advantage of
25 Robert Edward __
26 Tijuana cheer
29 Start
31 Gleamed faintly
34 Home: Abbr.
36 Track alternative
37 State of confusion
38 Buried-treasure direction
42 Love god
43 Wine cooler
44 "Poppycock!"
45 Aquatic sport
48 Workaholic sort
52 Get a load of
53 CT hours
54 Vietnamese New Year
56 Nav. rank
57 Take a nap
60 Idiosyncrasy
64 Rubs the wrong way
65 __ terrier
66 Correspondence
67 Like autumn leaves
68 Legs, so to speak
69 Attack
70 Musical Myra
71 Fr. holy women

DOWN

1 "__ Be Hard" ('69 song)
2 Perfume bottle
3 Church offerings
4 Crystal gazer
5 Wedges
6 Kayak cousins
7 "Oh dear!"
8 *2001...* stone
9 Use a coupon
10 Bunyan's tool
11 Sprightly dance
12 __ carte
13 "__ So Fine" ('63 tune)
21 Peripheral
22 Dues payer
26 Popular cookie
27 For fear that
28 Asner and Wynn
30 Clean the blackboard
32 Monopoly prop
33 Meaningless
35 __ grade (goes from 1st to 3rd)
38 Medical photo
39 Tiny bit
40 From Edinburgh
41 __ voce (softly)
42 Flock female
46 Calculate
47 Outsiders
49 Observe on the sly
50 Pepsin, e.g.
51 Take the measure of
55 Some curves
58 Algonquian language
59 E-mail contents
60 P-T link
61 Dubai's loc.
62 *Addams Family* cousin
63 __ *Bravo* ('59 film)

584   TINTED TUNES by Bob Lubbers

ACROSS

1 Sloop feature
5 Matinee __
9 Fit for a king
14 Sapporo sport
15 Completed
16 Actress Verdugo
17 Dorsey tune
19 Narratives
20 Unfair treatment
21 __ Paulo, Brazil
23 Nav. concern
24 Specks of land
26 Chopper blades
28 Common contraction
31 Fatty substance
33 Exist
34 Strauss opera
37 Facilitate a felony
40 Bottom of the barrel
42 California county
43 Very serious
44 Seal
45 Expressed a view
47 __ Tin Tin
48 Read the paper
50 *As You Like It* setting
52 Chance happenings
54 Rooms at the Ritz
57 __ Lingus
58 Tchrs. group
60 Church spire
64 Called strikes
66 Irving Berlin tune of '27
68 Nick of *Cape Fear*
69 Actor Neeson
70 Greek letters
71 Curl one's lip
72 Snaky fish
73 Architectural detail

DOWN

1 Ch. title
2 Atmosphere
3 Fish-eating duck
4 Nailed studs
5 Paragon
6 Moriarty's creator
7 Individual
8 Minus
9 Update the factory
10 Slangy suffix
11 Top-10 tune of '61
12 Keep __ to the ground
13 Endures
18 Robin roosts
22 Ms. Francis
25 Tales
27 Despicable one
28 Arrest
29 General vicinity
30 Bing Crosby tune
32 Obote's foe
35 "Are you a man or __?"
36 Drinks like a Doberman
38 New York county
39 Ark. neighbor
41 Go after
46 Palm produce
49 Provide
51 Smelled strongly
52 Rural deities
53 Crummy car
55 Run-of-the-mill
56 Stuff
59 Can-do
61 Bread with a pocket
62 Call the shots
63 Exxon's ex-name
65 When Strasbourg sizzles
67 Fib

585 FORGET IT! by Donna J. Stone

ACROSS

1 Olympic VIP
5 __ buddies
10 Scoundrels
14 *Lohengrin* soprano
15 It multiplies by dividing
16 "__ forgive those . . ."
17 Carol word
18 Column style
19 Analyze poetry
20 START OF A QUOTE BY RITA MAE BROWN
23 Biscayne Bay city
26 Offspring
27 Compass pt.
28 Ms. Huston
32 Ocean's motions
34 Newsman Pappas
35 Bulwark
38 MIDDLE OF QUOTE
42 Like a woodie
43 Inoperative
46 Stops trying
49 Like some ink
52 Checkout scan
53 Indian export
56 Hand out
57 END OF QUOTE
62 Japanese city
63 Donated
64 Tourists' neckwear
68 Friars, e.g.
69 Actor's rep
70 Forearm bone
71 Duck soup
72 Sonata movement
73 Mouthy miss

DOWN

1 Asian sect
2 "Xanadu" rockers
3 Exploit
4 Strauss opera
5 Commanded
6 Melville work
7 Manor worker
8 Newspaper notices
9 Virile
10 Cooper's concern
11 Rise
12 Actor Hickman
13 Has a hunch
21 Zip
22 __ nous
23 *Printemps* month
24 Sign
25 "Leaving on __ Plane"
29 Turkey neighbor
30 Topographic feature
31 Plenty of
33 __ a Living
36 "Bon voyage" site
37 *A Man __ Woman*
39 Make a choice
40 "¡__ luego!"
41 Whimpers
44 Winter bug
45 Professional charge
46 Marmalade fruit
47 New Jersey campus
48 Aviation pioneer?
50 Salutation word
51 Sanctuary
54 Mystery award
55 Chihuahua chum
58 Treat like a tot
59 Tied
60 Repair
61 Aware of
65 Elm City collegian
66 Rural hotel
67 Clinton's instrument

586 PLAY BALL! by Harvey Estes

ACROSS

1 Fizzy drink
5 Inclined planes
10 __ *Man Flint*
13 Ring results
14 Napoleon's fate
15 Western Indians
17 Work units
18 Snake poison
19 Prepares leather
20 Pol. contributor
21 Dairy container
23 Sorrowful word
25 Neither fish __ fowl
26 Gas ratings
29 Imitator
33 Cabdrivers
34 Hammers and saws
36 Long follower
37 Arthur of tennis
38 Make tapestries
39 Approve
40 Hwy.
41 *Being __* (Sellers film)
42 Fancy flapjack
43 Spray-can contents
45 Brushed off
47 Lass' counterpart
48 Bear in the stars
49 Blades on snow
55 Explosive: Abbr.
58 Inventor Elias
59 Lacks
60 Do a slow burn
61 Nights before
62 Public persona
63 Art __ ('20s style)
64 Superlative suffix
65 Carried around
66 Ticks off

DOWN

1 __ on it (hurry)
2 Pod veggie
3 Pound employee
4 Pack animal
5 Correct errors, e.g.
6 Ice skater's move
7 Wrap fur
8 Drop noisily
9 Florida collegian
10 Strong protest
11 Idaho neighbor
12 Descartes of math
16 Ukraine, formerly: Abbr.
21 "__ inhumanity to . . ."
22 Spinning toys
24 Blue spot on a map
26 Scarlett's maiden name
27 Social stratum
28 Foundry output
29 Sheltered places
30 Baker's material
31 With dropped jaw
32 Played cat and mouse
35 Canoe propeller
38 Novel genre
39 Heavenly bodies
41 Russian ruler
42 Scoundrels
44 Firstborn
46 Cared for
49 __ *Stoops to Conquer*
50 Tennis term
51 Lambs' moms
52 Verne character
53 In apple-pie order
54 Barely defeat
56 Bottle part
57 Ark complement
60 Star Wars defense program: Abbr.

BODY PAINTING by Fred Piscop

ACROSS
1 Piece of candy
5 SASE, for one
9 Tower of __
14 __ Man (Estevez film)
15 Spanish surrealist
16 Tabletop decoration
17 Give __ (care)
18 Music genre
19 __ und Drang
20 Military decoration
23 Language suffix
24 Cause by necessity
25 Egyptian amulet
27 CO clock setting
29 Blob
32 Liver, for one
36 Bar mitzvah dance
39 New York college
40 Phone line
41 Norton's workplace
42 __ War (1899-1902)

43 Having color
44 __-Lease Act
45 "... I __ my way"
46 "__ by Starlight"
48 Hockey great Bobby
50 __ a pin
53 Some navels
58 The __ Four (Beatles)
60 Coward
62 Mount the soapbox
64 Goalie's success
65 Dresden denial
66 Kitchen gadget
67 Radio message ender
68 Aware of
69 It __ a Thief
70 Waterman's wares
71 "A friend in __ ..."

DOWN
1 Window embellishment

2 Nick at Nite offering
3 Dizzying designs
4 Where's __? ('70 film)
5 '50s Fords
6 Lye, chemically
7 Crossword listings
8 Pale lavender
9 Small café
10 Picnic pest
11 Aristocrat
12 Wall features?
13 Old __, CT
21 Outline in detail
22 M*A*S*H role
26 Suspect's explanation
28 Quaker pronoun
30 "Dedicated to the __ Love"
31 Thespian's gig
32 Protest singer Phil
33 Beat decisively
34 Legal tender
35 Mix up
37 Have title to
38 Make over

41 Nominee listing
45 Beat decisively
47 Hens, e.g.
49 Galleon crew
51 Journalist Joseph
52 Drudge
54 Mortise mate

55 Actress Graff
56 Top-class
57 Church council
58 Army outpost
59 Opera solo
61 Pizzeria need
63 Placekicker's prop

EYE TEST by Dean Niles

ACROSS
1 __ Here To Eternity
5 Flat boats
10 "Dear me!"
14 Take a risk
15 "That's __" (Dean Martin tune)
16 Civil wrong
17 Prayer conclusion
18 Georgia city
19 Centers
20 Winnie-the-__
22 Rolaids rival
23 Okla. neighbor
24 90210 star
28 Pipe dregs
31 Eats lavishly
32 "Both Sides Now" composer
37 Lush
38 Cartoonist Wilson
39 Flub it
42 Nurses actress
46 Prefix for path
49 Some Arabs

50 1993 Nobel author
55 Atomic-particle suffix
56 Reptilian word form
57 Strikebreaker
60 Carry around
62 Van Gogh locale
64 Trumpeter Al
66 Wrathful feelings
67 New Hampshire city
68 Singer Adams
69 Backtalk
70 Our Miss Brooks star
71 Wise guy

DOWN
1 Regulatory agcy.
2 Kind of incline
3 Two-color cookie
4 Amahl and the Night Visitors composer
5 Zodiac animal

6 Stradivari's teacher
7 Point of attention
8 Step on
9 Feel vibes
10 Part of NATO
11 __ on (visit)
12 Esoteric
13 Bee barbs
21 Actress Celeste
25 Sit on the throne
26 The "bad" cholesterol: Abbr.
27 __ Abner
28 Spinners of a sort
29 Tic-tac-toe win
30 Cable network
33 Skater Babilonia
34 Chinese tea
35 Solo of Star Wars
36 "The __ near"
39 Atty.'s title
40 Louis XVI, e.g.
41 Med. staffers
42 Oahu welcome
43 __-pah band
44 Love god
45 Western spreads

46 Ear trouble
47 Mexican state
48 Govt. debt securities
51 Japanese metropolis
52 Less common

53 "If I __ the World"
54 Cara of Fame
58 Verdi heroine
59 Sea cell
61 Curvy letter
63 Sun Yat-__
65 Links platform

589 IN THE RED by Randolph Ross

ACROSS

1 Flower supports
6 Duck
11 Last section of the OED
14 Prevent legally
15 Runner-up
16 Wood chopper
17 Major no-no
19 Breadbasket st.
20 Forest peaks
21 Bounce
23 Actor Roger
24 Church feature
26 Hester wore one
31 Junks, e.g.
32 Circle of light
33 Social Register word
35 Chip in
36 Confidence
38 Gray's subj.
39 __ Tac Dough
40 Uniformed group
41 Free as __
42 Spring bloomer in D.C.
46 Butters
47 Noun ending
48 Houston or Austin
51 Meant
55 Flub one
56 Alabama's nickname
59 Lunes or martes
60 Bizarre
61 Mortise attachment
62 Wild blue yonder
63 Bridges
64 Sordid

DOWN

1 Religious group
2 Peter or Alexander
3 Raison d'__
4 Serve as emcee
5 Nasty ones
6 Go by
7 Tennessee footballers
8 Long-eared equine
9 "Agnus __"
10 Guevara's real first name
11 Western name
12 Corporate VIP
13 Red ink
18 A Christmas carol
22 Lear product
24 Word of woe
25 Throw stones at
26 Boom variety
27 Stumbling block
28 Seek a ride
29 Composer Morricone
30 Provide with new weapons
31 Mr. Masterson
34 Airport abbr.
36 Time in office
37 Sunbeams
38 Truant
40 Hypnotic states
41 Flight paths
43 Chapter in history
44 Frame inserts
45 Aware of
48 Danson and Weems
49 Actor Estrada
50 Picture of health?
51 "__ the Mood for Love"
52 Actress Merrill
53 Esau's alias
54 Disavow
57 Agent
58 Keogh cousin

590 MASTER QUOTE by William Lutwiniak

ACROSS

1 Cookie king Wally
5 Acts sullen
10 Dumbo's wings
14 Low blow
15 Disoriented
16 Squad ldrs.
17 START OF A QUOTE
20 Break
21 Insurers, for short
22 Frankfurt's river
23 Flick
24 Moved rudely
27 PART 2 OF QUOTE
31 Pluto's domain
32 Estonians, e.g.
34 Period
35 Continually
36 With 49 Across, source of quote
37 Principal
38 Summer sign
39 They may be counted
40 Founded
41 Likes a lot
43 Dillon portrayer
44 PART 3 OF QUOTE
45 "Too bad!"
46 Dissident Sakharov
49 See 36 Across
53 END OF QUOTE
56 "Vengeance is __ . . ."
57 Blue shade
58 1/16 ounce
59 Downhill racer
60 Ayn and Sally
61 Hardens

DOWN

1 Yonder
2 Song from Mondo Cane
3 Scoreboard info
4 Sort of sweater
5 Touched on the head
6 Supplementary
7 Function
8 Part of AT&T
9 Chew out
10 Bury
11 Sore
12 Way to travel
13 Aerospatiale products
18 Flanks
19 Fitzgerald et al.
23 Saws down
24 Book support
25 "__ nice day!"
26 Classical theater
28 Realty deal
29 Eastern Indians
30 __ of Iwo Jima
32 Opera voice
33 Actor Vigoda
36 Man of verse
37 Sloping roofs
39 Some Japanese-Americans
40 Moss leaf
42 Prepared hair
43 '86 sci-fi sequel
45 Plant pest
46 Jacket parts
47 Simon or Diamond
48 Moonrise actor Clark
50 In the bag
51 Sports datum
52 Certain meter reading
54 Frat letter
55 Prepare leather

LOVE AND KISSES by Shirley Soloway

ACROSS

1 School org.
4 Western height
8 Faux __
11 Word of woe
12 Asia's __ Sea
13 In any way
16 Mattress partner
18 Sitcom actress Roker
19 Book issue
20 Women warriors
22 __-mo replay
23 Heavy metal
24 Butter bit
25 Forbid
28 Not fooled by
30 Have a snack
32 "He's making __ and checking . . ."
34 Very annoying
38 Alluring
39 Actor Bean
40 Poker stake
41 Absolve from blame
43 Political ploy
44 Leningrad's river
45 Sailor's patron
47 __ Na Na
48 Lwyr.
50 Roman roadway
52 Mel of baseball
54 Church section
56 Lure
60 Go __ (deteriorate)
61 Sporting dogs
63 Singer Cara
64 Not active
65 Apple center
66 Pregrown grass
67 __-do-well
68 Naval off.

DOWN

1 Trudge
2 Car for hire
3 Office aides: Abbr.
4 Leave stranded
5 Ireland's nickname
6 __ Jose, CA
7 Pond growth
8 Logical contradiction
9 From __ (completely)
10 Jazz instruments
11 "Honest" nickname
14 Director Wertmuller
15 "__ we forget"
17 Boeing captain
21 Massenet opera
23 Popular seafood
25 Infield corner
26 Emcee Trebek
27 Watergate focus
29 Synagogue scroll
31 *The King and I* setting
33 "Auld Lang __"
35 Christmas carol
36 Mormons' mecca
37 Antitoxins
39 Make a speech
42 Forced to vacate
43 __ voce
46 __ superior (nuns' boss)
48 Play's start
49 Thunder god
51 Spritelike
53 Cessation of hostilities
55 Forbidden act
56 Wheel connector
57 After a while
58 Superiors of 68 Across: Abbr.
59 Mao __-tung
62 Keats creation

ALL BUSINESS by A.J. Santora

ACROSS

1 Lhasa __
5 "Phooey!"
8 Hair styles
13 Mythical birds
14 Tony-winner Merkel
15 Get in
16 Business-acquisition specialist
19 Company's tactic against 16 Across
20 Shooter ammo
21 Irritate
22 Bar crawler
23 Reproduce
25 Actor Voight
26 After expenses
28 __ polloi
29 Goes after apples
30 Prefix for physics
34 Building addition
35 Ogle
36 EMT technique
38 Selfish sort
39 "The __ Were"
41 Legal attachment
42 Plug's place
43 Psychic power
45 Little devil
46 Script direction
47 Mimic
49 Thompson of *Howards End*
51 Five-centime piece
52 Prey for 16 Across
57 Exec's insurance against 16 Across
58 Fabled Chicagoan
59 Adams or Ameche
60 Spanish 101 verb
61 Ruses
62 Chang's brother
63 Pentagram

DOWN

1 Compass drawings
2 Express contempt
3 In a gutsy way
4 Sea bird
5 Puppeteer Tillstrom
6 Microorganism
7 Women's weapons
8 Russian river
9 Men of the cloth
10 __ harm (was innocuous)
11 Runner Steve
12 Rev.'s recital
15 "Get Happy" composer
17 __ deal (initiate business)
18 Fish with a charge
23 Eat properly
24 Alley Oop's gal
25 Bliss
27 Have coming
29 Honey bunch
31 *Teahouse of __ Moon*
32 Thoroughfare
33 Monster
36 Ferber novel
37 Vitality
40 Work time for many
41 Citrus cooler
44 Garden flower
46 "__ a jolly good fellow"
47 Reef + lagoon
48 Word form for "fossil"
50 Sports award
51 Anatomical pouch
53 Users: Suff.
54 Sharp flavor
55 Singer James
56 Lacerate
57 House party: Abbr.

593 BREAKFAST MENU by Dean Niles

ACROSS

1 Texas city
5 __ *Entertainment!*
10 Small bog
14 Name that may ring a bell
15 Send a check
16 Unusual: Scot.
17 Jacks, for one
18 Love, to Luigi
19 Basics
20 Foundation of a sort
23 Azure, in Apulia
25 Oscar-winner Kingsley
26 Tightly packed
27 "__ luck!"
29 Ballet barre
32 Andrea __ Sarto
33 Vicinity
34 '50s car feature
37 English essayist
42 "__ Mom . . ." (teen attention-getter)
43 Elite or pica
44 Mil. address
47 __ *dixit*
48 Extra
49 Center of power
51 Mideast federation: Abbr.
53 WWII agency
54 Klutz
59 "Do __ once!" ("Hurry!")
60 Actor Delon
61 Continental prefix
64 Granular snow
65 People: Sp.
66 Green land
67 European river
68 Ltr. enclosures
69 Holiday

DOWN

1 Roguish wit
2 Ms. Gardner
3 Software utilizer
4 Draft rating
5 Vestige
6 Musclebound guy
7 Frenzied
8 Wear out
9 Pipe part
10 Fault phenomenon
11 Relax
12 Point a finger at
13 Music genre
21 Hoop grp.
22 Wing it, in a way
23 Gil __ (Le Sage hero)
24 Singer of *Fame*
28 Bank feature
29 Nouveau __
30 Set down
31 In that case
34 Canvas covering
35 Colony residents
36 Postwar alliance
38 Poker move
39 Attention-getter
40 Magnum __
41 Untouchables name
44 Inkless postage stamp
45 Acted sullenly
46 Musical interval
48 Bonnet buzzer
50 Out-and-out
51 Draw together
52 Actress Moorehead
55 Joplin pieces
56 Dog bane
57 Fleming and Smith
58 Hazard to navigation
62 Slow down: Mus.
63 Number or pronoun

594 JOLLY OLD ENGLAND by Matt Gaffney

ACROSS

1 Poetic contraction
4 Flowerless plants
9 __ Clemente
12 Hay portion
14 Ridiculous
15 L.A. thoroughfare
16 "Tower Bridge Ahead"?
19 Diner offerings
20 Escape capture
21 NASA name
22 Big __ outdoors
24 Stubborn sorts
27 Skier's transport
28 Sternward
31 Where most people live
32 Diviner's decks
34 Draw
35 Chaucer works?
38 Kept out of sight
39 He doesn't buy it
40 Spender, for one
41 Important period
42 Industrial containers
43 Word on a nickel
44 Upper-crust
46 P __ "pneumonia"
48 Enjoy
50 Providence neighbor
54 Lord Nelson?
57 Nonstandard contraction
58 Lot fillers
59 Structural suffix
60 Unseen substance
61 Kilimanjarolike
62 Rug rat

DOWN

1 Recipe amt.
2 Greet with pomp
3 Ms. Korbut
4 Tootled, perhaps
5 __ nous
6 Encouraging sounds
7 Vane dir.
8 Match part
9 Tryout of a sort
10 Passed easily
11 Winning margin
13 Beg
15 Become cloying
17 Singer Redding
18 Name in the news
22 "Plato is __": Nietzsche
23 Nymph chaser
24 Papier-__
25 Delta rival
26 Krystle Carrington portrayer
27 Bridge support
29 Steak cut
30 Battery components
32 Unexpected pleasure
33 Ease off
36 __ *Madigan*
37 Starts speaking candidly
43 Fifi's five
45 Artist's quarters
46 Street-sign shape
47 Fresh
48 Frat party
49 Puccini piece
50 Roman orator
51 Arcade infraction
52 Billion-selling cookie
53 Barber's call
55 Scale notes
56 Starter's need

595 ON TV by S.E. Booker

ACROSS

1 Dampen a stamp
5 Rendezvous
10 In vogue
14 Will-__-wisp
15 Uproar
16 __ Hashanah
17 Toe the line
18 With 62 Across, Billy Wilder quote on TV
20 Most advanced
22 "... __ singing birds": Johnson
23 That is, for long
25 Tour de force
26 Brooch
28 Head set?
30 Unwelcome winds
34 U.K. part
35 Clumsy one
37 Pleasure boat
38 Runner, maybe
39 Writer Jones
41 Deli bread
42 Early infatuation
45 Eighth word of "The Star Spangled Banner"
47 Trucking unit
48 Sewed an edge
50 __ colada
51 Newman/Neal film
52 __ impasse
54 Blake's nickname
56 "Guaranteed!"
59 California's motto
62 See 18 Across
65 Have __ for (crave)
66 "Ma, he's making eyes __"
67 Stared at
68 __ off (angry)
69 The best
70 "__ Fools Fall in Love?"
71 Make out

DOWN

1 Cuckoo bird?
2 "Let __" (Beatles tune)
3 With 31 Down, Frank Lloyd Wright quote on TV
4 __ up (tense)
5 "__, folks!"
6 Nonsense
7 "That hurts!"
8 Grain bundle
9 Made suede
10 *City Slickers* star
11 Cowboy Gibson
12 "There __ little enemy": Franklin
13 Pot holder
19 Rips apart
21 Go for
24 Aligned
26 Seafood
27 Toughen
29 Handbag holder
31 See 3 Down
32 "Happy Birthday __"
33 Use up
36 Campy exclamation
40 Sly hint
43 Breaks
44 Excited
46 Actor in *The Jungle Book*
49 Scopes' defender
53 Stable sound
55 Furious
56 Italian auto
57 Aware of
58 Sgt. Preston's group
60 Don't give up
61 *60 Minutes* name
63 Wily
64 Multi-vol. lexicon

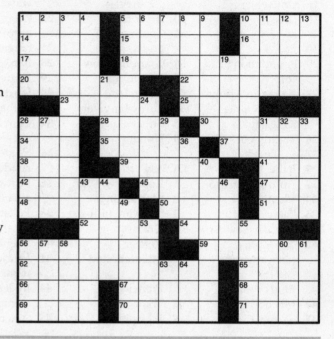

596 LENGTHWISE by Shirley Soloway

ACROSS

1 Ship's dock
5 In flames
10 Demeanor
14 Concerning
15 Carnival features
16 __-European (prototypical language)
17 Boy Scout beginner
19 Chem. and biol.
20 Sharon of Israel
21 Actress Lanchester
22 "__ went thataway!"
23 Riddle, e.g.
25 Melt
27 Marvin or Grant
28 Search for
31 Meadow males
34 Sincere
37 Happy
38 __ Baba
39 Fast cars
41 Atlas page
42 Taco topping
44 Prerecord
45 Capri, for one
46 Assumption
48 Dancer Miller
50 Pepper's partner
51 Wipes off
54 Makes believe
56 Alda of *M*A*S*H*
59 Stacked up
61 Winnie-the-__
62 Railroad boss
64 Sound of mind
65 Spread joy
66 Carryall
67 Bullfight bravos
68 Writer Runyon
69 Alps surface

DOWN

1 Pocket bread
2 Not moving
3 Comic Kovacs
4 Distributes again
5 Airport info: Abbr.
6 Drummer's companion
7 Role model
8 Early autos
9 Large homestead
10 Faux pas
11 Little crawlers
12 Singer Adams
13 Prone to snoop
18 Otherwise
24 Architect Saarinen
26 Alters pants
28 Hog food
29 Russian range
30 Use a keyboard
31 Scraping sound
32 Winglike
33 Major step
35 Diminutive ending
36 Coach Parseghian
39 Solid rain
40 Costly
43 Breaks to bits
45 Won't budge
47 Remained
49 Wine valley
51 Put an __ (stop)
52 Rock singer __ John
53 Take care of
54 Lhasa __ (dog)
55 Heat source
57 "Ooh __!"
58 Composer Khachaturian
60 Made a sketch
63 Half the honeymooners

597 FAMILY TREE by Eric Albert

ACROSS

1 Fast-food favorite
7 Shipmate of Jason
15 Shrewd-minded
16 Musical chestnut
17 English essayist
19 Betelgeuse, e.g.
20 Half of *dos*
21 Tiny circle
24 Thesaurus name
26 Sleeve fold
30 Not cool
33 Pooh pal's signature
34 Unimportant
35 In coastal Maine
37 Diverse
38 Famous sharpshooter
40 Chore
42 King David, for one
45 Feminist Friedan
46 Distress signal
47 __ Barbara, CA
48 Foundation
49 In a lather
51 Swindle
52 A ways away
53 Geezer
56 *Evening Shade* actress
64 Short piano piece
65 Split
66 Filament element
67 Tomboy

DOWN

1 Cave flier
2 Adjective ending
3 Racing-car initials
4 "__ the word!"
5 Rat-__
6 Señor Chavez
7 Inspire wonder in
8 Actress Welch
9 Sow sound
10 Buckeye state
11 Nantes negative
12 Bow line?
13 Manipulate
14 Mystery writer Josephine
18 Nod off
21 Defective bomb
22 Yoko __
23 Stymies
25 Degenerate
26 The pix biz
27 Eternal
28 Pro
29 Cook bacon
31 Natural-born
32 Candy cost, once
34 Cogitates
36 Help out
37 Jamaican music
39 In itself
40 Flow back
41 Stephen of *The Crying Game*
43 Pigpen
44 Phone bug
46 Undisturbed
49 Nun's wear
50 Fish unofficially
52 Thomas Waller
54 Skagerrak seaport
55 He and she
56 W. Va. setting
57 "Skip to My __"
58 Hostelry
59 Move at a sharp angle
60 Brown shade
61 Stripling
62 *All About __*
63 Strong longing

598 SCORE KEEPING by Dean Niles

ACROSS

1 Famous feminist
5 City rides
9 Did the lawn
14 Magical syllables
15 On the main
16 Spring up
17 See 51 Across
18 Small brook
19 Senator Helms
20 Diver's locale
22 Gave the willies to
24 Attention-getter
25 Expose
26 Genesis craft
29 Sills song
31 Brought down
36 German engraver
38 Bad-check marking
40 St. Theresa of __
41 Knock for __ (stun)
42 Cruet contents
43 Fix a street
44 Sean's family
45 Vitamin stat.
46 Savage
47 Hardly high-class
49 Sicilian spouter
51 With 17 Across, temp phrase
52 Poet's contraction
54 Glacial mass
56 Mexico neighbor
60 Art style
64 Hold firmly
65 Word of praise
67 Buffalo's county
68 Distress signal
69 Actress Sommer
70 Work alone
71 Tijuana title
72 Pit or stone
73 Reception interference

DOWN

1 Anti-DWI org.
2 Tony's cousin
3 Shoe stretcher
4 Buccaneer's home
5 Calling
6 Turkey's area
7 __ canto (singing style)
8 Nacho dip
9 Shaw play
10 Sweet treat
11 Fab rival
12 To be, to Ovid
13 Boy Scout act
21 Marksman
23 Ms. Zadora
26 Adjust to conditions
27 Foot-long device
28 Swedish money
30 Stage digression
32 Declare positively
33 Gym exercise
34 Overjoy
35 Brave one
37 Long times
39 Busted
48 Hankering
50 Had to have
53 Goes ape
55 *Cagney & Lacey* star
56 Poodle plaints
57 Stir up
58 A Karamazov
59 Goose egg
61 Wrinkle remover
62 Storage place
63 Catty remark
66 *Corrida* cry

599 PIOUS PEOPLE by Matt Gaffney

ACROSS
1. Riga residents
6. Toreador's "Bravo!"
9. Beer ingredient
13. Awesome hotel lobbies
14. Kook
15. Bring out dinner
16. Pious silents star?
19. Pious toon?
20. Under the weather
21. "__ was saying . . ."
22. Anytown, U.S.A. address
26. Cereal grain
28. Bring to naught
29. Act as facilitator
35. Stuck-up ones
37. This very minute
38. Newsperson Shriver
39. Galileo gadget
41. Sean Connery, e.g.
42. Grassy field
43. Mansion's grounds
45. Uncommon sense
47. Thirst
51. Pious novelist?
55. Reggie Jackson's pious nickname?
58. *My Fair Lady* character
59. Beatnik's interjection
60. Hair, in Hamburg
61. René's head
62. Hog's home
63. Went astray

DOWN
1. Fond du __, WI
2. Ordinal ending
3. Missile's path: Abbr.
4. Akron product
5. Spicy dips
6. Irish surname
7. Soaps star Susan
8. Fictional Frome
9. Thin, crispy bread
10. Some Semites
11. XXIX doubled
12. Midmorning
15. Fitness center
17. "Not from where __!"
18. Inert gas
22. Is forced to
23. Novelist Rice
24. Admired person
25. Economist's honor
27. USN officer
29. Yoko __
30. Mini-explosion
31. Ram's mate
32. Killer whale
33. Hilarious person
34. Quench completely
36. Vane dir.
40. West Pointer
43. Julia Roberts' brother
44. Boil with anger
45. Monsieur Zola
46. Trash-collecting dept.
48. Moppets' schools: Abbr.
49. Dieter of rhyme
50. Literary device
52. Beauregard's grp.
53. Fly high
54. Ski-lift type
55. Ran into
56. Before
57. Spectrum part

600 TOEING THE MARK? by A.J. Santora

ACROSS
1. Inhabitants: Suff.
5. Some chops
9. Boastful boxer
12. START OF A QUOTE
15. MIDDLE OF QUOTE
16. END OF QUOTE
17. Thompson of *Family*
18. Tom's mate
19. Sleep __ (decide later)
20. Incompetents
21. Mythical nymphs
23. Ventilated thoroughly
26. Massive
27. Vowel rhyme
28. Massachusetts motto word
29. *Casino* __
30. Make a blouse
31. Swizzle
33. Plays the ponies
35. Ecol. agcy.
38. Lauder et al.
40. Chervil or chive
44. Source of quote
46. Pin type
47. Forgiveness
48. A Finger Lake
49. Ancient serf
50. German coal area
52. Kiddie __ (*Jeopardy!* category)
53. Word form for "thought"
54. Magic words
57. Squirrel nosh
58. Harbor barrier
59. Some AMA members
60. Part of CBS
61. Polaroid part

DOWN
1. __ numbers (rounded)
2. Asian capital
3. They do their level best?
4. Bayh, Biden, or Boxer: Abbr.
5. Sundial numeral
6. Rapture
7. Half a Heyerdahl title
8. Computer perch, perhaps
9. Fabled warriors
10. Irma's epithet
11. Fretting
13. __ Island Red
14. Berry and Kercheval
17. Scotch partner
20. *Reader's Encyclopedia* compiler
22. Long time
24. Señora Perón
25. Actor's résumé
27. Cardiologist's adjective
29. Gotten up
32. Doctrine
34. Holmes' "One Hoss __"
35. Piece of artwork
36. Stacked high
37. Little chimps
39. Champs follower
41. Take after
42. What you eat
43. Straw hats
45. Melville novel
46. Cavalier poet
48. Heavy barrel
51. Med. subj.
54. Dict. abbr.
55. Use a crowbar
56. __ ammoniac

601   OUT WITH THE OLD by Shirley Soloway

ACROSS

1 Purchase price
5 Egg-shaped
10 Movie terrier
14 Opera solo
15 __ apparent reason
16 Sgts., for example
17 Balers' tools
19 Get bigger
20 Perfectly
21 Fill up
23 Upperclassman: Abbr.
24 Reading and B&O
26 Low down
27 Like some stomachs
30 Four-poster, for instance
33 Add up to
36 Shoshoneans
37 Dover __ (fish)
38 "__ to the wise . . ."
39 Review badly
40 Got up
41 Not so much
42 Composer Porter
43 Croissant creator
44 Asner and Wynn
45 Small carpet
47 Poet Teasdale
49 Bro's sibling
50 Impersonate
53 Out-and-out
56 Starts a tennis point
58 French composer
59 Dinner entrée
62 Author Hunter
63 Ghostlike
64 Tiny creature
65 Boggs of baseball
66 Golfer Sam
67 Otherwise

DOWN

1 Marvel and America: Abbr.
2 Mythical hunter
3 Shankar's instrument
4 Social asset
5 Proposes
6 "Hinky Dinky Parlay __"
7 Bobby of hockey
8 Prepares the presses
9 Square-dance call
10 Ms. Dickinson
11 Clippings holder
12 Horn sound
13 ". . . have mercy on such __"
18 Miami paper
22 __ *Little Indians*
25 Dazed state
27 Traffic jammers
28 Author Calvino
29 Extends a subscription
31 Actress Sommer
32 Forest forager
33 Anecdote
34 Had a debt
35 Dinner preparation step
37 Pirate's haul
40 One who mistreats
42 "__ Are" (Mathis tune)
45 Singer's syllable
46 Took a chance
48 Repent
50 Be of use
51 Annoyances
52 Lauder of lipstick
53 Used a bubble pipe
54 Volcanic flow
55 Afterwards
57 Capital of Italy
60 Noun suffix
61 FBI's counterpart

602   PHASES OF THE MOON by Dean Niles

ACROSS

1 Bide one's time
5 Eng. honor
8 Lawn growth
13 __ *of Green Gables*
14 __ and crafts
16 Hair-care activity
17 Harplike instrument
18 __ as a button
19 Reference list
20 Porky features
23 Three __ match
24 Southern sch.
25 Spills the beans
30 Pie piece
32 Turnstile opening
34 All __ (listening)
35 Literary collection
37 Nigerian town
38 Conclusions
39 Fanatical group
43 Cartel: Abbr.
44 Mork's home
45 Many mos.
46 "Somebody bet __ bay"
47 Role for Stack
49 With an __ (in consideration of)
53 Wifely
55 Preserve, as fruit
57 Geometry proof letters
58 Debussy piece
61 __ the Hutt (*Star Wars* series villain)
65 Sports org.
66 Whence sunrise is seen
67 Outsider
68 *Edward Scissorhands* star
69 Rescind a correction
70 Give rise to
71 Ready to go
72 Antitoxins

DOWN

1 Luxuriate
2 "__ Can Whistle"
3 Progress
4 High-schooler
5 *Miracle on 34th Street* store
6 Caesar's addressee
7 Caesar's question
8 Ground grain
9 __ Tin Tin
10 Here __ now
11 Point farthest from NNW
12 Dr. Ruth topic
15 Placed in the mail
21 Actress Verdugo
22 Mel's Diner, e.g.
26 Very small
27 "Auld __ Syne"
28 Earth: Ger.
29 Draft grp.
31 Male goose
33 Last __ (final at-bat)
36 Like some modern music
39 Bobcat
40 Negate
41 Limerick location
42 Cara of *Fame*
43 Old French coin
48 Difficult situation
50 Draw a parallel
51 More wound up
52 Folk-blues singer
54 "__ Get Started"
56 Adjust to conditions
59 Readies champagne
60 Negative suffix
61 Boxer's motion
62 Dark malt
63 Tom Hanks film
64 Stinging insect

603 — OPPOSITES by Wayne R. Williams

ACROSS
1 Tot holder
5 Fancy
9 Russian range
14 Protagonist
15 Lamb's pen name
16 Flier
17 Lawyer's cinch
20 Mount of Moses
21 Non-believer
22 Opposite of WSW
23 Witty reply
27 Scottish loch
29 Like Abner
30 More tense
35 Posed questions
37 Medieval-romance figure
38 Leaning
41 Explosive letters
43 Magic sticks
44 Dwarfed tree
46 Gray and Moran
48 Necessitate
49 Take first
50 Fish choice
54 Excuses
57 Holiday concoction
58 Cha-cha accompaniment
62 John Jacob or Mary
64 Quite plainly
68 Tizzies
69 Dueling tool
70 Ed or Nancy
71 Actor Davis
72 Drenches
73 Makes one

DOWN
1 Picked
2 Feel discontent
3 Cara and Papas
4 __ fide
5 Coop up
6 Antique
7 Boom-bah beginning
8 Lots of laughs
9 With 36 Down, Sandy Dennis movie
10 Texas university
11 Jai __
12 Setback
13 Editor's instruction
18 One of the four elements
19 Express vocally
24 Type
25 Painter Mondrian
26 Yesterday's papers
28 Latin beat
31 See-through material
32 Writer Fleming
33 *Howards __*
34 Sts.
36 See 9 Down
38 Presidential nickname
39 Heavy weight
40 Bank pymt.
42 Small combo
45 Of the intestine
47 Rural stopover
51 Punctual
52 Took spoils
53 Way out
55 To one side
56 Old saying
58 Japanese soup ingredient
59 Sothern and Sheridan
60 Slugger's stats
61 Word form for "height"
63 Major Barbara's creator
65 *The Naked __*
66 Profit
67 Since: Fr.

604 — ITALIAN TOUR by Randolph Ross

ACROSS
1 Teacher's deg.
5 Tourney winner
10 Goof
13 Orbit point
15 Actress Anouk
16 Social Register word
17 Italian eateries?
19 Surcharge
20 Italian utility?
22 "Moonlight" music
23 Cuts in two
25 List extending abbrs.
26 DDS group
28 Make a sharp turn
29 Mao __-tung
30 Prince Charles' game
32 Pumpkin relatives
34 Italian soul singer?
36 Agree (to)
39 Sermon topics
40 Reagan DOD project
43 Boxing venue
44 EMK's nickname
45 Alda's TV costar
46 Expurgate
49 Most ready for picking
51 Italian bug catcher?
54 Apiece
55 Italian sweet stuff?
57 *People __ Funny*
58 They're coded
59 "The best is __ be"
60 Dr. Leary's drug
61 Doesn't hide
62 Deer

DOWN
1 Cartographer's product
2 Taps
3 Main meaning
4 Ross and Rigg
5 Relief org.
6 San Juan or Blueberry
7 Microscope sight
8 Grenoble gratitude
9 Annoyers
10 Temptress
11 Did a double take
12 Reviewer Reed
14 Name for a Dalmatian
18 Top bond rating
21 Variety show
22 Go down
24 Next yr.'s alums
26 Norton nemesis
27 Search for water
30 Barrie character
31 Table scrap
32 Canasta cousin
33 Army sch.
34 Opened
35 Went underground
36 Parabolic path
37 Bilko portrayer
38 Looked villainous
40 Certify under oath
41 Question the truth of
42 Addams' cousin
44 Plains dwelling
45 More agile
47 Simone and Foch
48 Rumor result, maybe
49 Singer Cooder et al.
50 Teeny-weeny
52 Complaints
53 More, to Browning
54 Buddy
56 Battery abbr.

605 TABLE MANNERS by Donna J. Stone

ACROSS

1 Drug buster
5 *Rich Man, Poor Man* author
9 Kitchen kingpin
13 Geometry calculation
14 Seated Beatle
15 Hartman or Bonet
16 Beethoven's birthplace
17 __ Selassie
18 Jai __
19 START OF A QUIP BY HENNY YOUNGMAN
22 Ryan's *Love Story* costar
23 Short play
24 Like wreaths and pumpkins
29 Thickset
33 Current amount
34 Gen. Robt. __
36 Col. Tibbets' mother
37 Compete
38 MIDDLE OF QUIP
40 Litter sound
41 Bring bliss to
43 Pony
44 Cry over cards?
45 Illinois city
47 Reno residents
49 Dull
51 Ivy Leaguer
52 END OF QUIP
59 Home of Columbus
60 Transmission parts
61 Soho streetcar
63 *The Egg* __
64 Remove a Reebok
65 Othello's foe
66 Disposition
67 It came from Montana
68 Role for Liz

DOWN

1 Catch a crook
2 Graceland name
3 Monsieur Clair
4 Look for votes
5 Wild guess
6 It grows on you
7 Van Gogh locale
8 Inflicts
9 Moore of *The Lone Ranger*
10 Hawaiian city
11 Genesis redhead
12 Evenhanded
14 Fez wearer
20 "Evil Woman" rockers
21 Check cheat
24 Reserved, as a seat
25 Author Zola
26 "Silent, upon __ in Darien": Keats
27 Baldwin of *Malice*
28 Pick up
30 It may give you pause
31 Comic Robert
32 Tedium symptoms
35 Singer Adams
38 Last name in law
39 Heads
42 Gossipy paper
44 Not too bright
46 Outstanding
48 Smith and Yankovic
50 Serengeti scavenger
52 Wander
53 "What have I done?"
54 Fashionable resort
55 Feedbag contents
56 *Battle Cry* author
57 Orenburg's river
58 Kid at court
62 Bossy remark?

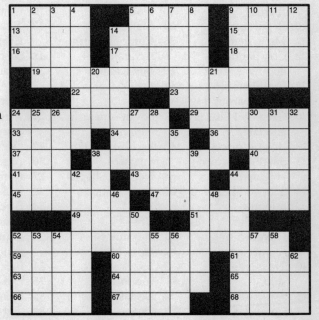

606 SPEAK UP! by Shirley Soloway

ACROSS

1 Adored one
5 Heavenly instrument
9 *Leave __ Beaver*
13 Neck part
14 Screenwriter James
15 Love, in Lille
16 Claire and Balin
17 Rickey requirement
18 Boxing arenas
19 Speak the truth
22 Map close-up
23 Stephen of *The Crying Game*
24 Suction tube
27 More briny
31 "__ Blue?"
32 Proportions
36 Singer Fitzgerald
37 Chatter on and on
40 Richard of films
41 Swamp creatures, for short
42 Insect egg
43 Pours a second cup, perhaps
45 Jane and Edmund
47 Casual shirt
48 War horse
51 Say something nice
57 *The Lady* __
58 Temperate
59 He loved Irish Rose
60 Sky lights?
61 "Ye __ Gift Shoppe"
62 Take a nap
63 May celebrants
64 Wintertime vehicle
65 Changes colors

DOWN

1 "What's __ for me?"
2 Victor Borge is one
3 Milky gemstone
4 Actor __ Howard
5 Brings to a stop
6 Nimble
7 Send in payment
8 Take a look
9 Did a takeoff on
10 Singer Tennille
11 Pulls hard
12 Hosp. areas
15 Sharon of Israel
20 Opening bars
21 Mistake remover
24 Latin dad
25 Reflection
26 Rice style
27 London neighborhood
28 Massey of the movies
29 Pixieish
30 River transports
33 Fisherman
34 Afternoon socials
35 Novel ending?
38 Sweater makers
39 Made a request
44 Yorkshire city
46 Playwright Albee
48 Ability
49 The squiggle in *señor*
50 Came to a close
51 "Do __ others . . ."
52 Mine car
53 Noted cookie maker
54 Follow orders
55 Get up
56 PD investigators
57 Doctrine

607   LITTLE CIRCLES by Wayne R. Williams

ACROSS

1 Night-sky sight
5 Jacob's brother
9 Not suitable
14 Sky bear
15 __ best friend
16 Showy flower
17 Halfway into a flight
20 Regulations
21 Menu item
22 Comparative ending
23 Protuberance
24 Wheels around
28 Gregory Hines specialty
29 River projects
33 Small, brownish antelope
34 Shaped like a rainbow
36 Night flier
37 Historical-movie requirement
40 Traveler's stop
41 Static
42 Composer Erik

43 Relative of "great" and "keen"
45 TV hardware
46 Bit of food
47 Alternative to a saber
49 Name a knight
50 Not noticed
53 Maladies
58 Computer-printer technology
60 Bay window
61 Pennsylvania port
62 South American nation
63 Reddish-brown quartzes
64 Neckline shapes
65 Air pollution

DOWN

1 Has dinner
2 Horse's pace
3 The largest continent
4 Declaim violently
5 Overacts

6 Morley of *60 Minutes*
7 Jillian and Beattie
8 GI entertainers
9 Overturn
10 Caught fish, in a way
11 Bridge quorum
12 Concerning
13 Newcastle's river
18 School fee
19 Examine a case again
23 Mother-of-pearl
24 Arrive unexpectedly
25 Goddess of peace
26 Actress __ Lisi
27 Kimono sash
28 Reliance
30 Borders on
31 Scientist Curie
32 Drum or wool material
34 Burning
35 Fail to heed
38 Museum guide
39 Old sailor

44 Came down in buckets
46 Rumples
48 Rings out
49 Southern anthem
50 Japanese vegetables
51 Writer Ephron
52 Be up and about
53 Ominous
54 Poisonous snakes
55 Part of a pipe
56 Architect Saarinen
57 Self-satisfied
59 Gun the motor

608   DOUBLE TAKES by Randolph Ross

ACROSS

1 A Baldwin boy
5 Mommy's mate
10 Frisbee, e.g.
14 *De __* (afresh)
15 Peruvian peaks
16 Famous next-to-last words
17 Gift for a Texan with a swelled head?
20 In moderation
21 Sonny and Cher numbers, e.g.
22 Genealogical construction
23 Beseeched
25 Like cows in India
28 Escaped a debt, with "out"
32 Hosiery shade
33 Small pies
34 Acapulco gold
35 Expanded Vivaldi opus?
39 EMK's nickname
40 Street show
41 Sooner of the '30s

42 Dashboard device
44 Provides shelter
46 All over
47 Roseanne's first last name
48 Man of Muscat
51 Proverbial place for hard labor
55 Indicator of very fast beard growth?
58 What the nose knows
59 Bring to mind
60 Dried up
61 Many, many years
62 Limey's pal
63 Clothes lines

DOWN

1 Unwelcome picnic guests
2 *Wayne's World* costar Rob
3 Tied
4 Draw a conclusion
5 Sleep sofa
6 Point of view

7 WWII turning point
8 __ Rio, TX
9 Fashion monogram
10 Strip
11 Spillane's __ *Jury*
12 RBI or ERA
13 Budget reductions
18 Become bored
19 Black Sea city
23 Intrinsically
24 Past the deadline
25 Fracas
26 Felt sore
27 Words to live by
28 Irrigate
29 Appearances
30 Bert's friend
31 Medicinal allocations
33 Tossed
36 Peaceful
37 Concert proceeds
38 Moonshiner's concoction
43 Estates
44 WWII admiral

45 Word form for "straight"
47 Scott : slavery :: __ : affirmative action
48 Midwestern tribesman
49 Beatles' "Love __"
50 Shortly
51 Highlander
52 __ *fixe*
53 *Cheers* character
54 Woolly females
56 Moon lander
57 Cato's eggs

609 SMOKE DETECTORS by Cathy Millhauser

ACROSS

1 Traversed the Tiber
5 Caesar's partner
9 Berry of *Jungle Fever*
14 "Eek!"
15 They give a hoot
16 Euclidean statement
17 Sneezing attack?
19 Tarantula toxin
20 Palos pal
21 Zilch
23 Cable network
24 Some Czechs' smellers?
28 Sha Na Na member
32 Odin's offspring
33 Mare fare
34 Sgt., e.g.
36 Forbidden
40 Nosy pair on TV?
44 Actor Davis
45 License plate
46 SSS status
47 Absorbs, with "up"
50 With caution
52 Bee's beezer?
56 Yoko __
57 Thicke of *Growing Pains*
58 Dame Edith
63 Corday's victim
65 "Congrats" to Schnozzola?
68 Soul
69 ". . . __ saw Elba"
70 Carryall
71 Windshield attachment
72 Ooze (out)
73 Portent

DOWN

1 Love seat partner
2 Impulse
3 Part of ABM
4 Synthesizer inventor
5 Corn holder
6 Keep one's balance?
7 Horseshoe game sound
8 Invite for a date
9 Indigents
10 *Wizard of Oz* prop
11 *Peanuts* kid
12 Relaxed, so to speak
13 Actresses Samms and Thompson
18 Dandies
22 Bible bk.
25 Casino city
26 Sunoco rival
27 Cicero, notably
28 "Jump," in computerese
29 Bowl cheers
30 Hot times in Toulouse
31 Italian town
35 Former Giants star
37 Proclivity
38 Pitcher Hershiser
39 Key opener?
41 Post-delivery
42 Swedish car
43 Hemispherical home
48 Bakker's TV club
49 Embarrasses
51 Jamesian biographer Leon
52 Lapp, for one
53 Fatuous
54 Antiseptic acid
55 Harden
59 Nix
60 Enrico Fermi's concern
61 Short letter
62 Cinematographer Nykvist
64 Doc bloc
66 Alphabetic ultimate
67 Nil

610 CANINE QUEST by Matt Gaffney

ACROSS

1 Chan phrase
5 It may be grand
9 Loser of '17
13 Angry mood
15 Toledo's water
16 Mrs. Chaplin
17 START OF A QUIP
20 Health club
21 With 30 Down, Porter tune
22 Minimal money
23 Charlotte NBAers
25 Ski-lift type
27 Pitcher part
28 Early VP
29 Ore. neighbor
32 Nag
34 Sports palaces
36 ". . . __ iron bars a cage"
37 PART 2 OF QUIP
40 Bustle
41 Trail users
42 Takes home
43 Bran variety
44 Small songbird
45 Knight title
46 Asian beasts
47 Gorbachev's successor
51 Berth place
53 Lug around
54 As well
55 PART 3 OF QUIP
59 Like crazy
60 Soothing plant
61 Couric of TV
62 Farmer's place
63 China buys
64 END OF QUIP

DOWN

1 Prone to imitation
2 Zoo favorite
3 Calculator button
4 No longer stylish
5 Kids
6 *Trinity* author
7 Nautical gear
8 Ginza gelt
9 Rapunzel's home
10 Augsburg offspring
11 Working without __ (acting riskily)
12 Sprinted
14 Swiss mathematician
18 Favorite
19 Egyptian amulet
24 Midday breaks
25 Home style
26 Sea cells
28 German region
29 Coast-to-coast road
30 See 21 Across
31 Part of BA
32 Borgia's "bye"
33 *M*A*S*H* star
34 Smug expression
35 Little shavers
38 Impede a plan
39 Troop group
45 Glossy
46 Barbra role
47 Team frames
48 Ordinal ending
49 Ancient Greek region
50 Eminent
51 Mucho money
52 Object of adulation
53 Harness race
55 Dear old one?
56 Used to be
57 Grand __ Opry
58 Sleeper, e.g.

611 GIVE UP? by Shirley Soloway

ACROSS
1 Attired
5 Mary's pet
9 Entertainers
14 Conceal
15 Iris layer
16 Kukla's pal
17 Up above
18 Price
19 Actress Davis
20 SURRENDER
23 Have a feeling about
24 Wine region of Italy
25 Boulevard liners
28 Rooftop structure
33 Swelled head
36 Counts calories
39 __ Romeo (car)
40 SURRENDERS
44 Actor Richard
45 Firm
46 Dads of Jrs.
47 Make a choice
50 Forget to include
52 Sound like a snake
55 Characteristic
59 SURRENDER
65 More or less
66 Cleo's river
67 TV handyman
68 Washer cycle
69 Church area
70 Roman road
71 Runs into
72 Have a strong odor
73 Respond rudely

DOWN
1 Converses casually
2 Graceful
3 Add embellishment
4 Put out of power
5 Lynda Bird's sister
6 Stratford's river
7 Hostess Perle
8 Washups
9 Render immobile
10 Butter alternative
11 Did in
12 Utensil point
13 Circus star
21 Attaches permanently
22 Greek vowel
26 Farrow of *Zelig*
27 Takes up a hem
29 Brit. fliers
30 Troubles
31 Distant, to Donne
32 Falls behind
33 Farm females
34 Redcoat general
35 Egg-shaped
37 However, for short
38 Grain housing
41 Chemical suffix
42 Comic Conway
43 Archie's mate
48 Skydivers' needs
49 Gratuity
51 Country singer Randy
53 Submarine system
54 Take potshots (at)
56 O'Day or Baker
57 Runs without moving
58 Ivan and Peter
59 Cause damage to
60 Theater award
61 Solitary
62 Homemaker's nemesis
63 "What __ is new?"
64 Look for

612 LONG TIME by Wayne R. Williams

ACROSS
1 Fill too tightly
5 *M*A*S*H* star
9 Tint
14 Protagonist
15 Dates
16 Atelier item
17 Long time
20 Track official
21 Hatcher of *Lois & Clark*
22 Park art
25 Flairs
30 Strike sharply
32 "The Raven" lady
33 Existed
36 Saudis, e.g.
38 Rafsanjani's land
39 Long time
43 Gold patch
44 Prefix for "sun"
45 Compass dir.
46 Puts up
49 Blockheads
51 Relatives of roads
53 Boat building area
57 Carpenter's need
59 French brother
60 Long time
66 Garden area
67 Hurries
68 Pennsylvania port
69 Rider's straps
70 Woodcutters
71 Mtg.

DOWN
1 Confabs
2 Send payment
3 Lure of the kitchen
4 Some impressionist paintings
5 Volcanic dust
6 August sign
7 Quick and skillful
8 Selling feature
9 Doddering
10 Possessed
11 Simile center
12 Susan of *L.A. Law*
13 Loop trains
18 Author Capote
19 Russian river
23 Ireland
24 Hidden supply
26 Novelist Bagnold
27 Ephron and others
28 TV dinner holders
29 Significance
31 Dropped back
33 Hand signals
34 Paying attention
35 More crafty
37 Met show-stoppers
40 Fairy-tale opener
41 Small brook
42 Let know
47 Domingo and Pavarotti, e.g.
48 Laurel or Getz
50 Spending frenzies
52 Indian sect members
54 "__ the World"
55 *Mrs. __ Goes to Paris*
56 Affirmative comments
58 *Star Wars* princess
60 A ways away
61 Mine find
62 Diamond stat
63 Put on
64 Evergreen tree
65 Draft letters

613 OUT OF THE WOODS by Dean Niles

ACROSS
1 Mild cigar
6 Lip
10 Moves it
14 *King Lear* daughter
15 On the sheltered side
16 Egyptian cross
17 Nitrogen compound
18 Hit the ground
19 Words of comprehension
20 Resign under fire
23 Sault __ Marie, Ont.
24 Vows
25 Of hearing
29 Snug
30 Track alternative
32 __ mode (stylish)
33 Juan Carlos' land
36 Fido fluff
37 The nights before
38 Long John Silver saying
41 Slender bristle
42 Lion's lair
43 Humble dwelling
44 *Home Improvement* home
45 Submissions to eds.
46 Family group
47 Boorish lout
49 Winter woe
51 Bishop's domain
54 College expense, often
57 Spill the beans
60 Grade option
61 Ike's rival
62 Sitarist Shankar
63 Caesarean phrase
64 Last, sometimes
65 Aid a felon
66 Gangbuster Eliot
67 Fills a hold

DOWN
1 Bird's crops
2 Paul of *Melvin and Howard*
3 Nimble-footed
4 Station
5 Corresponding completely
6 It should be first
7 Hebrew letter
8 Betrays the cause
9 Ward of *Sisters*
10 Japanese verse form
11 Election victors
12 __ out (supplement)
13 __ *Stoops to Conquer*
21 Ponds and bunkers
22 Apprehend
26 Shiny black
27 On one's toes
28 Cattle catcher
29 Vena __ (blood line)
31 Sang, in a way
33 Paine piece
34 Solomon's queenly visitor
35 Slope
36 Marshy area
37 Abba of Israel
39 Barracks buddy
40 Spaghetti may support it
45 Cow comment
46 1990 event
48 Sphere of influence
50 Endures
51 Side dish
52 Remove
53 Bleeps out
55 Straight-forward
56 Music halls
57 Swimsuit top
58 Guinea-pig place
59 Wide rd.

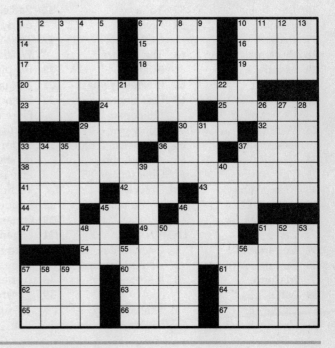

614 BOXING LEGENDS by Fred Piscop

ACROSS
1 Little brother, perhaps
5 Dizzying designs
10 Bonkers
14 Apropos of
15 Bandleader Shaw
16 __ about (circa)
17 Boxing legend?
19 Sleuth Wolfe
20 Sprite competitor
21 Pushed through the crowd
23 Put into action
24 Peculiarity
25 Extra goods
28 Mix up
32 *Critique of Pure Reason* writer
36 Motorists' org.
37 Haifa's locale
38 Actor Beery
39 Be frugal
41 Reo maker
42 __ straight (poker hand)
44 *Tic __ Dough*
45 Leaner's locale
46 Fluff up
47 South African politico P.W.
49 Muffed grounder, e.g.
51 Poolroom props
56 __ surfing (tube-watcher's activity)
59 Take back
61 Monetary unit for 47 Across
62 Boxing legend?
64 '84 Nobelist
65 Snack with milk
66 *Momma* cartoonist Lazarus
67 "Your __ is showing!"
68 Kemo Sabe's buddy
69 Thermometer type

DOWN
1 VCR button
2 Antique auto
3 Comic Martin
4 Copier additive
5 Honolulu's island
6 Stage gizmo
7 From __ Z
8 __ Island (NYC penitentiary)
9 Inventor Nikola
10 Boxing legend?
11 Once again
12 Driver's exhortation
13 Stepped on
18 Aware of
22 Prejudice
24 Arnold was one
26 Place for posies
27 Scarf down
29 Spanish surrealist
30 Digital displays
31 *Born Free* lioness
32 Heal, as bones
33 Tops
34 Shuttle grp.
35 Boxing legend?
37 Seven-year phenomenon
40 Natalie's pop
43 Bruce or Laura
47 Ravel composition
48 St. Louis sight
50 Transplant
52 Santa Anna took it
53 Highland Games missile
54 *To __ Mockingbird*
55 Limburger property
56 PC screens
57 Drive a semi
58 Opposed to
59 Civil disturbance
60 Former Sinclair competitor
63 Stimpy's pal

615 UP, UP, AND AWAY by Donna J. Stone

ACROSS
1 Used a playground piece
5 Ballerina Shearer
10 Grouch
14 Positions
15 Rock singer John
16 *Les Misérables* creator
17 People
18 Brick man
19 Making a crossing
20 START OF A COMMENT
23 Wind, essentially
24 Identical
25 Early epic
30 Responsible
34 Actor O'Neal
35 Improves, perhaps
37 Lox smith?
38 Summer setting in Conn.
39 MIDDLE OF COMMENT
41 Zsa Zsa's sister
42 Author Jong
44 Spanish painter
45 Makes out
46 Piano piece
48 Take up with an old flame?
50 Prepares leather
52 Yalie
53 END OF COMMENT
61 The O'Hara estate
62 Opening remark?
63 Scat singer Fitzgerald
64 Milky gem
65 Deep-seated hate
66 Actor Cobb
67 Cher film of '85
68 Golf club
69 Workout org.

DOWN
1 Uncultured one
2 Actress Anderson
3 It keeps things cool
4 That haughty feeling
5 D.C. sight
6 Norwegian king
7 __ *Wonderful Life*
8 Housetops
9 Temper, as metal
10 French castle
11 Parcel marking
12 *The Morning Watch* author
13 Big pig
21 Part of RSVP
22 Friend, in Florence
25 Locusts, e.g.
26 Water power, for short
27 Like some kitchens
28 Beside oneself
29 Ornamentation
31 Engender
32 Carpenter's tool
33 Wipe out
36 Terrier type
39 __ *Attraction* ('87 film)
40 Net
43 Backstage passage
45 With nastiness
47 Be that as it may
49 Tact ending
51 Nobel Prize panelist
53 Bit of matter
54 Wine region
55 Eventful periods
56 "Put __ on it!"
57 Funny money
58 Kadiddlehopper
59 Sir Guinness
60 Indian chief

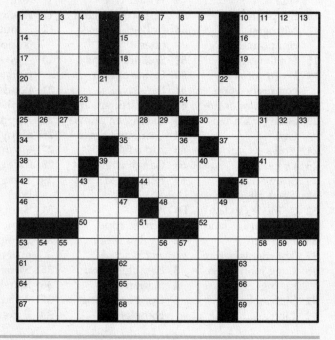

616 WORKING IT OUT by Shirley Soloway

ACROSS
1 Only
5 Figure-skater Thomas
9 The Devil
14 Related
15 *The Good Earth* character
16 Novelist Zola
17 Sail support
18 Shuttle org.
19 Pee Wee of baseball
20 Somehow
23 Agree
24 Trimmed of fat
25 P.I.
27 __ *Rides Again*
32 Make changes to
36 Put on board
39 Opera highlight
40 Somehow
43 Ireland's alias
44 And others: Abbr.
45 Carries on
46 Stretching muscle
48 Lamb's mom
50 Rugged rock
53 "__ *Fidelis*"
58 Somehow
63 Weekly pay
64 Underground growth
65 Mandlikova of tennis
66 __ a minute (fast)
67 Tommy of Broadway
68 Manages, with "out"
69 Baseballer Staub
70 Impersonated
71 Learning method

DOWN
1 Latin dance
2 Rubber-stamps
3 Shopping aids
4 __ nous (confidentially)
5 Contribute
6 Israeli airline
7 Kind of metabolism
8 Senseless
9 Cool and calm
10 From the U.S.
11 Stadium row
12 In addition
13 __-do-well
21 Opening bars of music
22 Mommy's mate
26 Coagulate
28 Roosevelt matriarch
29 Disney film of '82
30 Hilarious performance
31 Beasts of burden
32 Support
33 String instrument of yore
34 Lacking substance
35 Many centuries
37 "... man __ mouse?"
38 Talented
41 Tralee's county
42 Belief
47 Dramatist Sean
49 Had a yen for
51 The main artery
52 Aggregation
54 Anesthetic
55 Military headwear
56 Doctrine
57 Rub out
58 Man __ (racehorse)
59 __, *the Killer Whale* ('66 film)
60 Sponsorship
61 Shoe part
62 Tiptop

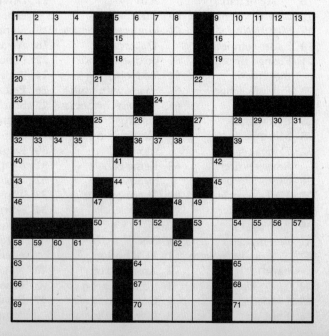

617 CREATURE FEATURE by Cathy Millhauser

ACROSS

1 Door post
5 Polite address
10 Do one's part?
14 *Siegfried* solo
15 Mrs. Kramden
16 Milky gem
17 Sugar source
18 Wallace family's *The Book of __*
19 Inclination to anger
20 What the over-the-hill man had?
23 Sneaker need
24 Least well
25 Mock
28 "Super!"
30 Elvis' middle name
31 Kid's sandwich leftover
32 AWOL pursuers
35 What the man who jumped to conclusions had?
39 "For shame!"
40 Less than a man?
41 The Sundance Kid's girlfriend
42 Spherical hairstyles
43 One of Santa's team
45 Routine-bound
48 Florence's river
49 What the propmaster for *The Sting* had?
54 They're inflatable
55 Usage expert Newman
56 Losers of '45
58 "Rule Britannia" composer
59 British novelist Charles
60 Scout quarters
61 Overlook
62 Makes an appointment
63 Nervous

DOWN

1 Fast punch
2 Realm
3 Appearance
4 At war
5 "With __ toward none . . ."
6 Skirt shape
7 Meal choice
8 *Othello* opener
9 Superlatively sloppy
10 Blue shade
11 Put one's two cents in
12 Fountain orders
13 Hallow'd
21 Blue
22 *The Bell Jar* author
25 Cuckoo
26 Fouls up
27 Chess castle
28 Looks like Carroll's cat
29 Stratagem
31 "Ah" follower
32 Closet undesirable
33 Top of the head
34 Film rater's unit
36 Jestingly
37 Our hemisphere
38 Echo
42 Springs
43 Bagpipe sounds
44 Author Beattie
45 Car-suspension piece
46 Valentino's girlfriend
47 Ages
48 Stomach
50 Mother of invention?
51 Did the crawl
52 Marked a ballot
53 High-pitched sound
57 Hog's home

618 SIX PIX by Wayne R. Williams

ACROSS

1 Ms. Midler
6 Pluto's tail
10 School grps.
14 Fictional Frome
15 Top-notch
16 Cry of distress
17 Marvin/March pic
20 Diligent insect
21 Supplemented, with "out"
22 Poolside place
23 Pen dwellers
25 Programmer's instruction
27 Old French coin
28 Pollution patrol grp.
30 Hacienda hats
34 Author Glasgow
36 Welfare
37 Opp. of SSW
38 Hamilton/Saint James pic
42 Whopper
43 Columnist Herb
44 Male voice
45 Alaskan harbor
48 Afr. nation
49 Solo of *Star Wars*
50 Fireside yarn
52 Verbal skirmish
55 Get on
57 Printer's measure
59 Señor's cheer
60 Turner/Gavin pic
64 Folktales
65 High beginner?
66 Kidney enzyme
67 Defeat
68 Malt-ed beverage?
69 *Them* author

DOWN

1 Greek letters
2 Word form for "race"
3 Ron Moody pic
4 Skater Babilonia
5 Noun ending
6 Brief appearances
7 Hope/Crosby pic
8 Actress Sheridan
9 Gumshoe
10 Pulpy refuse
11 MacLaine/Bancroft pic
12 Against
13 London area
18 Heart chart
19 Light work at the Met
24 *Pursuit of the Graf __*
26 Barbra's *Funny Girl* costar
29 Big snake
31 Lib. collection
32 Not fooled by
33 Prognosticator
34 Scatter Fitzgerald
35 Cut of meat
39 Black goo
40 Accomplishment
41 Uncle __ (rice brand)
46 Bret and others
47 *Sense and Sensibility* heroine
51 Coll. course
53 Caine film
54 The green years
55 Check
56 Herman Melville novel
58 '60s do
61 Slot filler
62 Bar rocks
63 Meadow

619 ONE-TRACK MIND by Donna J. Stone

ACROSS
1 Moonshine ingredient
5 __ Spumante
9 Throws in the towel
14 At rest
15 Rich soil
16 Lobbies for
17 Sophoclean tragedy
18 Fall rudely
19 *Roots* Emmy-winner
20 START OF A DEFINITION OF A BORE
23 "The Enlightened One"
24 Bit of Morse code
25 PC key
27 "__ you sure?"
28 Marsh birds
31 Old Chevy
32 Upcoming grad.
33 Celebratory suffix
34 Got one's feet wet
35 MIDDLE OF DEFINITION
38 Places for ports
41 Stewpot
42 Giant legend
45 Outer limits
46 Knight wear
48 Born yesterday
49 Bonanza material
50 __ Saud
51 Leisurely, to Liszt
53 END OF DEFINITION
57 Decent
58 Jai __
59 Social climber
61 Actress Verdugo
62 Poker-player's phrase
63 __ Taft Benson
64 Eleanor's uncle
65 Rambling
66 Hold up

DOWN
1 Actress Sara
2 Break up
3 Defame
4 Put the whammy on
5 Collected letters?
6 Go it alone
7 Kit Carson House site
8 Get in the way of
9 Peck part
10 Heavenly bear
11 Set afire
12 Adolescent
13 Ukr., formerly
21 Soupçons
22 Carol word
23 __-relief
26 Spoiled
29 Adjective suffix
30 *Cheers* chair
31 Napa vessel
34 "__ Say" ('59 tune)
35 Endorses
36 Einstein's birthplace
37 Lambent
38 __-Magnon
39 Igloo feature
40 Finger-painted
42 Crisp fabric
43 They'll keep you in stitches
44 Low card
46 Cable option
47 Have as a consequence
50 Furniture detail
52 Photographer Adams
54 Hourglass contents
55 Admiral Zumwalt
56 Eaves drops
57 Came upon
60 Halloween decoration

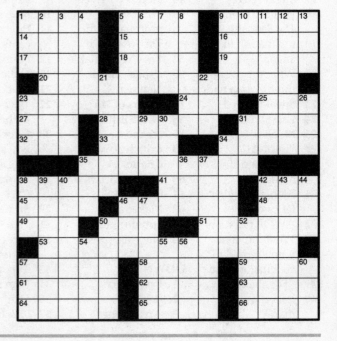

620 INTERSECTION by Bill Swain

ACROSS
1 Operatic voices
7 Economist Milton
15 Makes fit
16 Find and carry back
17 King of the Franks
18 Dashboard gauge
19 Dollar : penny :: ruble : __
20 DXXV quadrupled
21 Liqueur flavor
22 Seed: Prefix
23 One-time connection
24 Brains behind a UFO
25 Use a keyhole
28 Turkish money
30 Consumed
31 Speech impediment
32 Buddhist sect
33 Dead-center
39 Musician Montgomery
40 Chaplin's wife
41 Org. that supports sculptors
42 __-ski
45 Hating
47 Kanga's kid
48 Card game
49 Runner Zatopek
50 Maintained uprights
53 __ *Always Fair Weather*
54 Noted violin maker
55 Circumlocutory
57 Typewriter roller
58 Plot outline
59 Worked over
60 E-mail predecessor
61 Brings to bear

DOWN
1 Spot for a car critic
2 Medical practitioner
3 Way station
4 Forbidding
5 Composer Satie
6 Draft letters
7 Cap-a-pie
8 Railway worker
9 "Am __ understand . . ."
10 Columnist Bombeck
11 __ Bien Phu
12 Occupation
13 Zoroastrian sacred texts
14 Sea nymph
20 Wetland
26 Turns on a pivot
27 Hip pad
28 *Gypsy Love* composer
29 Chemical suffix
32 Greek philosopher
34 Have debts
35 Chuckles
36 Disney employee
37 Opposing stubbornly
38 Exit words
42 41 Across beneficiary
43 Swoop down
44 Short poem
45 Pianist de Larrocha
46 Started again from scratch
51 __ *kleine Nachtmusik*
52 Bummer
54 Mr. Trebek
56 Drop the ball, perhaps
57 __-game show

621 EURO MENU by Carol Blumenstein

ACROSS
1 Tranquil
5 Knight's mount
10 __ up (support)
14 Culture medium
15 Rex Stout detective
16 Lanyard
17 Dinner veggies
20 In the dumps
21 Vigorous
22 Most despicable
23 Computer monitors: Abbr.
24 Rat (on)
25 Zodiacal bull
28 Out of __ (antiquated)
29 Fourth mo.
32 Felonious flames
33 Recipe word
34 Bassoon kin
35 Dark dessert
38 Spider's octet
39 A son of Zeus
40 Like most new movies
41 Ending for Japan or Siam
42 Iowa city
43 Sovereigns
44 Slipped
45 Mountain lion
46 Matches up
49 __ mater
50 Spanish article
53 Dinner starter
56 Peel
57 Go in
58 __ Karenina
59 Against All __ ('84 film)
60 Titles to property
61 Favorites

DOWN
1 Taxis
2 Site of the Taj Mahal
3 Praise
4 Title for a married woman
5 Exercise attire
6 For Whom the Bell __
7 Otherwise
8 Failing grades
9 Uses up
10 Sneak about
11 Cad
12 Makes a choice
13 Nuisance
18 Reduced
19 Word with play or model
23 Kin to gators
24 Appropriates
25 Put off
26 City on the Rhone
27 Custom
28 Acts riskily
29 Wane
30 Fireplace tool
31 Tall grasses
33 Not interested
34 City near Gainesville
36 Starved
37 Author Capote
42 Baldwin of The Getaway
43 Tabloid tidbits
44 Dispatches
45 Practiced (a trade)
46 '60s hairstyle
47 Grillwork
48 Rip
49 Poker stake
50 The __ Ranger
51 Family member
52 Health farms
54 __-armed bandit
55 Patsy

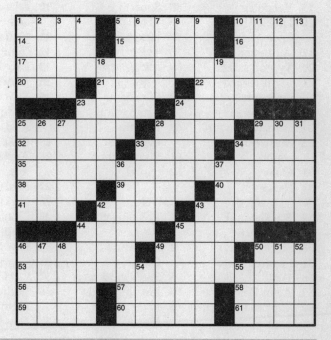

622 WAYS TO GO by Robert H. Wolfe

ACROSS
1 Israeli port
6 Bonanza role
10 The World According to __
14 Visibly happy
15 Caron film of '53
16 On __ with (equivalent to)
17 Laissez __
18 Nudge a little
19 Nutmeg relative
20 High range
22 Go __ (fall apart)
24 Take time off
26 Jodie and Stephen
27 Light-dimming device
31 Percent ending
32 Negotiations
33 Carried
35 Birth of a Nation grp.
38 Perry's penner
39 Go __ (deteriorate)
40 Port, for one
41 Workout place
42 Pounce on prey
43 See-through
44 Nectar collector
45 Potluck dinner item
47 Expected
51 Old phone feature
52 "Go __!" (oath)
54 Covers a cutlet
58 The good earth
59 Sinful
61 Pang
62 Christian Science founder
63 Take a train
64 Spoiler
65 Thumbs-ups
66 Snow rider
67 __ on (incited)

DOWN
1 Sword handle
2 Gelatin ingredient
3 Mr. Nastase
4 Go __ (risk all)
5 Not impressed
6 Swiss height
7 Scuttlebutt
8 Unconcerned
9 Linear center
10 Reproductive cell
11 Swiftly
12 Souped-up auto
13 Conference questioners
21 D.C. clock setting
23 Key, for instance
25 Unmentionable
27 US 76 and CA 101, e.g.
28 A Marx instrument
29 "A-Tisket, A-Tasket" singer
30 Fiddler on the Roof star
34 Caught cattle
35 Chicken __
36 Baby bouncer
37 Lancaster's love in From Here To Eternity
39 Stamp collector's tool
40 Go __ (plunge in)
42 __ precedent
43 Do the unexpected
44 Budd and Bigelow
46 Don't play it straight
47 Cruising
48 Arlo's dad
49 Stand
50 New Jersey iceman
53 Faction
55 Cut __ (dance)
56 Medicinal amount
57 Tournament ranking
60 Guided

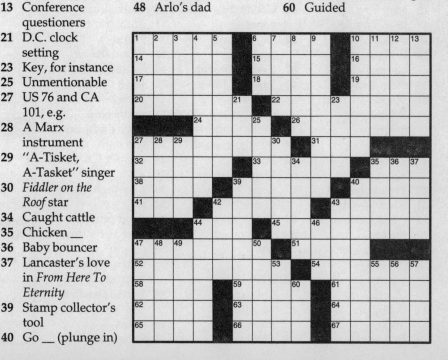

623 CHIEF LOCATIONS by Randolph Ross

ACROSS

1 Clothier Strauss
5 VIP's vehicles
10 Four-legged omnivore
14 Kitchen warmer
15 Vacuous
16 Hawks' home, once
17 Apple source
20 Tycoon's digs
21 Eight-legged creature
22 Be in store
24 French pronoun
25 Midwest capital
31 Quay
33 Raison __
34 __ kwon do
35 Bricklaying equipment
36 Stores (away)
37 Papered place
38 Wrath
39 Actor Delon
40 Superman's birth name
41 Robert James Waller locale
44 Actor Torn
45 German admiral
46 Cure
51 Rug source
55 Spot off Manhattan
57 Jackson or Tyler
58 *Middlemarch* author
59 First name in gymnastics
60 Acts the mendicant
61 Like bamboo
62 "Sure!"

DOWN

1 Rob of *Wayne's World*
2 Perón and Gabor
3 Suit's third piece
4 Breathing aids
5 *In the __ Fire* (Eastwood film)
6 Gerundial ending
7 First name in spydom
8 __ about (approximately)
9 State pair
10 Like certain arches
11 Gulf sultanate
12 Con
13 Laced
18 Knock __ (stop)
19 Tea cake
23 Middle of the road
25 Blasé
26 Archaeological find
27 Pool members
28 NATO member
29 Chaucer chapter
30 Let off steam
31 Caprice
32 Circle dance
36 Vertical-hold problem
37 Downfall
39 In private
40 Some joints
42 Spring bloomers
43 Snobbish
46 Riyadh resident
47 __ *But the Brave*
48 Chinese society
49 Conference opener
50 Nobelist Wiesel
52 Vaccine name
53 Actress Swenson
54 __ *at the Races*
56 Horror director Browning

624 WINDOW DRESSING by Dean Niles

ACROSS

1 Indian prince
6 Child or Beard
10 One mo.
14 Scarlett or John
15 Members list
16 Mag for *filles*
17 Jolson staple
18 Parkay is one
19 Economist Greenspan
20 Flow away
21 Mood
24 Eskimo neighbor
26 Ups the bet
27 Go through again
29 Trombone part
31 Slack-jawed
32 Church cry
33 Big bird
37 Adjective for the 1890's
38 Court conclusions
41 Bobby of hockey
42 Cheese choice
44 Postwar alliance
45 NC-17 moviegoer
47 Large tangelos
49 Prizes
50 40 winks
53 Goodman's genre
54 '60s singing family
57 Corp. takeover
60 James __ Jones
61 Ticket punishment
62 Fancy headdress
64 Mrs. Lou Grant
65 Push
66 Map feature
67 Comedienne Charlotte et al.
68 Onion kin
69 Throws out a line

DOWN

1 Colosseum city
2 Melville monomaniac
3 Creole dish
4 Shirt part
5 Sneezin' reason
6 Certain Slav
7 Actress Celeste
8 Robt. __
9 Tile, perhaps
10 More sleazy
11 Immigrants' island
12 Wood shaver
13 Leans (toward)
22 Wish undone
23 Hula hoops, e.g.
25 Bottle edge
27 High dudgeon
28 Old oath
29 Former *L.A. Law* actor
30 Late-night name
32 Jai __
34 Sand container
35 Perry's creator
36 __ and Entertainment Network
39 Forbidden, in a way
40 Cruel
43 Pecs and abs
46 Put on
48 Pontiac model
49 Shoemaker's tool
50 Use the rudder
51 "If __ Hammer"
52 Supernatural
53 Glossy
55 Father
56 *Picnic* playwright
58 Writer Harte
59 Cookie ingredients
63 Once __ blue moon

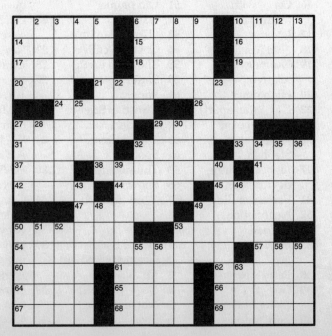

625 STAR-CROSSED by Wayne R. Williams

ACROSS
1 Declare untrue
5 Rudiments
9 Brazilian dance
14 Verdi number
15 Patsy
16 Two-toed sloths
17 *Bang the Drum Slowly* star
20 Ice-cream device
21 Remove from text
22 Inhabitant of: Suff.
23 Easy gait
25 Woodstock, e.g.
28 Compass pt.
30 Egyptian deity
32 Less than chipper
33 Samuel's teacher
34 Literary leader
35 Hawaiian hardwood
38 *Time After Time* star
42 Eskimotel?
43 Single thing
44 Author Rita __ Brown
45 4/15 addressee
46 Make amends
47 Bus. abbr.
48 Forcefully effective
51 Ollie's partner
53 Resistance unit
54 Arthur of the courts
56 *Enigma Variations* composer
59 *Black Like Me* star
63 Festoon
64 Model Macpherson
65 Cager Archibald
66 "A votre __!"
67 Roy Rogers' real surname
68 Ogled

DOWN
1 They'll hold water
2 Ambler or Blore
3 *The Seven Percent Solution* costar
4 Loudmouthed lummox
5 Mature
6 Blacker type
7 *Death of a Salesman* star
8 Creeper's stem
9 __ generis
10 Santa __, CA
11 *Manhattan* star
12 Projects forward
13 So far
18 Hardy horse
19 __ room
24 Actor Jannings
26 About .6 of a mile
27 Took off
28 Partial prefix
29 Smelting residue
31 May honoree
36 __ Bator
37 Composer Wilder
39 Taro tuber
40 Work with a soloist: Abbr.
41 Iniquity sites
46 Stadium pathways
48 Dickens' Spenlow et al.
49 Mary's friend from New York
50 Inventor's initials
52 Unchallenged
55 Slippery
57 Pot starter
58 Marsh growth
60 TV part
61 Single
62 Opie's aunt

626 DRINK UP! by Wayne R. Williams

ACROSS
1 Pepsi rival
5 "Home on the __"
10 Chair part
14 Norse god
15 Sacred images
16 Source of poi
17 Foundry form
18 "Night and Day" composer
20 Actress Dahl
22 Prehistoric
23 Flightless bird
24 Five-spot
26 Lab burners
27 Incur resentment
30 RN's specialty
31 Mr. Antony
32 Cellular substance: Abbr.
33 Director Eric
37 Dwight's nickname
38 Escape from prison
40 Actor Wallach
41 Tall buildings
43 Seabird
44 Hebrew letter
45 Ignited
46 Nevada attraction
48 Used a lariat
51 Writer Rand
52 Broadcast
53 Frozen regions
55 Horse's home
58 Snitch
61 "I've __ had!"
62 Nautical adverb
63 Fiction book
64 Allow to use
65 Orange-red mineral
66 Dirt path
67 Time periods

DOWN
1 Deep sleep
2 Aroma
3 Homer-hitter Harmon
4 Localized
5 Popular side dish
6 Fuss
7 Lon of Cambodia
8 Gather gradually
9 Sports cable network
10 Actress Elaine
11 Turn toward midnight
12 Show place
13 Law-school course
19 Spotted wildcat
21 Fanatic
24 Boggy grounds
25 In an angry way
27 Give off
28 Type of shark
29 Guardianship
30 Tree part
34 German composer
35 Novelist Kazan
36 Fruit covering
38 Wedding-related
39 Algerian seaport
42 Voted in
44 Friendly
47 Snack on
48 Moreno et al.
49 Central Florida city
50 An apostle
51 John Jacob __
54 Closely confined
55 Vend
56 Melodious Horne
57 Finishes up
59 Gardner of *Mogambo*
60 Maui garland

627 SCREEN SCORCHERS by Frank Gordon

ACROSS
1 Demean
6 Cleverness
9 Forgoes food
14 Grand Prix entrant
15 Wedding words
16 Say
17 Kate's TV housemate
18 Just out
19 Writer Ephron et al.
20 Mel Brooks film
23 Misplace
24 Houston hitter
25 Indy 500 tally
27 Aliens: Abbr.
28 Weasel's sound?
29 Penn. neighbor
31 Me, to Maurice
32 Papas' partners
34 "__ a Grecian Urn"
36 '74 disaster film, with *The*
41 Egg shapes
42 Govt. security
43 Obtain
44 Printer's measures
47 Sot's affliction
48 DDE's command
51 Paris landmark
53 Santa __
55 "Put __ on it!"
56 Best Picture of '81
59 Stallone role
60 Rainy
61 Greek letters
62 Office-communication system
63 Corn portion
64 College women
65 Al __ (pasta specification)
66 Kind of martini
67 Bewildered

DOWN
1 Fit for farming
2 Voter's paper
3 In __ by itself (unique)
4 Impound
5 ". . . __ saw Elba"
6 Bird or plane measure
7 That is: Lat.
8 Facing
9 Endow
10 South Pacific feature
11 Party decoration
12 Recipe measure
13 Last year's jrs.
21 Singer Judd
22 Unknown John
26 Word form for "Chinese"
28 Analyze a sentence
30 Yuppie apartments
32 Actor Gibson
33 Cpl.'s superior
35 Billy __ Williams
36 Roman garb
37 Surmounted
38 Night worker
39 Business activity
40 Untrue
45 AT&T rival
46 Put on the brake
48 Exclusive groups
49 Angry speech
50 Black Sea port
52 Nun's wear
54 On __ (rampaging)
55 "The game is __!"
57 Function
58 Pay-stub abbr.
59 Carpet color

628 PEOPLE FOOD by Randolph Ross

ACROSS
1 Dull-colored
5 Not glossy
10 Spielberg blockbuster
14 General's staffer
15 Young Jetson
16 __ Bator
17 Beef entrée
19 Flood wall
20 Painter Matisse
21 Pourer's problem
23 Actress Hagen
25 Hot times in Le Havre
26 Pass catcher
27 French dessert
32 Snitch
33 Upswing
34 Author Silverstein
38 Guild member
40 Shows up
43 Heavy hammer
44 Petri-dish contents
45 Inlet
46 Breakfast entrée
51 ASAP
54 Grub
55 Yale student
56 Cats and dogs
59 Atlas feature
63 Drop
64 Popular dessert
66 Head: Fr.
67 Prufrock's creator
68 Crowd sound
69 Nasal input
70 Fender flaws
71 Posted

DOWN
1 Élan
2 Ceremony
3 Arabia's Gulf of __
4 Endure
5 Club __ (vacation destination)
6 MacGraw and Baba
7 Circus swinger
8 Marquee word
9 Buttonhole
10 Karate cousin
11 Kicking partner
12 Rouse
13 Bergen voice
18 Check tamperers
22 D-Day craft
24 Home to billions
27 Study all night
28 __ avis
29 Caesarean phrase
30 Cmdr.'s org.
31 Compass pt.
35 Mata __
36 Author Ambler
37 Would-be atty.'s exam
39 Tact suffix
40 Epoch
41 Sheet of stamps
42 Main-event opener
44 Vote "present"
47 "Wow!"
48 Having spaces
49 Addison's colleague
50 Restaurant patrons
51 Passport requirement
52 Like the Capitol
53 South American capital
57 -arian relative
58 Highlander
60 Gin flavoring
61 Abba of Israel
62 Sour-tasting
65 Alts.

629 THE HARD STUFF by Dean Niles

ACROSS

1 Ballet leap
5 Medieval Danish king
9 It may waft
14 Gung-ho
15 Easy gait
16 Pickle palaces
17 Little thing
18 Part of
19 Unwelcome wind
20 Hide-and-seek cousin
23 "Big Blue"
24 Poetic dusk
25 Beelike
29 Fix, as in memory
32 "I __ Little Prayer"
36 Jumper's need
38 "If __ a Hammer"
40 __ generis
41 Out-of-the-mainstream music
44 Vane dir.
45 Test type
46 Show
47 Roll-call response
49 "Excuse me!"
51 Most of the earth
52 Turkey part
54 Hosp. area
56 Crisp greens
64 Pushy move
65 Glide along
66 __ Minor
67 He cares too much
68 __ Cong
69 "Shall we?" answer
70 Tuckered out
71 Specific advantage
72 Canadian Indian

DOWN

1 Window side
2 Bringing trouble
3 South American monkey
4 First home
5 Scale the ladder
6 Generic
7 Once __ a time
8 Sawbucks
9 Mix up
10 Summer features
11 Norwegian king
12 Offend
13 Nova Scotia clock setting: Abbr.
21 Moola
22 Act well
25 Make blush
26 Beat
27 Part of ICBM
28 Era
30 Front-page feature
31 NL or AL city
33 United
34 Southwestern plant
35 Poet Conrad
37 Infuriate
39 Pious
42 Sound of satisfaction
43 Mr. Ocasek
48 News time
50 Surroundings
53 Famous film critic
55 Tristan and Iseult, e.g.
56 Flapjack franchise
57 Sheep shelter
58 "Let's hear from you"
59 *Passages* author Sheehy
60 Skin powder
61 Manipulative one
62 Quote
63 Make less difficult
64 '60s campus org.

630 CLEANED OUT by Donna J. Stone

ACROSS

1 Lay an egg
5 Fearless Fosdick's creator
9 Parachute landing
13 Satan's bag
14 Jazzman Chick
15 Architect Saarinen
16 *Symphonie Espagnole* composer
17 Alliance
18 Wolf gang?
19 START OF A QUIP
22 Weimaraner's warning
23 Utters
24 Pass on
29 Bites
33 Get __ for one's money
34 *Hud* star
36 Actress Verdugo
37 Stole
38 Lesser Antilles isle
40 Capt.'s superior
41 '52 button name
43 Chopped
44 Go against Galahad
45 Prompt
47 *Agnes of God* actress
49 San __ Obispo, CA
51 Long time
52 END OF QUIP
60 Not quite closed
61 Accomplished, old-style
62 Spoken
63 Casino city
64 Great Lake natives
65 Bring down the house
66 WWII gun
67 Place a patch
68 Place for a patch

DOWN

1 Composer Bartók
2 Ellipse
3 Grain processor
4 Amazon weapon
5 Bean on the bean
6 Sills solo
7 Menial laborers
8 Black-and-white beasts
9 Coup d'état
10 Swing a sickle
11 Largest dolphin
12 Hardly hurried
14 Jelly fruit
20 Trams transport it
21 A Baby Bell
24 Kiddie-lit pachyderm
25 Carve a canyon
26 Misgiving
27 Part of MIT
28 Sultan's pride
30 Philanthropist Rhodes
31 Hillock
32 Like anchovies
35 Rob of *Masquerade*
38 Hole in your head
39 Absorbs
42 Wing thing
44 Tole
46 Highfalutin' headgear
48 Low digit
50 British county
52 Damages
53 "Leaving on __ Plane"
54 Carol of *Taxi*
55 Valhalla VIP
56 Hand-me-down
57 OPEC member
58 Shake up
59 Gen. Robert __

SHELL GAME by Shirley Soloway

ACROSS
1 Fastener
6 Bit of dew
10 Fizzy fluid
14 Less tinted
15 Intense anger
16 Adam Arkin's dad
17 Too big
18 Prophetic sign
19 Minor damage
20 Decorative border
23 Is under the weather
24 Everyone
25 Western mount
29 Patella
33 Neutral shade
36 Actress Gabor
37 Catfish catchers
38 Coop critter
39 Yemeni port
40 __ jiffy
41 Cropped pants
45 Child protection

47 Nice and warm
48 Tapper Miller
49 Diplomacy
51 Nighttime working hours
57 Folk follower
58 Estrada of TV
59 Actress Patricia et al.
61 Always
62 Ready to eat
63 Fortuneteller's card
64 Ms. Trueheart
65 Require
66 Make a speech

DOWN
1 USN man
2 Chem rooms
3 Guinness or Baldwin
4 Western sight
5 Bishop, e.g.
6 Salivate
7 Inclines

8 Curved molding
9 Necklace dangler
10 Riding seat
11 Cassini of design
12 Borge, e.g.
13 Picnic pest
21 Fabricator
22 Gen. Robert __
25 Kind of boom
26 Laughing mammal
27 "Swinging on __"
28 Aves.' kin
29 Good-natured
30 Yields
31 Turn away
32 Spring bloomer
34 "Huh?"
35 Garment bottom
39 Muslim ruler
41 100-yr. periods
42 Outdoor-party light

43 Annoying sensation
44 Penetrated
46 Duel tools
49 Worthless talk
50 Made a request
51 Be enamored of

52 Mine finds
53 Great Lake
54 Feeling of dread
55 Fictional estate
56 Narrow opening
57 Permit
60 Fr. holy woman

TRUNK SPACE by A.J. Santora

ACROSS
1 Drivel
4 Just fair
8 Electricity
13 Airline to Tokyo
14 Lab burner
15 Bower
16 Ancient harp
18 Composer Satie
19 Dolphins' home
20 One of Trump's exes
23 Pitcher Darling
24 A thousand G's
25 Delhi wrap
26 On the whole
29 Some GI's
34 Chicago airport
35 Pea coats?
37 Jannings of *The Blue Angel*
38 Passé
39 Slangy suffix
40 Hersey bell town

41 Buffalo's lake
42 Ifs follower
43 Knight weapon
44 Roof type
46 Fishing boats
47 Actor Max
49 Hosp. staffers
50 Caveman Alley __
53 Hughes aircraft
58 Fork partner
60 Burden
61 Dog's bane
62 Kremlin name
63 Formal letter opening
64 Fond du __, WI
65 Vigilant
66 Rooney or Williams
67 Olive-tree relative

DOWN
1 Tropical tree
2 Writer Seton
3 Young salmon

4 Attractive
5 Other: Sp.
6 Small cuts
7 AL team
8 Overcrowds
9 Sch. in the smallest state
10 Steel beam
11 Singer Perry
12 Ireland
17 New Haven sights
21 Felt poorly
22 Cupid
26 Computer adjunct
27 Colleen Maureen
28 Participated
30 __ Lebanon
31 Muscat man
32 Pie choice
33 Blackthorns
35 *Bonanza* ranch
36 Ancient
40 "I'll String __ With You"

42 "I don't give __!"
45 Missing
46 Stylish
48 Argument
50 N. Mex. neighbor
51 Like Nash's lama

52 Yearn
54 Cheese lump
55 __ podrida
56 Briny septet
57 Apiece
59 Douglas __

633   A CROSSWORD by Bill Swain

ACROSS
1 Tin Pan Alley org.
6 Can openers
10 Plays a part
14 Hood of *Our Gang*
15 Shakespearean plaint
16 "__ was no lady . . ."
17 Holy table
18 Winning quarterback in Super Bowl I
20 Grandmothers
22 Athens rival
23 "There oughta be __!"
26 *Raiders of the Lost __*
27 Baseballer Tony
28 "Nearer, My God to Thee" writer
32 Prom goers, in short
33 Rio de la __ (Argentine river)
34 Iron hook
37 Inhaler's target
40 Brilliant beetle
43 German river
44 Indian melodies
46 Author's output, briefly
49 "Teach Your Children" singer
53 Dismay
56 The old college cry
57 Sp. gal
58 Unwelcome winds
60 Grind teeth
62 *Broca's Brain* author
64 Gulf Coast city
68 Aleutian island
69 Black-tie bash
70 Saint honored on June 21
71 "Hey, you!"
72 Asian nursemaid
73 Peter and Ivan

DOWN
1 City in Oklahoma
2 Mineo or Maglie
3 Computer screen: Abbr.
4 *Way of Zen* author
5 Chute starter
6 Knight coat
7 Baked state?
8 Watering hole
9 Concorde fleet
10 Perfume from roses
11 Talismans
12 Fish sauce
13 Fake jewelry
19 Reducing club
21 Flight grp.
23 African snake
24 Song syllables
25 Coach Parseghian et al.
29 Some laughs
30 British autos
31 Kangaroo pouch
35 Cultivate
36 Dutch artist
38 *Cosmo*, e.g.
39 Schedule notation
41 Temple's first
42 Rope fiber
45 __ Na Na
46 Zany
47 Dieters of rhyme
48 Radioman's nickname
50 Asian stork
51 Actress Daryl
52 Triumphant cry
54 Black key
55 Mil. officers
59 *The Forsyte __*
61 Sports figure
63 Actress Rita
65 Finance deg.
66 Duffer's goal
67 Ques. response

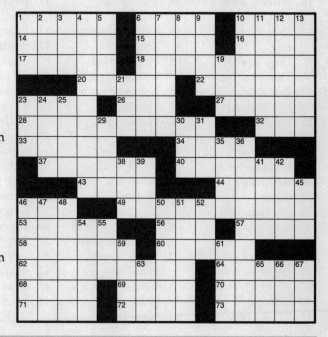

634   B CAREFUL by R.A. Sefick

ACROSS
1 Porky Pig, actually
5 Item from the horse's mouth?
8 Turkish title
11 Politico Abzug
12 One, in Avignon
13 Better than
15 Catcher cited in Bartlett's
17 Henry __ Lodge
18 Painting the town
19 Some cars
20 In addition
21 Didn't __ eye (took it calmly)
22 Chicago lines
23 Marketing software
26 Break out the books
29 Sissy talk?
30 Sweetums
31 "__ happen to you if you're young at heart"
32 Ventilate
33 Some D.C. buildings
36 Pinza, for one
38 Power-cell type
39 Seafarer
40 Bear homes
41 Crabby?
45 Good for crops
47 Telly
48 Platitudinous
49 Tropical flora
50 Four seasons, e.g.
51 NYC subway line
52 "I think I'm going to __!"
53 His: Fr.
54 Seeded privilege
55 Vegas figures

DOWN
1 End of "The Purple Cow"
2 Korbut et al.
3 Wouldn't take the blame
4 In a wild way
5 Small towns
6 As to
7 Social drink
8 "The __ Honeymoon"
9 Lose it
10 Outfit that chimes in
11 Invitation advisory
13 Perfume-factory ingredient
14 Aliens: Abbr.
16 Chemical endings
19 Smoothness symbol
21 Rum cakes
23 Perilous
24 39 Down and related subjs.
25 Saarinen of structures
26 NL stadium
27 Pyramid, essentially
28 Throw off
29 Swizzles
31 Rhone tributary
34 Moors' drums
35 "__ Nacht"
36 Baseballer Bonilla, for short
37 Touched up against
39 Rock study: Abbr.
41 *Affliction* actor
42 Like the tabloids
43 Rudolf and I.W.
44 Virginia dance
45 E-Z formula
46 Bright spots
47 __ the hatchet
49 Tot's coverup

635 — NEAR-MISS FILMS by Wayne R. Williams

ACROSS
1 Fluttery fliers
6 Photographer's order
11 Kipling book
14 Actor Hawke
15 Some down
16 Eddie Cantor's wife
17 Elvis Presley's dog?
20 Ump's cohort
21 Thorny shrub
22 *Pravda* source
23 __ Roberts U.
25 Wacky Wilson
27 Fits of pique
30 Drunkard
32 Creative forces
34 Art school subj.
35 Cast
38 Jolly laugh
40 Coll. exam
41 Teamster candidates?
44 Japanese honorific
45 Actress McClurg
46 Is frugal
47 Work units
49 Weapons
51 Healthy spot
52 Infield coverers
54 Popular pet name
56 Cartoon mail-order company
59 *My Favorite __*
61 Costa __
63 Pioneer director Browning
64 Unidentified female jogger?
68 Nabokov novel
69 Humiliate
70 Wear away
71 Place of confinement
72 Nerve-racking
73 Baseball's "Big Poison"

DOWN
1 French subway
2 Tryon novel, with *The*
3 Runner with a grudge?
4 "Eureka!"
5 Fargo forecast
6 Doddering
7 Dark queen?
8 Wedding vow
9 Remaining
10 Bombeck and others
11 Smooching manual?
12 Infamous Amin
13 Scottish-name prefix
18 TV band
19 Annapolis sch.
24 Takings
26 "Fiddlesticks!"
28 Card with a message
29 British guns
31 Yule buy
33 Females
35 Selling feature
36 Bow of the silents
37 Soft drink
39 Inning divisions
42 Evergreens
43 Palm thatch
48 *The Pursuit of the Graf __*
50 Evening gathering
53 Former Middle East leader
55 Fort Worth sch.
57 World according to Pierre
58 Gardening tool
60 Playwright David
62 Once again
64 Spring runner
65 Poetic piece
66 Game piece
67 Gun-owners' lobby

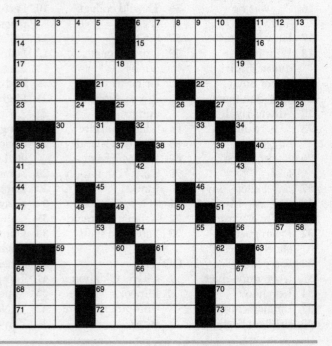

636 — TWO FIRSTS by Janie Lyons

ACROSS
1 Roseanne's former surname
5 Israeli native
10 Carpenter's tool
14 Mayberry moppet
15 Felt poorly
16 Appear
17 Hip '50s comic
19 Over with
20 Trial
21 Extra copies
23 Developed
25 Bad weather
26 Street noise
29 Donkey's uncle
31 Stiller's wife/partner
34 Nicholas, e.g.
35 Part of TGIF
36 Spanish city
37 __ Khan
38 *Wheel of Fortune*, basically
40 Scot's topper
41 Suppose, to Jed Clampett
43 Bobbysoxer's dance
44 Location
45 Old-time anesthetic
46 Civil War initials
47 Chinese cuisine
48 Negate
50 Political coalition
52 Treed
55 Foot components
59 Competent
60 *Family Affair* actor
62 Carol
63 In awe
64 Sea avian
65 Harper or Trueheart
66 Stockings stuff
67 *The Naked and the __*

DOWN
1 Western tie
2 Little or Frye
3 Melon leftover
4 Bridge botcher
5 Dark marten
6 Broadcast
7 Indistinct image
8 School break
9 Proficient
10 Had hopes
11 Ex-partner of Jerry Lewis
12 Pizazz
13 Ambulance personnel: Abbr.
18 Knitter's need
22 Type of type
24 Alert
26 Ogler's look
27 Map speck
28 R&B singer
30 Nostalgic sounds
32 Lasso
33 Commercial developers?
35 Ceiling device
36 Atlas page
38 Songstress Lena
39 Old kingdom
42 Dog sitters
44 Hit the top
46 Nuns and bishops
47 Goose talk
49 Municipal
51 Napery
52 Defeatist's word
53 A woodwind
54 Watch part
56 Engage
57 Italian volcano
58 Backyard structure
61 GI's mail abbr.

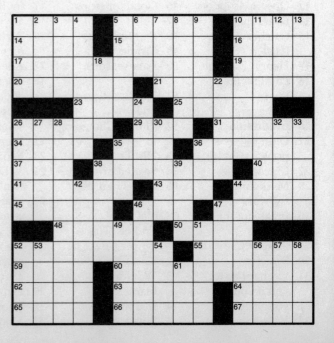

637 INTERNATIONAL GAMES by Fred Piscop

ACROSS
1 Polite forms of address
6 Cleaner brand
10 Ninnies
14 Cat's-eye relative
15 Paper quantity
16 Prima donna's tune
17 Board game
20 He can put you to sleep
21 New hire, perhaps
22 Singer James
24 Tire features
25 Rio Grande city
29 European coal region
31 Petri-dish stuff
32 Salt, chemically
34 Inventor Howe
39 High-risk game
42 Divs.
43 Wedding-cake part
44 Seward Peninsula city
45 Former Big Apple paper, for short
47 Made reparation
49 *Being and Nothingness* author
53 Sicilian spewer
55 Alexandra, for one
57 Two continents, collectively
62 Strength game
64 Jump
65 __-Contra hearings
66 Quickly, old-style
67 Messes up
68 Seeing things?
69 Rover

DOWN
1 Some Apples
2 Turkish title
3 Not "fer"
4 Obey
5 Appeared to be
6 Commentator Musburger
7 NRC predecessor
8 Bangkok coin
9 Sworn secrecy: It.
10 Comic actor Jack
11 Field of endeavor
12 Shot off
13 Envelope encls.
18 ". . . Muffet __ tuffet . . ."
19 Library cubicle
23 Attribute
25 Cooking fat
26 Fit of chills
27 File type
28 Prefix for while
30 Houseplant
33 Opposed
35 Letterman rival
36 *Blame __ Rio* ('84 film)
37 "Look __!" ("Pay attention!")
38 Tree-to-be
40 Adriatic peninsula
41 Planet discovered in 1781
46 Michael of *The Third Man*
48 Kilt design
49 Subway entrance
50 Grant portrayer
51 Nehi drinker
52 Loses footing
54 Most high-schoolers
56 Off-course
58 Fido fare
59 *The King and I* locale
60 Peruvian of yore
61 Made mellow
63 __ Dawn Chong

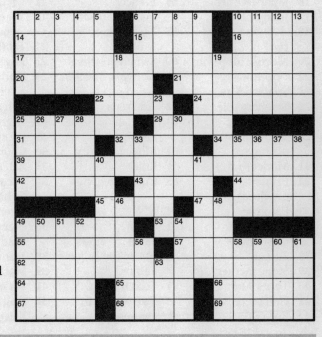

638 ON THE STREET by Bob Lubbers

ACROSS
1 Conference site
6 WWII soldier
10 __ de deux
13 __ Rogers St. Johns
14 Yippie Hoffman
16 Feeling of anger
17 TRAFFIC
19 A fifth of MV
20 "__ pig's eye!"
21 Latin I word
22 Kesey or Olin
23 Box with a bow
27 Fugue intro
29 Smoked salmon
30 Project part
32 Ooze
33 Tyrannical Ugandan
35 Coup d'__
37 Photo finish
40 Western alliance
41 Flies alone
43 Faucet flaw
44 Drum accessory
46 Barber's call
47 Fill to excess
48 Ayn or Sally
50 Barrel of laughs
52 "__ was only a bird . . ."
53 Oak-leaf arrangement
56 Well-worn witticisms
58 Lady lobster
59 Summer coolers
61 Anti-pollution grp.
62 Like steak tartare
63 PEDESTRIAN
68 "This __ stickup!"
69 Lake Indians
70 Martinelli and Lanchester
71 Pen type
72 Holy *femmes*, for short
73 Speaks hoarsely

DOWN
1 Owned
2 "__ to Billy Joe"
3 Crumpet partner
4 Island for immigrants
5 Cleo and Frankie
6 Bankroll
7 Incantation start
8 Like __ on a log
9 Burns props
10 POLICE
11 Traveled a curved path
12 It has two banks in Paris
15 High regard
18 Seaport on the Loire
23 Schemes
24 "The noblest __ of them all"
25 TAXI
26 Wyoming range
28 Goes first
31 Not as colorful
34 Bayes and Charles
36 Poisonous
38 Church contribution
39 Parrying pieces
42 Filched
45 Use allure
49 Interior settings
51 Mrs. Gore
53 Sportscaster Schenkel
54 Smallest amount
55 Mail a payment
57 Lovely lily
60 Hook's mate
64 CIA predecessor
65 Utter fool
66 Spending limit
67 Snaky letter

639 REAL ESTATERS by Wayne R. Williams

ACROSS
1 Legendary tales
6 Bias
11 Brief rest
14 Put into effect
15 Older companion?
16 Japanese sash
17 John or David
18 *A Shropshire Lad* poet
20 Mortise insertions
22 Wrathful
23 Spanish Mrs.
25 Smeltery pile
26 Lived (in)
28 Ado Annie portrayer
31 Model Kim
32 Printer's measures
33 Paradise
37 Responds to leavening
38 Top off
39 Stone marker
40 Tours summers
41 Golf score
42 Eucalyptus eaters
43 Earl Scruggs' partner
45 Dickers
49 Morse signal
50 Scale notes
51 Sci-fi thriller
52 Singer MacKenzie
54 French mathematician
57 Last inning, usually
60 Switch positions
61 Network honcho Arledge
62 Add data
63 Born, in Bordeaux
64 Moved little by little
65 College bigwigs

DOWN
1 Stitch
2 Santa __ winds
3 *Honor Thy Father* author
4 Teen trauma
5 Narrowing, in anatomy
6 Foster river
7 *sex, __, and videotape*
8 Cigar end
9 Modern prefix
10 Established fact
11 Wanderer
12 Let up
13 Yearned (for)
19 __ Lanka
21 Table scraps
23 Frighten
24 Started the fire again
26 Spree
27 High RRs
29 Former wives
30 Courage
33 Lat. list-ender
34 Oscar of fashion
35 Overjoy
36 Branch headquarters?
38 Mama __ Elliot
39 Mollified
41 For each
42 Singer/actor Kristofferson
43 Poe's lady
44 Worked on a manuscript
45 Omelet ingredient
46 Partnerless
47 Washer cycle
48 Turner or Williams
52 DNA component
53 Merchandise offering
55 Distance measure
56 Gear tooth
58 Midmorning
59 Many min.

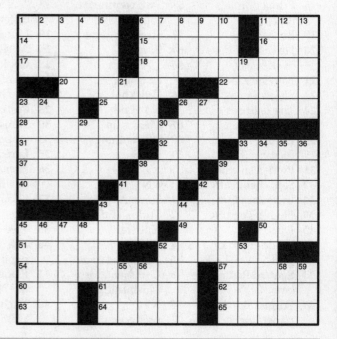

640 TEAM PLAYERS by Manny Nosowsky

ACROSS
1 Pint in a pub
4 Choose
7 Angry state
14 Webster's offering
16 Tiredness cause, perhaps
17 Concerns of 31 Across and 18 Down
19 Prepares for a new start
20 Pennsylvania city
21 Squealer
22 Red Sox old-timer Bobby
23 Cries of disapproval
24 Sagacious
25 Call a halt to
26 Abilene buddy
27 Eggs' partner
28 Banjo sound
30 President Ford
31 Half a comedy team
33 "I do," e.g.
35 Borscht basics
36 "__ for the sky!"
37 __-all (panacea)
38 Uncommon sense
41 Otherwise
42 "Comin' __ the Rye"
43 Screen image unit
45 Fall-sem. start
46 O'Casey or Penn
47 "The Raven" woman
48 Like 31 Across' persona
51 More sallow-looking
52 In mid-bombast, maybe
53 Fancy premises
54 Pot company?
55 Bee chaser

DOWN
1 Refer (to)
2 Pressure
3 Oozed out
4 Earth color
5 Pea, in Paris
6 Country cable channel
7 Cannon clearer
8 *Henry & June* character
9 Ending for check or play
10 Favorite
11 Part of AFL
12 It's a jewel
13 Area north of the Thames
15 Lab assistant name
18 Half a comedy team
23 __-Sadr
24 Merchandise
26 Rate of speed
27 Asteroid's region
28 Do tec work
29 Take a bath
30 Merriment
31 __ straws (makes a futile try)
32 Dynamic beginning
33 Take for granted
34 Author Hanff et al.
37 Meeting heads
38 Strikingly unusual
39 At peace
40 Promise
42 Bit of silly laughter
43 A real nut
44 __ the finish
46 "__ it out!" ("Say it!")
47 Change at Calabria
49 Slangy suffix
50 Go one better

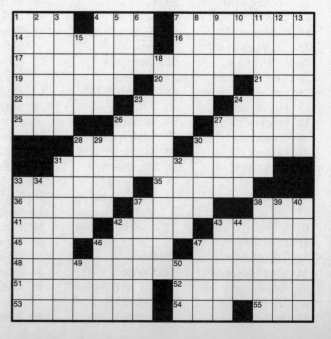

PLAYTIME by Shirley Soloway

ACROSS
1 *Jeanne d'__*
4 Air attacks
9 Citrus drinks
13 Stinging remark
15 Cook's coverup
16 Ali __
17 Concluded
18 Hidden character flaw
20 Jason's wife
22 Peter or Franco
23 Election winners
24 Loses control
28 Kingly address
29 Bag handles
33 Start of a Latin dance
36 Burdened beasts
39 Potpourri
40 Avoid
44 Brainstorm
45 Beauty establishment
46 However, for short
47 Feathered talker

50 Run off
52 Accommodate
58 Ecological org.
61 Love, in León
62 __ firma
63 "Get lost!"
67 April forecast
68 Clinton's choice
69 Russian ruler
70 Normandy town
71 Walk heavily
72 Sidled
73 Inventor Whitney

DOWN
1 Manhattan Project result
2 *Bolero* composer
3 Statement of belief
4 Brit. pilots
5 Imitate
6 Actress Dunne
7 Is overfond
8 Responds derisively

9 Easy as __
10 Spanish surrealist
11 Abba of Israel
12 Utters
14 Makes tea
19 A third of a yard
21 From China
25 Approximately
26 Makes a home
27 Ship's front
30 Landed
31 Solidity
32 London neighborhood
33 Computer element
34 "If I __ Hammer"
35 State as fact
37 The Fabulous '50s, e.g.
38 Germ fighter
41 Crime fighter Wyatt
42 Univ. part
43 Genuflected
48 Oil of __

49 Mexican food
51 Water holders
53 Harnessed
54 Take along
55 Angry
56 Singing style
57 Vietnam's capital

58 Quiche ingredients
59 Mosconi's game
60 '60s hairdo
64 Chicken part
65 Make a knot
66 Finale

FEATHER REPORT by A.J. Santora

ACROSS
1 Shocked
7 Palindromic name
10 Grassy field
13 Comic Wil
14 Fort __, NJ
15 Co. name add-on
16 Walter Lantz character
19 Rubbing liq.
20 Bk. writer
21 Prefix for dynamics
22 __-do-well
24 "Poetry Man" singer
28 '90s music form
30 Phone sound
31 De-bunk?
33 "__ Fly Now" (*Rocky* theme)
35 Poor grade
38 Grisham bestseller
41 Dawn goddess
42 Court orders
43 Escapades

44 Many eras
45 Superlative suffix
46 DeVito role
52 Basics
55 First-class
56 Namedropper
58 Anger
59 Padres' mascot
64 Part of TNT
65 Caustic solution
66 Most breezy
67 Asner and Ames
68 Moon vehicle, for short
69 Accentuate

DOWN
1 __ *in the Head* (Sinatra film)
2 Supermarket stuff
3 Secreted
4 Writer Seton
5 Gain a monopoly
6 Faithfulness
7 Combine numbers
8 Fall a bit

9 Chopper's tool
10 Compare
11 January in Juárez
12 __ to pick (argumentation)
13 Aquatic bird
17 Exulter's cry
18 In any __ (regardless)
23 Grate
25 Lab burners
26 Cold-war capital
27 Permit
29 Small fry
31 Munched on
32 Greek letter
33 Readying for inspection
34 World Series mo.
35 Motorized cycles
36 "A mouse!"
37 Gee preceders
39 Writer __ Hubbard
40 Tabula __ (clean slate)
44 Impersonated

46 Sample food
47 Stash away
48 Singer Skinnay
49 Service grp.
50 Peru natives
51 Like some Nolan Ryan performances

53 Culinary garnish
54 Mailed
57 Whirring sound
60 Not well
61 CBS logo
62 Treasure
63 Co., in Quebec

643 INSTRUMENTALS by Wayne R. Williams

ACROSS

1 *Paper Lion* star
5 Chatter
10 Hurok et al.
14 Stable tyke
15 Location of gutters
16 Say uncle
17 *Deuce Coupe* choreographer
19 Do-others separator
20 Change a title
21 *Sliver* author Levin
22 Word form for "height"
23 Stage classification
24 Rock-and-roll pioneer
26 Ornamental button
28 Mr. Baba
29 Stitch
32 Slot fillers
35 Follow as a consequence
39 1973-76 U.S. Open runner-up
43 Tippy boat
44 Old Testament book
45 Soft, wet ground
46 FDR's Blue Eagle org.
48 Creative drives
51 Infielder-turned-sportscaster
56 Patron saint of France
60 Wheel spindle
61 Cut the grass
62 Eclipse sight
63 Painter Mondrian
64 Prototypical muckraker
66 Author Ferber
67 Pluck
68 French islands
69 Close up
70 Collect bit by bit
71 Fictional terrier

DOWN

1 Broadcast talent org.
2 Downgrade
3 Singer Taylor __
4 Sherman and others
5 *Our Gang* dog
6 Team support
7 Benefit
8 __ incognita
9 Iberian *nación*
10 __ off (battling)
11 Light weight
12 Petrol unit
13 Tolerated
18 *Amo, amas,* __
24 Proverb
25 Minute circus star
27 Shoshonean
29 Wine description
30 __ Marie Saint
31 Took first
33 Singer Scaggs
34 Philosopher Kierkegaard
36 Blake Edwards movie
37 One, to Juan
38 Fabergé collectable
40 Carbon, e.g.
41 Claudius' nephew
42 Response time
47 Setting a timer
49 Olfactory trigger
50 Slavic land
51 Pokes fun
52 Zinc-__ ointment
53 Actress Verdugo
54 Mathematician Kurt
55 In the know
57 Coward and Harrison
58 Estuary
59 Latin beat
62 Columnist Herb
65 Dam-building grp.

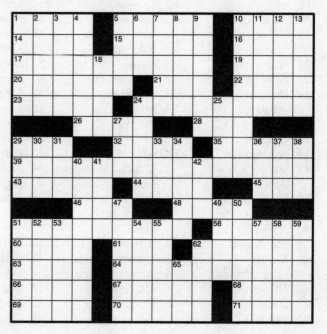

644 SYNTHETICS by Cathy Millhauser

ACROSS

1 Mrs. Warren's creator
5 More than passed
9 Curtain fabric
14 Singer of films
15 Conn of *Benson*
16 Island off Venezuela
17 Fritzi, to Nancy
18 Mayberry's sot
19 Symbol
20 BANLON
23 Don Juan's mother
24 Manet medium
25 Weekend wear
28 Down __ (Maine)
30 Greek peak
34 LL.B. holder
35 Museum vessels . . .
37 . . . and their openings
39 RAYON
42 Jeweler's measures
43 "Stop that!"
44 Compass pt.
45 Short cut
46 Macmillan's predecessor
48 Horse opera
50 Annapolis sch.
52 Sponges (up)
54 GORETEX
60 Basso Ezio
61 Joint effort?
62 Craze
63 *The Wind in the Willows* character
64 Otherwise
65 Neural transmitter
66 Oar pin
67 Batik artist, e.g.
68 Fuzz problem

DOWN

1 Rebuff
2 Appointed time
3 Florence's river
4 Contained by
5 Southwestern dwelling
6 Taxpayers
7 Word on some PC menus
8 Does the hustle
9 Birth-related
10 Settles
11 Zap in the microwave
12 Follow
13 Bert Bobbsey's twin
21 Dis
22 *Pelican Brief* character
25 One-eyed twosome
26 Allen of Vermont
27 Video-game name
29 "By the way" line
31 Play Scrooge
32 Shed light
33 *Roots* Emmy-winner
36 Feel bitter about
38 Squid kin
40 Long-locked lady
41 Tomfoolery
47 Applied plaster
49 Like a diamond in the sky
51 Make start
53 Law partner
54 Stem center
55 Proverbs preposition
56 Count (on)
57 Prepare to take off
58 *Ghostbusters* good guy
59 Flat charge?
60 Soup vessel

645 SHORT SPELLS by Richard Silvestri

ACROSS

1 Ambassador's title?
5 Marine creature?
10 Simple treatise?
14 Commuter line
15 Colorful horses
16 Just around the corner
17 Actress __ May Wong
18 Attack
19 Withstand
20 Alumnus memento
22 Iago's wife
24 Lodge members
25 __ moss
26 Small sofa
29 Well-acquainted
33 That girl
34 Men and women
36 Exile isle
37 Between __ and a hard place
39 Plant tub
40 "__ a Grecian Urn"
41 Actress Kedrova
42 Strictness of a sort
44 Harbor helper
45 Revealing
47 Greek goddess
49 Zhivago's love
50 Utah's state flower
51 Wisdom personified
54 "The Lost Continent"
58 Lend an ear
59 Wooden pin
61 Minor weakness
62 Genesis name
63 A Night at the __
64 Fencing piece
65 Uninhabited tent?
66 Advantageous-ness?
67 Bad news at the dentist?

DOWN

1 Picture of health?
2 Stroller's site
3 Designer Ricci
4 Red wine
5 Dishonest
6 Taboos
7 Disguise
8 Plane hdg.
9 Prizes
10 Authorized
11 Passion
12 Munro's pseudonym
13 Surface measurement
21 Gloomy
23 __ tai (rum drink)
25 Singer Page
26 Commandment verb
27 Spine-tingling
28 Billy Goats Gruff adversary
29 Warning light
30 "__ Song Go Out of My Heart"
31 Circa
32 Versatility
35 Palate part
38 Telephoned
40 Greek letter
42 Self-contradiction
43 Trounce
46 Shade of brown
48 Outwardly round
50 Inflexible
51 "Excuse me!"
52 Trial
53 Pressure
54 Intimidated
55 Waiter's rewards
56 Topped the cake
57 Go after
60 Top, to bottom: Abbr.

646 MOVIE PEOPLE by Robert H. Wolfe

ACROSS

1 Humor response
5 Mass ending
9 "I've __ up to here!"
14 Pizzeria need
15 Great review
16 Martini extra
17 Margarita extra
18 George Peppard film of '66
20 Where the money goes
21 __ Antonio, TX
22 Concurrence
23 Plums' kin
25 Cotton thread
27 Plummet
29 "New" prefix
30 Collude in crime
34 Sign of a hit
36 Cosmetic
38 Football coach Don
39 Actress Del Rio
41 Hair dressings
43 Ease
44 Political football
46 __ Plaines, IL
47 Deciding factors
48 Compass pt.
49 Ribald
51 Knight workers
53 African capital
56 They should be respected
60 Tailor of song
62 A lot
63 Eastwood film of '71
65 Jean Stein bestseller
66 Steamed
67 Eye drop
68 Chances
69 Starchy veggie
70 Author Ferber
71 Wall St. org.

DOWN

1 Runs the show
2 Benefit
3 Streisand film of '69
4 Bullwinkle feature
5 They may be liberal
6 Taj __
7 Dark hours
8 Neighbor of 34 Down
9 Blackjacker's opponent
10 Pub potions
11 Thin coin
12 The typical Russian
13 Student's burden
19 Composer Schifrin
24 Rueful
26 Flows in slowly
28 "Annabel Lee" creator
30 "Gotcha!"
31 Lemmon/Matthau film of '81
32 Gen. Robt. __
33 Soviet news agency
34 Mt. Rushmore's home
35 Part
37 Taking advantage of
38 Fingerpainter's stroke
40 U.S. alliance
42 __ Town
45 Gets mad
48 "Adam had 'em" poet
50 Entrained
51 Snoop
52 Transparent wrap
54 H_2SO_4 and HCl
55 Plural pronoun
56 Computer command
57 One coin in the fountain?
58 "Godfrey Daniels!"
59 Feminine suffix
61 Role for Raquel
64 Eroded

647   MONSTERMEISTERS by Wayne R. Williams

ACROSS

1 "Non più andrai," e.g.
5 Brown furs
11 "Gotcha!"
14 Remain undecided
15 Folkloric cave dwellers
16 San Francisco hill
17 Author of "The Colour Out of Space"
19 Collar
20 Worldwide workers' grp.
21 __ Downs (racetrack)
22 Alluring
23 Peace-loving
25 Broadway figure
28 Superlatively sugary
31 Price ceilings
34 Tuneful Travis
35 Polar region
36 USMC rank
39 Imperial Russian Ballet, today
41 Time remembered
42 Almighty, in Hebrew text
45 White Sea bay
48 Disarm a bull
49 Having a hissing sound
53 Gentle push
55 Flowering shrub
56 Deck officer
58 Buy new weapons
61 Rower's need
62 Nest-egg $$$
63 Author of Watchers
66 Greek cross
67 Toxic gas
68 On the briny
69 Pipe shape
70 Planting device
71 Actor Rip

DOWN

1 Garden pests
2 Do a farm job again
3 Smitten
4 Botheration
5 Author of Cujo
6 Trajectories
7 One of five in NYC
8 Camel kin
9 Mischievous creature
10 Mach topper
11 Author of The Mummy
12 Sham
13 Actress Dalton
18 Hearth goddess
22 Vague amount
24 Comparative ending
26 The Hellbound Heart author
27 Muscle spasm
29 "Star Wars" abbr.
30 New guys
32 Old salt
33 Healing waters
36 Frenzied
37 Fruity quaff
38 Author of Shadows
40 Sailors' spy grp.
43 Part of speech
44 Difficult, for a Cockney
46 Gadget
47 So. state
50 King in The Tempest
51 More cool
52 Jungle hunk
54 Wipe clean
56 Take the bait
57 Preacher Roberts
59 Author Bagnold
60 "Rule Britannia" composer
63 German article
64 Afore
65 Feedbag morsel

648   PASSION PLAY by Dean Niles

ACROSS

1 "Hey, you!"
5 Corn color
10 Secluded hollow
14 Slow payer's risk
15 Intentional fire
16 Wander about
17 Sacred image
18 Stirs up
19 Messiah section
20 Pontiac model
21 Betray a secret
23 Din
25 "__ you kidding?"
26 Code of silence
28 Spielberg title word
33 Lanai
34 Trio x 3
35 Cow comment
36 __ Minor
37 Very cold
38 Bad reviews
39 Bandleader Brown
40 Gave out hands
41 Implied
42 Pleasing proportion
44 Winter wraps
45 NATO cousin
46 Indian princess
47 Short musket
52 Slugger's stat
55 Completely absorbed
56 Lodes
57 Look listlessly
58 Pay one's share
59 Foy family father
60 Convivial
61 British slammer
62 Interminably
63 Some snakes

DOWN

1 Fussy sort
2 Religious faction
3 "White Horse souse" is one
4 Whole bunch
5 Actress Berenson
6 Came up
7 Fertility goddess
8 Dreyfus defender
9 Captured
10 Rubs the wrong way
11 Folktales
12 "See no __ ..."
13 Actress Patricia
21 __ and kin
22 "Dagnabbit!"
24 Killer whale
26 Iridescent stones
27 Saunter
28 Adjective for Roger
29 Constituent part
30 Moola
31 Aegean area
32 Amounts to
34 Close
37 Has one's revenge
38 Cut back
40 __ Poets Society
41 Catches rays
43 Talk-show host Williams
44 Left in the dust
46 Arrest
47 Talk big
48 Screen Turner
49 As far as
50 Make over
51 Wait awhile
53 Old toon Betty
54 Roadhouses
57 Grad. degree

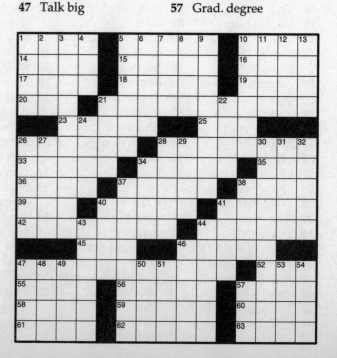

649 SOUNDS LIKE IT by Shirley Soloway

ACROSS

1 Green stroke
5 Knowledgeable
10 Proclivity
14 Orem's state
15 Actress Shire
16 Medicinal plant
17 Instruct an office worker?
19 Gets off one's feet
20 Mr. Agnew
21 Printer's mark
22 Classify
23 Paramedic: Abbr.
25 Performs in school
27 Do a little retail business?
32 Clamor
33 GI hangout
34 Wed in haste
36 Perry's right hand
40 Corner sign
42 Beneficial beam
44 Garage item
45 Mamas' mates
47 Day in Hollywood
49 Claire or Balin
50 Brit. military branch
52 Taunt a transgression?
54 Brings to mind
58 Attila, e.g.
59 *Duck Soup* prop
60 Elevator man
63 Untied
67 Oklahoma native
68 Select an Easter bloom?
70 Collision result
71 Thread holder
72 In the vicinity
73 Zeus' colleague
74 Streisand film
75 Large volume

DOWN

1 Stock options
2 Lone Star sch.
3 Anklebones
4 *And __ Stood With My Piccolo* (Willson book)
5 Pig's digs
6 Glove compartment items
7 Came down to earth
8 Day starter
9 Created lace
10 Fisherman's catch?
11 Writer T.S.
12 __ Dame
13 Finals
18 Ballet step
24 Statuesque
26 El __ (Heston role)
27 Tooth point
28 Spanish verb
29 Chicago's business area
30 Kermit's kin
31 __ Downs
35 Saarinen of architecture
37 __ *and Clark*
38 Burt's ex
39 King of comedy
41 Two goldfish?
43 Wealthy
46 Pitcher Maglie
48 Row, in a way
51 Story-time rabbit
53 Consecrate
54 Valerie Harper role
55 Buffet lover
56 Hag
57 Short stem
61 Revered object
62 Aberdeen native
64 Toast topper
65 Close with force
66 O'Casey's land
69 Everything

650 BATTLE OF THE SEXES by A.J. Santora

ACROSS

1 Stratagems
6 Dollops
10 What RNs give
13 Practice piece
14 Birthright seller
15 Small chuckle
16 Tom of *The Dukes of Hazzard*
17 Vermont tree
18 Mezzo-soprano Stignani
19 Biol. branch
20 With caution
21 Easter entrée
22 Outbreak
24 Writer Jong
25 Singer Tennille
26 With 42 Across, a Cervantes quote
28 "__ home right now, so when you hear the tone..."
30 *Pacem in __*
31 Most boring
32 Fuse unit
34 Snacked
35 Tiny metric meas.
36 Word of assent
37 Paucity
39 "__ in trying!"
41 School team
42 See 26 Across
45 Cash-filled conveniences
46 Singer LaBelle
48 Small bit
49 Omar Sharif role in a '69 film
50 Shatner's *T.J. Hooker* costar
51 Eur. land
52 Poe's time of day
53 Either *Paper Moon* star
54 Keep an __ (watch)
56 "Mona Lisa" singer
57 RBI, for one
58 Threshold
59 NFL scores
60 Existence: Lat.
61 Soothed

DOWN

1 Heat over
2 Literally, "not a place"
3 High cost of leaving?
4 Writer LeShan
5 Ready to go
6 Darlings
7 Clear jelly
8 Wifely attachment?
9 Chop __
10 Kramden saga
11 Like Danny Thomas
12 The Curies, for two
17 *My Little __* (old sitcom)
20 Show who's boss?
23 Trevi coin count
25 10-__ odds
27 Aroused to anger
29 Bach's instrument
32 Nearby
33 Archie's son-in-law
35 *The Producers* star
38 Motor homes, for short
39 Silents' film
40 *"Vive le __!"*
43 Underling
44 Part of ERA
47 Fields of expertise
50 Medicinal amount
54 First mate
55 "Verily!"

651 FLAG DAY by Dean Niles

ACROSS
1 Whole bunch
5 Disney deer
10 Squabble
14 Tiny bit
15 Verdi selections
16 Tan-lotion ingredient
17 Lei land
18 Wash cycle
19 Elvis __ Presley
20 Nabokov novel
21 Diversion
23 Author Silverstein
25 Certain curves
26 Guiding light
29 Kerrigan's footwear
32 Bring toward fruition
33 The pokey
34 Rocker Reed
37 Office work
41 Whole bunch
42 Straw in the wind
43 Protection
44 PC operating system
46 The President, sometimes
47 Westminster __
50 The __ of the Story (Paul Harvey book)
51 Show prize
55 Maybe, maybe not
59 Michael or Susannah
60 "__-porridge hot"
61 Father
62 Rice drink
63 Composer Erik
64 Baking place
65 Gang ending
66 Different
67 Fishermen's needs

DOWN
1 Fool
2 Monetary advance
3 Needle case
4 Wooden wall lining
5 Unproductive
6 Spirit of The Tempest
7 Obey
8 Wild party
9 "Uh-huh"
10 Few and far between
11 The City of Light
12 Have __ to pick (complain)
13 Strong flavors
22 Not active: Abbr.
24 Work on the edge
26 Cry loudly
27 Cavern effect
28 Go __ (contend)
29 Markdowns
30 See 64 Across
31 __ carte
33 Kenyatta of Kenya
34 Corporate identifier
35 Emmy's cousin
36 Gorbachev's realm
38 Food fish
39 Charlotte and kin
40 Cast away
44 More compliant
45 Isr. neighbor
46 Surface appearance
47 Bottomless pit
48 Puff up
49 Delta of TV
50 Riveter of WWII
52 __ facto
53 Totally exhausted
54 Shower site
56 Lincoln's bill
57 Stew
58 Urges

652 SIT ON IT by Shirley Soloway

ACROSS
1 Actress Ullmann
4 Former Surgeon General
8 Pitching ace Warren
13 Part to play
14 PBS science series
15 ". . . after they've seen __"
16 Object of devotion
17 "The __ Love"
18 Opening bars
19 Court order
22 Miles or Ferguson
23 Largest continent
24 __-mo replay
27 __ about
29 Ed of mystery
31 Ticked off
34 Evening working hours
37 In its present condition
39 Bud's sidekick
40 Pretty Woman star
41 Meeting conductor
46 Matched pieces
47 Actor Michael
48 Russian despot
50 Miner's discovery
51 Sonja Henie's birthplace
54 Move furtively
57 Informers
60 Outpouring
63 Pertaining to lyric poetry
64 Mr. Kringle
65 Famous fur merchant
66 Put on the market
67 Comical Kett
68 Nerds
69 Perry's penner
70 German article

DOWN
1 Sources of 50 Across
2 Massey of films
3 Fastening material
4 Smarts
5 Mrs. Chaplin
6 __ barrel (helpless)
7 Twosomes
8 Popeye's power source
9 Hyperventilate
10 Sculpture, for one
11 That girl
12 Prefix for "new"
13 Barbequed bone
20 Fictional Brinker
21 Points at the target
24 Cash keepers
25 Liquid measure, in London
26 Beginning
28 Exasperate
30 Tom Hanks film
31 Very large in scope
32 My Name Is __ Lev
33 Ms. Keaton
35 Negative conjunction
36 Surge of wind
38 Transgression
42 Some mob members
43 Mexican money
44 Small bone
45 Da __, Vietnam
49 Smelled bad
52 Untied
53 More mature
55 Main artery
56 Makes a muffler
57 Corner sign
58 Caplet, e.g.
59 Entitlement org.
60 Observed
61 Greek letter
62 24-hr. banking aid

653 IN THE DRINK by Bob Lubbers

ACROSS
1. __ 1 (the speed of sound)
5. Canadian Indian
9. Cellist Casals
14. Medicinal plant
15. Circle dance
16. Vane pointer
17. Seacoast
19. Performer's platform
20. Yalta conferee
21. The mater tongue?
23. James or Jimmy
26. Give the business to
29. Shakespeare's Moor
32. Actor Dan
33. Primp plumage
34. One who stares
36. "That __ no lady, that . . ."
37. Abel's dad
38. Laotian's neighbors
39. Having smarts
40. Agt.
41. Dashboard features
42. Road repair markers
43. Washed away
45. Jostled
47. Manorial property
48. Embattled European
49. Set the stage with props
51. Gone aloft
56. Exhibited
58. U. of West Florida home
61. Post payment
62. Novelist Leon
63. __ Well That Ends Well
64. Actress Papas
65. What's My Line? host
66. Ararat visitor

DOWN
1. Door accessories
2. Landed
3. Musical epilogue
4. Loaf end-piece
5. Last name in perfumes
6. Balderdash
7. Before, to Moore
8. Basketballer Monroe
9. Muni role
10. More showy
11. Battle site of 1777
12. Ship's diary
13. Run a tab
18. Add a lane
22. South American mountain chain
24. Hilo hail
25. Arizona town
27. Rented
28. Takes the heat off
29. Marching __ (walking papers)
30. Harding-administration scandal
31. Blouse border
33. "Gay" city
35. Cotton thread
38. Cinematic princedom?
39. "Oh, boy!"
41. Cold War respite
42. Hooded snake
44. Galápagos visitor
46. Loud and shrill
50. KP peelable
52. __ Get It For You Wholesale
53. Aviate alone
54. First name in scat
55. Last name in light verse
56. __ Lanka
57. Not him
59. Memorable period
60. Zilch

654 FILM OFFSPRING by Wayne R. Williams

ACROSS
1. Highlands hat
4. Let in
9. Howled
14. Be penitent
15. Type of linen
16. "Be-Bop-__" ('56 tune)
17. Curtis film of '66
20. Tropical tree
21. '60s protest grp.
22. Dress styles
23. Western Samoa capital
25. Small songbird
26. Ape film of '49
32. Felt (for)
33. Mars' equivalent
34. Caviar
35. Epochs
36. He's treating
38. Give as an example
39. JFK plane
40. Front of the calf
41. See-through
42. Eddie Murphy film of '89
46. Alien craft
47. Dash
48. Ariel, e.g.
51. Bishopric
52. Beef-rating org.
56. Bob Hope film of '51
59. Gobbled up
60. Acid in apples
61. Eur. land
62. Lock of hair
63. Contract details
64. Pokey

DOWN
1. Hidden snag
2. Faint glow
3. Blackbird
4. Jeep, e.g.: Abbr.
5. "Nobody __ Better"
6. Noon
7. French specks of land
8. Painter Gerard __ Borch
9. F. Lee and Pearl
10. Unpigmented
11. Chinese currency
12. German river
13. Work shift
18. Mental pictures
19. Life's work
24. Advanced deg.
25. Sported
26. Wetlands
27. Hot under the collar
28. Mansfield or Meadows
29. An archangel
30. Well-known
31. Actor Will
32. "__ la vie!"
36. Plant tissue
37. Helps out
38. "Hang in there!"
40. Thaws out
41. __ Na Na
43. Sneaky ways
44. Goad
45. Religious figure
48. Editor's directive
49. __ Lap (horse film)
50. Neural network
51. Crisp cookie
53. Pass over
54. Desperate
55. Arabian seaport
57. Mantras
58. Lt.-to-be's sch.

WORDS AT PLAY by Randolph Ross

ACROSS
1 GI hangouts
5 Fastener
9 Drum's partner
13 Summer weasel
14 Approve
15 Clark's co-worker
16 Where to take a sports suit?
19 __ The Head (Sinatra film)
20 Musical talent
21 Dining area
24 Shimon of Israel
28 Wimbledon gala?
32 Office sub
33 Compound word?
34 Not clerical
36 Little legume
37 Tach reading
38 Nested
41 __ Lingus
42 Lowe or Reiner
43 Walked over
44 Hideaways
46 Dot in the sea

48 Links lessons?
51 He went to town
53 Despot
54 Something to chew on
56 Not at all
60 Fielding gem?
65 Done
66 Reagan secretary of state
67 Pub contest
68 Turns the ship
69 Wheel connector
70 Hot times in Le Havre

DOWN
1 Jazz's home
2 Mediocre
3 West Coast city
4 Having the most nerve
5 Pal around
6 Wanted-poster initials
7 Soda starter
8 Nabors role

9 Broccoli cluster
10 Chit
11 Douglas' tree
12 Guinness Book suffix
13 Govt. agcy. for retailers
17 Muscular spasms
18 Put the lid on
22 With reason
23 Style
25 Fix
26 Arab princes
27 Thinly populated
28 Burning hot
29 Tell all
30 Like Jack of nursery rhymes
31 Ignited
35 Row of columns
39 Bit of work
40 Play the horn
45 Restaurant of yore
47 Gardening tools

49 Site often raided
50 "How __ Be Sure?"
52 Hero
55 Rajah starter
57 Donned

58 Army insects
59 NFL gain
60 Tarzan's kid
61 Frank's ex
62 Suture
63 Careless
64 __ Abner

DUTCH TREAT by Bob Lubbers

ACROSS
1 Floral oil
6 Big bash
10 Ore source
14 Cook onions
15 In the sack
16 Over again
17 Metric weights, for short
18 Former Netherlands inlet
20 Pointless
22 Church officers
23 African antelope
25 Taj Mahal site
27 Sent a wire
28 Gave
33 Grounded bird
34 Novelist Anya
36 Went by burro
37 Physically fit
39 Incites anger
41 Cereal holder
42 Elapse
43 Anglers' awakeners
45 Modern recording syst.

46 Hearts of the matter
49 Dancing Chita
51 Courtroom recitation
52 Makes powdery
53 Flight segments
57 Editor's marks
58 Things to tilt at
61 __ Majesty's Secret Service ('69 film)
64 Pedestal percher
65 Verne's captain
66 __ ear and out the other
67 Kelly or Hackman
68 Has
69 Wanting

DOWN
1 "__ not what your country . . ."
2 Mai __ (cocktail)
3 Spring sprouters
4 Keyless
5 Used-car deals
6 Stare

7 __ Dhabi
8 Aloha gift
9 Poisonous snakes
10 Animal fat
11 11, in France
12 Forest forager
13 Maa belles?
19 Aqaba port
21 Consumer advocate Ralph
23 Glacial epoch
24 Ballroom dances
25 Do away with
26 The Maids playwright
29 Sphere
30 Wynken and Blynken's boat
31 __ Scissorhands
32 River features
35 Shangri-La setting
38 Center of a hurricane
40 Lint-grabbing material
44 Steak cut

47 Comedian Crosby
48 Bettors' mecca
50 River to the Loire
53 Canteen mouthful
54 Neap or spring
55 Unknown auth.

56 Sit in neutral
57 Mil. decorations
59 Ben-Hur author Wallace
60 K-O link
62 Wind up
63 The Bridge of San Luis __

657 BLOW ME DOWN! by Fred Piscop

ACROSS
1 Slider, e.g.
6 Thom of shoedom
10 Designer Picone
14 Courtyards
15 Florence's river
16 Italian island resort
17 Coney Island coaster
19 School founded in 1440
20 Gram or decimal starter
21 Word form for "ear"
22 Wash basin
24 Vietnamese seaport
27 Retail transactions
28 Comic Chuck
31 Take five
33 In favor of
34 Conical abodes
37 "__ the ramparts . . ."
40 Boxer in a Dylan song
44 Last letter
45 Miniature mint
46 Drivers' org.
47 Former member of the UN
49 Mortar mate
51 Chief Justice, 1941-46
54 Most prudent
57 Marquee word
59 Martial-arts legend Bruce
60 The Beatles' "__ Love Her"
64 Way out
65 Chicago Bears great
68 "Have a __ day!"
69 Fed. agent
70 Composer Ned
71 Change for a five
72 Yemeni capital
73 Covered with white stuff

DOWN
1 Bike lane
2 Spillane's __ Jury
3 Dinosaur, for short
4 Noisy insect
5 "That ain't __!"
6 Island nation
7 Emulate Bing
8 Abby's twin
9 Mr. Coward
10 Otis invention
11 Like some statistics
12 Sun-dried brick
13 Verboten items
18 Hooks up
23 Silly person
25 Opposed to
26 Say "hi" to
28 Speedometer abbr.
29 Santa __, CA
30 Apple throwaway
32 Prison-wall jumpers
35 Noah's passengers
36 Business letter abbr.
38 Coup d'__
39 Not imaginary
41 Brings together again
42 Holes-in-one
43 Comic Charlotte
48 Prepare the table
50 Leave later
51 Office worker
52 Antidote target
53 In reserve
55 Edgar __ Poe
56 Actress Davis
58 Green __ and Ham
61 Cruel ruler
62 Took a card
63 God __ Co-Pilot
66 G.P. grp.
67 __ Gratia Artis

658 WORLD SERIES by Robert H. Wolfe

ACROSS
1 Tanning-lotion ingredient
5 Computer corrupter
10 Tale
14 Like 2 or 20
15 Banal
16 Slangy suffix
17 Baked clay vessels
20 Like some equations
21 Water pitcher
22 Teeny
23 More, to some
24 Competition sites
26 Getz's instrument
28 Yearn for
31 Feeling disgust
36 Do woodwork
38 Gulf of Lions port
42 Wildly
43 Mollycoddles
44 Blender settings
48 __ Boot ('81 German film)
49 Window treatments
51 PGA props
55 Drunkard
58 Snarl
59 Processed grain
61 In the manner of a nabob
64 Altar activity
65 Slalom curves
66 Sermon
67 __ Show of Shows
68 Feats
69 Caesar's being

DOWN
1 Role for Rigg
2 Use
3 Swiss capital
4 Pot builders
5 Contender
6 Place to stop
7 Less cooked
8 Not at all impressed
9 Quiet
10 Mouth, or mouth off
11 In __ (lined up)
12 Memorization method
13 Winning margin
18 Bother
19 Historical periods
24 Skating move
25 Strong fiber
27 He had a divine right
29 Signalled, in a way
30 Noun ending
31 Doctors' grp.
32 Dawber and Shriver
33 Type of plane, for short
34 Questioned
35 551, to Ovid
37 __ Moines, IA
39 Means justifiers?
40 Prescription agcy.
41 Rural
45 Therefore
46 Did the reel
47 Few and far between
50 Rub out
52 Make happy
53 Fitzgerald and Raines
54 Peddles
55 Nimble-footed
56 Mishmash
57 Ballet wear
59 Feel the loss of
60 Actor Dick Van __
62 Numerical word form
63 Danson or Kennedy

OLYMPIC GAMES by Walter Williams

ACROSS
1 Practice punching
5 Mr. Bumppo
10 Took a chair
13 Bean curd
14 Painter's pigment
15 Art __
16 Thicke or Cranston
17 Lose deliberately
18 "__ each life . . ."
19 Unable to decide
20 Morris' musing
21 VHS adjunct
22 Charlie Weaver's Mount __
24 Losers' consolation phrase
26 Actress Massey
29 Board a rush-hour subway
30 Filament element
32 Dressed for the Forum
36 Landed
37 Actress Samantha
39 "__ Excited" ('84 tune)
40 Metropolis menace Lex
42 Railroader
44 Rare __ (metallic elements)
46 Hearty brew
47 The cost of leaving
49 Toy merchant __ Schwarz
50 Singer Joplin
51 Second son
53 Sitcom radio station
57 Strong bugs
58 Avoid capture
59 Butter alternative
60 *Coma* author
61 Contradict
62 Hitchcock's __ *Window*
63 Barbie's beau
64 Slugs
65 Continued

DOWN
1 RBI, e.g.
2 Horse play?
3 A long ways off
4 Cliché Olympics event?
5 "It's __ cup of tea"
6 Sore spot
7 Cliché Olympics event?
8 Gardener's tool
9 Tree for bows
10 Have a feeling
11 Played a part
12 Whistle sound
15 Cliché Olympics event?
21 The Stooges, e.g.
23 German article
25 Tropical fish
26 Like *this*: Abbr.
27 Doozy
28 "Put a lid __!"
29 Wooden pin
31 __ firma
33 Arsenal stock
34 Isaac's eldest
35 Word of warning
38 __ *Gratia Artis* (MGM motto)
41 Bumblers
43 "This __ test"
45 Irish city
47 Lake boat
48 Sultry singer Susan
49 Skedaddles
50 Mr. Palance
52 Computer command
54 Swiss abstract painter
55 Gather up grain
56 Freighter's destination
58 Fade away

RUG PLUG by Donna J. Stone

ACROSS
1 English county
6 *Fanny* author
10 Improvise, in a way
14 Call up
15 Bass Pinza
16 Singer Redding
17 START OF A QUIP
19 Musical pause
20 Friendly ghost
21 Vasco __
23 Esau's wife
25 Sorts
27 Assail
28 Stands for
30 Fossey's friend
32 *Printemps* follower
33 Jazzman Louis
34 Exist
35 MIDDLE OF QUIP
41 Tree tool
42 Long Island town
45 Theorem initials
48 Pipe cleaner
49 Wave, for one
51 Pool
53 Fountain order
55 *Fort Apache* actor
56 This way
58 On the way up
60 Decline
61 END OF QUIP
65 *Three Men __ Baby*
66 Cleveland's lake
67 Drink slowly
68 __-poly
69 "The Swedish Nightingale"
70 Beast of Borden

DOWN
1 Morning moisture
2 Actress Le Gallienne
3 Hot-tempered
4 Eller's musical
5 Catches cod
6 Rocks for rings
7 Missouri's __ Mountains
8 Zilch
9 Sourdough's quest
10 Beat into shape
11 Colonel's command
12 Destiny
13 Graceland, e.g.
18 Mayberry moppet
22 Beame or Burrows
23 Business computer dept.
24 German article
26 Agra attire
29 Pine product
31 Barnyard enclosure
34 Dealt with dessert
36 Cough up the cash
37 Small businessman?
38 *M*A*S*H* extras
39 Constantinople, currently
40 Mays and Mantle
43 Author Levin
44 By means of
45 Faraway object
46 California town
47 Alpine outfit
48 Brown or Crane
49 Moved with grace
50 Orient
52 Hungarian wine
54 Senator Hatch
57 Cartoonist Silverstein
59 Skye of *Say Anything*
62 Jackie's second
63 "__ live and breathe!"
64 Placekicker's prop

661 COLORFUL STATIONERY by Harvey Estes

ACROSS
1 Church area
5 *Cabaret* singer
9 G-sharp's alias
14 Beethoven's birthplace
15 Eye part
16 Sister's girl
17 Bachelor's pride
19 Bride's follower
20 Sea life
21 Compass dir.
22 Goes on one's way
23 Denver clock setting: Abbr.
25 Rub a blade on stone
27 Circus swings
32 Boo-boo list
36 "__ Master's Voice"
37 Phone-book section
39 Follower of John
41 *Cheers* role
42 Beseech
43 Government reports
48 Poetic preposition
49 Shawl for a señor
50 Most cobra-infested
52 Truth stretcher
54 Racket
55 Produces 34 Down
58 __ in "Apple"
61 "Last of the Red Hot __" (Sophie Tucker)
65 Sneeze sound
66 Schematic
68 Correct
69 Cosby show
70 *Beetle Bailey* barker
71 "Walk Away __"
72 Measure of medicine
73 Produce 34 Down

DOWN
1 Eban of Israel
2 Roper report
3 Fly in the ointment
4 Pitch a tent
5 Ad __ (wing it)
6 Wedge or niblick
7 National park in Utah
8 Out of whack
9 Belgian city
10 Tinderbox
11 Tilt
12 Etching liquid
13 Perfect diving scores
18 Author Ken
24 __-kung (Chinese city)
26 Use an ax
27 Goes soft
28 Nouveau __
29 Up and about
30 *Born Free* name
31 Hits open-handed
33 See eye to eye
34 Eye drops?
35 So far
38 Portentous sign
40 He's had a Rocky career
44 Part of a serial
45 Soup ingredient
46 Totally awesome
47 Cut corners
51 Straight
53 Like a mad dog
55 Boxer Max
56 Highest point
57 "__ in Rome . . ."
59 Too
60 Has an evening meal
62 Bit
63 Penny, often
64 Word on an octagon
67 Needle hole

662 HIGH STEPPIN' by Shirley Soloway

ACROSS
1 Mold
6 FDR's pet
10 Kuwaiti native
14 Kid around with
15 Eddie or Richard
16 Ward of *Sisters*
17 Together (with)
18 Broadway light
19 Look over
20 Evades the issue
23 Takes one's leave
24 Finery
25 Pet tenders
29 Sandy substance
31 Possessing talent
32 Fire residue
33 Cereal grain
36 One isn't enough
41 Compass pt.
42 Roundish
43 Frozen desserts
44 Actress Meg
45 Without purpose
48 French farewell
51 As well
52 Completing easily
59 "Thanks __!"
60 Challenge
61 Courtyards
62 Nevada city
63 Concluded
64 Get to work
65 Actress Cannon
66 Majors and Marvin
67 Flies alone

DOWN
1 Mild argument
2 Luau entertainment
3 Surmounting
4 Toad abode
5 Hire
6 Real-estate markers
7 Tommie and James
8 Cambodia's neighbor
9 "Getting to Know You" singer
10 Classify
11 Happen again
12 __-Dale
13 Toss back and forth
21 Partner of neither
22 Singer Bonnie
25 Destiny
26 Abba of Israel
27 Actress Sommer
28 Poor grade
29 Obtained
30 Aussie jumper
32 Impresario Hurok
33 Fairy tale opener
34 Stone, Bronze, and Iron
35 Pitch
37 Soviet spaceship
38 Hydroelectric agcy.
39 Pale-faced
40 Feel under the weather
44 Gymnast Mary Lou
45 Makes changes to
46 __ Kabibble
47 Swampy place
48 Oscar or Tony
49 Chicago mayor Richard
50 Massey of the movies
51 Match up
53 Adored one
54 Church area
55 Director Preminger
56 Russian range
57 Copter relative
58 Head warmers

663 · AIRMEN by Dean Niles

ACROSS

1 React to a compliment
5 Farmland units
10 Work on the salad
14 Armbone
15 "Ta da!"
16 "__ us a child is born . . ."
17 Jeremy Irons film
19 Hold back
20 Fight
21 Chef's secret
23 Norma __
25 Hits on the noggin
26 Gene Barry series
33 Dismount
34 Carry around
35 Cook's meas.
38 Hecht and Franklin
39 Show (in)
41 Char
42 Bunyan's tool
43 Collar holder
44 Stone or Bronze?
46 Military comic strip
48 Delicious, e.g.
51 Fish-fetcher
52 Taylor film
56 "__ mañana!"
61 Aquarium
62 Saturday Night Fever group
64 In the old days
65 Exalted
66 Kind of incline
67 Blvds.
68 Blackbird
69 Mont Blanc range

DOWN

1 Brooklyn Dodgers, in cartoons
2 North Sea feeder
3 ". . . some kind of __?"
4 Actor Dillon
5 "__ Maria"
6 Girdle kin
7 Teeming
8 Jazz great's first name
9 States
10 Arouse
11 __ a million
12 Reek
13 Porter products
18 Synagogue scroll
22 Clarinet's cousin
24 Showing shrewdness
26 Rum cake
27 Host Trebek
28 Fork part
29 Booker T. & the __
30 It's a gas
31 __ v. Wade
32 Disco light
35 Freshwater duck
36 Wise guy
37 Sitting duck
40 Watched the tot
41 "Star Wars" abbr.
43 Ooze
45 Shaping machine
46 Jolly good fellows
47 Make possible
48 Equity member
49 Manufacturing place
50 Change for 46 Down
53 __ time (never)
54 "__ Swell"
55 Confederates
57 Taj Mahal site
58 Close up
59 Part-timer
60 Some snakes
63 Slippery one

664 · EQUAL SIDES by Wayne R. Williams

ACROSS

1 Color-changing lizard
6 Folklore being
11 Mule of song
14 __ lazuli
15 Mother-of-pearl
16 Status __
17 Mega-hit
19 Main numero
20 Pillager
21 Knight or Williams
22 Night fliers
23 Update, as a factory
25 Madame Curie
26 Provençal love song
30 __ Dawn Chong
31 Lurch and swerve
32 Wild times
34 Song stylist
36 Fabric
38 Grossly wicked
41 From Here to Eternity costar
43 Ring in the ocean
44 Marine raptor
46 Historic period
48 Stick it out
49 Removes rind
50 Get the ball rolling
52 Wallach and Whitney
53 __ Baba
54 Good, farmlandwise
59 Anaïs the diarist
60 Freezer adjunct
62 Chang's twin
63 Ships' lengths
64 Battery terminal
65 Scale notes
66 Senator Kefauver
67 Acted as a tug

DOWN

1 Priests' garments
2 Festive
3 Putative Bible bk.
4 Mr. Jagger
5 Interviewer
6 African antelope
7 More down-and-dirty
8 Band of a sort
9 Classic sitcom
10 Command conclusion
11 Calculator key
12 Family member
13 Untie
18 Rabbit's title
22 Sea east of Norway
24 Aspect
25 Current craze
26 Well-honed skill
27 Invent facts
28 Bed parts
29 Dresses
31 Miler Sebastian
33 Reciprocals of cosecants
35 Role for Leigh
37 Deposit
39 Form ending
40 Crafty
42 Cross hairs
44 First game
45 Salty
47 Saudi, e.g.
50 Icy rain
51 Cover the tab
53 Old pros
55 __ cost (free)
56 Forehead
57 Take on cargo
58 Ogled
60 "I Like __"
61 Amer. ship designation

665 ANIMAL HOUSING by Bob Lubbers

ACROSS
1 Social stratum
6 Pass twice
11 __ Mahal
14 Motorist's maneuver
15 Cover story?
16 Wedding words
17 Turned (away)
18 Photographic technique
20 NESTS
22 Rock producer Brian
23 Comedienne Charlotte
24 Pool pro
28 *Ste. Jeanne* __
30 Man from Qum
34 Green guarder
35 That girl
37 Adds more mist
39 BURROWS
42 Justice's domain?
43 Merry month
44 Flask
45 "Big Three" site
47 Some projectiles: Abbr.
51 Alan and Robert
53 Slippery swimmer
55 Road-map org.
56 HIVES
61 Hash houses
64 How Lindy flew
65 Utter fool
66 Exploding stars
67 Silver seeker
68 Erté's bag
69 Fatigued
70 Corp. helpers

DOWN
1 Swore at
2 Savvy goddess
3 Swain
4 Very, in Versailles
5 Biblical witch town
6 Rural pet, perhaps
7 Director Kazan
8 Branch
9 Genesis name
10 Pier posts
11 Helpful hint
12 Billboards, e.g.
13 Palooka
19 Casino glassware
21 Tee vista
25 Part of UAR
26 Comedienne Martha
27 Mess-hall workers: Abbr.
29 Padre
31 The Little Mermaid
32 Electron's chg.
33 Melville narrator
36 Pinkerton logo
38 Bake-sale org.
39 Marlo's mister
40 Principal role
41 Magnavox rival
42 Water-power agcy.
46 China group
48 Copland et al.
49 Attractive object
50 Football great Gale
52 British guns
54 Wool-coat owner
57 Soybeans or celery
58 Busy place
59 Have a little lamb
60 Yale team
61 Feathery stole
62 Pitcher part
63 Sternward

666 CAMERA READY by Dean Niles

ACROSS
1 Open one's big mouth
5 __ at (deride)
10 Biblical sufferer
13 Lord over
14 "Horrible" comics character
15 One of Hamlet's options
16 In a short time
17 Jane Curtin role
18 Hold back
19 38 Across' Oscar winner
22 1953 Alan Ladd western
23 Con job
24 Biological group
28 Not too swift
32 Letter writer's addenda: Abbr.
35 Russian range
37 Let up
38 Hollywood heavyweight
42 TV comic Bob
43 Church recess
44 Ruby or Sandra
45 Like some novels
47 Historic Crimean city
50 Slapstick projectiles
52 Intentional conflagration
56 Film directed by 38 Across
61 '60s musical
62 Relocation specialist
63 Celtic language
64 Chops down
65 Nitrogen compound
66 Root cause
67 Between, to Browning
68 Central points
69 Retton's scores

DOWN
1 Copper-zinc alloy
2 Out to __ (inattentive)
3 Islands hello
4 Mrs. Beatty
5 Herring kin
6 Use the phone
7 Give the eye
8 County occasions
9 Painting on plaster
10 Louis and Frazier
11 Newspaper notice
12 Painter Shahn
15 Airplane stabilizer
20 Maiden-name preceder
21 Tag
25 *Sister Act* extra
26 Sky bear
27 Mawkish
29 Took advantage of
30 Desiccated
31 Boundary
32 "Hey, you!"
33 __-crossed (ill-fated)
34 __ Genesis (Nintendo rival)
36 Actress Hartman
39 Evening service
40 Moral value
41 Slippery one
46 Naval petty officer
48 Greek cross
49 Put a stop to
51 Replay effect
53 Wild time
54 Merlin or Ole
55 Craves
56 Hirsch sitcom
57 Speeded
58 *Metamorphoses* poet
59 M. Descartes
60 CEO, often
61 Overdoer of a sort

667 OINK SPOTS by Robert Herrig

ACROSS
1 Anna's adopted land
5 "Big" burger
8 Plummeted
12 Small land mass
13 Nasty habits
15 Surface size
16 Market patron of rhyme
19 Calendar column heading
20 Nuptial site
21 Knack
24 Tart-tasting
25 Family MDs
28 Italian instrument
30 Rogue
32 Strauss of jeans
33 Plumber's joints
36 Standish's stand-in
37 Ozarkian grunters
40 Better fit
41 Shirley Temple's first husband
42 Senior member
44 Sentra maker
46 In accordance with truth
48 Expert
49 __ + tissue = makeshift kazoo
52 Rope loops
53 Zoo Story playwright
54 Econ. calculation
55 Storied homebuilders
62 Rock musical
63 Result
64 Daredevil Knievel
65 Fire man?
66 Spud sprout
67 Depend

DOWN
1 Command to Beethoven
2 Sort of a suffix?
3 "The Greatest"
4 Entrances
5 Cambridge coll.
6 Take the role of
7 Casals' instrument
8 Cloudless
9 Little bit of work
10 Hose filler
11 Install carpeting
13 Port authority?
14 Delivery extra
17 Actress Anderson
18 Avoided one
21 "My mama done __ me . . ."
22 Bitterly harsh
23 Ravel work
25 Kitchen wonders
26 Before the auction
27 Junior, for one
29 Goya patron
31 Heavy shoe
34 Fall behind
35 Lasting impression
38 Clairvoyant
39 Santa's alias
40 Trivia collection
43 Gov. Pataki's territory
45 __ House (Clavell epic)
47 Vanished
50 Potsdam possessive
51 Ms. Ross
53 Pertaining to planes
55 Article
56 Falstaff's pal
57 Periphery
58 Follower of 19 Across
59 I have shrunk?
60 Toothpaste type
61 Arch

668 MATCHING MONOGRAMS by Randolph Ross

ACROSS
1 Short summary
6 Petri-dish contents
10 Surrounded by
14 Bakery attraction
15 Toad feature
16 Spike the punch
17 Ulysses author
19 College exam
20 Went to Wendy's
21 Shoe bottoms
22 Bracelet site
23 "This early?"
25 Driver's lic. and dogtag
26 Archie's pal
33 Spartan slave
36 Icelandic works
37 Logger's tool
38 Exodus protagonist
39 Some haircuts
40 Watch junior
41 Narc's org.
42 Terra __
43 Vegetarian taboo
45 Cowboys' former coach
48 Bar opener
49 Start a paragraph
53 Poetic preposition
56 Harsh Athenian
59 Card game
60 Bee home
61 "Shoeless" ballplayer
63 Where some worship from
64 Armbone
65 Jungle vine
66 Till slot
67 Bucks, e.g.
68 Ford flop

DOWN
1 Punjab princes
2 Poetry muse
3 Arrives
4 Soul: Fr.
5 Faint
6 Off base?
7 Soulful Marvin
8 Circle sections
9 AAA suggestion
10 Ballerina Alicia
11 Grade
12 Myth ending
13 Take out of print?
18 Author of Fear of Flying
22 Pts. of speech
24 Iberian eye
25 Lupino et al.
27 Leave __ Heaven
28 Archie's mate
29 TV commercial maker
30 Apollo initials
31 Sixplex sign
32 Match divisions
33 Pilgrimage to Mecca
34 ". . . __ saw Elba"
35 Actor Neeson
39 WWII name
42 Sporelike cell
43 Erstwhile reading aid
44 Last word at the movies
46 Gregarious types
47 Director Vittorio De __
50 Lanchester and Schiaparelli
51 Not a soul
52 Related to sound quality
53 Just one of those things
54 "Take my __, please!"
55 Typical Russian
56 Republican name
57 Actor Auberjonois
58 Slightly open
61 Oklahoma! baddie
62 Josh

669 — WATCH AND WEAR by Wayne R. Williams

ACROSS

1 Wacky
5 Overcrowded
10 Help a crook
14 Computer image
15 Actress Massey
16 Seedy bar
17 Armor?
19 Old World wild goat
20 Golf gadget
21 Go-between
22 Composer of *The Planets*
23 Put in the effort
25 It comes out in *The Wash*
26 Hospital garment?
30 Purchase
33 Sample house
36 Hard to find
37 Joffrey jump
38 Merit
39 Plump
40 Enthusiastic vigor
41 Very: Fr.
42 Major landmass
43 Photographic solutions
44 Double bend
45 Wear a bandanna?
47 Ship's pole
49 Speaks scornfully
53 Ford __ Ford
55 Purview
58 Nonsense
59 God of love
60 Hosier's command?
62 Daily report
63 Craftiness
64 Polish border river
65 Hamlet, e.g.
66 Three-tone chord
67 Chrysler car

DOWN

1 Itemizes
2 Group of eight
3 Kitchen gadget
4 Mrs. Lennon
5 Miner
6 Otherwise
7 Part of speech
8 Agitated state
9 Corrode
10 Señorita's "So long!"
11 Part of a Sunday suit?
12 12/24 and 12/31
13 Written part
18 Seagoing
22 Cry's partner
24 Olympian Jesse
25 Toe the line
27 Some Syrians
28 CBer's "ears"
29 Body part
31 Western state
32 Cravings
33 Parcel (out)
34 Paddles
35 Criticize one's clothes?
37 Ex-ambassador Kirkpatrick
39 Twosome
43 Actress Lisa
45 Put a strain on
46 Saw
48 Western band
50 Wear away
51 Lover boy
52 Violin virtuoso
53 Repair
54 Neighborhood
55 Lemony?
56 One-fifth of MX
57 Neighbor of Tex.
60 Mil. rank
61 Heavy weight

670 — IRISH FOLK by A.J. Santora

ACROSS

1 Vipers
5 Ginny or Zoot
9 Casey and Kildare
13 Shea cover
14 Professor Hill
16 Ancient Greek verse form
17 Mrs. __ (alleged arsonist)
19 Repel, with "off"
20 Musicians of song
22 "Star Wars" abbr.
23 Forget-__
24 Surround firmly
26 Tempe coll.
28 "__ Grecian Urn"
29 Emerald kin
35 Former intelligence org.
36 Joyce novel
39 Village shader
40 Gorbachev policy
41 Shellfish that sticks
43 Periodical
46 Cable hub
47 TV comic Milt
52 High-tech X-ray: Abbr.
54 Home fries
57 "What's __ for me?"
58 Vivid shade
59 Sandwich shop
60 Flash of light
61 Saragossa's river
62 Taking a cruise
63 O'Hara mansion
64 Orient

DOWN

1 Specks
2 Lipton competitor
3 Concise summary
4 Bridge
5 "Say You, __" (Richie tune)
6 "I Left My Heart __ Francisco"
7 Mini relative
8 Dark ermine
9 Backbite
10 Type of test
11 Shorten
12 Theologian's deg.
15 Regretful cries
18 L.A. player
21 Moistens
25 Some attys.
27 Mil. branch
28 Approximately
30 Actress Pier
31 Linus Van __
32 Drivers' org.
33 Possesses
34 Wayfarer's stop
36 __ lid (lose control)
37 Frozen
38 S&L device
39 High lines
42 *The Merchant of Venice* heroine
44 Protozoan
45 Germaine et al.
47 Prepared to be knighted
48 Cop __
49 Permanent tooth
50 Root words
51 Pester
53 "A House __ a Home"
55 Heart chart
56 Locust, e.g.
57 "Apple Cider" girl

671   AYE-AYE by Shirley Soloway

ACROSS
1 Nonsense
5 Aspen transport
9 Asian desert
13 Art Deco artist
14 Attorney general Janet
15 Bodybuilder, perhaps
16 All over
17 Singer Anita
18 Prayer endings
19 Winter Olympics event
22 Aves.
23 Alias initials
24 Coffeemaker
25 Midwest Native Americans
31 Sign up
34 Dorothy's pet
35 __ Abner
36 Egg on
37 Animator Barbera's partner
39 Logical
40 Supply with weapons
41 __ Alto, CA
42 Stitch over again
43 Capital of *Campania*
47 Court divider
48 Short snooze
49 Skater Babilonia
52 Maui, for one
57 Turner and namesakes
58 Wise __ owl
59 __ time (never)
60 Pack away
61 Shade of green
62 Accessory for Salome
63 Take care of
64 Rude reply
65 Mars, to the Greeks

DOWN
1 Wampum units
2 "Ready __!"
3 Hearty entrées
4 Chopped down
5 Russian wagon
6 State of wild confusion
7 Job for a psych.
8 Rogers and Clark
9 Astrological sign
10 Portent
11 Loud sound
12 Election winners
15 Coiffure
20 Signal a cab
21 __ Kinte (*Roots* role)
25 Hip
26 "Let __ be said . . ."
27 Charged particle
28 Word of woe
29 Midevening
30 Did in
31 Actor Richard
32 Asta's mistress
33 Incline
37 Caribbean nation
38 Ring champ
39 Baltic or Bering
41 Make happy
42 Tears
44 Ahead
45 Historical records
46 Frankie and Cleo
49 Spud
50 Warbucks' charge
51 Role models
52 Abhor
53 In a while
54 Fleming and Paisley
55 Europe's neighbor
56 Volcanic flow
57 Mil. vehicle

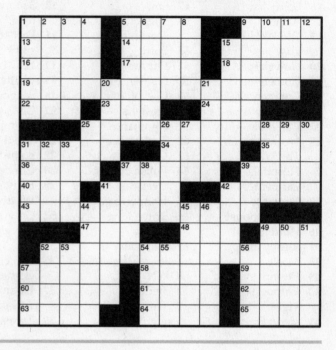

672   ON THE DIAL by Sally R. Stein

ACROSS
1 Tree branch
5 Showed fear
10 "Okey-__!"
14 Where Laos is
15 "__ a stinker?"
16 Andy's pal
17 Misfortunes
18 Sports data
19 Runners of song
20 Superman's dressing room
23 Bearing
24 Coffee vessel
25 Goes along
28 Compass point, in Paris
30 Mail-order regulators: Abbr.
33 Breakfast food
34 Bull or Bullwinkle
35 Seatless state, initially
36 Wheeler-dealer
40 Tune from *A Chorus Line*
41 Claude of *Casablanca*
42 Be overfond
43 QB's scores
44 Mean monster
45 Bowler's prize
47 Abby's sister
48 Burn a bit
49 Digital exercise book?
56 Mardi __
57 Jeweled headband
58 Party cheese
59 Greek liqueur
60 Tube preceder
61 Singular
62 Road Runner's syllable
63 Slide downhill
64 Water jug

DOWN
1 *Café au* __
2 South Seas site
3 Steel factory
4 Last place, figuratively
5 Military bands?
6 Discover, as an idea
7 __ uproar
8 Minimizing suffix
9 Pay out
10 Pythias' pal
11 Forget to include
12 Former mayor of New York
13 180 degrees from WNW
21 Missile for Soupy Sales
22 Waiter's request
25 Monastery man
26 Monotony
27 Goes ape
28 Not a soul
29 Klutz's remark
30 Lens setting
31 Promise to marry
32 Nutty professor Irwin __
34 Former Israeli prime minister
37 Literary twist
38 Rife with charisma
39 Darn cute
45 Ruin someone's plans
46 Culpability
47 Old-time storyteller
48 Apple trash
49 Multiple-choice answer
50 Morning weather
51 Floor covering, for short
52 Turner around Hollywood
53 Shoot up
54 __ kleine Nachtmusik
55 Future examiner
56 Sea dog

673 BEASTLY MOVES by Wayne R. Williams

ACROSS
1 Greek letter
4 Kind of play
9 Couches
14 Spherical object
15 Exterior
16 Flung
17 Military march
19 Native New Zealander
20 Oriental nursemaid
21 Tit for __
22 Actress Kidder
23 Devilish
25 Sheik's wives
26 Grouchoesque stride
28 Commercials, for instance
31 Cook's wardrobe
34 Mr. Linkletter
35 Nerd
36 Long nails
37 Chopping tool
38 Sacred city
39 Shiloh soldiers
40 Take to court
41 Hits on the head
42 Period of decline
43 Line dance
45 Not right
47 Aquarium attachment
51 French region
53 __-med student
54 Bulwer-Lytton heroine
55 Fool
56 Track event
58 Occupied
59 *A Lesson from* __
60 Flop
61 Polonius and Laertes, e.g.
62 Use a divining rod
63 "Sure thing!"

DOWN
1 Forum attire
2 Lure of an eatery
3 German sub
4 Forest female
5 Country folk
6 Raid
7 Encounter
8 French avant-garde artist
9 Gospel writer
10 Chicago airport
11 Propel with a forearm grip
12 Aircraft prefix
13 *M*A*S*H* costar
18 Dark spots
22 Beer ingredient
24 Religious women
25 Tortoise's rival
27 Polished, in a way
29 Las Vegas cubes
30 Health resorts
31 Piece of land
32 Commoner
33 Updike novel
35 Anagram of "praised"
37 Greene's *Travels with My* __
38 Othello, e.g.
40 Has dinner
41 Dairy products
43 Slugger Harold
44 Peter of Peter, Paul and Mary
46 Rope knot
48 Sycophant
49 When to enter
50 Oboes and bassoons
51 In the center of
52 Gossipy Barrett
53 Italian explorer
56 Possessed
57 Language ending

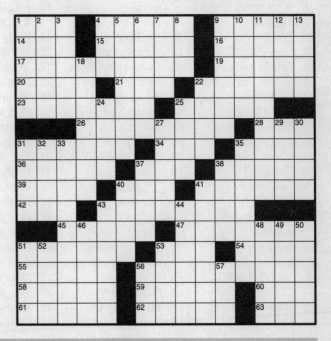

674 ON ICE by Randolph Ross

ACROSS
1 Timber tree
9 Fall flower
14 Not as heavy
15 Outfit
16 Anna's story, with *The*
17 Wet floor?
18 Indiana coll.
19 Intellectual trivia
21 Auction item
24 Pit contents
25 Alternatives to CDs
26 Noted skater
31 Unprepared
32 Gulf rival
36 Bond rating
37 Like radials
40 Group of atoms: Abbr.
41 Family member
43 Poet Moore
45 Noted skater
48 At sea
51 Neurological exam.
52 Baton Rouge sch.
53 Apollo crewman
56 Ship's record
59 Esprit de corps
60 Party game
64 "__ Restaurant" (Guthrie tune)
65 Be available
66 Ticket entitlements
67 Sort of

DOWN
1 "My, my!"
2 Related
3 Be bothered by
4 Bony
5 Genetics initials
6 Own: Scot.
7 Give up land
8 Noted skater
9 Suit to __
10 Fame
11 Shinbone
12 Put up
13 __ a beet
15 *Ad* __ *per aspera* (Kansas motto)
20 Nose-bag bit
22 Kind of punch
23 Slope transportation
26 __ Brith
27 Multicolored horse
28 Like *this*: Abbr.
29 Keats work
30 Rock bottoms
33 Where the Hawks used to play
34 Mass. neighbor
35 First name in fashion
38 Bit of Morse code
39 Of a time
42 Draw
44 Fawn over
46 Hawaiian state birds
47 "Verily!"
48 Fernando or Lorenzo
49 "__ Mio"
50 Streak
54 Music to a toreador's ears
55 Comparative word
57 Ruler of the Aesir
58 Topazes and tourmalines
61 Marilu on *Evening Shade*
62 Scale notes
63 Meet a bet

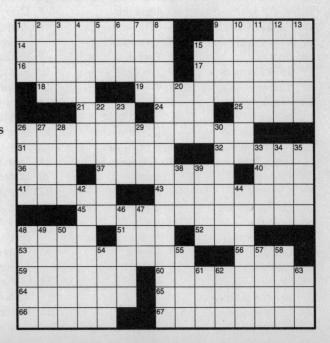

675 SOUNDS LIKE TROUBLE by Harvey Estes

ACROSS

1 Wax
5 Runs batted in, e.g.
9 Make into a ball
14 Barrett of talk shows
15 Runner-up to the tortoise
16 Too big
17 Seer's sighting
18 Tabriz's country
19 Indian, for one
20 ... TO A BACHELOR
23 Boston airport
24 Makeup name
25 Mercury or Saturn
28 Compass pt.
29 Jack Sprat forwent it
31 Costa Rican capital
33 Seabirds
35 Base opposite
36 ... TO A BACH LOVER
42 Fairy-tale fall guy
43 Milky gems
44 Tempestt of *The Cosby Show*
48 Ecol. org.
49 Defective firecracker
52 Pull some strings?
53 Like some eclipses
55 Pine Tree State
57 ... TO A THIEF
59 "Sherry" singer
62 Deep-voiced lady
63 Bread spread
64 Noted Newton
65 *The __ Earth*
66 Straight up
67 "It's possible"
68 *Jane __*
69 __ Stanley Gardner

DOWN

1 Makes tummy noises
2 Lover boys
3 Having the heebie-jeebies
4 Fish in a film
5 Leg part
6 Used the cross hairs
7 Arafat and Sadat, for two
8 Religious beliefs
9 Like some socks
10 Kindergarten lesson
11 Billy __ Williams
12 UN member
13 Cooler
21 Red leader
22 Thompson of *Back to the Future*
25 Comedienne Imogene
26 F __ "foxtrot"
27 Fred, on *Sanford and Son*
30 Landers of letters
32 Quick punches
33 __ out (got by)
34 Sellout letters
36 Rips off
37 Stare at
38 Tars and salts
39 Ernestine's job
40 Runner's round
41 Andes animal
45 Drainage channel
46 __ *Miss Brooks*
47 Hire
49 Phone user, perhaps
50 "Far out!"
51 Reduce in rank
54 Brass, e.g.
56 *Home __*
57 Spill the beans
58 Took a horse
59 Vigor
60 Free-bird link
61 Produce eggs

676 TAKE THE PLUNGE by Shirley Soloway

ACROSS

1 Bread unit
5 Lord's mate
9 John or Don
14 Swedish pop group
15 The Emerald Isle
16 Rocker David
17 Christmas carol
18 Fusses
19 1984 Kentucky Derby winner
20 The farmer's milieu
21 Short snooze
22 Submerged, as a doughnut
23 Lyric poem
25 Car part
27 Had a yen for
30 Surpass
31 Sanctuary
32 Lockhart of *Lassie*
33 Ski-lift feature
37 Baker's aide
38 Dove shelters
39 Sharpen
40 Peter of the piano
41 Wedding words
42 Hammer parts
43 "__ I can help it!"
45 Have second thoughts
46 Wigwams
48 Corn serving
49 Partial
50 Doctrine
52 Brewer's oven
56 Adjust
57 *The African Queen* writer
58 Arm bone
59 __ Rogers St. Johns
60 Herring
61 Lunchtime for some
62 Feudal workers
63 Give it __
64 Names, as a knight

DOWN

1 Touch down
2 Woodwind instrument
3 Cain's brother
4 Be excessively eager
5 Stood (against)
6 Verdi work
7 Disappears
8 Word of agreement
9 Ridiculous
10 Completely
11 Up and about
12 Bannister or Ryun
13 Burpee offering
22 Sees socially
24 Lion's lair
26 Melodies
27 Beard locale
28 Competition
29 State with conviction
32 Foster of *Maverick*
34 Certain South African
35 Bancroft or Boleyn
36 Musical pause
38 Referred to
42 Soup veggie
44 6 Down and others
45 Cure
46 Spanish mark
47 Refrige-raider
49 Sheep sounds
51 Seal in the juices
53 Baseball manager Felipe
54 Snooty one
55 Takes the sun
57 Cool __ cucumber

677 YOUR HIT PARADE by Bob Lubbers

ACROSS
1 Aunts: Sp.
5 Entice
9 After-shower wraps
14 Author Rice
15 Vicinity
16 Parriers' needs
17 Needle
19 Snitches (on)
20 Captivate
21 Holy one
23 Fewer
26 West Point freshmen
29 "Who's on first?" asker
33 Draw a new line
34 Tense, slangily
35 Had a pain
37 Crow call
38 Very dry
39 Polynesian carvings
40 __ terrier
41 Luau dip
42 Wove a chair seat
43 1040 submitter
44 Evelyn of *The Wolf Man*
46 Longing ones
48 Country singer Jim
49 Perry's creator
50 Tag, bridge, etc.
52 __ de corps
57 Word form for "red"
59 Joke ending
62 Greek physician
63 Estrada or Satie
64 Shoppe descriptor
65 Libyan gulf
66 Eugene V. __
67 Unskilled laborer

DOWN
1 Recording medium
2 Privy to
3 Singer Paul
4 Appear to be
5 Partner of Hardy
6 Coffee maker
7 Stephen of *Angie*
8 Diner sign
9 Redid the bathroom, perhaps
10 First game of a series
11 Clasp of a sort
12 Wriggly fish
13 Draft grp.
18 Onetime House Speaker Tom
22 After: Fr.
24 Done in
25 Kind of salmon
27 Ionospheric region
28 Underground ducts
29 One of the Magi
30 Nine-__ (emergency number)
31 Succeed
32 Mao __-tung
36 Escapee, maybe
39 Cup, in Calais
40 Envy or sloth, e.g.
42 Amati's hometown
43 Sassy
45 Tax cheat, perhaps
47 Smart __ (wise guys)
51 Went too fast
53 Drip sound
54 Steam up
55 __-European
56 College freshman, usually
57 Football linemen: Abbr.
58 "Bali __"
60 Ending for press
61 Penpoint

678 AT THE DAIRY by Dean Niles

ACROSS
1 Nodule
5 Ruth __ Ginsberg
10 Prosperity
14 Andy's TV son
15 Abrade
16 Morning mist
17 Indianapolis footballer
18 Parlance
19 "__ boy!"
20 Pen filler
21 Stomach bugs?
23 Hip-knee link
25 Soak
26 Protozoan
28 Supplicate
30 Secures the ship
31 Polar explorer
32 City conveyance
35 Division word
36 Campus greens
37 Peter, Paul and Mary, e.g.
38 Lah-di-__
39 Cumbersome
40 1498 sculpture
41 Tarnishes
42 Swampland
43 "Jelly Roll" __
46 Twig broom
47 Gauzy cotton
50 Ballet step
53 *La __ aux Folles*
54 Director Sergio
55 *Scarface* star
56 Type of exam
57 Chilean plain
58 Way over there
59 Hankerings
60 Birch cousin
61 Newts

DOWN
1 Sets of points
2 Put-__ (hassled)
3 Baby biter
4 Favorite
5 Kind of whale
6 Math. branch
7 "__ Be Cruel"
8 *The __ of Night*
9 Salesperson's goals
10 Sailed with Ahab
11 Dine at home
12 Montezuma subject
13 Restraint
21 Lobster eaters' protections
22 Skirmish
24 Main character, often
26 In the course of
27 __ *Lisa*
28 Mountaintops
29 __ *Chatterley's Lover*
31 Influence
32 Pushover
33 Islands in a stream
34 Feathery stoles
36 Exotic racetrack bet
37 Beginner
39 Hisses
40 Well-appointed
41 Makes inflexible
42 Streak in the sky
43 "Bones" on *Star Trek*
44 Chicago field
45 *King Lear* daughter
46 __ *amie* (sweetheart)
48 Prison unit
49 Fill up
51 Medical school subj.
52 Chaplin and Gielgud, e.g.
55 Ginnie __ securities

679   DOGGONE IT by Wayne R. Williams

ACROSS

1 Rachel of *The Thorn Birds*
5 Spring runner
8 Blubbered
14 *Inside __* (Gunther book)
15 Malay peninsula
16 Cylindrical
17 Dog food?
19 Trebek's namesakes
20 Scruffs
21 Muscle quality
22 Paddlers' org.
25 W.C. Fields' affliction
26 Easy pace
29 Expedition
31 Martin or McCarthy
32 Theater letters
33 Doggone belligerent?
35 Advanced degs.
36 Cultural values
37 Essence
38 Gin flavorings
39 Biggers' sleuth
40 Dog Caribbean capital?
42 X
43 First-class
44 Impact hole
45 Fish for eels
47 __ Na Na
48 '60s campus org.
49 Deep-orange quartz
50 Editor's markings
52 Principal course
54 Dog prize?
58 Works at an exchange
59 Botheration
60 Architect Saarinen
61 Most rational
62 Alternative wd.
63 __ moss

DOWN

1 Woman of WWII
2 Bat wood
3 *Blame It on __*
4 Natural alarm clock
5 Nonbeliever
6 Zodiac sign
7 Kitchen utensils
8 Machine parts
9 Study of birds' eggs
10 Spiner or Scowcroft
11 Dog underwear?
12 Language ending
13 Some: Fr.
18 Indian port
22 Facets
23 Derby winner on Affirmed
24 Dog country?
26 Dilettante's paintings
27 Alphabetized
28 Insomniacs, perhaps
30 Unsigned, for short
31 Computer clicker
34 Lacking substance
35 Entreaty
38 Horizontal clouds
40 Most forward
41 Flight formation
43 Thinks alike
46 Avant-__
47 Den
50 Health resorts
51 Dance movement
52 UFO pilots
53 FDR's Blue Eagle org.
55 Snore symbol
56 Time period
57 Go bad

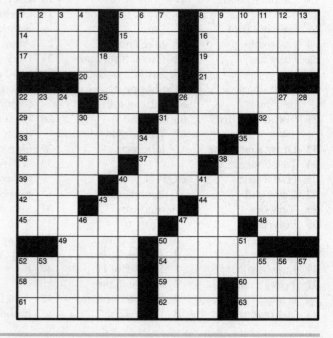

680   FAVORITE MONTHS by Robert H. Wolfe

ACROSS

1 To the stern
6 Summer place for kids
10 Complain
14 Tropical mammal
15 God of love
16 Opera highlight
17 Fox, for one
18 Wan
19 Sitarist Shankar
20 Succinct
22 Minister's favorite month?
24 __-friendly
26 Major meals
27 Eban and Dayan
31 "Smoking or __?"
32 Precious ones
33 Angry moods
35 Salt
38 Greed's cousin
39 Spores
40 Roman counterpart of Zeus
41 Fr. holy woman
42 Fountain-coin count
43 With full faculties
44 Common article
45 Ponderosa activity
47 Big fans
51 *The __ in Winter*
52 Gambler's favorite month?
54 Bully
57 __ Hari
58 A Great Lake
60 Unsophisticated
62 Without __ (riskily)
63 Hue
64 Sea birds
65 Earns after taxes
66 Pop
67 Colorists

DOWN

1 Phone co.
2 Maverick or Simpson
3 "... baked in __"
4 Liar's favorite month?
5 Locks of hair
6 Tam
7 *__ Called Horse*
8 Canine relative
9 Averts
10 Trolley driver
11 Stately steeds
12 Fasten securely
13 Skating category
21 Moray
23 Homer's forte
25 Stair part
27 Bad day for Caesar
28 Transmitted
29 Pan's opposite
30 Villainous look
34 Perfect
35 Mongolian desert
36 Kitchen need
37 *Titanic* stopper
39 Cold desserts
40 Hancock's favorite month?
42 Giant-ant horror film
43 Disdained
44 Pays for all
46 Pen tip
47 Spot maker
48 Keaton of *The First Wives Club*
49 Group of eight
50 Comic's intro
53 Skin
55 Fork part
56 Always
59 Greek vowel
61 Half of a figure-eight

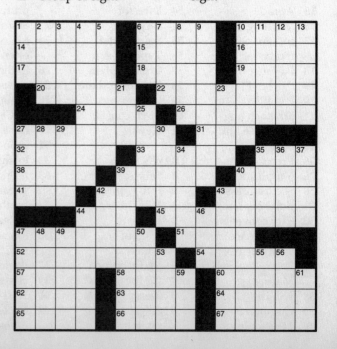

INITIAL REACTION by Ray Smith

ACROSS
1 *I Remember __*
5 Toddlers
10 Does sums
14 Desertlike
15 "__ of robins"
16 Dull sound
17 Short sprint
18 Tobacco manufacturer
20 Never-captured hijacker
22 Turner and Cantrell
23 Not van. or straw.
24 Tendon
25 Campaign '64 letters
28 Pre-cable need
30 Cincinnati baseballer
33 Commands
35 Make a hole
36 Toy-block brand
37 Costume jewelry
38 Pepper or York: Abbr.

39 Dance that "takes two"
40 Perón and Gabor
41 Actor's prompt
42 Relief
43 Our sun
44 Stogie
46 USNA grad
47 Wight and Capri
49 Learning method
51 Put in a chip
52 Former Giants quarterback
56 Tire magnate
58 Signal (a cab)
59 Hurler Hershiser
60 Fruit for cider or sauce
61 Miss Fitzgerald
62 Put to sleep?
63 *The Sun Also __*
64 Curb

DOWN
1 Road-safety org.
2 Saudi, for one
3 Catchall abbr.
4 Kind of committee

5 Florida game fish
6 Inoculate
7 Deborah or Jean
8 Language suffix
9 Teasing, as hair
10 Make up (for)
11 *Sons and Lovers* author
12 Lemons
13 '60s campus grp.
19 *Peter Pan* dog
21 Busy airport
24 Testy state
25 Easy strides
26 Theater cheer
27 Holden Caulfield's creator
29 Gardening tool
31 Prod
32 Portals
34 ALF et al.
36 Fond du __, WI
38 Brings to court
39 __-frutti ice cream

41 Aged yellow cheese
42 Comforts
44 Role for Liz
45 Seer
48 Fur wrap
50 Anesthetic
51 Bushy hairdo

52 Kennel sounds
53 Yarn
54 "__ Marlene" (WWI song)
55 Enthusiasm
56 Newhart or Cousy
57 Troy, NY coll.

DISNEY WORLD by S.N.

ACROSS
1 Impassive
6 G.P.'s grp.
9 Big shot
14 *Your Show of Shows* host
16 Political event
17 Disney's first sound cartoon: 1928
19 The "white" in Great White Way
20 Curved letter
21 Variety show VIPs
24 Joplin creation
25 Deep black
26 Mid.
29 This __ (choice words)
31 Beat walker
32 Kingston, e.g.
33 Ricochet
34 Temporary
36 Best Song Oscar recipient: 1947
38 Marginalia
39 "Ditto!"
41 Donna or Robert

42 Shaving-cream type
43 Dressy hat
44 Fed. collectors
45 Driller's deg.
46 Noticed
47 Ward healers?
48 Large lake
49 Epithet for Earl Hines
51 With *The*, TV series: 1955-59
58 Foul-smelling
59 Rake over the coals
60 Drudges
61 Penultimate letter
62 Like knives

DOWN
1 Draft org.
2 __ for tat
3 Shelley opus
4 "__ See Clearly Now"
5 Film-crew member
6 "With __ in My Heart"
7 Lea sounds

8 Illustration
9 Watch place for many
10 Haarlem painter
11 Plumber's piece
12 Yalie
13 Soap ingredient
15 PT's opposite number
18 "__ more, my lady . . ."
21 Summer shoe, for short
22 More wacko
23 Walks broadly
25 Steinbeck family
26 Disney, vis-à-vis 17 Across
27 Small-time
28 Decay
30 Trusted
31 Angler's need
32 __ over (saw through difficulty)
34 French noodles?
35 *West Side Story* tune
37 __ *Afternoon* (Pacino film)
38 __ Lanka

40 W. Hemisphere alliance
43 Dom DeLuise movie of '80
45 Exploits
46 Pasta topping
48 Wiener covering
49 Arch

50 Sulfuric or carbolic
51 Work by Mercator
52 Cola cooler
53 __-Magnon
54 Kittenish remark
55 Fall behind
56 Western Indian
57 Murphy, for one

683 FROM A TO Z by Wayne R. Williams

ACROSS
1 __-ski (after the slopes)
6 Locks with pins
11 Wood-finishing tool
14 Spacious
15 Mongolian range
16 Composer Delibes
17 Bennett tune, with "The"
19 Fire
20 Q-U connection
21 Permission slip
22 Fulmination
24 Took lunch
25 *Uno + due*
26 *Terrace at Le Havre* painter
27 Lethargy
29 TV Captain
32 Author of *A Perfect Peace*
34 Dred Scott, e.g.
35 Comparative word
38 Sajak's spinner
40 Arrow rival
41 Glacial peak
43 Zany Jimmy and Harry's brother
45 Protest posters
47 Uses a broom
51 Hawaiian geese
52 Kimono sash
53 Expected
54 Western desert
56 Highlander
57 Israeli gun
58 __ Darya (Asian river)
59 Fosse flick
62 A: Fr.
63 Old robe
64 "Harlem Nocturne" composer Hagen
65 Designer Claiborne
66 Trap
67 *The Age of Innocence* star

DOWN
1 Turkish peak
2 Basis of operations
3 Despicable cad
4 Flightless bird
5 Indication
6 Part of a ship's bow
7 "Woe is me!"
8 Letters on Cardinals' caps
9 Scott role
10 Graded classifications
11 Former island prison
12 With *The* and 13 Down, King novel
13 See 12 Down
18 Cramped
23 Achieve
26 Wooden goblet
28 Cure-all
29 Cuckoo birds
30 Word form for "egg"
31 Brit. ref.
33 Herrings
35 Recipe abbreviation
36 Loki's daughter
37 City in Spain
39 Portuguese capital, to natives
42 Solicit votes
44 Giggle
46 "__ and Rockin' "
48 Czech statesman Beneš
49 Conundrum
50 Grabber
52 Earth pigment
54 Heavy hammer
55 Present starter?
56 Julie Andrews movie
60 *Little Women* monogram
61 Johnny's successor

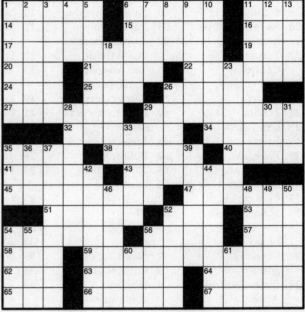

684 DARN IT by Bob Lubbers

ACROSS
1 Seashell pinks
7 Felon, in cop-speak
11 Young fellow
14 Slow, to Solti
15 Sharif or Bradley
16 Tankard filler
17 NEEDLE
19 Brokaw's bailiwick
20 Oklahoma town
21 Strong acid
22 German article
23 "Heavens to __!"
24 Borden bovine
26 Not as stiff
30 See lightbulbs?
31 Call off, as a mission
32 Energize
35 Muck's mate
36 Lays asphalt
37 Big bender
40 Daytime performance
42 Mrs. Helmsley
43 Hercule's creator
45 Plump piggie
46 Rope a bull
47 Add breadth to
50 Circle segment
51 East African republic
53 "Smooth Operator" singer
57 Diamond boss: Abbr.
58 HOLE
60 Music to Manolete
61 Baloney
62 Ogle
63 Stitch up
64 Nicholas I, for one
65 Soda sippers

DOWN
1 Canary condo?
2 Norse god
3 Physics Nobelist
4 Like fine wines
5 Fleur-de-__
6 Oklahoman
7 Frost and Eliot
8 Atlanta campus
9 Indian queen
10 Go before
11 SOCKS
12 Even if
13 Judicial decision
18 RPI rival
23 Play the ponies
25 Bandleader Lanin
26 Nunn or Ervin
27 Japanese sash
28 THREAD
29 Candies and such
30 Tax org.
32 Skipped town
33 *All About __*
34 Service charge
36 Singer Zadora
38 "__, two, buckle my shoe"
39 Cigarette substance
41 Believed
42 Chaney of cinema
43 Los __, NM
44 Use mouthwash
45 Organic gemstones
47 "__ Mile In My Shoes"
48 Conclude
49 ETO commander
52 Sticky liquids
53 Ending for road or young
54 Halo
55 Gunfighter's dare
56 Land newts
59 Complete collection

685 OVERRIPE by Donna J. Stone

ACROSS
1 Diner coffee
5 Lethargy
10 Convertible, e.g.
14 Whiff
15 Superman's target
16 Barbra's *A Star Is Born* costar
17 Singer Tennille
18 De Mille of dance
19 Itches
20 START OF A QUIP BY GEORGE BURNS
23 Surrender
25 Pro foe
26 Amount
30 Inn
34 Egg on
35 __-do-well
37 Mississippi mound
38 Out of sorts
39 MIDDLE OF QUIP
41 Ames and Asner
42 "Lovergirl" singer __ Marie
44 Recipe instruction
45 "That's __ of baloney!"
46 Mock
48 __ pie (simple)
50 Indigence
52 Immerse
53 END OF QUIP
59 Following
60 *Rawhide* prop
61 Biblical preposition
65 Blind as __
66 *Inter* __ (among other persons)
67 From the top
68 Like Gentle Ben
69 Successful dieter
70 Favor, with "toward"

DOWN
1 Smidgen
2 Fuss and feathers
3 Max __ Sydow
4 She handed Theseus a line
5 Racket
6 Rowdy party
7 __ colada
8 Plato's last letter
9 Feel hurt about
10 Travel by air, in a way
11 Cookie with contrast
12 Twain character
13 Man Fri.
21 Lunar new year
22 NATO member
23 Salon item
24 Bald birds
26 Considerably
27 Edison or Bell: Abbr.
28 Links litter
29 Busybody
31 One of the Waughs
32 North American tree
33 Heron homes
36 Sluggers' stats
39 Gobbled up
40 Noun suffix
43 Tony winner Fabray
45 Habitually
47 Serengeti beasts
49 Drillers' org.
51 Newspaper type
53 A speck with wings
54 Big name in country music
55 Final, for one
56 Collar
57 Perched on
58 Punny poet
62 Plane hdg.
63 Sri Lanka crop
64 Be responsible for

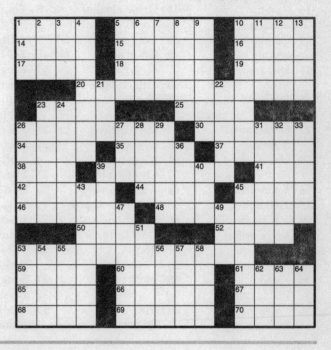

686 WILD WEST by Deborah Martin

ACROSS
1 Quite bright
6 Commercial creator
11 Wager
14 Thespian
15 Idaho's capital
16 Midwest Indian
17 Western desperado
19 Government agcy.
20 "Michael, Row Your Boat __"
21 From a distance
22 Gregorian singers
25 Heathens
27 Glove insert
28 Spot for a boutonniere
29 Coffeepot
30 Ozzie and Harriet
34 __ Yeller
37 Three: Pref.
38 Superimpose
39 Spelling contest
40 Give the __ (ogle)
41 Madmen
42 "__ Got a Crush on You"
43 Forebodings
45 Toboggan
46 Hears (of)
48 Peter and Paul
52 Vessels
53 Topnotch
54 Nev. neighbor
55 He rode with Jesse James
60 Compass dir.
61 Solo
62 Frightening
63 Susan of *L. A. Law*
64 Preclude
65 Marsh plant

DOWN
1 Day of rest: Abbr.
2 Sprint competitor
3 Part of NATO
4 *Chanson de* __
5 Assignation
6 Loathe
7 Movers and shakers
8 Newsman Wallace
9 "__ was saying . . ."
10 Actor Beatty
11 Wild West Show organizer
12 __ *Frome*
13 Rips
18 Useful article
21 Ripen
22 Skydiver's need, for short
23 Ike's predecessor
24 Western markswoman
25 Lose control
26 Church areas
28 Singer Falana
30 "__ allowed" (ladies only)
31 Cowgirl Dale
32 Camera part
33 __ Lanka
35 River embankment
36 Property titles
44 *The Ghost and __ Muir*
45 Point of view
46 Spiked, as punch
47 Wipe out
48 Stadium
49 He treats
50 Meter preceder
51 Children's-book pseudonym
53 Clump
55 Scoundrel
56 Bullfight cheer
57 Wander
58 Unit of work
59 Deli bread

687   WASH DAY by Dean Niles

ACROSS

1 Some saxes
6 Futures exchange, for short
10 Word of relief
14 Deception
15 Unexciting
16 Past the deadline
17 Certain line segments
18 He loved an Irish Rose
19 Pilaster
20 __ kind (unique)
22 Ornamental flower
24 One's salary, to an accountant
26 Vitamin stats.
27 Tied up
29 __ Cruces, NM
30 Voice origin
34 __ Kabibble
35 "For shame!"
36 Plead
37 Poet's eternity
38 "Agnus __"
39 Salt's response
40 Oscar-winning composer Francis __
41 Span. lady
42 Work unit
43 Mil. branch
44 Bustle
45 Green climber
46 Top type
48 Gold source
49 Grant and Madigan
50 Litigate against
51 North African
53 Send along
57 Most definite
60 Desire
61 It's easy
63 Climbing vine
64 Atlanta arena
65 Author Godwin
66 Stevedore, e.g.
67 Dick and Jane's dog
68 __ account
69 More wily

DOWN

1 Frizzy top
2 Director David
3 Blondie song
4 Spicy, in a way
5 Unyielding
6 Grad. degree
7 Pushes aside
8 Train track
9 Sidelines yellers
10 2-D
11 It's given in marriage
12 Suffix for kitchen
13 Put on
21 Encouraging words
23 Slow tempo
25 Of a hard wood
27 Basinlike fixture
28 Those who partake
31 Song of '65
32 Brash
33 Medical photos
35 Ford model
36 Racket
47 "__ Romantic?"
48 Garner
49 Auto appendage
52 Chicago cagers
53 Pairs
54 Slanting surface
55 __ Domini
56 __ uproar
58 Snicker-__
59 Region: Abbr.
62 Arafat grp.

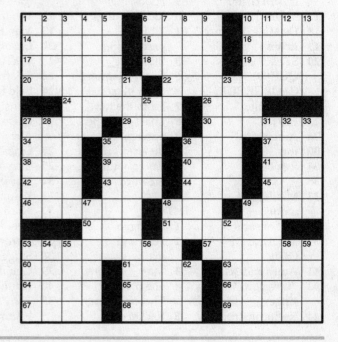

688   TOUGH PUZZLE by Robert H. Wolfe

ACROSS

1 Singer Laine
5 Copy, in a way
10 Urban vehicle
13 Without much fat
14 Winter-hat adjunct
16 Actress Hagen
17 TOUGH
19 Abner's adjective
20 Employer's obligation
21 Brain part
23 Eared seals
25 Tool house
26 __ Julius Caesar
29 Switch positions
30 *The Waste Land* monogram
31 Telescope need
32 Exclamation of delight
33 Unreal image
36 Word from Sandy
37 TOUGH
39 Performed
40 Enlarge, as a pupil
42 Outmoded title
43 Give in
44 Summer in Nice
45 Actress Zetterling
46 Encumbered
47 __-Coburg-Gotha
49 Feldspar, for one
51 Crinkler
53 Most worthy
57 Massage
58 TOUGH
60 Building wing
61 Director Spielberg
62 Takes advantage of
63 Teeny
64 Slyly malicious
65 Posted

DOWN

1 Paper holder
2 Musical Horne
3 Simple
4 TOUGH
5 Inventor Nikola __
6 One of four in Monopoly
7 Prado display
8 Meteorological regions
9 Roof edges
10 TOUGH
11 Functional
12 Tossed item
15 __ XING (urban sign)
18 Have-__ (needy ones)
22 Stalin's land
24 TOUGH
26 In a happy mood
27 Word form for "atmosphere"
28 TOUGH
30 "My country, __ of thee . . ."
32 Part of "to be"
33 Greek consonants
34 Writer of *The Immortalist*
35 Anthony or Barbara
37 Partook of
38 Having one's bearings
41 "Up and __!"
43 TOUGH
45 Helen of *Prime Suspect*
46 Chem rooms
47 Metal fastener
48 As __ (generally)
49 Butcher's offerings
50 Arledge of ABC
52 Acidity measures
54 Otherwise
55 Cinematographer Nykvist
56 Trial
59 XXII x XXIII

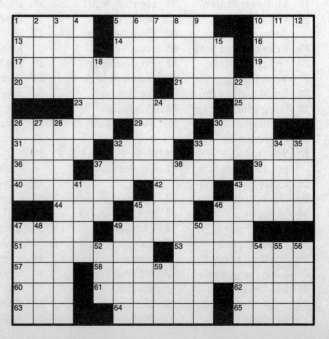

689 MIXED BAG by Manny Nosowsky

ACROSS

1 Witticism
5 Sea dogs
9 Hardly appropriate
14 Auto part
15 Bread spread
16 "Vive __!"
17 Office message-taker
19 Frankie or Cleo
20 Do sums
21 Unplanned sequence
23 All __ (mistaken)
24 Wise one
25 Furthermore
28 Act __ hunch
31 Belted
35 See 20 Across
37 Of Nehru's land
39 Comic Philips
40 Busman's holiday, perhaps
43 Film-box letters
44 Defeat, in a way
45 State fund-raiser
46 Edit
48 Reb general
50 Hearing: Law
51 Noun suffix
53 Little I topper
55 Like some vegetables
60 Move quickly
63 Bicycle spokes
64 Theme of this puzzle
66 "This is only __"
67 Former Chevy
68 "Oh sure!"
69 Scouting covers
70 Chimp in space
71 A real clown

DOWN

1 Asian island
2 O.T. book
3 Came home, in a way
4 Pulp-fiction shamus
5 Salad ingredient
6 Astronaut Shepard
7 Collins of CNN
8 Goes it alone
9 Preposterous
10 More convenient
11 Dry as a desert
12 Baked corn bread
13 Stadium section
18 Before
22 Earvin Johnson
23 He wrote The Caine Mutiny
25 Battling
26 Unfettered
27 Fine fiddle
29 Close, to a poet
30 Blacksmith's device
32 Supreme being
33 Act too much
34 Philanthropic one
36 Substitutes
38 Take out
41 "__ I see you first!"
42 Blow the whistle
47 Help out
49 Plant swellings
52 Show
54 "Sail __ Ship of State!"
55 College group, for short
56 Merit
57 First lady's home
58 "Olly, olly __ free!"
59 Word form for "yoke"
60 Rail rider
61 Don Juan's mother
62 This: Sp.
65 Tease a bit

690 PROMOTIONAL by Bob Carroll

ACROSS

1 Disney World fun
6 Oater meal
10 Tablets
14 VIPs on 3/17
15 "The Eternal City"
16 Hydrox competitor
17 Over-exclusive functions?
20 Captivate
21 Porgy and Bess, e.g.
22 Ultimatum ending
23 Took a liner
25 Flows out
28 Stood out, quality-wise
29 How to cook your goose
31 Greek epic
32 "Calling all cars . . ."
35 Over-powerful magnate?
38 __ glance (instantly)
39 Singer Baker
40 Burgundy grape
41 Golden Boy playwright
42 Chucklehead
43 Lady with lines
46 Grimm bad guy
49 Overeater's remedy, for short
50 Contemporary
54 Over-entrepreneurial student?
57 Keats feats
58 Filmdom's Pasteur
59 True-blue
60 Drivers' supports
61 County place
62 Wipe clean

DOWN

1 Lestat's creator
2 Press
3 Scandal-sheet stuff
4 Trattoria drink
5 Sand bar
6 Dinner prayer
7 Function
8 He cleans his plate
9 "Luck __ Lady"
10 Homey entrée
11 Celestial butter?
12 Farm-equipment name
13 "__, so fresh, the days that are no more": Tennyson
18 Hosp. workers
19 Cowboy work
23 The good dishes
24 Hog's habitat?
25 Humorist Bombeck
26 Bathtub toy
27 __ California
28 Skirt features
30 Exploit
31 __ Tuesday, This Must Be Belgium
32 __ cost (free)
33 Cane, for Chaplin
34 Computer storage unit
36 Some person's
37 One way in
41 Hit-__ (haphazard)
43 Big brother?
44 Uncultured
45 "We're Off __ the Wizard"
46 Footnote abbr.
47 Sports car in a '64 tune
48 Actress Esther
50 Carter's coll.
51 Writer Seton
52 Herbal drinks
53 Fashion mag
55 Typesetting widths
56 Take to court

691 — BE A DEER by Shirley Soloway

ACROSS

1 Rum cakes
6 Lettuce relative
10 A long way off
14 Make happy
15 Nutritional need
16 Pasternak heroine
17 "He's somebody __ problem . . ." (L. Hart lyric)
18 "Bye!"
19 Do the backstroke
20 Shift blame
23 Short snooze
24 "When I Take My Sugar __"
25 British weapons
27 Smart
30 Madrid missus
33 Crack pilot
36 Jamie of *M*A*S*H*
38 At no time
39 Linden or Holbrook
40 "Get lost!"
42 NY zone in August
43 Leg joint
45 Simplicity
46 Rogers or Clark
47 Command
49 John __ Garner
52 Cowboy flick
54 Things to be done
57 Comedian Erwin
59 Prenuptial get-togethers
63 Salad fish
65 "__ Clock Jump"
66 Capable
67 Remnants
68 Wimpy one
69 Fur-bearing swimmer
70 Intertwine
71 Gets the point
72 Jury members

DOWN

1 Electronic sound
2 __ sea (confused)
3 Opera singer
4 Bikini events
5 Six-line verse
6 Franklin's flier
7 Part of UAR
8 Water lily
9 Passes, as a bill
10 Hirt and Pacino
11 Dotes on
12 Diva's solo
13 Incline
21 Israeli metropolis
22 New Hampshire city
26 Map dir.
28 Identify
29 React to a bad joke
31 Make over
32 Affected
33 *Moby-Dick* captain
34 Sugar source
35 Norwegian canines
37 *Madame __* (Signoret film)
40 Sleeveless jackets
41 *I __ Letter to My Love*
44 Actress Thompson
48 Wyoming range
50 Drive-in employee
51 House and grounds
53 Hindu queen
55 Kunta __ of *Roots*
56 Passover dinner
57 Flower holder
58 Melody
60 Richard of *Primal Fear*
61 Pea containers
62 Damascus citizens: Abbr.
64 Cigar end

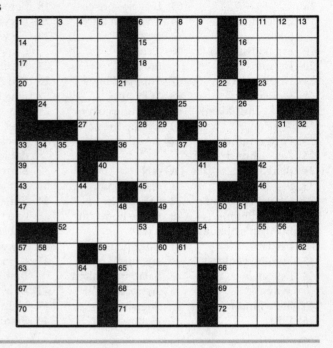

692 — SHIP SHAPE by Richard Silvestri

ACROSS

1 Gangplank, e.g.
5 Lazarus and Thompson
10 Expended
14 Brainstorm
15 Press-release addressees
16 Hang around
17 Censorship of a sort
19 Possess
20 Lode stuff
21 Let down
23 Imitating
26 Echo, for short
27 Home shopping network?
28 Multi-faced one of film
30 Distribute
33 Yukon, for one: Abbr.
34 Banish
36 Tire filler
37 Try a contest
39 Moose kin
40 Start a set
42 I.D. info
43 Less difficult
46 "*Et tu*" time
47 Consolidates
49 Pinkerton's logo
50 Five from New Jersey
51 Gave a bash
53 Impolite looks
55 Plunderers
57 Terse prez
58 Be next to
59 Violin virtuoso
65 Teddy's mom
66 Closely compacted
67 Surface extent
68 Enthusiastic
69 Berlin's "The Song Is __"
70 Coddle

DOWN

1 Barbecued bit
2 Hoo-ha
3 Sound of a Siamese
4 Digs for a beatnik
5 Stepped forth
6 "A __ bagatelle!"
7 Half of MMMII
8 Bridal path
9 Russian Tea Room server
10 Theater group
11 Rooming-house VIP
12 Roof edge
13 Prepared Easter eggs
18 *The Ghost of Frankenstein* name
22 Nathanael and Rebecca
23 Get even for
24 Prime-rib neighbor
25 About
26 Made a response
27 First-stringers
29 Two-finger signs
31 Holds one's attention
32 Hank of hair
35 __-doke
38 Teammate of Campanella
41 __ *kleine Nachtmusik*
44 Riding a horse
45 Tightened the shoestrings
48 Acquired
52 German city
54 High rails
55 Good clean fun
56 Reed instrument
57 Job for Mason
60 &
61 Boxtop piece
62 Diamond stat
63 Gray soldier
64 Negative vote

693 OLD-TIME OUTING by Bob Lubbers

ACROSS
1 Gen. __ E. Lee
5 Jack of TV
9 Role for Michael Caine
14 Medicinal plant
15 Taj Mahal site
16 Armstrong and Simon
17 Char
18 Land parcels
19 Nostrils
20 STARTING POINT
23 Zealous
24 Chronic thief, for short
27 Fleur-de-__
28 Malign, in street lingo
30 Bosses: Abbr.
31 Nol of Cambodia
32 __ Mame
34 Certain
35 MODE OF TRAVEL
39 Didrikson or Ruth
40 Colorful colonist?
41 Lubricate
42 Colleague of Curly
44 Alias indicator
45 Skill
48 Mild oath, across the sea
50 Pencil tip
52 DESTINATION
56 Not moving
58 Wood strip
59 Regrets
60 Maine city
61 Low woman's voice
62 Coup d'__
63 Muscle power
64 Tide type
65 Collections

DOWN
1 Imp
2 Fabled Chicago cow owner
3 Enplanes
4 Pied-à-__
5 One of the hills of Rome
6 All aflutter
7 Comic Johnson
8 Unduly hasty
9 Cancels
10 Car document
11 Hydrant
12 __ de France
13 Curve
21 Pakistan river
22 Approved
25 Whig opponent
26 In agreement
29 Gape (at)
30 Ms. Hopper
32 "__ you awake?"
33 Chemical ending
34 Mil. rank
35 "__ and farewell"
36 Forgotten state
37 Pastry place
38 Strip of weapons
39 Barker or Vila
42 Laid back
43 Thimble Theater name
45 Shrewd
46 Prepare leftovers
47 Secret meetings
49 Pooh creator
51 Buenos __
53 Thicke or Arkin
54 Strong wind
55 Singer James
56 Distress call
57 Three: Pref.

694 THE STING by Wayne R. Williams

ACROSS
1 Detection device
6 Comprehend
11 Canadian prov.
14 Residence
15 Edmonton skater
16 UN member
17 Waters off Cape Cod
19 Poetic adverb
20 Suffix for expert
21 Come up short
22 Paramours
24 Ball/Arnaz production company
26 Exodus name
27 Fop
30 Memo abbreviation
33 Doff a derby
36 Artistic work
37 Arctic surface
38 Equipment
39 Evenings: Abbr.
40 Does nothing
42 Sothern or Sheridan
43 Writer on film
44 Cast off
45 Command to Fido
47 Italian innkeeper
49 1941 and 2001, for two
51 Sprayed plants
55 Masquerade mask
57 Top rating
59 Comic Olsen
60 Spanish gold
61 Parent's Day event
64 Coll. course
65 Way from a man's heart
66 Hamper
67 Jose or Juan preceder
68 Long-answer exam
69 Himalayan legends

DOWN
1 Zealous
2 Willful destruction
3 Rests fitfully
4 Carpentry tool
5 Changes the distribution
6 Valhalla inhabitants
7 Get up
8 Priest's vestment
9 Underwater facilities
10 The Toy star
11 Bed choice
12 Software buyer
13 Jug handles
18 Sauce thickener
23 Shortwave org.
25 Adjective-forming suffix
26 Entertainer
28 Latin American dances
29 Made a choice
31 High cards
32 Pain in the neck
33 Home of the Jazz
34 Zilch
35 First family vacation
40 Act of mercy
41 Matures
43 Pertinent
46 Floral ring
48 Former Atlanta arena
50 Handlelike parts
52 Book of the Apocrypha
53 Varnish ingredient
54 Submarine areas
55 Accomplishes
56 Killer whale
57 Utah city
58 Oil of __
62 Hesitation syllables
63 Coll. sr.'s test

ACROSS

1 Distort
5 Actor Willem
10 Ticket leftover
14 Subj. for Gore
15 Swashbuckling Flynn
16 Crosby's *Road* companion
17 Management headaches?
19 "__ Rhythm"
20 Leave school
21 *Nación*
23 Attacks
24 Ashen
26 Actress Oberon
28 Haven
32 Captain Pierce portrayer
36 __ *of Our Lives*
37 Slap spot?
38 Constructed
40 Wee hour
41 Munster or Haskell
42 Make joyful
43 Surpasses
45 __ packing (dismissed)
46 Barkin or Burstyn
47 Takes second place
49 Worked the oars
51 Fateful spinner
56 Shutterbug's need
59 Once-popular movie site
60 Shake __ (hurry)
61 What currency speculators do?
64 Double negative?
65 Go __ for (support)
66 Shoe shaper
67 Knight and Danson
68 Stands pat
69 Bridge seat

DOWN

1 Merges metals
2 Without __ in the world
3 *Lost in Space* role
4 Wishing-well sounds
5 Named as a representative
6 Smell __ (be suspicious)
7 Part of TGIF
8 Ending for ball or drag
9 "That's someone __, not mine"
10 What textile merchants do?
11 Roman wrap
12 Familiar with
13 Gamma preceder
18 Wander
22 Skiing spot
24 What lumber salesmen do?
25 __ *Fables*
27 Disconcert
29 "Us" or "Them"
30 "The doctor __"
31 Undo a dele
32 Busy as __
33 Period of inactivity
34 Coast rival
35 What psychiatrists do?
39 Domingo, for one
44 Confidences
48 Actor Pickens
50 Units of power
52 Egg-shaped
53 __ firma
54 Long walks
55 Beginning
56 "__ Buy Me Love"
57 Medicinal plant
58 Do some darning
59 6/6/44
62 Flapdoodle
63 Lawyers' org.

ACROSS

1 Cadabra preceder
5 Suffix for special or final
8 Imitation
12 Runs in neutral
13 Not pro
14 Architect Saarinen
15 Harmonica
17 Treats leather
18 Vicinity
19 Laundry additive
21 On the __ (exactly)
22 Progression
24 Not moving
26 Cleo or Frankie
29 Go bad
31 Brit. fliers
34 Tall grasses
36 Reno or Leigh
38 Jean of *Arsenic and Old Lace*
40 Muslim title
41 Final Greek letter
42 XLIX sqvared?
43 "... emblem of the __ love"
45 Yanks' Boston rivals
46 "__ evil ..."
48 Equestrian's controls
50 Unclear
52 Like some modern music
56 Coach Parseghian
58 Exertion
61 FDR's dog
62 Scrabble piece
64 Stevie Wonder oldie
66 Musical composition
67 Eight: Pref.
68 Change for a ten
69 Chick's sound
70 Charlotte of TV
71 Astute

DOWN

1 Worship
2 Sadder
3 Not wholesale
4 Cigar residue
5 Swenson of *Benson*
6 Night-sky sights
7 Dyes: Poet.
8 Tennis match unit
9 Front-page screamers
10 Florence's river
11 Largest amount
12 "__ corny as Kansas ..."
13 Museum offering
16 Davis of *Evening Shade*
20 Swinging nightspot
23 Jewelry items
25 Sandy soil
27 Actress Patricia
28 Writer __ Rice Burroughs
30 Kids' block brand
31 St. Louis footballer
32 Navy VIPs
33 Apparent worth
35 Rational
37 April 15 concern
39 Brainstorm
44 Sawyer or Ladd
47 Looking to obtain
49 Easy mark
51 Writer Jong
53 Uninformed
54 Of the Tyrol
55 Gaelic girl
56 Over
57 Ready to eat
59 Poker entry fee
60 "__ to Rio" (Peter Allen song)
63 Clairvoyant's talent: Abbr.
65 D.C. stadium

697 KNOCKING ABOUT by Dean Niles

ACROSS
1 Popular '70s hairdo
5 Comics Viking
10 Unappetizing stuff
14 High wind
15 Last of a series
16 Casino city
17 Rowdy group
20 Sectors
21 Perfect grade
22 Civil War monogram
25 Debussy's sea
26 Highest
30 Washington's Kennedy __
32 Dad's boys
33 Colorado Native American
34 __ Thompson (Maugham character)
35 Ike's ex
36 Footnote phrase
37 Group members
40 Hem in
41 Clears
42 Best man's offering
44 Poet's contraction
45 Poet's tributes
46 Grass variety
47 Stuck
49 Sleeve filler
50 Ecol. org.
51 "__ Day Will Come"
52 Hardly right
54 Group's forte
61 Rani's garment
62 City near Gainesville
63 Pennsylvania port
64 Paired
65 Gallo products
66 Old horses

DOWN
1 Preston or Pepper: Abbr.
2 "Gotcha!"
3 Dark malt
4 Jazzman Stan
5 Little Jack __
6 Turkish title
7 The Bee __
8 Cabinet lawyers: Abbr.
9 Clear-thinking
10 Bride's mate
11 Without a __ to stand on
12 Impersonal pronoun
13 Batt. terminal
18 Family prep. course
19 Klutz's cry
22 Dosage amts.
23 More sleazy
24 Pyrenees nation
26 Theater honors
27 Beat Andretti, e.g.
28 Waits for Santa, perhaps
29 __ Aviv
31 Even-steven
32 Some sediments
35 Cornered
36 Love god
38 Surf phenomenon
39 Music marking
40 Procured
43 Pekoe or Earl Grey, e.g.
45 Magnum __ (masterpiece)
46 Uproar
48 Visit unexpectedly
49 Foot-leg link
52 See 60 Down
53 Govt. agents
54 JFK arrival
55 __ & Order
56 Jackie's second
57 Here, in Toulouse
58 Distinct period
59 Use a shovel
60 With 52 Down, Sammy Davis autobiography

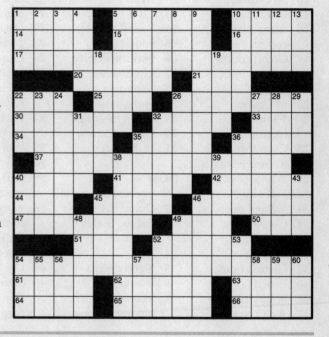

698 ON THE HOUSE by Wayne R. Williams

ACROSS
1 Eban et al.
6 Perimeter measurement: Abbr.
10 Three-handed card game
14 List of candidates
15 Sailing
16 Hawaiian haven
17 Table sprinkler
19 Elevator man
20 Neighborhood
21 First Hebrew letter
22 Exploits
23 Songwriter Johnny
25 Swear word
27 Gold stamping
31 Chicago trains
34 Bit of bedding
37 Doone of fiction
38 The Confessions of __ Turner
39 Kept back
40 Mantle's teammate
41 Tableland
42 Powerful sphere
43 Watercraft
44 Squalid
45 Excessively
46 Daniel's whereabouts
48 Pained cry
50 Eaves sight
54 God of war
56 Pub pints
60 Drink voucher
61 Plenty
62 Unshakeable belief
64 Entrance
65 Group of mobsters
66 Cornhusker city
67 Sample tape
68 Scoria
69 Ruhr Valley city

DOWN
1 Indian state
2 Sound loudly
3 Harvest worker
4 Fond of, with "to"
5 Dry, as wine
6 Telephone
7 Capri, for one
8 Gather crops
9 Traffic noises
10 Young pig
11 Earl of Khartoum
12 Landed
13 Heave
18 Justice Warren
24 Sup
26 Police file abbreviation
28 Pampas kin
29 Chucklehead
30 Zodiac sign
32 Stand up
33 Sojourn
34 Worn out
35 Rescuer, maybe
36 Maneuverability
40 Letter holders
41 Personal recorders
43 Half of CCCII
44 Winter mo.
47 Part of CD
49 Houston player
51 Sill "pets"
52 Flexible
53 Actor Hawke
54 Road safety grp.
55 __ vera
57 Latin abbr.
58 Sicilian peak
59 1994 Tony winner Diana
63 Adversary

699 HIT THE DECK by S.E. Booker

ACROSS
1 Clean up
5 Low-tech snowmobile
9 Dr. Salk
14 Concerning
15 Fleet member
16 Not suitable
17 Lab tube
18 Sommelier's cooler
19 Go off course
20 Adams or Brickell
21 JACK
23 Margaret Thatcher's husband
25 Cash substitute
26 Riviera resort
29 Whole bunch
30 Fall guy
33 Violent outburst
37 Get canines
39 Smooth out
40 Cut out
42 Genie's home
43 Fanciful
45 Night shift?
47 Asian bean
48 Mars or Jupiter
50 Stan of jazz
51 Thrashed
53 Powell/Keeler film of '34
57 KING
62 It's drawn with water
63 Civil War side
64 Penny, perhaps
65 Sound copy
66 Berlin specialty
67 Music maker
68 "Younger __ Springtime"
69 Secret meeting
70 Diamond crew
71 Make sharp

DOWN
1 Greeted the crowd
2 Out of the way
3 Cabinetmaker's finish
4 ACE
5 Blend drinks
6 Interweave
7 Members of the board, for short
8 Call the shots
9 Bateman of *Family Ties*
10 Ready to be used
11 Drug cop
12 "Oh! What __ Was Mary"
13 Orb anomaly
22 Mentor's concern
24 Die high
27 Twister kin
28 Compass dir.
30 Mr. Deer
31 Exclamation of regret
32 Cartoon skunk LePew
33 World War II pope
34 Cartoonist Peter
35 Calhoun of westerns
36 "__ your battle stations"
38 QUEEN
41 Piece: Abbr.
44 Contrary to
46 Sign of a Commonwealth corp.
49 Repeat performance of a sort
51 Wooden shoes
52 Jeans material
54 Virile
55 Frome of fiction
56 Excelled
57 California alternative?
58 "__ out? Make up your mind!"
59 Striped
60 Surmounting
61 *I Remember Mama* son

700 CALL OF THE WILD by Bob Lubbers

ACROSS
1 Head coverings
5 Compact recording medium
9 Actress Normand
14 Latin trio member
15 Wee bit
16 __ of Two Cities
17 How the *Cats* cast is paid?
19 Greenish blues
20 Real __
21 Avers
23 Breathe
25 Unconnected
26 Trudges on
28 Dappled feline
31 Marseilles militia
34 Moxie
36 __ du Diable (penal colony)
37 Roe source
38 Pulls in
39 Film spool
40 __ Lingus
41 Inch indicator
42 Crusoe creator
43 Matched (up)
45 Spring blossom
47 More current
49 Chivalrous
53 "Be __" (Scout motto)
56 Basic dive
57 Kitchen tool
58 Hogtier's order?
60 Chan portrayer
61 Split-level cookie
62 Queen of scat
63 Salamanders
64 Dizzy or Daffy
65 Take five

DOWN
1 Frolic
2 Give pleasure to
3 Segments
4 Cash-deficient
5 Monterrey moola
6 Charged particle
7 Poker variety
8 WWI Sopwith fighter
9 Role for Griffith
10 "Relax!"
11 Silence of the lambs?
12 *La femme*
13 Fewer
18 Scrabble vowel
22 Possum cousins
24 Ford flop
27 Tout's talk
29 Margarine
30 Prefix meaning "far"
31 PDQ
32 Perlman of *Cheers*
33 Where crows mark time?
35 Strip a ship
38 More coarse
39 Tilting chair
41 Bounties
42 __ Lama
44 Make amends
46 Pondlike body of water
48 Fix lawn defects
50 Bracelet site
51 Carter and Gwyn
52 Spring for the tab
53 You or me, for short
54 Tick off
55 Challenge
59 Vote for

701 OFFICEWORK by Dean Niles

ACROSS
1 Beer ingredient
5 Dieter's concern
10 Ax stroke
14 Mr. Nastase
15 "Live Free __" (NH motto)
16 Musical sample
17 Pigeonhole
19 Actor James
20 Bain or Hilton
21 Wood strip
23 Like the desert
24 European capital
26 Get ready to play golf
28 Doesn't get it, in a sense
32 More reckless
35 French friend
36 Winter precipitation
37 Mrs. Helmsley
38 Penny
40 Bore a hole
43 Close-fitting
44 __ the Horrible (comics Viking)
46 Fruit-filled desserts
48 Poetic preposition
49 Sign up
51 Gung-ho
53 Pixies
55 Valhalla resident
56 Ump kin
58 Special-interest orgs.
60 Prescribes
64 Allies' opponent
66 Ad creator
68 Thurber's The __ Animal
69 Labor group
70 Coup d'__
71 Church outcry
72 Sean and Arthur
73 Koran chapter

DOWN
1 Var. topics
2 Sax type
3 Legal claim
4 Overwhelming fear
5 Forest
6 Actor Carney
7 Pastoral poem
8 Nurse, as a drink
9 Fluctuate
10 Atlanta health agcy.
11 Walkman part
12 Mr. Sharif
13 Small horse
18 Relieves
22 Mend
25 Stink
27 Exploits for gain
28 Papier-__
29 Words of clarification
30 One way to march
31 Filch
33 Accustom
34 Vented one's spleen
39 End piece
41 Oilcloth, in Britain
42 Disappointments
45 Invitation letters
47 Bake eggs
50 China piece
52 Lingerie
54 British biscuit
56 "__ Lama Ding Dong"
57 Midterm, e.g.
59 Whirl around
61 "__, Brute?"
62 Bring up
63 Mlle. in Madrid
65 E.M. Kennedy's title
67 At that place

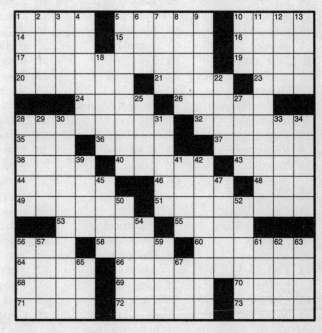

702 COLOR TELEVISION by Harvey Estes

ACROSS
1 Life sketch
4 Jazz phrase
8 Bullets, for short
12 Sea birds
13 Walk __ (be elated)
15 Tail end
16 Gemini org.
17 "Be quiet!"
18 Is human?
19 '60s crime show
22 Show host
23 Word of cheer?
24 Gymnast Comaneci
26 Inform
27 Weed chopper
29 Words of surprise
31 Travelers' stop
32 "It" game
33 San Diego attraction
34 Editor's direction
35 '70s police show
39 Heart of the matter
40 Conclusion
41 Fall mo.
42 Singer Shannon
43 Salt Lake City setting: Abbr.
44 "Either he goes __ go!"
45 Friend of de Gaulle
48 Some circus performers
50 Actor Charleston
52 Agnew's nattering one
54 '80s sitcom
57 Puff-of-smoke sound
58 Pakistan neighbor
59 Allie's ally
60 Catch sight of
61 Takes it easy
62 Garden spot
63 Culp/Cosby program
64 Red mark
65 Beatty of Deliverance

DOWN
1 Hindu deity
2 Bug
3 Orange type
4 Got up
5 Not out there
6 Beasts in the flora
7 End of the line?
8 The MCI Center, for one
9 Burgess of Rocky
10 Strict disciplinarian
11 Hosp. theaters
12 Computer key
14 Greek letter
20 Betty Ford Clinic work
21 Workers in 11 Down
25 Picnic pest
28 Stares at
30 Integrity
32 Singer Ritter
33 Last letter in London
34 An NCO
35 Where Tarzan swings
36 '50s toy
37 Up to this point
38 Cake cover
39 S&L concerns
43 Food-flavor enhancer: Abbr.
44 Big name in drama
45 Rub raw
46 Shed feathers
47 Hedda Gabler writer
49 Grove of baseball
51 Discombobulate
53 Conrad of verse
55 Black gold
56 Cartoonist Thomas
57 Pressure meas.

703 BIG GUYS by Bob Lubbers

ACROSS
1 Memory gaps
7 Go out with
10 Technique for Torme
14 Acid ester
15 Make lace
16 Story
17 Runway surface
18 Not permanent, as ink
20 Jazz composer
22 __ effort (WWII slogan)
24 Brenneman of *NYPD Blue*
25 Facing the pitcher
29 Rocky crag
30 Yang's counterpart
32 Sortie
33 Pitcher's pride
34 Best or Millay
36 Hexes
38 Silents star
41 Fix a loose board
42 *Charley's* __
43 Many mos.
45 *Casablanca* role
46 Dollar sign, basically
47 __ polloi
48 Precipitous
50 Bic product
52 Family group
53 Rock legend
57 Mound prop
60 Beethoven symphony
63 Tel __
64 Pub quaff
65 Oland or Baxter
66 Margot Fonteyn, e.g.
67 Apt. units
68 Folksinger Pete

DOWN
1 Realty unit
2 __ mode
3 Theatrical presentation
4 Philippine island
5 Coup d'__
6 French state
7 Water vapor
8 Ahead of schedule
9 Encompassing abbr.
10 Show for Shatner
11 Urban vehicle
12 Totally
13 Football holder
19 Ocean
21 "I __ Be Around" (Bennett tune)
22 Greek vowel
23 Lose by default
26 Raucous advertising
27 Wing flap
28 6-pointers
30 Himalayan legend
31 Romantic interlude
35 Coach Parseghian
36 Works on one's tan
37 Agents' cuts: Abbr.
39 Rest
40 Good, in Mexico
41 B&O and others
44 "__ boom bah!"
49 Bad review
50 Sacred song
51 Rims
52 Make z's
54 Ski lift
55 Stables
56 *"Dies* __*"*
57 "Cool!"
58 Eggs: Lat.
59 Actor Alastair
61 Passing grade
62 JFK info

704 BELL, BOOK, AND CANDLE by Frank Gordon

ACROSS
1 This might be saved for last
5 Broom __ of the comics
10 Proper partner
14 Rights org.
15 Standouts
16 "I __ Song Go . . ."
17 Marker
18 Halloween option
19 Summer coolers
20 BELL followers
23 "The Lady __ Tramp"
24 Brit. military arm
25 Inflation stat.
28 Barber's sharpener
32 1992 role for Nicholson
36 Attila's group
38 Apiece
39 Sandwich snacks
40 BOOK followers
43 Man the helm
44 Gone by
45 Wineglass part
46 Burdened
47 Campaign tactic
49 Compass pt.
50 Shamus
52 Cell material
54 CANDLE followers
63 Privy to
64 Hoopster Shaq
65 Like Mother Hubbard's cupboard
66 Wee one
67 *Gremlins* director Joe
68 Highly excited
69 Canned
70 Spirited horse
71 AAA offerings

DOWN
1 *Brandenburg Concerti* composer
2 Reverberation
3 Give the __ to (elude)
4 __-frutti
5 Bathful of trouble?
6 About
7 Lascivious look
8 Dull as dishwater
9 Famous fur merchant
10 Political programs
11 Decorate anew
12 List component
13 Religious ceremony
21 CIA predecessor
22 Western resort
25 Word after war or hope
26 Pedro's point
27 Directory
29 Parking garage features
30 Razor-sharp philosopher?
31 Stage in development
33 Daring deeds
34 Golfers' shouts
35 "__ no questions . . ."
37 Honeyed
41 In apple-pie __ (neat)
42 Shocked
48 Hosp. pros
51 Clumsy ones
53 Facing the pitcher
54 Pocket bread
55 Dark black mineral
56 Roused
57 __ the finish
58 Hackman or Kelly
59 Can't stand
60 *Othello* baddie
61 Raven's cousin
62 Beer barrels

705 NIGHTWEAR by Manny Nosowsky

ACROSS
1 Copies
7 Tennessee defendant of '25
13 Early visionary
14 Ogler's phrase
15 Like plywood
17 Substituted (for)
18 Stretch a bit
19 Imitate Romeo and Juliet
21 Latin she-bears
22 Made one's voice carry
24 Be concerned (about)
27 Fur source
28 OPEC unit
31 WWII vessel
33 Rocker Billy
34 Actress Charlotte
35 *Life* employee
39 Not neg.
40 Israeli leader of the '70s
41 Architectural order
42 "But is it ___?"
43 Author Ephron et al.
46 Cal ___
47 Fops
49 One way to get information
52 Old oaths
53 "That's a joke, ___!"
56 Circumscribed or detached
58 In a cheerful way
60 Striped marbles
61 Ecclesiastic groups
62 Indian soldiers of old
63 Hogan relative

DOWN
1 Race distance
2 Author Dinesen
3 Noted auntie
4 Clock numeral
5 Chair specialist
6 Middle East greeting
7 Drunkard
8 Onetime Chinese premier
9 Start of a prayer
10 Steno's items
11 Director Kazan
12 Sensible
16 Red: Sp.
17 Military region
20 Courtroom illegality
22 Moss material
23 Ump follower
24 Coffee serving
25 Detest
26 Fowl place
28 Salt water
29 Fundamental
30 Wolf
32 Noted jungle doctor
36 *M*A*S*H* transport
37 More slick
38 Large quantities
44 Open a bit
45 Cruel one
47 Disney dog
48 Belgian violinist/composer
49 Days, in Durango
50 *Picnic* playwright
51 Right away, in a way
53 Octagonal sign
54 Shoppe descriptor
55 Wall St. org.
57 Burro
59 Plane hdg.

706 STORMY WEATHER by Shirley Soloway

ACROSS
1 Offer a chair to
5 ___ Major (Great Bear)
9 Greek letters
14 Wheel support
15 Tailor's line
16 Repent
17 Sounds from a comedy club
20 Land or sea follower
21 Nile snake
22 Consume
23 Robert Mitchum miniseries
28 Durango direction
29 Slangy denial
30 Health resort
33 Spring beauty
36 Taken-back purchases
40 Hi and bye?
44 Calm, as fears
45 The Elephant Boy
46 Mystery writer Josephine
47 Scottish denial
49 Concerned with
52 Summer night sights
58 ___ capita
59 Pull a scam
60 ___ *Grows in Brooklyn*
62 Car make
67 Belief
68 Broadway light
69 "___ Old Cowhand"
70 Bob of *Full House*
71 Sp. miss
72 Oscar ___ Renta

DOWN
1 Droops
2 Precise
3 God of Islam
4 Indian tent
5 GI aid org.
6 Ring ump
7 Dinner course
8 Gather together
9 Groceries holder
10 Archaic verb ending
11 "When I Take My Sugar ___"
12 Lend ___ (listen)
13 Spanish artist
18 Plies a needle
19 Atop
24 "Put ___ writing"
25 School outcasts
26 Cab cost
27 Sound of relief
30 ___ Na Na
31 Buddy
32 Feel sick
34 ___ *Man Answers* ('62 film)
35 Polio pioneer
37 Housecat, e.g.
38 Bullring cheer
39 Wily
41 Singer k.d. ___
42 Indian nanny
43 Ladder step
48 Engrave
50 Ski lift
51 Offer more money
52 Martin Arrowsmith's wife
53 Not perf., as clothing
54 Verbs' subjects
55 ___ *Sanctum*
56 Soot
57 Ecological adjective
58 Promoted pvts.
61 Author Ferber
63 '50s pres.
64 Little one
65 Period
66 Queen of Spain

707 YANKEE DOODLES by Richard Silvestri

ACROSS
1 Echelon
5 Jefferson's belief
10 Big chunk
14 "This one's __!"
15 "Moldy" tune
16 Flag holder
17 Yankee Hall-of-Famer
19 Serenader's instrument
20 What enemies have lost?
21 Ring around the collar?
22 Dr. Frankenstein's assistant
23 In a snit
25 Outstanding
27 Corporate cow
29 Restraint
32 Stephen and William of Hollywood
35 Darth __
37 Fink
38 "Xanadu" group
39 Western scenery
40 "__ Got a Crush on You"
41 Silly Putty container
42 A bit more normal
43 Racing sleds
45 Hem maker
47 Take hold
49 "__ Ha'i"
50 $$$
54 Mass conclusion
56 Architectural deg.
59 Sun circler
60 High in alcohol
61 Yankee Hall-of-Famer
63 Zoning unit
64 San Antonio landmark
65 Differently
66 Minimal wampum
67 David's weapon
68 Report-card woes

DOWN
1 Burgs
2 __ water (trouble-bound)
3 Author Zola
4 Hauled again
5 Senior members
6 Subordinate Claus?
7 Admiree
8 Kingly address
9 Gets both sides together
10 First-aid item
11 Yankee Hall-of-Famer
12 Sort of sax
13 "The amber nectar"
18 What Pandora released
24 Specified
26 "__ the ramparts . . ."
28 Unburdens
30 Icicle locale
31 AAA selections
32 Exemplar of redness
33 Ms. Korbut
34 Yankee Hall-of-Famer
36 Challenged
39 Mexican music makers
42 The sun's name
43 Actress Palmer
44 Took sneakers off
46 Splashed down
48 Numero uno
51 Spat's spot
52 Singer Della
53 Eye infections
54 Gregory Peck's *Moby Dick* role
55 Anti-mugger weapon
57 Pervade
58 Jai __
62 K-O interior

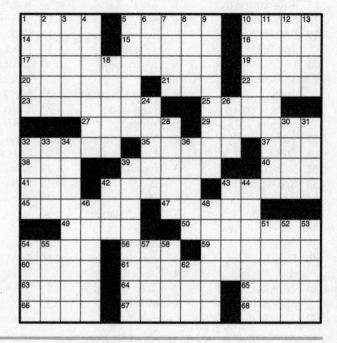

708 CALLING DR. RICHTER by Bob Lubbers

ACROSS
1 Words of possibility
5 Leer at
9 "Oh, sure!"
13 __ avis
14 Yarn amount
15 Actress Naldi
16 SHAKE
18 NCOs
19 "__ Nightingale"
20 Stuffed entrées
22 Writer Alison
24 Indian queen
25 Monetary incentives
28 Under
31 Simpson or Greenspan
32 Mexican city
34 Ms. Farrow
35 Ebb or flood
36 D.C. figure
37 Yearn (for)
38 Ike's WWII command
39 Worshiped
42 Actress Swenson
43 Made graffiti
45 Less straight
47 Sea: Ger.
48 La __ Vita
49 Liquidate, as a mortgage
52 Cheers up
56 Olin or Horne
57 RATTLE
59 Stocking stuffers?
60 Broad collars
61 Tra __
62 Terrier type
63 Location
64 French river

DOWN
1 Jason's ship
2 Reddish-brown quartz
3 "Dies __"
4 High life, slangily
5 Russian river
6 Art category
7 Italian beach resort
8 Guarantor
9 Off one's rocker
10 ROCK
11 Feminine ending
12 USIA rival
14 Pottery fragments
17 Rain and rain and rain and rain and rain and rain and rain and rain and rain and rain and rain and rain and rain and rain and rain and rain and . . .
21 Cantrell or Turner
23 Crustacean
25 Evaluated
26 Upper crust
27 ROLL
28 Ravel composition
29 Trace
30 Comics Viking
33 "Neither rain __ . . ."
37 How family trees branch
39 Word form for "vinegar"
40 Takes (from)
41 Stingy distributors
44 Add oxygen
46 USC rival
48 Train station
49 Landon et al.
50 Milquetoasty
51 Tube-shaped pasta
53 Afternoon socials
54 Perry's creator
55 Twinkler
58 Compass pt.

709 LETTER-PERFECT by Wayne R. Williams

ACROSS
1. Gaseous state
6. Greek letters
11. British letter
14. *Dallas* matriarch
15. Losing streak
16. Shoshone Indian
17. Parents' Day event
19. Resident's suffix
20. "__ she blows!"
21. RR stop
22. Likely winner
24. Pain lover
26. Inch sideways
27. Ball holder
30. Concoct
33. Tire support
36. Eagle's dwelling
37. Ornamental vase with a pedestal
38. Scheduled next
40. "__ Now or Never"
41. Unable to act
42. Portion
43. Portion
45. End one's hunger
46. Set aside
47. "Wow!"
49. Bombeck and others
51. One way to graft a plant
55. Disinfectant agent
57. *Newhart* setting
59. Green shade
60. __ *Quartet* (Paul Scott tetralogy)
61. Flower of South Carolina?
64. Doctors' org.
65. __ *Gay*
66. Groovy
67. Might possibly
68. More sensible
69. "Stormy Weather" composer

DOWN
1. British undershirts
2. Greek letter
3. Entreat
4. North Sea structure
5. Fam. member
6. Doesn't exist
7. Gymnast Korbut
8. Vat
9. French woman's name
10. Pace
11. Inlet of the North Sea
12. Diminutive ending
13. Antelope playmates?
18. Agave fiber
23. Composer Berg
25. Full of suds
26. Playground device
28. Upholstery fabrics
29. Church contribution
31. Old Testament book
32. Inventor of the steam engine
33. Cones' partners
34. Cetacean genus
35. Certain cable announcer
37. Related product
39. Affirms
44. German river
47. Lead ore
48. More wacky
50. Feels sorry for oneself
52. Alternative beau
53. Baseballer Boyer
54. Wading bird
55. Study late
56. *Rendezvous With* __ (sci-fi novel)
57. Inactive
58. In the neighborhood
62. Long time
63. Genetic letters

710 FLOWERY LANGUAGE by Robert H. Wolfe

ACROSS
1. Elevs.
5. __ Domini
9. Long tales
14. Kennel coop
15. Former costar of Ebsen and Ryan
16. Game site
17. Actor Jannings
18. Unoccupied
19. Insertion mark
20. Silly flowers?
22. Army station
23. Cash conclusion
24. Schisms
26. Innards
30. Shiny fabric
32. Williams or Anka
33. S.A. mountain range
34. Dockworkers' grp.
37. Peculiarity
39. "The Raven" author
40. More steadfast
42. Sun. homily
43. Maturing elements
45. Give out
46. Ridicule
48. Elegant
50. Spielberg or Seagal
52. Jack of *Barney Miller*
53. Burt's ex
54. Ariose flowers?
60. Cat-__-tails
62. Always
63. Came down
64. Serenity
65. Reasons for overtime
66. Carnival attraction
67. German industrial city
68. Model Macpherson
69. Ooze

DOWN
1. Served well
2. Monk
3. Week-ending cry
4. "To thine own __ . . ."
5. Remains
6. Low point
7. Actress Carter
8. Metallic rocks
9. Cul-de-__
10. Fit for crops
11. Well-watered flowers?
12. "__ of robins . . ."
13. Satisfies
21. Yang's partner
24. Sault __ Marie
25. Aphid, for one
26. Chooses
27. Seldom seen
28. Shielded flowers?
29. Former heavyweight champ
30. Sound of sleep
31. Fruit drinks
33. Mimicked
35. Kauai keepsakes
36. Pretentious
38. Shipping-container weight
41. *The Crying Game* star
44. Card game
47. Make clear
48. Dessert, e.g.
49. Chaney Sr. or Jr.
50. Incline
51. Phone-machine sounds
52. Author Danielle
54. Rose or Hamill
55. Iniquitous
56. Canal zones?
57. Netman Nastase
58. Assistant
59. Stair part
61. Blake's dusk

IN PURSUIT by Shirley Soloway

ACROSS
1 Days gone by
5 Arizona river
9 Scent sensors
14 Man __ (racehorse)
15 Eden resident
16 Patriot Allen
17 Thompson of *Family*
18 Gaucho's weapon
19 Video-game name
20 Pathfinder
23 "Spring forward" time: Abbr.
24 Small sofa
25 First month, in Madrid
27 Approximately
30 Fishes with a net
33 Squelched
37 Landing place
39 Wading bird
40 "Holy cow!"
41 French director Louis
42 Classify
43 Tim of *Frank's Place*
44 Unit
45 Male and female
46 Composer Harold et al.
48 Lady of Spain
50 Welcome
52 Blake or Plummer
57 Lawyers' org.
59 List of accomplishments
62 Word before larceny or point
64 Burn
65 Yuletide buy
66 Eydie's mate
67 Casino game
68 Racetrack shape
69 Let up
70 Goulash
71 Baking apple

DOWN
1 Sends by mail
2 Cognizant
3 Mubarak's predecessor
4 Characteristic
5 Tongue wagger
6 Object of worship
7 Singing sounds
8 Stun
9 More reachable
10 Hall-of-Famer Mel
11 Spar solo
12 Corn servings
13 Foul mood
21 Writer Uris
22 __ nous (confidentially)
26 Lift up
28 Mild disagreement
29 Lubricated
31 Money in Milan
32 Overseas planes
33 Medical fluids
34 Teen follower
35 Football-party sites
36 More unusual
38 Seaman's saint
41 Penny-pincher
45 Identical
47 Retained after expenses
49 Not wide
51 Fasteners
53 Thespian
54 Vibes player Red
55 Sleep experience
56 Fred Astaire's sister
57 Church space
58 Letter after alpha
60 Newsman Huntley
61 Role for Welles
63 "__ Got Sixpence"

AS EASY AS . . . by Fred Piscop

ACROSS
1 Castle protection
5 Chinchilla, e.g.
8 Country singer Charley
13 Chan's comment
14 Norwegian monarch
16 Sieved potatoes
17 ABC
20 Short vocal solo
21 Diplomats' quest
22 Kind of 26 Across
23 Had on
24 Prompter's lead-in
26 Fisherman
31 Former Sinclair competitor
35 Vaughn role
37 Duffer's shot
38 PIE
41 Lama land
42 Author Ephron
43 Sufficiently cooked
44 Lucky charm
46 Brewer's need
48 Actress Skye
50 Errand runner
55 Write scores
59 Bring in
60 1-2-3
62 Nine-headed serpent
63 Pâté de __ gras
64 Defeat
65 Lamb product
66 Draft agcy.
67 Sp. women

DOWN
1 Goya subjects
2 Chicago airport
3 Computer-code abbr.
4 Straphanger's purchase
5 Recliner part
6 Forearm bone
7 Spitfire fliers
8 Make-believe
9 Shine's partner
10 Computer-screen symbol
11 Fender bender
12 Leading __ (vanguard)
15 Pooch's name
18 Editor's mark
19 Actress Miles
23 Mat word
25 Beef cut
27 Tickled pink
28 Suction starter
29 Friedman's subj.
30 Actor Auberjonois
31 "¿Cómo __ usted?"
32 Singer Whitman
33 Star of India
34 German auto
36 Gumbo veggie
39 Big name in pianos
40 Game fish
45 Frat-party wear
47 Blue shade
49 Soft ball
51 Amorphous masses
52 Cut obliquely
53 California city
54 Fits together
55 Tennis great Arthur
56 Rogers and Acuff
57 Backwoods P.O. routes
58 Razor brand
59 Slugger's stats
61 Dawn goddess

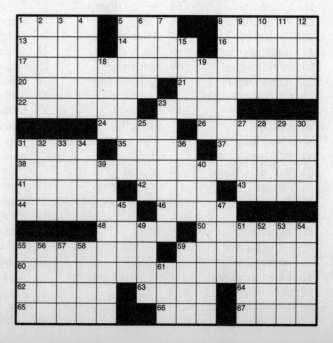

713 ANIMAL AX by Bob Lubbers

ACROSS
1 Auto fuel
4 Garden denizen
8 "__ With Me"
13 Job-safety org.
15 Greek letter
16 Nostrils
17 Diamond double
19 Ounce fractions
20 Bunny barbers?
22 Allergic reaction
23 *Of __ I Sing*
24 Scratch the surface
27 Asian holidays
29 Fats Domino's real first name
31 Curved path
34 Anchor man?
36 Arles aunt
37 Bruin basics?
42 __ *Warbucks* (musical sequel)
43 "Phooey"
44 Compass dir.
45 Citrus hybrid
48 Sergeants et al.
51 TV's Tarzan
52 __ ex machina (plot device)
54 Caner's material
58 Laryngitic pony?
60 Make happy
63 Marquee word
64 Bravery
65 Fairy-tale opener
66 Grounded bird
67 Tests
68 Clark and Orbison
69 Upperclassmen: Abbr.

DOWN
1 Early Germans
2 Nile dam site
3 Seaside
4 Feathery headpiece
5 Venetian official
6 Alamogordo event
7 Mason of *Chapter Two*
8 Racecar driver Mario
9 Taverns
10 Keogh kin
11 Party member: Abbr.
12 Snake shape
14 As red as __
18 Wood-shaping tool
21 Poetic time
24 Short skirts
25 Puts in a chip
26 Songstress Della
28 Fluid pouch
30 Cereal grain
31 Lessen
32 Kidney-related
33 Cautious
35 TKO caller
38 Fix, as a game
39 Barb throwers
40 Gluttony, for one
41 Hides away
46 Flower garland
47 __ blood (seeking revenge)
49 Hawaiian island
50 Mall unit
53 Office worker, for short
55 Snips off
56 *Thunder Alley* star
57 Spicy wine drink
58 Molecule part
59 Like some lingerie
60 See 4 Across
61 Careless
62 Words before carte or mode

714 TURNABOUT by Wayne R. Williams

ACROSS
1 Container
5 Surrendered formally
10 Linkletter and Fleming
14 Realty sections
15 Model Stewart
16 Actress Garr
17 Wedding vows
18 Soccer player?
20 Chart
21 Nincompoop
22 Bring up
23 Small cafés
25 Lose evolutionary ground
27 Family catastrophe?
29 Imitate Revere
31 Caviar source
32 Squabble
36 Author of "The Luck of Roaring Camp"
37 Morse signal
38 Uncommunicative ones
39 Industrious ones
40 Harris or Gibson
41 Err
42 Dinner at eight reservation?
44 Knight of the Round Table
48 More than two
51 "Für __"
52 Words of understanding
53 Actor Wheaton
54 Masseur, at times?
57 Incarnation of Vishnu
58 Soreness
59 Singer Cleo
60 Grade sch.
61 Suffix for mob or young
62 Put a stop to
63 Pit-bull biter

DOWN
1 Scale
2 Vietnamese costume
3 Not go far enough?
4 Double bend
5 Ultimate car
6 Go by
7 Chip's cartoon partner
8 Blowup of a pic.
9 Tap gently
10 __ of roses
11 Fasten wingtips again
12 Lock or shock
13 Male parents
19 Press
21 Lebanese group
24 Recommends
25 Civil unrest
26 Afore
28 Ruffled border
29 Cry of discovery
30 Operated
32 Slippery buildup
33 Part of a Japanese house?
34 __ Darya
35 Recipe abbreviation
37 Obligation
38 Novelist/film-maker Barker
40 Game piece
41 Took the helm
42 Level
43 Ancient ascetic
44 Rowlands and others
45 Choose
46 Nouveau __
47 Requester
49 *A Man and a Woman* star
50 Domesticated guanaco
52 In the same place: Lat.
55 Diminutive ending
56 Outlaw
57 Penalty caller

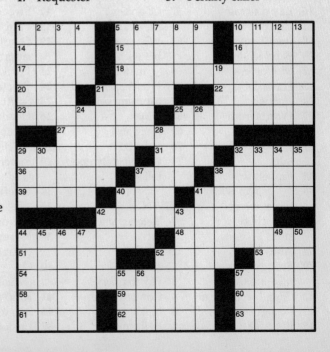

715 CHANGE OF PACE by S.E. Booker

ACROSS
1 Fort __, NC
6 Nicely
10 Hook attachment
14 Montez et al.
15 Baseball family name
16 Where the Hawks used to play
17 Writer __ Rogers St. Johns
18 Outfitted
19 Folk tales
20 *Hud* star
21 Coyote's quarry
23 Indiana town
25 Bro or sis
26 Bog material
28 Horselaugh
33 Creole stew
38 "My mama done __ . . ."
39 Without __ (broke)
40 Plastered
42 Bring up
43 Enamor
45 Simple and modest

47 From Nairobi
49 Threesome
50 Seek the affections of
52 Decline
56 Lenin's opponent
62 Hindu teacher
63 Car bar
64 Rowlands of *Gloria*
65 Mosquito, frequently
66 Flow (forth)
67 Working hard
68 Choice words
69 Clothing
70 Lug around
71 Feeling of defeat?

DOWN
1 Unwritten-on
2 Western show
3 Spring __
4 British city
5 Govt. purchasing agcy.
6 Baylor home
7 Scat name

8 An awful lot
9 Beethoven's first
10 Weevil nosh
11 Frenzied
12 Concerning
13 Wedding-cake section
21 Explorer Amundsen
22 Juxtapose
24 __ *culpa*
27 It's saved for a rainy day
29 "These Boots Are Made __" (Nancy Sinatra tune)
30 Pooch pest
31 __ *for All Seasons*
32 Had being
33 Auto hoist
34 Arthur of tennis
35 Sound of distress
36 Mongkut portrayer
37 Med. sch. subj.
41 Bruno of *City Slickers*
44 Bryn __

46 Never: Ger.
48 Candy-bar filling
51 "You're a fine __ talk!"
53 Surpass
54 Cold chemical?
55 Like a hobbit's feet

56 Endure
57 Montreal's __ '67
58 Cassini of fashion
59 Hot info
60 Peevish mood
61 Shakespeare's shrew
65 Pasture sound

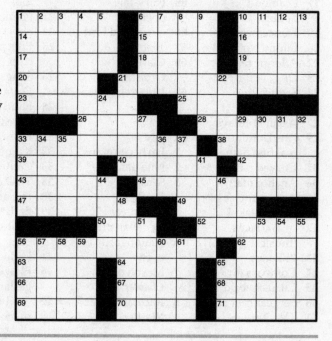

716 WISE WORDS by Ann Seidel

ACROSS
1 Latin abbr.
5 Delhi's land
10 Strip of concrete
14 Actress Turner
15 Broadway lights
16 Lay concrete
17 Crafts' partner
18 Inspiration
20 Band leader
22 Motionless
23 Have debts
24 Carried
27 Words from experience
31 __ *Dog* (Terhune tale)
35 Embellish
36 "__ a man with seven wives"
37 K-6 school, for short
38 Auto
39 Brought the meeting to order
42 "Egg" word form
43 Recognized
45 El __, TX

46 Encounter
48 Jerk's offering
49 Corner that's less than 90 degrees
51 Throat problem
53 Steelers' org.
54 Artistic judgment
57 Of ancient Mexicans
61 What insiders bet with
65 __ mater
66 French girlfriend
67 Morning sound
68 Dines
69 Rock and __
70 Lake craft
71 "For __ jolly good fellow"

DOWN
1 Veteran actor Jack
2 O'Haras' residence
3 Pay to play
4 Cowboy, often
5 Not acquired
6 Evil emperor

7 "__ make myself clear?"
8 Gerund suffix
9 Cigar residue
10 "Do not fold, __ or mutilate"
11 Put on cargo
12 Swear
13 Patrol area
19 Overtime situation
21 Plucked sound
24 Proctor's call
25 Spotted wildcat
26 Head: Fr.
27 Baseball bases
28 *A Bell for* ___
29 Pierced, in a way
30 Lively, in music
32 "Take Me __"
33 Flavor eggs
34 Nitrogen compound
40 On __ with (equal to)
41 Kind of beer
44 Squanderer
47 Let loose

50 Digestive protein
52 Vietnamese New Year
54 Nicholas or Alexander
55 Bombs and bullets
56 Glide along

57 Dynamic beginning
58 Inkling
59 Fuse units
60 Gemini org.
62 PC alternative
63 Pay or scram ending
64 A Bobbsey

717   ASSUME THE POSITION by Dean Niles

ACROSS
1 Photo holder
6 Bric-a-__
10 High-school equiv.
13 Famous frontiersman
14 Luxury car
15 Certain Semite
17 Actor Kathy or Alan
18 P __ "pneumatic"
19 Garrison of tennis
20 CPR giver
21 Adverse reactions
24 Earth tone
26 Shop tools
27 Argentine plain
29 Amidst
31 Rope fiber
32 Stylish
33 Goes down
37 Actor Erwin
38 Devotion
41 *You __ There*
42 Cook's portions: Abbr.
44 Talk wildly
45 Footnote abbr.
47 Slammer
49 Three-wheelers
50 F to F, e.g.
53 Encrusted
54 Back-row cry
57 CD-__ (computer device)
60 Oklahoma city
61 Comet part
62 Muscat resident
64 Slender bristle
65 Russian designer
66 Communion piece
67 Fashion monogram
68 Performs
69 Crook's "soup"

DOWN
1 Singer Lane
2 Sand, silt, and clay
3 "Cheers!"
4 French article
5 Military eatery
6 Razor filler
7 __ to the occasion
8 Girlfriend: Fr.
9 Be at loggerheads
10 Newspaper name
11 Author Segal
12 *Inferno* poet
16 Mingus' instrument
22 Tax agcy.
23 Modern communications machine
25 Numbers cruncher: Abbr.
27 "Hey, you!"
28 River islands
29 __-you note
30 Shrivel
32 Greenish blue
34 1991 Ron Howard film
35 Creamy cheese
36 Puts in place
39 Got one's bearings
40 Site of Cornwallis' surrender
43 Big stink
46 Boston cream __
48 56, in old Rome
49 Catch some rays
50 Poet's tributes
51 __ Island, NY
52 Gibes
53 Nat and Natalie
55 Betting game
56 Religious ceremony
58 Unique fellow
59 Spanish painter
63 A month in Montmartre

718   BRIDGE WORK by Mel Rosen

ACROSS
1 Start of many titles
4 Corrosive chemical
8 Paris eatery
12 Arsenal stock
13 Generous one
15 Spanish stewpot
16 Work place
17 Omar Sharif's command in a '74 film
19 "__ Love Her" (Beatles tune)
20 __ tree (in trouble)
21 On edge
22 Floor models
24 "What __ doing here?"
25 Type style
26 Hard workers
31 ". . . the grace of God __"
33 AMPAS award
35 Coffee-break time, perhaps
36 Doctors' lobby: Abbr.
37 Past
38 Match end, often
39 Goes quickly
42 Zoo beast
45 Line of thought?
46 Diplomatic aides
48 Rwy. worker
50 Deng's predecessor
51 Chick's calls
53 Fish or fur
55 Actress Gardner
57 Djellabah wearer
59 Captain Hook's command
61 Overrun (with)
62 Attorney Bailey
63 Air-freshener asset
64 Pre-owned
65 Tell's partner
66 Koppel and Kennedy
67 In accordance with

DOWN
1 The way things are going
2 Alec Guinness' command in a '62 film
3 His home is a dome
4 Rolls with the punches
5 Masterstroke
6 Swenson of *Benson*
7 Pointer, e.g.
8 Make schemes
9 Word of regret
10 Channel through the roof
11 Grandma's command
12 Oklahoma town
14 Pave over
18 Fork over
23 Sean Lennon's mama
26 Grand-scale adventures
27 Disney sci-fi film
28 Captain Picard's command
29 Fall tool
30 Dirty air
31 Strip in the Middle East
32 Neglect
34 Batman's wear
40 Takes the odds
41 Snakelike
43 Takes off
44 Actress Sue __ Langdon
47 Farmers, often
49 Prepare
52 Less risky
53 Arias, for example
54 British brews
55 Author James
56 Sell via machine
58 Night spot
59 Oliver Stone film
60 Fall mo.

719   BOOM! CRASH! BANG! by Fred Piscop

ACROSS
1 Rocker Clapton
5 Child, e.g.
9 One-__ bandit
14 Aswan Dam site
15 Actor Cronyn
16 Norman Vincent __
17 Singer Billy
18 Leave unmentioned
19 __ Selassie
20 BOOM
23 *Concentration* picture
24 Lawyer's letters
25 Taped-eyeglasses wearer
28 Maintain
33 Computer-code abbr.
37 It may be Far or Near
39 Barbra's *Funny Girl* costar
40 CRASH
43 Tortoise adversary
44 Ronny Howard role
45 Singers Hall and __
46 Puzzler's need
48 Brings home
50 Baton Rouge sch.
52 Eat voraciously
56 BANG
62 "Gay" city
63 Layer
64 Radio "good buddy"
65 Portents
66 *Gentlemen Prefer Blondes* writer
67 Sax type
68 What "i.e." stands for
69 Or __ (ultimatum words)
70 Mexican money

DOWN
1 Author Bagnold
2 *Easy __* (1969 film)
3 The Beatles' "P.S. __ You"
4 Tabloid target, for short
5 __ up sides (select teams)
6 Camel feature
7 Mideast bigwig
8 Obstetrical adjective
9 Plant pests
10 Peruse
11 Postal delivery
12 __ May Clampett
13 Sandra or Ruby
21 Russian launch
22 Diamond spot
26 Gather
27 "If I Were a Carpenter" singer
29 Soft drink
30 Give off
31 Stellar review
32 Very, in Versailles
33 1975 Wimbledon champ
34 Red dwarf, e.g.
35 Mrs. Dithers
36 Summer treats
38 __-Ball (arcade game)
41 Code inventor
42 Puccini opera
47 First-born
49 African fly
51 Fester or Wiggly
53 Songwriters' org.
54 Murmansk moola
55 Guitar parts
56 Port __, Egypt
57 Goad
58 Cub Scout units
59 Mosconi's game
60 Vientiane's land
61 Suffix with switch
62 Air-pump abbr.

720   ABOUT TIME by Robert H. Wolfe

ACROSS
1 Ballroom dances
7 Murphy Brown's home
10 Tress
14 Consecrate
15 Coronado's quest
16 Netman Nastase
17 Batter's position
18 Time to proceed along?
20 Censure
22 Deft
23 "No ifs, __ or buts"
24 Student paper
26 Not healthy
29 Stream
30 Humor
32 Hook's mate
33 Whichever
34 Dark brews
35 Some collegians, once
36 Dry time?
39 Shellfish eater
42 "If __ a Hammer"
43 RN's forte
46 Victuals
47 Those trying to escape
49 Tolstoy topic, in part
50 Oolong, for one
51 *Scent of a Woman* director
52 Be overfond
53 Remains
55 Swears (to)
58 Time for fauns?
61 "Stop everything!"
62 Sign
63 In time past
64 Tie
65 Broad
66 Strong desire
67 Approved

DOWN
1 Lash darkener
2 Justice Scalia
3 Time to complain?
4 Ties
5 Tale starter
6 Plant part
7 Intimidate
8 Fried-chicken selection
9 Time for Junior?
10 Speech impediment
11 Characteristic of the past
12 Spy grp.
13 Crucial
19 Susan of *L.A. Law*
21 Strong "no"
25 Cowards
27 Paced the field
28 __ *Misérables*
30 Cowardly Lion portrayer
31 Wallach of *Tough Guys*
32 Sauce source
35 Bounders
36 Danson or Husing
37 Eta follower
38 Patriotic org.
39 Frequently, poetically
40 __ the line (behave)
41 Raised a glass
43 Time for pairs?
44 Trelliswork
45 __ Butte, CO
47 Time to sauté?
48 Novelist Alain
51 Taproom
52 Perry's aide
54 Actress Daly
56 Huxtable or Kojak
57 *Honky __* (Gable western)
58 Spread seeds
59 Pierre's pal
60 Hither's companion

721　BEASTLY by Eileen Lexau

ACROSS

1 Showed up
5 Ravine
10 '60s hair style
14 Tel __
15 Separated
16 City map
17 Supreme Court number
18 Naive ones
19 Left, on a ship
20 Snoozed a bit
22 Mystery board game
23 "This is only __"
24 Off one's nut
26 Gridders' org.
28 Composer Rorem
29 Bandleader Brown
32 Rock-band tour assistant
34 Soup cracker
37 Track event
38 Doesn't have much food
41 __ mater
42 Put up
43 Peggy Fleming, e.g.
45 Berry or Kercheval
46 Prevent
49 Kazakhstan, once: Abbr.
50 Soap ingredients
53 Not a soul
55 Convent room
57 Fortunate ones
60 Palo __, CA
61 Was wearing
62 Look leeringly at
63 Courage
64 In a __ (excited)
65 Civil disturbance
66 Symphony woodwind
67 High-strung
68 Mtg.

DOWN

1 High-kicking dance
2 Navigate the air
3 Manufactured coins
4 Ties the score
5 Irving character
6 "__ and Away" (5th Dimension song)
7 Tag
8 Statement of belief
9 Elevs.
10 Not theoretical: Abbr.
11 Flatfish
12 Exalted
13 Baseball great Mel
21 Map book
22 Bill's partner
25 Produce
27 Allow
30 Mystery writer Queen
31 Cooking direction
33 Amongst
34 RBI, e.g.
35 "I Like __"
36 Place for a tie
38 Fraternal group
39 Almond-flavored liqueur
40 Rochester's boss
41 Burro
44 Building extension
46 __-woogie
47 North Americans, to Latinos
48 Bowling-alley buttons
51 Fill with happiness
52 North African nation
54 Smells
56 Come in second
58 Barracks beds
59 Leg joint
60 "Long __ and Far Away"
61 FDR's third veep

722　WATERLOGGED by Shirley Soloway

ACROSS

1 The Charleses' pet
5 Words before "happens" or "were"
9 "__ the night before . . ."
13 Turns to the right
14 Warwick and Westheimer
16 In this spot
17 Experiencing bad trouble
19 "I cannot tell __"
20 Wise goddess
21 Lubricated again
23 Enter, as a crowd
26 Crafty
27 Unworkable item
30 Part in a play
31 Tide type
33 Run off to wed
35 Memorable times
37 MacMurray or Allen
40 "__ Laurie" (Scottish air)
41 C.P.A.'s forte
42 Every 24 hours
43 Echelon
44 Throw out a line
45 Corbin on L.A. Law
46 1994, e.g.
48 Sty cry
50 Automotive fuel
51 Recede
53 Hustler's hangout
56 Disney production
58 Doing nothing
62 Clarinet cousin
63 Holds off
66 Writer Uris
67 As of
68 Point out
69 Wapitis
70 Retains after expenses
71 Pay attention to

DOWN

1 Water in Juárez
2 Labor Day mo.
3 Hebrew letter
4 Fire remains
5 Jockey Eddie
6 Big __, CA
7 Resident suffix
8 Unit of heat
9 East Asian
10 Fountainhead
11 Sharon of Israel
12 Run-down
15 Hanks of wool
18 Menu item
22 Single
24 Actress Verdugo
25 Pressurized container
27 Costly
28 Arm bone
29 Free-for-all
32 At a distance
34 Food fish
36 Up and about
38 Kazan of Hollywood
39 Changes color
42 Half of ND
44 Thieves
47 Mil. address
49 Looped ropes
51 School: Fr.
52 Biblical city
54 __ a million
55 Bandleader Miller
57 Change for a twenty
59 Theater award
60 Fill up
61 Spotted
64 Compass pt.
65 Interest amt.

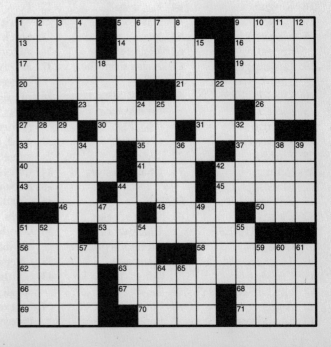

723 HAVE IT BOTH WAYS by Harvey Estes

ACROSS
1 Held onto
5 Skins
10 Paid players
14 Pita sandwich
15 Hirsute
16 Litter's tiniest
17 Bellyache
18 Mr. Bean
19 Land in the water?
20 School trainee
23 Marsha on *Night Court*
24 Dict. abbr.
25 Hardtop
26 "Don't move!"
28 Matures, as wine
31 __ *Got a Secret*
32 Do research
33 Do a slow burn
34 Crystal-ball gazer
35 Reversed
38 Effrontery
41 "No pain, no __"
42 Terminal
46 __ Grande
47 *Beetle Bailey* dog
48 *In Cold Blood* author
49 Church instrument
51 "That's __ she wrote"
52 Rangers' org.
53 Sweet delicacy
58 Plumb crazy
59 Stale show
60 GI Joe, for example
62 Oomph
63 Speechify
64 Washington bigwig
65 Strike out
66 Nat and Natalie
67 See 5 Down

DOWN
1 USSR's CIA
2 Unmowed lawn, maybe
3 Bar snack
4 Bean product
5 With 67 Across, "Poetry Man" singer
6 Pulls down
7 *Schindler's* __
8 Pony pace
9 "Auld Lang __"
10 Spooky Vincent
11 Controversial author
12 Absent from duty
13 More by the book
21 Baker's quantity
22 Pack animal
23 Country postal letters
27 Wicked
28 Sound
29 Fed. agents
30 Fair-hiring letters
33 Sports car
34 __ up (accelerate)
36 U.S. Army rank
37 Kennedy's Secretary of the Interior
38 Spoke harshly
39 Animal-carrier opening
40 Sensible
43 Bridge supporter
44 Shakespearean Moor
45 __ Aviv
47 Pronoun
48 They may be beside themselves
50 Make up (for)
51 Not quite right?
54 Gator cousin
55 *Last Action* __
56 Reverend Roberts
57 Throws in
61 Ayres or Wallace

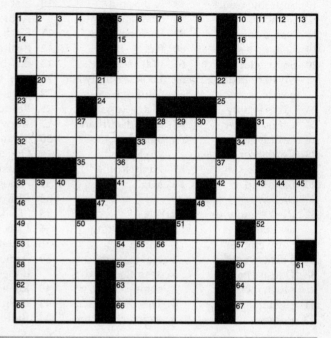

724 WHO'S WHO by Bob Lubbers

ACROSS
1 "__ aching back!"
5 Capacious
10 Health resorts
14 Cad
15 Worship
16 Ring up
17 __ Nostra
18 More appealing
19 Le Bourget alternative
20 HIS PROFESSION
23 Mineo or Viscuso
24 Hill dwellers
25 Enrolls
29 Painter Matisse
31 Enzyme suffix
32 Twist the truth
33 HIS INTEREST
37 Ollie's pal
40 Teachers' org.
41 Cruising
42 HIS DISCOVERY
47 Anger
48 GI address
49 Snooped (around)
52 Booze brand
54 Hammer end
56 Museum offering
58 HIS NAME
61 After-shower wear
64 "__ it up" ("It's not true")
65 Jacob's brother
66 Vicinity
67 Away from the office
68 May Whitty, for instance
69 "'__ I Do" (1926 song)
70 Welcome
71 Charon's river

DOWN
1 Killer whales
2 Cheer word
3 Pumper's pride
4 Slangy affirmative
5 Terse
6 Full-grown
7 Sunday sections
8 Eldest Brady son
9 Most spooky
10 Patton portrayer
11 Regulation score
12 Everyone
13 Foxy
21 Merit
22 Snick's partner
26 Actor Ron et al.
27 Ready for harvest
28 Bristle
30 Da __ (Vietnamese port)
31 Med. school subject
34 Involved with
35 Shoe widths
36 Chatters
37 Slide
38 Goodrich product
39 Over again
43 South Seas staple
44 Marked increase
45 "Not __ for tribute"
46 "__ Lisa"
50 Annoys
51 Really good-looking
53 In the lead
54 Babble
55 Murphy or Bracken
57 Actor Ernest
59 Love god
60 Cincinnati team
61 Cool
62 Mine yield
63 Stinging insect

725 UP FRONT by Ann Seidel

ACROSS
1 Gibson of the screen
4 Surmount
9 63 Across counterpart
13 Bar brew
14 Supply-__ (certain economist)
15 Feel (for)
16 Winter transport
18 Senator Alfonse D'__
19 Steer clear of
20 Certain Louisianan
22 "Goodnight, __"
24 Font widths
25 Flash Gordon portrayer
28 The Gypsies
31 Ringlet
32 Type of romance novel
37 Christian letters
38 Colorful fish
39 Edmond O'Brien suspense film
42 Velvet-collared coat
46 Chicago destination
49 Blubbered
50 Tom Hanks sitcom
55 Took a chair
56 Blender setting
57 Arrangement
61 German river
63 Tariff pact
65 __ of the above
66 Father
67 Robert of *Hogan's Heroes*
68 Sporty model
69 Passed along
70 Appliance maker
71 Dad's lad

DOWN
1 Not fem.
2 Actress Raines
3 Actor Cobb
4 Jeff Davis' territory
5 Curb
6 "Do __ to eat a peach?"
7 Cab clock
8 Mustang
9 Neon, for one
10 Nigerian novelist
11 Hitches (a ride)
12 Strains
17 United Arab Emirate
21 Now: Lat.
23 Art Deco designer
26 Seven, in Sonora
27 Flight stat
28 Baseball stat
29 Cry of awe
30 GP and OB-GYN, e.g.
33 Legal matter
34 Addams Family cousin
35 Grand __, Nova Scotia
36 Zoroastrian
39 Society newcomer
40 Tijuana tribute
41 Total
42 __-Magnon
43 Rope fiber
44 Rivals
45 *Hedda Gabler* dramatist
46 Preoccupy
47 Submarine
48 Aft
51 Swindle
52 Russian range
53 Get the lard out
54 Raison __
58 Garb
59 "Do __ others . . ."
60 Unskilled worker
62 On a pension: Abbr.
64 Scottish county

726 BB'S by Fred Piscop

ACROSS
1 Sharp ache
5 Circuit
10 __ Eban
14 Like two peas in __
15 Island nation
16 Do another hitch
17 *Mikrokosmos* composer
19 Fourth planet
20 Unvoiced
21 Beginning stage
23 __ Na Na
24 Genesis album of 1981
26 Pole-vaulter Sergei
29 Road sign
30 *The Woman __* (Wilder film)
33 "__ live and breathe!"
34 Sweet wine
37 Power, in combinations
38 __-de-sac
39 "Open sesame" speaker
41 Tempe sch.
42 Newsman Marvin
44 Egyptian talisman
45 Well-used pencil
46 As __ a fox
48 CPR expert
49 Fills to the gills
51 Fictional Starr
53 Go for apples, perhaps
54 '50s pitcher Ralph
56 Popular dolls
60 Knowledge
61 Baseball star
64 LL.B. holder
65 '60s tune, e.g.
66 Godunov was one
67 Lads
68 More meanspirited
69 Some turkeys

DOWN
1 Sunscreen ingredient
2 *Planet of the __*
3 __ contendere
4 Solidarity city
5 Appliance name
6 Trade center
7 Diner offering
8 Skater Midori
9 __ powder (run off)
10 Uniform accessory
11 Long-time coach at 24 Down
12 __ the hatchet
13 Lhasa __
18 Grand __ Island (vacation spot)
22 Sprint rival
24 Dixie state
25 He married Bacall
26 Supports
27 "The __" (regular's bar order)
28 Player of small parts?
29 Prepared apples, perhaps
31 Follow
32 Smears paint
35 Pacino et al.
36 Lawyers' org.
40 Suck up
43 Rubble and Fife
47 Dry, as wine
50 Comic Bud
52 Natterer, to Agnew
53 Anacin rival
54 Spill the beans
55 __-Rooter
56 Soft cheese
57 __ many words
58 Dutch cheese
59 Baltic states, once: Abbr.
62 In the manner of
63 Ave. crossers

727 DELIVERANCE by Ann Seidel

ACROSS
1 Cellist __ Ma
5 "__ Nice Clambake" (*Carousel* tune)
10 Use the molars
14 Repute
15 Bagel relative
16 Sign of sanctity
17 Overwhelming victory
18 Wears
19 Moslem honorific
20 Ens' preceders
21 Old mail system
23 Tennis star Chris
25 Young bird of prey
26 Talk-show groups
28 Singer Taylor __
30 Gide or Previn
31 Painter Claude
32 Shade source
35 Meek one
36 Hankered
37 French girlfriend
38 Sault __ Marie, Ontario
39 Big, noisy bird
40 Spring up
41 Chores
42 Carve in stone
43 Costello's foil
46 Windowpane adhesive
47 Gridiron tactic
50 Non-commercial notice: Abbr.
53 Birch or beech
54 Buenos __, Argentina
55 Weaving machine
56 Angler's aid
57 Bullwinkle, for one
58 __ of Wight
59 Tabulates
60 Back-of-the-book reference
61 English prep school

DOWN
1 The old days
2 Baseball's Blue Moon
3 Sam Cooke song
4 Food scrap
5 Loathes
6 Cheerful
7 Like pie, perhaps?
8 Skin moisturizer
9 Sharp-sighted
10 Use Visa
11 Actress Veronica
12 "Für __"
13 Least desirable
21 Soccer great
22 Breathe hard
24 Action word
26 Bosom friends
27 Med. school subject
28 Portuguese titles
29 From the top
31 Singer Jagger
32 Miss Manners predecessor
33 Talk like Daffy Duck
34 __ the Press
36 Deli beef
37 In __ (stuck)
39 __ Hari
40 Stops procrastinating
41 Shower linen
42 English region
43 Entertainers' union
44 Yawning
45 Animal category
46 Bel __ cheese
48 "Runaround Sue" singer
49 Urge on
51 Napoleon or Han
52 Prayer finish
55 Untruth

728 EEK! by Eileen Lexau

ACROSS
1 Gators' cousins
6 Extreme
11 Catch on to
14 Loose turf
15 Asian capital
16 Aerobic prefix
17 Terrified
19 "__ the ramparts . . ."
20 Writer Horatio
21 Outdoors
23 Shah's land
25 Flour sifter
26 Slugger's need
29 Bible book
31 Southwestern abodes
34 Wood for 26 Across
35 Boy: Fr.
37 Waldheim or Russell
38 Embarrassing situation
40 Bribe
41 *Cherchez la* __
42 Hawkeye State
43 Special K, e.g.
45 Golfer's benchmark
46 Sew up
48 Singer Fitzgerald
49 Compass dir.
50 "__ Theme" (*Doctor Zhivago* tune)
52 King's address
54 Words to a gas jockey
57 Smart society
60 Actor Wallach
61 What the frenzied may push
64 "What's the __?" ("I give up")
65 Bring out
66 Likely
67 German article
68 Calyx part
69 Made a dress, perhaps

DOWN
1 Successors to LPs
2 Costa __
3 Roundish
4 Welsh dog
5 Cheap sea accommodations
6 Amer. ship letters
7 "__ Smile Be Your Umbrella"
8 Works like a slave
9 Violent guy
10 *Batman* butler
11 Manifestation of fear
12 Naval second-in-command
13 First-timer
18 Pulitzer category
22 Conjure up
24 From Oslo
26 Foundation
27 Fancy neckwear
28 Spooked feeling
30 Game result
32 *Aunt __ Cope Book*
33 Cubic meter
36 German cars
39 Of birth
41 Sudden recurrences
43 Grant/Hepburn film
44 Go out on __ (dare)
47 French flapjacks
51 Dawn
53 __ nous
54 Longstanding quarrel
55 Ingrid, in *Casablanca*
56 Type size
58 Put away
59 Top-notch
62 Animation unit
63 Actor Beatty

729 FELLOW PUZZLERS by William Lutwiniak

ACROSS

1 "Not a chance!"
5 Shredded, in a way
10 Alka-Seltzer sound
14 Iridescent gem
15 Plot twist
16 Wander
17 TOM
20 Tangles up
21 Voice regret
22 __ XING (street sign)
23 An Untouchable
24 Sun shields
28 Alluring
29 Part of HMS, sometimes
32 Muscateer?
33 Half an illness?
34 New Rochelle college
35 DICK
38 Stone, Bronze, etc.
39 __ Named Joe (Spencer Tracy film)
40 Funt or Ludden
41 Forewent
42 Meager
43 Biker's selections
44 Leaves gatherer
45 Take a bough
46 Expunge
49 Not at all compelling
54 HARRY
56 Subordinate staffer
57 Speak in the Senate
58 Polaroid inventor
59 Mullins of the comics
60 Egg order
61 Singer Kristofferson

DOWN

1 Wine-tasting quality
2 Unobstructed
3 Handy tree?
4 High-fashion magazine
5 Alger ending?
6 Pestered
7 Whispers sweet nothings
8 Register for sch.
9 Reading difficulty
10 London strollers
11 "A many-splendored thing"
12 Pizza place?
13 Sassy
18 Lively wit
19 A snap
23 Bold
24 Opinionated
25 What you see
26 In reserve
27 Folks
28 Vaccine
29 Card-game authority
30 Signed a contract
31 Composer Saint-__
33 "Just like __ and Bacall"
34 Pointless
36 Discussed
37 Siesta taker
42 H.H. Munro
43 Did mail work
44 Up
45 Singer Lenya
46 GI entrée
47 Tom, Dick, and Harry
48 Start from scratch
49 __ B'rith
50 Be a sore loser
51 Sharif or Khayyám
52 "The __ Love"
53 Windups
55 Make mistakes

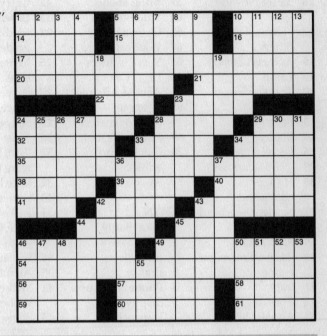

730 DEER ME by Randy Sowell

ACROSS

1 "I __ Symphony"
6 Savory smell
11 Snead or Spade
14 Ole or Merlin
15 Trite
16 Mao __-tung
17 Outrun a deer?
19 Al Jolson's real first name
20 __ the Woods (Sondheim musical)
21 He gave us a lift
22 Broadway backer
24 Capone's nemesis
26 Flora
27 Mind one's p's and q's
30 Starch digester
32 Give a speech
33 Casa rooms
34 Label
37 Sink in mud
38 Cat's hangout
39 Quote
40 Place a wager
41 "Get __ on!"
42 Oven setting
43 West Indies island
45 Contaminates
46 Dough
48 Evict
49 Exercise aftermath
50 Retained
52 "¿Cómo __ usted?"
56 Boston jetsam
57 Deer coin?
60 Attention
61 Eastern potentate
62 Mirthful
63 Canadian prov.
64 Begins to appear
65 Aunt, in Arles

DOWN

1 Southwestern tribe
2 Ardor
3 ADC, e.g.
4 Sound loudly
5 Tiny colonist
6 Furthers a felony
7 1944 Nobelist in physics
8 Burden
9 Big __ (burger choice)
10 Acid neutralizers
11 Deer country?
12 Plus
13 Lunch and dinner
18 Stockings
23 Part of USNA
25 Seth's mother
26 Drama, e.g.
27 Long pass
28 Huron neighbor
29 How some deer talk?
30 Series of shots
31 Nautical adverb
33 Plod
35 Keep __ (persevere)
36 Sets
38 Chinese nurse
39 Standards
41 Disconcerted
42 College degs.
44 Corrida cheer
45 Nobel-winning bishop
46 San __, CA
47 Singer Billy
48 N-T filler
50 Was aware of
51 Home for 25 Down
53 Ollie's sidekick
54 Revival setting
55 Comic Johnson
58 "__ Believer" (Monkees song)
59 Medium of expression

731 FOUR-BAGGER by Ann Seidel

ACROSS
1 Rhyme scheme
5 Lively
9 Actress Jaclyn
14 Singer/politico Sonny
15 Hint
16 Sierra Nevada lake
17 "Do __ others . . ."
18 Actress Lenska
19 Lasso
20 Traveler's bags
22 Born first
23 Forgo
24 Booby __
26 Joie de vivre
29 __ out (exposes)
33 Hunger hankerings
37 Nuclear-warhead acronym
39 Arm bone
40 Baseball manager Felipe
41 Irate
42 Corp. bigshots
43 Aquatic bird
44 Wallet fillers
45 Enjoys gum
46 Sparse
48 Not faked
50 Abominable Snowman
52 Bahamas seaport
57 Bring about
60 Student bags
63 Open a bottle
64 Window ledge
65 Yawn inducer
66 La __ Vita
67 Actress Adams
68 __ about (approximately)
69 Plumber's tool
70 Catches forty winks
71 Sawbucks

DOWN
1 Treat badly
2 Employee's reward
3 Prank
4 Phone enclosure
5 Sloppy John Hancock
6 Definite asset
7 Hold sway
8 Bread necessity
9 Small river
10 Postal bag
11 "If __ a Hammer"
12 Carry around
13 Listen to
21 Mediocre grades
25 Invitation letters
27 Prayer conclusion
28 Saltpeter part
30 Swiss modernist
31 "Ah, Wilderness were Paradise __!"
32 Give lip to
33 Butter squares
34 Actor Baldwin
35 Nick Charles' mate
36 Burlap bag
38 Artful dodge
41 Pitcher __ Wilhelm
45 Show approval
47 Indian dwelling
49 Places for some bracelets
51 Norwegian dramatist
53 Wooden shoe
54 British biscuit
55 Buckeye State city
56 Manipulative people
57 Cows masticate them
58 Soon
59 Home of the Bruins
61 Verdi opera
62 Paper fastener

732 WONDERFUL by Norma Steinberg

ACROSS
1 Coke and Pepsi, e.g.
6 "Yay, maestro!"
11 Actor Mineo
14 Scene of the action
15 Caesar or Brutus
16 Opposite of sing.
17 Majestic ending
19 Shade tree
20 Run in neutral
21 Convene
22 NYPD Blue character
23 Actress Lansbury
26 Dress fabric
28 Pavement material
29 Implant
33 Farrow or Sara
34 "Little piggie"
35 South Sea island
36 D-sharp alias
39 "__ corny as Kansas . . ."
41 Inventor Howe
43 Put away alphabetically
44 Referred to
46 Burt's ex
47 Sermon subject
48 Patriotic org.
49 Nos. for athletes
51 Holyfield feat: Abbr.
52 Happy faces
55 Posse, e.g.
57 "Mazel __!"
58 Sea plea
60 Impoverished
61 Yalie
62 Food source
67 Total (up)
68 Employment
69 "High Noon" singer
70 Caustic liquid
71 Sharp pains
72 Riders to the Sea playwright

DOWN
1 Droop
2 Hockey great
3 Antidrug org.
4 __ Get Your Gun
5 Equestrian gear
6 Cheese-store choice
7 Howard or Reagan
8 Amo, __, amat
9 Legally binding
10 Former
11 Neurologists and OB-GYNs
12 Apportion out
13 Like bad gravy
18 Afire, in a restaurant
23 Storage room
24 Wynonna's mother
25 Rocky Mountain watershed
27 Get one's goat
30 Spheres
31 Prufrock's creator
32 Dors or Sands
37 Share and share __
38 Choir voice
40 Close an envelope
42 Roseanne or Coach
45 Put on the Ritz
50 Sand bars
52 Unbelievable bargain
53 Like old bread, perhaps
54 The March King
56 Display
59 Straddle
60 Corporate exec.
63 Omelet ingredient
64 Family reunion attendees
65 School subj.
66 Casual shirt

CITY STUFF by Randolph Ross

ACROSS
1 Advance after a fly ball
6 Snarl
10 March and Van Fleet
13 __ acid
14 Piece of 45 Down
15 Bat wood
16 Alabama abodes?
18 Fidel's amigo
19 Gets weary
20 Smelled bad
22 Ferrets
25 Dances and sauces
26 Rebels
27 Word form for "sun"
28 Operated
29 "I'm __" (*Nashville* song)
32 Ferber and Best
35 Andean people
38 Marked a ballot
39 Put off
40 Heisted
41 Like summertime tea
43 NYC subway line
44 Huey and Shelley
46 *Twelfth Night* maiden
49 NATO member
51 Daytime shows
53 100% behind
54 "__ my case"
55 Arafat's org.
56 Michigan gems?
61 Joplin music
62 Detonates
63 Related to mom
64 Sounds of the satisfied
65 Lasting mark
66 Lear's daughter

DOWN
1 Highland hat
2 Latin I verb
3 Male cat
4 Joins
5 Force in blue
6 Shine
7 __ de plume
8 Reluctant
9 Closed up again
10 Mississippi quintet?
11 Actor Milo
12 Toolhouses
14 David's co-anchor, once
17 Rub out
21 Slur together
22 "City of Light"
23 Praying figure
24 Nebraska firewood?
27 __ Park, NY
30 Graph line
31 "Just a __!" ("Wait!")
33 High house
34 Mlles. of Mallorca
36 "Half __ is better . . ."
37 Bon-voyage parties, e.g.
42 Gives too much attention
45 Pizza topper
47 Antiseptic discoverer
48 Chant
49 *It's a Wonderful Life* director
50 God of Islam
51 Ore worker
52 Liberal __
57 Keogh cousin
58 Be a shrew
59 Hellenic H
60 D.C. VIP

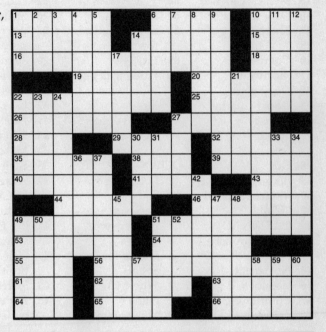

ANIMAL ANATOMY by Harvey Estes

ACROSS
1 Globe Theatre offering
8 City of Washington
15 Brew ingredient
16 "Golden" state
17 Most brief
18 Provoked
19 Corn units
20 *2001* computer
21 Pipe bowl, maybe
23 Military mission
27 Molten iron's "head"
31 Gumbo ingredient
33 Stern or Newton
35 Promising words?
36 Small vessel
37 Corrects text
38 Royal sphere
39 Mind-bender
41 Breadwinner
43 Brown from the sun
44 "It's a deal!"
48 "Woe is me!"
49 She-sheep
50 Old-fashioned writer
51 Snoot
52 June honorees
54 Lure into lawbreaking
57 Pub potable
58 Orange drink
60 Nonsense-verse writer
62 Bad-luck look
66 Ballot brandisher
69 Dukakis running mate
70 Light source
71 Adjective for manner
72 Guts

DOWN
1 Giant outfielder
2 Where drivers swing
3 Dimwitted
4 *Born Free* lioness
5 Nasty looks
6 Cow collar
7 Time and time again
8 U-turn from NNW
9 Stubborn
10 Gymnast Korbut
11 Boat bottoms
12 "__ then I wrote . . ."
13 Sgt., e.g.
14 Adverb in verse
21 Much desired
22 Ryukyu island
24 Hoop edge
25 Mao __-tung
26 Scottish John
28 Like Richard
29 Ductless gland
30 Bust
32 Geom. and trig. companion
34 R.E. Lee's country
37 Visually sharp
40 Classroom wall hanging
42 Director Reiner
45 Baseball score
46 CPR expert
47 Professional suffix
53 Tars
55 Edgar __ Poe
56 Hammer parts
59 Hubby of Lucy
61 Show starter
62 Flow's partner
63 Singer Bobby
64 J. Danforth Quayle's state
65 Chemical suffix
66 Inventor Whitney
67 Unrefined metal
68 Patient attendants: Abbr.

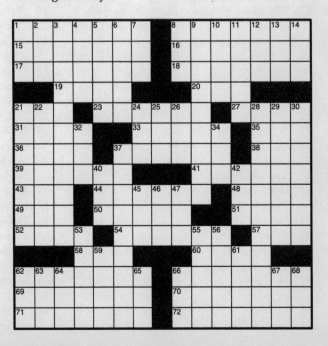

735 MULTIPLE MEANINGS by Shirley Soloway

ACROSS
1 Afternoon socials
5 Shouts of surprise
9 Runs without moving
14 Make a fuss
15 Musical cadence
16 Dancer Shearer
17 Therefore
18 "__ boy!"
19 Composer Morricone
20 CARDINAL
23 Goes to market
24 Peruse
25 Gets off one's feet
28 Got
33 Bikini top
36 Mother-of-pearl
39 "Uh-uh"
40 CARDINAL
44 Eve's significant other
45 Not so hot
46 Capitol VIP
47 Contribute
50 Safecracker
52 Singer Guthrie
55 "__ Was a Lady" (Porter song)
59 CARDINAL
64 Kim of films
65 Reagan Secretary of State
66 __ even keel
67 Ridiculous
68 Indian tourist town
69 Pro __
70 Fitted with glass
71 Woodwind insert
72 "__ a Woman" (Beatles song)

DOWN
1 Lock of hair
2 Soil
3 __-Saxon
4 Bends over
5 Jai __
6 Successful at-bats
7 Where vows are made
8 Make a remark
9 Mrs. Marcos
10 Finished
11 Fiber fuzz
12 Northern Native American
13 __ Paulo, Brazil
21 Employing
22 Old crone
26 Skater Babilonia
27 Aberdeen resident
29 Actress Balin
30 Dozes off
31 Duel tool
32 Laura of *Jurassic Park*
33 Headless nail
34 Make over
35 King of comedy
37 Actress McClanahan
38 Notice
41 "__ Fool to Want You"
42 Golf-ball position
43 Sidled
48 Posted on a bulletin board
49 Go awry
51 Eva and Magda
53 Operetta composer
54 Missouri river
56 Shore or Manoff
57 Ticked off
58 Best et al.
59 Columnist Barrett
60 Author Hunter
61 Niels Bohr, e.g.
62 Lose energy
63 "Holy cow!"
64 Chill

736 TIMELY CHOICES by Dean Niles

ACROSS
1 Cry like a baby
5 Mrs. Gorbachev
10 Pops
14 Sore spot
15 Boo-boo
16 Drama award
17 '70s rock group
19 Step to the __
20 El Salvador neighbor
21 *The Most Happy __*
22 Stimpy's pal
23 __ in (get closer)
25 *Hair* star
31 Defeated overwhelmingly
33 Did a garden chore
34 Lah-di-__
35 Poker contribution
36 Coal enclosure
37 *The Thin Man* woman
38 Favorite
39 Window ledge
41 James Bond's nemesis
43 Deceptive remark
46 Get up
47 Hippie home
48 Jazz form
51 Work periods
56 Gabor and Perón
57 Date arrangement
59 Belgrade resident
60 Car pedal
61 Where the gold is
62 Do in
63 Bottomless pit
64 Astronaut Shepard

DOWN
1 Speed-of-sound name
2 Sound reflection
3 "Where or __"
4 Starring role
5 Certain tire
6 Downright
7 Rainbow
8 Part of ASPCA
9 Early vessel
10 Money
11 Cain's brother
12 "Don't touch that __!"
13 Antitoxins
18 Blender result
21 Crease
23 __ National Park, Utah
24 Spanish cheer
25 __-frutti
26 Blvd., e.g.
27 In a __ (later)
28 Embellish
29 The red planet
30 Former Irani leader
31 Transported
32 Unique fellow
36 Down in the dumps
37 Modernist
39 Jump over
40 Mensa measures
41 Hides away
42 The thick of things
44 Bing or David
45 Little bits
48 Armstrong or Myerson
49 Daredevil Knievel
50 Actress Theda
51 Stick around
52 __ la Douce
53 Trompe l'__ (visual deception)
54 Granny
55 Submachine gun
57 Trade-name abbr.
58 City, informally

737 WEAR AM I? by Norma Steinberg

ACROSS
1 Collins or Donahue
5 "My Way" singer
9 Endow with godhood
14 Author Jaffe
15 Appear to be
16 Additional
17 "__ Around" (Beach Boys song)
18 Montreal baseballer
19 Buffalo kin
20 North Carolina area
23 Way in
24 Conflicts
28 Literary selection
32 __ de France
33 Started the PC
37 Leather with a nap
39 "Natural" hairdo
40 Shatter
43 Plant stand?
44 Falls in drops
46 Reason for overtime
48 Sense of self
49 Symphony conductor
52 Thickly
54 In __ (neither here nor there)
59 Prodigies' opposites
63 George Burns prop
66 Weaving machine
67 __-a-brac
68 Up
69 Early Peruvian
70 M*A*S*H star
71 Gas-powered bike
72 Way out
73 Bambi, e.g.

DOWN
1 Cost
2 __'s Heroes
3 Bumbling
4 "See ya!"
5 On a cruise
6 Barber's cry
7 Retained
8 One-celled animal
9 Campaign events
10 Be
11 __ Always Fair Weather ('55 film)
12 To and __
13 PBS' __ Can Cook
21 Exaggeration
22 Scott Joplin creation
25 Try to deceive
26 __ statesman
27 "Come up and __ sometime"
29 Help-wanted notices
30 Total
31 Shoe coverings
33 Revealed
34 Coming __ in Samoa
35 Celestial hunter
36 Heavy weight
38 Western sch.
41 Pose
42 That girl
45 Bedaubed
47 Perform alone
50 High, in music
51 Place for shadow
53 Quench
55 Phrase from a Michael Jackson tune
56 Singer Haggard
57 Newlywed
58 Felix's roommate
60 Cher's surname, once
61 In __ parentis
62 General Bradley
63 Projection on a wheel
64 __ Jima
65 Wide divergence

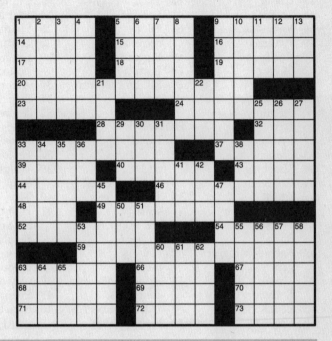

738 IN YOUR FACE by Ann Seidel

ACROSS
1 Quirks
5 Spud
10 Depletes
14 Repeat
15 Donald's ex
16 Hard journey
17 Appear
18 Kid's gift-bearer
20 Home-repair stuff: Abbr.
21 Fleur-de-__
22 Speechify
23 Took it easy
25 Unwell
27 Verandas
29 At work
33 Med. specialty
34 Money players
35 Good review
36 Carp
37 Party drawing
40 Card game
41 Overabundance
43 Exodus author
44 Easy gait
46 Shameless
48 Big name in publishing
49 Rich supply
50 Director Louis
51 Deep dread
54 Chatter on
55 GWTW estate
58 Lawyer, slangily
61 __ out a living (got by)
62 Pre-stereo sound
63 Asian country
64 Pass along
65 Wretched excess
66 Conjecture
67 Love god

DOWN
1 Hart's cohost
2 On the rocks
3 Wrigley's wares
4 When "my prince will come"
5 Bookstore offerings
6 Keep away from
7 Artsy Southwestern town
8 Med. specialty
9 Word of cheer
10 More severe
11 Opera offering
12 Saucily assured
13 Kind of terrier
19 WWI marshal
24 Ding-a-__
25 Pretentious ones
26 "__ Long Way to Tipperary"
27 Word form for "length"
28 "One pours out __ upon the world": Keats
29 Once around the planet
30 Hard candy
31 Racetracks
32 Cloth cap
34 Work out the grammar of
38 Lamented
39 Celt
42 Anna Karenina author
45 The __ Falcon
47 "Through the eyes the heart __ speak"
48 __ corpus
50 Ceremonial clubs
51 Bullets, e.g.
52 Jordan's queen
53 __-ho (avid)
54 Cindy Crawford's spouse
56 Sagebrush State city
57 Tacks on
59 Parcel: Abbr.
60 Chit

739   DRIVER'S ED by Bob Lubbers

ACROSS

1 However, for short
4 Give up, as territory
8 Chow chain
13 Burner base
15 Chou __
16 TURN
18 Very sharp
19 Wakens
20 Really rad
22 Slugger Williams
23 Paisley or Fleming
26 For all time
27 PARK
33 French river
34 Shocking fish?
35 Get ready, for short
38 Skater Henie
41 Wrestlers' pads
42 Former Mideast grp.
43 Trevor's *Brief Encounter* costar
45 BACK UP
52 Vicinity
53 Puts down for the count
54 Soldier in gray
56 Trig function
59 Florida city
61 Social stratum
62 STOP
65 Foreign
66 Pilot's command
67 Big party
68 Portray
69 Militant campus grp.

DOWN

1 Have faith in
2 "I __ to add . . ."
3 New York city
4 Thermometer scale
5 JFK notice
6 i topper
7 Hebrew measure
8 Apartment contracts
9 Extra number?
10 Skin shrinker
11 Overfill
12 Make tracks
14 Needle-nosed fish
17 Washstand crockery
21 Arden or Plumb
24 War god
25 Sleuth Wolfe
28 Gratuity
29 Change for a pound
30 Actor Stephen
31 Dog doc
32 Trains on high
35 Darts place
36 *Norma* __
37 Historic time
39 Weightlifting term
40 Too
41 Half the name of an African revolutionary
44 "Say __ a paper moon"
46 City on the Loire
47 Pressing
48 Society column word
49 McGarrett's assistant
50 Sink features
51 Cried out
55 Max and Bugs
56 Skyscraping
57 Most populous continent
58 Sink feature
60 Cost-of-living letters
61 Singer Calloway
63 Hodges of the Dodgers
64 Coach Parseghian

740   WRY READING by Sally R. Stein

ACROSS

1 Looked over
5 Health hangout
8 Hosiery shade
13 Enjoy Stephen King
14 Notice
15 Beauty expert Adrien
16 Bibles, hymnals etc.?
19 "We __ not amused"
20 French girlfriend
21 Solo
22 Sci-fi author Hubbard
23 "Up and __!"
24 Sizing, spray starch, etc.?
28 Apr. payee
31 Indian chief
32 __ *Abner*
33 Got a load of
34 "Oh yeah, sure!"
35 Suggest
37 Wine spot
38 TV inits.
39 Batman and Robin, e.g.
40 Song style
41 Northeastern U. neighbor
42 Inspector Clouseau, to some film buffs?
45 Ritzy
46 Beseech
47 Mr. Marner
49 NE state
50 Feel poorly
53 What Bond had to kill?
56 Wide
57 *Vogue* rival
58 Unforeseen obstacle
59 Ships out
60 Deletes
61 Disburses

DOWN

1 Ms. Bombeck
2 Planetary lap
3 Relaxation
4 Driller's degree
5 Slinky, e.g.
6 Little nudge
7 Did lunch
8 Postpones a motion
9 E.M. Forster's __ *With a View*
10 Fairy tale's second word
11 Small dog, for short
12 Overhead trains
14 Mead hangout
17 Mystery writer Ngaio __
18 Be a fink
22 Pre-law exam: Abbr.
23 Have __ with (know well)
24 King of Troy
25 Kemelman's sleuth
26 VCR button
27 *Cats* "lyricist"
28 Publish
29 Book reviewer, for example
30 __ *Family Robinson*
35 Forsyth's *The __ File*
36 Impel
37 Comrade
40 Voice of Bugs Bunny
42 Entrains
43 Stretches
44 Sergeant Bilko
45 Answer a charge
47 King's address
48 Lay __ thick (exaggerate)
49 Nabors role
50 *Call Me __* (Duke book)
51 Londoner's exclamation
52 Chair parts
53 UPS units
54 Reviewer Reed
55 Uncommon sense

741 INCENDIARY by Shirley Soloway

ACROSS
1 Saudi citizen
5 Tortoiselike
9 Own up
14 Libertine
15 Mandlikova of tennis
16 Weepy
17 "Bye-bye!"
18 In a while
19 Weasel relative
20 Misleading device
23 Navy VIP
24 Art Deco name
25 Hurries off
27 South American rodent
30 Tumult
32 Woke up
33 Food store, for short
34 Western alliance
37 British title
38 Hot under the collar
41 Berry or Kercheval
42 Author of *The Nazarene*

44 Crimson and cerise
45 Perfect
47 Employers
49 With an even hand
50 Composer Mahler
52 __ *Misbehavin'*
53 Soldiers' org.
54 July 4 noisemaker
60 City dept.
62 Astringent
63 Mata __
64 Parisian wild cat
65 Distribute, with "out"
66 Ardor
67 1987 world champion figure skater
68 Jury member
69 Writing place

DOWN
1 Cultural pursuits
2 Wander about
3 Roadster
4 Lab vessels

5 California peak
6 Galahad's weapon
7 __ about (approximately)
8 Diminish
9 Like some modern music
10 P.I.
11 Dolly Levi, e.g.
12 Dunne or Papas
13 Novices
21 Eastern Indians
22 Comedian Murphy
26 __ Jose, CA
27 Space agcy.
28 Writer Leon
29 Heartsick ballads
30 Necklace units
31 Shade trees
33 Forest forager
35 Blue-green
36 "My One and __"
39 Fountain of Rome
40 Singer Ross

43 Big success
46 Jilted
48 Ceiling support beam
49 More solid
50 Zest
51 United competitor

52 Keen
55 Incline
56 Gen. Robert __
57 Leafy green
58 Distinctive periods
59 Ice arena
61 Dudgeon

742 BOARING by Dean Niles

ACROSS
1 Shop shaper
6 Roseanne's surname, once
10 Music-score notation
14 Collection
15 Sheriff Andy's son
16 Tortoise competitor
17 Lowlife
18 Alight
19 __-de-camp
20 Part of MIT
21 Senate bill of a sort
23 Skulks
25 Pick, with "for"
26 Good __ Policy
30 "__ was saying . . ."
33 Forest clearing
36 Chess piece
37 Nerve
38 Split apart
39 Fish-eating eagle
40 Fable ender
41 In the course of

42 Floral vessel
43 Chicago airport
44 "Certainly!"
45 Decisive defeat
47 Funding source in D.C.
48 Christmas quaff
52 Uninformed buy
58 Had on
59 Pure black
60 __ *bene*
61 Blend
62 To be, to Babette
63 Potter's need
64 Escapee
65 __ and die
66 Cellist Ma
67 Mix up

DOWN
1 Endures
2 Senator Specter
3 In a __ (quickly)
4 Clumsy
5 Take a gander at
6 Western tie
7 On __ with (equal to)

8 Skating floor
9 Women's magazine
10 Map
11 Hideaway
12 *"Das Lied von der __"* (Mahler work)
13 Experience
21 Tire-pressure inits.
22 Tax mo.
24 Supercool
27 *The __ Gatsby*
28 Flicka, for one
29 Goof
30 Heavenly glow
31 Headliner
32 Man or Capri
33 Overcast
34 Whitewash component
35 Hertz competitor
37 Run riot
40 Synthesizer eponym
42 Motel sign
45 Pallid

46 Spike or Bruce
47 TV-screen element
49 Famous
50 Bay window
51 Comedy or tragedy, e.g.
52 Yeats or Keats

53 Absorbed by
54 Stabilizer, for short
55 Mallet sport
56 Buckwheat's affirmative
57 Flatten in the ring
61 Rural grp.

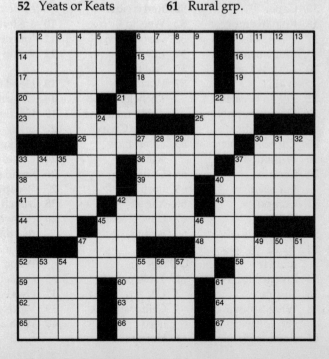

743 SPACE MOVIES by Wayne R. Williams

ACROSS
1 __ Kid (Western hero)
6 Erroll Garner tune
11 Afore
14 French love
15 French goodbye
16 Cambridge sch.
17 Chuck Norris movie
20 Temporary expedient
21 Way from a man's heart
22 Novelist Murdoch
24 WWII arena
25 Paul Newman movie
33 Off-peak periods
34 Reclined
35 __ Plaines, IL
36 ... Alive and Well ... man
37 Lithograph, e.g.
39 Is sick
40 "We __ the World"
41 Non-cleric
42 Working-class member
43 Tom Hanks movie
47 24 Across leader
48 Sour-tasting
49 The Bat or The Cloak
52 Quiz giver
57 Frank Sinatra movie
61 Self
62 Bolivian beast
63 The __ One (Waugh novel)
64 "Help!"
65 Like some kitchens
66 Pitchers

DOWN
1 Machine parts
2 Faux, briefly
3 Just fair
4 Zodiacal border
5 Geneses
6 Heckle or Jeckle, e.g.
7 Infamous Amin
8 Religious wrong
9 Herbal drink
10 New World peninsula
11 Middle East chieftain
12 Run wild
13 Sicilian peak
18 DEA employee
19 Implement
23 Importune
24 Give off
25 Composer Berg
26 Pack animal
27 Inclement weather
28 Building wing
29 Bleacher bum
30 Language nuance
31 Casals' instrument
32 Ruhr Valley city
37 Piece of glass
38 Trucker's truck
39 Appendage
41 Simpatico
42 Fit to drink
44 Employ
45 Runyon's Detroit
46 Canadian tribe
49 Change for a five
50 Okefenokee resident
51 Slaughter in the Hall of Fame
53 Toot one's own horn
54 Own
55 At any time
56 Cincinnati sluggers
58 Form ending
59 Make lace
60 PA reactor

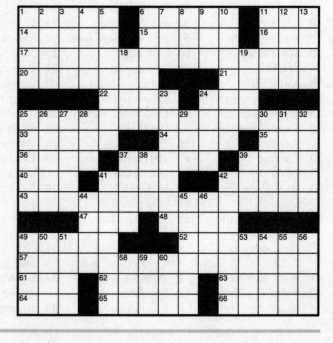

744 PARADOXES by Robert H. Wolfe

ACROSS
1 Word form for "fat"
5 Film holders
10 Naturalist Fossey
14 Ht.
15 Caper
16 Roman emperor
17 What Selznick's film wasn't
20 Actress Foch et al.
21 Yoked beasts
22 Energy-supplying nucleoside
25 Corneal cover
26 Without a shirt
29 Certain Louisianian
31 Composer Schifrin
32 Be sorry about
33 "... a __'clock scholar"
34 Practice for a bout
36 Disgrace
38 What Sabin's vaccine wasn't
41 Keats, e.g.
42 Editor's req.
43 Rivulets
45 Part of RPM
46 Gabor et al.
48 Father Damien's wards
50 Red citadel
52 Wee, to Burns
53 Part of CBS
54 Egyptian river
55 Nut tree
57 What Michelangelo didn't do at the Sistine Chapel
63 Casablanca woman
64 Obliterate
65 Portrayal
66 Minus
67 Gave a score to
68 Scout's feat

DOWN
1 Table part
2 UN grp.
3 Calligrapher's need
4 Hot spot
5 Most pluvial
6 Inward
7 Numerical suffixes
8 Ignited
9 Word before days or ties
10 Fastening peg
11 Journey plans
12 Philip of Kung Fu
13 Head move
18 Determination
19 Uncover
22 Sister __
23 Walker
24 Dreamy quality
26 Small pies
27 Recapitulation
28 Match the bet
30 Fireworks reactions
31 Turner and Wood
35 Galileo, for one
37 Dwell (on)
39 Verdi opera
40 With a protected head
41 Mork's home
44 Draft org.
47 Nielsen subject
49 Every one
51 Touchy king?
52 Rationality
55 Sea vessel
56 What sheepdogs do
57 Abner's adjective
58 __ de France
59 Blue Eagle org.
60 Friday or Palooka
61 Bravo, in Barcelona
62 Flower plot

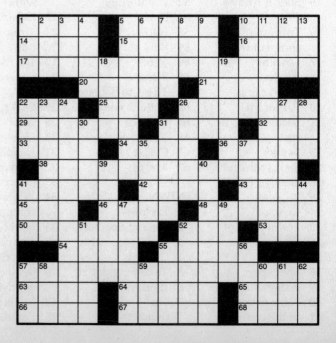

745 WORD CHAIN by Karen Hodge

ACROSS

1 Snake's sound
5 Not nuts
9 Ad bug's shout
13 Lubricate twice
14 Second son
15 MacDonald's Mountie
16 START OF THE CHAIN
19 How the sedate behave
20 Not exempt
21 Wheat meat?
23 Times for *vacances*
24 Bumper-to-bumper
28 Really mad
31 Columbus' home
32 Where *Hamlet* once played
33 Wharton deg.
36 MORE OF THE CHAIN
40 Hydroxide solution
41 Construction site beams
42 Actress Sommer
43 Sarcastic
44 Texas A&M attendees
46 Actor Everett
48 Uninspired
50 "Catch of the Day," e.g.
53 Bell tower
58 END OF THE CHAIN
60 Invites
61 *God's Little __*
62 Asian capital, old-style
63 Unsurpassed
64 Demand for electricity
65 Frenzied

DOWN

1 Intensity of feeling
2 Cedar Rapids' state
3 Eduardo's emphatic agreement
4 Yucky stuff
5 Rake in the forest?
6 *Nightline's* network
7 Nicely done
8 Ms. Lanchester
9 Purchase incentive
10 Brick type
11 Stars, to some
12 Dick Van __
13 *Kidnapped* initials
17 "Where Is the Life That Late __?"
18 Devonshire town
22 __ *Pierce*
24 Cheek's neighbor
25 Ocean hail
26 Entangle
27 "__ always liked you best!"
29 Cornfield units
30 Blood grouping
32 Needle
33 Thrice DXVII
34 Microwave, maybe
35 Votes for
37 Get __ (learn about)
38 Geisha's sash
39 Beer order of a sort
43 Most reliable
44 Utah resort
45 Jackson of *Hopscotch*
46 Hold it
47 Listens
49 Seated, slangily
50 Strikebreaker
51 Kind of exam
52 Art __
54 Hard cheese
55 Slightly, to Solti
56 Uncontrollable circumstances
57 Greek vowel
59 Tide competitor

746 BREAKFAST TIME by Lee Weaver

ACROSS

1 They play for pay
5 Large aquatic mammal
10 Singe
14 *Charley's __*
15 Music hall
16 Angel topper
17 Breakfast fare
19 Muslim religious leader
20 Stadia
21 Cravat holder
23 Conks out
25 Beer mug
26 Appalling
29 Hibachi residue
31 Fix the sound track again
34 Instrument for a Marx brother
35 Grande or Bravo
36 Spanish coin
37 __ *Ventura: Pet Detective*
38 Diminishes
40 Sloe __ fizz
41 Acted like a dictator
43 "Here Comes the __" (Beatles tune)
44 Stare at
45 Pelvic joint
46 __ diem
47 Melts together
48 A Little Rascal
51 Very dry, as Champagne
53 Area for Old MacDonald
55 Quiver contents
59 With 64 Across, John Wayne film
60 Breakfast fare
62 Sponsorship
63 Official proclamation
64 See 59 Across
65 Learning method
66 Errata
67 "I'm all __"

DOWN

1 Sobriquet for Hemingway
2 Regretful one
3 In the past
4 __ and be counted
5 Mountie's mount
6 Altar response
7 Pepper with pebbles
8 Spit and __
9 Beginning
10 Hot peppers
11 Breakfast fare
12 "Too bad!"
13 Frolic boisterously
18 Carpenter's need
22 Goddess of grain
24 Spoke
26 Moby Dick seeker
27 Texas city
28 Breakfast fare
30 Toper
32 Practical
33 *Bêtes noires*
35 Eric the __
36 Bill-signing need
38 Answer an invitation
39 Sidewalk's edge
42 Like Anna's King
44 Abominable act
46 Send-up
47 Roll up, as a flag
48 Later than
49 Slow and majestic, in music
50 Aspect
52 River floaters
54 Faucet problem
56 Gumbo ingredient
57 River dam
58 Orly arrivals
61 Sgt., e.g.

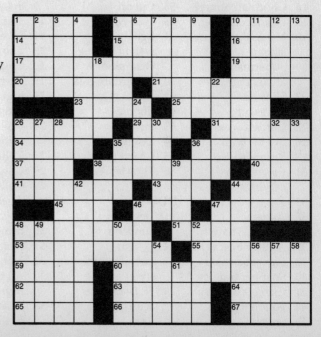

747 OVER YOUR HEAD by Fred Piscop

ACROSS
1 Violet variety
6 Indy 500 entrant
11 Hole-punching gadget
14 Teddy Roosevelt's daughter
15 Athens marketplace
16 Cedar Rapids college
17 Mars phenomenon
19 __ Sharkey (Rickles sitcom)
20 Appear
21 Skating place
22 It's a wrap
24 Sole-related
27 Deserve
28 Dash competitor
31 Take advantage of
32 Track figure
34 Sam of Jurassic Park
36 More despicable, perhaps
39 Racetrack event
43 Dreamy state
44 Hall of Famer Banks
45 Modify text
46 Opening Day mo.
48 CIA precursor
49 DeVito series
52 Most lemonlike
55 1936 Olympics star
57 Actress Swenson
58 Dynamic start
62 Poor review
63 Leo G. Carroll role
66 In favor of
67 Starts the pot
68 Source of annoyance
69 Sun Yat-__
70 Irascible
71 Lock of hair

DOWN
1 Soft foods
2 __ vera
3 Aswan Dam site
4 Rascal
5 Law or saw ender
6 Wisconsin city
7 Ten-percenter
8 Crested parrot
9 Bullpen ace's stat
10 Hard knocks
11 Ghana's capital
12 Tom of The Dukes of Hazzard
13 Sierra __
18 Tax-deferred accts.
23 More pretentious
25 Put to sleep
26 Red horse
28 "__ how!"
29 Impolite look
30 Lawn chemical
33 Milkers' handfuls
35 "__ Bloom"
36 Popular June gift
37 Mr. Rubik
38 Slugger's stats
40 Eye part
41 Followers of Josip Broz
42 "Permission granted!"
46 Merchant ship
47 Bog material
49 Baseball card company
50 Cognizant
51 Noble gas
53 Not dealt with
54 Slender candle
56 Command to Socks
59 Fencer's weapon
60 Guns the engine
61 Galena et al.
64 Singleton
65 Make a choice

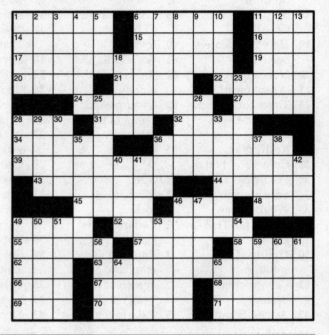

748 GROUND CREW by S. E. Booker

ACROSS
1 Actor Vigoda
4 Prince Harry's mummy
9 Light of heel
14 Goddess: Lat.
15 __ a high note
16 Chocolate source
17 Drum container
18 Mississippi blues singer
20 Superman's archenemy
22 Slips by
23 Gives off
25 Garden areas
26 Put up with
27 Rumor source
31 Polynesian carvings
33 Tax
35 Anger
36 Writer Wharton
37 Author Buscaglia
38 Cheers barmaid
40 Snapper trapper
41 Cuzco's country
42 Following
43 Snitch
46 Grant __ of execution
48 Towel word
49 Directed on the gridiron
52 "So foul __": Shak.
55 Cut off
56 1960 Olympic light heavyweight boxing champion
60 Heyerdahl craft
61 Agent Ness
62 Jimmies
63 Hwys.
64 DeVito of Hoffa
65 Characteristic
66 Thus far

DOWN
1 Designer Simpson
2 __-Arts (architectural style)
3 St. Louis Blues actress/singer
4 Raze
5 Accustomed to difficulty
6 Get to the bottom line
7 Affirmative action
8 Whichever
9 Subjects to steam
10 Sixties dance
11 Like some tea
12 Cab cost
13 Chuck
19 Teeny-__
21 Ingrained activity
24 Real-estate principals
25 Military camp
28 Clint role
29 Colleague of Agatha and Ellery
30 Bring up
31 Nomad's pad
32 Notion
34 All the time, in rhyme
38 Reaction facilitator
39 Make __ (grimace)
41 Concealed
44 Trinity member
45 Gentleness
47 Rival's retort
50 Dodge
51 Pragmatic believer
52 Waltzed through
53 Eleanor's pooch
54 "The doctor __"
57 Lush
58 Red Cross course: Abbr.
59 Farmland

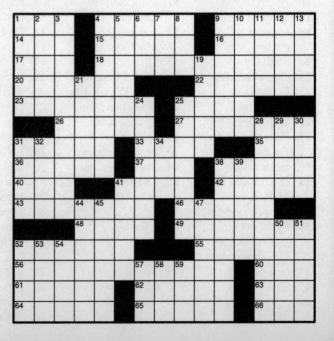

749 GRATEFULLY YOURS by Dean Niles

ACROSS
1 World-weary
6 "__ Ha'i"
10 Fitzgerald or Raines
14 In existence
15 Oboe, e.g.
16 Summer tops
17 Around half of us
18 __ Minor
19 "What __ God wrought?"
20 Sault __ Marie, Ontario
21 IN ENGLISH
24 Kemo __
25 Kimono tie
26 IN FRENCH
32 Hits or kisses
34 Talk wildly
35 Anecdotal collection
36 Imparted
37 Part of AC
38 __ were
39 Prefix meaning "one"
40 Mauna Loa matter
42 Decadent
44 IN SPANISH
47 Business abbr.
48 "__ she blows!"
49 IN GERMAN
53 Water-__ (dental device)
56 Director Fritz
57 Inner-tube outsides
58 Went for
60 Sea bird
61 Lay __ the line
62 Black wood
63 Tend the garden
64 Tea portions
65 Out of __ (irritable)

DOWN
1 Vise parts
2 Oodles
3 Couple of nickels
4 All About __
5 Hamlet's home
6 Oil-rich sultanate
7 High home
8 "__ we forget"
9 Person from Pocatello
10 Racial
11 Faucet flaw
12 "__ Fall In Love"
13 __ Wednesday
22 Basics
23 Meet edge to edge
24 Religious group
26 Frenzied
27 Pipe type
28 Corn portion
29 Desert stops
30 Troop group
31 Head
32 Rundown area
33 Offerings list
37 Part of GPA
38 Over there
40 Thin
41 Self-denying one
42 Sound reflection
43 Engaged men
45 Depended (upon)
46 Sparta rival
49 Challenge
50 Mrs. Lindbergh
51 In __ (correctly located)
52 Harvest
53 Low-quality
54 "__ It Romantic?"
55 Florida islets
56 Actor Ayres
59 Cable network

750 SPECIAL K by Randolph Ross

ACROSS
1 Member of the stork family
5 Down
9 IOU
13 Film composer Nino
14 Otic
16 Crazed
17 Was able to give tours south of the border?
19 Sills solo
20 Icon
21 Affirmed, parliamentarily
23 Element
25 Brings to a boil?
26 Smith of the NBA?
31 Canal chambers
32 Lively dances
33 Silent approval
36 Holiday preceders
37 Raid
38 Singer Mitchell
39 Corrode
40 Curative drink
41 Postman's path
42 Tangled-up flower?
44 Posers, perhaps
47 Not out
48 Nitrous oxide, slangily
51 Convent resident
55 Angry, with "off"
56 King Arthur's era?
58 Actress Russo
59 Ace Rickenbacker
60 Home of Phillips U.
61 Mimic
62 Itches
63 Sinking-ship deserters

DOWN
1 Peeves
2 Emaciated
3 Couple in the news
4 Tenners
5 Dublin tongue
6 Bit of illumination
7 Trinity author
8 Self-defense spray
9 Trolley sounds
10 Multitude
11 More dangerous for driving
12 Frog relatives
15 Nearby
18 Friars
22 Binary digits
24 Crowd
26 Swiss etcher Paul
27 Superstar of a sort
28 Cool rapper
29 High house
30 Does a double take
33 "Heart" or "soul"
34 Aware of
35 Japanese legislature
37 Abandon
38 Comic
40 Civil offense
41 Update equipment
42 Birdcage device
43 Prepares potatoes
44 Ad __ per aspera
45 Win every game
46 Nancy Drew series author
49 Dr. Jones, familiarly
50 "Ticket to __"
52 Frank, Jr.'s sister
53 Send out
54 Movie about John Reed
57 Knocking game

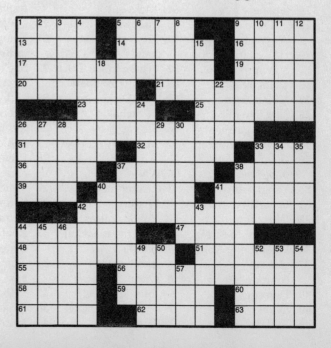

751 BRILLIANCY by Shirley Soloway

ACROSS
1 Shoots out
6 Worry
10 First-grade lesson
14 Yankee Yogi
15 Take out, to an ed.
16 Perry's creator
17 Loss of creative talent
19 100 dinars
20 Return addressee
21 West or Clarke
22 Folklore meanie
23 Love god
25 Hoards
27 Break of day
30 Corrida shout
32 Pigeonhole
33 Touched down
34 Egyptian cotton
36 Martini additive
39 __ Vegas
40 Cosmetic-pencil target
42 Female deer
43 Lying still
45 Tim of *WKRP*
46 Spill the beans
47 Coin . . .
49 . . . and its color
50 Ingests
51 Positive
54 Ward of *Sisters*
56 Actor Sharif
57 Puppy bite
59 Ferguson and Miles
63 *Of __ and Men*
64 Wise investors
66 Chase of films
67 River in Spain
68 Corn concoctions
69 "__ la vie!"
70 Told a tall tale
71 Little fish

DOWN
1 Recedes
2 Like a pittance
3 Where to spend 19 Across
4 Neptune's staff
5 More logical
6 Four-term pres.
7 Paper pack
8 Inventor Howe
9 Principles
10 Pressurized can
11 Inspired thought
12 County in Ireland
13 Monica of tennis
18 Sagging
24 More wily
26 In the ship's hold
27 Spanish surrealist
28 Greenspan or Shepard
29 Sarcastic remarks
31 Burning particle
35 First zodiac sign
37 Electrical unit
38 Morays
40 Sicilian hot spot
41 Most unusual
44 Fall back
46 Specialized restaurant
48 Christmas tree enhancement
51 Humorous
52 Author Zola
53 Rain clouds
55 Nightstand items
58 Remove a covering
60 Jackson or Meara
61 Command to Rover
62 Meth.
65 Serling of suspense

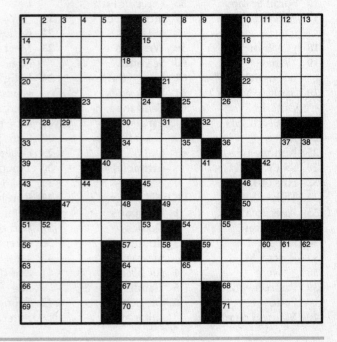

752 APT NAMES by Norma Steinberg

ACROSS
1 Church service
5 Hayworth or Coolidge
9 Economic indicator: Abbr.
12 "So long, Pierre"
14 Japanese fare
15 __ *Bravo* (John Wayne film)
16 He's a Hollywood bigwig
18 Years: Fr.
19 Maine town
20 Sing like Ella
21 Forum garments
24 Nicks or Wonder
26 *Greed* and *Intolerance*, e.g.
28 Yangtze boat
31 Desertlike
32 Diner sign
35 Chelsea, to Roger
36 Washroom: Abbr.
37 Hawaii components
39 Fish eggs
40 Skilled
42 Buffalo's water
43 Condor or finch
44 Flotsam and jetsam
46 Clientele
48 Allergic reactions
51 Byways
52 Stick around
54 Kicks out
56 Follower of Attila
57 She's got great hands
62 Where to see *Coach*
63 Clarinetist Shaw
64 Poet Dickinson
65 "Gotcha!"
66 Strong __ ox
67 Mayberry moppet

DOWN
1 Leader met by Nixon
2 Public notices
3 [Not my mistake]
4 Bering __
5 Ladder steps
6 *Once __ Enough* (Susann novel)
7 "__ a Small Hotel"
8 Tire filler
9 She'll be patient
10 Columbus' smallest ship
11 Hitching __
13 Of the city
14 Sermon subject
17 Spends foolishly
20 __ Valley, CA
21 Temper tantrum
22 She's a peacemaker
23 H.S. diploma alternative
25 Moving vehicles
26 Pre-entrée course
27 Vendition
29 Squirrel food
30 Requisites
33 Roofing material
34 Trim the bangs, e.g.
37 "How sweet __!"
38 Absence
41 Speak to God
43 Swimsuit part
45 Clippers
47 ". . . __ the Wizard"
49 Webber/Rice opus
50 Stay-put protest
52 Pahlavi's title
53 Oompah horn
55 Fidel's co-revolutionary
57 Fed. airport monitor
58 __, *amas, amat*
59 Pitcher part
60 Actor Wallach
61 Bar or bakery order

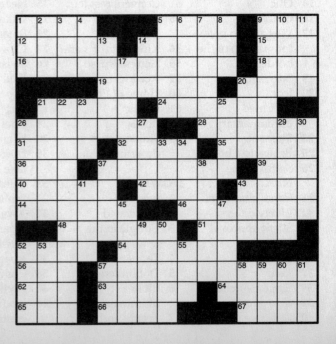

TYKES by Wayne R. Williams

ACROSS

1 Sour flavor
6 Fire
9 "Lonesome George"
14 Really dig
15 Playwright Burrows
16 Miffed to the max
17 Cautious handlers
19 The Scales
20 Chemical ending
21 Fuse, as ores
22 Senior member
23 Cantina
25 Band of hoods
26 Metal cutters
30 Yankee's foe
33 Oodles
36 Mother of Clytemnestra
37 W. alliance
38 "Dies __"
39 Corporate stages
40 __ even keel
41 Mixed bag
42 Gym org.
43 With regrets
44 High __
45 The Bambino
47 Highland group
49 Racers' grp.
53 "Over There" composer
55 Lag behind
58 Actress Hagen
59 Mimicry
60 Language with clicking consonants
62 Bushwa
63 GI entertainers
64 Paris' water
65 Passover meal
66 Precious one
67 Inflections

DOWN

1 Louise and Victoria
2 Twin Cities suburb
3 Catalogue subject
4 Assoc.
5 Ozzie and Harriet
6 Underground opening
7 Genesis character
8 Branch structure?
9 Radner and others
10 Heavenly hunter
11 Piano type
12 To be, in Toulouse
13 Low-fat
18 Atlanta arena
24 Bone: Pref.
25 Mardi __
27 Absolutely
28 Pieces of a pound
29 Winter of the blues
31 Latin list ender
32 Skinny
33 Mob melee
34 Woody's son
35 Actress Morgan
37 Beery, Jr. and Sr.
39 Hurler Nolan
43 Supremely trite
45 British sausage
46 Component
48 Actress Hope
50 Jump the line
51 Make amends
52 Merits
53 Hacks
54 Early role for Ron
55 Hoodlum
56 Charlie of PBS
57 Particle
61 Modernist's prefix

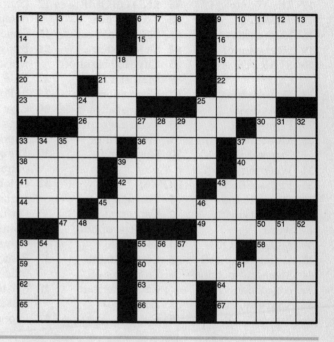

NOT SO GREAT by Matt Gaffney

ACROSS

1 Bachelor party
5 Vail visitor
10 Blue shade
14 Comment from Chan
15 File, as a complaint
16 Stubborn sort
17 Eastern landmark
20 Heliotrope's need
21 Showed again
22 Corral
23 Potion holder
25 Ruhr valley city
28 Got down
29 Infamous Amin
32 Put one's 2¢ in?
33 Wine quantity
35 Sister Act extra
36 Coral Sea sight
39 Goof
40 Things to strive for
41 Pertinent words
42 Dream-time phenom.
43 Cafeteria item
44 Cap adjunct
45 Pop hits?
47 Chick's ma
48 Kitchen wear
50 Waffle irons
55 Family elder
58 Ancient inscription
59 Ordinary
60 Gawk
61 Aesthete's passion
62 Sassy girl
63 H.S. test

DOWN

1 Collapses, in a way
2 Singular ye
3 ". . . unto us __ is given"
4 Parting word
5 Done in
6 German city, to its residents
7 Eric of Monty Python
8 Freudian concern
9 Ump's relative
10 Dull hurts
11 Nonconformist's trait
12 MD institution
13 Simile center
18 At such time as
19 __ Lake, OR
23 Horsewhip
24 "Outcast from __ feast": Joyce
25 Champing at the bit
26 Sleep loudly
27 Leading edge of bad weather
28 Deck out
30 Because of
31 Going to get (it)
33 Unified group
34 Bailiwicks
37 Like some wit
38 Storm unit
44 Hindu sacred text
46 Gold mines
47 In a cool way
48 Taj Mahal's home
49 Decant
50 Wildebeests
51 Nutritional amts.
52 Race segments
53 __ noche (at night)
54 Editor's mark
56 Molasses product
57 "__ was saying . . ."

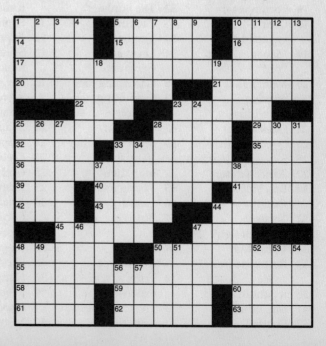

755 KNEADING THE BARD by Frank Gordon

ACROSS
1 Crooning name
5 Sourpuss
9 Marsh bird
14 __ about
15 Take on
16 __ of the Year
17 The Thompson Twins, e.g.
18 High cards
19 Steer clear of
20 START OF A QUIP
23 Trap for tuna
24 Bears do it
25 Feline foot
28 Moore of *Indecent Proposal*
31 Watering hole
35 Furnace fleck
36 Decorate anew
38 College key word
39 MORE OF QUIP
43 Wreck completely
44 Meat-and-potatoes concoction
45 That guy, in France
46 "... have to fear is fear __"
48 Ollie's partner
50 Wee, in Dundee
51 Redaction retraction
53 Keg party need
55 END OF QUIP
62 Go gaga over
63 Pain in the neck
64 Sit for a shot
65 City Hall big shot
66 *Mask* star
67 Nonconformists swim against it
68 Verse alternative
69 Turn partner
70 Norse king

DOWN
1 This and that
2 Concerning
3 Roulette option
4 Sprouted
5 Certain flights
6 Proprietor of Café Américain
7 Zone
8 Defeats
9 Tchaikovsky classic
10 Shortish works of fiction
11 "__ Fire" (Springsteen song)
12 Canceled-check notation
13 Conclude
21 British ref. work
22 Loser to DDE
25 LuPone or Page
26 Give it __ (try)
27 Uses an oilstone
29 Interlock
30 Think-tank output
32 October birthstones
33 Perfume brand
34 Gymnast Comaneci
37 Remove from office
40 Masterful musicians
41 In one's right mind
42 Goes to pieces?
47 Bank charge
49 Slangy negative
52 Plot of land
54 __-Bismol
55 Month after Shebat
56 Toy on a string
57 Sonic boomerang
58 __ *Gotta Have It*
59 Muddy the waters
60 A govt. agcy . . .
61 . . . inspects this
62 Band booster

756 OKAY by Shirley Soloway

ACROSS
1 Trunk item
6 Took off
10 Dick and Jane's dog
14 Attacks
15 Rajah's wife
16 Forum wear
17 Coarse-leafed vegetables
19 Manages, with "out"
20 Monty Hall offering
21 Individual
22 Goes along
24 __-of-mouth
26 Sidelong glances
27 African desert
30 Baseball's __ Fame
32 Tactics
33 Circle of light
34 Vocalized
37 Response from space
38 Japanese island
41 Mil. officer
42 Footfall
44 Prepares the press
45 Actress Garbo
47 Leaveners
49 Did farm work
50 Mimics
51 Shopping aid
52 The Bunkers' daughter
53 Ventilate
54 Levin and Gershwin
58 Gardening tool
59 Swimming motion
62 Singer Ed
63 Money in Milan
64 Varnish ingredient
65 Young men
66 Heavenly spot
67 Birth cert., e.g.

DOWN
1 Roe source
2 Trim, as expenses
3 The Charleses' terrier
4 Train line
5 List-ending abbr.
6 Palm branch
7 Ontario or Michigan
8 Map dir.
9 Refuse, as testimony
10 Sound systems
11 Expressionless
12 S-shaped moldings
13 Soviet news agency
18 Circle dance
23 Solidify
25 Approximately
27 Dieters' retreats
28 Greatly
29 Alley Cat step
30 *Philadelphia* Oscar-winner
31 Word of woe
33 Suggestion
35 Short message
36 Happy
39 Ready for smooching
40 Matures
43 Noblewoman
46 No longer working
48 Hero of *Exodus*
49 Knightly addresses
50 Memorable mission
51 Compare
52 Snatch
53 Land measure
55 Billy or Pete
56 Related
57 Dispatched
60 Lend a hand
61 Prefix for angle or color

757   GO WITH THE FLOW by Frank Gordon

ACROSS

1 Jazz singer Vaughan
6 Result of a conking
10 Angry
13 Inflationary __
15 Jacob's twin
16 Indefinite pronoun
17 Colonial silversmith
18 Puma's pad
19 Rap sheet abbr.
20 Dakar's country
22 Bee's quest
24 CD-__ (computer adjunct)
25 Inferior
27 Word with sell or shell
29 In a tizzy
30 Rub-__
34 Train unit
35 Naval rank: Abbr.
36 Raising __ ('87 film)
38 "I'd like to propose __"
40 Lineup at Lillehammer
41 Horse-race measures
43 Bolger or Charles
44 Coll. basketball event
45 "¿Cómo __ usted?"
46 __ salts
48 Singer Lovett
49 Recite magic words
51 Wail
52 Horner's milieu
55 JFK or O'Hare
58 Gold, to Gomez
59 Stink
61 Ceylonese teas
63 Krazy __
64 Billy Budd's captain
65 Completely
66 Overhead trains
67 __ out (just got by)
68 Symbol

DOWN

1 Azerbaijan, once: Abbr.
2 Large primates
3 Reds' stadium
4 "We __ amused"
5 Seraglio
6 Starr et al.
7 Cable network
8 Having prevalent attitudes
9 Blender setting
10 Medieval defense
11 Pop singer Paul
12 Letter opener
14 Drumstick
21 Kal Kan rival
23 Fad
26 Vast expanse
27 Grocer's need
28 Author Joyce Carol __
29 In a tough spot
31 Free-for-all
32 Up to
33 Moisten meat
35 Winter time in Chi.
37 Garden climber
39 Once more
42 Bath or Bad Ems
43 French roast
47 Twisted and turned
48 Seek advice from
50 Brass
51 All in
52 Pepsi rival
53 Spoken
54 Decays
56 Troy, NY coll.
57 Head overseas?
60 Poetic preposition
62 "That's a joke, __"

758   GLOBAL WARMING by Dean Niles

ACROSS

1 Ran, as colors
5 Picket-line crosser
9 Fussbudgets
14 Adore
15 Detective's job
16 Lumberjack
17 Was in debt
18 Tel __
19 Treeless plain
20 Ceremonial tributes
23 CIO partner
24 Part of some business phone nos.
25 Cave dweller of lore
29 Thick piece
32 Recedes
36 Fill with fizz
38 Burden
40 Fish eggs
41 On dangerous ground
44 Gobble up
45 Inkling
46 Earlier than later
47 Colors
49 Memorial Day event
51 Donna and Robert
52 FedEx rival
54 Newt
56 Controversial topics
65 Protection
66 Old one: Ger.
67 Poker share
68 Approaches
69 Caboose position
70 Flirt
71 "No man is an island" poet
72 Nosegay
73 Don't go

DOWN

1 Political interest group
2 Rob of Wayne's World
3 Mr. Knievel
4 "__ Dinah" (Avalon tune)
5 Neck-warmer
6 Splits hairs
7 __ were
8 Collection
9 Flame-colored plant
10 Tell about
11 __ a Teenage Werewolf
12 Old-fashioned guy
13 Sellout signs
21 Monopoly avenue
22 Counters
25 Used the VCR
26 Pass on
27 Speechify
28 Put down pipe
30 Sounded like Elsie
31 Black cuckoo
33 Salt water
34 Unamused
35 Psychic-hotline staff
37 Sign up
39 Summer wear
42 Smith & Wesson, e.g.
43 Enemy
48 Induce, as perjury
50 Busybodies
53 Handbag
55 Like a furnace
56 Wrist extension
57 Popular cookie
58 Govt. agent
59 Canvas covering
60 Bread spread
61 Donaldson and Spade
62 Component
63 Sicilian spouter
64 Alluring

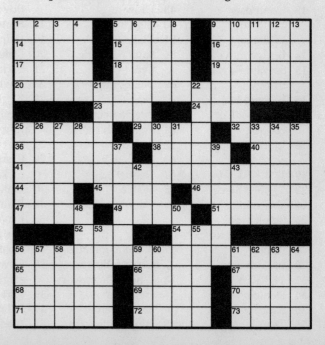

759 TRUE TO FORM by Wayne R. Williams

ACROSS

1 Houston university
5 Like ears and lungs
10 Wild guess
14 "Elsa's Dream," e.g.
15 Where *élèves* learn
16 Followers of tra
17 Ticket purchase
19 Cart pullers
20 Compass pt.
21 British school
22 *The __ of the Night* (Mailer book)
24 Make smaller
26 Stable lad
27 Twenty to eleven
30 Ecological watchdog grp.
33 *The Kiss* sculptor
36 Showy flower
37 British gun
38 Vote in
39 Be under the weather
40 Fabric fold
41 Robert or Alan
42 Functions
43 Merry sprees
44 City near Lourdes
45 Poster guy
47 Poem part
49 Solution
53 Improve
55 Otherwise
57 Epoch
58 Hodgepodge
59 Outer covering
62 Filch
63 Wipe clean
64 Garfield's foil
65 Without
66 Polonius and Ophelia, e.g.
67 Windows to the soul

DOWN

1 Less likely
2 Dancing Castle
3 Commended
4 Vichy water
5 Of the Pre-Easter season
6 Numerical prefix
7 "__ in the USA"
8 Samuel's teacher
9 Takes off
10 Great play replay, often
11 Hack machine
12 Nautical direction
13 Prohibits
18 Like news
23 Country singer Clark
25 City on the Mohawk
26 Young salmon
28 Unqualified failure
29 Bay window
31 High point
32 Acacia crawlers
33 Harvest
34 __ podrida
35 Holmes' specialty
37 Lambastes
40 Altair IV, e.g.
42 Not attempted
45 French one
46 Gives lip
48 Tiny particles
50 Overgrown
51 One of the Muppets
52 Schedule figures
53 Marshlands
54 Logan or Raines
55 Novelist Hunter
56 __ *majesté*
60 FDR's Blue Eagle
61 Shemp's brother

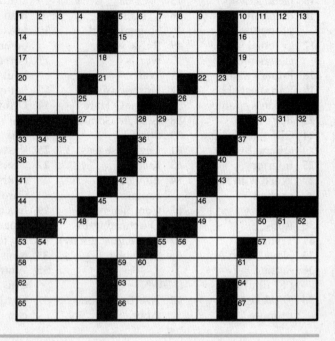

760 TURKEY LEFTOVERS by Ann Seidel

ACROSS

1 Knights' weapons
6 Slamming sound
10 Stick to chew on
13 Composer Vaughan Williams
14 Bridge move
15 Satyajit Ray trilogy
16 His and her
17 __ the side of caution
18 Inquiring sounds
19 TURKEY
22 "__ She Sweet?"
24 Twice LI
25 Small brook
26 Lunchtime for some
28 Impediment
32 TURKEY
34 Denials
35 Sauce source
36 Tear
37 Black cuckoo
40 TURKEY
43 Make a new connection
46 Calm times
47 "__ a man with seven wives"
48 Draw
50 Liquefy
51 TURKEY
56 Sault __ Marie, Ont.
57 Photographer Diane
58 Bye, to Brigitte
61 Poet's adverb
62 At hand
63 Baseball bases
64 Dentist's deg.
65 Seabird
66 Curved letters

DOWN

1 A-Team member
2 Ooh's follower
3 Where the unwary are taken
4 Formal letter
5 Hindu title
6 Klingon, e.g.
7 Take on
8 Throw __ to the masses
9 Options list
10 Celtic tongue
11 Against the flow
12 Brawn
14 Italian artist
20 Defeats, in a way
21 Bikini tops
22 Envelope abbr.
23 "__ Have Nothing" (Tom Jones song)
27 Suit parts
29 Charlie Parker's nickname
30 Gilligan's boss
31 Plains frame
33 Do office work, perhaps
37 Abstinent ones
38 Coward of the stage
39 Part of MIT
40 Fill fully
41 Meddle
42 Dome-shaped shelters
43 Got rid of shampoo
44 Hammed it up
45 High temperatures
49 "She wore an __-bitsy . . ."
52 Filly's mom
53 __ Rabbit
54 Israeli statesman
55 Comfort
59 __ out a living
60 __ *Nimitz*

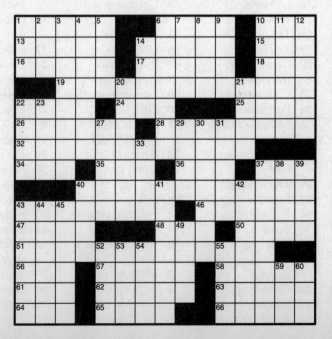

FORE THOUGHT by Frank Gordon

ACROSS
1 Single
5 Segment
9 *77 Sunset __*
14 "__ old cowhand . . ."
15 Not quite closed
16 Snapshot
17 Painter Chagall
18 __ dancer (disco worker)
19 Robbery
20 O'Connor role
23 Oklahoma city
24 Construct
27 Turner of *Northern Exposure*
30 "Right you __!"
31 Captain's diary
33 Nondrinker
35 Soccer great
36 French cap
37 Notes after dos
38 Composer Copland
39 Eager
40 Red Cross event
42 Stephen of *The Crying Game*

43 Bale contents
44 Royal residence
45 Glossy
47 Groceries holder
48 1963 Dick Van Dyke film musical
55 Stared, in a way
58 Pianist __ "Fatha" Hines
59 Liberal __
60 Beyond what's required
61 "I cannot tell __"
62 Pod fillers
63 Substantial
64 Clarinetist's need
65 Hawaiian port

DOWN
1 Peru's capital
2 Sharif or Bradley
3 DEA agent, for short
4 Under a spell
5 Beauty contest, e.g.

6 "This is __ for Superman!"
7 Prego rival
8 1982 Disney sci-fi film
9 Globe
10 In that place
11 King: Fr.
12 "__ about time!"
13 Kettle
21 Featherbrain
22 Deborah, John, or Graham
25 Ordained one
26 "Easy __" (Porter tune)
27 Wodehouse butler
28 TV antenna
29 Ahead of schedule
30 Fable guy
32 Chromosome unit
33 Ski lift
34 MGM's lion
35 Article part
38 He opposed Dwight twice

40 Cook cookies
41 Played (at)
43 Prime time
46 Partner of Siskel
49 Abide
50 New Haven campus

51 A Great Lake
52 *Eins* plus *zwei*
53 Type of type: Abbr.
54 Exxon, once
55 Jewel
56 Give the __ (fire)
57 School grp.

GETTING EVEN by Dean Niles

ACROSS
1 Southern university, for short
5 Brooklet
10 Bleacher or bench
14 "Dear me!"
15 Mountie's mount
16 Ike Turner's ex
17 Revolver
19 Culture medium
20 Here, in Toulouse
21 Actress Sommer
22 "There __ be a law!"
24 Always: Mus.
26 Selling point
27 Adrenaline and ACTH
30 __ canto (singing style)
33 Bring toward fruition
36 Pakistan neighbor
37 __ Morgana (mirage)

38 Cut, as wood
39 __ *of Two Cities*
40 Common astringent
41 Michigan city
42 "Tell __ the Marines"
43 Improvise
44 Politician Landon
45 Pinball reward
47 "Who Can __ To?"
49 Edible root
53 Composer Ferruccio __
55 Jacques of *Traffic*
57 Menlo Park initials
58 Italian wine town
59 Tie knot
62 Angler's aid
63 ID tag
64 Couturier Cassini
65 Tacks on
66 Think piece
67 *Jane* __

DOWN
1 Foundation

2 Mrs. Kramden
3 Saying
4 Beast of burden
5 Wrath
6 Chess piece
7 Art Deco designer
8 Point opposite WNW
9 Lamp oil
10 Theater platform
11 Pool game
12 Med. school subject
13 O'Hara home
18 Wading bird
23 __ *Nimitz*
25 Counterfeit
26 Not digital
28 Hand warmer
29 Hold forth
31 Needle case
32 Meek one
33 Movie terrier
34 Poet Sandburg
35 Vigorous
37 Sun-bleached

39 Certain gun
43 With full force
45 Enjoyment
46 In a showy way
48 Works hard
50 Home of Rome
51 More logical

52 Line of shrubs
53 Actress Theda
54 Took advantage of
55 Oleo holders
56 Vicinity
60 NATO cousin
61 Tilling tool

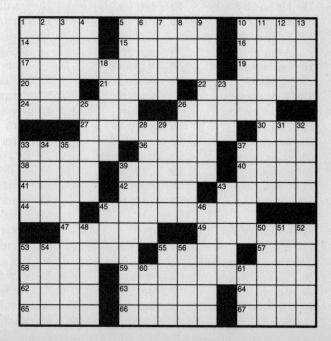

FAMOUS FATHERS by Harvey Estes

ACROSS
1 Free tickets
7 Exotic scent
14 Go by
15 "__ Beethoven" (Berry tune)
16 Make a gift of
17 Descartes' deductions
18 Picnic intruders
19 Right __ and there
21 El __, TX
22 Actress Thompson
23 Sticky stuff
24 Touch
26 KGB counterpart
28 Kitty comment
30 Did the backstroke
34 Notre Dame coach Lou
36 Was human?
38 "__ Maria"
39 Riled up
40 They assist in 13 Down

41 *Hedda Gabler* playwright
43 T in Sparta
44 Smart-alecky
46 Gandhi friend
47 *Born Free* feline
49 Catcher's glove
50 Chiang __-shek
51 Read rapidly
53 "Yoo-hoo!"
55 Gridders' org.
58 Fear or Cod
60 Asked on one's knees
62 Make eyes at
63 Pentagon on a diamond
65 Chin tuft
67 Guacamole needs
68 RESOUNDED . . . ounded . . . ounded
69 Treaty topic
70 Shenanigans

DOWN
1 Foot lever
2 Solo
3 Father Christmas

4 Health resorts
5 Superlative suffix
6 Take care of
7 Bachelor father
8 Pub output
9 Hillside
10 Ethical rules
11 Folksinger Burl
12 Fictional sub captain
13 Hospital areas
15 St. or rd.
20 Cartoon father
23 Looks at stars, maybe
25 She-sheep
27 *Addams Family* cousin
29 Painter Max
31 National father
32 State positively
33 Computer choice list
34 Author Shere
35 Spoken
37 Small-time
42 Arthur or Lillie
45 Bordeaux buddy

48 Facet
52 Steak stuck on a stick
54 Barely beats
56 Fast on one's feet
57 English town
58 Small bay

59 Famous cookiemaker
61 Bandleader Brown
62 Diamond Head's home
63 Headgear
64 Nabokov novel
66 Halloween mo.

SOUND EFFECTS by Robert H. Wolfe

ACROSS
1 From Havana
6 Poet Ezra
11 Chess pieces
14 Vacuous
15 Walking __ (elated)
16 He had a divine right
17 Keaton or Arbus
18 Feline's genetic accident?
20 Yogi's family
22 '50s First Lady
23 *Anything* __
25 Expert
28 Song or gab suffix
29 Circle part
30 Kitchen tool
31 Fracas
32 Marinara, for one
34 French composer
36 Makes happy
39 Cowhide
43 Dressed for the bench

45 Revolutionary pamphleteer
46 On the Indian
49 "__ Restaurant"
52 Sault __ Marie
53 Salon job
54 Of armadas
55 Starting
56 *The Woman* __ (Wilder film)
58 Sign up
60 Of a dove's cooking?
63 Reach the plate, perhaps
66 ETA part
67 Left page
68 Ponti's mate
69 __ Palmas
70 Jingle folks
71 Word roots

DOWN
1 El __ (Heston role)
2 Cycle prefix
3 Lamb cookout?
4 Rice and Archer

5 __-do-well
6 Mousse predecessor
7 All by __ (alone)
8 Detroit-based org.
9 NCAA rival
10 Small amount
11 Hurtful one
12 "Epistle From __ to Abelard" (Pope work)
13 X less than C
19 Crisp fabric
21 *Norma* __
23 Pant
24 Type of exam
26 Bell sound
27 Undeniable
30 Cancún coin
33 Chewy candy
35 Emulates Ice-T
37 Abba of Israel
38 Ward of *Sisters*
40 Python's past?
41 Word form for "inner"
42 Coral structure
44 Varied

46 Of the tip
47 *Madame's* Spanish cousin
48 Mistakes
50 Steve of the comics
51 Kay's follower
55 Fancy neckwear

57 Moffo or Sills
59 Man, for one
61 Beatty or Rorem
62 Equip with weapons
64 Sleep stage
65 Spanish queen

765 ALPHABET SOUP by Joe Clonick

ACROSS
1 OPEC representative
6 Jazz performances
10 Utter
13 Wine/hot water concoction
14 Rind remover
16 Card game
17 Smith, at times
18 Like lambs
19 90-degree shape
20 Sour
21 Gloomy guy in *Li'l Abner*
23 Mideast markets
25 Suits
26 Puts it to
27 In the chips
30 Body rhythm?
32 Decided upon
33 From then to now
34 __ Gang
35 Platter-cleaning family name
36 Easy chairs' extras
38 Albright and Falana

39 Fable relative
40 Anecdotal knowledge
41 Hun king
42 Eastern Indians
45 Adjusting the vise
48 "Oh, how I __ to get up . . ."
50 Sort
51 P, R, N, D, 1 and 2
52 Made out
53 Grand __ Opry
54 Result
55 In unison
56 One of Abe's boys
57 First-rate
58 TV tube element

DOWN
1 *Meet Me __ Louis*
2 Make-well process
3 Greek marketplace
4 Aztec serpent god

5 Haifa's country: Abbr.
6 Animal tracks
7 Roof edges
8 Paper's nickname
9 Summoned
10 Water-activated clock
11 Get going
12 Sunny side?
15 Does smeltery work
21 Copacetic
22 *National Velvet* event
24 Gathering
27 Half of GM
28 Greek vowels
29 .
30 Middle Eastern bread
31 Out of one's rut
32 Vienna's nation: Abbr.
33 Absorb, with "up"
34 Half-company?

37 Food
38 "The Kingfish"
40 Eyewear inventory
42 Breakfast topping, alternatively
43 Moses' brother
44 Pad's purpose
45 Funny fellow
46 Jazz singer Fitzgerald
47 El __, TX
49 Garden spot
52 Office need

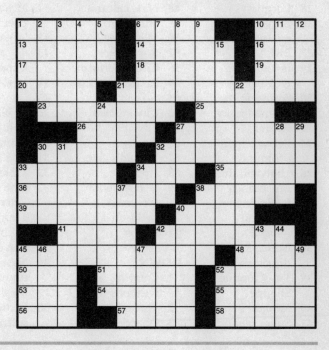

766 MASH NOTES by A.J. Santora

ACROSS
1 Actress Lili
7 Rogue
10 Magazine stand
14 Captivate
15 A person
16 Concerning
17 *M*A*S*H* role
20 Dan or span ending
21 Stumbles
22 __ one's eye (favorite)
25 Nosh
26 Actress Remick
27 Pigeon sound
28 Rainbow shapes
30 Mess place
31 What *M*A*S*H* was
34 Recolor
36 *M*A*S*H* role
40 Top of a certain scale
41 Portrayer of 36 Across
43 Seat groups

46 __ end (over)
47 Part of a car's elec. syst.
48 "__ Lazy River"
49 Neighbor of Mich.
51 Ached
54 Most polished
57 Fond du __, WI
58 *M*A*S*H* role
62 "So *that's* it!"
63 Spanish diminutive suffix
64 In dishonorable fashion
65 Geek
66 Inexperienced
67 Existing: Lat.

DOWN
1 St. Nick's mo.
2 "It's __-win situation!"
3 Western lily
4 Force
5 Peter O'__
6 Part of ETA
7 Pop drink
8 Leg joints

9 Perry's secretary
10 Lemon skin
11 African nation
12 Embroidery yarn
13 Bit of corn
18 Brawl
19 Doer: Suff.
22 Otto's exclamation
23 *Winnie-the-__*
24 Based on a grain
29 Baseball-shoe piece
30 Zeus' wife
32 Gold amts.
33 Turner or Eisenhower
34 Sawyer of the news
35 Yokohama moola
37 __ win (compete intensively)
38 Embraces
39 Nose (out)
42 Useful connector
43 "Fools __"

44 Resist
45 Supper server
46 "__ Fideles"
49 "__ Ruled the World"
50 __ the bud
52 Song parodist Sherman
53 Poker play
55 Escaped
56 Theater work
59 Where: Lat.
60 Haig and Capp
61 Actress Carrie

767 BODIES IN MOTION by Ann Seidel

ACROSS

1 Bye-bye, in Bordeaux
6 Push down
10 After-bath wear
14 Showed again
15 Location
16 Bringing misfortune
17 BREAST
19 Is under the weather
20 Sea eagle
21 Plumb wacky
22 Center
24 Become more profound
26 High and thin
28 Mil. branch
30 Is nothing to __ (matters)
34 Elevate
37 *Norma Rae* director Martin
39 Ye __ Junque Shoppe
40 Xanadu's river
41 Sugar plants
42 Warren Beatty film
43 Readily, old-style
44 Gargantuan
45 Flooded
46 Sponsored with funds
48 NYC cultural attraction
50 Martini & __
52 Royal color
56 Circus performers
59 Actress Patricia
61 Go bad
62 City in *Italia*
63 FINGER
66 Assert
67 Buffalo's lake
68 Uptight
69 __ one's way (proceed)
70 In the area
71 Rip off

DOWN

1 Carrying weapons
2 Tractor name
3 "Good-night, __"
4 Chow down
5 Wicked
6 Skin powder
7 Passion
8 Comic Brooks
9 Remittances
10 ARM
11 *Metamorphoses* poet
12 Moyers of PBS
13 ". . . or __!" (threat ender)
18 Mrs. Chaplin
23 General Amin
25 NOSE
27 Value
29 Scams
31 Dog's bane
32 Tacks on
33 John of *Entertainment Tonight*
34 Big bundle
35 Ken or Lena
36 Newspaper's comment page, for short
38 Participial suffix
41 King and queen
45 Charms
47 Conquered
49 Milky mineral
51 Madras' country
53 Folksinger John
54 "__ luck!"
55 Fred Mertz's wife
56 Bird's stomach
57 It conquers all
58 Harbinger
60 German river
64 Prior to
65 Soaked

768 THIS BUD'S FOR YOU by Raymond Hamel

ACROSS

1 Commoner
5 *Lion King* villain
9 Not as much
13 "Weird Al" Yankovic song parody
15 Bagel center
16 Marlene, in *The Blue Angel*
17 Cremona violinmaker
18 Tel __
19 Cameo stone
20 Tabernacle site
23 Swirl
24 Dodgers
28 Showed leniency to
31 Yonder
32 Hair holder
33 Blanches
34 October birthstone
35 WWII battle site
36 Thicke or Sues
37 Skirmishes
38 Trompe l'__ (visual deception)
39 Drawstring
40 Hard to find
41 Clinic employee
42 Aussie bird
43 Predilection
44 Gold weight units
45 *Hawaii Five-O* actor
47 Heroic
48 Bob Fosse musical
53 Chipper
56 Comet part
57 *Moll Flanders* author
58 Sandwich cookie
59 Notion
60 North Pole name
61 Moist
62 "__ la vie"
63 Want back

DOWN

1 Soup vegetables
2 Buddhist monk
3 Catchall abbr.
4 Unpleasant conclusion
5 Not too sturdy
6 Sheltered bay
7 *In Old Chicago* star
8 Tent meetings
9 Bentsen or Bridges
10 Long time
11 Foxlike
12 Kenny G's instrument
14 Diacritical marks
21 Insert
22 Cigarette ingredient
25 Alimentary canals
26 Enumerate again
27 Mink wraps
28 Actress Sissy
29 Picasso's daughter
30 Warning sound, old-style
31 Take __ (disassemble)
34 Summer drink
35 Burrito topping
37 More than busy
41 Nymphs of myth
43 Violinist's need
44 Metric speed abbr.
46 Camera setting
47 Striking effect
49 Cravats
50 Moroccan region
51 Bib wearers
52 Pro votes
53 Home for 1 Down
54 Notable period
55 Sleep phenom.

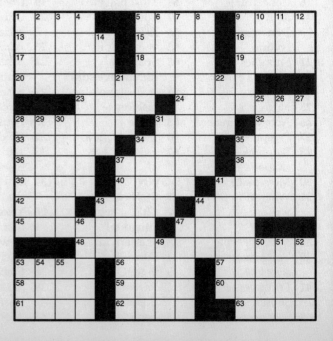

769 THIS SPUD'S FOR YOU by Randolph Ross

ACROSS

1 Wedding vows
5 Chest wood
10 Possesses
13 Cooking appliance
14 Unique
15 Dadaist painter
16 Potatoes for cobblers?
18 Hot Springs, for one
19 Planetary surfaces
20 Engraved
22 *Hook* character
23 Bother
24 Roast masters
27 Author of *Berlin Diary*
28 Merchandise
29 Book part
30 Go (for)
33 Actress Gray
34 Auctioneer's penultimate word
35 *Bridge on the River __*

36 Sun Yat-__
37 Fights
38 Ballpark boundary
39 Gold measures
41 Steam show
42 Optimistic, in a way
44 Get moving
45 Brunch serving
46 In reach
50 Jackson 5 song
51 Potatoes for Pierre?
53 Robert Morse role
54 Annoy
55 Bad guys
56 Watched Junior
57 Fabric workers
58 Cones' mates

DOWN

1 __ *Jury* (Spillane novel)
2 Way in
3 Supervised
4 Bun seeds

5 Chili ingredient
6 Wallach and Lilly
7 Put on
8 Causing to boil
9 Bring back
10 Leftover potatoes?
11 Lauder rival
12 Bogie role
13 JFK visitor
17 Affiliations
21 Signal
23 Dilutes
24 Woolly ones
25 Mrs. Ed?
26 Potatoes for an accordionist?
27 Barbecue equipment
29 Lee's side
31 Tempo
32 Wedding-cake feature
34 Take a wrong turn
35 Bogart film

37 Informed one's superior
38 Empathized with
40 100%
41 Ancient barbarian
42 Junks, e.g.
43 Shadow

44 Geom. figures
46 Snarl
47 Jay, for one
48 Majors and Horsley
49 Slalom shape
52 Hot time on the Riviera

770 REPEAT OFFENDER by Donna J. Stone

ACROSS

1 One-liner
5 Silents vamp
9 Left open
13 List ender
14 "Over There" composer
15 Its HQ is in Brussels
16 Kierkegaard, for one
17 Catalyst
18 Back talk?
19 START OF A 1 ACROSS
22 President Taylor
25 Figure at prayer
26 Queen of mystery
27 Kukla's colleague
30 __ Palmas
31 Strained
32 Novelist Lurie
34 MIDDLE OF THE 1 ACROSS
40 "Aha!"
41 Hatcher of *Lois & Clark*
42 Butter bit
45 Sound quality

46 Horse color
48 Decoration
50 Mocks
51 END OF THE 1 ACROSS
55 Got by, with "out"
56 "We __ please"
57 Stargazer's sight
61 "__ smile be your . . ."
62 Sulky horse
63 Disney sci-fi film
64 Soon
65 *Diary of __ Housewife*
66 Alluring

DOWN

1 Proof letters
2 Actress Hagen
3 Smith of Rhodesia
4 Linden costar
5 One over par
6 "Harrumph!"
7 Rampur royalty

8 Social workers?
9 Lend __ (listen)
10 Forsyth predator
11 Wise goddess
12 Sits on a perch
14 Toyota model
20 Paddle
21 Like a __ bricks
22 It follows epsilon
23 Fruit-tree spray
24 Hint
27 Stroke of luck
28 Costa __
29 Lava particles
32 Mass word
33 Good things in foods
35 Run circles around
36 Goya's gold
37 Propeller-head
38 Shade source
39 Art medium
42 Richardson novel
43 Get up

44 Start liking
46 Uruguayan title
47 Tolkien villain
49 Kind of fortification
50 Acted like a grandma

52 Winemaking region
53 Author O'Flaherty
54 Village People tune
58 Nev. neighbor
59 __ populi
60 Whichever

771 RISKY BUSINESS by Shirley Soloway

ACROSS

1 Colorless
5 "Get lost!"
9 Chef James
14 Thespian's pursuit
15 Service station job
16 "__ Was a Lady" (Porter tune)
17 Thomas __ Edison
18 Composer's output
19 Used a ballpoint
20 Take a chance
23 Perfect rating
24 Bolsheviks
25 Before, to a poet
26 Knight's title
27 Ralph Waldo __
31 Attacked
34 Wise men
36 Ripen
37 Taking a chance
41 Broadcast
42 Mars' alias
43 Birch tree
44 Wicker trees
47 Life story, for short
48 SASE, perhaps
49 From (that date)
51 Police order: Abbr.
54 Took a chance
59 Man-made fabric
60 Hanger supports
61 Italian wine region
62 Lift up
63 Talented
64 Tailor's concern
65 "Dearly beloved" spot
66 Sport shirts
67 *Laughing Cavalier* artist

DOWN

1 Conscript
2 Esther of *Good Times*
3 Singing chipmunk
4 Put up with
5 More leisurely
6 Bow bearer
7 Is adjacent to
8 TV host John
9 "Proceed with caution"
10 Breadwinner
11 Sick as __
12 Ceremony
13 Bambi's kin
21 Singer Lopez
22 Resign
26 Salty sauce
27 Protection
28 Uttered
29 Bad guy of legend
30 __-do-well
31 Woman of the Coast Guard
32 Kazan of Hollywood
33 Pielet
34 Bosses: Abbr.
35 Intense respect
38 John __ Garner
39 Israeli city
40 Showman Ziegfeld
45 Brewer or Wright
46 13 Down outgrowth
47 Employers
49 Western home style
50 Edge around
51 Confused
52 Flower segment
53 Hat edges
54 "Fame" singer Irene
55 Vocal
56 Section
57 "Nuts!"
58 Waist cincher

772 FILMS UNLIMITED by Mark Ryder

ACROSS

1 Tool's partner
4 Big bite
9 Roughnecks
14 Rural hotel
15 *Key __* (Bogart film)
16 Talk-show name
17 Experienced
18 Matt Dillon film of 1979
20 Does a brake job
22 Chance to act
23 Even-__
24 Uncle in the supermarket
25 Awfully long time
29 Unfortunate
30 Paul Newman title role
31 Elvis' "Don't Be __"
32 Part of NAACP
34 Appearance
35 He gets the boot
36 The Bakkers' former grp.
37 Say twice
39 Unexpected
40 Show-biz mag
42 Feedbag bit
43 Art degrees: Abbr.
44 Montreal suburb
45 United rival
46 Show sorrow
47 Gets by, with "out"
48 *48 __* (Murphy/Nolte film)
49 Relay-race props
52 G
54 Court business
55 Buster Keaton film of '30
59 Lt. saluter
60 Foreshadow
61 Appearance
62 Univ. div.
63 Bad weather
64 Boo-boo
65 Grads-to-be: Abbr.

DOWN

1 Designer dresses
2 Inter-island passage
3 Brooke Shields film of '81
4 Made copies, in a way
5 Safe place
6 Valuable rocks
7 Supvr.
8 Drunk
9 Attendee
10 Bottle accessories
11 Fort __, CA
12 Remind too often
13 Yon lady
19 Terrible guy
21 "Terrible" guy
24 Foxes' homes
26 Anthony Michael Hall film of '86
27 "We __ Little Christmas"
28 Has fun in the snow
30 Rush
31 Signal on the set
32 Pie flavor
33 Rib eye, e.g.
34 Wolfed down
35 Baseball great Mel
37 "__ Never Smile Again"
38 Trip-routing org.
41 Noted micro-biologist
43 Bons __ (clever comments)
45 Walk wearily
46 Diane of ABC
48 Sweetie
49 Choral member
50 Less unpleasant
51 Cuts out
53 Damage
54 Hideaway
55 Notes on the scale
56 Dull situation
57 Self-image
58 KLM destination

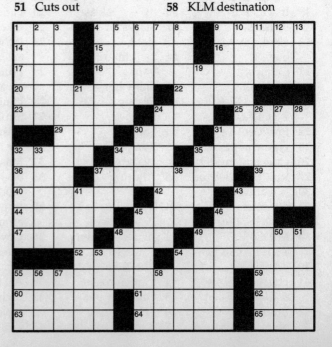

AT YOUR SERVICE by Dean Niles

ACROSS

1 Tennis need
4 Droops
8 "__ Stop Loving You"
13 Norwegian king
15 Prosperity
16 "If you knew __ like . . ."
17 Countertenor
18 Wild revelry
19 Step up a wall
20 Family treasure
22 Gave what-for
23 Barbie's beau
24 Actress Barrymore
26 Clean the blackboard
29 __ Pea
30 Irani title
34 Ms. Evert
35 Spiel
36 Mustard greens cousin
37 Forsaken
38 Bishop's cap
39 __ Stanley Gardner

40 Mine passage
41 German eight
42 Hay hunks
43 Mary Hart's cohost
44 Some receptions
45 Authoritative decree
46 Water vessels
48 __ Arbor, MI
49 Spanish city
52 Imitative work
57 Truism
58 One-person performances
59 Muscle verb
60 Summary
61 Campus figure
62 Freedom from fretting
63 Goes downhill, perhaps
64 *Picnic* playwright
65 British raincoat

DOWN

1 Arkwright
2 Women's magazine

3 French comic actor
4 Faint away
5 Dynamic beginning
6 Valley Girl "request"
7 Stallone, familiarly
8 Matter at hand
9 Bryan Adams song
10 Without modification
11 Longest river
12 __ off (angry)
14 Times of decision
21 Spike and Brenda
22 Tide competitor
25 Guiding principles
26 Kudos
27 __ Island Red
28 *Mrs. __ Goes to Paris*
29 Deli machine
31 Mrs. Trump
32 *"Deutschland über __"*
33 Reagan cabinet member

38 Beat at chess
42 Batter's ploy
47 Non-macho types
48 Out of the way
49 Red planet
50 Kerrigan move
51 Monopoly needs

53 Without __ to stand on
54 Happy mollusk?
55 "__ real nowhere man"
56 Corp. VIP
58 __-fi

PARAMILITARY by Harvey Estes

ACROSS

1 Available, as a book
8 Cotton material
15 Watch over
16 Sign of imperfection
17 Enliven
18 None at all
19 Pop star?
20 City in 41 Across
22 '60s radical org.
23 Does "sum" math
25 "Take a bite!"
28 Provide provender to
30 R.E. Lee's nation
31 Okra dish
35 McClanahan of *The Golden Girls*
36 Ruckus
38 The __ of the law
40 Before
41 Neighbor of Belg.
42 Knot-tying words
43 Game beginning
44 Carrot cousin
46 Grandpa Walton
47 Neighbor of Minn.

48 Commercial spokescow
49 Miners dig it
51 Commons' counterpart
53 Use peepers piercingly
55 Unimportant
56 66, for short
59 Third Greek letter
61 To be, on the Riviera
64 Envelope inscription
67 Put on a pedestal
69 Ferry chaser
70 Tea root
71 It will open doors for you
72 __ International (rights group)

DOWN

1 *Yes __* (Sammy Davis memoir)
2 Second starter
3 Pirates
4 Done again

5 "__ man answers . . ."
6 So and so?
7 Very: Fr.
8 Speak broadly
9 Literary device
10 Cole of song
11 Govt. purchasing org.
12 Where spokes meet
13 Like the Sahara
14 Shea team
21 Peter, Paul and Mary, for short
24 Friday's program
26 Mean
27 Ship shover
28 Paper type
29 Ear-oriented
30 About the body
32 Baton twirlers
33 Do a ranch job
34 Leaves out
37 *"Agnus __"*
39 Poet's product
45 __ boom bah
50 Dream-state occurrence

52 End of a threat
54 Surefooted
55 Saw
56 Say with a gravelly voice
57 "__ yellow ribbon . . ."
58 Pitching stats
60 Beginning of bucks
62 Tore apart
63 Like a nervous Nellie
65 BMW challengers
66 Northern bird
68 Landers of letters

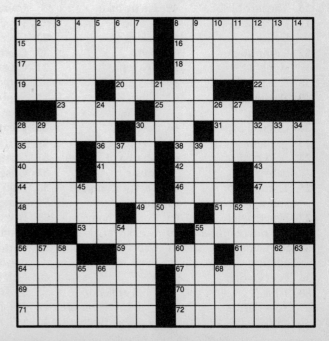

775   LOOK BOTH WAYS by Matt Gaffney

ACROSS

1 Capp and Pacino
4 Stroke
7 Yellow vehicle, often
10 Angels or Devils
12 Literally, "upstream people"
15 First name in cubes
16 '78 Peace Nobelist
18 PED __
19 Pub amounts
20 Holy cups
22 __ Gay
23 Unite
24 Bits of info
26 The alternative
28 Loud horns
31 *Splash* star
35 Pasture comment
36 Commit a hockey violation
37 '81 Grammy winner
38 Band's need
39 Period
40 1991-92 U.S. Open winner
42 Notwithstanding
44 How-to helpers
45 Any time now
46 Boom bah preceder
48 Smarts dully
52 Tan-lines avoider
54 Park activity
55 Swizzle
57 Sarah Purcell TV show
59 Savages
60 *Thunder Alley* star
61 Garden problem
62 Vandal's missile
63 Susan of *L.A. Law*
64 They assist MDs

DOWN

1 Dickens title start
2 *Pravda*'s founder
3 Took care of
4 Famous flagmaker
5 Actress Thurman
6 Cop's ID
7 Panama Canal city
8 Miller or Reinking
9 Peat spot
11 Scrooge's partner
13 Tough "school"
14 __ standstill
15 Metamucil competitor
17 "I don't __" ("It's no bother")
21 Pocatello campus
23 Exploitable qualities
25 "What's in __?"
27 Bamboo bit
29 Maui neighbor
30 Fall guys
31 Conked out
32 *U.S. __* (Jim Davis comic)
33 Logic
34 Coveted NCAA ranking
41 Third-party account
43 Rains hard
47 "Try __ see!"
49 He's gotta believe
50 Actress Barkin
51 Winter rides
53 Lyricist Gershwin
54 Agile
55 Andress role
56 Harbor craft
58 *Malcolm X* director

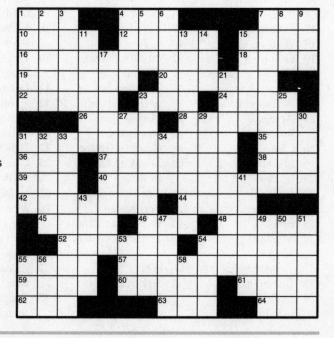

776   JEWELRY BOXES by Shirley Soloway

ACROSS

1 Bridge player's bonus
5 Great review
9 Religious groups
14 Oahu dance
15 The terrible one
16 J.R.'s mom on *Dallas*
17 Computer symbol
18 Essence
19 To the right or left
20 Circus hosts
23 __ diem
24 Bald bird's baby
25 Therapy, for short
27 Flee to wed
30 Put out of office
33 Soviet news agency
36 Poet Ogden
38 Tilts
39 Superlative suffix
40 River duck
42 Séance sound
43 Chopin piece
45 In shreds
46 Uptight
47 Cindy Crawford et al.
49 Go by bike
51 Movie
53 Like some beds
57 "Gotcha!"
59 Illegal mail
62 Gibbs or Maples
64 Men-only
65 Nevada city
66 Mischa of music
67 The __ Diamond
68 Ingests
69 Builds a home
70 Greek war god
71 Gaelic

DOWN

1 Talia of *Rocky*
2 __ di Lammermoor
3 Together (with)
4 Botches
5 Ridged pasta
6 Hertz rival
7 Spacious
8 "Come in!"
9 Shore souvenir
10 Aboveground trains
11 Paper holder
12 Ocean motion
13 Clairvoyant
21 Gibson of *Maverick*
22 Sunburned
26 Mimic
28 Breathe fast
29 Bar, in law
31 Obstruction
32 Observe
33 Rain heavily
34 Concerning
35 Horses' homes
37 Tortoise's opponent
40 Fish-eating birds
41 Caters to
44 Md. neighbor
46 Stately shader
48 Univ.
50 Chemical ending
52 Coarse grain
54 Shed __ (weep)
55 Bumper marks
56 Notched, as leaves
57 Prayer finale
58 Patriot Nathan
60 *Believe __ Not*
61 Back of the neck
63 Atlas abbr.

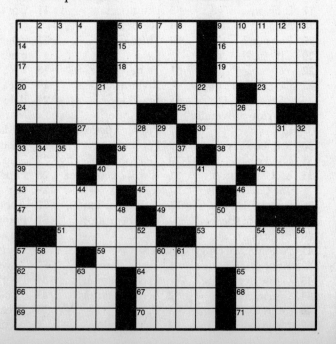

777 BOARD MEMBERS by John Leavy

ACROSS

1 Struck down
6 Italian town
11 Beanie
14 Turkish bigwig
15 Satirist's tool
16 French friend
17 Fictional sleuth
19 Regret
20 "Vaya Con __"
21 Loopholes
22 Chicken's seat
24 Narrative
26 Sailor's kitchen
27 Commandeer
30 Great Plains Indian
32 Separated
33 Prepared steak, perhaps
34 Frat-party need
37 __ off (angry)
38 General Powell
39 Dog's name
40 Pig's digs
41 Raise, as a flag
42 Door part
43 Lennon or McCartney
45 Smithies
46 Horse's headgear
48 Carry
49 Martini partner
50 Noble rank
52 Cuts wood
56 Bat wood
57 Noted basketball coach
60 GM economy car
61 Europe/Asia divider
62 Image of perfection
63 Cobra's kin
64 Core principle
65 Green sauce

DOWN

1 Floored it
2 African nation
3 Cold capital
4 Stephen King novel
5 Corn portion
6 Resentment
7 In __ (stuck)
8 Accomplishes
9 French article
10 The Fountainhead author
11 "So Far Away" composer
12 Divert
13 Sanctity
18 Flan ingredient
23 __ Miss
25 Pet detective Ventura
26 Dancer Verdon
27 They may be checked
28 "__ a Song Go Out of ..."
29 Rat Pack comedian
30 Sign of life
31 Not much
33 Spring
35 The Razor's __ (Maugham novel)
36 Takes a powder
38 __ d'Azur
39 FDR's __ chats
41 Fish dish
42 Like a day in June?
44 Ames and Grimley
45 People
46 Actress Sonia
47 Bouquet favorite
48 Romantic rendezvous
50 Israeli statesman Abba
51 Qualified
53 Ripens
54 "Say again?"
55 WWII battle site
58 Prospector's quest
59 Small swig

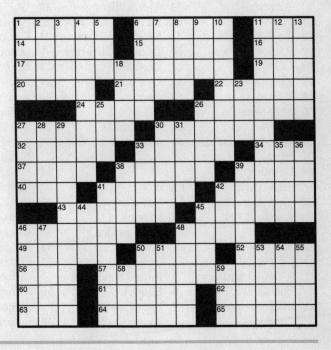

778 CAHN JOBS by Dean Niles

ACROSS

1 Take on
6 LBJ or WJC
10 Stops up
14 Less refined
15 Senator Trent
16 Great Lakes port
17 Chou __
18 "__ boy!"
19 Color-copier company
20 Sammy's romantic advice
23 Food scrap
24 Provokes
25 Sammy's Chicago tribute
31 Scram
32 Costello et al.
33 Silents actress Clara
36 Past due
37 Swell
39 PBS science show
40 Before
41 Sorry, as an excuse
42 __ up (assessed)
43 Sammy's salute to solitude
46 Goofed in golf
49 German article
50 Sammy's Our Town smash
57 Horse breed
58 Ireland
59 __ on (incited)
60 Actress Rowlands
61 Playing with a full deck
62 Mary Tyler __
63 Fly in the ointment
64 Cookbook instruction
65 Court command

DOWN

1 Cain's brother
2 Linda of Another World
3 Norway's capital
4 Summit
5 Musical interval
6 __ win (compete hard)
7 __-Rooter
8 Question to Brutus
9 Commence the journey
10 Humiliate
11 Kathleen Battle selections
12 British joint
13 They're between aisles
21 Fort __, CA
22 Cleaves
25 Fr. girl
26 Año, in Anaheim
27 Singer Smith
28 "__ Gotta Be Me"
29 Plants of a region
30 One __ customer
33 TV clown
34 Microwave, e.g.
35 Walk in water
37 Courage
38 __ comedy (slapstick)
39 Nothing at all
41 Bargain, maybe
42 Italian port
43 Cold remedy?
44 Not as stout
45 Wine apéritif
46 Metal drosses
47 Sophia of Two Women
48 Donald's ex
51 "Fiddlesticks!"
52 Skirt start
53 Composer Stravinsky
54 "Thou art __ ready to pardon"
55 Actor Richard
56 German river

779   GO OUT by Raymond Hamel

ACROSS
1 AAA giveaways
5 Wooden shoe
10 Volume
14 Sore spot
15 Hersey hamlet
16 Tennis pro Arthur
17 Hold sway
18 Copier need
19 Rack's partner
20 GO OUT
23 Fate
24 Whammy
25 Malachite and azurite
26 Well-behaved kid
28 Storage unit
29 Cough syrup ingredient
32 Choreographer Ailey
35 Expand
37 Tel __
38 GO OUT
41 Richards and Rutherford
42 Magazine magnate Condé
43 Of the kidneys
44 Strength
46 Something to chew on
47 Hero
48 *Pequod*'s skipper
50 Menagerie
53 The works
55 GO OUT
58 Bennett or Baez
60 Lorna of literature
61 Well off
62 One opposed
63 Recall
64 "*Dies* __"
65 Film holder
66 Type of butterfly
67 Aquaman's wife

DOWN
1 Cattail's site
2 Sharp
3 Rock-garden favorite
4 Ooze
5 Jupiter neighbor
6 Like a lot
7 Engagement announcement
8 "Dedicated to the __ Love"
9 Demolished
10 Captain's insignia
11 Weissmuller costar
12 Glenn's home
13 Artist Rockwell
21 Cartoon sound effect
22 Burns role
27 Like some gasoline
28 Oblique
29 Ducklike bird
30 Silents star Naldi
31 First name in cycle jumping
32 PDQ
33 Carson's successor
34 Air out
35 *Little Orphan Annie* cartoonist
36 *Kidnapped* author's monogram
39 Embraces
40 Island off Venezuela
45 Postman's Creed word
46 Life's work
48 In process
49 __-tonk
50 African nation
51 Film trophy
52 Music-hall star Tessie
53 Not completely closed
54 Unescorted
56 Blazing star
57 Stiffly formal
59 Zero

---

780   BEASTLY by Manny Nosowsky

ACROSS
1 Top of the line
5 Each
9 *R.U.R.* writer
14 Southern arena
15 Beastly retreat
16 Piece of the *casa*
17 Annoying movie for Mr. Ed?
20 Prepare to fire
21 Ob-__ (medical specialty)
22 Animation frame
23 Have a bite
24 Animated character
26 Punch lines, often
27 Golda of Israel
29 Ironic
30 Over
32 Golfer Woosnam
33 Isle of Man man
34 Crazy guy
37 Discount
39 Olive stuffer
40 Sigh, perhaps
41 Comic Johnson
42 Sub. for the unlisted
43 Lasting introduction
44 Line of jive
45 Pastel color
46 Push for
48 *The King and I* setting
50 Teutonic war god
51 Office seeker
52 Ticker tape?
53 Struggle (over)
57 SPCA concern?
60 Borden's ruminant
61 Copycat
62 G.N.P., e.g.
63 "We're Off __ the Wizard"
64 Actress Pitts
65 Scandinavian city

DOWN
1 Gravy holder
2 Actress Samms
3 What a cad sees while shaving?
4 Musical deficit
5 Jai __
6 Where to get dates
7 It floats on water
8 Please, in Palermo
9 "High Hopes" lyricist
10 Bit of a fuss
11 Sharp blankets?
12 Buddy of film
13 Falls (over)
18 Roscoe
19 Explosive
25 Popeye's love
26 Corn bread
27 Nursery-rhyme trio
28 Waters of Vichy
29 Follow a boat, perhaps
31 Break a bronc
33 High wind
35 Aleutian island
36 Caesar costar
38 Act like a 34 Across, maybe
39 Men and apes
41 Pie __ mode
45 Slangy denial
46 Unexpected win
47 Rich kid in *Nancy* comics
49 Hungarian name
50 Rocky peak
52 Duel gear
54 Spiritual leader
55 Ardor
56 This: Sp.
58 Humble meal?
59 UCLA stat

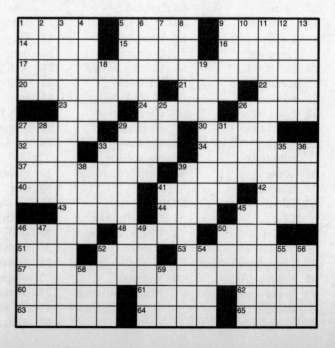

781 TOOLING UP by Shirley Soloway

ACROSS
1 Satirist Mort
5 Accumulate
10 Plays a part
14 Potpourri
15 Go from __ worse
16 Big boat
17 Itch scratcher
19 Singer Turner
20 Actress Lansbury
21 Archie Bunker, e.g.
23 Get the point
24 Actress/director Lupino
26 Dunce-cap shape
27 Enjoyed a playground ride
30 House site
33 Church alcove
36 Night twinkler
37 Abrasive material
39 More pleasant
41 Suffix for press
42 More unusual
43 __ firma
44 Little people
46 Vacation resort
47 Compass pt.
48 Pulled forcefully
51 Sound of joy
53 Sandwich meat
54 Train depot: Abbr.
57 William Randolph __
59 Panoramas
61 Young blooms
62 Hogan hold
65 Water: Sp.
66 More mature
67 Actor Tamiroff
68 Back-to-school mo.
69 Tries out
70 Tennis pro Sampras

DOWN
1 Couches
2 Garment cut
3 Door holder
4 Theater section
5 Irritates
6 "The __ I Love"
7 Actress Maris of Nurses
8 Mix
9 Consolation
10 A Gomez Addams portrayer
11 Cheaters
12 Hue
13 Calorie counters' retreat
18 Nobelist Wiesel
22 Cryptogram maker
25 Keen
27 Prognosticator
28 Composer Copland
29 Miserable one
31 Hurler Hershiser
32 Lebanon town
33 Colony builders
34 Pizza and Boston cream
35 Made a mess of things
38 Household worker
40 Less cooked
45 Beard busters
49 Filmed again
50 Kuwaiti chief
52 Attacks
54 Tend the furnace
55 Implied
56 "__ no questions . . ."
57 Oversized
58 Anecdote
60 __ on the wrist (punish mildly)
61 __-relief
63 Drs.
64 Shea player

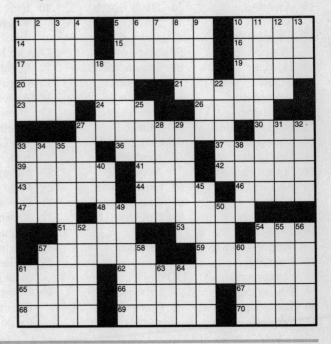

782 ICE FOLLIES by Dean Niles

ACROSS
1 Unhappy
5 Young ram
9 One on the move
13 __ avis
14 Like an excited crowd
16 Russian designer
17 Surrounded by
18 __ the Conqueror (Von Sydow film)
19 Hoses down
20 Not fem.
21 Skater's tiff?
23 Sports org.
25 __ long way toward (help)
26 Skater's serenade?
34 Ingest
35 Up and about
36 __ of Troy
38 Actresses Farrow and Sara
40 Actress Merkel
41 __ on (fuss over)
42 Small bay
44 Does a fall chore
47 That guy's
48 Decline, as a skater?
51 "__ Believer" (Monkees song)
52 Get a load of
53 Inept skater?
59 "__ See Clearly Now"
63 Husband's mate
64 Hang (over)
65 Wise one
66 Wrinkle remover
67 Acrylic fiber
68 For real
69 Examination
70 Transmitted
71 The four seasons

DOWN
1 Metric unit
2 Tibetan monk
3 Exodus author
4 Wild and crazy
5 What sitting Santas can support
6 General location
7 __ Flanders
8 Sphere
9 Laden with baubles
10 Sandwich cookie
11 "__, Brute?"
12 Sack out
15 Hold the scepter
22 Ark master
24 __ rule (usually)
26 18-wheeler
27 British psychiatrist
28 Author Calvino
29 "__ my back to the East": Blake
30 Singer Shore
31 Baghdad resident: Var.
32 Islands salutation
33 Abominable Snowmen
37 Bird bed
39 The dregs
43 King Tut's __
45 Oxygen or helium
46 Foxy
49 Where's __?
50 Pugnacious
53 Loretta of M*A*S*H
54 Wear out
55 Sky saucers
56 Strays
57 Big bundle
58 "Once __ a time . . ."
60 Safekeeping
61 Water, in Juárez
62 __-do-well

783 CRAWLIES by Wayne R. Williams

ACROSS
1 Aboveboard
6 Pisa's river
10 Skiers' lift
14 City south of Gainesville
15 Stead
16 Architect Saarinen
17 Financially irresponsible
19 Hardens
20 Russian chessmaster
21 NL team
22 Hills separator
24 Martin and Allen
26 Uris bestseller
27 Poison remedy
30 And so forth: Abbr.
33 Whimpers
36 1993 Tom Berenger movie
37 Vocalize displeasure
38 Disney dog
40 Tooth topper
41 Perplex
43 Poultry product
44 Petite piano
47 Periods of diminution
48 Diplomat Hammarskjöld
49 Carpentry device
51 Day's march
53 Study of light and vision
57 Made over
59 Trigonometric function
61 Fly-fish
62 North Carolina college
63 Parade "rain"
66 Kind of mile: Abbr.
67 Quiz answer
68 Gray-faced
69 Not fooled by
70 Grub
71 Have on

DOWN
1 Urban studios
2 Conspicuous success
3 Singer Crystal
4 Priest's vestment
5 Non-priests
6 Landed
7 Puts in the fix
8 O.T. book
9 Gain a majority
10 Unit of magnetic flux density
11 Old Nick
12 Comic Johnson
13 Optimistic
18 Aspen abodes?
23 Mimics
25 Extensive
26 Leo G. Carroll role
28 Stir up
29 Ladd or Lane
31 Pyramid, e.g.
32 Urban officers
33 Hightailed it
34 Gymnast Korbut
35 Broke camp quickly
39 Ottoman Empire's founder
42 Speech in writing
45 Lab straw
46 Steak cut
50 Wagner works
52 Silverheels role
54 Western state
55 Frolic
56 Exhausted
57 Nevada destination
58 Flair
59 Rabbit's tail
60 Turner and others
64 Novelist Levin
65 Recipe meas.

784 TELEVISED ADDRESSES by Merl H. Reagle

ACROSS
1 Orange skin
5 "__ an arrow . . ."
10 Actor Dillon
14 Grimace causer
15 Murder by __ (Neil Simon film)
16 "I wouldn't do that!"
17 1313 __ (address of 25 Across)
20 On __ knee
21 Commercial interviewee, e.g.
22 Football field
24 Coleridge's "Dejection," for one
25 Sitcom hubby
31 Raucous sound
32 Felt: Fr.
33 Grass-skirt accessory
35 Where cranberries grow
36 Clyde or Forth
37 Rick's love
38 VW preceders
39 Seaweed
40 ACLU, for instance
41 Sitcom hubby
44 Point (at)
45 Sneaky __ (hooch)
46 Read superficially
51 Using planes
55 1313 __ (address of 41 Across)
57 Biblical son
58 Could kill for
59 Mass response
60 San __, CA
61 Paddled
62 Deviates from the course

DOWN
1 Virginia politico Charles
2 Put out of work
3 Mad Libs need
4 Kitchen devices
5 "__ with my little hatchet"
6 "Satisfied?"
7 Laugh-In star
8 Mr. Preminger
9 Bluecoats' side
10 Bip's portrayer
11 At the drop of __
12 Baja snack
13 Irving Wallace's __ Document
18 Burma Shave creation
19 Spokes
23 Accident's antonym
25 Clergy
26 The __, Netherlands
27 Butt again
28 Fill the pot
29 Barbara on Dallas
30 Answer __ No (old game show)
31 Air-rifle shot
34 Actor McShane
36 Foot-stompin' music?
37 Sandwich between
39 __ curiae
40 Second person, to Pablo
42 Irk
43 Came up to
46 One-sharp key sig.
47 Timber wolf
48 Cheater's sleeveful
49 Taj Mahal's location
50 Ski lift
52 __ Camera
53 For a second time
54 An eyeful, for some
56 "Lord knows __ tried!"

785 AVON CALLING by Frank Gordon

ACROSS

1 Corn lover
5 Cup rims
9 VCR button
14 Backpacker's activity
15 Gauguin's greeting
16 Fibber McGee's medium
17 Some land
18 Pants cut
19 Avoid
20 Mishandles a six-pack?
23 "Behold, Brutus!"
24 Prevaricate
25 Like some oats
27 A familiar ring?
31 Weather-map areas
32 Staring
33 Succumb to a seam stress
37 Old wives' tales
38 Word before clip or cut
39 Wiesel or Abel
40 Tough breaks
42 Mrs. Gorbachev
43 Rounds up
44 __ in the Cathedral
45 Boilermaker components
48 Racket
49 Beef cut
50 Moslem ruler's equal?
56 How some tuna is packed
58 Menlo Park name
59 Start from scratch
60 Takes the wraps off
61 Peruse a palm
62 "Step __!"
63 Bergen bumpkin
64 Chihuahua cash
65 Old legend

DOWN

1 Cartoonist Addams
2 Like fudge cake
3 Podded plant
4 Common pay period
5 Dog star
6 "__ There" (Jackson 5 tune)
7 Swan Lake movement
8 Now and then
9 Indecision sounds
10 LaMotta's lance?
11 Ukase
12 Legendary enchantress
13 Schlepped
21 Vogue rival
22 Toon rabbit
26 "Gotcha!"
27 Little dogie
28 Borodin subject
29 __ avis
30 Brno resident's dock?
31 Aspirations
33 Ace hider
34 "Put __ on it!"
35 Gentle slope
36 Tissue target
38 Functions smoothly
41 Pigskin prop
42 Diamond tally
44 Nanki-Poo's papa
45 Corn holders
46 Chinese province
47 Love, Italian-style
48 Prima donnas
51 Gen. Robert __
52 Gym event
53 Start of a count
54 Redact
55 Portnoy's creator
57 Initials associated with Dr. Leary

786 IN THE MAIL by Shirley Soloway

ACROSS

1 Cavalry weapon
6 Sporty hats
10 Walk in water
14 Neighborhoods
15 __ ben Adhem
16 Roll-call response
17 Acceptable rating
20 British radial
21 Touch softly
22 Hazards
23 News service: Abbr.
25 "__ Be Cruel" (Elvis tune)
26 Supplying ongoing information
32 Naval off.
33 Peaceful
34 Musical composition
37 "__ luck!"
39 Coach Parseghian
40 Open courtyards
41 Story line
42 Israeli welcome: Var.
44 Under the weather
45 Essence
48 Precipitate heavily
49 Common title starter
50 Unsusceptible
53 Babilonia of the ice
55 Hernando's house
59 Bank approvals
62 Aromatic herb
63 Scat queen
64 Take as one's own
65 Pub orders
66 Fabric worker
67 Untidy

DOWN

1 At the end of the line
2 Pretentious
3 Close at hand
4 Arose
5 Seer's talent
6 Paris eatery
7 Blind as __
8 Dad
9 Guess
10 Most concise
11 Jeans maker Strauss
12 Spoken
13 Hair applications
18 Give one's view
19 Monthly payment
24 Tower town
25 Marla's spouse
26 Seaweed
27 Organic compound
28 Bar legally
29 Choreographer Martha
30 Juan or Eva
31 Column style
35 River from Lake Victoria
36 Nerve
38 Laws
40 Chinese nanny
42 Had the helm
43 Of the eye
46 Auberjonois of Deep Space Nine
47 Ebb
50 Ingrid's Casablanca role
51 Supper, e.g.
52 Home buyer's debt: Abbr.
53 Enameled metal
54 A long way off
56 Commotions
57 Uses a straw
58 Matlock or Mason: Abbr.
60 Wily
61 Los Angeles gridder

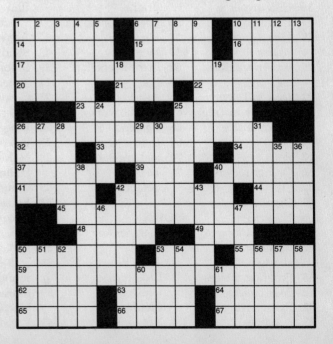

787 CELESTIAL by Frank Gordon

ACROSS
1 Whip
5 Receive, as news
9 Land of the Rising Sun
14 __ of Man
15 Mustang or Colt
16 Wield words like Webster
17 Result of surveying the heavens?
20 Plaything
21 Actress Moran
22 Apartment papers
23 Australian rock group
24 Atlas pages
25 Astronaut's home course?
29 TV watchdog
32 "To __ human . . ."
33 Majors or Iacocca
34 Distinctive air
35 Exploits
36 Etchers' needs
38 Aspiring M.B.A.'s hurdle
39 Ice cream holder
40 Tavern
41 Radio soap heroine Helen
42 USNA grad
43 Space Shuttle dessert?
46 Refinery input
47 Cork's country
48 Like the Six Million Dollar Man
51 Luncheon ending
52 Mork's home
55 Celestially ecstatic?
58 Nick of *Weeds*
59 Elm or ash
60 Letterman rival
61 Uppity one
62 Buffalo group
63 One more time

DOWN
1 Shopper's aid
2 In re
3 Do in
4 That woman
5 Coif
6 __ Kennedy Shriver
7 Like __ of bricks
8 Director Howard
9 Coat-of-many-colors wearer
10 Spheres
11 Is profitable
12 Fits to __
13 Role for Stack
18 Religious offshoots
19 Makes merry
23 Licorice-flavored spice
24 Eloquent equine
25 Low card
26 Welles or Bean
27 Songbirds
28 Excuse
29 Gets steamed
30 Model T feature
31 Spiteful
34 Come to terms
36 Per person
37 Pool equipment
41 *My __ Sons*
43 Topiarist's target
44 On the __ side (under)
45 Contributed a tenth
46 __ a customer
48 Storeroom items
49 Privy to
50 European capital
51 Raison d'__
52 Where rolls rise
53 Painter Magritte
54 Have down cold
56 Extreme degree
57 Tenn. neighbor

788 LEGALESE by Wayne R. Williams

ACROSS
1 Brief sample
5 Alpine needs
9 1989 French Open winner
14 Oxfordshire
15 Breathe shallowly
16 Cliff dwelling
17 Power unit
18 Like a developed country
20 Brown and Rice, e.g.
22 One, in Toledo
23 Summer, in Tours
24 Tuscaloosa's home
27 Pol. party
30 Orange rocks
32 "It"
34 Greek letter
36 Hwy. sign abbreviation
37 Japanese aborigine
38 Program choices
40 Pearl collector
42 Ex-superpower
43 __ breve
44 Regular guy
45 Legal action grp.
47 Tennis surface
50 Way from a man's heart
53 Chop
54 Black __ (Kahlua drink)
56 Poetic monogram
57 Big __, CA
58 Increases
60 In the event that
65 Car
66 Also known as
67 Artistic work
68 Contends
69 Door stopper
70 Red vegetable
71 To be, in Toulouse

DOWN
1 Searches for water
2 Track bet
3 Lady Bird Johnson, to Charles Robb
4 Not fooled by
5 Tanker leak
6 Toto's home
7 Unaffiliated voter: Abbr.
8 Actor Erwin
9 Bit of shuteye
10 1992 Hoffman film
11 *Exodus* hero
12 Actress Peeples
13 Solidify
19 Indonesian island
21 Tobacco kiln
25 Cleaver and others
26 Wheel bar
27 Disco attire
28 McKellen and Holm
29 Cloud
31 Version of the Bible
33 São __
35 End a session
38 __ 1 (speed of sound)
39 Model Macpherson
41 Valuable notes
46 Sugar source
48 Kidman's husband
49 Sneezer's need
51 Less loose
52 Place side by side
55 Bomb blast, in headlines
57 Men-only event
59 Do road work
60 Yammer
61 Diminutive ending
62 Caesar of comedy
63 Corn holder
64 Mimic

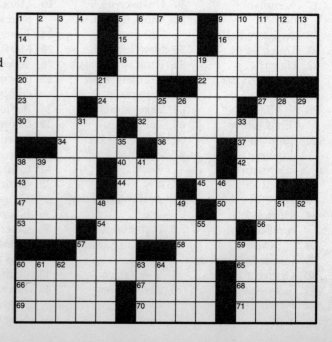

789 SIX-PACK by Dean Niles

ACROSS

1 Sarah Bernhardt role
6 PACK
10 Big deals
14 Spin around
15 Glow
16 __ monster
17 PC chip maker
18 PACK
20 Stickum
21 71% of the earth
23 Medical professional
24 Chimney ducts
26 Cassette format
27 *Little Women* woman
29 Joined, in a way
34 Table extender
35 Pads
37 B-F link
38 Civil wrong
39 Missile parts
40 Farmer's concern
41 Not to mention
42 Vergil's hero
43 Tap on the green
44 Booming
46 First name in mystery
48 __ Tin Tin
49 Smart or Solo
50 Sphere of influence
53 High land
55 *In medias* __
58 PACK
60 Baby bird?
62 __ facto
63 Egyptian sacred bird
64 Subtle sarcasm
65 Spotted
66 PACK
67 Tent of skins

DOWN

1 Offshoot
2 Expression of disbelief
3 PACK
4 Middling mark
5 No-holds-barred
6 Neon and Freon
7 Actress Lee
8 Golf club
9 Animal appendage
10 Rabbitlike rodent
11 Couture tag
12 GM make
13 Mail enc.
19 Midges
22 Flipper or Willy
25 Hay space
26 Horse obedience
27 Place for sacrifice
28 Director Sergio
29 Painter Claude
30 Music halls
31 PACK
32 __ Ann (Tomlin character)
33 River feature
36 Beethoven's birthplace
40 C-__ (cable service)
42 Santa __ (California track)
45 Sacred plea
47 Sees the light
49 Bottomless pit
50 Japanese sashes
51 Ready for plucking
52 Despicable
53 Band biggie
54 Rainbow
56 Eagle of the sea
57 Type of terrier
59 Henson or Croce
61 *Uno + due*

790 PLASTIC RAP by Donna J. Stone

ACROSS

1 Camel cousin
6 Swedish import
10 Curly coif
14 Moral man?
15 Helper
16 Appealed
17 START OF A QUIP
19 Monsieur Le Pew
20 Pickable
21 Warning device
23 Harsh-sounding
28 Sanctify
29 Fire up
30 Dictionary abbr.
32 Actress Wallace
33 __ hasty retreat
34 Tennis term
35 MIDDLE OF QUIP
41 Pantry pest
42 Violinist Mischa
45 Gossip
48 Typesetting units
49 Pick up
51 Bikini event
53 Dancer's maneuver
55 Fanatic
57 Rampur royalty
58 Actor Billy of *Only You*
59 END OF QUIP
65 Hand-me-down
66 Barrie dog
67 Kinglike?
68 Hosiery buy
69 Manuscript imperative
70 Dais covering

DOWN

1 Composer Francis
2 Aspin or Crane
3 Ski material
4 Bossy remark?
5 Sanction
6 WWII site
7 Poet Conrad
8 Citrus cooler
9 Schnoz
10 Dismay
11 Bent
12 Dignified calm
13 Andersen's birthplace
18 Reinforce a raincoat
22 Presidential monogram
23 Society miss
24 Chemical suffix
25 Concrete base
26 In __ (archaeology term)
27 RPM indicator
31 Narcs' org.
34 Opera division
36 On the __ (fleeing)
37 Police rank: Abbr.
38 Avenged
39 It's often tacky
40 Give off
43 Humorist Buchwald
44 Born
45 Embellish
46 Colonel's command
47 Withdrew (from)
48 Monty's milieu
49 Ark park?
50 Rabbit
52 Runners carry them
54 Castle or Cara
56 Bills
60 Napa vessel
61 "And I Love __"
62 Author Levin
63 Snort
64 "Well, I'll be!"

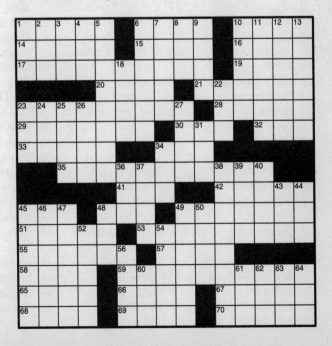

791   AT THE WHEEL by Shirley Soloway

ACROSS

1 Rat-__
5 Pen name of H.H. Munro
9 More mature
14 Walesa of Poland
15 Give off
16 Stop temporarily
17 Art deco artist
18 "See ya!"
19 Double-__ sword
20 Go too far
23 Continuing drama
24 Primitive urges
25 Big fuss
28 Avoid
32 Ghostly sound
35 Jacob's twin
36 Steinbeck's __ Eden
37 *Symphonie Espagnole* composer
39 Comic Conway
41 Fragrant tree
42 "Finally!"
45 Zola novel
48 Always, in verse
49 Changed one's course of action
52 Mao __-tung
53 Corn portion
54 Show again
58 Mislead
61 Expert group
64 Grain keeper
65 Forever __ day
66 Tilted, at sea
67 Cabbage salad
68 "__ Around" (Beach Boys tune)
69 Canine restraint
70 Urges
71 Dozes (off)

DOWN

1 Baldwin and Guinness
2 __ Haute, IN
3 Baldwin or Guinness
4 College paper
5 Sinks to the bottom
6 Beijing nanny
7 Franklin's flier
8 Type of type
9 Middle of the Atlantic
10 Put on board
11 Made a hole
12 Linguistic suffix
13 Hot shade
21 Fill up
22 Not in use
25 Clarinetist Shaw
26 *Lorna* __
27 Make a bid
29 Have a bite
30 Feeling regretful
31 Dangerous snake
32 Explosion
33 Vows
34 Kukla's pal
38 Dolt
40 Daisy __ Yokum
43 Furtiveness
44 Light wood
46 Tapers
47 Vicinity
50 Formal, in a way
51 Muscle injury
55 Jargon
56 Found the sum
57 Irish poet
58 Polanski film
59 Nail shaper
60 Pearl Buck heroine
61 Good buddy
62 Stout alternative
63 Peeples of TV

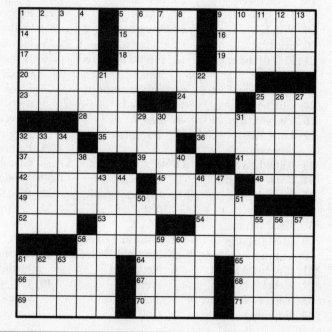

792   CAREERS by Raymond Hamel

ACROSS

1 Partially open
5 Boston fish
10 Ewe's partner
13 Automaton
15 Chart indication
16 *For Love of __* (Poitier film)
17 Rock star
19 Decimal number
20 Set up
21 Black-eyed bean
22 "Rabbi Ben __" (Browning poem)
23 Nero's teacher
25 Word of regret
27 *Baby Doll* actress
33 VIP vehicle
36 Sea signal
37 Actress Anders
38 Pay dirt
39 Disastrous collapse
42 Wayne's word
43 Friendly hombre
45 Kipling serpent
46 Porgy's love
47 Cookbook author
51 Architectural pier
52 Lose color
56 Simpson kid
59 "I __ Rumour" (Bananarama song)
62 In the manner of
63 Fire-fighting tool
64 *Chapter Two* actress
66 Pollinator
67 Licorice flavor
68 *Unsolved Mysteries* host
69 Sprite
70 Calvin of the PGA
71 Lodge members

DOWN

1 Lab media
2 Beautiful, in Bordeaux
3 Straighten
4 VCR-button abbreviation
5 Put away
6 Cut short
7 Abrogate
8 Soccer tie
9 East Germany: Abbr.
10 "Puttin' On the __"
11 Assert
12 Talking bird
14 Pilgrim's goal
18 Unpolished
22 One of Rebekah's sons
24 *Foucault's Pendulum* author
26 Up to snuff
28 Filch
29 1970 World's Fair site
30 Rosebud owner
31 Genesis name
32 Hamelin's headache
33 Rye unit
34 __ *la Douce*
35 Chow __
39 Polish off
40 Train unit
41 Greek letter
44 Pesky bug
46 Bikini part
48 Natural gas component
49 *The __ Queene*
50 Western actor Jack's family
53 Sounding congested
54 Radio partner
55 He played Gump
56 Blue ox
57 Kerrigan move
58 Boating hazard
60 Aide: Abbr.
61 Leader exiled in 1960
64 Mall display
65 Took as a loss

793 TAKING A POSITION by Harvey Estes

ACROSS
1 Computer choice list
5 Cajun Tuesday
10 Crease
14 Pub potables
15 Weaver film
16 *Ars Amatoria* author
17 Sitarist Shankar
18 Knight weapon
19 Take five
20 Ongoing rule
23 Waffle
24 Destroyer
27 Happy-clam heart
28 Old hat
33 In unison
34 Parking by a pier
36 Greek vowel
37 Easy target
39 Lt. trainer
41 Motives
42 Call forth
44 Egyptian statesman
45 Wager
48 Walking the floor
50 J.R.'s mom
52 Pew attachments
57 Parts of ovals
59 Gymnast Comaneci
60 "Leave it as it was"
61 Ta-ta, in Turin
62 Butler in a mansion?
63 King James pronoun
64 Dumb jokes
65 Remove chalk
66 Ship off

DOWN
1 Mason of *The Goodbye Girl*
2 Tickles pink
3 It has 4 electoral votes
4 Employing
5 Bamako's country
6 King or Alda
7 Pugilists' place
8 Art follower
9 Like helium
10 Legal science
11 Burn the beans
12 Fleur-de-__
13 Banned bug spray
21 Where passengers wait
22 Day, to Diego
25 Rubber-tree mover of song
26 Teachers' org.
29 Play beginning
30 D.C. NFLers
31 Noel name
32 __ on (provoked)
34 Amherst poet
35 *Giant* author Ferber
37 Race vehicle
38 Absolute
39 Agt.
40 Eggs: Lat.
43 Plane hdg.
45 Lighthearted
46 Brennan of *Private Benjamin*
47 Gave an exam to
49 Sci-fi, e.g.
51 Hangs on
53 Cowardly Lion portrayer
54 "What's the big __?"
55 Picky ones pick them
56 Fence entrance
57 Part of C.P.A.
58 Hope/Crosby destination

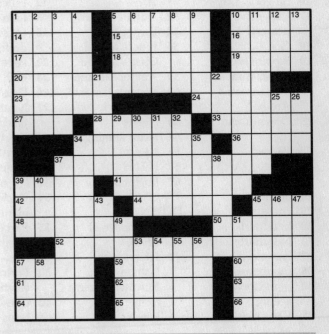

794 MATCHING PAIRS by Wayne R. Williams

ACROSS
1 Bo of *10*
6 Intrigue, metaphorically
9 Discomforts
14 Greek weights
15 Tiller's tool
16 Use timber for support
17 Lack of sensitivity
19 Twilled cloth
20 Grassy ground
21 Our sun
22 Cut, in a way
24 Cut corners
26 Selling features
27 Battleship site of the Japanese surrender
31 Thelma's partner in crime
32 J.F. Cooper novel, with *The*
33 Slug or song ending
37 Christmas songs
38 Draft letters
39 Having wings
40 Pay into the pot
41 One of the Stooges
42 Loan shark
43 Vicksburg's home
45 Gives lip to
49 Spirited mount
50 Stalemate
52 NL stat
53 Antidrug agcy.
56 Cash drawers
57 Like Communist utopias
60 Licorice flavor
61 __ jacet
62 __ 2 (sci-fi TV show)
63 British work schedules
64 Pay ending
65 Romp

DOWN
1 MDs
2 Spanish river
3 Street
4 Overhead trains
5 Roald Dahl collection
6 Engulfs
7 Goddess of the dawn
8 One of the Trumans
9 Birthplace of St. Francis
10 Capablanca's game
11 Quagga kin
12 Grain fungus
13 Clairvoyants
18 Cacophony
23 Grant or Elwes
24 Funt's order
25 Have
27 Arm bone
28 Any day now
29 Tallow base
30 Boom times
33 Mutable
34 Costner role
35 Dance movement
36 Actress Garr
38 "Help!"
39 Takes stock of
41 Wide shot
42 Software buyers
43 Sticky wickets
44 New York college town
45 Indian instrument
46 __ acids
47 Bowling challenge
48 Latin beat
51 Call back
53 Earl __ Biggers
54 Ferrara patron
55 Arthur of the courts
58 Abner's adjective
59 Kiddie seat?

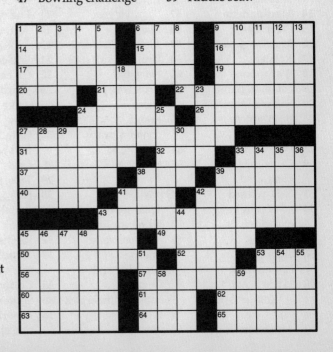

795 CROSSBREEDS by Fred Piscop

ACROSS
1 __ soap (flattery)
5 Bugle tune
9 Thicket
14 __ breve
15 *Fish Magic* painter
16 Singer O'Day
17 Expensive dessert?
19 Gist
20 5-point type
21 Music from a sore-throated Aretha?
23 Down-under flier
25 Pickled
26 Miss __ (Archie's teacher)
28 Singer Joan
29 Grasslands
30 Back part
33 Nonconformist
37 News org.
38 Lumberjacks
40 __ of Good Feeling
41 Very, musically
43 Ray of Hollywood
44 Farm wagon
45 Europe-Asia border range
47 Paved, perhaps
49 Points the finger at
52 Author Gibran
54 Escape hole?
56 Where to find Ouagadougou
59 Author Calvino
60 Barber's lament?
62 Drew back
63 Newts
64 Actor Jannings
65 Logic
66 H H H
67 Jib, for one

DOWN
1 Thompson of *Family*
2 First name in fashion
3 Run away from a former veep?
4 Plaids
5 Bout ender
6 Hilo hello
7 Acapulco cash
8 Tarot reader
9 Wedding figures
10 "__ fits all"
11 Pine nut
12 Lifted
13 Like some seals
18 Do some darning
22 Federal agcy.
24 Bath radial
26 Dejected
27 Nonpayment takeback, for short
28 Born and __
31 Mideast carrier
32 "__ of Me"
34 Unclothed holy man?
35 Part of HOMES
36 Hit the runway
38 Presage
39 Portnoy's creator
42 Goes head over heels
44 Squirms
46 Sun Devils sch.
48 What there oughta be
49 Happy state
50 Shape wood
51 At full speed
52 Big name in cheese
53 Vessel from the left ventricle
55 Syngman __
57 It follows *et*
58 __ out (turn traitor)
61 Slalom curve

796 ROUND-THE-CLOCK by Frank Gordon

ACROSS
1 Oscar Madison, e.g.
5 Pat an infant
9 Word before potato or Alaska
14 Macadamize
15 Over: Ger.
16 Martini garnish
17 Related
18 It's taboo
19 *Laugh-In* name
20 Sailor's omen
23 Bran source
24 Selfish sort
25 Pub
29 Gunslinger's command
31 Nos. wizard
34 "Goodnight" gal of song
35 Wild pig
36 Slips up
37 Pacino film
40 "Woe is me!"
41 __-Romeo (sports car)
42 Atmospheric gas
43 __ *Misérables*
44 Sherbets
45 Frat party
46 Hardwood tree
47 RR depot
48 Dizzy Gillespie tune
57 "__, *c'est moi*"
58 Black: Fr.
59 *M*A*S*H* actor
60 United rival
61 Narrated
62 Criticism, so to speak
63 Freud contemporary
64 Part of SRO
65 Longings

DOWN
1 Train for a fight
2 Huron or Erie
3 *Metamorphoses* poet
4 Kingsley and Gazzara
5 Fabled lumberjack
6 Wolf-pack member
7 Monthly payment
8 High-school event
9 Use temporarily
10 "__ came a spider . . ."
11 Fuzzy fruit
12 Author Hunter
13 __ Xiaoping
21 '50s conflict site
22 Chicago airport
25 Word before wave or basin
26 Play __ (act)
27 Gambling place, for short
28 Odds' partner
29 Tips, as a cap
30 Pro __ (proportionally)
31 Hook alternative
32 Predisposed (to)
33 *Thunder Alley* star
35 Cotton measure
36 Singer Stuarti
38 America's Cup vessel
39 Antony, e.g.
44 Beatty bomb
45 Well-built
46 Shooting marble
47 Moonshiner's device
48 *M*A*S*H* actor
49 Require
50 "__ never work!"
51 Division word
52 Midday
53 Uncertain
54 Print-ad word
55 Oil exporter
56 Large vessels

797 BUYING OPTIONS by Harvey Estes

ACROSS
1 Pulls out plumage
7 Pertaining to Easter
14 Cry of delight
15 See 40 Across
16 Adenoid neighbor
17 Metric area units
18 Hall-of-Fame pitcher Warren
19 Moisten
20 Deliver a tirade
21 Battlefield healer
23 Canine command
25 Small taste
28 Fraternal order member
29 Like the acid in vinegar
33 Bouquet
34 Stout relative
35 "Forget it!"
36 *The Way We __*
37 Pub game
39 Ugandan exile
40 With 15 Across, 1943 movie
42 Skeptical remark
43 Dactyl and spondee
44 Lento
45 Mine material
46 Some evergreens
47 __ out (manage)
48 Boxing place
50 *Born Free* lioness
53 Use one's nose?
54 Slicked up
58 Giggled
61 Actress Jeanne
62 Climbing plants
63 African fly
64 Hall hanging
65 Boat or barge

DOWN
1 Pans' companions
2 Chicago area
3 Humerus neighbor
4 Wool garment
5 Kevin of *Dave*
6 Actor Mineo
7 Pound, for one
8 Former auto co.
9 Game, __, and match
10 Subordinate diplomat
11 Israeli dance
12 Hemsley sitcom
13 For fear that
15 Squares full of squares
19 Author Cather
22 Good shot
23 Wailing woman
24 Author Umberto
25 Hangs out in alleys
26 Paragon
27 Trunk
30 "By the __ Get to Phoenix"
31 More frosty
32 Cheap Lincoln pics
38 Hang back
41 Sort
49 Rope loop
50 Cut with acid
51 Italian bread?
52 Editor's note
53 Concoct coffee
55 "Why don't we!"
56 Facility
57 One-on-one event
59 Ecol. org.
60 __ room (play area)
61 Rock network

798 POSITIONAL PAIRS by Dean Niles

ACROSS
1 Inflexible
6 Lively
10 Not fem. or neut.
14 "Ditto!"
15 Tavern choices
16 Way over there
17 Area of exploration
19 __ contendere
20 Pontiac model
21 Fashionable
22 Q-X link
24 Numb
26 Van __ (rock group)
27 Somewhat behind
30 Clown of fame
32 Actress Lena
33 Not capital letters
38 Rummy game
41 Whole number
42 Powers that be
44 Fontanne's partner
45 *Jane __*
46 Taste
48 "__ to the wise . . ."
52 Tomfoolery
54 Anne __ (wife of Henry VIII)
56 General location
57 Chinese chairman
60 Idi of infamy
61 Current psychology concern
64 Hole in a hill
65 __ Raton, FL
66 Matter in contest
67 Understood
68 Rescind a revision
69 Scintillas

DOWN
1 L.A. weather feature
2 Ger.
3 "Take __ the Limit" (Eagles song)
4 Adversary
5 Military might
6 Flavorful
7 Sugar pill
8 Cassette-deck button
9 Belgian river
10 __ ray (devilfish)
11 Run __ of (cross)
12 Soothing lotion
13 Regal headgear
18 Persian ruler
23 Lacking
24 Singer Shore
25 "__ the time for all good . . ."
27 Ness, for one
28 Jai __
29 Bell-like sound
31 Buddhism branch
33 Designer Ashley
34 Body parts
35 Water, in Juárez
36 Passed along
37 Russian designer
39 Disreputable
40 Test the patience of
43 Contrition
46 Breakwater
47 Yellow-flowered shrub
48 Taken __ (disconcerted)
49 "A __ Is a Sometime Thing"
50 Ms. Oyl
51 Extend the library loan
53 Pay the tab
55 His __ (authority figure)
57 Soybean mixture
58 Common astringent
59 Poet's tributes
62 "__ on your life!"
63 DDE predecessor

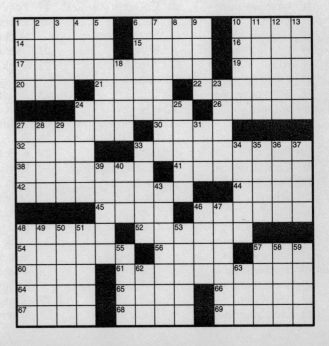

799 TOUCH OF CLASS by Wayne R. Williams

ACROSS

1 Soak (up)
4 Category
9 Make happy
14 Big galoot
15 Poisonous
16 First name in gymnastics
17 Dance class?
19 Seth's brother et al.
20 Opposed to, at first?
21 Butter kin
22 Free-for-all
23 Bed canopy
25 Share the load
26 No sweat, with class?
30 Short jaunt
33 Stood very still
36 "Sorry!"
37 Silent performer
38 Actor Rob
39 Units of force
40 Bacterial culture base
41 Congregational feedback
42 Familiar with
43 Former Indian leader
44 Place of confinement
45 Gets rough, with class?
47 Sailors
49 Come to terms
53 Caribbean island
55 Stain
58 Chef's thickener
59 Evil one
60 TV show, with class?
62 *Jagged Edge* star
63 Make one
64 Solidify
65 Johnny's intro
66 *The Screens* dramatist
67 Presidential letters

DOWN

1 Mubarak's predecessor
2 State one's view
3 Naggers
4 Former Pontiac
5 Turning parts
6 Eddie's cop character
7 Yahtzee need
8 Parrot
9 Glossy paint
10 Manufacturer's sticker
11 College, with class?
12 Scrabble piece
13 Nonchalance
18 U.S. voter, for one
24 Summer: Fr.
25 *Bonanza* character
27 Aquatic rodent
28 Peer recognition
29 Bids first
31 Barbra's *Funny Girl* costar
32 Llama land
33 Social stink
34 European capital
35 First of Elizabeth's dynasty, with class?
37 Music teacher
39 Twosomes
43 Compass pt.
45 Machines with movable booms
46 Heir's inheritance
48 Humiliate
50 Gritty
51 Pear-shaped instruments
52 Rejoice triumphantly
53 Writer Sholem
54 Breathing sound
55 Complacent
56 Window element
57 Valhalla VIP
61 Chip in chips

800 PRIZE HOLDINGS by A.J. Santora

ACROSS

1 Marriott competitor
7 Mites
14 Like two peas __
15 Peter Weller film
16 Onetime door prize
18 German article
19 *Of Mice and Men* role
21 Hand bone
26 SW Conference team
27 A *numero*
28 Avails oneself of
29 Rare air
31 Crowd around
32 Bartók and Schick
33 Belief
34 Prize won by Bill Koch
37 Killer whales
39 Synthetic ruby
40 Med. republic
43 Texas river
44 Breathing sound
45 Relatives
46 Have __ at (try)
47 Unshackled
50 Woolly
53 Fencing sword
54 Harness-racing prize
60 Costar of Rue and Betty
61 Hat for Bear Bryant
62 Attic function
63 Improvises

DOWN

1 Actor Torn
2 Literary miscellany
3 Half the name of a Kenyan group
4 Cop __
5 Column style
6 Face on a two-mark coin
7 "All the Things You __"
8 Tenor oboe
9 "Does that ring __?"
10 Pre-bout attire
11 Computer graphic
12 Someday
13 Married
17 Poetic style
20 Dollar or bond starter
21 Silent
22 Rock producer Brian
23 Panatela purveyor
24 Sailor's jacket
25 D-Day soldier
29 Behold, to Livy
30 Robert Morse role
32 Myerson or Armstrong
35 Red leader
36 "The __ laboring man is sweet": Eccles.
37 Gemstone
38 Entertains
41 Bro's sib
42 Hosp. staffers
47 *The Most Happy* __
48 Take a second?
49 '80s tennis star
51 Kruger or Klemperer
52 -arian relative
55 Taina of *Les Girls*
56 Spelldown
57 TV actress Lansing
58 City area
59 Home-heating fuel

GREAT LENGTHS by Norma Steinberg

ACROSS

1 Memo abbr.
5 Stage-curtain material
10 Cries of triumph
14 Carson's successor
15 Ruling class
16 *Striptease* name
17 Gave temporarily
18 Piano technician
19 Head covering
20 Curbside markers
23 Porcine sound
24 Fleming and Carney
25 Flicker
28 Similar
31 Pollock medium
32 Take it in __
34 Actress Arthur
37 Good first impression
40 NW state
41 Collaborators
42 "__ it my way"
43 Eat away at
44 Leg joints
45 DeMille genre
47 '60s event
49 Alden's friend
55 Lion's glory
56 Belt's place
57 Linguist Chomsky
59 Nibble
60 Word before child or sanctum
61 Spiritual teacher
62 Bates or Thicke
63 Like many teens' rooms
64 Svelte

DOWN

1 Winner's take
2 Ooze
3 Actress Magnani
4 Braised beef dish
5 Arrive, as fog
6 Dull sound
7 Boxing enclosure
8 Unit
9 Unimportant __
10 Stick (to)
11 Central area
12 Out of kilter
13 Term of respect
21 Kipling hero
22 Buyer
25 Asian desert
26 Committed perjury
27 Actress Lanchester
28 Clarinetist Shaw
29 A bowl of cherries?
30 Wedding vows
32 Fly alone
33 Snitched
34 Commanded
35 Buffalo's lake
36 Annexes
38 Humorous play
39 Atlantic City gains
43 Actress Heckart
44 Josh
45 PC-to-PC correspondence
46 Ship of 1492
47 First and home, e.g.
48 The way in
50 Do the crawl
51 Rational
52 Metal containers
53 James Brown's genre
54 Mata __
55 Advanced degree: Abbr.
58 "__'s the word!"

WHAT'S THE SCOOP? by Mary Brindamour

ACROSS

1 Cadabra preceder
5 Farmer's place?
9 Quick look
13 Supporting bracket
15 Sills solo
16 Perry's creator
17 Florida city
18 Ice-cream flavor
20 Car-radiator parts
22 Tree growths
23 Sign of spring?
24 Life savers
25 Quaker
27 Bedsheets
28 Palmas or Vegas starter
29 Urge
31 Wooden shoe
35 Diva's rendition
37 Lets up
39 Olympic sled
40 Agent's cut
42 Affirmatives
44 Jerry's partner
45 Drinks too much
47 Patted lightly
49 Carpenter, at times
51 Flower part
52 Enhanced
53 Servicemen
55 Ice-cream flavor
57 Had a fit
59 Words of comprehension
60 Done with
61 Become accustomed to: Var.
62 Geek
63 Mail-order enc.
64 Iowa college town

DOWN

1 Dershowitz or Kunstler: Abbr.
2 Crow
3 Ice-cream flavor
4 Be ambitious
5 Coolidge's VP
6 Epochs
7 Actress Ullmann
8 Clergy nonmembers
9 Private
10 Clear a tape
11 North Pole workers
12 Florida isles
14 Salty
19 Political family
21 Projection
24 Dancer Gregory
25 Like a pancake
26 One in a million
27 Misses out on
30 More cheerful
32 Ice-cream flavor
33 Molding type
34 Take care of
36 Pounced upon
38 Passover event
41 "A Taste of __"
43 Literary form
46 Almadóvar et al.
48 Split ingredient
49 Ordinary language
50 Shoe seller, at times
51 Spanish priest
52 Broad smile
53 Actresses West and Questel
54 Dried out
56 Eggs: Lat.
58 __ Plaines, IL

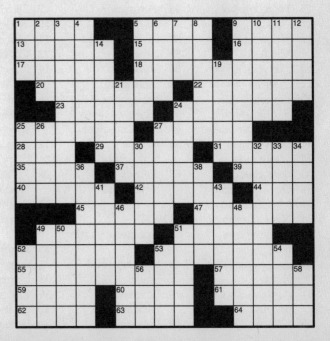

803 LITERARY SEASONING by Dean Niles

ACROSS
1 Pre-Columbian empire builder
5 Savory jelly
10 CPR-giver
13 Close
14 Wine source
15 __ and Order
16 Tennessee Williams play
19 Ignited
20 Hog feed
21 Short putt
22 Taj Mahal site
24 __ Charity
27 Good fellow
28 Drum type
30 Sound of disgust
31 Wild excess
32 Carson book
36 NATO cousin
37 Mideast federation: Abbr.
38 Freud topic
39 Publisher's incoming mail: Abbr.
42 Arthur Miller play
45 Shepard and Spade
48 Far from WSW
49 Maui porch
50 Star __
51 Got a lasso around
54 Frewer or Dillon
55 Trod the boards
57 Rat residences, often
59 What $$ are made of
60 Shakespeare play
64 End of a kid's song
65 Library stickum
66 Central European river
67 __ Spiegel
68 Keanu Reeves movie
69 Part of PTA

DOWN
1 Colonel's eagle, e.g.
2 White and beige
3 Rotating disk
4 A Farewell to __
5 Tell's weapon
6 "Ship out" alternative
7 Bowler's target
8 Not Dem. or Rep.
9 "__ Magnifique" (Porter tune)
10 Romeo or Juliet, e.g.
11 The __ of the President: 1960
12 Jackson's bill
17 Loop conveyances
18 Biblical nation
19 Cattle corraller
23 "Just the Way You __"
25 Marsh bird
26 Hip-knee link
29 Sufficient, slangily
33 Spud
34 "__ evil . . ."
35 Coward of the stage
39 Stocks or bonds
40 Untidy woman
41 Peepholes
42 Cockeyed
43 Well-stocked
44 Kinfolk: Abbr.
45 Averred
46 Nero Wolfe's scribe
47 Streak in the sky
52 Having flaps
53 Sound measures: Abbr.
56 Drops down
58 Greek portico
61 40 winks
62 Poet's monogram
63 Classifieds

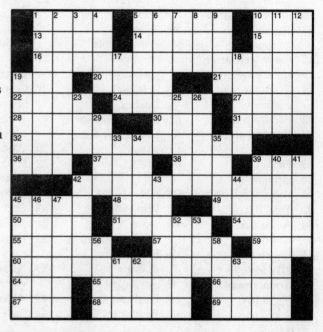

804 THE ANIMALS by Michael Selinker

ACROSS
1 Theater sign
4 XXVIII x L
7 "__ tree falls . . ."
10 Sunshine st.
13 Pull a rabbit out of a hat, e.g.
15 More macho
17 Gypsy __
18 Home of The Masters
19 '70s rock group
21 __ gin fizz
22 Tijuana coin
23 Shriek sound
25 Contract details
27 Lab burners
29 Many mos.
30 Beer glasses
32 Dusk, poetically
33 Mrs. Truman
34 Nat Cole song
37 "__ you were here"
40 Salesperson, for short
41 Assert without proving
45 Chemical suffix
46 Love Boat bartender
48 Architect Aalto
49 Touches down
51 Depots, in skeds
53 Enthusiasm
54 #1 tune for 19 Across
57 Make desolate
58 Bars
60 Student
61 Mechanic, sometimes
62 Increases
63 AMA members
64 Stimpy's housemate
65 Sounds of hesitation

DOWN
1 Apothecary unit: Abbr.
2 Underground branch
3 Beached
4 Pack animal
5 Lowlife
6 Onetime White House spokesperson Myers
7 Sitting duck's lament
8 Goat-man
9 Dickinson et al.
10 Wide-angle lens
11 Much of the mail
12 Coach Parseghian
14 Name heard in 54 Across
16 Sled event
20 Bone-and-muscle specialist
21 Ave. crossers
24 Curve
26 "Weekend Update" pgm.
28 Author Seton
31 Simple cameras, briefly
33 What 14 Down was
35 Gourmands
36 Pay ender
37 Shriner or Wheaton
38 Four Jills __ (1944 Martha Raye film)
39 Mexican women
42 Satan
43 Perry Mason's creator
44 Shakespeare's "before"
46 "__ corrected"
47 He crossed the Rubicon
50 British poet John
52 Valley
55 Finished
56 Ken or Lena
57 Italian color
59 Last year's jrs.

805 REED IT AND WEEP by A.J. Santora

ACROSS

1 Fannie __
4 Injury
8 Do a knee jerk
13 Invoice
14 Mixture
15 Grouch of TV
16 START OF A DEFINITION OF AN OBOE
18 Domingo's domain
19 __ U.S. Pat. Off.
20 Copier chemicals
22 The youngest Cratchit
23 Metaphysical poet John
25 Tender
26 Prosperous period
27 Bread spread
28 Prepayment
30 Ankle-related
33 Heavenly
34 MIDDLE OF DEFINITION
36 Accounts-payable stamp
39 Bookstore statistic
43 Emergency force
44 Drink too much
45 Mouth-to-mouth
46 Jazzman Getz
49 Elementary computer language
50 Squeal
51 Beret, e.g.
53 Nationality suffix
54 Job for an emcee
56 END OF DEFINITION
58 The flock
59 Musical Horne
60 Hosiery shade
61 Past the deadline
62 Snappish?
63 Western Amerind

DOWN

1 Big Apple suburb
2 Straight man?
3 Kay follower
4 "__ I doin'?": Ed Koch
5 Alternative name
6 Beatle with the sticks
7 Faster than andante
8 Aussie jumpers
9 Predictive power, initially
10 Paint solvent
11 *Flying Down to Rio* dance
12 Restrain
13 *. . . And God Created Woman* star
17 Golf ball position
21 Frank
24 Little breather
26 Robert Blake TV role
29 Start of Caesar's boast
31 "There'll be __ time . . ."
32 Extravagant
33 Cut off
35 Service support?
36 Lover of love
37 Dangerous swimmer
38 Lunch order
40 Miss an opportunity
41 Serial part
42 Withdraw
47 Cop __
48 Nitery lights
49 Kramden's workplace
51 Reproduce
52 Out of here
55 Embarrassed
57 Antelope type

806 WHOOPS! by Shirley Soloway

ACROSS

1 Voice-master Mel
6 Venomous snakes
10 Pro __ (pro-portionally)
14 Farmlike
15 Card game
16 Adam Arkin's dad
17 Having hard times
19 Abel's brother
20 Tiny
21 Coral deposit
22 Airplane walkway
23 Jackpots
26 Storage areas
29 Strong singers
33 Church seats
34 Tour of duty
36 i topper
37 Vocal gaffe
41 Overhead trains
42 Skin openings
43 __ of Eden
44 Fill up
46 Moms of Madrid
48 TV-image defects
51 Western ties
54 Fem. opposite
55 Model Carol
58 Baseball manager Felipe
59 Heavy tool
62 Bridle control
63 Voice range
64 *Lorna* __
65 Bank purchase
66 Onetime atlas initials
67 School assignment

DOWN

1 Eye topper
2 "*Clair de* __"
3 Johnson of comedy
4 Slangy refusal
5 Man of the cloth
6 Made a request
7 Sailing ship
8 Cushion
9 Ave. crossers
10 Archie Bunker, e.g.
11 "Too bad!"
12 Kite appendage
13 Actress Bancroft
18 Capitol VIPs
22 __ the good (desirable)
23 Thin streak
24 __ *Irish Rose*
25 Pre-Easter season
26 Church recesses
27 "I cannot __ lie"
28 Entwine
30 Bergen or Poe
31 Wake up
32 Editors' marks
34 Type of germ, for short
35 One article
38 Semiprecious stones
39 Snapshot, in product names
40 Sparks and Beatty
45 "Blueberry Hill" opener
46 Openwork fabric
47 Mall area
49 Fails to include
50 Kettle output
51 Fence defense
52 Bread spread
53 Beef cut
55 Cookie king
56 Olin or Horne
57 Low card
59 Sigma follower
60 *Treasure Island* monogram
61 Parts of yrs.

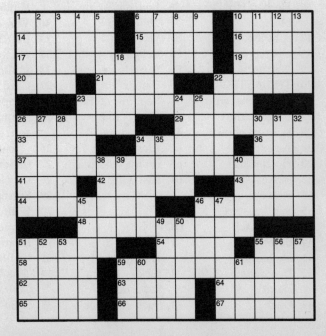

807 — INTEMPERANCE by Randolph Ross

ACROSS
1 USN rank
4 Thom of shoedom
8 Peer
13 Talk like Fudd
15 Mobil competitor
16 Reach, as a total
17 Word form for "Mars"
18 Impolite look
19 Dangerous gas
20 Fusspot
22 Synthetic materials
23 Intemperate vegetables?
25 Batting failures
26 Eva's half-sister?
27 What *le* means
30 Yell
33 Opposite of post-
34 Pants unit
35 Intemperate entrée?
39 Unwelcome picnic guests
40 Brain-wave picture: Abbr.
41 Broad neckwear
42 Ref's call, for short
43 E.T. craft
44 "Who __?" (doorbell response)
46 Intemperate fruit?
51 Treacher or Miller
54 Star's part
55 Doctor, at times
56 Happy
57 Author Hunter
58 Noncitizen
59 Head of France
60 Match divisions
61 High-school books
62 Wallet fillers
63 Golfer Trevino

DOWN
1 Envelope device
2 Serial opener
3 Fatty acid
4 Barrel-headed hammer
5 Sets of beliefs
6 Sour
7 Hide-hair connector
8 Publishing problems
9 Piers
10 Disassemble
11 Like __ of bricks
12 Chaney and Nol
14 Anti-labor actions
21 Jane Fonda film
22 Bowler's button
24 Poet Pound
27 After-bath application
28 Hawaiian port
29 Prefix for while
30 Quarrel
31 Goose greeting
32 Palindromic name
33 Cribbage piece
34 Cow-feterias?
36 Put off
37 Cat call
38 Puppeteer Bil
43 Reversals of a sort
44 Conceptualize
45 A suit
46 Piece of paper
47 Barkin or Burstyn
48 Innovative
49 Bring joy to
50 Logic
51 ". . . to skin __"
52 Reign
53 Kids' cereal
56 Beach Boys' car

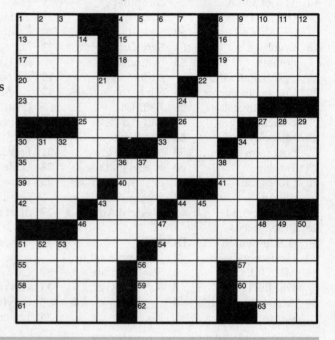

808 — WHODUNIT HIT by Cynthia Lyon

ACROSS
1 Does logging
5 __ off (occasionally)
10 __ *Lap* ('83 film)
14 Touched the turf
15 Tijuana title
16 Herbert Hoover's birthplace
17 A little force?
18 Open boat
19 Icky terrain
20 THE ACTRESS
23 Traditional stuff
24 Take to court
25 Western shows
28 Actor Sharif
30 Holemaker
33 Make a statement
34 Sea cells
35 Sudden start
36 THE ROLE
40 Be a thorn
41 Desiccated
42 Dog owner's shout
43 Duct
44 Carson's successor
45 __ *From a Marriage*
47 Suite piece
48 Emmy winner, maybe
49 THE SHOW
56 Prefix meaning "billionth"
57 "Never!"
58 Religious symbol
59 Sartre's *No __*
60 Democratic Republic of the Congo, once
61 Have coming
62 Alongside of
63 Set for a skirmish
64 Last word of the year?

DOWN
1 Actress Thompson
2 Kirk __ (a film Superman)
3 Buck's partner
4 Four-time Super Bowl champs
5 Hepburn's quartet
6 Tennis pro Fraser
7 __ *Karenina*
8 Lunch time, often
9 Equestrian exhibition
10 Vexed feeling
11 Lunch time, often
12 On the road
13 Joplin piece
21 Card game
22 Popped
25 Indira's son/successor
26 __ barrel (helpless)
27 Office furniture
28 Gluck role
29 Springlike
30 White, in a way
31 A question of location
32 Old-time strings
34 TV's Barbara or Conrad
37 Didn't work
38 Legless sideboard
39 Slot-machine fruits
45 Beyond tipsy
46 Blackbird's comment
47 Soup base
48 Seaside
49 Long skirt
50 Troop group
51 React to a riot?
52 Wedge
53 Authorize
54 Ripped
55 Feminine suffix
56 Inexperienced

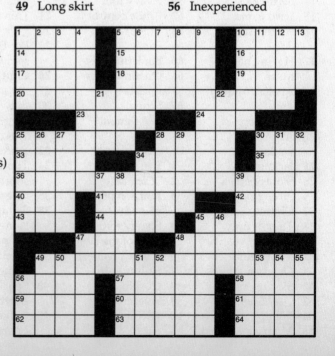

809 NOT QUITE by Raymond Hamel

ACROSS

1 *The Planets* composer
6 Musante role
10 Pin kin
14 Wife of Prince Valiant
15 Deserter's status
16 Coin of Iran
17 Surgical tool
18 Send back to Congress
19 Economist Smith
20 Not quite an all-star
23 Writer Wiesel
24 Praise
25 Indy 500 time
27 Breathing sound
30 Mechanical pieces
33 Work unit
34 *Billy Budd* character
35 Jobs around the house
37 Not quite magic
40 Most angry
41 Rayburn or Roddenberry
42 Coffeepot
43 Fernando and Aldo
44 Ubangi tributary
45 *Emerald Point __* (TV series)
46 Pile
48 Anti-DWI org.
51 Not quite real happiness
56 Suave
57 A dimension
58 Whopper
60 Mist
61 Man with a lift
62 Become accustomed (to)
63 Iowa city
64 Nikita's negative
65 Coup __

DOWN

1 Linden of *The Boys Are Back*
2 Norwegian name
3 "Judy's Turn To Cry" singer
4 Shoplift
5 Foot bones
6 "Rikki-Tikki-__"
7 Author Wister
8 Mark with spots
9 Wahine's hello
10 Stage exit
11 Operatic slave
12 *For the Boys* star
13 Dutch airline
21 Because of this
22 Game with a five-card hand
25 Service chow
26 Iron clothing
28 Son of 14 Across
29 Pigeon's landing site
31 Hits an infield one-hopper, perhaps
32 Missionary Junipero
34 Container
35 The movies
36 9-digit IDs: Abbr.
38 Sites for snoopers
39 Tillis or Tormé
44 Snobbish
47 __ Martin (007's auto)
49 Extra
50 One of Saturn's satellites
51 Pillow filler
52 Move like The Blob
53 French confidante
54 Break
55 Biblical scribe
56 Dance syllable
59 As __ (so far)

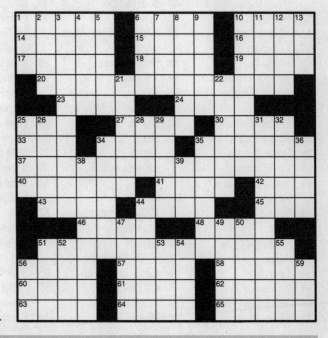

810 TACTFULLY PUT by Donna J. Stone

ACROSS

1 Coll. hotshot
5 *R.U.R.* dramatist
10 Samoa studier
14 Morning wear
15 '60s baseballer Tony
16 Part of TAE
17 "Alphabet Song" gamut
18 Flight segment
19 Simpleton
20 DIPLOMACY DEFINITION: PART 1
23 Comedian Louis
24 Bone-dry
25 Scales of *Fawlty Towers*
30 Five iron
34 Stud site
35 *Shane* star
37 Martin and Stockwell
38 Flap
39 DEFINITION: PART 2
41 Circle
42 Pageant prop
44 Request
45 Raison d'__
46 Unexpurgated
48 Make a guess
50 Macadamize
52 Sleet, essentially
53 DEFINITION: PART 3
61 Rely (on)
62 Actor Alain
63 Tender
64 Palomino's pride
65 Soap star Slezak
66 Face shape
67 Floored it
68 Fortify
69 Foster film

DOWN

1 Wild child
2 Butterfly kin
3 Bassoon relative
4 Post-Impressionist painter
5 Singer Elvis
6 Countertenor
7 Chanteuse Edith
8 Ills
9 Big name in basketball
10 Toy terrier
11 Wells race
12 Revlon rival
13 "__ Me" (Roger Miller tune)
21 Bread or booze
22 Swap
25 Service member?
26 *The Kiss* sculptor
27 *Kapitän's* command
28 Reader's need
29 Mr. Rochester's ward
31 "__ luego"
32 Motionless
33 Helena's competitor
36 *Bambi* extras
39 Miles or Purcell
40 Citizen
43 Aged
45 "The Sage of Concord"
47 Dodges
49 Hosp. area
51 Turn inside out
53 *Desire Under the __*
54 Bound
55 Sound
56 Nobelist Wiesel
57 Draft device
58 Emulated Arachne
59 Asian inland sea
60 Say "Hey!"

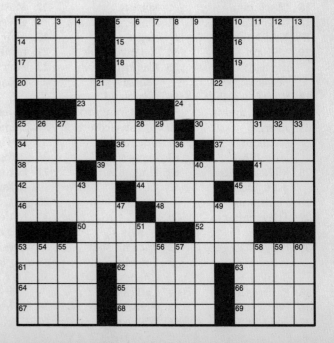

811 COLORIZATION by Bob Lubbers

ACROSS

1 Take down __ (belittle)
5 Mad rush
9 Prefix for marine or sonic
14 Carson predecessor
15 Butter substitute
16 Master, in India
17 Dietrich film, with *The*
19 Take a whiff
20 Kind of vine
22 Stare at
23 Dispute decider
26 Hardened (to)
28 French port
29 Enticement
31 Stretch, as one's neck
32 Wave hello
33 Sup
36 Makes a tape: Abbr.
37 Terrific
38 Baxter or Boleyn
39 Ararat arrival
40 Three-note chord
41 Pistol provider
42 Puffs up
44 Rose oils
45 Hibernates
47 Eye parts
48 Afternoon parties
49 North Star
52 Awaken
54 Gary Cooper film of '28
58 Starts a pot
59 Moolah
60 Zest
61 Star of 32 Down
62 "__ sow, so shall . . ."
63 Go to __ (deteriorate)

DOWN

1 Police dept. radio message
2 Chum
3 __ de Cologne
4 Corinth citizens
5 Gift recipients
6 Writer Horatio __
7 Flow slowly
8 Golfer's target
9 Amer. vessel designation
10 Costar of Hope and Crosby
11 Sim film
12 Moon valley
13 Otherwise __ (differently qualified)
18 Clarinetist Shaw
21 Signed a new tenant
23 Capital of Ghana
24 Less common
25 Horsy film of '46
27 Bolt fastener
29 Vicinities
30 Like a __ balloon
32 *True __* ('69 western)
34 "It's the end of __"
35 Short and sweet
37 Hold, as a handrail
38 Performers
40 "You're the __" (Porter tune)
41 Storage space
43 Abate
44 Add fizz to
45 Malt-shop freebie
46 Hotelier Helmsley
47 Mass meeting
50 Gymnast Korbut
51 Is situated
53 Linguistic suffix
55 __ de France
56 West or Murray
57 Finish

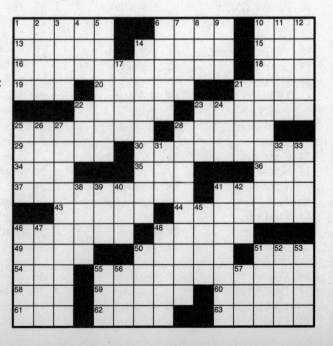

812 THE HARD STUFF by Robert H. Wolfe

ACROSS

1 Tracking system
6 Helper
10 TV overseer
13 Get out of bed
14 Eve or Enoch
15 __-di-dah
16 Music genre
18 Chemical suffix
19 NASA remark
20 Military memento, perhaps
21 Winter weather
22 Max Sr. and Jr.
23 *Altered __* (William Hurt film)
25 Make the turkey even juicier
28 Finds fault
29 They matter in matter
30 Height or age, e.g.
34 Without a __ (broke)
35 Distress letters
36 Poetic form
37 Some joiners
41 Fiscal penalties
43 Sturdy carts
44 Solemn
46 Refrigerants
48 The Ram
49 Bring in
50 Dean Martin song subject
51 Undergraduate degs.
54 Relative of Inc.
55 California golf course
58 Grassland
59 U.S. Grant's foe
60 __ nous (confidentially)
61 Navy VIP
62 Unique person
63 Curves

DOWN

1 __ avis
2 Buck finisher
3 Powell or Cheney
4 Call (for)
5 Gather again
6 Wall hanging
7 Adored one
8 Neighbor of Penna.
9 Blow up a photo: Abbr.
10 Rubble's buddy
11 Lake craft
12 Masticates
14 Gives a talk
17 Nair rival
21 Lunkheads
22 Sound of impact
23 What Miss Muffet did
24 Three: Pref.
25 Demolish, in Devon
26 British school
27 Former Colorado River name
28 Baking dish
31 Little piggy
32 Bad day for Caesar
33 "__ la vie!"
38 Do a laundry chore
39 __ Mateo, CA
40 Cobb and Hardin
41 Giveaway
42 Electees
45 Leeds' river
46 *The Most Happy __*
47 Emulated Ebert
48 Yellowish
50 Competent
51 Belfry denizens
52 Farm measure
53 "__ a Lady" (Tom Jones song)
55 Money player
56 Evening, to Noyes
57 Pulver's rank: Abbr.

813 BATMAN VILLAINS by Dean Niles

ACROSS

1 Niger neighbor
5 Some snakes
9 Strikebreakers
14 Old __, CT
15 Rachel's sister
16 River embankment
17 Cassandra portrayer on *Batman*
19 Stage digression
20 Calendar abbr.
21 *Les* __ (musical, for short)
22 Score intervals
24 Specialty periodicals
27 Poet's contraction
28 Oil-can letters
29 Make too much of
34 Pipe up
37 Sharp-tongued
38 "Fine by me!"
39 Crackerjack
40 Nongeneric swabs
41 Bog down
42 Hauteur
43 Colorado Indians
44 Dollar divisions
45 Felicitous
47 Controversial coat
48 Gloomy __
49 Like old paper
54 Crusades opponent
58 Once around
59 Govt. agency
60 Common people
61 The Archer portrayer on *Batman*
64 Tippy boat
65 Castle
66 Genesis place
67 Court decision
68 Pros and __
69 NASDAQ rival

DOWN

1 Clavin or Huxtable
2 Largest constellation
3 Full-force
4 __ Monte pineapple
5 Elevated
6 Take hold of
7 Bad notice
8 "Beat it!"
9 Actor Christian
10 The Joker portrayer on *Batman*
11 Tel __
12 Venerable monk
13 Calls on
18 Aleut craft
23 Dorm group
25 Minerva portrayer on *Batman*
26 Part of 54 Down
30 Mr. and Ms. Big
31 Related
32 Sour-tasting
33 Takes in
34 Cashless transaction
35 Donahue or Spector
36 Word on Irish coins
37 Memo opener
40 Resembling
44 *Mea* __
46 Made soap bubbles
47 Publicity seekers
50 First name in rock
51 Playwright Wasserstein
52 Fencing needs
53 Singer Taylor
54 Pet org.
55 "There oughta be __!"
56 Actress Olin
57 DEA agent
62 'Supial
63 Stimpy's pal

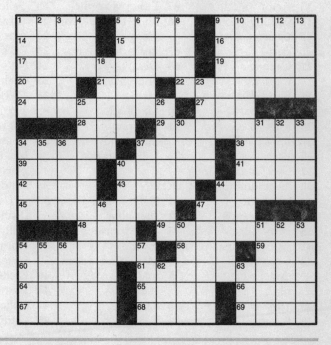

814 HOLY by Fred Piscop

ACROSS

1 '30s boxing champ
5 Ignore
9 Contemptuous remark
14 Land measure
15 Actress Skye
16 It fell in 1836
17 Three holy items
20 Type of poem
21 TV scan lines
22 FedEx rival
23 Kind of tent
24 Place for a small house
25 Nincompoops
28 Change drastically
30 Bachelor's last words?
31 Add
32 Rio Grande city
36 Two holy items
40 Ace's home, perhaps
41 Actress Hagen
42 *Le* __ *Soleil*
43 Major meals
45 Ward off
47 Café au __
50 Dollar divs.
51 Foreman beater
52 Painter Maurice
54 Chemist Lavoisier
58 Five holy items
60 Monogram ltrs.
61 "Good Lord!"
62 __ *kleine Nachtmusik*
63 Not exactly brilliant
64 Take out
65 Frog kin

DOWN

1 Bases
2 Advil target
3 Cupid counterpart
4 Take it easy
5 Inks
6 Mrs. Charles
7 Actress Merkel
8 Mediterranean seaport
9 Handles clumsily
10 Female Oscar Madison
11 Bigoted one
12 "__ bagatelle!"
13 More severe
18 They come to those who wait?
19 California city
23 Stats for Mattingly
25 Letter starter
26 Graven image
27 Dermatologist's target
28 Comfy shoe
29 Greek letter
31 Oversweet sentimentality
33 De Valera's land
34 Portal
35 "Step __!"
37 Radicals of a sort
38 Arden of *Our Miss Brooks*
39 Rainier and others: Abbr.
44 Used the overhead
45 Meter starter
46 Part of Roy G. Biv
47 All there
48 Make reparation
49 Novelist Shaw
51 Battery terminal
53 __ majesty (sovereign crime)
54 What the suspicious smell
55 Word form for "personal"
56 Grandma
57 Took notice of
59 Turkish VIP

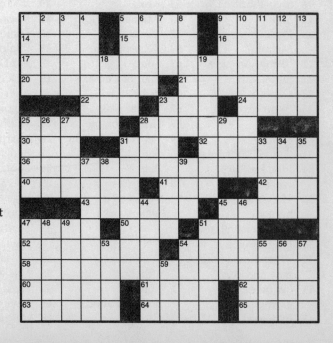

815 TOWN TALK by Michael Selinker

ACROSS
1 Ditty singer Doris
4 Gym surface
7 Vessel
10 A-E link
13 Binding words
14 Jeff Lynne's grp.
15 Actor Vigoda
16 Old high note
17 *Calamity Jane* ditty, part 1
21 Caliban's tormentor
22 Blind parts
23 Ditty, part 2
28 Ruckus
29 Bill's partner
30 Past
31 Shocking swimmer
32 Northumbrian's neighbor
34 Unique sorts
36 Ditty, part 3
41 Ancient Persians
42 *Guarding __* (MacLaine film)
45 Time
48 Buddy
49 Cub org.
52 Caviar source
53 Ditty, part 4
57 Caroline Islands group
58 Mountain ridge
59 Ditty, part 5
65 Ethiopian prince
66 Short word before "long"
67 Peace, to Akihito
68 Discovery cry
69 Superman's emblem
70 Mr. Spade
71 Program interruptors
72 Ditty, part 6

DOWN
1 Half of MIV
2 Dict. abbr.
3 "The sunshine of my life"
4 Measuring system
5 Inkless postage stamp
6 Klinger's hometown
7 Cat's dog
8 Kimono closer
9 About 100 feet high
10 Tongue-lash
11 Provide attire
12 Distressed one?
18 Called with chips
19 Tarzan player Ron
20 Soar
23 QB's stats
24 Sot's syllable
25 Archaic adverb
26 "Who __ Turn To?"
27 "__ no kick . . ."
33 Conway or Allen
34 Mil. training place
35 Tend the kids
37 *__ Daughter* (Esther Williams film)
38 Normandy time
39 Squeal
40 Eastern European
43 Worthless coin
44 Collection
45 Ottoman's pride
46 Cow ropes
47 *Through __, Darkly*
49 Howitzer sobriquet
50 Blotto
51 __ time (now)
54 "Bali __"
55 Gandhi successor
56 Affirmative vote
60 Musical syllable
61 Amethyst, e.g.
62 Touching game
63 *Tommy* group, with "The"
64 Chow down

816 THE CAMPBELLS by Bill Hendricks

ACROSS
1 Edition
6 Chan remark
10 Game-show VIP
14 Ten-__ odds
15 Hope/Crosby movie milieu
16 Sweet sandwich
17 Soup
20 Prefix meaning "whole"
21 "Kingly" name
22 Simoleons
23 Choose
25 "You're putting __!"
26 Soup
31 Guess: Abbr.
34 Like Harvard walls
35 *The Good __* (Buck book)
37 Altar constellation
39 Ling-Ling, e.g.
40 When lunch hour may end
41 Carpenter's garment
43 Bad deed
44 Approach dawn
46 First American-born saint
47 Sodium hydroxide
49 Soup
51 Layer
53 Klutz
54 Auto emporium
57 Use a +
59 '77 sea thriller
63 Soup
66 Start of Caesar's boast
67 Marsh grass
68 Get out of line
69 "Is You __ Is You Ain't Ma Baby?"
70 Cravings
71 Turns on the waterworks

DOWN
1 Septennial affliction?
2 London neighborhood
3 Ground
4 Raw
5 "A mouse!"
6 "Rule Britannia" composer
7 Humbug
8 __ Diego, CA
9 Leftover
10 It's funny
11 Vocal
12 Some vaccines
13 "Baloney!"
18 Art Deco artist
19 Jack of *Barney Miller*
24 Go biking
25 Leatherneck
26 Sharp barks
27 Benefit
28 Fool
29 "Scram!"
30 Ingested
32 Andrea del __
33 Scottish golf town
36 "__ la vista"
38 Ms. Meara
42 Necessarily
45 Lovey?
48 Cylindrical pastry
50 Repairs the lawn
52 __ pah pah
54 A quarter of DCCCXXIV
55 Warmonger of myth
56 "The Biggest Little City in the World"
57 Mass conclusion
58 Clothing
60 Learning method
61 Clever accomplishment
62 Rock-band equipment
64 Admission charge
65 Hem's partner

817 FOR GOOD MEASURE by Shirley Soloway

ACROSS

1 Ice and Iron
5 Sky light?
9 Strong string
14 Pre-Easter season
15 Milan money
16 Duck down
17 "__ boy!"
18 Whale of a movie
19 Adds and deletes
20 Close call
23 TV sleuth Remington __
24 Arnold's crime
28 Small amount
31 Ed Norton's concern
32 Russian news agency
35 Grain keeper
37 Indian tourist town
38 Curved opening
39 Squelch
40 __ over (faint)
41 Philippine native
42 Difficult
43 Matched pieces
44 Cook too much
46 Liffey's land
48 Work on an old painting, perhaps
50 Mrs. Marcos
55 Math subject
58 Thread holder
61 Actress Lollobrigida
62 Cozy
63 Golfer Palmer, to fans
64 Wicked
65 Border
66 Showy blossom
67 P.I.s
68 Satirist Mort

DOWN

1 Thicke and Bates
2 Reach
3 __ nous
4 Gaze intently
5 More leisurely
6 Grow weary
7 Circle segments
8 Show feeling
9 Indian abode
10 Very alert
11 General Amin
12 Court divider
13 Hosp. areas
21 Car maker
22 Fiery felony
25 Bob of *Full House*
26 Folklore villains
27 *Hud* actress
29 Europe's neighbor
30 British bishop's hat
32 Treasure find
33 *Green __* (old sitcom)
34 Cut of meat
36 City near Sacramento
38 Latin love
39 Stripped of wool
43 Trucking rig
45 "Hang down your head, Tom __"
47 Adversaries
49 Urged (on)
51 Road curves
52 Evangelista or Evans
53 Unbaked bread
54 Jockey Cordero
56 Seedy establishment
57 "What's __ for me?"
58 Syrup source
59 Ante- kin
60 Mrs. Lennon

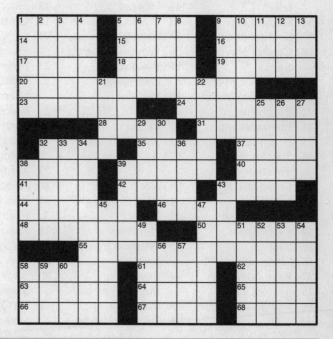

818 CLEAN UP YOUR ACT by Ray Smith

ACROSS

1 __ Kadiddlehopper
5 Bloomingdale's rival
9 Pixyish
14 Mystic writing
15 Sight from the Strait of Messina
16 Mrs. Gorbachev
17 "Put __ on it!"
18 Energy source
19 Lubricated
20 Blues great
23 Numerical prefix
24 Producer Norman
25 More elevated
27 Nutria, e.g.
30 Down in the dumps
32 __ Amin
33 Smooth transition
35 Nostrils
38 "The __ From Ipanema"
40 Hits the fridge
42 Robert De __
43 Joins the game, in a way
45 __ du jour (daily specials)
47 Langley org.
48 Ran on
50 Anchor of note
52 Clubs carrier
54 "__ to Love" (Porter song)
55 In the past
56 Crummy diner
62 Nonmusician's instrument
64 Leftovers category: Abbr.
65 Fascinated by
66 Happening
67 Toon's lightbulb
68 Defeats a bridge contract
69 Parking lot souvenirs
70 Speak wildly
71 Ilium

DOWN

1 Burn the midnight oil
2 "Little" cartoon character
3 Geraint's wife
4 Be a snoop
5 Brine
6 Rose oil
7 Slip or square item
8 "Ditto"
9 Wearing away
10 Chou En-__
11 More than well off
12 Grenoble's river
13 Low point
21 Urges
22 Letter after pi
26 Fed. agent
27 Baltic seaport
28 Asgard resident
29 Trini Lopez, Jim Brown, Ernest Borgnine, etc.
30 Craftsmen's group
31 Mother of Castor and Pollux
34 Stare in wonder
36 Eastern canal
37 Emulate Yeager
39 Coveted role
41 Pound denizen
44 Keg taps
46 Smart talk
49 Part of RPM
51 Office worker
52 Crusted
53 Century plant
54 Big Bertha's birthplace
57 Mideast title
58 Verdi heroine
59 Special person
60 Preminger or von Bismarck
61 Like a yenta
63 Mich. neighbor

819 BUTTERFINGERS by Ann Seidel

ACROSS
1 Leno or Letterman
5 Misbehave
10 Whimpers
14 Opera highlight
15 Eighth Hebrew letter
16 Singer Laine
17 Beatles movie
18 Certain movie role
19 Be in charge of
20 Comics caveman
22 Bird claw
24 Insurance claim
25 __ to pass (occur)
26 Stay for the duration
29 Broadcast boo-boos
33 Shady recess
34 Excursions
35 Rim
36 Grate upon
37 Baby carriages
38 __-item veto
39 Enzyme suffix
40 Idaho capital
41 Loyal Order of __
42 Farm structures
44 Kicked (out)
45 Make a wish
46 Nurse in *Martin Chuzzlewit*
47 Piece of pottery
49 '50s fad
53 Potion container
54 Send by computer
56 Words of despair
57 Put out of commission
58 Popular lily
59 Half of CVI
60 Pizzazz
61 Struck, in a way
62 Ages upon ages

DOWN
1 "That's a laugh!"
2 Pitcher Hershiser
3 Window frame part
4 Replay mechanism
5 Confront
6 Total confusion
7 Office sub
8 Colorado Native American
9 Certain staged events
10 Lug around
11 Toast spread
12 Fiber source
13 Ground cover
21 "__ Cheatin' Heart"
23 Bible book
25 Weather, in poems
26 Beatrice's mother
27 Clean the blackboard
28 Actor Buddy
29 Military officers
30 Nobel poet
31 Wash cycle
32 Hightail it
34 Rubbish
37 Ship area
38 Way out
40 Rude, crude dude
41 NYC cultural attraction
43 Swiss cottage
44 "__ of the Green Berets"
46 Cunning treachery
47 "Them" or "us"
48 Holbrook and Linden
49 Fit as a fiddle
50 Buckeye State
51 From here __ (henceforth)
52 French veggies
53 That is to say, briefly
55 __ of La Mancha

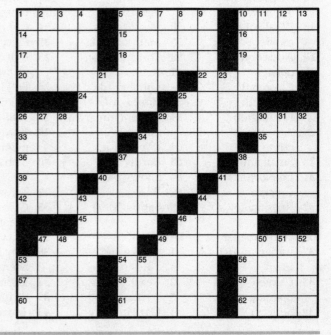

820 NAP TIME by Fred Piscop

ACROSS
1 Man with a touch
6 *Kidnapped* monogram
9 Sergeant Garcia's quarry
14 Put up with
15 Second-sequel indicator
16 Self-evident truth
17 Tacked
19 Rodeo rope
20 The two Begleys
21 Dash feature
22 Harmonica virtuoso Larry
23 Current strength
25 Pollute
29 Tom of *Newhart*
33 Darth Vader-like
34 Squirt
38 __-Wan Kenobi
39 Bandleader Prado
41 Prescription agcy.
42 Biblical brother
44 Lode stuff
45 Secret stuff
48 Restrain
49 Power of filmdom
51 Vixen's partner
53 Autocrats' realms
57 Prickly plants
60 Underworld
61 School grp.
64 Recovery process, for short
65 Oxygen converters
67 Battlefield
68 __ Bingle (Crosby)
69 Sources of irritation
70 Errandperson
71 Western beast
72 Souvenir

DOWN
1 Pencil puzzle
2 Footnote abbr.
3 Pad
4 Wood shaper
5 *Hard to Kill* star
6 Construct haphazardly
7 Faithful
8 Partisan
9 City in España
10 Rust et al.
11 Iranian coin
12 Learning method
13 Barbra's costar in '68
18 Fun's partner
24 Prone
25 Bus station
26 "__ dog has his day"
27 Kiln operator
28 __ de France
30 Shul scroll
31 Amin deposed him
32 San Francisco footballer
35 Cpl.'s inferior
36 Dietary initials
37 Actor McShane
40 Big island
43 Pecs' partners
46 New Deal agcy.
47 Madison Avenue workers
50 Gas-pump word
52 Hoopster's stat
54 Valerie Harper sitcom
55 Knocks for a loop
56 Stinks
57 Rugged rock
58 Dynamic start
59 __ Boyardee
61 Make coffee
62 Baobab or banyan
63 Org.
66 Chaotic scene

821 PYRO TECHNIQUES by Frank Gordon

ACROSS
1 Workplace- safety grp.
5 Skiffs and sloops
10 Durham institution
14 Picnic spoiler
15 Come next
16 Opera highlight
17 End prior alliances
20 Snooze
21 Wild guesses
22 First lady
23 Ply a needle
25 Rest stop
27 FDR's last VP
30 Cherish unreturned feelings (for)
37 Birds' partners
39 Cad
40 Scant
41 Look at longingly
42 __ with faint praise
44 King or Alda
45 Timbuktu locale
46 De __ (old car)
47 Part of CD-ROM
48 Be pioneering
52 Revolutionary Guevara
53 Dumbo's wing
54 Apply salve
56 Veneration
59 Piano practice
63 Minimal
67 Incite to action
70 Gymnast Korbut
71 Geena or Miles
72 Sugar source
73 Toward the Pacific
74 Not supine
75 Stevenson character

DOWN
1 Poet's peepers
2 Author Bellow
3 Engage
4 Archer and Rice
5 Actor Gazzara
6 Till compartment
7 Prof.'s aide
8 Oompah instrument
9 Belgrade's region
10 June honoree
11 Importune
12 Ukrainian city
13 Comfort
18 Oil cartel
19 "__ It Romantic?"
24 One in custody
26 Wanderer
27 Teller's brainchild
28 *Love Story* author
29 "I cannot __ lie"
31 Prepare chestnuts, perhaps
32 Grapevine yield
33 Meddler
34 Surviving trace
35 Collision
36 It follows that
38 __ the Day (novel by 2 Down)
43 Evening: Fr.
49 Toward the Atlantic
50 Pinballer's mecca
51 Humdinger
55 Park pew
56 Keep __ profile (shun the limelight)
57 __ E. Coyote
58 Breakfast option
60 A long way off
61 Exist
62 Guitarist Clapton
64 "An apple __ keeps. . ."
65 Dispatch
66 Shoe shaper
68 Fedora or beret
69 NYC setting

822 COUNTRY STARS by Bill Hendricks

ACROSS
1 Puppeteer Bil
6 Roundup device
10 Patch up
14 Play part
15 Light overhead?
16 Otherwise
17 "Elvira" singers
20 Cloth border
21 Average
22 Jimmies
23 Sennett squad
24 Spice or club
26 "All Tied Up" singer
32 Made pay
33 Theater sign
34 Mode
35 Isolated water
36 Möbius creation
38 Antler branch
39 Emulated Jack Horner
40 Strings member
41 Sorts
42 *Dukes of Hazzard* balladeer
46 "__ anywhere for your smile . . ."
47 Charlie's lady
48 Grating noise
51 Gloating
52 Move after swerving
55 "Crossword Puzzle" singer
59 Malefic
60 "And giving __, up . . ."
61 Jack of the late show
62 Director Clair
63 Dangerfield's stock-in-trade
64 Reagan cabinet member

DOWN
1 British resort
2 Feel sore
3 Gossipy tidbit
4 Cruise port
5 Hard rock
6 Word group
7 Fall from the sky
8 Ancient
9 Hound
10 Mideast language
11 *The Time Machine* race
12 "__ sow, so shall . . ."
13 Minus
18 Military topper
19 Orlando-area attraction
23 Footballer's trouble spot
24 1111
25 Go for __ (swim)
26 Rodeo rope
27 Getting the notes right
28 Singer Haggard
29 Southfork surname
30 Explorers' finds
31 Caustic substances
32 Crack
36 Vocalize
37 WWII general
38 Turner of rock
40 Screwdriver need
41 Realm
43 Apt
44 Wandering ones
45 Parser's part
48 Radio-active trucker
49 Great review
50 One of the Walton kids
51 Urban woe
52 Rural nickname
53 MacGraw et al.
54 __ club (chorus)
56 Cleaning cloth
57 Get __ for effort
58 *Norma* __

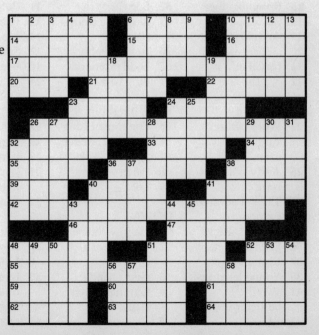

THROUGH THE WEEK by Raymond Hamel

ACROSS
1 Uncover
6 He loves: Lat.
10 Family members
14 Japanese city
15 Racer Yarborough
16 Dummy's perch
17 *Double Indemnity* author
19 Raison d'__
20 Be indebted to
21 *Pretty Poison* star
23 Singing Mama
24 Santa __, CA
25 Spanish king
26 Rado/Ragni musical
29 Curved letter
31 Start of "Jabberwocky"
33 Whether __ (in any case)
34 Vintage auto
35 Real things, in metaphysics
38 Macabre kid
42 Oedipus' father
43 Doozy
44 Coup d'__

45 Abbreviated aide
47 Gary Cooper's affirmative
48 City west of Sparks
49 Barley beard
51 Bond rating
53 Cup edges
55 Ballplayer turned evangelist
58 Mode preceder
61 __ at the Races
62 Disneyland offerings
64 RC competitor
65 Take home
66 French student
67 Dazzles
68 Type of racing
69 Ohio tornado town of '74

DOWN
1 Karate school
2 Middle of Caesar's statement
3 Clue, for one
4 Guitar kin

5 Ziti, e.g.
6 Reached
7 *Serpico* author
8 Italian actress Valli
9 Apartment renter
10 Throw out of whack
11 Major highway
12 "Mr. Television"
13 Ragged
18 They who ruminate
22 Changed course
23 Titan of myth
26 Ginsberg poem
27 Field of expertise
28 Cowsills tune
30 Ready for rinsing
32 Actress Luana
36 Mrs. David Bowie
37 About
39 Blue-book entry
40 Giving way
41 __ Way (Roman road)
46 Sampled

49 Hemp plant
50 *The Merry __* (Léhar work)
52 Icelandic coins
54 Measuring-cup material
56 Strong cleaners

57 Early capital of Japan
58 Yemeni seaport
59 Son of Jacob
60 Drifting on the Sargasso
63 Seine sight

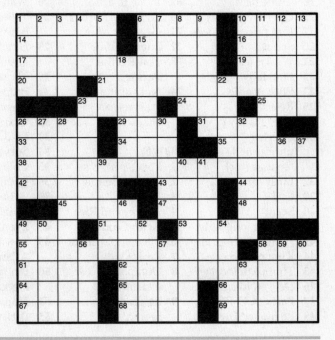

HEAVENLY MUSIC by Shirley Soloway

ACROSS
1 God of thunder
5 Shea player
8 As such
13 Roof overhang
14 Onetime White House pet
15 Bring together
16 Ray Charles song
19 Animal restraints
20 __ Cruces, NM
21 Naval off.
22 "__ the ramparts we watched . . ."
23 Word before surgeon or exam
25 Andy Williams song
30 Taken-back items
34 Category
35 Aachen article
36 State for certain
37 Bismarck's st.
39 Young herring
41 WWII battleground
42 Banish

44 Make a choice
45 Leibman or Perlman
46 Take a shot (at)
47 Temptations song
50 Insult
52 Born
53 Response from space
56 Actress Balin
57 Food extenders
61 Bing Crosby song
64 Sailing ship
65 The simian King
66 Lyricist Harbach
67 __ in the Dark
68 Patch of lawn
69 Loch __

DOWN
1 Hebrew letter
2 Sounds for a comic
3 Gem shape
4 Gymnast Mary Lou
5 Raincoats

6 Certain lodge member
7 Liz or Rod
8 Sources of radio waves
9 Finale
10 Stand up
11 Put into shock
12 Poetic nights
14 Most hairy
17 Sidelong glance
18 Boat propeller
24 __ Than Zero
25 Obeys
26 Of the past
27 Giraffe kin
28 Bigwig, for short
29 Join up
31 __ dish (lab holder)
32 Synthetic fabric
33 Sly or Sharon
36 Harmonizing
38 Keystone group
40 Mil. address
43 Ignite one more time
47 Complainers
48 Oscar __ Renta

49 Wrestling hold
51 Prefix for cycle or corn
53 "__ silly question . . ."
54 Has payments to make

55 Friends and neighbors
57 Is __ of (likes)
58 Suffix for kitchen
59 "Oh, no!"
60 Theater signs
62 Sgt., e.g.
63 Sticky stuff

825 LOOK SHARP by Ann Seidel

ACROSS
1 Air Force org.
4 Indian chief
9 Fido's four
13 __ Flanders
14 Lucci role
15 Russian range
16 Hidden
18 __ Genesis (Nintendo rival)
19 Toast word
20 Horrified
22 City on the Ruhr
23 Sound option
26 Disapprove
31 __-pitch softball
34 Luxury car
35 Joliet discovery
36 Simple machine
38 Bailed out
40 Et __ (and others)
41 Indonesian island
44 Classical prefix
45 Narrow-mindedness
49 Mystical knowledge
50 Petunia's suitor
54 League of Nations home
57 Don't panic
58 Affirm
59 Computing concept
63 "Hi __, Hi Lo"
64 Turkish official
65 Capital of Yemen
66 Women's magazine
67 Forward-looking dept.
68 Half a fly

DOWN
1 Whiskey mixes
2 Some saxes
3 Storage space
4 Sack out
5 Exodus name
6 It may be up
7 "Oh, Hans!"
8 1962 Hawks film
9 Easy mark
10 Neighborhood
11 Jokers
12 Blind part
13 Sulk
17 Conclusion
21 Sparkler
23 Madonna work
24 Greek letter
25 Asner et al.
27 West is one
28 Pakistan neighbor
29 Bach's a
30 ". . . it's off to work __"
31 Tiff
32 Pip
33 Actress Lena
37 Buy at Frederick's
38 __-disant (self-styled)
39 Drive
41 Sets in the house
42 Clock numeral
43 Rough drafts: Abbr.
46 Part of SASE
47 You can't tie one on
48 Free
51 Shankar selections
52 Actor Kevin
53 Swimming-pool site
54 Unit of laughter
55 Bringing trouble
56 Old Curiosity Shop heroine
57 Explorer or Senator
60 Actress Thurman
61 Buddhism branch
62 A __ and Two Noughts (Greenaway film)

826 PIECES OF CAKE by Stanley B. Whitten

ACROSS
1 Steady look
5 Actress Merrill
9 Does an usher's job
14 Diva's song
15 Coup d'__
16 Arm of the sea
17 Invigorates
18 World Series winners in '86
19 Each
20 Elvis film of '67
23 Actor Mineo
24 Museum material
25 At war
30 "__ Falling Star"
35 Stench
36 Connection line
38 Sand bar
39 Chad of Life Goes On
40 Realtor's listings
42 Oklahoma city
43 __ Irish Rose
45 Nifty
46 Closely pressed package
47 End a strike
49 Colander
51 Stowe character
53 Branch of math.
54 Jack Nicholson film of '70
62 Man of morals
63 Expressway access
64 Smell __ (suspect trickery)
65 Condition
66 In the past
67 Indisputable
68 Underground duct
69 At hand
70 Canine cry

DOWN
1 Open wide
2 Region
3 Goes quickly
4 Worry-free address
5 Raze
6 List element
7 Hoopster Archibald
8 Completely confused
9 Afternoon naps
10 One of the deadly sins
11 Shake __ (hurry)
12 Mr. T's real last name
13 Piggery
21 Coolidge's nickname
22 Part of a comet's path
25 Gaucho's weapons
26 Southwestern building material
27 Namely
28 Inert gas
29 Fun's partner
31 Quaid/Barkin film of '87
32 Barbarian of comics
33 __ Selassie
34 Birch family member
37 Gist
41 Big fellow
44 Railroad car
48 New Year's __
50 Three-time boxing champ
52 Moses' brother
54 Give a party for
55 "__ Mommy Kissing Santa Claus"
56 Choose a ticket
57 Showing sense
58 Swimming-class offerer: Abbr.
59 Motley __ (rock group)
60 Jazzman Hines
61 Plan portion
62 Donkey's uncle?

ACROSS

1 Actor Sharif
5 T-men
9 Master, in Swahili
14 Sandwich filler
15 "__ the Light" (Hank Williams song)
16 Unbending
17 A party to
18 Film composer Nino
19 "__ Mio"
20 Murphy Brown, for one
23 "I agree"
24 Knights' weapons
26 Draft org.
29 Bee Gees' surname
32 Lethargy
35 Post-N lineup
36 First vice president
38 "Dies __"
39 Oxymoronic game

43 Asian sea
44 Tea biscuit
45 Rorem or Beatty
46 Light, as fireworks
49 Prod
50 Companion of svcs.
51 Goggle
53 Govt. undercover group
55 Thick sandwich
61 Confusion of voices
64 Mrs. Dithers
65 Urban cruiser
66 Idolize
67 Leave out
68 Army group
69 Peter Rabbit sibling
70 Box office total
71 Sampras of tennis

DOWN

1 Elevator inventor

2 Pasteur portrayer Paul
3 Soon
4 Long-limbed
5 FDR's __ chats
6 Workers' share in the co.
7 Computer input
8 Bee group
9 Rodeo ride
10 Climbing shrub
11 In the past
12 Nothing
13 Summer refresher
21 Within the law
22 Consume
25 Growing season
26 Pops
27 Seed
28 Hunkers down
30 String-section member
31 Univ. bigshots
33 Rowed
34 Marsh growths
37 Wet mud
40 Desk accessories

41 Flood
42 Of few words
47 Chris of comedy
48 Part of TGIF
52 Disney site
54 Be a brat
56 __ Linda, CA

57 Composer Satie
58 Citizen __
59 The way out
60 Baptism, e.g.
61 Dull thud
62 Fuss
63 Jazz type

ACROSS

1 Vincent van __
5 Suitably
10 Display
14 Skin moisturizer
15 Western resort
16 Cougar
17 Singer Horne
18 Senator Lott
19 Sacred image
20 Ripened
21 Tax-return agcy.
22 Tea type
23 Cry loudly
25 Toward the summit
28 My Friend __
30 Pin (down)
31 Flub it
34 Shaping machine
35 Social class
36 Long snake
37 Wimbledon winner in '75
38 Shapes clay
39 Leftovers
40 Adjust a Swatch
41 Diagram a sentence

42 Pointed
43 Prince Charles' title: Abbr.
44 Jason's ship
45 Isabella's mother
46 Magic potion
48 "Don't go!"
49 Scattered seed
51 "__ to Extremes" (Joel tune)
53 Sky saucers, briefly
56 Turkish title
57 Nose-related
59 Maiden
60 Cabinet name
61 Jung rival
62 Prefix meaning "within"
63 Warhol or Rooney
64 Cotton thread
65 Elitist

DOWN

1 Festive affair
2 Yves' rival
3 SOUTHERN BELLE SCORNED!

4 Annoyance
5 Hun head
6 Young salmon
7 A LOST GENERATION EXPOSED!
8 Nol of Cambodia
9 Thus far
10 Sales pitch
11 MAN AND BOY ALONE ON A RAFT!
12 Melville romance
13 Fade away
22 Heap
24 Adlai's opponent
26 __ deux (ballet piece)
27 Box-office smashes
28 Pizazz
29 Concentrated beam
32 Martini & __
33 Given a G or R
35 Welsh breed
38 Engels colleague

39 Calibrates anew
41 Forked over
42 Cable channel
45 Tristan and __
47 "Bad, Bad __ Brown"
49 Antitoxins

50 Straw in the wind
52 Part of the Roman Empire
54 Word on a dollar
55 Messy one
57 Super Bowl org.
58 Magnate Onassis

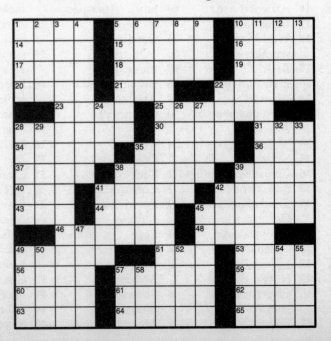

LITHOLOGY by Wayne R. Williams

ACROSS

1 Ling-Ling is one
6 Athens market
11 Govt. nutrition watchdog
14 Bay window
15 Makes cuts
16 Grouped merchandise
17 California course
19 Gomez's cousin
20 Singer Sheena
21 *Aladdin* prince
22 Against
23 Mel et al.
25 Pencil substance
27 Shortened wd.
30 Flightless bird
32 Like Coast Guard rescues
33 __ Tomé (African island)
34 Workplace for 11 Down
36 Drummer Gene
38 Apollo vehicle
39 Wed without warning
42 Lights of the '60s
45 Singer Peeples
46 Infuriate
48 Patriotic grp.
49 Copper
50 Partial concurrence
52 Nothing to write home about
54 Lose energy
55 Shirt style
57 Star of *My Favorite Year*
61 Hoodwinked
62 West Virginia senator
64 Sked letters
65 *A Lesson From __*
66 Strip city
67 ZZZ letters
68 Author Hermann
69 Backspace, perhaps

DOWN

1 Bishop of Rome
2 Living space
3 Birds' bills
4 One in the red
5 Apportion
6 PD alert
7 Greek goddess of the earth
8 Some tests
9 Student's performance
10 Blond shade
11 1994 role for Goodman
12 Country singer West
13 Athens' region
18 Input data
22 Shower time
24 Petty
26 "Egads!"
27 Invite
28 Stand in the way
29 Construction project completed in '36
31 Parts of eyes
34 Court prop
35 Peel and Bovary
37 California ballplayer
40 Wrestling success
41 Break fast
43 Nobelist France
44 Indisputable evidence
46 Convent head
47 Take to the air
49 Picnic tote
51 Rio Grande feeder
53 Pitcher Carlton
56 Just gets by, with "out"
58 First name in gymnastics
59 Pastures
60 Highland tongue
62 Bleacher bleat
63 Tongue ending?

BIRDLAND by Bob Lubbers

ACROSS

1 *The Forsyte __*
5 Well-appointed
9 Amiss
13 St. crossers
14 Have __ in one's bonnet
15 Binge
16 Avian designer?
18 Certain newspaper pages
19 Connected to a computer
20 Burstyn or Barkin
22 Corp. abbrs.
25 Skirt
27 Purposely sink
30 Savage
32 Ernest's Oscar role
33 *Les __-Unis*
35 Singing syllable
36 __ vera
37 Heiress Hearst
38 Decree
39 To-do
40 Fills fully
41 Maneuvers through muck
42 Tailed wonders
44 Call again
46 Exploding stars
47 First name in pound cake
48 Flatfish
50 Early Nebraskans
55 Wheel part
57 Stylishly avian?
60 *The Gulf Stream* painter
61 Starting
62 __ *kleine Nachtmusik*
63 Mimicked
64 Bradlee et al.
65 Actor Hale

DOWN

1 Maine waterway
2 Stratford waterway
3 Coll. subject
4 Wine region
5 Rearer
6 Sash
7 "Get it?"
8 Roll-call response
9 Seem
10 Avian trilogy?
11 Muleta color
12 Pro vote
15 Works a puzzle
17 Oneness
21 Pitcher Grove
23 Shoe spike
24 Hunting dogs
26 Make angry
27 Beer joint
28 Bit of avian genetics?
29 American Indian
31 Devours
32 *Julius Caesar* name
34 Lost
37 Outmoded
38 Alice's co-worker
40 Not as fresh
41 Sea World whale
43 Brought forth
45 First prints
49 Swedish auto
51 Zone
52 Frozen pellets
53 First name of 54 Down
54 *Nana* actress
55 __ Na Na
56 Cereal sound
58 "What's the __?"
59 Heyerdahl's __-*Tiki*

831 CUPFULS by Lee Weaver

ACROSS
1 Hits head-on
5 Chicago gridders
10 Battle memento
14 Operatic highlight
15 Looked leeringly at
16 Mexican munchie
17 Herbal refresher
19 Frizzy hairdo
20 Menlo Park name
21 Type of deer
22 Symbol of Wales
23 Close by
25 Actress Farrow
26 *Pygmalion* playwright
30 Come out even
31 Coffee go-withs
34 Dad
36 Concoct, with "up"
38 *Burke's* __
39 Dead end
41 Kettledrums
43 __ Aviv
44 Turkish title
46 Put in a row
47 Hole edged by stitching
49 Police alert: Abbr.
51 Siouan
52 Soda container
53 Geek
55 Guzzle
57 Just awful
59 Spring holiday
64 Beach resort
65 Hot, spiced claret
67 Cookie favorite
68 Mountain nymph
69 Says more
70 Sea swallow
71 Finds fault
72 Aerie, e.g.

DOWN
1 Ire
2 Like the Mojave
3 Skirt length
4 Speak rudely
5 Hat for 59 Across
6 Omelet need
7 Tailor, at times
8 Film holder
9 Pierre's st.
10 Former Russian leader
11 French brew with milk
12 Ranch unit
13 Chess piece
18 Long time
24 General helpers
25 Mate of 34 Across
26 Malice
27 Comfy-cozy
28 Fall drink
29 New Deal org.
31 Doris or Dennis
32 Dance that takes two
33 Boars, e.g.
35 Quaking tree
37 Troop camp
40 Posed
42 Arafat's org.
45 Political manager
48 Water enclosed by an atoll
50 Engenders
54 Another name for 34 Across
55 Vending-machine opening
56 Send a cable
57 Univ. hotshot
58 Atmosphere
60 Word before dive or song
61 Ocean's motion
62 Calls a halt to
63 Musical silence
66 Drink like a dog

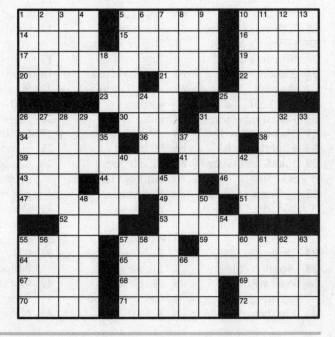

832 ON THE JOB by Shirley Soloway

ACROSS
1 Long nail
5 Rigging support
9 Signature song
14 Singer Julius La __
15 Wheel holder
16 Furies
17 Culture, with "the"
18 Genuine
19 Point of view
20 Where authors live?
23 Unruffled
24 Social insect
25 Bikini top
28 Midmonth day
31 Cotton fabrics
33 Make changes to
37 Officer's outfit?
39 Ward of *Sisters*
40 "O Sole __"
41 Carson's successor
42 Where office workers live?
45 Romero of films
46 Jockey Eddie
47 Word form for "gas"
49 On the __ (punctual)
50 Charged particle
52 __-Lorraine (French region)
57 Policeman's weapon?
60 Valuable violin
63 Church section
64 "__ fair in love . . ."
65 Lose control
66 Preceding nights
67 Brood
68 Uptight
69 Monthly payment
70 Getz of jazz

DOWN
1 Birds' crops
2 Mr. Moto portrayer
3 Up and about
4 Squander
5 Damaged
6 Wood choppers
7 Thick slice
8 "I cannot __ lie"
9 Farm machine
10 Snow or Williams
11 Nog ingredient
12 Tormé or Tillis
13 Direction: Abbr.
21 Writer Bagnold
22 Not fooled by
25 B.B. King specialty
26 Spanish queen
27 Mary of *The Maltese Falcon*
29 Ms. Bovary
30 "You __ mouthful!"
32 Capri, e.g.
33 Syrian leader
34 Parisian underground
35 Put in office
36 Grandma
38 Slugger Canseco
43 Aperture
44 Small explosive sound
45 Mil. ranks
48 Most difficult to find
51 S.F. gridder, for short
53 Con games
54 Apportion
55 *Mea* __
56 He played Clampett and Jones
57 Singer Redding
58 Mountain hideaway
59 Tied up
60 Fitting
61 Daisy __
62 Jillian or Miller

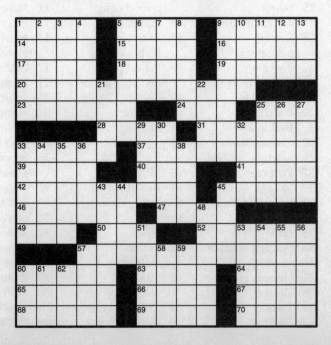

833 PRE-TV by Arnold Moss

ACROSS
1 Big rig
5 Silent actors
10 Butts into
14 Prayer word
15 ". . . and __ grow on"
16 Will's river
17 Liquor over cracked ice
18 Stagger
19 Heavy reading?
20 '30s radio documentary series
23 Tough to find
24 Speed-trap device
25 Tailless cat
27 Take, as advice
30 Rum cake
31 Biblical prophet
33 Old oath
36 '40s radio mystery
39 Ltd., in Lyons
40 Goes along
41 Dumbo's wings
42 "Cross of Gold" man
43 New England campus
44 Temple's *Captain January* dance partner
47 *Misery* star
49 '30s radio "soap"
55 Part of QED
56 Even though
57 Vincent Lopez's theme
59 Guitar gadget
60 Gymnast Comaneci
61 Cheshire Cat trademark
62 Not now
63 Writer Danielle
64 Sports datum

DOWN
1 American uncle
2 Send out
3 Interlock
4 IRS leader?
5 Grinding tooth
6 Accustom
7 Thermometer liq.
8 Engrave
9 Where Carnaby Street is
10 Wickerwork
11 Steer clear of
12 *Throw __ From the Train*
13 Contemptuous look
21 Nth degree, slangily
22 *The Art of Loving* author
25 Site of Haleakala National Park
26 Baker's pal?
27 Longfellow go-between
28 Relief org.
29 St. Anthony's crosses
30 English channel
31 Hobgoblin
32 Taj Mahal site
33 Colt or filly
34 About
35 Press staffers, for short
37 Mends socks
38 "Set" has nearly 200 of them
42 Muralist Thomas Hart __
43 Go off course
44 Expel
45 Idaho senator of the '30s
46 Physique
47 Whoopi's role in *The Color Purple*
48 "He's __ nowhere man"
50 Makes the last payment on
51 Just one of those things?
52 Pelt
53 __ Collins, CO
54 Director Kazan
58 Opp. of syn.

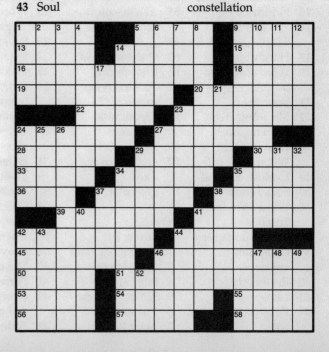

834 GOOD BOOKS by Randolph Ross

ACROSS
1 Strikebreaker
5 Junction point
9 Rent-__
13 Taboo
14 *M*A*S*H* setting
15 Alaskan port
16 Half the integers
18 Hawaiian baking pits
19 Ken Burns subject
20 Least volatile
22 Folk history
23 '50s and '60s
24 Optimistic
27 Just
28 Honor with insults
29 Bagel alternative
30 "Today I __ man!"
33 Circle sections
34 "Gee whiz!"
35 Trash boat
36 Albanian coin
37 Gold unit
38 Montana city
39 '63 physics Nobelist
41 Lubitsch and Mach
42 Praise
44 Pillage the refrigerator
45 Mitchell of NBC News
46 Protests
50 Latvian capital
51 Armand Assante film, with *The*
53 Ness' squad
54 Dress carefully
55 Part of QED
56 Kiln
57 Without: Fr.
58 Cub Scout groups

DOWN
1 Elitist
2 Musical postscript
3 Clause connectors
4 Filleted
5 High-minded
6 Pitcher Hershiser
7 __ *Spiegel*
8 Meteorological adverb
9 Twenty Questions category
10 Improv routines
11 Tickle
12 Takes five
14 Retail giant
17 WWII sub
21 __-deucey
23 Gave out cards
24 Russian river
25 Little breather?
26 Football officials
27 La Scala's city
29 Dull ones
31 Feminist Lucretia
32 Leaves open-mouthed
34 Erstwhile illuminators
35 Like some tomatoes
37 Patella's place
38 Oven material
40 Like some knights
41 Shirley of *Goldfinger*
42 Key name
43 Soul
44 Goldberg et al.
46 Augury
47 Memo phrase
48 Character actor Richard
49 Heathrow jets
52 Southern constellation

ACROSS

1 Exhausted
6 Small number
9 Dynamite inventor
14 Have a cow
15 Mr. Baba
16 French school
17 '91 NFL first draft pick
19 Loose wrap
20 Western actor Jack
21 Not only that
22 "__ alive!"
23 Less trouble
25 Forgo
27 Appropriates
30 Blow a gasket
33 Just
36 Hot drinks
38 Town near Caen
39 Actress Merkel
40 Quarterback great
41 Big bankroll
42 Quick pace
44 "Render __ Caesar . . ."
45 Softly, in music
47 Scouts, often
49 Name meaning "bearlike"
51 Heads for the wings
53 Commandeer
57 Coe's rival in the mile
59 Part of TAE
62 Stare at
63 Change the machinery
64 Querier re Santa Claus
66 Ransack
67 Columbus Day mo.
68 Most tiny
69 Show contempt
70 Caraway seed holder
71 __ Park, CO

DOWN

1 Rocky debris
2 Funny Poundstone
3 "__ Dream" (*Lohengrin* song)
4 McQueen role
5 Hole starter
6 Camus novel, with *The*
7 Shade sources
8 *The Merry __*
9 Monster's nickname
10 Scale spans
11 Founder of Tuskegee Inst.
12 Model Macpherson
13 Wine sediment
18 For-the-fun-of-it act
24 Erode
26 ADC, e.g.
28 English boys' school
29 Take care of
31 Dash
32 Dull-witted one
33 Book after Naomi
34 Letters on the cross
35 *Cow's Skull* painter
37 *Omnia vincit __*
40 Barely
43 Material
45 Luau fare
46 Ford role
48 Singer Tex
50 Persian potentate
52 Relish
54 Lace tip
55 In the ballpark
56 Superman's stepparents
57 Bobby and kin
58 Bonanza, perhaps
60 Gossamer
61 Plebiscite
65 Dumbstruck wonder

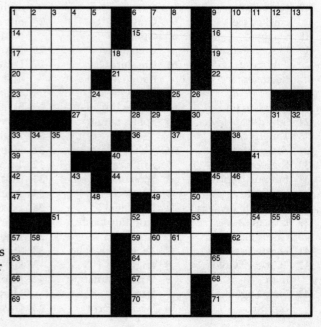

ACROSS

1 Gilbert of *Roseanne*
5 Title of India
10 Composer Khachaturian
14 Seaweed product
15 Florida city
16 The Eternal City
17 Handy guy
20 *Wheel of Fortune* buy
21 Bounder
22 Ms. Rubinstein
23 Gold measure
25 Heavyweight Willard
27 Explosive sound
30 Social class
35 Word form for "high"
38 Roman emperor
39 Computer operators
40 Ready guy
43 Let up
44 Polish border river
45 Diminutive ending
46 Turning part
47 Successful dieters
49 Pointed arch
51 Movie award
55 At a discount
59 Scout Carson
61 __ Khan III
62 Ordinary guys
66 Brainstorm
67 Divided Asian nation
68 Algonquian language
69 Appear to be
70 Author Joyce Carol __
71 Leered at

DOWN

1 Emcee Pat
2 Capital of Guam
3 Indy driver
4 Biblical boat
5 Seat for several
6 Private sch.
7 Actor Linden
8 Under the weather
9 Spa units
10 Inland sea of Asia
11 Took a cab
12 Closing word
13 Butte kin
18 Word form for "eight"
19 Save from a pickle
24 Like
25 Unknown guy
26 Gets all melodramatic
28 Young man
29 *Lawrence of Arabia* star
31 Determine the amount of
32 Back-to-school mo.
33 Quick step
34 East: Sp.
35 Open a bit
36 Gray wolf
37 The one there
41 Perfumery essence
42 Otto I's realm: Abbr.
48 Author Philip
50 Small lizard
52 Tote
53 Be as one
54 Having spokes
55 Elevator man
56 Junction point
57 Hook's mate
58 Garden dweller
59 Down on one __ (proposing)
60 Lupino and others
63 Hawaiian tree
64 Fine work
65 Poker card

837 FIVE KINGS by Shirley Soloway

ACROSS
1 Skiers' resort
6 Actor Pitt
10 Ring stats
14 Moviemaker Ponti
15 Judge's garb
16 Blood carrier
17 KING
19 Angelic light
20 Foxy
21 Wisk rival
22 Word-twisting reverend
24 Gem holder
26 Make certain
27 Bigoted belief
30 Plumed heron
32 Baldwin of *The Shadow*
33 __ about (approx imately)
35 Pen name, e.g.
39 Adds color
41 Mine material
42 Tureen utensil
43 Sting operation
44 Quiche need
46 Singer McEntire
47 Long arm?
49 Annoy repeatedly
51 Stick
54 Home of 14 Across
56 Detectives, at times
58 Onassis, familiarly
59 New start?
62 Volcanic flow
63 KING
66 Imitator
67 Gen. Robert __
68 Racket
69 Transmit
70 Decays
71 Monica of tennis

DOWN
1 Sales rep's clients: Abbr.
2 Satirist Mort
3 Victim
4 Overhead trains
5 Snoops
6 Boitano of the ice
7 Caviar source
8 Early teachings
9 More profound
10 KING
11 Reeves of *Speed*
12 Fuel carrier
13 Nap loudly
18 TV teaser
23 Ryan or Tatum
24 KING
25 KING
27 Pied Piper's followers
28 "I cannot tell __"
29 Smallest coin
31 Pro golfer Norman
34 Caroler's offering
36 Notion
37 Church vestments
38 Red and Black
40 Steeple top
45 Lamb Chop's mistress
48 *Show Boat* author
50 Foreigners
51 Map collection
52 Window covering
53 Sanctuary
55 Stories
57 Grain warehouse
59 Diamond or Simon
60 Simplicity
61 Individuals
64 Give permission to
65 Pesci or Piscopo

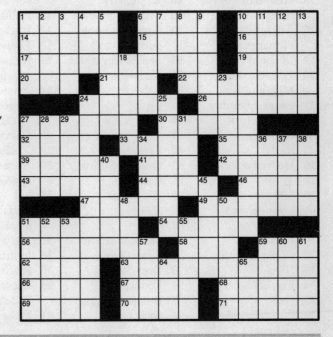

838 JEOPARDY by Bob Klahn

ACROSS
1 Military council
6 Bushy thicket
11 Feminist's foe: Abbr.
14 Bellowing
15 Diminish
16 "Great idea!"
17 New-business funds
19 White wine aperitif
20 Breaks bread
21 Seafood order
23 "To do" list
26 That guy's
27 Woodwind
28 Morse morsel
29 Inventor Howe
31 Goblet part
32 Get __ (exact revenge)
34 Night bird
35 __ 17 (Holden film)
37 Classic silent film serial, with *The*
40 Bits of color
41 Come out ahead
42 Splinter group
43 Garment attachments
44 Supermarket chain
46 Doggie doc
47 "Long __ Sally"
48 Practice diligently
49 Full of brambles
51 19th-century Seminole chief
53 Pugilist Max
54 Greek letter
55 *Caddyshack* star
60 Kitty
61 Stratosphere layer
62 Incense
63 Grunter's grounds
64 "The mouse __ the clock"
65 Like clown's clothing

DOWN
1 Mayo holder
2 William Tell's canton
3 Turndowns
4 Spoken for
5 Teen hangout
6 Mortarboards
7 *Shogun* sash
8 Argot
9 Sticks it out
10 Reef wrigglers
11 Song from *Show Boat*
12 Palmist
13 Dissect a sentence
18 Nonplussed
22 Wrecks completely
23 Highly skilled
24 Try
25 Epithet for Rome
26 Equidistant
30 *Sands of __ Jima*
31 Alphabetic trio
33 Carp
35 Boater's hazard
36 Big name in oil
38 Guitarist Paul
39 Brooch
44 Offshoot of AA
45 Ready-to-assemble, for short
47 Baseball card company
48 Tollbooth area
50 Mother in *The Sea Gull*
52 Sniffer's whiff
53 Road Runner's sound
56 Wildebeest
57 Quiche ingredient
58 Competition component
59 Like zinfandel

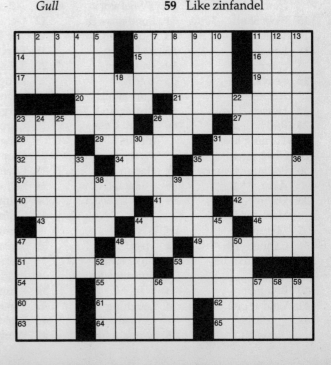

ATTRACTIVE by Randolph Ross

ACROSS

1 Puccini opus
6 Wall hanging, for short
11 Bit of work
14 Love, in Limoges
15 Actor Flynn
16 Hide-hair connector
17 Attractive, like a kidnapper?
19 IRS employee
20 Where to find MDs and RNs
21 Family member
22 Alberta fruit
24 Birth announcement
26 Heavenly strings
27 __ acid
30 Lettuce arrangement
31 Murray or Hooks
32 GOP meeting
33 100%
34 Egg holder
37 Dub
39 Purplish-red

40 French existentialist
41 Stocking stuffer
42 Ancient Peruvian
43 Sundial numeral
44 Diamond girl
45 Tick off
46 Placard
48 KP activity
50 Mercury models
52 Guinness Book suffix
53 Sen. Shelby's state
56 Verse starter
57 Attractive, like a bride?
60 Cacophony
61 Cream of the crop
62 Rope knot
63 Give in to gravity
64 Coasters
65 Harnesses

DOWN

1 Mexican snack
2 Actor Sharif
3 Drenches
4 Reduce
5 British noble, for short

6 Not requiring ownership
7 NYC subway
8 Camera stand
9 Tea sweetener
10 Gymnast Korbut
11 Attractive, like a sorceress?
12 Gallup rival
13 Understanding
18 Latin power
23 Attractive, like a jeweler?
24 Attractive, like a hostess?
25 __ canto
27 Sleeve cards
28 __ Lisa
29 Attractive, like a spy?
31 Jolt
33 British brew
34 Small island
35 Fairy tale start
36 Intimate
38 Angle prefix
39 Vassar and Radcliffe
41 Make a bow

44 Mr. Nielsen
45 Shakespearean eulogist
46 Gulf War weapons
47 Ancient Greek land
48 Shampoo name

49 Peres' home: Abbr.
51 Leaves open-mouthed
53 How the crazed run
54 __ majesté
55 Lemon coolers
58 Inc., in the UK
59 Tic-tac-toe win

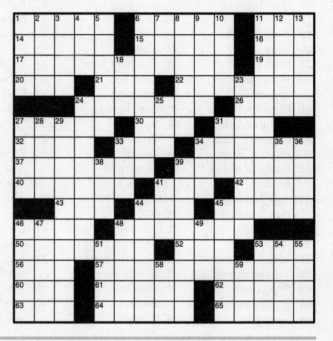

WHAT'S SO FUNNY? by Bob Lubbers

ACROSS

1 Llama kin
7 Morse code word
10 Barge
14 __ mind (remember)
15 "We Shall __"
17 Taste sense
18 Laughing composer?
19 Leave
21 Art form
22 Hersey town
24 Pull strings?
25 Turning tool
28 Govt. agents
30 Pedigree issuers: Abbr.
33 Orange-and-black bird
35 Mature
36 Canned fish
37 Rome invader
38 Detest
40 Bouquet
41 Cold capital
42 __ Maria (liqueur)

43 Three's Company actress
45 Call a bet
46 Reverb
48 "__ Were the Days"
49 TV network
51 Pond growth
53 Hokkaido port
56 Reader's __
59 Laughing craft?
63 Cure again
65 Rise again
66 __ Last Case (Bentley mystery)
67 Handouts
68 __ Rafael, CA
69 Took to heart

DOWN

1 Msgr.'s supervisor
2 Run ahead
3 Wan
4 Laughing plainsman?
5 Stronghold

6 "It's the end of __"
7 U.S. money
8 Hail, to Caesar
9 Derisive snicker
10 Wood fastener
11 Attorney Roy
12 General Bradley
13 The Way We __
16 Fury
20 TV network
23 Laughing tribesman?
24 Bergen dummy
25 Corporate insignias
26 Came up
27 Owner's proof
29 Self
30 Sound
31 Granny's relatives
32 Menu, in Marseilles
34 Eroded
36 Laughing bird?
39 Pen name
44 Bric-a-brac stand
47 Worn

49 Studies hard
50 Microwave
52 Circumference
53 Gumbo green
54 Far East weight
55 Morning, to Winchell
57 Fax, perhaps
58 London gallery
60 Many mos.
61 __ Khan
62 Maynard or Murray
64 Hallucinogenic initials

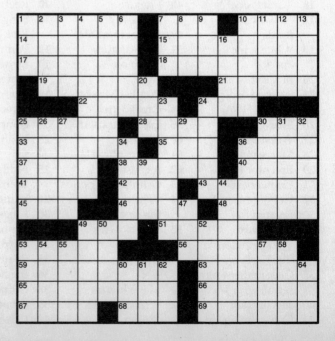

841 FOUR OF A KIND by Bob Lubbers

ACROSS
1 Copied
5 Cop a __
9 Arthur of tennis
13 __ to (awaken)
14 Be nomadic
15 Greek letters
16 Garment-care direction
18 As __ (generally)
19 Says
20 Cotton fabric
22 Drome starter
25 Most Egyptians
27 Robert of *The Music Man*
30 Ornamental column
32 Piccolo kin
33 Deli choices
35 Ike's command: Abbr.
36 Hindu god
37 Puts in the post
38 Newspaper notice
39 Horseplayers' HQ
40 Comics adoptee
41 Accustom
42 Thawed
44 College life
46 Wait on
47 Dry
48 "Red __ in the Sunset"
50 Spelling and Copland
55 Close on Broadway
57 What error admitters eat
60 Dove's goal
61 List-shortening abbr.
62 Bit of dialogue
63 Area
64 Remove from the galleys
65 Word after fiscal or leap

DOWN
1 Play parts
2 Look sullen
3 Poet Lazarus
4 Entry in red
5 Have ready in advance
6 Mideast airport
7 Musical sense
8 Carter and Vanderbilt
9 Up in the sky
10 Guy with two left feet
11 *2001* computer
12 Linguistic suffix
15 *The Gong Show* host
17 Renter's contract
21 Bligh and Kidd, for short
23 __ *Holiday* (Hepburn film)
24 New York Indians
26 Political humor, often
27 Dishes
28 Early Ford feature
29 LAX datum
31 Repetition
32 As of
34 Author Walker
37 Replica
38 United
40 Western sidekick Andy
41 Perfect
43 Hypnotic state
45 Good for farming
49 Backyard building
51 Depend (on)
52 Mayberry character
53 *Pinta*'s fleet-mate
54 Soothsayer
55 Some MDs
56 Flower garland
58 Plains Indian
59 __ *de mer* (seasickness)

842 PARK IT by Lee Weaver

ACROSS
1 *Moonstruck* star
5 Bends in the middle
9 Affirmative votes
13 *Damn Yankees* vamp
14 Ajax competitor
15 Draw with acid
16 Michigan national park
18 Fishline adjunct
19 Lawyer's due
20 Western state
21 Leaned (on)
23 Snarl
25 __ Domingo
27 Take five
29 Little ones
33 Comics conqueror
36 Rascals
38 *Family* actress Thompson
39 Dark, poetically
40 Grown-up
41 Barbershop service
42 Still sleeping
43 Daiquiri need
44 Three-card __ (street scam)
45 Sheet cloth
47 Bridge reach
49 Bright-eyed and bushy-tailed
51 Reply to the Captain
55 Gleason cohort
58 Hawaiian city
60 Schisgal play
61 Not home
62 Oregon national park
65 Lily family member
66 Capp lad
67 Latin love
68 Paradise
69 Wedding-cake feature
70 Word of warning

DOWN
1 *Freud* actor Montgomery
2 Biblical prophet
3 DeGeneres sitcom
4 *Norma* __
5 Popular bean
6 Asian nursemaids
7 Hair dressing
8 Most severe
9 Wyoming national park
10 Needle case
11 Ranch unit
12 Molt
14 Pigeon coops
17 Pencil-box accessory
22 Summer in Lyons
24 Arizona national park
26 Orchard product
28 Not as messy
30 Bring in
31 Brush up copy
32 "Ditto"
33 Jalopy
34 Singer Lane
35 Traveler
37 Corsage flower
40 '60s line dance
44 Munchkin official
46 Pub potable
48 More washed out
50 Macbeth's title
52 Hertz rival
53 Canadian territory
54 Chris of tennis
55 Container
56 Profoundly impressed
57 Uncontrolled anger
59 Roman road
63 Baseball stat
64 Young boy

843 — NOUN SENSE by Wayne R. Williams

ACROSS

1 Threaded pin
6 Very bad
10 Urban renewal site
14 Preminger classic
15 Sugar source
16 Petty of *A League of Their Own*
17 Bet-it-all wager
20 Make one
21 Birdbrain
22 Too big
23 Black goo
24 Cornerstone abbr.
26 Gleason/Hanks film
35 Duck and dodge
36 Catholic calendar
37 Villain of Venice
38 Speck
39 Dock device
40 Stick-to-itiveness
41 Hgt.
42 Actress Lena
43 Clear the stubble
44 Envier's hope
47 Abu Dhabi's grp.
48 One or more
49 Hypothesize
53 Architect Saarinen
55 Corn holder
58 Grodin/Gielgud film of '74
62 Cartoon lightbulb
63 Main dish, often
64 Set sights
65 Far from the flock
66 Pea cases
67 *JFK* director

DOWN

1 Great amount
2 Mammoth, e.g.
3 Thought better about
4 Mess up
5 Buttonholed
6 Yodeling effect
7 Mirror-loving
8 B&B, e.g.
9 Tour segment
10 Mess maker
11 Actor Rob
12 *Trinity* author
13 Where to go for the gold
18 *The Larry Sanders Show* costar
19 Dorothy's dog
23 Engage in pillaging
24 Upshot
25 Highlander
26 Identifies
27 Convex molding
28 Indian carving
29 Hockey player
30 Humorist __ S. Cobb
31 Powerful
32 French Revolution name
33 Pointed arch
34 Observer
39 Capital of Qatar
43 León ladies
45 Exclamation of disdain
46 Word form meaning "pressure"
49 Inventor Borden
50 Loosen and remove
51 Seeing things
52 Photo repro
53 "Holy smoke!"
54 Newts
55 Italian lake
56 Hot chamber
57 Venerable saint
59 Fiendish little one
60 Modernist's opener
61 Came to rest

844 — FOUR WEDDINGS by Ann Seidel

ACROSS

1 Treat crops
5 Soccer great
9 Rapidly
14 *To Live and Die __*
15 Folk singer Phil
16 Eggs' partner
17 Crackerjacks
18 Castle trench
19 No-holds-barred crusade
20 WEDDING
22 ". . . the lamb was __ go"
23 Show up for
24 Video-game name
26 Corp. exec.
28 Got back for
32 Forward
36 Wash
38 Arizona river
39 Civil-rights figure Parks
40 Ceremonies
41 *The __ Duckling*
42 Salt's word
43 Declare positively
44 Eavesdroppers
45 Seder fish
47 Comedian Louis
49 Bête __ (bugaboo)
51 Raise a design
56 Sinatra in *From Here to Eternity*
59 WEDDING
61 Northern people
62 Mouth-administered
63 Father
64 __ Nast
65 __ time (never)
66 Crucifix
67 Belgian artist
68 Irish dramatist
69 Dennis' *NYPD Blue* role

DOWN

1 Rigg of *The Avengers*
2 Full-length
3 Dozed
4 Discernment
5 Hair goo
6 Green subj.
7 Capital of Tibet
8 Superlative ending
9 Swear off
10 WEDDING
11 Feel sore
12 Winter wear
13 Prefix meaning "within"
21 Foot piece
22 Stashes away
25 Where to get a boilermaker
27 Twist or North
29 Caron musical
30 Fashion mag
31 Calendar squares
32 Talk big
33 Mies van der __
34 Beginning
35 WEDDING
37 Chomped on
40 Proportion
44 18-wheeler
46 Hang around
48 Canary
50 Mars neighbor
52 Iraqi port
53 Hamburger helper
54 White fish
55 Run-down
56 Jerry's kin
57 Author unknown: Abbr.
58 Revs
60 Turner of the screen
62 NATO cousin

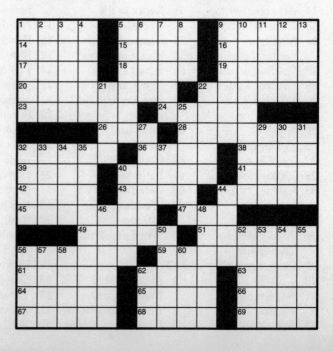

845 TENNIS TIME by Karen Hodge

ACROSS
1 Peter Benchley book
5 Castaways' transportation
10 "El Condor __" (Simon tune)
14 Parrot
15 Hair-raising
16 Statesman Abba
17 Wimbledon?
20 Make ready
21 Office wear
22 Open, as sneakers
23 Becker's backhands?
26 Hardy buddy
28 Arafat's grp.
29 Grp. that trains at Quantico
32 Sneaky __ (hooch)
33 You're working on it
35 Baselines?
39 "And the __ not cloudy all day"
40 Candy shape
41 1/6 fl. oz.
42 Coll. at Troy, NY
43 Basic beliefs
46 Tournament director?
48 Mobile home
51 Helps out
52 Shriner's topper
55 Tie score?
59 Little biter
60 "__ Lakes" (Minnesota license-plate phrase)
61 *Madama Butterfly* selection
62 Beanery chow
63 News medium
64 Market order

DOWN
1 Super Bowl III winners
2 Pain in the neck
3 Stimulate
4 Brillo rival
5 Distinction
6 Dish ancestor
7 Gets worried
8 Conway or Allen
9 Visualize
10 Unskilled laborers
11 Just touch
12 Delhi wear
13 Penny, perhaps
18 PC owner
19 Clip
23 Nine: Sp.
24 Pet name
25 Fitzgerald of music
26 Scallions' cousins
27 "Come Take __ In My Airship" (old song)
29 Norway bay
30 Sonny and Cher, in the '60s
31 Clouseau, for instance: Abbr.
32 "Hey, you!"
33 Compass dir.
34 __ over (helped out, in a way)
36 Nation since '48
37 USN off.
38 Leif's pop
43 Ancient Greek garment
44 Frankfurter
45 Simplicity
46 Sandwich fillers
47 Asian capital
48 Shoe dog
49 Sicilian landmark
50 Exam for H.S. jrs.
52 Cost of leaving
53 Early Oscar winner Jannings
54 Enthusiasm
56 Where gloss goes
57 Comparative ending
58 Freon or neon

846 METALLURGY by Bob Lubbers

ACROSS
1 Greek consonant
6 Terra __
11 Actress Lupino
14 E.T., for one
15 Sky hunter
16 St. Louis gridder
17 Kids' cable channel
19 Bullring cheer
20 *Star Wars* trilogy creature
21 Hit the hay
23 Perform
26 Trailways vehicle
28 Part of GE
29 Half of CIV
30 Hat, slangily
32 Bathroom fixture
34 Oakley and Hall
36 Set an example for
38 Fall mos.
39 Judge Lance
40 Russian cooperative
42 Huge
44 SALT, e.g.
45 Santa __, CA
46 Starts a point, in tennis
48 Ailing
49 __ breve
51 Transgress
52 Maiden name indicator
53 Enclosed
55 Top-rated
58 Heating fuel
59 Goof-off
65 Lyric poem
66 Galahad's quest
67 Newlywed
68 "You don't __!"
69 Marsh plant
70 Egypt neighbor

DOWN
1 Kal-__ (dog food)
2 Mr. Baba
3 Snapshot
4 Lap dog, for short
5 From the beginning
6 Hatch, as a plan
7 California fort
8 Dead heat
9 Toy-horn blowers
10 Negate
11 Obsolete European barrier
12 Spanish surrealist
13 Prayer ender
18 Wolves
22 Hit the hay
23 __ and alack
24 The film world
25 Pop music source
27 Malicious ones
30 D'Urberville lass
31 Music producer Brian
33 Scarab
35 "__ Right With Me" (Porter tune)
37 Golf scores
39 __ *Got a Secret*
41 Talbot or Waggoner
43 Izzy's real name
44 Pavarotti or Domingo
47 Capable of living
50 Hanes rival
53 Courts
54 Verdi opera
56 Penpoints
57 Tan tint
60 Young boy
61 Excavate
62 The Sundance __
63 Author LeShan
64 Stimpy's pal

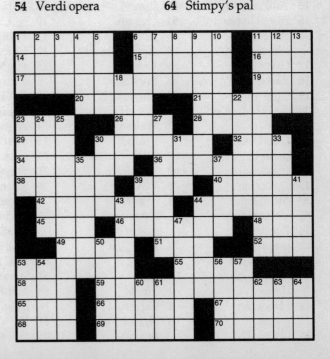

847 ALL GONE by Norma Steinberg

ACROSS
1 Tip one's cap
5 *Enemy of the People* playwright
10 Café au __
14 Singer Fitzgerald
15 Cacophony
16 Gymnast Korbut
17 Poetic form
19 Cool it
20 Robbins or Conway
21 Pitcher part
22 Mag bigwigs
24 Appeared
26 Being dragged
27 Like neon
29 __ kind (unique)
33 Barrels into
36 Hope/Crosby locale
38 Ed Norton's workplace
39 *__ a Teenage Werewolf*
40 Witch-hunt town
42 Boat's bottom
43 Orderly thinking
45 *Venus de __*
46 Exxon, formerly
47 Actress Donahue
49 Circus performer
51 Macon breakfast
53 Train-station employee
57 Actress Dietrich
60 Feel poorly
61 Linden of *The Boys Are Back*
62 Jai __
63 Bomb's target
66 Rent
67 Taking advantage of
68 "... pretty maids all in __"
69 Look for
70 Rains blows upon
71 Brooches

DOWN
1 Obligations
2 Stan's pal
3 Burning gas
4 *Lady Windermere's __*
5 Huns, e.g.
6 Certain South African
7 Term of respect
8 Ruhr Valley city
9 Must
10 Milland movie, with *The*
11 Kind of sax
12 Composer Stravinsky
13 Bugle call
18 Word after peachy
23 Charged particles
25 Paleontologist's quest
26 *This type*
28 Travel aimlessly
30 Has 1 Down
31 Service charges
32 Woody's son
33 Get one's goat
34 Playing hooky, militarily
35 Early Christmas visitors
37 The Farmer's location
41 Marina units
44 Apple part
48 Register a cash sale
50 Join metals
52 To the point
54 Parisian darling
55 Composer Copland
56 Farm tools
57 Wrestling surfaces
58 Skin lotion ingredient
59 Steakhouse specification
60 Mom's sister
64 Salad dressing ingredient
65 Cook in the microwave

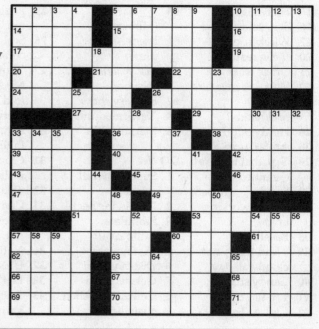

848 IN POSITION by Dean Niles

ACROSS
1 Sacred cow
5 __ of the Jungle ('50s series)
10 Grad. degree
13 Docile
14 Author Jong
15 Sorrel horse
16 Sheet-music symbol
17 Gives over
18 Part of MIT
19 Clue
20 "__ I Love Her"
21 Thwart
23 Onetime Chevy model
26 In advance
27 __ Doone
30 MCP, e.g.
32 Certain classes
34 Poetic preposition
35 Woodwind
39 Genie's grant
40 Range piece
42 Hawaiian goose
43 "Okey-__"
44 Little one
45 Eastern European village
47 Abominate
50 "That's great!"
51 Cancel
54 Fizz up
56 Beehive, e.g.
58 Apt. offerings
59 Defaces
63 Fuel cartel
64 Three, to Marie
66 Got off
67 Walesa of Poland
68 Cockamamie
69 Indelicate
70 WNW opp.
71 "Smooth Operator" singer et al.
72 Fort __, KY

DOWN
1 Tingle
2 Surrealist
3 Sign of the future
4 Abandoned
5 Summary
6 Stadia
7 Political stance
8 Swell serve
9 Impetuous
10 __ Carlo
11 Polish singer
12 Chipped in
15 Highly accurate
22 NATO cousin
24 Actress West
25 Witt move
27 Salacious
28 Stew
29 Strategy game
31 Righteous wraths
33 Spanish Ms.
36 BBC nickname
37 Aware of
38 Hard to pin down
41 Bit
46 Sweltering
48 Pre-Columbian
49 White fur
51 __ in the Head (Sinatra film)
52 Neck backs
53 Brother's daughter
55 Beasts of burden
57 Redding of song
60 Actor Arkin
61 Puerto __
62 Underworld river
65 Protein synthesizer

849 POLITICAL NEWS by Wayne R. Williams

ACROSS
1 Starlet's dream
6 Duffer's dream
9 Coptic bishops
14 Sculptor Henry
15 Old-time comic Olsen
16 Pesto, e.g.
17 Frighten
18 Gumshoe
19 Noodles
20 "Ex-Prez Turned Down"
23 Worker's wedge
24 Site of Baylor U.
25 Born
27 Feathery scarf
28 Fairy queen
31 "Ex-Senator Shut Out"
34 Overhead
36 City in France
37 Car for hire
38 Fact fabricators
40 Mets' home
43 Straying
45 Menu lines

46 "Veep Loses Badly"
50 Expected
51 Sphere of power
52 For each
53 "Un bel dì," e.g.
55 God: Sp.
57 "Senator Shoulda Won"
62 Increases
64 Mentalist Geller
65 Pope's crown
66 Bungling
67 Pizza order
68 Language quirk
69 Loathsome
70 Signal of distress
71 Swing a thurible

DOWN
1 Middle Eastern nation
2 Singular performances
3 Cajole
4 Turn signal
5 Carpet leftover
6 Elixir

7 Game-show name
8 Go back to caucus
9 Small snake
10 Sheep sounds
11 "Ex-Prez Needs a Vacation"
12 Bettor's quest
13 Swabby
21 Mil. rank category
22 Inert gases
26 Sea flier
28 Welcome site
29 Just like
30 "Senator Pulls No Punches"
32 Poetic muse
33 Branch headquarters?
35 Cannon command
38 Light weapon
39 Cliques
41 Flightless bird
42 Chemical suffix
44 What to let 'er do

45 Preposterous
46 __ Austen (second highest mountain)
47 Writer Fallaci
48 Pasteur's foe
49 Misdo

54 Tolerate
56 Cal. abbr.
58 Vivacity
59 Actor Conrad
60 Cupid
61 British title
63 Farm enclosure

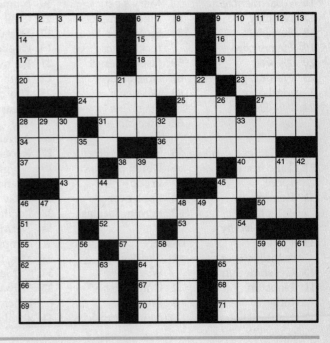

850 PRYER ASSISTANCE by Randolph Ross

ACROSS
1 Nile reptile
4 Carnivore's target
8 Free-for-all
13 Strengthen
15 Poet Teasdale
16 Set of keys
17 __ about (approximately)
18 START OF A QUIP
20 Disney uncle
22 Actor Jacques
23 PART 2 OF QUIP
30 Slalom shape
31 __ tai (cocktail)
32 France of fiction
33 Breathing spaces
35 Woolly ones
36 PART 3 OF QUIP
42 Oil of __
43 Round of fire
44 Stream barrier
48 Louis ou Charles
49 Part of Q&A

52 PART 4 OF QUIP
55 Space starter
56 Artless
57 END OF QUIP
63 Words of comprehension
64 Divided
65 Symbol: Var.
66 Offer temporarily
67 Pooh creator
68 Tidings
69 KLM cousin

DOWN
1 Greek malls
2 Tendons
3 TV ads
4 Greek letter
5 WWII fliers
6 Urania's sister
7 Motorcycle maker
8 Type of paper
9 Hellenic H
10 __ Alamos
11 Lodge member

12 Trains above
14 Something to beat
19 "__ o'clock scholar"
21 Dr. Mead's study area
24 DEA agent
25 Wedding-cake feature
26 Wing combiner
27 __ Won the War
28 "__ a song go..."
29 GI dining room
33 Biological groupings
34 USCG signal
36 Interior
37 Rival of Bjorn
38 After-bath application
39 Hard finish
40 Voting group
41 For the birds
45 1980s Salvadoran leader
46 Cruising

47 King Arthur's advisor
49 Liqueur flavorings
50 Catholic devotion
51 Mighty mounts
53 He discovered the cell

54 Catch in the act
57 Fugitive's flight
58 Prefix for center
59 Kilmer of The Doors
60 East ender
61 Present-tense
62 USN rank

851 AT THE MALL by Shirley Soloway

ACROSS
1 Long narrative
5 Ink stain
9 Lunch fish
13 Russian river
14 Chart over again
16 Apartment, e.g.
17 Nothing
18 Senseless
19 Heavy cord
20 As well
23 Natural-gas ingredient
24 "__ Clear Day . . ."
25 __-la-la
28 Sp. ladies
31 Take from the spool
33 Remark of acceptance
38 Not fooled by
39 Plow manufacturer
40 Get some sun
41 Houston hitter
42 Nautical shout
43 Had a business conversation
45 Actress Daryl
47 Touch down
48 "Are you a man __ mouse?"
49 Sound from Mary's pet
51 Like chenille
56 Suffers for recklessness
59 Jason's vessel
62 Anesthetic
63 Women's magazine
64 Like McCoy, perhaps
65 Songstress Della
66 Dutch cheese
67 Brood
68 Look over
69 Filming locales

DOWN
1 *The World of __ Wong*
2 Don't exist
3 Brooks of country music
4 Welcome in Waikiki
5 Venal crime
6 Olin or Horne
7 Actor Sharif
8 Latin dance
9 Rotate
10 Numero __
11 Chill
12 Had dinner
15 Goober
21 Follow
22 Author Fleming
25 "Lords a-leaping" day
26 Active starter
27 Knocked for __
29 "__ girl!"
30 Intends to
32 Betsy or Diana
33 Potato state
34 *The Merry Widow* composer
35 Mrs. Helmsley
36 __ Mawr College
37 "My Way" lyricist
41 Total
43 *Matlock* actress Brynn
44 Came in
46 Legal org.
50 Star-shaped flower
52 Lets go
53 Spanish mark
54 Brilliance
55 Believes
56 Warsaw native
57 You, once
58 "For __ jolly . . ."
59 Supply weapons to
60 Collector's car
61 Separation

852 SPRING TIME by Bob Lubbers

ACROSS
1 Craze
4 DEA agent
8 Of an extremity
13 George's brother
14 Second name?
16 Too big
17 Do cable work, in a way
19 Hostess Perle
20 Set afire
21 1996 or 2004
23 __ "Fatha" Hines
25 Hoopsters' grp.
26 Swing-era tune
31 Chart
32 Inventor or Rubik
33 Pentateuchs
36 Tower town
38 New Deal agcy.
40 Oklahoma Indian
41 Catchphrase
44 "__ corny . . ."
47 Seine spot
48 Like some books
51 Gal of song
52 Cologne, to Kohl
53 Fly low
58 Tiller attachment
62 Foreign
63 Pub hanging
65 Royal headgear
66 The Man of __ (Superman)
67 Edmond O'Brien film
68 Maid of the comics
69 "Smooth Operator" singer
70 Dolt

DOWN
1 Pacific island group
2 Cut __ (dance)
3 __ *Yankees*
4 Connors contemporary
5 Tailor, often
6 Inlet
7 Sagan or Reiner
8 __ Beach, FL
9 Mind
10 __ majesté
11 Movie terrier
12 Raise up
15 Dictation pro
18 Berth place
22 Border on
24 Redgrave or Fontanne
26 Hoosegow
27 __ Downs
28 __ acid (antiseptic)
29 __-Magnon
30 Dine at home
31 GI cops
34 Ship's storage area
35 Get the point
37 Have __ at (try)
39 Out of control
42 Weapons cache
43 Beery or Webster
45 Cut short
46 Capable of liquefaction
49 Clumsy ones
50 Take apart
53 Possess, old-style
54 Director Kazan
55 Former Mexican president
56 *Pretty Woman* star
57 New England team, for short
59 Art genre
60 Valentine archer
61 Vitamin abbr.
64 Actor Stephen

853 OUCH! by Randolph Ross

ACROSS

1 __ Romeo
5 1985 Glenn Close film
10 Sloppy spot
13 Discourage
15 Cake covering
16 *Padre's hermano*
17 Not-too-subtle persuasion
19 Pipe joint
20 Attendance
21 Up the __ (in trouble)
23 Cobb and Hardin
24 Flightless bird
25 For two
26 Very, very funny
31 One of your contacts
33 Pilot's pace
34 Composer Edouard
35 Director Lubitsch
37 Beliefs
38 Diamond size
40 Division word
41 Physically taxing
44 Miss Trueheart
45 Addams' cousin
46 Southern constellation
49 *Saturday Night Live* announcer
51 Ninja, e.g.
53 "How was __ know?"
54 Very tasty
57 Scam
58 Band together
59 Josh
60 GIs' duties
61 Unspoken
62 Cabinet dept.

DOWN

1 Modify
2 Artist/musician Rivers
3 Stews
4 Military insects?
5 Goof
6 Entr'__
7 Clock numeral
8 Tavern
9 Breakfast holders
10 With the most nerve
11 Mah-jongg piece
12 Egg part
14 Middle-schoolers
18 "I've Got the Music __"
22 Performing like Ice-T
25 Pointed weapon
26 Criticized
27 December temp
28 Fleur-de-__
29 Captain of the *Nautilus*
30 Mdse.
31 Lang of *Smallville*
32 Atomic orbiters
34 Tennis tactic
35 Blows the play
36 Comedienne Charlotte
39 Smirnoff rival
40 Whole
42 Fate
43 "__ boy!"
46 Korean, for one
47 Dentist's order
48 Tick off
49 Play the banjo
50 Over
51 Italian wine area
52 __-ball (arcade game)
55 Actress Claire
56 Film, to *Variety*

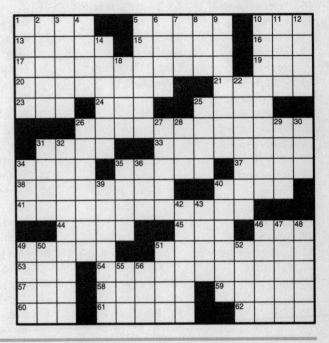

854 UNCOMMONWEALTH by Mary M. Murdoch

ACROSS

1 Swedish rock foursome
5 Loses out to gravity
9 Lobbying grps.
13 Frame of mind
14 Falling sound
15 Wall hanging
16 Contribute communally
17 Distaste, and then some
18 Beyond the limit
19 Parts of Westminster?
22 Casey or Cartwright
23 Org. acid
24 Hobo, for short
27 Line of rotation
30 Available
35 Alternatively called
37 Stadium section
39 Classical theaters
40 Air Canada fleet?
43 Porcine plaint
44 Trousers irritant?
45 Head for the J.P.
46 Delay
48 Frat party
50 Mid.
51 __ Claire, WI
53 Insolence
55 Cardiff art?
62 Either star of *Six Weeks*
63 Met music
64 Wheel holder
66 Under protection
67 __-bitty
68 Ardency
69 Numerical suffix
70 "Touch Me in the Morning" singer
71 Dangerous snakes

DOWN

1 Fuse word
2 Insensitive one
3 Insensitive one
4 Groucho's specialty
5 Exemplar of mystery
6 Word of regret
7 Barbarian
8 Broccoli bit
9 Nudnik
10 Pay to play
11 Mongrels
12 Exercise establishment
15 Korean port
20 Ride
21 Encircle
24 It's a gas
25 Kate's mate
26 King-size
28 Pour __ (exert oneself)
29 Separates
31 Diamond, once
32 Improvised
33 Acted rashly
34 Debussy masterpiece
36 "Diana" singer
38 Dawnward
41 Peace Prize sharer of '78
42 Aqua __ (powerful acid)
47 Avoid expiration
49 Irving Berlin standard
52 Carrier's ex-name
54 Shopping mall
55 Southern bread
56 One way to learn
57 Fe
58 "__ take arms . . ."
59 Things to throw
60 Marks a ballot
61 Open-handed treatment
62 Engr.'s sch.
65 Right-angle shapes

855 THE BOND MARKET by A.J. Santora

ACROSS

1 Abundance
4 Catch __ (misstroke)
9 Not together
14 Barbarian
15 Bond player
16 Actress Laurie
17 Authentic works
19 Palindrome center
20 Schlep
21 Scornful one
23 Tarmac area
25 Disconnected
29 Garden bush
32 MTV figure
33 Sweet stuff
36 Fume
37 Bond player
39 Truck
41 Ionian strait
42 Loosey-goosey
44 Fall guys
48 Enlivens
51 Cinematic Hall
52 Bliss
55 Pas __ (ballet step)
56 Contest, e.g.
59 POWs
61 Oblivion
62 Non-pros
63 New Year in Nha Trang
64 Butterfly
65 Eagle nest
66 __-Cat (winter vehicle)

DOWN

1 Have a __ (try)
2 Old World expanse
3 Grieg dancer
4 "__ Blue?"
5 Bilks
6 Horse color?
7 Site for van Gogh
8 Hem in
9 For one
10 Bond player
11 Spring mo.
12 Dakota Indian
13 Cycle starter
18 Bond player
22 Italian city
24 Arndt song
26 ". . . beauty is __ forever"
27 Asian tongue
28 Segar surname
30 Dismal
31 Behold, to Cato
34 Comics caveman
35 Fastener
37 Egyptian port
38 Sundance's girlfriend
39 Uris title word
40 One __ time
43 War-zone area
45 Small arms
46 Actress Brennan
47 Takes care of
49 Of service
50 Philippine island
53 __-fry vegetables
54 Himalayan legend
56 Overhead rails
57 Through
58 Ambulance tech.
60 Whiskey type

856 FOOD PROCESSOR by Norma Steinberg

ACROSS

1 Police calls, for short
5 Bikini atoll event
10 "Yo! Ship!"
14 Masculine
15 Coupe de __
16 Inlet
17 ORBWINE
19 Sign of foreboding
20 Bachelor's last two words
21 Pontiac product
22 Mature married women
24 Garfield, e.g.
26 Stalin's predecessor
27 Western author Bret
29 Opening word?
33 Dear: It.
36 Pumping __
38 Zilch
39 "__ and away!"
40 Colorless gas
42 "Do __ others . . ."
43 As-needed helpers
45 Ms. Hepburn, familiarly
46 Bus. letter abbr.
47 Kicks out
49 Raises
51 Passé
53 To have and __
57 Satchmo's instrument
60 Genetic building block
61 Born
62 Kennedy matriarch
63 SEAP
66 Think-tank output
67 Smells
68 Sunbathe
69 Heckler
70 Broadway lights
71 British brews

DOWN

1 Scope
2 TV announcer Don
3 Flower
4 Make a blouse
5 Earhart, for one
6 Row of seats
7 Shade tree
8 Ghostbusters goo
9 Perot and Richards
10 CRONA
11 __ sapiens
12 Kitchen appliance
13 Compulsions
18 College sports grp.
23 Neckwear
25 TEAM
26 Composer Bernstein
28 Hike
30 Mom's sister
31 Actor Dillon
32 British prep school
33 Adorable
34 Pinnacle
35 Beef cut
37 Memo
41 It often counts
44 Strike
48 Tread
50 Highway
52 Musical form
54 Actor Ryan
55 Renter's paper
56 Office furniture
57 Stumble
58 Went on horseback
59 Employs
60 Jurassic Park actress Laura
64 Kanga's son
65 Cops' org.

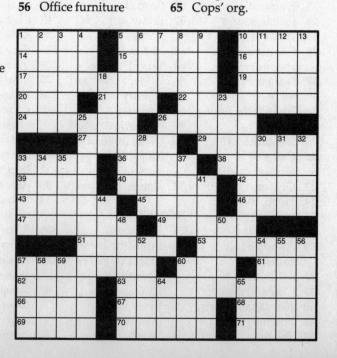

857 QUADRUPLE U by Randolph Ross

ACROSS

1 Kramden's co-workers
7 "Hey you!"
11 Wrestling surface
14 Prompt
15 Lotion additive
16 *Exodus* protagonist
17 Former Bay State governor
19 "__ Get By" (1928 song)
20 Road divider
21 Full
23 Hindu honorific
26 Northern herder
28 Playing with a full deck
29 1940 election loser
34 Protects
35 Negative vote
36 Bouncer's order
37 Vacuum tube
42 H.S. organization
44 Of interest to Richter
45 Columnist of the '30s
49 Evening in Roma
50 Horse control
51 Social Register word
52 Does damage to
54 Kind of punch
58 Bar opener
59 *Leaves of Grass* poet
64 Original
65 Petri dish contents
66 Camden Yards player
67 Overhead trains
68 Deuce beater
69 Made sloppy

DOWN

1 Present topper
2 Verse starter
3 Cardinal insignia
4 Tiny lengths
5 Emanate
6 At hand
7 Tropical fruit tree
8 Stay in bed late
9 Note before la
10 Danson and Williams
11 Rum cocktail
12 Francis of *What's My Line?*
13 Spanish squiggle
18 Hayley or Donna
22 Invite
23 Gulp of gin
24 Actor Auberjonois
25 Part of MIT
27 Typewriter roller
30 Pair
31 Blow one's top
32 Missive
33 Melody's words
38 "Sort of" suffix
39 Augury
40 Roy's mate
41 *Vogue* rival
43 Circles of color
44 Strength
45 Slimy sort
46 Quiver fill
47 Fugitive's flight
48 Freezing
49 Polish
53 Ruth's sultanate
55 Shoe man McAn
56 Set up a stereo
57 Inventor Elisha
60 Cabinet dept.
61 Jan. and Dec.
62 Beer relative
63 Buntline or Beatty

858 FACE THE MUSIC by Dean Niles

ACROSS

1 Acorn : oak :: bulb : __
6 Overhead curve
10 Make puffs?
14 Blazing
15 Actress __ Flynn Boyle
16 Stew
17 Nadir
19 Cathay visitor
20 Question
21 The Isleys, for short
22 What's next
24 __ *Sylphides*
25 "__, Brute?"
26 Diving birds
30 Example
34 Gads about
35 Heavyweight Max
36 Greek philosopher
37 Largest continent
38 Becomes dim
39 Nothing whatsoever
40 Jr.-year exam
41 Down with, in Dijon
42 Board
43 Suggested
45 Minor mayhem
46 Coal scuttles
47 Tittle
48 Certain Arab
51 Cad
52 Coll. degrees
55 At any time
56 Self-analyze
59 One of a nautical trio
60 Like some tales
61 Part
62 Feed, as pigs
63 Don't go
64 Filled up

DOWN

1 Scarlett's home
2 Sky sights
3 Whup
4 Bug
5 Bamm Bamm's playmate
6 Some voices
7 "Phooey!"
8 __-Magnon
9 Pet rodents
10 Surprise tests
11 Expos manager Felipe
12 Longest river
13 Saw or file
18 Mine extracts
23 And so on: Abbr.
25 Fencing implements
26 Represent, in a way
27 Martini & __
28 Perrier rival
29 Escape blame
30 Mubarak predecessor
31 Joins
32 Sign up
33 Not a soul
35 Raisiny cakes
38 Trend followers
42 Cowardly
44 Forever and a day
45 Pedal extremities
47 __ Roll Morton
48 Hankerings
49 Wicked
50 *Send __ Flowers*
51 Hippy dance
52 Spoiled kid
53 Lot size, often
54 Cast off
57 Breakfast grain
58 "Caught you!"

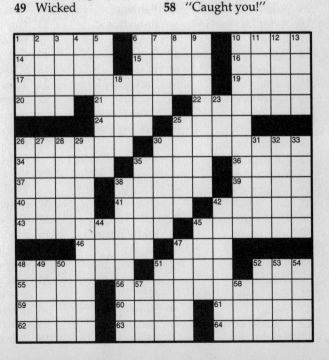

859   CARDINAL FILMS by Wayne R. Williams

ACROSS
1 Deli sandwich
4 Madagascar primate
9 Unit of capacitance
14 "__ la la!"
15 __ acids
16 Spring (from)
17 Ava Gardner movie
20 Stout: Fr.
21 All other drivers?
22 Aid in crime
23 Clique
25 Dog classes
28 Poker take
29 European fish
31 __ vs. Wade
32 Robert Mitchum movie
37 Abu Dhabi leader
38 Racing world
39 Woodward film, with *The*
46 Dander
47 Oenone's husband
48 Ducats
49 Sticky situations
53 Digit on the line
54 Hit the road
55 Gas figure
57 "__ Lisa"
58 Richard Barthelmess movie
63 Actress Taylor
64 Paris underground
65 Fruit drink
66 Viper
67 Dough
68 "No way!"

DOWN
1 Surprising word
2 Robin's weapon
3 Bit of legalese
4 Asian nation
5 Cassowary kin
6 O.T. book
7 Do a buckboard chore
8 Cross
9 Tend towards
10 Craggy crest
11 Kitchen helpers
12 Sun Devils sch.
13 Some, on the Somme
18 Littl'un
19 Kind lie
22 Appropriate
23 Line of a letter
24 Capture
26 O'Brien or Quaid movie
27 Put in stitches
29 Weighty reading
30 Word form for "different"
33 Cost to participate
34 "Wake Up Little __"
35 God of love
36 Flunk letter
39 McCarver or Allen
40 Otto I's realm: Abbr.
41 Echo
42 Banquet pro
43 Old-school-tie guy
44 Italian Baroque master
45 Devonshire river
50 Rocky debris
51 Clear sky
52 __ Tomé
54 South Korean soldier
56 Unfeeling
57 Ambiance
58 Lobster __ Diavolo
59 Brit. ref.
60 Sault __ Marie, MI
61 __ la la
62 Latin law

860   CAPITAL GANG by Bob Lubbers

ACROSS
1 Pet rocks and pogs
5 Chest muscles
9 Aesopian output
14 Soothing plant
15 Algerian port
16 Actor Leon
17 Lease
18 Painter of Catalan landscapes
19 Certain tides
20 Venezuelan dunkers?
23 Giant giant
24 Seahawks' turf
25 RR depot
28 Part of A&P
29 Dinghy direction
31 Se __ español
34 Husky group
37 Irish island group
38 Norwegian freighter?
41 Kick target
42 Swell
43 Loamy deposit
44 Razz maker
46 Letter enc.
47 Flag, e.g.: Abbr.
48 Stuffed pasta
52 Famous Pharaoh
55 Irish insurance?
58 Panama palindrome start
60 Singer Adams
61 Evil Idi
62 Partaken of
63 Oxidize
64 Cast starter
65 Della or Pee Wee
66 Loses moisture, perhaps
67 Mine finds

DOWN
1 Wells' partner
2 Awake
3 Oscar-winner for *Goodbye, Mr. Chips*
4 Horologist Thomas
5 Saddle horn
6 Susan on *All My Children*
7 Jeweler's weight
8 Short shot
9 *Picket* __
10 Zone
11 Unpretentious restaurant
12 Cut off
13 Raised trains
21 Take __ at (try)
22 Memorable mission
26 Part of TWA
27 Freud and Held
28 "__ the Santa Fe Trail"
30 Resort lake
31 Trebek and Sajak
32 "Suddenly __ rang out"
33 Willis/Basinger movie
34 Skater Babilonia
35 Catchall abbr.
36 Devoured
39 McEnroe's ex
40 Aver
45 Polished
46 Icy falls
49 Contenders
50 __ time (eventually)
51 Lyric poet
52 Oven gadget
53 Useful
54 Actress Daly et al.
56 French article
57 SEATO counterpart
58 __ Lingus
59 Marsh or Clarke

AUTO SUGGESTION by Raymond Hamel

ACROSS

1 Withdraw (from)
5 Manitoba Indian
9 Noted chef
14 Wagner role
15 Sham
16 Float in the air
17 Tibetan monk
18 Practicality
20 Car-lot cost
22 Soup warmer
23 One __ time (singly)
24 Batting avg. figure
27 Seal baby
30 Like eyes of fury
32 Commuters' crush time
36 Desert stop
37 Sudden wind
38 Goatlike antelope
40 First name in Solidarity
41 Diarist Nin
43 Car-value reference
45 Holocaust event
47 Blood fluids
48 Compass pt.
49 __ Tse-tung
51 Northern native
56 Minor car mishap
59 Caroline Islands' region
62 Sow one's wild __
63 Dress smartly
64 Soft mineral
65 "Comin' __ the Rye"
66 Hollow stone
67 Mope
68 Movie trailer promise

DOWN

1 From Cardiff
2 Sister of Clio
3 Let on
4 Civil-rights org.
5 Fast felines
6 Crowd sound
7 Western Wyatt
8 Left over
9 Home of the *Sun-Times*
10 Sharpen
11 "__ Gotta Be Me"
12 Brown or Paul
13 AMA members
19 __ snag (get stuck)
21 Former Big Apple mayor
24 Promenade
25 Mini-river
26 Hart's former cohost
28 Darrow client of 1924
29 Rolls up a flag
31 Film composer Schifrin
32 Like a multiclause sentence
33 Practice
34 Move about
35 Cad
37 Stare open-mouthed
39 Returnees' phrase
42 "__ to Watch Over Me"
44 Headquarters
46 Jazz flutist Herbie
50 Playwright Clifford
52 Ship-speed measure
53 Sun Valley location
54 Paris subway
55 Bean or Welles
56 Wilma's hubby
57 One of Rebekah's sons
58 Moonscape feature
59 EPA figure
60 Intense anger
61 *Fortune* subject: Abbr.

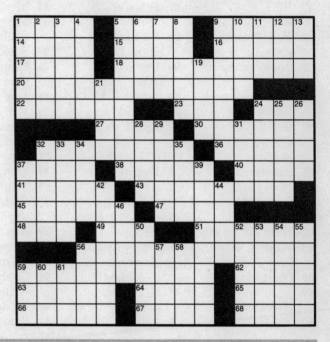

LITERARY SETTING by Dean Niles

ACROSS

1 Infinitive for Hamlet
5 Runs on at the mouth
10 __ *Timberlane* (Lewis novel)
14 Figurine stone
15 "__ the Riveter"
16 Go __ (contend)
17 Westheimer or Roman
18 Bring toward fruition
19 Pro __ (proportionally)
20 Workplace agcy.
21 A cinch
23 Top-drawer
25 Wanton looks
26 Planetary path
28 Spicy stew
32 *60 Minutes* commentator
34 Rescue
35 40 winks
38 Air dirtier
39 More than enough
41 '50s crooner
42 Acorn source
43 *The Bridge on the River __*
44 Jitters
46 Glass ingredient
48 Lilliputian
49 Gradient
52 Outspoken
54 Informed
58 Jazzman Jackson
61 "__ Love Her"
62 Raison __
63 Actress Adams
64 "Don't dele!"
65 That is: Lat.
66 Painter Magritte
67 __ d'oeuvres
68 Musical sounds
69 Asian oxen

DOWN

1 Bull, in the ring
2 Burden
3 Scrupulously
4 Letting go, in a way
5 Leaf of a flower
6 Pulitzer cartoonist Dick
7 __ spumante
8 Sci. subject
9 Transport
10 Floor cover
11 __ *of Two Cities*
12 Indian lute
13 Hangs around
22 Swing around on an axis
24 Rock suffix
26 Thereabouts
27 *Italia* city
29 Meat garnish
30 "My __ Sal"
31 Kiln
33 Ketch cousin
35 Brainstorm
36 Prayer word
37 Nosegay
40 __ tai (cocktail)
41 Butter plant
43 Ukraine capital
45 Handy abbr.
46 Gymnast's moves
47 Ill-disposed
49 How buckling may begin
50 Slowly, to Solti
51 More mature
53 *Waiting For Lefty* playwright
55 Prepare for publication
56 Try again
57 Submachine gun
59 Hookup
60 Shirts seen in summer

863 COLOR ME . . . by Shirley Soloway

ACROSS
1 "__ Doll"
6 Picnic pests
10 Tiptop
14 Actress Massey
15 Asta's mistress
16 Tennis ace Lendl
17 RED
20 Rainproof cover
21 In its present state
22 Toolbox items
23 Tax mo.
25 How some food is ordered
27 BLUE
34 Comedienne Merkel
35 Pale-faced
36 More costly
38 Secluded hollow
40 A, in Bonn
42 *Pinta's* sister ship
43 Western watering hole
46 Short snoozes
49 __ *Hollywood* (Fox film)
50 YELLOW
53 Actress Jurado
54 Whitney or Wallach
55 Lock holder
57 Misplace
60 Simplicity
64 GREEN
67 Felipe or Moises
68 "Walk a Mile __ Shoes"
69 Dodger Pee Wee
70 Julep additive
71 "Got it!"
72 Knight wear

DOWN
1 Prepare flour
2 Actress Nazimova
3 Guided trip
4 Harness
5 Slangy refusal
6 Companion of ifs & buts
7 "__ lay me down . . ."
8 *Valse __*
9 Pulled up a chair
10 Earhart, e.g.
11 Gem shape
12 Henpecks
13 Chemical suffix
18 Merits
19 The __, Holland
24 Singer Zadora
26 Unusual
27 They fizzle
28 *Love Story* star
29 Half a WA city
30 Common title starter
31 Taking off
32 Lion group
33 Madrid mister
37 Slightly improper
39 Prevents access
41 Make a collar
44 Giraffe's relative
45 NCAA rival
47 Primp
48 Pitcher Maglie
51 Hosiery
52 TV watcher
55 Word form for "sun"
56 English waterway
58 "Dream a Little Dream __"
59 __ terrier
61 Attention-getter
62 Mediocre
63 Water holder
64 Beaver's project
65 MIV halved
66 Mouths: Lat.

864 CONSTRUCTION ZONE by Bob Lubbers

ACROSS
1 Director Frank
6 Michelangelo work
11 Fam. member
14 Distiller Walker
15 Hoops star Shaquille
16 Compass pt.
17 Contractor's favorite sitcom?
19 Part of USSR
20 End
21 Olympian Zaharias
22 Fuss
24 Contractor's favorite film?
28 Rich cakes
31 Madden's old team
32 Stage salesman
33 Dens
35 Contractor's favorite couple?
40 Foundry material
41 Track shapes
43 Guitar cousin
47 Posts via computer
48 Siding contractor's tests?
51 "Unforgettable" name
52 Actress Suzy
53 Marsh plant
56 Building site
57 Contractor's favorite song?
62 French article
63 Battery terminal
64 Emits light beams
65 Dawn goddess
66 Bennett and Randall
67 Tree houses

DOWN
1 Part of a dance
2 Assist
3 In a perfunctory manner
4 Physics Nobelist
5 So be it
6 French trench warrior
7 Passage to the sea
8 Sea shocker
9 Randy's skating partner
10 Gore and Green
11 Roll topping
12 Weather line
13 Natural throws
18 Openings
21 Physique, for short
22 Part of NATO
23 Destiny
25 Court action
26 Tall tale
27 Sagacity
29 Second X?
30 Cloisonné
33 Chicle source
34 *I __ Camera*
36 Strike out
37 A Gabor sister
38 Overflowing pride
39 Queen of scat
42 JFK arrival
43 Heat-loss measurement
44 Geisha garb
45 Weds
46 Fleur-de-__
47 Spanish compass point
49 Sourish
50 Ship's officers
54 Potter's oven
55 "*Dies __*"
57 Hood's heater
58 Important numero
59 __ sequitur
60 Seine
61 Part of a dollar sign

865   MUSICAL NUMBERS by A.J. Santora

ACROSS

1 Man-mouse link
4 Gets off the fence
8 Conflict
14 Debussy's sea
15 Fine-edged
16 Western dam
17 Justice Fortas
18 Janis Ian tune
20 Singer Ferlin
22 Sign of summer
23 Tobacco ovens
24 Part of SEATO
25 Justify
27 Pictures of health?
29 Baby place of rhyme
33 Office recorder
34 Sandra of *Gidget*
35 New Deal org.
36 Beatles '67 tune
40 __ *Haw*
41 __ *a Fugitive From a Chain Gang*
42 Warms up
43 Giving the hook
46 __ Domingo
47 Swallows
49 Fissionable material
52 Jean of *Upstairs, Downstairs*
55 Weaken
56 Work too hard
57 Jimmy Savo tune
60 Easter starter
61 Beer hall
62 Ho do
63 Band job
64 __ Island, NY
65 Alternatively
66 Adorer's poem

DOWN

1 Home of Ak-Sar-Ben Coliseum
2 Picture puzzle
3 "You __" (*Sound of Music* tune)
4 Sanction
5 Ugly mood
6 Electrical units
7 Disdainful look
8 __ *Done Him Wrong*
9 Second __ (nonpareil)
10 Take turns
11 Currier's partner
12 Tape measures
13 Fish-eating birds
19 Eddy
21 Valentine of TV
25 Last state in the roll call
26 Singer Franklin et al.
28 *Wheel of Fortune* purchase, often
30 "Takes __" (Pearl Bailey tune)
31 Composition
32 Duffer's dream
33 National park?
34 Not at all clear-cut
36 A question of motive
37 Most wise
38 Longing
39 *Attraction* or *Instinct* preceder
44 Destiny
45 "Psst!" follower
46 City on the Mississippi
48 Fur or fish
50 Egg-shaped
51 Bring together
52 Clever remarks
53 Veterinary school subj.
54 TV actress __ Rose
56 Swing around
58 Dancer Miller
59 Spanish article

866   FESTIVITIES by Eileen Lexau

ACROSS

1 Assign roles
5 Spanish appetizer
9 Ransacks
14 Regulation
15 Microwave, for one
16 Detach, in a way
17 Valhalla bigwig
18 "*Bei Mir __ Du Schön*"
19 "__ say more?"
20 Oenophile gathering
23 Bottom line
24 GI identification
25 Slangy agreement
27 Gat
31 Fights
34 Delighted mightily
38 Football play
39 Continental currency
40 Dress up
41 B&O et al.
42 Lawyers' burdens
43 Smelting leftover
44 Harvard rival
45 __ hooks (carton admonition)
46 Overdone publicity
47 R-month food
49 Entreat
51 Cowboys' ropes
56 Antipollution agcy.
58 Halloween gathering
62 Retiring Hollywood star
64 Word form for "equal"
65 Luau entertainment
66 Make a change
67 Ayatollah's land
68 Oil cartel
69 Senior member
70 Scheherazade offering
71 Smell awful

DOWN

1 Three may be one
2 TV element
3 Singapore __ (cocktail)
4 Belief
5 Trinidad and __
6 Budget rival
7 Nuisance
8 Not for
9 Fencing ploy
10 Song from *A Chorus Line*
11 New Year's Day gathering
12 Detergent brand
13 Bad temper
21 Not punctual
22 Russian denial
26 Geometry calculations
28 Apply perfume, perhaps
29 Shirley Temple feature
30 Beginning
32 Small songbird
33 Just okay
34 Bundle of laundry
35 Paris airport
36 Hollywood gathering
37 Ardent
42 Nobelist Marie
44 Spinning toy
48 Elegant fur
50 Oak-to-be
52 Detest
53 Brownish gray
54 Lane: Fr.
55 "Cut me some __!"
56 Major Hoople's oath
57 __ Alto, CA
59 Barbecue item
60 O'Hara home
61 Russia's __ Mountains
63 Good grade

867 TIGHT SPOTS by Ann Seidel

ACROSS
1 Shows approval
6 Water form
11 Medic
14 Automation fixture
15 Scarlett __
16 Three __ match
17 Like some celebs
19 Crowded area, in Britain
20 Tumult
21 *Crying Game* star Stephen
22 Author unknown: Abbr.
23 Suit feature
25 Treeless plain
26 Paycheck remainder
30 Indeed
31 Official seal
32 Bolivian city
34 __ up (gathered)
36 Impose (upon)
38 *Rocky and His Friends* dog
41 Best policy
43 Salad-oil bottle
44 Like the Grand Canyon
46 Mars or Mercury
48 Just __ (little bit)
49 Acts worried
50 Shed tears
52 Wounded
53 Keystone Konstable
54 Act like a baby?
59 Compass pt.
60 Hardly unsullied
62 *Norma* __
63 They're the pits
64 Broadcast
65 Big deer
66 '92 and '96 candidate
67 Weill's wife

DOWN
1 Brag
2 It conquers all
3 Biblical shepherd
4 Sweet wine
5 Author Danielle
6 Soak (up)
7 Walden visitor
8 Artist's aid
9 General location
10 Unhinged
11 Destitute
12 Early tie score
13 Is unable to
18 Medical photo
22 Geometry cousin
24 Name in Israeli politics
25 Redolent shrub
26 __-pitch softball
27 Actor Hunter
28 In trouble
29 Rank above knight
31 Sault __ Marie, Ont.
33 New Mexico Indians
35 *Heidi* author
37 Nov. follower
39 Govt. narcs
40 Acctg. benchmark
42 Missile type
44 Realm of influence
45 Relating to a motive
47 Greek letter
50 One who disguises
51 License plate sticker
53 Patella
55 Nobelist Wiesel
56 In shreds
57 Rocker Lewis
58 Icelandic epic
60 Letters on drug labels
61 Q-U filler

---

868 GOOD SPORTS by Bob Lubbers

ACROSS
1 Lodges
5 Table staple
9 Mr. Newhart
12 Tidy
13 Zone
14 Coup d'__
16 NFL battle-ground
18 Aboveboard
20 From __ Z
21 Newsstand
22 FDR's Interior Secretary
23 Ricky or Willie
25 __ Got a Secret
27 Ret. check distributor
28 __ the Red
29 German count
31 Mix
32 Conscious
35 Boca __, FL
37 Yachting prize
39 Plains tent
40 Prince Valiant's wife
41 Indian wrap
42 Zilch
44 Tough file
48 "So *that's* it!"
49 Pants-too-long guy
50 Tricky
52 Shangri-la land
54 Sun-dried brick
57 Fifth of CCLX
58 Toll stop
59 Baseball action site
61 Cake inscriber
62 Med. sch. subj.
63 Love god
64 Brunei coin
65 *All My* __ (Miller play)
66 That lady's

DOWN
1 Bonkers
2 Like "it"
3 City of *Italia*
4 *Jeanne d'Arc*, for one
5 Vaccine developer
6 Slangy suffix
7 Ayres and Grade
8 '27 film first
9 Refute
10 Of the ear
11 Catcher's nickname
15 Fits
17 Picture-palace chain
19 Despot
24 Shrimp __
26 Poem part
29 Downhill runner
30 Pie nut
31 Washington portraitist
33 Like Willie Winkie
34 Boxing center
36 Play segment
37 Fitness exercises
38 Pub draw
39 *Bounty* stop
41 Topers
43 Western Indians
45 On fire
46 Wooer
47 Handy grabbers
49 Violin virtuoso Isaac
50 Helps in a crime
51 Agt.
53 Gen. Robert __
55 "The king can __ wrong"
56 Mideast sultanate
60 __-di-dah

869 DUTCH TREAT by Dean Niles

ACROSS
1 Chess act
5 Remove a no-no
10 Impersonated
14 Russian river
15 Not mainstream
16 Field mouse
17 Word from the Dutch for "pirate"
19 Church recess
20 Sock part
21 Poker contribution
22 Painter Johns
24 Firmly fixed
26 Underdeveloped
27 Travel stops
30 Crow call
33 Really the pits
36 __ at first sight
37 Venetian magistrate
38 Sound of failure
39 Panatela, e.g.
40 Chilled
41 Unimportant
42 Egg cell
43 Earns
44 Night flier
45 Stays abed
47 Cisco Kid vehicle
49 Female warrior
53 Distracts
55 18-wheeler
57 Solemn vow
58 Sprees
59 Word from the Dutch for "tracts"
62 Tooth trauma
63 __ acids
64 Precious
65 Catch a snooze
66 Character in Wagner's *Ring*
67 Noble poem

DOWN
1 Out-of-uniform garb
2 Hunter constellation
3 Personal attendant
4 Actor Wallach
5 Tribute
6 Craving
7 Cigar end
8 Before
9 False witness
10 "Stop, matey!"
11 Word from the Dutch for "garbage"
12 Otherwise
13 Moose, for one
18 Trite
23 Response: Abbr.
25 Sidestep
26 Overhaul
28 Dickens hero
29 *Elle* rival
31 *Let Us Now Praise Famous Men* author
32 Says 57 Across
33 Prefix meaning "air"
34 Sigh of relief
35 Word from the Dutch for "leaves"
37 Ross or Spencer
39 Picnic dish
43 Make fun of
45 Sault __ Marie, MI
46 Biblical longhair
48 Selling point
50 Close, in a way
51 "__ a Nightingale"
52 Proboscides
53 Partly open
54 Mugger deterrent
55 Hissy fit
56 Pulitzer-winner Ferber
60 Latin lover's word
61 Hole in one

870 WHO'S ZOO by Robert H. Wolfe

ACROSS
1 Fernando of filmdom
6 Faux pas
11 Slangy suffix
14 Like a lot
15 Like lettuce
16 Postman's Creed word
17 Gelt
18 Feline monster?
20 Dealt in
22 Lariat loop
23 Premeditate
25 Plumbing problems
28 Pieces of 11?
29 Chem room
30 Sonnets' endings
32 Short time?
33 Pour __ troubled waters
35 Reacts to rudeness
37 Not C.O.D.
40 Apprentice
44 They may be biased
46 Ultimate aim
47 Valueless talk
50 Ointment ingredient
53 "It __" ("Who's there?" response)
54 Uninteresting
56 Scarecrow's stuffing
57 Iron and Stone
58 Gave (out)
60 Low-pressure area
62 Teddy Roosevelt's dog?
65 Got snoopy
68 Linguist's suffix
69 High-interest activity
70 Preposterous
71 Rev.'s remarks
72 Sharon of *Cagney and Lacey*
73 Polk's predecessor

DOWN
1 Sudden flight
2 Bustle
3 Like a bovine feast?
4 "Get Happy" composer
5 Penn name
6 Gantry et al.
7 Corrects twice
8 Uncooked
9 Frequently, in verse
10 Fastballer Nolan
11 Like some dips
12 Not so secure
13 Matt Dillon portrayer
19 Excessively
21 White House initials
23 "Splat!" kin
24 Hideout
26 Throw stones at
27 Have the lead
30 Slow mover
31 NATO member
34 Make a choice
36 Imogene's colleague
38 Gershwin and Levin
39 Bend a fender
41 Like a horse with hay fever?
42 Calm state
43 Yale students
45 Postal workers
47 San Diego baseballers
48 Stimulate
49 Filch
51 Fine and Bird
52 __ Jima
55 Telephonic 3
57 Defeated feeling?
59 Doctor's prescription
61 Army group
63 St. Kitts, e.g.
64 Coming
66 Compass pt.
67 __ *Stern* (German mag)

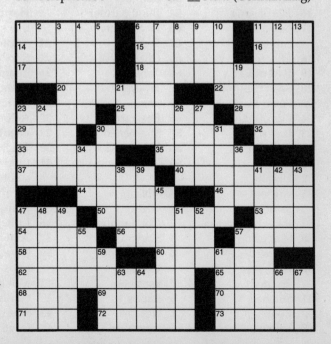

871 OUT ON A LIMB by Norma Steinberg

ACROSS
1 With it
5 Comic Martin
10 Bambi, for one
14 Farmer's measurement
15 British royal house
16 Words of understanding
17 Lent event
19 Spiffy
20 They sang "Evil Woman"
21 Printer's buy
22 Wild cats
24 Watering hole
26 Paratrooper's need
27 Janet or Vivien
29 Stephen King's genre
33 Baby's bed
36 Shem's dad
38 Incline
39 Trademark
40 Al and Tipper
42 Largest continent
43 Swears to
45 Discharge a gun
46 Retain
47 Became one
49 Make a speech
51 Move to stimuli
53 Famous TV street
57 WWII battle site
60 Hither and __
61 Kernel holder
62 Entreaty
63 Gardener's digit
66 Charged atoms
67 Coffeehouse order
68 "Stop looking __!"
69 Head: Fr.
70 Heston role
71 Studier of Samoa

DOWN
1 French royal house
2 Florida city
3 Russian noble family
4 Moon-visit vehicle
5 Gorgeous
6 Thick piece
7 Unusual
8 Household pest
9 Audition
10 New York State region
11 ". . . against __ of troubles"
12 Have on
13 Takes home after taxes
18 Father
23 Southwestern Indians
25 Exertion
26 *Ben-Hur* vehicle
28 Make a mistake
30 Popular bloom
31 Sheriff Taylor's son
32 Harvest
33 Oyster kin
34 Wander
35 Composer Stravinsky
37 *Frau*'s husband
41 Experienced
44 Fortuneteller
48 Twist in the wind
50 Bivouac shelter
52 Reef material
54 Severe
55 Female parent
56 Diminished slowly
57 Barbecue part
58 Skin-cream ingredient
59 Gave temporarily
60 Abominable Snowman
64 Collective abbr.
65 Easter-season entrée

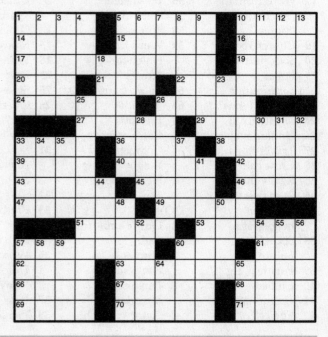

872 SPOOKY by Bob Lubbers

ACROSS
1 Kin of PDQ
5 Small weight
9 Twine fiber
14 Actress Teri
15 Vegas alternative
16 Isle of song
17 Norway's capital
18 Filly food
19 Part of BTUs
20 Secret author
23 Actor Stephen
24 Fits of pique
25 Is of use
27 Squatter
30 Rid
32 Urchin
33 Ancient ascetic
35 Joke response
38 Claims on property
40 All __ up (excited)
41 Stitched
42 Robt. __
43 Sullen
45 Part of "to be"
46 Ridicule
48 __ words (pun)
50 Stashed
52 Marsh and West
53 Summer quaff
54 Blind partner
60 Florida city
62 Press
63 Chess piece
64 Tabernacle group
65 Snout
66 Pot starter
67 Sharpened
68 Mimicked
69 Military meal

DOWN
1 Eager
2 Obi, for one
3 Singer Guthrie
4 Relative of "Skoal!"
5 Farmers
6 Raises
7 Not pro
8 Nearly all
9 Winding turn
10 Writer Fleming
11 Kidnap
12 Russian cooperative
13 Bonet and Hartman Black
21 Kilmer poem
22 Roof edge
26 Tennis great Arthur
27 African river
28 Actor Jannings
29 Leadfoot
30 Tractor maker
31 Involved with, as a hobby
34 Wearing pumps
36 Protagonist
37 Arabian gulf
39 On a __-to-know basis
41 Monica of tennis
43 Short skirt
44 Gave rise to
47 Lost-and-found offering
49 Guru's retreat
50 Concoct, as a plan
51 Potato type
52 Elk cousin
55 Ship of 1492
56 Let fall
57 Tops
58 Tiny circles
59 Supplements, with "out"
61 Tart kin

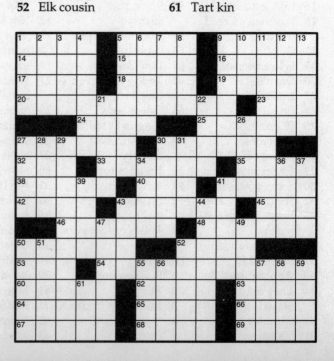

873 NO BIG DEAL by Dean Niles

ACROSS

1 Authority
6 Little terror
10 Fort Peck and Hoover
14 Hit hard
15 Architect Saarinen
16 Fuel cartel
17 Got in shape
18 Singer Barbara Mc__
19 "Look at me!"
20 Like Clark Kent
23 Curly's brother
26 Go by
27 Blood lines
28 Dump
30 Fusses
31 Slow sort
34 S&L device
37 Low joint
38 "Hail!"
39 Skin moisturizer
40 "__ out!" (ump's call)
41 Fictional detective
45 Creamy cheese
46 Literally, "my masters"
47 Operation
50 Diplomatic trait
52 Distinctly unfriendly
53 Like some police
56 Wound up
57 Depose
58 __ à clef
62 Eagle of the sea
63 Killer whale
64 Social stratum
65 The Grateful __
66 "Calico Pie" poet
67 Nodded off

DOWN

1 JFK arrival
2 Latin lover's word
3 That place
4 Pipe part
5 Like a tragic Greek king
6 Shows flexibility
7 Paper measures
8 50 Down selection
9 Violent weather
10 They care too much
11 Separate
12 Euripides play
13 A whole bunch
21 Put on cargo
22 High time
23 Like some deer
24 Cat-__-tails
25 Mr. Fudd
29 "To __ their golden eyes": Shak.
30 Part of ACLU
32 Mail enc.
33 College climber?
34 Provide an excuse
35 Picker-upper
36 Unkempt
39 Priestly vestment
41 Land of the Shannon
42 Chill out, in a way
43 Roguish
44 __ down (diluted)
45 Prepared the hook
47 Gorky Park director
48 Distress signal
49 Creatures of a region
50 Puccini favorite
51 Oil from petals
54 Draw hither
55 Without accompaniment
59 Les __ (musical's nickname)
60 Took in
61 Actor Beatty

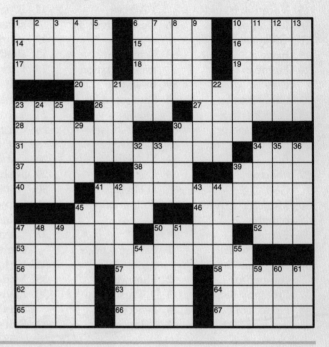

874 SPOONERISMS by Shirley Soloway

ACROSS

1 RBI, e.g.
5 Caesar's partner
9 Fall
14 German auto
15 __ Well That . . .
16 City of Light, in song
17 Volcanic matter
18 Blind unit
19 Williams of Happy Days
20 Witnesses injustice?
23 __ dish (lab container)
24 Japanese sash
25 West of Hollywood
28 Trig functions
31 Donny or Marie
33 Monk's title
36 What the caught fish did?
38 NY university
40 Actress Carrere
41 Perry's creator
42 Opposes fabrication?
47 Moray
48 Character actor Cook
49 Banks or Ford
51 Compass pt.
52 Levin of lit
54 Luther or Stella
57 Rate one's household help?
61 Calms down
64 Softening agent
65 MacDonald's costar
66 Nautical shout
67 Skirt style
68 Latvian capital
69 Small-minded
70 Appear
71 Observed

DOWN

1 Impudence
2 Spring bloom
3 Wise saying
4 Robin Hood: Men in __
5 Oleg of design
6 Ceramic pot
7 Talon
8 Jetsons' dog
9 Taxco tongue
10 Ache
11 Tax org.
12 Summer sign
13 Mr. Deighton
21 Former NY paper
22 Mitch Miller's instrument
25 Onetime James Bond portrayer
26 Place for a bracelet
27 Defunct car
29 Songstress James
30 Fence access
32 Miney follower
33 Marching instruments
34 Stirs up
35 Actress Dickinson
37 It's over your head
39 Expressions of pleasure
43 Dry-throated
44 Two Mules for Sister __
45 Site of Disneyland
46 Astronaut Sally
50 Rice and Gantry
53 Jefferson's predecessor
55 "__ Was a Lady" (Porter tune)
56 Mountain crest
57 Adventure story
58 Nobelist Wiesel
59 Musical quality
60 Cannon of films
61 Faucet
62 St. crosser
63 Welcoming item

875 SOUND EFFECTS by Randolph Ross

ACROSS
1 Old city
5 Harness race
9 The __ Kid (Western hero)
14 Tied
15 Vacation island
16 Jordan's capital
17 Great work
19 Extra
20 Home of the Braves
21 Other names
23 Let him do it
24 Assure victory
25 Barry Levinson film
27 "Nearer, My God, __"
30 More recently bought
33 Earned
35 Agree (with)
36 AP's erstwhile competitor
37 Pro-shop display
40 Up to, poetically
41 For fear that
43 Wallach and Lilly
44 Overhead
46 Looked impolitely
48 Hebrew month
50 Treating meat
52 Thirty in 1 Across
56 Destructive wind
58 Temporary transportation
59 Byways
60 Sources of loud music
62 *Tante*'s mate
63 Table light
64 Melody
65 Uncovered
66 H H H
67 Ballpark figs.

DOWN
1 Pack groceries again
2 Elliptical
3 __ Park, NJ
4 Fencer's cry
5 Letterman list
6 Punjab prince
7 Discoverer's remark
8 Cylindrically shaped
9 __ *Royale*
10 Has an effect on
11 Broadway successes
12 Worry
13 Wallet fillers
18 Loosen one's belt
22 Soda quantity
24 Yen
26 Czech runner Zatopek
28 Correct copy
29 Sushi serving
30 Not in effect
31 Rapier's relative
32 Uncalled-for commentary
34 He loved Lucy
38 Made over
39 Egyptian amulet
42 Roll along
45 Musically monotonous Johnny
47 Deleted electronically
49 Jazz dances
51 High-minded
53 Link
54 Roman Catholic council site
55 Donkey's uncles?
56 Disney sci-fi film
57 Mrs. Chaplin
58 __ Linda, CA
61 Feedbag morsel

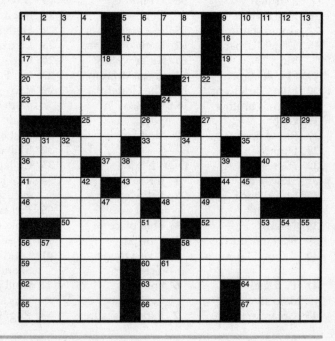

876 IN A HURRY by Randolph Ross

ACROSS
1 Groucho's brother
6 Sleeve cards?
10 U.S.' Civil War foe
13 __ a kind (unique)
14 Walks heavily
15 Leon Uris' *The* __
16 Good buddies
18 Lawyers' org.
19 Erstwhile interjection
20 Facilitated
21 Heart of the matter
22 Oregon city
24 Sworn promise
27 Log-cabin luxury
32 Visit Nod
35 *Archie* girl
36 "A mouse!"
37 Veep Agnew
39 *Wayne's World* interjection
40 Cause of overtime
43 Bald bird?
45 British dish
48 Ledger entry
49 Like live TV
53 WWII general
56 Folger's rival
58 UN agency
59 Three __ match
60 Mercury
63 Pince-__ (glasses)
64 Bored feeling
65 Sierra __
66 Red Sox great, for short
67 Faxed, perhaps
68 College protest

DOWN
1 Nicholson role
2 Author Nin
3 Bowler's button
4 Poker winnings
5 Propose as a sacrifice
6 Out of the wind
7 One who tacitly approves
8 Teacher's deg.
9 Sound of a slow leak
10 Burn slightly
11 Elephant boy of film
12 Comet competitor
14 Galileo was one
17 Picnic spoiler
21 Oland role
23 Mine find
25 Word form for "soil"
26 Company quorum
28 Like Harvard's walls
29 Triangle sound
30 Environmental sci.
31 Make the grade
32 Adam's third
33 *Star Wars* princess
34 Supplements, with "out"
37 Drenches
38 Shade of blue
41 Norman WWII battle site
42 YMCA cousin
43 Involves
44 Turkish VIP
46 Dips a donut
47 India and invisible
50 Whirl on one foot
51 Nicholas Gage book
52 Charles Van __ (*Quiz Show* character)
53 Oscar's cousin
54 Draftable status
55 Carmen McRae's specialty
57 Eight, in Ulm
60 TD passers
61 Glob ending
62 Hawaiian souvenir

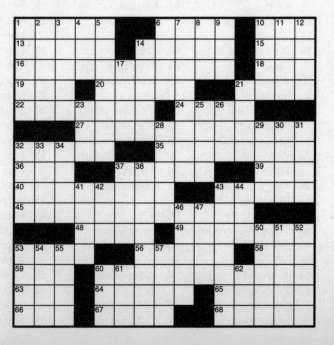

877 EEK! by Bob Lubbers

ACROSS

1 Photo finish
5 Pigeonhole
9 Height extender
14 Woody's son
15 Carson's predecessor
16 Kitchen tool
17 Wild tusker
18 Gam or Moreno
19 "What's in __?"
20 Singular method
23 Put to work
24 Star of *The Crying Game*
25 Apr. collector
26 Lariats
29 Hawaiian skirt material
32 Lyricist Gershwin
33 Fall guys
37 Left-handed compliment?
43 Paybacks
44 Fled
45 Actress Bara
47 Persian Gulf port
49 Purple Heart req.
50 Squealer
53 Like Abner
54 Where to buy old knickknacks
61 Start of a challenge
62 Fall guy
63 Shore bird
64 Caravan stop
65 Concerning
66 Actress Foch
67 Singer Lopez
68 Cong. meeting
69 C-__ (cable channel)

DOWN

1 *Jungle Book* star
2 Disney sci-fi film
3 Jai __
4 Rotational force
5 Wild time
6 Café au __
7 Western film
8 Vestige
9 Read a UPC
10 Pop singer Tennille
11 Natives of 47 Across
12 Madagascar primates
13 Ashes and oaks
21 Battleship letters
22 Scottish dish
26 Dolores Del __
27 Globe
28 Chum
30 Inactive: Abbr.
31 "__ was saying . . ."
33 Auto import
34 Afternoon drink
35 Fall mo.
36 Unrefined rock
38 Anger
39 Proof conclusion: Abbr.
40 "Alphabet Song" group
41 Former Mideast alliance: Abbr.
42 *Bambi* character
45 Kindling
46 Wayne film set in Africa
47 Nipped
48 Straightens
49 Belt area
51 Sponsorship
52 Steak choice
53 Guitar relatives
55 Modern Persia
56 Cunard ship, for short
57 Bireme needs
58 Bon mot
59 Arm bone
60 Ardor

878 TWICE-TOLD by Ann Seidel

ACROSS

1 Young salmon
6 Initials in a proof
9 Kind of finish
14 Vietnam capital
15 Suffix for press
16 "Hi, Don Ho!"
17 *Take Me __* (musical)
18 Feel feverish
19 Covers with frost
20 What a rebuker says
22 "Later!"
23 Holiday in 14 Across
24 Petty officer
25 Kingsmen song
30 Short distance
34 Barbeque garb
35 Go-__ (four-wheeler)
37 Protein synthesis letters
38 Transition
39 Hemispheric alliance
40 Leaves out
42 *Uno, due,* __
43 God of *España*
45 Swabbed
46 "Smooth Operator" singer
48 Words of comfort
50 Platform at the front
52 Derisive cry
53 Perfect situation
56 "I'll be!"
61 Homeric tome
62 __-relief
63 Chills-inducing
64 Petrol measure
65 Play about Capote
66 Science writer Carl
67 West Yorkshire town
68 Increases
69 Film technique

DOWN

1 Persian ruler
2 Tom or bull
3 __ about (around)
4 Single
5 Made fast
6 Book size
7 Great Lake
8 The first st.
9 *The Bells of St. __*
10 E.T.s
11 __ of the Unknown Soldier
12 He and she
13 Leisure
21 Lampreys
22 Afrikaner
24 Prejudice
25 Hangs in
26 *Faust*, e.g.
27 Pressed
28 Chit
29 Proclamation
31 Balderdash
32 Come on stage
33 __ deux (dance for two)
36 Ineffectual
39 Appreciative sounds
41 Speedometer letters
44 "Put __ writing!"
45 One of three squares
47 Artist Hopper
49 Indian monkey
51 Helpers
53 Mental power
54 First name in tennis
55 Marquee word
56 Twist
57 Prosperity
58 Therefore
59 Actor Neeson
60 TV host Jay
62 A/C unit

879   DUDS by Dean Niles

ACROSS

1 Action figure
5 Real hunk?
9 Butler on screen
14 Taj Mahal site
15 __ contendere
16 Above it all
17 Thongs
19 Chicago playwright
20 __ one (long odds)
21 *Northern Exposure* beast
23 Some ammo
24 Tijuana tribute
26 Apportions
28 Belgian surrealist
33 Ballpark fare
36 Flub it
37 Luck of the draw
39 *Pretty Woman* star
40 'supials
42 Singer John
43 Pizazz
44 "Your time __"
45 Offended the nose

47 Inc. equivalent
48 Teacher's protection
50 Lets out
52 "Life is but a __"
54 Lyricist Harburg
55 Wood tool
57 Cover story?
60 Large hooks
64 Bailiwicks
66 Trini Lopez tune
68 Musical Marx
69 Rachins or Rickman
70 Cad
71 Bound by oath
72 Celebrity
73 Speak out

DOWN

1 Nutty
2 Leer at
3 Land of the Shannon
4 *Jurassic Park* denizen

5 NBC staple
6 Weaving machine
7 Purina rival
8 Intimate, as a friend
9 Specialized cell
10 __ carte
11 Courtroom surprises
12 Leopold's co-defendant
13 Terrestrial newts
18 __ acid (B vitamin)
22 With great tranquility
25 Sublime
27 Border
28 Raise reason
29 Came up
30 Detonation point
31 Long story
32 Inscribe
34 Hold forth
35 Inclines
38 Coal product

41 Goad
46 Condescend
49 Use your head
51 Ho-hum feeling
53 Italian city
55 Oohs and __
56 Ring result

58 Composer Bartók
59 Muslim priest
61 Unfettered
62 Sense
63 Act like a bear?
65 Borrower's fig.
67 Indivisible

880   END TO END by Harvey Estes

ACROSS

1 Angora product
7 Sign of things to come
14 One who decorates
16 Turned aside
17 Circles of light
18 Cash back
19 Hoffman flick
21 MacLeish's "__ Poetica"
22 Chow down
23 Twitches
26 Capp and Capone
27 Common canines
32 Actress Gardner
33 Range infant
35 London landmark
36 Grasp at straws
39 Threat's last words
40 Nut's best part
41 Pedagogues' grp.
42 Steve's singing partner

43 Hula hoop, e.g.
44 Try to find
45 Palooka, for one
46 Long snake
48 The best
56 Putting in the pot
57 Where butts rest
58 Dollars-and-sense subject
59 Like surgeons' instruments
60 Rattled metallically
61 Puts up

DOWN

1 Truck name
2 What noses notice
3 Hour, to Hernando
4 Bouquets
5 Deeply felt
6 Arises on hind legs
7 Windy-day wear
8 In the open

9 "Queen of Country" McEntire
10 Soho streetcar
11 Cigar tip
12 __-do-well
13 NFL stat
15 Bible version: Abbr.
20 How I see me
23 Resort lake
24 Key material
25 Like Batman
26 Carte start
27 Catcher's glove
28 Word of disgust
29 Steakhouse offering
30 Mobile home?
31 Weaselly one
33 "Get off my __!"
34 Mature
35 Good-deed grp.
37 Actor Wallach
38 Beatty of *Homicide*
43 Cheated on a diet?

44 *No Exit* playwright
45 Coppers
46 Moisten in the pan
47 Earthy yellow
48 Roll of postage stamps
49 Barrett of gossip

50 Dash
51 Weasellike animal
52 West end of Vegas?
53 Philosopher Hoffer
54 Soda-fountain treat
55 Potato parts
56 Cpl.'s underling

881 PLACEMENT by Bob Lubbers

ACROSS
1 Damage
5 Broad-beamed
9 Portends
14 Gen. Robt. __
15 Actor Tamiroff
16 Met production
17 Hideaway
18 Be unsuccessful
19 Stadium levels
20 The Met's locale
23 __ kick (football ploy)
24 Pitcher Hershiser
25 "__ De-Lovely"
27 Changes, as a clock
32 Family car
36 Preschool project
39 Arab sultanate
40 Roger Rabbit et al.
41 Part of the eye
42 Unpleasant conclusion
44 That is: Lat.
45 Arm covering
46 "Of course"
48 Art-school subj.
51 Meal
56 The heartland
59 Furlough
61 Sandwich shop
62 General Bradley
63 Make a change
64 Soon
65 Singer Jerry
66 Give the benediction
67 Fill
68 French summers

DOWN
1 Phone greeting
2 Actor Delon
3 Jockey's straps
4 Polite word, in France
5 Money holder
6 Image: Var.
7 Dance club, for short
8 Arab chief
9 "99 __ of beer on the wall . . ."
10 Mayberry moppet
11 Bambi, for one
12 Foul up
13 KLM rival
21 Norse god
22 Unhip ones
26 Brogan or pump
28 Poker variety
29 Roof edge
30 Very, in Versailles
31 RBI, e.g.
32 Weeps
33 '20s actor Jannings
34 Engagement
35 Pot starter
37 Long time
38 Griffith or Rooney
40 Tendency
43 Dodgers
44 "It's clear to me now!"
47 Royal fur
49 Alan and Robert
50 Singer __ Marie
52 Demonstrate the truth of
53 Get in one's sights
54 Bathroom device
55 Counterweights
56 Ship's officer
57 Folksinger Burl
58 "Thanks __!"
59 Chem room
60 Pipe angle

882 FOWL PLAY by Dean Niles

ACROSS
1 Soda-shop orders
6 Café au __
10 Yard divisions
14 "Move it!"
15 Footnote abbr.
16 Give the eye
17 Horn voyager
20 Gave the meaning of
21 Poet Nash
22 Family room
23 Safekeeping
25 Synagogue language
29 Easy thing
33 Potpourris
34 Paint the town
35 Hot tub
36 Woodwind instrument
37 Encumbers
38 Manipulative one
39 Ante destination
40 Type options
41 Verge
42 Popular ballet
44 Isn't colorfast
45 Clear liqueur
46 __ Lanka
47 Inert gas
50 Cackle snidely
54 Futile efforts
58 EPA concern
59 Gorge
60 Giant
61 British title
62 Former political initials
63 Fishhook attachment

DOWN
1 Eds.' concerns
2 Corrosive liquid
3 Folk tales, e.g.
4 Fashion plate
5 Advances
6 Flax cloth
7 All before E
8 Clock numeral
9 6-pointers, for short
10 Beats into shape
11 "Good golly!"
12 Actress Sommer
13 Ninth-grade student
18 Over again
19 Socially inept
23 Whey mate
24 Bible book
25 Barrel parts
26 Poke, in a way
27 Flora and fauna
28 Fish eggs
29 Italian poet
30 Actor Davis
31 Flip
32 Emcee Bert
34 Left-winger
37 Ruth's husband
38 Actress Mary
40 Threw with force
41 Scourges
43 Head
44 __-a-brac
46 Curl the lip
47 Impressed
48 Costa __
49 Pilfer
50 Jet-set jets
51 Progress
52 Spanish compass direction
53 Not faked
55 Columbus sch.
56 NATO cousin
57 NBC show since '75

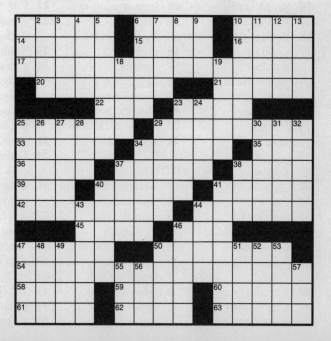

883   WHO J? by Randolph Ross

ACROSS

1 Rub-__
5 Surf motion
9 Wet weather
13 Garage event
14 Writer Anita
15 Tub spreads
17 B.J. of *M*A*S*H*
19 NY Mets and LA Dodgers
20 Scott of *Charles in Charge*
21 Writer P.J.
23 Asian desert
26 Pen friends
27 Corporate R.J.
31 TV cop T.J.
35 Rock producer Brian
36 Washington's state motto
38 Give marks to
39 James Brown's kingdom
41 Food biz H.J.
43 Belgian river
44 __ once (suddenly)
46 Hook's mate
47 Big bird
48 J.J. on *Good Times*
50 Humorist S.J.
53 Nobelist Wiesel
55 Major-__
56 Heisman-winner O.J.
59 Baseball honchos: Abbr.
62 On __ (spreeing)
63 The Fresh Prince's DJ
68 Tara's owner
69 Singer Redding
70 Rhyme scheme
71 __'acte
72 Eastern discipline
73 Long skirt

DOWN

1 Olive relative
2 Paint sloppily
3 Radius neighbor
4 Harmless
5 What RNs dispense
6 Marker
7 Period
8 Bar legally
9 Stand-up routine
10 Like magic
11 Fortuneteller
12 Peter of The Monkees
16 Pilot's hdg.
18 M
22 Bowl cheer
24 Ho-hum
25 Runs in neutral
27 Make firewood smaller
28 __ *Gay*
29 "__ be sorry!"
30 Economize
32 *America's Top Forty* host
33 Plant swelling
34 Summer TV offering
37 "You're All __ to Get By"
40 Cleveland or Buffalo
42 Nil
45 Communications satellite
49 Spanish river
51 TV prize
52 Backup
54 Relish
56 __ Paulo
57 Spillane's __ *Jury*
58 Spooky sound
60 First name in country music
61 Tunisian city
64 From __ Z
65 Half a turn
66 Half a Gabor
67 Freeh's org.

---

884   POLITICKING by Shirley Soloway

ACROSS

1 Eastwood film
5 Lettuce choice
9 Edison's middle name
13 Clinging vines
15 Winglike
16 Set (down)
17 African native
18 Betting setting
19 Cabinet member
20 When the third party wins?
23 Bro., e.g.
24 Private instructors
25 __ glance
28 Editor
32 __ *Noël*
34 Center
35 Stan's pal
40 Presidential desserts?
43 Sportscaster Rusty
44 Popular bean
45 Corner sign
46 Reveals oneself
49 Some
50 Religious ram's horn
54 CCLI doubled
56 New Congressional levy?
63 Iron and Stone
64 Survey
65 Understandable
66 Hair line
67 Sinister
68 "I __ Symphony"
69 Historic periods
70 Singer McEntire
71 Low card

DOWN

1 Actress Osterwald
2 Court star Lendl
3 Lemon zest
4 Hold back
5 Farm structure
6 __ *Three Lives*
7 Bugaboo
8 Any of three 19th-century novelists
9 Roster of the best
10 *Star Wars* series character
11 Clergyman
12 "All in __ work!"
14 "Great!"
21 Put in office
22 *Presumed Innocent* author
25 Tailless beasts
26 Printed material
27 Neighborhood
29 Sheer fabric
30 Humorist __ S. Cobb
31 Appears
33 Old French coin
36 Brown of renown
37 "__ Smile Be Your Umbrella"
38 *Blame __ Rio*
39 Notice
41 WWII sub
42 __ Arabia
47 Correct
48 Bit of salt
50 Land or sea follower
51 Comics conqueror
52 Puccini production
53 Clenched hands
55 Small spot of land
57 Be mad about
58 Fast-talking
59 Actress Nazimova
60 Eye drop
61 Swiss river
62 Med. photo

885   NO CAN DO by Dean Niles

ACROSS

1 Mrs. Simpson
6 Palaver
10 Impart
14 Once more
15 King of Thailand
16 Place
17 T, e.g.
18 They cannot jump
20 Vile rumors
22 Slender cat
23 Accomplishments
25 Eggs
26 French architect
29 Old Peruvian
31 Afternoons: Abbr.
34 Traditional knowledge
35 From Calcutta
37 In the know
38 Hide away
40 Excluding none
41 St. Theresa's birthplace
43 "__ the Walrus"
44 Begrudged
47 __ Bator
48 Compass reading
49 Property right
50 "The Wah Watusi" group
52 Chair part
53 Rub it in
55 Measured out, one way
59 Dose holders
63 They cannot walk backwards
65 Wrathful
66 __ of Wight
67 "__ bigger than a breadbox?"
68 Salamanders
69 Kid stuff
70 Feels poorly
71 Some bends in the road

DOWN

1 Not fem.
2 Turkish title
3 Drizzle
4 They cannot swim
5 Access
6 Wave top
7 2001 computer
8 Brother-act surname
9 Pudding type
10 Camel kin
11 __ kleine Nachtmusik
12 Takes home, as wages
13 Actress Eleonora
19 Choice cigar
21 Melting-watch artist
24 Moving furtively
26 Beast of Borden
27 Smidgens
28 Physique
30 Shade of blue
31 Word form meaning "loving"
32 Lombardy city
33 Runs the gamut
36 Church area
39 First name in cosmetics
42 They can't make a sound
45 Lagos' land
46 Gloom's mate
51 Plunder
52 Stadium levels
54 Shoe forms
55 Funny bit
56 El __, TX
57 As recently as
58 __-do (square-dance move)
60 Code contents
61 Leather end
62 Congressional mtg.
64 It's refined

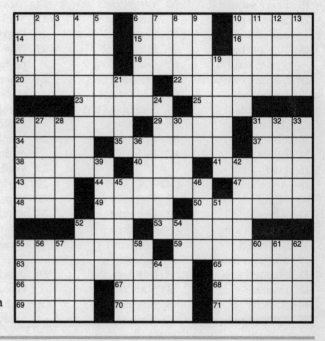

886   PAY UP by Robert Land

ACROSS

1 Wane
4 Phase
9 Play start
13 Word form for "height"
14 Rice dish
15 Sharp
16 Embassy official
19 Bible bk.
20 Winter hazard
21 Pro __ (hypothetical)
22 Reuners
24 Garr or Hatcher
25 Hes
28 Marsh bird
29 Cut, as a lawn
31 Gauguin's retreat
33 Purse closer
34 French seasons
36 Better than lite
37 Whitsunday
40 Like some breakfast foods
43 Headliner
44 Helps
48 Bandleader Phil
50 List-ending abbr.
51 Concerning
52 __ tai (cocktail)
53 Agitate, with "up"
55 Set
57 Car parker
59 __ Cruces, NM
60 CIA predecessor
61 Awards-show vote counter
65 Bring up
66 Veldt antelope
67 In the sack
68 New Haven campus
69 Dimwits
70 Knox and Ord: Abbr.

DOWN

1 Blue Angels formation
2 Skillful
3 NYC div.
4 Sample
5 Water movement
6 Pie __ mode
7 Faux pas
8 Attempt
9 Actor Tamiroff
10 Tile material
11 Shirt shape
12 Election winners
13 In __ by itself
17 Rummy game
18 Supporters' suffixes
23 Chart maker
24 Woofer partner
26 Greek letter
27 Zilch
30 Giant great and kin
32 Balloon filler
35 Ella's specialty
38 Strand, in a way
39 Groves
40 Resistance unit
41 Drivers' org.
42 __ Pursuit
45 Unsure
46 Dons duds
47 Felt
49 Prepared prunes, perhaps
54 Novelist Calvino
56 Hardwood tree
58 Farm parcel
59 Letterman competitor
61 Snoop
62 Crying Game actor
63 Little bit
64 Bumpkin

TAKE THAT! by Norma Steinberg

ACROSS
1 Slightly open
5 Large truck
9 Burrows and Vigoda
13 Uris' __ 18
14 Hero
15 Perry's assistant
17 Soothsayer's aid
18 "...in the pot, __ days old"
19 Sammy or Geena
20 Unlawful payments
22 Arrests
23 Ceremony
24 Brave
25 Leaf
28 Angelic higher-up
30 "Bye!"
32 Absorb
33 Mme. Bovary
37 Swiveled
39 Summer fruit
41 Strong __ ox
42 Ensnare
44 Scarcity
45 Kind of piano
48 Gibbons
49 Use the tub
51 Potpourri: Abbr.
53 __ firma
54 Libation container
59 "To __ human"
60 West Point monogram
61 Gumbo ingredient
62 *Golden Hind* captain
63 Authentic
64 Mortgage, e.g.
65 Yes votes
66 Writer Ferber
67 Be inclined

DOWN
1 Frenzied
2 Guitarist Hendrix
3 William Baldwin's brother
4 Standing
5 Egyptian peninsula
6 Decrees
7 Tork, Nesmith et al.
8 Islands, to Pierre
9 Makes sense
10 Get off
11 Santa's helpers
12 Yucky
16 Burro
21 *Dark Victory* costar
24 Stared slack-jawed
25 French veggie choice
26 Menlo Park middle name
27 Walk out
29 Carl Reiner's son
30 Fitness center
31 *Aladdin* character
34 Swamp
35 Series winners in '69
36 Baseball-bat wood
38 Aykroyd or Quayle
40 Stretch (for)
43 Puzzled
46 Stages of development
47 Jack Haley part
49 Oft-quoted catcher
50 Display
52 La __ (opera house)
53 Danson or Knight
54 Immaculate
55 Dash off
56 Tom Joad, e.g.
57 Small brown bird
58 Come to earth

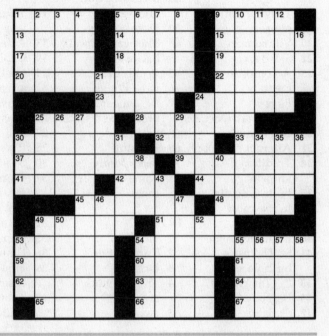

GONG SHOW by Ann Seidel

ACROSS
1 Revolver guy
5 Street actor
9 Vaccine discoverer
14 Capital of Western Samoa
15 Love, to Luis
16 __ France
17 Kook
19 Thousand, in France
20 Compass pt.
21 Lean
22 More exalted
23 Wound up
25 Like some endings
27 __, the Beloved Country
28 Like some losers
29 City on the Danube
32 Fancy tie
35 Chew the fat
36 Runny cheese
37 Name of two presidents
39 Puts away
41 "I cannot tell __"
42 Media mogul Zuckerman
44 Calls for
45 CD-__ (computer-disk type
46 Fill to excess
47 __ mot (witticism)
48 Prickled
50 Meadows or Hepburn
54 Biological subdivisions
56 Viet __
58 Kimono sash
59 Seaweed
60 Chocolate-chip cookie
62 "Für __"
63 Villain in *Othello*
64 Darmstadt donkey
65 Country roads
66 Bandleader Kenton
67 Tear apart

DOWN
1 Military-school student
2 Give one's views
3 Bedding
4 Kid's game
5 What ails you
6 "__ the Mood for Love"
7 Solitary
8 Work unit
9 Cinema's Signoret
10 Excuse
11 Graphic distribution
12 Unemployed
13 __-do-well
18 Puts on notice
22 1994 Rob Reiner film
24 Tea biscuit
26 Cook beef
30 Fibbed
31 Army meal
32 Open a bit
33 Go it alone
34 Speaking up
35 Big bill
36 Intermingle
38 Missouri River city
40 Adequate
43 1776 soldier
46 Masses of loose rock
47 Knit-shirt material
49 Needle
51 Get out of bed
52 TV's Jed Clampett
53 Bond return
54 Highlander
55 Scat name
57 Gymnast Korbut
60 "__ the season to be jolly"
61 On top of, poetically

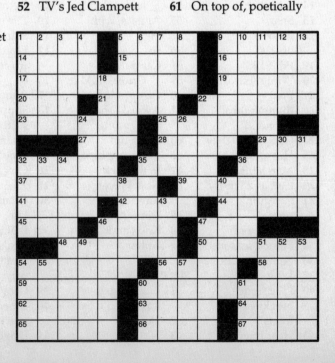

889 CLOSE CALLS by Dean Niles

ACROSS
1 Bettor's tactic
6 Seniors grp.
10 Surfer's surface
14 Eskimo relative
15 Blackjack prop
16 Tel __
17 Tithing portion
18 CLOSE
20 "__ Jude"
21 Tabloid twosomes
23 Ponders
24 English racing venue
26 Grunts
27 Disqualify, in court
29 German capitalist?
34 Letter openers
35 Reporter Bly
37 Comic Philips
38 Beats it
39 Mr. T's group
40 "Just the facts, __"
41 Loop conveyances
42 Foreboding aura
43 Joliet discovery
44 Extracts, in a way
46 Waterways
48 Possesses
49 Tycoon from Texarkana
50 Vapor
53 Swarming throng
55 Hawaiian Punch rival
58 CLOSE
60 Under, to a poet
62 Spiny plant
63 Saturn or Mercury
64 *Inferno* poet
65 Porgy's love
66 Fall rudely
67 "Bloody Mary" was one

DOWN
1 "Hell __ no fury . . ."
2 Robt. __
3 CLOSE
4 Stomach
5 B-school topic
6 Black-ink item
7 "Might I interrupt?"
8 Mythical birds
9 For each
10 '60s dance
11 Budget competitor
12 Long live: Fr.
13 12/24 and 12/31
19 Rousseau work
22 Pedicurist's concern
25 Beer
26 Smirked
27 Displayed ire
28 Italian town
29 Consecrate
30 Veteran actor Jack
31 CLOSE
32 Internet missive
33 Some apples
36 Footnote phrase
40 Less, in music
42 Where US 95 ends
45 London river
47 "Banality of evil" philosopher
49 Hospital area, for short
50 Pierce
51 The T in TV
52 Love god
53 Truckers do it
54 __ von Bismarck
56 "Take __ the Limit" (Eagles tune)
57 *Mask* star
59 40 winks
61 __ *de vie* (brandy)

890 THE SOUND OF MUSIC by Bob Lubbers

ACROSS
1 Pol.'s money source
4 Tendon
9 Senegal capital
14 He played Tarzan
15 Doe follower
16 Portrait
17 Shade tree
18 Couch potato's complaint?
20 Shul teacher
22 Cul de __
23 Stone or Gless
25 Steady currents
29 Singer Julius
31 Originate
33 __-relief
35 Prepare to take off
37 Bayes and Ephron
38 Sacro ending
41 GI address
42 Stumbling blocks
43 Small band
44 Repetition method
46 Bee follower
47 "I __ Care"
49 Battleground of 1943
52 Reel men?
54 Southwestern bricks
57 Santa __, CA
58 *Lorna* __
59 Dessert?
66 Western Indian
67 Eaglets' nursery
68 Drew or DeGeneres
69 Actor Beatty
70 Mix
71 Doesn't walk
72 Towel (off)

DOWN
1 Equals
2 Islam's Almighty
3 Pieman's customer?
4 Rescuer
5 General Amin
6 Classic beginning
7 Slithery swimmer
8 Watch place
9 Detects
10 Latin 101 word
11 Auntie Em's st.
12 T-man, e.g.
13 Run up an engine
19 DEA man
21 Bikini part
24 Like it or __
25 Star personas?
26 Uncountable years
27 Leather-covered?
28 __ *Door Canteen*
30 German river
32 Latin being
33 Pen names
34 Kauai "Bye!"
36 Bit
39 Snug as __ . . .
40 Nabbed
45 Memorable period
48 Declare false
50 Accessories
51 Court
53 It's built for speed
55 Enroll
56 Squalid
59 Bandleader Calloway
60 Norse goddess
61 Before, poetically
62 __-Tin-Tin
63 Yalie
64 Lawyer's deg.
65 Peggy or Pinky

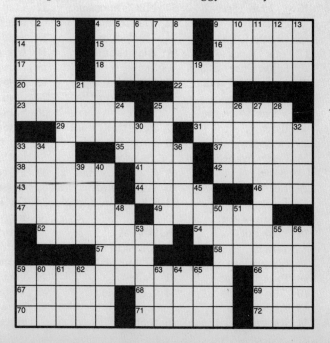

891 ???? by Norma Steinberg

ACROSS
1 Sound of a guffaw
5 Shore spot
10 In __ (lined up)
14 Composer Stravinsky
15 Cornered
16 Jacob's first wife
17 Ex-Speaker Gingrich
18 Heat unit
19 Ricki or Veronica
20 Conclusion
21 Question from Lou Costello
23 Tales
25 Hive resident
26 Three feet
27 Theater street
32 Mick Jagger, e.g.
34 Elevator stop
35 Hurry
36 *The Winds of War* author
37 Invigorating
38 Baby's first word, perhaps
39 Annex
40 VCR button
41 Irrigate
42 Marina slots
44 Earth's neighbor
45 Actress MacGraw
46 Truthful
49 Kids' picture-game book
54 In favor of
55 Leave the path
56 Hang around
57 Bloodhound's clue
58 Genesis son
59 Writer Jong
60 Capitol topper
61 Small horse
62 Office furniture
63 Read, as a bar code

DOWN
1 Dancer Gregory
2 Representative
3 Words upon meeting
4 "Wherefore __ thou?"
5 Soaked
6 Group's personality
7 Burrows and Vigoda
8 Dear: It.
9 Churchgoer's carry-along
10 Connected by treaty
11 Hindmost part
12 Grown acorns
13 Sharpen
21 Current conduit
22 Phobia
24 Hierarchical standing
27 Ecstasy
28 Kennedy matriarch
29 Mel Blanc line
30 Adjutant
31 Part of a decade
32 Did the crawl
33 Brouhaha
34 Kin of the twist
37 Sent into exile
38 Pub missile
40 Heap
41 Texas town
43 Once in a blue moon
44 Cotton cloth
46 Speckle
47 Bouquet
48 *Two Women* star
49 Prepare presents
50 King of the road
51 Not odd
52 Had on
53 Hertz rival
57 "__ bodkins!"

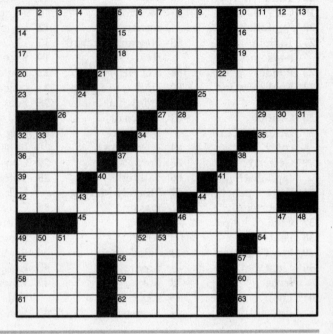

892 TV LAWMEN by Rich Norris

ACROSS
1 Shopper's burden
5 Spiny-leaved plant
10 Touch on
14 Scandinavian capital
15 __ fours (French cookies)
16 Create
17 '60s TV cops
20 Salon rinse
21 Most small and round, as eyes
22 Turns down the light
25 In no way
26 Clairvoyance, for short
29 Let down
32 Birdman of Alcatraz, e.g.
36 Leak out slowly
38 Showed up
39 French verse
40 '70s TV cops
43 Artist's need
44 Rigatoni relative
45 "__ pin, pick it up . . ."
46 Allen or Martin
47 Choose democratically
49 Society girl, for short
50 NRC's ancestor
52 Classic cars
54 Think over
59 Island south of Sicily
63 '80s TV cops
66 Away from the wind
67 Powerfully built
68 Drive the getaway car
69 Used 20 Across
70 Agreements
71 *Ghost* star Moore

DOWN
1 This and that?
2 Arthur of tennis
3 Valley
4 Like a good argument
5 Suitable
6 Metro or Prizm
7 ". . . three men in __"
8 __ versa
9 Patriot Allen
10 Upwardly mobile
11 Hay unit
12 Luau strings, briefly
13 Student's concern
18 Use a hammer
19 Lyricist Green
23 Poke fun at
24 *Ghost* star Patrick
26 Sharp curves
27 Attack
28 "__ porridge hot . . ."
30 PC communication
31 Lessee
33 Gave a banquet for
34 Quiz host
35 Detox, perhaps
37 Came out on top
41 Frozen rainfalls
42 Vegas cubes
48 Pyramid, essentially
51 Cartoonist Guisewhite
53 Dinner course
54 Country south of Libya
55 Slick
56 Jocularity
57 Quiz answer
58 Congers
60 Garage job
61 Pour
62 Italian wine region
64 __ out a living
65 Cobb and Hardin

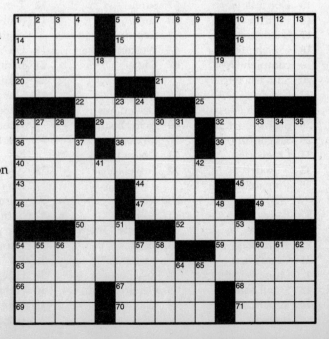

893 CROSS-SWORD PUZZLE by Dean Niles

ACROSS
1 Before deductions
6 "Get __ of that!"
11 Cold War org.
14 Part of USNA
15 Worth
16 That girl
17 Caribbean resort
18 Put an __ (terminate)
19 Santa __, CA
20 Liquefy again
22 Powdery residue
23 Comic scene
24 Virginia senator
26 Dice-game bugs
28 Like some undershirts
31 Goad
32 Israeli dance
33 Transfixed
35 Prier's need
39 Discharges
41 Pa. neighbor
42 Marry on the run
43 March, e.g.
44 Historic times
46 Exultation
47 TV producer Norman
49 Went off, in a way
51 Former Romanian president
54 Freight hauler
55 Aggregation
56 Sturm __ Drang
58 Disconnect
62 "Peggy __" (Holly tune)
63 Parking penalties
65 Textile fiber
66 Goof up
67 Particulars
68 Slow gaits
69 Rebel Turner
70 English poet
71 Donkeys

DOWN
1 Growl
2 Out of the ordinary
3 Egg cell
4 Flexed one's muscles
5 Zigzag course
6 "__ Maria"
7 Singer Cantrell
8 Midsize car
9 Poet or playwright
10 __ volente (God willing)
11 Coarse fabric
12 Bottle occupant
13 Little terrors
21 Ski lift
23 Uke kin
25 Harrison Ford film
27 Give the eye
28 '54 sci-fi film
29 __ sapiens
30 Land of the Shannon
34 For each
36 Electrical unit
37 Fencer's arm
38 Grass stalk
40 "__ Always a Woman"
45 Tore off
48 Keenness
50 Oath of silence
51 *Peer Gynt* playwright
52 Actress Dern
53 Like some gases
57 Spec recording
59 Singer Tori
60 Summon to court
61 Dame Myra
63 Fish story
64 123-45-6789, e.g.: Abbr.

894 BEASTLY by Bob Lubbers

ACROSS
1 "__ the ramparts . . ."
4 Does sum work
8 Hide
13 John and Maureen's daughter
14 Go bad
15 Squander
16 Missile path, e.g.
17 Uproar over a bear?
19 Start a Model T again
21 Classic start
22 Innie opposite
23 Alphonse's partner
27 EPA concern
29 Engine pt.
31 "You're __" (Porter tune)
33 Brinker or Conried
34 Dumbarton __
36 Words from Caesar
37 Some MDs' specialties
38 Poetic conjunction
39 Pitch detector
40 Per-__ worker
42 Greek goddess
43 Part of A&E
44 Grads
46 Hearst's captors
48 Swiss abstractionist
49 Secret
51 Intermission follower
53 Paths: Abbr.
54 Pruned
57 Musical king?
62 Ore. neighbor
63 Sink unclogger
64 Discharge
65 Allen of *Home Improvement*
66 Muscle
67 Nitti nemesis
68 Understand

DOWN
1 Ike contemporary
2 The Auld Sod
3 Masked storyteller?
4 "It's __!" ("Very funny!")
5 Burdened idealist?
6 Carried out
7 Street talk
8 Sound of speed
9 Treat hide
10 __ *Lay Dying*
11 R-V connectors
12 Dress end
14 Mini-feud
18 Deli slices
20 Runners, e.g.
24 Driver's peg
25 Mammal boundaries?
26 Jot
27 "I did not think to __ tear": Shak.
28 Envelope material
30 John and Bert
32 Prize money
35 Cuddly one's traits?
41 End of the next century
42 Vedas reader
43 Actor Tamiroff
45 Straight's partner
47 Not like this clue
50 German city
52 Apply color
55 Sedgwick or Brickell
56 May Whitty, e.g.
57 TV spots
58 Dernier __
59 Role for Harrison
60 Single
61 Bigger than med.

895 NUMEROUS THINGS by Harvey Estes

ACROSS
1 Save companion
7 Least risky
13 Mined find
15 Recover from
16 Delivery room worker?
17 Reporter's fix-up
18 Card game
20 Book of legends?
21 Poet's product
22 Hear a case
23 __ up (make sense)
26 Fidgety
28 Bay baby, maybe
32 Some combos
34 Taco need
36 The __ Bears
39 Fans of the cotton bole?
40 He can't remember
42 Denim pants
43 Poet Allen
44 General Patton
47 Workplace-fairness abbr.
48 Tag pursuers
50 Mauna __
51 Fairway border
54 Girls' mag
60 They take a bow
62 Like a rubber band
63 Israel-Jordan divider
64 He did it his way
65 __ out (exhausted)
66 Lifework

DOWN
1 Riverbank deposit
2 Where it may stick
3 Pajama coverer
4 Privy to
5 Comedian Sahl
6 Victimize
7 Exercise the eyes
8 Engaged in hostilities
9 Two-tune record
10 Eye opener?
11 __ good example
12 Very, in Verdun
14 Eat at
15 Coll. sr.'s test
19 Unmixed
22 Phoenician city
23 Near home?
24 O'Neill work
25 "I __ Get to Sleep at All"
26 Purposes
27 Miss Piggy, for one
29 Popeye's goyl
30 Kate & __
31 Capture in a loop
33 U-turn
35 Phone front
37 Spare hair
38 Unstamped enc.
41 Merry king
45 Wanders
46 Highlanders' language
49 Objects nearby
51 Grating sound
52 Reverend Roberts
53 '95 NCAA champ
54 FICA funds it
55 Singer Mouskouri
56 Pre-revolution ruler
57 Kitchen extension
58 Land of Yeats
59 Former CSA state
61 Football great Grange

896 HOLD IT by Shirley Soloway

ACROSS
1 Tree fluids
5 Tartan design
10 Sore feeling
14 Busy as __
15 Mexican rope
16 New York stadium
17 Go to bed
19 Get wind of
20 Baking potatoes
21 Truthful
23 Barbara __ Geddes
24 Musical notes
26 Add color to
27 Sure to happen
30 Reno's st.
33 Claims
36 Cache box?
37 Get away from
39 __ Gay (WWII plane)
41 Hacienda Mrs.
42 "__ Be Me"
43 Of an insect part
44 Care for
46 Regarding
47 Hosp. areas
48 Whodunit devices
51 Grass-animal name
53 Genetic initials
54 747, e.g.
57 Most flirty
59 Recessed area
61 Challenge
62 Social service employer
65 Pizza cooker
66 Japanese dog
67 Poetic dusks
68 Western plateau
69 Artist Neiman
70 33 Down artist

DOWN
1 Indian term of address
2 Tolerate
3 Posy part
4 Son of Adam
5 Adjusts ahead of time
6 Fleur-de-__
7 Motorists' org.
8 Annoying sensation
9 Former U.S. territory
10 Pale-faced
11 Stale jokes
12 Summer discomfort
13 Pitcher part
18 Brass instrument
22 Actor Bruce or Hawthorne
25 Daisy type
27 Cuba, e.g.: Sp.
28 Actor Zimbalist
29 Socked on the head
31 Revise
32 Turn down
33 Art __
34 "Are you __ out?"
35 Sports stats
38 Grazing grounds
40 Michael Caine role
45 Actress Faye
49 Mischief-maker
50 __ Alto, CA
52 Laughing mammal
54 Batman's nemesis
55 Occasion
56 Short and sweet
57 Hideaway
58 Accept
60 Northern native
61 Funnyman DeLuise
63 Knightly title
64 WWII region

897 PARTY TIME by Mary Brindamour

ACROSS
1 Vessel for wine
5 Music symbols
10 During
14 Hurt
15 Springfield or carbine
16 Space grp.
17 Persia, today
18 Deli patron
19 Prof.'s helper
20 Party time
23 Prov. of Canada
24 Gore and D'Amato
25 Used more Elmer's
27 Muffin ingredient
32 Casanova
33 Live
34 Satellite's path
36 Fire-truck adjunct
39 Pro __ (proportionally)
41 Assail
43 Rice drink
44 Boat berths
46 Word before firma or cotta
48 __ Plaines, IL
49 Vintage cars
51 Most theatrical
53 Delinquent
56 Moving vehicle
57 Carnes or Novak
58 Party time
64 On the briny
66 Put into words
67 Foil kin
68 Over there, old-style
69 Noses (into)
70 Special-interest grp.
71 Sp. miss
72 Hearing or sight
73 Witty sayings

DOWN
1 Dean of *Lois & Clark*
2 Land measure
3 Bernard or George Bernard
4 Native of Nairobi
5 Folders
6 Pseudologist
7 Newts
8 Escapee
9 Tennis starter
10 *Wheel of Fortune* buy
11 Party time
12 Magazine unit
13 Out of vogue
21 Sailors' saint
22 Psyche segments
26 San __ Obispo
27 Gridlock causers
28 By mouth
29 Party time
30 Encourage
31 Lo-fat foods
35 Bakery item
37 __ out a living (gets by)
38 TV sitcom *Empty __*
40 Mimic
42 Go across
45 Cola or tonic
47 Food stabilizer
50 Morning events
52 Trousers measurement
53 Gives the nod to
54 Brim
55 __ nous
59 Pack __ (quit)
60 Victory signs
61 Lhasa __
62 Take five
63 Longings
65 Periodontists' grp.

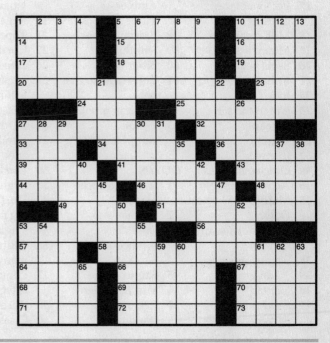

898 BUZZ WORDS by Bob Lubbers

ACROSS
1 Ring official
4 Aroma
9 __ lazuli
14 Wallach or Lilly
15 Turkic native
16 Papas or Cara
17 Small bus
18 Solo
19 *I Remember Mama* mama
20 Orthographic contest
23 Snow __ (deception)
24 Actor Davis
25 Conducted
26 One, in Arles
27 Knicks' rivals
28 Iron alloy
31 Gratis
32 Needy
33 Sows
34 Slender at the belt
38 Watchful
40 Remain
41 Not present?
42 Helps in crime
44 Slot fillers
48 Favorite
49 Health resort
50 Eagle's nest
51 Palindromic preposition
52 Big trouble
56 ". . . poem lovely as __"
58 Street kid
59 "__ in my backyard!"
60 Logic
61 M. Zola
62 Single
63 Westphalian city
64 Inhibit
65 Mao __-tung

DOWN
1 Cosmetics king Charles
2 Go by
3 Best-quality
4 Passé
5 Colombian city
6 Ian Fleming's alma mater
7 Da __, Vietnam
8 Tweeter range
9 Sweetened the sod
10 Southern constellation
11 Swore falsely
12 Sang
13 U.S. Navy battalion
21 Lily, in Lille
22 Moray
28 Bribe
29 Tug's chore
30 Rub out
31 Lawyer's charge
32 L.A. clock setting
33 Pigpen
34 Horse operas
35 Garfunkel or Linkletter
36 Addams Family cousin
37 Airline to Sweden
38 Mollify
39 Hamlet's attacker
42 GI address
43 Brought by scow
44 X
45 "We __ alone"
46 Oxlike mammals
47 Sofa
49 Luster
50 *Roots* Emmy-winner
53 Application information
54 Give off
55 Ceramic square
57 Pilot's hdg.

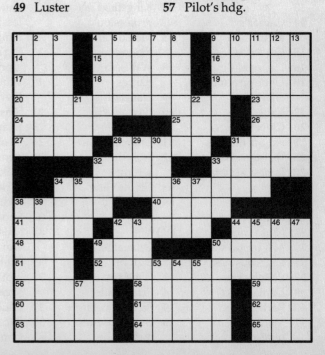

899 — SODA-JERK JARGON by Ann Seidel

ACROSS
1 Chicago team
5 Risked
10 Stickum
14 Competent
15 Cheer up
16 Well-ventilated
17 Person, place, or thing
18 Milk measures
19 Miami's county
20 Scots negative
21 Coffee
23 Jock
25 Not in the pink
26 A snap
27 Common buzzer
32 Intended
34 Office machines
35 Actress Ullmann
36 Middle of 57 Down
37 Took the measure of
38 Senate presider
39 __-de-France
40 Heptad
41 Sand ridges
42 Sewer entrances
44 Western buddy
45 Canine comment
46 One who abstains
49 No ice
54 Uno, due, __
55 Gung-ho
56 Clapton and Ambler
57 Turner of rock
58 Pastrami palace
59 Sinuous
60 Bitter
61 Contribute to the pot
62 Mexican moola
63 __ out (supplements)

DOWN
1 Showy tropical plant
2 German sub
3 Dose of Bromo-Seltzer
4 Sun Yat-__
5 Sheriff's aide
6 Mrs. Kramden
7 Relative standing
8 Diminutive ending
9 Foreordained
10 Irksome critic
11 Irish writer O'Flaherty
12 Pakistani language
13 Regarded
21 Topnotch
22 Corrida cries
24 Screen Turner
27 Confused feelings
28 Beasts of burden
29 Vanilla ice cream cone
30 Land of Tara
31 Nights before
32 Hurt badly
33 Big name in jazz singing
34 Quitting time for many
37 Popular book category
38 Wise guy
40 Classify
41 Pioneer Boone, for short
43 Finnan __ (smoked dish)
44 Balances evenly
46 Cheesy chip
47 A Muppet
48 Peruses
49 "If I __ Hammer"
50 Roaster
51 Cadence
52 Pennsylvania port
53 Smacks
57 Inventor's monogram

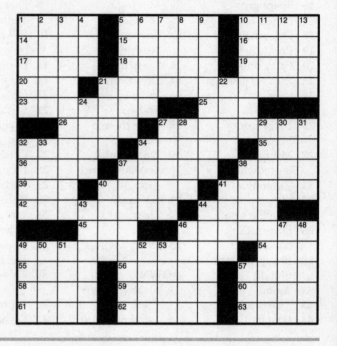

900 — ACROSS THE BOARD by A.J. Santora

ACROSS
1 "Daniel Boone" poet
6 Where Anna was governess
10 Sweatshop?
13 __ at Eight
14 Caesar's accusation
15 Cat's dog
16 Fictional sleuth
18 Underground element
19 Yalie
20 CNN reporter
22 Adjournments
25 Extinguished
27 James and Place
28 Dud
30 __ Dawn Chong
32 Close friend
33 MA motto start
34 Loan business
37 Poker game
39 Denial word
40 Part of Q&A
41 Medicinal plants
43 Evil spirit
47 Line dance
48 Heat
51 The Day Kennedy Was Shot author
54 Kingsfield's profession
55 Menlo Park monogram
56 WWI-era dancer
59 Naval off.
60 Post-WWII alliance
61 Chaplin in-law
62 NC winter setting
63 Clothes line
64 Hotsy-__

DOWN
1 Official order
2 Sign up
3 Wind dir.
4 Profit ender
5 Secret meeting
6 Geisel, pseudonymously
7 Willow genus
8 "__ o'clock scholar"
9 Saki's kin
10 Making fun of
11 Mary-Louise and Sarah Jessica
12 Amaze
13 Big name in farm machines
17 What, in Paris or Madrid
21 Sins
23 Example
24 Vidi
26 Poor grade
28 Jacket style
29 Writer Chase
31 Sicilian city
32 Snoop
34 Most clever with words?
35 Coll. degrees
36 Not Dems. or Reps.
37 Pouch
38 Pac-10 team
42 Compartments
44 Schematically colored items
45 By swallowing
46 Stairpost
48 __ Penh
49 Fish eggs
50 Florida mecca
52 "Dies __"
53 Bristle
55 Placekicker's prop
57 "It's __-win situation!"
58 Stage decor

901 OINK SPOTS by Lee Weaver

ACROSS
1 Weird
4 Declare
8 __ glider
12 Place for a rodeo
15 VIP's wheels
16 MP's headache
17 __ Holiday (Hepburn film)
18 Champagne bucket
19 Tortilla dough
20 Place to put coins
22 Wilbur's talkative friend
23 Hiding spot
24 Fencing swords
26 Bell or jalapeño
30 Alumnus
31 Mixed bag
32 __ and void
35 Greedy king
39 Not even once, to a poet
40 Caviar source
41 Outfit for Nero
42 Office furniture
44 Gossip tidbit
46 Colo. Springs letters
47 Leader
49 Electric current unit
51 Singer Ross
53 Norway's capital
55 Part of NWT
56 Happy place to wallow
61 Ending for young or hip
62 Alan of M*A*S*H
63 Home to Governor Bush
65 British composer
66 Oboist's need
67 63 Across, e.g.
68 Film holder
69 Top rating
70 Do lawn work

DOWN
1 Boat mover
2 Bit of rain
3 Half: Pref.
4 Excuse
5 Clergyman
6 Sign
7 Laborer
8 Got carried away on stage
9 __ of (onto)
10 Facial features
11 Delighted
13 Washed-up horse
14 Point of view
21 Sea dog's tale
25 Actress Dawber
26 Small lake
27 Robt. __
28 Some desserts
29 Government patronage source
30 Merriment
33 Exodus author
34 Land parcel
36 B_{12} amount
37 Lab medium
38 Snugly secure
43 Junior, e.g.
45 Stag or stallion
48 African desert
50 Palace protectors
51 Raison __
52 Cara or Castle
53 Poet Nash
54 Tint
55 Ivan was one
57 Margarine
58 Dog doc
59 School test
60 Western alliance: Abbr.
64 Make a seam

902 LOOMING by Robert W. Land

ACROSS
1 Tel __
5 Roman's 1650
9 Sounds of surprise
14 Vittorio De __
15 Like __ of sunshine
16 Kind of committee
17 Exaggerate, story-wise
19 Dolphins coach
20 Comedienne Coca
22 Relative of etc.
23 Transatlantic message senders
26 Polite bow
28 French schools
29 Rabbi of yore
31 Of a curved projection
32 Sired
33 Hesitant syllables
36 Ret. accounts
37 Steer
38 Take a glance at
39 Landers or Blyth
40 Manufacturer
41 Actress Sharon
42 Impelled
44 Typewriter bar
45 Update the outlets
47 Showed gratitude
48 Hot spot
49 Gere or Rodgers
52 Endymion author
54 Enterprise pace
58 Smithy's shaper
59 Sunburn balm
60 Woody's son
61 Office worker
62 Family members
63 Box-office figure

DOWN
1 Dolt
2 Celeb
3 Here: Fr.
4 Ice-cream flavorings
5 City heads
6 Hauls
7 Give a hoot
8 Actress Fontanne
9 Vapor
10 Stick (to)
11 Badminton bird
12 Negri namesakes
13 Armadillo-like
18 Arab chieftain
21 Social radiance
23 Johnson of Brief Encounter
24 Oak seed
25 Boxing technique
27 The nth degree: Abbr.
29 Hayes or Hunt
30 Doctor Frankenstein's assistant
32 Two-wheeler
34 Indian queen
35 Bergen dummy
37 Road worker
38 Play 'em as they are
40 Russian space station
41 Sail supports
43 2/3 of a movie dog
44 Molds
45 Cheese choices
46 Happening
47 Pulsate
50 "__ only kidding!"
51 Colombian city
53 __-mo
55 Time period
56 Wapiti
57 John or Jane

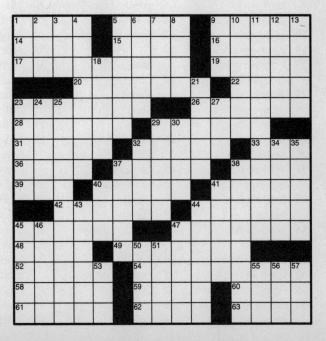

903   IN THE RING by Bob Lubbers

ACROSS
1 Paradise
5 Cavil
9 Part of RSVP
12 Ann __, MI
14 Gen. Robt. __
15 Check out
16 What an unsteady boxer has
18 Pueblo pot
19 Inner quality
20 Consumes
21 Ballgame official
25 Asian holiday
26 Condé __
27 One who hurls
29 Lemony
31 Aunt Millie's competitor
32 Author Deighton
34 "__ boy!"
37 Ring agility
41 Linemen
42 "Oh, boy!"
43 Mitchell mansion
45 Left-turn commands
48 Cabin piece
50 Durango money
53 Owns
55 Temporary resident
56 Honolulu's home
57 Llama cousin
59 RR depots
60 Ring protector
65 Kingly address
66 Day start
67 Broadcast
68 Compass pt.
69 Not fooled by
70 Bargain time

DOWN
1 Canal locale
2 Joanne of *Red River*
3 Recede
4 __ Hill
5 Boston NBAer
6 Certain Alaskan
7 Rue
8 Madrid money
9 Saucy music?
10 Ocean specks
11 Smallest
13 Pick up a lease
15 Do a 28 Down's job
17 Hardly ever
21 *Clermont*, e.g.: Abbr.
22 Abrade
23 Grinder's gear
24 Ring punch
28 Ring figure
30 Uncooked
33 Right away
35 Song syllables
36 Ohio city
38 14 Across' country: Abbr.
39 Cartoon caveman
40 Jerk rapidly
44 T-man
46 Explosive sound
47 Watering place
49 Certain tides
50 Deputized riders
51 Kitchen descriptor
52 Take part in
54 Gush
58 __ extra cost (free)
61 "__ a deal!"
62 Epoch
63 Animation unit
64 Wool-coat owner

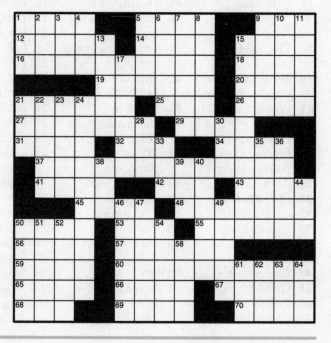

904   ON THE RUN by Raymond Hamel

ACROSS
1 Xavier's ex
5 Muzzle
9 Fumbles
14 Main point
15 About
16 Get __ in the face
17 Ireland symbol
18 Light gas
19 Rhone feeder
20 Company picnic competition
23 Third word of "America"
24 Broadside
25 Sea: Fr.
26 Swearing
31 White House Scottie
33 Dolly's last name
34 Made a rug
36 Ilk
38 Pimlico contest
42 Chip in
43 Apollo's mother
44 Small amount of progress
45 Phoenix suburb
47 Heartbreakers' head
49 François' friend
51 Delta rival
53 Inclement
54 Ten-second event
61 Bestow a gift
62 Peace symbol
63 "... wish __, wish ..."
64 Covering the vicinity
65 River to the Elbe
66 Package binder
67 Clarinetist-bandleader Johnny
68 Puerto __
69 Toledo's lake

DOWN
1 Tooth problem
2 Crow
3 Small town
4 Exile
5 Stitched without machines
6 Plays for a fool
7 Cool it
8 Pay tribute to
9 Sloop structure
10 "Back in the __" (Beatles tune)
11 Bargain place
12 Mockery
13 *Inside the Third Reich* author
21 Counting game
22 Bumbler
26 Yodeler's perch
27 Miles of film
28 Not easily perturbed
29 Mr. Coward
30 Electronic babysitter
32 Cheater's cubes
35 Last word of Missouri's motto
37 Camper's need
39 Small falcons
40 Large floppy hat
41 Piggery
46 Reverent fear
48 Walk like a dog
49 In the future
50 Saki's real name
52 Venomous bookkeeper?
55 Twosome
56 Boo-Boo's buddy
57 With, in Avignon
58 Crosby tune of '44
59 Indian wrap
60 __ Park, NY

905   HEAR HEAR by Dean Niles

ACROSS
1 Lobster extremity
5 At a distance
9 More frosted
14 Pantomime dance
15 Water sport
16 "It takes a __ raise a boy"
17 Persia, now
18 "Splash!" to a Greek
20 Acted like a nag?
22 Santa's entryway
23 Captured
24 Shoe width
25 Ben Casey portrayer
29 Henry or Dennis
33 Complains
34 Precipitate
36 Skedaddle
37 Cask stopper
38 Shul scroll
39 Summon to court
40 Compass pt.
41 Not domesticated
42 Talk show host O'Donnell
43 1776 fighter
45 Scrounged
47 Planet
48 Judge Lance
49 Circus attraction
53 Notified
57 "Kitchy koo!" to a Russian
59 "Dies __"
60 Boosted the signal
61 Lendl of tennis
62 Home, to Jorge
63 Marsh growth
64 Singer k.d.
65 Unobstructed

DOWN
1 Place to take it on?
2 Decoy
3 Jai __
4 "Bow-wow" to a Chinese
5 Tack on
6 Dog-ear
7 __ Baba
8 Coll. marchers
9 Irreverence
10 Less frazzled
11 __ instant (immediately)
12 Novel ending
13 Optimistic
19 Knife holder
21 __ d'oeuvres
25 Live coal
26 Submerge
27 Subsided
28 Lacking cash
29 Hymn of praise
30 From Cork
31 Attractive one
32 Attacked, in a way
35 Altar constellation
38 Pekoe holder
39 "Cock-a-doodle-doo!" to a Frenchman
41 Interdicts
42 Fixed procedure
44 Got less hot
46 Giving a lube
49 Culture medium
50 Arrive
51 Bind together
52 Labor
53 Thicke of TV
54 Booby __
55 Leisure
56 Faculty head
58 Eggs

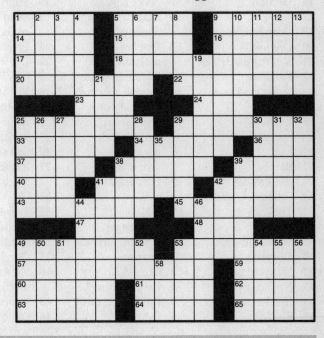

906   ROOM SERVICE by Bob Lubbers

ACROSS
1 Buenos __
6 Van Gogh's home
11 Gives a thumbs-up
14 Twerp
15 Beltline
16 "But __ for Me"
17 Social butterfly
19 Song syllable
20 49 Across, e.g.
21 Knockout gas
23 Releases, as a spring
27 Ogle
29 Came over the horizon
30 Really tiny
31 Tie tightly
32 Stews
33 USN officer
36 Ruin's partner
37 London newspaper
38 Release
39 Etna dust
40 Bundled cotton
41 Records
42 Combined, as resources
44 Eamon de __
45 Multiplication result
47 Campaign events
48 Like some cereals
49 Scot
50 The end of an __
51 Committee head
58 Lunar New Year
59 Two under par
60 Royal headgear
61 Box off. sign
62 Goes berserk
63 Have on

DOWN
1 Performance
2 Lyricist Gershwin
3 Upriser, for short
4 Slithery fish
5 Genus division
6 MP's collars
7 Awed
8 Cup edge
9 Compass dir.
10 Mini-rivers
11 Facing a scolding
12 M*A*S*H setting
13 Begin
18 Embraced
22 Part of TNT
23 Extreme
24 Bayes and Dunn
25 TV nut
26 Russian city
27 Spirited horse
28 Little ones
30 __ and dangerous
32 Debone
34 Tractor name
35 Flat hills
37 Bath powder
38 FDR's dog
40 Saloon guard
41 Pills
43 Kind of poem
44 Nickname for Alben Barkley
45 Keats and Burns
46 Harder to come by
47 Challenges
49 Gold veneer
52 "Bali __"
53 In the past
54 Tear
55 __ Paulo
56 Legendary Bruin
57 Singer Cole

TEAMWORK by Raymond Hamel

ACROSS

1 Cellist Casals
6 Knitted throw
11 Likely
14 Once more
15 Heroine of *The Color Purple*
16 Dernier __
17 Ally
19 Corn holder
20 Leg joint
21 Not fulfilled
22 Relocate
23 Slow, musically
25 Ant
26 Carter's hometown
29 Lug
32 Barely discernible
33 Curie or Osmond
34 Took up the baton
37 Pain reliever
39 Dullness
41 Nautical hdg.
42 Not soggy
44 Bead material
45 Bleak
47 Pith helmets
48 Pita, e.g.
50 India's first prime minister
52 Suggestive
53 Civil War general
55 Rosalind of *Deep Space Nine*
59 Marilu's *Evening Shade* role
60 One lending assistance
62 Valuable stone
63 Pindar, for one
64 Piebald pony
65 Sight from Albertville
66 Medicine amounts
67 Displease

DOWN

1 Cub group
2 Ancient Greek contest
3 Curse
4 Palm etching?
5 Bill passed daily
6 Odor
7 __ Beach, CA
8 Amor's wings
9 Debi Thomas rival
10 Golfer Trevino
11 Lookout, maybe
12 Show true
13 High land
18 Sends a bill collector
22 French Mrs.
24 Drew in
25 '40s First Lady
26 USMC ranks
27 Vietnam neighbor
28 Military assistant
30 Cut short
31 It's above the thigh
33 '70s world leader
35 To be, in Bordeaux
36 Recolors
38 Gun lobby org.
40 New World monkey
43 Nerve juncture
46 Dancer Bolger
47 Afterwards
48 Brazilian actress Sonia
49 Composer of *Bolero*
51 Redacts
53 "Love __" (Beatles tune)
54 New Haven students
56 Put in the closet
57 Prefix with room or date
58 Stench
60 Brick carrier
61 Dean's-list fig.

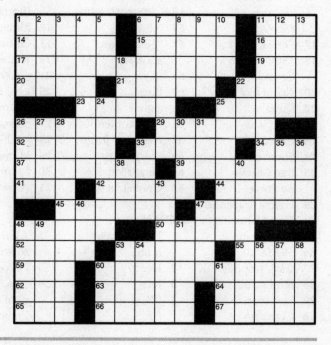

SOME OF THE GUYS by Robert W. Land

ACROSS

1 Bodybuilder's bane
5 Burst forth
10 Partly open
14 Verdi opera
15 Take to court again
16 Barrett or Jaffe
17 Wisenheimers
19 Penny
20 British royalists
21 Repeats one's steps
23 Small combos
25 Architect Saarinen
26 Gets back to
29 Benedict or Hap
31 "__ go bragh!"
32 Most willing
34 Durocher's sobriquet
36 *Pistolets et épées*
38 Great thing, to a hipster
39 Rocket stage
41 Went first
42 Eugene's home
45 Ripened
46 Newsman Townsend
48 Card concealers
50 King Hussein's wife
51 Cosmetician Lauder
52 Pleasure doctrine
55 Aching
59 P __ "phony"
60 Hijinks
62 "Oh, yeah"
63 Actor Delon
64 War god
65 Promising
66 Snouts
67 Ecliptic intersection

DOWN

1 Speedy
2 Wheels of fortune?
3 Nisan preceder
4 Dick Haymes, e.g.
5 Getting the lead out?
6 Fam. member
7 Computer clientele
8 Dark purple
9 Inspectors of a sort
10 Jockey Eddie
11 Prototypical undergrad
12 __ of Cleves
13 "Nuts!"
18 Garr or Hatcher
22 Oscar de la __
24 Missouri Indians
26 Not ersatz
27 Goofed
28 Great stuff
29 __ *Fables*
30 Informal eatery
33 *Us* or *W*
35 Shoulder enhancers
37 Athenian lawgiver
40 Strategy
43 Rutgers' river
44 Part of UN
47 __ *Tunes* (cartoon series)
49 Carson's replacement
51 Lazarus and Thompson
52 Winning margin, maybe
53 Exxon, formerly
54 Fly alone
56 Nautical prefix
57 Angry
58 Wall St. big board
61 Old oath

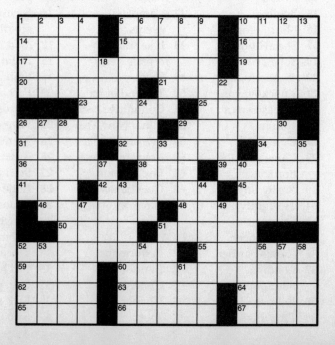

909 NET WORK by Shirley Soloway

ACROSS

1 Former Egyptian leader
6 Coddle
10 To-do
14 Fighting ___ (Notre Dame)
15 McClurg of sitcoms
16 Folk follower
17 NETS
20 Tie adornment
21 Day segment
22 "Ready ___!"
23 Choral voice
24 Theater balcony
26 NETS
33 King Mongkut's nanny
34 Position, in golf
35 Bumped into
36 "Get ___ writing!"
37 Uses a low phaser setting
39 Fit
40 Decay
41 Author Deighton
42 "Step ___"
43 NETS
49 "Excuse me"
50 In its present state
51 Aromatic flavoring
54 Mardi ___
55 Skater Babilonia
58 NETS
62 *Coffee, Tea ___?*
63 Heedless
64 Devoured
65 Wild pig
66 Auto-
67 Pick up the tab

DOWN

1 Prepare flour
2 Diva's feature
3 Recording medium
4 Cigar end
5 *The Cat in ___*
6 Perplex
7 Hebrew month
8 Storage drawer
9 Last word of Joyce's *Ulysses*
10 Small bloom
11 Minnesota bird
12 Alice's troubadour
13 Nuisance
18 Writer Macdonald
19 Roman garb
23 Grain part
24 Set down
25 Bauxite and galena
26 Lorre, in *The Maltese Falcon*
27 Ahead
28 Get together
29 Drop abruptly
30 Muscat native
31 Old thing
32 Printers' marks
37 Blackthorn fruit
38 Semester
39 ___ de combat
44 1 Across' predecessor
45 "Whoopee!"
46 A long ways away
47 PDQ
48 *The Deep* actress
51 "Get ___" (1958 song)
52 Pianist Peter
53 ___ la Douce
54 Purpose
55 Head: Fr.
56 Vicinity
57 Doesn't exist
59 3-ft. lengths
60 Bray start
61 Pavement material

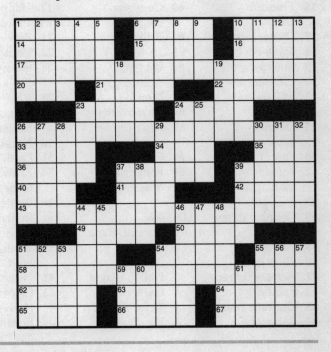

910 QUESTIONABLE by Robert H. Wolfe

ACROSS

1 Dr. Dre's forte
4 Former map abbr.
8 Sounded like a crow
13 Actress Moran
15 Before long
16 Centrist leader
17 Trig function
18 Questionable daywear
20 Bring into agreement
22 Ogrish
23 Questionable hookah
27 "How sweet ___!"
30 More hoarse
31 Word before brand or recognition
32 Hit flies
34 Burn the edges
36 Major unrest
37 Drag
39 Take on
41 Metal *por* Pizarro
42 Clad
46 Comedienne Martha
47 Opera star
49 Polish leader's family
51 Tore
52 Questionable goblet
56 Word form for "flow"
58 Compass pointer
59 Questionable lingerie
64 Witnessed
65 Pick up
66 Actor Stoltz
67 Bob tail?
68 Library items
69 ___ Doc Duvalier
70 SAT preparers

DOWN

1 Cut again
2 Math. branch
3 Noted 15th-century caravel
4 Movie guides?
5 Jack of *Barney Miller*
6 Farm female
7 E.R. workers
8 Sign over
9 NYC transport
10 Left, questionably
11 Nav. rank
12 Windows alternative
14 Uncommitted
19 Come forth
21 Not so messy
24 Second addendum, for short
25 Second sequel, cinematically
26 Enclosure
28 Spitting ___
29 Dry
32 Paper money
33 Questionable barrier
35 Steam up
37 Outfield covers
38 Conference
40 Like a vacuum
43 Scrooge word
44 Ron of *Tarzan*
45 Lair
48 Remain loyal
50 Roman philosopher
53 Fred Astaire's sister
54 February hazard
55 Ships off
57 They have eagle eyes
59 Nth: Abbr.
60 Word form for "recent"
61 Wise, man
62 Christian, for one
63 Lacerate

911 ON THE MOVE by Bob Lubbers

ACROSS
1 Thickening agent
5 Lusterless
9 Morley of *60 Minutes*
14 Puerto __
15 Stir (up)
16 Treasure cache
17 Oyster relative
18 State: Fr.
19 Buenos __
20 Clothier
23 MD specialty
24 Tatters
25 Dodges
27 Salary, e.g.
30 Part of FBI
32 Aussie marsupial
33 Snoopers
35 Country singer Hank
38 Gather
40 Short joke
41 Actress Berger
42 Peddle
43 Unpretentious
45 Long time
46 Four-baggers
48 Saw the sights
50 Ad phrase
52 Speaker's table
53 Diner's add-on
54 Battery booster
60 Copy, for short
62 British peer
63 Ex-senior
64 On __ (romping)
65 Moniker
66 Roof overhang
67 After-dinner wines
68 Old oath
69 Freberg or Musial

DOWN
1 Curved shape
2 River in Arizona
3 Hail __ (flag a taxi)
4 Actor Cesar
5 Big digger
6 Moreno and Hayworth
7 Partner of alack
8 A Little Woman
9 Go hungry
10 Jackie's ex
11 Harbinger
12 Happening
13 Takes five
21 Parkway exits
22 Corn spikes
26 Soften
27 Ret. accounts
28 Alaska city
29 Bituminous hauler
30 Necklace units
31 Prod
34 Frankenstein's helper
36 Western Indian
37 Magic stick
39 Trudge in mud
41 Impassive
43 Café card
44 Hollywood hopeful
47 Captains' superiors
49 Practices
50 Watchband
51 "I wouldn't __ you" ("Honest!")
52 Word form for "skin"
55 Repair
56 Carson predecessor
57 Pesky child
58 Molten rock
59 Genesis spot
61 __-a-tat

912 KEEP SMILING by Gerald R. Ferguson

ACROSS
1 *Ne plus ultra*
5 Mixer for rum
9 NaCl
13 Felt flu-ish
15 Bartlett's attrib.
16 Lover of 71 Across
17 Football coach Don
18 Macduff, for one
19 Performs
20 1981 Neil Simon film
23 That lady
24 Kitchen ending
25 Vaulted alcove
29 Most unusual
33 Part of CPO
35 Not fooled by
36 Heavy-hearted
39 Titillate
43 Class
44 Conductor Klemperer
45 "My Old __"
46 Tot's toy
49 Mellowed, as wine
50 Defendant's offering
53 Under the weather
55 Art Linkletter program
62 Hard to find
63 Ran, in a way
64 __ *Now* (Murrow program)
66 Land area
67 Linger
68 St. Pete's twin
69 Golfer's props
70 Alpha Centauri, e.g.
71 Broadway title character of 1922

DOWN
1 __-relief
2 Sonic bounce
3 Steer clear of
4 Swiss hero
5 Redeemed, as a check
6 In the old days
7 Great northern diver
8 Contrary one
9 Anwar or Jihan
10 More or less
11 Feudal superior
12 TV host/musician John
14 Week units
21 He's on first
22 Emit, as steam
25 Overture follower
26 Donahue or Esposito
27 See 53 Across
28 Scaredy-cat's shout
30 "I __ choose to run": Coolidge
31 Yacht hdg.
32 Ave. crossers
34 Deodorizer scent
36 Plan staller
37 Crowning point
38 Gave a new color to
40 Zeta follower
41 Baseball's Ed or Mel
42 In the manner of
47 German ditties
48 Santa's helper
50 Tolstoy title word
51 *M* star
52 Blunted swords
54 Insatiable desire
55 Prefix for fall
56 Recedes
57 Found a perch
58 Hester Prynne's decoration
59 At hand
60 Fictional commander
61 Shrill barks
65 __ kwon do

913 — THE "IN" GROUP by Shirley Soloway

ACROSS

1 Germ fighters
5 Maui greeting
10 Resident of Aberdeen
14 Sharif of films
15 Franchise exerciser
16 Day segment
17 In __ (hale and hearty)
19 Fairy-tale start
20 Poseidon's son
21 Flamboyance
23 Therefore
25 Determination
26 *Great Expectations* name
29 In __ (commonly)
32 Western tribe member
35 Remove, as an error
37 Emulate Saint George
38 Osiris' spouse
39 Posed a challenge
40 Anne Jackson's spouse
41 Swoon
42 "__ boy!"
43 Penn. and Grand Central
44 Hole __ (ace)
45 Tropical garland
46 In __ (by the way)
48 Actress Carrie
49 Grease deposit
51 Patricia of *Hud*
53 Like otters
56 Military units
60 Uninteresting
61 In __ (quickly)
64 Use an old phone
65 Aunt: Fr.
66 Hammett or Ibsen character
67 Agile
68 Reeves/Bullock film
69 Cultural subjects

DOWN

1 Fluffy
2 Mideast leader
3 Hindu noblewoman
4 Mountain ridge
5 Settle a score
6 Home site
7 Diamond great Mel
8 "Mayday!"
9 Small passage
10 Sandbank
11 In __ (finally)
12 "That hurts!"
13 Holly or walnut
18 Processed iron
22 Zero
24 Beginnings
26 Go by bike
27 Ticked off
28 In __ (specifically)
30 Raines and Fitzgerald
31 Muffin ingredient
33 Having a metallic sound
34 Makeup maven Lauder
36 Bering or Baltic
38 Writer Fleming
41 Opera barber
43 Cruel ones
46 Place
47 Kept after expenses
50 Political gathering
52 Judy's second daughter
53 Inserts
54 Humorous remark
55 Fellow
57 Nose detection
58 Saucy
59 Sp. ladies
62 *A Chorus Line* finale
63 Hwy.

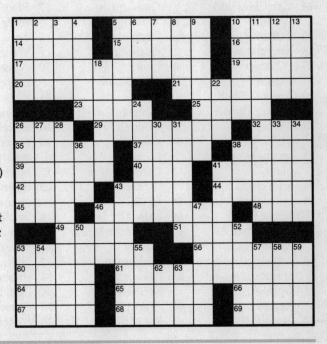

914 — WHAT'S ON TONIGHT by Dean Niles

ACROSS

1 Staff starter
5 Milk drink
10 Partly closed
14 Million suffix
15 __ in (surrendered)
16 Fixed procedure
17 Doc's predecessor
20 Doddering
21 Make money, maybe
22 MD employer
23 Groove in a board
25 NYC summer setting
27 Thurman of *Pulp Fiction*
30 Conduit
32 Angel
36 Zhivago's love
38 Most August folks
40 TV sound
41 Johnny's magic act
44 Home, to a cowboy
45 Intellectual, to some
46 Very: Fr.
47 Nissan model
49 Amulet
51 Superlative suffix
52 Slippery fellow
53 Break of day
55 *Exodus* hero
58 Lamb's pen name
61 Calls it quits
65 1969 event
68 Gymnast Korbut
69 Stay home for dinner
70 Revise
71 High point
72 Restrict in amount
73 Beatty film

DOWN

1 Singing Mama
2 Resembling
3 Actress Moran
4 Smelly
5 Plan for
6 Hoo-__ (to-do)
7 With, on the Oise
8 Vegas game
9 Whirlpools
10 Timetable abbr.
11 Kid around
12 Small matter?
13 Janet in the Cabinet
18 Attired
19 Make beloved
24 Indian, e.g.
26 Rely on
27 Excessive
28 Taj __
29 "__ You Glad You're You?"
31 Aleut carving
33 Think the world of
34 Cone-bearing trees
35 Lift up
37 Texas A&M athlete
39 Atlantic haddock
42 Encounter again
43 Contiguous
48 Axis enemies
50 Was indebted
54 Consumer voice
55 Over
56 Irritate
57 Actress Swenson
59 "__ the end of my rope!"
60 Wine region
62 A Möbius strip has only one
63 Oklahoma city
64 Some NCOs
66 Talk like an animal?
67 Capture

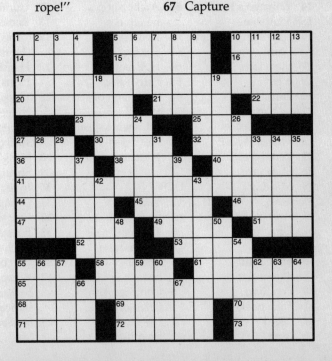

915 NAME GAME by Henry Hook

ACROSS
1 Titanic downfall?
4 Slightly
8 Wholesale
12 Sullivan's presentation?
13 King's mad dog
14 Carnegiea and opuntia
15 TOM
18 Rd. relative
19 "Oysters __ season"
20 Actor O'Brien
21 Paul or Brown
22 Dueler : second :: diplomat : __
25 Japanese salad plant
26 Rote chant
28 "Comment allez-__?"
29 Opposite of 31 Across
30 After-shave application
31 Opposite of 29 Across
32 Bingo call
33 DICK
37 Namath's alma mater
40 Tree lead-in
41 "Stupid __ stupid does"
44 Director Jean-__ Goddard
45 Very dry
46 Campaign catchphrase
48 Live
49 __ de Monte Cristo
51 Incense
52 Doddering
54 Horace's __ Poetica
55 Center square, perhaps
56 HARRY
60 Lam it for love
61 One of the Dalton gang?
62 Western Indians
63 Diamond borders?
64 "Has 1001 __"
65 Rat of film

DOWN
1 Fielder's cry
2 Piano's cousin
3 Lamb's mama
4 Keenness
5 Overcooked
6 H-L link
7 Placekicker's pride
8 Teacher, in oaters
9 Write-up
10 A late bus passenger . . .
11 . . . can't do this
12 Humiliated
14 Secret writing
16 Complete absorption
17 Maestro Menuhin
23 Essence of guacamole
24 Stable kid
27 Filmdom's Joe Tynan
32 "How can you __ stubborn?"
34 Buffet piece
35 Grand-scale
36 Most ignoble
37 @#?&*!!
38 Radiance
39 '84 U.S. Open champ
42 Get one's dander up
43 Crusader's foe
45 Parisian path
46 Mavericks
47 Woody areas?
50 Possibly
53 Mighty mites?
57 Greek letter
58 Hardly the big shot
59 Seagoing bucket of bolts

916 STATE FARE by Bob Lubbers

ACROSS
1 Recedes
5 Opposite the mouth
11 Compete, as for apples
14 Zhivago's love
15 Movable
16 Supplement, with "out"
17 State fare
19 Exist
20 Family car
21 __ Nidre
22 Art sch. class
23 Tim of WKRP
25 Pedal digits
28 State fare
33 Midday
35 Mai __ (cocktail)
36 And others: Lat.
37 Directional suffix
38 Fitzgerald's namesakes
40 Pen fluid
41 Take back
44 "Bird" word form
45 Constructed
46 State fare
49 Long for
50 Affirmatives
51 Average grades
54 Topper
56 Archbishop's headpiece
60 Drumstick
61 State fare
64 H.S. math
65 Fairy king
66 Anderson of WKRP
67 Ed.'s worksheets
68 Not finished
69 Matching outfit

DOWN
1 Yalies
2 Beckoned
3 Thin nail
4 Like a desert
5 Rock-band need
6 Contract with Crichton, e.g.
7 Director Preminger
8 Theater district
9 Supermodel Carol
10 August birth sign
11 Fiber-rich food
12 Gumbo base
13 Borscht base
18 "The __ Love" (Dorsey tune)
22 Hammett terrier
24 Plans (to)
26 Physician's concern
27 Superlative suffix
28 Ming's planet
29 Spring bloomer
30 Inventor Howe
31 Orange peel
32 Rice wine
33 Foam-ball brand
34 Pitcher Hershiser
39 Part of FAA
42 Weapons
43 Second-sequel indicator
45 Baseballer Stan's kin
47 Not __ of evidence
48 Do-fa filler
51 Chowder chunk
52 Morays
53 Easter items
55 Word form for "soil"
57 You, once
58 Hindu queen
59 Send forth
61 Expense receipt: Abbr.
62 __ Saud
63 Pilot's hdg.

917 CUTTING EDGE by Gregory E. Paul

ACROSS
1 "The Georgia Peach"
5 __ Boothe Luce
10 Ski lift
14 Again
15 Ontario Indian
16 Taboo
17 Bamako's country
18 Audibly
19 Small branch
20 '82 Harrison Ford film
23 Graph add-on
24 "My __ Sal"
25 Business clothes, perhaps
27 Soprano Peters et al.
32 Stink
33 "__ Believer" (Monkees tune)
34 __ It ('83 Cruise film)
36 Rationality
39 Tweety, for one
41 Dressed to the __
43 Thoughtful
44 War horse
46 Eagle's nest
48 Tropical fruit
49 Candy units
51 Temperance
53 Proportionately
56 Part of TGIF
57 Done with, with "of"
58 Hugh Beaumont role
64 Actress Sommer
66 She plays Fran on Mad About You
67 Senator Grassley's state
68 Epidermis
69 Donna of fashion
70 ". . . __ o'clock scholar"
71 Fax, perhaps
72 Snoozed
73 Ride __ on (control)

DOWN
1 Hair-care need
2 Track shape
3 Oscar role for Martin
4 River crosser
5 Actor Heston
6 Berg opera
7 Elvis __ Presley
8 Without corners
9 Make beloved
10 Explosive letters
11 Alamo weapon?
12 Singer O'Day
13 Walkie-talkie word
21 Pianist Hines
22 Deli breads
26 "Eight Days a __"
27 Barbecued food
28 Exclude
29 Soliloquy prop
30 Korea's continent
31 Trig terms
35 Detective Wolfe
37 Tizzy
38 Uptight
40 Letter opener?
42 Hissing
45 Dead heat
47 Art Deco designer
50 Corn holders
52 Bible book
53 Fourth estate
54 German poet
55 "And we'll have __ good time"
59 Calamitous
60 Show approval
61 Suffragist's quest
62 Jug
63 McNally's partner
65 Tackle's teammate

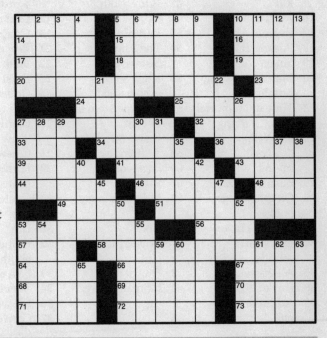

918 THOU SWELLS by Dean Niles

ACROSS
1 Kathie Lee's cohost
6 Place
11 Sound of disgust
14 Happening
15 See 10 Down
16 Actor Stephen
17 Abdominal dimple
19 A/C unit
20 Gave an excuse for
21 Bucket
22 Query response
25 College board
27 Bugle tune
28 B-F link
31 __ Fifth Avenue
32 IRS time
33 Newswoman Connie
35 Braided cord
37 Power, in a way
39 Uproar
40 Uncle Miltie
42 First name in cheesecake
43 State drawing
45 Singular contribution?
46 Not sim.
48 "__ Can I Turn To?"
49 '40s conflict
50 French chemist
53 Trumpet, at times
55 Pain in the neck
56 Sets right
59 Sault __ Marie
60 Final phase
64 Shade
65 Actress Ekland
66 __ branch (peace sign)
67 Likely
68 Word form for "bone"
69 Poet Elinor

DOWN
1 Confederate
2 Christmas predecessor
3 Coagulate
4 Acquired family
5 Mode of expression
6 Check piece
7 Comic Jacques
8 Walk in
9 Battery terminals
10 With 15 Across, Vega$ private eye
11 City's spread
12 "Come and __!"
13 Tugs along
18 Canoe-bark source
21 Black tea
22 Rat-__
23 Neck parts
24 Planning software
26 Camille star
29 Twofold
30 Furnish, as with funds
33 Rub the wrong way
34 Barbarian
36 Miss __ (Dallas role)
38 Well-worn
41 Arab prince
44 Namely
47 Rages
49 With sapience
50 Turkish official
51 Malfunction
52 Send in payment
54 Bow missile
57 Singer Seeger
58 Concerning
60 Cinemax rival
61 Twice-shortened preposition
62 LIII doubled
63 __ Haw

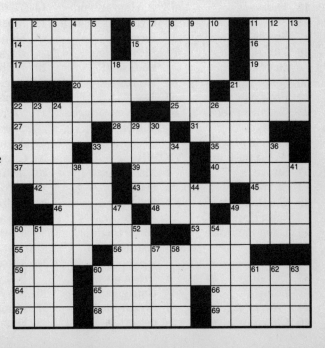

919 WHEN IN ROME by Norma Steinberg

ACROSS
1 Pigs' digs
5 Monk's room
9 From Geneva
14 Dairy-case choice
15 Sheriff Taylor's kid
16 Kind of bean
17 Region: Abbr.
18 Pocket contents
19 Singer John
20 Man's grooming problem
23 Time immemorial
24 __ out a living
25 Mr. Yeltsin
27 "__ was saying . . ."
29 Business AKA
32 *On the Frontier* poet
33 Parts of circles
34 Dairy-farm sounds
35 All gussied up
38 Part of NEA
39 Additive to *café*
40 Debbie or Ethan
41 Some cal. pgs.
42 Yes vote
43 Oversatiates
44 Large container
46 Give up, in poker
47 Pride, sloth, etc.
53 Part of a poem
54 The Andrews Sisters, e.g.
55 Klutz's exclamation
57 Hammerstein or Levant
58 Bump into
59 __-friendly
60 Back-comb
61 Father
62 Makes a blouse

DOWN
1 Cook's purchase
2 Hgt.
3 Pianist Peter
4 Morgan le Fay, e.g.
5 : : :
6 DeMille output
7 Part of a chain
8 "Oh, why not?"
9 Put into words
10 Dorian Gray's creator
11 Long-division word
12 Cache
13 Offspring
21 Beef cuts
22 Bank job
25 Beast of burden
26 *Golden Boy* playwright
27 Clarinetist Shaw
28 Glaswegian, e.g.
29 Furniture protector
30 Contends in the ring
31 Org.
32 Economist Smith
33 "An apple __ . . ."
34 Tuneful
36 Fill with joy
37 Corridors
43 Road Runner's pursuer
44 Tennis star Gerulaitis
45 Put on a pedestal
46 Frequent __ program
47 Flower container
48 Early Peruvian
49 Bank conveniences
50 *Eins, zwei, __*
51 Schnozz
52 Cast forth
53 Portable bed
56 Jrs.' parents

920 POSSESSIVENESS by Rich Norris

ACROSS
1 Brokaw or Rather
7 Revise extensively, as a novel
13 First name in gospel
15 Hide
16 Speedily
17 Scouts' concerns
18 Philosopher's clay?
20 Señor Guevara
22 Food fish
23 Gazetteer abbr.
24 Nasty
27 Dad, in Mayfair
29 Acted the ham
31 Stroke
32 St. crossers
36 Continued a subscription
38 Devil-may-care
40 Host
41 Virgo preceder
43 '50s singer Julius
44 "Ain't," e.g.
46 Chan portrayer
47 Mild epithet
50 Word form for "skin"
52 Salt or glass ender
53 President's futuristic toy?
57 Asylum seeker
58 Overconcern with form
61 Most under-nourished
62 Expresses
63 Tax
64 *Illness as Metaphor* author

DOWN
1 Medical grp.
2 Pester
3 Field-trip guide
4 Office corridor
5 Southwestern stewpot
6 Urban unrest
7 Unfeigned
8 Cream-filled dessert
9 Plunders, with "upon"
10 Ivan of tennis
11 Four German kings
12 Sellecca's husband
14 To the rear, at sea
15 Epistle author
19 Shot or happy starter
20 With 35 Down, singer's investment?
21 Veronica of *Hill Street Blues*
25 Agonize
26 Chop
28 Inclusive term
30 Actor Gabriel
32 Bushy hairstyle
33 Anne-Sophie Mutter, for one
34 Museum Folkwang site
35 See 20 Down
37 Firmly decided
39 Skim milk's lack
42 Unique item
44 Long looks
45 Understanding
47 Sale items, often
48 Falls, perhaps
49 Longhorn rival
51 Old stories
53 Singer McEntire
54 Stack role
55 Greek sandwich
56 __ Bator
59 ". . . a __ of troubles": Shakespeare
60 Food additive

921   SWEET DREAMS by Robert H. Wolfe

ACROSS
1 Endures
6 Neigh's relative
10 Hardly snaillike
14 Seething
15 Marcello's money
16 Stare at
17 Alabama city
18 Profess
19 A __ of One's Own (Woolf novel)
20 One ready for bed
22 Pitfall
23 Botherer
24 Nolan and Irene
25 __ Boulevard (Swanson film)
29 Deli side dish
31 Beg
32 Nonviolent ones
37 Once more
38 Dinner course
39 Spruced up
40 Soaked, in a way
42 Glide, in a way
43 Beatty and Rorem
44 Prynne of fiction
45 Aphorism
48 Strong __ ox
50 Black bird
51 Go to sleep
57 Picador's prey
58 __ about (approximately)
59 Actress Leslie
60 Not fooled by
61 Humorist Bombeck
62 Kate's TV partner
63 Peruse
64 Breathing, to an MD
65 Appropriated

DOWN
1 Maiden
2 Second son
3 Food fish
4 Newsweek rival
5 Smacked on the face
6 The __ (boredom)
7 Rosie's fastener
8 Zone
9 Lawn spot
10 Short snooze
11 Greek marketplace
12 Wake of the Ferry painter
13 Fill-ins, for short
21 Although
24 Brit. fliers
25 Lunch meat
26 Arm bone
27 Not even once, to Blake
28 Snoring
29 Large number
30 Lash holder
32 Butter portions
33 Lager relative
34 Do an usher's job
35 London art gallery
36 Brit. currency
38 Blue
41 Society-page word
42 New York Indians
44 "So there!"
45 Role player
46 Pilotless craft
47 Blood line
48 Basic parts
49 Watchband
51 Gardener, at times
52 About
53 Shaker's grains
54 Woody's son
55 Wind
56 Leg joint

922   VOWEL PLAY by Bob Lubbers

ACROSS
1 Dalai __
5 Skirt bottoms
9 Bud rival
14 Right away: Abbr.
15 Latin verb form
16 Talk big
17 Italian prime minister Aldo
18 Soccer great
19 Agitator
20 Political stump
23 Atty.'s degree
24 Floral greetings
25 Chekhov's "Uncle" et al.
27 Filet
30 Piano practice
32 "__ was saying . . ."
33 Poseidon's son
35 Perlman of Cheers
38 Spicy sauce
40 At this moment
41 Catcalls
42 Ship's body
43 Alien heroine
45 Silkworm
46 Big cruisers
48 Poems
50 Kingston music genre
52 Curse
53 Spanish gold
54 Exotic entertainer
60 Keaton or Ladd
62 The Auld Sod
63 Roof edge
64 Keaton or Ladd
65 Eros alias
66 Toothy smile
67 Tweed-basher's kin
68 Criticizes
69 Glamour rival

DOWN
1 Essays of Elia author
2 Without __ (broke)
3 Clayey deposit
4 Moon-landing program
5 More elated
6 Ostrich cousins
7 Shopping center
8 Ladder segment
9 Door
10 Onassis, for short
11 Imported footwear
12 Carved slab
13 Conditions
21 Rumormonger
22 Nagy or Lendl
26 Sleuth Wolfe
27 Speed burst
28 Rebekah's son
29 Bewhiskered bleaters
30 Organ devices
31 Head covering
34 Monogram pt.
36 Raison d'__
37 Sale stipulation
39 Volcano output
41 Scavenging mammal
43 Former president of South Korea
44 Dodgers
47 Scottish poles
49 Bridge blunder
50 1957 movie monster
51 Writer Jong
52 Childe Harold poet
55 Jump
56 Peru's capital
57 Reiner or Sagan
58 Satanic
59 M. Descartes
61 "She loves me __"

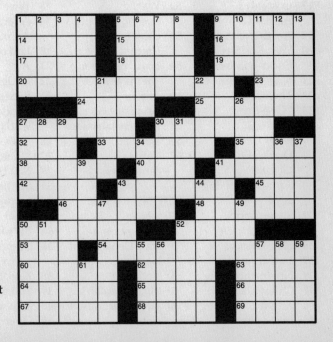

923 THROUGH THE RANKS by Christopher Page

ACROSS

1 Mountaintop
5 No longer in
10 Meander
14 Princess of India
15 Nile dam site
16 Etcher's need
17 Roman road
18 Beet variety
19 Following
20 Some E-mail transmissions
22 Teary
24 One person buying stock
30 FICA grp.
31 __ canto (singing style)
32 Hand movement
33 Rings
35 List leader
36 Dodger Stadium offering
42 "__ Rhythm"
43 Greenstreet costar
44 Spruces (up)
48 Mature
49 Texas coll.
52 Primary follower
55 Arrested
56 Former Portuguese colony
57 Tennis pro Fernandez
60 Available
63 Flag
64 Deuce follower, perhaps
65 Central Vermont ski area
66 Pub offerings
67 __ the Drum Slowly
68 Liturgical prayer
69 Hotbed

DOWN

1 Dresses carefully
2 Trenchermen
3 Lack of iron
4 Bolshoi rival
5 Campaign contributor
6 Bat wood
7 Hindu pundit
8 Malay garb
9 Salad herb
10 "Who __ a Millionaire?" (Porter tune)
11 Drink cooler
12 86
13 Banned insecticide
21 Scimitar kin
23 French possessive
25 Blue-green shade
26 Model Macpherson
27 Chicken of the sea
28 Russian city
29 Honest-to-goodness
33 __ about (meandering)
34 Pitcher Maglie
36 Chinese for "luminous"
37 Writer James
38 Artist Miró
39 Orr score
40 Prod
41 Put up
45 Stat for 34 Down
46 __ of the North
47 Staircase-walking toy
49 Literary device
50 Dudley and Demi
51 Riot cause
53 PC key
54 Moon of Jupiter
57 The gift of __
58 Lupino or Cantor
59 Boll cleaner
61 Pierre's pal
62 Baltimore bard

924 TOUGH TWOSOME by Rand H. Burns

ACROSS

1 Forage crop
8 Poe title
15 More temperamental
16 Too much hair, medically
17 Costars of 37 Across
19 Academic stat
20 West Side Story Oscar-winner
21 Singer Axton
23 Threadlike
24 "One-hoss __"
28 Heavenly body
29 Derek and Jackson
30 Anti-price-fixing agcy.
32 Silver source
33 York portrayer
35 Hairdressers
37 1946 film
39 Not forthcoming
41 Galley slave's activity
44 In the past
45 Homburg or Panama
46 Son of Jacob
47 Sri Lanka export
48 Volume
50 Info-gathering mission
52 Wacky
53 Bosses, in Africa
55 Gibson or Brooks
56 17 Across, soon after filming 37 Across
62 Undisturbed
63 Renders harmless
64 Hawked
65 Callas companion

DOWN

1 UN rep.
2 Card game
3 State Department locale
4 Acclimate
5 Milan moolah
6 Tire-price add-on: Abbr.
7 A Musketeer
8 Air movements
9 WWI bond
10 Thicke of Hope & Gloria
11 Madrid madmen
12 '96 Olympics host
13 Wire measure
14 Alien's course: Abbr.
18 Lon of Cambodia
21 Ad __ committee
22 El Dorado's lure
23 Patience
25 London chaplains who tend the ill
26 __ Deco
27 "Fine!"
29 Nut tree
31 Spotless
34 Honor-society letter
35 PD rank
36 Comparative suffix
38 Betrothed
39 Snitch
40 Trip taker?
42 Open fabric
43 Chitchat
46 Dance step
49 Flowed back
51 Crow sound
52 Old VCRs
54 Dutch river
55 High land
56 Aware, so to speak
57 French article
58 What MPH quantifies
59 Half a sawbuck
60 "__ Blue?"
61 Orig. texts

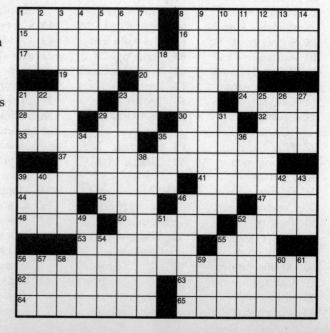

925   DANCE FEVER by Gregory E. Paul

ACROSS

1 IRS employees
5 Clean a chimney
10 Dogie
14 Gap
15 Pet rocks, e.g.
16 Russian city
17 Whit
18 Amber or mastic
19 Casa __ Orchestra
20 '20s dance
22 Actor Sharif
23 Porridge grain
24 Treat with carbon dioxide
26 Kind of drum
30 Colonist William
32 Forster title start
33 '40s dance
38 Ponce de __
39 Sport shirts
40 Sharpen
41 Lively dance
43 United rival
44 Gasp
45 Silver-tongued speaker
46 Part of AWOL
50 Harem room
51 Great Northern diver
52 Ragtime dance
59 Churchill Downs denizen
60 Needle cases
61 Unctuous
62 MA's motto start
63 Breathing sounds
64 Boo-boo
65 Bring up
66 "__ Lady" (Tom Jones song)
67 Gin flavor

DOWN

1 Cartoonist Young
2 Word of disparagement
3 Neighbor of Mont.
4 Char
5 Something very funny
6 Take by force
7 Bridge position
8 Singer Pinza
9 Stadium souvenirs
10 Silver or gold
11 Scent
12 Paul of *Melvin and Howard*
13 Emergency signal
21 Pend
25 Buffalo-to-Rochester dir.
26 #1 on the Mohs scale
27 Chocolate cookie
28 Debatable
29 Nobelist Morrison
30 Oven light
31 Thames town
33 Merge
34 Big bird
35 *A Man for All Seasons* playwright
36 Golden Rule word
37 Accoutrements
39 "The Great Pretender" group, with "The"
42 ANA member
43 Cart
45 Black Sea port
46 Modify
47 Wilderness Road warrior
48 March man
49 Sign up for
50 Steinbeck characters
53 The 45th state
54 Hold sway
55 Easy throw
56 Lunar trench
57 Mélange
58 Input data, perhaps

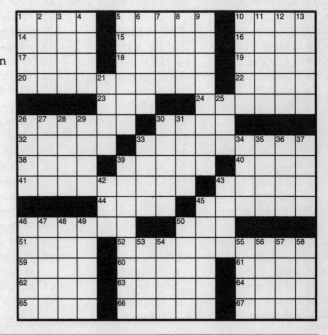

926   OPEN-DOOR POLICY by Gerald R. Ferguson

ACROSS

1 Molecule part
5 Frost
9 Send a package
13 Fizzy drinks
15 List ender
16 Type size
17 "Who's there?" gags
20 Graham or Lorne
21 Dangerous falls
22 Morning moisture
23 Chapter's partner
24 Asian sea
28 Word before hatch or clause
32 __ the house (husband)
34 Mother-of-pearl source
38 Mail option
42 Used a baton
43 Medical aide
44 __ pie (a snap)
47 Witticisms
48 Song of David
52 40 winks
54 Hubbubs
57 Cross-hairs sight
61 Jack Lemmon film of '64
64 Perry's creator
65 Robt. __
66 Basie's instrument
67 Golf-ball stands
68 Physique
69 Beer holders

DOWN

1 Inquire
2 Chinese secret society
3 Aroma
4 War club
5 Extends, as a subscription
6 L.A. judge Lance
7 Speed-of-sound word
8 Actress Sommer
9 Fine china
10 Scout, at times
11 Bakery workers
12 Out of date
14 Travel-info sheet, for short
18 Leg joint
19 It's tossed in track
24 Morning hrs.
25 Engrossed
26 Once more
27 Places, to Pliny
29 Course worker
30 Presidential nickname
31 Buddy
33 *Backdraft* extra
35 Egg cell
36 Ruler before Galba
37 Prefix for while
39 __ carte
40 Bandleader Brown
41 "Indeed!"
45 National song
46 Swedish automaker
48 __ Sound, WA
49 Mushroom-to-be
50 Played __ (acted)
51 Ore sources
53 Play thing?
55 Coral ridge
56 Fodder holder
58 Uncompromising
59 Birthright seller
60 Zest
62 Cologne's loc.
63 Yr. components

927   HOLD IT! by Bob Lubbers

ACROSS

1 Singer Vikki
5 Speaker's platform
9 Civvies
14 To the sheltered side
15 Icelandic epic
16 Burger topper
17 Croat or Serb
18 Diet target
19 Big nicks
20 Coiled ruler
23 ''Golly!''
24 Rajah's consort
25 Prince of Monaco
27 Astaire's frequent partner
30 Celestial radiation source
32 Center or cure starter
33 Entertain lavishly
35 __-slapper (joke)
38 Fop
40 MA cape
41 Wal-Mart competitor
42 Ms. Korbut
43 Chicken part
45 Little devil
46 Abdicator of 1936
48 Combination at the track
50 Upper-body passage
52 Mishmash
53 He opposed DDE
54 Lightning partner
60 Fork fingers
62 Set of laws
63 __-friendly
64 Literary bell town
65 Mortgage, e.g.
66 Gin additive
67 Age
68 JFK postings
69 Shade

DOWN

1 Assign roles
2 __ breve
3 Gather, as a harvest
4 Midnight rider
5 Coach's concern
6 Part of 53 Across
7 Lupino et al.
8 *Elephant Boy* actor
9 Posers
10 One: Fr.
11 Itch reliever
12 Schlepper
13 Map close-up
21 Wed
22 Breathing sound
26 Make cake
27 Decorate again
28 October stone
29 Crisp cookie
30 Like some windows
31 Forearm bone
34 Actress Teri
36 Writer Bombeck
37 Spot
39 Pedestal section
41 Set of steps
43 Chaucer's Wife of __
44 Bad tempers
47 Doyle doctor
49 Hearty
50 Turkic tongue
51 *The __ Chronicles* (Wasserstein play)
52 More unusual
55 Bruins' sch.
56 Black: Fr.
57 Norway's capital
58 Spinks or Trotsky
59 Corner
61 Compass dir.

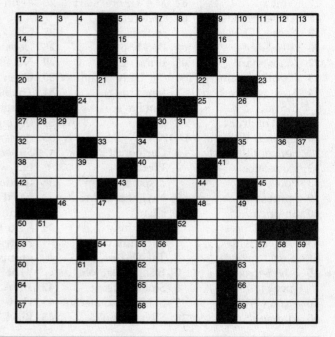

928   HIGHMINDEDNESS by Rich Norris

ACROSS

1 __ loco
6 Shower alternative
10 FDR follower
13 Conform
14 Veranda, on Maui
15 Skater Midori
16 Camera attachment
18 Fundamental
19 Place to live
20 Ointment
22 Dues payers
25 Made a goof
27 Surfeited
28 Rum-and-curaçao drink
29 Abundances
30 *The Web and the Rock* author
31 WWII vessel
34 __ kleine Nachtmusik
35 Throttle
36 Happiness
37 NY time
38 Uses a horizontal bar
39 Pours
40 City in Ohio or Georgia
42 Attempt, old-style
43 Repose
45 He played Nabors' cousin
46 Visceral
47 Bridal path
48 Traditional tattoo subject
49 Saturday-matinee device
55 Small land mass: Fr.
56 Big name in hotels
57 Ant-sized
58 Brown shade
59 Urges
60 Wear away

DOWN

1 Eagle plus two
2 NYC airport
3 Samovar
4 Computer-memory unit
5 Ammunition of a kind
6 Scourge
7 &
8 Menlo Park inits.
9 Woolly
10 The Clampetts, e.g.
11 Fend (off)
12 Pulled from behind
14 Covers
17 Jack Ryan portrayer
21 Attorney's org.
22 Fibber of radio
23 Immigrant's island
24 Pioneers
25 Columbo portrayer's kin
26 Magazine cofounded by Luce
28 Satellites
30 Complain
32 Horse follower
33 Petulant
35 '87 Oscar-winner
36 Lawn tender
38 Strictly religious
39 Got behind
41 Mao __-tung
42 Ice-cream holder
43 Cap
44 __ Gay
45 Hitchhiker's need
47 Midday pds.
50 Cleaning substance
51 Author Fleming
52 Prizm maker
53 Goal
54 Deli choice

929 DOUBLE MEANINGS by Shirley Soloway

ACROSS
1 Singer Laine
5 Mars' alias
9 Cross the plate
14 Dwell (on)
15 Take out
16 Product 19 rival
17 Capri, e.g.
18 *All __* (Martin/Tomlin film)
19 Up to
20 What a librarian must do?
23 Highway marker
24 Always, to an odist
25 Chinese leader
27 Fall guy
31 Tiny fall flowers?
36 *Les __-Unis*
37 Some seniors
39 Diminutive ending
40 Beef dishes
42 *Cutty __*
43 Earring sellers, at times
45 Author Plain
46 Ship layoffs?
48 Valuable possession
49 Giant Mel
50 Pds. before noon
52 Mom's sister
55 Underwater assignment?
62 Collar inserts
64 Boston orchestra
65 Home lot
66 Iota follower
67 Arcade foul
68 San __, Italy
69 Word after cookie or crib
70 Corrida cheers
71 Yemeni gulf

DOWN
1 Elegantly stylish
2 Cat-o'-nine-tails
3 Author Gardner
4 Oil org.
5 Western home style
6 Change
7 Saint of seamen
8 Look for
9 Actor Erwin
10 Subjects for inmates?
11 Kruger or Kahn
12 Joan Crawford classic
13 Pronoun for *une femme*
21 Types (in)
22 Jimmy of *NYPD Blue*
26 "What Kind of Fool __?"
27 Chick talk
28 Storage area
29 Spud
30 Kind of sound system?
32 "__ my case"
33 Just purchased
34 Ground grains
35 Function (as)
38 Card game
40 Religious groups
41 Capote, to pals
44 100 lbs.
45 Ray Brown's ax
47 Salesman's item
51 Light drizzles
52 Poses, in a way
53 Provo's state
54 Neck area
56 "I'll leave it __ you"
57 Bring to a bubble
58 FDR's mom
59 Frosted
60 *Coffee, Tea __?*
61 Marquee light
63 Took a chair

930 DOUBLE FEATURE by Randolph Ross

ACROSS
1 Lhasa __
5 Arose (from)
11 Sen. Kerrey's state
14 Fellow
15 Monopoly square
16 Poetically ajar
17 Jolson tune
20 Lwyr.
21 Sign of a smash
22 Baltic natives
23 Number cruncher
28 Lined up
29 Tony of the links
30 Assad's nation
31 Ohio bean?
32 "Never pry – lest we lose our __": Browning
34 Proof word
36 Villain Luthor
37 Samaritan's work
41 Oklahoma city
44 Mrs. Copperfield
45 Backs
49 Celtic great
51 Ways to go
54 Place for an ornament
55 Hectare kin
56 Chocoholic's problem
58 Moonshine machine
60 Mexican Mrs.
61 Word alphabetizers ignore
62 Presents good qualifications
67 Hellenic H
68 Independent (of), perhaps
69 Party pooper
70 First st.
71 *No Exit* playwright
72 Ticked off

DOWN
1 Suitable for the stage
2 Snapped
3 Island off Gabon
4 Make a choice
5 Sportscast info
6 "Yecch!"
7 Squealer
8 Picnic pest
9 Sgt. or cpl.
10 Earth sci.
11 Hole in the head
12 Best example
13 "None of your __!"
18 Reprover's comment
19 Small duck
24 North Korean premier __ Song San
25 Come before
26 Cork's country
27 Boil over
33 Grass square
35 Eccentric
38 Clod's cry
39 Tie
40 London neighborhood
41 Embarrassed
42 Impose
43 Incoming plane
46 Take sides
47 "Take that!"
48 Stuck (to)
50 Strike out
52 *__ Street* (Carol Kane film)
53 Took big steps
57 Chinese belief
59 Statutes
63 Pasture
64 Paddle
65 Cable choice
66 Ness' grp.

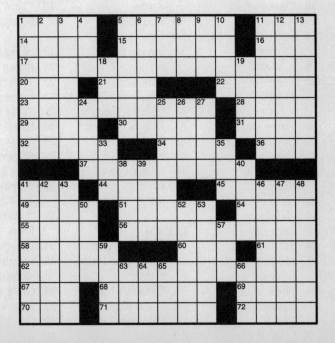

931 BREAKFAST CLUB by Gerald R. Ferguson

ACROSS
1 Lloyd Webber musical
5 Date source
9 Boulder
13 War god
14 Words of understanding
15 Anesthetic gas
17 Gusted
18 Truth-stretcher
19 Howdy __
20 Tennis unit
21 Beatnik's hangout
23 Pitch a dream game
25 The sun
26 Emcees
32 Culture medium
34 Paella ingredient
35 __ Baba
37 Wahine's dance
38 Descartes et al.
39 Etcher's need
40 Malt drink
41 "If __ I Would Leave You"
42 Comedienne Mabley
43 17th-century English philosopher
48 Co. kingpin
49 Gary and Mary
51 "Queen of Hearts" singer
57 Summer, on the Seine
59 Brought to a close
60 Entryway
61 Sword fight
62 Spanish diacritical mark
63 Charged particles
64 Vocal
65 __ off (angry)
66 Advantage
67 Inquires

DOWN
1 Urban vehicles
2 "Over the Rainbow" composer
3 Nondrinker
4 Compass pt.
5 Cockpit figures
6 "__ by magic..."
7 Table extension
8 Unimportant
9 Ardent
10 *Lawrence of Arabia* star
11 __ En-lai
12 Sneaker brand
16 Bread option
21 Spy grp.
22 Curved letters
24 Israeli dance
27 Rome fountain
28 Quarry kin
29 Harsh in temper
30 Storytellers
31 Willowy
32 "Now I see!"
33 Sea extension
36 Psyche sections
38 Scout's job
39 Cupid's alias
44 Agree (to)
45 Requisite
46 Richard III's request
47 Sauce holder
50 T-bone or porterhouse
51 Boeing product
52 Part of BTU
53 Standing by
54 Singer Adams
55 Desk material
56 Chinese protective society
58 Plumbers' fittings
61 __ good deed

932 NO-BRAINER by Eileen Lexau

ACROSS
1 Actress Thompson
5 Trousers
10 Ski lift
14 Grad
15 Santa __, CA
16 Deserve
17 Alaska city
18 Ingredient of 64 Across
19 __ mater
20 Paget or Winger
22 Type of woodpecker
24 Spare hair
26 Drying oven
27 Jack or king, e.g.
30 Firefighter, at times
34 Director Kazan
35 Galena or bauxite
36 Make fun of
37 Mouthpiece for Dobbin
38 "Beautiful __" (Foster song)
40 Sass
41 City of Germany
43 Undercover org.
44 Choir voice
45 *77 Sunset* __
46 Staunch supporters
48 At once, to a doctor
50 Boutique
51 Iron pyrite
56 Spring snow result
59 Sooner st.
60 Above the fray
62 "Sock __ me!"
63 Knight's consort
64 Pasta sauce
65 Flabbergast
66 Easter-egg needs
67 Go in
68 Jekyll's alter ego

DOWN
1 Smooth wood
2 Word on a lotion bottle
3 Caterer's lift
4 "God Bless __"
5 EPA concern
6 "Ah, me!"
7 Space grp.
8 Photographer's device
9 Latin beat
10 Farm machine
11 Baseball no-no
12 "Don't throw bouquets __..."
13 Bring up
21 Ripen
23 Theater aide
25 Contempt
27 Trifle (with)
28 Exist
29 Show a response
31 Clay in an egg
32 Prepares for publication
33 __ *Man* (Estevez film)
34 Recedes
36 Martin and Koontz
38 Govt. agencies
39 Actress Farrow
42 Can't find
44 Do away with
46 Taken illicitly
47 Some AL batters
49 One way to stare
51 Drop out of the betting
52 Sign off on
53 Shoppe adjective
54 Misplaced
55 Be too fond
57 Large-headed rivet
58 Sharpen
61 In favor of

933 SHADES OF MEANING by Bob Lubbers

ACROSS

1 __ of tears (the world)
5 Praise
9 Precipice
14 PDQ cousin
15 Taj Mahal site
16 Biblical prophet
17 Bashful one
20 Actor Danson
21 Morays
22 Canvas supports
23 Skin
24 Writer Tyler
25 Dry-cleaning jobs
28 Stopper
29 *2001* computer
32 Spooky
33 Parking-scofflaw stopper
34 Word form for "self"
35 Guinness film, with *The*
38 Wallach and Whitney
39 "¿Cómo __ usted?"
40 Without help
41 9-digit ID
42 Saxophone range
43 Nooses
44 Wraps
45 __ 500
46 Aft
49 Sills solo
50 Grain
53 Of royal blood
56 Actress Massey
57 Sharpen
58 Lowlife
59 Mary Baker and Nelson
60 Ogler
61 Previously

DOWN

1 Far-reaching
2 Court legend
3 Rendered fat
4 Cure beginner
5 L.A. hoopsters
6 Nimble
7 Coffee servers
8 Hammarskjöld of the UN
9 __ Kai-shek
10 Unfastened
11 Global dot
12 Sense
13 Domino or Waller
18 Straighten (up)
19 Jazz violinist Joe
23 Snoops
24 Waikiki welcome
25 Monica of tennis
26 Cures
27 Monte of Cooperstown
28 __ Alegre, Brazil
29 Mollify
30 Make amends
31 Stud sites
33 Dog-show winners
34 Ease
36 Part of FDR
37 Oscar-winner as Lugosi
42 Blood lines
43 Sharpshooter
44 Burns contemporary
45 Castle or Cara
46 Rose's guy
47 Auction ender
48 Beat a path
49 Sea greeting
50 Ready for trade
51 First name of 35 Across' star
52 Vision start
54 Common article
55 Greek letter

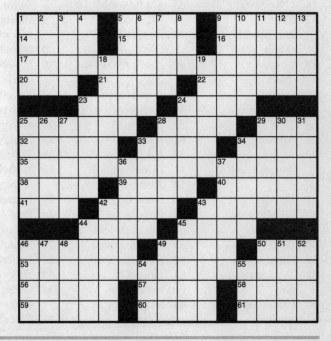

934 NONSTOP ACTION by William A. Hendricks

ACROSS

1 Retain
5 Minor disagreement
9 Severe
14 __ *fixe*
15 "It must've been something __"
16 Salad spheroid
17 Helsinki native
18 Designer Von Furstenberg
19 Alma __
20 With 38 Across, '84 action film
23 St. Paul's home
24 On behalf of
25 __ *Wiedersehen!*
28 Army mule, e.g.
30 RBI or ERA
34 The ones here
36 SAT fill-in
37 Kansas city
38 See 20 Across
42 Christmastime
43 Completely
44 "Grease __ word"
45 *Pygmalion* playwright
46 Add spices to
49 Fooled
50 Snake with a squeeze
51 One-__ (ball game)
53 Director of 20 Across
61 "__ Theme" (*Doctor Zhivago* tune)
62 Scatter Fitzgerald
63 Elliptical
64 State one's view
65 Scottish river
66 What a certain stitch saves
67 Professional doctrine
68 Has title to
69 Sommer in the movies

DOWN

1 Audiophile's equipment
2 Norse god
3 Grant a mortgage
4 Jeans material
5 Pigment color
6 Heathens
7 More than a third of the files
8 12:50
9 Base clearer
10 "Too bad!"
11 *Rio* __
12 Cinematographer Nykvist
13 Rancher's responsibility
21 Evangelist McPherson
22 Untrue
25 Bar men: Abbr.
26 "Yeah"
27 "I __ Song Comin' On"
29 Greenhouse lily
30 Caesar's namesakes
31 Biblical exchange unit?
32 Wahine welcome
33 Broke a bronc
35 One-pot dinner
39 *Lolita* actor
40 "Go right ahead!"
41 Ultimate
47 "__, O Ship of State!"
48 Continental separators
50 Harass
52 Steak leftover, sometimes
53 Pigeonhole
54 Use the VCR
55 Green land
56 Rooster on the roof?
57 Snow remover
58 Like Darth Vader
59 Naval station?
60 Elation

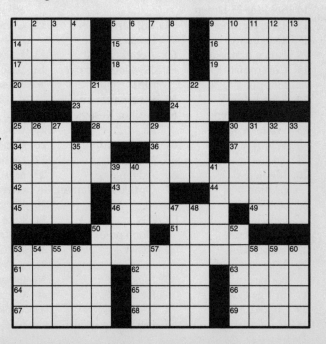

935 STRANGE WEATHER by Randolph Ross

ACROSS

1 Like some tales
5 Cheer for the diva
10 Need an aspirin
14 Potpourri
15 Chicago 7 name
16 "Now hear __"
17 In the laundromat, I saw it __
19 Cougar, for short
20 Hermits
21 Inside info
23 That *muchacha*
24 Animator Tex
25 At the pancake house, I saw it __
28 Tousle
29 Elisabeth or Andrew
30 Terre __, IN
31 Hosp. areas
32 "__ a song go . . ."
33 Passed on the track
34 On the farm, I saw it __
36 Make a difference in
39 Falls behind
40 Quite loud, in music
43 Ma has one
44 Ma has one
45 Dean's *Lois & Clark* costar
46 In church, I saw it __
48 Actor Alain
49 Adherent's suffix
50 Before
51 JFK's sister
52 Kitchen extension
54 At the bank, I saw it __
57 Prexy's no. 2
58 Texas athlete
59 Relationships
60 Icelandic story
61 Hoops maneuver
62 Singer from Nigeria

DOWN

1 Culpable
2 Kaput
3 Elsa, for one
4 Reduces
5 Forbids
6 Baseball stat
7 Actor Vigoda
8 It's its own reward
9 Norse pantheon
10 Sun. banking convenience
11 Encouraging words
12 Hairy
13 Leaked out
18 Thirsty
22 Disbeliever's comments
25 Sound of relief
26 Beat
27 Big mouths
29 Pigeonhole
32 Revenue
33 Sluggish
34 Order to a broker
35 Test sites
36 Get done
37 Ate like a king
38 Darted
40 Mrs. Jack Lemmon
41 Wearing clerical garb
42 Diplomatic skill
44 Chicken serving
45 Doctrines
47 Polonius' hiding spot
48 Unintelligent remark
51 Earth sci.?
53 L.A. smog monitor
55 Mineral suffix
56 New Deal org.

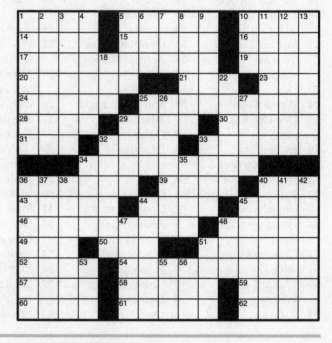

936 OUT OF THE KITCHEN by Norma Steinberg

ACROSS

1 One of the Three Bears
5 Crow sounds
9 Bank adjuncts: Abbr.
13 Bates or Arkin
14 Solo for 25 Down
15 Take pictures
17 Thin board
18 Fancy dance
19 Columnist Hopper
20 Schedule
22 Indian, for one
23 Wallach and Whitney
24 Trolleys
25 Medicinal portion
28 Spider's creation
30 In existence
32 Never: Ger.
33 Like summer coffee
37 Brings to a tie
39 Snookums, e.g.
41 Unlit
42 Body of water
44 Argument
45 From do to do
48 List-ending abbr.
49 Tote
51 Against
53 "Things could be __"
54 Big variety
59 Swears
60 Actress Lena
61 1994 Jodie Foster film
62 Send payment
63 Author Kesey et al.
64 *Exodus* author
65 NFL team
66 Advantage
67 Option for Hamlet

DOWN

1 Sloop pole
2 "That's __ know"
3 "Just the facts, __"
4 Feed the kitty
5 Intriguing group?
6 Arafat's language
7 *Music Man* composer Meredith
8 Price reduction
9 On land
10 Presidential advisors
11 Computer-phone link
12 Fizzy drinks
16 Beachgoer's quest
21 Adolescence
24 Bird sound
25 Opera singer
26 Concluded
27 Critical test
29 Marceau character
30 Conducted
31 Like some winds
34 Pedro's house
35 Actor Jannings
36 __ Moines, IA
38 Often-split veggie
40 Plural pronoun
43 Took advantage (of)
46 Comes to a head
47 Finale
49 Quilt, for one
50 Fragrance
52 Stressed out
53 Armed conflict
54 Heeded the alarm
55 ". . . some kind of __?"
56 Roman emperor
57 Silver-tongued
58 Word in an ultimatum

937 '94 FILMS by Mary E. Brindamour

ACROSS

1 Green gemstone
5 Arrive at
10 __ Alto, CA
14 Hertz rival
15 Neutral shades
16 Unique person
17 Plane part
18 Stadium sounds
19 Famous spouter
20 Letter insert: Abbr.
21 '94 Travolta film
23 Frankie or Cleo
25 Part of TGIF
26 Propped (up)
28 Sweet buns
33 Strips corn
34 Repose
35 Cereal grain
36 Burden
37 Swung around
38 Bishop Desmond
39 This dir.
40 Purloiner
41 Gave some medicine to
42 Math proofs
44 Termites, e.g.
45 Mauna __
46 Fork feature
47 '94 Loren film
52 Employ
55 "__ Need" (Temptations tune)
56 Aristide's country
57 Fells, as a tree
58 Drain or peace follower
59 Snaky roads
60 Sale condition
61 Russian news source
62 Metric measure
63 "Tell __ the Marines"

DOWN

1 Fonda or Pauley
2 English river
3 '94 Douglas film
4 Compass dir.
5 Noun ending in -ing
6 Place for an *élève*
7 Mouse catcher
8 Sod
9 Opposed to change, in a way
10 Written in verse
11 Not pro
12 Letterman rival
13 Algerian port
21 Dessert options
22 Trim, as a photo
24 Clumsy boats
26 Young hog
27 Intuitive feeling
28 Sad feeling
29 Coral deposit
30 '94 Sinbad film
31 Snacker
32 Terkel or Lonigan
34 Unlikely, as odds
37 Puts in a case
38 Rip of Hollywood
40 New York city
41 Way in
43 Nostalgic records
44 Cook, in a way
46 Nero or Falk
47 Engrossed
48 Director Kazan
49 European mountains
50 Kiln relative
51 Sagacious
53 Loretta of *M*A*S*H*
54 Exxon, once
57 "Bali __"

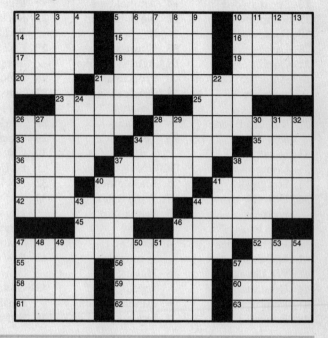

938 JUVENILE by Bob Lubbers

ACROSS

1 Conical kiln
5 Roseanne's maiden name
9 Indian prince
14 Suit to __
15 Section
16 Break out
17 African language
19 Low regions
20 Supported
21 Defendant's excuse
23 Farrow and Sara
26 Of birds
28 Met texts
32 Signal light
34 Studio sign
35 Taken-back cars
37 Owl remark
38 Western wolf
39 Kuwaiti money
40 Participates at Sotheby's
41 Some quantity
42 Colorful horses
43 Western Starr
44 Sonnet part
46 Saw (to)
48 Marsh bird
49 County center
50 Rare folks
52 Shark clinger
57 1 Down farewell
59 Gentleness, so to speak
62 Ancient Mayan city
63 Netman Nastase
64 Profound
65 Tries
66 Barber's call
67 Winds up

DOWN

1 Hawaiian island
2 On
3 Timely Thomas?
4 Head: Fr.
5 Masked man
6 School subject
7 Olds classic
8 Pro __
9 Wakes up
10 Saudi __
11 TV chef
12 Goon
13 Alts.
18 Fudd or Gantry
22 Toil
24 Courtyards
25 Burnt and raw shades
27 Brain, slangily
28 Albright and Falana
29 __ cups (soused)
30 Fanny Brice character
31 Hope/Crosby locale
33 Snooped (around)
36 Kiddie stickum
39 Spoiler of a sort
40 Kingsley or Bradlee
42 Abrogates
43 Pepper plant
45 Helmet
47 What you're aiming at
51 Onion covering
53 Current fashion
54 1 Across, for one
55 Oboist's need
56 Vipers
57 ABA member
58 Commit perjury
60 Seine spot
61 Reformer Dorothea

939   MIXED DOUBLES by Dean Niles

ACROSS

1 Fuming over
6 "__ Breaky Heart"
10 Apparel
14 NBA's Thomas
15 Crestfallen
16 Sport sword
17 Rubberneck
18 Space-time __
20 Last
22 Cold
23 American Legion member
24 Swami, e.g.
27 Richard Boone role
31 Sweet snack
35 Composer Stravinsky
36 Dorothy Lamour wrap
38 O.T. book
39 Kitchen areas
41 Parker product
42 Wit Levant
44 Decorated vase
45 Elvis epithet
48 Robust
49 Entryway
51 Linked together
53 Dull
55 __-Wan Kenobi
56 Schenkel of TV sports
59 Thought process
64 Animal boss
67 Novelist John le __
68 Church recess
69 Actress Lenska
70 Proclamation
71 Crack a book
72 Crooner Williams
73 Toledo title

DOWN

1 Mash preceder
2 Wine region
3 Primatologist Fossey
4 Snouted mammal
5 Having a specific topic
6 Fundamentals
7 Dry goods
8 Raider of old
9 Thus far
10 Einstein
11 "Since Hector was __"
12 Enlist again
13 "__ Valentine"
19 Blue hue
21 Rock singer Redding
25 Like some story lines
26 A Bobbsey twin
27 Betty Grable, once
28 Marketplace
29 Wackos
30 City in Italy or Florida
32 Ancient Peruvian
33 Author Zora __ Hurston
34 Scrap
37 Crank up
40 Few and far between
43 Gourmet mushroom
46 Self-regard
47 Brogan, e.g.
50 Like maces
52 Early calculator
54 Bond return
56 Autocrat
57 Expectation
58 Soprano Ponselle
60 Low cart
61 Persia, now
62 Phrase of approximation
63 __-do-well
65 Failed amdt.
66 Wordplay

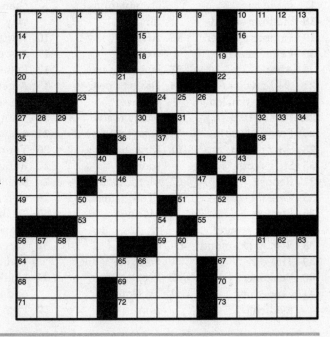

940   ON-OFF SWITCH by Henry Hook

ACROSS

1 Yawning
5 *Art of the Fugue* composer
9 1979 Len Deighton novel
13 Frizzy do
14 Toast enhancement
15 Prima follower
16 Susan of CNN
17 Quarters of a school year
18 Gone by
19 Greeted silently
22 Environment
23 St. __ (city near Montreal)
26 Blackbird
27 He's living on the edge
28 Borders
31 Fleming and Ziering
32 Use plastic
33 Breakfast duo
37 Haunch
38 Portrayer of Big Daddy
39 Some saxophones
40 They're open for public display
43 Reggae's cousin
44 Settles
45 Joy: Sp.
49 "Me and Bobby McGee" writer
51 Product made by bees
53 Stage statuary
54 Author Morrison
55 Big Band leader Skinnay
56 Effortless victory
57 "*Chacun __ goût*"
58 Feet
59 The Red and the Black
60 See

DOWN

1 *En* follower
2 Start of an aphorism re prodigality
3 Back up
4 Dasher, to Dancer
5 Painter/typeface designer
6 High up
7 Random House cofounder
8 Native nations
9 Jungle jaunt
10 Examined
11 Hodges of diamond fame
12 Hotel offering
15 Movie stars can usually be seen in it
20 Compact
21 Final authority
24 Unfamiliar with
25 Lock
27 Gets (through) laboriously
28 Was sore
29 Nightclub
30 Post-vacation chore
31 Backers
34 Buenos __
35 Charlatan
36 She debuted at the Met in 1935
41 "The __ Mine" (Jackson/McCartney tune)
42 Takes out of context?
43 Pulls a Van Winkle
45 Inner personality, to Jung
46 Astronaut Stuart
47 Otherwise
48 "__ Romance"
50 Cylindrical instrument
51 Proof notation
52 Top *número*

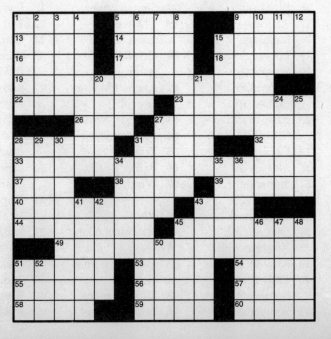

941   COUNTRY BREAKFAST by Rich Norris

ACROSS

1 Betty Ford Clinic purpose
6 Possess
10 Appends
14 Hersey town
15 "An apple __ ..."
16 Search (for)
17 Russian Communist Party founder
18 Department store event
19 Amiss
20 Breakfast bread
23 Catchall abbr.
24 Afr. neighbor
25 Kazakhstan, formerly: Abbr.
28 Nourished
31 Vocal
34 Asian fruit tree: Var.
36 State confidently
38 Employs
40 Heads alternative
41 Breakfast beverage
44 Japanese dog
45 "Oh! What __ Was Mary"
46 Sicilian spouter
47 Deteriorates
49 Zoomed
51 Arranged the table
52 Historic period
53 Cry of discovery
55 Ooh's partner
57 Breakfast side dish
64 Faucet problem
66 Intimidates
67 Stalwart
68 Versatile vehicle
69 Actor Kristofferson
70 Flood preventer
71 Method: Abbr.
72 Dispatched
73 Make corrections to

DOWN

1 Raspy sound
2 Biblical garden
3 __ around (linger)
4 Doddering
5 Tuna relative
6 Miscellany
7 Resident of 2 Down
8 Esteem
9 Something to behold
10 Jai __
11 Slows, in a way
12 *Le Coq __* (Rimsky-Korsakov opera)
13 Heavens
21 Wash vigorously
22 Fried: Sp.
26 Moon goddess
27 Move to a new table
28 False front
29 One who elicits
30 Fancy foods
32 Land west of the Pacific
33 Bounds
35 Sidewalk eatery
37 Composer Nino
39 Cereal sound
42 Ancient language
43 Spotless
48 Rickety structures
50 Fool around
54 Cherish
56 Sultan's wives
58 Scheduled time: Abbr.
59 Victor's shout
60 Aide: Abbr.
61 Bat's home
62 Kitchen need
63 Require
64 CD players
65 Spanish king

942   NO-FLY ZONE by Gerald R. Ferguson

ACROSS

1 Booty
5 Cambodia neighbor
9 Like a cryptogram
14 VIP's wheels
15 Incantation start
16 Without peer
17 Slangy suffix
18 Tub toy
20 Sawbuck
22 Undo
23 Landscaper's equipment
24 Pitchman's payoff
25 Bingo variant
27 Grommet
32 Hibachi residue
35 At any time
37 Autobahn auto
38 Sitcom producer Norman
39 Burger partner
40 Show pleasure
41 Former Israeli leader
42 One waiting in ambush
43 Street in London
44 Sock pattern
46 Baseball manager Joe
48 Rotation line
50 Hoses down
54 Gas alternative
58 Eyelash coloring
59 Kind of tournament
61 Word before exam or thermometer
62 Peace goddess
63 Sell
64 Capable of
65 __ up (excited)
66 Writer O'Brien
67 Roger Rabbit, for one

DOWN

1 Election roster
2 Sent a cable to
3 Included with
4 Spiny European shrub
5 Singer Julius
6 Touch
7 Moon, e.g.
8 Native-born Israeli
9 *Wayne's World* costar
10 Ye __ Shoppe
11 Sullen
12 Ref. books
13 Hockey ploy
19 Some anglers
21 HST or RMN
24 Russians, once
26 St. Philip __
28 Troop VIP
29 Entice
30 Singer Brickell
31 Windshield feature
32 __ mater
33 Prognosticator
34 Reagan secretary of state
36 Architect Saarinen
39 Joint muscle
43 Monks' titles
45 *The Eagle Has __*
47 Kigali's land
49 __ *Trouble* (Nolte/Roberts film)
51 Musical Marx
52 Muse of lyric poetry
53 Upscale shop
54 Estrada or Satie
55 Ripped
56 Long or Lewis
57 Last of the Stuarts
58 Duluth's st.
60 "And so to __"

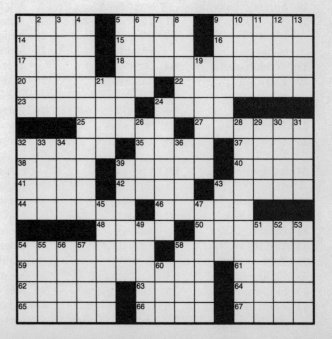

943   HAPPY OURS by Daniel R. Stark

ACROSS

1 Without a __ (smoothly)
6 River in Tibet
11 Truck compartment
14 007, in *Moonraker*
15 Not a soul
16 Pussycat's partner
17 Investment choices
19 1940 costar of W.C.
20 Conscious
21 18-wheelers
23 Sonny's costar
24 Narrow-minded ones
25 __ off (wrote hastily)
28 Chimp cousin
30 __ *People's Money*
31 Templar or Legree
32 Mgmt. biggie
35 Word before runner or work
36 Li'l Abner's dad
37 Beer head
38 The cruelest mo.?
39 Rickey additives
40 Oil center
41 Wed on the run
43 Food supply
44 High-stepping horses
46 Belgrade native
47 Sensational
48 Most like monsoons
52 Hubbub
53 Chef's cut
56 Topple (over)
57 Preposterous
58 Sudden incursion
59 Dawn goddess
60 Tunnel makers
61 Pigs

DOWN

1 Sound of deep thought
2 Chits
3 Big purse
4 Ground noisily
5 Actress Locklear
6 Derive as a conclusion
7 Subject or object
8 Warning word
9 *Et*, for Hans
10 Conference part
11 Sneezin' reason
12 Be pending
13 Sanctify
18 Told fibs
22 Vanity
24 Rap music fan
25 Mrs. Copperfield
26 Upon
27 Farms, in a way
28 Two-footed creature
29 Rock-concert gear
31 Ditto
33 "At __!"
34 Khayyám or Sharif
36 Gladys Knight & the __
37 Skirt ruffle
39 Joseph Conrad novel
40 Export duties
42 Kauai souvenir
43 Letterman rival
44 License or home follower
45 TV signal component
46 Places
48 Mideastern money
49 __ of Cleves
50 Rani's wear
51 Fed. agent
54 Yoko __
55 "Later!"

944   MENTAL FITNESS by Bob Lubbers

ACROSS

1 Okinawa's capital
5 Actor Jacques
9 "Rock of __"
13 Notched
15 Signed a chit for
16 Singer Fitzgerald
17 "A __ than kin . . .": Shakespeare
19 Writer Greene
20 Patrician-wannabe's exercise?
22 She-bear: Sp.
23 Unaccounted-for GI
24 Songwriters' grp.
26 *Cheers* role
28 Bottom line
32 Balin or Claire
33 WWII spy org.
36 Table of __
38 Retail exercise?
40 Sidewalk area
42 Point of no return?
43 Fit __ tee
44 Stock (up)
46 Settee
50 Saguaros
52 "I see!"
55 Sty
56 Couch potato's exercise?
61 *Moonstruck* star
62 What tickets provide
63 Damsel saver
64 Rational
65 Direct
66 Off. aide
67 Eros alias
68 Goes wrong

DOWN

1 Harriet or Horatio
2 Musical passage
3 Auto thief's booty
4 __ spumante
5 Alley howler
6 GI on the lam
7 Garr or Hatcher
8 Same, to an annotator
9 Auspices
10 Bouncing (off)
11 Splendidly tasteful
12 Maglie or Mineo
14 Actor Jack
18 Yalie
21 Monopoly avenue
25 __ de deux
27 Eve's opposite
29 Earth tone
30 French pronoun
31 "Lonely Boy" singer
34 Joins a jam session
35 Forte of 16 Across
37 Chemical endings
38 Veldt violators
39 Self
40 Ad agcy. of a sort
41 Urban pests
45 Simpler
47 View giver
48 Certain Olympian
49 Riles
51 Seer's card
53 Cadence beginning
54 Part of A&E
57 Letters on *Atlantis*
58 Wax-coated cheese
59 Alphabet's core
60 Destiny
61 Dance step?

FABULOUS FIFTIES by Matt Gaffney

ACROSS
1 Inspire to action
7 Metal dross
11 Play dumb, perhaps
14 Tax category
15 Earthquake site of 1/95
16 Wall Street name
17 Milestone of a sort
19 Inventor Whitney
20 Radio fare
21 Marsh growths
22 Baseballer Dykstra
23 Forget to include
24 Connecticut senator
25 Soak up the sun
26 __ room (play area)
27 NBA giant
28 Speaker of the '80s
30 Actress Braga
32 Float alternative
33 Local broadcast
37 Obliquely

38 Sticky
39 Close shaves
40 Gore et al.
41 Mine stuff
44 Tiny bits
45 Prima donna
47 Actor Baldwin
48 Dernier __
49 Nintendo predecessor
51 Pennsylvanian sect
52 Crest competitor
53 Lord's show
55 Charlemagne, par exemple
56 Perfect, as a curio
57 Garfield, for one
58 Ship on the Pac.
59 Otherwise
60 Jogger's wear

DOWN
1 Track visitor
2 Dig up
3 Naturally beautiful

4 Where the Dalai Lama is from
5 Wife of Osiris
6 __ U.S. Pat. Off.
7 Schussed
8 The __ One (Waugh book)
9 Not up yet
10 Some Chevrolets
11 Capital of South Australia
12 Side order
13 Emulates the stars
18 Play
24 No-nos
25 Hilarious Hill
27 Famous frontiersman
28 Sponge holes
29 Puts in the microwave
30 Scorches
31 Neighbor of Tun.
33 Status symbols of a sort
34 Biblical traitor

35 Humbert's creator
36 Patron saint of Norway
41 John's Grease costar
42 Take offense at
43 Canyon sounds

45 Era beginnings
46 Really ticked
47 Talk __ a minute
49 Rueful sigh
50 Follow
51 __ Good Men
54 Preconditions

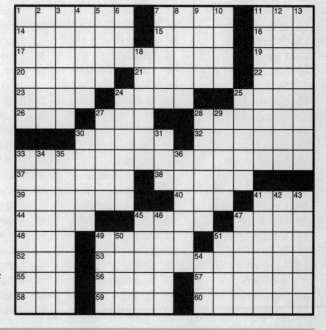

PARKS DEPARTMENT by Gregory E. Paul

ACROSS
1 Movie award
6 Side dish
10 "The Gift of the __"
14 Osmond or Dressler
15 Recording medium
16 Dry
17 National park
19 Blackbird
20 Unused
21 Tim of WKRP
22 Sonora snack
24 2000, e.g.
25 Grete Waitz's birthplace
26 Separate wheat from chaff
29 Beer's partner
33 Pump parts
34 Stated
35 To __ and Back (Audie Murphy film)
36 Of a time period

37 W. __ Burpee (seed magnate)
38 Deep unconsciousness
39 Lamebrain
40 Dallas cagers, for short
41 Painter Édouard
42 In no special location
44 Longfellow subject
45 Desiccated
46 Ore site
47 Word form for "middle"
50 Wizard of Oz dog
51 Poorly lit
54 Toast spread
55 National park
58 Related
59 Commuter's choice
60 Helpful one
61 __ up (get fit)
62 At hand
63 Wiesbaden's state

DOWN
1 Sign
2 Except for
3 Yacht squad
4 Football filler
5 Backslide
6 Part of a flight
7 Alan or Cheryl
8 Imitate
9 Chicago neighborhood
10 National park
11 Section
12 Working __ (Griffith film)
13 Not working
18 Jacob's wife
23 Elev.
24 National park
25 Steinbeck characters
26 Actress Bara
27 Wading bird
28 Primed
29 Balm
30 Sierra __
31 Playwright Rice
32 Roofing tile
34 Rubberneck

37 United competitor
41 Hanukkah candelabra
43 LBJ beagle
44 Religious ceremony
46 Power source
47 Paint application
48 Nevada city

49 Nürnberg negative
50 "Cheerio!"
51 Pops
52 Turner and Pappas
53 Unimportant
56 Regret
57 Prevaricate

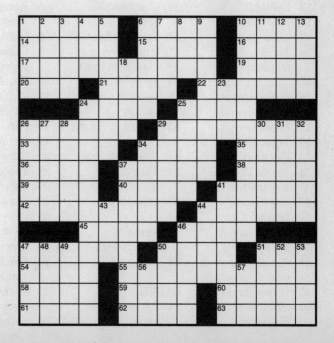

947 STORAGE SPACE by Bob Lubbers

ACROSS

1 Con game
5 Stocking problem
9 Matched furniture set
14 Nautical direction
15 Musical quality
16 Implied
17 Sure thing
19 Fight site
20 Stylist
22 Male ox
23 Sprawling evergreen
24 __ Hari
28 Bathday cake
31 Fixed a coat
33 24-hr. cashier
36 Seine spots
38 Opening bars
39 Catchers' pads
43 Of the kidneys
44 Robert De __
45 Maiden-name indicator
46 Attempted
49 Delhi dress
51 Char
52 __ de mer
54 Prefix meaning "between"
58 Newspaper honcho
61 Eucalyptus eater
65 Illiterate one
66 Passion
67 Privy to
68 Stow cargo
69 Pick up the tab
70 Cures hide
71 Threat ender

DOWN

1 Goldman's partner
2 Sport-shoe feature
3 Condor condo?
4 London lengths
5 Agitate
6 Zilch
7 Jittery
8 Spouting spring
9 Have the lead
10 Defunct Mideast abbr.
11 Cooling cubes
12 __ Lizzie
13 Greek letter
18 Skillfully
21 Meadow mom
24 In perfect condition
25 Chekhov or Bruckner
26 Pied-à-__
27 Get __ of one's own medicine
29 Swiss peak
30 __ diem
32 Candy stick
33 Land units
34 Not those
35 Brainy group
37 Favorite __ (candidate)
40 Moselle feeder
41 "__ the season . . ."
42 Memorable time
47 Ostrich cousin
48 "Dang!"
50 Draw a breath
53 Mrs. Helmsley
55 Cyclic, in a way
56 Woodwinds
57 "It's __ country"
58 Homer and Marge's kid
59 Of unknown authorship: Abbr.
60 Coffee makers
61 Krazy __
62 Bruin giant
63 Cool drink
64 Mauna __

948 COPING by Diane C. Baldwin

ACROSS

1 "Eureka!"
4 Mess up
9 Sty resident
12 Dancers cut them
14 D-Day beach
15 Dullard
16 Skip over
17 __ in (gathers)
18 Inventor Sikorsky
19 "__ Lisa"
20 Pulled toward
21 Make amends
22 Fancy sock
24 Rope fiber
26 Doctrine
28 Tex or Thelma
32 Use the tub
35 American Beauty, e.g.
37 Actor Cronyn
38 Milan moola
39 __ Get Your Gun
40 Writer Bagnold
41 Ambler or Bogosian
42 Gives the go-ahead to
43 Helps a crook
44 Lower in rank
46 Vishnu worshipper
48 Remus or Vanya
50 Cartographic speck
54 Without funds
57 Israeli port
59 Hawaiian feast
60 Spare hair
61 Set of moral values
62 Moran of Happy Days
63 Run in neutral
64 Take a __ to (like)
65 Whopper
66 "Golly!"
67 Remains undecided
68 Draft org.

DOWN

1 Bakery come-on
2 Laughing matter
3 Maturing
4 Notorious Lizzie
5 Bradley or Sharif
6 Accept defeat
7 Masticates
8 Holds
9 Comic-strip possum
10 Flatten wrinkles
11 Richard of First Knight
13 Persevere
15 Be brave
21 "The Greatest"
23 Grant foe
25 Shoe support
27 Sea eagle
29 Ditty
30 Send forth
31 Cincinnati team
32 Ran, like madras
33 Yorkshire river
34 Barber job
36 Mexican affirmation
39 Sir Guinness
43 Sale proclaimers
45 Explosive item
47 Female kin
49 Woodshop tool
51 Emanations
52 Brads, e.g.
53 Coastal high spots
54 Quick guzzle
55 Lay low
56 Lothario's look
58 Orange wrap
61 Sixth sense

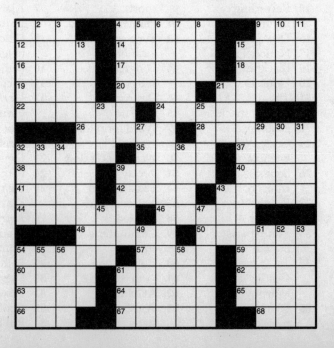

949 — DOUBLE-O FOUR by Christopher Page

ACROSS
1 __ au rhum
5 Gentleman's gentleman
10 First part of 49 Across' boast
14 Imported auto
15 Dramatic device
16 Crimea's Sea of __
17 Clinton or Bradley
18 African river
19 Turkish currency
20 __ Night Live
22 Taft, for example
24 Arms of a river
25 Oklahoma city
26 Verdict follower, often
29 Child's game
33 Hilo garland
34 Also-ran
36 Certain jackets
37 "__ boy!"
39 Eye-related
41 Branch of eng.
42 Hag
44 Sandwich treats
46 __ Khan
47 Wallaby, e.g.
49 Eminent emperor
51 Roasting spot
52 Sideslip
53 D.C. airport
56 Hearty
60 Vicinity
61 Namely
63 Mr. Eban
64 __ Bien Phu
65 Word form for "heavens"
66 Reformer Jacob
67 Issues an invitation
68 __-Bismol
69 Office item

DOWN
1 Weaves' partner
2 Samoan city
3 Slug of hooch
4 Fascination
5 Indian dish
6 Songs for Sills
7 Sluggish
8 Compass pt.
9 Power of films
10 Confirm
11 Pinza of *South Pacific*
12 Actress Dunn
13 Dreaded czar
21 Irani coin
23 Long walk
25 Weird
26 Old expression of grief
27 Ancient Levantine city
28 Mountaineer's need
29 Word form for "rock"
30 Pampas weapons
31 Russian lake
32 Felix's roomie
35 Dish's cohort
38 Luanda natives
40 Colorful parrot
43 Roof part
45 Ship out
48 Take it easy
50 English royal name
52 Spell of duty
53 Modern art form
54 *Battle Cry* author
55 Symbol of Wales
56 Exchange
57 Irish Rose lover
58 Stats for Ripken
59 Job to be done
62 Silver source

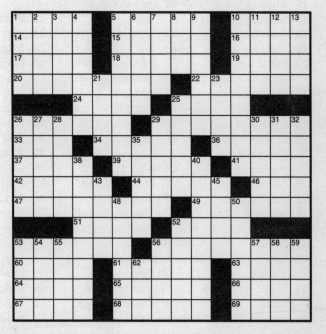

950 — MUSICAL JOKE by Dean Niles

ACROSS
1 Flex
5 Reeves of *Johnny Mnemonic*
10 SASEs, e.g.
14 Margarine
15 Swimming mammal
16 It arrives once a day
17 Melville novel
18 PART 1 OF JOKE
20 Witticism
22 Loan shark
23 Comfort
27 The way it's going
28 PART 2 OF JOKE
32 __ day (vitamin dose)
33 Sleep scene
34 Chicken __ king
37 Writer Damon
40 Talented
42 NC zone
43 Most Irish
47 Moistureless
48 PART 3 OF JOKE
51 Sound of the '70s
54 Spotted cat
55 Pops the top
57 *La __* (Puccini opera)
61 THE PUNCH LINE
65 Actor/director Dixon
66 Opposed
67 Straight shot
68 Verne captain
69 Capital of Elam
70 Wind blasts
71 Matured

DOWN
1 Inept one
2 Sailor's saint
3 Gaudy sign
4 Pessimistic scenario
5 Grovel
6 Old verb ending
7 __ snail's pace
8 After-tax
9 Pakistani language
10 Tough it out
11 __ Dame
12 Comic Myron
13 Bergen dummy
19 Narrow passages
21 Tic-tac-toe win
24 Seminary deg.
25 That girl
26 Compass dir.
28 Apple heart
29 Responsibility
30 Left
31 Hang down
34 Razor brand
35 Kauai souvenirs
36 Tacks on
38 Some mollusks
39 Born: Fr.
41 Old British coin
44 Takeover maneuver: Abbr.
45 Great pains, for short
46 "A Boy Named __" (Cash song)
48 National park in Maine
49 Acts pushy
50 Sticky stuff
51 Aramis' creator
52 '40s Turkish president
53 Mary's subjects
56 Catch
58 Always
59 *Auntie __*
60 "Oh, Wilderness were Paradise __!"
62 Actress Joanne
63 4/15 org.
64 Came down with

951 SHOCKING! by Norma Steinberg

ACROSS
1 Sharpens
6 Harbor craft
10 Ping-__
14 Easy out at Shea
15 Right away: Abbr.
16 Missing GI
17 Singer Baker
18 __ and kin
19 Arizona river
20 What's going on
23 Emulated Streisand
24 Chains of hills
25 Come to pass
29 Eternally, poetically
30 "Dies __"
31 Burn slightly
34 African country
39 Like a lot
42 Must
43 Computer-screen picture
44 Word form for "one"
45 Joplin piece
47 More profound
49 Director's cry
53 Wearing loafers
55 With no time left
59 Newsman Sevareid
60 Tax-deferred svgs.
61 Tennis star Evert
64 Former Clinton cabinet member
65 Brokaw's beat
66 __ firma
67 Very: Fr.
68 Vision starter
69 Impertinent

DOWN
1 FDR program
2 Sweetie
3 The *Iliad*, e.g.
4 Ballerina's skirt
5 Scanty
6 Filched
7 Taking advantage of
8 Intl. trade pact
9 Orb
10 Beeped
11 Due (to)
12 *Jefferson in Paris* star
13 Tumbler
21 "Meanwhile, back at the __ ..."
22 Zodiac sign
25 Elevated
26 Vicinity
27 Benatar and Buchanan
28 __ moss
29 Therefore
32 Nixon aide
33 Part of a circle
35 Actor Cronyn
36 On
37 Zilch
38 Get an __ effort
40 French painter
41 Provide with funds
46 Sanctify
48 Official proclamations
49 Skillful
50 Kitchen tool
51 Bundle binder
52 Early Peruvians
53 Whistler's mother's wrap
54 Novelist Hermann
56 Word after shoe or family
57 Actress Perlman
58 Blunders
62 Treas. Dept. agcy.
63 "You don't __!"

952 MOVIE TIME by Rich Norris

ACROSS
1 In need
5 Dinner course
10 Genie offering
14 USC rival
15 Lacking sense
16 Involved with
17 '86 Fonda/Bridges film
20 Full-length garments
21 Trapped
22 Story line
25 Until now
26 Galena or feldspar
27 Witness
31 Shade tree
33 Dobbs of CNN
34 WWII foe
36 Is deserving of
40 '75 Pacino film
44 Yarn measure
45 Comic Laurel
46 "__ Clear Day..."
47 Vent
49 Evade deftly
52 Musical notes
55 Debussy's "La __"
57 Invitation letters
58 Atones for
61 Rub out
65 '82 Scheider/Streep film
68 Long haul
69 Supply with weapons anew
70 Banana, e.g.
71 Display disrespect to
72 Rendezvous
73 Goes fast

DOWN
1 Golf stroke
2 Esteban's eight
3 First name in fashion
4 NYC suburb
5 Letter opener?
6 Landers or Miller
7 Not of the cloth
8 Pester
9 Educational pursuit
10 Kim, to Alec
11 Emcee's responsibility
12 Bum follower
13 Throng
18 Scandinavian capital
19 Buck feature
23 Give the go-ahead to
24 Michener novel
27 Automobile pioneer
28 Cozy spot
29 Sled of a sort
30 Schisms
32 Fellow
35 Way up
37 Plant anchor
38 Not any
39 Fastener
41 Diego's day
42 20 Questions category
43 Terminals
48 Snappy comeback
50 Tied
51 Use a mister
52 Musical notations
53 Unbilled performer
54 Paid informants
56 Allude
59 Types
60 Hang around
62 Farming word form
63 Police dog's name
64 Summers abroad
66 Day divs.
67 CPR giver

953   SLIGHT SOUNDS by Daniel R. Stark

ACROSS
1 Femur joiners
5 Department store founder
9 Wedge
13 Bridge support
14 Decorator's shade
15 Stratagem
16 Formal affairs
17 Group of horses
18 General Bradley
19 Just made it
21 Color Easter eggs
22 Stamen's counterpart
23 Raw fish dish
26 Funny money
29 Pitchers' places
32 Chatter
35 *The Wind in the Willows* character
37 Bar of gold
38 Exploit
39 Copper ore
41 Stretch (out)
42 Of poor quality
44 Berth place
45 Corded fabric
46 Noted astronomer
48 Wild guesses
51 Bewitches
53 Like fresh chips
57 Egg __ yung
59 Cartoon bird
62 Cheery tune
64 Verdi role
65 Wry
66 Toast topper
67 Lodges
68 Thin porridge
69 Furtive whisper
70 Not diluted
71 Nibbles on

DOWN
1 Baghdad native
2 Dillies
3 Keys
4 Launch an attack on
5 Dole (out)
6 Served perfectly
7 Some hermits
8 Murmur of enjoyment
9 Sign of a B'way hit
10 Doozy
11 Polite attention-getter
12 Insignificant
13 Cook's meas.
20 Clumsy one
24 French silk
25 Attila follower
27 Rise
28 Rani's wardrobe
30 Okey-__
31 "That's one small __ for a man . . ."
32 "That's really gross!"
33 Tennis great
34 Front-door features
36 Bookstore category
39 Tip of a pyramid
40 Piece of land
43 Dark brew
47 Hold onto
49 Reach across
50 Saw-toothed mountain range
52 Louts
54 Lip
55 Lotsa loot
56 School cheer
57 Turkey of a show
58 Van Gogh products
60 Writer Ferber
61 Cardinal point
63 Two-year-old

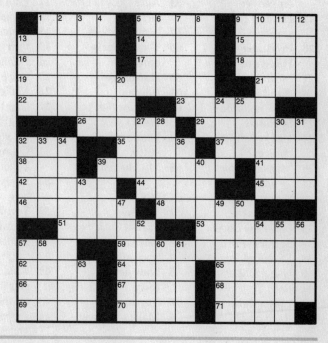

954   OVEN-FRESH by Bob Lubbers

ACROSS
1 Nile bird
5 Slanted type: Abbr.
9 Semolina product
14 Nothing
15 French Sudan, today
16 Hosni's predecessor
17 Pushover
19 Arises (from)
20 Actress Renée
21 Church donation
23 Icelandic epic
26 Sway
29 Sea cows
33 New York city
34 Leans against
35 British cleaning women
37 Erode
38 Love too much
39 Reads a UPC
40 Vaulted area
41 Circle part
42 Pepsodent rival
43 Trickier
44 Boater's motel
46 Film-clip previews
48 Tilts
49 Fresh kids
50 Kadiddle-hopper's namesakes
52 Digressions
57 Smitten (with)
59 Tots' game
62 Assists in crime
63 Beehive State
64 On a par
65 Prize money
66 __ a one (none)
67 Relax

DOWN
1 Pizarro victim
2 Poet
3 Word form for "concept"
4 German river
5 Block
6 Greek letter
7 TV alien
8 Pick-me-up
9 Artist's option
10 National song
11 Darlin'
12 Scot's topper
13 __ *gratia artis*
18 Encounters
22 Anatomical passages
24 Old record label
25 Ghanaian
27 Rubber rectifier
28 PG givers
29 Polite terms of address
30 Opposite the mouth
31 Shell shatterer
32 Dined
36 Costs __ and a leg
39 Twitch
40 100%
42 Zealous
43 Actress Spacek
45 Bay openings
47 Indifference
51 Told, as a yarn
53 Cake finisher
54 Jazz pianist Brubeck
55 Squeezes (out)
56 Mailed
57 Bar pull
58 __ Dhabi
60 __ glance
61 Roof sealer

955 SPORTY by Shirley Soloway

ACROSS
1 Crucifix
5 Ski-lift type
9 Send
13 Therefore
14 Let up
16 Capitol employee
17 Hit and run statistics?
20 Producer Hayward
21 *Medical Center* star
22 Nev. neighbor
23 Sprinted
24 Hockey draft choices?
29 Made a home
34 __ *du pays* (home-sickness)
35 Japanese dogs
37 Sonora snorter
38 Discompose
40 Use a Singer
41 *Born Yesterday* playwright
42 Race place
43 On a slant
45 Hosp. area
46 Puts in office
48 Hip bowler?
50 "Master Melvin"
52 Actress MacGraw
53 *Alice Doesn't Live Here* __
57 Movie shoots
60 Tennis star's entrance?
63 Harmless
64 Jumped
65 Food or fish
66 Food fish
67 Diminutive suffix
68 Mil. decorations

DOWN
1 Johnny __
2 Part of ORU
3 Gaze at
4 Spoonful
5 New Jersey town
6 Versifier
7 Make a request
8 Direct attention (to)
9 Sidetrack?
10 Word in many Bugs Bunny cartoon titles
11 "__ it!" ("Oh!")
12 Pain in the neck
15 Sofas
18 Outcast
19 Barry or Tierney
24 Public persona
25 Secret group
26 Make glad
27 Light carom
28 Engraved stone
30 RR stop
31 Quinine beverage
32 Susan's soap role
33 Toroid shape
36 Errant GI's status
39 "Just a __!"
41 *42nd Street* star
43 Of the stars
44 Appease
47 Binge
49 __ yang
51 *F Troop* structure
53 Bible book
54 Big name in lexicography
55 Arizona city
56 Loquacious equine
57 When sch. starts
58 Slaughter of the diamond
59 Lowlifes
61 One way to stand
62 Naval off.

956 URBAN EATS by Gregory E. Paul

ACROSS
1 Former ruler of 18 Across
5 "Auld Lang __"
9 Starter for chip or phone
14 Mandlikova of tennis
15 Legal equal
16 Kind of committee
17 NC college
18 Persia, today
19 Singer Bonnie
20 Sliced steak
23 Bus. honcho
24 Actress Bonet et al.
25 Small plateau
27 Make amends
30 Scarlet bird
33 Tin Man's prop
34 Nairobi's country
37 __ *Gay*
38 Kid's transport
40 Scuttlebutt
42 Ella's specialty
43 Dress shape
45 Surgical beam
47 Badlands Indian
48 Plant part
50 Covered, as with sugar
52 "Anything __"
53 Plastic-wrap name
55 Lend a hand
57 Poultry dish
62 Full force
64 O'Hara's home
65 Rose Murphy's man
66 Roast host
67 Do a washday chore
68 Ali's arena
69 California cager
70 Mailed
71 On the Aegean

DOWN
1 Author Silverstein
2 Angel's topper
3 Of unknown authorship: Abbr.
4 "__ with care"
5 Miss Havisham, e.g.
6 __ Buena (S.F. Bay island)
7 Approaches
8 Cube inventor Rubik
9 Dietrich of filmdom
10 "Apple cider" girl
11 Strip steak
12 Learning method
13 Numerical word form
21 Porcine cry
22 "__ Yankee Doodle Dandy"
26 Opposite of *avec*
27 Capital of Morocco
28 Banish
29 Poultry dish
30 Resort near Santa Fe
31 Delight
32 Evaluated
35 Void's partner
36 Singer Sumac
39 Word form for "within"
41 Disloyal
44 Barn raiser
46 Speckled horse
49 Fool ending
51 Turkish capital
53 Terrify
54 Ohio city
55 A son of Adam
56 __ *la Douce*
58 "How sweet __!"
59 Nile bird
60 German article
61 Star in Lyra
63 Once named

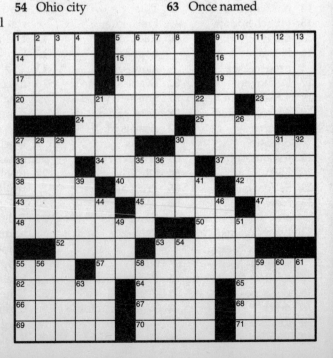

957 — AT POOLSIDE by Randolph Ross

ACROSS

1 Pod contents
5 Close or Burma follower
10 Headliner
14 Prefix for while
15 Trivialize
16 Peter, Paul and Mary, e.g.
17 Loses purposely
19 Sushi serving
20 Taken by surprise
21 Inextricable situation
23 *True __* (1994 film)
24 Marked for removal
25 Lacquers
28 Nighttimes
31 Chopping down
32 After-dinner offering
33 Motorists' org.
34 Piquant taste
35 Ceremonies
36 Busy
37 Lodge member
38 1959 Frankie Avalon record
39 Martin or Allen
40 Ensiled
42 Secured the boat
43 Waves of laughter
44 Former European capital
45 New Jersey college
47 Mutual interest group
51 Arguments
52 Get help from the bank
54 Skirt feature
55 Freeze (up)
56 "__ we forget"
57 Charity
58 Dutch painter
59 Belgian river

DOWN

1 Favorites
2 Part of QED
3 "__ silly question . . ."
4 Magnificent
5 Piano practice
6 Pluto's turf
7 Enthusiastic
8 Actress Vance's nickname
9 Gold and tin
10 Binaural effect
11 Stay in place
12 Is ill
13 Author Macdonald
18 Cause a twinge
22 Ransom Eli __
24 Cape Cod features
25 Charges
26 Put on a pedestal
27 Extreme alternatives
28 Take notice
29 Artless
30 Full
32 Drawback
35 Writes a new version of
36 In a non-musical manner
38 Cutlet meat
39 Actress Braga
41 Teasing sessions
42 Like lava
44 Jaded
45 Sky bear
46 Roper's report
47 Top-rated
48 Refusals
49 Example
50 __'acte
53 Tennis do-over

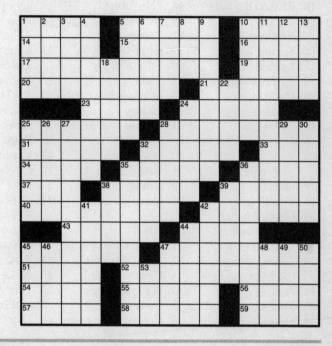

958 — WHO'S WHO by Bob Lubbers

ACROSS

1 Open-mouthed
6 Lucie's dad
10 Jab target
13 Palindromic honorific
14 Teheran resident
16 Show to a seat, slangily
17 Real name of 10 Down
19 Roman 502
20 Sea shocker
21 Light punishment
22 NFL gains
23 Muddied
27 Bull's-eye place
29 Beam
30 Night light
32 Director Kazan
33 Totes (up)
35 Organic compound
37 When the first 100 days end
40 Plant pests
41 Scout's mission, for short
43 "What __ is new?"
44 Indian "master"
46 Stocking color
47 Tweed basher
48 Soon
50 Fairy-tale opener
52 New beginning?
53 Actress Rita
55 Lamp owner
57 Greek magnate's nickname
58 Midmonth date
61 Memorable period
62 Neon, e.g.
63 Real name of 25 Down
68 "__ a date!"
69 True up
70 Two under par
71 Average grade
72 Latin being
73 Don clothes

DOWN

1 Pinsetter co.
2 Needlefish
3 Oklahoma city
4 Do the den
5 TV hosts
6 Insult, so to speak
7 Work units
8 Man of Tarsus
9 Cell-dweller
10 Reel name of 17 Across
11 Stage whisper
12 Bridge ancestor
15 Veldt vaulter
18 Click beetle
23 Russian mountains
24 Gymnast Comaneci
25 Reel name of 63 Across
26 Indian queen
28 Age
31 __ *and His Brothers* (Visconti film)
34 Paris river
36 __ *Doone*
38 Japanese immigrant
39 Reveal
42 Galaxy centers
45 Actress Granville
49 Small knob
51 Warranted
53 Legerdemain
54 Speechify
56 Senegal's capital
59 Yale University students
60 __ *souci*
64 Charge
65 More than med.
66 Raised trains
67 Loser to DDE

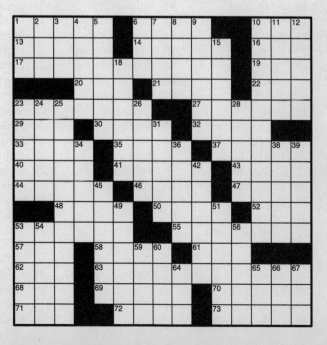

959 SPARE NO EXPANSE by Dean Niles

ACROSS
1 Londoner
5 Glasses
10 Certain noncom: Abbr.
14 Stereo predecessor
15 City on the Nile
16 Capital of Western Samoa
17 Latitude
19 Firmly in place
20 Dad's sister
21 Flamboyance
23 Silver-gray
26 Underworld river
28 Weight deduction
29 Outfit
31 Buildings
35 Phone opener
36 Way to dial
38 Lumber cutter
39 Former president of Egypt
41 Ad follower
42 Lent a hand
44 Submachine gun
45 "Life is like __ chocolates"
48 Big party
49 Wife in *The Odyssey*
51 TV test pattern
53 Trinket
54 "No more!"
56 Jrs., next year
57 Tournament-name word
60 Is indebted to
62 Mata __
63 Every-game victory
68 Pitcher Hershiser
69 Spooky
70 Jason's ship
71 Singer Anita
72 Grassy turf
73 Drive around

DOWN
1 Imported auto
2 King of France
3 Gerund ending
4 Frat-party wear
5 Perfumed
6 Get-together
7 End of Old MacDonald's song
8 Harvest
9 Physical
10 Kenya trek
11 Unfocused group
12 Film legend Lillian
13 London art gallery
18 Verdant
22 1993 treaty
23 Causes a stir
24 Lowlife
25 Place to wait
27 Copies, in a way
30 Devon drink
32 Art __
33 Capital of Devonshire
34 Passover ceremonies
37 Pancake chain
40 Anklebone
43 Partners of ands and buts
46 Dress parts
47 Looked askance
50 Without effort
52 Chimps
55 Surface-__ missile
57 Half of baby's train
58 Grease
59 Hint, to a 1 Across
61 Big blow
64 Time period
65 __ e Leandro (Mancinelli opera)
66 The I has it
67 Office seeker

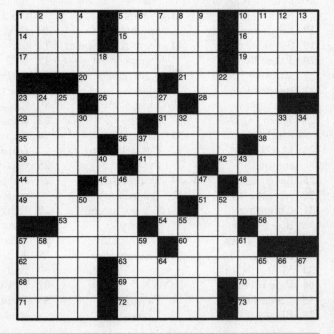

960 I'LL TAKE THE CAESAR by Michael Selinker

ACROSS
1 Exploitative pieces?
6 Anteing site
9 Alaska politico
13 Where to learn French
14 Seize
15 Junction point
16 Rose product
17 Slant, maybe
19 Portuguese-speaking resort
20 Tank
22 Log ingredient
23 START OF A T-SHIRT SLOGAN
28 Lavin title role
29 Think
30 Actor Villechaize
33 Arab garments
35 Pitch
36 '58 Pulitzer winner
37 PART 2 OF SLOGAN
38 Leslie Caron role
39 Slangy negative
40 See
41 See 3 Down
42 Black Sea city
45 Join up
47 END OF SLOGAN
51 Inflexibility
52 Misbehaving
53 Tarzan's kid
55 After labor day?
58 Public persona
60 Kim's hubby
61 Midevening
62 Corroded
63 Net component
64 Word with the most definitions
65 Habiliments

DOWN
1 Char
2 Part of *Julius Caesar*
3 Confront, with 41 Across
4 Chicken-king link
5 Fawning
6 Bit of butter
7 Giraffelike animal
8 Air
9 Box
10 Fighting
11 Cooper's tool
12 Wedding announcement word
14 Peru-Bolivia border lake
18 On the rocks
21 Word form for "bird"
24 Church section
25 Emulated Buckley
26 Futurist Calvino
27 Spooky
30 Ho Chi Minh's base
31 Mild oath
32 Performs before the audience?
34 Docile
37 Some potato farmers
38 Lounge
41 Was 5 Down
43 Albert/Wagner TV series
44 Leo, e.g.
46 Cape Town's nation: Abbr.
48 Bandleader Shaw
49 Lessen
50 Venetian magistrates
54 Desires
55 Dawber or Tillis
56 Bullfight cheer
57 Farm resident
59 Scratch

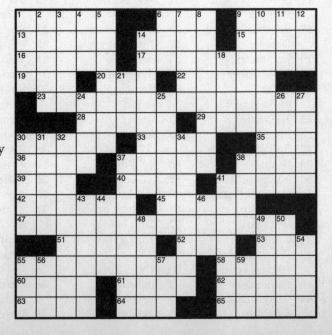

961 VOCAL ENSEMBLE by Bob Lubbers

ACROSS
1 Corn holders
5 Paris' subway
10 Boar or swine
13 Caper
15 Once more
16 Yoko __
17 Nitrous oxide
19 Spare hair
20 Author Anaïs
21 Arctic abode
23 Conch collector
27 Beer mugs
28 Actor Erwin
29 Bathe
30 High schooler, usually
31 Point (at)
32 Drugstore item
34 Noncoms: Abbr.
37 Be unwilling
39 Insect egg
40 Kitten, at times
41 Sale stipulation
42 "__ Goes By"

44 "__ baaaad boy!": Lou Costello
45 Da __, Vietnam
47 Mideast airline
48 Yosemite mgr.
49 Jamaican beat
51 Dishonor
53 Brown shade
54 "Alley-__!"
55 Sprint rival
56 Pitiful thing
64 "__ the fields . . ."
65 Chicago airport
66 Down source
67 Grange or Skelton
68 Planted
69 Costly

DOWN
1 Coolidge, for short
2 "__ Clear Day . . ."
3 Heat measure: Abbr.

4 Actress Hasso
5 Isle of __
6 Urge (on)
7 Kids' game
8 Estuary
9 Kind of inspection
10 Storm sound
11 Burger topper
12 Disco dancers
14 Scary movie
18 Cavity filler
22 Silly ones
23 Pig places
24 Tiny flier
25 Ties up
26 Read aloud
27 Gas additive
28 Thompson of *Family*
33 Useful
35 Arizona city
36 Sp. ladies
38 Procedure
40 __ *Place* (Fox series)
42 Mellow

43 Satanic nation of the Bible
46 DEA agents
49 Unfounded gossip
50 Show host
52 Plant parasite

57 Greek P
58 Go off-course
59 Anger
60 Actor Beatty
61 Juice drink
62 __ culpa
63 Flub

962 PUNCH BOWL by Gerald R. Ferguson

ACROSS
1 Job-safety org.
5 Big shot
10 *Cape __* (Nolte film)
14 *Pequod* skipper
15 Frigidaire rival
16 Ranch unit
17 Bear the brunt
20 __ salts
21 Crystal-lined rock
22 Ship's record
23 Off-key
25 Tuckered out
28 In a snit
29 Scepter's partner
32 Sing like Bing
33 Bond rating
34 Pacific Rim area
35 Trouble-bound
38 Charles' sister
39 Onetime Hagman costar
40 Synonym specialist
41 No longer is
42 Journey man?

43 Paddled
44 Beethoven's birthplace
45 Gambling initials
46 Ford flop
49 West Indies island group
54 Knocked out
57 Land of the Kurds
58 Base clearer
59 Plant panacea
60 Notice
61 Bakery by-products
62 Has to

DOWN
1 Cheerios ingredient
2 Inauthentic
3 Codlike fish
4 Cain's brother
5 Republic
6 Intermingled with
7 Shot sound
8 Canadian prov.
9 "Harrumph!"

10 Diamond plane
11 Reverberation
12 Very dry
13 Actor Auberjonois
18 Fighting __ (Big Ten school)
19 "Holy moley!"
23 Refrigerant gas
24 Father of Regan
25 Field of combat
26 Bank transactions
27 Rich supply
28 Use logic
29 Orange variety
30 Irritated
31 Native of Latvia
32 Tobacco plug
33 Poet Nash
34 Get an __ effort
36 Vegas light
37 Mideast language
42 Pebble Beach game
43 Water rascals
44 Hill or Goodman

45 __ *Majesty's Secret Service* (Bond film)
46 Singer Brickell
47 Actress Diana
48 Exchange
49 Word form for "air"

50 Friable soil
51 Doozy
52 Slaughter of baseball
53 Correction canceler
55 Cry of discovery
56 Laver of tennis

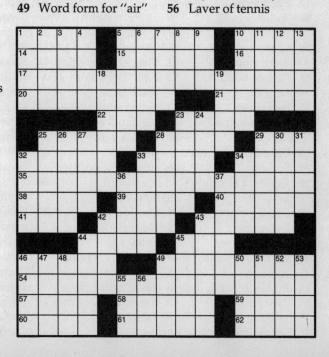

963 NOBODY SPECIAL by Dean Niles

ACROSS

1 Verne hero
5 Spanish dance
9 "I __ for animals" (bumper sticker)
14 Object of reverence
15 Adam Smith subj.
16 Unyielding
17 Ballet leap
18 Moon vehicles
19 Legend's maker
20 Like some alibis
22 Hebrew toast
23 Burt's ex
24 "Give __ rest!"
25 Spiritualist's board
29 Glaswegian
31 "__ Lama Ding Dong"
35 Bugs
37 Fast-food letters
38 Wrestling result
39 __ of passage
40 Shrubby wasteland
42 __ avis
43 Somme summers
44 Plant bristle
45 Weather-map feature
47 Loxland
48 Comic Foxx
50 Beau __
51 Eliminated, in a way
53 Import
55 Plains of Argentina
58 Standouts
63 Fields of expertise
64 Fact-based
65 Not aweather
66 As of
67 Prod
68 Opening day?
69 Things to do
70 Yeltsin denial
71 Pet-food brand

DOWN

1 South Pacific island group
2 Baltic feeder
3 __ the head of the class
4 Valley
5 Wiggly dessert
6 Arctic et al.
7 Three anybodies
8 Part of Q&A
9 Leaflike plant part
10 Legal anybody
11 Water, in Juárez
12 __ Te Kanawa
13 Round cheese
21 Ali, once
22 Chinese tree
25 Rowed
26 Bring together
27 Chip maker
28 Voting anybody
30 Frequently, poetically
32 Some Lebanese
33 French revolutionary
34 Cognizant
36 Bits and pieces
41 Farm female
46 Some NCOs
49 Inundation
52 Soft-pedals
54 Rapid
55 Yesteryear
56 Tosca tune
57 __ store (haberdashery)
59 Hailed auto
60 __ mater
61 Paper quantity
62 Legis. meeting
64 Wine cask

---

964 WEATHER ALERT by Rich Norris

ACROSS

1 Old gas name
5 Kansas motto word
10 Radio buff
13 Keeps cool
14 Loafers, e.g.
15 Spanish eye
16 Adjunct to 58 Across
18 Glove compartment item
19 "There ought to be __!"
20 Beef order
21 River into the Rhone
23 Cause amazement
25 Scenery
26 Deposed ruler's lot
27 Greek poetry
30 Drive crazy
34 Chafes
35 Onetime alliance: Abbr.
38 Emulate Cicero
39 Pre-Q queue
40 Litigant
41 Dupe
43 At an angle
45 Southern style of cooking
49 Greek god
50 Treat royally?
53 Smart set
55 Blackthorn
56 Sailorly: Abbr.
57 __ Baba
58 Torrents
61 Pres. military role
62 Friend of Kukla and Fran
63 Singer Murray
64 Tibetan beast
65 Chris Cagney portrayer
66 Improved, perhaps

DOWN

1 Outflow
2 Deli offering
3 Small fall
4 Bear, in Barcelona
5 City on the Nile
6 Small, sharp piece
7 Bag or board starter
8 VCR button
9 Paler
10 Not pretentious
11 Slightly open
12 Have a long face
17 See 46 Down
19 Citrus drink
22 Red flag, maybe
24 Word form for "wine"
25 High-priced
27 PFC's superiors
28 Showtime competitor
29 Clairvoyance
31 Magic word
32 "Dies __"
33 Rebel Turner
35 WWII morale booster
36 Big sandwich, for short
37 Gone With the Wind producer
42 Johann's exclamation
44 Chowder ingredient
46 With 17 Down, All the King's Men actress
47 Factory fresh
48 Circus safety device
50 Rock legend on a stamp
51 "The Torchbearer" poet
52 Numerical prefix
53 Bill of Maude
54 Literary pen name
55 Store event
59 Hospital wing
60 Motorist's org.

965 ALL 64 ACROSS by A.J. Santora

ACROSS
1 Generic name
4 From
8 Watch area
13 I love, to Ovid
14 __ acid
15 You may be dyeing to get it
16 Was valid
18 Deduce
19 Singer Paula
20 Brown, as a 22 Across
22 Grassy area
23 Curie title
24 Station end
25 Fashionable tie
27 "__ lay me . . ."
29 Balmoral, e.g.
31 Grant, or Grant's foe
32 Crude railway
36 Vernon's partner
38 Needle
39 Rivulets
42 "Come as you __"
44 Shooting marble
45 Harness race
46 Lash of oaters
48 Engine part
51 Melodize
53 Bunker
56 CNN newsman
58 National Leaguer
59 Stop, in Quebec
60 Pool
62 Impolite look
63 Sidestep
64 Showery
65 Not as ruddy
66 Dickens girl
67 Plane heading

DOWN
1 Taj __
2 Unicellular being
3 Throw __ on (nix)
4 Drs.' grp.
5 Position
6 Erect
7 "__ of a nail . . ."
8 Rapids
9 Russo of *Outbreak*
10 It means "below"
11 Look scornfully at
12 Late
14 Pick tool
17 Presses for payment
21 Cupid
23 Miney's follower
26 City near Tampa
28 __ *Mine* (Harrison book)
29 Your guy's
30 Knack
33 Dilute
34 Smart-whip filler
35 Evergreen shrub
37 Meshwork
40 Castle protector
41 Scattered
42 Top pro
43 Charlotte of sitcoms
47 D-Day beach
48 Fastener
49 Blood vessel
50 Rivera work
52 Cultural cable channel
54 Senator Specter
55 Calvin of the PGA
57 "The Way We __"
58 Grand __, Nova Scotia
61 *The Lobster Reef* playwright LeShan

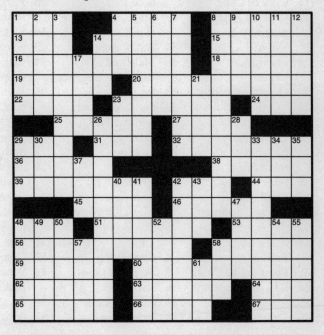

966 IRON SUPPLEMENT by Bob Lubbers

ACROSS
1 River blocker
4 Drywall coat
11 *A __ Good Men*
14 Amin of Uganda
15 Dawdled
16 Hockey star Bobby
17 Washington slept here in 1777
19 Light beam
20 Comes in
21 After-dinner treats
23 Teacake
24 "Darn it!"
26 Portnoy's creator
29 Camping need
30 Hired thug
31 Garry or Demi
32 Chow
33 Fries lightly
34 Longfellow subject
38 Sow again
39 Crucifix
40 Irving's Ichabod
41 Men-only
42 Off. aide
46 Ann Landers' sister
47 Sound of shock
48 Solo
49 Artist's stand
51 Director's cry
52 Totally
54 Part of *Il trovatore*
57 __ *Abner*
58 Make ready
59 Sorbonne summer
60 Pod occupant
61 Tranquilized
62 Curvy letter

DOWN
1 Rid (oneself of)
2 "Ten Cents __" (Rodgers & Hart song)
3 Comic Berle
4 Cubic meter
5 Picks up the tab
6 Collie comment
7 __-Magnon
8 Persian rug
9 Kosher
10 First garden
11 Truly, old-style
12 Pitcher's stat
13 Ironically humorous
18 Pre-Easter time
22 Salmon relative
24 Henning or McClure
25 Evangelist Oral
27 Deuce topper
28 "For __ a jolly . . ."
30 Last year's senior
31 Hotel employee
32 Merriment
33 Dirty air
34 Action word
35 Columbus' sponsor
36 Singer Lotte
37 Bath bar
38 NBC's former parent
41 Assuaged
42 Sax type
43 Evening party
44 Noses
45 Verb categories
47 Art category
48 Pined (for)
50 Tree fluids
51 Farm parcel
52 Mont Blanc, for one
53 Misstatement
55 Symbolic alphabet: Abbr.
56 Long. partner

967 VERSIFICATION by Diane C. Baldwin

ACROSS
1 Fancy dance
5 Doled (out)
10 Goof
14 Miscellany
15 Island off Venezuela
16 Coty or Clair
17 With 54 Across, poem by 10 Down
20 Instrument panels
21 Cowboys' ropes
22 "__ the season . . ."
23 Coin factory
24 Crocodile relative
28 Fury
29 Draft org.
32 Neck adornment
33 "That hurts!"
34 Computer fodder
35 Poem by 10 Down
38 Roll call response
39 Property claim
40 Strainer
41 Age meas.
42 In addition
43 Lower in significance
44 Appear to be
45 Favored one
46 __ Sun (Crichton book)
49 Think some more about
54 See 17 Across
56 Male heirs
57 Actor Christopher
58 In __ (stuck)
59 Panda or Hardy
60 Affirmatives
61 Cribbage markers

DOWN
1 Pear variety
2 Glee-club voice
3 Disney's The __ King
4 Chops off
5 Remit by post
6 Sea eagles
7 Harbor boats
8 Tidal term
9 What dawn brings
10 American poet
11 Most August babies
12 Ruin, in a way
13 Mrs. Truman
18 Pancake ingredient
19 Diminish
23 Georgia city
24 Guisewite comic strip
25 Jacob's eighth son
26 Bakery workers
27 An additional amount
28 Mysterious symbols
29 Benefits
30 Baseballer Garvey
31 Less inane
33 Detestation
34 Speaker's platform
36 Symbolic story
37 African fly
42 Actor Sean
43 Table extenders
44 Wimp
45 Irritation
46 Sub __ (secretly)
47 Privy to
48 Gobi grains
49 Grain varieties
50 Break sharply
51 Green land
52 Comfy-cozy
53 Bilko and Pepper, for short
55 Tiny

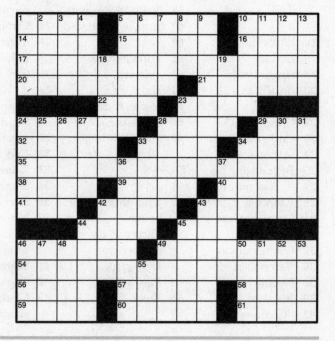

968 MUSIC, MUSIC, MUSIC . . . by Randy Sowell

ACROSS
1 Footnote abbr.
5 Smash musical
9 37 Across work
13 Callas, e.g.
14 The Merry Widow composer
16 Pride noise
17 Unconventional composer
18 Town in Maine
19 To be, in Toulon
20 "Liza" composer
22 Musical form
24 __ kleine Nachtmusik
25 "__ silly question . . ."
26 Marchers of song
29 Mesozoic period
33 March fliers
34 Like April weather
35 Brother of 20 Across
36 "The wolf __ the door"
37 Operatic composer
38 Applaud
39 Kay chaser
40 French river
41 Dish
42 Troop group
44 Stops
45 __ the finish
46 Lacerate
47 Messiah man
50 Gilbert's partner
54 "Waiting for the Robert __"
55 Factotum
57 Singer Simone
58 Swizzle
59 Writer Calvino
60 Coll. subj.
61 Hurok et al.
62 Mine output
63 Singer Turner

DOWN
1 "__ Rock 'n' Roll Music"
2 Seedy bar
3 At any time
4 Manon composer
5 "Send in the __"
6 Eagle's home
7 Long-running suffix
8 __ Remo, Italy
9 Sports sites
10 Greek letter
11 Pub projectile
12 Field
15 William Tell composer
21 Smash songs
23 Give approval
25 "Hitchin' __"
26 Phil Mahre, e.g.
27 Path to the altar
28 Slanted types: Abbr.
29 Mountain pools
30 Marner of fiction
31 Angry
32 Superheroes' wear
34 VCR button
37 The Four Seasons composer
38 Goodman's instrument
40 "Rule Britannia" composer
41 Ring
43 Certain ducks
44 Some strings
46 Veil material
47 Pianist Dame Myra
48 Voice range
49 Singer Diamond
50 European river
51 Veni, vidi, __
52 Soon, poetically
53 Grandma
56 Siouan Indian

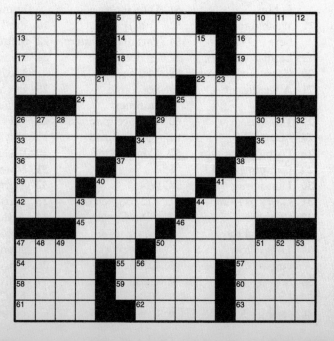

969 TV TWOSOMES by Randolph Ross

ACROSS
1 Burst of energy
6 Certain office shape
10 Mideastern strip
14 Mame in Marseilles?
15 Cracker topper
16 Israeli carrier
17 Church council
18 Computer figure
19 Diamond or Armstrong
20 *General Hospital* couple
23 It's said to a photographer
26 Word form for "nose"
27 Mystery writer Josephine
28 Metropolis couple
31 Hot mo.
32 Stocking stuffer
33 Sugar-free, perhaps
37 Futile
40 Evoking "Wow!"
42 Canary cousin
43 Part of TGIF
44 *6 Rms __ Vu*
45 Sci-fi sitcom couple
50 IRS mo.
53 Installed carpeting
54 Past and present
55 Lucy's landlords
58 Discovery
59 Garfield's friend
60 Giant
64 Tiny bit
65 Penalty of sorts
66 *Invierno* month
67 Medical picture
68 He played Dan'l and Davy
69 Made over

DOWN
1 Peter, Paul and Mary: Abbr.
2 Make worthwhile
3 Raggedy name
4 Wraps
5 Perseus' victim
6 Ronny Howard role
7 Motel sign
8 Lacking a key
9 __ hand (helps out)
10 Actress Rowlands
11 Alaskan islander
12 Belgian Congo, now
13 Put at ease
21 Smallville family
22 Michaels of *SNL*
23 North Pole name
24 DeLay's domain
25 Trevanian's *The __ Sanction*
29 Peruvian pair
30 Fight finishes
34 Toe travails
35 Compound containing NH2
36 Comic Eugene et al.
38 Boundary: Abbr.
39 __ *Gay*
40 Prince Valiant's son
41 Rectangular dimension
43 Movie shots
46 Eloped
47 __ lit (children's books)
48 Committee member
49 Kind of skates
50 Stick on
51 Before
52 __-car
56 WWII turning point
57 Ball holders
61 EMK's nickname
62 *Exodus* protagonist
63 Silent approval

970 SOUND THINKING by Dean Niles

ACROSS
1 Gearshift position
5 Esau's alias
9 Church height
14 Venue
15 Author Anita
16 Birch tree
17 Protect, in a way
19 Ft. __, IN
20 What every story has
21 Fashions
22 Teachers' grp.
23 Setback
24 Cattle breed
28 __ avis
30 Activist Parks
34 Eye part
36 Volleyball barrier
37 Novelist Murdoch
38 Did some gardening
39 Raison __
41 Band dates
42 Town near Padua
43 __-Wan Kenobi
44 Blueprint
46 Beloved
47 *B Minor Mass* composer
49 Rand's shrugger
50 "Stop pouring"
52 "Here, Henri!"
54 Colorful fabric
57 Aped
62 Prodigy service
63 Space object on Earth
64 Strike down
65 Modem speed unit
66 Mardi __
67 Waters down
68 Not to mention
69 It's often scrambled

DOWN
1 Treaty
2 In __ (lined up)
3 Taken-back auto
4 Kyser and Starr
5 Slur
6 Bookmark of a sort
7 Sounds of delight
8 Wyo. zone
9 Took responsibility for
10 Aristophanes or Albee
11 Pastoral poem
12 Painter Magritte
13 "__ Tu" ('74 tune)
18 Washer cycle
21 Party offerings
23 __ Rabbit
24 Had the flu, perhaps
25 Rope loop
26 Scacchi or Garbo
27 Back
29 Bit of sport
31 Bay window
32 "Sweetheart of __ Chi"
33 Donkeys
35 Pueblo structures
40 Abba of Israel
45 Egyptian port
48 Break
51 Compels, as to court
53 Moral tenet
54 Interweave
55 Shot
56 Speaker's platform
57 Ring out
58 Wild revelry
59 Novice
60 And others: Abbr.
61 Office space
63 Finance deg.

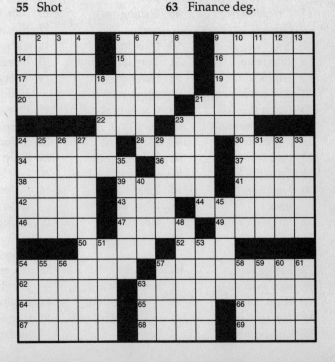

971 O PAIRS by Shirley Soloway

ACROSS
1 Cleaning cloths
5 Went white
10 Tiff
14 Taj Mahal site
15 Fred's dancing sister
16 Tiptop
17 Ottomans
19 Plant protuberance
20 Pencil end
21 By itself
23 Tried for office
24 Musician's jobs
27 Part of NWT
28 Make light of
30 Pumpkin mo.
33 __ Romeo (car)
36 Seabird
37 Oahu greeting
39 Religious
41 Asian holiday
42 Caesar, for one
43 __ Gay
44 Cambodian's neighbors
46 Egyptian snakes
47 Marina __ Rey
48 Happy frame of mind
51 Juicy fruit
53 Part of IRS
54 Syrup source
57 Skulls
59 Tell (on)
61 Barn sounds
62 Student's text
65 Soothing agent
66 Japanese port
67 British composer Thomas
68 Umps' kin
69 Unfamiliar with
70 Deli breads

DOWN
1 Olympian Johnson
2 Marketplace
3 Sound of discomfort
4 Pre-coll. exams
5 Loyal countryman
6 Fuss
7 Zodiac sign
8 Room extensions
9 Spanish explorer
10 More rational
11 Billiards halls
12 Actor Garcia
13 Undershirt type
18 Lily variety
22 Operetta composer
25 City area
26 Jam and jelly
28 Newman or Anka
29 Punctual
31 Fellow
32 Brown shades
33 Imitated
34 Queue
35 Completely reliable
38 Put on board
40 Françoise or Carl
45 Get unconfused
49 Prayer
50 Egg-shaped
52 Abates
54 Short fiction
55 "All __" (Berlin tune)
56 Snub-nosed dogs, for short
57 Nat or Natalie
58 Part of a Parisian play
60 Skier's lift
61 Damage
63 Hee partner
64 "Are you a man __ mouse?"

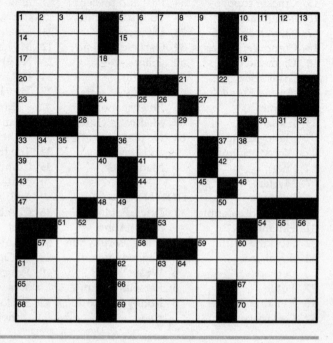

972 WING IT by Daniel R. Stark

ACROSS
1 __ May, NJ
5 Sphere of influence
10 Finish the laundry
14 Cranston or Bates
15 Nary a soul
16 17th state
17 Alphabetize
18 Shivery feeling
20 Up in the sky
22 Tin or titanium
23 Eightsome
25 Beat soundly
28 Took the helm
30 Nocturnal insect
32 Stops stalling
33 Hindu garments
35 Father, to tot
36 Not worth a __
37 Food fish
38 Tennis shot
39 Road charge
41 Brake parts
43 Something extra
44 Get __ of the action
46 New England pro
48 Fishing-reel parts
50 Muscle
51 Turn on a point
53 Drive-in employee
56 Gadding about
60 Soap unit
61 Marsh bird
62 Bottled spirit
63 Literary Gardner
64 Raised
65 Whodunit award
66 Pierre's st.

DOWN
1 José's house
2 __ vera lotion
3 Spectacular bulb
4 Lures
5 Fly tiers
6 Bossy comment
7 Economic upswing
8 Dress panel
9 Grows canines
10 Soft, light silk
11 Electrical unit
12 Canyon edge
13 Durango duo
19 Theda of the silents
21 Patronized a bistro
24 Indoctrinate
26 Gulp
27 Lay low
28 Ice-cream servers
29 Lack good posture
31 Yaks it up
32 Hammett pooch
34 Notions
40 Conductor Stokowski
41 Fabric edge
42 Car-price label
43 Drills through
45 Invent, as a word
47 Genetic strand
49 Cobbled
52 Sharp taste
54 Tulsa's st.
55 Steal a glimpse
56 Poetic eye
57 Distant
58 "For shame!"
59 Narrow inlet

973   KEEP FIT by Rich Norris

ACROSS
1 Leave out
5 Comparative diagram
10 Came down
14 Shop clamp
15 Sonja of skating
16 Take it easy
17 Be prudent
20 Hospital employee
21 Regional military dictators
22 Accelerate
25 Guzzler
26 Part of QED
28 Clenched, as hands
33 Give a nudge to
37 Joyful
39 Joyful
40 Be under the weather
43 __ a customer
44 Storage locale
45 Spandau's last inmate
46 Helmet attachments
48 Straight up
50 Witch
52 Grabs for oneself
57 Transmission media
62 Game of chance
63 Extremely frightened
66 Golden __ (Drake's ship)
67 Study aids
68 Arden and Plumb
69 Son of 29 Down
70 Helium and oxygen
71 Very dry

DOWN
1 Pizzeria cookers
2 Confusion
3 River into the Rhone
4 Short and sweet
5 4 on a phone
6 Home: Abbr.
7 Once more
8 Print widths
9 Receive word about
10 Choir member
11 Animal abode
12 Big name in clothing
13 Wallet fodder
18 Sign over
19 Last syllable of a word
23 Give encouragement to
24 California trees
27 Hoop shot
29 Adam's third
30 Undeniable
31 Says "oops," perhaps
32 Does a salon job
33 Cons' antitheses
34 Litter's littlest
35 Humdinger
36 Facts
38 Takes out
41 Astaire prop
42 Bookbinder's leather
47 Part of DST
49 Like some tales
51 City southeast of Turin
53 Gdansk natives
54 Comics adventurer Canyon
55 Out-and-out
56 Bad-guy chasers
57 Tennis great
58 Victor's cry
59 Janet of the cabinet
60 Considerable amounts
61 Cpls.' orderers
64 Busy one
65 Oceangoing initials

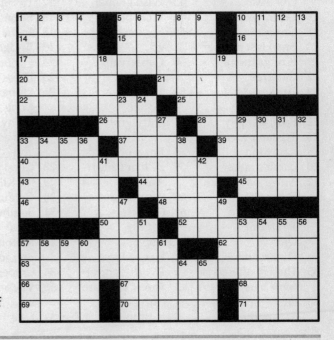

974   LOSE IT by Bob Lubbers

ACROSS
1 Stephen of Angie
4 Algerian port
8 Former First Lady
13 Spheres
15 M. Descartes
16 With it
17 Russian river
18 Head-swellers
19 Visit again
20 Lose it
23 Muse of poetry
24 Like Milquetoast
25 Used to be
29 Achy
31 Argues
33 Iron-pumper's pride
36 Understandings
38 Spew lava
39 Lose it
43 Slow, in music
44 Warts and all
45 Needle hole
46 Stuff (oneself)
49 Parisian pate
51 Lime drinks
52 Winged
54 Potato place
58 Lose it
60 HI hi
64 Canary's home
65 Fashion mag
66 Wall art
67 Cake topper
68 Rollicking rhythm
69 Last letter
70 Take care of, with "to"
71 Three dits, codewise

DOWN
1 Moulin __
2 Booted ball
3 Addis __
4 Pitcher Hershiser
5 Large military unit
6 Have __ for news
7 Like some tables
8 Painter Chagall
9 Pub pint
10 French pronoun
11 Pique
12 Printemps follower
14 Chair parts
21 "__ the union label . . ."
22 Husband of 8 Across
25 Sound the alarm
26 Chopin selection
27 Answer
28 Cosmetician Lauder
30 Ring master?
32 Critter
33 "Send him hence with __ in his ear"
34 Meld
35 Playboy of the Western World poet
37 __ Na Na
40 Western Indians
41 Female hormone
42 Hasten
47 "My __ Sal"
48 Draw forth
50 '50s Ford
53 Quickly
55 '50s pitcher Reynolds
56 Rolling land
57 Golden Boy playwright
58 FDR's dog
59 Geek
60 __, amas, amat
61 __ and Abner (old radio show)
62 Lead source
63 Crone

20 QUESTIONS by Manny Nosowsky

ACROSS
1 Boring
5 Yawned, like a canyon
10 Strong flavor
14 Chantilly, for one
15 Lermontov's __ of Our Time
16 Germ, perhaps
17 Charisma
20 Breakfast partner
21 It rings the castle
22 Carefree
23 Ford model, for short
25 Face, slangily
26 Tristan's love
28 Army kid
29 Lamb's father
32 Auberjonois and Descartes
33 Word before sesame or wide
34 Eliot's Adam
35 They're offered at some bars
38 First words of the day, perhaps

39 Word of substance?
40 *To __ Mockingbird*
41 Banns word
42 Loco
43 Adds color to
44 One for the book
45 Wish granter
46 More nervous
49 "__ a song go . . ."
50 Conservative start
53 Mined-over matter
56 Nitty-gritty
57 Pooh's creator
58 Buzzi or Roman
59 Belli or Bailey: Abbr.
60 *Gypsy* scorer
61 On a cruise

DOWN
1 Have a big mouth
2 *Planet* reporter
3 Shrew's feature
4 Curtain fold
5 In profusion

6 Rashad of NBC Sports
7 Fen fuel
8 Bit of work
9 Romeos
10 __ *Andronicus*
11 Score after deuce
12 Hornbill home
13 Strong-flavored
18 In the thick of
19 Bridge seat
24 __ out (censor)
25 Dress sharply
26 Humorist __ S. Cobb
27 "Why don't you come up and __"
28 Good grade
29 '85 Kilmer film
30 Confuse
31 Southwestern rises
33 Milton who preceded Idi
34 Crepes
36 Vile and evil, e.g.
37 Like

42 Max Jr. or Sr.
43 *Dances With Wolves* structure
44 Filial follower
45 Astronaut/senator
46 Peel or Samms
47 Losing proposition?

48 Flying pest
49 In a lazy fashion
51 Feminizing suffix
52 Workplace watchdog: Abbr.
54 Hit with a beam
55 Sp. title

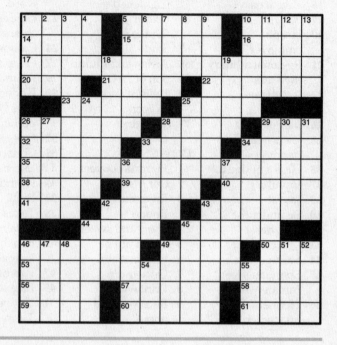

FOWL PLAY by Norma Steinberg

ACROSS
1 Kathie Lee's cohost
6 Debatable
10 Patches the roof
14 In solitude
15 Bullets
16 Medicinal plant
17 Exact double
18 Prong
19 Do, re, or mi
20 "Okay!"
21 Obvious target
24 Overjoy
26 Pub order
27 Arm joints
29 Come out on top
33 Nye or Calhern
34 In one piece
35 "How dry __ . . ."
37 Columns of additions
38 Greets
39 Give the once-over to
40 Sixth sense
41 Judy of *Laugh-In*

42 Villain's expression
43 Runaway
45 Crooner Vic
46 African snake
47 Flaxen material
48 Paltry sum
53 Stayed out of sight
56 Songbird
57 Nick Charles' wife
58 Make up (for)
60 Spoken
61 Smoothed-out
62 Shade of purple
63 Wilder or Hackman
64 Pops
65 "__ evil . . ."

DOWN
1 Risqué
2 Pronoun for Françoise
3 Nervous reaction
4 Rural hotel
5 Playground equipment

6 Flat finish
7 Leave out
8 Starter for bus or potent
9 Polish site
10 In __ (together)
11 Felipe of baseball
12 Campus mil. unit
13 Look for
22 "__ Impossible" (Como tune)
23 Mucilage
25 Actress Nettleton
27 Otherwise
28 Bad guy
29 Old-time pronoun
30 Part in a play
31 Classify
32 Guitarist Eddie Van __
34 Bit of merchandise
36 Insignificant
38 Came to pass
39 "This one's __!"
41 Wine barrel

42 Summer footwear
44 Fowl laugh?
45 Gaming cube
47 Is inclined
48 Plumbing problem
49 Tortoise's rival
50 Iraq's neighbor

51 PBS science program
52 Wilma's husband
54 __ instant (quickly)
55 Erté's style
59 Reason for overtime

TABLE SERVICE by Bob Lubbers

ACROSS

1 Baby's word
5 Dear: It.
9 Enticers
14 Strasbourg summers
15 Ran up a tab
16 Computer messages
17 Gondolier's song
19 Couric's bailiwick
20 Tank covering
22 Theater district
23 __ Kippur
24 Forum fashion
28 Urgent
30 Coin-op eatery
32 Sounds of surprise
35 Colombian city
37 __ of Two Cities
38 TV-signal receivers
42 Dior style
43 List-ending abbr.
44 Picnic pest
45 Wisconsin city
48 Actress San Juan
50 Music and painting, for two
51 Prefix for center
53 Prepares potatoes
57 "Only You" singers
59 Golfer Palmer
63 Getting proficient at
64 Acquire knowledge
65 Pro opponent
66 Mine passage
67 Swung along
68 Space org.
69 Tells stories

DOWN

1 Preclude
2 Arcade game name
3 Skin layer
4 __ as ice
5 Two-striper
6 MP's catch
7 Pass along
8 "__ Nightingale" (Keats work)
9 Animal docs
10 Latin I word
11 Bonkers
12 Pop singer Zadora
13 Tricky
18 Mag pieces
21 No-fly bird
24 Wee ones
25 Nebraska city
26 Greek physician
27 "This is only __"
29 Yale student
31 Parking-lot party site
32 Honshu port
33 More robust
34 Pinch pennies
36 Resident's suffix
39 Slugger Slaughter
40 Ike's command
41 Balkan region
46 Nasty chortle
47 Tarzan, e.g.
49 Star-related
52 Pepsodent rival
54 Role for Shirley Temple
55 Sesame Streeter
56 Some GIs
57 Take care of
58 WWII craft
59 Everyone
60 Olds creation
61 40 winks
62 Wrath

PLACES, PLEASE by Manny Nosowsky

ACROSS

1 "The Georgia Peach"
5 Las Vegas attraction
10 Poet Whitman
14 Other things: Lat.
15 Resembling
16 Hydrox rival
17 Big shot
20 Denier's remarks
21 Light in manner
22 Become angry
23 Velvet cloth
25 The Ugly Duckling, really
26 Like wood for construction
28 Pokey
29 Young fellow
32 Michigan town
33 Gravy holder
34 Moore of *Ghost*
35 Political position
38 Frothy fluids
39 Memo
40 Slow, to Solti
41 Lith. or Lat., once
42 Part of Muffet's meal
43 Equilibrium
44 Equipment
45 Bite hard (on)
46 Knit blanket
49 Burn a bit
50 Devil's disciple
53 It's south of San Diego
56 "Olly olly __ free!"
57 Praise to the skies
58 Gumbo ingredient
59 Ibsen character
60 18-wheelers
61 Belgian river

DOWN

1 "It's Magic" lyricist
2 Minstrel-show medley
3 Sport
4 Scornful expletive
5 Strained look
6 Reward
7 Pleasant-smelling, as a forest
8 Mao __-tung
9 Takes the spot next to
10 Two of the Supreme Court
11 In __ (going nowhere)
12 Mr. Walesa
13 Casino tip
18 New user's guide
19 Time between birthdays
24 They counteract lyes
25 Condition
26 Arizona Indians
27 Stirs (up)
28 Easily cowed one
29 Heavyweight champ in '78
30 Fine fiddlemaker
31 Pranks
33 Unhappy fan, maybe
34 __ *On* (HBO sitcom)
36 Augments
37 Matador's nemesis
42 Have on
43 Mine passages
44 War of 1812 treaty site
45 Hot dish
46 Like a bump on __
47 Sly
48 Dancer Verdon
49 Dollar
51 Bog down
52 Carson forerunner
54 Cutting tool
55 Bean or Campanella

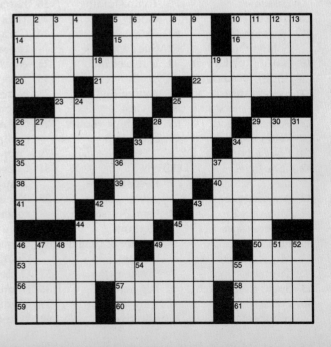

979   PEN NAMES by Dean Niles

ACROSS

1 Reach
6 Outlaws
10 Fluid bags
14 Once more
15 Actor Baldwin
16 Not care __
17 Unseasoned
18 Japanese wrestling
19 Musical quality
20 Chloe Wofford
23 Chi Chi's grp.
26 Euripides drama
27 Used a blender, perhaps
28 Passionate
30 Shoe glow
32 Mary Ann Evans
34 Favorite
37 To be, to Babette
38 Ripken of the Orioles
39 Meter reading
40 Rowan or Rather
41 David Cornwell
45 Assembly-line worker
46 Soothing liquid
47 Welcomes
50 Latin lover's verb
51 Cunning
52 Charles Dodgson
56 "It's __ to Tell a Lie"
57 *E pluribus* __
58 Theater walk
62 Underground mag
63 Hoarfrost
64 Hiding nothing
65 B&O position
66 View
67 Secret huddle

DOWN

1 Carefree
2 Self-regard
3 Greek T
4 Shade
5 Unbroken
6 Washbowl
7 Grad
8 Verne captain
9 Sign of November
10 Swift genre
11 Part of a Stein line
12 Slim boat
13 Go out-of-pocket
21 Keep in mind
22 Little squirt
23 Called
24 Ms. Garbo
25 Embellish
29 Poetic preposition
30 Bias
31 Rise
33 Resound
34 Helen's abductor
35 Swashbuckler Flynn
36 Minute
39 Butter, essentially
41 Tittles
42 Faint
43 *Sesame Street* character
44 Antifreeze
45 *A Few Good Men* director
47 Donut covering
48 Varnish ingredient
49 NBA star Patrick
50 Man of the House
53 Black cuckoos
54 Beef cut
55 Prevaricator
59 The limit, sometimes
60 Guitar whiz Paul
61 NYC summer setting

980   TEAM PLAY by Randolph Ross

ACROSS

1 Leave the flock
6 SAT relative
9 College exam
13 Musical refrain
14 Sector
15 Frat party costume
16 Like Cheerios
17 Skeletons at Soldier Field?
19 NBAers Oakley or Smith, formerly?
21 System starter
22 Parking place
23 Article of food
27 Boxer or Biden
30 Long adventure
32 "She loves me __"
33 Ivy Leaguer
34 Mineral suffix
35 Phoenix sitcom?
39 Friend of France
41 Musical talent
42 Turin trio
43 Sugar from starch
46 Political commentators
50 Saloon seat
51 Something to shoot for
52 Sticky stuff
53 Florida actor/baseball player?
58 Tampa folding money?
61 Float __
62 Buck ending
63 Unpleasant to touch
64 Author Bret
65 Go fast
66 Wild blue yonder
67 Nasty look

DOWN

1 Keeps the fire going
2 Hypnotic state
3 Mete out
4 Brother of Daniel, William, and Stephen
5 Tug hard
6 Tony the Tiger's adjective
7 Bring up
8 Hines of jazz
9 Mishearing
10 Director Howard
11 Epoch
12 __ Cruces, NM
14 Revile
18 Large group
20 Togs
24 Garage-sale caveat
25 After taxes
26 Turn colors
28 Nonspecific amount
29 Nursery occupant
30 Opry adjective
31 Cause a commotion
33 Auction conclusion
35 *Venus de* __
36 Comedienne Charlotte
37 Coffee server
38 Buntline or Beatty
39 Morning hrs.
40 Wrestling surface
44 Drum of a sort
45 Oil of __
46 Mammy Yokum
47 Snub
48 As of now
49 Cornhusker rival
51 Hard to please
54 Diamond stats
55 Gambler's need
56 Super Bowl sounds
57 King of comedy
58 Tasseled topper
59 Acapulco gold
60 Outback hopper

981 LOFTY by Eileen Lexau

ACROSS

1 Crèche trio
5 Cry like a baby
9 Practices boxing
14 Andy's pal
15 Ronny Howard role
16 Snafu
17 Is unable to
18 *Pinta* companion
19 Cub Scout leader
20 Horseplay
22 Lease again
23 Vote out of office
24 Arises (from)
26 *Wizard of Id* exclamation
28 Mediterranean island
32 On the __ (broken)
36 Neighbor of Ore.
39 Actor Holliman
40 Shakespearean baddie
41 Printing process, for short
42 Jason's ship
43 "Hold your horses!"
44 Pulitzer winner James
45 Shooting sport
46 Guided the sheep
48 Former Chinese leader
50 __ the hills
53 Comedy routine
58 Song of David
61 Difficult project
63 Monte __
64 Entreaty
65 Jai __
66 Dim from tears
67 Bard's river
68 Pigsty
69 Gape
70 Torn apart
71 Half of VP

DOWN

1 __ Picchu
2 With full force
3 Shallow bells
4 "Now __ time for all . . ."
5 Mackerel relative
6 Neat as __
7 Flirts, in a way
8 Smallest
9 Unctuous
10 Colorado attraction
11 Figure skater's move
12 Reign
13 Small fight
21 Marsalis' medium
25 Canyon phenomenon
27 Branchlet
29 Steak order
30 Yen
31 Opening
32 5 Down, e.g.
33 Appraise
34 Inventor Sikorsky
35 Highest price
37 Dined
38 Ark passenger
41 Alan or Cheryl
45 London district
47 Author __ Leonard
49 Obliquely
51 One way to buy bonds
52 Balm
54 Kind of steamer
55 Do-nothing
56 See 43 Across
57 Mr. Kringle
58 EPA no-nos
59 Diet concern
60 Vicinity
62 Panetta or Spinks

982 ANIMAL ACT by Gerald R. Ferguson

ACROSS

1 Pal
5 Orange-red stone
9 Schlep
13 Jay of late-night TV
14 Toast topper
15 "What's in __?"
17 Like the Gobi
18 Not of the clergy
19 Jeopardy
20 Prokofiev piece
23 ROTC's kin
24 Singer Ponselle
25 Advantageous aspect
29 Fiver
30 Jabbers
34 Time being
35 Hollywood crosser
36 Feminist org.
37 Paul Hogan film
41 From __ Z
42 Portentous March day
43 Bellini heroine
44 Boston music group
46 Profit word
47 Least covered
48 *Othello* tormentor
50 Canoe paddle
51 Fictional gumshoe
59 Make pigtails
60 Part of UAE
61 Hardly __ (rarely)
62 As of
63 Pepper grinder
64 Identical
65 Affix a brand to
66 Foil's cousin
67 Like molasses

DOWN

1 Thank the cast
2 This spot
3 Troop group
4 Fashion or form
5 Provide comfort
6 Greenspan et al.
7 Tim of *Frank's Place*
8 Principles of law
9 Binding strips
10 Street sign
11 Poi source
12 Actor Jannings
16 Keebler creature
21 Bronco buster's milieu
22 Used the strop
25 Remove the lid from
26 __ Alegre, Brazil
27 Nosy Parker
28 Trucking agcy.
29 Boned portion
31 Pianist Previn
32 Frost products
33 No __ (easy)
35 Pac Man, for one
38 Australian wild dog
39 Divest of weapons
40 Postal-creed word
45 Glass ingredient
47 Trinket
49 European viper
50 Papal cape
51 Air-rifle ammo
52 *Topaz* author
53 Country byway
54 Sign of a thaw
55 Organizer's challenge
56 Flattened circle
57 Fictional captain
58 Sketched

983 EXPLOSIVE by Daniel R. Stark

ACROSS
1 RNs' group
4 Umpire's call
8 Lunch order
11 Doll word
13 Bridge fees
14 __ gin fizz
15 Kind of collar
16 Follow
17 Bring home the bacon
18 First-rate work
20 Altar end
21 Saharan land
22 Curriculum part
23 Showing shame
24 Aversion
28 Monastery
31 Confronts
32 Tin Man's need
33 Frame of mind
34 Supply the food
35 NCO wannabes
36 *Wheel of Fortune* buy
37 Claire of *My So-Called Life*
38 *Metamorphosis* author
39 Felt hats
41 Energy
42 Piece on a string
43 Plunders
47 Christmas song
48 Malt-shop buy
50 Exam base
51 Sanctify
52 *The Thin Man* pooch
53 Mars, to Alexander
54 Idaho city
55 Clairvoyant
56 Egos' relatives
57 Agile
58 Impatient cluck

DOWN
1 Microscopic swimmer
2 City north of Recife
3 "__ My Souvenirs" (1927 song)
4 Skater Henie
5 To boot
6 Goof up
7 Compass pt.
8 Heads for space
9 Folk tail?
10 X
12 Riled up
13 Moderately warm
14 Photo tint
19 Heavy-hydrogen discoverer
20 Aardvark snacks
22 Computer owner
24 Sees
25 Frozen treats
26 Mark time?
27 Actress Martinelli
28 Asian nursemaid
29 Sonny of Sonny and Cher
30 Oversize radios
31 Diller's husband
34 Witty person
35 Tropical fruits
37 Two-way
38 *Quo Vadis* costar
40 Veggies for pickling
41 Dissect, grammatically
43 Disheveled
44 Surprise win
45 Shows much fondness
46 Fire starter
47 Dweeb
48 Hoof sound
49 He may be apparent
50 Mai __ cocktail
51 Little shots

984 MAG TUNES by Bob Lubbers

ACROSS
1 Open-mouthed
6 Actress San Juan
10 Dweeb
14 Admiral's concern
15 Dread
16 __ vera
17 Dietz/Schwartz tune
20 Fable finishes
21 Tennis plays
22 "Step __!"
23 SASE, e.g.
24 Sob
27 Whichever
29 Free ticket
33 O'Hare abbr.
34 Cassio's rival
36 Opposite the mouth
38 Stevie Wonder tune
41 Air valve
42 Comic actress Martha
43 Call a bet
44 Tracy's Trueheart
45 Spanish king
46 Musical silence
47 Signal
49 Go along (with)
52 "The Waltz King"
56 Flier Earhart
59 Loesser/ Carmichael tune
62 Emulate Daffy Duck
63 Storm
64 Rustler chasers
65 Singles
66 Headliner
67 Spy

DOWN
1 Yes vote: Abbr.
2 Swipe, slangily
3 Plane starter
4 Fuel for a Bentley
5 Allen or Frome
6 In the wings
7 Waikiki welcome
8 Civil-rights activist Marcus
9 Fire crime
10 Part of NASA
11 Author Wiesel
12 Actress Schneider
13 Poor grades
18 Yalie
19 RN's treatment
24 Suit
25 Make amends
26 __ and all (as is)
28 Bête __
29 PAC beneficiary
30 Get up
31 Yegg's targets
32 Icy rain
34 Publicity
35 Humorist Goodman
36 Jimmy and Rosalynn's daughter
37 Tournament exemption
39 W. Hemisphere group
40 Skeptic
45 Usher again
46 Try to tie once more
47 __-de-sac
48 Manipulative ones
50 Little troublemaker
51 Ocean trenches
52 Town on the Vire
53 Abby or Ann
54 Got up
55 Vipers
57 __ facto
58 Too
60 Links grp.
61 "I'm frightened!"

985 DEIFICATION by Robert H. Wolfe

ACROSS
1 Gasconades
6 Bar orders
11 Coll. class
14 Boston airport
15 Macho group
16 Arab org.
17 Early video-game maker
18 One from Qum
19 Jogged
20 What one could do in predawn Sparta?
22 Second sequel suffix
23 Pool members?
24 Archer or Boleyn
25 Stood tall (over)
28 Comes out
31 Like two peas in __
32 Biblical landing spot
33 Debussy's sea
34 Make move
37 2001 computer
40 Works hard
42 Oliver's request
43 Painters' gear
45 Quinine target
48 Start of a tot's tune
49 Whopping goof
50 Anger
51 Pharaohs' favorite dessert?
57 Train unit
58 Betray
59 Current source
60 Cooler in the summer
61 Make up (for)
62 Cuts back
63 Bandleader Brown
64 Mails out
65 Senator Kefauver

DOWN
1 Dull
2 Learning method
3 Culture goo
4 Sheltered, in a way
5 Hidden shooter
6 Polished
7 Cowboys' concerns
8 Actor Sharif
9 "A __ 'clock scholar"
10 Barbershop sound
11 Annual Valhalla event?
12 Seinfeld role
13 Capitalizations
21 Hero follower
24 Ex-coach Parseghian
25 Tufted hat
26 Unseal, to Blake
27 Olympic games?
28 Period
29 Surface for Hulk Hogan
30 Palindromic preposition
32 Mornings: Abbr.
34 Justice Fortas
35 Common connector
36 Apr. collectors
38 Meyers of Kate & Allie
39 Grassy plain
41 Summer's verb
42 They cover the waterfront
43 Of non-clergymen
44 Chafe
45 Des __, IA
46 Airline to Tokyo
47 Delaware Indian
49 Redford, for one
51 Levin and Gershwin
52 London gallery
53 Like __ of bricks
54 Segregate
55 French notion
56 Cong. meeting

986 FLOUR POWER by Norma Steinberg

ACROSS
1 Feedbag contents
5 Thick slice
9 Young seal
12 Detonates
14 Filched
15 Fury
16 Squander, as time
18 Henhouse find
19 Reed or Hardy
20 Good cards in blackjack
21 Rose from a chair
24 Royal fur
26 Came to a halt
28 She __ to Conquer
31 Used to be
32 Peddled
35 Prefix for "below"
36 Museum offering
37 Outpourings
39 Title for the Pres.
40 Midler or Davis
42 Short skirt
43 Actor Nicholson
44 Skyrocketed
46 Golf shots
48 Most tender
51 "And so __"
52 Responsibility
54 On the couch
56 __ Baba
57 Elvis' music
62 Rustic motel
63 Say
64 Cry of glee
65 Droop
66 Overseer
67 J. Edgar Hoover, e.g.

DOWN
1 Switch position
2 Ventilate
3 Word form for "three"
4 Prepared
5 Barrel slat
6 __ the boom
7 Frightens
8 Actor Turhan
9 "A cinch!"
10 Compulsion
11 Wooden pins
13 Milkmaid's chair
14 __ Lanka
17 First-born
20 Soon, in poems
21 Sound system
22 Like a lemon
23 Grand __ Opry
25 "How sweet __!"
26 Mops the deck
27 Campus quarters
29 Checked the cost of
30 Paper bags
33 Flower garland
34 Marino and Quayle
37 Fortuneteller
38 Glove kin
41 City near Albany
43 Occupation
45 Spanish explorer
47 Actor McDowall
49 Religious subdivisions
50 Film shoots
52 Speaker's platform
53 Forearm bone
55 Roofing material
57 "Ay, there's the __"
58 Tatter
59 Electrical unit
60 Mauna __
61 Actor Chaney

987 KNOCK ON WOOD by Robert H. Wolfe

ACROSS

1 Living: Ger.
6 Hurried
10 Overhead trains
13 Solo
14 Dog bane
15 NY college
16 Brood over
18 French sea
19 Weizman of Israel
20 1040 grp.
21 Sniffler's need
23 Like Asia
25 Girder holder
26 Comic Kabibble
27 Lab work
30 Misplaces
33 Some quadrilaterals: Abbr.
34 Before
35 Mont Blanc et al.
36 Center of activities
37 Malt product
38 To __ With Love
39 Indian lute
40 Jennings or Arnett
41 Roof
43 Morning drops
44 Nurse, perhaps
45 Boat basins
49 Before '39
51 Writer Fleming
52 Actress Turner
53 __ Alamos, NM
54 Fortuneteller's activity
57 __ Dhabi
58 Place and James
59 Embankment
60 "Righto"
61 Cong. meeting
62 Lock of hair

DOWN

1 Boutonniere site
2 My Fair Lady ingenue
3 Big mistake
4 Vitalities
5 PBS benefactor
6 Robert of Airplane!
7 To be, e.g.: Abbr.
8 Swelled-headed ones
9 Extracts (from)
10 Horror film locale
11 In __ of (instead of)
12 Certain
14 Trading center
17 Birthday expression
22 __ of Galilee
24 Curve
25 Happen again
27 Synopsize
28 Algonquian
29 What to call Kohl
30 Mascara target
31 Mixed bag
32 Neatens
33 Chopper topper
36 Well-educated
37 Leave at sea
39 Mexican wraps
40 For each
42 Carpenter's tool
43 Bohr or Borge
45 The fourth planet
46 Gullible
47 Jackson and Meara
48 Wise guys?
49 Rialto event
50 After-bath wear
51 "__ corny as Kansas . . ."
55 Capt.'s underlings
56 Supermodel Carol

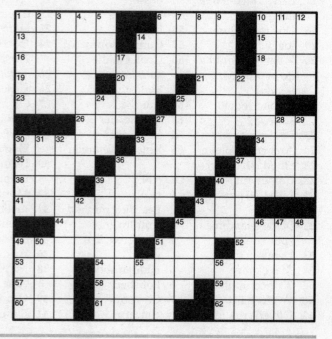

988 HOUSEHOLD STAFF by Bob Lubbers

ACROSS

1 Footnote abbr.
5 Tennis shots
9 Lahr and Wheeler
14 __ Geste
15 Flightless bird
16 __ as a pistol
17 Babysitter brouhaha
19 Cubic meter
20 Readies for production
22 Kitchen addition
23 Renounce
26 Engrossed
28 __ about
29 Sidewinder track
32 Ewe's pride
33 Heckler
35 Comic-strip frame
37 Scanner input: Abbr.
40 Actress Sommer et al.
41 Mrs. Lennon
42 Musical lead-in
44 Bao __ (former Vietnamese leader)
45 Cast a ballot
47 Actor Alain
48 Next year's jr.
50 Actor Stephen
52 "Houston, __ got a problem"
53 Jazzman Mose
56 Holy
58 Repast
59 Writer Alger
62 Bancroft and Baxter
64 Ticket issuer
68 Word form for "water"
69 Love god
70 Author Ferber
71 Rancher's rope
72 Puts on
73 Tear

DOWN

1 __ Saud
2 "__ Clown"
3 Songwriter Janis
4 Denim
5 Papal representative
6 Poet Khayyám
7 Wagers
8 Lucille Le __ (Joan Crawford)
9 __ relief
10 Regard
11 Gable role
12 Rich cake
13 War horse
18 Desire
21 Stack
23 Sporting a caftan
24 __ Gay
25 South Pacific archipelago
27 Meaningful
30 Jane's dog
31 More lucid
34 Formal answers
36 Knot, e.g.
38 Show true
39 Like some road markers
43 The latest arrival
46 "Whoops!"
49 Tankers
51 Fall blooms
53 __ and the Night Visitors
54 Weill's wife
55 Wanderer
57 Televise
60 San __, Italy
61 "This weighs __!"
63 Jack of Barney Miller
65 Juicy cooler
66 Lodging
67 June honoree

989 — THE OTHER OJ by Dean Niles

ACROSS
1 Title for 3 Down
4 Hang together
10 Linger
14 Half of *dos*
15 Worn by all
16 Actor Ray
17 Banned chem.
18 Tarantino film
20 Better than others
22 With firmness
23 Ticks off
24 __ de deux
25 Tropical fish
27 Tough
32 Trade shows, e.g.
33 Ratchet-wheel catches
34 Sean Lennon's mom
35 *Jeanne et Anne*
36 Watch part
37 Change for a Jackson
38 Three, in Turin
39 Took a chance
40 "If You Knew __"
41 Crunchy crackers
43 Was penalized in pinball
44 Groovy
45 Book page
46 Franklin production
50 Slips by
53 "Queen of Hearts" singer
55 W. Va. summer setting
56 Qualified
57 Not under any circumstances
58 Self-image
59 Oboe adjunct
60 Remarks to the audience
61 Morning condensation

DOWN
1 Sch. boss
2 Move slowly
3 One of Victoria's prime ministers
4 Domes
5 Burdens of proof
6 Sword handles
7 Uncommon sense
8 Ring judges
9 Election Day activity
10 '60s dance
11 Landed
12 Object of reverence
13 Crooner Bennett
19 Embers, once
21 Abstract works
25 Tries out
26 Special edition
27 Visibility problems
28 Was indebted to
29 Deteriorates
30 Photographer Leibovitz
31 Snooped
33 Father of France
36 Scarf style
37 Bell-shaped bloom
39 Sawyer of news
40 Gases used in electronics
42 Ran down
43 "Freedom's just another word for nothing left __"
45 Rank
46 Partly open
47 Oil job
48 Eight furlongs
49 Corp. bosses
51 Hem
52 Put away
54 1914-18 event

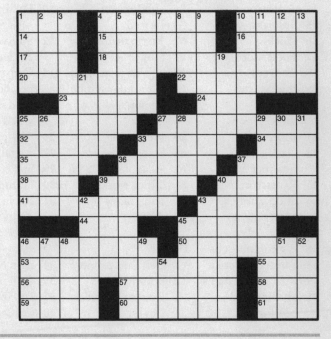

990 — TRIPLE PLAY by Shirley Soloway

ACROSS
1 "Presto" prop
5 Élan
9 Marinate
14 "Are you __ out?"
15 Nobelist Wiesel
16 Ricardo's former sidekick
17 Songstress Horne
18 __-lease (WWII program)
19 First zodiac sign
20 SUIT
23 Superlative suffix
24 Finale
25 Tax org.
28 Ballet move
31 Tristan's love
36 Nick of flicks
38 Grocery carryall
40 Resolve, with "down"
41 SUIT
44 Arm bone
45 Peter or Franco
46 Teheran native
47 Feel sorry about
49 School jacket
51 Graph or mason ender
52 Cut
54 A third of MDCCCIII
56 SUIT
65 Make happy
66 Muscovite, generically
67 Heavenly place
68 Up and about
69 Skips the ads, perhaps
70 *Inter* __
71 Unpleasant
72 "Waiting for the Robert __"
73 Faxed

DOWN
1 Lose vigor
2 Over again
3 Forbidden thing
4 Sheathe
5 Remove
6 Wilder or Guinness
7 Math function
8 Privet greenery
9 Dish fragments
10 Semester
11 Eastern port
12 At deuce
13 Pain in the neck
21 Tropical spots
22 Bryant or Ekberg
25 Bring about
26 Esther of *Driving Miss Daisy*
27 Tossed
29 160 square rods
30 Chaplain, familiarly
32 __ close to schedule
33 Oahu patio
34 "If I __ Care"
35 Borden's bovine
37 Ski lift
39 It's hysterical
42 Victorious
43 Holiday pie ingredient
48 Queen of mystery
50 City in Denmark
53 Value greatly
55 Brainstorms
56 Fat-free
57 Designer Schiaparelli
58 Hoods' weapons
59 Going __ (battling)
60 Track shape
61 May or Horn
62 Run in place
63 *Fräulein*'s refusal
64 Tiny insect

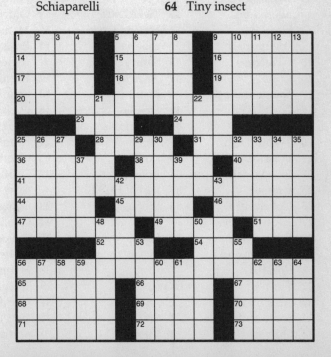

991 TUTTI FRUTTI by Lee Weaver

ACROSS

1 Computer mfr.
4 Dashboard instrument, for short
8 Social class
13 Astronaut Armstrong
15 Take on
16 Duck
17 Food shop
18 Concept
19 Intends (to)
20 Piece of information
21 Bronx cheer
23 Desirable qualities
25 Russian autocrat
26 Shop spinner
28 Most recent
33 *Sister Act* costume
36 Big commotions
38 Sandwich cookie
39 Mrs. John Adams
41 Huffing and puffing
43 "__ a Song in My Heart"
44 Sound from Simba
46 Assists a felon
47 Snuggle
49 Cowboy's rope
51 Military subdivision
53 Leased
57 Rumor source
61 Singer Guthrie
62 __ *Vice* (cop show)
63 Computer symbol
64 Person, place, or thing
65 Frequently
66 Famous lioness
67 Alan of *M*A*S*H*
68 Office worker
69 Bad grades
70 Allow

DOWN

1 Gandhi's country
2 Borscht needs
3 Jazz trumpeter Davis
4 Craving
5 Verdi opera
6 Crowned, as a bird
7 Clunky cars
8 Paparazzo's prop
9 State firmly
10 Fly like an eagle
11 Insignificant
12 Sullivan and Begley
14 Conspicuous position
22 Model-airplane wood
24 "So long!"
27 Angel topper
29 Star comic
30 Huron's neighbor
31 Put in the mail
32 Attire
33 *Private Benjamin* star
34 Irish Rose lover
35 Drill parts
37 Folklore villain
40 Castle or Cara
42 Fill to the brim
45 Newspaper account
48 Actress Ida
50 Fields of play
52 Like some college walls
54 Folklore villain
55 Give the slip to
56 Robert of *The 39 Steps*
57 Talent
58 Assess
59 Prayer ender
60 Scent finder
62 Yr. divisions

992 HURRY UP by Randolph Ross

ACROSS

1 Medicinal medium
5 Root for Hawaiians
9 Do some more alterations
14 Hawk's counterpart
15 GI offense
16 Chou __
17 Dangerous bed
19 Office pool member
20 Tropical fish
21 Pressure
22 Filled (with)
25 Dresser
26 Got close to
27 Files an appeal
30 Stengel or Jones
31 Fountain and Rozelle
32 Turin trio
33 ABA member
34 Some sculptures
35 Operated
36 Arbitrator, for short
37 Prepared apples
38 Exhaust
40 Matriculated
42 Per
43 Ticked off
44 Having more aspartame
45 Satisfy
47 Anesthetic liquid
48 Dressing choice
49 Black Hills tourist center
53 Confuse
54 Roundish
55 Part of HOMES
56 Proposition votes
57 Ration (out)
58 Moist

DOWN

1 ASAP
2 Chit
3 VII x VIII
4 Homily
5 Went on a wine tour
6 Tony or Edgar
7 Author Jaffe
8 Antique
9 Outcomes
10 Menu item
11 British news center
12 Fleming et al.
13 Spanish relatives
18 *Cuckoo's Nest* creator
21 Hamlet's countrymen
22 __ of (entrusted to)
23 Straighten up
24 Good buddies
25 Pulled the lever
27 Gave up
28 Hypnotic state
29 Telegraph tapper
31 Blender output
34 1995 Jefferson portrayer
37 Doesn't go (with)
38 Do 70
39 Stuck
41 Delphi VIP
42 For some time
44 3/17 honoree
45 Wish (for)
46 Stow cargo
47 Icicle holder
49 CD follower
50 Keogh cousin
51 Conway or Allen
52 "Uh-huh"

993 FROSTY FILMS by Rich Norris

ACROSS
1. Stretch across
5. Blue
8. Leverage
13. Mulgrew of *Star Trek: Voyager*
14. Victorian, maybe
16. Region of Spain
17. 1960 Richard Burton film
19. Czar foe
20. Stout relative
21. Went with
23. Ransacker's activity
27. Building material
28. Opposite of vert.
29. Dutch cheese
31. Avoids
34. Compass dir.
35. Famous
37. Islam's Almighty
38. Even
40. Pave anew
42. South American capital
43. Ricky's dad
45. 1995 tennis returnee
47. Hiatus
48. Keanu of *Johnny Mnemonic*
50. Art __ ('20s style)
51. Charlemagne's realm: Abbr.
52. Wades across
54. Beethoven works
56. Keillor of radio
59. Pooh's pal
60. Swiftly
61. 1989 Martin Sheen film
66. Brings under control
67. Seat for junior?
68. Shoe insert
69. Aviary sound
70. Finis
71. In the sack

DOWN
1. Hit the slopes
2. D.C. fundraiser
3. Dined on
4. High land
5. Magnificence
6. Parseghian of football
7. Prepare onions, perhaps
8. Oaf
9. Invoice too much
10. 1962 Ingmar Bergman film
11. Nobelist Wiesel
12. *The Fountainhead* author
15. __ Verde National Park
18. E.T., e.g.
22. Music buy
23. Socrates, for one
24. Put a charge into
25. 1992 Shannen Doherty film
26. Computer mogul Bill
30. Dealt (out)
32. Dobson of *Cleopatra Jones*
33. Influences, as opinions
36. Low-lying areas
39. *The Gay __* (Astaire film)
41. Made a tape
44. Most spooky
46. Start of a sequel title
49. '60s radical grp.
53. It's something over a foot
55. Main artery
56. NAFTA predecessor
57. "Give me __" (request to Fido)
58. Zilch
62. Dawson of the NFL
63. Sphere
64. Born: Fr.
65. Kennedy or Koppel

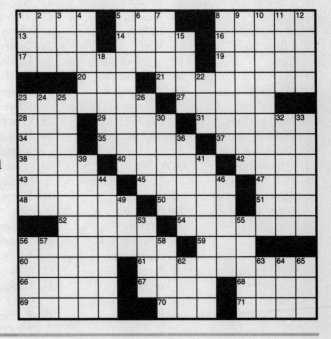

994 WE GOT TROUBLE by Raymond Hamel

ACROSS
1. Tell's companion
5. A singing Stone
9. Talks like Sylvester
14. Musical finale
15. Cooking vessel
16. Prank
17. Wishes undone
18. Ken of *thirtysomething*
19. Biological classifications
20. Facing trouble
23. Farm team
24. Dentist's deg.
25. Butt
26. Treat icy roads
28. Wheedled
30. Greeley phrase
34. Show approval
37. Genesis name
39. Excedrin rival
40. Sword handles
42. Long opening
43. Gregg expert
44. Fred Astaire's hometown
45. Modem transmission
47. Swirling water
48. One with an affected manner
50. 4-time Wimbledon winner
52. Dirt clump
54. Hanoi holiday
55. School contest
58. Bock, e.g.
61. Facing trouble
64. Gaveler's cry
66. Large antelope
67. Dresden's river
68. Like some real estate
69. Author of *The Neverending Story*
70. Ripening agent
71. Kobe's bay
72. Lip
73. Vivacious

DOWN
1. Boston entrée
2. Harass
3. *Waiting for Lefty* playwright
4. Clean up
5. Marina fee
6. Doomed
7. Football no-no
8. Charles Foster and Erica
9. Two pool lengths
10. Facing trouble
11. Charon's river
12. Carpet quality
13. Speedread
21. Blunder
22. Become flaccid
27. High balls
28. Facing trouble
29. PGA's __ Ryder Open
31. Espied
32. Ship out
33. New York city
34. Karate blow
35. VIP's vehicle
36. "Too bad!"
38. Be in opposition
41. Israel's first king
46. Wide thoroughfares
49. Aussie jumper
51. Greek letter
53. Some peers
55. Naval hogwash
56. Coal residue
57. Critic Roger
58. A real clown
59. Bow-toting tot
60. Actress Best
62. Salad fish
63. Illogical conclusion
65. Vitamin amt.

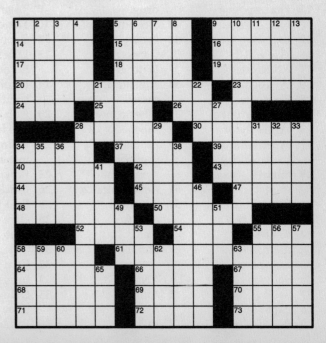

IN THE KITCHEN by A.J. Santora

ACROSS
1 Wait
5 Genetic initials
8 Adam of *Chicago Hope*
13 Pamper
15 Bel __ (cheese)
16 Unsuitable
18 Entice
19 Ship's spine
20 Lunar New Year
21 Wt. units
22 Mideast airline
24 Deal partner
27 Flabbergast
31 Tidal flooding
32 Uncommon
33 Hebrew month
35 Taina of *Les Girls*
36 Out-of-__ (tourists, perhaps)
39 See 5 Across
40 Something owed
42 Too-hot room
43 Crack up
45 Wooden expressions
47 Bombeck et al.
48 Doesn't care __
49 Small part
50 Rubbish
52 Blunder
55 Dakota Indian
59 Bet
62 __ Haute, IN
63 Distributes
64 Big name in auto racing
65 Giant Mel
66 Mil. awards

DOWN
1 Lodge letters
2 Smidgen
3 Scribbler
4 Exalts
5 __ Plaines, IL
6 Bottle part
7 Together, in music
8 Artemis' twin
9 Brit. fliers
10 Tympanist's target
11 "Oh"
12 Unmixed
13 NBC show since '75
14 Swamps
17 Kitchen tool
23 Two-way name
24 Lawn bane
25 Summonsed
26 Whirlybirds
27 Cheer for Sills
28 Of a cereal
29 British service-women
30 __ bell (seemed familiar)
34 Pep squad cries
37 Unseat
38 Went o'er the fields
41 Gob
44 Lacking guile
46 Zanier
49 Two together
50 Post-Q queue
51 Author Wister
53 Erase
54 "__ ever so humble, . . ."
56 Unconfirmed Bibl. writings
57 Dobbs and Waters of CNN
58 Half of DA
60 Before
61 "Spring forward" hrs.

FOOD STUFF by Diane C. Baldwin

ACROSS
1 Actress Andersson
5 House pet
8 Skycap's burden
12 Blue-pencil
13 Prepared apples
15 Hodgepodge
16 NASA negative
17 Express a view
18 Bright star
19 RN's forte
20 Wage earner
22 Keep after
24 Wine sediment
25 With candor
27 Word before badge or pay
29 Smart __ (wise guy)
30 Showroom cars
31 Woolen cap
34 Kennedy matriarch
35 Bulb bloom
36 Soliloquy start
37 Sault __ Marie
38 Paper unit
39 Building overseer
40 Use a divining rod
41 Distort one's words
42 Grand musical production
44 Bacteria-fighting drug
45 Nobody's fool
48 Doze (off)
51 Garr or Hatcher
52 Afghanistan capital
53 Tibetan monk
54 Ripened
55 Ermine, in summer
56 Army group
57 Acid neutralizer
58 "__ a real nowhere man . . ."
59 Entrance barrier

DOWN
1 Affinity
2 Admired one
3 VIP
4 "How was __ know?"
5 Managed
6 42 Across highlight
7 Be inclined (to)
8 Easter topper
9 Together (with)
10 Has elasticity
11 Zoom skyward
13 Like some humor
14 Bit of morning condensation
20 Heft
21 Eye feature
23 A single instance
25 Rowing needs
26 Garden area
27 Free-for-all
28 Give off
30 Club fees
31 Star
32 Cain's brother
33 Insignificant
35 Delivers a heavy blow
36 Layer of earth
38 Put in order
39 Auctioneer's aim
40 Heap scorn on
41 Jury's determination
42 Psi follower
43 Whittles (down)
44 Gull-like birds
45 Attempt
46 Court ritual
47 Clarinet cousin
49 Fail to include
50 Palm fruit
53 Carry, in a way

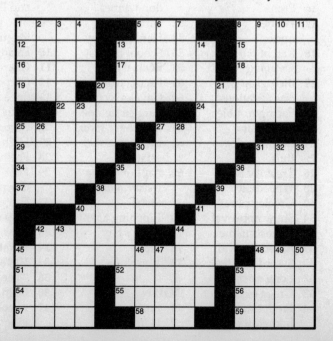

997   REPTILIAN by Shirley Soloway

ACROSS
1 Necklace unit
5 Strongman Charles
10 Regarding
14 Interest consideration
15 Barbecue surface
16 Short drive
17 Actress Gray
18 Cowboy convention
19 *Citizen* __
20 Avocado
23 Hold back
24 Slugger Williams
25 Top gymnastics score
28 Soars
32 Obliterate
34 Asner and Wynn
37 Casual garments
40 Tibetan priest
42 Computer messages
43 Tune for two
44 Indian rituals
47 Most Soc. Sec. recipients
48 Asian creed
49 Shooting game
51 Moray
52 Sort of: Suff.
55 Big volumes
59 Eyeglass-frame material
64 Mix (up)
66 Litters' littlest
67 Potpourri
68 Actor Cronyn
69 Composers' org.
70 "__ we forget"
71 Skating maneuver
72 Arctic explorer
73 Sandra and Ruby

DOWN
1 Staff of life
2 Composer Hagen
3 On a slant
4 One who says "no"
5 Taj Mahal city
6 Jog
7 Italian resort
8 Wide awake
9 Incline
10 "__ silly question, . . ."
11 Kirk Douglas role
12 Soft metal
13 Indivisible
21 *True* __
22 '50s British prime minister
26 Sandy ridge
27 Makes a home
29 Took to court
30 Columnist Bombeck
31 Laurel and Getz
33 Beet-colored
34 Borden mascot
35 "__ *Macabre*"
36 Petty
38 Defeat
39 Gen. Robt. __
41 Alias initials
45 Asian ruler
46 Tennis divisions
50 "To have and __"
53 Belt
54 Dwelling
56 Confused fight
57 Beethoven dedicatee
58 Openings for tabs
60 Pitcher Hershiser
61 Peruvian native
62 Top performer
63 Catch sight of
64 __ Na Na
65 Formal wear, informally

---

998   HEAVE HO by Randolph Ross

ACROSS
1 Hindu honorific
4 *M*A*S*H* corporal
9 Cardinal insignias
13 Golden Gate, e.g.
14 Express one's feelings
15 __ En-lai
16 Chorus needs
18 Saharan
19 Cold storage
20 Sharp claws
22 Despots
23 Colorful bird
24 '50s nickname
25 Postponement
28 Andy and Crunch
31 Sailing hazards
32 Juan's one
33 Word of woe
34 Smelling __ (revivers)
35 NCOs
36 Spanish article
37 They're put up in a fight
38 Church areas
39 Communiqués
41 Fr. holy woman
42 First Oscar-winning movie
43 Actress Holm
47 Orbital extreme
49 Smokey Robinson's group
50 Bus garage
51 Kids' weapons
53 Pakistani language
54 Spanish squiggle
55 Raison d'__
56 Stunned response
57 Collar stiffeners
58 __ Na Na

DOWN
1 Like Cajun cooking
2 Star giver
3 Enslaved
4 Good name
5 Not right
6 "The Gentleman Is a __"
7 Consumed
8 Hires new workers
9 Ladderlike
10 Floor coverings
11 Cut of beef
12 Beer
13 Barbecue item
17 Car calls
21 Sleeve cards
23 Convenes
25 Removes from the galleys
26 Chip in
27 Ledger entry
28 Pre-storm situation
29 Lotion additive
30 Entrance requirements
31 Garden gear
34 Hints at
35 Addresses
37 Great dog?
38 Map collection
40 Enroll
41 Suit materials
43 Penny's sitcom costar
44 Lazy creature
45 Tropical fish
46 Latin being
47 "Snug as __ . . ."
48 Legal opening
49 __ *18* (Uris book)
52 Ignited

999 FOR A RAINY DAY by Dean Niles

ACROSS
1 Minus
5 Drinks like a dog
9 One who gives examples
14 Word form for "within"
15 Water, in Juárez
16 Japanese poetry form
17 Door position
18 Party pooper
20 Unsmiling
22 Russian river
23 Boy or girl ending
24 Laughing carnivore
25 James of *White Palace*
27 Taken-back car
29 __ 17 (Holden film)
33 Blissful place
38 Nerve beginning
39 Aggressive
40 Give off
43 Women's mag
44 Outerwear brand
46 Ruddy
49 Invitation request
50 Not __ (in no way)
52 See 48 Down
57 Sp. lady
60 Call attention to
61 Narrow-minded
62 Hendrix tune
65 Rouse
66 "Farewell!"
67 Over
68 Coll. major
69 Brought back
70 Charged atoms
71 Imparted

DOWN
1 Tether
2 Relish
3 Like old bread
4 Theologian Kierkegaard
5 Grass en masse
6 Mature
7 Taken advantage of
8 Native Israeli
9 Alpine lodge
10 Bond creator Fleming
11 Kon-__
12 __ out a living (makes do)
13 "The Bambino"
19 Little fellows
21 __ Gras
25 Harangue
26 Arrested
28 Blow up: Abbr.
30 Paper piece
31 Four-wheeler
32 Diver Louganis
33 White-hat wearer
34 Lounge
35 Scandinavian capital
36 In __ (unborn)
37 Collagist Max
41 Pt. of speech
42 Silent dwarf
45 Pizza topping
47 Arrival
48 With 52 Across, "The Queen of the West"
51 Middle Eastern religion
53 U or I
54 Quickly
55 Canon competitor
56 Perfume
57 Bandy words
58 Uncouth
59 Very dry
61 Kitten cries
63 Little, in Lyons
64 Branch of Buddhism

1000 FOUR IN A ROW by Fred Piscop

ACROSS
1 Bank org.
5 Whitish gem
9 Cheesed it
13 Jot
14 Garden walk
15 Writer Jong
16 Asian inland sea
17 Rug descriptor
18 Ciphers
19 Florida fish
22 Not as naive
23 Puts a strain on
24 It may be raw
27 Quarterback Y.A.
31 One of the Aleutians
34 Flat occupant
37 Stovepipe, e.g.
38 North Carolina ruminant
41 Ducats, in headlines
42 Human
43 Writes a note, perhaps
44 *Opus 300* writer
46 European capital
48 Varsity
51 Cool digs?
55 Iowa tea
59 Tree-dwelling mammal
60 Dr. Pavlov
61 Sacked out
62 Civil-rights leader Medgar
63 TV knob
64 Overfill
65 Wilder in the movies
66 Sinclair rival
67 '82 Disney film

DOWN
1 Imported autos
2 PGA event
3 Bologna is found here
4 Drafted
5 Brilliantly colored fish
6 Chute opener
7 Alamogordo event
8 The Forbidden City
9 Least restrained
10 Dough from 3 Down
11 Environmentalist's subj.
12 __ Boot
15 Bible book
20 Live
21 Getty of *The Golden Girls*
25 Here, there, and everywhere
26 Annealing oven
28 Easing of tension
29 Like some excuses
30 HHH
31 Official records
32 The one here
33 DeVito series
35 Ride the bench
36 Thick slice
39 Hams
40 At __ (finally)
45 Like some movie audiences
47 Del __, TX
49 "Look __!"
50 P-K4 et al.
52 Of a rounded projection
53 __ a customer
54 Utah city
55 "__ Only Just Begun"
56 Mass ender
57 Galley propellers
58 Aware of
59 Turkey part

RANDOM HOUSE CROSSWORD ORDER FORM

VOL.	ISBN	QUANT.	PRICE	TOTAL

NEW YORK TIMES CROSSWORDS

New York Times Crossword Omnibus
Vol.10 0812931653 _____ $11.50 _____

New York Times Daily Crosswords
Vol.56 0812933869 _____ $9.95 _____

New York Times Easiest Crosswords
Vol.1 0812932927 _____ $9.95 _____

New York Times Large Type Omnibus
Vol.2 081293069X _____ $13.00 _____

New York Times Sunday Crosswords
Vol.25 0812932080 _____ $14.00 _____
Vol.26 0812933818 _____ $9.95 _____

New York Times Sunday Crossword Tribute to Eugene T. Maleska
0812933842 _____ $13.95 _____

New York Times Sunday Crossword Omnibus
Vol.5 0812932935 _____ $12.50 _____

New York Times Toughest Crosswords
Vol.7 0812930703 _____ $10.00 _____

New York Times Toughest Crossword MegaOmnibus
Vol.1 0812931661 _____ $13.95 _____

DELL CROSSWORDS

Dell Crossword Puzzles
Vol.11 0812934482 _____ $9.95 _____
Vol.12 0812934652 _____ $9.95 _____

Dell Sunday Crossword Puzzles
Vol.2 0812934385 _____ $9.95 _____
Vol.3 0812935063 _____ $9.95 _____

LOS ANGELES TIMES CROSSWORDS

Los Angeles Times Sunday Crosswords
Vol.21 0812934490 _____ $9.95 _____
Vol.22 0812934210 _____ $9.95 _____

Los Angeles Times Sunday Omnibus
Vol.3 0812933575 _____ $12.95 _____

WASHINGTON POST CROSSWORDS

Washington Post Sunday Crosswords
Vol.10 0812934172 _____ $9.95 _____
Vol.11 0812934547 _____ $9.95 _____

Washington Post Sunday Omnibus
Vol.2 0812934415 _____ $12.95 _____

BOSTON GLOBE CROSSWORDS

Boston Globe Sunday Crosswords
Vol.11 0812934342 _____ $9.95 _____
Vol.12 0812934857 _____ $9.95 _____

Boston Globe Sunday Omnibus
Vol.1 0812934318 _____ $12.95 _____

NEW YORK MAGAZINE CROSSWORDS

New York Magazine Crosswords
Vol.3 081293430X _____ $9.95 _____
Vol.4 0812934601 _____ $9.95 _____

CHICAGO TRIBUNE CROSSWORDS

Chicago Tribune Daily Crosswords
Vol.1 0812934067 _____ $9.95 _____
Vol.2 0812934261 _____ $9.95 _____

Chicago Tribune Sunday Crosswords
Vol.1 0812934075 _____ $9.95 _____
Vol.2 081293427X _____ $9.95 _____

RANDOM HOUSE CROSSWORDS

Random House Summer Vacation Crosswords
0812934792 _____ $6.95 _____

Random House Spring Training Crosswords
0812934784 _____ $6.95 _____

Random House Cabin Fever Crosswords
0812934776 _____ $6.95 _____

Random House Back to the Beach Crosswords
0812934768 _____ $6.95 _____

Random House Bedtime Crosswords
0812934679 _____ $6.95 _____

Random House Cozy Crosswords
0812934326 _____ $6.95 _____

Random House Crosswords
Vol.2 0812934504 _____ $9.95 _____
Vol.3 0812934997 _____ $9.95 _____

Random House Club Crosswords
Vol.5 0812932900 _____ $13.00 _____

Random House Crossword MegaOmnibus
Vol.2 0812930258 _____ $13.95 _____

Random House Mammoth Crossword Puzzle Omnibus
081293394X _____ $16.95 _____

Random House Sunday Monster Omnibus
Vol.1 0812930592 _____ $17.50 _____

Random House Masterpiece Crossword Collection
0812934946 _____ $12.95 _____

Random House Sunday Crosswords
Vol.7 0812934164 _____ $9.95 _____

Random House Sunday Crossword Omnibus
Vol.1 0812933982 _____ $12.95 _____

Random House Sunday MegaOmnibus
Vol.2 081292908X _____ $13.95 _____

Random House UltraHard Crossword Omnibus
Vol.1 0812931262 _____ $12.50 _____

WALL STREET JOURNAL CROSSWORDS

Wall Street Journal Crosswords
Vol.1 0812932056 _____ $9.95 _____
Vol.2 0812934636 _____ $9.95 _____

SPECIALTY CROSSWORDS

Atlantic Monthly Cryptic Crosswords
0812935128 _____ $9.95 _____

The Crosswords Club Collection
Vol.8 0812934431 _____ $9.95 _____
Vol.9 081293444X _____ $9.95 _____

Henry Hook's Guess the Celebrity Crosswords
0812934121 _____ $10.95 _____

Henry Hook's Film-in-the-Blanks Crosswords
0812934598 _____ $10.95 _____

Random House Guide to Cryptic Crosswords
0812935454 _____ $12.95 _____

Random House Golf Crosswords
0812933966 _____ $6.95 _____

Stanley Newman's Literary Crosswords: Something Novel
0812935047 _____ $8.95 _____

Stanley Newman's Movie Mania Crosswords
0812934687 _____ $7.95 _____

Stanley Newman's Sitcom Crosswords
0812934695 _____ $7.95 _____

Stanley Newman's Sunday Crosswords
Vol.1 0812934512 _____ $9.95 _____
Vol.2 0812935144 _____ $9.95 _____

Will Shortz's Tournament Crosswords
0812929349 _____ $13.00 _____

Will Weng's Crossword Omnibus
Vol.3 0812919351 _____ $12.95 _____

SPECIALTY PUZZLES

Games Magazine Presents Best Pencil Puzzles
Vol.2 081292553X _____ $13.95 _____

Games Magazine's Paint by Numbers
0812923847 _____ $14.00 _____

The Puzzlemaster Presents
0812963865 _____ $12.95 _____

Stanley Newman's Coffee Time Word Games
0812934539 _____ $7.95 _____

Will Shortz's Best Brain Busters
0812919521 _____ $12.95 _____

World-Class Puzzles from the World Puzzle Championships
Vol.3 0812933087 _____ $13.95 _____
Vol.4 0812935055 _____ $14.95 _____

ACROSTIC PUZZLES

Henry Hook's Crostics with a Twist
0812934393 _____ $10.95 _____

Henry Hook's Trivia Crostics
Vol.1 081293413X _____ $10.95 _____

Random House Crostics
Vol.6 0812933907 _____ $9.95 _____
Vol.7 0812933915 _____ $9.95 _____

PUZZLES FOR CHILDREN

Funtime Family Puzzles
Vol.1 0812935071 _____ $8.95 _____
Vol.2 0812935080X _____ $8.95 _____

New York Times Children's Word Games (ages 7-9)
Vol.1 0812935217 _____ $6.95 _____
Vol.2 0812935225 _____ $6.95 _____
Vol.3 0812935233 _____ $6.95 _____

New York Times Children's Word Games (ages 9 & up)
0812935241 _____ $6.95 _____

PUZZLE REFERENCE

New York Times Crossword Puzzle Dictionary
(mass market)
081293122X _____ $7.99 _____

New York Times Square One Crossword Dictionary
(hardcover)
0812930436 _____ $23.00 _____

More Random House crossword puzzle books are available through your local bookstore, or fill out this coupon and return to:

Random House, Inc., 400 Hahn Road, Westminster, MD 21157
Attention: Order Processing

☐ Enclosed is my check or money order payable to Random House

☐ Charge my credit card (circle type): AMEX Visa MasterCard

EXP DATE _____

NAME _____ SIGNATURE _____

ADDRESS _____ CITY _____ STATE _____ ZIP _____

To order, call toll-free 1-800-733-3000

POSTAGE & HANDLING		
CARRIER	**ADD**	
USPS	$5.50	
UPS	$7.50	

Total Books _____
Total Dollars $ _____
Sales Tax * $ _____
Postage & Handling $ _____
Total Enclosed $ _____

* Please calculate according to your state sales tax rate.

Prices apply to US and territories only. In Canada write: Random House of Canada, 2775 Matheson Blvd., Mississauga, Ontario L4W 4P7 (Prices subject to change)

2003

ANSWERS

1
```
ALPS SCRAM CAST
CALM QUOTA ONOR
INAUGURATIONDAY
DEN REED NADIR
    GOAD ALTO
ATRISK BLAH ANT
TAILS ARON WOO
OFFTOAGOODSTART
NFL MEAN ARISE
EYE LAND PROTEM
PORT SLOT
MARIE DOIN DUD
BEGINTHEBEGUINE
BRED TAMER MATE
CEDE ODORS PLOP
```

2
```
CLAW OTIS EDNAS
LIMA PETE GRATE
ELAN ELSE GUILE
FINGERLAKES LAM
LEES SHREWS
INTENT RESEND
FAHD TOUT LAD
STU PALMOIL OLE
MEL DONS TWIN
BRAYER GRANDS
FLEECE SOAR
REL KNUCKLEHEAD
OVINE CLAD ELSA
SENAT LATE EMIT
TRAPS AMEN LOSE
```

3
```
SNIP AMMO LEA
COATOFPAINT INS
CITYSLICKER QTS
SLO SEN ERASURE
SEDGE HOES
GOOP PASTURES
YELLOWJACKET
PRAIRIE TINTERS
CAPEHATTERAS
REVELERS RANT
AUER THATS
TRESSES AMA EVA
SOR TRAILBLAZER
OPE PLASTICWRAP
NED ERRS SEAL
```

4
```
HALT MARLO HAIL
OMOO IVIED UGLY
RABBIDAVIDSMALL
ADOANNIE SPARSE
GAIL MOON
STRONG TENUOUS
AAA HARA SITKA
SPIRITUALMEDIUM
EISEN DISC CLI
READMIT CREAKS
LIAT CAIN
MALIGN WORLDWAR
PRISONERATLARGE
AINT ERICH LAUD
ADDS RATTY LYES
```

5
```
THEM BLOBS SOCK
WAXY AIMEE ALAI
AHEM BRAGA NERD
ACAREERISAJOB
MER NOLO
SWIMSUIT NOSHOW
CODY TRIO SEINE
ORE THATHAS VEE
LEACH QUIP BEAK
DASHES SOPHISTS
ASTI RAG
GONEONTOOLONG
TROT IGETA TARA
HAZE CONIC EVAN
OBEY STASH DEFY
```

6
```
LAGS JUAN DAME
ABOU MAGMA EVEN
BYEBYEBLACKBIRD
SENSEN INHOUSE
ENOS SOOT
PART THE SLITS
ADA STARE ANAME
CHICHIRODRIGUEZ
TOSEA EDGED PAR
CANNY EAT HERA
TAOS RITE
BRINGON RIALTO
MAUMAUREBELLION
ELSE REMUS TROT
TIES TROD HALO
```

7
```
AHAB IBIS SPIKE
MAMA TUNA TATER
PHINEASTBLUSTER
SANDAL OUI TOP
STY BRA
CASTS HIRE CAM
UCLA CLARABELLE
STAN OILER ROLL
HOWDYDOODY GNAT
YRS SINS POETS
TLC SUN
MAO ISA ABODES
BUFFALOBOBSMITH
ASTIN DUNE ISTO
TESTY AMER CHEW
```

8
```
APORT LIMB FEW
RARER IDOL ONIN
CREPE ALLI USDA
HILLSTREETBLUES
ASH SHUBERT
ABLY IOC ERA
IRA CELLO SLIME
ROCKOFGIBRALTAR
SWEAR AMOUR SRI
RNS BEN TAKE
EAGLETS OER
THEMARCHOFDIMES
CENA IRON IVORY
HAIR POLL TITAN
DIX EDDY HASTE
```

9
```
ARTEMIS DELIVER
DUEDATE ORINOCO
ARTICLE WINSLOW
MARCELMARCEAU
SLAT CYAN NBC
ACDC ETAL
ESQ CHROME NERO
MAUREENMCGOVERN
IVAN TOPMAN RYE
TOSS AIDE
SRI FRAN OCHS
MARILYNMONROE
PRORATA AIRTIME
ABDOMEN STEAMER
LIONESS HELPERS
```

10
```
SLANT STOWS TAT
HONOR THROW HRS
AROSE OUIJA ERE
WINESBURGOH HAT
TETS IRONS
METTLE PLATTE
MAHRE CASUITE
DREI WAIST ILLS
TXVILLE SONIA
PINION MESHED
ROWEL RHEA
IDA LIFEONTHEMS
NIL EDIES TOQUE
TNT YEAST LOUSE
SEZ SATES EDITS
```

11
```
BMI SADA DOMO
HEAR ELAN ERODE
MARKSDOWN NINOS
ORK PANG SMEARS
ICING CHAN
CLEATS SHORTAGE
LOPES CHINK CAN
ATON TORTE SCUD
ITS ROVES SIEGE
MOTHERED FANNED
OMAR CRUET
FARRAH GRIT MET
ANEAR TRADEMARK
STACK RANG BRIO
IDES ISEE AKC
```

12
```
ABUTS MAST TREK
CAROL ASIA OOZE
TRAFALGARSQUARE
ENLIVEN ETERNAL
VETO NED
ACHE LAS WADS
BRA OTIS SPINET
BERMUDATRIANGLE
OTTERS RENT ELI
TEEN TAD FRAN
BOA FATE
MISCAST ARRAIGN
ANTARCTICCIRCLE
ROUT AONE SNEER
ENDS ROAD HOSED
```

13
```
POKES BUMP EZRA
AGILE AREA GIAN
CLEVELANDBRONZE
ELIDE SILO CON
SEXY CONCORD
PEG RIOTS DAR
ATOP CUR WORSTS
ARLO AROMA TWIT
REDIAL LOY SITE
FLU FLOWS MOP
STRUDEL DATA
IOO IMAS RADII
TINCOMMANDMENTS
ALTO ABLE PACES
REST SETA SLAMS
```

14
```
JAKE ISLES COPS
AVIV CHANT CROP
POTEMKINVILLAGE
EWE OINK LIELOW
SMEE JEFF
ZITHER BITE DOT
ASWAN WELT SABU
PAINTTHETOWNRED
PACK AIRS RATSO
ACE SPRY CIPHER
BYES TATS
APPEND OUCH FEE
PRINCEOFTHECITY
EAST CHLOE AJAR
XMAS KMART PILE
```

15
```
MOAB CAM SABER
APPLETREE OCOME
ZEITGEIST SHOAL
UNA GABORS ETNA
MERV SPOOL CAT
ARYANS PLACATE
MORSEL GAMED
ESPRITDECORPS
ALTER VOXPOP
HOUDINI ONALOG
END SANDS LORI
AGES SCOTIA SIM
DANTE ELANVITAL
OTTER NECTARINE
FESTA TSK ANAT
```

16
```
CODE ELSE PELTS
ABEL TERN ELIOT
ROBINHOOD LITER
LESSON SAINT
LIFT SCOLD
MANACLE PARERS
SALON ELLEN JOE
WILT RESIN LONE
ALA HASTE COHEN
BENTON AGROUND
DARLA REEL
DELTA COSTAS
BLAME FRIARTUCK
VALOR RUIN ANTI
DYERS OMIT REST
```

17
```
WEAK STEVE SHAG
ARON TOTAL NINE
WININAWALK ETTA
ACETATES HARPER
MEL GOTTA
HASTEN BAUM YEA
ALTOS TWIN ADAM
SORE BRAND LITE
THIS EONS PARTS
OAK TATA FRITOS
EVERS DRU
PAGODA LIONIZES
ALOT BREEZEHOME
PALE LANGE ONIT
ANDS ENDON PETS
```

18
```
GAGE SEDER OGRE
IRON AMILE FRAT
LAUD FICKLEFETA
ABDICATE ABYSS
AVER SABRE
ALGERIA MANACLE
PERSE PLUS THEM
AMI SPOILED EVE
COED AGEE ELDER
ENFORCE TEPIDLY
PETER COMA
EERIE ESOTERIC
BRIEFORALL ABBA
BITS CURIE DOLT
SCAT TEMPS EXES
```

19
```
LIONS AJAR FILE
ENVOI DOPE ODOR
SCALEDMTEVEREST
SALARIES INMATE
RAN GETA
CLEAN TOWELOFF
SOUL AUGER PIE
WORKINGFORSCALE
UKE TORTS ELMS
MESDAMES GROSS
ALIE ZOE
DOWNIN MOLLUSKS
ONASCALEOFITOIO
NYRO TEAM CALLA
OXEN EELS SHOOK
```

20
```
DECIMAL ETC SHE
IRONAGE TWO TEX
MADAMEX TIN RAP
MAN HANGFIVE
DAZE TAO BOOKER
OPART RUDE RENT
GENIE CREDIT
EXECS ALF SYNCH
ATONAL OMAHA
OLEO BASE FITIN
BARNES TAB NECK
STHELENS LOU
EVA FRY RAGTIME
SIR IVE AILERON
SAD NET DRESSED
```

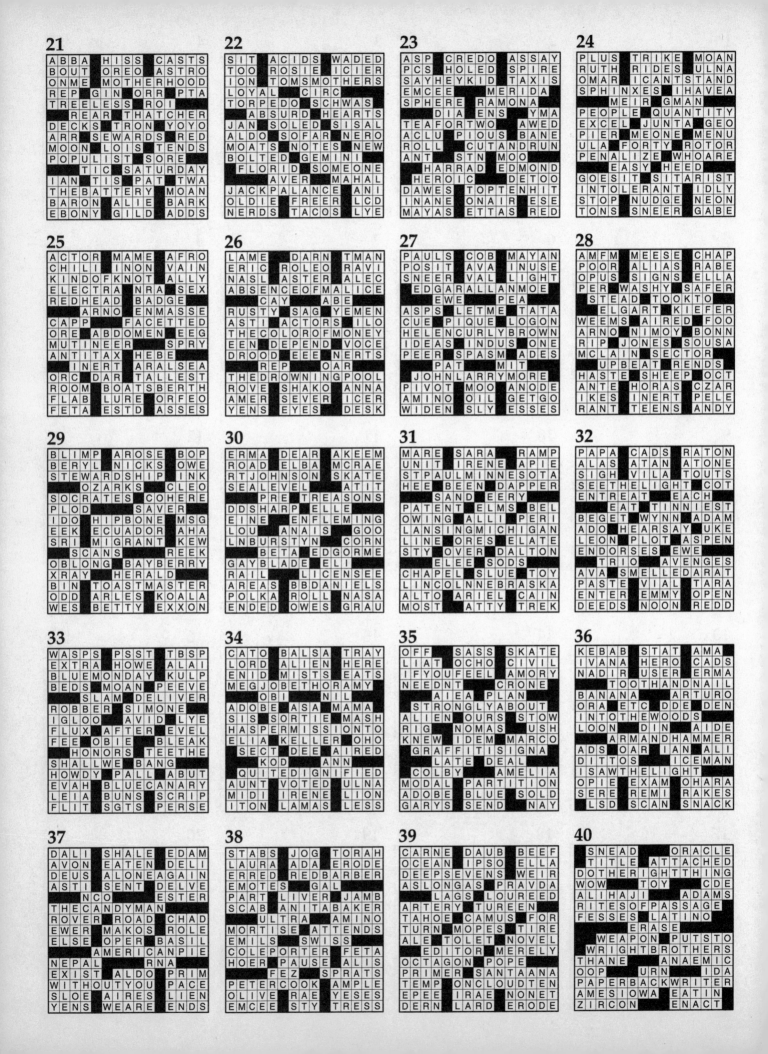

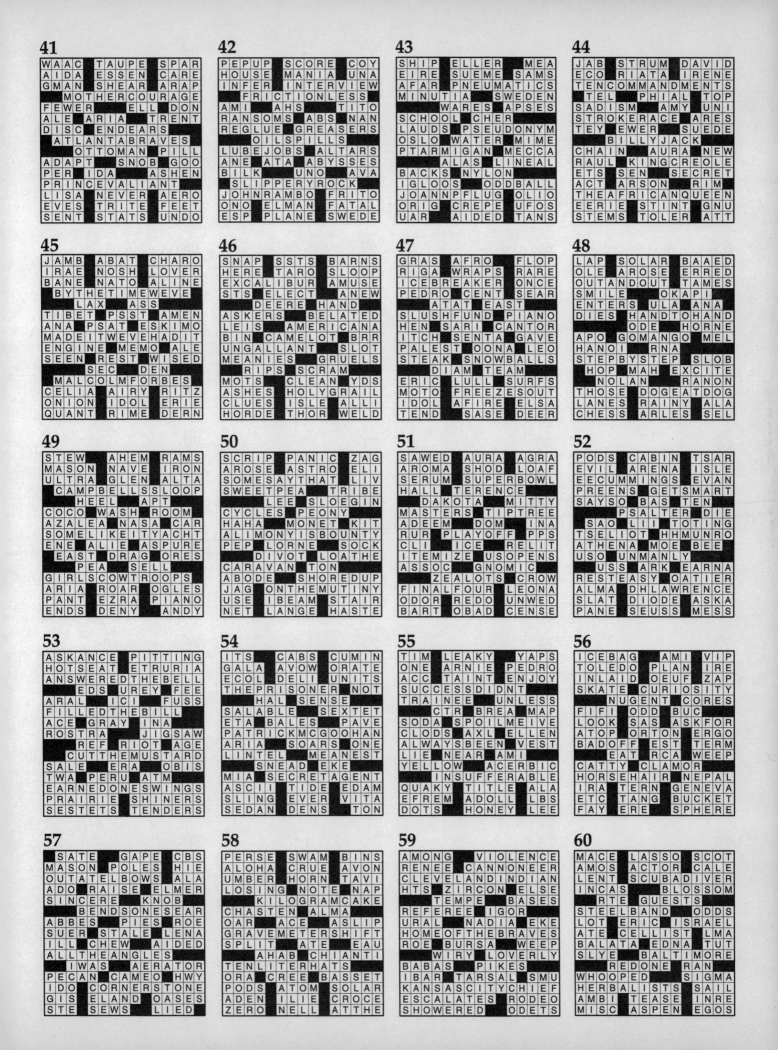

41

```
WAAC  TAUPE  SPAR
AIDA  ESSEN  CARE
GMAN  SHEAR  ARAP
  MOTHERCOURAGE
FEWER   ELL   DON
ALE  ARIA  TRENT
DISC  ENDEARS
  ATLANTABRAVES
  OTTOMAN  PILL
ADAPT   SNOB   GOO
PER   IDA   ASHEN
  PRINCEVALIANT
LISA  NEVER  AERO
EVES  TRITE  FEET
SENT  STATS  UNDO
```

42

```
PEPUP  SCORE   COY
HOUSE  MANIA   UNA
INFER  INTERVIEW
  FRICTIONLESS
AMI   AHS   TITO
RANSOMS  ABS  NAN
REGLUE  GREASERS
  OILSPILLS
LUBEJOBS  ALTARS
ANE  ATA  ABYSSES
BILK   UNO   AVA
  SLIPPERYROCK
JOHNRAMBO  FRITO
ONO  ELMAN  FATAL
ESP  PLANE  SWEDE
```

43

```
SHIP  ELLER   MEA
EIRE  SUEME  SAMS
AFAR  PNEUMATICS
MINUTIA   SWEDEN
  WARES  APSES
SCHOOL   CHER
LAUDS  PSEUDONYM
OSLO  WATER  MIME
PTARMIGAN  MECCA
  ALAS  LINEAL
BACKS  NYLON
IGLOOS   ODDBALL
JOANNPFLUG  OLIO
ORIG  CREPE  UFOS
UAR   AIDED  TANS
```

44

```
JAB  STRUM  DAVID
ECO  RIATA  IRENE
TENCOMMANDMENTS
TEL   PHIAL   TOP
SADISM   AMY   UNI
STROKERACE  ARES
TEY   EWER  SUEDE
  BILLYJACK
CHAIN   AURA   NEW
RAUL  KINGCREOLE
ETS   SEN   SECRET
ACT   ARSON   RIM
THEAFRICANQUEEN
EERIE  STINT  GNU
STEMS  TOLER  ATT
```

45

```
JAMB  ABAT  CHARO
IRAE  NOSH  LOVER
BANE  NATO  ALINE
  BYTHETIMEWEVE
LAX   ASS
TIBET   PSST  AMEN
ANA  PSAT  ESKIMO
MADEITWEVEHADIT
ENGINE  MEMO  ALE
SEEN  REST  WISED
  SEC   DEN
  MALCOLMFORBES
CELIA  AIRY  RITZ
ONION  IDOL  ERIE
QUANT  RIME  DERN
```

46

```
SNAP  SSTS  BARNS
HERE  TARO  SLOOP
EXCALIBUR  AMUSE
STS  ELECT   ANEW
  DEERE  HAND
ASKERS  BELATED
LEIS  AMERICANA
BIN  CAMELOT  BRR
UNGALLANT  SLOT
MEANIES  GRUELS
  RIPS  SCRAM
MOTS  CLEAN  YDS
ASHES  HOLYGRAIL
CLUES  ISLE  ALLI
HORDE  THOR  WELD
```

47

```
GRAS  AFRO  FLOP
RIGA  WRAPS  RARE
ICEBREAKER  ONCE
PEDRO  CENT  SEAR
  ATAT  EAST
SLUSHFUND  PIANO
HEN  SARI  CANTOR
ITCH  SENTA  GAVE
PALEST  OONA  LEO
STEAK  SNOWBALLS
  DIAM  TEAM
ERIC  LULL  SURFS
MOTO  FREEZESOUT
IDOL  AFIRE  ELSA
TEND  SASE  DEER
```

48

```
LAP  SOLAR  BAAED
OLE  AROSE  ERRED
OUTANDOUT  TAMES
SMILE   OKAPI
ENTERS  ULA  ANA
DIES  HANDTOHAND
  ODE   HORNE
APO  GOMANGO  MEL
HANOI   RNA
STEPBYSTEP  SLOB
HOP  MAH  EXCITE
  NOLAN  RANON
THOSE  DOGEATDOG
LANES  RAINY  ALA
CHESS  ARLES  SEL
```

49

```
STEW  AHEM  RAMS
MASON  NAVE  IRON
ULTRA  GLEN  ALTA
CAMPBELLSSLOOP
  HEEL   APT
COCO  WASH  ROOM
AZALEA  NASA  CAR
SOMELIKEITYACHT
ENE  ALIE  ASPURE
EAST  DRAG  ORES
  PEA   SELL
GIRLSCOWTROOPS
ARIA  ROAR  OGLES
PANT  EZRA  PIANO
ENDS  DENY  ANDY
```

50

```
SCRIP  PANIC  ZAG
AROSE  ASTRO  ELI
SOMESAYTHAT  LIV
SWEETPEA  TRIBE
  LEE  SLOEGIN
CYCLES   PEONY
HAHA  MONET  KIT
ALIMONYISBOUNTY
PEP  LORNE  SOCK
  DIVOT  LOATHE
CARAVAN   TON
ABODE  SHOREDUP
JAG  ONTHEMUTINY
USE  IBEAM  STAIR
NET  LANGE  HASTE
```

51

```
SAWED  AURA  AGRA
AROMA  SHOD  LOAF
SERUM  SUPERBOWL
HALL  TERENCE
  DAKOTA  MITTY
MASTERS  TIPTREE
ADEEM  DOM  INA
RUR  PLAYOFF  PPS
CLI  ICE  RELIT
ITEMIZE  USOPENS
ASSOC  GNOMIC
  ZEALOTS  CROW
FINALFOUR  LEONA
ODOR  REDO  UNWED
BART  OBAD  CENSE
```

52

```
PODS  CABIN  TSAR
EVIL  ARENA  ISLE
EECUMMINGS  EVAN
PREENS  GETSMART
SAYSO  BAS   TEN
  PSALTER  DIE
SAO  LII  TOTING
TSELIOT  HHMUNRO
ATHENA  MOE  BEE
USO  UNMANLY
USS  ARK  EARNA
RESTEASY  OATIER
ALMA  DHLAWRENCE
SLAT  DIODE  ASKA
PANE  SEUSS  MESS
```

53

```
ASKANCE  PITTING
HOTSEAT  ETRURIA
ANSWEREDTHEBELL
EDS  UREY   FEE
ARAL  ICI  FUSS
FILLEDTHEBILL
ACE  GRAY   INA
ROSTRA   JIGSAW
REF  RIOT  AGE
  CUTTHEMUSTARD
SALE  ERA  OBIS
TWA  PERU  ATM
EARNEDONESWINGS
PRAIRIE  SHINERS
SESTETS  TENDERS
```

54

```
ITS  CABS  CUMIN
GALA  AVOW  ORATE
ECOL  DELI  UNITS
THEPRISONER  NOT
  HAL  SENSE
SALABLE  SEXTET
ETA  BALES  PAVE
PATRICKMCGOOHAN
ARIA  SOARS  ONE
LINTEL  MEANEST
  SNEAD  EKE
MIA  SECRETAGENT
ASCII  TIDE  EDAM
SLING  EVER  VITA
SEDAN  DENS  TON
```

55

```
TIM  LEAKY  YAPS
ONE  ARNIE  PEDRO
ACC  TAINT  ENJOY
SUCCESSDIDNT
TRAINEE  UNLESS
  CTR  BREA  MAP
SODA  SPOILMEIVE
CLODS  AXL  ELLEN
ALWAYSBEEN  VEST
LIE  NEAR  AMI
YELLOW  ACERBIC
  INSUFFERABLE
QUAKY  TITLE  ALA
EFREM  ADOLL  LBS
DOTS  HONEY  LEE
```

56

```
ICEBAG  AMI  VIP
TOLEDO  PLAN  IRE
INLAID  OEUF  ZAP
SKATE  CURIOSITY
NUGENT   CORES
FIFI  ODD  BUC
LOOK  SAS  ASKFOR
ATOP  ORTON  ERGO
BADOFF  EST  TERM
  EAT  RCA  WEEP
CATTY   CLAMOR
HORSEHAIR  NEPAL
IRA  TERN  GENEVA
ETC  TANG  BUCKET
FAY  ERE  SPHERE
```

57

```
  SATE  GAPE  CBS
MASON  POLES  HIE
OUTATELBOWS  ALA
ADO  RAISE  ELMER
SINCERE   KNOB
  BENDSONESEAR
ABBES  PIES  ROE
SUER  STALE  LENA
ILL  CHEW  AIDED
  ALLTHEANGLES
IWAS   AERATOR
PECAN  CAMEO  HWY
IDO  CORNERSTONE
GIS  ELAND  OASES
STE  SEWS  LIED
```

58

```
PERSE  SWAM  BINS
ALOHA  CRUE  AVON
UMBER  HORN  TAVI
LOSING  NOTE  NAP
KILOGRAMCAKE
CHASTEN  ALMA
OAR  ACE  ASLIP
GRAVEMETERSHIFT
SPLIT  ATE  EAU
  AHAB  CHIANTI
TENLITERHATS
ORA  CREE  BASSET
PODS  ATOM  SOLAR
ADEN  ILIE  CROCE
ZERO  NELL  ATTHE
```

59

```
AMONG  VIOLENCE
RENEE  CANNONEER
CLEVELANDINDIAN
HTS  ZIRCON  ELSE
  TEMPE  BASES
REFEREE   IGOR
URAL  NADIA  EKE
HOMEOFTHEBRAVES
ROE  BURSA  WEEP
WIRY  LOVERLY
BABAS   PIKES
IBAR  TARSAL  SMU
KANSASCITYCHIEF
ESCALATES  RODEO
SHOWERED  ODETS
```

60

```
MACE  LASSO  SCOT
AMOS  ACTOR  CALE
LENT  SCUBADIVER
INCAS   BLOSSOM
RTE  GUESTS
STEELBAND  ODDS
LOT  ERIC  ISRAEL
ATE  CELLIST  LMA
BALATA  EDNA  TUT
SLYE  BALTIMORE
  REDONE  RAN
WHOOPED   SIGMA
HERBALISTS  SAIL
AMBI  TEASE  INRE
MISC  ASPEN  EGOS
```

61

```
ASSUME GAGA  LIV
REPLAY URIS  ACE
CLAUDERAINS  RIN
EMIL  SAVE   GEO
DANAS GALESTORM
      TOW    TEA
GONEWITHTHEWIND
EUR  SHEAN   NED
MIAMIHURRICANES
     PSI     COP
LIGHTNING  GRAPH
ERA  NOON   ILEO
GAP  THUNDERCLAP
ATE  NERO  OTOOLE
LED  TEES  NETTED
```

62

```
ACTS    KIM  CAGE
LAIT    EINE ONYX
SENSE   STUN RAPT
SPOKESPERSON
WHEELERDEALERS
        TERI ALIAS
AHA  RITE  AFLAME
MOD  ASLIP   NOW
PRIMAL ONEA  TAN
SEEIT   ARBS
BUSINESSCYCLES
PEDALPUSHERS
PEAL  ATOI MENAT
JAVA  LIEN  AMIS
SUEY  ENS   LANE
```

63

```
AMS  SILAS  FACES
LAP  ATIME  OMEGA
AGE  MAKEAFOOLOF
MING LENTIL  TSE
OCTOPI  DOAS
     PLATE TRADER
RAE  ANODE  UNITE
ARROYOS  MISDEAL
SNERT SMITH  SLY
HEIGHT  ITSIN
      EARL ANIMAL
MAE FRIEND  LAZE
ALLFOOLSDAY  MUD
POLLO ETATS  ARG
STEAL YOKEL  SEE
```

64

```
SHEM ABORT  SKAT
PUPA LONER  LUNE
ELIS ARENA  IRON
WASHINGTONADAMS
OILS WISP   LIE
MODEL FOR  ESTER
FRI   NOT    PAT
ABCDEFGHIJKLMNO
AXL   RMS    AND
HASNT PEP  FINED
IRA   RISE  EDGE
JANUARYFEBRUARY
ABIT ICONS  ATIE
CITE SHUTE  NEON
KAYS HERON  ARTS
```

65

```
ATLAS   JAB  LAMA
SWIPE   BOIL IGOR
POKER   ANDA VAIN
EXPERIENCEISA
ABA EDS   CHINTZ
GORING  ASHEN
GOODTEACHER  FOP
INCA  LAA   LARA
EEK BUTSHESENDS
CANOE   RIOTED
MOGULS  AER  ARE
ENORMOUSBILLS
LEAF  URAL OUTDO
DUPE  NILE ILIAD
SPEW  DST  NACRE
```

66

```
DESKS   LED  ATOP
ELLIS  FIREALARM
SAINTLOUISBLUES
PIP  SON    CIAO
ONUS PDQ   SUSAN
TEPEE  UNSETTLE
ELATION    YOW
AFRICANVIOLET
AFL   ESCAPEE
CREVASSE   RAMPS
TOWEL  SEC  PALE
NINA   TAB   KEN
RHODEISLANDREDS
PERENNIAL  RIDGE
MEAD   END  MOOED
```

67

```
BLAS  BASRA  ADES
RIPE  AREAS  MAGI
ISAACSTERN  AVON
MARSHA  SEEDLING
      HELD  RAID
MAJOR ESS  DEBUG
USER APIECE  ONA
RISE POLAR  SWIT
ADS DESTRY  TITO
LEERY EYE  GREER
     HAEC  DARE
ANECDOTE  RIALTO
FALK HOWARDKEEL
ATME ARENA  ETRE
REST NERDY  DANG
```

68

```
SELF CREW  SCOTT
ETUI ZITI  HAZER
ACRE AVON  EBONY
THESTRANGER  NOS
     TAIL ALPERT
HEART  METOO
TUX  ZEAL  CLARA
WEIRDALYANKOVIC
OSTEO LONI   ODE
EGGAR  CLAWS
CUCKOO  SKIP
AVA ODDSANDENDS
TUNED IOTA  MORE
CLIVE SLIM  ANEW
HATER CONE  NODS
```

69

```
SCOLD  RAFT  BUS
TAPER  ELIA  ENT
DEREKJACOBI  AIR
ANON  DANE  NATE
TOBEHOOPER  CREW
DOA    SPAT
PEA RHONE  RAHAL
URN RUBYDEE  UTE
BANJO SCARF  REX
BARN   LAS
LADY  EUBIEBLAKE
IDAS  ENOS  AMEN
NEV EDWARDALBEE
ELI  VEER  ATOLL
DES  ADDS  DAMES
```

70

```
RAJAH  FAZE  DEJA
ONICE  EXAM  ONES
NEVERKEEPUPWITH
AWE  RIBS  ANGLE
PILL  WISEMAN
THEJONESESDRAG
WURST   TREES
ODE  SPREE   FAT
TIARA   MELBA
THEMDOWNTOYOUR
CHEEPED   IONE
ORATE  TASK  OFF
LEVELITSCHEAPER
OWER  THAI ELATE
RADS  TURN SPLAT
```

71

```
GASH  SEGAL  FESS
IDLE  HAITI  LEAP
BEERBARRELPOLKA
ENDEARED   LOSER
       RED  THAR
SIPPED SOON  ARM
CORE  STORE  BAA
ANYPORTINASTORM
RIO  FEELS  IDEA
FAR  FEAT COMERS
       PILL  LOA
ASSES  LASTSTEP
CATCHERINTHERYE
ARIA RAVEL  LEER
BARN REEDY  LEST
```

72

```
GRAS  RAPS  RACES
LENO  ALAI  CRYME
ACEY  POND  ATRIA
SAABSISTER  FELT
SPREADS   BOSUN
ABS      MILANO
PAYNE GOFER   UAR
ONUS  LINES  SLOE
ENG  PYLON  PATHS
TOOTER     PIN
BORIC   PREFACE
CALF CAMEOROLLS
LEAFY BOLT   RIIS
ARCED OREO   DANE
POKES TEEN   SSTS
```

73

```
ACHE  SMEAR  ABEL
BLUR  HEADY  NERO
BUSINESSSECTION
REHEARSE  BLONDE
PRY    GRANGER
POPFLY   KEEN
AGREE TINA   SKEW
CROSSWORDSWITH
KEPT  WISE  PATTI
BASK    MAKEUP
RADIANT    SOW
ADONIS  STUNTMAN
FORGOODNESSSAKE
TRIO NOONE   AMIS
SECT GABOR   RANT
```

74

```
ASAP  MEETS  PAST
LOGE  ALLAH  INKY
BLUEONBLUE   SNIP
SOANDSOS   DOCILE
DEW      PEELS
AVAIL    ASHES
BOBBYVINTON  MAR
CLEM  INNER  GABE
STD ROSESARERED
PHLOX   HEXED
IDAHO    BRO
REPAST  PRANCERS
ALPS  BLUEVELVET
TALE  SERVE  EELY
EYED  POLED  ONYX
```

75

```
AFRAME  CLEO   IQS
DRIVEN  ROTC  MUM
SOMESTRETCH  BOA
MARES    SHIRR
DADA EASES  ABUT
EXERTED  ALCHEMY
SEPIA   UTAH
PANTSHAVENO
GULF    RIGBY
JAWBONE  EPIGRAM
ARIA ADOVE  HERA
CREDO   BEAST
KIN OTHERCHOICE
EVE  ZEUS  HOWLER
DER  EDGE  YELLER
```

76

```
MASK  USURY  AJAR
EREI  MAFIA  GALA
DONNYBROOK  ACTS
IMAGER STEP   KOP
CATSPAW   STROP
SSE  GAB  YOHOHO
SCENES   ASTIR
AMATI  EAT  MASTS
MELON   DRESSY
ALFRED  SAP   EDS
REMAP   DRIBLET
EWE  AURA ARRIVE
NOSE BOBBYSOXER
DOCS EMCEE   MIRE
SLOT DOSED   OREO
```

77

```
WADE  SASS  HORSY
EDEN  ACHE  ALOHA
AMAN  AMEX  NEWEL
VITUSBERING   SSE
ETHIC   BEAUT
ROBERTPEARY
ROD OBIT    AVOW
ALADDIN  HAWKISH
MEMO   PUMA   SEA
PONCEDELEON
SCENA   EARED
MEN LIVINGSTONE
AROMA INAN   ODDS
SINAI ELBA   MEEK
SNEER SYST   SODS
```

78

```
LAPS  BRIDE  ATNO
ALOE  RELET  VIOL
NOTCRICKET   ACTI
COTTEN   PIGSKIN
EFS  AIM   NITE
FLEABAGS    DEB
HOWE  RILL  TOORA
ORALS  SUB  SOFIA
CESTA ISEE  PFCS
KOP   BEEHIVES
IRON  TIL   IDA
PESETAS  CLONES
ACHE MBUTTERFLY
SOLD ELSIE   COLE
SLYS LINED   ARAT
```

79

```
CROP  SERGE  NANA
AONE  PRIED  EBAN
PUMPKINPOI  NEST
ETE  ALIE  TEETHE
KYLE    SINN
SEPIAS  QUOVADIS
CRANK RUIN   NEMO
ARUG  QUITS  ETAL
ROLL  USES  STAGE
FLAUTIST  JETTED
ADZE   CUTE
SCHUSS GRIT   AMP
HOAX HULACOPTER
AVIV OZONE   JOMO
DELI WIPER   SNOW
```

80

```
DIPS  YECCH  MICE
INLA  EVERY  ONYX
SCAN  AIDED  CHAP
TICKERTAPE  KANE
USE  GLARE  RUBIN
ROBROY    RAPIDS
BROOM STRAW   TEE
TACKINESS
PJS  NAILS  CROPS
RANCID    BOOBOO
OMAHA BLUER   VIM
GAPE TOETHELINE
RIPE IRATE   OATH
ACES RAVES   OTTO
MARY EXERT   MEOW
```

81
```
MONA  SARAH  BAWL
ORAL  ERODE  ASIA
SEVENDEADLYSINS
TOY  EGAD  POISES
     AGES  BMWS
PAMPAS  DEAL  BBC
ABORT  COAT  PLEA
THREEMUSKETEERS
TONS  ARES  ASSET
YRS  KRIS  KNOTTS
     FAKE  LIDS
ASSAYS  VINE  IQS
TENCOMMANDMENTS
MEAT  EASEL  SKIT
ERGS  NEEDY  TSPS
```

82
```
ESSES  SELF  GEMS
LUCRE  IDEO  ALIT
BERET  NEAR  MILA
ATE  THUNDERBOLT
   WALES  MILTIE
ROBBER  THANE
OPAL  DARING  BOW
OILER  VAN  SARGE
MEL  EJECTS  DALE
AVERT  AMAZED
STATUE  SWAMI
WASHERWOMAN  LSU
ASWE  ERLE  TINAS
STAN  RIGA  LOUSE
HENS  STAR  ENTER
```

83
```
FIN  ALUM  STAIRS
ONO  RONA  TIPTOE
RHO  INST  ALTAIR
MADMAGAZINE
ELLA  LOS  SHAG
DEEPEST  MISTAKE
   GWEN  REEDIT
ALFREDENEUMAN
ADORED  TONS
MANATEE  VESSELS
OMIT  TSE  ARAT
WHATMEWORRY
REDSEA  ABLE  ASL
ATONER  FESS  TEE
DECODE  FRET  AND
```

84
```
WILDS  CHAT  ERMA
ADIEU  HYPE  COUP
ROMANNUMERALONE
PLAN  INN  INAFIX
SANK  IGET
STELLA  GNAW  PRO
AWAIT  BAER  BLOW
PERSONALPRONOUN
PELT  ABET  MATTE
YDS  YVES  KAISER
TOYS  BARB
ADVERB  SET  RISE
GREEKLETTERIOTA
EARN  USES  ATWAR
SWAY  ESPY  THARP
```

85
```
DEADAS  MALE
ELBOWMACARONI
ARTICHOKEHEART
SMOG  ITALO  OAR
PAN  ALE  GRILLE
EYE  CAITLIN
SOME  FRONTSEAT
DAVE  CRONY  TENS
OVERLOADS  AHSO
BARGAIN  ESE
INTERN  ACH  TEA
ENO  SUTRA  BOAT
ANGELHAIRPASTA
HEADOFLETTUCE
SPAT  SEAMAN
```

86
```
EBRO  ALDA  REAP
SNEER  SEAS  ANYA
ITSYBITSYSPIDER
DOES  SISSIES
EMT  FAN  GLANCE
ABSORB  TUNE  OAR
TEEDUP  ANKA
LITTLEBOYBLUE
DINO  PANELS
OFF  UMPS  LOOKER
GEORGE  TLC  ONO
ALLEGRO  SOTS
WEEWILLIEWINKIE
OVAL  OLGA  LAIRS
WETS  WAIT  EPEE
```

87
```
PELT  MAIL  SWAT
ONOR  RANDY  IAGO
AONE  ASTER  STOP
CLEARTHEAIR  EGO
HARDER  SCOUR
LOANS  SANDER
FIFE  COAT  MOOLA
ARI  GERBILS  GET
LORNE  AIDE  ASEA
KNEELS  NEGEV
BOILS  IRIDIC
CAR  DOWNTOEARTH
ALAS  PAEAN  TAME
RANT  PLOPS  OMAR
ANDY  YENS  RAYE
```

88
```
ESTA  ABACI  SLAW
LOOT  RIPEN  TARO
BARRYMGOLDWATER
ARNIE  DPL  ATEAM
ALTI  ABLE
MER  LITERAL  CAR
ALAN  PCT  LOCALE
HUBERTHHUMPHREY
ADAGIO  ANI  AONE
LET  LEANDER  MES
KIDD  ERIC
ARDEN  EAR  COSTA
GEORGESMCGOVERN
APER  STOUT  EXIT
RORY  PESTO  TYPE
```

89
```
FACTS  PROP  GAME
AGENT  LOPE  OVAL
CASTE  ATEARFELL
EVA  TRYON  EERIE
TERESABREWER
LONI  REV  MAP
ABSENTLY  DERIDE
LOON  LIL  ODDS
UNFAIR  POPULIST
MET  RUS  NONE
LETMEGOLOVER
BRYAN  ULTRA  ENE
YOUSENDME  CARTE
RULE  AGER  ENDED
DEER  PERM  DAIRY
```

90
```
ADDICT  BUGABOO
LAUGHS  ICECOLD
APPLEPIALAMODE
SPOOF  CLARET
KENO  ROY  NFL
ART  HEN  TAGSALE
DID  SOCRATES
TOUGHRHOTOHOE
LOOPHOLE  OWL
ASPECTS  CNN  BOP
MSS  CHE  MATE
RETIRE  SENOR
WHATSNUWITHYOU
POSTAGE  TOTALS
APPAREL  SWANEE
```

91
```
ANTE  STOOD  CHAD
COOT  ORIBI  RIGA
HIGHTAILIT  ITEM
ERASURES  TASTES
NED  LYMPH
CAMBER  BEBE  EDS
AWARD  CUTANDRUN
BAKE  SHRUG  ROLE
BREAKCAMP  PEACE
YET  OONA  MADDER
REBUT  SAO
STARER  STILETTO
COCO  GETAMOVEON
ARKS  ELATE  ELSE
BASE  SIRED  NESS
```

92
```
EBBS  BOARD  DDAY
RENE  ALLEY  ERIE
GEAR  NIECE  TURN
FIELDOFDREAMS
NOS  SCI
CAGER  PER  UNBAR
OCR  NAILED  ERGO
THEBADNEWSBEARS
TEAR  DENOTE  SEE
ASTOP  DAN  LOSES
WIL  SLR
CASEYATTHEBAT
MAGI  ROMEO  IRIS
OPEN  INANE  TUNA
BERG  CENTS  STEW
```

93
```
HAD  PAT  GEL  PAW
USO  ELUSIVE  ORI
HAWAIIFIVEO  MRT
CNN  TEEN  SPIN
FLEECES  SLEEVE
EARWAX  GOALIES
EMS  TERRA  WEISS
JACOBRIIS
CANAL  TINTS  DAS
ARAMAIC  ENMESH
LAZING  OROURKE
ILIE  USSR  NBA
PSI  WATERSKIING
HES  ANYTIME  ECO
SAM  SAX  NUN  SEA
```

94
```
FANG  PELE  LARGO
AROW  ETON  ONION
DALY  ATOZ  RETRO
STONECANYONWAY
NAH  MEA
ASSET  LIEU  ASHE
CPA  SEEM  VALLEY
MOCKINGBIRDLANE
ERRAND  USED  BIO
STET  RHEA  IBSEN
QUE  ACE
CHAUNCEYSTREET
OUIJA  ALES  TAXI
ARLES  TINA  IRED
SLOTH  EASY  ELSE
```

95
```
SHIRK  ESSAY  JAM
EERIE  AWARE  AWE
ARACETRACKS  PAT
MONOPOLY  STAKE
CRY  THINNER
BATBOY  SHORT
YAHOO  SWAP  LOU
THEPLACEWINDOWS
ESE  CADS  EAGLE
AFIRE  CARESS
OLDLADY  MRT
CLIFT  MOONBEAM
CAP  CLEANPEOPLE
UMP  AISLE  SUEDE
RAY  TVSET  STEAK
```

96
```
ACHE  SPA  CELT
NOOK  SPENT  ADAM
NINE  CRANE  NAVE
OLE  THECANDYMAN
YAHWEH  DUO
DAHLIA  REFUSAL
ATOMS  SMURF  USO
TONS  DAMNS  AGIN
ENE  WINES  BLADE
REYNARD  POORER
ERN  PLUSES
SWEETDREAMS  UAR
LARD  LETUP  OGRE
AKIN  SEARS  FAIL
MEET  FLA  FRAY
```

97
```
TWIG  PLEAD  EGGS
ORCA  LEASE  JILT
SAKSFIFTHAVENUE
SPY  RATS  DECAMP
PONY  CHET
ABJECT  BAER  JOB
CREAK  OLGA  GOBI
HILLSTREETBLUES
EELS  OBEY  LASSO
DRY  SNIP  LISTEN
MEET  BETS
AGEOLD  MOTH  CHI
MIDDLEOFTHEROAD
OBIE  ALOHA  DAZE
SEEM  FERAL  AXES
```

98
```
DDTS  DAB  NAPE
MORITA  EMU  EGAN
APEMAN  GEN  LEND
NEWENGLAND  LESS
ESS  CUES  LAY
VELA  HEPBURN
BETA  ATTA  TEPEE
LAWN  RHINE  LTDS
OVINE  ECOL  LOOT
BENATAR  VICE
WES  METE  STA
MATH  HARRINGTON
EREI  ALB  STOPIT
NEXT  ROI  METALS
DATE  PEG  ROTS
```

99
```
DEBORAH  SAG  ITS
ELEVATE  PRAIRIE
MATEHANDAIDNAME
OMAR  NOR  GLESS
DEBAR  CEO
NATURESIGHTWIND
OTHERS  SHA  NEE
MOO  SIP  IRK  NIL
ANN  DAR  GISELE
DEGREERATEWORLD
AMS  TURIN
ABATE  VIN  ASST
DIMENSIONESTATE
DOORDIE  ENRAGED
SSS  SSW  LEASERS
```

100
```
SWAG  MEDAL  TABS
OHIO  UTILE  ALLI
DIDYOUHEARABOUT
REALM  MINGLERS
DUG  ERE
THEMURDERATTHE
KOALA  OWNS  HOW
ORRIN  WAD  ADELE
PIE  CURE  TOILS
SODAPOPFACTORY
LOU  ROE
ASSIGNEE  UNZIP
THEBOTTLERDIDIT
VENI  ERECT  NONO
SATS  DEMOS  CLAW
```

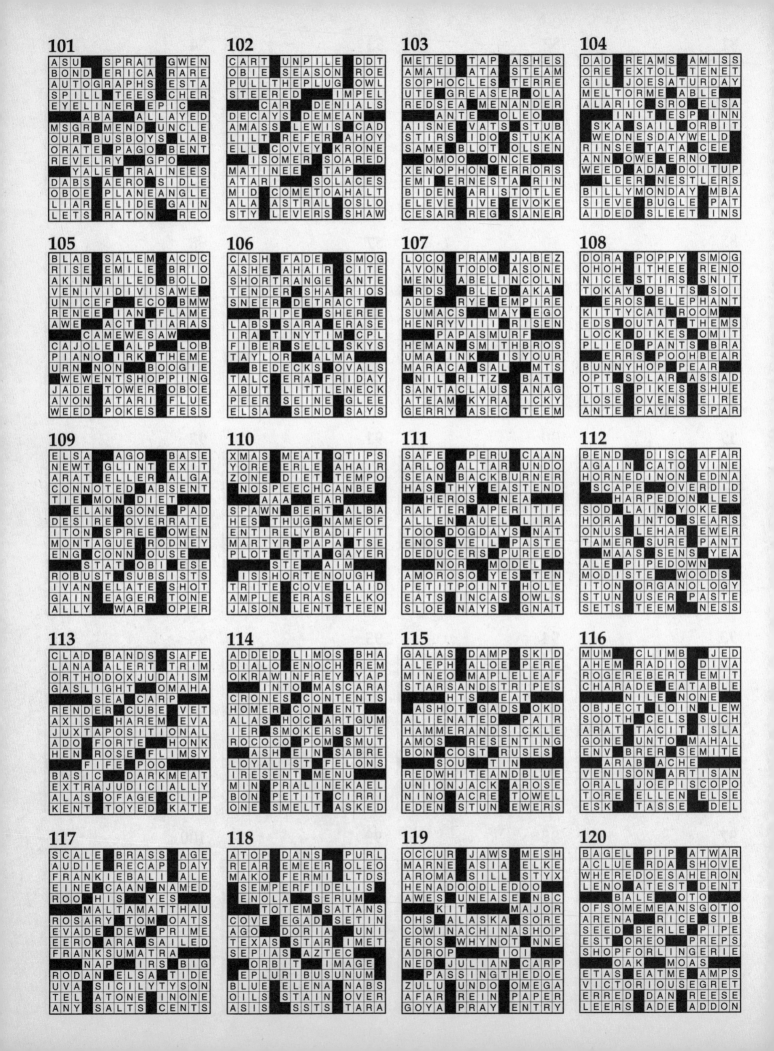

101
```
ASU . SPRAT . GWEN
BOND . ERICA . RARE
AUTOGRAPHS . ESTA
SPILL . TEES . CHER
EYELINER . EPIC . .
ABA . ALLAYED . .
MSGR . MEND . UNCLE
OUR . BUSBOYS . LAB
ORATE . PAGO . BENT
REVELRY . GPO . .
. YALE . TRAINEES
DABS . AERO . SIDLE
OBOE . PLANEANGLE
LIAR . ELIDE . GAIN
LETS . RATON . REO
```

102
```
CART . UNPILE . DDT
OBIE . SEASON . ROE
PULLTHEPLUG . OWL
STEERED . IMPEL
CAR . DENIALS
DECAYS . DEMEAN
AMASS . LEWIS . CAD
LILT . REFER . AHOY
ELL . COVEY . KRONE
ISOMER . SOARED
MATINEE . TAP
ATARI . SOLACES
MID . COMETOAHALT
ALA . ASTRAL . OSLO
STY . LEVERS . SHAW
```

103
```
METED . TAP . ASHES
AMATI . ATA . STEAM
SOPHOCLES . TERRE
UTE . GREASER . OLA
REDSEA . MENANDER
ANTE . OLEO
AISNE . VATS . STUB
STIRS . IDO . STUKA
SAME . BLOT . OLSEN
OMOO . ONCE
XENOPHON . ERRORS
EMI . ERNESTA . RIN
BIDEN . ARISTOTLE
ELEVEN . IVE . EVOKE
CESAR . REG . SANER
```

104
```
DAD . REAMS . AMISS
ORE . EXTOL . TENET
GIL . JOESATURDAY
MELTORME . ABLE
ALARIC . SRO . ELSA
INIT . ESP . INN
SKA . SAIL . ORBIT
WEDNESDAYWELD
RINSE . TATA . CEE
ANN . OWE . ERNO
WEED . ADA . DOITUP
LEER . NESTLERS
BILLYMONDAY . MBA
SIEVE . BUGLE . PAT
AIDED . SLEET . INS
```

105
```
BLAB . SALEM . ACDC
RISE . EMILE . BRIO
AKIN . RILED . BOLD
VENIVIDIVISAWE
UNICEF . ECO . BMW
RENEE . IAN . FLAME
AWE . ACT . TIARAS
CAMEWESAW
CAJOLE . ALP . LOB
PIANO . IRK . THEME
URN . NON . BOOGIE
WEWENTSHOPPING
JADE . TOWER . OBOE
AVON . ATARI . FLUE
WEED . POKES . FESS
```

106
```
CASH . FADE . SMOG
ASHE . AHAIR . CITE
SHORTRANGE . ANTE
TENDER . SHA . RIOS
SNEER . DETRACT
RIPE . SHEREE
LABS . SARA . ERASE
IRA . TINYTIM . CPL
FIBER . SELL . SKYS
TAYLOR . ALMA
BEDECKS . OVALS
TALC . ERA . FRIDAY
ABUT . LITTLENECK
PEER . SEINE . GLEE
ELSA . SEND . SAYS
```

107
```
LOCO . PRAM . JABEZ
AVON . TODO . ASONE
MENU . ABELINCOLN
RDS . BLED . AKA
ADE . RYE . EMPIRE
SUMACS . MAY . EGO
HENRYVIII . RISEN
PAPASMURF
HEMAN . SMITHBROS
UMA . INK . ISYOUR
MARACA . SAL . MTS
NIL . RITZ . BAT
SANTACLAUS . ANAG
ATEAM . KYRA . ICKY
GERRY . ASEC . TEEM
```

108
```
DORA . POPPY . SMOG
OHOH . ITHEE . RENO
NICE . STIRS . SNIT
TOKAY . OBITS . SOI
EROS . ELEPHANT
KITTYCAT . ROOM
EDS . OUTAT . THEMS
LOCK . DIKES . OMIT
PLIED . PANTS . BRA
ERRS . POOHBEAR
BUNNYHOP . PEAR
OPT . SOLAR . ASSAD
OTIS . PIKES . SHUE
LOSE . OVENS . EIRE
ANTE . FAYES . SPAR
```

109
```
ELSA . AGO . BASE
NEWT . GLINT . EXIT
ARAT . ELLER . ALGA
CONNOTED . ABSENT
TIE . MON . DIET
ELAN . GONE . PAD
DESIRE . OVERRATE
ITON . SPREE . OWEN
MONTAGUE . RODNEY
ENG . CONN . OUSE
STAT . OBI . ESE
ROBUST . SUBSISTS
IVAN . ELATE . SHOT
GAIN . EAGER . TONE
ALLY . WAR . OPER
```

110
```
XMAS . MEAT . QTIPS
YORE . ERLE . AHAIR
ZONE . DIET . TEMPO
NOSPEECHCANBE
AAA . EAR
SPAWN . BERT . ALBA
HES . THUG . NAMEOF
ENTIRELYBADIFIT
MARTYR . PAPA . TSE
PLOT . ETTA . GAYER
STE . AIM
ISSHORTENOUGH
TRITE . COVE . LAID
AMPLE . ERAS . ELKO
JASON . LENT . TEEN
```

111
```
SAFE . PERU . CAAN
ARLO . ALTAR . UNDO
SEAN . BACKBURNER
HAS . THY . EASTEND
HEROS . NEA
RAFTER . APERITIF
ALLEN . AUEL . LIRA
TOO . DOGDAYS . NAT
ENOS . VEIL . PASTE
DEDUCERS . PUREED
NOR . MODEL
AMOROSO . YES . TEN
PETITPOINT . HOLE
EATS . INCAS . OWLS
SLOE . NAYS . GNAT
```

112
```
BEND . DISC . AFAR
AGAIN . CATO . VINE
HORNEDINON . EDNA
SCAPE . OVERDID
HARPEDON . LES
SOD . LAIN . YOKE
HORA . INTO . SEARS
ONUS . LEHAR . EWER
TAMER . SURE . PANT
MAAS . SENS . YEA
ALE . PIPEDOWN
MODISTE . WOODS
ITON . ORGANOLOGY
STUN . USER . PASTE
SETS . TEEM . NESS
```

113
```
CLAD . BANDS . SAFE
LANA . ALERT . TRIM
ORTHODOXJUDAISM
GASLIGHT . OMAHA
SEA . CARP
RENDER . CUBE . VET
AXIS . HAREM . EVA
JUXTAPOSITIONAL
ADO . FORTE . HONK
HEN . ROSE . FLIMSY
FIFE . POO
BASIC . DARKMEAT
EXTRAJUDICIALLY
ALAS . OFAGE . CLIP
KENT . TOYED . KATE
```

114
```
ADDED . LIMOS . BHA
DIALO . ENOCH . REM
OKRAWINFREY . YAP
INTO . MASCARA
CRONES . CONTENTS
HOMER . CON . ENT
ALAS . HOC . ARTGUM
IER . SMOKERS . UTE
ROCOCO . POM . SMUT
ASH . EIN . SABRE
LOYALIST . FELONS
IRESENT . MENU
MIN . PRALINEKAEL
BON . PETIT . CIRRI
ONE . SMELT . ASKED
```

115
```
GALAS . DAMP . SKID
ALEPH . ALOE . PERE
MINEO . MAPLELEAF
STARSANDSTRIPES
HTS . EAT
ASHOT . GADS . OKD
ALIENATED . PAIR
HAMMERANDSICKLE
AMOS . RESENTING
BON . COST . RUSES
SOU . TIN
REDWHITEANDBLUE
UNIONJACK . AROSE
NINO . ACRE . TOWEL
EDEN . STUN . EWERS
```

116
```
MUM . CLIMB . JED
AHEM . RADIO . DIVA
ROGEREBERT . EMIT
CHARADE . EATABLE
NILE . NONE
OBJECT . LOIN . LEW
SOOTH . CELS . SUCH
ARAT . TACIT . ISLA
GONE . UNTO . MAHAL
ENV . BRER . SEMITE
ARAB . ACHE
VENISON . ARTISAN
ORAL . JOEPISCOPO
TORE . ELLEN . ELSE
ESK . TASSE . DEL
```

117
```
SCALE . BRASS . AGE
AUDIE . RECAP . DAY
FRANKIEBALI . ALE
EINE . CAAN . NAMED
ROO . HIS . YES
MALTAMATTHAU
ROSARY . TOM . OATS
EVADE . DEW . PRIME
EERO . ARA . SAILED
FRANKSUMATRA
NAP . IRS . BIG
RODAN . ELSA . TIDE
UVA . SICILYTYSON
TEL . ATONE . INONE
ANY . SALTS . CENTS
```

118
```
ATOP . DANS . PURL
REAR . EMEER . OLEO
MAKO . FERMI . LTDS
SEMPERFIDELIS
ENOLA . SERUM
TOTEM . SATANS
COVE . EGAD . SETIN
AGO . DORIA . UNI
TEXAS . STAR . IMET
SEPIAS . AZTEC
ORBIT . IMAGE
EPLURIBUSUNUM
BLUE . ELENA . NABS
OILS . STAIN . OVER
ASIS . SSTS . TARA
```

119
```
OCCUR . JAWS . MESH
MARNE . ASIA . ELKE
AROMA . SILL . STYX
HENADOODLEDOO
AWES . UNEASE . NBC
KIT . MAJOR
OHS . ALASKA . SORE
COWINACHINASHOP
EROS . WHYNOT . NNE
ADROP . IOI
NED . JULIAN . CARP
PASSINGTHEDOE
ZULU . UNDO . OMEGA
AFAR . REIN . PAPER
GOYA . PRAY . ENTRY
```

120
```
BAGEL . PIP . ATWAR
ACLUE . RDA . SHOVE
WHEREDOESAHERON
LENO . ATEST . DENT
BALE . OTO
OFSOMEMEANSGOTO
ARENA . RICE . SIB
SEED . BERLE . PIPE
EST . OREO . PREPS
SHOPFORLINGERIE
OAK . MOAS
ETAS . EATME . AMPS
VICTORIOUSEGRET
ERRED . DAN . REESE
LEERS . ADE . ADDON
```

121

```
NAIL BLAME AFEW
AGRO REPOS LAPD
SEAR ATEST PSIS
CONNECTTHEDOTS
ALIEN EEL TOR
RDS EDAM MIKADO
ARABIA ALEC
COLORINGBOOKS
DANA GORERS
EMERGE SAGS SRS
LPS ART OSHEA
FINGERPAINTING
AIDE COALS ANTE
CREW TOPOL RTES
TEDS SPATE TORT
```

122

```
PAJAMAS SLACKED
ADULATE MACHETE
PONTIACMICHIGAN
APTED ALIEN
STAR MELEE ANTS
SMUG RESORT
ALI ALAN AERIE
LINCOLNNEBRASKA
DECOR WREN EEL
AGARIC MASC
SESS ADMAN REEL
ANNAS BASRA
DODGECITYKANSAS
ANNEXES EERIEST
BEASTLY TYRONES
```

123

```
TILDE SIT FRAN
AGAIN SUMO IOWA
DOING CRAB CLAP
ATROOPOFMONKEYS
RON GEL
AGAGGLEOFGEESE
BELIE NEAR ADD
ENOS PREEN ALSO
TOO RIOT RIVER
AFLOCKOFCAMELS
OAK LAD
ABANDOFGORILLAS
CLOD FLAP COACH
RENO FIRS ANNIE
EDEN STY LEADS
```

124

```
ATRA AVAST LISP
HOAR CISCO IOOI
EPSILONTAU STAG
MOHAIR INC TAPS
MNO THROB
REALIST MINERS
ILLAT HAREM TUT
TIPS EWE HALO
ASH PAREE TIMER
SEANCE STATURE
TETRA EER
COAT ORB POTASH
ABUT BETAETATAU
LIME INUSE ROBE
FEUD CASKS OPUS
```

125

```
BASH JADE IAMBS
YIPE EROS SPOIL
FRIARTUCK LANGE
OFGREEN ITERATE
ROOSTS SMUT RIP
CITER ETON ACME
ELS EAVE ESTHER
SATELLITE
RIYADH LANA EGG
IDOL OKAY TAMIL
PEU OMAR BULOVA
OARSMEN AERATES
STALE SUNDERING
TENON ASTI MOTO
EDGES SEEM SNOW
```

126

```
BETA SHES AJAR
RAHS TAMPS TELE
EVIL ADMIN VAIN
RENEETAYLOR NET
ECU TOUCANS
COMPORTS TBAR
ABA LEAPS ENTRE
TORT SNEAD SHOW
VENUS GENIE USE
ICED DECLARES
TINKERS TEN
AMI KATEJACKSON
MAXI MAMET LIME
EGOS AGILE ELIS
DENT ELLS TOTS
```

127

```
PAM URIS RINSED
ALA PANE ENTREE
YAK KINGOFSWING
ERE ELO SLIT
EMOTE VALID WED
ROPEADOPE IDO
EBBS ETA RINGO
PERCALE BESMEAR
CLEAR NOR BARS
OLA RUNFORFUN
TSK EPICS REDDY
ASST TAI DOE
FILLTHEBILL INN
TOOTOO ONEL NOT
HUBERT AGES ERA
```

128

```
SLO BEDECKS DRJ
PIC UXORIAL ROO
ABC GEORGIABUSH
GRAILS ASPIRIN
HASTE TORE RYES
ERIE OWN RAN
TIO SKILL TENAM
TENNESSEEANYONE
ISSUE TANGO CNN
TDS VIE POET
CHEM AMEN SANTA
REVENUE DACTYL
OREGONDONOR ELI
WON PAIRING SET
DDS ESCAPEE TRY
```

129

```
MALABO TEA SOP
ANIMAL HAY APE
PAMELA ARRESTER
PEELFRUITSKINS
SPARS ITCH ERNO
OLDS ACHE TWEEN
TEE SOHO GUESTS
POKERHAND
STRAUS DURA FRY
HHOUR DUMP BLED
ARON DEMO BRASS
BOSCORBARTLETT
BATHMATS RANCOR
ATE ECO ORDARE
TYD NOR NEARED
```

130

```
SLASH CROW MEAD
HARTE LOVE ANNE
RUMOR ABEL EDNA
IDONOTMIND POD
MERE RUN PIOUS
PRY DIP PAULINE
MUG DISTINCT
LYINGBUTIHATE
POUNCEON AID
ALLEARS STP BUD
CLEON PEI GENA
KIT INACCURACY
EPIC SORT METOO
TODO OLEO PATON
SPEW FARR STYLE
```

131

```
ADAMS TAPE ELSA
REBET ALAN TAIL
INBLACKANDWHITE
ATA RAES ANDES
REST HADI
BLOWSHOTANDCOLD
RAZE RICE GOO
ANA ASPIRED LON
WAR ROES DERN
LIKENIGHTANDDAY
NETS OTOS
ATLAS ARNO BEA
FROMSTEMTOSTERN
RILE AGEE EATIN
OPAL MOSS SPACE
```

132

```
AJAR LAPS CHRIS
TACO EMIT HAITI
OPUS VEGEBURGER
NAPE ENS ATE
ENRAGED FRESCOS
ETAS DABS OUT
CASES AIDE UTE
ALS PEPPERY CRT
FLU VIPS ASHES
EAR WINY PREP
SHEBANG CONNOTE
INC GAL ATOP
GLITTERATI TAXI
NOLTE IMET OTIC
PALED PARE ROCS
```

133

```
PORE GLEAM EMUS
AHEM AORTA RARA
RAGINGBULL RIND
ERATO PATTON
DAN SLITS ALERT
THESETUP VIE
TORI AND RECESS
OXIDANT BARONET
REPEAT SON STRS
TYP ROCKYIIII
SEETO AIDAN TEM
DONALD CRAVE
OMOO KIDGALAHAD
RIFT ICEUP CODA
OAFS NORSE KEEL
```

134

```
HAIGS LALAW RCA
ACCRA OLIVA ORG
RHEAPERLMAN BEN
MESS UNAPT AIDE
STRAY ACTNOW
ENCORE FRAIL
RAH OKAPI LEEDS
ASI JAYLENO ARI
SACRA LOSER CAL
KINDA RIGHTO
INCASE CAVER
TOOL LARUE URIS
ERR RAVENSYMONE
MAE INEPT APACE
SSA BORES MYNAS
```

135

```
BASK ELBOW OLGA
ETTA DIANE NEON
THOR INLET COLD
REPARTEE BRENDA
ANITA SWAN URN
YAT JAG IRA RUT
TAVERN WISE
ISWHATYOUWISH
ONTO SEURAT
AHA ALE TIN PSI
REM GOTH EARLS
LAPDOG YOUDSAID
OVER JUMPS WIDE
CEDE ANNIE ASEA
KNEW MUSES NERD
```

136

```
EWES PHNOM TWI
ROTO ABODE SRAS
GRACENOTES TELL
ONSIDE SAVABLE
EDS ASSAIL
AMITY RCA GREET
DENY BIC MUSCLE
ADV CADENCE LIE
PIEMAN NED LEON
TAROT ATV LEFTY
SUEDES AAA
STIRRER CODGER
TOON FORTISSIMO
ANNS EBBED OBIS
YES REINS NETS
```

137

```
SPA OWLET PHONE
LEI VIOLA IONIA
EASYASPIE ENACT
ERLE TET SCENES
PLEASE ETRE
SIR HOOTERS
OSS TIARA FIDEL
LIKETAKINGCANDY
AMATI INTRA ADE
FISHNET AKC
GNAT NEURAL
WORLDS ODD REBA
ADIEU FROMABABY
CIVIC OSCAR DEE
SNEAK POSSE SYR
```

138

```
ATOLL SIBS SLAB
LANAI ENOL MOLE
FRANZKAFKA ACTA
SANG UFO KALKAN
USDO CALLERS
THEOHUXTABLE
SABRE ELL RISE
ANO DRUMMER REL
RANG ESP AMORE
ONEMILLIONBC
MANDELA LYNN
EVOLVE OAR INGA
HONE DONMARQUIS
TICS IDEA OUTRE
ADES NESS TESLA
```

139

```
FIFE CLIMB FLAB
LOLL LORCA SABU
ATALEOFIICITIES
WAX NUTS KNOTTY
EDDY PLOP
IRAQIS WEAN JAB
BEGUN SIRS BARE
SLAUGHTERHOUSEV
EATS ORLY CLONE
NYE AMID ATONAL
CROP BLOW
ATTAIN WEEP VOW
FRIDAYTHEXIIIITH
REND MAORI MATE
OKAY STAYS PLOT
```

140

```
SLOT TULIP PDQ
TENAM ERIKA LOU
EVENAWAITER ALE
PIAZZAS ONICE
ADIEU EXETER
SIGNAL SONYA
ALAI LORDS ASH
FINALLY COMESTO
EEG AORTA STOW
AMBER ESCAPE
THISBE YALTA
BORIC SMELLSA
ONA HIMWHOWAITS
NET ORFEO STRAP
EYE PAGET EARS
```

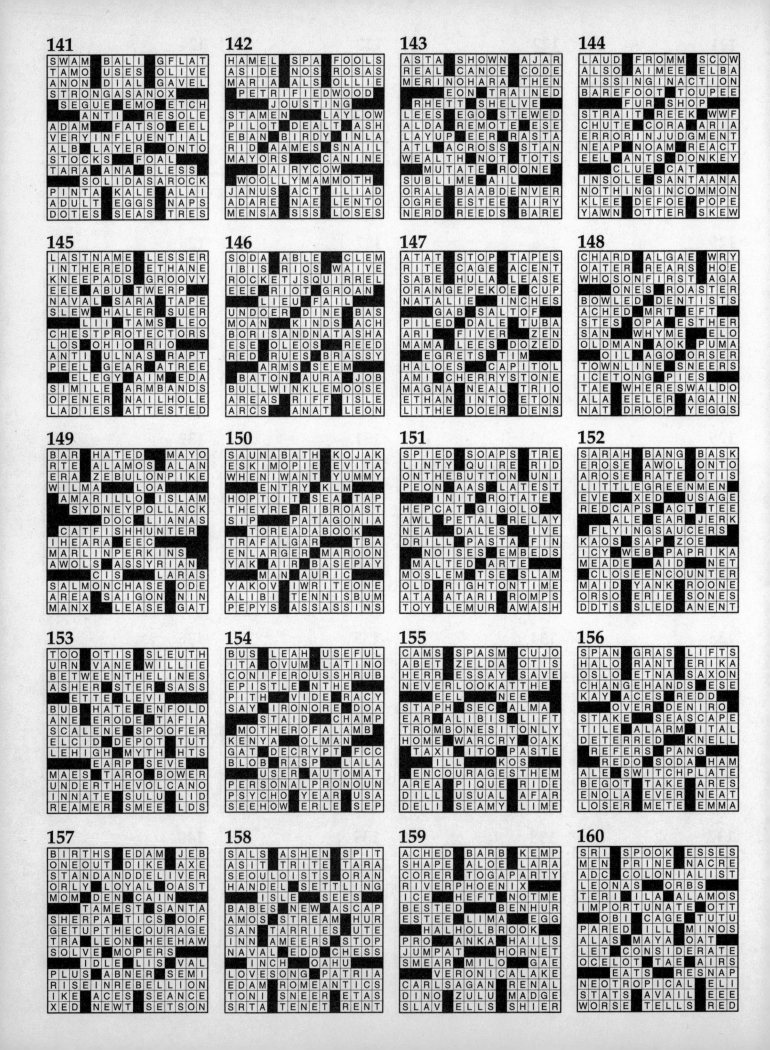

141
```
SWAM BALI GFLAT
TAMO USES OLIVE
ANON DIAL GAVEL
STRONGASANOX
SEGUE EMO ETCH
ANTI RESOLE
ADAM FATSO EEL
VERYINFLUENTIAL
ALB LAYER ONTO
STOCKS FOAL
TARA ANA BLESS
SOLIDASAROCK
PINTA KALE ALAI
ADULT EGGS NAPS
DOTES SEAS TRES
```

142
```
HAMEL SPA FOOLS
ASIDE NOS ROSAS
MARIA ALS OLLIE
PETRIFIEDWOOD
JOUSTING
STAMEN LAYLOW
PILOT DEALT ASH
EBAN BIRDY INLA
RID AAMES SNAIL
MAYORS CANINE
DAIRYCOW
WOOLLYMAMMOTH
JANUS ACT ILIAD
ADARE NAE LENTO
MENSA SSS LOSES
```

143
```
ASTA SHOWN AJAR
REAL CANOE CODE
MERINOHARA THEN
EON TRAINED
RHETT SHELVE
LEES EGO STEWED
ALDA REMOTE ESE
LAYUP EER RASTA
ATL ACROSS STAN
WEALTH NOT TOTS
MUTATE ROONE
SUBLIME AIL
ORAL BAABDENVER
OGRE ESTEE AIRY
NERD REEDS BARE
```

144
```
LAUD FROMM SCOW
ALSO AIMEE ELBA
MISSINGINACTION
BAREFOOT TOUPEE
FUR SHOP
STRAIT REEK WWF
CHUTE CORA ARIA
ERRORINJUDGMENT
NEAP NOAM REACT
EEL ANTS DONKEY
CLUE CAT
INSOLE SANTAANA
NOTHINGINCOMMON
KLEE DEFOE POPE
YAWN OTTER SKEW
```

145
```
LASTNAME LESSER
INTHERED ETHANE
KNEEPADS GROOVY
EEE ABU TWERP
NAVAL SARA TAPE
SLEW HALER SUER
LII TAMS LEO
CHESTPROTECTORS
LOS OHIO RIO
ANTI ULNAS RAPT
PEEL GEAR ATREE
ELEGY AIM EDA
SIMILE ARMBANDS
OPENER NAILHOLE
LADIES ATTESTED
```

146
```
SODA ABLE CLEM
IBIS RIOS WAIVE
ROCKETJSQUIRREL
EEE RIOT GROAN
LIEU FAIL
UNDOER DINE BAS
MOAN KINDS ACH
BORISANDNATASHA
ESE OLEOS REED
RED RUES BRASSY
ARMS SEEM
BATON AURA JOB
BULLWINKLEMOOSE
AREAS RIFF ISLE
ARCS ANAT LEON
```

147
```
ATAT STOP TAPES
RITE CAGE ACENT
SABE HULA LEASE
ORANGEPEKOE CUP
NATALIE INCHES
GAB SALTOF
PILED DALE TUBA
ARI FIVER ZEN
MAMA LEES DOZED
EGRETS TIM
HALOES CAPITOL
AMI CHERRYSTONE
MAGNA NEAL TRIO
ETHAN INTO ETON
LITHE DOER DENS
```

148
```
CHARD ALGAE WRY
OATER REARS HOE
WHOSONFIRST AGA
ONES ROASTER
BOWLED DENTISTS
ACHED MRT EFT
STES OPA ESTHER
SAN WHYME ELO
OLDMAN AOK PUMA
OIL AGO ORSER
TOWNLINE SNEERS
ICETONG PIES
TAE WHERESWALDO
ALA EELER AGAIN
NAT DROOP YEGGS
```

149
```
BAR HATED MAYO
RTE ALAMOS ALAN
ERA ZEBULONPIKE
WILMA LOA
AMARILLO ISLAM
SYDNEYPOLLACK
DOC LIANAS
CATFISHHUNTER
IHEARA EEC
MARLINPERKINS
AWOLS ASSYRIAN
CIS LARAS
SALMONCHASE ODE
AREA SAIGON NIN
MANX LEASE GAT
```

150
```
SAUNABATH KOJAK
ESKIMOPIE EVITA
WHENIWANT YUMMY
ENTRY KLM
HOPTOIT SEA TAP
THEYRE RIBROAST
SIP PATAGONIA
TOREADABOOK
TRAFALGAR TBA
ENLARGER MAROON
YAK AIR BASEPAY
MAN AURIC
YAKOV IWRITEONE
ALIBI TENNISBUM
PEPYS ASSASSINS
```

151
```
SPIED SOAPS TRE
LINTY QUIRE RID
ONTHEBUTTON UNI
PEON AAS LATEST
INIT ROTATE
HEPCAT GIGOLO
AWL PETAL RELAY
NEA DALES IVE
DRILL PASTA FIN
NOISES EMBEDS
MALTED ARTE
MOSLEM TSE SLAM
OLD RIGHTONTIME
ATA ATARI ROMPS
TOY LEMUR AWASH
```

152
```
SARAH BANG BASK
EROSE AWOL ONTO
AROSE RATE OTIS
LITTLEGREENMEN
EVE XED USAGE
REDCAPS ACT TEE
ALE EAR JERK
FLYINGSAUCERS
KAOS SAP ZOE
ICY WEB PAPRIKA
MEADE AID NET
CLOSEENCOUNTER
MAID YANK ROONE
ORSO ERIE SONES
DDTS SLED ANENT
```

153
```
TOO OTIS SLEUTH
URN VANE WILLIE
BETWEENTHELINES
ASHER STER SASS
ETTE LEVI
BUB HATE ENFOLD
ANE ERODE TAFIA
SCALENE SPOOFER
ELCID DEPOT TUT
LEHIGH MYTH HTS
EARP SEVE
MAES TARO BOWER
UNDERTHEVOLCANO
INNATE SULU LID
REAMER SMEE LDS
```

154
```
BUS LEAH USEFUL
ITA OVUM LATINO
CONIFEROUSSHRUB
EPISTLE NTHE
PITH VIDE RACY
SAY IRONORE DOA
STAID CHAMP
MOTHEROFALAMB
KENYA OLMAN
GAT DECRYPT FCC
BLOB RASP LALA
USER AUTOMAT
PERSONALPRONOUN
PSYCHO YEAR USA
SEEHOW ERLE SEP
```

155
```
CAMS SPASM CUJO
ABET ZELDA OTIS
HERR ESSAY SAVE
NEVERLOOKATTHE
EEL NEE
STAPH SEC ALMA
EAR ALIBIS LIFT
TROMBONESITONLY
HOME WARCRY OAK
TAXI ITO PASTE
ILL KOS
ENCOURAGESTHEM
AREA PIQUE RIDE
DILL USUAL AFAR
DELI SEAMY LIME
```

156
```
SPAN GRAS LIFTS
HALO RANT ERIKA
OSLO ETNA SAXON
CHANGEHANDS ESE
KAY ACES REDD
OVER DENIRO
STAKE SEASCAPE
TILE ALARM ITAL
DETERRED KNELL
REFERS PANG
REDO SODA HAM
ALE SWITCHPLATE
BEGOT TAKE ARES
ENOLA EVER NEAT
LOSER METE EMMA
```

157
```
BIRTHS EDAM JEB
ONEOUT DIKE AXE
STANDANDDELIVER
ORLY LOYAL OAST
MOM DEN CAIN
TAMEST SANTA
SHERPA TICS OOF
GETUPTHECOURAGE
TRA LEON HEEHAW
SOLVE MOPERS
IDLE LIS VAL
PLUS ABNER SEMI
RISEINREBELLION
IKE ACES SEANCE
XED NEWT SETSON
```

158
```
SALS ASHEN SPIT
ASIT TRITE TARA
SEOULOISTS ORAN
HANDEL SETTLING
ISLE SEES
BABES NEW ASCAP
AMOS STREAM HUR
SAN TARRIES UTE
INN AMEERS STOP
NAVAL EDD CHESS
INCH OAHU
LOVESONG PATRIA
EDAM ROMEANTICS
TONI SNEER ETAS
SRTA TENET RENT
```

159
```
ACHED BARB KEMP
SHAPE ALOE LARA
CORER TOGAPARTY
RIVERPHOENIX
ICE HEFT NOTME
BESTED BENHUR
ESTEE LIMA EGG
HALHOLBROOK
PRO ANKA HAILS
JUMPAT HORNET
SMEAR MILO GAE
VERONICALAKE
CARLSAGAN RENAL
DINO ZULU MADGE
SLAV ELLS SHIER
```

160
```
SRI SPOOK ESSES
MEN PRINE NACRE
ADC COLONIALIST
LEONAS ORBS
TERI ILA ALAMOS
IMPORTUNATE OTT
OBI CAGE TUTU
PARED ILL MINOS
ALAS MAYA OAT
LET CONSIDERATE
OCELOT TAE AIRS
EATS RESNAP
NEOTROPICAL ELI
STATS AVAIL EEE
WORSE TELLS RED
```

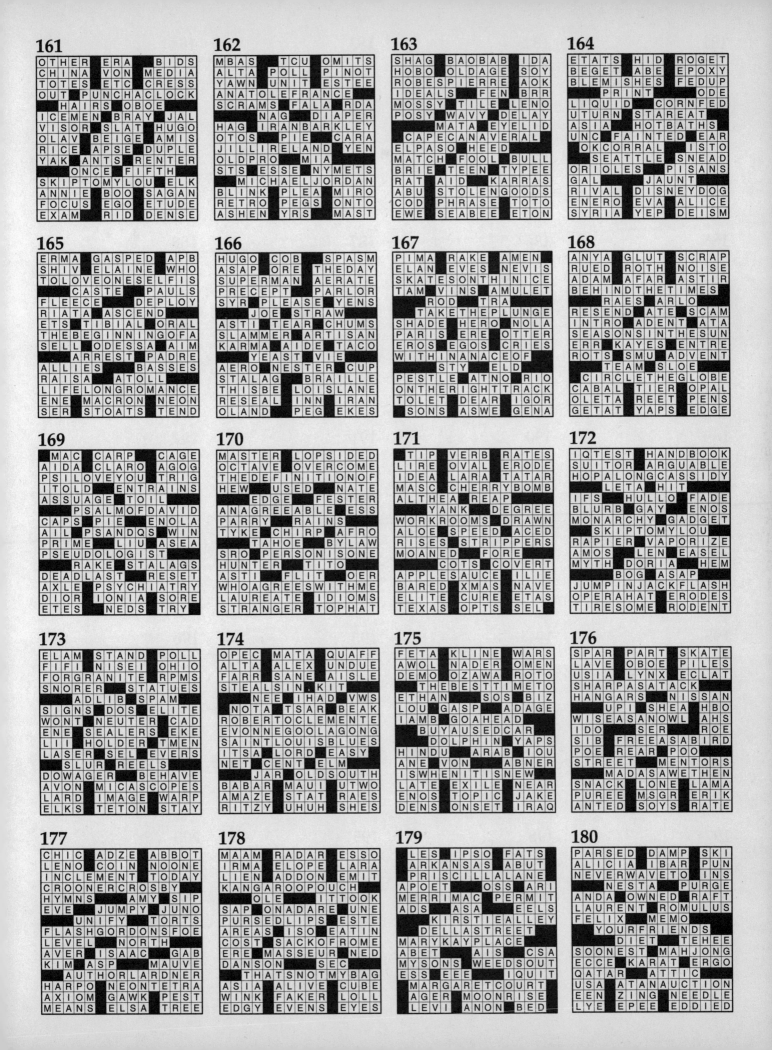

161

```
OTHER  ERA  BIDS
CHINA  VON  MEDIA
TOTES  ETC  CRESS
OUT PUNCHACLOCK
    HAIRS  OBOE
ICEMEN  BRAY  JAL
VISOR  SLAT  HUGO
OLAV  BEIGE  AMIS
RICE  APSE  DUPLE
YAK  ANTS  RENTER
   ONCE  FIFTH
SKIPTOMYLOU  ELK
ANNIE  BOO  SAGAN
FOCUS  EGO  ETUDE
EXAM  RID  DENSE
```

162

```
MBAS  TCU  OMITS
ALTA  POLL  PINOT
YAWN  UNIT  ESTEE
ANATOLEFRANCE
SCRAMS  FALA  RDA
    NAG  DIAPER
HAG  IRANBARKLEY
OTOS  PIE  CARA
JILLIRELAND  YEN
OLDPRO  MIA
STS  ESSE  NYMETS
MICHAELJORDAN
BLINK  PLEA  MIRO
RETRO  PEGS  ONTO
ASHEN  YRS  MAST
```

163

```
SHAG  BAOBAB  IDA
HOBO  OLDAGE  SOY
ROBESPIERRE  AOK
IDEALS  FEN  BRR
MOSSY  TILE  LENO
POSY  WAVY  DELAY
    MATA  EYELID
CAPECANAVERAL
ELPASO  HEED
MATCH  FOOL  BULL
BRIE  TEEN  TYPEE
RAT  AID  KARRAS
ABU  STOLENGOODS
COD  PHRASE  TOTO
EWE  SEABEE  ETON
```

164

```
ETATS  HID  ROGET
BEGET  ABE  EPOXY
BLEMISHES  FEDUP
   PRINT    ODE
LIQUID  CORNFED
UTURN  STAREAT
ASIA  HOTBATHS
UNC  FAINTED  EAR
OKCORRAL  ISTO
SEATTLE  SNEAD
ORIOLES  PISANS
GAL    JAUNT
RIVAL  DISNEYDOG
ENERO  EVA  ALICE
SYRIA  YEP  DEISM
```

165

```
ERMA  GASPED  APB
SHIV  ELAINE  WHO
TOLOVEONESELFIS
   CASTE  PAULS
FLEECE  DEPLOY
RIATA  ASCEND
ETS  TIBIAL  ORAL
THEBEGINNINGOFA
SELL  ODESSA  AIM
   ARREST  PADRE
ALLIES  BASSES
RAISA  ATOLL
LIFELONGROMANCE
ENE  MACRON  NEON
SER  STOATS  TEND
```

166

```
HUGO  COB  SPASM
ASAP  ORE  THEDAY
SUPERMAN  AERATE
PRECEPT  PARLOR
SYR  PLEASE  YENS
   JOE  STRAW
ASTI  TEAR  CHUMS
SLAMMER  ARTISAN
KARMA  AIDE  TACO
   YEAST  VIE
AERO  NESTER  CUP
STALAG  BRAILLE
THISBE  LOISLANE
RESEAL  INN  IRAN
OLAND  PEG  EKES
```

167

```
PIMA  RAKE  AMEN
ELAN  EVES  NEVIS
SKATESONTHINICE
TAM  VINS  AMULET
    ROD  TRA
TAKETHEPLUNGE
SHADE  HERO  NOLA
PARIS  ERE  OTTER
EROS  EGOS  CRIES
WITHINANACEOF
    STY  ELD
PESTLE  ATNO  RIO
ONTHERIGHTTRACK
TOLET  DEAR  IGOR
SONS  ASWE  GENA
```

168

```
ANYA  GLUT  SCRAP
RUED  ROTH  NOISE
ADAM  AFAR  ASTIR
BEHINDTHETIMES
    RAES  ARLO
RESEND  ATE  SCAM
INTRO  ADENT  ATA
SEASONSINTHESUN
ERR  KAYES  ENTRE
ROTS  SMU  ADVENT
   TEAM  SLOE
CIRCLETHEGLOBE
CABAL  TIER  OPAL
OLETA  REET  PENS
GETAT  YAPS  EDGE
```

169

```
MAC  CARP  CAGE
AIDA  CLARO  AGOG
PSILOVEYOU  TRIG
ITOLD  ENTRAINS
ASSUAGE  TOIL
PSALMOFDAVID
CAPS  PIE  ENOLA
AIL  PSANDQS  WIN
PRIME  LIU  ASEA
PSEUDOLOGIST
   RAKE  STALAGS
DEADLAST  RESET
AXLE  PSYCHIATRY
DIOR  IONIA  SORE
ETES  NEDS  TRY
```

170

```
MASTER  LOPSIDED
OCTAVE  OVERCOME
THEDEFINITIONOF
HEW  USED  NATE
    EDGE  FESTER
ANAGREEABLE  ESS
PARRY  RAINS
TYKE  CHIRP  AFRO
   TAHOE  BYLAW
SRO  PERSONISONE
HUNTER  TITO
ASTI  FLIT  OER
WHOAGREESWITHME
LAUREATE  IDIOMS
STRANGER  TOPHAT
```

171

```
TIP  VERB  RATES
LIRE  OVAL  ERODE
IDEA  LARA  TATAR
MASC  CHERRYBOMB
ALTHEA  REAP
   YANK  DEGREE
WORKROOMS  DRAWN
ALOE  SPEED  ACED
RISES  STRIPPERS
MOANED  FORE
   COTS  COVERT
APPLESAUCE  ILIE
BARED  XMAS  NAVE
ELITE  CURE  ETAS
TEXAS  OPTS  SEL
```

172

```
IQTEST  HANDBOOK
SUITOR  ARGUABLE
HOPALONGCASSIDY
   LETA    HIT
IFS  HULLO  FADE
BLURB  GAY  ENOS
MONARCHY  GADGET
SKIPTOMYLOU
RAPIER  VAPORIZE
AMOS  LEN  EASEL
MYTH  DORIA  HEM
   BOG  ASAP
JUMPINJACKFLASH
OPERAHAT  ERODES
TIRESOME  RODENT
```

173

```
ELAM  STAND  POLL
FIFI  NISEI  OHIO
FORGRANITE  RPMS
SNORER  STATUES
   ADLIB  SPAM
SIGNS  DOS  ELITE
WONT  NEUTER  CAD
ENE  SEALERS  EKE
LII  HOLDER  TMEN
LASER  SEL  EVERS
   SLUR  REELS
DOWAGER  BEHAVE
AVON  MICASCOPES
LARD  IMAGE  WARP
ELKS  TETON  STAY
```

174

```
OPEC  MATA  QUAFF
ALTA  ALEX  UNDUE
FARR  SANE  AISLE
STEALSIN  KIT
NEE  IHAD  VWS
NOTA  TSAR  BEAK
ROBERTOCLEMENTE
EVONNEGOOLAGONG
SAINTLOUISBLUES
ITSA  LORD  EASY
NET  CENT  ELM
   JAR  OLDSOUTH
BABAR  MAUI  UTWO
AMAZE  STAT  RAES
RITZY  UHUH  SHES
```

175

```
FETA  KLINE  WARS
AWOL  NADER  OMEN
DEMO  OZAWA  ROTO
THEBESTTIMETO
ETHAN  SOS  BIZ
LOU  GASP  ADAGE
IAMB  GOAHEAD
BUYAUSEDCAR
DOLPHIN  YAPS
HINDU  ARAB  IOU
ANE  VON  ABNER
ISWHENITISNEW
LATE  EXILE  NEAR
ENOS  TOPIC  JAKE
DENS  ONSET  IRAQ
```

176

```
SPAR  PART  SKATE
LAVE  OBOE  PILES
USIA  LYNX  ECLAT
SHARPASATACK
HANGARS  NISSAN
UPI  SHEA  HBO
WISEASANOWL  AHS
IDO  SER  ROE
SIB  FREEASABIRD
POE  REAR  POO
STREET  MENTORS
MADASAWETHEN
SNACK  LONE  LAMA
PUREE  MSGR  ERIK
ANTED  SOYS  RATE
```

177

```
CHIC  ADZE  ABBOT
LENO  COIN  NOONE
INCLEMENT  TODAY
CROONERCROSBY
HYMNS  AMY  SIP
EVE  JUMPY  JUNO
   UNIFY  TORTS
FLASHGORDONSFOE
LEVEL  NORTH
AVER  ISAAC  GAB
KIM  ASP  MAUVE
AUTHORLARDNER
HARPO  NEONTETRA
AXIOM  GAWK  PEST
MEANS  ELSA  TREE
```

178

```
MAAM  RADAR  ESSO
IRMA  ELOPE  LARA
LIEN  ADDON  EMIT
KANGAROOPOUCH
OLE    ITTOOK
SAP  ONADARE  UNE
PURSEDLIPS  ESTE
AREAS  ISO  EATIN
COST  SACKOFROME
ERE  MASSEUR  NED
DANSON  SEC
THATSNOTMYBAG
ASIA  ALIVE  CUBE
WINK  FAKER  LOLL
EDGY  EVENS  EYES
```

179

```
LES  IPSO  FATS
ARKANSAS  ABUT
PRISCILLALANE
APOET  OSS  ARI
MERRIMAC  PERMIT
ADS  ASA  EELS
KIRSTIEALLEY
DELLASTREET
MARYKAYPLACE
ABET  AIS  CSA
MYSONS  WEEDSOUT
ESS  EEE  IQUIT
MARGARETCOURT
AGER  MOONRISE
LEVI  ANON  BED
```

180

```
PARSED  DAMP  SKI
ALICIA  IBAR  PUN
NEVERWAVETO  INS
NESTA  PURGE
ANDA  OWNED  RAFT
LAURENT  ROMULUS
FELIX    MEMO
YOURFRIENDS
DIET  TEHEE
SOONEST  MAHJONG
ECCE  KARAT  ERGO
QATAR  ATTIC
USA  ATANAUCTION
EEN  ZING  NEEDLE
LYE  EPEE  EDDIED
```

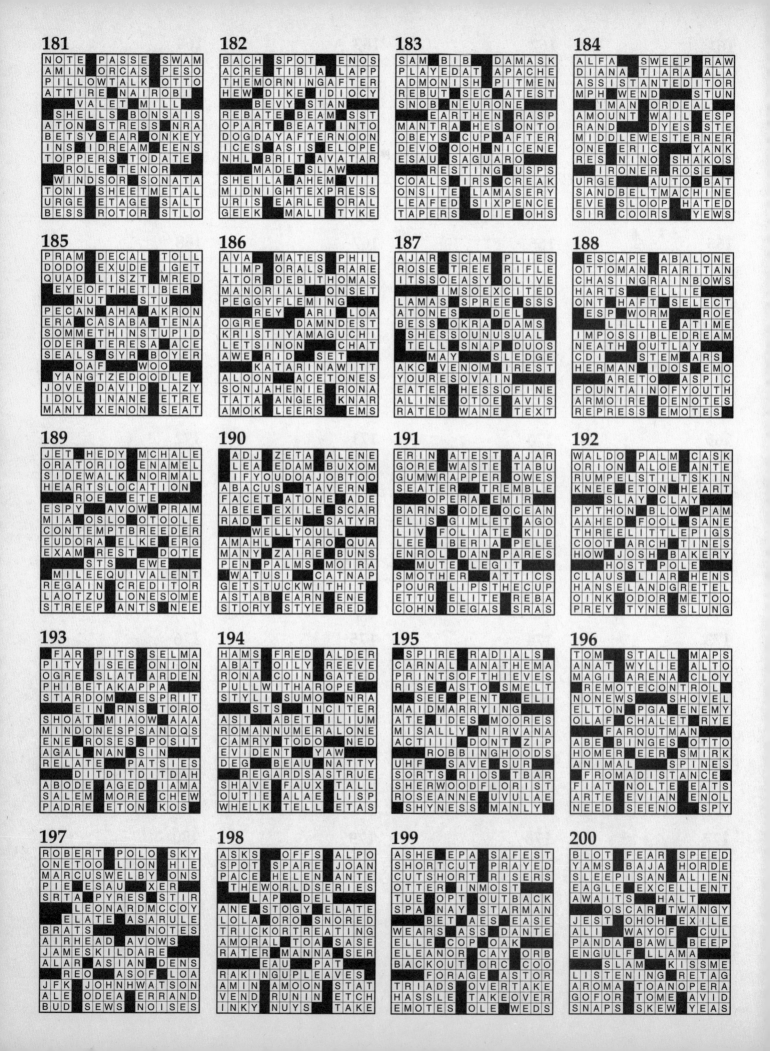

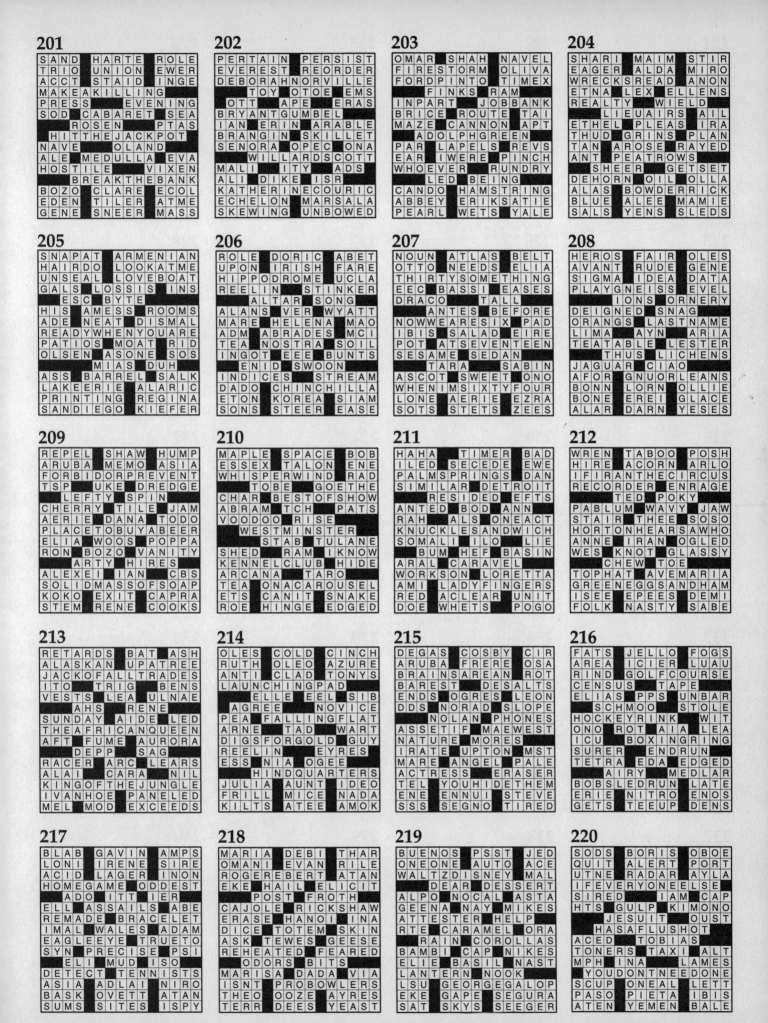

221
```
ECCE ETTAS BIAS
DOAS DEARS ANNE
DUSTJACKET NATE
ANTHEM ENSLAVES
STEER CST ANA
REAR APACHE
CAWS SEDANS UAR
ASA STOOLIE URN
LES CANNOT AMES
MAHLER FARR
BEN FAT ERIKA
FRONTIER ADORES
LEAS SWEEPSWEEK
INRE LENDS ENNE
PODS ERASE DEED
```

222
```
RICK SPEND SPAR
ASHE EAGER PATE
PLUMBCRAZY ASEA
TEMPERED DENTED
RED MORSE
PARENT DICE BSA
IMAGE KINK GOAL
LIZA SENDS RANI
ETON TREY CARTE
SYR MARS MADDEN
BEANS KID
SHARED INTERACT
PICA PAPERTIGER
ILKS AISLE TARA
NOSE TROTS ARTY
```

223
```
CHAPS STICH UPS
HELEN HENRI NEE
EAGERBEAVER DAN
WREN ADS DESERT
TREVI WISER
DINGBAT EDEN
EFF ASIAN INONE
RURAL DST NOGOS
GRABS ERECT SST
OLIO ROADHOG
DUGAN AWARD
MAYTAG MAN MORE
ARC FLYINGTIGER
ALA FAINT ANEAR
SOT ENNIS PERMS
```

224
```
CANT ENGIRD AVA
USER PEEDEE MEX
LSHAPEDMOOR OIL
PORCHES SPACKLE
ACUTE ENE
SWIMMINGLOOP
DIP LOOS ELOPE
ERA MANTLED ZAP
BALSA DIAG ELS
TEMPLEOFMOOD
ADS BULGE
MAGNETO LIONELS
ALA MACHINELOOT
JET ETHELS INRE
AXE RESEAT NAYS
```

225
```
RAREGAS WAFFLED
ELEVATE PRELUDE
GIVEMEA ATLARGE
ABUSE HONKED
LIE PRONOUN
ESS LAUNDRYLIST
SACRED ERIE
ALBANY OCTANE
GEEK PECKAT
ANDILLSETIT FEE
OUTGREW RAJ
FRACAS OBESE
RISOTTO TOMUSIC
EPITHET DRAGNET
DESSERT SENSORS
```

226
```
GAFFE OHNO OOPS
AWAIT DOOR CLAP
PRIVATEPRACTICE
EYRE ITEM RENEW
CANS ABUT
ASSERT AJAX BOW
SHANE USER BOZO
CAPTAINKANGAROO
ALPS SPIN ASONE
PLY PEON BURNER
WEEP MILE
AWARE UPON LIMP
GENERALHOSPITAL
OAKS PAIR RETIE
GNAT ERLE OFOLD
```

227
```
KISS TWAS JADED
ANTE RAJA OLIVE
PLIE URAL BAGEL
PENNANTRACES
ATTACK DOT BAH
OSLO CHARGE
POLAR OTTO BAER
ABANNERHEADLINE
PEST VEER RENTS
ASSISI RIPE
LEO ETE EASTER
STANDARDTIME
POSIT DOOM ABBA
AWARE OMNI PIER
NEWER FEET HARM
```

228
```
SPA WIZ SLR JOS
TURBINE EYETEST
ARRANGE INGRATE
GEORGESAND UNIT
SEWN NEA AMAS
SWAMIS RNA
ELM ALIT BETRAY
MOO RADAMES SHE
PULSES HOSE HAS
LES SIESTA
PAYS PTL FLEE
ANYA SALLYFIELD
STAMMER OVERAGE
TOREOUT VETERAN
AND ADS ESE YRS
```

229
```
SALAD MET APT
ADONIS ASIA RAH
FOOTSTOMPER MNO
ESP BRAINBUSTER
FAIRE ABOWL
ONLAND IRANI
REINDEERS ESME
AMP SWUNG TIL
LOST ENTREMETS
MARCS OMERTA
MANIA ALVIN
BACKSTABBER SSW
ELK KNEESLAPPER
ALE SIRE STOOGE
MER POT ELTON
```

230
```
ACETIC LAM UVEA
LAREDO IVY PADS
IBERIA AIR ALES
MOTHRANATURE
WED TRI RAT ELS
OREL AERY APSES
WISEACRE SMA
KINGKONGTABLE
NAS IRONSIDE
GREYS INAN TOIL
ION SOS TEA NEY
GODZILLAACRE
OMOO DAS ONAGER
TIRE INK LITERS
SEAS EDS DESERT
```

231
```
SHES SWAIN CAKE
EAVE HORNE ANNA
THELIONINWINTER
HALFNOTE LOOSEN
TIS TYNE
MATRON MOWS CBS
ORBIT PIKE SALK
CROCODILEDUNDEE
HONK ICON NURSE
AWE TSKS ATBEST
POKY ERR
SCRIBE INCUBATE
PLANETOFTHEAPES
RENT TOWEL LIRA
YOKO EMERY MENU
```

232
```
TILDE POOR SRA
OCEAN UPTO STEP
TONYCURTIS HAVE
SNOCONE STERNER
ARIES EVILLY
TURRET EUREKA
KNEE EVER REUPS
ODD ESO GIS RAH
SOBER WREN AERO
UNREST VALLEE
PATTON EMIRS
ATTIRES AVIANCA
CROC RINGOSTARR
TINE GLEN TIBET
SAS YOGA OASES
```

233
```
PAAR SCAB USDA
ARNO HOLE SNOOT
REED ELIA ETUDE
ANGELALANSBURY
AGOUTI TOUT
THEDORMOUSE
SABRES AWE RNAS
ARLES AYN SETAT
WAAC AMO FODORS
ALBERTBFALL
SEMI FIASCO
FUSSOVERTRIVIA
CURIE EDIT LILI
INGOT RICE LIED
ADEN TEAR SIRE
```

234
```
SEAS ABASH APSE
HARP CARLO LAOS
ERGO DROIT ASWE
IFYOUCANTDOIT
LULLS SON REO
ALE HADA GALAXY
MEDUSA EMIL
CORRECTLYDOIT
JOVE TAVERN
ONEDGE RATE UPC
GER OTT ABNER
BYTHEDEADLINE
ZERO ATARI AQUA
EVER NOTIN SULK
DADE ENACT SETS
```

235
```
CASTRO STROKER
OCARINA LIEDOWN
PARAPET AMASSES
IDOLS RAVEL
NINA DABS GOGET
GAG MEND SEDUCE
CONDOMINIUM
CONDOMEDIUM
CONDORMINIUM
ORTEGA NUNS RED
DORSA HAIG BALI
MOULT CAVER
TASTING ELUSIVE
INHASTE MARINES
STENTOR DECENT
```

236
```
ERA JAVA YAWNED
LOM URIS ADRIAN
ICESTATIONZEBRA
JOCASTA UKES
ACHY MISE TACT
HOE TWISTER COO
GRANT INLAW
WATERCHESTNUT
WAGON MAIZE
EVE DEBUSSY TWO
BEEP VEST WHEN
LOIS WINERED
STEAMLOCOMOTIVE
PASCAL HOOT VIC
ARTERY EDNA ELK
```

237
```
RIDE GASP COMA
ANON TABOO OVER
CANDLEPINS NANA
ENAMOR EAT CLUB
RESOUND RATE
STARS GARAGE
HART LANTERNJAW
USA WAY ALE
LAMPOONING PRES
APPEAR LARGE
DRAG NEATASA
MRED CRO EVADES
COLL LIGHTERMEN
ABLE ELLIS DIME
NEER SLED STER
```

238
```
SWAP GRAS MARGO
PAVE RAIN ABEAM
ARES UNDO GLAZE
MRTANGERINEMAN
ODD TRE
MAA OYEZ ATHOME
EDGAR GOON AVIS
THELEMONSISTERS
RONS ONEL PENTA
OCTOPI DODO SHY
ASP AKA
WICHITALIMEMAN
AGAIN CARP AXIS
ROGET TIME ZENO
PRESS STAR EDEN
```

239
```
AHAB ABASH DEMI
PALL MACHO OXEN
ESAU BEDEW MATA
NEVERCALLAMAN
FMAJOR AISLE
AURAL BECKON
INKY WELLES GPA
TRIS AFOOL CURL
HON TRIPUP HAIL
JOTTED MITZI
UMBER SPLEEN
BORROWFROMHIM
OLEO OLIVE DAZE
ADAM REPEL OLEG
TYKE EXERT GANG
```

240
```
CANASTA ARILS
COWORKER CRANIA
ABETTING AINTNO
ROSE MOUSTACHE
SPREE HES
THAT EAR DCI
THEMANINTHEMOON
ORDERINTHECOURT
DOGSINTHEMANGER
DUE SEE NAHS
GSA ROGET
HARDENING STLO
SOBEIT LOGICIAN
BUENOS EMERALDS
ATTAR REDATED
```

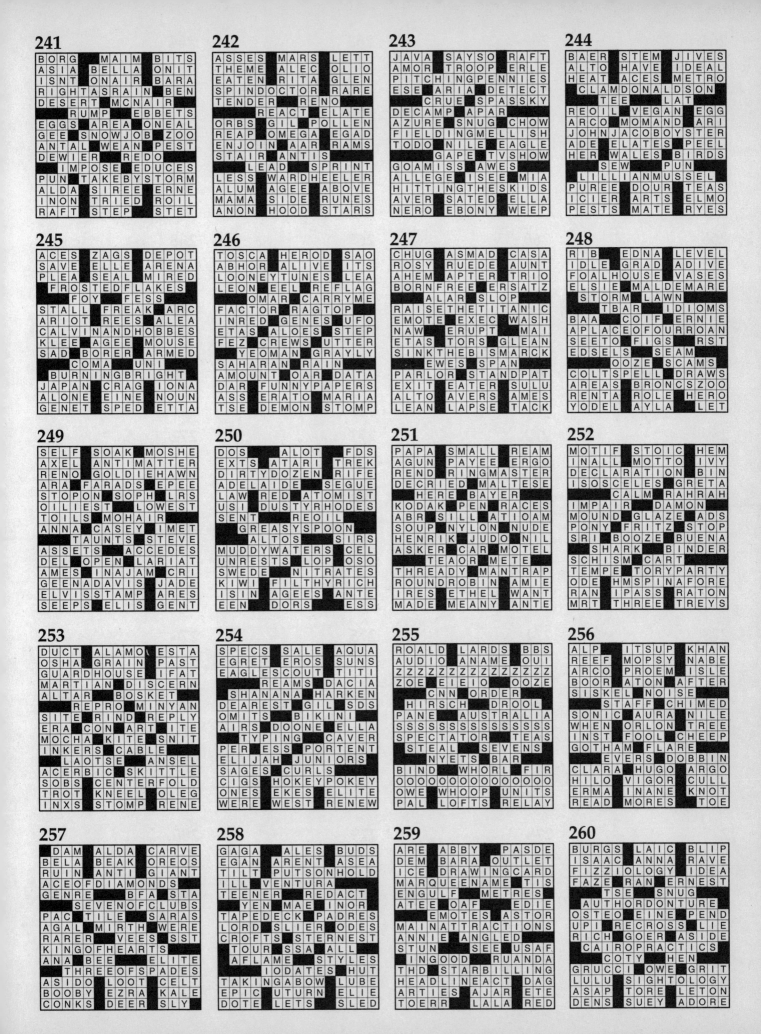

261

```
CARD  AGAPE  OFFS
OMOO  ROMAN  LILT
CATCHERINTHERYE
ONT  USE  DEE  EPA
ADELE  BARE  BAM
SADA  PRESS  DUPE
  NOSES   CAGED
BACKINTHEUSSR
PANES   MONTH
ALTS  STAND  ERRS
LIE  SCAN  GREAT
ANN  SAC  OOP  STA
CENTEROFGRAVITY
ESAU  AMORE  IDEE
SEEN  BABES  NERD
```

262

```
SHAM  AMID  BEARD
TAPE  RARE  LAGER
ELAN  OXEN  TRIBE
EECUMMINGS  OLES
RYE  EASE  LABELS
    TASK  LONI
ADMEN  INAPTNESS
BOIL  PROSE  SNAP
CIGARETTE  RODDY
WITS  REIN
CHARGE  ABAD  SCI
LAME  SJPERELMAN
INONE  ALAN  AIRS
NONCE  DEMI  SLOE
TIGER  EAST  TENT
```

263

```
COCA  PASS  MAKO
AMOS  TONIC  ARID
TART  OLDER  REDD
CHERRYYOGURT
HADIT   REBOILED
  DESK   SNIDE
LOBE  PAPPYYOKUM
ABE  ATRIA  ECO
YEARBYYEAR  ADES
ESTEE   SNOB
RESOLUTE  RAILS
  CANARYYELLOW
TALC  ILIAD  OLGA
ALOU  TICKS  NEAL
BLUR  SASS  ERNE
```

264

```
SITUP  ACTS  FAO
ALONG  PLAIT  ALP
CLEARHEADED  ILE
  WAITS   ERROR
LOCATES  CANASTA
AZORES   SHRINK
DOLED  THATS  ISA
ENDS  FIERY  GNUS
DEB  HILLY  RANTS
LIONEL  CETERA
SPOOLED  BAGHDAD
IRONY   TORRE
ROD  WARMHEARTED
EVE  AROAR  DEERE
NED  REIN  EDNAS
```

265

```
DADA  DEFER  OFIT
AMIS  OLIVE  VIVA
IMAFIRMBELIEVER
SOLACES   CREST
   TOM  HAWED
INFAMILYVALUES
PARSE  OMIT  BLAB
SOI  ANNAS  ELI
EMMA  GEAR  ASNOT
ILLSELLYOUMINE
LADYS   FRA
ABOOK   ARALSEA
FORFIFTYDOLLARS
ADAM  GROOM  EGOS
RYNE  HANSE  REST
```

266

```
DREW  CARR  COSTS
CARE  ALDA  ANKLE
CRABGRASS  PLACE
CASBAH   HITIT
   SOAR  SANER
STIPPLE  LIEBER
SHUNS  ELLEN  OLE
ERRS  TREAT  MAID
NOT  SRTAS  DARED
TULANE  SECONDS
DEMON  EROS
  NERDS   NESSIE
SMELT  LOANSHARK
LUCIE  ABLE  ALOE
OSKAR  MILD  MEND
```

267

```
ITCH  RAZOR  SCOW
NILE  ALEUT  NOVA
HEADSTARTS  OMER
UPS  TENOR  WORD
MOPPED  UAE  RAE
ALERT  HANDSDOWN
NODE  SET  DAISES
  FOURHCLUB
APPEAL  ORE  BALK
HEARTFELT  OLLIE
ERR  HAS  CREATE
AVOW  STOIC  BEN
DALE  HEALTHCARE
ODES  ANODE  AMAS
FEET  YESES  MALT
```

268

```
SOS  PRO  RADIAN
CHI  SHOW  ONEOUT
RAT  HIDEANDSIKH
AROMA   NEAP
GANDHICANE  ONCE
ISDONE   STOOL
OVA  ERA  TRICKY
DELHISANDWICHES
EXTORT  GEO  ESE
TEAMS   SEABED
ODIE  JOLLYRAJAH
  BEAU   INURE
AGRACULTURE  DIG
POISON  SKIS  GEE
RODENT  KEG  ELL
```

269

```
EMPTY  WEPT  LIAR
LOUIE  AMOS  ALTE
ENTERANELECTION
MASC  GERE  STALE
   LARRY  NEEDLE
ARMADAS   BOAR
ROUSE  CEL  MAI
COMPETEONATRACK
SDS  ESQ  HENCE
  SEES  TEAPOTS
EVENTS   MANIA
LOGAN  MARV  ISTO
MIGRATEUPSTREAM
ELEE  BONO  BERRA
RADS  SWAN  ARBOR
```

270

```
LAST  USER  SAPID
ECHO  NOLO  PRADO
THENOBLESTOFALL
MEDICO  NERO  RYE
EDS   TREASON
  MONA  USMAIL
ATEUP  RANG  ENDE
DOGSISTHEHOTDOG
ATOI  CHAR  URALS
HONCHO  VETO
  ITFEEDS  THE
CHE  NCOS  DEMEAN
HANDTHATBITESIT
OLDIE  MERE  ALTE
POSED  YEAS  LAIR
```

271

```
MATS  REVS  ISEE
ATIT  REPEL  AMES
COLA  EVITA  MART
SPLITSECOND  LIE
  NOEL  DEALER
RECENT  SPEECH
EVADE  APER  TOUR
NIL  REGRESS  URE
OLLA  MEAL  LARGE
  INGEST  RINSED
PATTER   SETA
ONA  MINUTESTEAK
LIDS  TIROS  ONTO
ATAT  UTILE  LION
RAYS  SASE  EDNA
```

272

```
BALE  SOS  SCROD
OVAL  PITA  OHARA
METS  ALUM  IAMBS
BREADWINNERS
ESE  ENE  ENEMIES
DENEB  ROSIE  NAH
  RUM  CIG  ETRE
MARGECHAMPION
EELS  TOR  AIR
TWO  TRUES  ZEBRA
ASPIRIN  TOZ  RAT
  VICTORMATURE
BASIA  EPEE  HIES
EXPEL  DRAG  ASST
LEADS  YMA  WETS
```

273

```
SPREAD  JAMS  ADD
AIELLO  IDEA  LEE
INSIDE  GOLDLEAF
LATHES   LAXLY
   URNS  STEW
DEERSTALKER  WED
ARLO  TOAD  BIDE
INTO  EDITS  UZIS
RIOT  TORE  DECK
YEN  POWERPLANTS
PENN   SHEB
PUMAS   RABBIT
STEMTURN  AVOUCH
SAD  ESAU  SETTEE
THE  RENT  ENTERO
```

274

```
LAMB  CBER  SASS
RODEO  RELY  ONTO
OCEAN  OGLE  UTAH
SALTSAWAY  PREGO
ALE  AINT  PEG
  SIR  BARROOM
STEW  STARS  AMMO
ARTE  TREES  PAIN
KITE  RECAP  ERTE
SPUTNIK   OKS
  TOP  DARE  BIO
MAJOR  BITTEREND
OLEO  GOAL  POLLO
DART  ANNA  UTTER
SIKH  BEES  PEST
```

275

```
JAMB  VICAR  HOBO
ELAL  ENOLA  EVER
DEMI  RIDOF  NILE
ICANNOTAFFORDTO
   TIN  TIDY
QUIZKIDS  ADVISE
ASHE  CUED  LINUS
TAE  WASTEMY  CAT
AGATE  TUBA  LOVE
REREAD  PILLAGES
LIRA   IAN
TIMEMAKINGMONEY
ONYX  MELON  LOPE
OGRE  ALENE  IDEA
LEAD  SATED  NEER
```

276

```
PECK  CAEN  AGNEW
ARLO  ALDA  DRAMA
BRAN  JOEY  EATIN
LONGJOHNSILVER
ORK  ALA  ALLY
  BYE  PYLE  WHO
INFUN  REY  COAX
GOLDENPARACHUTE
OVID  AYN  AIKEN
RAP  CORK  AMP
FUME  ABE  GAB
PLATINUMBLONDE
JOYCE  ERIE  HOLT
AGNES  EGGS  OMIT
MONTY  SEAS  HEBE
```

277

```
TIME  PLAIN  SAL
AGER  RONDOS  ALA
ROMENEWYORK  FEZ
PROCESS   ELEGY
   TAT  PLIE
CAIROILLINOIS
HORNS  NYETS  SUP
IBEG  ASIDE  USTA
ERN  BRING  INERT
ATHENSGEORGIA
SCOT   BAR
QUITO   FINANCE
URN  MOSCOWIDAHO
AGO  EROICA  EVEN
YEN  CUTIN  DEWS
```

278

```
LAD  NORAD  ACED
ICED  ELATE  SURE
MACEBEARER  CRIB
PROBED  ETA  ORES
  AGES  ENJOY
PECTORAL  GOLFER
INLET  VALET  AMI
ATOR  PEPYS  EVIL
NEV  ERROR  STOLE
ORELSE  FESTERED
NIECE   SAAR
RAFT  EXO  TINGED
ALOT  DILLYDALLY
VIOL  ELDER  LOBE
ETTE  DEEDS  WAD
```

279

```
JOSE  HELPS  MOMA
EATS  ELENI  ANEW
TRAPAFOXINAHOLE
ESTAB   NANA
  NIOBE   INTROS
BROADCAST  EMERY
REO  EARTHA  AGIN
AFL  DLI  ILL  GAT
QUIP  ANGELO  ANA
UNTIL  GIVETHEAX
EDENIC  GENIE
  ETRE   OCULO
USETHESPRINKLER
ZASU  SAINT  LANE
ITEM  TINAS  ENOS
```

280

```
  BASES   SAGEST
SAMPLER  SCULLED
AREAWAY  ORDAINS
SIXWASAFRAID
  NYC  REM  IDA
BRAS  APER  JOINS
LAS  EPEE  ROLLIE
OFSEVEN  BECAUSE
ATONES  LACK  TED
TERMS  TOTE  BESS
RTE  OHO  PEA
  SEVENATENINE
FIGHTER  DILATOR
INTERNE  EVENING
GEODES   ERASE
```

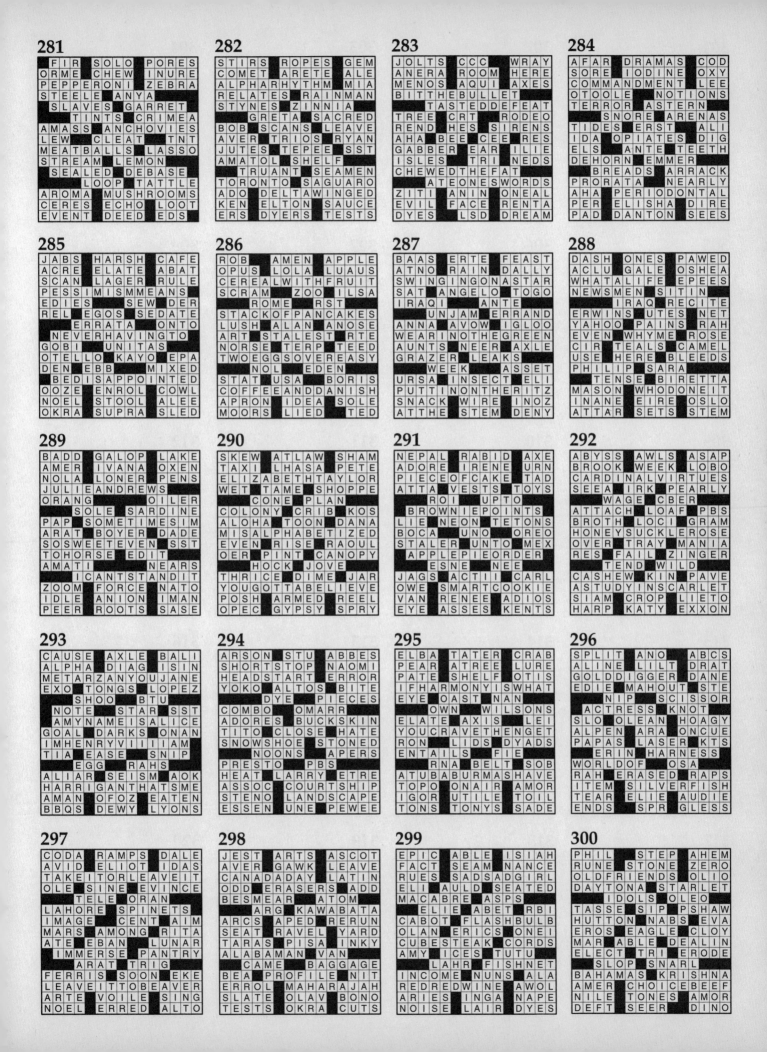

301
GMC TONKA RUMOR
EAU ERROR ENTRE
NYC LOCOMOTIVES
TAKES PERI
SNOUTED SCRUBS
ORATOR AERATE
BBC RAZOR SALON
AILS LEGOS LMNO
STOIC NEVER YES
SECTOR REVERB
SKEWED REPORTS
ABES ABEET
NUTCRACKERS EPA
BRAID CIVET ZIG
ANNAS ADAMS EDS

302
RUFF SKIM SWISH
ORAL WIDE CARLA
MALECATORTURKEY
ANTEUP MUD SES
NIECE STAB POPE
CURE MAIN JAMIE
EMS CAFE TAGEND
DETECTIVE
DAMONE LAMA LOD
OPART WIPE REAR
GRIM JAPE MUCKY
SIT DAN DONATE
TORMENTANDWORRY
ARENA ASIA FREE
RIDOF DALY FEED

303
MILKS EAR MADE
ONAIR OGLE USED
SANDALWOOD LIND
ENID ENSUE EASY
SENECAS EST
REV PUMPEDUP
PIC METER LEAFY
ADOBE AKA ERROL
LEMON NOLTE TSE
SABOTAGE INS
TSP ABSENCE
BOSC PEALE MEAL
ALTA OXFORDIANS
SLAM SIRE ATRIA
HARP ETO BESTS

304
PROM LESS ADALE
AIDA AXEL NEGEV
STOLESECONDBASE
STRIKERS ERASES
GERT USES
SANDS EST ERLE
STLEO ETHOS EER
HELDUPTHERUNNER
ANO TONER NEEDS
HOWL WAR CRIES
AIDS HAIG
ATTUNE AIRSHIPS
MURDEREDTHEBALL
PRIER LIMO OGEE
SNORT STEP ROAD

305
SCAB SEPT BEERS
LATE AVER ALAIN
ONES LEEIACOCCA
TOAST STARK HEP
HEMMER EDGED
YEAS ORATES
ANNEMEARA NOVA
COORS GUY ANTES
ENOS ARIMEYERS
SENORA NASA
NOTES POISED
RIO NOLTE PETER
EDWINMEESE LORE
ELENI CETA LOIS
DENSE TRET ODES

306
CANS MALES ARAB
ABET AROLE LURE
POLA INGOT ETTE
PULLONESPUNCHES
EAT EPA
ANA TAIL SCRIPT
LOVE INIT RODEO
INARINGSIDESEAT
NOSIR ELLE EASE
ESTEEM ETCH LED
NAT KIT
HITBELOWTHEBELT
AREA TIARA ALOE
TONY ELLEN RISE
ENDS DELED SEEN

307
CAMP HAIRS TGIF
OMAR EGRET ARNE
MAYONNAISE PARE
ONAGER STRIPPED
ROYS UNTIE
ETHAN LAP ANJOU
FROM DUB ALGERS
RUT AIRBAGS LGE
ERMINE ODE CLAN
MOUND PTA SAYNO
STORE MAID
WATERING CLEARS
IVAN APRICOTJAM
FORD TAINT TALE
ENDS ALDAS ERLE

308
ADOPT OPP SPRAT
MEDEA ROO ALINE
PLOWRIGHT RANTS
SER TESLA ANDES
CAR TACT
SAVOR CROPEARED
AGIO PLO ENGAGE
RASP RUDER ETRE
AMOEBA IRS NEED
HARROWING TESTS
ANNS BET
ABATE ALIEN ALI
VALID BARNACLES
ASTOR ETA NOLTE
STONY LEN TEASE

309
VOWS BOCA LAMA
ADEN CARAT ETES
LIEU ABELL OWLS
EDGARALLANPOET
GUT ENCORES
MAILROOM TALKS
ROSEANNEBARD
TKO TAE ALI
WINONAWRITER
EDINA TRAINEES
STYLING TOP
CHESTERAAUTHOR
UNDO TENDS AXED
DOIN TAKEI SEND
SSNS ETAS ENDS

310
PAM YUM JEDI
ALCAPONE SHAVEN
QUINQUAGENARIAN
UNDER CIG DDE
AGIT MIGHT LESE
SEC PEROT PINED
BANAL INCA
ALBUQUERQUE
RDAS CLAUS
BEAST SKATE STA
ACME DOYLE ELEM
SOW RIO ASONE
QUEBECNORDIQUES
UNSAFE CONDUCTS
ETTA TWA EHS

311
SPAR MAC CRASS
PALE EARL EERIE
ISAW ATTU LAINE
THROWTHEBULL
AKRON MATURE
KNOWTHEROPES
DEIST ROOK REDS
ELL PARTI NYE
MELT ATAT ALDEN
ONAHIGHHORSE
SATIRE ATALE
RIDEFORAFALL
BRASS BONE LIVE
SUITE BEAR EKES
ANDYS SSN TASS

312
STAMP SELF MALT
MARIE LIAR ELIE
OCEAN ARIA MOON
GOA COVERGROUND
FIXE GIRDS
SHILLYSHALLY
LAMAS ELEE COT
ARAB WRAPS PAPA
PEN BEAT EATEN
RUSHHEADLONG
VAULT RBIS
FIDDLEABOUT ETC
LODE RHOD OMAHA
OLES NONE ROVER
PART SPED SWEET

313
WIDE CAMEL NOVA
ABUT ANAGE ALAN
FATHERKNOWSBEST
TRY XRAYS OBOE
APO ELI
THEMOTHERSINLAW
WARPS ASIS GALE
ERA TATTLER PTS
ESSO SLOE UPSET
THESNOOPSISTERS
TON GSA
TIES LAINE FBI
DRJOYCEBROTHERS
TIKI BABAR ORAL
SOLD CHASE ONCE

314
MESTA ALUMS JAM
ICHOR NATES UTE
CHINARIVERA LOA
HONK ETAPE SILL
IOTAS SHOALS
FRONTAL TALC
LAM CRANI TAHOE
ARAM DOURO NINA
GENOA STABS LES
STIR NEAREST
ASHORE CLYDE
STAR SCREE BAAL
IER POLANDJOFFE
DEI ELAND OZARK
ELF NEWEL TOROS

315
ELMO PESO ADHOC
DOIN AVER GEENA
WASTETIME ALLOW
AFLASHLIGHTIS
REAPS OWE ITS
DRY CORNY KNEW
SPORE TAKEI
ACANFORCARRYING
DORIC OXEYE
ACCT AGNES FOP
MAH RIO FORCE
DEADBATTERIES
SAUDI BROWNBELT
ARKIN LAMA IDOL
PIETY EBBS TATE

316
SHOT SLAB LOTTO
PUMA LALA ELIOT
URAL AMOS ADEPT
MONKEYBUSINESS
ENISLE ONE
ERMA TRAGIC
ASWAN AMOR GENA
THEMARXBROTHERS
MIRE HIES OAKIE
EVENSO ROAN
ADS PISTOL
ANIMALCRACKERS
STAMP ALIT ANNA
CANAL MATH TOOT
INANE SWAY ENTS

317
DETAT STAR ICES
AZURE POLE WILE
LITER ITIS ODIN
YOUARELOVE NETS
EXT ELMTREE
QUAY AMP LTD
URGE MILE MATZO
ASIS SLASH NOON
DANTE KITE COOT
ELK DIM ELMO
GSTRING MAD
OPED OLMANRIVER
TUNA WAIT ASIDE
TREY IDLE FANGS
ANTS TEDS TWEET

318
CRAB MAJA HASUP
LETO AFOR EXALT
INTO IFAT LEXUS
FAITHDANIELS
FIL ASI SNO IQS
SLANT ROTC MAUI
ETH DIORAMAS
HOPEANDCROSBY
REPARTEE EMU
OREL TARS ARMED
ZEN SIR OWN ANA
SWEETCHARITY
KAFKA ARIA ALIT
ALLEY SEAL ZERO
YEOWS TELE EDEN

319
YAMS MULE HERON
ALAW ASIA ELATE
WAXINGNOSTALGIC
PRINCE NEED ASK
GOLF LARK
PAS SLOG SOREST
ESPO AGRA OUNCE
SHININGEXAMPLES
TOTEM YELP PANT
STEPPE DEPP ITY
MIRA SALK
AUG SERE ROASTS
FLUSHINGNEWYORK
ANSEL EGON ALAI
RATTY LOST KEPT

320
MAS GOLF DALLAS
IDOLATER ORIENT
DOLOROSO OCTANE
ARFS MINSTREL
SNEE STER ESSE
GRACE SCAR
BOG SHEA LESLIE
ELI TIMBRES ARK
ADORES MUNI RAE
ERMA SCRAG
BRAT WASH PHDS
REFRAINS LEAP
ALTAIC FALSETTO
NEEDLE OPERATED
STRESS REDO ODE

321

```
SLAG  SHUN  SPOIL
HIRE  COSA  HENCE
ALAS  ROSS  ARTIE
HITTHETRAIL  HER
     ABES  ELMERS
COUPON   UPROAR
ALPO  ETRE  TROOP
RET  ERASERS  CPO
ASHEN  LANE  AKIN
ENABLE   AMUSED
TACOMA   SCAT
RRR  OVERTHEHILL
ATEAR  LEAF  OLAY
LIEGE  MILO  RISE
ASKED  ONER  SETS
```

322

```
SHAKE  FLAB  SPEW
TOLET  IOWA  NOAH
AMANCALLEDHORSE
BENT  MEL  MARKET
     HOOT  PORT
ADORNS  CHUM  SIT
GARBO  SHOT  KANE
AFTERTHETHINMAN
TOOK  WACO  COOLS
EEN  JOCK  LOCALE
     BACK  PINK
ACTIVE  WIZ  DEMO
TARZANTHEAPEMAN
OPIE  TOOT  HAIKU
PEST  SWAY  IDLES
```

323

```
RPM  BLOWIT  WAT
LEAN  EATERY  IDO
SPRINGSTEEN  NUN
EXPO       NEATLY
   PROBATE  LETS
DUTY  DELI  WAR
ICH  INAT  ONTHE
OLE  GETBACK  HOW
RAFER  SANE  USE
ALE  EMIL  ARES
ILLS  ENACTED
SOLEIL    MAIN
EGG  DONNASUMMER
EAU  OPIATE  SAVE
ANY  LEANER  NAB
```

324

```
BLOW  SINK  RIGS
YODA  CRUE  EDNA
EXAM  HAMEL  DEAL
   PINEBLUFFARK
ACURA     NBA
PALMSPRINGSCA
ORE  SINES  ERMA
TORS  STE  DRAT
SNIT  WEEDS  EMT
CEDARRAPIDSIA
EEN       ROUTE
OAKRIDGETENN
AREA  SONIA  CUJO
RING  BIND  EGOS
SATE  IDES  SHES
```

325

```
ANTI  ADAM  SCAB
MOON  NINES  PASO
PROPAGANDA  ANTS
SALUTE   ELASTIC
   TELECAST  ENS
HUP  EVA  ABEL
ERIC  SINS  AGOOD
ASCOT  LSU  YOURE
PACER  SENS  SPAN
ADAR  CUT  ELY
STD  CANOPIES
CHINESE   GRATIS
RELY  PARAMEDICS
IDLE  STELA  ALOT
MAYS  ODES  TENS
```

326

```
DIME  CHIRP  URAL
ISIS  HONOR  NONE
CAMPAIGNBUTTONS
EYE  IMAS  NOISES
   WREN  BELL
STEAMS  NULL  AKA
TANTE  DELL  ARAP
ABSENTEEBALLOTS
FOUR  OLDS  ALLIE
FOE  CRAY  STOLES
   ARTY  ALIT
BOOHOO  JUAN  SEE
UNDECIDEDVOTERS
DEEM  SADIE  EXIT
SASS  EMITS  DYNE
```

327

```
PAGE  SOLD  ADAM
OLAN  ELIAS  CORE
LAIC  TASSE  REAL
ONTOPOFTHEWORLD
     DAN  DAS
RACER  STS  STAMP
ERA  ORNATE  IDEA
MIDDLEAMERICANS
USER  DIPPED  MIT
SETUP  LAS  ILENE
     TOT  BOO
ONTHEBOTTOMLINE
MORE  ARIEL  ISAY
EVER  RELET  TIRE
NAYS  LESS  ASKS
```

328

```
ABCS  SHAMU  LAZE
BOUT  NOLAN  OMAN
BASEBALLDIAMOND
ART  LIES  VASES
   ONEL  AMEN
JAMESSPADER  RES
ELMOS  ELVIS  ELI
ALA  ARLEN  TID
NED  ELMER  BRAHE
EYE  JOINTHECLUB
   BEET  ALAI
ADHOC  ZINC  AHA
HEARTBREAKHOTEL
ALTO  BINGE  NEAP
BIEN  SPOOR  OSLO
```

329

```
FALLS  OGLED  SAW
AWAIT  FROME  ARA
RACKETFACES  DEN
GREENE   FOREHAND
ODDS  MST  GRETAS
     APT  SETS
BACKCOURT   TAIL
OLLIE  FIR  AISLE
SAUL   FOOTFAULT
     MISS  KIT
MEREST  EEL  SCAN
OVERHEAD   TROUPE
NET  TENNISELBOW
ARR  ALTAR  AVERT
STY  REESE  PESTS
```

330

```
CAJUN  FLEW  ALEC
ANITA  LOKI  BAJA
WOTAN  EDEN  APES
   THEREISNOSUCH
ATE  TUT  INEPT
BERATE   PEPYS
AMBLE  CODEX  CUP
SPUE  THING  BOHR
HOG  LHASA  PIQUE
   KEENE  TENURE
OLIVA  BAT  IAN
ASALITTLEDULL
BAUM  ERIN  NOLAN
OGRE  RAZE  ISERE
YEAR  SPAT  ASSET
```

331

```
ASTO  SIMP  TAMPA
CAMS  ODIE  OREOS
THESUNALSORISES
ELNINO  TORS  ATT
     ETRE  SNOB
MAD  RAGU  ISRAEL
ADIEU  GNAT  ISLA
PLANETOFTHEAPES
LENA  UNIT  ARENT
ERECTS  TAMS  NAS
   TOCK  RAES
ABC  WAIT  RUCKUS
MOONANDSIXPENCE
POLAR  DARE  NELL
STAND  SRAS  TEAL
```

332

```
HASPS  RESET  SST
OLSEN  IMPEI  MAE
PIECEOFCAKE  ARM
   KEPLER  WRAP
REPARTEE   BLITHE
EXIT     BLANC
VIE  HIPBOOT  OAK
ELI  ONEINCH  ODE
LEN  VANDYKE  KAY
   TREND  LIME
ADHERE   SEAMLESS
SEED     BORNEO
CBS  THECANDYMAN
ARK  SOAKS  IDAHO
PAY  PERSE  ASWAN
```

333

```
MATS  TROT  LOANS
ALIT  RENE  INDIA
SOLO  IBIS  TOOTS
CUTOFBUTTER  GAS
     PIES  LENO
FIFERS   ABSORBS
ANODE  SINO  DART
MOO  SETDOWN  CUE
ENDS  LEON  ORATE
RECORDS   DIETER
   OBIE  SASE
AGO  FRUITCENTER
BIKEL  STAR  TOBE
ALENE  NERO  EGAN
BARED  AMEN  RAND
```

334

```
SAS  DRABS  ANJOU
ELO  RADON  SEALS
LIL  SHOWOFHANDS
MAEVE    SUET
ASSAULT   TARIFF
   UNSEAT  RADIAL
LAP  SARIS  YENTA
EXPO  PIETA  AGAR
ALONG  QUAKE  ELK
HEROES  PRIMER
   STREEP  KNEEPAD
WEAK     REACH
MOUTHPIECES  ITO
OMANI  NEATO  NOT
MERTZ  ELLEN  TRI
```

335

```
FAP  BEAN  CLASP
KIWI  RENO  LANCE
IFATFIRST  ANTES
STRIDE   YOUDONT
SEDER  EDENS  NEL
MEED  BLUTO  WIRE
END  PEEK  AHOY
   SUCCEEDSO
ABIT  DRIP  CIO
FUEL  AWORD  MANN
AGA  ADAMS  FENCE
MUCHFOR   IRONED
ISHOT  SKYDIVING
STAKE  AWEE  ELSE
HAMER  WHAM  RYE
```

336

```
LAMP  CASAS  THUD
AREA  OMEGA  EERY
WINDSHIELD  RAGE
SADDLE   RETARDED
   LINT  TOTALS
ASSET  ADS  LII
REPS  ACE  MANGOS
CPA  AGONIES  HAM
STRICT  SON  ETTE
   ECT  DEN  PASSE
STEELE   SLUR
CHILDISH  ALFRED
RARE  SPARKPLUGS
APES  TORTE  ADAM
MESS  STEER  PEDS
```

337

```
RIMS  PACT  ESTOP
OTIC  ALLA  AMALE
MOMANDPOPSTORES
PRIMER  YEA  OAST
     POEM  VAT
DALE  SISTERHOOD
OMAR  SHADE  HIE
RINSE  HER  STALL
ISA  DIALS  OREL
CHILDSPLAY  REDS
     AAA  LADE
SPAT  IDS  PRIEST
LIKEADUTCHUNCLE
ICING  CLUE  TRON
TANTE  TORT  OUTS
```

338

```
NEST  LOX  FOCAL
EXPO  VARY  ATARI
CHIEFCRAZYHORSE
TAT  IRV  ODOR
ALERT  ACLU  LYES
REDO  TERI  HEIDI
   AIR  OLGA  NIX
CURTISSTRANGE
BOP  BOOS  AGE
AISLE  FUZZ  HOME
ANTE  PAPA  MILAN
AGOG  PAL  IRA
WEIRDALYANKOVIC
ERRED  PUTT  DENT
BASES  SPA  EROS
```

339

```
NAP  BOLD  ELGAR
IBIS  ASIA  MEARA
NECK  WHEW  MAMMY
JEKYLLANDHYDE
ATSEA  LOS  CPA
   SPORTED  TOES
SRS  EDNA  DICES
HECKLEANDJECKLE
ALOES  DEAL  SSS
PITY  LAYAWAY
ETC  EEL  NESTS
   HIDEANDGOSEEK
AGING  SORE  ETTE
RANGE  KANE  SURE
CIGAR  AMOK  PAT
```

340

```
EVEN  AMASS  AVON
MIRO  LANCE  DEMO
INAMILLION  HEIR
ROSALIE  ROBERTA
   DES  ACRES
CELS  ONTHEAISLE
RYE  SNIT  SMOKED
ADAPT  BIO  ENURE
MIRIAM  RETD  LON
PENNYOPERA  ELIS
   TONES  LAM
ANDANTE   SLEIGHT
HARI  ONTHEFLOOR
EVEL  YESES  IOWA
MEWS  ADEPT  ONLY
```

341
```
CONS  SLAP  SODAS
AHEM  TARA  HAITI
MAGI  AMIN  ARMOR
PRETTYPENNY  ENS
SEVERE  LEANON
    EDD  MELONS
TOQUE  AIDE  IVEY
ABUT  INKED  VERN
COAT  REEL  WELDS
TERESA  ABA
TRINES  ACORNS
HOE  NICKELODEON
APRON  RIDS  OBIE
WILDE  ULNA  RUSE
KEYED  SLAM  STER
```

342
```
HEMP  DIANE  AMEN
AVER  INCAN  MAMA
REMOTEFEED  AKIN
PROMOTES  ESTERS
OER  BASIC
SECOND  TARS  HAG
CLANS  MAKE  MALL
ATTU  PAWED  ONTO
ROSS  INNS  LOGES
ENC  MANY  ROGERS
ROANS  MIT
ADAGIO  SALTINES
MODE  LITTLEROCK
MOLE  ACUTE  ASHE
ORES  SINES  SHOW
```

343
```
LEAD  EMMA  OMNI
AXLE  AVOID  RUIN
PIANOBENCH  ISNO
TITLE  GEORGIAN
IDLER  CHIC
ALOSS  REF  ONSET
VERT  LOLLED  TEE
AVG  KID  USA  ARS
SEA  NIECES  SNIT
TENSE  DAN  LODES
PEER  STAID
SKILLETS  WEAVE
TAPE  GUITARPICK
ALEC  ANNOY  ONCE
NEST  NEIN  PEEN
```

344
```
SHAH  REAR  SCRAP
LOLA  ENDE  THEME
OVAL  DEAF  RENEW
PERFORMMUSICON
ELM  NAY  SACK
KEW  NEXT  ADO
ADIEU  BONO  AJAX
TAKEPARTINAGAME
TWIN  BUCK  LOREN
AND  BASH  NAG
BOSH  TOM  PJS
SCOPEFORMOTION
DUANE  IDEA  AQUA
MERGE  RIND  RUSK
ZZTOP  ENDS  PETE
```

345
```
SARI  AZTEC  VIAL
OPEN  PEONY  ENDE
FRESHBROOD  DECAF
TILTA  OKS  ORANT
ARPS  STENOS
ANTLER  SAWED
FOWLMOUTHED  ELM
AVIS  SPOON  BRAE
RAN  SPORTSCOOPS
SCENE  ORLOPS
ONECAR  ENID
ROMAN  SOD  SNEAD
BUILTUPHERPECKS
ISLE  SUNNY  SHIM
TEES  AROSE  SONS
```

346
```
TANS  RILED  ADAM
ABEE  EDINA  LIRA
BOWLEDOVER  ISEE
OUTLAW  KASHA
OTO  ROTS  ETTE
SNOOPERS  DAN
ALFA  DORA  EBONY
LEONA  BIT  ARUDE
DARED  INST  ATAT
ARK  MUGGIEST
LAIT  SNAP  BIN
PINTO  SALINE
DEFT  PLATEMAKER
ASTI  ILLER  REPO
BOSS  ABIES  ARTS
```

347
```
SOLAR  ORA  BARED
ERODE  ROB  AWARE
LEGAL  GOB  LAIRS
FLORIDAMARLINS
EON  HOT
ARRIVE  SPIT  PTL
SHERE  OPEN  SOHO
COLORADOROCKIES
ODIN  COOK  RINSE
TAC  WORK  CENTER
OER  BOA
EXPANSIONTEAMS
ACRES  ADS  UNLIT
SHARE  LEO  ROONE
LOYAL  SAX  ESTES
```

348
```
TONED  PAP  COCOA
ANODE  IRA  LEAKY
LEWIS  EEL  ARTIE
CUTSCORNERS  AES
SPOORS  TROPIC
NILE  ASTORS
AMS  BOLGER  EMEU
GEESE  BAR  EMBED
ANTI  SADISM  SDS
RUSSIA  NOUS
FINITO  BLAMES
USO  FLUFFSALINE
SPREE  BTU  TANTE
METER  BED  EMEER
ACHES  SND  DIORS
```

349
```
MALT  ACAD  TEAM
ARIA  SABIN  HIRE
TEMPTPROVIDENCE
ASPERITY  ARREST
ARE  AGEE
RESIDE  CLAW  ALI
ORATE  THOR  SNIT
GOTOSEAINASIEVE
EDEN  MILE  CLAIM
RED  LOLL  CHORDS
SITS  MAO
ASSISI  CAROUSAL
SLEEPONAVOLCANO
HANG  NOVEL  LINT
ETTE  DENS  ALAS
```

350
```
SPELLS  AMERICA
STADIUM  BOLIVAR
TASTELESSREMARK
ARS  DULL  EVENT
IVES  LOSSES
RESURGE  ION  ASK
SEADOG  GLUE
JUDICIALHEARING
ISEE  RETIRE
MEN  PEA  UNTAMED
SULTAN  TEAR
LHASA  ISAK  ATO
TOUCHTELEPHONES
ANGRIER  ERASERS
RESENDS  NINERS
```

351
```
JUDO  PCT  TACOS
ASAP  ALOE  APORT
ROPERPOLL  CIRCE
NARWALS  EDAM
SALINES  ACCESS
OPINES  HANSEL
LANGE  KORDA  LAD
ACES  TASTY  AHSO
REB  THREE  BRUCE
AFIELD  PARLOR
SACRED  BASALTS
TIKI  ASPIRIN
ARENA  STRINGERS
VERGE  TADS  ERIK
ESSES  SSS  DENY
```

352
```
CHIP  CALM  ASPIE
HALE  OPIE  MYERS
ASIA  RHEA  ANTES
THERESISTANCE
WED  LLD  RAP
GAMBIT  COLA  LEI
OCEAN  LAO  PONG
CHARGEDAFFAIRES
AILS  LIP  SPRAT
RET  UMPS  CHEESY
TRISES  SUE
COURTANDSPARK
FAKIR  IHAD  ORAL
OBESE  COIL  SIZE
EATER  KYLE  HAZE
```

353
```
MERGE  POP  IHAVE
ONEAL  EMU  TEPID
ZIPPINGONESLIPS
ASAS  EGOTRIP
RLS  CEY  INSEAM
TETRAD  TSE  DNA
ARETHA  CONKS
ZIPADEEDOODAH
NESTS  AMECHE
BAA  ALE  TASSEL
ALKALI  RON  NNE
TENSEUP  SEGA
ZIPPYTHEPINHEAD
ATEAT  OLE  FORGE
PADRE  EYE  LOSER
```

354
```
BOPS  CLAD  SEERS
ADEN  LAMA  ELLIE
ROSA  OVER  ALIVE
BROKENARROW  TAM
ESE  ENAMELS
ALIST  NINETY
NAT  POD  AERATE
THEMIRRORCRACKD
ERMINE  NET  HOI
TESTED  WREST
ALBERTA  TAI
LOA  TORNCURTAIN
GARNI  TELL  TOTO
ATRIA  ARAL  ENOS
SHELL  ROME  RENE
```

355
```
PAST  RAJA  SNIP
RUER  ADULL  HERE
OREOCOOKIE  EWES
ANJOU  ESPRESSO
ADLIB  TERP
AETNA  DOS  USAGE
PRES  MIXERS  PEA
HAL  POO  ROE  ENG
ISE  INCHED  BRIE
DEVIL  YON  POSER
INAN  REBEL
PASTRAMI  ERODE
ERIE  PUZZLEGRID
PEON  STOOL  NERD
SAND  ENOS  AWES
```

356
```
IRMA  PROS  SARAH
REAL  RARE  ELATE
ARNE  EVER  REPOS
QUICKSILVER  INS
NASAL  ELAND
NEST  STAFFS
ELSA  YEAR  EMILE
RIPS  SAXES  ERIN
ONEND  RENT  SETS
STEERS  SERE
DRAPE  ELOPE
DOS  FASTTALKERS
ITHOT  TOOK  ALAN
STOLE  EDGE  YESI
COPED  ROAD  SEEP
```

357
```
HANA  MACAW  FACT
AJAX  ABASH  ALOU
LAVENDERHILLMOB
FRY  ADEE  TUSSLE
DUET  GERE
RESIGN  COCK  CAT
URIAH  SOFA  BALE
BORNTOTHEPURPLE
IDEA  NEAR  BARON
KEN  CLAN  CAVITY
GOOD  ARNO
ARTURO  SNAG  CBS
SHRINKINGVIOLET
PEAL  EMILE  WARY
SAME  RATED  LYNX
```

358
```
PAID  SAFES  TART
ONTO  DIANA  ALAI
SNOW  ALLOF  KONG
HANNA  ELLA  INGE
TOKYO  RINGER
REVOKE  VYING
ALIT  ABEE  ATLAS
MASH  NORAS  HASH
SNEER  ROSA  ESTE
GALEN  SOPHIA
CHARGE  ETHEL
HALO  CASE  RUMOR
ASOU  TREND  NAVE
STUN  OILED  GLAD
MADD  RAFTS  ELLS
```

359
```
TAPED  BOOS  MAID
STARR  AIDE  ATTA
KITTY  LOOT  HOLM
THECOLORPURPLE
EDS  ORE
STIFLE  TWIN  ESS
CANAL  GRIN  MATA
ARAISININTHESUN
DOLT  NABS  ONEND
STL  ACRE  GLOSSY
SOL  SAD
KNOCKONANYDOOR
ROTO  VERA  OARED
INTO  ERIK  WHINE
SOOT  RODE  NUTTY
```

360
```
GUM  LAIC  SIDES
ONO  PASCH  TBOLT
OBRIANTHEHUNTER
DEADSEA  YEN  EVA
SAVE  BREAKODAY
ORISON  END  NOTE
NSA  PECAN  BYNER
OTOOLEBOX
AMANS  NISAN  SIR
RACE  ACS  NOTONE
OHAIRCUTS  MOSS
UAR  ERR  PIMENTO
SLIPPERYASONEAL
AIDER  EMILE  STE
LASSO  DANE  TED
```

361
```
BMW   CANST BOX
SARAH ELATE RUM
OPENANDSHUT ICE
ISE TORO DRJOHN
MENOTTI  BEAU
  THICKANDTHIN
TOPTEN ANT UNO
ODEON UPS CANTO
SIE OSU BOSTON
HEREANDTHERE
  INSA ABRADES
MAINST LUAU RAP
IQS WARANDPEACE
SUM EGYPT TOTHE
TAS REEDS SSS
```

362
```
MAMA OHARA JAR
AVES RERAN PANE
REDHERRING ACTS
TRIAD SAIL SKIT
STAMEN  SEATS
  ENOLA SLOPES
LAPD RIGS ARROW
ALI SMELTER ANA
BIKEL NOLA ITSY
STENOS WORDS
  STEWS SERIAL
ROPE OPIE PANDA
OVER OLDCAPECOD
MAAS PAEON LARD
ELK STAND INNS
```

363
```
LAC MASSE TACOS
ISH ARYAN UPPER
LTA SINGLESBARS
ARIAS  EARS
CONGEAL ISLETS
LAYLOW TETHER
ESE STORM SAUTE
ROTH STOOL SNUB
ALTOS SNOOP DPS
SIESTA GRILLE
DREAMS SNEERED
  REAR AMBLE
AUBURNLOCKS OBL
MAINE EMCEE LOT
BROOD SPINS TWA
```

364
```
TANS RAPID ADDA
NOAH EMILY LRON
UNIONJACKS AERO
TELECAST LASSEN
  TAIS PECKS
AMORAL TAXTABLE
NAVE FOLIO AID
THEELGINMARBLES
ERR ERNES ALTO
DETRAINS BENSON
HARMS MARK
STERNA PARANOIA
LITE CELLBLOCKS
AMOS ELATE THEY
WEPT DINAR ESSE
```

365
```
LAPS NOLTE BOLL
ARLO OMAHA OKIE
VIOLINBOWS TREE
AZTEC SAT TASK
  MEGA REDO
WINDINSTRUMENT
EAN LIL ASNER
LID ILLEGAL AAA
AVION POE CRY
LEADGUITARISTS
  DENS LOST
WEBB ARE IONIA
AQUA BASSSTRING
LULL LETIT ELSE
KILL ELATE SETS
```

366
```
AMAD FLOP ARCED
ROTO RIME LAURA
CHOWLINES LIRAS
HANNA ENTRUST
EVA SONS IDEATE
RELETS AMERIND
  GETUPS LTD
  BOXERSHORTS
ASU STEREO
SULTANA SANDER
PELOTA IDOL ALA
PROPANE TAMER
CREEL PUPPYLOVE
ANNUL ISTO ONES
RASPS GEST WENT
```

367
```
AGOG ARISE PLAT
LUPE TENON RAMA
FRENCHCUFF ITIN
SUNDAE STORMING
  ANISE LOAN
BEDREST DOLLAR
ALUM MEREST ORE
LITE NAV AVON
SAC BLOWER VEST
ASHORE REVERES
TMAN STAIR
PARENTAL CASALS
REEL IRISHLINEN
IRAE LUCIE ONEI
MOTT SNERD NEST
```

368
```
LADLE ABRAM CHI
AVAIL WAYNE AIM
WOLFMANJACK RGT
SWEETPEA HOHOHO
  RED RONALD
ARGUES GURGLE
BOONE TABE SKID
CLOD CUPID TITO
DODY OXEN BONZO
MITRED HANGAR
CANONS MOR
JUNGLE PALOALTO
AKA ELLERYQUEEN
DOC DIARY UNCLE
ARE OAKES ETHER
```

369
```
SCAM CHAW CASAS
AONE LIMO APPLE
WATCHEDPOTSBOIL
SLICER SEE IBM
  ARID REGALIA
COQ SHUT SALS
IOUS ERAT TOPAZ
THECOWSCOMEHOME
ESSAY TONE ARMS
ALLS STEM TOT
MODESTY OKIE
ANI AIL NAVAJO
HELLFREEZESOVER
AMLIT LIES KIEL
LOADS DADS ESPY
```

370
```
POISE SHIFT PIG
ALLEN TORRE ORE
WISECRACKER KIN
SOAK ARK ERNEST
  EMITS POUR
FISTED CORNCOB
ANKHS ONOR SHOE
IDI HEXNUTS IZE
TINA VEEP UPPER
HANGTEN BRASSY
YARN SIREN
MADRAS ANA CARP
OUI DOUBLEDATES
PEP EUBIE IKONS
ELS STINT DEPOT
```

371
```
SPAS PRONG SOAP
HELP LONER TART
ATLI AMUSE ETTA
GRANITESTARE
SINES STALLED
  TIARA REEVE
LTD STONEMARTEN
ARE NAIVE TNT
ROCKCONCERT STS
KOALA ELVIS
SPLURGE CHORE
GRAVELVOICED
CLAM MARIA NAPA
AIDA EDITS ELAM
MEAN RENEE SAYS
```

372
```
BLOC SLOP VOCAL
LANE CARE AMUSE
EYEOPENER LITHE
ELI UNDO PUTTER
DANGLE FRESH
ASSAILED RAG
ADORE TRAP SOSO
LINT SHAMS CAST
MOTH COTE COTTA
ASH NAMEDROP
ELIDE OMELET
TENONS BEAM AXE
ELOPE EARMARKED
ASSET BRIE NERD
REEDY BRED ARTY
```

373
```
SLAW MALT ROONE
TOSH OBEY ACRES
ACHYBREAKYHEART
MAO ALTHEA ANDA
PLEASES HANG
REY TAOS EAT
SUIT SAMOA ANA
ITSYBITSYSPIDER
PAL UNITS NEWT
SHA SERE SAN
NUTS TENSPOT
ODDS SAVORY RAE
DEMISEMIQUAVERS
EVANS BAUM IGET
SONGS ILES CODY
```

374
```
HEMI PIGS STEM
ITALS AWOL AERO
FALLINLOVE LEIS
ITISTOO TIRADES
PERMA GEM
CHE MARCHWINDS
CLANG THEO OOH
HOSTAGE ADVERSE
OTT GROW EAVES
CHARGECARD SOD
ALA COATI
FAUCETS GLENDAS
LICK FIREENGINE
IDLE UNIT TUNER
PEAT NEDS PETE
```

375
```
FUDD SEMI STRAD
ASEA PROM HAILE
VERYHARDPROBLEM
ERASER ASOF EXO
SST YELL TAD
MYRA STRANGE
AEREO BATE LOUS
PROTUBERANTLUMP
BITE ALAR WASPY
SNORERS ICES
SIR ASHE LST
AWL LENS ITLIKE
SEAVELOCITYUNIT
ALLIE DOLT NEMO
PLAIN STAY ASSN
```

376
```
MITTS INLET MAP
IDIOT OFAGE IDO
NEPLUSULTRA NAM
KASDAN HER UMP
SLY RACE TOSS
ITZHAK FOCUS
JOHN ZETA FLUSH
ALAS YACHT OLEO
VIRUS TRUE NEST
ANDRE SONTAG
TEND WARD EBB
CHI EEL AVOWAL
HEM GREATDIVIDE
IRE ABODE SINGE
CBS LYNDE EDGED
```

377
```
CLAP SLOOP BLOW
HARI LEAVE RULA
EDIT OTTER ELEC
REACT THROWRUGS
INSHAPE STY
FRERE SESTET
BABO LEX SLAVE
AGAR EDICT IKES
JERKS TUB NESS
ADESTE STANG
ILL EROSION
FIREFLIES SHOVE
ONEAL MAIL ONES
ERASE EVEL TINT
SIRES SERB SASS
```

378
```
GAGA GUSTO CHAS
ENOS ENTER HOLY
LENT MIRED ERIN
TWERP TIMER NCO
WARDEN ROUSED
BOILED GASTRO
AFT FATAL SAFER
JOHN YALTA LALO
AZTEC KOALA DEN
HARDEN ULTIMA
CHERIE GAMBOL
HEW BLOWN ADEPT
IRIS UNION AMIE
NONO DITTO TMEN
ANDY ETHER EAST
```

379
```
BOTH SLAVS SINO
ABRA PUREE KNOB
COATHANGER ERIE
HEP ERGO ELLERY
CASE KNEE
SMOTE BLASTOFF
WHIM LIED OVAL
ARAB CUTIE NIKE
DEMI OMEN KNEW
SWINDLES SPEED
ANON SPRY
BANTAM FARO FAD
ALAI BRUTEFORCE
DINO IONIA REEF
ETON AIDED BEST
```

380
```
REYKJAVIK ISA
AMERICANAS NEW
TONIGHTSHOW SRO
SGT ENNE TIL
NAB LUST TARIFF
ABILENE ASET
DOLE GEORGEBUSH
IDLER IRA LOTTO
RECREATING LIAR
LEND DOCTORS
ABIDED MICA NEE
HEN ESAI ARM
MIT SUMMERHOMES
AGO PUERTORICO
DEN ROSSPEROT
```

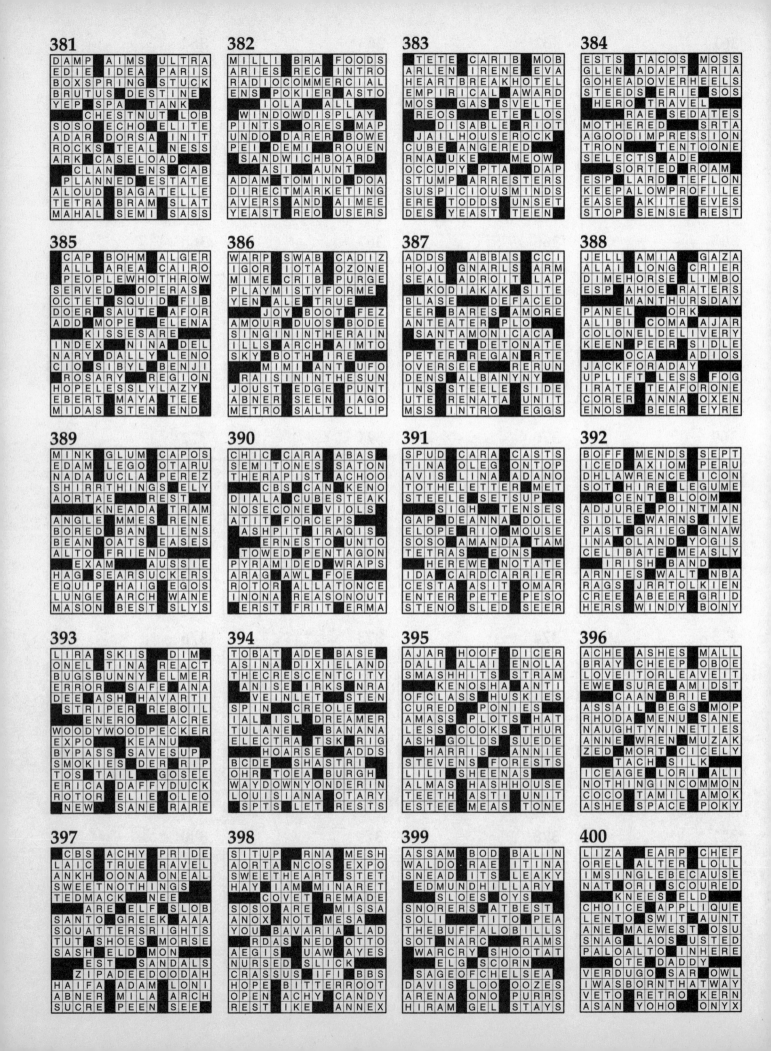

381
```
DAMP  AIMS  ULTRA
EDIE  IDEA  PARIS
BOXSPRING  STUCK
BRUTUS  DESTINE
YEP  SPA  TANK
  CHESTNUT  LOB
SOSO  ECHO  ELITE
ADAR  DORSA  INIT
ROCKS  TEAL  NESS
ARK  CASELOAD
  CLAN  ENS  CAB
PLANNED  ESTATE
ALOUD  BAGATELLE
TETRA  BRAM  SLAT
MAHAL  SEMI  SASS
```

382
```
MILLI  BRA  FOODS
ARIES  REC  INTRO
RADIOCOMMERCIAL
ENS  POKIER  ASTO
   IOLA  ALL
 WINDOWDISPLAY
PINTS  ORES  MAP
UNDO  DARER  BOWE
PEI  DEMI  ROUEN
SANDWICHBOARD
   ASI  AUNT
ADAM  TOMIND  DOA
DIRECTMARKETING
AVERS  AND  AIMEE
YEAST  REO  USERS
```

383
```
TETE  CARIB  MOB
ARLEN  IRENE  EVA
HEARTBREAKHOTEL
EMPIRICAL  AWARD
MOS  GAS  SVELTE
REOS  ETE  LOS
  DISABLE  RIOT
JAILHOUSEROCK
CUBE  ANGERED
RNA  UKE  MEOW
OCCUPY  PTA  DAP
STUMP  ARRESTERS
SUSPICIOUSMINDS
ERE  TODDS  UNSET
DES  YEAST  TEEN
```

384
```
ESTS  TACOS  MOSS
GLEN  ADAPT  ARIA
GOHEADOVERHEELS
STEEDS  ERIE  SOS
 HERO  TRAVEL
  RAE  SEDATES
MOTHERED  SRTA
AGOODIMPRESSION
TRON  TENTOONE
SELECTS  ADE
  SORTED  ROAM
ESP  LARD  TEFLON
KEEPALOWPROFILE
EASE  AKITE  EVES
STOP  SENSE  REST
```

385
```
 CAP  BOHM  ALGER
 ALL  AREA  CAIRO
PEOPLEWHOTHROW
SERVED  OPERAS
OCTET  SQUID  FIB
DOER  SAUTE  AFOR
ADD  MOPE  ELENA
  KISSESARE
INDEX  NINA  DEL
NARY  DALLY  LENO
CIO  SIBYL  BENJI
ROSARY  REGION
HOPELESSLYLAZY
EBERT  MAYA  TEE
MIDAS  STEN  END
```

386
```
WARP  SWAB  CADIZ
IGOR  IOTA  OZONE
MIME  CRIB  PURGE
PLAYMISTYFORME
YEN  ALE  TRUE
  JOY  BOOT  FEZ
AMOUR  DUOS  BODE
SINGININTHERAIN
ILLS  ARCH  AIMTO
SKY  BOTH  IRE
 MIMI  ANT  UFO
RAISININTHESUN
JOUST  EDGE  PUNT
ABNER  SEEN  IAGO
METRO  SALT  CLIP
```

387
```
ADDS  ABBAS  CCI
HOJO  GNARLS  ARM
SEAL  ADROIT  LAP
 KODIAKAK  SITE
BLASE  DEFACED
EER  BARES  AMORE
ANTEATER  PLO
SANTAMONICACA
  TET  DETONATE
PETER  REGAN  RTE
OVERSEE  RERUN
DENS  ALBANYNY
INS  STEELE  SIDE
UTE  RENATA  UNIT
MSS  INTRO  EGGS
```

388
```
JELL  AMIA  GAZA
ALAI  LONG  CRIER
DIMEHORSE  LIMBO
ESP  AHOE  RATERS
  MANTHURSDAY
PANEL  ORK
ALIBI  COMA  AJAR
COLONELDELIVERY
KEEN  PEER  SIDLE
   OCA  ADIOS
 JACKFORADAY
UPLIFT  LESS  FOG
IRATE  TEAFORONE
CORER  ANNA  OXEN
ENOS  BEER  EYRE
```

389
```
MINK  GLUM  CAPOS
EDAM  LEGO  OTARU
NADA  UCLA  PEREZ
SHIRRTHINGS  ELY
AORTAE  REST
  KNEADA  TRAM
ANGLE  MMES  RENE
BORED  BAN  LIENS
BEAN  OATS  EASES
ALTO  FRIEND
  EXAM  AUSSIE
HAG  SEARSUCKERS
EQUIP  HAIG  EGOS
LUNGE  ARCH  WANE
MASON  BEST  SLYS
```

390
```
CHIC  CARA  ABAS
SEMITONES  SATON
THERAPIST  ACHOO
 CBS  CAN  KENO
DIALA  CUBESTEAK
NOSECONE  VIOLS
ATIT  FORCEPS
 ASHPIT  IRAQIS
  ERNESTO  UNTO
 TOWED  PENTAGON
PYRAMIDED  WRAPS
ARAG  AWL  FOE
ROTOR  ALLATONCE
INONA  REASONOUT
ERST  FRIT  ERMA
```

391
```
SPUD  CARA  CASTS
TINA  OLEG  ONTOP
AVIS  LINA  ADANO
TOTHELETTER  MET
STEELE  SETSUP
  SIGH  TENSES
GAP  DEANNA  DOLE
ELOPE  RIO  MOUSE
SOSO  AMANDA  TAM
TETRAS  EONS
 HEREWE  NOTATE
IDA  CARDCARRIER
CESTA  ASIT  OMAR
ENTER  PETE  PESO
STENO  SLED  SEER
```

392
```
BOFF  MENDS  SEPT
ICED  AXIOM  PERU
DHLAWRENCE  ICON
SOT  HIRE  LEGUME
  CENT  BLOOM
ADJURE  POINTMAN
SIDLE  WARNS  IVE
PAST  GRIEG  GNAW
INA  OLAND  YOGIS
CELIBATE  MEASLY
  IRISH  BAND
ARNIES  WALT  NBA
RAGS  JRRTOLKIEN
CREE  ABEER  GRID
HERS  WINDY  BONY
```

393
```
LIRA  SKIS  DIM
ONEL  TINA  REACT
BUGSBUNNY  ELMER
ERROR  SAFE  ANA
DEE  ASH  HAVARTI
 STRIPER  REBOIL
 ENERO  ACRE
WOODYWOODPECKER
EXPO  KEANU
BYPASS  SAVESUP
SMOKIES  DER  RIP
TOS  TAIL  GOSEE
ERICA  DAFFYDUCK
ROTOR  ELIE  OLEO
NEW  SANE  RARE
```

394
```
TOBAT  ADE  BASE
ASINA  DIXIELAND
THECRESCENTCITY
 ANISE  IRKS  NRA
 VEINLET  STEN
SPIN  CREOLE
IAL  ISL  DREAMER
TULANE  BANANA
ELECTRA  TSK  RIG
 HOARSE  ADDS
BCDE  SHASTRI
OHR  TOEA  BURGH
WAYDOWNYONDERIN
LOUISIANA  OTARY
SPTS  LET  RESTS
```

395
```
AJAR  HOOF  DICER
DALI  ALAI  ENOLA
SMASHHITS  STRAM
 KENOSHA  ANTI
OFCLASS  HUSKIES
CURED  PONIES
AMASS  PLOTS  HAT
LESS  COOKS  THUR
ASH  GOLDS  SUEDE
 HARRIS  ANNIE
STEVENS  FORESTS
LILI  SHEENAS
ALMAS  HASHHOUSE
TEETH  ASTI  UNIT
ESTEE  MEAS  TONE
```

396
```
ACHE  ASHES  MALL
BRAY  CHEEP  OBOE
LOVEITORLEAVEIT
EWE  SURE  AMIDST
  CAAN  BRIE
ASSAIL  BEGS  MOP
RHODA  MENU  SANE
NAUGHTYNINETIES
ANNE  WREN  MUZAK
ZED  MORT  CICELY
  TACH  SILK
ICEAGE  LORI  ALI
NOTHINGINCOMMON
COCO  TAMIL  AMOK
ASHE  SPACE  POKY
```

397
```
 CBS  ACHY  PRIDE
LAIC  TRUE  RAVEL
ANKH  OONA  ONEAL
SWEETNOTHINGS
TEDMACK  NEE
 ARE  ELF  SLOB
SANTO  GREEK  AAA
SQUATTERSRIGHTS
TUT  SHOES  MORSE
SASH  ELD  MON
   EST  SANDALS
ZIPADEEDOODAH
HAIFA  ADAM  LONI
ABNER  MILA  ARCH
SUCRE  PEEN  SEE
```

398
```
SITUP  RNA  MESH
AORTA  NCOS  EXPO
SWEETHEART  STET
HAY  IAM  MINARET
  COVET  REMADE
SOSO  ARE  MISSA
ANOX  NOT  MESA
YOU  BAVARIA
RDAS  NED  OTTO
AEGIS  UAW  AYES
NURSED  SLICK
CRASSUS  IFI  BBS
HOPE  BITTERROOT
OPEN  ACHY  CANDY
REST  IKE  ANNEX
```

399
```
ASSAM  BOD  BALIN
WALDO  RAE  ITINA
SNEAD  ITS  LEAKY
EDMUNDHILLARY
SLOES  OYS
SNORERS  ATBEST
SOLI  TITO  PEA
THEBUFFALOBILLS
SOT  NARC  RAMS
WARCRY  SHOOTAT
  ELG  SCORN
SAGEOFCHELSEA
DAVIS  LOO  OOZES
ARENA  ONO  PURRS
HIRAM  GEL  STAYS
```

400
```
LIZA  EARP  CHEF
OREL  ALTER  LOLL
IMSINGLEBECAUSE
NAT  ORI  SCOURED
  KNEES  ELD
CHOICE  APPLIQUE
LENTO  SWIT  AUNT
ANE  MAEWEST  OSU
SNAG  LAOS  USTED
PALOALTO  INHERE
  OTE  DADDY
VERDUGO  SAR  OWL
IWASBORNTHATWAY
VETO  RETRO  KERN
ASAN  YOHO  ONYX
```

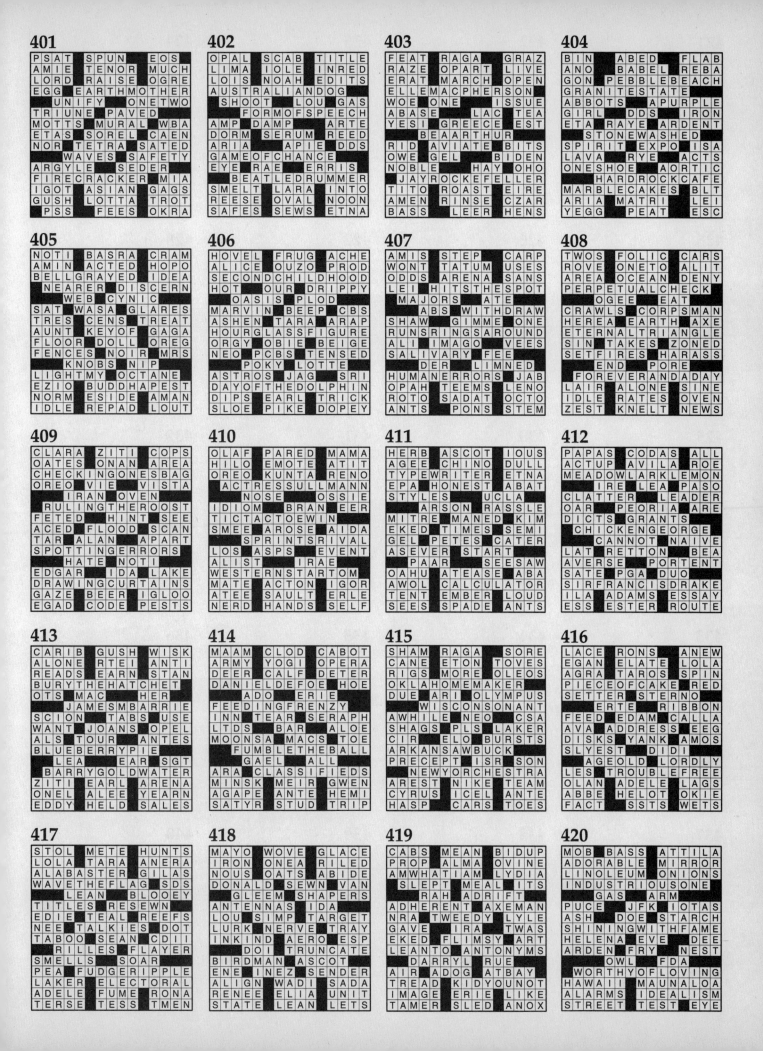

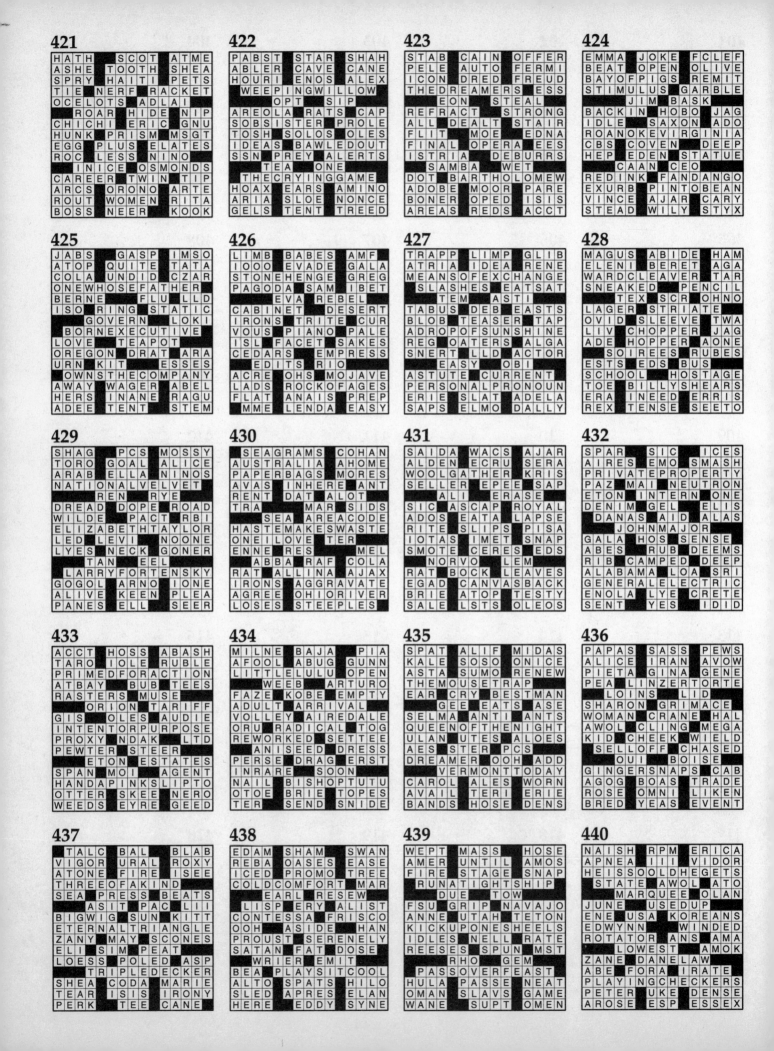

421
HATH·SCOT·ATME
ASHE·TOOTH·SHEA
SPRY·HAITI·PETS
TIE·NERF·RACKET
OCELOTS·ADLAI·
·ROAR·HIDE·NIP
CHICHI·ERIC·GNU
HUNK·PRISM·MSGT
EGG·PLUS·ELATES
ROC·LESS·NINO·
·INICE·OSMONDS
CAREER·TWIN·TIP
ARCS·ORONO·ARTE
ROUT·WOMEN·RITA
BOSS·NEER·KOOK

422
PABST·STAR·SHAH
ABLER·CAVE·CANE
HOURI·ENOS·ALEX
WEEPINGWILLOW·
·OPT···SIP··
AREOLA·RATS·CAP
SOBSISTER·PROLE
TOSH·SOLOS·OLES
IDEAS·BAWLEDOUT
SSN·PREY·ALERTS
··TEA···ONE·
·THECRYINGGAME
HOAX·EARS·AMINO
ARIA·SLOE·NONCE
GELS·TENT·TREED

423
STAB·CAIN·OFFER
PELE·AUTO·FERMI
ICON·DRED·FREUD
THEDREAMERS·ESS
··EON·STEAL··
REFRACT·STRONG
ALL·DEALT·STAIR
FLIT·MOE·EDNA
FINAL·OPERA·EES
ISTRIA·DEBURRS
··SAMBA·WET··
DOT·BARTHOLOMEW
ADOBE·MOOR·PARE
BONER·OPED·ISIS
AREAS·REDS·ACCT

424
EMMA·JOKE·FCLEF
BEAT·OPEN·OLIVE
BAYOFPIGS·REMIT
STIMULUS·GARBLE
···JIM·BASK··
BACKIN·HOBO·JAG
IDLE·SAXON·ADO
ROANOKEVIRGINIA
CBS·COVEN·DEEP
HEP·EDEN·STATUE
··CAAN·CEO···
REDINK·FANDANGO
EXURB·PINTOBEAN
VINCE·AJAR·CARY
STEAD·WILY·STYX

425
JABS·GASP·IMSO
ATOP·QUITE·TATA
COLA·UNDID·CZAR
ONEWHOSEFATHER·
BERNE·FLU·LLD
ISO·RING·STATIC
··GOVERN·LOKI·
·BORNEXECUTIVE
·LOVE·TEAPOT··
OREGON·DRAT·ARA
URN·KIT·ESSES
·OWNSTHECOMPANY
AWAY·WAGER·ABEL
HERS·INANE·RAGU
ADEE·TENT·STEM

426
LIMB·BABES·AMF
1000·EVADE·GALA
STONEHENGE·GREG
PAGODA·SAM·IBET
··EVA·REBEL··
CABINET·DESERT
IRONS·TRITE·CUR
VOUS·PIANO·PALE
ISL·FACET·SAKES
CEDARS·EMPRESS
··EDITS·RIO··
ACRE·OHS·MOJAVE
LADS·ROCKOFAGES
FLAT·ANAIS·PREP
MME·LENDA·EASY

427
TRAPP·LIMP·GLIB
ATRIA·IDEA·RENE
MEANSOFEXCHANGE
·SLASHES·EATSAT
·TEM···ASTI··
TABUS·DEB·EASTS
BLOB·TEASER·TAP
ADROPOFSUNSHINE
REG·OATERS·ALGA
SNERT·LLD·ACTOR
··EASY·OBI···
ASTUTE·CURRENT
PERSONALPRONOUN
ERIE·SLAT·ADELA
SAPS·ELMO·DALLY

428
MAGUS·ABIDE·HAM
ELENI·BERET·AGA
WARDCLEAVER·TAR
SNEAKED·PENCIL
TEX·SCR·OHNO
LAGER·STRIATE·
OVID·SLEEVE·TWA
LIV·CHOPPER·JAG
ADE·HOPPER·AONE
·SOIREES·RUBES
ESTS·EDS·BUS
SCHOOL·HOSTAGE
TOE·BILLYSHEARS
ERA·INEED·ERRIS
REX·TENSE·SEETO

429
SHAG·PCS·MOSSY
TORO·GOAL·ALICE
ARAB·ELLA·NINOS
NATIONALVELVET·
··REN···RYE··
DREAD·DOPE·ROAD
WILDE·PACT·RBI
ELIZABETHTAYLOR
LED·LEVI·NOONE
LYES·NECK·GONER
··TAN·EEL···
·LARRYFORTENSKY
GOGOL·ARNO·IONE
ALIVE·KEEN·PLEA
PANES·ELL·SEER

430
SEAGRAMS·COHAN
AUSTRALIA·AHOME
PAPERBAGS·MORES
AVAS·INHERE·ANT
RENT·DAT·ALOT
TRA·MAR·SIDS
··SEA·AREACODE
HASTEMAKESWASTE
ONEILOVE·TER··
ENNE·RES·MEL
·ABBA·RAF·COLA
RAT·ALLINA·AJAX
IRONS·AGGRAVATE
AGREE·OHIORIVER
LOSES·STEEPLES

431
SAIDA·WACS·AJAR
ALDEN·ECRU·SERA
WOOLGATHER·KRIS
SELLER·EPEE·SAP
··ALI·ERASE··
SIC·ASCAP·ROYAL
ADOS·EATA·LAPSE
RITE·SLIPS·PISA
IOTAS·IMET·SNAP
SMOTE·CERES·EDS
··NORVO·LEM··
RAT·BOCK·LEAVES
EGAD·CANVASBACK
BRIE·ATOP·TESTY
SALE·LSTS·OLEOS

432
SPAR·SIC·ICES
AIRES·EMO·SMASH
PRIVATEPROPERTY
PAZ·MAI·NEUTRON
ETON·INTERN·ONE
DENIM·GEL·ELIS
DANAS·AID·ALAS
·JOHNMAJOR···
GALA·HOS·SENSE
ABES·RUB·DEEMS
RIB·CAMPED·DEEP
ALABAMA·LOA·SRI
GENERALELECTRIC
ENOLA·LYE·CRETE
SENT·YES·IDID

433
ACCT·HOSS·ABASH
TARO·IOLE·RUBLE
PRIMEDFORACTION
ATBAY·BUB·TEES
RASTERS·MUSE··
··ORION·TARIFF
GIS·OLES·AUDIE
INTENTORPURPOSE
PROXY·NDAK·LTD
PEWTER·STEER··
·ETON·ESTATES
SPAN·MOI·AGENT
HANDAPINKSLIPTO
OTTER·SKEE·NERO
WEEDS·EYRE·GEED

434
MILNE·BAJA·PIA
AFOOL·ABUG·GUNN
LITTLELULU·OPEN
··WEEB·ARTURO
FAZE·KOBE·EMPTY
ADULT·ARRIVAL
VOLLEY·AIREDALE
ORU·RADICAL·TOG
REWORKED·SETTEE
·ANISEED·DRESS
PERSE·DRAG·ERST
INRARE·SOON··
NAIL·BISHOPTUTU
OTOE·BRIE·TOPES
TER·SEND·SNIDE

435
SPAT·ALIF·MIDAS
KALE·SOSO·ONICE
ASTA·SUMO·RENEW
THEMOUSETRAP··
EAR·CRY·BESTMAN
··GEE·EATS·ASE
SELMA·ANTI·ANTS
QUEENOFTHENIGHT
ULAN·UTES·ALOES
AES·STER·PCS··
DREAMER·OOH·ADD
··VERMONTTODAY
CAROL·ALES·WORN
AVAIL·TERI·ERIE
BANDS·HOSE·DENS

436
PAPAS·SASS·PEWS
ALICE·IRAN·AVOW
PIETA·GINA·GENE
PEA·LINZERTORTE
·LOINS···LID··
SHARON·GRIMACE
WOMAN·CRANE·HAL
AWOL·CLING·MEGA
KID·CHEEK·WIELD
SELLOFF·CHASED
··OUI···BOISE
GINGERSNAPS·CAB
AGOG·BOAS·TRADE
ROSE·OMNI·LIKEN
BRED·YEAS·EVENT

437
·TALC·BAL·BLAB
VIGOR·URAL·ROXY
ATONE·FIRE·ISEE
THREEOFAKIND··
SEA·PRESS·BEATS
··ASIT·PAC·LII
BIGWIG·SUN·KITT
ETERNALTRIANGLE
ZANY·MAY·SCONES
ELI·SIM·PEAT··
LOESS·POLED·ASP
··TRIPLEDECKER
SHEA·CODA·MARIE
TEAR·ISIS·IRONY
PERK·TEE·CANE

438
EDAM·SHAM·SWAN
REBA·OASES·EASE
ICED·PROMO·TREE
COLDCOMFORT·MAR
··EARL·RESEW··
LISP·ERY·ALIST
CONTESSA·FRISCO
OOH·ASIDE·HAN
PROUST·SERENELY
SATAN·FAT·DOSE
··WRIER·EMIT··
BEA·PLAYSITCOOL
ALTO·SPATS·HILO
SLED·APRES·ELAN
HERE·EDDY·SYNE

439
WEPT·MASS·HOSE
AMER·UNTIL·AMOS
FIRE·STAGE·SNAP
RUNATIGHTSHIP·
···DUE···TOW·
FSU·GRIP·NAVAJO
ANNE·UTAH·TETON
KICKUPONESHEELS
IDLES·NELL·RATE
REESES·SPUN·MST
·RHO···GEM···
·PASSOVERFEAST
HULA·PASSE·NEAT
OMAN·SLAVS·GAME
WANE·SUPT·OMEN

440
NAISH·RPM·ERICA
APNEA·III·VIDOR
HEISSOLDHEGETS
STATE·AWOL·ATO
·MARQUEE·OLAN·
·JUNE·USEDUP··
ENE·USA·KOREANS
EDWYNN·WINDED
ROTATOR·ANS·AMA
··LOWEST·AMOK·
·ZANE·DANELAW·
ABE·FORA·IRATE
PLAYINGCHECKERS
PETER·UKE·DENSE
AROSE·ESP·ESSEX

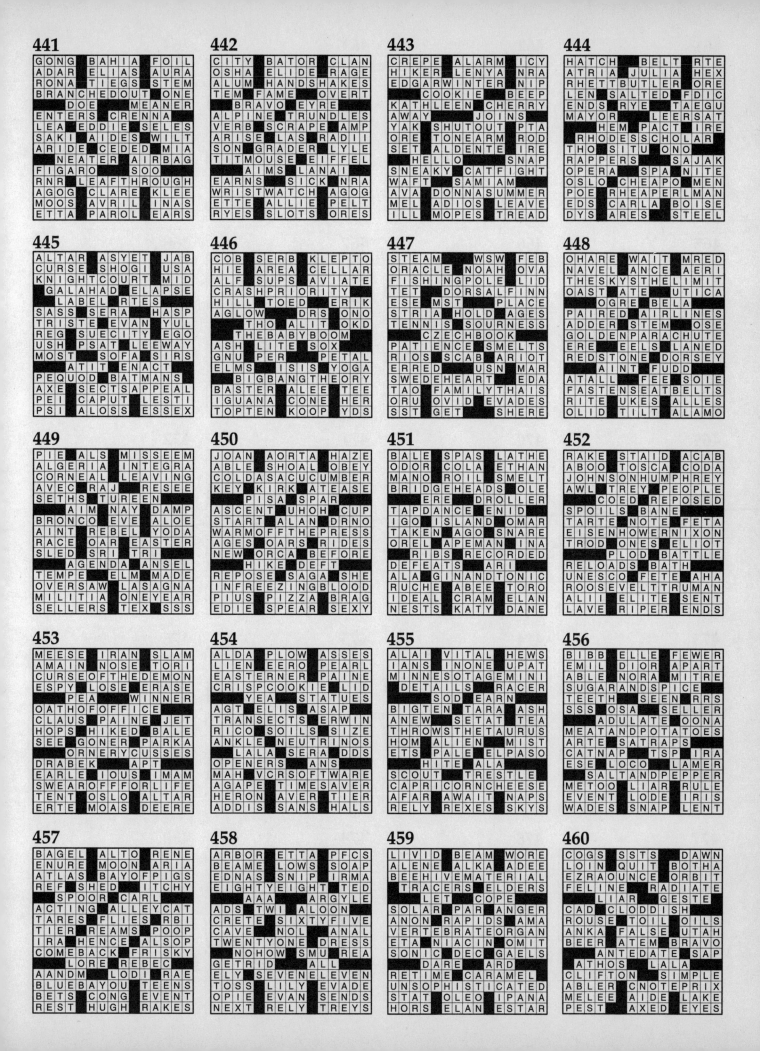

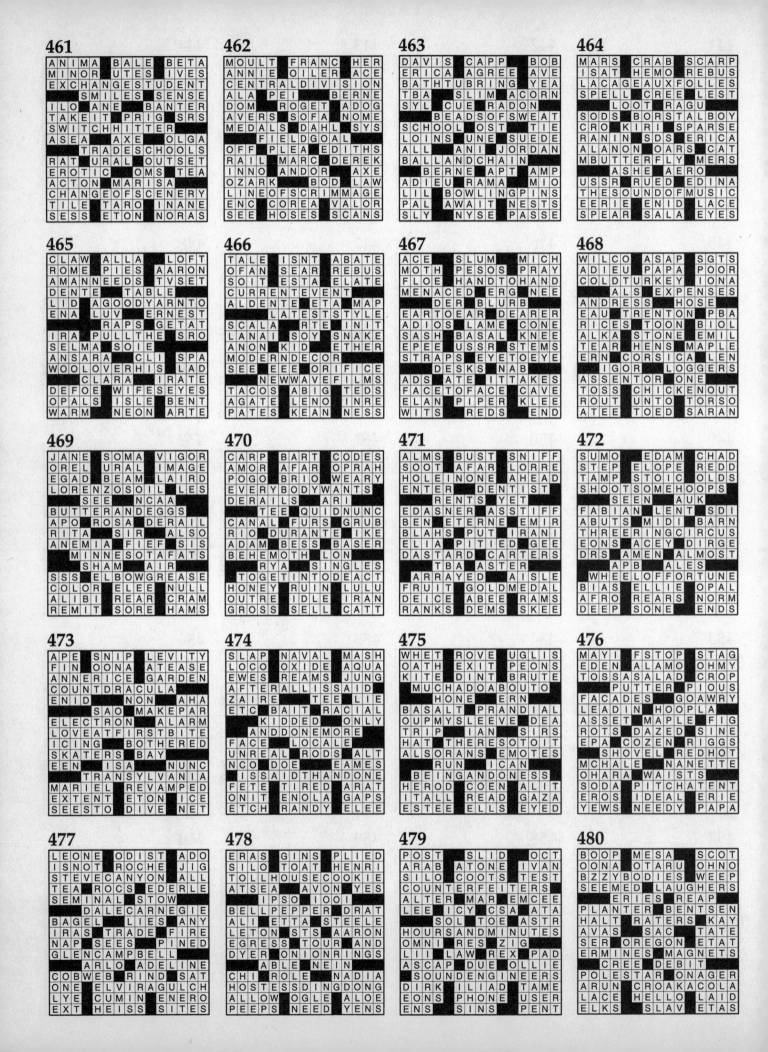

481

```
LAPIS BRAT   ASA
ALECK EERO  TRES
MAKEACLEANSWEEP
ENE  TOLD  KINTE
   DEL  GAINSON
SCOURAROUND
HOLES EMIT  SALS
OVAL  EVADE ATEE
TENS  GENE DINAR
POLISHEDOFF
REDRESS   OFA
ALIAS ACRE   IDA
WASHONESHANDSOF
ENCS  ALTO DELLA
RDS   PLOP SNEER
```

482

```
GUY SETAT  HELOT
ATE ERATO  ANICE
BAA QUICKSILVER
SHROUD OIL  IRAN
   RIIS LESSENS
SEVENTHFLEET
TAE  EEE  PEELED
EVERS ARC  PROVO
PESETA RUR   NAN
HASTYPUDDING
REGENTS   SLOE
AREA AHS  EWINGS
FASTFRIENDS  OAT
ESTER REBBE  OLE
REEDY TRAYS  NAT
```

483

```
LIMB CHER   VELD
ODOR LAVE  GELID
MYNA AREA  UNITE
LADYMARMALADE
   YAMS  BALES
CID  WYSIWYG
ADORN RES   BORA
FORESTPRESERVES
ELAN ROE   XRAYS
VULGATE    LST
EMAIL   TURF
JELLYSLASTJAM
HEDGE AIMS  OMIT
ICIER REAL  ROLE
STAR  ANNE  DRED
```

484

```
SEMI PRIMP  SLAM
EVIL RIDEA  MILA
WILLROGERS  YEAS
UTE  ITSA THRUSH
PARADE    ADEN
JIMMYDURANTE
MESA RODEO   OIL
EXTRA MUS  DRUNK
APE  SCOTT  ANTE
LOWELLTHOMAS
NOIO    AGHAST
STREWN GINO  GAB
HOER GRETAGARBO
OLEG TURIN  SEEN
EDDY ONEND  HERE
```

485

```
ETNA  SCI  TOGAS
GOON DULL  OKAPI
GRAZ OPAL  BRITS
THIEVESSTEAL
OVERHANG    DER
ASH ABBEYS   ERA
SCANDALS   PIVOT
SORCERY  PIECEDE
ERROR  BANTERED
REI  DIAPER  SSR
TDS   CONVEXES
BURGLARALARM
ROUTE ERIC  JUAN
AURAS TINT  ASIA
MIGHT SAG   KELP
```

486

```
SCALA  DOM  TRIP
ELLIS COCA  OONA
REACHFORTHEMOON
BOSH INSOLE  TNT
   EAST  PEEL
UPINTHEAIR  ORCA
PAN  SYNS  ALARM
PULSE TSP  LANAI
ELENA ALAI   DIS
DATA FLYINGHIGH
PARA   NINA
ASK CARETS  LOSS
THESKYSTHELIMIT
NERO EONS  UTILE
OARS  DNA  GETON
```

487

```
RITA CAAN  USHER
ADAM YWCA  STELE
EAROFCORN  CRASS
ROLLOUT    EDIE
SPHERES  OMELET
TEETER   DENOTE
ETATS RAVEN  THE
NERO EATER  STAG
ORT  UTTER CHUTE
OMAHAS   TRACES
SAFARI  COOLEST
PIPS   CAPITAL
IDAHO POTATOEYE
CELIE OREL   TOES
ARMED SESS  SNAP
```

488

```
HARP ONCE  MAVEN
IBAR KEEN  CLOVE
DEVILSADVOCATES
ELENA LIETO   ENS
CPA   LITON
ANGELFALLS  ALFS
DOO  AREA  STALL
MORENOS  ESTONIA
INAND ALEE   CNN
TENO DEVILEDEGG
LEONI    FLO
MAE LEGGY  IRWIN
ANGELSINAMERICA
STAVE NORA  INKY
SEDAN ENDS  TOYS
```

489

```
CAMP AWED   RAZZ
FUROR LIVE  ADUE
OREOS STOP  RANK
IVAN COCKAMAMIE
LESSOR    HERO
TRAY   STANDUP
STARKMAD  NOISE
LULU  PAR   BEEP
ABACK  BUGHOUSE
MAWKISH   MOOD
TWOS    ANYWAY
OFFTHEWALL  HIMA
HAIR ANNA  GONER
OKRA ROTS  AMEND
HEEP SWAT   BESS
```

490

```
LEEJ CIGAR  AMOS
ALDA ASIDE  VALE
PLAN LINED  OREL
AMAPISAPIECEOF
COG    TARA
AQUEDUCT  LADDER
SUNK RIATA  TOILE
TAJ PAPERTO  XES
OSAKA PAIR  CINE
RIMINI  DEADHEAT
PAST   CEO
HELPYOUGETLOST
ALOE BRAVO  SIAM
WEIR ABLER  EZRA
NESS ROARS  YETI
```

491

```
SASS APHID  COOS
TROT ARENA  PART
ECHO COLDTURKEY
WHOOSH MIAS  SOX
LIES   ABEE
HISPANIC  ARARAT
ASWIM NATS  GORE
SLAG CANOE  LADD
TETE LISP  RESOD
ASHORE TAPESTRY
NEAT   ZINC
ACE EVEN  STOKES
CHICKENOUT  UNIT
TINA RETRO  TERI
SPED STEEL  SEER
```

492

```
HAGAR PLED  BRAG
INANE ROLE  LETO
PASTA OGLE  ENTO
LICENSEPLATES
ALI  HAT  ERASE
WIGS ROCKET  LTD
ETHOS   RIATA
THEPLATTERS
OCEAN   RAMBO
SAC UNDEAD  BAIL
AROAR  DUH   ROD
DISHESTHEDIRT
ISTO WRAP  MOSES
STAY AUNT  OPERA
TASS BEGS  METAL
```

493

```
SASS  ILL   MEL
PINTA SEAT  TILE
ALEUT ACTA  IAMA
ROWDYYATES  GMEN
RICE   TSHIRT
ELAPSE   RHETT
VERA LYNE  ARNIE
INCLUDE  RAGOUTS
LOSES TSAR  PIET
REFIT   MEETME
STRIDE   ANON
PROD UNFORGIVEN
LOVE DEFT  IRONY
AVER SEER  NAIVE
YES   DDE   EDDY
```

494

```
SKIP ADLIB  WALL
ANNE SAYNO  OBOE
NEGATIVECOMMENT
EWE OTIS  BEATIT
PAID   STAN
DUCATS SPUD  STS
ABATE SNUB  OPEC
NOISEINANENGINE
ZANY RACK  ELLEN
ATE WORK  SVELTE
SANK   CHAD
ADONIS SLID  COB
RAPAFISTONADOOR
CZAR DIANE  DOZE
SELL EMBER  SKEW
```

495

```
ANGLER PINT  YAP
MARINE OWAR  ITA
AMANDA IAMABEAR
PEELS  SEVILLE
MAE ALIF  ELDER
OFVERYLITTLE
TRIES GRIS   UHF
HONK BRAIN  ONEA
SSE  SEER  SHOAL
ANDLONGWORDS
LIBRA SORE   DYE
INACRES   MEADE
BOTHERME  ATARIS
ENE  RIIS SENECA
LED  SETS ERODED
```

496

```
BASIS SLAV  SWAP
ABATE NINE  RANI
MEDEA ENTR  OTIS
STEMTHETIDE  ETA
SEAR   ULTRA
TOW  RLS  OGLES
SPARSE  BUOYEDUP
PAVE  BAR   MOVE
SHELLOUT  ANSWER
LEANS   PRO   NAT
GETME   ECTO
PAN BEINTHESWIM
ORGS YSER  PAIGE
ONTO ELIE  AGLOW
HIHO DELL  DEERS
```

497

```
SMEAR  HMS  BOBS
CARLA FOCH  AMOK
AMATI REDO  RAZE
LIT SPARETHEROD
AEOLIAN    RUED
INS  UMPS    AFT
TEAM TOPO  SADIE
STRIKEUPTHEBAND
ANITA TETE  AMES
RAD  ROOD    NRC
GAFF    SNEAKER
SPLITTHETAB  ALE
SUEZ HARE  ASPIN
GRAM ENGR  TRUST
TENO  EDS  ESTES
```

498

```
SHED DAFT  CACHE
LYLE IDLE  AFROS
APSE SAAR  LOADS
WEEPINGWILLOW
WEE   OUTLET
STRAY BRAS   SSW
TEAL TEAM   SPCA
TRACKSOFMYTEARS
RAKE UFOS   WACO
ATE SMUG   CAREW
MATTEA   LAN
THECRYINGGAME
RULED EAST  ALAN
ISERE ELLE  LARD
POSED DEER  ASKS
```

499

```
DSCS SAWTO  JEEP
OTOE AGAIN  URGE
REBA IRATE  NEON
SPATULACLARK
APLOMB ELY   BAA
LET BOOT  SECOND
TRALEE    UNTO
GRATERGARBO
HALO   OSIRIS
ELUDES ESTA  APB
WEE  RCA  ITALIA
FARRAHFAUCET
ABLE ADLAI  DOMO
TROT MEDIC  IVAN
EASE SNORE  TENS
```

500

```
ALAI BORO   APPT
TENDERNAME  MAHA
ENDEARMENT  ERRS
ERSE   IAN   EAS
CADS   MALIGNS
ONE  DOLE   PETE
LOC IMELDA   AHS
ARLENES  ENTREES
AAR NEGATE   STP
LRON AREA    III
EASIEST    ISNT
EDT  ESQ   DAHS
RIIS PUNISHMENT
NCOS NINETHUMPS
ETNA DEMI  DORE
```

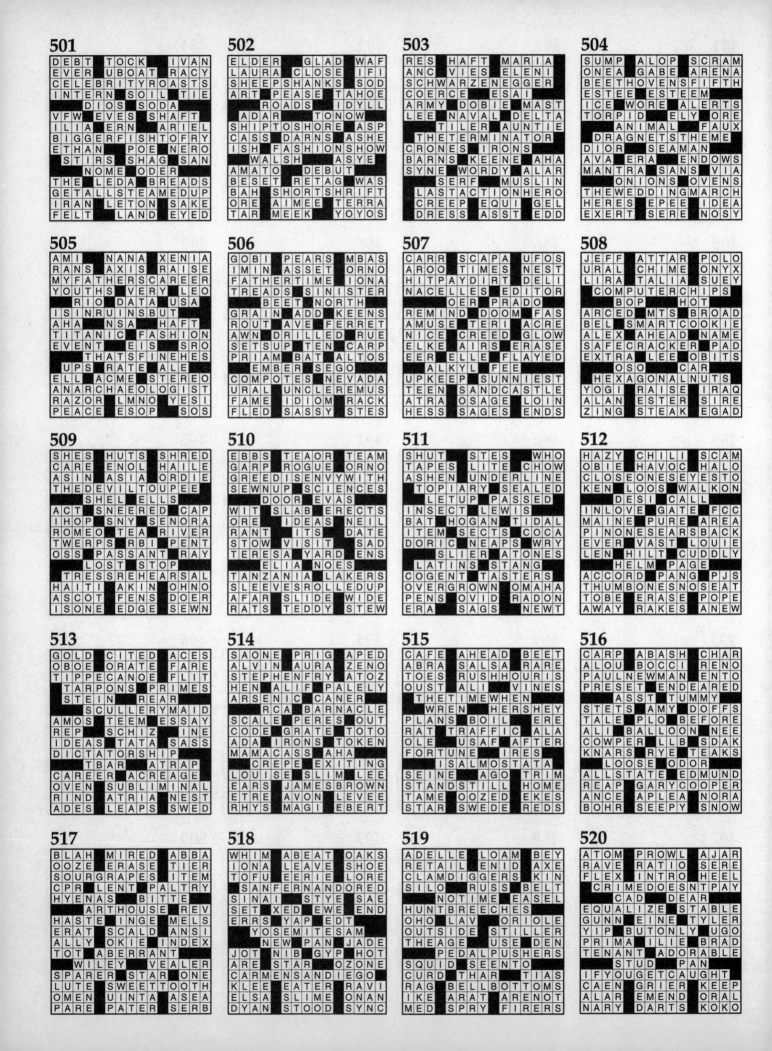

521

```
AGES  RAVES ATTA
MOLE  ALIKE SWAB
PAIROFACES  TIRE
STAIR NEST  ANTS
      AMISS EMIT
LADLES  STAROF
EROS ABUT  MEWLS
STU TWOTONE  EEE
TIBER NAPE  TRAM
ELAINE  AGASSI
ERGO  HELEN
ATTN OLEG  NAILS
SOIE SINGINGDUO
POMS ELIOT  ELMS
STET STENO  REPO
```

522

```
CORN BASIC  EPEE
ABOO AROMA  SODA
MOUSETRAPS  STIR
PEEWEE  RETREATS
      ELSA  LEANT
TOGAS PAS  SCORN
HURT HES  SPECIE
ATE EARTHLY  HOW
IDEALS ROY  PITS
SONGS BOB  TIPSY
AGILE  OFIT
INCREASE  RECAPS
TIRE  BUNKERHILL
ONES ORDIE  ERIE
NESS RESTS  DYED
```

523

```
LASTS AHAB  FLEE
IDIOT RUSE  OAST
FORTYEIGHT  UNTO
ERE MASH  WARDEN
RESTIVE  WISH
EEE  BOXLUNCH
GRAND KART  NOLO
REST OLD  DRAM
OATH PREY  BRADY
GROOVIER  DYE
UCLA  BELDAMS
MESSRS SEMI  BAL
ACTA NINEONEONE
SHUN ENUF  EDDIE
TODD RAGS  STEAK
```

524

```
CRIT SAVOR  OMAR
HANA ALIBI  NICE
ETAL DANSE  EDEN
WILLIAMCONRAD
SOLOS BEL  ALLIN
RES  EST  ERE
DOMDELUISE  SMEE
OBOE INICE  HAND
POUR CASEYJONES
ETS GEL  AER
SEEKS TAS  ATLAS
HEAVENCANWAIT
IDOL ORDER  AGRA
DULL TEENA  VEER
OBEY EDSEL  ERSE
```

525

```
SNIP CAMEL  COG
LOCO AROSE  BLOW
ATOP LOTTA  RAZE
VINCE WHENWOMEN
ORO  SETON
GOWRONG  MORTALS
IRONSOUT  SEESAW
FIR MEN  ORE
TESTED  DEFIANCE
SLEEVES  GORIGHT
HEAPS  PAR
AFTERTHEM  SWAMI
DIRE HEWER  OXEN
ARID IREAD  LEND
MEX NERDS  FLUE
```

526

```
ALAS OHARA  CHUB
SADE RATON  HARI
SIMMERDOWN  OLGA
ANAIL AMS  FIFES
DENTISTS  CURB
EAT  FORBADE
LEE SEALED  OKRA
ELMS AMEND  YEAR
ABBE MIDDLE  DBL
PARADED  EDS
OWED  BADGERED
TRIAL FAR  ENOLA
MALL BOILEDOVER
EVEL RAZES  RECT
NEDS AMENS  ARTS
```

527

```
ABCS CIRCA  ORAL
DOLE ODIUM  RARE
ONEARMEDBANDITS
BSA AMASS  TAN
EARSHOT  CHICLE
SISI NEATH  NOOK
LIS LION  ACE
TWOCENTSWORTH
IRE INRE  DNA
NESS SARGE  TIER
KETTLE  ORLANDO
ERE LIGHT  HID
THREELEGGEDRACE
IONA ENOLA  ALTO
DESK GORED  MESS
```

528

```
AVER SSTS  SHOT
MOJO PILAU  POLO
BLED ATURN  AUDI
ETC OVERABARREL
RATTLES  ALS
HES  MATTERED
ECCE CACHE  ELI
THROUGHTHERANKS
TOO TRITE  DESK
APPETITE  DOA
LEM  HORMONE
UNDERACLOUD  MEX
KIEV COORS  TAXI
ELLE ELUDE  SHUT
SEEN DADE  PASS
```

529

```
IQS MCA  UPSIDE
NUT BEON  NETHER
VIA OCHO  STARER
ITMAYCONCERN
TIENDAS  ARIZONA
ETNA TAR  ARES
RYE BLOT  IDS
AMISPEAKING
GEM PELE  SEE
OMOO ATE  GOBI
OURTOWN  CLARION
THEBELLTOLLS
ENRAGE MAAM  MET
DOOWOP PINE  ARE
TRIADS SRO  NOP
```

530

```
GAGS SONE  LEADA
ATRA QUAD  IMPEL
STAB UTNE  FIRST
APLEASURETRIP
SCHELL LOS  CAT
SHE PLEBES  JOIE
TED AERO  AUTRY
ISDRIVING
ZORRO LACE  APB
ERIK SYSTEM  NEB
NAG SRO  TIGERS
THEKIDSTOCAMP
NITTI ELON  WOLF
SNORT LUNG  KNEE
AGNES SEES  SEXY
```

531

```
ECHO MASON  AJAR
FLOP ANKLE  RULE
TAPE SNIDE  TMEN
SPAN HEP  PIPED
LIVE  AZALEA
CLONED GERE  TSP
RANGE MESTA  TWO
EGGS MONTY  SHES
SEC CONEY  FEELS
TRA HOER  ORACLE
SIESTA  BACH
VISOR TAJ  HAIG
EDIT LOIRE  ENRY
LEDA STOIC  SCAN
DAYS DONAT  TENT
```

532

```
RIGEL PEER  ABCS
ADORE ELEE  PILE
GEORGESAND  OLIN
SAP ATOM  BALLOT
PTAS  GAILY
SAMUEL  BARROOMS
AGAPE KILOS  COO
LIRA CONAN  MERL
ELK CORDS  CEASE
MESDAMES  WARNED
TAMPA  CANE
CORNEA ILSA  TAN
AMAD DINAHSHORE
LONI RATS  TIMEX
MODE ENOS  ATEST
```

533

```
GAFF SKI  ELSE
ALLOT CHIN  RIIS
STORE HOWE  IMPS
HAWKEYEPIERCE
TENS  DEALT
SARAHS TYP  IHS
ATIT ASHOE  GEE
HOTLIPSHOULIHAN
INA LAKER  ITGO
BAM IRS  WEISER
LOFAT  DIAN
RADARO'REILLY
SUEZ KARL  RAISA
ANNE EVIL  ONTAP
WOOD SIS  SETS
```

534

```
BONES ALAS  CST
AGENT PETAL  OAR
TRITECOMEDY  UNA
HELENA  ALLERGY
ROMP  SEEIT
SEAS PAPER  DSCS
ENC PYRE  DEPOT
NOTRE ART  AROSE
SLOOP ORBS  RTE
EARL MONEY  STAR
OLLAS  ETTE
HEROISM  HOSTEL
ALS SHOOTERAMMO
RIO TENSE  AMAIN
PEN DDAY  HENRI
```

535

```
JOT AHAB  TOTS
UNUM LINO  HAITI
DELI BENZVEREEN
ORACLE SOIL  REG
KER  COHERE
RAMJETS  FARAD
AMIA  TEARDUCTS
SONG SARIS  DARE
PROUSTIAN  IKON
RAPID  TRIDENT
IMPROV  EGO
NOA KISS  DOOFUS
GORBACHEVY  DORA
ASTON ELIE  YOGI
ESSE ALPS  LED
```

536

```
WEST AIMS  HANS
HAIR WRIT  HABIT
ACRE AONE  ELENA
THEMORNINGAFTER
OSE  RPM
SMART BOA  OAST
ION IMPEND  OFNO
DOGDAYAFTERNOON
OREO OTIOSE  ORE
NELL PET  VOTER
PSI  CUR
NIGHTANDTHECITY
ANNIE ARIA  HORA
STUNT PINS  INON
HOSS EPEE  DANK
```

537

```
BELL DEBS  EBSEN
OLEO AERO  LOTTO
BEACHHEAD  LORAN
SERIAL  ALIBI
RIAS  ASONG
ANIMATE  DOOGIE
IGORS EATEN  BAN
ALOE SATES  FEND
NED REMIT  DRATS
SALTED  NOTIONS
MEUSE  GNAT
SLURP  UTMOST
SHOAL  ASTRODOME
COUNT CHOU  CLOD
HOPES EYES  LAGS
```

538

```
SARA FALA  AMAN
PRES SOLAR  RULE
ACTI ARENA  EDGE
CHINESECABBAGE
EEN LES  USURP
DRANO TORTS  AIR
EPI CEO  BRAY
FRENCHBREAD
TRIO CUR  ONT
SOL SHEEP  OHARE
POISE OWL  BAA
SPANISHPEANUTS
ATIT VIOLA  ESTE
RENE ADMAN  HELL
TROD NEER  IDES
```

539

```
PRY ROBUST  DIAL
TAO TRENCH  ISEE
BUDGETDIRECTORS
ONEA STAIR  LAT
ACLEAR  PRORATE
THEALAMO  SPITER
SYR INITS  TESS
MEGAHERTZ
SOSO SETAE  AVA
EVENTS  RARAAVIS
REDTAPE  ELLENS
ERA MIXES  ONCE
NATIONALLEAGUER
ETES ELBOWS  ENT
REDO STATES  STS
```

540

```
MIKADOS  MARIAH
ARIZONAN  EXACTA
COLORADO  DENIED
ONTV  ATLAS
NIE ASTRAL  TOPO
SCRAPE EMS  ADEN
RINGSA  SKOAL
PRIVATEPROPERTY
LOGAN  WARREN
USED KGS  BAOBAB
SETA NASSER  RBI
LOWIQ  BOAC
LAYSIT  NUISANCE
ANOINT  GAVEITUP
STURDY  WETNESS
```

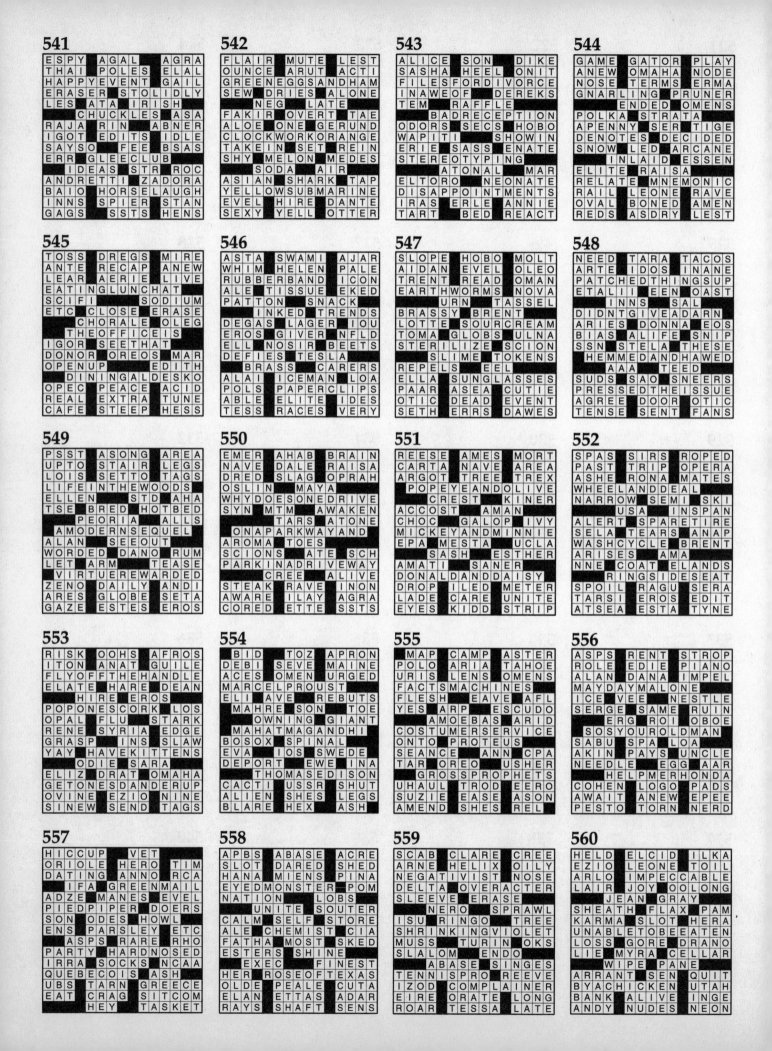

541
```
ESPY AGAL  AGRA
THAI POLES ELAL
HAPPYEVENT GAIL
ERASER STOLIDLY
LES  ATA  IRISH
   CHUCKLES ASA
RAJA RIN  ABNER
IGOT EDITS IDLE
SAYSO FEE  BSAS
ERR GLEECLUB
  IDEAS STR ROC
ANDRETTI ZADORA
BAIO HORSELAUGH
INNS SPIER STAN
GAGS SSTS  HENS
```

542
```
FLAIR MUTE  LEST
OUNCE ARUT  ACTI
GREENEGGSANDHAM
SEW DRIES  ALONE
    NEG   LATE
FAKIR OVERT  TAE
ALOE ONE  GERUND
CLOCKWORKORANGE
TAKEIN SET  REIN
SHY MELON  MEDES
    SODA  AIR
ASIAN SHARK  TAP
YELLOWSUBMARINE
EVEL HIRE  DANTE
SEXY YELL  OTTER
```

543
```
ALICE SON  DIKE
SASHA HEEL  ONIT
FILESFORDIVORCE
INAWEOF DEREKS
TEM   RAFFLE
BADRECEPTION
ODORS SECS  HOBO
WAPITI SHOWIN
ERIE SASS  ENATE
STEREOTYPING
ATONAL MAR
ELTORO NEONATE
DISAPPOINTMENTS
IRAS ERLE  ANNIE
TART BED  REACT
```

544
```
GAME GATOR  PLAY
ANEW OMAHA  NODE
NOSE TERMS  ERMA
GNARLING PRUNER
ENDED OMENS
POLKA STRATA
APENNY SER  TIGE
DENOTES DECIDED
SNOW LED  ARCANE
INLAID ESSEN
ELITE RAISA
RELATE MNEMONIC
RAIL LEONE  RAVE
OVAL BONED  AMEN
REDS ASDRY  LEST
```

545
```
TOSS DREGS  MIRE
ANTE RECAP  ANEW
LEAR AERIE  LIVE
EATINGLUNCHAT
SCIFI   SODIUM
ETC CLOSE  ERASE
CHORALE OLEG
THEOFFICEIS
IGOR SEETHAT
DONOR OREOS  MAR
OPENUP  EDITH
DININGALDESKO
OPEC PEACE  ACID
REAL EXTRA  TUNE
CAFE STEEP  HESS
```

546
```
ASTA SWAMI  AJAR
WHIM HELEN  PALE
RUBBERBAND ICON
ALE TISSUE  EKED
PATTON  SNACK
INKED  TRENDS
DEGAS LAGER  IOU
EROS GIVER  NFLD
ELL NOSIR  BEETS
DEFIES  TESLA
BRASS  CARERS
ALAI ICEMAN  LOA
POLS PAPERCLIPS
ABLE ELITE  IDES
TESS RACES  VERY
```

547
```
SLOPE HOBO  MOLT
AIDAN EVEL  OLEO
TRENT READ  OMAN
EARTHWORMS NOVA
URN   TASSEL
BRASSY  BRENT
LOTTE SOURCREAM
TOMA GLOBS  ULNA
STERILIZE SCION
SLIME TOKENS
REPELS EEL
ELLA SUNGLASSES
PAAR ASEA  CUTIE
OTIC DEAD  EVENT
SETH ERRS  DAWES
```

548
```
NEED TARA  TACOS
ARTE IDOS  INANE
PATCHEDTHINGSUP
ETALII EEN  OAST
INNS   SAL
DIDNTGIVEADARN
ARIES DONNA  EOS
BIAS ALIFE  SNIP
SSN STELA  THESE
HEMMEDANDHAWED
AAA   TEED
SUDS SAO  SNEERS
PRESSEDTHEISSUE
AGREE DOOR  OTIC
TENSE SENT  FANS
```

549
```
PSST ASONG  AREA
UPTO STAIR  LEGS
LOIS SETTO  TAGS
LIFEINTHEWOODS
ELLEN   STD AHA
TSE BRED  HOTBED
PEORIA  ALLS
AMODERNSEQUEL
ALAN  SEEOUT
WORDED DANO  RUM
LET ARM  TEASE
VIRTUEREWARDED
ZENO DAILY  ANDI
ARES GLOBE  SETA
GAZE ESTES  EROS
```

550
```
EMER AHAB  BRAIN
NAVE DALE  RAISA
DRED SLAG  OPRAH
OSLIN   MAYA
WHYDOESONEDRIVE
SYN MTM  AWAKEN
TARS  ATONE
ONAPARKWAYAND
AROMA  TOES
SCIONS ATE  SCH
PARKINADRIVEWAY
CREE  ALIVE
STEAK RAVE  INON
AWARE ILAY  AGRA
CORED ETTE  SSTS
```

551
```
REESE AMES  MORT
CARTA NAVE  AREA
ARGOT TREE  TREX
POPEYEANDOLIVE
CREST  KINER
ACCOST  AMAN
CHOC GALOP  IVY
MICKEYANDMINNIE
EPA MESTA  UCLA
SASH  ESTHER
AMATI  SANER
DONALDANDDAISY
DROP ILED  METER
LADE CARE  UNITE
EYES KIDD  STRIP
```

552
```
SPAS SIRS  ROPED
PAST TRIP  OPERA
ASHE RONA  MATES
WHEELANDDEAL
NARROW SEMI  SKI
USA   INSPAN
ALERT SPARETIRE
SELA TEARS  ANAP
WASHCYCLE BRENT
ARISES  AMA
NNE COAT  ELANDS
RINGSIDESEAT
SPOIL RAGU  SERA
TARSI EROS  EDIT
ATSEA ESTA  TYNE
```

553
```
RISK OOHS  AFROS
ITON ANAT  GUILE
FLYOFFTHEHANDLE
ELATE HARE  DEAN
HIRE  EROS
POPONESCORK LOS
OPAL FLU  STARK
RENE SYRIA  EDGE
GRASP INS  SLAW
YAY HAVEKITTENS
ODIE  SARA
ELIZ DRAT  OMAHA
GETONESDANDERUP
OVINE EZIO  NINE
SINEW SEND  TAGS
```

554
```
BID TOZ  APRON
DEBI SEVE  MAINE
ACES OMEN  URGED
MARCELPROUST
ELI AVE  REBUTS
MAHRE SON  TOE
OWNING  GIANT
MAHATMAGANDHI
BOSOX  SPINAL
EVA IOS  SWEDE
DEPORT EWE  INA
THOMASEDISON
CACTI USSR  SHUT
ALIEN SHES  LEGS
BLARE HEX  ASH
```

555
```
MAP CAMP  ASTER
POLO ARIA  TAHOE
URIS LENS  OMENS
FACTSMACHINES
FLESH EAVE  AFL
YES ARP  ESCUDO
AMOEBAS  ARID
COSTUMERSERVICE
ONTO  PROTEUS
SEANCE ANN  CPA
TAR OREO  USHER
GROSSPROPHETS
UHAUL TROD  EERO
SUZIE EASE  ASON
AMEND SHES  REL
```

556
```
ASPS RENT  STROP
ROLE EDIE  PIANO
ALAN DANA  IMPEL
MAYDAYMALONE
ICE VEE  NESTLE
SERGE SAME  RUIN
ERG ROI  OBOE
SOSYOUROLDMAN
SABU SPA  LOA
AKIN PAYS  UNCLE
NEEDLE EGG  AAR
HELPMERHONDA
COHEN LOGO  PADS
AWAIT ANEW  EPEE
PESTO TORN  NERD
```

557
```
HICCUP   VET
ORIOLE HERO  TIM
DATING ANNO  RCA
IFA  GREENMAIL
ADZE MANES  EVEL
PIEDPIPER DOERS
SON ODES  HOWL
ENS PARSLEY  ETC
ASPS RARE  RHO
PARTY HARDNOSED
IRRA SOCKS  NCAA
QUEBECOIS ASH
UBS TARN  GREECE
EAT CRAG  SITCOM
HEY   TASKET
```

558
```
APBS ABASE  ACRE
SLOT DARED  SHED
HANA MIENS  PINA
EYEDMONSTER POM
NATION  LOBS
UNITE  SOUTER
CALM SELF  STORE
ALE CHEMIST  CIA
FATHA MOST  SKED
ESTERS  SHINE
EXEC  FINEST
HER ROSEOFTEXAS
OLDE PEALE  CUTA
ELAN ETTAS  ADAR
RAYS SHAFT  SENS
```

559
```
SCAB CLARE  CREE
ARNE HELIX  OILY
NEGATIVIST NOSE
DELTA OVERACTER
SLEEVE ERASE
NERO  SPRAWL
ISU RINGO  TREE
SHRINKINGVIOLET
MUSS TURIN  OKS
SLALOM  ENDO
ABASE  SINGES
TENNISPRO REEVE
IZOD COMPLAINER
EIRE ORATE  LONG
ROAR TESSA  LATE
```

560
```
HELD ELCID  ILKA
EZIO LEONE  TOIL
ARLO IMPECCABLE
LAIR JOY  OOLONG
JEAN  GRAY
SHEATH FLAX  PAM
KARMA SLOT  HERA
UNABLETOBEEATEN
LOSS GORE  DRANO
LIE MYRA  CELLAR
WIPE  PANE
ARRANT SEN  QUIT
BYACHICKEN UTAH
BANK ALIVE  INGE
ANDY NUDES  NEON
```

561
```
GOTO  IZZY  EMIT
AUER  SEEIT NICE
DRYCLEANER  INON
   HURL  LESSENS
INCITE  IDEALS
TARDE  INS  LEWD
AMOS  AMS  REDEEM
LIP  ASPIRES  ELI
ONDECK  DAD  APEX
GURU  JET  SIETE
SITTER  TARRED
SETTEES  AILS
OVER  SUNBATHERS
MIRE  TIBER  OREO
ELSA  TATA  WAXY
```

562
```
ESSE  IRA  IQS
APHID  MESA  CUTS
SQUEEZEDIN  HIRE
ERNIES  MATS  ZEE
   ORATE  SCAMPS
HIQ  EZRA  YOGA
ONUS  SITS  TASKS
PREHEAT  EATITUP
SIZES  ESPN  NERO
ORSO  ITIS  RAT
TINMEN  GAMER
ARC  SCAM  ARABIA
SKIT  EQUALIZING
SETS  AUNT  FORCE
DYE  ADE  RDAS
```

563
```
AHAS  PATER  MASH
TOWN  LORRE  ARLO
TWOOFAKIND  RIIS
ALLOUT  WAKEME
   PEER  TITTLES
ERA  LAO  ENOW
ZEROSUM  DEPARTS
REED  IAMA
ALADDIN  PRINTER
CINE  REM  END
STROPHE  SCAB
THEUSA  EGOISM
EARP  BODYDOUBLE
ANAL  IRATE  TEUT
MENE  TENDS  STES
```

564
```
JADE  ALSOP  CHEW
ORAL  LOIRE  OATH
SKIFALLCRESSLOO
ESS  POLK  KIMONO
   OPUS  NATO
PIGLET  CUBE  CBS
AROMA  KATO  ALEC
COLORPISTOLGATE
ENDS  INKY  AARON
RYE  ANTS  MUTANT
HIKE  GERE
CLOUDS  KALE  ABE
LOGMELONPOLOBED
ARLO  IVIED  FLAG
PEER  PATSY  FETE
```

565
```
DRAB  HEAL  ASCAP
MOLE  ILSA  BOOLA
VELDTHATS  ENNIS
REALITY  OGEE
IMPORT  SALMONS
MILO  SIS  LOAM
ANAME  DALLY  IMP
MOIST  ONO  ARNIE
SSN  HILTS  LAINE
READ  ASH  RUER
CHANNEL  ALAMOS
LAPD  MALARIA
ASPIC  TABLEVINE
STEVE  HILO  ICON
PAREE  STEW  SYNE
```

566
```
TWA  CIVET  RADAR
REG  ICIER  ATONE
AGE  TALKINGHEAD
CONVENE  COMESTO
ETTA  STYRON
RUSTIC  PATCH
ATTIRE  PLO  EAU
SINGINGTELEGRAM
ICU  DOO  DRAINS
ASTAR  VESSEL
PALEST  OSAY
IMPOSER  ADOPTEE
LAUGHINGGAS  ARM
EMCEE  OPENS  VIE
TAKER  RODEO  EEN
```

567
```
RAW  BETH  BACKS
ELAM  EPEE  ATRIA
AONE  VIAL  TEENY
CHEESECLOTH  ADS
TASSEL  STREAM
ERIN  ADOPTS
BAM  GNARL  KURT
ALI  EGGHEAD  FIE
ISLE  SONIA  FOR
TOKENS  ARLO
GRATIS  CAROLS
CAL  BUTTERINGUP
ALAMO  HORA  OLGA
MISER  OLAF  TEEN
PESTS  TEST  DRS
```

568
```
MAPS  GAMMA  SCAM
ABEL  ORION  PUMA
REAR  SILTY  ORES
ETC  ATALOWPOINT
HALAS  HIKED
REFLAG  GWENS
AGUES  QUARK  NOD
GAZE  OUTRE  SOMA
ADZ  AVAST  DOTED
ELEGY  CASINO
MOTOR  HERON
CASHUPFRONT  PAD
LILI  ALERT  ALPO
ALEC  SENSE  BAEZ
WARS  SEDER  EYRE
```

569
```
SAGAS  JERICHO
TRENT  TAXATION
OPENER  HIAWATHA
PEN  TOTELL  LYON
SLAP  NHL  TOY
SDI  REMISS  WAS
ANGOLAN  RAITT
LAVERNE&SHIRLEY
OXIDE  FLEECED
YES  ASTORS  AFC
ETC  UTA  SLAM
HEAL  RAISIN  ONE
ORDINALS  DARWIN
PIZZAPIE  BUENO
ICEAGES  STREW
```

570
```
HARE  BLED  MOTEL
EDEN  YALE  EVADE
LOLA  LISA  DEBIT
PRACTICALNURSE
SEXTON  TESS
REST  PATTON
MOTTA  ORCA  URGE
ONEWHOFALLSFORA
MUNI  NAME  AFTER
SPASMS  POND
TOES  EASYAS
WEALTHYPATIENT
MAYBE  ROOT  LAIR
GIRLS  ERLE  ARTE
SLEET  DEER  SNAP
```

571
```
WILD  AROMA  TSAR
ASEA  GELID  APSO
NEARATHAND  DECO
TEPID  EVEL  AOK
NAPA  RETORTS
ARC  MITLA  ISH
GOLDEN  ALLCLEAR
EPEE  CRUST  IAMA
REAPPEAR  GANDER
ROO  GALEN  SSA
ABATING  ENDS
BAS  OISE  TIARA
ARMS  TEARSOFJOY
BOUT  ESTEE  TAME
ANDY  STERN  SRAS
```

572
```
PAPA  APSO  ATIME
AVER  LAIR  SIRES
LIKEGANGBUSTERS
EVEARDEN  SEANCE
OYL  GURNEYS
ATOMS  SMART
MORASS  ESP  IPSO
PULLOUTTHESTOPS
STYE  POE  RITUAL
SPARK  TORSO
SEAFOOD  OBI
INLETS  EBONIZES
FULLHEADOFSTEAM
TRALA  SELF  ARTE
SENAT  INDO  LOSE
```

573
```
OOMPAH  JOB  SAG
STOOGE  HALE  NIL
LIPTON  AVES  ALI
OSSA  NEWAGE  FED
TWYLA  ETUDE
HANOI  FIASCO
ELECTS  INCHOATE
ESTH  PLATO  TURN
POSITION  TESTED
PINUPS  RIOTS
QUEST  USAGE  PEER
URN  ADONIS  POODLE
AGA  NARC
SEC  INCH  ESPIED
IST  CSA  NESTED
```

574
```
DEARIE  DEPARTS
INBORN  ENTREAT
MADAMESOUSATZKA
AMUSE  HOCUS  OER
YORE  ARMEE  INIT
ONE  SLIPS  KNELL
RDS  PENH  SADDLE
LIRE  SPRY
ABSENT  SHAM  ORB
DIODE  OHARA  NEA
EZRA  TRUNK  SOLD
LAG  BHANG  APRIL
MRHULOTSHOLIDAY
ARUSTLE  AWAKEN
NEMESES  INSERT
```

575
```
BREW  SLY  DECIDE
REMINTED  ONAGER
IWITNESS  SIDLES
BILLETS  WED  APE
ERIE  ETAS  SSN
REOS  DREG  LOSES
SHE  NEPALESE
IDI  ISHADOW  SST
SEDATION  ENL
HARES  STRS  ILET
DOS  PESO  MELO
ALP  DES  STEIGER
TIPTOE  ICONTACT
ONEACT  CORVETTE
PERUSE  YEN  ROSS
```

576
```
LISI  CREDO  TOOL
OLIN  PAPER  EDNA
OLDS  ARIEL  ADES
MALTESECROSS
STEEL  SNAPAT
PLIED  NOVAE
DOT  ANGORAGOATS
UVEA  GAYER  NITS
PERSIANLAMB  LYE
ERRED  EDSEL
TENORS  SADIE
SIAMESETWINS
EDIE  DAVID  SETS
LENO  ILENE  OGRE
LEAF  OLSEN  NOON
```

577
```
BLED  LOPED  REST
AIDE  ORATE  ERIE
CLIP  RASTA  LIND
HITTHEROADJACK
OLE  SOX
SABLE  TEEN  AMI
PLAYITAGAINSAM
TILL  HUG  OKRA
BEAMMEUPSCOTTY
ASH  URGE  OREOS
SNO  ONT
SAYITAINTSOJOE
BOLL  INDIE  PABA
BLIP  COLON  UNIT
BOTH  ANENT  SETS
```

578
```
TRIAD  CARB  CAPO
ROLLE  ALAR  OMAN
ILLITERATESMARK
GESTATE  SWEETIE
INTO  NOISY
PAMELA  LEMON
YEAR  LEVER  SRI
ROMANNUMERALTEN
ONE  AESIR  OINK
SPATS  OSPREY
OMAHA  SOME
ROZELLE  CARAMIA
BLUEMOVIERATING
EAST  LIRA  PANDA
DRAY  ALAN  ETHOS
```

579
```
MARNIE  THEBIRDS
AROUND  SAYONARA
TIPTHE  ARRANGES
ADE  ENTREE  SEWS
RIIS  BOSSY
FLEECE  LEAF
LEIA  ROTC  FBI
ALFREDHITCHCOCK
BLT  ZOOM  AIDE
MICE  LITTLE
MACAO  FICA
ETAL  BRAVER  BBC
SABOTEUR  CORRAL
ALANALDA  ATEASE
SELECTED  PSYCHO
```

580
```
PAST  PICAS  ECHO
ITCH  AMAZE  RAIN
GEAR  GATOR  ERTE
ROMESERVICE
CHEWS  REENTERS
PARISITES  KOREA
ASSN  LAD  PERSON
SAX  BED
FLESHY  FOR  ABBA
LOVER  SEOULFOOD
UNIQUELY  AFINE
DUBLINCUBES
OLEO  ADMAN  CEST
LONI  TEASE  TIES
DATA  ERNES  SDAK
```

581
```
AMOS GARDE AMEN
DONT ALIEN GAME
ARIA BEGET EXIT
MACROSCOPIC ITS
SNEER  RERUNS
  CAP REBUKES
COMPARES EDITH
ODER CRATE ERTE
NOGOS DESISTED
GRANTEE DEL
BEETLE SAMMS
SMU MULTIRACIAL
TACO DENNY RARA
ANKA ERASE IMIN
GEST SYSTS DIET
```

582
```
 ALAN JAY ROSS
OLIVE ONO LEAHS
NAMEOFADDRESSEE
ERE NAN AUDITS
  DAK  NOD
COATING GUESTS
NUMBERANDSTREET
ARI NAE IRE
CITYSTATEANDZIP
LOSETO SPRUCES
ARA AMI
TOREST ICE JAM
USPOSTALSERVICE
MAILS LIL AMBER
PRED LEE LIED
```

583
```
EFTS SCAM RAJAH
ALIE HALO EXILE
SATE INAN DEGAS
YCHROMOSOME
TOE USE LEE OLE
ONSET SHIMMERED
RES OTB MESS
XMARKSTHESPOT
EROS ICE ROT
WATERPOLO TYPEA
EYE EST TET ENS
CATCHSOMEZS
QUIRK IRES SKYE
RATIO SERE GAMS
SETON HESS STES
```

584
```
MAST IDOL ROYAL
SUMO DONE ELENA
GREENEYES TALES
RAWDEAL SAO LAT
ISLES ROTORS
HADNT TALLOW
ARE SALOME ABET
LEES MARIN DIRE
TAPE OPINED RIN
PERUSE ARDEN
FLUKES SUITE
AER NEA STEEPLE
UMPED BLUESKIES
NOLTE LIAM ETAS
SNEER EELS DADO
```

585
```
ZEUS BOSOM CADS
ELSA AMEBA ASWE
NOEL DORIC SCAN
ONEOFTHEKEYS
MIAMI SON NNE
ANJELICA TIDES
IKE RAMPART
TOHAPPINESS
PANELED OFF
QUITS ERASABLE
UPC TEA ISSUE
ISABADMEMORY
NARA GIVEN LEIS
CLUB AGENT ULNA
EASY RONDO MINX
```

586
```
SODA RAMPS OUR
TKOS EXILE UTES
ERGS VENOM TANS
PAC MILKPITCHER
ALAS NOR
OCTANES COPYCAT
HACKS TOOLS AGO
ASHE WEAVE OKAY
RTE THERE CREPE
AEROSOL SNUBBED
LAD URSA
SLEDRUNNERS TNT
HOWE NEEDS STEW
EVES IMAGE DECO
EST TOTED IRKS
```

587
```
DROP ENCL BABEL
REPO DALI INLAY
ARAP SOUL STURM
PURPLEHEART ESE
ENTAIL SCARAB
MST DOLLOP
ORGAN HORA IONA
CORD SEWER BOER
HUED LEND DIDIT
STELLA ORR
NEATAS OUTIES
FAB YELLOWBELLY
ORATE SAVE NEIN
RICER OVER ONTO
TAKES PENS NEED
```

588
```
FROM RAFTS ALAS
DARE AMORE TORT
AMEN MACON LOCI
POOH TUMS KAN
TORISPELLING
DOTTLE DINES
JONIMITCHELL
SOT GAHAN ERR
LONIANDERSON
OSTEO IRAQIS
TONIMORRISON
INO SAUR SCAB
TOTE ARLES HIRT
IRES KEENE EDIE
SASS ARDEN SAGE
```

589
```
STEMS EVADE ZED
ESTOP LOSER AXE
CARDINALSIN NEB
TREETOPS EJECT
REES APSE
SCARLETLETTER
BOATS HALO NEE
ANTE TRUST ANAT
TIC TEAM ABIRD
CHERRYBLOSSOM
RAMS ENCE
TEXAN INTENDED
ERR CRIMSONTIDE
DIA EERIE TENON
SKY SPANS SEAMY
```

590
```
AMOS POUTS EARS
FOUL ATSEA NCOS
ARTISTHELIETHAT
RESPITE LLOYDS
ODER FILM
SHOVED ENABLES
HADES BALTS ERA
EVER PABLO MAIN
LEO NOSES BASED
FANCIES ARNESS
USTO ALAS
ANDREI PICASSO
REALIZETHETRUTH
MINE ETAIN DRAM
SLED RANDS SETS
```

591
```
PTA MESA PAS
ALAS ARAL ATALL
BOXSPRING ROXIE
EDITION AMAZONS
SLO LEAD PAT
BAN ONTO NOSH
ALIST OBNOXIOUS
SEXY ORSON ANTE
EXONERATE SMEAR
NEVA ELMO SHA
ATT ITER OTT
CHANCEL ATTRACT
TOPOT FOXHOUNDS
IRENE IDLE CORE
SOD NEER ENS
```

592
```
APSO BAH UPDOS
ROCS UNA ARRIVE
CORPORATERAIDER
SHARKREPELLENT
PEA RILE SOT
COPY JON NET
HOI BOBS ASTRO
ELL EYE CPR HOG
WAYWE LIEN EAR
ESP IMP FADE
APE EMMA SOU
TAKEOVERTARGET
GOLDENPARACHUTE
OLEARY DON ESTA
PLOYS ENG STAR
```

593
```
WACO THATS QUAG
AVON REMIT UNCO
GAME AMORE ABCS
PANCAKEMAKEUP
BLU BEN DENSE
LOTSA RAIL DEL
AREA TAILFIN
SIRFRANCISBACON
EARTHTO TYPE
APO IPSE BONUS
LOCUS UAE OSS
BUTTERFINGERS
ITAT ALAIN EURO
NEVE GENTE ERIN
ODER SASES FETE
```

594
```
THO FERNS SAN
BALE INANE PICO
SIGNOFTHETHAMES
PLATTERS ELUDE
RIDE ASALL
MULES TBAR AFT
ASIA TAROTS TIE
CANTERBURYTOILS
HID LEASER POET
ERA VATS CENTS
ELITE ASIN
SAVOR CRANSTON
TRAFALGARSQUIRE
AINT AUTOS PLEX
GAS SNOWY TOT
```

595
```
LICK TRYST CHIC
OTHE HOOHA ROSH
OBEY ATWENTYONE
NEWEST ANESTOF
IDEST FEAT
PIN EARS DRAFTS
ENG KLUTZ SLOOP
RUG LEROI RYE
CRUSH DAWNS TON
HEMMED PINA HUD
ATAN EUBIE
FORSURE EUREKA
INCHPRISON AYEN
ATME OGLED TEED
TOPS WHYDO ESPY
```

596
```
PIER AFIRE MIEN
INRE RIDES INDO
TENDERFOOT SCIS
ARIEL ELSA THEY
TEASER THAW
LEE SEEKOUT
RAMS REAL MERRY
ALI HOTRODS MAP
SALSA TAPE ISLE
PREMISE ANN
SALT ERASES
ACTS ALAN PILED
POOH YARDMASTER
SANE ELATE TOTE
OLES DAMON SNOW
```

597
```
BIGMAC ARGONAUT
ASTUTE WARHORSE
THOMASDEQUINCEY
STAR UNO
DOT ROGET CUFF
UNHIP WOL MINOR
DOWNEAST SUNDRY
ANNIEOAKLEY
ERRAND PSALMIST
BETTY SOS SANTA
BASE HETUP GYP
FAR COOT
ELIZABETHASHLEY
SONATINA CLEAVE
TUNGSTEN HOYDEN
```

598
```
MOTT CABS MOWED
ABRA ASEA ARISE
DIEM RILL JESSE
DEEPSEA SPOOKED
AHEM AIR
ARK ARIA ABASED
DURER NSF AVILA
ALOOP OIL RETAR
PENNS RDA BRUTE
TRASHY ETNA PER
OER BERG
ARIZONA REALISM
RIVET GOOD ERIE
FLARE ELKE SOLO
SENOR SEED SNOW
```

599
```
LETTS OLE MALT
ATRIA NUT SERVE
CHARLIECHAPLAIN
JESSICARABBI
AILING ASI
MAINST OAT
UNDO OPENDOORS
SNOBS NOW MARIA
TELESCOPE SCOT
LEA ESTATE
ESP DESIRE
MARCELPRIEST
MINISTEROCTOBER
ELIZA MAN HAARE
TETE STY ERRED
```

600
```
ITES VEAL ALI
NEVERKICKA MAN
WHENHEISUP SADA
HEN ONIT BOZOS
OREADS AIREDOUT
LARGE ASSONANCE
ENSE ROYALE SEW
STIR BETS
EPA ESTEES HERB
TIPONEILL CAMEO
CLEMENCY CAYUGA
HELOT SAAR LIT
IDEO OPENSESAME
NUT BREAKWATER
GPS SYST LENS
```

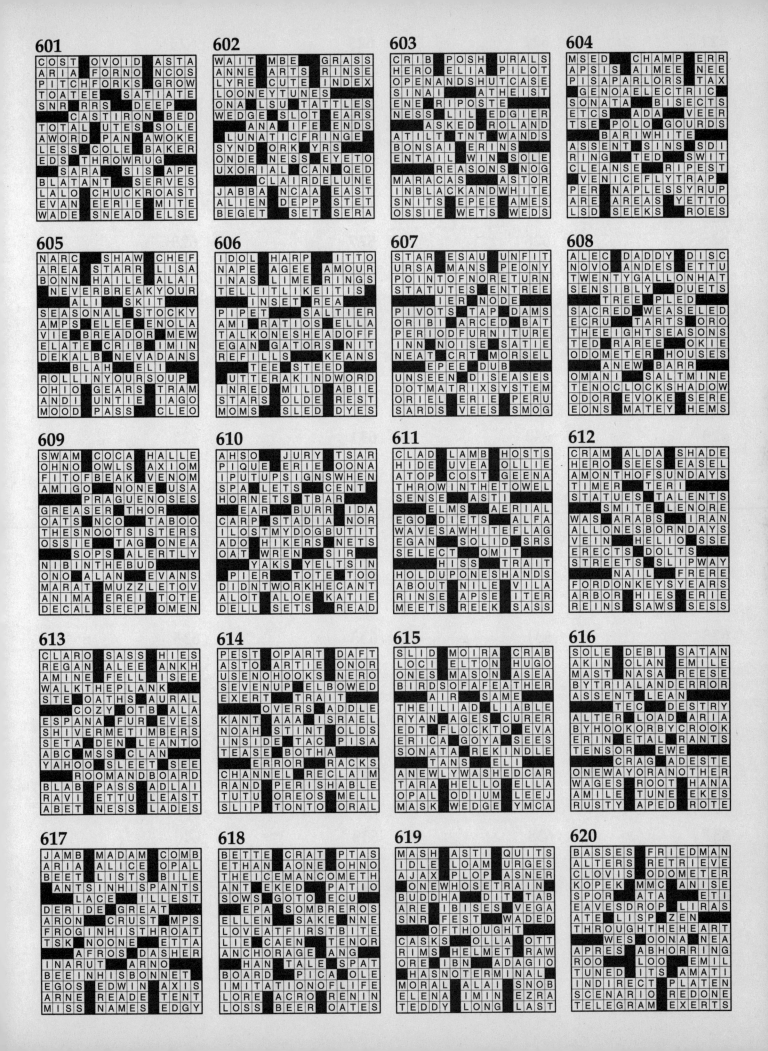

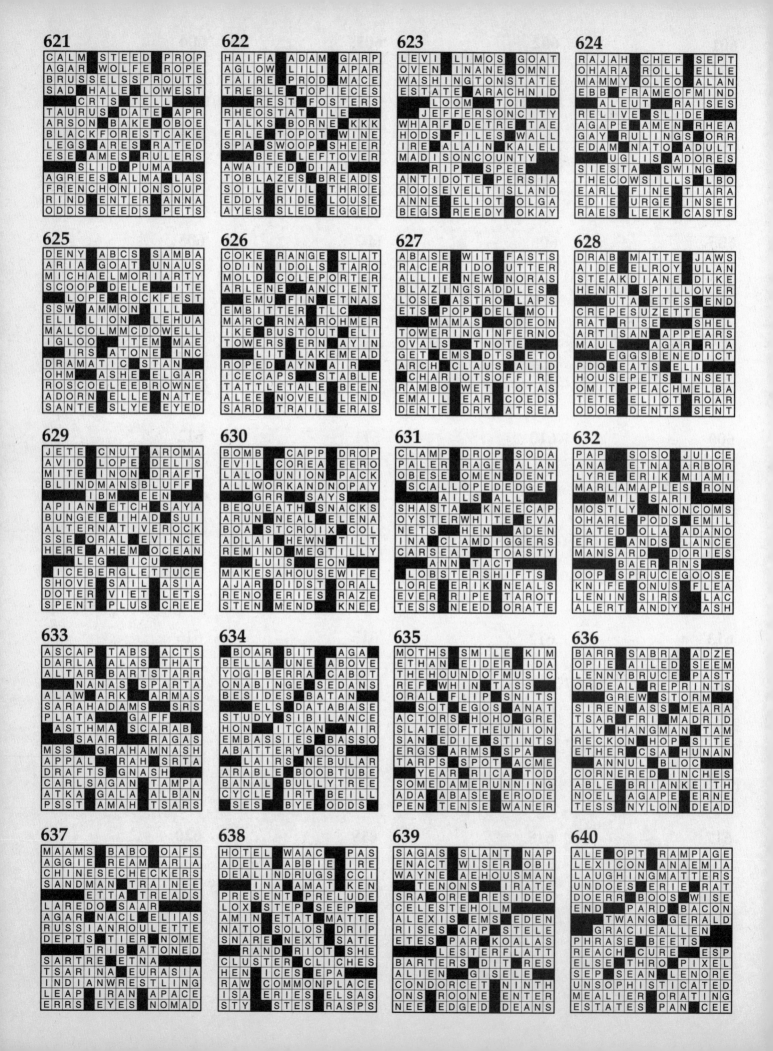

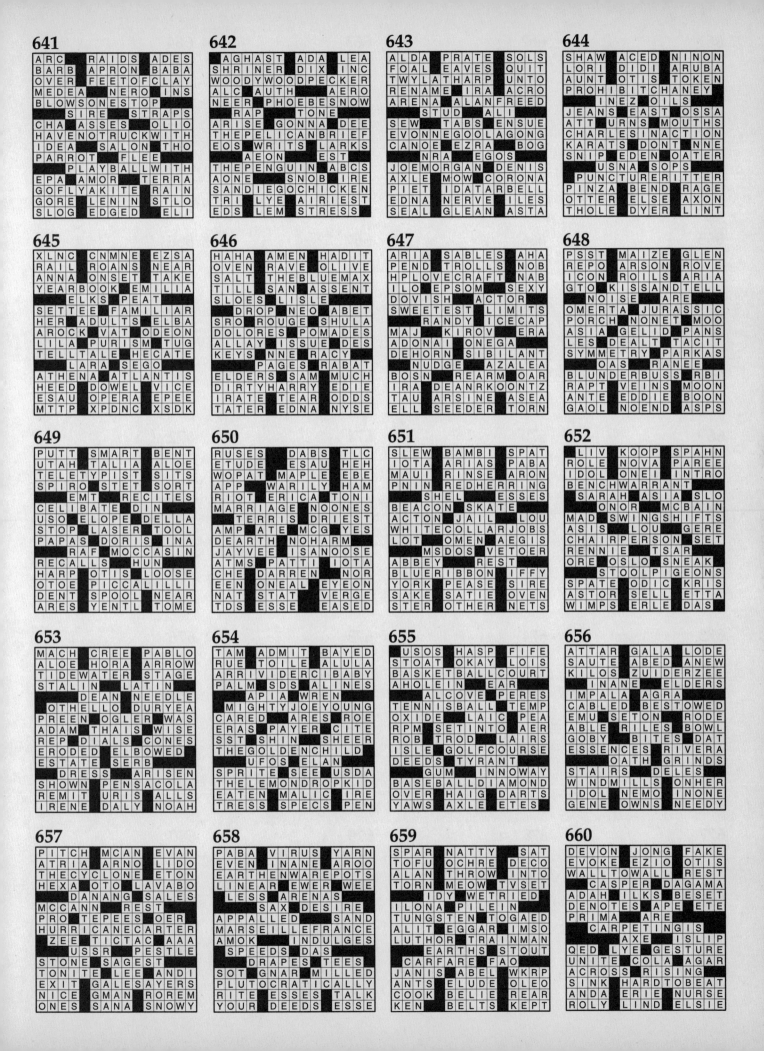

661

```
APSE  LIZA  AFLAT
BONN  IRIS  NIECE
BLACKBOOK  TRAIN
ALGAE  NNE  WENDS
      MST  WHET
TRAPEZES   ERRATA
HIS  YELLOWPAGES
ACTS   SAM   PRAY
WHITEPAPERS  ERE
SERAPE   SNAKIEST
     LIAR  DIN
BAWLS  AAS  MAMAS
ACHOO  BLUEPRINT
EMEND  ISPY  OTTO
RENEE  DOSE  WEEP
```

662

```
SHAPE  FALA  ARAB
PUTON  EGAN  SELA
ALONG  NEON  SCAN
TAPDANCESAROUND
      GOES  ARRAY
FEEDERS   GRIT
ABLE  SOOT   OAT
TAKESTWOTOTANGO
ENE  OVAL   ICES
RYAN   AIMLESS
ADIEU   ALSO
WALTZINGTHROUGH
ALOT  DARE  ATRIA
RENO  OVER  START
DYAN  LEES  SOLOS
```

663

```
BEAM  ACRES  TOSS
ULNA  VOILA  UNTO
MBUTTERFLY  REIN
SETTO  SEASONING
       RAE  BONKS
BATMASTERSON
ALIGHT  TOTE  TSP
BENS  USHER  SEAR
AXE  STAY  OLDAGE
BEETLEBAILEY
APPLE    NET
CLEOPATRA  HASTA
TANK  THEBEEGEES
ONCE  NOBLE  RAMP
RTES  OUSEL  ALPS
```

664

```
AGAMA  GNOME  SAL
LAPIS  NACRE  QUO
BLOCKBUSTER  UNO
SACKER  TED  BATS
REFIT   MARIE
ALBA  RAE  CAREEN
RIOTS   CROONER
TEXTILE  HEINOUS
SINATRA   ATOLL
OSPREY  ERA  STAY
PARES   START
ELIS  ALI  ARABLE
NIN  ICECUBETRAY
ENG  KEELS  ANODE
RES  ESTES  TOWED
```

665

```
CASTE  RELAP  TAJ
UTURN  ALIBI  IDO
SHIED  TIMELAPSE
SETSOFTABLES
ENO  RAE  SHARK
DARC  IRANI  TRAP
HER  RESPRAYS
PLAYWRIGHTABE
THEPEACE   MAY
VIAL  YALTA  SAMS
ALDAS  EEL  AAA
ITCHYALLERGY
BEANERIES  ALONE
OAF  NOVAE  MINER
ART  SPENT  ASSTS
```

666

```
BLAB  SCOFF   JOB
RULE  HAGAR  TOBE
ANON  ALLIE  REIN
SCHINDLERSLIST
SHANE    SCAM
GENUS  OBTUSE
PSS  URAL  EASED
STEVENSPIELBERG
SAGET  APSE   DEE
TRASHY   YALTA
PIES   ARSON
THECOLORPURPLE
HAIR  MOVER  ERSE
AXES  AMINE  SEED
MID  NODES  TENS
```

667

```
SIAM  MAC   FELL
ISLE  VICES  AREA
THISLITTLEPIGGY
MON    ALTAR
TALENT  SOUR  GPS
OCARINA   PICARO
LEVI  ELLS  ALDEN
RAZORBACKHOGS
ABLER  AGAR  DEAN
NISSAN   RIGHTLY
ACE  COMB  NOOSES
ALBEE    GNP
THREELITTLEPIGS
HAIR  ENSUE  EVEL
ELMO  EYE   RELY
```

668

```
RECAP  AGAR  AMID
AROMA  WART  LACE
JAMESJOYCE  ORAL
ATE  SOLES  ANKLE
SOSOON    IDS
JUGHEADJONES
HELOT  EDDAS  AXE
ARI  TRIMS   SIT
DEA  COTTA  MEATS
JIMMYJOHNSON
ISO    INDENT
TWIXT  DRACO  LOO
HIVE  JOEJACKSON
AFAR  ULNA  LIANA
TENS  DEER  EDSEL
```

669

```
LOCO  DENSE  ABET
ICON  ILONA  DIVE
STRONGSUIT  IBEX
TEE  AGENT  HOLST
STROVE    OUSE
WARDROBE   BUY
MODEL  RARE  JETE
EARN  PUDGY  ELAN
TRES  ASIA  BATHS
ESS  TIEONEON
SPAR   SNEERS
MADOX  SCOPE  ROT
EROS  SOCKITTOME
NEWS  GUILE  ODER
DANE  TRIAD  NEON
```

670

```
ASPS  SIMS  DOCS
TARP  ANITA  EPOS
OLEARYSCOW  FEND
MACNAMARASBAND
SDI  MENOT  EMBED
ASU   ODEONA
SAPPHIRE   OSS
FINNEGANSWAKE
ELM  GLASNOST
LIMPET    MAG
SPOOL  KAMEN  MRI
OBRIENPOTATOES
INIT  KELLYGREEN
DELI  GLEAM  EBRO
ASEA  TARA  EAST
```

671

```
BOSH  TBAR  GOBI
ERTE  RENO  HEMAN
ANEW  ODAY  AMENS
DOWNHILLSKIING
STS  AKA   URN
MIAMIINDIANS
ENROL  TOTO  LIL
GOAD  HANNA  SANE
ARM  PALO  RESEW
NAPOLIITALIA
NET   NAP  TAI
HAWAIIANISLAND
LANAS  ASAN  ATNO
STORE  NILE  VEIL
TEND  SASS  ARES
```

672

```
LIMB  SHIED  DOKE
ASIA  AINTI  AMOS
ILLS  STATS  MICE
TELEPHONEBOOTH
MIEN    URN
AGREES  NORD  FTC
BRAN  MOOSE  SRO
BIGTIMEOPERATOR
ONE  RAINS  DOTE
TDS  OGRE  TROPHY
ANN    CHAR
THEYELLOWPAGES
GRAS  TIARA  BRIE
OUZO  INNER  LONE
BEEP  COAST  EWER
```

673

```
TAU  DRAMA  SOFAS
ORB  OUTER  THREW
GOOSESTEP  MAORI
AMAH  TAT  MARGOT
SATANIC   HAREM
DUCKWALK   ADS
APRONS  ART  DRIP
CLAWS  AXE  MECCA
REBS  SUE  COSHES
EBB  BUNNYHOP
INAPT   AERATOR
ARTOIS  PRE  IONE
MORON  HORSERACE
INUSE  ALOES  DUD
DANES  DOWSE  YES
```

674

```
TAMARACK   ASTER
SKINNIER  ATTIRE
KINGANDI  SEABED
NDU   ESOTERICA
LOT  TAR  DATS
BRIANBOITANO
NOTREADY   AMOCO
AAA  TREADED  MOL
INLAW  MARIANNE
TONYAHARDING
LOST  EEG  LSU
ASTRONAUT   LOG
MORALE  CHARADES
ALICES  HAVETIME
SEATS  INASENSE
```

675

```
GROW  STAT  WADUP
RONA  HARE  OBESE
OMEN  IRAN  OCEAN
WEDDINGBELLS
LOGAN  ESTEE  CAR
SSE  FAT  SANJOSE
ERNES   ACID
ROCKANDROLLBAND
OGRE   OPALS
BLEDSOE  EPA  DUD
SEW  LUNAR  MAINE
BURGLARALARM
VALLI  ALTO  OLEO
ISAAC  GOOD  NEAT
MAYBE  EYRE  ERLE
```

676

```
LOAF  LADY  ADAMS
ABBA  EIRE  BOWIE
NOEL  ADOS  SWALE
DELL  NAP  DUNKED
ODE   STARTER
CRAVED   OUTDO
HAVEN  JUNE  TBAR
ICER  COTES  HONE
NERO  IDOS  PEENS
NOTIF   REGRET
TEEPEES   EAR
BIASED  ISM  OAST
ALTER  AGEE  ULNA
ADELA  SHAD  NOON
SERFS  ATRY  DUBS
```

677

```
TIAS  LURE  ROBES
ANNE  AREA  EPEES
POKEFUNAT  TELLS
ENAMOR   SAINT
LESS   PLEBES
COSTELLO  RERULE
ANTSY  ACHED  CAW
SERE  TIKIS  SKYE
POI  CANED  FILER
ANKERS  YEARNERS
REEVES   ERLE
GAMES   ESPRIT
RHODO  PUNCHLINE
GALEN  ERIK  OLDE
SIDRA  DEBS  PEON
```

678

```
LUMP  BADER  WEAL
OPIE  ERODE  HAZE
COLT  LINGO  ATTA
INK  BUTTERFLIES
THIGH   DRENCH
AMOEBA   PLEAD
MOORS  PEARY  CAB
INTO  QUADS  TRIO
DAH  BULKY  PIETA
SOILS   MORASS
MORTON   BESOM
CHEESECLOTH  PAS
CAGE  LEONE  MUNI
ORAL  LLANO  AFAR
YENS  ALDER  EFTS
```

679

```
WARD  SAP  SOBBED
ASIA  KRA  TOROSE
CHOWMEIN  ALEXES
NAPES    TONE
ACA  DTS  DOGTROT
SAFARI  MARY  SRO
PUGNACIOUS  PHDS
ETHOS  NOB  SLOES
CHAN  BASSETERRE
TEN  AONE  CRATER
SNIGGLE  SHA  SDS
SARD   STETS
ENTREE  PULITZER
TRADES  ADO  EERO
SANEST  SYN  PEAT
```

680

```
ABAFT  CAMP  CARP
TAPIR  AMOR  ARIA
TRIBE  PALE  RAVI
TERSE  NAVEMBER
USER   REPASTS
ISRAELIS   NON
DEARS  SNITS  GOB
ENVY  SEEDS  JOVE
STE  THREE  SOBER
THE   RANCHING
ADORERS   LION
DICEMBER  BRUTE
MATA  ERIE  NAIVE
ANET  TINT  ERNES
NETS  SODA  DYERS
```

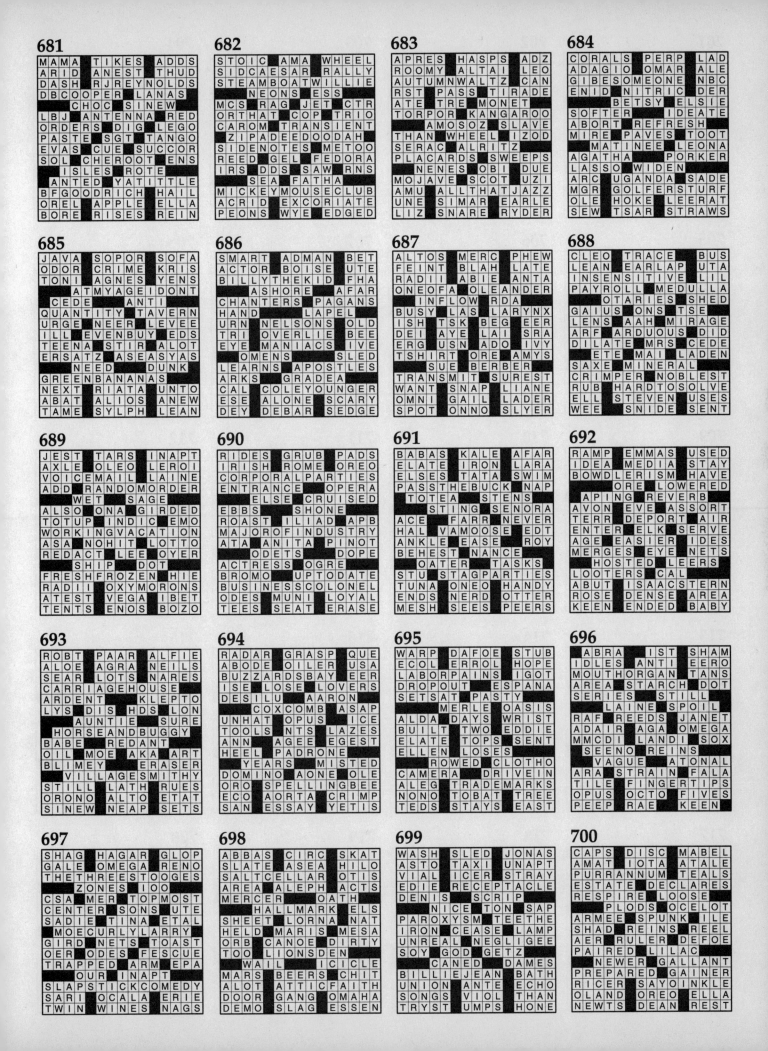

701
```
MALT  WAIST  CHOP
ILIE  ORDIE  DEMO
STEREOTYPE   CAAN
CONRAD   LATH  DRY
    OSLO  TEEUP
MISREADS   RASHER
AMI  SNOW   LEONA
CENT  DRILL  SNUG
HAGAR  PIES   ERE
ENLIST  ENTHUSED
   ELVES  ODIN
REF  PACS  ORDERS
AXIS  COPYWRITER
MALE  UNION  ETAT
AMEN  PENNS  SURA
```

702
```
BIO  RIFF   AMMO
ERNS  ONAIR  REAR
NASA  SHUSH  ERRS
THEGREENHORNET
EMCEE  RAH  NADIA
RAT  HOE  OHS  INN
   TAG  ZOO  STET
THEBLUEKNIGHT
CRUX  END  OCT
DEL  MST  ORI  AMI
SEALS  IAN  NABOB
THEGOLDENGIRLS
POOF  INDIA  KATE
SPOT  LOLLS  EDEN
ISPY  WELT   NED
```

703
```
LAPSES  SEE  SCAT
OLEATE  TAT  TALE
TARMAC  ERASABLE
    FATSWALLER
EFOR  AMY  ATBAT
TOR  YIN   RAID
ARM  EDNA  SPELLS
FATTYARBUCKLE
RENAIL  AUNT  YRS
RICK  ESS   HOI
STEEP  PEN  SONS
    FATSDOMINO
ROSINBAG  EROICA
AVIV  ALE  WARNER
DAME  RMS  SEEGER
```

704
```
BEST  HILDA  PRIM
ACLU  ONERS  LETA
CHIT  TREAT  ADES
HOPTOWERBOTTOMS
    ISA  RAF
CPI  STROP  HOFFA
HUNS  EACH  OREOS
ENDWORMCASEMARK
STEER  PAST  STEM
TAXED  SMEAR  SSE
    TEC  RNA
POWERLIGHTSTICK
INON  ONEAL  BARE
TYKE  DANTE  AGOG
AXED  STEED  TOWS
```

705
```
MIMICS     SCOPES
ISAIAH     OHLALA
LAMINAR  STOODIN
EKE  ELOPE  URSAE
   PROJECTED
CARE  MARTEN  BBL
UBOAT  JOEL   RAE
PHOTOJOURNALIST
POS  MEIR  IONIC
ART  DELIAS  TECH
   POPINJAYS
DIALO  EGADS  SON
INSULAR  RIANTLY
AGATES     SYNODS
SEPOYS     TEEPEE
```

706
```
SEAT  URSA  BETAS
AXLE  SEAM  ATONE
GALESOFLAUGHTER
SCAPE  ASP   EAT
THEWINDSOFWAR
ESTE   NAH
SPA  IRIS  REPOS
HAILANDFAREWELL
ALLAY  SABU   TEY
NAE   INTO
LIGHTNINGBUGS
PER  CON  ATREE
FORDTHUNDERBIRD
CREDO  NEON  IMAN
SAGET  SRTA  DELA
```

707
```
TIER  DEISM  SLAB
ONME  OLDIE  POLE
WHITEYFORD  LUTE
NOLOVE  LEI  IGOR
STEWING   AONE
   ELSIE  TETHER
BOYDS  VADER  RAT
ELO  MESAS   IVE
EGG  SANER  LUGES
TAILOR   SETIN
BALI  DOLLARS
AMEN  MFA  PLANET
HARD  BILLDICKEY
ACRE  ALAMO  ELSE
BEAD  SLING  DEES
```

708
```
ASIF  OGLE  IBET
RARA  SKEIN  NITA
GRASPHANDS  SGTS
ODETOA  ROULADES
   LURIE  RANI
REWARDS  BENEATH
ALAN  SONORA  MIA
TIDE  POL   LONG
ETO  ADORED  INGA
DEFACED  ROUNDER
   MEER  DOLCE
AMORTIZE  ELATES
LENA  VIPERALERT
FEET  ETONS  LALA
SKYE  SITE  YSER
```

709
```
VAPOR  IOTAS  ZED
ELLIE  SLUMP  UTE
SPELLINGBEE  ITE
THAR  STA  LEADER
SADIST   SIDLE
GOLFTEE   BREW
RIM  AERIE  TAZZA
ONTAP  ITS  INERT
DIVVY  SHARE  EAT
SAVE  GEEWHIZ
ERMAS   INARCH
CRESOL  INN  NILE
RAJ  PEEDEERIVER
AMA  ENOLA  NEATO
MAY  SANER  ARLEN
```

710
```
ALTS  ANNO  SAGAS
CAGE  BAER  ARENA
EMIL  IDLE  CARET
DAFFYDILS   BASE
   IER  SPLITS
ORGANS   SATEEN
PAUL  ANDES   ILA
TRAIT  POE  TRUER
SER  AGERS  EMIT
DERIDE  CLASSY
STEVEN  SOO
LONI  PETUNEIAS
ONINE  EVER  ALIT
PEACE  TIES  RIDE
ESSEN  ELLE  SEEP
```

711
```
PAST  GILA  NOSES
OWAR  ADAM  ETHAN
SADA  BOLA  ATARI
TRAILBLAZER  DST
SETTEE   ENERO
   ORSO  TRAWLS
SATON  PIER  IBIS
EGAD  MALLE  SORT
REID  ITEM  SEXES
ARLENS   DONA
GREET  AMANDA
ABA  TRACKRECORD
PETIT  CHAR  TREE
STEVE  KENO  OVAL
EASED  STEW  ROME
```

712
```
MOAT  FUR   PRIDE
AHSO  OLAF  RICED
JACKSONFIVESONG
ARIETTA  DETENTE
SEINER   WORE
   TELE  ANGLER
ESSO  SOLO  SLICE
SLAPSTICKWEAPON
TIBET  NORA  DONE
AMULET   MALT
IONE  LEGMAN
ARRANGE  REALIZE
SOFTWAREBYLOTUS
HYDRA  FOIE  BEST
ESSAY  SSS  SRAS
```

713
```
GAS  ADAM  ABIDE
OSHA  IOTA  NARES
TWOBAGGER  DRAMS
HAREDRESSERS
SNEEZE  THEE  MAR
TETS   ANTOINE
ARC  TAR  TANTE
BEARNECESSITIES
ANNIE  FIE   SSE
TANGELO   NCOS
ELY  DEUS  RATTAN
ALITTLEHORSE
ELATE  FEATURING
VALOR  ONCE  EMEU
EXAMS  ROYS  SRS
```

714
```
CASE  CEDED  ARTS
LOTS  ALANA  TERI
IDOS  BALLBUTTER
MAP  DOPE  RAISE
BISTROS  REGRESS
   HOUSEFIRE
AROUSE  ROE  SPAT
HARTE  DIT  CLAMS
ANTS  MEL  SLIPUP
   TABLETIME
GERAINT  SEVERAL
ELISE  ISEE   WIL
NECKRUBBER  RAMA
ACHE  LAINE  ELEM
STER  ENDED  FLEA
```

715
```
BRAGG  WELL  BAIT
LOLAS  ALOU  OMNI
ADELA  CLAD  LORE
NEAL  ROADWALKER
KOKOMO   SIB
   PEAT  GUFFAW
JAMBALAYA  TOLME
ASOU  DRUNK  REAR
CHARM  PLAINJANE
KENYAN   TRIO
WOO   BEGOFF
LEONRUNSKY  GURU
AXLE  GENA  BITER
SPEW  ATIT  ANDOR
TOGS  TOTE  AGONY
```

716
```
ETAL  INDIA  SLAB
LANA  NEONS  PAVE
ARTS  BRIGHTIDEA
MAESTRO   INERT
   OWE  TOTED
SAGEADVICE  LADA
ADORN  IMET  ELEM
CAR  GAVELED  OVI
KNEW  PASO  RUNIN
SODA  ACUTEANGLE
STREP  NFL
TASTE   AZTECAN
SMARTMONEY  ALMA
AMIE  ALARM  SUPS
ROLL  CANOE  HESA
```

717
```
ALBUM  BRAC  GED
BOONE  LIMO  ARAB
BATES  ASIN  ZINA
EMT  SIDEEFFECTS
   OCHRE  LATHES
PAMPAS   TWIXT
SISAL  CHIC  EBBS
STU  LOYALTY  ARE
TSPS  RANT  OPCIT
CLINK  TRIKES
OCTAVE   CAKED
DOWNINFRONT  ROM
ENID  TAIL  OMANI
SETA  ERTE  WAFER
YSL  DOES  NITRO
```

718
```
THE  ACID   CAFE
ARMS  DONOR  OLLA
DESK  JUGGERNAUT
ANDI  UPA  TENSE
   DEMOS  AMI
   FONT  STRIVERS
GOI  OSCAR  TENAM
AMA  AGO   TKO
ZINGS  PANDA  EEG
ATTACHES  ENGR
MAO   PEEPS
SABLE  AVA  ARAB
JOLLYROGER  RIFE
FLEE  SCENT  USED
KISS  TEDS   PER
```

719
```
ERIC  CHEF  ARMED
NILE  HUME  PEALE
IDOL  OMIT  HAILE
DEVELOPRAPIDLY
REBUS   LLD
   NERD  ASSERT
ASCII  EAST  OMAR
STOCKMARKETDIVE
HARE  OPIE  OATES
ERASER   NETS
LSU   SCARF
SUDDENPLEASURE
PAREE  COAT  CBER
SIGNS  LOOS  ALTO
IDEST  ELSE  PESO
```

720
```
MAMBOS  CBS  LOCK
ANOINT  ORO  ILIE
STANCE  WENDSDAY
CONDEMN   ADEPT
ANDS  ESSAY   ILL
RIA  LEVITY  SMEE
ANY  ALES  COEDS
   THIRSTDAY
OTTER  IHAD  TLC
FOOD  FLEERS  WAR
TEA  BREST  DOTE
STAYS   ATTESTS
SATYRDAY  HOLDIT
OMEN  AGO  ENLACE
WIDE  YEN  OKAYED
```

721
```
CAME  GULCH  AFRO
AVIV  APART  PLAT
NINE  RUBES  PORT
CATNAPPED   CLUE
ATEST   LOCO   NFL
NED  LES  ROADIE
  SALTINE  MEET
  EATSLIKEABIRD
  ALMA  ERECTED
SKATER  KEN  BAR
SSR  LYES  NOONE
CELL  LUCKYDOGS
ALTO  HADON  OGLE
GUTS  STATE  RIOT
OBOE  TENSE  SESS
```

722
```
ASTA  ASIT  TWAS
GEES  RUTHS  HERE
UPTHECREEK  ALIE
ATHENA  REOILED
  STREAMIN  SLY
DUD  ROLE  NEAP
ELOPE  ERAS  FRED
ANNIE  NOS  DAILY
RANK  CAST  ARNIE
  YEAR  OINK  GAS
EBB  POOLROOM
CARTOON  OTIOSE
OBOE  KEEPSATBAY
LEON  SINCE  CITE
ELKS  NETS  HEED
```

723
```
KEPT  PELTS  PROS
GYRO  HAIRY  RUNT
BEEF  ORSON  ISLE
STUDENTTEACHER
ROZ  OBS  SEDAN
FREEZE  AGES  IVE
DELVE  FUME  SEER
  INSIDEOUT
GALL  GAIN  DEPOT
RIO  OTTO  CAPOTE
ORGAN  ALL  NHL
WHITECHOCOLATE
LOCO  RERUN  DOLL
ELAN  ORATE  DOLE
DELE  COLES  SNOW
```

724
```
OHMY  LARGE  SPAS
ROUE  ADORE  CALL
COSA  CUTER  ORLY
ARCHEOLOGIST
SAL  ANTS  ENTERS
HENRI  ASE  LIE
  ANCIENTEGYPT
STAN  NEA  ASEA
KINGTUTSTOMB
IRE  APO  NOSED
DEWARS  PEEN  ART
  HOWARDCARTER
ROBE  IMADE  ESAU
AREA  NOTIN  DAME
DEED  GREET  STYX
```

725
```
MEL  CLIMB  GATT
ALE  SIDER  ACHE
SLED  AMATO  SHUN
CAJUN  IRENE  EMS
  BUSTERCRABBE
ROMANI   TRESS
BODICERIPPER
IHS  TETRA  DOA
  CHESTERFIELD
OHARE   SOBBED
BOSOMBUDDIES
SAT  PUREE  SETUP
EGER  NAFTA  NONE
SIRE  CLARY  GTO
SENT  OSTER  SON
```

726
```
PANG  AMBIT  ABBA
APOD  MALTA  REUP
BELABARTOK  MARS
ASONANT  EMBRYO
  SHA  ABACAB
BUBKA  SLO  INRED
ASI  MALAGA  DYNA
CUL  ALIBABA  ASU
KALB  SCARAB  NUB
SLYAS  EMT  SATES
  BRENDA  BOB
BRANCA  BARBIES
LORE  BARRYBONDS
ATTY  OLDIE  TSAR
BOYS  BASER  TOMS
```

727
```
YOYO  AREAL  CHEW
ODOR  BIALY  HALO
ROUT  HASON  AMIR
EMS  PONYEXPRESS
  EVERT  EAGLET
PANELS  DAYNE
ANDRE  MONET  ELM
LAMB  PINED  AMIE
STE  MACAW  ARISE
  TASKS  SCULPT
ABBOTT  PUTTY
FORWARDPASS  PSA
TREE  AIRES  LOOM
REEL  MOOSE  ISLE
ADDS  INDEX  ETON
```

728
```
CROCS  ULTRA  GET
DIVOT  SEOUL  OXY
SCAREDSTIFF  OER
ALGER  ALFRESCO
  IRAN  SIEVE
BAT  AMOS  ADOBES
ASH  GARCON  KURT
SCENE  SOP  FEMME
IOWA  CEREAL  PAR
STITCH  ELLA  SSE
  LARAS  SIRE
FILLERUP  MENSA
ELI  PANICBUTTON
USE  EDUCE  PRONE
DAS  SEPAL  SEWED
```

729
```
NOPE  RICED  PLOP
OPAL  IRONY  ROVE
SELLECKORSEAVER
ENMESHES  LAMENT
  PED  NESS
VISORS  SEXY  HIS
OMANI  BERI  IONA
CAVETTORVANDYKE
AGES  AGUY  ALLEN
LED  SLIM  SPEEDS
  RAKE  LOP
STRIKE  BORESOME
PRESIDENTTRUMAN
AIDE  ORATE  LAND
MOON  FRIED  KRIS
```

730
```
HEARA  AROMA  SAM
OLSEN  BANAL  TSE
PASSTHEBUCK  ASA
INTO  OTIS  ANGEL
  NESS  PLANTS
BEHAVE  SALIVA
ORATE  SALAS  TAG
MIRE  ALLEY  CITE
BET  AMOVE  BROIL
  TOBAGO  TAINTS
MOOLAH  OUST
ACHES  KEPT  ESTA
TEA  HINDQUARTER
EAR  EMEER  RIANT
ONT  DAWNS  TANTE
```

731
```
ABAB  SPRY  SMITH
BONO  CLUE  TAHOE
UNTO  RULA  RIATA
SUITCASES  ELDER
ESCHEW   TRAP
  ELAN  SMOKES
PANGS  MIRV  ULNA
ALOU  HETUP  CEOS
TERN  ONES  CHEWS
SCANTY  REAL
  YETI  NASSAU
CAUSE  BACKPACKS
UNCAP  SILL  BORE
DOLCE  EDIE  ONOR
SNAKE  NAPS  TENS
```

732
```
SODAS  BRAVO  SAL
ARENA  ROMAN  PLU
GRANDFINALE  ELM
  IDLE  SIT  COP
ANGELA  DIMITY
TAR  EMBED  MIA
TOE  BALI  EFLAT
IMAS  ELIAS  FILE
CITED  LONI  SIN
  DAR  STATS  TKO
SMILES   CHASER
TOV  SOS  POOR
ELI  SUPERMARKET
ADD  USAGE  LAINE
LYE  PANGS  SYNGE
```

733
```
TAGUP  GNAR  JOS
AMINO  CLOVE  ASH
MOBILEHOMES  CHE
TIRES   REEKED
POLECATS  SALSAS
ARISES   HELIO
RAN  EASY  EDNAS
INCAS  XED  DEFER
STOLE  ICED  IRT
  LONGS  OLIVIA
CANADA  MATINEES
ALLFOR  IREST
PLO  FLINTSTONES
RAG  FIRES  ENATE
AHS  SCAR  REGAN
```

734
```
OTHELLO  SPOKANE
TEALEAF  SILENCE
TERSEST  EGGEDON
  EARS  HAL
COB  SORTIE  SLAG
OKRA  ISAAC  IDO
VIAL  EMENDS  ORB
ENIGMA  EARNER
TAN  AGREED  OHNO
EWE  PLUME  BEAK
DADS  ENTRAP  ALE
  ADE  LEAR
EVILEYE  ELECTOR
BENTSEN  LANTERN
BEDSIDE  INSIDES
```

735
```
TEAS  AHAS  IDLES
RANT  LILT  MOIRA
ERGO  ATTA  ENNIO
STLOUISATHLETE
SHOPS   READ
  SITS  GAINED
BRA  NACRE  NOPE
RELIGIOUSLEADER
ADAM  TEPID  SEN
DONATE  YEGG
  ARLO  EADIE
REDCRESTEDBIRD
NOVAK  HAIG  ONAN
INANE  AGRA  RATA
PANED  REED  SHES
```

736
```
MEWL  RAISA  DADS
ACHE  ERROR  OBIE
CHEAPTRICK  REAR
HONDURAS  FELLA
  REN  ZOOM
  TREATWILLIAMS
ROUTED  HOED  DAH
ANTE  BIN  NORA
PET  SILL  SMERSH
TRICKQUESTION
  RISE  PAD
BEBOP  SESSIONS
EVAS  DUTCHTREAT
SERB  BRAKE  MINE
SLAY  ABYSS  ALAN
```

737
```
PHIL  ANKA  DEIFY
RONA  SEEM  EXTRA
IGET  EXPO  BISON
CAPEHATTERAS
ENTRY   BATTLES
  PASSAGE  ILE
BOOTEDUP  SUEDE
AFRO  SMASH  STEM
RAINS  TIESCORE
EGO  MAESTRO
DENSELY   LIMBO
  LATEBLOOMERS
CIGAR  LOOM  BRIC
AWAKE  INCA  ALDA
MOPED  DOOR  DEER
```

738
```
TICS  TATER  SAPS
ECHO  IVANA  TREK
SEEM  TOOTHFAIRY
HDWE  LIS  ORATE
  IDLED  SICK
LANAIS  ONTHEJOB
OBGYN  PROS  RAVE
NAG  GRABBAG  WAR
GLUT  URIS  AMBLE
IMMODEST  HEARST
  LODE  MALLE
ANGST  GAB  TARA
MOUTHPIECE  EKED
MONO  KOREA  SEND
ORGY  GUESS  EROS
```

739
```
THO  CEDE  LEASH
RANGETOP  ENLAI
USEALATHE  ACUTE
STIRS  AWESOME
TED  IAN  EVER
NATUREPRESERVE
  ISERE  EEL
PREP  SONJA  MATS
UAR  CELIA
BEANUNDERSTUDY
AREA  KOS  REB
TANGENT  OCALA
CASTE  ORGANPIPE
ALIEN  AIRLINER
BLAST  PLAY  SDS
```

740
```
EYED  SPA  TAUPE
READ  SPOT  ARPEL
MASSMARKETBOOKS
ARE  AMIE  ALONE
  LRON  ATEM
PRESSAGENTS  IRS
RAJAH  LIL  SAW
IBET  OPINE  ASTI
ABC  DUO  BLUES
MIT  BESTSELLERS
  POSH  PRAY
SILAS  PENN  AIL
LITERARYLICENSE
BROAD  ELLE  SNAG
SENDS  XES  PAYS
```

741

A	R	A	B	■	S	L	O	W	■	A	D	M	I	T
R	O	U	E	■	H	A	N	A	■	T	E	A	R	Y
T	A	T	A	■	A	N	O	N	■	O	T	T	E	R
S	M	O	K	E	S	C	R	E	E	N	■	C	N	O
■	■	■	E	R	T	E	■	■	D	A	S	H	E	S
N	U	T	R	I	A	■	B	E	D	L	A	M	■	■
A	R	O	S	E	■	D	E	L	I	■	N	A	T	O
S	I	R	■	S	T	E	A	M	E	D	■	K	E	N
A	S	C	H	■	R	E	D	S	■	I	D	E	A	L
■	■	H	I	R	E	R	S	■	F	A	I	R	L	Y
G	U	S	T	A	V	■	■	A	I	N	T	■	■	■
U	S	O	■	F	I	R	E	C	R	A	C	K	E	R
S	A	N	I	T	■	A	L	U	M	■	H	A	R	I
T	I	G	R	E	■	M	E	T	E	■	E	L	A	N
O	R	S	E	R	■	P	E	E	R	■	D	E	S	K

742

L	A	T	H	E	■	B	A	R	R	■	C	L	E	F
A	R	R	A	Y	■	O	P	I	E	■	H	A	R	E
S	L	I	M	E	■	L	A	N	D	■	A	I	D	E
T	E	C	H	■	P	O	R	K	B	A	R	R	E	L
S	N	E	A	K	S	■	■	■	O	P	T	■	■	■
■	■	■	N	E	I	G	H	B	O	R	■	A	S	I
G	L	A	D	E	■	R	O	O	K	■	G	U	T	S
R	I	V	E	N	■	E	R	N	■	M	O	R	A	L
A	M	I	D	■	V	A	S	E	■	O	H	A	R	E
Y	E	S	■	W	A	T	E	R	L	O	O	■	■	■
■	■	■	P	A	C	■	■	■	E	G	G	N	O	G
P	I	G	I	N	A	P	O	K	E	■	W	O	R	E
O	N	Y	X	■	N	O	T	A	■	F	I	T	I	N
E	T	R	E	■	C	L	A	Y	■	F	L	E	E	R
T	O	O	L	■	Y	O	Y	O	■	A	D	D	L	E

743

C	I	S	C	O	■	M	I	S	T	Y	■	E	R	E
A	M	O	U	R	■	A	D	I	E	U	■	M	I	T
M	I	S	S	I	N	G	I	N	A	C	T	I	O	N
S	T	O	P	G	A	P	■	■	■	A	O	R	T	A
■	■	■	■	I	R	I	S	■	E	T	O	■	■	■
A	B	S	E	N	C	E	O	F	M	A	L	I	C	E
L	U	L	L	S	■	■	L	A	I	N	■	D	E	S
B	R	E	L	■	P	R	I	N	T	■	A	I	L	S
A	R	E	■	L	A	I	C	■	■	P	R	O	L	E
N	O	T	H	I	N	G	I	N	C	O	M	M	O	N
■	■	■	I	K	E	■	T	A	R	T	■	■	■	■
O	P	E	R	A	■	■	■	T	E	A	C	H	E	R
N	O	N	E	B	U	T	T	H	E	B	R	A	V	E
E	G	O	■	L	L	A	M	A	■	L	O	V	E	D
S	O	S	■	E	A	T	I	N	■	E	W	E	R	S

744

L	I	P	O	■	R	E	E	L	S	■	D	I	A	N
E	L	E	V	■	A	N	T	I	C	■	O	T	H	O
G	O	N	E	W	I	T	H	T	H	E	W	I	N	D
■	■	■	N	I	N	A	S	■	O	X	E	N	■	■
A	T	P	■	L	I	D	■	T	O	P	L	E	S	S
C	R	E	O	L	E	■	L	A	L	O	■	R	U	E
T	E	N	O	■	S	P	A	R	■	S	H	A	M	E
■	A	S	H	O	T	I	N	T	H	E	A	R	M	■
O	D	I	S	T	■	S	A	S	E	■	R	I	A	S
R	E	V	■	E	V	A	S	■	L	E	P	E	R	S
K	R	E	M	L	I	N	■	S	M	A	■	S	Y	S
■	■	N	I	L	E	■	B	E	E	C	H	■	■	■
L	I	E	D	O	W	N	O	N	T	H	E	J	O	B
I	L	S	A	■	E	R	A	S	E	■	R	O	L	E
L	E	S	S	■	R	A	T	E	D	■	D	E	E	D

745

■	H	I	S	S	■	S	A	N	E	■	R	A	I	D
R	E	O	I	L	■	A	B	E	L	■	E	D	D	Y
L	A	W	S	U	I	T	C	A	S	E	B	O	O	K
S	T	A	I	D	L	Y	■	T	A	X	A	B	L	E
■	■	■	■	G	E	R	M	■	■	E	T	E	S	■
J	A	M	M	E	D	■	I	R	A	T	E	■	■	■
O	H	I	O	■	■	G	L	O	B	E	■	M	B	A
W	O	R	M	W	O	O	D	W	O	R	K	D	A	Y
L	Y	E	■	I	B	A	R	S	■	■	E	L	K	E
■	■	■	S	N	I	D	E	■	A	G	G	I	E	S
■	C	H	A	D	■	■	D	U	L	L	■	■	■	■
S	E	A	F	O	O	D	■	S	T	E	E	P	L	E
C	A	R	E	F	R	E	E	H	A	N	D	O	U	T
A	S	K	S	■	A	C	R	E	■	D	A	C	C	A
B	E	S	T	■	L	O	A	D	■	A	M	O	K	■

746

P	R	O	S	■	H	I	P	P	O	■	C	H	A	R
A	U	N	T	■	O	D	E	O	N	■	H	A	L	O
P	E	C	A	N	R	O	L	L	S	■	I	M	A	M
A	R	E	N	A	S	■	T	I	E	C	L	A	S	P
■	■	■	D	I	E	S	■	S	T	E	I	N	■	■
A	W	F	U	L	■	A	S	H	■	R	E	D	U	B
H	A	R	P	■	R	I	O	■	P	E	S	E	T	A
A	C	E	■	R	E	D	U	C	E	S	■	G	I	N
B	O	S	S	E	D	■	S	U	N	■	O	G	L	E
■	■	H	I	P	■	P	E	R	■	F	U	S	E	S
A	L	F	A	L	F	A	■	B	R	U	T	■	■	■
F	A	R	M	Y	A	R	D	■	A	R	R	O	W	S
T	R	U	E	■	C	O	R	N	F	L	A	K	E	S
E	G	I	S	■	E	D	I	C	T	■	G	R	I	T
R	O	T	E	■	T	Y	P	O	S	■	E	A	R	S

747

P	A	N	S	Y	■	R	A	C	E	R	■	A	W	L
A	L	I	C	E	■	A	G	O	R	A	■	C	O	E
P	O	L	A	R	I	C	E	C	A	P	■	C	P	O
S	E	E	M	■	R	I	N	K	■	S	A	R	A	N
■	■	■	P	L	A	N	T	A	R	■	R	A	T	E
A	L	L	■	U	S	E	■	T	O	U	T	■	■	■
N	E	I	L	L	■	■	T	O	A	D	I	E	R	■
D	E	M	O	L	I	T	I	O	N	D	E	R	B	Y
■	R	E	V	E	R	I	E	■	■	E	R	N	I	E
■	■	■	E	D	I	T	■	A	P	R	■	O	S	S
T	A	X	I	■	S	O	U	R	E	S	T	■	■	■
O	W	E	N	S	■	I	N	G	A	■	A	E	R	O
P	A	N	■	C	O	S	M	O	T	O	P	P	E	R
P	R	O	■	A	N	T	E	S	■	P	E	E	V	E
S	E	N	■	T	E	S	T	Y	■	T	R	E	S	S

748

A	B	E	■	D	I	A	N	A	■	S	W	I	F	T
D	E	A	■	E	N	D	O	N	■	C	A	C	A	O
E	A	R	■	M	U	D	D	Y	W	A	T	E	R	S
L	U	T	H	O	R	■	■	■	E	L	U	D	E	S
E	X	H	A	L	E	S	■	B	E	D	S	■	■	■
■	■	A	B	I	D	E	■	I	N	S	I	D	E	R
T	I	K	I	S	■	L	E	V	Y	■	■	I	R	E
E	D	I	T	H	■	L	E	O	■	C	A	R	L	A
N	E	T	■	■	P	E	R	U	■	A	F	T	E	R
T	A	T	T	L	E	R	■	A	S	T	A	Y	■	■
■	■	■	H	E	R	S	■	C	O	A	C	H	E	D
A	F	I	E	N	D	■	■	■	C	L	E	A	V	E
C	A	S	S	I	U	S	C	L	A	Y	■	R	A	I
E	L	I	O	T	■	O	P	E	N	S	■	R	D	S
D	A	N	N	Y	■	T	R	A	I	T	■	Y	E	T

749

J	A	D	E	D	■	B	A	L	I	■	E	L	L	A
A	L	I	V	E	■	R	E	E	D	■	T	E	E	S
W	O	M	E	N	■	U	R	S	A	■	H	A	T	H
S	T	E	■	M	A	N	Y	T	H	A	N	K	S	■
■	■	■	S	A	B	E	■	■	O	B	I	■	■	■
■	■	M	E	R	C	I	B	E	A	U	C	O	U	P
S	M	A	C	K	S	■	R	A	N	T	■	A	N	A
L	E	N	T	■	■	A	I	R	■	■	A	S	I	T
U	N	I	■	L	A	V	A	■	E	F	F	E	T	E
M	U	C	H	A	S	G	R	A	C	I	A	S	■	■
■	■	■	I	N	C	■	■	T	H	A	R	■	■	■
■	D	A	N	K	E	S	C	H	O	N	■	P	I	K
L	A	N	G	■	T	I	R	E	■	C	H	O	S	E
E	R	N	E	■	I	T	O	N	■	E	B	O	N	Y
W	E	E	D	■	C	U	P	S	■	S	O	R	T	S

750

I	B	I	S	■	G	L	U	M	■	■	C	H	I	T
R	O	T	A	■	A	U	R	A	L	■	L	O	C	O
K	N	E	W	M	E	X	I	C	O	■	A	R	I	A
S	Y	M	B	O	L	■	S	E	C	O	N	D	E	D
■	■	■	U	N	I	T	■	■	A	N	G	E	R	S
K	N	I	C	K	C	H	A	R	L	E	S	■	■	■
L	O	C	K	S	■	R	E	E	L	S	■	N	O	D
E	V	E	S	■	F	O	R	A	Y	■	J	O	N	I
E	A	T	■	T	O	N	I	C	■	R	O	U	T	E
■	■	■	F	O	R	G	E	T	M	E	K	N	O	T
A	S	K	E	R	S	■	■	S	A	F	E	■	■	■
S	W	E	E	T	A	I	R	■	S	I	S	T	E	R
T	E	E	D	■	K	N	I	G	H	T	T	I	M	E
R	E	N	E	■	E	D	D	I	E	■	E	N	I	D
A	P	E	R	■	■	Y	E	N	S	■	R	A	T	S

751

E	M	I	T	S	■	F	R	E	T	■	A	B	C	S
B	E	R	R	A	■	D	E	L	E	■	E	R	L	E
B	R	A	I	N	D	R	A	I	N	■	R	I	A	L
S	E	N	D	E	R	■	M	A	E	■	O	G	R	E
■	■	■	E	R	O	S	■	S	T	A	S	H	E	S
D	A	W	N	■	O	L	E	■	S	L	O	T	■	■
A	L	I	T	■	P	I	M	A	■	O	L	I	V	E
L	A	S	■	E	Y	E	B	R	O	W	■	D	O	E
I	N	E	R	T	■	R	E	I	D	■	T	E	L	L
■	■	C	E	N	T	■	R	E	D	■	E	A	T	S
C	E	R	T	A	I	N	■	S	E	L	A	■	■	■
O	M	A	R	■	N	I	P	■	S	A	R	A	H	S
M	I	C	E	■	S	M	A	R	T	M	O	N	E	Y
I	L	K	A	■	E	B	R	O	■	P	O	N	E	S
C	E	S	T	■	L	I	E	D	■	S	M	E	L	T

752

M	A	S	S	■	■	■	R	I	T	A	■	G	N	P
A	D	I	E	U	■	S	U	S	H	I	■	R	I	O
O	S	C	A	R	W	I	N	N	E	R	■	A	N	S
■	■	■	■	B	A	N	G	O	R	■	S	C	A	T
■	T	O	G	A	S	■	S	T	E	V	I	E	■	■
S	I	L	E	N	T	S	■	■	S	A	M	P	A	N
A	R	I	D	■	E	A	T	S	■	N	I	E	C	E
L	A	V	■	I	S	L	A	N	D	S	■	R	O	E
A	D	E	P	T	■	E	R	I	E	■	B	I	R	D
D	E	B	R	I	S	■	■	P	A	T	R	O	N	S
■	■	R	A	S	H	E	S	■	R	O	A	D	S	■
S	T	A	Y	■	E	V	I	C	T	S	■	■	■	■
H	U	N	■	F	A	I	T	H	H	E	A	L	E	R
A	B	C	■	A	R	T	I	E	■	E	M	I	L	Y
H	A	H	■	A	S	A	N	■	■	■	O	P	I	E

753

L	E	M	O	N	■	C	A	N	■	G	O	B	E	L
A	D	O	R	E	■	A	B	E	■	I	R	A	T	E
K	I	D	G	L	O	V	E	S	■	L	I	B	R	A
E	N	E	■	S	M	E	L	T	■	D	O	Y	E	N
S	A	L	O	O	N	■	■	■	G	A	N	G	■	■
■	■	■	S	N	I	P	P	E	R	S	■	R	E	B
R	A	F	T	S	■	L	E	D	A	■	N	A	T	O
I	R	A	E	■	R	U	N	G	S	■	O	N	A	N
O	L	I	O	■	Y	M	C	A	■	S	A	D	L	Y
T	O	R	■	B	A	B	E	R	U	T	H	■	■	■
■	■	C	L	A	N	■	■	■	N	A	S	C	A	R
C	O	H	A	N	■	T	R	A	I	L	■	U	T	A
A	P	I	N	G	■	H	O	T	T	E	N	T	O	T
B	I	L	G	E	■	U	S	O	■	S	E	I	N	E
S	E	D	E	R	■	G	E	M	■	T	O	N	E	S

754

S	T	A	G	■	S	K	I	E	R	■	A	Q	U	A
A	H	S	O	■	L	O	D	G	E	■	C	U	S	S
G	O	O	D	W	A	L	L	O	F	C	H	I	N	A
S	U	N	S	H	I	N	E	■	■	R	E	R	A	N
■	■	■	P	E	N	■	■	F	L	A	S	K	■	■
E	S	S	E	N	■	■	A	L	I	T	■	I	D	I
A	N	T	E	■	C	A	R	A	F	E	■	N	U	N
G	O	O	D	B	A	R	R	I	E	R	R	E	E	F
E	R	R	■	I	D	E	A	L	S	■	A	S	T	O
R	E	M	■	T	R	A	Y	■	■	V	I	S	O	R
■	■	F	L	I	E	S	■	■	H	E	N	■	■	■
A	P	R	O	N	■	■	G	R	I	D	D	L	E	S
G	O	O	D	G	R	A	N	D	P	A	R	E	N	T
R	U	N	E	■	U	S	U	A	L	■	O	G	L	E
A	R	T	S	■	M	I	S	S	Y	■	P	S	A	T

755

B	I	N	G	■	C	R	A	B	■	S	N	I	P	E
O	N	O	R	■	H	I	R	E	■	W	O	M	A	N
T	R	I	O	■	A	C	E	S	■	A	V	O	I	D
H	E	R	W	O	R	K	A	T	A	N	E	N	D	■
■	■	■	N	E	T	■	■	S	E	L	L	■	■	■
P	A	W	■	D	E	M	I	■	S	A	L	O	O	N
A	S	H	■	■	R	E	D	O	■	K	A	P	P	A
T	H	E	M	A	S	S	E	U	S	E	S	A	I	D
T	O	T	A	L	■	H	A	S	H	■	■	L	U	I
I	T	S	E	L	F	■	S	T	A	N	■	S	M	A
■	■	■	S	T	E	T	■	■	T	A	P	■	■	■
■	A	Y	T	H	E	R	E	S	T	H	E	R	U	B
A	D	O	R	E	■	A	C	H	E	■	P	O	S	E
M	A	Y	O	R	■	C	H	E	R	■	T	I	D	E
P	R	O	S	E	■	T	O	S	S	■	O	L	A	F

756

S	P	A	R	E	■	F	L	E	D	■	S	P	O	T
H	A	S	A	T	■	R	A	N	I	■	T	O	G	A
A	R	T	I	C	H	O	K	E	S	■	E	K	E	S
D	E	A	L	■	O	N	E	■	A	G	R	E	E	S
■	■	■	W	O	R	D	■	■	L	E	E	R	S	■
S	A	H	A	R	A	■	H	A	L	L	O	F	■	■
P	L	O	Y	S	■	H	A	L	O	■	S	A	N	G
A	O	K	■	O	K	I	N	A	W	A	■	C	O	L
S	T	E	P	■	I	N	K	S	■	G	R	E	T	A
■	■	Y	E	A	S	T	S	■	S	E	E	D	E	D
■	A	P	E	R	S	■	■	L	I	S	T	■	■	■
G	L	O	R	I	A	■	A	I	R	■	I	R	A	S
R	A	K	E	■	B	A	C	K	S	T	R	O	K	E
A	M	E	S	■	L	I	R	E	■	R	E	S	I	N
B	O	Y	S	■	E	D	E	N	■	I	D	E	N	T

757

S	A	R	A	H	■	■	B	U	M	P	■	M	A	D
S	P	I	R	A	L	■	E	S	A	U	■	O	N	E
R	E	V	E	R	E	■	L	A	I	R	■	A	K	A
■	S	E	N	E	G	A	L	■	N	E	C	T	A	R
■	■	R	O	M	■	L	E	S	S	E	R	■	■	■
S	O	F	T	■	U	P	S	E	T	■	A	D	U	B
C	A	R	■	C	P	O	■	A	R	I	Z	O	N	A
A	T	O	A	S	T	■	■	■	E	V	E	N	T	S
L	E	N	G	T	H	S	■	R	A	Y	■	N	I	T
E	S	T	A	■	E	P	S	O	M	■	L	Y	L	E
■	■	■	I	N	C	A	N	T	■	S	O	B	■	■
C	O	R	N	E	R	■	A	I	R	P	O	R	T	■
O	R	O	■	R	E	E	K	■	P	E	K	O	E	S
K	A	T	■	V	E	R	E	■	I	N	T	O	T	O
E	L	S	■	E	K	E	D	■	■	T	O	K	E	N

758

B	L	E	D	■	S	C	A	B	■	P	R	I	G	S
L	O	V	E	■	C	A	S	E	■	H	E	W	E	R
O	W	E	D	■	A	V	I	V	■	L	L	A	N	O
C	E	L	E	B	R	I	T	Y	R	O	A	S	T	S
■	■	■	■	A	F	L	■	■	E	X	T	■	■	■
T	R	O	L	L	■	S	L	A	B	■	E	B	B	S
A	E	R	A	T	E	■	O	N	U	S	■	R	O	E
P	L	A	Y	I	N	G	W	I	T	H	F	I	R	E
E	A	T	■	C	L	U	E	■	S	O	O	N	E	R
D	Y	E	S	■	I	N	D	Y	■	R	E	E	D	S
■	■	■	U	P	S	■	■	E	F	T	■	■	■	■
H	O	T	B	U	T	T	O	N	I	S	S	U	E	S
A	R	M	O	R	■	A	L	T	E	■	A	N	T	E
N	E	A	R	S	■	R	E	A	R	■	M	I	N	X
D	O	N	N	E	■	P	O	S	Y	■	S	T	A	Y

759

R	I	C	E	■	L	O	B	E	D	■	S	T	A	B
A	R	I	A	■	E	C	O	L	E	■	L	A	L	A
R	E	T	U	R	N	T	R	I	P	■	O	X	E	N
E	N	E	■	E	T	O	N	■	A	R	M	I	E	S
R	E	D	U	C	E	■	■	G	R	O	O	M	■	■
■	■	■	T	E	N	F	O	R	T	Y	■	E	P	A
R	O	D	I	N	■	I	R	I	S	■	S	T	E	N
E	L	E	C	T	■	A	I	L	■	P	L	E	A	T
A	L	D	A	■	U	S	E	S	■	L	A	R	K	S
P	A	U	■	U	N	C	L	E	S	A	M	■	■	■
■	■	C	A	N	T	O	■	■	A	N	S	W	E	R
B	E	T	T	E	R	■	E	L	S	E	■	E	R	A
O	L	I	O	■	I	N	V	E	S	T	M	E	N	T
G	L	O	M	■	E	R	A	S	E	■	O	D	I	E
S	A	N	S	■	D	A	N	E	S	■	E	Y	E	S

760

M	A	C	E	S	■	■	W	H	A	M	■	G	U	M
R	A	L	P	H	■	R	A	I	S	E	■	A	P	U
T	H	E	I	R	■	E	R	R	O	N	■	E	H	S
■	■	A	S	I	A	N	R	E	P	U	B	L	I	C
A	I	N	T	■	C	I	I	■	■	■	R	I	L	L
T	W	E	L	V	E	■	O	B	S	T	A	C	L	E
T	H	R	E	E	S	T	R	I	K	E	S	■	■	■
N	O	S	■	S	O	Y	■	R	I	P	■	A	N	I
■	■	■	S	T	U	P	I	D	P	E	R	S	O	N
R	E	F	A	S	T	E	N	■	P	E	A	C	E	S
I	M	E	T	■	■	■	T	I	E	■	M	E	L	T
N	O	V	E	M	B	E	R	T	R	E	A	T	■	■
S	T	E	■	A	R	B	U	S	■	A	D	I	E	U
E	E	R	■	R	E	A	D	Y	■	S	A	C	K	S
D	D	S	■	E	R	N	E	■	■	E	S	S	E	S

761
```
LONE PART STRIP
IMAN AJAR PHOTO
MARC GOGO HEIST
ARCHIEBUNKER
ADA      ERECT
JANINE ARE LOG
TEETOTALER PELE
BERET RES AARON
AVID BLOODDRIVE
REA HAY PALACE
SLEEK      BAG
BYEBYEBIRDIE
GAPED EARL ARTS
EXTRA ALIE PEAS
MEATY REED HILO
```

762
```
BAMA CREEK SEAT
ALAS HORSE TINA
SIXSHOOTER AGAR
ICI ELKE OUGHTA
SEMPRE ASSET
HORMONES BEL
ACTON IRAN FATA
SAWN ATALE ALUM
TROY ITTO ADLIB
ALF FREEGAME
ITURN RADISH
BUSONI TATI TAE
ASTI FOURINHAND
REEL LABEL OLEG
ADDS ESSAY EYRE
```

763
```
PASSES JASMINE
ELAPSE ROLLOVER
DONATE THEOREMS
ANTS THEN PASO
LEA GOO FEEL
CIA MEOW SWAM
HOLTZ ERRED AVE
IRATE RNS IBSEN
TAU SASSY NEHRU
ELSA MITT KAI
SKIM HEY NFL
CAPE PLED OGLE
HOMEBASE GOATEE
AVOCADOS ECHOED
TESTBAN STUNTS
```

764
```
CUBAN POUND MEN
INANE ONAIR ALI
DIANE MEWTATION
BERRAS MAMIE
GOES ADEPT FEST
ARC PEELER FRAY
SAUCE FAURE
PLEASES LEATHER
ROBED PAINE
ASEA ALICES STE
PERM NAVAL ASOF
INRED ENLIST
COOLINARY SCORE
ARR VERSO LOREN
LAS ADMEN ETYMA
```

765
```
IRAQI SETS CRY
NEGUS PARER LOO
SHOER OVINE ELL
TART JOEBTFSPLK
BAZAARS FITS
ASKS MONEYED
PULSE AGREEDTO
SINCE OUR SPRAT
OTTOMANS LOLAS
PARABLE LORE
ATLI SENECAS
RECLAMPING HATE
ILK GEARS FARED
OLE ENSUE ASONE
TAD TOPS XENON
```

766
```
DAMITA CAD RACK
ENAMOR ONE INRE
CORPORALKLINGER
IEL FALLSDOWN
APPLEOF EAT LEE
COO ARCS HALL
HOSPITAL DYE
HAWKEYEPIERCE
TEN ALANALDA
ROWS ATAN IGN
UPA IND YEARNED
SPIFFIEST LAC
HOTLIPSHOULIHAN
ISEE ITO BASELY
NERD NEW INESSE
```

767
```
ADIEU TAMP ROBE
RERAN AREA EVIL
MEETBOLDLY AILS
ERN LOCO MIDDLE
DEEPEN REEDY
USAF SNIFFAT
BOOST RITT OLDE
ALPH CANES REDS
LIEF HUGE AWASH
ENDOWED MOMA
ROSSI PURPLE
CLOWNS NEAL ROT
ROMA MEDDLEWITH
AVER ERIE TENSE
WEND NEAR STEAL
```

768
```
PLEB SCAR LESS
EATIT HOLE LOLA
AMATI AVIV ONYX
SALTLAKECITY
EDDY EVADERS
SPARED AFAR NET
PALES OPAL STLO
ALAN FRAYS OEIL
CORD RARE NURSE
EMU BENT KARATS
KAMFONG EPIC
SWEETCHARITY
PERT TAIL DEFOE
OREO IDEA SANTA
DAMP CEST MISS
```

769
```
IDOS CEDAR HAS
STOVE ALONE ARP
SHOESTRINGS SPA
TERRAINS ETCHED
SMEE TROUBLE
EMCEES SHIRER
WARES SPINE OPT
ERIN GOING KWAI
SEN BOUTS FENCE
KARATS GEYSER
BULLISH ROLL
OMELET GETTABLE
ABC FRENCHFRIES
TRU EATAT OGRES
SAT DYERS RODS
```

770
```
QUIP BARA AJAR
ETAL COHAN NATO
DANE AGENT ECHO
SOMEMISTAKES
ZACHARY ORANT
ELLERY FRAN LAS
TAUT ALISON
ARETOOMUCHFUNTO
EUREKA TERI
PAT TONE SORREL
AWARD DERIDES
MAKEONLYONCE
EKED AIMTO NOVA
LETA PACER TRON
ANON AMAD SEXY
```

771
```
DRAB SCAT BEARD
ROLE LUBE EADIE
ALVA OPUS WROTE
FLIRTWITHDANGER
TEN REDS ERE
SIR EMERSON
SETON MAGI AGE
PLAYINGWITHFIRE
AIR ARES ALDER
RATTANS BIO
ENC ASOF APB
COURTEDDISASTER
ARNEL RODS ASTI
RAISE ABLE SEAM
ALTAR TEES HALS
```

772
```
DIE CHOMP GOONS
INN LARGO OPRAH
OLD OVERTHEEDGE
RELINES TURN
STEVEN BEN EONS
SAD HUD CRUEL
ASSN AIR OUSTEE
PTL ITERATE ODD
PEOPLE OAT MFAS
LAVAL TWA SOB
EKES HRS BATONS
THOU LAWSUIT
FREEANDEASY NCO
AUGUR GUISE DEP
STORM ERROR SRS
```

773
```
NET SAGS ICANT
OLAF WEAL SUSIE
ALTO ORGY STILE
HEIRLOOM CUSSED
KEN ETHEL
ERASE SWEE IMAM
CHRIS LINE KALE
LORN MITER ERLE
ADIT ACHT BALES
TESH TEAS UKASE
EWERS ANN
MADRID PASTICHE
AXIOM SOLI FLEX
RECAP COED EASE
SLEDS INGE MAC
```

774
```
INPRINT GINGHAM
CAREFOR ERASURE
ANIMATE NOTABIT
NOVA ESSEN SDS
ADDS TRYIT
CATER CSA GUMBO
RUE ADO LONGARM
ERE GER IDO JAI
PARSNIP ZEB ONT
ELSIE ORE LORDS
STARE MERE
RTE GAMMA ETRE
AIRMAIL EXALTED
SEAGULL GINSENG
PASSKEY AMNESTY
```

775
```
ALS RUB CAB
TEAM OMAHA ERNO
ANWARSADAT XING
LITRES GRAILS
ENOLA WED DATA
ELSE KLAXONS
DARYLHANNAH BAA
ICE YOKOONO AMP
ERA MONICASELES
DESPITE KITS
SOON SIS ACHES
NUDIST STROLL
STIR REALPEOPLE
HUNS ASNER WEED
EGG DEY RNS
```

776
```
SLAM RAVE SECTS
HULA IVAN ELLIE
ICON GIST ASIDE
RINGMASTERS PER
EAGLET REHAB
ELOPE DEPOSE
TASS NASH LEANS
EST PINTAIL RAP
ETUDE TORN EDGY
MODELS PEDAL
FLICK UNMADE
AHA CHAINLETTER
MARLA STAG RENO
ELMAN HOPE EATS
NESTS ARES ERSE
```

777
```
SMOTE PADUA CAP
PASHA IRONY AMI
ELLERYQUEEN RUE
DIOS OUTS ROOST
TALE GALLEY
HIJACK PAWNEE
ALONE CUBED KEG
TEED COLIN FIDO
STY HOIST HINGE
BEATLE FORGES
BRIDLE TOTE
ROSSI EARL SAWS
ASH BOBBYKNIGHT
GEO URALS IDEAL
ASP TENET PESTO
```

778
```
ADOPT PRES DAMS
BASER LOTT ERIE
ENLAI ATTA MITA
LOOKTOYOURHEART
ORT TEASES
MYKINDOFTOWN
LEAVE LOUS BOW
LATE BLOAT NOVA
ERE POOR SIZED
ILLWALKALONE
SLICED EIN
LOVEANDMARRIAGE
ARAB ERIN EGGED
GENA SANE MOORE
SNAG STIR ORDER
```

779
```
MAPS SABOT BOOK
ACHE ADANO ASHE
RULE TONER RUIN
STOPBURNING LOT
HEX ORES DOLL
BIN CODEINE
ALVIN GROW AVIV
SEEAGIRLONADATE
ANNS NAST RENAL
POTENCY CUD
IDOL AHAB ZOO
ALL RUNFORAPASS
JOAN DOONE RICH
ANTI EVOKE IRAE
REEL SATYR MERA
```

780
```
BEST APOP CAPEK
OMNI LAIR ADOBE
AMANGALLEDHORSE
TAKEAIM GYN CEL
EAT TOON PUNS
MEIR WRY ATOP
IAN GAEL MANIAC
CUTRATE PIMENTO
EXHALE ARTE ETC
EVER LIE AQUA
URGE SIAM TIU
POL EKG AGONIZE
SLAPPINGTURTLES
ELSIE APER STAT
TOSEE ZASU OSLO
```

781
```
SAHL AMASS ACTS
OLIO BADTO SHIP
FINGERNAIL TINA
ANGELA  RACIST
SEE IDA CONE
  SEESAWED LOT
APSE STAR EMERY
NICER URE RARER
TERRA TOTS ISLE
SSE WRENCHED
 WHEE HAM STA
HEARST  VISTAS
BUDS HAMMERLOCK
AGUA OLDER AKIM
SEPT TESTS PETE
```

782
```
GLUM LAMB  GOER
RARA AROAR ERTE
AMID PELLE WETS
MASC FALLINGOUT
   AAU GOA
SLIPSLIDINAWAY
EAT ASTIR HELEN
MIAS UNA DOTE
INLET RAKES HIS
GODOWNHILLFAST
   IMA EYE
STUMBLEBUM ICAN
WIFE DRAPE SAGE
IRON ORLON TRUE
TEST SENT YEAR
```

783
```
LEGAL ARNO TBAR
OCALA LIEU EERO
FLYBYNIGHT SETS
TAL METS VALLEY
STEVES  TOPAZ
 ANTIDOTE ETC
SOBS SNIPER BOO
PLUTO CAP STUMP
EGG SPINET EBBS
DAG MITERBOX
 ETAPE OPTICS
REDONE SINE DAP
ELON TICKERTAPE
NAUT TRUE ASHEN
ONTO EATS SPORT
```

784
```
RIND ISHOT MATT
ODOR DEATH AHAH
BLUEVIEWTERRACE
BENDED NONACTOR
   GRID ODE
CHESTERARILEY
BLARE SENTI LEI
BOGS FIRTH ILSA
STU ALGAE UNION
HERMANMUNSTER
   AIM PETE
GLANCEAT AERIAL
MOCKINGBIRDLANE
ABEL CRAVE AMEN
JOSE OARED YAWS
```

785
```
CROW LIPS EJECT
HIKE ALLO RADIO
ACRE SLIM SKIRT
SHAKESBEER ECCE
 LIE TOASTED
CIRCLE HIGHS
AGAZE COMEAPART
LORE PAPER ELIE
FRACTURES RAISA
 HERDS MURDER
CHASERS DIN
RUMP SHEIKSPEER
INOIL ALVA REDO
BARES READ ONIT
SNERD PESO MYTH
```

786
```
LANCE CAPS SLOG
AREAS ABOU HERE
STAMPOFAPPROVAL
TYRE PET PERILS
   UPI DONT
KEEPINGPOSTED
ENS SERENE SONG
LOTSA ARA ATRIA
PLOT SHOLOM ILL
PARTANDPARCEL
 TEEM THE
IMMUNE TAI CASA
LETTERSOFCREDIT
SAGE ELLA ADOPT
ALES DYER MESSY
```

787
```
LASH HEAR JAPAN
ISLE AUTO ORATE
STARSINONESEYES
TOY ERIN LEASES
 ACDC MAPS
DOWNTOEARTH FCC
ERRIS LEE AURA
USES ACIDS GMAT
CONE PUB TRENT
ENS PIEINTHESKY
 ORES EIRE
BIONIC ETTE ORK
INSEVENTHHEAVEN
NOLTE TREE LENO
SNOOT HERD ANEW
```

788
```
DEMO SKIS CHANG
OXON PANT AERIE
WATT INDUSTRIAL
SCHOOLS  UNO
ETE ALABAMA LIB
SARDS SEXAPPEAL
 IOTA ALT AINU
MENU DIVER USSR
ALLA JOE ACLU
CLAYCOURT AORTA
HEW RUSSIAN EAP
 SUR STEPSUP
JUSTINCASE AUTO
ALIAS OPUS VIES
WEDGE BEET ETRE
```

789
```
TOSCA GRIP ADOS
WHEEL AURA GILA
INTEL STOWGOODS
GOO OCEAN NURSE
 FLUES DAT
ALCOTT MORTISED
LEAF ABODES CDE
TORT CONES SOIL
AND AENEAS PUTT
RESONANT AGATHA
 RIN AGENT
ORBIT TIBET RES
BIASAJURY STORK
IPSO IBIS IRONY
SEEN MASS TEPEE
```

790
```
LLAMA SAAB AFRO
AESOP AIDE PLED
ISHOPLIKEA PEPE
 RIPE KLAXON
DISSONANT BLESS
ENLIVEN ADJ DEE
BEATA ACE
 BULLICHARGE
  ANT ELMAN
JAW EMS ACQUIRE
ATEST PIROUETTE
ZEALOT RANI
ZANE EVERYTHING
USED NANA EERIE
PEDS STET DRAPE
```

791
```
ATAT SAKI OLDER
LECH EMIT PAUSE
ERTE TATA EDGED
CROSSTHELINE
SERIAL IDS ADO
 STEERCLEAROF
BOO ESAU EASTOF
LALO TIM PINE
ATLAST NANA EER
SHIFTEDGEARS
TSE EAR REPLAY
 TAKEFORARIDE
PANEL SILO ANDA
ALIST SLAW IGET
LEASH YENS NODS
```

792
```
AJAR SCROD RAM
GOLEM TREND IVY
ALICECOOPER TEN
RIG COWPEA EZRA
SENECA  ALAS
 CARROLLBAKER
LIMO SOS LUANA
ORE DEBACLE NOT
AMIGO KAA BESS
FANNIEFARMER
 ANTA BLANCH
BART HEARDA ALA
AXE MARSHAMASON
BEE ANISE STACK
ELF PEETE ELKS
```

793
```
MENU MARDI FOLD
ALES ALIEN OVID
RAVI LANCE REST
STANDINGORDER
HEDGE  TINCAN
ASA PASSE ASONE
 DOCKAGE IOTA
 SITTINGDUCK
ROTC INTENTS
EVOKE SADAT BET
PACING  ELLIE
 KNEELINGRAILS
ARCS NADIA STET
CIAO RHETT THEE
CORN ERASE SEND
```

794
```
DEREK WEB ACHES
OBOLI HOE SHORE
CRASSNESS SERGE
SOD SOL SCISSOR
 SKIMP ASSETS
USSMISSOURI
LOUISE SPY FEST
NOELS SSS ALATE
ANTE MOE USURER
 MISSISSIPPI
SASSES STEED
IMPASSE HRS DEA
TILLS CLASSLESS
ANISE HIC EARTH
ROTAS OLA SPREE
```

795
```
SOFT TAPS COPSE
ALLA KLEE ANITA
DEERMOOSE TENOR
AGATE HORSESOLE
 QANTAS BRINED
GRUNDY  BAEZ
LEAS REAR REBEL
UPI FELLERS ERA
MOLTO ALDO WAIN
 URAL TARRED
BLAMES KAHLIL
LAMBBURRO ATLAS
ITALO HAREWHALE
SHIED EFTS EMIL
SENSE ETAS SAIL
```

796
```
SLOB BURP BAKED
PAVE UBER OLIVE
AKIN NONO ROWAN
REDSKYATMORNING
   OAT HOG
TAVERN DRAW CPA
IRENE BOAR ERRS
DOGDAYAFTERNOON
ALAS ALFA OZONE
LES ICES SMOKER
 ASH STA
ANIGHTINTUNISIA
LETAT NOIR FARR
DELTA TOLD FLAK
ADLER ONLY YENS
```

797
```
PLUCKS  PASCHAL
OOLALA COMEHOME
TONSIL HECTARES
SPAHN WET RANT
 MEDIC BEG
BITE ELK ACETIC
ODOR ALE NODICE
WERE DARTS AMIN
LASSIE BAH FEET
SLOWLY ORE FIRS
 EKE ARENA
ELSA PRY OILED
TITTERED MOREAU
CREEPERS TSETSE
HATRACK  VESSEL
```

798
```
STIFF SPRY MASC
METOO ALES AFAR
OUTERSPACE NOLO
GTO CHIC RSTUVW
 DEADEN HALEN
LATISH BOZO
OLIN LOWERCASE
CANASTA INTEGER
HIGHERUPS LUNT
 EYRE PALATE
AWORD ANTICS
BOLEYN AREA MAO
AMIN INNERCHILD
CAVE BOCA ISSUE
KNEW STET ATOMS
```

799
```
SOP GRADE ELATE
APE TOXIC NADIA
DISCOTECH ABELS
ANTI OLEO MELEE
TESTER  HELP
 ITSCHOOL HOP
FROZE OOPS MIME
LOWE DYNES AGAR
AMEN UPON NEHRU
PEN COURSENS
TARS SETTLE
ARUBA SPOT ROUX
SATAN MADABOUTU
CLOSE UNITE GEL
HERES GENET HST
```

800
```
RAMADA ACARIDS
INAPOD ROBOCOP
PAULREVEREBOWL
 EINE LENNIE
METACARPAL TCU
UNO USES ETHER
MOB BELAS CREDO
 AMERICASCUP
ORCAS BOULE ISR
PECOS RALE KIN
AGO FETTERLESS
LANOSE EPEE
LITTLEBROWNJUG
ESTELLE FEDORA
STORAGE ADLIBS
```

801

```
ASAP  SCRIM  AHAS
LENO  ELITE  DEMI
LENT  TUNER  HAIR
   PARKINGMETERS
     OINK    ARTS
GLEAM      ALIKE
OILS  STRIDE  BEA
BESTFOOTFORWARD
IDA  ALLIES  IDID
   ERODE   KNEES
EPIC       BEIN
  MILESSTANDISH
MANE  WAIST  NOAM
BITE  INNER  GURU
ALAN  MESSY  SLIM
```

802

```
ABRA   DELL   PEEK
TRUSS  ARIA   ERLE
TAMPA  WAVYGRAVY
GRILLES   MOSSES
ARIES    HEROES
FRIEND     LINEN
LAS  EGGON  SABOT
ARIA  EASES  LUGE
TENTH  YESES  BEN
   TOPES  DABBED
PLANER    PETAL
GRACED   MARINES
ROCKYROAD  RAGED
ISEE  OVER  ENURE
NERD  SASE  AMES
```

803

```
INCA  ASPIC  EMT
NEAR  RHINE  LAW
SUMMERANDSMOKE
LIT  SLOP  TAPIN
AGRA  SWEET  GENT
SNARE  UGH  ORGY
 SILENTSPRING
OAS UAE EGO MSS
  AFTERTHEFALL
SAMS  ENE  LANAI
TREK  ROPED  MATT
ACTED  LABS  CTS
THEWINTERSTALE
EIO  PASTE  ODER
DER  SPEED  ASSN
```

804

```
SRO MCD IFA FLA
CONJURE  MANLIER
ROSELEE  AUGUSTA
  THREEDOGNIGHT
SLOE  PESO  EEEEE
TERMS  ETNAS  YRS
STEINS  EEN  BESS
    ALLFORYOU
WISH  REP  ALLEGE
INE  ISAAC  ALVAR
LANDS  STAS  FIRE
  JOYTOTHEWORLD
BEREAVE  SALOONS
LEARNER  ALIGNER
UPS DRS REN ERS
```

805

```
MAE  HARM  REACT
BILL  OLIO  OSCAR
ANILLWIND  OPERA
REG  IMAGERS  TIM
DONNE  SORE  BOOM
OLEO    ADVANCE
TARSAL  ETHEREAL
   THATNOONE
APPROVED  TITLES
MILITIA    TOPE
ORAL  STAN  BASIC
RAT  CHAPEAU  ESE
INTRO  BLOWSGOOD
SHEEP  LENA  NUDE
TARDY  EASY  UTE
```

806

```
BLANC  ASPS  RATA
RURAL  SKAT  ALAN
ONTHESKIDS  CAIN
WEE  REEF  AISLE
    WINDFALLS
ATTICS   BELTERS
PEWS  STINT  DOT
SLIPOFTHETONGUE
ELS  PORES  EAST
SATIATE   MADRES
   FLOPOVERS
BOLOS  MASC  ALT
ALOU  TRIPHAMMER
REIN  ALTO  DOONE
BOND  USSR  ESSAY
```

807

```
CPO  MCAN  EQUAL
LALL  ARCO  RUNTO
AREO  LEER  RADON
STICKLER  RAYONS
 PICKLEDBEETS
OUTS  ZSA  THE
SHOUT  PRE  PAIR
POTTEDMEATBALLS
ANTS  EEG  ASCOT
TKO  UFO  ISIT
  STEWEDPRUNES
ARTHUR  LEADROLE
CURER  GLAD  EVAN
ALIEN  TETE  SETS
TEXTS  ONES  LEE
```

808

```
SAWS  ONAND  PHAR
ALIT  SENOR  IOWA
DYNE  CANOE  QUAG
ANGELALANSBURY
     LORE   SUE
RODEOS  OMAR  AWL
AVER  BRIGS  SHY
JESSICAFLETCHER
IRK  DRIED  HERE
VAS  LENO  SCENES
     BED   STAR
 MURDERSHEWROTE
NANO  NOHOW  IKON
EXIT  ZAIRE  EARN
WITH  ARMED  SYNE
```

809

```
HOLST  TOMA  TACK
ALETA  AWOL  RIAL
LASER  VETO  ADAM
 FLASHINTHEPAN
ELIE    LAUD
MAY  RALE  COGS
ERG  VERE  CHORES
SMOKEANDMIRRORS
SOREST  GENE  URN
REYS  UELE  NAS
HEAP    MADD
 FOOLSPARADISE
COOL  TIME  DOOZY
HAZE  OTIS  ENURE
AMES  NYET  DETAT
```

810

```
BMOC  CAPEK  MEAD
ROBE  OLIVA  ALVA
ATOZ  STAIR  LOON
THEARTOFLETTING
     NYE   SERE
PRUNELLA  MASHIE
LOBE  LADD  DEANS
ADO  SOMEONE  SET
TIARA  PLEA  ETRE
ENTIRE  ESTIMATE
    PAVE   ICE
ELSEHAVEYOURWAY
LEAN  DELON  SORE
MANE  ERIKA  OVAL
SPED  STEEL  NELL
```

811

```
APEG  DASH  ULTRA
PAAR  OLEO  SAHIB
BLUEANGEL  SMELL
 CREEPER   OGLE
ARBITER   ENURED
CALAIS   ALLURE
CRANE  GREET  EAT
RECS  GREAT  ANNE
ARK  TRIAD  ARMER
  BLOATS  ATTARS
SLEEPS   RETINAE
TEAS    POLARIS
ROUSE  LILACTIME
ANTES  DIET  ELAN
WAYNE  SIDE  SEED
```

812

```
RADAR  AIDE  FCC
ARISE  ARDEN  LAH
ROCKANDROLL  INE
AOK  MEDAL  SNOW
BAERS   STATES
REBASTE   CARPS
ATOMS  STATISTIC
SOU   SOS   ODE
ENLISTEES  FINES
DRAYS   EARNEST
FREONS   ARIES
EARN  AMORE  BAS
LTD  PEBBLEBEACH
LEA  RELEE  ENTRE
ADM  ONER  ESSES
```

813

```
CHAD  ASPS  SCABS
LYME  LEAH  LEVEE
IDALUPINO  ASIDE
FRI  MIZ  OCTAVES
FANZINES    OER
SAE   OVERRATE
SPEAK  ACID  OKAY
WHIZ  QTIPS  MIRE
AIRS  UTES  CENTS
PLEASANT    FUR
GUS   YELLOWED
SALADIN  LAP  EPA
PLEBS  ARTCARNEY
CANOE  ROOK  EDEN
AWARD  CONS  NYSE
```

814

```
BAER  SNUB  PSHAW
ACRE  IONE  ALAMO
GHOSTGRAILWATER
SESTINA  RASTERS
   UPS  PUP  TREE
SIMPS   MUTATE
IDO  TOT  LAREDO
ROLLERCOMMUNION
SLEEVE  UTA  ROI
   FEASTS  AVERT
LAIT  CTS  ALI
UTRILLO   ANTOINE
COWSEEWAROILDAY
INITS  EGAD  EINE
DENSE  DATE  TOAD
```

815

```
DAY MAT POT BCD
IDO ELO ABE ELA
IJUSTBLEWINFROM
    ARIEL  SLATS
THEWINDYCITYTHE
DIN COO AGO EEL
SCOT     ONERS
   WINDYCITYIS
MEDES     TESS
ERA PAL BSA ROE
MIGHTYPRETTYBUT
PALAU     ARETE
ITAINTGOTWHATWE
RAS ERE HEI AHA
ESS SAM ADS GOT
```

816

```
ISSUE  AHSO  HOST
TOONE  ROAD  OREO
CHICKENANDSTARS
HOLO  REX  MOOLAH
     OPT  MEON
YANKEEBEAN   EST
IIVIED  EARTH  ARA
PANDA  ATI  APRON
SIN  LATEN  SETON
LYE  MINESTRONE
     COAT   OAF
CARLOT  ADD  ORCA
CREAMOFMUSHROOM
VENI  REED  ACTUP
ISOR  YENS  WEEPS
```

817

```
AGES  STAR  TWINE
LENT  LIRE  EIDER
ATTA  ORCA  EDITS
 NARROWESCAPE
STEELE   TREASON
DRAM    SEWAGE
TASS  SILO  AGRA
ARCH  SITON  KEEL
MORO  HARD  SETS
OVERDO    EIRE
RESTORE   IMELDA
  LONGDIVISION
SPOOL  GINA  SNUG
ARNIE  EVIL  EDGE
PEONY  DETS  SAHL
```

818

```
CLEM  SAKS  ELFIN
RUNE  ETNA  RAISA
ALID  ATOM  OILED
MUDDYWATERS  TRI
   LEAR   HIGHER
RODENT    GLOOMY
IDI  SEGUE  NARES
GIRL  RAIDS  NIRO
ANTES  PLATS  CIA
YAPPED   RATHER
CADDIE    EASY
AGO  GREASYSPOON
KAZOO  MISC  INTO
EVENT  IDEA  SETS
DENTS  RANT  TROY
```

819

```
HOST  ACTUP  SOBS
ARIA  CHETH  CLEO
HELP  CAMEO  HEAD
ALLEYOOP   TALON
   LOSS   COME
SEEOUT  BLOOPERS
ARBOR  TRIPS  LIP
RASP  PRAMS  LINE
ASE  BOISE  MOOSE
HENCOOPS  BOOTED
   HOPE   GAMP
SHARD   HULAHOOP
VIAL  EMAIL  OHNO
IDLE  CALLA  LIII
ZEST  KNEED  EONS
```

820

```
MIDAS  RLS  ZORRO
ABIDE  III  AXIOM
ZIGZAGGED  RIATA
EDS  GAUGE  ADLER
    AMPERAGE
DEFILE    POSTON
EVIL  SPRITZ  OBI
PEREZ  FDA  AARON
ORE  ARCANA  BATE
TYRONE    DASHER
    CZARDOMS
CACTI  HADES  PTA
REHAB  OZONIZERS
ARENA  DER  SORES
GOFER  ASS  TOKEN
```

821
```
OSHA BOATS DUKE
RAIN ENSUE ARIA
BURNONESBRIDGES
SLEEP STABS EVE
      SEW   INN
HST CARRYATORCH
BEES ROUE  MERE
OGLE DAMNS ALAN
MALI  SOTO DISC
BLAZEATRAIL CHE
      EAR RUB
AWE  SCALE LEAST
LIGHTAFIREUNDER
OLGA DAVIS CANE
WEST ERECT HYDE
```

822
```
BAIRD PROD HEAL
ACTII HALO ELSE
THEOAKRIDGEBOYS
HEM MEAN  PRIES
    KOPS MACE
RONNIEMCDOWELL
FINED EXIT  WAY
LAKE STRIP TINE
ATE  VIOL KINDS
WAYLONJENNINGS
    IDGO OONA
CREAK SMUG  ZAG
BARBARAMANDRELL
EVIL ANOD OAKIE
RENE GAGS MEESE
```

823
```
DIGUP AMAT SIBS
OSAKA CALE KNEE
JAMESMCAIN ETRE
OWE TUESDAYWELD
    CASS ANA REY
HAIR ESS  TWAS
ORNO REO ENTIA
WEDNESDAYADDAMS
LAIUS PIP  ETAT
ASST  YEP  RENO
AWN  AAA  LIPS
BILLYSUNDAY ALA
ADAY TRAINRIDES
COKE EARN ELEVE
AWES DRAG XENIA
```

824
```
THOR MET  PERSE
EAVE FALA UNITE
THATLUCKYOLDSUN
HALTERS LAS  ENS
    OER   ORAL
MOONRIVER REPOS
ILK  EIN ASSERT
NDAK SPRAT STLO
DEPORT OPT  RON
SNIPE CLOUDNINE
      SLUR  NEE
AOK  INA FILLERS
SWINGINGONASTAR
KETCH KONG OTTO
ASHOT SOD  NESS
```

825
```
SAC RAJAH PAWS
MOLL ERICA URAL
OUTOFSIGHT SEGA
PROSIT   AGHAST
ESSEN  STEREO
   TAKEADIMVIEW
SLO LEXUS  ERIE
PULLEY   SPRANG
ALII  TIMOR  NEO
TUNNELVISION
  GNOSIS PORKY
GENEVA   BECALM
AVER FUZZYLOGIC
LILI EMEER SANA
ELLE RANDD  TSE
```

826
```
GAZE DINA SEATS
ARIA ETAT INLET
PEPS METS EVERY
EASYCOMEEASYGO
    SAL   ART
BATTLING CATCHA
ODOR SEAM SHOAL
LOWE HOMES  ENID
ABIES NEAT BALE
SETTLE STRAINER
   EVA ALG
FIVEEASYPIECES
AESOP RAMP ARAT
STATE ONCE SURE
SEWER NEAR YELP
```

827
```
OMAR FEDS BWANA
TUNA ISAW RIGID
INON ROTA OSOLE
SINGLEPARENT
   YES   MACES
SSS GIBB TORPOR
OPQ ADAMS  IRAE
DOUBLESOLITAIRE
ARAL SCONE  NED
SETOFF SPUR GDS
      STARE NSA
TRIPLEDECKER
BABEL CORA TAXI
ADORE OMIT UNIT
MOPSY TAKE PETE
```

828
```
GOGH APTLY SHOW
ALOE TAHOE PUMA
LENA TRENT ICON
AGED IRS  PEKOE
  WAIL  UPHILL
FLICKA NAIL  ERR
LATHE CASTE BOA
ASHE MOLDS REST
SET PARSE TERSE
HRH ARGO INGRID
  ELIXIR STAY
SOWED IGO  UFOS
EMIR NASAL GIRL
RENO FREUD ENDO
ANDY LISLE SNOB
```

829
```
PANDA AGORA FDA
ORIEL PARES LOT
PEBBLEBEACH ITT
EASTON ALI ANTI
   OTTS STYPTIC
ABBR EMU AIRSEA
SAO GRAVELPIT
KRUPA LEM ELOPE
  LAVALAMPS NIA
MADDEN SAR CENT
OVERLAP  SOSO
TIRE TEE OTOOLE
HAD ROCKEFELLER
ETA ALOES VEGAS
REM HESSE ERASE
```

830
```
SAGA POSH  AWRY
AVES ABEE SPREE
COOTURIER OPEDS
ONLINE  ELLEN
   INCS EVADE
SCUTTLE FERINE
MARTY ETATS TRA
ALOE PATTY FIAT
ROW SATES SLOGS
COMETS REPHONE
NOVAS  SARA
  SOLES OMAHAS
SPOKE AUKOURANT
HOMER ASOF EINE
APED BENS ALAN
```

831
```
RAMS BEARS SCAR
ARIA OGLED TACO
GINSENGTEA AFRO
EDISON ELK LEEK
   NEAR MIA
SHAW TIE DONUTS
POPPA DREAM LAW
IMPASSE TYMPANI
TEL PASHA ALIGN
EYELET APB OTOE
  CAN  NERD
SWIG BAD EASTER
LIDO MULLEDWINE
OREO OREAD ADDS
TERN CARPS NEST
```

832
```
CLAW MAST THEME
ROSA AXLE RAGES
ARTS REAL ANGLE
WRITERSBLOCK
SERENE ANT  BRA
   IDES TOILES
AMEND MAJORSUIT
SELA MIO  LENO
STENOPADS CESAR
ARCARO  AERO
DOT ION ALSACE
OFFICERSCLUB
AMATI NAVE ALLS
PANIC EVES MOPE
TENSE RENT STAN
```

833
```
SEMI MIMES RAMS
AMEN ONETO AVON
MIST LURCH TOME
THEMARCHOFTIME
RARE   RADAR
MANX   ACTON
BABA BALAAM FIE
BULLDOGDRUMMOND
CIE AGREES EARS
  BRYAN  YALE
EBSEN   CAAN
JOHNSOTHERWIFE
ERAT WHILE NOLA
CAPO NADIA GRIN
THEN STEEL STAT
```

834
```
SCAB NODE ACAR
NONO KOREA NOME
ODDNUMBERS IMUS
BASEBALL TAMEST
LORE DECADES
UPBEAT MERELY
ROAST BIALY AMA
ARCS GOLLY SCOW
LEK KARAT BUTTE
JENSEN ERNSTS
LAURELS RAID
ANDREA OUTCRIES
RIGA MAMBOKINGS
GMEN PREEN ERAT
OAST SANS DENS
```

835
```
SPENT FEW NOBEL
CALVE ALI ECOLE
RUSSELLMD STOLE
ELAM ALSO SAKES
EASIER  WAIVE
  TAKES SEERED
RIGHT TEAS STLO
UNA JOEMT  WAD
TROT UNTO PIANO
HIKERS ORSON
  EXITS HIJACK
OVETT ALVA OGLE
REFIT VAOHANLON
RIFLE OCT WEEST
SNEER RYE ESTES
```

836
```
SARA SAHIB ARAM
AGAR OCALA ROME
JACKOFALLTRADES
ANE CAD HELENA
KARAT  JESS
  KABOOM CASTE
ALTI OTHO USERS
JOHNNYONTHESPOT
ABATE ODER ETTE
ROTOR LOSERS
  OGEE  OSCAR
ONSALE KIT  AGA
TOMDICKANDHARRY
IDEA KOREA CREE
SEEM OATES EYED
```

837
```
ASPEN BRAD TKOS
CARLO ROBE VEIN
CHESSPIECE HALO
SLY ERA SPOONER
  PRONG ENSURE
RACISM EGRET
ALEC ONOR ALIAS
TINTS ORE LADLE
SETUP EGGS REBA
  RIFLE HARASS
ADHERE ITALY
TRACERS ARI NEO
LAVA BILLIEJEAN
APER ELEE NOISE
SEND ROTS SELES
```

838
```
JUNTA COPSE MCP
AROAR ABATE AHA
RISKCAPITAL KIR
   EATS OYSTERS
AGENDA HIS OBOE
DIT ELIAS  STEM
EVEN OWL STALAG
PERILSOFPAULINE
TINGES WIN SECT
TAGS AANDP VET
TALL PLY BRIERY
OSCEOLA  BAER
PHI DANGERFIELD
POT OZONE ANGER
STY RANUP BAGGY
```

839
```
TOSCA LITHO ERG
AMOUR ERROL NOR
CAPTIVATING CPA
ORS SIS PEACHES
ITSABOY  HARP
AMINO BED  JAN
CONV ALL CARTON
ENTITLE CARMINE
SARTRE TOY INCA
III  LIL  ANGER
SIGN PEELING
COUGARS EST ALA
UNI WELLGROOMED
DIN ELITE NOOSE
SAG SLEDS YOKES
```

840
```
ALPACA DAH SCOW
BEARIN OVERCOME
PALATE LEHARHAR
DEPART   GENRE
   ADANO  SEW
LATHE TMEN  AKC
ORIOLE AGE TUNA
GOTH ABHOR ODOR
OSLO TIA DEWITT
SEE ECHO THOSE
  CNN ALGAE
OTARU   DIGEST
KAYAKYAK REHEAL
REEMERGE TRENTS
ALMS SAN HEEDED
```

841
```
APED  PLEA  ASHE
COME  ROAM  BETAS
TUMBLEDRY   ARULE
STATES      SCRIM
     AERO   ARABS
PRESTON     PILLAR
FLUTE  MEATS  ETO
RAMA   MAILS  OBIT
OTB  DONDI   INURE
MELTED      ACADEME
SERVE       SERE
     SAILS  AARONS
GLENN  HUMBLEPIE
PEACE  ETAL  LINE
SITE   DELE  YEAR
```

842
```
CHER   SAGS   YEAS
LOLA   COMET  ETCH
ISLEROYALE    LURE
FEE  UTAH   RELIED
TANGLE      SANTO
     REST   PEEWEES
HAGAR  IMPS  SADA
EBON   ADULT TRIM
ABED   LIME  MONTE
PERCALE     SPAN
ALERT       AYEAYE
CARNEY HILO  LUV
AWAY   CRATERLAKE
SEGO   ABNER AMOR
EDEN   TIER  DONT
```

843
```
SCREW  EVIL  SLUM
LAURA  CANE  LORI
EVERYTHINGTOWIN
WED  LOON   OBESE
     TAR    EST
NOTHINGINCOMMON
AVOID  ORDO  IAGO
MOTE   DAVIT GRIT
ELEV   OLIN  SHAVE
SOMETHINGBETTER
UAE         ANY
GUESS  EERO  COB
ANYTHINGFORLOVE
IDEA   MEAT  AIMED
LOST   PODS  STONE
```

844
```
DUST   PELE  APACE
INLA   OCHS  BACON
ACES   MOAT  JIHAD
NUPTIALS    SURETO
ATTEND      ATARI
     CEO    AVENGED
BRASH  LAVE  GILA
ROSA   RITES UGLY
AHOY   AVER  SPIES
GEFILTE     NYE
NOIRE       EMBOSS
MAGGIO      ALLIANCE
INUIT  ORAL  SIRE
CONDE  ATNO  ROOD
ENSOR  SHAW  ANDY
```

845
```
JAWS   RAFTS PASA
ECHO   EERIE EBAN
THESUPREMECOURT
SET  SUIT   UNTIE
     NETASSETS
LAUREL PLO   FBI
PETE        SOLUTION
SERVICESTATIONS
SKIESARE    DROP
TSP  RPI    CREEDS
     MATCHHEAD
TEPEE  AIDS  FEZ
ITSALLINTHEGAME
GNAT   IOOOO ARIA
EATS   PRINT SELL
```

846
```
KAPPA  COTTA IDA
ALIEN  ORION RAM
NICKELODEON   OLE
EWOK        TURNIN
ACT  BUS    ELEC
LII  TOPPER TUB
ANNIES      INSPIRE
SEPTS  ITO  ARTEL
MASSIVE     TREATY
ANA  SERVES ILL
ALLA   SIN   NEE
WALLED      AONE
OIL  GOLDBRICKER
ODE  GRAIL  BRIDE
SAY  SEDGE  SUDAN
```

847
```
DOFF   IBSEN LAIT
ELLA   NOISE OLGA
BLANKVERSE    STOP
TIM  EAR    EDITORS
SEEMED      INTOW
     INERT  ONEOFA
RAMS   ROAD  SEWER
IWAS   SALEM KEEL
LOGIC  MILO  ESSO
ELINOR      CLOWN
     GRITS  REDCAP
MARLENE AIL  HAL
ALAI   GROUNDZERO
TORN   USING AROW
SEEK   PELTS PINS
```

848
```
IDOL   RAMAR MBA
TAME   ERICA ROAN
CLEF   CEDES INST
HINT   AND   HOGTIE
     IMPALA AHEAD
LORNA       SEXIST
ELITES OER   OBOE
WISH   RIFLE NENE
DOKE   TOT   SHTETL
LOATHE      OHBOY
ANNUL       AERATE
HAIRDO RMS   MARS
OPEC   TROIS ALIT
LECH   INANE RACY
ESE    SADES KNOX
```

849
```
OSCAR  PAR   ABBAS
MOORE  OLE   SAUCE
ALARM  TEC   PASTA
NIXONNIXON    SHIM
     WACO   NEE  BOA
MAB  NONEFORNUNN
ALOFT       RENNES
TAXI   LIARS SHEA
     ERRANT ITEMS
GOREISGORED   DUE
ORB  PER    ARIA
DIOS   ROBBROBBED
WAXES  URI   TIARA
INEPT  PIE   IDIOM
NASTY  SOS   CENSE
```

850
```
ASP    PREY  MELEE
GIRD   SARA  ATOLL
ONOR   IFAMANASKS
REMUS       TATI
AWOMANTOHELPHIM
ESS  MAI    ANATOLE
PORES       EWES
WITHACROWBARITS
OLAY        SALVO
MILLDAM ROI  ANS
BECAUSEHECANNOT
     AERO   NAIVE
LEVERALONE    ISEE
APART  IKON  LEND
MILNE  NEWS  SAS
```

851
```
SAGA   BLOT  TUNA
URAL   REMAP UNIT
ZERO   INANE ROPE
INTHEBARGAIN
ETHANE ONA   TRA
     SRAS   UNREEL
ILLBUYTHAT    ONTO
DEERE  TAN   ASTRO
AHOY   TALKEDSHOP
HANNAH      LAND
ORA  BAA    TUFTED
     PAYSTHEPRICE
ARGO   ETHER ELLE
REAL   REESE EDAM
MOPE   READ  SETS
```

852
```
FAD    NARC  POLAR
IRA    ALIAS OBESE
JUMPSTART     MESTA
IGNITE      LEAPYEAR
     EARL   NBA
JERSEYBOUNCE
MAP    ERNO  TORAHS
PISA   NRA   OTOE
SLOGAN IMAS  ILE
MOROCCOBOUND
SAL         KOLN
HEDGEHOP    RUDDER
ALIEN       DARTBOARD
TIARA  STEEL DOA
HAZEL  SADE  ASS
```

853
```
ALFA   MAXIE STY
DAUNT  ICING TIO
ARMTWISTING   ELL
PRESENCE    CREEK
TYS  EMU    DUAL
     KNEESLAPPING
LENS        AIRSPEED
LALO   ERNST ISMS
ONECARAT    INTO
BACKBREAKING
TESS        ITT  ARA
PARDO       ASSASSIN
ITO  LIPSMACKING
CON  UNITE  TEASE
KPS  TACIT  ENER
```

854
```
ABBA   SAGS  PACS
MOOD   PLOP  PINUP
POOL   HATE  ULTRA
BRITISHAISLES
BEN         RNA
VAG  AXIS   ONCALL
ALIAS  TIER  ODEA
PLANESOFABRAHAM
OINK   ANTS  ELOPE
RETARD STAG  CTR
     EAU    LIP
PRINTSOFWALES
MOORE  ARIA  AXLE
INTOW  ITTY  ZEAL
TEEN   ROSS  ASPS
```

855
```
SEA    ACRAB APART
HUN    MOORE PIPER
ORIGINALS     IEREI
TOTE        SNEERER
APRON       STACCATO
TEAROSE     VEEJAY
GLUCOSE     BOIL
SEANCONNERY
HAUL        LEPANTO
ATEASE      PATSIES
JAZZESUP    ANNIE
ECSTASY     ALLE
EVENT       INTERNEES
LIMBO  LAITY TET
SATYR  EYRIE SNO
```

856
```
APBS   ATEST AHOY
MALE   VILLE COVE
BROWNIEMIX    OMEN
IDO  CAR    MATRONS
TOMCAT      LENIN
     HARTE  SESAME
CARO   IRON  SQUAT
UPUP   XENON UNTO
TEMPS  KATE  ATTN
EXPELS      REARS
     DATED  TOHOLD
TRUMPET     DNA  NEE
ROSE        PUREEDPEAS
IDEA   ODORS BASK
PEST   NEONS ALES
```

857
```
BUSMEN PSST  MAT
ONTIME ALOE  ARI
WILLIAMWELD   ILL
STRIPE      SATED
SRI  LAPP   SANE
WENDELLWILLKIE
INSURES     NAY
GETOUT      TRIODE
PTA         SEISMAL
WALTERWINCHELL
SERA        REIN NEE
HARMS       ONETWO
ISO  WALTWHITMAN
NEW  AGAR   ORIOLE
ELS  TREY   MESSED
```

858
```
TULIP  ARCH  PANT
AFIRE  LARA  OLIO
ROCKBOTTOM    POLO
ASK  BROS   SEQUEL
LES         ETTU
GREBES      SPECIMEN
ROVES  BAER  ZENO
ASIA   FADES ZERO
PSAT   ABAS  GETON
HINTEDAT    TUSSLE
HODS        JOT
YEMENI HEEL  BAS
EVER   SOULSEARCH
NINA   TALL  SHARE
SLOP   STAY  SATED
```

859
```
BLT    LEMUR FARAD
OOH    AMINO ARISE
ONETOUCHOFVENUS
GROS        IDIOTS
ABET   SET   BREEDS
POT    TENCH ROE
TWOFORTHESEESAW
EMIR        TURF
THREEFACESOFEVE
IRE         PARIS TIX
MESSES TOE   ROVE
OCTANE      MONA
FOURHOURSTOKILL
RENEE  METRO ADE
ADDER  BREAD NIX
```

860
```
FADS   PECS  FABLE
ALOE   ORAN  ERROL
RENT   MIRO  NEAPS
GRAHAMCARACAS
OTT  SEATTLE STA
     ATL    ASTERN
HABLA  TEAM  ARAN
OSLOBOATTOCHINA
SHIN   NICE  LOESS
TONGUE      SAE
STD  RAVIOLI TUT
     DUBLINDEMNITY
AMANA  EDIE  AMIN
EATEN  RUST  TELE
REESE  SETS  ORES
```

861
```
WEAN CREE CHILD
ERDA HOAX HOVER
LAMA EARTHINESS
STICKERPRICE
HOTPOT ATA PCT
CALF AGLARE
RUSHHOUR OASIS
GUST SEROW LECH
ANAIS BLUEBOOK
POGROM SERA
ENE MAO ESKIMO
FENDERBENDER
MICRONESIA OATS
PREEN TALC THRO
GEODE SULK SOON
```

862
```
TOBE BLABS CASS
ONYX ROSIE ATIT
RUTH ACTON RATA
OSHA CHILDSPLAY
ELITE LEERS
ORBIT RAGOUT
ROONEY SAVE NAP
SMOG AMPLE COMO
OAK KWAI NERVES
SILICA TEENY
SLOPE VOCAL
WELLVERSED MILT
ANDI DETRE EDIE
STET IDEST RENE
HORS TONES YAKS
```

863
```
SATIN ANTS AONE
ILONA NORA IVAN
FLUSHEDWITHRAGE
TARP ASIS AWLS
APR TOGO
DOWNINTHEDUMPS
UNA ASHY DEARER
DELL EIN NINA
SALOON NAPS DOC
LACKINGBRAVERY
KATY ELI
HASP LOSE EASE
DEVOIDOFKNOWHOW
ALOU INMY REESE
MINT ISEE ARMOR
```

864
```
CAPRA PIETA SIS
HIRAM ONEAL ESE
ADOBEGILLIS SOV
FINALE BABE
ADO PUTTYWOMAN
TORTES RAIDERS
LOMAN LAIRS
MACADAMANDEVE
METAL OVALS
UKULELE EMAILS
VINYLEXAMS NAT
AMIS CATKIN
LOT GUNITEIRENE
UNE ANODE LASES
EOS TONYS NESTS
```

865
```
ORA OPTS STRIFE
MER KEEN HOOVER
ABE ATSEVENTEEN
HUSKY LEO OASTS
ASIA WARRANT
XRAYS TREETOP
STENO DEE WPA
WHENIMSIXTYFOUR
HEE IAM HEATS
YANKING SANTO
INGESTS ATOM
MARSH SAP SLAVE
ONEMEATBALL NOR
TAVERN LUAU GIG
STATEN ELSE ODE
```

866
```
CAST TAPA LOOTS
RULE OVEN UNPIN
ODIN BIST NEEDI
WINETASTING NET
DOGTAG YEAH
ROSCOE ROWS
WOWED PUNT EURO
ARRAY RRS CASES
SLAG YALE USENO
HYPE OYSTER
PRAY RIATAS
EPA COSTUMEBALL
GARBO PARI HULA
ALTER IRAN OPEC
DOYEN TALE REEK
```

867
```
CLAPS STEAM DOC
ROBOT OHARA ONA
OVEREXPOSED WEN
WELTER REA ANON
LAPEL LLANO
STUB YEA SIGNET
LAPAZ RUSTLED
OBTRUDE PEABODY
HONESTY CRUET
SCENIC ORB ATAD
PACES CRIED
HURT KOP TEETHE
ESE UNDERACLOUD
RAE SEEDS AIRED
ELK PEROT LENYA
```

868
```
INNS SALT BOB
NEAT AREA ETAT
SUPERBOWL LICIT
ATO KIOSK ICKES
NELSON IVE SSA
ERIC SPEE STIR
AWAKE RATON
AMERICASCUP
TEPEE ALETA
SARI NONE RASP
OHO SAM ARTFUL
TIBET ADOBE LII
STILE HOMEPLATE
ICER ANAT AMOR
SEN SONS HERS
```

869
```
MOVE BLEEP APED
URAL OUTRE VOLE
FILIBUSTER APSE
TOE ANTE JASPER
INTENT RUNTY
LAYOVERS CAW
AWFUL LOVE DOGE
THUD CIGAR ICED
MERE OVUM MAKES
OWL SLEEPSIN
OATER AMAZON
AMUSES SEMI IDO
JAGS LANDSCAPES
ACHE AMINO CUTE
REST WOTAN EPOS
```

870
```
LAMAS ERROR OLA
ADORE LEAFY NOR
MOOLA MEWTATION
VENDED NOOSE
PLAN DRIPS ONES
LAB SESTETS YRS
OILON SLAPS
PREPAID TRAINEE
TIRES IDEAL
PAP LANOLIN ISI
ARID STRAW AGES
DOLED TROUGH
RUFFRIDER NOSED
ESE USURY INANE
SER GLESS TYLER
```

871
```
COOL SHORT FAWN
ACRE TUDOR ISEE
PALMSUNDAY NEAT
ELO INK COUGARS
TAVERN CHUTE
LEIGH TERROR
CRIB NOAH SLOPE
LOGO GORES ASIA
AVOWS FIRE KEEP
MERGED ORATE
REACT SESAME
SALERNO YON COB
PLEA GREENTHUMB
IONS LATTE ATME
TETE ELCID MEAD
```

872
```
ASAP GRAM SISAL
GARR RENO CAPRI
OSLO OATS UNITS
GHOSTWRITER REA
IRES AVAILS
NESTER DIVEST
IMP ESSENE HAHA
LIENS HET SEWED
ELEE MOROSE ARE
DERIDE PLAYON
HIDDEN MAES
ADE WINDOWSHADE
TAMPA IRON ROOK
CHOIR NOSE ANTE
HONED APED MESS
```

873
```
SAYSO BRAT DAMS
SMOTE EERO OPEC
TONED NAIR TADA
MILDMANNERED
MOE PASS AORTAS
UNLOAD ADOS
SIMPLESIMON ATM
KNEE AVE ALOE
YER EASYRAWLINS
BRIE RABBIS
AFFAIR TACT ICY
PLAINCLOTHES
TAUT OUST ROMAN
ERNE ORCA ELITE
DEAD LEAR DOZED
```

874
```
STAT COCA SPILL
AUDI ALLS PAREE
SLAG SLAT ANSON
SIGHTSAWRONG
PETRI OBI MAE
SINES OSMOND
FRA BITTHEHOOKS
IONA TIA ERLE
FIGHTSALIAR EEL
ELISHA ERNIE
SSE IRA ADLER
GRADETHEMAID
TAMES ALOE EDDY
AVAST MINI RIGA
PETTY SEEM SEEN
```

875
```
ROME TROT CISCO
EVEN OAHU AMMAN
BANGUPJOB SPARE
ATLANTA ALIASES
GEORGE CLINCH
DINER TOTHEE
NEWER MADE SIDE
UPI DRIVERS TIL
LEST ELIS COSTS
LEERED NISAN
CURING TRENTA
TORNADO LOANERS
ROADS BOOMBOXES
ONCLE LAMP TUNE
NAKED ETAS ESTS
```

876
```
HARPO ACES CSA
ONEOF PLODS HAJ
FASTFRIENDS
FIE EASED CRUX
ASTORIA OATH
RUNNINGWATER
SLEEP VERONICA
EEK SPIRO NOT
TIESCORE EAGLE
HASTYPUDDING
LOSS UNTAPED
TOJO SANKA ILO
ONA QUICKSILVER
NEZ BLAHS LEONE
YAZ SENT SITIN
```

877
```
STAT SLOT STILT
ARLO PAAR CORER
BOAR RITA ANAME
UNIQUETECHNIQUE
USE REA IRS
ROPES GRASS
IRA STOOGES
OBLIQUECRITIQUE
REBATES RAN
THEDA BASRA
WIA RAT LIL
ANTIQUEBOUTIQUE
IDARE GOAT GULL
SERAI INRE NINA
TRINI SESS SPAN
```

878
```
SMOLT QED MATTE
HANOI URE ALOHA
ALONG AIL RIMES
HEREHERE BYEBYE
TET BOSN
LOUIELOUIE STEP
APRONS KART RNA
SEGUE OAS OMITS
TRE DIOS MOPPED
SADE THERETHERE
DAIS HAH
WINWIN WELLWELL
ILIAD BAS EERIE
LITRE TRU SAGAN
LEEDS UPS SLOMO
```

879
```
DOER SLAB GABLE
AGRA NOLO ALOOF
FLIPFLOPS MAMET
TENTO MOOSE BBS
OLE METES
MAGRITTE REDHOT
ERR CHANCE GERE
ROOS ELTON ELAN
ISUP REEKED LTD
TENURE RELEASES
DREAM YIP
ADZ ALIBI GAFFS
AREAS LEMONTREE
HARPO ALAN HEEL
SWORN NAME YELL
```

880
```
MOHAIR PORTENT
ADORNER AVERTED
CORONAS REBATES
KRAMERVSKRAMER
ARS EAT
TICS ALS MUTTS
AVA CALF BIGBEN
HOPEAGAINSTHOPE
ORELSE MEAT NEA
EYDIE FAD SEEK
PUG BOA
CREMEDELACREME
POOLING ASHTRAY
FINANCE STERILE
CLANKED ERECTS
```

881
```
HARM WIDE BODES
ELEE AKIM OPERA
LAIR LOSE TIERS
LINCOLNCENTER
ONSIDE OREL
ITS RESETS
SEDAN HEADSTART
OMAN TOONS UVEA
BITTEREND IDEST
SLEEVE YES
ANAT REPAST
MIDDLEAMERICA
LEAVE DELI OMAR
ALTER ANON VALE
BLESS SATE ETES
```

882
```
MALTS LAIT FEET
SCOOT IBID OGLE
SIRFRANCISDRAKE
DEFINED OGDEN
DEN CARE
HEBREW DUCKSOUP
OLIOS PARTY SPA
OBOE BINDS USER
POT FONTS BRINK
SWANLAKE BLEEDS
OUZO SRI
ARGON SNIGGER
WILDGOOSECHASES
ECOL SATE TITAN
DAME USSR SNELL
```

883
```
ADUB TIDE MIST
SALE LOOS OLEOS
HUNNICUTT NLERS
BAIO OROURKE
GOBI PALS
REYNOLDS HOOKER
ENO ALKI GRADE
SOUL HEINZ YSER
ALLAT SMEE EMU
WALKER PERELMAN
ELIE DOMO
SIMPSON MGRS
ATOOT JAZZYJEFF
OHARA OTIS ABAB
ENTR YOGA MAXI
```

884
```
BIRD BIBB ALVA
IVIES ALAR LAID
BANTU RENO INCA
INDEPENDENTSDAY
REL TUTORS
ATA REVISER
PERE CORE OLLIE
EXECUTIVESWEETS
STAUB LIMA STOP
OPENSUP ANY
SHOFAR DII
CAPITOLGAINSTAX
AGES POLL CLEAR
PART EVIL HEARA
ERAS REBA TREY
```

885
```
MARGE CHAT LEND
AGAIN RAMA LIEU
SHIRT ELEPHANTS
CANARDS SIAMESE
FEATS OVA
EIFFEL INCA PMS
LORE INDIAN HIP
STASH ALL AVILA
IAM ENVIED ULAN
ESE LIEN ORLONS
LEG GLOAT
SPOONED AMPULES
KANGAROOS IRATE
ISLE ISIT NEWTS
TOYS AILS ESSES
```

886
```
EBB STAGE ACTI
ACRO PILAF KEEN
CHARGEDAFFAIRES
LEV ICE FORMA
ALUMNI TERI MEN
SORA MOW TAHITI
SNAP ETES NOCAL
PENTECOST
OATEN STAR AIDS
HARRIS ETC INRE
MAI STIR HARDEN
VALET LAS OSS
PRICEWATERHOUSE
REAR ELAND ABED
YALE DODOS FTS
```

887
```
AJAR SEMI ABES
MILA IDOL DELLA
OMEN NINE DAVIS
KICKBACKS STEMS
RITE GUTSY
PAGE SERAPH
SOLONG SOP EMMA
PIVOTED BERRIES
ASAN NAB DEARTH
SPINET APES
BATHE MISC
TERRA PUNCHBOWL
ERRIS USMA OKRA
DRAKE REAL LIEN
AYES EDNA TEND
```

888
```
COLT MIME SABIN
APIA AMOR ILEDE
DINGALING MILLE
ENE LANK NOBLER
TENSED IRONIC
CRY SORE ULM
ASCOT CHAT BRIE
JOHNSON SHELVES
ALIE MORT NEEDS
ROM SATE BON
ITCHED AUDREY
GENERA CONG OBI
ALGAE TOLLHOUSE
ELISE IAGO ESEL
LANES STAN REND
```

889
```
HEDGE AARP WAVE
ALEUT SHOE AVIV
TENTH SECRETIVE
HEY ITEMS MUSES
ASCOT GIS
RECUSE BERLINER
ABCD NELLIE EMO
GOES ATEAM MAAM
ELS MIASMA ERIE
DISTILLS CANALS
HAS PEROT
STEAM HORDE HIC
TERMINATE NEATH
ALOE AUTO DANTE
BESS PLOP TUDOR
```

890
```
PAC SINEW DAKAR
ELY ADEER IMAGE
ELM VIOLINSONTV
RABBI SAC
SHARON STREAMS
LAROSA CREATE
BAS TAXI NORAS
ILIAC APO SNAGS
COMBO ROTE CEE
SHOULD TARAWA
ANGLERS ADOBES
ANA DOONE
CHERRYCELLO UTE
AERIE ELLEN NED
BLEND RIDES DRY
```

891
```
HAHA BEACH AROW
IGOR ATBAY LEAH
NEWT THERM LAKE
END WHOSONFIRST
STORIES BEE
YARD BROADWAY
STONE FLOOR HIE
WOUK BRISK DADA
ADD PAUSE WATER
MOORINGS MARS
ALI FACTUAL
WHERESWALDO PRO
ROVE HOVER ODOR
ABEL ERICA DOME
PONY DESKS SCAN
```

892
```
BAGS AGAVE ABUT
OSLO PETIT MAKE
THEUNTOUCHABLES
HENNA BEADIEST
DIMS NOT
ESP LOWER LIFER
SEEP CAME POEME
STARSKYANDHUTCH
EASEL ZITI SEEA
STEVE ELECT DEB
AEC REOS
COGITATE MALTA
HILLSTREETBLUES
ALEE HULKY ABET
DYED YESES DEMI
```

893
```
GROSS ALOAD KGB
NAVAL VALUE HER
ARUBA ENDTO ANA
REMELT ASH SKIT
ROBB COOTIES
THERMAL URGE
HORA RAPT LEVER
EMITS DEL ELOPE
MONTH ERAS GLEE
LEAR SPOUTED
ILIESCU SEMI
BAND UND DETACH
SUE FINES RAMIE
ERR ITEMS TROTS
NAT BYRON ASSES
```

894
```
OER ADDS STASH
MIA SPOIL WASTE
ARC PANDAMONIUM
RECRANK NEO
OUTIE GASTON
SMOG CYL THETOP
HANS OAKS ETTU
ENT THO EAR
DIEM HERA ARTS
ALUMNI SLA KLEE
ARCANE ACTII
RDS TRIMMED
ACHORUSLION IDA
DRANO EGEST TIM
SINEW NESS SEE
```

895
```
SCRIMP SAFEST
IRONORE GETOVER
LABORER REWRITE
TWENTYONE ATLAS
ODE TRY
ADD UNEASY FOAL
TRIOS TORTILLA
BADNEWS WEEVILS
AMNESIAC LEVIS
TATE GEORGE EEO
ITS LOA
ROUGH SEVENTEEN
ARCHERS ELASTIC
SALTSEA SINATRA
PLAYED CAREER
```

896
```
SAPS PLAID ACHE
ABEE RIATA SHEA
HITTHESACK HEAR
IDAHOS HONEST
BEL RES TINT
INTHEBAG NEV
DIBS SAFE ELUDE
ENOLA SRA LETIT
COXAL TEND ASTO
ORS FRAMEUPS
CHIA DNA JET
COYEST ALCOVE
DARE CASEWORKER
OVEN AKITA EENS
MESA LEROY ERTE
```

897
```
CASK CLEFS AMID
ACHE RIFLE NASA
IRAN EATER ASST
NEWYEARSEVE QUE
ALS REGLUED
CORNMEAL ROUE
ARE ORBIT SIREN
RATA SETAT SAKE
SLIPS TERRA DES
REOS STAGIEST
OVERDUE VAN
KIM ANNIVERSARY
ASEA UTTER EPEE
YOND PRIES ASSN
SRTA SENSE MOTS
```

898
```
REF SCENT LAPIS
ELI TATAR IRENE
VAN ALONE MARTA
SPELLINGBEE JOB
OSSIE LED UNE
NETS STEEL FREE
POOR SEEDS
WASPWAISTED
ALERT STAY
PAST ABETS TABS
PET SPA AERIE
ERE HORNETSNEST
ATREE GAMIN NOT
SENSE EMILE ONE
ESSEN DETER TSE
```

899
```
CUBS DARED GLUE
ABLE ELATE AIRY
NOUN PINTS DADE
NAE BUCKETOFMUD
ATHLETE ILL
EASY HONEYBEE
MEANT FAXES LIV
ALVA SIZED GORE
ILE SEVEN DUNES
MANHOLES PARD
ARF NONUSER
HOLDTHEHAIL TRE
AVID ERICS TINA
DELI LITHE ACID
ANTE PESOS EKES
```

900
```
BENET SIAM SPA
DINNER ETTU PAW
ELLERYQUEEN ORE
ELI SUSANROOK
RESPITES OFFED
ETTAS MISFIRE
RAE PAL ENSE
PAWNBROKING
STUD NAY ANS
ARNICAS DEMON
CONGA PRESSURE
JIMBISHOP LAW
TAE IRENECASTLE
ENS NATO ONEILL
EST SEAM TOTSY
```

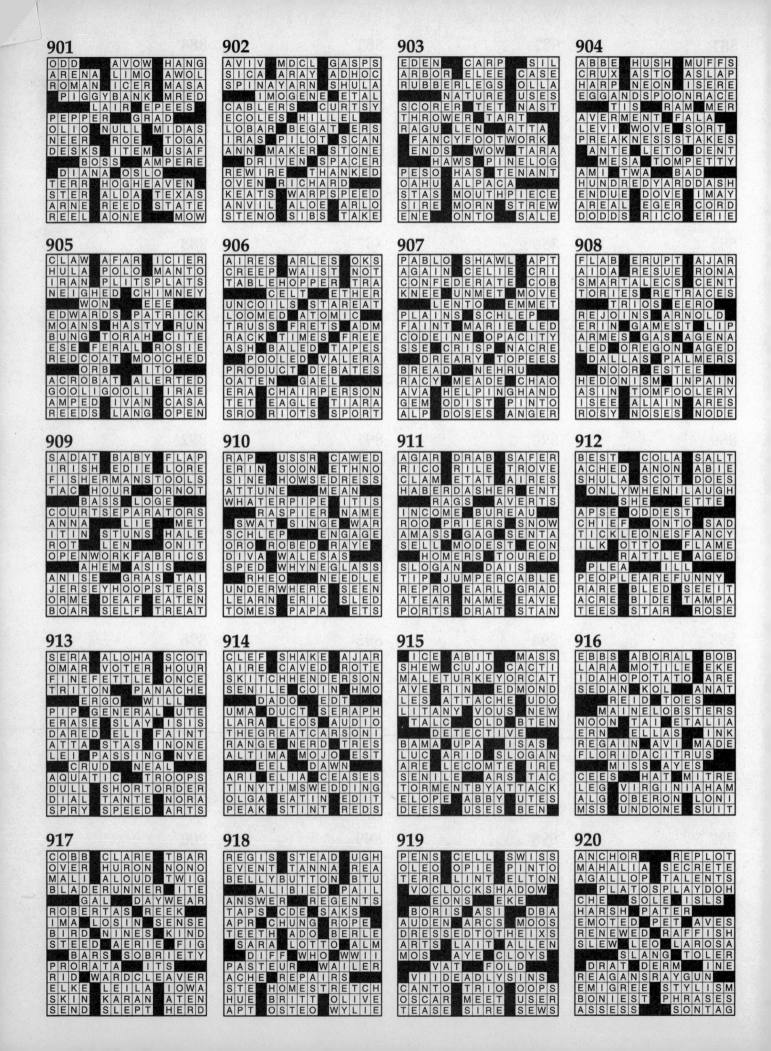

921
```
LASTS BRAY FAST
ABOIL LIRA OGLE
SELMA AVER ROOM
SLEEPYHEAD TRAP
     PEST  RYANS
SUNSET  SLAW
PLEAD PACIFISTS
ANEW SALAD NEAT
MARINATED SKATE
  NEDS  HESTER
ADAGE  ASAN
CROW HITTHESACK
TORO ONOR CARON
ONTO ERMA ALLIE
READ RESP STOLE
```

922
```
LAMA HEMS PABST
ASAP AMAT ORATE
MORO PELE RILER
BULLYPULPIT LLM
   LEIS  VANYAS
DEBONE SCALES
ASI TRITON RHEA
SALSA NOW HOOTS
HULL RIPLEY ERI
YACHTS VERSES
REGGAE  BANE
ORO BELLYDANCER
DIANE EIRE EAVE
ACTOR AMOR GRIN
NASTS PANS ELLE
```

923
```
PEAK PASSE WIND
RANI ASWAN ACID
ITER CHARD NEXT
MEMOS  MOIST
PRIVATEINVESTOR
SSA BEL GESTURE
  PEALS  ONEA
MAJORLEAGUEBALL
IGOT  LORRE
NEATENS AGE SMU
GENERALELECTION
  RANIN  TIMOR
GIGI ONTAP TIRE
ADIN OKEMO ALES
BANG KYRIE NEST
```

924
```
ALFALFA ULALUME
MOODIER PILOSIS
BOGARTANDBACALL
  GPA MORENO
HOYT FILAR SHAY
ORB BOS FTC ORE
COOPER STYLISTS
  THEBIGSLEEP
RETICENT OARING
AGO HAT DAN TEA
TOME RECON BATS
  BWANAS MEL
HUSBANDWIFETEAM
INPEACE DISARMS
PEDDLED ONASSIS
```

925
```
CPAS SWEEP CALF
HOLE CRAZE OREL
IOTA RESIN LOMA
CHARLESTON OMAR
   OAT  AERATE
TOMTOM PENN
AROOM JITTERBUG
LEON POLOS HONE
COTILLION DELTA
PANT ORATOR
ABSENT  ODA
LOON TURKEYTROT
TOUT ETUIS OILY
ENSE RALES SLIP
REAR SHESA SLOE
```

926
```
ATOM RIME SHIP
SODAS ETAL PICA
KNOCKKNOCKJOKES
GREENE HEADERS
  DEW  VERSE
ARAL ESCAPE
MANOF ABALONE
SPECIALDELIVERY
TWIRLED NURSE
EASYAS MOTS
PSALM  NAP
UPROARS TARGET
GOODNEIGHBORSAM
ERLE ELEE PIANO
TEES FORM MUGS
```

927
```
CARR DAIS MUFTI
ALEE EDDA ONION
SLAV FLAB DENTS
TAPEMEASURE GEE
  RANI  ALBERT
ROGERS PULSAR
EPI REGALE KNEE
DANDY ANN SEARS
OLGA BREAST IMP
EDWARD PARLAY
THROAT OLIO
AES THUNDERBOLT
TINES CODE USER
ADANO LIEN SLOE
RIPEN ARRS TONE
```

928
```
PLUMB BATH HST
AGREE LANAI ITO
RANGEFINDER LAW
  ABODE SALVE
MEMBERS FLUBBED
CLOYED MAITAI
GLUTS WOLFE LST
EINE CHOKE GLEE
EST CHINS RAINS
ATHENS DAREST
LEISURE LINDSEY
INNER  AISLE
MOM CLIFFHANGER
ILE HYATT TEENY
TAN YENS ERODE
```

929
```
CLEO ARES SCORE
HARP DELE TOTAL
ISLE OFME UNTIL
CHECKBOOKS CONE
  EER  MAO
PATSY MINIMUMS
ETATS RETIREES
ETTE STEWS SARK
PIERCERS BELVA
CREWCUTS ASSET
OTT  AMS
AUNT SUBMISSION
STAYS POPS ACRE
KAPPA TILT REMO
SHEET OLES ADEN
```

930
```
APSO SPRANG NEB
CHAP CHANCE OPE
TOOTTOOTTOOTSIE
ATT SRO LETTS
BOOKKEEPER AROW
LEMA SYRIA LIMA
EDENS ERGO LEX
GOODDEEDS
ADA DORA DORSA
BIRD PATHS HOOD
ACRE SWEETTOOTH
STILL SRA THE
HAVEALOTTOOFFER
ETA WEANED BORE
DEL SARTRE IRED
```

931
```
CATS PALM ROCK
ARES ISEE ETHER
BLEW LIAR DOODY
SET COFFEEHOUSE
NOHIT SOL
TOASTMASTERS
AGAR RICE ALI
HULA RENES ACID
ALE EVER MOMS
FRANCISBACON
CEO HARTS
JUICENEWTON ETE
ENDED DOOR DUEL
TILDE IONS ORAL
TEED EDGE ASKS
```

932
```
SADA PANTS TBAR
ALUM CLARA RATE
NOME BASIL ALMA
DEBRA SAPSUCKER
WIGS OAST
FACECARD HOSER
ELIA ORE DERIDE
BIT DREAMER LIP
BREMEN CIA ALTO
STRIP STANDBYS
STAT SHOP
FOOLSGOLD SLUSH
OKLA ALOOF ITTO
LADY PESTO STUN
DYES ENTER HYDE
```

933
```
VALE LAUD CLIFF
ASAP AGRA HOSEA
SHRINKINGVIOLET
TED EELS EASELS
PARE ANNE
SHIRTS PLUG HAL
EERIE BOOT AUTO
LAVENDERHILLMOB
ELIS ESTA ALONE
SSN ALTO SNARES
BOAS INDY
ASTERN ARIA OAT
BORNTOTHEPURPLE
ILONA HONE HEEL
EDDYS EYER ONCE
```

934
```
HOLD SPAT HARSH
IDEE IATE OLIVE
FINN EGON MATER
INDIANAJONESAND
MINN FOR
AUF MASCOT STAT
THESE ANS IOLA
THETEMPLEOFDOOM
YULE ALL ISTHE
SHAW SEASON HAD
BOA ACAT
STEVENSPIELBERG
LARAS ELLA OVAL
OPINE DOON NINE
TENET OWNS ELKE
```

935
```
TALL BRAVA ACHE
OLIO ABBIE THIS
BLOWDRIERS MERC
LONERS TIP ESA
AVERY POURSYRUP
MESS SHUE HAUTE
ERS ILET LAPPED
SNOWPLOWS
AFFECT LAGS FFF
CELLO BABY TERI
HAILMARYS DELON
IST ERE EUNICE
ETTE RAINCHECKS
VEEP ASTRO TIES
EDDA STEAL SADE
```

936
```
MAMA CAWS ATMS
ALAN ARIA SHOOT
SLAT BALL HEDDA
TIMETABLE OCEAN
ELIS TRAMS
DOSE COBWEB
LIVING NIE ICED
EVENSUP PETNAME
DARK SEA THESIS
OCTAVE ETAL
CARRY ANTI
WORSE WIDERANGE
AVOWS OLIN NELL
REMIT KENS URIS
RAMS EDGE TOBE
```

937
```
JADE GETTO PALO
AVIS ECRUS ONER
NOSE ROARS ETNA
ENC PULPFICTION
LAINE FRI
SHORED BRIOCHES
HUSKS SLEEP OAT
ONUS SLUED TUTU
ACR THIEF DOSED
THEOREMS BORERS
LOA PRONG
READYTOWEAR USE
ALLI HAITI HEWS
PIPE ESSES ASIS
TASS STERE ITTO
```

938
```
OAST BARR RAJAH
ATEE AREA ERUPT
HOTTENTOT VALES
UPHELD ALIBI
MIAS AVIAN
LIBRETTI BEACON
ONAIR REPOS HOO
LOBO DINAR BIDS
ANY ROANS BELLE
SESTET ATTENDED
SNIPE SEAT
ONERS REMORA
ALOHA KIDGLOVES
TIKAL ILIE DEEP
TESTS NEXT ENDS
```

939
```
MADAT ACHY GARB
ISIAH BLUE EPEE
STARE CONTINUUM
HINDMOST NIPPY
VET HINDU
PALADIN RAISINS
IGOR SARONG NEH
NOOKS PEN OSCAR
URN PELVIS HALE
PASSAGE CHAINED
PROSY OBI
CHRIS IDEATION
ZOOKEEPER CARRE
APSE RULA UKASE
READ ANDY SENOR
```

940
```
GAPY BACH SSGB
AFRO OLEO FACIE
ROOK DORM OFOLD
DONEDOFFESCAP
ELEMENT LAURENT
ANI WAYSIDER
ABUTS IANS OWE
CONEEANDDOFFUTS
HIP IVES ALTOS
ETAGERES SKA
DECIDES ALEGRIA
KRISTONERSOFF
QUILT OBIE TONI
ENNIS ROMP ASON
DOGS SEAS DATE
```

941
```
REHAB HAVE ADDS
ADANO ADAY LOOK
LENIN SALE AWRY
ENGLISHMUFFIN
    ETC EUR SSR
FED ORAL LICHEE
AVER USES TAILS
COLOMBIANCOFFEE
AKITA APAL ETNA
DECAYS SPED SET
ERA AAH
  CANADIANBACON
DRIP COWS BRAVE
JEEP KRIS LEVEE
SYST SENT EMEND
```

942
```
SWAG LAOS CODED
LIMO ABRA ALONE
AROO RUBBERDUCK
TENSPOT REVERSE
EDGERS SALE
  BEANO EYELET
ASHES EVER AUDI
LEAR FRIES GRIN
MEIR LIER FLEET
ARGYLE TORRE
  AXIS WASHES
ETHANOL MASCARA
ROUNDROBIN ORAL
IRENE VEND UPTO
KEYED EDNA TOON
```

943
```
HITCH INDUS CAB
MOORE NOONE OWL
MUTUALFUNDS MAE
 SENTIENT SEMIS
  CHER BIGOTS
DASHED BABOON
OTHER SIMON CEO
ROAD PAPPY FOAM
APR LIMES TULSA
 ELOPED LARDER
PACERS SERB
LURID RAINIEST
ADO JOINTOFLAMB
TIP INANE FORAY
EOS MOLES SWINE
```

944
```
NAHA TATI AGES
EROSE OWED ELLA
LITTLEMORE GAEL
SOCIALCLIMBING
OSA MIA ASCAP
NORM TOTAL INA
   OSS CONTENTS
   PRICEHIKING
FRONTAGE ACE
TOA STORE SOFA
CACTI AHA PEN
 CHANNELSURFING
CHER ADMITTANCE
HERO SANE STEER
ASST AMOR ERRS
```

945
```
BESTIR SLAG ACT
EXCISE KOBE DOW
THEBIGFIVEO ELI
TUNES REEDS LEN
OMIT DODD BASK
REC BOL ONEILL
 SONIA SUNDAE
FIVEOCLOCKNEWS
ASLANT GLUEY
SCARES ALS ORE
TADS DIVA ALEC
CRI ATARI AMISH
AIM HAWAIIFIVEO
ROI MINT FELINE
STR ELSE SWEATS
```

946
```
OSCAR SLAW MAGI
MARIE TAPE ARID
EVERGLADES MERL
NEW REID TAMALE
 YEAR OSLO
THRESH SKITTLES
HEELS SAID HELL
ERAL ATLEE COMA
DODO MAVS MANET
ANYWHERE REVERE
SERE MINE
CENTRI TOTO DIM
OLEO CRATERLAKE
AKIN AUTO AIDER
TONE NEAR HESSE
```

947
```
SCAM SNAG SUITE
ALEE TONE TACIT
CERTAINTY ARENA
HAIRDRESSER
STEER YEW MATA
 SOAP RELINED
ATM ILES INTRO
CHESTPROTECTORS
RENAL NIRO NEE
ESSAYED SARI
SEAR MAL INTRA
 BUREAUCHIEF
KOALA NONREADER
ARDOR INON LADE
TREAT TANS ELSE
```

948
```
AHA BOTCH PIG
RUGS OMAHA BORE
OMIT RAKES IGOR
MONA DREW ATONE
ARGYLE ISTLE
 TENET RITTER
BATHE ROSE HUME
LIRE ANNIE ENID
ERIC LETS ABETS
DEMOTE HINDU
 UNCLE ISLAND
SHORT ACRE LUAU
WIGS ETHIC ERIN
IDLE SHINE TALE
GEE PENDS SSS
```

949
```
BABA VALET VENI
OPEL IRONY AZOV
BILL NIGER LIRA
SATURDAY OHIOAN
 RIAS ENID
APPEAL PEEKABOO
LEI LOSER ETONS
ATTA OPTIC ELEC
CRONE OREOS AGA
KANGAROO CAESAR
 OVEN SKID
DULLES STALWART
AREA TOWIT ABBA
DIEN URANO RIIS
ASKS PEPTO DESK
```

950
```
BEND KEANU ENCS
OLEO OTTER NOON
OMOO WHATDIDTHE
BONMOT USURER
 SOOTHE TREND
COWDOWHENSHE
ONEA DREAM ALA
RUNYON GIFTED
EST CELTS ARID
 ATEBLUEGRASS
DISCO OCELOT
UNCAPS BOHEME
MOODINDIGO IVAN
ANTI ARROW NEMO
SUSA GUSTS GREW
```

951
```
WHETS TUGS PONG
POPUP ASAP AWOL
ANITA KITH GILA
 CURRENTEVENTS
 SANG RIDGES
HAPPEN EER
IRAE CHAR GHANA
GETACHARGEOUTOF
HASTO ICON MONO
 RAG DEEPER
ACTION SHOD
DOWNTOTHEWIRE
ERIC IRAS CHRIS
PENA NEWS TERRA
TRES TELE SASSY
```

952
```
POOR SALAD WISH
UCLA INANE INTO
THEMORNINGAFTER
TOGAS CORNERED
 PLOT YET ORE
ONLOOKER ELM
LOU AXIS EARNS
DOGDAYAFTERNOON
SKEIN STAN ONA
 AIR SIDESTEP
RES MER RSVP
EXPIATES ERASE
STILLOFTHENIGHT
TREK REARM TREE
SASS TRYST ZIPS
```

953
```
ILIA MACY SHIM
TRUSS ECRU RUSE
BALLS TEAM OMAR
SQUEAKEDBY DYE
PISTIL SUSHI
 SLUGS MOUNDS
YAP TOAD INGOT
USE AZURITE EKE
CHEAP PIER REP
KEPLER STABS
 HEXES CRISPY
FOO TWEETIEPIE
LILT AIDA DROLL
OLEO INNS GRUEL
PSST NEAT EATS
```

954
```
IBIS ITAL PASTA
NADA MALI ANWAR
CREAMPUFF STEMS
ADOREE TITHE
 EDDA TEETER
MANATEES ELMIRA
ABUTS CHARS EAT
DOTE SCANS APSE
ARC IPANA SLIER
MARINA TRAILERS
SLANTS IMPS
 CLEMS ASIDES
TAKEN PATTYCAKE
ABETS UTAH EVEN
PURSE NARY REST
```

955
```
ROOD TBAR SHIP
ERGO EASED PAGE
BALLPARKFIGURES
LELAND EVERETT
 ORE RAN
ICEPICKS NESTED
MAL AKITAS TORO
ABASH SEW KANIN
GATE ASLOPE ICU
ELECTS ALLEYCAT
 OTT ALI
ANYMORE SCENES
COURTAPPEARANCE
TAME LEAPT NOUN
SHAD ETTE DSMS
```

956
```
SHAH SYNE MICRO
HANA PEER ADHOC
ELON IRAN RAITT
LONDONBROIL CEO
 LISAS MESA
REPENT TANAGER
AXE KENYA ENOLA
BIKE RUMOR SCAT
ALINE LASER UTE
TENDRIL COATED
 GOES SARAN
AID CHICKENKIEV
BRUNT TARA ABIE
EMCEE IRON RING
LAKER SENT ASEA
```

957
```
PEAS SHAVE STAR
ERST CAVIL TRIO
TAKESADIVE EELS
STARTLED MORASS
LIES DELED
RESINS SUNDOWNS
AXING MINTS AAA
TANG RITES ATIT
ELK VENUS STEVE
STOREDUP MOORED
 ROARS BONN
UPSALA ALLIANCE
ROWS FLOATALOAN
SLIT TENSE LEST
ALMS STEEN YSER
```

958
```
AGAPE DESI JAW
MADAM IRANI USH
FRANCESGUMM DII
 EEL SLAP YDS
UNCLEAR TARGET
RAY STAR ELIA
ADDS ENOL APRIL
LICE RECON ELSE
SAHIB ECRU NAST
 ANON ONCE NEO
MORENO ALADDIN
ARI IDES ERA
GAS TULAFINKLEA
ITS ALINE EAGLE
CEE ESSE DRESS
```

959
```
BRIT SPECS SSGT
MONO CAIRO APIA
WIGGLEROOM FAST
 AUNT PANACHE
ASH STYX TARE
CLOTHE EDIFICES
TELE DIRECT AXE
SADAT HOC AIDED
UZI ABOXOF FETE
PENELOPE RASTER
 GAUD STOP SRS
CLASSIC OWES
HARI CLEANSWEEP
OREL EERIE ARGO
ODAY SWARD TOOL
```

960
```
SAGAS POT EGAN
ECOLE TAKE NODE
ATTAR ITALICIZE
RIO VAT PECAN
 VENIVIDIVEGGIE
 ALICE IDEATE
HERVE ABAS TAR
AGEE ICAME LILI
NAH DATE TOTOE
ODESSA ENROL
 ISAWIHADASALAD
 RIGOR BAD BOY
POSTNATAL IMAGE
ALEC NINE EATEN
MESH SET DRESS
```

961
```
COBS  METRO  HOG
ANTIC AGAIN  ONO
LAUGHINGGAS  WIG
      NIN  IGLOO
SHELLER  STEINS
STU  LAVE  TEEN
AIM EYECUP SGTS
DEMUR NIT  MEWER
ASIS ASTIME  IMA
NANG  ELAL  NPS
REGGAE  DEGRADE
UMBER       OOP
MCI CRYINGSHAME
OER OHARE  EIDER
RED SOWED   DEAR
```

962
```
OSHA NABOB  FEAR
AHAB AMANA  ACRE
TAKEITONTHECHIN
SMELLING  GEODE
     LOG  FLAT
ALLIN IRED   ORB
CROON ONEA  ASIA
HEADINGFORAFALL
ANNE EDEN  ROGET
WAS  GOER  OARED
     BONN   OTB
EDSEL   ANTILLES
DOWNFORTHECOUNT
IRAN HOMER  ALOE
ESPY ODORS  MUST
```

963
```
FOGG JOTA  BRAKE
IDOL ECON  RIGID
JETE LEMS  ACURA
IRONCLAD  LCHAIM
    LONI  ITA
OUIJA SCOT  RAMA
ANNOYS KFC  DRAW
RITE HEATH  RARA
ETES AWN  ISOBAR
DELI REDD  GESTE
     XED  HEFT
PAMPAS  ALLSTARS
AREAS TRUE  ALEE
SINCE URGE  XMAS
TASKS NYET  IAMS
```

964
```
ESSO ASTRA  HAM
FANS SHOES  OJO
FLOODWATCH  MAP
ALAW RARE  ISERE
DUMFOUND   SETS
EXILE   STROPHE
UNHINGE    RUBS
USSR ORATE  MNOP
SUER   CATSPAW
OBLIQUE   CAJUN
ZEUS   ENTHRONE
MENSA SLOE  NAUT
ALI  HEAVYRAINS
CIC OLLIE   ANNE
YAK GLESS   AGED
```

965
```
MAC  ASOF  WRIST
AMO AMINO  HENNA
HELDWATER  INFER
ABDUL  UNWATERED
LAWN MADAME  ARY
ASCOT     NOWI
HAT LEE  TRAMWAY
IRENE      TEASE
STREAMS  ARE  TAW
     TROT  LARUE
CAM WARBLE  TRAP
LOUWATERS  PADRE
ARRET  WATERHOLE
STARE EVADE  WET
PALER DORA   NNE
```

966
```
DAM SPACKLE  FEW
IDI TARRIED  ORR
VALLEYFORGE  RAY
ENTERS     MINTS
SCONE DRAT  ROTH
TENT GOON  MOORE
     GRUB  SAUTES
VILLAGESMITHY
RESEED     ROOD
CRANE STAG  ASST
ABBY GASP  ALONE
EASEL     ACTION
ALL ANVILCHORUS
LIL PREPARE  ETE
PEA SEDATED  ESS
```

967
```
BALL METED  FLUB
OLIO ARUBA  RENE
STOPPINGBYWOODS
CONSOLES  LASSOS
     TIS  MINT
CAIMAN RAGE  SSS
ASCOT OUCH  DATA
THEROADNOTTAKEN
HERE LIEN  SIEVE
YRS PLUS  LESSER
    SEEM  PET
RISING  REASSESS
ONASNOWYEVENING
SONS REEVE  ARUT
ANDY YESES  PEGS
```

968
```
IDEM CATS  AIDA
DIVA LEHAR  ROAR
IVES ORONO  ETRE
GERSHWIN  SONATA
     EINE  ASKA
SAINTS  TRIASSIC
KITES RAINY  IRA
ISAT VERDI  CLAP
ELL AISNE  PLATE
RESERVES  CEASES
INAT       TEAR
HANDEL  SULLIVAN
ELEE DOALL  NINA
STIR ITALO  ECON
SOLS ORES   TINA
```

969
```
SPASM OVAL  GAZA
TANTE PATE  ELAL
SYNOD ICON  NEIL
LUKEANDLAURA
CHEESE NASO  TEY
LOISANDCLARK
AUG  TOY  NOCAL
USELESS  AWESOME
SERIN FRI   RIV
MORKANDMINDY
APR LAID  TENSES
FREDANDETHEL
FIND ODIE  TITAN
IOTA FINE  ENERO
XRAY FESS  REDID
```

970
```
PARK EDOM  SPIRE
AREA LOOS  ALDER
COPYRIGHT  WAYNE
TWOSIDES  STYLES
     NEA  BLOW
ANGUS RARA  ROSA
CORNEA NET  IRIS
HOED DETRE  GIGS
ESTE OBI  SCHEME
DEAR BACH  ATLAS
     WHEN  ICI
MADRAS  PARROTED
EMAIL  METEORITE
SMITE BAUD  GRAS
HOSES ALSO  YOLK
```

971
```
RAGS PALED  SPAT
AGRA ADELE  AONE
FOOTSTOOLS  NODE
ERASER   SOLELY
RAN GIGS  TERR
POOHPOOH    OCT
ALFA TERN  ALOHA
PIOUS TET  ROMAN
ENOLA TAIS  ASPS
DEL GOODMOOD
PEAR SERV   SAP
CRANIA   TATTLE
MOOS SCHOOLBOOK
ALOE OTARU  ARNE
REFS NEWAT  RYES
```

972
```
CAPE AMBIT  FOLD
ALAN NOONE  OHIO
SORT GOOSEBUMPS
AERIAL     METAL
OCTET    THRASH
STEERED   EARWIG
ACTS SARIS  DADA
SOU  COD    LOB
TOLL SHOES  PLUS
APIECE  PATRIOT
SPOOLS    SINEW
PIVOT   CARHOP
OFFONALARK  CAKE
RAIL GENIE  ERLE
BRED EDGAR  SDAK
```

973
```
OMIT GRAPH  ALIT
VISE HENIE  LAZE
EXERCISECAUTION
NURSE   WARLORDS
SPEEDUP    SOT
ERAT     FISTED
PROD GLAD  MERRY
RUNATEMPERATURE
ONETO SILO  HESS
STRAPS    NEAT
HAG     SNAPSUP
AIRWAVES   LOTTO
SWEATINGBULLETS
HIND NOTES  EVES
ENOS GASES  SERE
```

974
```
REA  ORAN  MAMIE
ORBS RENE  ALERT
URAL EGOS  RESEE
GOBALLISTIC
ERATO MEEK  WERE
SORE    DEBATES
ABS KENS  ERUPT
FLYOFFTHEHANDLE
LENTO ASIS   EYE
ENGORGE    TETE
ADES ALAR  IDAHO
FLIPONESLID
ALOHA CAGE  ELLE
MURAL ICER  LILT
OMEGA TEND   ESS
```

975
```
BLAH GAPED  TANG
LACE AHERO  IDEA
ANIMALMAGNETISM
BED MOAT  JAUNTY
TBIRD    PUSS
ISOLDE BRAT  RAM
RENES OPEN  BEDE
VEGETABLESALADS
IMUP NOUN  KILLA
NEE BATS  TINGES
PAGE    GENIE
EDGIER ILET  NEO
MINERALDEPOSITS
MEAT MILNE  RUTH
ATTY STYNE  ASEA
```

976
```
REGIS MOOT  TARS
ALONE AMMO  ALOE
CLONE TINE  NOTE
YES SITTINGDUCK
ELATE      ALE
ELBOWS   TRIUMPH
LOUIS WHOLE  IAM
SUMS HAILS  OGLE
ESP CARNE  SNEER
ESCAPEE   DAMONE
ASP       LINEN
CHICKENFEED  HID
LARK NORA  ATONE
ORAL EVEN  LILAC
GENE DADS  SEENO
```

977
```
DADA CARO  VAMPS
ETES OWED  EMAIL
BARCAROLE  TODAY
ARMORPLATES
RIALTO YOM  TOGA
DIRE    AUTOMAT
OHS CALI  ATALE
SATELLITEDISHES
ALINE ETAL   ANT
KENOSHA    OLGA
ARTS EPI  MASHES
THEPLATTERS
ARNIE  MASTERING
LEARN ANTI  ADIT
LOPED NASA  LIES
```

978
```
COBB SLOTS  WALT
ALIA QUASI  OREO
HIGHMUCKETYMUCK
NOS AIRY  SEETHE
PANNE     SWAN
PRECUT STIR  LAD
IONIA BOAT  DEMI
MIDDLEOFTHEROAD
ALES NOTE  LENTO
SSR WHEY  STASIS
GEAR    CHOMP
AFGHAN CHAR  IMP
LOWERCALIFORNIA
OXEN EXALT  OKRA
GYNT SEMIS  YSER
```

979
```
GETTO BANS  SACS
AGAIN ALEC  ARAP
YOUNG SUMO  TONE
TONIMORRISON
PGA ION  PUREED
ARDENT    SHINE
GEORGEELIOT  PET
ETRE CAL   FARE
DAN JOHNLECARRE
ROBOT    LOTION
GREETS AMO   SLY
LEWISCARROLL
ASIN UNUM  AISLE
ZINE RIME  NAKED
ENGR ESPY  TRYST
```

980
```
STRAY GRE   ORAL
TRALA AREA  TOGA
OATEN BEARBONES
KNICKCHARLES
ECO LOT   VIAND
SENATOR  ODYSSEY
NOT  ELI    ITE
MYTHREESUNS
AMI EAR    TRE
MALTOSE  PUNDITS
STOOL PAR   GOO
MARLINBRANDO
FORTYBUCS  ALOAN
EROO ICKY  HARTE
ZOOM SKY   SNEER
```

981
```
MAGI  BAWL  SPARS
AMOS  OPIE  MIXUP
CANT  NINA  AKELA
HIGHJINKS   RELET
UNSEAT   STEMS
    ZOT  CYPRUS
FRITZ  WASH   EARL
IAGO  LITHO  ARGO
STOP  AGEE  SKEET
HERDED    MAO
  OLDAS  SHTICK
PSALM  TALLORDER
CARLO  PLEA  ALAI
BLEAR  AVON  MESS
STARE  RENT  PRES
```

982
```
CHUM  SARD  TOTE
LENO  OLEO  ANAME
ARID  LAIC  PERIL
PETERANDTHEWOLF
     OCS  ROSA
UPSIDE  FIN  YAPS
NONCE  VINE  NOW
CROCODILEDUNDEE
ATO  IDES  NORMA
POPS  NET  BAREST
    IAGO  OAR
BULLDOGDRUMMOND
BRAID  ARAB  EVER
SINCE  MILL  SAME
SEAR  EPEE  SLOW
```

983
```
ANA  SAFE  BLT
MAMA  TOLLS  SLOE
ETON  ENSUE  EARN
BANGUPJOB   APSE
ALGERIA   UNIT
RED  DISTASTE
ABBEY  FACES  OIL
MOOD  CATER  PFCS
ANO  DANES  KAFKA
HOMBURGS   PEP
  BEAD  MARAUDS
NOEL  CHERRYPOP
TEXT  BLESS  ASTA
ARES  BOISE  SEER
IDS  SPRY  TSK
```

984
```
AGAPE  OLGA  NERD
FLEET  FEAR  ALOE
FORTHEFIRSTTIME
MORALS  VOLLEYS
  ONIT  ENC
BAWL  ANY  PASS
ETA  IAGO  ABORAL
FORONCEINMYLIFE
INTAKE  RAYE  SEE
TESS  REY  REST
   CUE  SIDE
STRAUSS  AMELIA
TWOSLEEPYPEOPLE
LISP  RAGE  POSSE
ONES  STAR  SPOOK
```

985
```
BRAGS  SHOTS  SEM
LOGAN  HEMEN  PLO
ATARI  IRANI  RAN
HERAPINDROP   III
  GENES   ANNE
TOWERED  EMERGES
APOD   ARARAT
MER  ANIMATE  HAL
  LABORS   MORE
LADDERS  MALARIA
ABCD   BONER
IRE  ITALIANISIS
CAR  RATON  ANODE
ADE  ATONE  PARES
LES  SENDS  ESTES
```

986
```
OATS  SLAB  PUP
FIRES  STOLE  IRE
FRITTERAWAY  EGG
  OLIVER  ACES
STOOD  ERMINE
STALLED  STOOPS
WERE  SOLD  INFRA
ART  STREAMS  CIC
BETTE  MINI  JACK
SOARED  STROKES
  SOREST  TOBED
DUTY  SEATED
ALI  ROCKANDROLL
INN  UTTER  YAHOO
SAG  BOSS  GMAN
```

987
```
LEBEN  HIED  ELS
ALONE  MANGE  LIU
PINEAWAYFOR  MER
EZER  IRS  TISSUE
LARGEST  RIVET
  ISH  RESEARCH
LOSES  RECTS  ERE
ALPS  LOCUS  BEER
SIR  SITAR  PETER
HOUSETOP   DEW
  CARER  MARINAS
PREWAR  IAN  LANA
LOS  PALMREADING
ABU  ETTAS  LEVEE
YEP  SESS  TRESS
```

988
```
IBID  LOBS  BERTS
BEAU  EMEU  ASHOT
NANNYGATE  STERE
  GEARSUP  ETTE
RECANT  RIVETED
ONOR  ESS  LAMB
BOOER  PANEL  UPC
ELKES  ONO  INTRO
DAI  VOTED  DELON
  SOPH  REA  WEVE
ALLISON  SACRED
MEAL  HORATIO
ANNES  METERMAID
HYDRO  AMOR  EDNA
LASSO  DONS  REND
```

989
```
SIR  COHERE  WAIT
UNO  UNISEX  ALDO
PCB  PULPFICTION
THEMOST  STOUTLY
  RILES   PAS
TETRAS  HOOLIGAN
EXPOS  PAWLS  ONO
STES  BEZEL  TENS
TRE  DARED  SUSIE
SALTINES  TILTED
  RAD  FOLIO
ALMANAC  ELAPSES
JUICENEWTON  EDT
ABLE  NOWISE  EGO
REED  ASIDES  DEW
```

990
```
WAND  DASH  STEEP
INOR  ELIE  HERVE
LENA  LEND  ARIES
TWOPIECEGARMENT
   EST  END
IRS  LEAP  ISOLDE
NOLTE  CART  NAIL
CLUBSORDIAMONDS
ULNA  NERO  IRANI
REGRET  ETON  ITE
  LOP  DCI
LEGALPROCEEDING
ELATE  IVAN  EDEN
ASTIR  ZAPS  ALIA
NASTY  ELEE  SENT
```

991
```
IBM  TACH  CASTE
NEIL  HIRE  AVOID
DELI  IDEA  MEANS
ITEM  RASPBERRY
ASSETS   TSAR
  LATHE  LATEST
HABIT  ADOS  OREO
ABIGAIL  GASPING
WITH  ROAR  ABETS
NESTLE   REATA
  UNIT  RENTED
GRAPEVINE  ARLO
MIAMI  ICON  NOUN
OFTEN  ELSA  ALDA
STENO  DEES  LET
```

992
```
PILL  TARO  REFIT
DOVE  AWOL  ENLAI
QUICKSAND  STENO
  TETRA  DURESS
INFUSED  VALET
NEARED  CONTESTS
CASEY  PETES  TRE
ATT  NUDES  RAN
REF  CORED  SPEND
ENROLLED  APIECE
  IRATE  SWEETER
PLEASE  ETHER
RANCH  RAPIDCITY
ADDLE  OVAL  ERIE
YESES  METE  DAMP
```

993
```
SPAN  SAD  POWER
KATE  PRIM  AVILA
ICEPALACE  LENIN
  ALE  ESCORTED
RIFLING  ADOBE
HOR  EDAM  SKIRTS
ENE  NOTED  ALLAH
TIED  RETAR  LIMA
OZZIE  SELES  GAP
REEVES  DECO  HRE
  FORDS  SONATAS
GARRISON   ROO
APACE  COLDFRONT
TAMES  KNEE  TREE
TWEET  END  ABED
```

994
```
SHOW  MICK  LISPS
CODA  OLLA  ANTIC
RUES  OLIN  PHYLA
ONTHEROPES  OXEN
DDS  RAM  SALT
  URGED  GOWEST
CLAP  ENOS  BAYER
HILTS  ERE  STENO
OMAHA  DATA  EDDY
POSEUR  LAVER
  CLOD  TET  BEE
BEER  OUTONALIMB
ORDER  KUDU  ELBE
ZONED  ENDE  AGER
OSAKA  SASS  PERT
```

995
```
BIDE  DNA  ARKIN
SPOONFEED  PAESE
NOTONESCUPOFTEA
LEADON  KEEL  TET
   LBS  ELAL
WHEEL  BOWLOVER
EAGRE  RARE  ADAR
ELG  STATERS  RNA
DEBT  OVEN  LAUGH
DEADPANS  ERMAS
  ARAP  BIT
ROT  FLUB  OGLALA
SWEETENEDTHEPOT
TERRE  DISHESOUT
UNSER  OTT  DSCS
```

996
```
BIBI  CAT  BAGS
EDIT  CORED  OLIO
NOGO  OPINE  NOVA
TLC  BREADWINNER
  HOUND  DREGS
OPENLY  MERIT
ALECK  DEMOS  TAM
ROSE  TULIP  TOBE
STE  SHEET  SUPER
  DOWSE  GARBLE
OPERA  SULFA
SMARTCOOKIE  NOD
TERI  KABUL  LAMA
AGED  STOAT  UNIT
BASE  HES  GATE
```

997
```
BEAD  ATLAS  ASTO
RATE  GRILL  SPIN
ERIN  RODEO  KANE
ALLIGATORPEAR
DETER  TED  TEN
  RISES  ERASE
EDS  TURTLENECKS
LAMA  EMAIL  DUET
SNAKEDANCES  SRS
ISLAM   SKEET
EEL  ISH  TOMES
TORTOISESHELL
STIR  RUNTS  OLIO
HUME  ASCAP  LEST
AXEL  PEARY  DEES
```

998
```
SRI  RADAR  STLS
SPAN  EMOTE  CHOU
PITCHPIPES  ARID
ICEHOUSE  TALONS
TYRANTS  MACAW
  IKE  DEFERRAL
CAPNS  REEFS  UNO
ALAS  SALTS  SGTS
LOS  DUKES  APSES
MESSAGES  STE
  WINGS  CELESTE
APOGEE  MIRACLES
BARN  SLINGSHOTS
URDU  TILDE  ETRE
GASP  STAYS  SHA
```

999
```
LESS  LAPS  CITER
ENTO  AGUA  HAIKU
AJAR  WETBLANKET
SOLEMN  URAL  ISH
HYENA  SPADER
  REPO  STALAG
CLOUDNINE  NEUR
HOSTILE  RADIATE
ELLE  LONDONFOG
FLORID  RSVP
  ONABET  EVANS
SRA  FLAG  MYOPIC
PURPLEHAZE  WAKE
ADIEU  ANEW  ECON
REDUX  IONS  LENT
```

1000
```
FDIC  OPAL  FLED
IOTA  PATH  ERICA
ARAL  AREA  ZEROS
TALLAHASSEEEEL
SLYER  TASKS
  DEAL  TITTLE
ATTU  LESSEE  HAT
CHAPELHILLLLAMA
TIX  MORTAL  OWES
ASIMOV   BERN
  ATEAM  IGLOO
WATERLOOOOLONG
LEMUR  IVAN  ABED
EVERS  VERT  SATE
GENE  ESSO  TRON
```